KU-664-044

PRODUCTION FILE COPY

SERIES/TITLES Wilbur Smith

PROD NO 9046.2 EDITION Chancellor

RAP DATE 15-x-93 BOARD WEIGHT 1100

PRINTER Bath Press PAPER 55gsm Snowdown

PRINTED 1x1 NOTES

WITHDRAWN

WILBUR SMITH

WILBUR SMITH

WHEN THE LION FEEDS

THE DARK OF THE SUN

HUNGRY AS THE SEA

CHANCELLOR PRESS

When the Lion Feeds first published in Great Britain in 1964 by William Heinemann Ltd
The Dark of the Sun first published in Great Britain in 1965 by William Heinemann Ltd
Hungry as the Sea first published in Great Britain in 1978 by William Heinemann Ltd

This collected volume first published in Great Britain in 1993 by
Chancellor Press an imprint of
Reed Consumer Books Ltd
Michelin House, 81 Fulham Road, London SW3 6RB
and Auckland, Melbourne, Singapore and Toronto

Reprinted 1993
ISBN 1 85152 383 9

When the Lion Feeds © copyright Wilbur A. Smith 1964
The Dark of the Sun © copyright Wilbur Smith 1965
Hungry as the Sea © copyright Wilbur Smith 1978

A CIP catalogue record for this book is available from the British Library

Printed in Great Britain by the Bath Press

CONTENTS

WHEN THE LION FEEDS

This book is for

Elfreda and Herbert James Smith

with love

ONE

Natal

1

A single wild pheasant flew up the side of the hill almost brushing the tips of the grass in its flight. It drooped its wings and hung its legs as it reached the crest and then dropped into cover. Two boys and a dog followed it up from the valley: the dog led, with his tongue flopping pink from the corner of his mouth, and the twins ran shoulder to shoulder behind him. Both of them were sweating in dark patches through their khaki shirts, for the African sun still had heat although it stood half-mast down the sky.

The dog hit the scent of the bird and it stopped him quivering: for a second he stood sucking it up through his nostrils, and then he started to quarter. He worked fast, back and forth, swinging at the end of each tack, his head down and only his back and his busy tail showing above the dry brown grass. The twins came up behind him. They were gasping for breath for it had been a hard pull up the curve of the hill.

'Keep out to the side, you'll get in my way,' Sean panted at his brother and Garrick moved to obey. Sean was his senior by four inches in height and twenty pounds in weight: this gave him the right to command. Sean transferred his attention back to the dog.

'Put him up, Tinker. Seek him up, boy.'

Tinker's tail acknowledged Sean's instructions, but he held his nose to the ground. The twins followed him, tensed for the bird to rise. They carried their throwing sticks ready and moved forward a stealthy pace at a time, fighting to control their breathing. Tinker found the bird crouched flat in the grass; he jumped forward giving tongue for the first time, and the bird rose. It came up fast on noisy wings, whirling out of the grass.

Sean threw; his kerrie whipped past it. The pheasant swung away from the stick, clawing at the air with frantic wings and Garrick threw. His kerrie cartwheeled up, hissing, until it smacked into the pheasant's fat brown body. The bird toppled, feathers flurried from it and it fell. They went after it. The pheasant scurried broken-winged through the grass ahead of them, and they shouted with excitement as they chased it. Sean got a hand to it. He broke its neck and stood laughing, holding the warm brown body in his hands, and waited for Garrick to reach him.

'Ring-a-ding-a-doody, Garry, you sure gave that one a beauty!'

Tinker jumped up to smell the bird and Sean stooped and held it so he could get his nose against it. Tinker snuffled it, then tried to take it in his mouth, but Sean pushed his head away and tossed the bird to Garrick. Garrick hung it with the others on his belt.

'How far do you reckon that was – fifty feet?' Garrick asked.

'Not as much as that,' Sean gave his opinion. 'More like thirty.'

'I reckon it was at least fifty. I reckon it was farther than any you've hit today.' Success had made Garrick bold. The smile faded from Sean's face.

'Yeah?' he asked.

'Yeah!' said Garrick. Sean pushed the hair off his forehead with the back of his hand, his hair was black and soft and it kept falling into his eyes.

'What about that one down by the river? That was twice as far.'

'Yeah?' asked Garrick.

'Yeah!' said Sean truculently.

'Well, if you're so good, how did you miss this one – hey? You threw first. How come you missed, hey?'

Sean's already flushed face darkened and Garrick realized suddenly that he had gone too far. He took a step backwards.

'You'd like to bet?' demanded Sean. It was not quite clear to Garrick on what Sean wished to bet, but from past experience he knew that whatever it was the issue would be settled by single combat. Garrick seldom won bets from Sean.

'It's too late. We'd better be getting home. Pa will clobber us if we're late for dinner.' Sean hesitated and Garrick turned, ran back to pick up his kerrie then set off in the direction of home. Sean trotted after him, caught up with him and passed him. Sean always led. Having proved conclusively his superior prowess with the throwing sticks Sean was prepared to be forgiving. Over his shoulder he asked, 'What colour do you reckon Gypsy's foal will be?'

Garrick accepted the peace-offering with relief and they fell into a friendly discussion of this and a dozen other equally important subjects. They kept running: except for an hour, when they had stopped in a shady place by the river to roast and eat a couple of their pheasants, they had run all day.

Up here on the plateau it was grassland that rose and fell beneath them as they climbed the low round hills and dropped into the valleys. The grass around them moved with the wind: waist-high grass, soft dry grass the colour of ripe wheat. Behind them and on each side the grassland rolled away to the full range of the eye, but suddenly in front of them was the escarpment. The land cascaded down into it, steeply at first then gradually levelling out to become the Tugela flats. The Tugela river was twenty miles away across the flats, but today there was a haze in the air so they could not see that far. Beyond the river, stretched far to the north and a hundred miles east to the sea, was Zululand. The river was the border. The steep side of the escarpment was cut by vertical gulleys and in the gulleys grew dense, olive-green bush.

Below them, two miles out on the flats, was the homestead of Theunis Kraal. The house was a big one, Dutch-gabled and smoothly thatched with combed grass. There were horses in the small paddock: many horses, for the twins' father was a wealthy man. Smoke from the cooking fires blued the air over the servants' quarters and the sound of someone chopping wood carried faintly up to them.

Sean stopped on the rim of the escarpment and sat down in the grass. He took hold of one of his grimy bare feet and twisted it up into his lap. There was a hole in the ball of his heel from which he had pulled a thorn earlier in the day and now it was plugged with dirt. Garrick sat down next to him.

'Man, is that going to hurt when Ma puts iodine on it!' gloated Garrick. 'She'll have to use a needle to get the dirt out. I bet you yell – I bet you yell your head off !'

Sean ignored him. He picked a stalk of grass and started probing it into the wound. Garrick watched with interest. Twins could scarcely have been less alike. Sean was already taking on the shape of a man: his shoulders were thickening, and there was hard muscle forming in his puppy fat. His colouring was vivid: black hair, skin brown from the sun, lips and cheeks that glowed with the fresh young blood beneath their surface, and blue eyes, the dark indigo-blue of cloud shadow on mountain lake.

Garrick was slim, with the wrists and ankles of a girl. His hair was an undecided brown that grew wispy down the back of his neck, his skin was freckled, his nose and the rims of his pale blue eyes were pink with persistent hay fever. He was fast losing interest in Sean's surgery. He reached across and fiddled with one of Tinker's pendulous ears, and this broke the rhythm of the dog's panting; he gulped twice and the saliva dripped from the end of his tongue. Garrick lifted his head and looked down the slope. A little below where they were sitting was the head of one of the bushy gullies. Garrick caught his breath.

'Sean, look there – next to the bush!' His whisper trembled with excitement.

'What's it?' Sean looked up startled. Then he saw it.

'Hold Tinker.' Garrick grabbed the dog's collar and pulled his head around to prevent him seeing and giving chase. 'He's the biggest old inkonka in the world,' breathed Garrick. Sean was too absorbed to answer.

The bushbuck was picking its way warily out of the thick cover. A big ram, black with age; the spots on his haunches were faded like old chalk marks. His ears pricked up and his spiral horns held high, big as a pony, but stepping daintily, he came out into the open. He stopped and swung his head from side to side, searching for danger, then he trotted diagonally down the hill and disappeared into another of the gullies. For a moment after he had gone the twins were still, then they burst out together.

'Did you see him, hey – did you see them horns?'

'So close to the house and we never knew he was there –'

They scrambled to their feet jabbering at each other, and Tinker was infected with their excitement. He barked around them in a circle. After the first few moments of confusion Sean took control simply by raising his voice above the opposition.

'I bet he hides up in the gulley every day. I bet he stays there all day and comes out only at night. Let's go and have a look.'

Sean led the way down the slope.

On the fringe of the bush, in a small cave of vegetation that was dark and cool and carpeted with dead leaves, they found the ram's hiding-place. The ground was trampled by his hooves and scattered with his droppings and there was the mark of his body where he had lain. A few loose hairs, tipped with grey, were left on the bed of leaves. Sean knelt down and picked one up.

'How are we going to get him?'

'We could dig a hole and put sharpened sticks in it,' suggested Garrick eagerly.

'Who's going to dig it – you?' Sean asked.

'You could help.'

'It would have to be a pretty big hole,' said Sean doubtfully. There was silence while both of them considered the amount of labour involved in digging a trap. Neither of them mentioned the idea again.

'We could get the other kids from town and have a drive with kerries,' said Sean.

'How many hunts have we been on with them? Must be hundreds by now, and we haven't even bagged one lousy duiker – let alone a bushbuck.' Garrick hesitated and then went on. 'Besides, remember what that inkonka did to Frank Van Essen, hey? When it finished sticking him they had to push all his guts back into the hole in his stomach!'

'Are you scared?' asked Sean.

'I am not, so!' said Garrick indignantly, then quickly, 'Gee, it's almost dark. We'd better run.'

They went down the valley.

2

Sean lay in the darkness and stared across the room at the grey oblong of the window. There was a slice of moon in the sky outside. Sean could not sleep: he was thinking about the bushbuck. He heard his parents pass the door of the bedroom; his stepmother said something and his father laughed: Waite Courtney had a laugh as deep as distant thunder.

Sean heard the door of their room close and he sat up in bed. 'Garry.' No answer.

'Garry.' He picked up a boot and threw it; there was a grunt. 'Garry.'

'What you want?' Garrick's voice was sleepy and irritable.

'I was just thinking – tomorrow's Friday.'

'So?'

'Ma and Pa will be going into town. They'll be away all day. We could take the shotgun and go lay for that old inkonka.'

Garrick's bed creaked with alarm.

'You're mad!' Garrick could not keep the shock out of his voice. 'Pa would kill us if he caught us with the shotgun.' Even as he said it he knew he would have to find a stronger argument than that to dissuade his brother. Sean avoided punishment if possible, but a chance at a bushbuck ram was worth all his father's right arm could give. Garrick lay rigid in his bed, searching for words.

'Besides, Pa keeps the cartridges locked up.'

It was a good try, but Sean countered it.

'I know where there are two buckshots that he has forgotten about: they're in the big vase in the dining-room. They've been there over a month.'

Garrick was sweating. He could almost feel the sjambok curling round his buttocks, and hear his father counting the strokes: eight, nine, ten.

'Please, Sean, let's think of something else. . . .'

Across the room Sean settled back comfortably on his pillows. The decision had been made.

3

Waite Courtney handed his wife up into the front seat of the buggy. He patted her arm affectionately then walked around to the driver's side, pausing to fondle the horses and settle his hat down over his bald head. He was a big man, the buggy dipped under his weight as he climbed up into the seat. He gathered up the reins, then he turned and his eyes laughed over his great hooked nose at the twins standing together on the veranda.

'I would esteem it a favour if you two gentlemen could arrange to stay out of trouble for the few hours that your mother and I will be away.'

'Yes, Pa,' in dutiful chorus.

'Sean, if you get the urge to climb the big blue gum tree again then fight it, man, fight it.'

'All right, Pa.'

'Garrick, let us have no more experiments in the manufacture of gunpowder – agreed?'

'Yes, Pa.'

'And don't look so innocent. That really frightens the hell out of me!'

Waite touched the whip to the shiny round rumps in front of him and the buggy started forward, out along the road to Ladyburg.

'He didn't say anything about not taking the shotgun,' whispered Sean virtuously. 'Now you go and see if all the servants are out of the way – if they see us, they'll kick up a fuss. Then come round to the bedroom window and I'll pass it out to you.'

Sean and Garrick argued all the way to the foot of the escarpment. Sean was carrying the shotgun across one shoulder, hanging onto the butt with both hands.

'It was my idea, wasn't it?' he demanded.

'But I saw the inkonka first,' protested Garrick. Garrick was bold again: with every yard put between him and the house his fear of reprisal faded.

'That doesn't count,' Sean informed him. 'I thought of the shotgun, so I do the shooting.'

'How come you always have the fun?' asked Garrick, and Sean was outraged at the question.

'When you found the hawk's nest by the river, I let you climb for it. Didn't I? When you found the baby duiker, I let you feed it. Didn't I?' he demanded.

'All right. So I saw the inkonka first, why don't you let me take the shot?'

Sean was silent in the face of such stubbornness, but his grip on the butt of the shotgun tightened. In order to win the argument Garrick would have to get it away from him – this Garrick knew and he started to sulk. Sean stopped among the trees at the foot of the escarpment and looked over his shoulder at his brother.

'Are you going to help – or must I do it alone?'

Garrick looked down at the ground and kicked at a twig. He sniffed wetly; his hayfever was always bad in the mornings.

'Well?' asked Sean.

'What do you want me to do?'

'Stay here and count to a thousand slowly. I'm going to circle up the slope and wait where the inkonka crossed yesterday. When you finish counting come up the gulley.

Start shouting when you are about halfway up. The inkonka will break the same way as yesterday – all right?'

Garrick nodded reluctantly.

'Did you bring Tinker's chain?'

Garrick pulled it from his pocket, and at the sight of it the dog backed away. Sean grabbed his collar, and Garrick slipped it on. Tinker laid his ears flat and looked at them reproachfully.

'Don't let him go. That old inkonka will rip him up. Now start counting,' said Sean and began climbing. He kept well out to the left of the gulley. The grass on the slope was slippery under his feet, the gun was heavy and there were sharp lumps of rock in the grass. He stubbed his toe and it started to bleed, but he kept on upwards. There was a dead tree on the edge of the bush that Sean had used to mark the bushbuck's hide. Sean climbed above it and stopped just below the crest of the slope where the moving grass would break up the silhouette of his head on the skyline. He was panting. He found a rock the size of a beer barrel to use as a rest for the gun, and he crouched behind it. He laid the stock of the gun on the rock, aimed back down the hill and traversed the barrels left and right to make sure his field of fire was clear. He imagined the bushbuck running in his sights and he felt excitement shiver along his forearms, across his shoulders and up the back of his neck.

'I won't lead on him – he'll be moving fairly slowly, trotting most probably. I'll go straight at his shoulders,' he whispered.

He opened the gun, took the two cartridges out of his shirt pocket, slid them into the breeches and snapped the gun closed. It took all the strength of both his hands to pull back the big fancy hammers, but he managed it and the gun was double-loaded and cocked. He laid it on the rock in front of him again and stared down the slope. On his left the gulley was a dark-green smear on the hillside, directly below him was open grass where the bushbuck would cross. He pushed impatiently at the hair on his forehead: it was damp with sweat and stayed up out of his eyes.

The minutes drifted by.

'What the hell is Garry doing? He's so stupid sometimes!' Sean muttered and almost in answer he heard Garrick shout below him. It was a small sound, far down the slope and muffled by the bush. Tinker barked once without enthusiasm; he was also sulking, he didn't like the chain. Sean waited with his forefinger on one trigger, staring down at the edge of the bush. Garrick shouted again – and the bushbuck broke from cover.

It came fast into the open with its nose up and its long horns held flat against its back. Sean moved his body sideways swinging the gun with its run, riding the pip of the foresight on its black shoulder. He fired the left barrel and the recoil threw him off balance; his ears hummed with the shot and the burnt powder smoke blew back into his face. He struggled to his feet still holding the gun. The bushbuck was down in the grass, bleating like a lamb and kicking as it died.

'I got him,' screamed Sean. 'I got him first shot! Garry, Garry! I got him, I got him!'

Tinker came pelting out of the bush dragging Garry behind him by the chain and, still screaming, Sean ran down to join them. A stone rolled under his foot and he fell. The shotgun flew out of his hand and the second barrel fired. The sound of the explosion was very loud.

When Sean scrambled onto his feet again Garrick was sitting in the grass whimpering

– whimpering and staring at his leg. The blast of the shotgun had smashed into it and churned the flesh below the knee into tatters – bursting it open so the bone chips showed white in the wound and the blood pumped dark and strong and thick as custard.

'I didn't mean it. . . . Oh God, Garry, I didn't mean it. I slipped. Honest, I slipped.' Sean was staring at the leg also. There was no colour in his face, his eyes were big and dark with horror. The blood pumped out onto the grass.

'Stop it bleeding! Sean, please stop it. Oh, it's sore! Oh! Sean, please stop it!'

Sean stumbled across to him. He wanted to vomit. He unbuckled his belt and strapped it round the leg, and the blood was warm and sticky on his hands. He used his sheathed knife to twist the belt tight. The pumping slowed and he twisted harder.

'Oh, Sean, it's sore! It's sore. . . .' Garrick's face was waxy-white and he was starting to shiver as the cold hand of shock closed on him.

'I'll get Joseph,' Sean stammered. 'We'll come back quickly as we can. Oh, God, I'm sorry!' Sean jumped up and ran. He fell, rolled to his feet and kept running.

They came within an hour. Sean was leading three of the Zulu servants. Joseph, the cook, had brought a blanket. He wrapped Garrick and lifted him and Garrick fainted as his leg swung loosely. As they started back down the hill Sean looked out across the flats: there was a little puff of dust on the Ladyburg road. One of the grooms was riding to fetch Waite Courtney.

They were waiting on the veranda of the homestead when Waite Courtney, came back to Theunis Kraal. Garrick was conscious again. He lay on the couch: his face was white and the blood had soaked through the blanket. There was blood on Joseph's uniform and blood had dried black on Sean's hands. Waite Courtney ran up onto the veranda; he stooped over Garrick and drew back the blanket. For a second he stood staring at the leg and then very gently he covered it again.

Waite lifted Garrick and carried him down to the buggy. Joseph went with him and they settled Garrick on the back seat. Joseph held his body and Garrick's stepmother took the leg on her lap to stop it twisting. Waite Courtney climbed quickly into the driver's seat: he picked up the reins, then he turned his head and looked at Sean still standing on the veranda. He didn't speak, but his eyes were terrible – Sean could not meet them. Waite Courtney used the whip on the horses and drove them back along the road to Ladyburg: he drove furiously with the wind streaming his beard back from his face.

Sean watched them go. After they had disappeared among the trees he remained standing alone on the veranda; then suddenly he turned and ran back through the house. He ran out of the kitchen door and across the yard to the saddle-room, snatched a bridle down from the rack and ran to the paddock. He picked a bay mare and worked her into a corner of the fence until he could slip his arm around her neck. He forced the bit into her mouth, buckled the chin strap and swung up onto her bare back.

He kicked her into a run and put her to the gate, swaying back as her body heaved up under him and falling forward on her neck as she landed. He gathered himself and turned her head towards the Ladyburg road.

It was eight miles to town and the buggy reached it before Sean. He found it outside Doctor Van Rooyen's surgery: the horses were blowing hard, and their bodies were dark with sweat. Sean slid down off the mare's back; he went up the steps to the surgery door and quietly pushed it open. There was the sweet reek of chloroform in the room. Garrick lay on the table, Waite and his wife stood on each side of him, and the doctor was washing his hands in an enamel basin against the far wall. Ada Courtney was crying silently, her face blurred with tears. They all looked at Sean standing in the doorway.

'Come here,' said Waite Courtney, his voice flat and expressionless. 'Come and stand here beside me. They're going to cut off your brother's leg and, by Christ, I'm going to make you watch every second of it!'

= 4 =

They brought Garrick back to Theunis Kraal in the night. Waite Courtney drove the buggy very slowly and carefully and Sean trailed a long way behind it. He was cold in his thin khaki shirt, and sick in the stomach with what he had seen. There were bruises on his upper arm where his father had held him and forced him to watch.

The servants had lanterns burning on the veranda. They were standing in the shadows, silent and anxious. As Waite carried the blanket-wrapped body up the front steps one of them called softly in the Zulu tongue. 'The leg?'

'It is gone,' Waite answered gruffly.

They sighed softly all together and the voice called again. 'He is well?'

'He is alive,' said Waite.

He carried Garrick through to the room that was set aside for guests and sickness. He stood in the centre of the floor holding the boy while his wife put fresh sheets on the bed; then he laid him down and covered him.

'Is there anything else we can do?' asked Ada.

'We can wait.'

Ada groped for her husband's hand. 'Please, God, let him live,' she whispered. 'He's so young.'

'It's Sean's fault!' Waite's anger flared up suddenly. 'Garry would never have done it on his own.' He tried to disengage Ada's hand.

'What are you going to do?' she asked.

'I'm going to beat him! I'm going to thrash the skin off him!'

'Don't, please don't.'

'What do you mean?'

'He's had enough. Didn't you see his face?'

Waite's shoulders sagged wearily and he sat down on the armchair beside the bed. Ada touched his cheek.

'I'll stay here with Garry. You go and try to get some sleep, my dear.'

'No,' Waite said. She sat down on the side of the chair and Waite put his arm around her waist. After a long while they slept, huddled together on the chair beside the bed.

5

The days that followed were bad. Garrick's mind escaped from the harness of sanity and ran wild into the hot land of delirium. He panted and twisted his fever-flushed face from side to side; he cried and whimpered in the big bed; the stump of his leg puffed up angrily and the stitches were drawn so tight it seemed they must tear out of the swollen flesh. The infection oozed yellow and foul-smelling onto the sheets.

Ada stayed by him all that time. She swabbed the sweat from his face and changed the dressings on his stump, she held the glass for him to drink and gentled him when he raved. Her eyes sunk darkly into their sockets with fatigue and worry, but she would not leave him. Waite could not bear it. He had the masculine dread of suffering that threatened to suffocate him if he stayed in the room: every half hour or so he came in and stood next to the bed and then he turned away and went back to his restless wandering around the house. Ada could hear his heavy tramp along the corridors.

Sean stayed in the house also: he sat in the kitchen or at the far end of the veranda. No one would speak to him, not even the servants; they chased him when he tried to sneak into the bedroom to see Garrick. He was lonely with the desolate loneliness of the guilty – for Garry was going to die, he knew it by the evil silence that hung over Theunis Kraal. There was no chatter nor pot-clatter from the kitchens, no rich deep laughter from his father: even the dogs were subdued. Death was at Theunis Kraal. He could smell it on the soiled sheets that were brought through to the kitchen from Garrick's room; it was a musky smell, the smell of an animal. Sometimes he could almost see it: even in bright daylight sitting on the veranda he sensed it crouched near him like a shadow on the edge of his vision. It had no form as yet. It was a darkness, a coldness that was gradually building up around the house, gathering its strength until it could take his brother.

On the third day Waite Courtney came roaring out of Garrick's room. He ran through the house and out into the stable yard. 'Karlie. Where are you? Get a saddle onto Rooiberg. Hurry, man, hurry – damn you. He's dying, do you hear me, he's dying.'

Sean did not move from where he sat against the wall next to the back door. His arm tightened around Tinker's neck and the dog touched his cheek with a cold nose; he watched his father jump up onto the stallion's back and ride. The hooves beat away towards Ladyburg and when they were gone he stood up and slipped into the house: he listened outside Garrick's door and then he opened it quietly and went in. Ada turned towards him, her face was tired. She looked much older than her thirty-five years, but her black hair was drawn back behind her head into a neat bun and her dress was fresh and clean. She was still a beautiful woman despite her exhaustion. There was a gentleness about her, a goodness that suffering and worry could not destroy. She held out her hand to Sean and he crossed and stood beside her chair and looked down at Garrick. Then he knew why his father had gone to fetch the doctor. Death was in the room – strong and icy cold hovered over the bed. Garrick lay very still: his face was yellow, his eyes were closed and his lips were cracked and dry.

All the loneliness and the guilt came swelling up into Sean's throat and choked him into sobs, sobs that forced him to his knees and he put his face into Ada's lap and cried.

He cried for the last time in his life, he cried as a man cries – painfully, each sob tearing something inside him.

Waite Courtney came back from Ladyburg with the doctor. Once more Sean was driven out and the door closed. All night he heard them working in Garrick's room, the murmuring of their voices and the scuff of feet on the yellow wood floor. In the morning it was over. The fever was broken and Garrick was alive. Only just alive – his eyes were sunk into dark holes like those of a skull. His body and his mind were never to recover completely from that brutal pruning.

It was slow – a week before he was strong enough to feed himself. His first need was for his brother, before he was able to talk above a whisper it was, 'Where's Sean?'

And Sean, still chastened, sat with him for hours at a time. Then when Garrick slept Sean escaped from the room, and with a fishing-rod or his hunting sticks and Tinker barking behind him went into the veld. It was a measure of Sean's repentance that he allowed himself to be contained within the sick-room for such long periods. It chafed him like ropes on a young colt: no one would ever know what it cost him to sit quietly next to Garrick's bed while his body itched and burned with unexpended energy and his mind raced restlessly.

Then Sean had to go back to school. He left on a Monday morning while it was still dark. Garrick listened to the sounds of departure, the whicker of the horses outside on the driveway and Ada's voice reciting last minute instructions: 'I've put a bottle of cough mixture under your shirts, give it to Fräulein as soon as you unpack. Then she'll see that you take it at the first sign of a cold.'

'Yes, Ma.'

'There are six vests in the small case – use a new one every day.'

'Vests are sissy things.'

'You will do as you're told, young man.' Waite's voice, 'Hurry up with your porridge – we've got to get going if I'm to have you in town by seven o'clock.'

'Can I say goodbye to Garry?'

'You said goodbye last night – he'll still be asleep now.'

Garrick opened his mouth to call out, but he knew his voice would not carry. He lay quietly and listened to the chairs scraping back from the dining-room table, the procession of footsteps out onto the veranda, voices raised in farewells and at last the wheels of the buggy crunching gravel as they moved away down the drive. It was very quiet after Sean had left with his father.

After that the weekends were, for Garrick, the only bright spots in the colourless passage of time. He longed for them to come and each one was an eternity after the last – time passes slowly for the young and the sick. Ada and Waite knew a little of how he felt. They moved the centre of the household to his room: they brought two of the fat leather armchairs from the lounge and put them on each side of his bed and they spent the evenings there. Waite with his pipe in his mouth and a glass of brandy at his elbow, whittling at the wooden leg he was making and laughing his deep laugh, Ada with her knitting and the two of them trying to reach him. Perhaps it was this conscious effort that was the cause of their failure, or perhaps it is impossible to reach back down the years to a small boy. There is always that reserve, that barrier between the adult and the secret world of youth. Garrick laughed with them and they talked together, but it was not the same as having Sean there. During the day Ada had the running of a large household and there were fifteen thousand acres of land and two thousand head of cattle that needed Waite's attention. That was the loneliest time for Garrick. If it had not been for the books, he might not have been able to bear it. He read everything that Ada brought to him: Stevenson, Swift, Defoe, Dickens and even Shakespeare. Much of it he didn't understand, but he read hungrily and the opium of the printed word helped him through the long days until Sean came home each Friday.

When Sean came home it was like a big wind blowing through the house. Doors slammed, dogs barked, servants scolded and feet clattered up and down the passages. Most of the noise was Sean's, but not all of it. There were Sean's followers: youngsters from his class at the village school. They accepted Sean's authority as willingly as did Garrick, and it was not only Sean's fists that won this acceptance but also the laughter and the sense of excitement that went with him. They came out to Theunis Kraal in droves that summer, sometimes as many as three on one bare-backed pony: sitting like a row of sparrows on a fence rail. They came for the added attraction of Garry's stump. Sean was very proud of it.

'That's where the doc sewed it up,' pointing to the row of stitch marks along the pink fold of scar tissue.

'Can I touch it, man?'

'Not too hard or it'll burst open.' Garrick had never received attention like this in his life before. He beamed round the circle of solemn, wide-eyed faces.

'It feels funny – sort of hot.'

'Was it sore?'

'How did he chop the bone – with an axe?'

'No.' Sean was the only one in a position to answer technical questions of this nature. 'With a saw. Just like a piece of wood.' He made the motions with his open hand.

But even this fascinating subject couldn't hold them for long and presently there would be a restlessness amongst them.

'Hey, Sean, Karl and I know where there's a nest of squawkers – you wanta have a look?' or 'Let's go and catch frogs,' and Garrick would cut in desperately.

'You can have a look at my stamp collection if you like. It's in the cupboard there.'

'Naw, we saw it last week. Let's go.'

This was when Ada, who had been listening to the conversation through the open kitchen door, brought in the food. Koeksusters fried in honey, chocolate cakes with peppermint icing, watermelon konfyt and half a dozen other delicacies. She knew they wouldn't leave until it was finished and she knew also that there'd be upset stomachs when it was, but that was preferable to Garrick lying alone and listening to the others riding off into the hills.

The weekends were short, gone in a breathless blur. Another long week began for Garrick. There were eight of them, eight dreary weeks before Doctor Van Rooyen agreed to let him sit out on the veranda during the day. Then suddenly the prospect of being well again became a reality for Garrick. The leg that Waite was making was nearly finished: he shaped a leather bucket to take the stump and fitted it to the wood with flat-headed copper nails; he worked carefully, moulding the leather and adjusting the straps that would hold it in place. Meanwhile, Garrick exercised along the veranda, hopping beside Ada with an arm around her shoulder, his jaws clenched with concentration and the freckles very prominent on his face that had been without the sun for so long. Twice a day Ada sat on a cushion in front of Garrick's chair and massaged the stump with methylated spirits to toughen it for its first contact with the stiff leather bucket.

'I bet old Sean'll be surprised, hey? When he sees me walking around.'

'Everyone will,' Ada agreed. She looked up from his leg and smiled.

'Can't I try it now? Then I can go out fishing with him when he comes on Saturday.'

'You mustn't expect too much, Garry, it's not going to be easy at first. You will have to learn to use it. Like riding a horse – you remember how often you fell off before you learned to ride.'

'But can I start now?'

Ada reached for the spirits bottle, poured a little into her cupped hand and spread it on the stump. 'We'll have to wait until Doctor Van Rooyen tells us you're ready. It won't be long now.'

It wasn't. After his next visit Doctor Van Rooyen spoke to Waite as they walked together to the doctor's trap.

'You can try him with the peg-leg – it'll give him something to work for. Don't let him overtire himself and watch the stump doesn't get rubbed raw. We don't want another infection.'

'Peg-leg.' Waite's mind echoed the ugly word as he watched the trap out of sight. 'Peg-leg': he clenched his fists at his sides, not wanting to turn and see the pathetically eager face behind him on the veranda.

6

'Are you sure that's comfortable?' Waite squatted in front of Garrick's chair adjusting the leg and Ada stood next to him.

'Yes, yes, let me try it now. Gee, old Sean will be surprised, hey? I'll be able to go back with him on Monday, won't I?' Garrick was trembling with eagerness.

'We'll see,' Waite grunted non-committally. He stood up and moved round beside the chair.

'Ada, my dear, take his other arm. Now listen, Garry, I want you to get the feel of it first. We'll help you up and you can just stand on it and get your balance. Do you understand?'

Garrick nodded vigorously.

'All right, then up you come.'

Garrick drew the leg towards him and the tip scraped across the wooden floor. They lifted him and he put his weight on it.

'Look at me – I'm standing on it. Hey, look I'm standing on it.' His face glowed. 'Let me walk, come on! Let me walk.'

Ada glanced at her husband and he nodded. Together they led Garrick forward. He stumbled twice but they held him. Klunk and klunk again the peg rang on the floor boards. Before they reached the end of the veranda Garrick had learned to lift the leg high as he swung it forward. They turned and he stumbled only once on the way back to the chair.

'That's fine, Garry, you're doing fine,' laughed Ada.

'You'll be on your own in no time,' Waite grinned with relief. He had hardly dared to hope it would be so easy, and Garrick fastened on his words. 'Let me stand on my own now.'

'Not this time, boy, you've done well enough for one day.'

'Oh, gee, Pa. Please. I won't try and walk, I'll just stand. You and Ma can be ready to catch me. Please, Pa, please.'

Waite hesitated and Ada added her entreaty. 'Let him, dear, he's done so well. It'll help build up his confidence.'

'Very well. But don't try to move,' Waite agreed. 'Are you ready, Garry? Let him go!' They took their hands off him cautiously. He teetered slightly and their hands darted back.

'I'm all right – leave me.' He grinned at them confidently and once more they released him. He stood straight and steady for a moment and then he looked down at the ground. The grin froze on his face. He was alone on a high mountain, his stomach turned giddily within him and he was afraid, desperately unreasonably afraid. He lurched violently and the first shriek tore from him before they could hold him. 'I'm falling. Take it off! Take it off!'

They sat him in the chair with one swift movement.

'Take it off! I'm going to fall!' The terrified screams racked Waite as he tore at the straps that held the leg.

'It's off, Garry, you're safe. I'm holding you.' Waite took him to his chest and held him, trying to quieten him with the strength of his arms and the security of his own big body, but Garrick's terrified struggling and his shrieks continued.

'Take him to the bedroom, get him inside.' Ada spoke urgently and Waite ran with him, still holding him against his chest.

Then for the first time Garrick found his hiding-place. At the moment when his terror became too great to bear he felt something move inside his head, fluttering behind his eyes like the wings of a moth. His vision greyed as though he was in a mist bank. The mist thickened and blotted out all sight and sound. It was warm in the mist – warm and safe. No one could touch him here for it wrapped and protected him. He was safe.

'I think he's asleep,' Waite whispered to his wife, but there was a puzzled expression in his voice. He looked carefully at the boy's face and listened to his breathing.

'It happened so quickly though – it isn't natural. And yet – and yet he looks all right.'

'Do you think, we should call the doctor?' Ada asked.

'No.' Waite shook his head. 'I'll just cover him up and stay with him until he wakes.'

He woke in the early evening, sat up and smiled at them as though nothing had happened. Relaxed and shyly cheerful, he ate a big supper and no one mentioned the leg. It was almost as though Garrick had forgotten about it.

7

Sean came home on the following Friday afternoon. He had a black eye – not a fresh one; it was already turning green round the edges of the bruise. Sean was very reticent on the subject of how he had obtained it. He brought with him also a clutch of flycatchers' eggs which he gave to Garrick, a live red-lipped snake in a cardboard box which Ada immediately condemned to death despite Sean's impassioned speech in its defence, and a bow carved from M'senga wood which was, in Sean's opinion, the best wood for a bow.

His arrival wrought the usual change in the household of Theunis Kraal – more noise, more movement and more laughter.

There was a huge roast for dinner that evening, with potatoes baked in their jackets. These were Sean's favourite foods and he ate like a hungry python.

'Don't put so much in your mouth,' Waite remonstrated from the head of the table, but there was a fondness in his voice. It was hard not to show favouritism with his sons. Sean accepted the rebuke in the spirit it was given. 'Pa, Frikkie Oberholster's bitch had pups this week, six of them.'

'No,' said Ada firmly.

'Gee, Ma, just one.'

'You heard your mother, Sean.' Sean poured gravy over his meat, cut a potato in half and lifted one piece to his mouth. It had been worth a try. He hadn't really expected them to agree.

'What did you learn this week?' Ada asked. This was a nasty question. Sean had learned as much as was necessary to avoid trouble – no more.

'Oh, lots of things,' he replied airily and then to change the subject. 'Have you finished Garry's new leg yet, Pa?'

There was a silence. Garrick's face went expressionless and he dropped his eyes to his plate. Sean put the other half of the potato in his mouth and spoke around it.

'If you have, me and Garry can go fishing up at the falls tomorrow.'

'Don't talk with your mouth full,' snapped Waite with unnecessary violence. 'You've got the manners of a pig.'

'Sorry, Pa,' Sean muttered. The rest of the meal passed in uneasy silence and as soon as it finished Sean escaped to the bedroom. Garry went with him hopping along the passage with one hand on the wall to balance himself.

'What's Pa so mad about?' Sean demanded resentfully as soon as they were alone.

'I don't know.' Garrick sat on the bed. 'Sometimes he just gets mad for nothing – you know that.'

Sean pulled his shirt off over his head, screwed it into a ball and threw it against the far wall.

'You'd better pick it up, else there'll be trouble,' Garrick warned mildly. Sean dropped his pants and kicked them after the shirt. This show of defiance put him in a better mood. He walked across and stood naked in front of Garrick.

'Look,' he said with pride. 'Hairs!'

Garrick inspected them. Indisputably they were hairs.

'There aren't very many.' Garrick couldn't disguise the envy in his voice.

'Well, I bet I've got more than you have,' Sean challenged. 'Let's count them.'

But Garrick knew himself to be an outright loser; he slipped off the bed and hopped across the room. Steadying himself against the wall he stooped and picked up Sean's discarded clothing, he brought it back and dropped it in the soiled linen basket beside the door. Sean watched him and it reminded him of his unanswered question.

'Has Pa finished your leg yet, Garry?'

Garry turned slowly, he swallowed and nodded once, a quick jerky movement.

'What's it like? Have you tried it yet?'

The fear was on Garrick again. He twisted his face from side to side as though seeking an escape. There were footsteps in the passage outside the door. Sean dived at his bed and snatching up his nightgown pulled it over his head as he slid between the sheets. Garrick was still standing beside the clothes basket when Waite Courtney came into the room. 'Come on, Garry, what's holding you up?'

Garrick hurried across to his bed and Waite looked at Sean. Sean grinned at him with all the charm of his good looks and Waite's face softened into a grin also. 'Nice to have you home again, boy.' It was impossible to be angry with Sean for long.

He reached out and took a handful of Sean's thick black hair. 'Now I don't want to hear any talking in here after the lamp's out – do you understand?'

He tugged Sean's head from side to side gently, embarrassed by the strength of his feeling for his son.

8

The next morning Waite Courtney rode back to the homestead for his breakfast when the sun was high. One of the grooms took his horse and led it away to the paddock and Waite stood in front of the saddle room and looked around him. He looked at the neat white posts of the paddock, at the well-swept yard, at his house filled with fine furniture. It was a good feeling to be rich – especially when you knew what it was like to be poor. Fifteen thousand acres of good grassland, as many cattle as the land would carry, gold in the bank. Waite smiled and started across the yard.

He heard Ada singing in the dairy.

'How rides the farmer
Sit, sit, so
Sit, sit, so – tra la
The Capetown girls say
Kiss me quick
Kiss me quick – tra la.'

She had a clear sweet voice and Waite's smile broadened – it was a good feeling to be rich and to be in love. He stopped at the door of the dairy; because of the thick stone walls and heavy thatch it was cool and dark in the room. Ada stood with her back to the door, her body moving in time to the song and the turning of the butter churn. Waite watched her a moment, then he walked up behind her and put his arms around her waist.

Startled, she turned within his arms and he kissed her on the mouth. 'Good morning, my pretty maid.'

She relaxed against him. 'Good morning, sir,' she said.

'What's for breakfast?'

'Ah, what a romantic fool I married!' She sighed, 'Come along, let's go and see.'

She took off her apron, hung it behind the door, patted her hair into place and held her hand out to him. They walked hand-in-hand across the yard and into the kitchen. Waite sniffed loudly.

'Smells all right. Where are the boys?'

Joseph understood English though he could not speak it. He looked up from the stove.

'Nkosi, they are on the front veranda.'

Joseph had the typical moon-round face of the Zulu, when he smiled his teeth were big and white against the black of his skin.

'They are playing with Nkosizana Garry's wooden leg.'

Waite's face flushed. 'How did they find it?'

'Nkosizana Sean asked me where it was and I told him you had put it in the linen cupboard.'

'You bloody fool!' roared Waite. He dropped Ada's hand and ran. As he reached the lounge he heard Sean shout and immediately there was the sound of someone falling heavily on the veranda. He stopped in the middle of the lounge floor; he couldn't bear to go out and face Garrick's terror. He felt sick with dread and with his anger at Sean.

Then he heard Sean laugh. 'Get off me, man, don't just lie there.'

And then, incredibly, Garrick's voice. 'Sorry, it caught in the floor boards.'

Waite walked across to the window and looked out onto the veranda. Sean and Garrick lay in a heap together near the far end. Sean was still laughing and on Garrick's face was a set nervous smile. Sean scrambled up. 'Come on. Get up.'

He gave Garrick his hand and dragged him to his feet. They stood clinging to each other, Garrick balancing precariously on his peg. 'I bet if it was me I could just walk easy as anything,' said Sean.

'I bet you couldn't, it's jolly difficult.'

Sean let go of him and stood back with his arms spread ready to catch him. 'Come on.'

Sean walked backwards in front of him and Garrick followed unsteadily, his arms flapping out sideways as he struggled to keep his balance, his face rigid with concentration. He reached the end of the veranda and caught onto the rail with both hands. This time he joined in Sean's laughter.

Waite became aware that Ada was standing beside him; he glanced sideways at her and her lips formed the words 'come away.' She took his arm.

9

At the end of June 1876 Garrick went back to school with Sean. It was almost four months since the shooting. Waite drove them. The road to Ladyburg was through open forest, two parallel tracks with the grass growing in between – it brushed the bottom of the buggy. The horses trotted in the tracks, their hooves silent on the thick powder dust. At the top of the first rise Waite slowed the horses and turned in his seat to look back at the homestead. The early sun gave the whitewashed walls of Theunis Kraal an orange glow and the lawns around the house were brilliant green. Everywhere else the grass was dry in the early winter and the leaves of the trees were dry also. The sun was not yet high enough to rob the veld of its colour and light it only with the flat white glare of midday. The leaves were golden and russet and red-brown, the same red-brown as the bunches of Afrikander cattle that grazed among the trees. Behind it all was the back-drop of the escarpment, striped like a zebra with the green black bush that grew in its gullies.

'Look, there's a hoopoe, Sean.'

'Yeah, I saw it long ago. That's a male.'

The bird flew up from in front of the horses: chocolate and black and white wings, its head crested like an Etruscan helmet.

'How do you know?' challenged Garrick.

''Cause of the white in its wings.'

'They've all got white in their wings.'

'They haven't – only the males.'

'Well, all the ones I've seen got white in their wings,' said Garrick dubiously.

'Perhaps you've never seen a female. They're jolly rare. They don't come out of their nests much.'

Waite Courtney smiled and turned back in his seat. 'Garry's right, Sean, you can't tell the difference by their feathers. The male's a little bigger, that's all.'

'I told you,' said Garrick, brave under his father's protection.

'You know everything,' muttered Sean sarcastically. 'I suppose you read it in all those books, hey?'

Garrick smiled complacently. 'Look, there's the train.'

It was coming down the escarpment, dragging a long grey plume of smoke behind it. Waite started the horses into a trot. They went down to the concrete bridge over the Baboon Stroom.

'I saw a yellow fish.'

'It was a stick, I saw it too.'

The river was the boundary of Waite's land. They crossed the bridge and went up the other side. In front of them was Ladyburg. The train was running into the town past the cattle sale pens; it whistled and shot a puff of steam high into the air.

The town was spread out, each house padded around by its orchard and garden. A thirty-six ox team could turn in any of the wide streets. The houses were burnt brick or whitewashed, thatched or with corrugated-iron roofs painted green or dull red. The square was in the centre and the spire of the church was the hub of Ladyburg. The school was on the far side of town.

Waite trotted the horses along Main Street. There were a few people on the side walks; they moved with early morning stiffness beneath the flamboyant trees that lined the street and every one of them called a greeting to Waite. He waved his whip at the men and lifted his hat to the women, but not high enough to expose the bald dome of his head. In the centre of town the shops were open, and standing on long thin legs in front of his bank was David Pye. He was dressed in black like an undertaker.

'Morning, Waite.'

'Morning, David,' called Waite a little too heartily. It was not six months since he had paid off the last mortgage on Theunis Kraal and the memory of debt was too fresh in his mind; he felt as embarrassed as a newly released prisoner meeting the prison governor on the street.

'Can you come in and see me after you've dropped off your boys?'

'Have the coffee ready,' agreed Waite. It was well known that no one was ever offered coffee when they called on David Pye. They went on down the street, turned left at the far end of Church Square, passed the courthouse and down the dip to the school hostel.

There were half a dozen Scotch carts and four-wheelers standing in the yard. Small boys and girls swarmed over them unloading their luggage. Their fathers stood in a group at one end of the yard – brown-faced men, with carefully brushed beards, uncomfortable in their suits which still showed the creases of long hanging. These men lived too far out for their children to make the daily journey into school. Their land sprawled down to the banks of the Tugela or across the plateau halfway to Pietermaritzburg.

Waite stopped the buggy, climbed down and loosened the harness on his horses and Sean jumped from the outside seat to the ground and ran to the nearest bunch of boys. Waite walked across to the men; their ranks opened for him, they smiled their welcomes and in turn reached for his right hand. Garrick sat alone on the front seat of the buggy, his leg stuck out stiffly in front of him and his shoulders hunched as though he were trying to hide.

After a while Waite glanced back over his shoulder. He saw Garrick sitting alone and he made as if to go to him, but stopped immediately. His eyes quested among the swirl of small bodies until they found Sean. 'Sean.'

Sean paused in the middle of an animated discussion. 'Yes, Pa.'

'Give Garry a hand with his case.'

'Aw, gee, Pa – I'm talking.'

'Sean! 'Waite scowled with both face and voice.

'All right, I'm going.' Sean hesitated a moment longer and then went back to the buggy.

'Come on, Garry. Pass the cases down.'

Garrick roused himself and climbed awkwardly over the back of the seat. He handed the luggage down to Sean who stacked it beside the wheel, then turned to the group that had followed him across.

'Karl, you carry that. Dennis, take the brown bag. Don't drop it, man, it's got four bottles of jam in it.' Sean issued his instructions.

'Come on, Garry.'

They started off towards the hostel and Garrick climbed down from the buggy and limped quickly after them.

'You know what, Sean?' said Karl loudly. 'Pa let me start using his rifle.'

Sean stopped dead, and then more with hope than conviction, 'He did not!'

'He did,' Karl said happily. Garrick caught up with them and they all stared at Karl.

'How many shots did you have?' asked someone in an awed voice.

Karl nearly said, 'Six' but changed it quickly.

'Oh, lots – as many as I wanted.'

'You'll get gun-shy – my Pa says if you start too soon you'll never be a good shot.'

'I never missed once,' flashed Karl.

'Come on,' said Sean and started off once more – he had never been so jealous in his life. Karl hurried after him.

'I bet you've never shot with a rifle, Sean, I bet you haven't, hey?' Sean smiled mysteriously while he searched for some new topic; he could see that Karl was going to kick the subject to death.

From the veranda of the hostel a girl ran to meet him.

'It's Anna,' said Garrick.

She had long brown legs, skinny; her skirts fussed about them as she ran. Her hair was black, her face was small with a pointed chin. 'Hello, Sean.'

Sean grunted. She fell in beside him, skipping to keep pace with him.

'Did you have a nice holiday?'

Sean ignored her, always coming and trying to talk to him, even when his friends were watching.

'I've got a whole tin of shortbread, Sean. Would you like some?' There was a flash of interest in Sean's eyes; he half turned his head towards her, for Mrs Van Essen's shortbread was rightly famous throughout the district, but he caught himself and kept grimly on towards the hostel.

'Can I sit next to you in class this term, Sean?'

Sean turned furiously on her. 'No, you can't. Now go away – I'm busy.'

He went up the steps. Anna stood at the bottom; she looked as though she was going to cry and Garrick stopped shyly beside her.

'You can sit next to me if you like,' he said softly.

She glanced at him, looking down at his leg. The tears cleared and she giggled. She was pretty. She leaned towards him.

'Peg-leg,' she said and giggled again. Garrick blushed so vividly, and suddenly his eyes watered. Anna put both hands to her mouth and giggled through them, then she turned and ran to join her friends in front of the girls' section of the hostel. Still blushing, Garrick went up the steps after Sean; he steadied himself on the banisters.

Fräulein stood at the door of the boys' dormitory. Her steel-rimmed spectacles and the iron grey of her hair gave her face an exaggerated severity, but this was relieved by the smile with which she recognized Sean.

'Ah, my Sean, you have come.' What she actually said was, 'Ach, mein Sean, you haf gom.'

'Hello, Fräulein.' Sean gave her his number one very best smile.

'Again you have grown,' Fräulein measured him with her eyes. 'All the time you grow, already you are the biggest boy in the school.'

Sean watched her warily, ready to take evasive action if she attempted to embrace him as she did sometimes when she could no longer contain her feelings. Sean's blend of charm, good looks and arrogance had completely captured her Teutonic heart.

'Quickly, you must unpack. School is just now starting.' She turned her attention to her other charges and Sean, with relief, led his men through into the dormitory.

'Pa says that next weekend I can use his rifle for hunting, not just targets,' Karl steered the conversation back.

'Dennis, put Garry's case on his bed.' Sean pretended not to hear.

There were thirty beds arranged along the walls, each with a locker beside it. The room was as neat and cheerless as a prison or a school. At the far end a group of five or six boys sat talking. They looked up as Sean came in but no greetings were exchanged – they were the opposition.

Sean sat down on his bed and bounced experimentally, it was hard as a plank, Garrick's peg thumped as he walked down the dormitory and Ronny Pye, the leader of the opposition, whispered something to his friends and they all laughed, watching Garrick. Garrick blushed again and sat down quickly on his bed to hide his leg.

'I guess I'll shoot duiker first before Pa lets me shoot kudu or bushbuck,' Karl stated and Sean frowned.

'What's the new teacher like?' he asked.

'He looks all right,' one of the others answered. 'Jimmy and I saw him at the station yesterday.'

'He's thin and got a moustache.'

'He doesn't smile much.'

'I suppose next holiday Pa will take me shooting across the Tugela,' Karl said aggressively.

'I hope he's not too keen on spelling and things,' Sean declared. 'I hope he doesn't start all that decimal business again, like old Lizard did.'

There was a round of agreement and then Garrick made his first contribution. 'Decimals are easy.'

There was a silence while they all looked at him.

'I might even shoot a lion,' said Karl.

= 10 =

There was a single schoolroom to accommodate the youngest upwards of both sexes. Double desks; on the walls a few maps, a large set of multiplication tables and a picture of Queen Victoria. From the dais Mr Anthony Clark surveyed his new pupils. There was a hushed anticipation; one of the girls giggled nervously and Mr Clark's eyes sought the sound, but it stopped before he found it.

'It is my unfortunate duty to attempt your education,' he announced. He wasn't joking. Long ago his sense of vocation had been swamped by an intense dislike for the young: now he taught only for the salary.

'It is your no more pleasant duty to submit to this with all the fortitude you can muster,' he went on, looking with distaste at their shining faces.

'What's he saying?' whispered Sean without moving his lips.

'Shh,' said Garrick.

Mr Clark's eyes swivelled quickly and rested on Garrick. He walked slowly down the aisle between the desks and stopped beside him; he took a little of the hair that grew at Garrick's temple between his thumb and his forefinger and jerked it upwards. Garrick squeaked and Mr Clark returned slowly to his dais.

'We will now proceed. Standard Ones kindly open your spelling books at page one. Standard Twos turn to page fifteen. . . .' He went on allocating their work.

'Did he hurt you?' breathed Sean. Garrick nodded almost imperceptibly and Sean conceived an immediate and intense hatred for the man. He stared at him.

Mr Clark was a little over thirty years old – thin, and his tight three-piece suit emphasized this fact. He had a pale face made sad by his drooping moustache, and his nose was upturned to such a degree that his nostrils were exposed; they pointed out of his face like the muzzle of a double-barrelled shotgun. He lifted his head from the list he held in his hand and aimed his nostrils straight at Sean. For a second they stared at each other.

'Trouble,' thought Mr Clark; he could pick them unerringly. 'Break him before he gets out of control.'

'You, boy, what's your name?'

Sean turned elaborately and looked over his shoulder. When he turned back there was a little colour in Mr Clark's cheeks. 'Stand up.'

'Who, me?'

'Yes, you.'

Sean stood.

'What's your name?'

'Courtney.'

'Sir!'

'Courtney, sir.'

They looked at each other. Mr Clark waited for Sean to drop his eyes but he didn't.

'Big trouble, much bigger than I thought,' he decided and said aloud, 'All right, sit down.'

There was an almost audible relaxation of tension in the room. Sean could sense the respect of the others around him; they were proud of the way he had carried it off. He felt a touch on his shoulder. It was Anna, the seat behind him was as close as she could sit to him. Ordinarily her presumption would have annoyed him, but now that small touch on his shoulder added to his glow of self-satisfaction.

An hour passed slowly for Sean. He drew a picture of a rifle in the margin of his spelling book then rubbed it out carefully, he watched Garrick for a while until his brother's absorption with his work irritated him.

'Swot,' he whispered, but Garrick ignored him.

Sean was bored. He shifted restlessly in his seat and looked at the back of Karl's neck – there was a ripe pimple on it. He picked up his ruler to prod it. Before he could do so Karl lifted his hand as if to scratch his shoulder but there was a scrap of paper between his fingers. Sean put down the ruler and surreptitiously reached for the note. He held it in his lap, on it was written one word.

'Mosquitoes.'

Sean grinned. Sean's imitation of a mosquito was one of the many reasons why the previous schoolmaster had resigned. For six months old Lizard had believed that there were mosquitoes in the room – then for the next six months he had known there were not. He had tried every ruse he could think of to catch the culprit, and in the end it had got him. Every time the monotonous hum began the tic in the corner of his mouth became more noticeable.

Now Sean cleared his throat and started to hum. Instantly the room was tense with suppressed laughter. Every head, including Sean's, was bent studiously over a book. Mr Clark's hand hesitated in writing on the blackboard but then went on again evenly.

It was a clever imitation; by lowering and raising the volume Sean gave the effect of an insect moving about the room. A slight trembling at his throat was the only sign that he was responsible.

Mr Clark finished writing and turned to face the room. Sean did not make the mistake of stopping, he allowed the mosquito to fly a little longer before settling.

Mr Clark left his dais and walked down the row of desks furthest from Sean. Once or twice he paused to check the work of one of his pupils. He reached the back of the room and moved across to Sean's row. He stopped at Anna's desk.

'It is unnecessary to loop your L's like that,' he told her. 'Let me show you.' He took her pencil and wrote, 'You see what I mean. To show off when writing is as bad as showing off in your everyday behaviour.'

He handed her back her pencil and then pivoting on one foot he hit Sean a mighty crack across the side of the head with his open hand. Sean's head was knocked sideways and the sound of the blow was very loud in the quiet room.

'There was a mosquito sitting on your ear,' said Mr Clark.

11

In the following two years Sean and Garrick made the change from child to young manhood. It was like riding a strong current, being swept with speed along the river of life.

There were parts of the river that flowed steadily:

Ada was one of these. Always understanding, with the ability to give her understanding expression, unchanging in her love for her husband and the family she had taken as her own.

Waite was another. A little more grey in his hair but big as ever in body, laugh and fortune.

There were parts of the river that ran faster:

Garrick's reliance on Sean. He needed him more strongly each month that passed, for Sean was his shield. If Sean was not there to protect him when he was threatened, then he used his final refuge: he crawled back into himself, into the warm dark mists of his mind.

They went to steal peaches: the twins, Karl, Dennis and two others. There was a thick hedge around Mr Pye's orchard and the peaches that grew on the other side of it were as big as a man's fist. They were sweet as honey but tasted even sweeter when taken on the plunder account. You reached the orchard through a plantation of wattle trees.

'Don't take too many off one tree!' Sean ordered. 'Old Pye will notice it as sure as anything.'

They came to the hedge and Sean found the hole.

'Garry, you stay here and keep cats for us. If anyone comes give a whistle.' Garrick tried not to show his relief, he had no stomach for the expedition.

Sean went on. 'We'll pass the peaches out to you – and don't eat any until we're finished.'

'Why doesn't he come with us?' asked Karl.

''Cause he can't run, that's why. If he gets caught they'll know who the rest of us are for sure and we'll all get it.'

Karl was satisfied. Sean went down on his hands and knees and crawled into the hole in the hedge and one at a time the others followed him until Garrick was left alone.

He stood close to the hedge, drawing comfort from its protecting bulk. The minutes dragged by and Garrick fidgeted nervously – they were taking an awfully long time.

Suddenly there were voices, someone was coming through the plantation towards him. Panic beat up inside him and he shrank back into the hedge, trying to hide; the idea of giving a warning never even entered his head.

The voices were closer and then through the trees he recognized Ronny Pye: with him were two of his friends. Each of them was armed with a slingshot and they walked with their heads thrown back, searching the trees for birds.

For a time it seemed they would not notice Garrick in the hedge; but then, when they had almost passed, Ronny turned his head and saw him. They stared at each other, ten paces apart, Garrick crouched against the hedge and Ronny's expression of surprise slowly changing to one of cunning. He looked around quickly, to make sure that Sean was not there.

'It's old Hobble-dee-hoy,' he announced and his friends came back and stood on each side of him.

'What're you doing, Peg-leg?'

'Rats got your tongue, Peg-leg?'

'No, termites got his leg!' – laughter aimed to hurt.

'Talk to us, Peg-leg.' Ronny Pye had ears that stood out on each side of his head like a pair of fans. He was small for his age which made him vicious and his hair was ginger.

'Come on. Talk to us, Peg-leg.'

Garrick moistened his lips with his tongue, already there were tears in his eyes.

'Hey, Ronny, make him walk for us, like this.' One of the others gave a graphic imitation of Garrick's limp. Again laughter, louder now, more confident and they closed in on him. 'Show us how you walk.'

Garrick swung his head from side to side searching for an escape.

'Your brother's not here,' crowed Ronny. 'No good looking for him, Peg-leg.'

He caught a hold of Garrick's shirt and pulled him out of the hedge.

'Show us how you walk.'

Garrick plucked ineffectually at Ronny's hand.

'Leave me, I'll tell Sean. I'll tell Sean unless you leave me.'

'All right, I'll leave you,' agreed Ronny and with both hands shoved him in the chest. 'Don't come my way – go that way!' Garrick stumbled backwards.

One of the others was ready for him. 'Don't come my way – go that way!' and pushed him in the back. They formed a ring around him and kept him staggering between them.

'Go that way!'

'Go that way!'

The tears were streaked down his cheeks now. 'Please, please stop.'

'Please, please,' they mimicked him.

Then, with a rush of relief, Garrick felt the fluttering start behind his eyes – their faces dimmed, he hardly felt their hands upon him. He fell and his face hit the ground, but there was no pain. Two of them stooped over him to lift him, and there was dirt mixed with the tears on his cheeks.

Sean came through the hedge behind them; the front of his shirt bulged with peaches.

For a second he crouched on his hands and knees while he took in what was happening, then he came out of his crouch at a run. Ronny heard him, dropped Garrick and turned.

'You've been pinching Pa's peaches,' he shouted. 'I'll tell –'

Sean's fist hit him on the nose and he sat down. Sean swung towards the other two but they were already running, he chased them a few paces and then came back for Ronny, but he was too late. Ronny was dodging away between the trees holding his face and his nose was bleeding onto his shirt.

'Are you all right, Garry?' Sean knelt beside him, trying to wipe the dirt off his face with a grubby handkerchief. Sean helped him to his feet, and Garrick stood swaying slightly with his eyes open but a remote and vacant smile on his lips.

There were landmarks along the course of the river. Some of them small as a pile of rocks in shallow water:

Waite Courtney looked at Sean across the breakfast table at Theunis Kraal. The fork-load of egg and grilled gammon stopped on the way to his mouth.

'Turn your face towards the window,' he commanded suspiciously. Sean obeyed. 'What the hell is that on your face?'

'What?' Sean ran his hand over his cheek.

'When did you last bath?'

'Don't be silly, my dear.' Ada touched his leg under the table. 'It isn't dirt – it's whiskers.'

'Whiskers, are they?' Waite peered closely at Sean and started to grin, he opened his mouth to speak and Ada knew instantly that he was going to make a joke – one of those ponderous jokes of his, as subtle as an enraged dinosaur, that would wound Sean deep in his half-formed manhood. Quickly she cut in, 'I think you should buy him a razor, don't you, Waite?'

Waite lost the thread of his joke, he grunted and put the egg into his mouth.

'I don't want to cut them,' said Sean and flushed scarlet.

'They'll grow quicker if you shave them a bit at first,' Ada told him.

Across the table from her Garrick fingered his jowls wistfully.

Some of the landmarks were big as headlands:

Waite fetched them from school at the beginning of the December holidays. In the confusion of loading their cases onto the buggy and shouting farewells to Fräulein and to their friends, some of whom they would not see for another six weeks, the twins did not notice that Waite was acting strangely.

It was only later when the horses were heading for home at twice their normal speed that Sean asked, 'What's the hurry, Pa?'

'You'll see,' said Waite, and both Garrick and Sean looked at him with sudden interest. It had been an idle question of Sean's but Waite's answer had them immediately intrigued. Waite grinned at the bombardment of questions but he kept his answers vague. He was enjoying himself. By the time they reached Theunis Kraal the twins were in a frenzy of curiosity.

Waite pulled the horses up in front of the house and one of the grooms ran to take the reins. Ada was waiting on the veranda and Sean jumped down and ran up the steps to her. He kissed her quickly. 'What's happening?' he pleaded. 'Pa won't tell us but we know it's something.'

Garrick hurried up the steps also. 'Go on, tell us.' He caught hold of her arm and tugged it.

'I don't know what you're talking about,' Ada laughed. 'You'd better ask your father again.'

Waite climbed up after them, put one arm around Ada's waist and squeezed her.

'I don't know where they got this idea from,' said Waite, 'but why not tell them to go and have a look in their bedroom? They might as well have their Christmas presents a bit earlier this year.'

Sean beat Garrick to the lounge and was far in the lead by the time he reached the door of their bedroom.

'Wait for me,' called Garrick desperately. 'Please wait for me.'

Sean stopped in the doorway.

'Jesus Christ,' he whispered – they were the strongest words he knew. Garrick came up behind him and together they stared at the pair of leather cases that lay on the table in the middle of the room – long flat cases, heavy polished leather with the corners bound in brass.

'Rifles!' said Sean. He walked slowly to the table as though he were stalking the cases, expecting them at any moment to vanish.

'Look!' Sean reached out to touch with one finger the gold lettering stamped into the lid of the nearest case. 'Our names on them even.'

He sprung the locks and lifted the lid. In a nest of green baize, perfumed with gun oil, glistened a poem in steel and wood.

'Jesus Christ,' said Sean again. Then he looked over his shoulder at Garrick. 'Aren't you going to open yours?'

Garrick limped up to the table trying to hide his disappointment: he had wanted a set of Dickens so badly.

In the river there were whirlpools:

The last week of the Christmas holidays and Garrick was in bed with one of his colds. Waite Courtney had gone to Pietermaritzburg for a meeting of the Beef Growers' Association and there was very little work to do on the farm that day. After Sean had dosed the sick cattle in the sanatorium paddock and ridden an inspection around the south section he returned to the homestead and spent an hour talking to the stableboys, then he drifted up to the house. Garry was asleep and Ada was in the dairy making butter. He asked for and got an early lunch from Joseph and ate it standing in the kitchen. While he ate he thought over the problem of how to fill the afternoon. He weighed the alternatives carefully. Take the rifle and try for duiker along the edge of the escarpment or ride to the pools above the White Falls and fish for eels. He was still undecided after he had finished eating so he crossed the yard and looked into the cool dimness of the dairy.

Ada smiled at him across the churn. 'Hello, Sean, I suppose you want your lunch.'

'Joseph gave it to me already, thanks, Ma.'

'Joseph has already given it to me,' Ada corrected mildly. Sean repeated it after her and sniffed the dairy smell – he liked the cheesy warmth of new butter and the tang of the cow dung smeared on the earth floor.

'What are you going to do this afternoon?'

'I came to ask you if you wanted venison or eels – I don't know if I want to go fishing or shooting.'

'Eels would be nice – we could jelly them and have them for dinner tomorrow when your father comes home.'

'I'll get you a bucket full.'

He saddled the pony, hung his tin of worms on the saddle and with his pole over his shoulder rode towards Ladyburg. He crossed the Baboon Stroom bridge and turned off the road to follow the stream up to the falls. As he skirted the wattle plantation below the Van Essens' place he realized he had made a mistake in picking this route. Anna, with her skirts held up to her knees, came pelting out from among the trees. Sean kicked the pony into a trot and looked straight ahead.

'Sean – hey, Sean.'

She was ahead of him, running to intercept him; there was no chance of evading her so he stopped the pony.

'Hello, Sean.' She was panting and her face was flushed.

'Hello,' he gruffed.

'Where are you going?'

'There and back to see how far it is.'

'You're going fishing – may I come with you?' She smiled appealingly. Her teeth were small and white.

'No, you talk too much; you'll frighten the fish.'

He started the pony.

'Please, I'll be quiet; honest I will.' She was running next to him.

'No.' He flicked the reins and pulled away from her. He rode for a hundred yards then looked round and she was still following with her black hair streaming out behind her. He stopped the pony and she caught up with him.

'I knew you'd stop,' she told him through her gasps.

'Will you go home? I don't want you following me.'

'I'll be quiet as anything – honest I will.'

He knew she'd follow him right up to the top of the escarpment and he gave in. 'All right, but if you say a word, just one single word, I'll send you home.'

'I promise – help me up, please.'

He dragged her onto the pony's rump and she sat sideways with her arms round his waist. They climbed the escarpment. The path ran close beside the White Falls and they could feel the spray blowing off them fine as mist. Anna kept her promise until she was sure they'd gone too far for Sean to send her back alone. She started talking again. When she wanted an answer from him, which wasn't very often, she squeezed his waist and Sean grunted. Sean knee-haltered the pony, and left him among the trees above the pools. He hid his saddle and bridle in an ant-bear hole and they walked down through the reeds to the water. Anna ran ahead of him and when he came out on to the sandbank she was throwing pebbles into the pool.

'Hey, stop that! You'll frighten the fish,' Sean shouted.

'Oh. I'm sorry. I forgot.'

She sat down and wriggled her bare toes into the sand. Sean baited his hook and lobbed it out into the green water – the current drifted his float in a wide circle under the far bank and they both watched it solemnly.

'It doesn't seem as though there are any fish here,' Anna said.

'You've got to be patient – you can't expect to catch one right away.'

Anna drew patterns in the sand with her toes and five minutes passed slowly. 'Sean –'

'Ssh!'

Another five minutes.

'Fishing's a silly old thing.'

'Nobody asked you to come,' Sean told her.

'It's hot here!' Sean didn't answer

The high reed beds shut out any breeze and the white sand threw the sun's heat back at them. Anna stood up and wandered restlessly across the sand to the edge of the reeds. She picked a handful of the long spear-shaped leaves and plaited them together.

'I'm bored,' she announced.

'Well, go home then.'

'And I'm hot.'

Sean pulled his line in, inspected the worms and cast them out again. Anna stuck her tongue out at his back.

'Let's have a swim,' she suggested.

Sean ignored her. He stuck the butt of his rod into the sand, pulled his hat down to shield his eyes from the glare and leaned back on his elbows with his legs stretched out in front of him. He could hear the sand crunching as she moved and then there was another silence. He started to worry what she was doing, but if he looked around it would be a show of weakness.

'Girls!' he thought bitterly.

There was the sound of running feet just behind him. He sat up quickly and started to turn. Her white body flashed past him and hit the water, with a smack like a rising trout. Sean jumped up. 'Hey, what're you doing?'

'I'm swimming,' laughed Anna, waist-deep in green water, with her hair slicked wetly down her shoulders and over her breasts. Sean looked at those breasts, white as the flesh of an apple and nippled in dark pink, almost red. Anna dropped onto her back and kicked the water white.

'*Voet sak,* little fishes! Scat, little fishes,' she gurgled.

'Hey, you mustn't do that,' Sean said half-heartedly. He wanted her to stand up again, those breasts gave him a strange tight feeling in his stomach, but Anna knelt with the water up to her chin. He could see them through the water. He wanted her to stand up.

'It's lovely! Why don't you come in?' She rolled on her stomach and ducked her head under the water; the twin ovals of her bottom broke the surface and Sean's stomach tightened again.

'Are you coming in?' she demanded, rubbing the water out of her eyes with both hands. Sean stood bewildered – within a few seconds his feelings towards her had undergone a major revolution. He wanted very much to be in the water with all those mysterious white bulges – but he was shy.

'You're scared! Come on, I give you guts to come in.' She teased him. The challenge pricked him.

'I'm not scared.'

'Well, come on then.'

He hesitated a few seconds longer, then he threw off his hat and unbuttoned his shirt. He turned his back on her while he dropped his pants then spun round and dived into the pool, thankful for the cover it gave him. His head came out and Anna pushed it under again. He groped and caught her legs, straightened up and threw her on her back. He dragged her towards the shallows, where the water wouldn't cover her. She was thrashing her arms to keep her head out and screaming delightedly. Sean's heels snagged a rock and he fell, letting go of her; before he could recover she had leapt on him and straddled his back. He could have thrown her off, but he liked the feel of her flesh on his – warm through the cool water, slippery with wetness. She picked up a handful of sand and rubbed it into his hair. Sean struggled gently. She threw her arms round his neck and he could feel the whole length of her body along his back. The tightness in his stomach moved up into his chest and he wanted to hold her. He rolled over and reached for her but she twisted out of his hands and dived back into the deep again. Sean splashed after her but she kept out of his reach, laughing at him.

At last they faced each other, still chin deep, and Sean was getting angry. He wanted to hold her. She saw the change of his mood and she waded to the bank, walked to his clothes and picked up his shirt. She dried her face on it, standing naked and unashamed – she had too many brothers for modesty. Sean watched the way her breasts changed shape as she lifted her arms, he looked at the lines of her body and saw that her once skinny legs had filled out; her thighs touched each other all the way up to the base of her belly and there she wore the dark triangular badge of womanhood. She spread the shirt out on the sand and sat down upon it, then she looked at him.

'Are you coming out?'

He came out awkwardly, covering himself with his hands. Anna moved over on the shirt. 'You can sit down, if you like.'

He sat hurriedly and drew his knees up under his chin. He watched her from the corner of his eye. There were little goose-pimples round her nipples from the cold water. She was aware that he was watching her and she pulled back her shoulders, enjoying it. Sean felt bewildered again – she was so clearly in control now. Before she had been someone to growl at but now she was giving the orders and he was obeying.

'You've got hairs on your chest,' Anna said, turning to look at him. Sparse and silky though they were, Sean was glad that he had them. He straightened out his legs.

'And you're much bigger there than Frikkie.' Sean tried to pull up his knees again but she put her hand on his leg and stopped him.

'Can I touch you?'

Sean tried to speak but his throat had closed and no sound came through it. Anna did not wait for an answer.

'Oh, look! It's getting all cheeky – just like Caribou's.'

Caribou was Mr Van Essen's stallion.

'I always know when Pa is going to let Caribou service a mare, he tells me to go and visit Aunt Lettie. I just hide in the plantation. You can see the paddock jolly well from the plantation.'

Anna's hand was soft and restless, Sean could think of nothing else.

'Do you know that people service, just like horses do?' she asked.

Sean nodded, he had attended the biology classes conducted by Messrs Daffel and Company in the school latrines. They were quiet for a while, then Anna whispered.

'Sean, would you service me?'

'I don't know how,' croaked Sean.

'I bet horses don't either the first time, nor people for that matter,' Anna said. 'We could find out.'

They rode home in the early evening, Anna sitting up behind Sean, her arms tight round his waist and the side of her face pressed between his shoulders. He dropped her at the back of the plantation.

'I'll see you at school on Monday,' she said and turned to go.

'Anna –'

'Yes?'

'Is it still sore?'

'No,' and then, after a moment's thought, 'it feels nice.'

She turned and ran into the wattle trees.

Sean rode slowly home. He was empty inside; it was a sad feeling and it puzzled him.

'Where are the fish?' asked Ada.

'They weren't biting.'

'Not even one?'

Sean shook his head and crossed the kitchen.

'Sean.'

'Yes, Ma.'

'Is something wrong?'

'No' – quick denial – 'No, I'm fine.' He slipped into the passage.

Garrick was sitting up in bed. The skin around his nostrils was inflamed and chapped; he lowered the book he was reading and smiled at Sean as he came into the room. Sean went to his own bed and sat on it.

'Where have you been?' Garrick's voice was thick with cold.

'Up at the pools above the falls.'

'Fishing?'

Sean didn't answer, he leaned forward on the bed with his elbows on his knees. 'I met Anna, she came with me.'

Garrick's interest quickened at the mention of her name and he watched Sean's face. Sean still had that slightly puzzled expression.

'Garry,' he hesitated; he had to talk about it. 'Garry, I screwed Anna.'

Garrick drew in his breath with a small hiss. He went very pale, only his nose was still red and sore-looking.

'I mean,' Sean spoke slowly as though he were trying to explain it to himself, 'I mean really screwed her, just like we've talked about. Just like. . . .' He made a helpless gesture with his hands, unable to find the words. Then he lay back on the bed.

'Did she let you?' Garrick's voice was almost a whisper.

'She asked me to,' Sean said. 'It was slippery – sort of warm and slippery.'

And then later, long after the lamp was out and they were both in bed, Sean heard Garrick's soft movements in the darkness. He listened for a while until he was certain.

'Garry!' He accused him loudly.

'I wasn't, I wasn't.'

'You know what Pa told us. Your teeth will fall out and you'll go mad.'

'I wasn't, I wasn't.' Garrick's voice was choked with his cold and his tears.

'I heard you,' said Sean.

'I was just scratching my leg. Honestly, honestly, I was.'

And at the end the river plunged over the last waterfall and swept them into the sea of manhood.

Mr Clark had not been able to break Sean. He had provoked instead a bitter contest in which he knew himself to be slowly losing ground, and now he was afraid of Sean. He no longer made Sean stand, for Sean was as tall as he was. The contest had been on for two years; they had explored each other's weaknesses and knew how to exploit them.

Mr Clark could not bear the sound of anyone sniffing; perhaps subconsciously he took it as mockery of his own deformed nose. Sean had a repertoire that varied from a barely audible connoisseur testing-the-bouquet-of-brandy sniff to a loud hawking in the back of his throat.

'Sorry, sir, I can't help it. I've got a bit of a cold.'

But then, to even the score, Mr Clark had realized that Sean was vulnerable through Garrick. Hurt Garrick even a little and you were inflicting almost unbearable agony on Sean.

It had been a bad week for Mr Clark. His liver, weakened by persistent bouts of malaria, had been troubling him. He bad suffered with a bilious headache for three days now; there had been unpleasantness with the Town Council about the terms on which his contract was to be renewed; Sean had been in good sniffing form the day before and Mr Clark had had about as much as he was prepared to take.

He came into the schoolroom and took his place on the dais; he let his eyes move slowly over his pupils until they came to Sean.

'Just let him start,' thought Mr Clark. 'Just let him start today and I'll kill him.'

The seating had been rearranged in the last two years. Sean and Garrick had been separated and Garrick was now at the front of the room where Mr Clark could reach him easily. Sean was near the back.

'English Readers,' said Mr Clark. 'Standard Ones turn to page five. Standard Twos turn to –'

Garrick sniffed wetly, hayfever again.

Mr Clark shut his book with a snap.

'Damn you!' he said softly, and then, his voice rising, 'Damn you!' Now he was shaking with rage, the edges of his nostrils were white and flared open.

He came down from the dais to Garrick's desk. 'Damn you! Damn you – you bloody little cripple,' he screamed and hit Garrick across the face with his open hand. Garrick cupped both hands over his cheek and stared at him.

'You dirty little swine,' Mr Clark mouthed at him. 'Now you're starting it too.'

He caught a handful of Garrick's hair and pulled his head down so that his forehead hit the top of the desk. 'I'll teach you. By God, I'll teach you.'

'I'll show you.' Bump.

'I'll teach you.' Bump.

It took Sean that long to reach them. He grabbed Mr Clark's arm and pulled him backwards. 'Leave him alone! He didn't do anything!'

Mr Clark saw Sean's face in front of him – he was passed all reason – the face that had tormented him for two long years. He bunched his fist and lashed out at it.

Sean staggered back from the blow, the sting of it made his eyes water. For a second he lay sprawled across one of the desks, watching Clark and then he growled.

The sound sobered Clark, he backed away but only two paces before Sean was on him. Hitting with both hands, grunting with each punch, Sean drove him against the blackboard. Clark tried to break away but Sean caught the collar of his shirt and dragged him back – the collar tore half loose in his hand and Sean hit him again. Clark slid down the wall until he was sitting against it and Sean stood panting over him.

'Get out,' said Clark. His teeth were stained pink by the blood in his mouth and a little of it spilled out onto his lips. His collar stood up at a jaunty angle under one ear.

There was no sound in the room except Sean's breathing.

'Get out,' said Clark again and the anger drained out of Sean leaving him trembling with reaction. He walked to the door.

'You too,' Clark pointed at Garrick. 'Get out and don't come back!'

'Come on, Garry,' said Sean.

Garrick stood up from his desk and limped across to Sean and together they went out into the school yard.

'What are we going to do now?' There was a big red lump on Garrick's forehead.

'I suppose we'd better go home.'

'What about our things?' asked Garrick.

'We can't carry all that – we'll have to send for them later. Come on.'

They walked out through the town and along the road to the farm. They had almost reached the bridge on the Baboon Stroom before either of them spoke again.

'What do you reckon Pa will do?' asked Garrick. He was only putting into words the problem that had occupied them both since they left the school.

'Well, whatever he does, it was worth it.' Sean grinned. 'Did you see me clobber him, hey? Smackeroo – right in the chops.'

'You shouldn't have done it, Sean. Pa's going to kill us. Me too and I didn't do anything.'

'You sniffed,' Sean reminded him.

They reached the bridge and leaned over the parapet side by side to watch the water.

'How's your leg?' asked Sean.

'It's sore – I think we should rest a bit.'

'All right, if you say so,' Sean agreed.

There was a long silence, then, 'I wish you hadn't done it, Sean.'

'Well, wishing isn't going to help. Old Nose-Holes is as punched up as he'll ever be and all we can do is think of something to tell Pa.'

'He hit me,' said Garrick. 'He might have killed me.'

'Yes,' agreed Sean righteously, 'and he hit me too.'

They thought about it for a while.

'Perhaps we should just go away,' suggested Garrick.

'You mean without telling Pa?' The idea had attraction.

'Yeah, we could go to sea or something,' Garrick brightened.

'You'd get seasick, you even get sick in a train.'

Once more they applied their minds to the problem. Then Sean looked at Garrick, Garrick looked at Sean and as though by agreement they straightened up and started off once more for Theunis Kraal.

Ada was in front of the house. She had on a wide-brimmed straw hat that kept her face in shadow and over one arm she carried a basket of flowers. Busy with her garden, she didn't notice them until they were halfway across the lawn and when she did she stood motionless. She was steeling herself, trying to get her emotions under control; from experience she had learned to expect the worst from her stepsons and be thankful when it wasn't as bad as that.

As they came towards her they lost momentum and finally halted like a pair of clockwork toys running down.

'Hello,' said Ada.

'Hello,' they answered her together.

Garrick fumbled in his pocket, drew out a handkerchief and blew his nose. Sean stared up at the steep Dutch-gabled roof of Theunis Kraal as though he had never seen it before.

'Yes?' Ada kept her voice calm.

'Mr Clark said we were to go home,' announced Garrick.

'Why?' Ada's calm was starting to crack.

'Well –' Garrick glanced at Sean for support. Sean's attention was still riveted on the roof.

'Well . . . You see Sean sort of punched him in the head until he fell down. I didn't do anything.'

Ada moaned softly, 'Oh, no!' She took a deep breath. 'All right. Start at the beginning and give me the whole story.'

They told it in relays, a garbled rush of words, interrupting each other and arguing over the details. When they had finished Ada said, 'You better go to your room. Your father is working in the home section today and he'll be back for his lunch soon. I'll try and prepare him a little.'

The room had the cheery atmosphere of a condemned cell.

'How much do you reckon he'll give us?' asked Garrick.

'I reckon until he gets tired, then he'll rest and give us some more,' Sean answered.

They heard Waite's horse come into the yard. He said something to the stable boy and they heard him laugh; the kitchen door slammed and there was half a minute of suspense before they heard Waite roar. Garrick jumped nervously.

For another ten minutes they could hear Waite and Ada talking in the kitchen, the alternate rumble and soothing murmur. Then the tap of Ada's feet along the passage and she came into the room.

'Your father wants to see you – he's in the study.'

Waite stood in front of the fireplace. His beard was powdered with dust and his forehead as corrugated as a ploughed land with the force of his scowl.

'Come in,' he bellowed when Sean knocked and they filed in and stood in front of him. Waite slapped his riding-whip against his leg and the dust puffed out of his breeches.

'Come here,' he said to Garrick and took a handful of his hair. He twisted Garrick's face up and looked at the bruise on his forehead.

'Hmm,' he said. He let go of Garrick's hair and it stood up in a tuft. He threw the riding-whip on the stinkwood desk.

'Come here,' he said to Sean. 'Hold out your hands – no, palms down.'

The skin on both hands was broken and one knuckle was swollen and puffy looking.

'Hmm,' he said again. He turned to the shelf beside the fireplace, took a pipe out of the rack and filled it from the stone jar of tobacco.

'You're a pair of bloody fools,' he said, 'but I'll take a chance and start you on five shillings a week all found. Go and get your lunch . . . we've got work to do this afternoon.'

They stared at him a moment in disbelief and then back towards the door.

'Sean.' Sean stopped, he knew it was too good to be true. 'Where did you hit him?'

'All over, Pa, anywhere I could reach.'

'That's no good,' Waite said. 'You must go for the side of his head – here,' he tapped the point of his jaw with his pipe, 'and keep your fists closed tight or you'll break every finger in your hands before you're much older.'

'Yes, Pa.'

The door closed softly behind him and Waite allowed himself to grin.

'They've had enough book learning anyway,' he said aloud and struck a match to his pipe; when it was drawing evenly he blew out smoke.

'Christ, I wish I could have watched it. That little pen-pusher will know better than to tangle with my boy again.'

= 12 =

Now Sean had a course along which to race. He was born to run and Waite Courtney led him out of the stall in which he had fretted and gave him his lead. Sean ran, unsure of the prize, unsure of the distance; yet he ran with joy, he ran with all his strength.

Before dawn, standing with his father and Garrick in the kitchen, drinking coffee with hands cupped around the mug, Sean felt excitement for each coming day.

'Sean, take Zama and N'duti with you and make sure there are no strays in the thick stuff along the river.'

'I'll only take one herdboy, Pa, you'll need N'duti at the dipping tank.'

'All right, then. Try and meet us back at the tank before midday, we've got to push through a thousand head today.'

Sean gulped the remains of his coffee and buttoned his jacket. 'I'll get going then.'

A groom held his horse at the kitchen door. Sean slid his rifle into the scabbard and went up into the saddle without putting his foot into the steel; he lifted a hand and grinned at Waite, then he swung the horse and rode across the yard. The morning was still dark and cold. Waite watched him from the doorway.

'So goddamned sure of himself,' thought Waite. Yet he had the son he had hoped for and he was proud.

'What you want me to do, Pa?' Garrick asked beside him.

'Well, there are those heifers in the sick paddock –'

Waite stopped. 'No. You'd better come with me, Garry.'

Sean worked in the early morning when the sunlight was tinted as a stage effect, all golden and gay, and the shadows were long and black. He worked in the midday sun and sweated in the heat; in the rain; in the mist that swirled down grey and damp from the plateau; in the short African twilight, and came home in the dark. He loved every minute of it.

He learned to know cattle. Not by name, for only the trek oxen were named, but by their size and colour and markings, so that by running his eye over one of the herds he knew which animals were missing.

'Zama, the old cow with the crooked horn. Where is she?'

'Nkosi,' no longer the diminutive Nkosizana – little lord.

'Nkosi, yesterday I took her to the sick paddock, she has the worm in her eye.'

He learned to recognize disease almost before it started. The way a beast moved and held its head. He learned the treatment for them. Screw worm – kerosene poured into the wound until the maggots fell out like a shower of rice. Ophthalmia – rinse the eye with permanganate. Anthrax and quarter-evil – a bullet and a bonfire for the carcass.

He delivered his first calf among the acacia trees on the bank of the Tugela; he did it alone with his sleeves rolled up above the elbows and the soapy feel of the slime on his hands. Afterwards, while the mother licked it and it staggered at each stroke of the tongue, Sean felt a choking sensation in his throat.

All this was not enough to burn up his energy. He played while he worked.

Practising his horsemanship: swinging from the saddle and running beside his horse, up again and over the other side, standing on the saddle at full gallop and then opening his legs and smacking down on his backside – his feet finding the stirrups without groping.

Practising with his rifle until he could hit a running jackal at a hundred and fifty paces, cutting the fox-terrier-sized body in half with the heavy bullet.

Then there was much of Garrick's work to do also.

'I don't feel very well, Sean.'

'What's, wrong?'

'My leg's sore, you know how it chafes if I ride too much.'

'Why don't you go home, then?'

'Pa says I've got to fix the fence round the Number Three dip tank.' Garrick leaned forward on his horse to rub his leg, giving a brave little smile.

'You fixed it last week,' Sean protested.

'Yes – but the wires sort of came loose again.' There was always a strange impermanency about any repairs that Garrick effected.

'Have you got the wire cutters?' and Garrick produced them with alacrity from his saddle bag.

'I'll do it,' said Sean.

'Hell, man, thanks a lot,' and then a second's hesitation. 'You won't tell Pa, will you?'

'No – you can't help it if your leg's sore,' and Garrick rode home, sneaked through to his bedroom and escaped with Jim Hawkins into the pages of *Treasure Island*.

From this work came a new emotion for Sean. When the rain brought the grass out in green and filled the shallow pans on the plateau with water it was no longer simply a sign that the birdnesting season had begun and that the fishing in the Baboon Stroom would improve – now it meant that they could take cattle up from the valley, it meant that there would be fat on the herds they drove into the sale pens at Ladyburg, it meant that another winter had ended and again the land was rich with life and the promise of life. This new emotion extended to the cattle also. It was a strong, almost savage feeling of possession,

It was in the late afternoon. Sean was sitting on his horse among trees, looking out across open vleiland at the small herd that was strung out before him. They were feeding, heads down, tails flicking lazily. Between Sean and the main body of cattle was a calf – it was three days old, still pale-beige in colour and unsure of its legs. It was trying them out, running clumsy circles in the short grass. From the herd a cow lowed and the calf stopped dead and stood with its legs splayed awkwardly under it and its ears up. Sean grinned and picked up the reins from his horse's neck; it was time to start back for the homestead.

At that moment he saw the lammergeyer: it had already begun its stoop at the calf, dropping big and dark brown from the sky, wings cocked back and its talons reaching for the strike. The wind rustled against it with the speed of its dive.

Sean sat paralysed and watched. The eagle hit the calf and Sean heard bone break, sharp as the snap of a dry stick, and then the calf was down in the grass struggling feebly with the eagle crouched on top of it.

For a second longer Sean sat, dazed with the speed at which it had happened. Then hatred came on him. It came with a violence that twisted his stomach. He hit his horse with his heels and it jumped forward. He drove it at the eagle and as he rode he screamed at it, a high-pitched formless sound, an animal expression of hate.

The eagle turned its head, looking at him sideways with one eye. It opened its great yellow beak and answered his scream, then it loosed its claws from the calf and launched itself into the air. Its wings flogged heavily and it moved low along the ground, gaining speed, lifting, drawing away from Sean.

Sean pulled his rifle from the scabbard and hauled his horse back onto its haunches. He threw himself out of the saddle and levered open the breech of the rifle.

The eagle was fifty yards ahead of him rising fast now. Sean slipped a cartridge into the breech, closed it and brought the rifle up in one continuous movement.

It was a difficult shot. Moving away from him and rising, the beat of its wings jerking its body. Sean fired. The rifle jumped back into his shoulder and the gunsmoke whipped away on the wind, so he could watch the bullet connect.

The eagle collapsed in the air. It burst like a pillow in a puff of feathers and fell with its six-feet-long wings fluttering limply. Before it hit the ground Sean was running.

It was dead when he reached it, but he reversed his rifle: holding it by the muzzle, he swung the butt down from above his head onto its body. At the third blow the butt of his rifle broke off, but he kept on hitting. He was sobbing with fury.

When he stopped and stood panting the sweat was running down his face and his body was trembling. The eagle was a squashy mess of broken flesh and feathers.

The calf was still alive. The rifle was jammed. Sean knelt beside it with tears of anger burning his eyes and killed it with his hunting-knife.

13

So strong was this new feeling that Sean could hate even Garrick. He did not hate for long, though. Sean's anger and his hatred were quick things, with flames like those of a fire in dry grass: hot and high but soon burnt out and afterwards the ashes dead with no smouldering.

Waite was away when it happened. For three consecutive years Waite Courtney had been nominated for the chairmanship of the Beef Growers' Association and each time he had stood down. He was human enough to want the prestige the office carried with it, but he was also sensible to the fact that his farm would suffer from his frequent absences. Sean and Garrick had been working for two years when the annual election of office bearers came around again.

The night before Waite left for the meeting in Pietermaritzburg he spoke to Ada. 'I had a letter from Bernard last week, my dear,' he was standing before the mirror in their bedroom trimming his beard. 'They insist that I stand for the chair this year.'

'Very wise of them,' said Ada. 'They'd have the best man if you did.'

Waite frowned with concentration as he snipped at his whiskers. She believed so unquestioningly in him that he seldom doubted himself. Now looking at his face in the mirror he wondered how much of his success was owed to Ada's backing.

'You can do it, Waite.' Not a challenge, not a question, but a calm statement of fact. When she said it he believed it.

He laid the scissors down on the chest of drawers and turned to her. She sat cross-legged on the bed in a white nightgown, her hair was down in a dark mass around her shoulders. 'I think Sean can look after things here,' she said, and then quickly, 'and of course Garry.'

'Sean's learning fast,' Waite agreed.

'Are you going to take the job?'

Waite hesitated. 'Yes,' he nodded and Ada smiled.

'Come here,' she held out her hands to him.

Sean drove Waite and Ada to the station at Ladyburg: at the last minute Waite had insisted that she go with him, for he wanted her to be there to share it with him.

Sean put their luggage into the coach and waited while they talked with the small group of cattlemen who were going up to the meeting. The whistle blew and the travellers scattered to their compartments. Ada kissed Sean and climbed up. Waite stayed a second longer on the platform.

'Sean, if you need any help go across to Mr Erasmus at Lion Kop. I'll be back on Thursday.'

'I won't need any help, Pa.'

Waite's mouth hardened. 'Then you must be God, he's the only one who never needs help,' Waite said harshly. 'Don't be a bloody fool – if you run into trouble ask Erasmus.'

He climbed up after Ada. The train jerked, gathered speed and ran out towards the escarpment. Sean watched it dwindle, then he walked back to the buggy. He was master of Theunis Kraal and he liked the feeling. The small crowd on the platform was dispersing and out of it came Anna.

'Hello, Sean.' She had on a green cotton dress that was faded with washing, her feet were bare. She smiled with her small white teeth and watched his face.

'Hello, Anna.'

'Aren't you going up to Pietermaritzburg?'

'No, I've got to look after the farm.'

'Oh!'

They waited in silence, uncomfortable before so many people. Sean coughed and scratched the side of his nose.

'Anna, come on. We've got to get home.' One of her brothers called from in front of the ticket office and Anna leaned towards Sean.

'Will I see you on Sunday?' she whispered.

'I'll come if I can. But I don't know – I've got to look after the farm.'

'Please try, Sean.' Her face was earnest. 'I'll be waiting for you, I'll take some lunch and wait all day. Please come, even if it's only for a little while.'

'All right, I'll come.'

'Promise?'

'Promise.'

She smiled with relief. 'I'll wait for you on the path above the waterfall.'

She turned and ran to join her family and Sean drove back to Theunis Kraal. Garrick was lying on his bed reading.

'I thought Pa told you to get on with the branding of those new cattle we bought on Wednesday.'

Garrick laid down his book and sat up. 'I told Zama to keep them in the kraal until you got back.'

'Pa told you to get on with it. You can't keep them there all day without feed or water.'

'I hate branding,' muttered Garrick. 'I hate it when they moo like that as you burn them, and I hate the stink of burning hair and skin – it gives me a headache.'

'Well someone's got to do it. I can't, I've got to go down and mix new dip into the tanks for tomorrow.' Sean was losing his temper. 'Hell, Garry, why are you always so damn helpless?'

'I can't help it, I can't help it if I've only got one leg.' Garrick was close to tears again. The reference to his leg had the desired effect – Sean's temper steadied instantly.

'I'm sorry,' Sean smiled his irresistible smile. 'I tell you what. I'll do the branding – you fix the tanks. Get the drums of dip loaded onto the Scotch cart, take a couple of the stable boys with you to help. Here are the keys of the storeroom.' He tossed the bunch onto the bed beside Garrick. 'You should be finished before dark.'

At the door he turned.

'Garry, don't forget to do all six tanks – not just the ones near the house.'

So Garrick loaded six drums of dip onto the Scotch cart and went off down the hill. He was home well before dark. The front of his breeches was stained with the dark, tarry chemical and some of it had soaked into the leather of his single riding-boot. As he came out of the kitchen into the passage Sean shouted from the study. 'Hey, Garry, did you finish them?'

Garrick was startled. Waite's study was a sacred place, the inner sanctum of Theunis Kraal. Even Ada knocked before going into it and the twins went there only to receive punishment. Garrick limped along the passage and pushed open the door.

Sean sat with his boots on top of the desk and his ankles neatly crossed. He leaned back in the swivel chair.

'Pa will kill you,' Garrick's voice was shaky.

'Pa's in Pietermaritzburg,' said Sean.

Garrick stood in the doorway and looked around the room. It was the first time he had really seen it. On every previous visit he had been too preoccupied with the violence to come and the only item in the room he had studied closely was the seat of the big leather easy chair as he bent over the arm of it and exposed his backside to the sjambok.

Now he looked at the room. The walls were panelled to the ceiling, the wood was dark yellow and polished. The ceiling was fancy plaster, in a pattern of oak leaves. A single lamp hung from the centre of it on a brass chain. You could walk into the fireplace of brown chipped stone and there were logs laid ready for the match.

Pipes and tobacco jar on the ledge beside the fireplace, guns in a rack along one wall, a bookcase of green and maroon leather bound volumes: encyclopaedias, dictionaries, books on travel and farming, but no fiction. There was an oil painting of Ada on the wall opposite the desk, the artist had captured a little of her serenity: she wore a white dress and carried her hat in her hand. A magnificent set of Cape buffalo horns above the fireplace dominated the room with their great crenellated bosses and wide sweep to the tips.

It was a man's room, with loose dog-hairs on the leopard-skin rugs, and the presence of the man strongly there – it even smelled of Waite. It was as distinctively his as the tweed coat and Terai hat that hung behind the door.

Next to where Sean sat the cabinet was open and a bottle of brandy stood on top of it. Sean had a goblet in his hand.

'You're drinking Pa's brandy,' Garrick accused.

'It's not bad.' Sean lifted the glass and inspected the liquid; he took a careful sip and held it in his mouth, preparing himself to swallow. Garrick watched him with awe and Sean tried not to blink as it went down his throat.

'Would you like some?'

Garrick shook his head and the fumes came up Sean's nose and his eyes ran.

'Pa will kill you!' said Garrick again.

'Sit down,' ordered Sean, his voice husky from the brandy. 'I want to work out a plan for the time Pa's away.'

Garrick advanced on the armchair, but before he reached it he changed his mind – the associations were too painful. He went to the sofa instead and sat on the edge.

'Tomorrow,' Sean held up one finger, 'we'll dip all the cattle in the home section. I've told Zama to start bringing them early – you did do the tanks, didn't you?'

Garrick nodded and Sean went on.

'On Saturday,' Sean held up his second finger, 'we'll burn fire breaks along the top of the escarpment. The grass is dry as hell up there. You take one gang and start near the falls, I'll ride down to the other end, near Fredericks Kloof. On Sunday. . .' Sean said and then paused. On Sunday Anna.

'I want to go to church on Sunday,' said Garrick quickly.

'That's fine,' agreed Sean. 'You go to church.'

'Are you going to come?'

'No,' said Sean.

Garrick looked down at the leopard-skin rugs that covered the floor – he didn't try to persuade Sean for Anna would be at the service. Perhaps afterwards, if Sean wasn't there to distract her, he could drive her home in the buggy. He started a day dream and wasn't listening as Sean went on talking.

In the morning it was full daylight by the time Sean reached the dip tank. He pushed a small herd of stragglers before him and they came out through the trees and stirrup high grass into the wide area of trampled earth around the tank. Garrick had started running cattle through the dip and there were about ten head already in the draining kraal at the far end, standing wet and miserable, their bodies dark with dip.

Sean drove his herd through the gates of the entrance kraal into the solid pack of brown bodies that were already there. N'duti slid the bars of the gate back into place to hold them.

'I see you, Nkosi.'

'I see you, N'duti. Plenty of work today!'

'Plenty,' agreed N'duti, 'always plenty of work.'

Sean rode around the kraal and tied his horse beneath one of the trees, then walked across to the tank. Garrick was standing by the parapet and leaning against one of the columns that supported the roof.

'Hello, Garry, how's it going?'

'Fine.'

Sean leaned over the parapet next to Garry. The tank was twenty feet long and eight wide, the surface of the liquid was below ground level. Around the tank was a low wall and over it a roof of thatch to prevent rain diluting the contents.

The herdboys drove the cattle up to the edge and each beast hesitated on the brink.

'E'yapi, E'yapi,' screamed the herdboys and the push of bodies behind it forced it to jump. If one was stubborn, Zama leaned over the railing of the kraal, grabbed its tail and bit it.

Each beast jumped with its nose held high and its forefeet gathered up under its chest; it disappeared completely under the oil black surface and came up again swimming frantically along the tank until its hooves touched the sloping bottom at the far end and it could lumber up into the draining kraal.

'Keep them moving, Zama,' shouted Sean.

Zama grinned at him and bit with big white teeth into a reluctant tail.

The ox was a heavy animal and it splashed a drop up onto Sean's cheek as he leaned over the wall. Sean did not bother to wipe it off, he went on watching.

'Well, if we don't get top prices for this lot at the next sale then the buyers don't know good cattle,' he said to Garry.

'They're all right,' agreed Garry.

'All right? They're the fattest oxen in the district.' Sean was about to enlarge on the theme, but suddenly he was aware of discomfort – the drop of dip was burning his cheek. He wiped it off with his finger and held it to his nose; the smell of it stung his nostrils. For a second he stared at it stupidly and the spot on his cheek burned like fire.

He looked up quickly. The cattle in the draining kraal were milling restlessly and as he looked one of them staggered sideways and bumped against the railing.

'Zama!' shouted Sean, and the Zulu looked up. 'Stop them. For God's sake don't let any more through.'

There was another ox poised on the edge. Sean snatched off his hat and jumped up onto the wall, he beat the ox in the face with his hat trying to drive it back, but it sprang out into the tank. Sean caught hold of the railing and stepped into the space it had left on the edge of the tank.

'Stop them,' he shouted. 'Get the bars in, don't let any more through.'

He spread his arms across the entrance, holding onto the railing on each side, kicking at the faces of the cattle in front of him.

'Hurry, damn you, get the bars in,' he shouted. The oxen pressed towards him, a wall of horned heads. Pushed forward by those behind and held back by Sean they started to panic; one of them tried to jump over the railing. As it swung its head its horn raked Sean's chest, up across the ribs, ripping his shirt.

Behind him Sean felt the wooden bars being dropped into place, blocking the entrance to the tank, and then Zama's hands on his arm pulling him up out of the confusion of horns and hooves. Two of the herdboys helped him over the railing and Sean shrugged their hands off as soon as he was on the ground.

'Come on,' he ordered and ran to his horse.

'Nkosi, you are bleeding.'

Blood had splotched the front of Sean's shirt but he felt no pain. The cattle that had been through the dip were now in terrible distress. They charged about the kraal, bellowing pitifully; one of them fell and when it got to its feet again its legs were shaking so that it could barely stand.

'The river,' shouted Sean, 'get them down to the river. Try and wash it off. Zama, open the gate.'

The Baboon Stroom was a mile away. One of the oxen died before they could get them out of the kraal, another ten before they reached the river. They died in convulsions, with their bodies shuddering and their eyes turned back into their heads.

Sean drove those that remained down the bank into the river. The water was clear and as each beast went into it, the dip washed off in a dark brown cloud.

'Stand here, Zama. Don't let them come out.'

Sean swam his horse to the far bank and turned back the oxen that were trying to climb it.

'Nkosi – one is drowning,' called N'duti and Sean looked across the river. A young ox was in convulsions in the shallows: its head was under water and its feet thrashed the surface.

Sean slid off his horse and waded out to it. The water was up to his armpits. He tried to hold its head out and drag it to the bank.

'Help me, N'duti,' he shouted, and the Zulu came into the river. It was a hopeless task: each time the ox lunged it pulled them both under with it. By the time they got the ox to the bank it was dead.

Sean sat in the mud beside the body of the ox: he was exhausted and his lungs ached with the water he had breathed.

'Bring them out, Zama,' he gasped. The survivors were standing in the shallows or swimming in aimless circles. 'How many?' asked Sean. 'How many are dead?'

'Two more while you were in the water. Altogether thirteen, Nkosi.'

'Where's my horse?'

'It ran, and I let it go. It will be back at the house.'

Sean nodded.

'Bring them up to the sick paddock. We must watch them for a few days.'

Sean stood up and started walking back towards the dip tank. Garrick was gone, and the main herd was still in the kraal. Sean opened the gate and turned them loose. He felt better by then, and as his strength returned with it came his anger and his hatred. He started along the track towards the homestead. His boots squelched as he walked and he hated Garrick more strongly with each step. Garrick had mixed the dip. Garrick had killed his cattle and Sean hated him,

As Sean came up the slope below the house he saw Garrick standing in the yard. Garrick saw him also; he disappeared into the kitchen and Sean started to run. He went in through the kitchen door and nearly knocked down one of the servants,

'Garrick,' shouted Sean. 'Damn it – where are you?'

He searched the house; once quickly and then again thoroughly. Garrick was gone, but the window of their bedroom was open and there was a dusty boot print on the sill. Garrick had gone over it.

'You bloody coward,' howled Sean and scrambled out after him. He stood a second, with his head swinging from side to side and his fists opening and closing.

'I'll find out,' he howled again. 'I'll find you wherever you're hiding.'

He started across the yard towards the stables and halfway there he saw the door of the dairy was closed. When he tried it he found it was locked from inside. Sean backed away from it and then charged it with his shoulder – the lock burst and the door flew open. Sean skidded across the room and came up against the far wall. Garrick was trying to climb out of the window, but it was small and high up. Sean caught him by the seat of his pants and pulled him down.

'Whatcha do to the dip, hey? Whatcha do to it?' He shouted in Garrick's face.

'I didn't mean to. I didn't know it'd kill them.'

'Tell me what you did.' Sean had hold of the front of his shirt and was dragging him towards the door.

'I didn't do anything. Honest I didn't know.'

'I'm going to hammer you anyway, so you might as well tell me.'

'Please, Sean, I didn't know.'

Sean jammed Garrick against the doorway and held him there with his left hand – his right hand he drew back with the fist bunched.

'No, Sean. Please, no.'

And suddenly the anger was gone from Sean, his hands sank back to his sides.

'All right – just tell me what you did,' he said coldly. His anger was gone but not his hatred.

'I was tired and it was getting late and my leg was hurting,' whispered Garrick, 'and there were still four more tanks to do, and I knew you'd check that all the drums were empty, and it was so late . . . and . . .'

'And?'

'And so I emptied all the dip into the one tank . . . but I didn't know it would kill them, truly I didn't.'

Sean turned away from him and started walking slowly back towards the house. Garrick stumbled after him.

'I'm sorry, Sean, honest I'm sorry. I didn't know that. . .'

Sean walked ahead of him into the kitchen and slammed the door in his face. He went through into Waite's study. From the bookshelf he lifted down the heavy leather-covered stock register and carried it to the desk. He opened the book, picked up a pen and dipped it. For a moment he stared at the page and then in the 'deaths' column he wrote the number *13* and after it the words 'dip poisoning'. He pressed down so hard with the pen that the nib cut the paper.

It took Sean and the herdboys all the rest of that day and the next to bale out the tank, refill it with clean water and mix in fresh dip. He saw Garrick only at meals and they didn't speak.

The next day was Sunday. Garrick went into town early, for the church service started at eight o'clock. When he had gone Sean began his preparations. He shaved – leaning close to the mirror and handling the cut-throat gingerly, shaping his side burns and clearing the hair from the rest of his face until his skin was smooth and fresh-looking. Then he went through to the master-bedroom and helped himself to a generous portion of his father's brilliantine, taking care to screw the lid back on the bottle and replace it exactly as he had found it. He rubbed the brilliantine into his hair and sniffed its perfume appreciatively. He combed his hair over his forehead, parted it down the centre and polished it into a gloss with Waite's silver-backed brushes. Then a clean white shirt, breeches worn only once before, boots as shiny as his hair – and Sean was ready.

The clock on the mantelpiece in the lounge assured him that he was well ahead of time. To be exact, he was two hours early. Eight o'clock now: church didn't end until nine and it would be another hour before Anna could escape from under the eyes of her family and reach the rendezvous above the falls. He settled down to wait. He read the latest copy of the *Natal Farmer*. He had read it three times before for it was a month old, and now even the excellent article on 'Stomach parasites in Cattle and Sheep' had lost much of its punch. Sean's attention wandered – he thought about the day ahead and felt the familiar movement within his breeches. This necessitated a rearrangement for the breeches were tight fitting. Then fantasy palled; Sean was a doer not a thinker, and he went through to the kitchen to solicit a cup of coffee from Joseph. When he had finished it, there was still half an hour to go.

'The hell with it,' said Sean and shouted for his horse. He climbed the escarpment, letting his horse move diagonally up the slope and at the top he dismounted and let it blow. Today he could see the course of the Tugela river out across the plain – it was a belt of dark green. He could count the roofs of the houses in Ladyburg and the church spire, copper clad, shone in the sunlight like a beacon fire.

He mounted again and rode along the edge of the plateau until he reached the Baboon Stroom above the falls. He followed it back and forded it at a shallow place, lifting his feet up on the saddle in front of him to keep his boots dry. He off-saddled next to the pools and knee-haltered his horse, then he followed the path until it dropped over the edge of the plateau into the thick forest that surrounded the falls. It was cool and damp in the forest with moss growing on the trees, for the roof of leaves and creepers shut out the sun. There was a bottle-bird in the undergrowth.

'Glug, glug, glug,' it said, like water poured from a bottle, and its call was almost drowned in the ceaseless thunder of the falls.

Sean spread his handkerchief on a rock beside the path, sat down on it and waited.

Within five minutes he was fidgeting impatiently – within half an hour he was grumbling aloud.

'I'll count to five hundred. . . . If she hasn't come by then I'm not going to wait.'

He counted and when he reached the promised figure he stopped and peered anxiously down the path. There was no sign of Anna.

'I'm not going to sit here all day,' he announced and made no effort to stand up. A fat yellow caterpillar caught his eye; it was on the trunk of a tree farther down the slope. He picked up a pebble and threw it. It bounced off the tree an inch above the caterpillar.

'Close,' Sean encouraged himself and stooped for another stone. After a while he had exhausted the supply of pebbles around his feet and the caterpillar was still moving leisurely up the trunk. Sean was forced to go out on a foraging expedition for more pebbles. He came back with both hands full and once more took up his position on the rock. He piled the pebbles between his feet and reopened the bombardment. He aimed each throw with the utmost concentration and with his third pebble he hit squarely and the caterpillar popped in a spurt of green juice. Sean felt cheated. He looked around for a new target and instead found Anna standing beside him.

'Hello, Sean.' She had on a pink dress. She carried her shoes in one hand and a small basket in the other. 'I brought some lunch for us.'

'What took you so long?' Sean stood up and wiped his hands on his breeches. 'I thought you weren't coming.'

'I'm sorry – everything went wrong.'

There was an awkward pause and Anna, flushed slightly as Sean looked at her. Then she turned and started up the path. 'Come on – I'll race you to the top.'

She ran fast on bare feet, holding her skirts up to her knees and she was out in the sunshine before Sean caught her. He put his arms around her from behind and they fell together into the grass beside the path. They lay holding each other, laughing and panting at the same time.

'The service went on and on – I thought it would never finish,' said Anna, 'and afterwards –'

Before she could finish Sean covered her mouth with his and immediately her arms came up around his neck. They kissed with the tension building up steadily between them until Anna was moaning softly and moving her body against his. Sean released her mouth and moved his lips down across her cheek to her neck.

'Oh, Sean, it's been so long. It's been a whole week.'

'I know.'

'I've missed you so – I thought about you every day.'

Sean had his face pressed into her neck, he didn't answer.

'Did you miss me, Sean?'

'Hmm,' Sean murmured and lifted his mouth to take the lobe of her ear between his teeth.

'Did you think about me while you were working?'

'Hmm.'

'Tell me properly, Sean, say it properly.'

'I missed you, Anna, I thought about you all the time,' lied Sean and kissed her on the mouth. She clung to him and Sean's hand went down, right down to her knee and then up again under her clothes. Anna caught his wrist and held his hand away. 'No, Sean, just kiss me.'

Sean waited until her grip relaxed and then tried again, but this time she twisted away from him and sat up. 'Sometimes I think that's all you want to do.'

Sean felt his temper coming up, but he had the good sense to check it.

'That's not true, Anna. It's just that I haven't seen you for so long and I've missed you so much.'

She softened immediately and reached out to touch his cheek. 'Oh, Sean, I'm sorry. I don't mind really, it's just that – oh, I don't know.' She scrambled to her feet and picked up the basket. 'Come on, let's go on to the pools.'

They had a special place. It was walled in by the reeds and shaded by a big tree that grew on the bank above; the sand was washed clean and white. Sean spread his saddle blanket for them to sit on. They could hear the river, close by but hidden, and the reeds rustled and nodded their fluffy heads with each breath of the wind.

'– and I couldn't get rid of him,' Anna chattered as she knelt on the blanket and unpacked the basket. 'He just sat there and every time I said something he blushed and wriggled on his seat. In the end I just told him, "I'm sorry, Garry, I have to go!" '

Sean scowled. The mention of Garrick had reminded him of the dip; he hadn't forgiven him yet.

'And then when I got into the house I found that Pa and Frikkie were fighting. Ma was in tears and the other kids were locked in the bedroom.'

'Who won?' asked Sean with interest.

'They weren't really fighting – they were just shouting at each other. They were both drunk.'

Sean was always slightly shocked at Anna's casual reference to her family's drinking habits. Everybody knew about Mr Van Essen and his two eldest boys but Anna didn't have to talk about it. Once Sean had tried to correct her. 'You shouldn't say things like that about your Pa. You should respect him.'

And Anna had looked at him calmly and asked, 'Why?' which was a difficult question. But now she changed the subject.

'Do you want to eat yet?'

'No,' said Sean and reached for her. She fought back, shrieking demurely until Sean held her down and kissed her. Then she lay quietly, answering his kisses.

'If you stop me now I'm going to get mad,' whispered Sean and deliberately unfastened the top button of her dress. She watched his face with solemn eyes and her hands stayed on his shoulders until he had undone her blouse down to the waist and then with her fingers she traced the bold black curves of his eyebrows.

'No, Sean, I won't stop you. I want to as well, I want to as much as you do.'

There was so much to discover and each thing was strange and wonderful and they were the first to find it. The way the muscles stood out down the side of his chest beneath his arms and yet left a place where she could see the outline of his ribs. The texture of her skin, smooth and white with the faint blue suggestion of veins beneath. The deep hollow down the centre of his back – pressing her fingers into it she could feel his spine. The down on her cheeks, so pale and fine he could see it only in the sunlight. The way their lips felt against each other and the tiny flutter of tongues between. The smell of their bodies, one milky warm and the other musky and vigorous. The hair that covered his chest and grew thicker under his arms, and hers: startlingly dark against white skin, a small silky nest of it. Each time there was something new to find and greet with soft sounds of delight.

Now, kneeling before her as she lay with her head thrown back and her arms half-raised to receive him, Sean suddenly bowed his head and touched her with his mouth. The taste of her was clean as the taste of the sea.

Her eyes flew open. 'Sean, no, you mustn't – oh no, you mustn't.' There were lips within lips and a bud as softly resilient as a tiny green grape. Sean found it with the tip of his tongue.

'Oh, Sean, you can't do that. Please, please, please.' And her hands were in the thick hair at the back of his head holding him there.

'I can't stand it any more, come over me . . . quickly, quickly, Sean.'

Filling like a sail in a hurricane, swollen and hard and tight, stretched beyond its limit until it burst and was blown to shreds in the wind and was gone. Everything gone. The wind and the sail, the tension and the wanting, all gone. There was left only the great nothingness which is peace. Perhaps a kind of death; perhaps death is like that. But, like death, not an ending – for even death contains the seeds of resurrection. So they came back from peace to a new beginning, slowly at first and then faster until they were two people again. Two people on a blanket among reeds with the sunlight white on the sand about them.

'Each time it's better and better – isn't it, Sean?'

'Ah!' Sean stretched, arching his back and spreading his arms.

'Sean, you do love me, don't you?'

'Sure. Sure I love you.'

'I think you must love me to have done' – she hesitated – 'to do what you did.'

'I just said so, didn't I?' Sean's attention wandered to the basket. He selected an apple and polished it on the blanket.

'Tell me properly. Hold me tight and tell me.'

'Hell, Anna, how many times have I got to say it?' Sean bit into the apple. 'Did you bring any of your Ma's shortbread?'

It was coming on night when Sean got back to Theunis Kraal. He turned his horse over to one of the grooms and went into the house. His body tingled from the sun, and he felt the emptiness and sadness of after-love, but it was a good sadness, like the sadness of old memories.

Garrick was in the dining-room, eating alone. Sean walked into the room and Garrick looked up nervously.

'Hello, Garry.' Sean smiled at him and Garrick was momentarily dazzled by it. Sean sat down in the chair beside him and punched him lightly on the arm.

'Have you left any for me?' His hatred was gone.

'There's plenty,' Garrick nodded eagerly. 'Try some of the potatoes, they're jolly good.'

— 14 —

'They say the Governor sent for your Pa while he was in Pietermaritzburg. Had him alone for nearly two hours.' Stephen Erasmus took the pipe out of his mouth and spat down onto the railway lines. In his brown homespun and *veldschoen* he did not look like a rich cattleman. 'Well, we don't need a prophet to tell us what it was about, do we?'

'No, sir,' Sean agreed vaguely. The train was late and Sean wasn't listening. He had an entry in the stock register to explain to his father and he was mentally rehearsing his speech.

'*Ja,* we know what it's about all right.' Old Erasmus put the pipe back between his teeth and spoke around it. 'It's been two weeks now since the British Agent was recalled from Cetewayo's kraal at Gingindhlovu. *Liewe Here!* in the old days we'd have called out the Commando long ago.' He packed his pipe, pushing down onto the glowing tobacco with a calloused forefinger. Sean noticed that the finger was twisted and scarred by the trigger-guards of a hundred heavy rifles.

'You've never been on commando have you, *Jong*?'

'No, sir.'

'About time you did then,' said Erasmus, 'about bledy time.'

Up on the escarpment the train whistled and Sean started guiltily.

'There she is.' Erasmus stood up from the bench on which they were sitting and the station master came out from his office with a rolled red flag in his hand. Sean felt his stomach sink slowly until it stopped somewhere just above his knees.

The train ran in past them, whooshing steam and brake-whining. The single passenger coach stopped precisely opposite the wooden platform. Erasmus came forward and took Waite's hand.

'*Goeie More,* Steff.'

'*More,* Waite. They tell me you're the new chairman now. Well done, man.'

'Thanks. Did you get my telegram?' Waite spoke in Afrikaans.

'*Ja.* I got it. I told the others, we'll all be out at Theunis Kraal tomorrow.'

'Good,' Waite nodded. 'You'll stay for lunch, of course. We've got a lot to talk about.'

'Is it what I think it is?' Erasmus grinned wickedly. The tobacco had stained his beard yellow around his mouth and his face was brown and wrinkled.

'I tell you all about it tomorrow, Steff.' Waite winked at him, 'but in the meantime you'd better get that old muzzle-loader of yours out of moth-balls.'

They laughed, one deep down and the other a rusty old laugh.

'Grab the bags, Sean. Let's get home.' Waite took Ada's arm and they walked with Erasmus to the buggy. Ada had on a new dress, blue with leg o'mutton sleeves and a picture hat; she looked lovely but a little worried as she listened to them talking. It's strange how women can never face the prospect of war with the same boyish enthusiasm as their men.

'Sean!' Waite Courtney's roar carried clearly from his study along the corridor and through the closed door of the sitting-room. Ada dropped her knitting into her lap and her features set into an expression of unnatural calm. Sean stood up from his chair.

'You should have told him earlier,' Garrick said in a small voice. 'You should have told him during lunch.'

'I didn't get a chance.'

'Sean!' Another blast from the study.

'What's happened now?' asked Ada quietly.

'It's nothing, Ma. Don't worry about it.'

Sean crossed to the door.

'Sean,' Garrick's stricken voice, 'Sean, you won't – I mean you don't have to tell –' He stopped and sat hunched in his chair, his eyes full of desperate appeal.

'It's all right, Garry, I'll fix it.'

Waite Courtney stood over the desk. Between his clenched fists the stock register lay open. He looked up as Sean came in and closed the door.

'What's this?' He prodded the page with a huge square-tipped finger. Sean opened his mouth and then closed it again.

'Come on. I'm listening.'

'Well, Pa –'

'Well, Pa – be buggered. Just tell me how you've managed to massacre half the cattle on this farm in a little over a week?'

'It's not half the cattle – it's only thirteen.' Sean was stung by the exaggeration.

'Only thirteen,' bellowed Waite, '*only* thirteen. God Almighty, shall I tell you how much that is in cash? Shall I tell you how much that is in hard work and time and worry?'

'I know, Pa.'

'You know,' Waite was panting. 'Yes, you know everything. There's nothing anyone can tell you, is there? Not even how to kill thirteen head of prime oxen.'

'Pa –'

'Don't Pa me, by Jesus.' Waite slammed the heavy book closed. 'Just explain to me how you managed it. What's "dip poisoning"? What the bloody hell is "dip poisoning"? Did you give it to them to drink? Did you stick it up their arses?'

'The dip was too strong,' said Sean.

'And why was the dip too strong? How much did you put in?'

Sean took a deep breath, 'I put in four drums.'

There was silence and then Waite asked softly, '*How much?*'

'Four drums.'

'Are you mad? Are you raving bloody mad?'

'I didn't think it would harm them.' His carefully rehearsed speech forgotten, Sean unconsciously repeated the words he had heard from Garrick. 'It was getting late and my leg was –' Sean bit the sentence off and Waite stared at him, then the confusion cleared from his face.

'Garry!' he said.

'No,' shouted Sean. 'It wasn't him, I did it.'

'You're lying to me.' Waite came round from behind the desk. There was a note of disbelief in his voice. To his knowledge it was the first time it had ever happened. He stared at Sean and then his anger was back more violently than before. He had forgotten the oxen – it was the lie that concerned him now. 'By Christ, I'll teach you to tell the truth.' He snatched up his sjambok from the desk.

'Don't hit me, Pa,' Sean warned him, backing away. Waite threw up the sjambok and swung it down overarm. It hissed softly and Sean twisted away from it, but the tip of the lash caught his shoulder. Sean gasped at the pain and lifted his hand to it.

'You lying little bastard!' shouted Waite and swung the whip sideways as though he were scything wheat, and this time it curled around Sean's chest under his uplifted arm. It split his shirt like a razor cut and the cloth fell away to expose the red ridged welt across his ribs and around his back.

'Here's some more!' Waite lifted the sjambok again and as he stood with his arm thrown back and his body turned off balance he knew he had made a mistake. Sean was no longer clutching the whip marks; his hands were held low and his fists were bunched. At the corners his eyebrows were lifted, giving an expression of satanical fury to his face. He was pale and his lips were drawn back tight, showing his teeth. His eyes, no longer blue but burning black, were on a level with Waite's.

'He's coming for me.' Waite's surprise slowed his reflexes, he couldn't bring his whip-arm down before Sean was on him. Sean hit him, standing solidly on both feet, bringing the full weight of his body into the punch, hurling it into the middle of Waite's exposed chest.

Heart punched, strength oozing out of him, Waite staggered back against the desk. The sjambok fell out of his hand and Sean went after him. Waite had the sensation of being a beetle in a saucer of treacle: he could see and think but he could barely move. He saw Sean take three quick paces forward, saw his right hand cocked like a loaded rifle, saw it aimed at his defenceless face.

In that instant, while his body moved in slow motion but his mind raced, the scales of paternal blindness dropped from Waite Courtney's eyes and he realized that he was fighting a man who matched him in strength and height, and who was his superior in speed. His only advantage lay in the experience he had gathered in forty years of brawling.

Sean threw his punch: it had all the power of the first one and Waite knew that he could not survive that in his face – and yet he could not move to avoid it. He dropped his chin onto his chest and took Sean's fist on the top of his head. The force of it flung him backwards over the desk, but as it hit he heard the brittle crackle of Sean's fingers breaking.

Waite dragged himself to his knees, using the corner of the desk as a support, and looked at his son. Sean was doubled up with pain, holding his broken hand against his stomach. Waite pulled himself to his feet and sucked in big breaths of air, he felt his strength coming back.

'All right,' he said, 'if you want to fight – then we fight.' He came round the desk, moving slowly, his hands ready, no longer underestimating his man.

'I am going to knock the daylights out of you,' announced Waite. Sean straightened up and looked at him. There was agony in his face now, but the anger was there also. Something surged up inside Waite when he saw it.

He can fight and he's game. Now we'll see if he can take a beating. Rejoicing silently Waite moved in on him, watching Sean's left hand, disregarding the broken right for he knew what pain was in it. He knew that no man could use a hand in that condition.

He shot out his own left hand, measuring with it, trying to draw Sean. Sean side-stepped, moving in past it. Waite was wide open for Sean's right, his broken right, the hand he could not possibly use – and Sean used it with all his strength into Waite's face.

Waite's brain burst into bright colours and darkness, he spun sideways, falling, hitting the leopard-skin rug with his shoulder and sliding with it across the floor into the fireplace. Then in the darkness he felt Sean's hands on him and heard Sean's voice.

'Pa, oh, my God, Pa. Are you all right?'

The darkness cleared a little and he saw Sean's face, the anger gone from it and in its place worry that was almost panic.

'Pa, oh, my God! Please, Pa.'

Waite tried to sit up, but he could not make it. Sean had to help him. He knelt next to Waite holding him, fumbling helplessly with his face, trying to brush the hair back off his forehead, stroking the rumpled beard into place. 'I'm sorry, Pa, truly I'm sorry. Let me help you to the chair.'

Waite sat in the chair and massaged the side of his jaw. Sean hovered over him, his own hand forgotten.

'What you want to do – kill me?' asked Waite ruefully.

'I didn't mean it. I just lost my temper.'

'I noticed,' said Waite, 'I just happened to notice that.'

'Pa – about Garry. You don't have to say anything to him, do you?'

Waite dropped his hand from his face and looked at Sean steadily.

'I'll make a bargain with you,' he said, 'I'll leave Garry out of it if you'll promise me two things. One: You never lie to me again.'

Sean nodded quickly.

'Two: If anybody ever takes a whip to you again you swear to me you'll give him the same as you just gave me.'

Sean started to smile and Waite went on gruffly. 'Now let's have a look at your hand.'

Sean held it out and Waite examined it, moving each finger in turn. Sean winced.

'Sore?' asked Waite. *He hit me with that. Sweet Jesus, I've bred me a wild one.*

'A little.' Sean was white-faced again.

'It's a mess,' said Waite. 'You'd better get into town right away and let Doctor Van have a go at it.'

Sean moved towards the door.

'Hold on.' Sean stopped and Waite pulled himself out of his chair. 'I'll come with you.'

'I'll be all right, Pa, you stay and rest.'

Waite ignored this and walked towards him.

'Really, Pa, I'll be all right on my own.'

'I'm coming with you,' Waite said harshly; and then softly, almost inaudibly, 'I want to, dammit.'

He lifted his arm as though to put it around Sean's shoulders, but before it touched him he let it drop back to his side and together they went out into the corridor.

= 15 =

With two fingers in splints Sean handled his knife awkwardly at lunch the next day, but his appetite was unimpaired. As was only right and fitting he took no part in the conversation except on the rare occasions that a remark was addressed directly to him.

But he listened, his jaws chewing steadily and his eyes moving from speaker to speaker. He and Garry sat side by side in a backwater of the luncheon board while the guests were grouped in order of seniority around Waite.

Stephen Erasmus by age and wealth was in the right-hand seat; opposite him Tim Hope-Brown, just as wealthy but ten years younger; below him Gunther Niewenhuizen, Sam Tingle and Simon Rousseau. If you added it all together you could say that Waite Courtney had about a hundred thousand acres of land and half a million sterling sitting around his table. They were brown men – brown clothing, brown boots and big brown, calloused, hands. Their faces were brown and battered-looking and now that the meal was in its closing stages their usual reserve was gone and there was a tendency among them to talk all at the same time and to perspire profusely. This was not entirely a consequence of the dozen bottles of good Cape Mossel that Waite had provided nor of the piles of food they had eaten – it was more than that. There was a sense of expectancy among them, an eagerness they were finding it difficult to suppress.

'Can I tell the servants to clear away, Waite?' Ada asked from the end of the table.

'Yes, thank you, my dear. We'll have coffee in here, please.'

He stood up and fetched a box of cigars from the sideboard and carried it to each of his guests in turn. When the ends were cut and the tips were glowing, every man leaning back in his chair with a recharged glass and a cup of coffee in front of him, Ada slipped out of the room and Waite cleared his throat for silence.

'Gentlemen.' They were all watching him. 'Last Tuesday I spent two hours with the Governor. We discussed the recent developments across the Tugela.'

Waite lifted his glass and sipped at it, then held it by the stem and rolled it between his fingers as he went on.

'Two weeks ago the British Agent at the Zulu king's kraal was recalled. Recalled is perhaps the wrong word – the king offered to smear him with honey, and tie him over an ant-hill, an offer that Her Britannic Majesty's Agent declined with thanks. Shortly thereafter he packed his bags and made for the border.'

There was a small ruffle of laughter.

'Since then Cetewayo has collected all his herds which were grazing near the Tugela and driven them into the north; he has commanded a buffalo hunt for which he has decided he will need *all* his impis – twenty thousand spears. This hunt is to be held along the banks of the Tugela, where the last buffalo was seen ten years ago.' Waite sipped at his glass, watching their faces. 'And he has ordered that all wounded game is to be followed across the border.'

There was a sigh then, a murmur from them. They all knew that this was the traditional Zulu declaration of war.

'So, man, what are we going to do about it. Must we sit here and wait for them to come and burn us out?'

Erasmus leaned forward watching Waite.

'Sir Bartle Frere met Cetewayo's Indunas a week ago. He has given them an ultimatum. They have until January the eleventh to disband the impis and take the Queen's Agent back into Zululand. In the event that Cetewayo disregards the ultimatum, Lord Chelmsford is to command a punitive column of regulars and militia. The force is being assembled now and will leave Pietermaritzburg within the next ten days. He is to cross the Tugela at Rorke's Drift and engage the impis before they break out. It is intended to end this constant threat to our border and break the Zulu nation for ever as a military power.'

'It's about bledy time,' said Erasmus.

'His Excellency has gazetted me full colonel and ordered me to raise a commando from the Ladyburg district. I have promised him at least forty men fully armed, mounted and provisioned who will be ready to join Chelmsford at the Tugela. Unless any of you object I am appointing you gentlemen as my captains and I know I can rely upon you to help me make good my promise to His Excellency.'

Suddenly Waite dropped his stilted manner and grinned at them. 'You will collect your own pay. It will be in cattle, as usual.'

'How far north has Cetewayo driven his herds?' asked Tim Hope-Brown.

'Not far enough, I'll warrant,' cackled Stephen Erasmus.

'A toast,' said Simon Rousseau jumping to his feet and holding up his glass. 'I give you a toast: the Queen, Lord Chelmsford and the Royal Herds of Zululand.'

They all stood and drank it, and then suddenly embarrassed by their display they sat down again, coughing awkwardly and shuffling their feet,

'All right,' said Waite, 'let's get down to details. Steff, you'll be coming and your two eldest boys?'

'*Ja,* three of us and my brother and his son. Put down five, Erasmus.'

'Good. What about you Gunther?'

They began the planning. Men, horses and wagons were marshalled on paper; each of the captains was allotted a series of tasks. There was question, answer and argument that filled the hours before the guests left Theunis Kraal. They rode in a bunch, trippling their horses, sitting slack and long-legged in the saddles, moving up the far slope along the road to Ladyburg. Waite and his sons stood on the front step and watched them go.

'Pa –' Garry tried tentatively for Waite's attention.

'Yes, boy?' Waite kept his eyes on the group. Steff Erasmus turned in the saddle and waved his hat above his head, Waite waved back.

'Why do we have to fight them, Pa? If the Governor just sent somebody to talk to them, then we wouldn't have to fight.'

Waite glanced at him, frowning slightly.

'Anything worth having is worth fighting for, Garry. Cetewayo has raised twenty thousand spears to take this from us –' Waite swept his arm in a circle that took in the whole of Theunis Kraal. 'I think it's worth fighting for – don't you, Sean?'

'You bet,' Sean nodded eagerly.

'But couldn't we just make a treaty with them?' Garry persisted.

'Another cross on a piece of paper.' Waite spoke with fierce disdain. 'They found one like that on Piet Retrief's body – hell of a lot of good it did him.'

Waite walked back into the house with his sons following him.

He lowered himself into his armchair, stretched his legs out in front of him and smiled at Ada. 'Damn good lunch, my dear.' He clasped his hands over his stomach, belched involuntarily and was immediately contrite. 'I beg your pardon – it just slipped out.'

Ada bent her head over her sewing to hide her smile.

'We've got a lot to do in the next few days.' He turned his attention back to his sons. 'We'll take one mule wagon and a pair of horses each. Now about ammunition. . . .'

'But, Pa, couldn't we just –?' Garry started again.

'Shut up,' said Waite, and Garry subsided miserably into one of the other chairs.

'I've been thinking,' announced Sean.

'Not you as well,' growled Waite. 'Damn it to hell, here's your chance to win your own cattle and. . . .'

'That's just what I've been thinking,' Sean cut in. 'Everybody will have more cattle than they know what to do with. The prices will drop way down.'

'They will at first,' admitted Waite, 'but in a year or two they'll climb back again.'

'Shouldn't we sell now? Sell everything except the bulls and breeding cows, then after the war we'll be able to buy back at half the price.'

For a moment Waite sat stunned and then slowly his expression changed.

'My God, I never thought of that.'

'And Pa,' Sean was twisting his hands together in his enthusiasm, 'we'll need more land. When we bring the herds back across the Tugela there won't be enough grazing to go round. Mr Pye has called the mortgages on Mount Sinai and Mahoba's Kloof. He's not using the land. Couldn't we lease them from him now before everybody starts looking for grazing?'

'We had a lot to do before you started thinking,' said Waite softly, 'but now we've really got to work.'

He searched his pockets, found his pipe and while he filled it with tobacco he looked at Sean. He tried to keep his face neutral but the pride kept showing.

'You keep thinking like that and you'll be a rich man one day.' Waite could not know how true his prophecy would prove – the time was still remote when Sean could drop the purchase price of Theunis Kraal across a gaming table, and laugh at the loss.

= 16 =

The Commando was moving out on New Year's Day. New Year's Eve was set down for a double celebration: 'Welcome 1879', and 'God speed the Ladyburg Mounted Rifles'. The whole district was coming into town for the *braaivleis* and dancing that was being held in the square. Feast the warriors – laugh, dance and sing, then form them up and march them out to war.

Sean and Garry rode in early. Ada and Waite were to follow later in the afternoon. It was one of those bright days of a Natal summer: no wind and no clouds, the kind of day when the dust from a wagon hangs heavy in the air. They crossed the Baboon Stroom and from the farther ridge looked down across the town and saw the wagon dust on every road leading into Ladyburg.

'Look at them come,' said Sean; he screwed up his eyes against the glare and stared at the north road. 'That will be the Erasmus wagon. Karl will be with them.'

The wagons looked like beads on a string.

'That's the Petersens',' said Garry, 'or the Niewehuisens'.'

'Come on,' shouted Sean, and slapped the free end of his reins across his horse's neck. They galloped down the road. The horses they rode were big glossy animals, with their manes cropped like English hunters.

They passed a wagon. There were two girls sitting beside mama on the box seat, the Petersen sisters. Dennis Petersen and his father were riding ahead of the wagon.

Sean whooped as he raced past the wagon and the girls laughed and shouted something that was lost in the wind.

'Come on, Dennis,' howled Sean as he swept past the two sedately trotting outriders. Dennis's horse reared and then settled in to run, chasing Sean. Garry trailed them both.

They reached the cross roads, lying flat along their horses' necks, pumping the reins like jockeys. The Erasmus wagon was trundling down to meet them.

'Karl,' Sean called as he held his horse a little to stand in the stirrups. 'Karl. Come on, man, catch a wayo, Cetewayo!'

They rode into Ladyburg in a bunch. They were all flush-faced and laughing, excited and happy at the prospect of dancing and killing.

The town was crowded, its streets congested with wagons and horses and men and women and girls and dogs and servants.

'I've got to stop at Pye's store,' said Karl, 'come with me – it won't take long.'

They hitched their horses and went into the store; Sean, Dennis and Karl walked noisily and talked aloud. They were men, big sun-burned raw-boned men, muscled from hard work, but uncertain of the fact that they were men. Therefore, walk with a swagger and laugh too loud, swear when Pa isn't listening and no one will know you have your doubts.

'What are you going to buy, Karl?'

'Boots.'

'That'll take all day – you'll have to try them on. We'll miss half the fun.'

'There'll be nothing doing for another couple hours,' protested Karl. 'Wait for me, you chaps.'

Karl sitting on the counter, trying boots on his large feet, was not a spectacle that could hold Sean's interest for long. He drifted away amongst the piles of merchandise that cluttered Pye's store. There were stacks of pick handles, piles of blankets, bins of sugar and salt and flour, shelves of groceries and clothing, overcoats and women's dresses and hurricane-lamps and saddles hanging from the roof, and all of it was permeated by the peculiar smell of a general dealer's store: a mixture of paraffin, soap and new cloth.

Pigeon to its coop, iron to magnet. . . . Sean's feet led him to the rack of rifles against the far wall of the room. He lifted down one of the Lee Metford carbines and worked the action; he stroked the wood with his fingertips, then he weighed it in his hands to feel the balance and finally brought it up to his shoulder.

'Hello, Sean.' His ritual interrupted, Sean looked up at the shy voice.

'It's Strawberry Pie,' he said smiling. 'How's school?'

'I've left school now. I left last term.'

Audrey Pye had the family colouring but with a subtle difference – instead of carrot her hair was smoked copper with glints in it. She was not a pretty girl, her face was too broad and flat, but she had that rare skin that too seldom goes with red hair: creamy unfreckled purity.

'Do you want to buy anything, Sean?'

Sean placed the carbine back in the rack.

'Just looking,' he said. 'Are you working in the store now?'

'Yes.' She dropped her eyes from Sean's scrutiny. It was a year since he'd last seen her. A lot can change in a year; she now had that within her blouse which proved she was no longer a child. Sean eyed it appreciatively and she glanced up and saw the direction of his eyes; the cream of her skin clouded red. She turned quickly towards the trays of fruit.

'Would you like a peach?'

'Thanks,' said Sean and took one.

'How's Anna?' asked Audrey.

'Why ask me?' Sean frowned.

'You're her beau, aren't you?'

'Who told you that?' Sean's frown became a scowl.

'Everybody knows that.'

'Well, everybody's wrong.' Sean was irritated by the suggestion that he was one of Anna's possessions. 'I'm nobody's beau.'

'Oh!' Audrey was silent a moment, then, 'I suppose Anna will be at the dance tonight?'

'Most probably.' Sean bit into the furry golden peach and studied Audrey. 'Are you going, Strawberry Pie?'

'No,' Audrey answered wistfully. 'Pa won't let me.'

How old was she? Sean made a quick calculation . . . three years younger than he was. That made her sixteen. Suddenly Sean was sorry she wouldn't be at the dance.

'That's a pity,' he said. 'We could have had some fun.' Linking them together, with the plural 'we', Sean threw her into confusion again. She said the first words she could think of, 'Do you like the peach?'

'Hmm.'

'It's from our orchard.'

'I thought I recognized the flavour.' Sean grinned and Audrey laughed. Her mouth was wide and friendly when she laughed. 'I knew you used to pinch them. Pa knew it was you. He used to say he'd set a mantrap in that hole in the hedge.'

'I didn't know he'd found that hole – we used to cover it up each time.'

'Oh, yes,' Audrey assured him, 'we knew about it all the time. It's still there. Some nights when I can't sleep I climb out of my bedroom window and go down through the orchard, through the hedge into the wattle plantation. It's so dark and quiet in the plantation at night – scary, but I like it.'

'You know something,' Sean spoke thoughtfully. 'If you couldn't sleep tonight and came down to the hedge at ten o'clock, you might catch me pinching peaches again.'

It took a few seconds for Audrey to realize what he had said. Then the colour flew up her face again and she tried to speak but no words came. She turned with a swirl of skirt and darted away among the shelves. Sean bit the last of the flesh off the peach pip and dropped it on the floor. He was smiling as he walked across to join the others.

'Hell's teeth, Karl, how much longer are you going to be?'

= 17 =

There were fifty or more wagons outspanned around the perimeter of the square but the centre was left open, and here the braaivleis pits were burning, the flames already sinking to form glowing beds. Trestle-tables stood in two lines near the fires and the women worked at them cutting meat and boerwors, buttering bread, arranging platoons of pickle bottles, piling the food on trays and sweetening the evening with their voices and laughter.

In a level place a huge buck-sail was spread for the dancing and at each corner a lantern hung on a pole. The band was tuning with squeaks from the fiddles and preliminary asthma from the single concertina.

The men gathered in knots amongst the wagons or squatted beside the braaivleis pits, and here and there a jug pointed its base briefly at the sky.

'I don't like to be difficult, Waite,' Petersen came across to where Waite was standing with his captains, 'but I see you've put Dennis in Gunther's troop.'

'That's right.' Waite offered him the jug and Petersen took it and wiped the neck with his sleeve.

'It's not you, Gunther,' Petersen smiled at Gunther Niewehuisen, 'but I would be much happier if I could have Dennis in the same troop as myself. Keep an eye on him, you know.'

They all looked at Waite to hear what he would say. 'None of the boys are riding with their fathers. We've purposely arranged it that way. Sorry, Dave.'

'Why?'

Waite Courtney looked away, over the wagons at the furious red sunset that hung above the escarpment. 'This isn't going to be a bushbuck shoot, Dave. You may find that you'll be called upon to make decisions that will be easier for you if you're not making them about your own son.'

There was a murmur of agreement and Steff Erasmus took his pipe out of his mouth and spat into the fire. 'There are some things it is not pretty for a man to see. They are too hard for him to forget. He should not see his son kill his first man, also he should not see his son die.'

They were silent then, knowing this truth. They had not spoken of it before because too much talk softens a man's stomach, but they knew death and understood what Steff had said. One by one their heads turned until they were all staring across the square at the gathering of youngsters beyond the fires. Dennis Petersen said something but they could not catch the words and his companions laughed.

'In order to live a man must occasionally kill,' said Waite, 'but when he kills too young, he loses something . . . a respect for life: he makes it cheap. It is the same with a woman, a man should never have his first woman until he understands about it. Otherwise that too becomes cheap.'

'I had my first when I was fifteen,' said Tim Hope-Brown. 'I can't say it made them any cheaper; in fact I've known them to be bloody expensive.'

Waite's big boom led the laughter.

*

'I know your old man pays you a pound a week but what about us, Sean?' protested Dennis, 'we aren't all millionaires.'

'All right, then,' Sean agreed, 'five shillings in the pool. Winner takes the lot.'

'Five bob is reasonable,' Karl opined, 'but let's get the rules clear so there's no argument afterwards.'

'Kills only, woundings don't count,' said Sean.

'And they have to be witnessed,' insisted Frikkie Van Essen. He was older than the others; his eyes were already a little bloodshot for he had made a start on the evening's drinking.

'All right, dead Zulus only and a witness to each kill. The highest score takes the pool.' Sean looked around the circle of faces for their assent. Garry was hanging back on the fringe. 'Garry will be banker. Come on, Garry, hold out your hat.'

They paid the money into Garrick's hat and he counted it.

'Two pounds – from eight of us. That's correct.'

'Hell, the winner will be able to buy his own farm.'

They laughed.

'I've got a couple of bottles of smoke hidden in my saddle bags,' Frikkie said. 'Let's go and try them.'

The hands of the clock on the church tower showed quarter before ten. There were silver-edged clouds around the moon, and the night had cooled. Rich meaty smelling steam from the cooking pits drifted across the dancers, fiddles sawed and the concertina bawled the beat, dancers danced and the watchers clapped in time and called encouragement to them. Someone whooped like a Highlander in the feverish pattern of movement, in the fever of fun. Dam the dribble of minutes with laughter, hold the hour, lay siege against the dawn!

'Where are you going, Sean?'

'I'll be back just now.'

'But where are you going?'

'Do you want me to tell you, Anna, do you really want to know?'

'Oh, I see. Don't be long. I'll wait for you by the band.'

'Dance with Karl.'

'No, I'll wait for you, Sean. Please don't be long. We've got such a little time left.'

Sean slipped through the circle of wagons, he kept in the tree shadow along the sidewalk, round the side of Pye's store and down the lane, running now, jumped the ditch and through the barbed wire fence. It was dark in the plantation and quiet as she had said; dead leaves rustled and a twig popped under his feet. Something ran in the darkness, scurry of small feet. Sean's stomach flopped over: nerves, only a rabbit. He came to the hedge and searched for the hole, missed it and turned back, found it and through into the orchard. He stood with his back against the wall of vegetation and waited. The trees were moon grey and black below. He could see the roof of the house beyond them. He knew she'd come, of course. He had told her to.

The church clock chimed the hour and then later the single stroke of the quarter hour. Angry now, damn her! He went up through the orchard, cautiously staying in shadow. There was a light in one of the side windows, he could see it spilling out into a yellow square on the lawn. He circled the house softly.

She was at the window with the lamp behind her. Her face was dark but lamplight lit the edges of her hair into a coppery halo. There was something of yearning in her attitude, leaning forward over the sill. He could see the outline of her shoulders through the white cloth of her gown.

Sean whistled, pitching it low to reach her only, and she started at the sound. A second longer she stared out from light into the dark and then she shook her head, slowly and regretfully from side to side. She closed the curtains and through them Sean saw her shadow move away. The lamp went out.

Sean went back through the orchard and the plantation. He was trembling with anger. From the lane he heard the music in the square and he quickened his pace. He turned the corner and saw the lights and movement.

'Silly little fool,' he said out loud, anger still there but something else as well. Affection? Respect?

'Where have you been? I've waited nearly an hour.' Possessive Anna.

'There and back to see how far it is.'

'Funny! Sean Courtney, where have you been?'

'Do you want to dance?'

'No.'

'All right, don't then.'

Karl and some of the others were standing by the cooking pits. Sean started for them.

'Sean, Sean, I'm sorry.' Penitent Anna. 'I'd love to dance, please.'

They danced, jostled by other dancers, but neither of them spoke until the band stopped to wipe their brows and wet dry throats.

'I've got something for you, Sean.'

'What is it?'

'Come, I'll show you.'

She led him from the light among the wagons and stopped by a pile of saddles and blankets. She knelt and opened one of the blankets and stood up again with the coat in her hands.

'I made it for you. I hope you like it.'

Sean took it from her. It was sheepskin, tanned and polished, stitched with love, the inside wool bleached snowy white.

'It's beautiful,' Sean said. He recognized the labour that had gone into it. It made him feel guilty: gifts always made him feel guilty.

'Thank you very much.'

'Try it on, Sean.'

Warm, snug at the waist, room to move in the shoulders; it enhanced his considerable bulk. Anna stood close to him, arranging the collar.

'You look nice in it,' she said. Smug pleasure of the giver.

He kissed her and the mood changed. She held him tight around the neck. 'Oh, Sean, I wish you weren't going.'

'Let's say goodbye properly.'

'Where?'

'My wagon.'

'What about your parents?'

'They've gone back to the farm. Pa's coming in tomorrow morning. Garry and I are sleeping here.'

'No, Sean, there are too many people. We can't.'

'You don't want to,' Sean whispered. 'It's a pity because it might be the last time ever.'

'What do you mean?' She was suddenly still and small in his arms.

'I'm going away tomorrow. You know what might happen?'

'No. Don't talk like that. Don't even think it.'

'It's true.'

'No, Sean, don't. Please don't.'

Sean smiled in the darkness. So easy, so very easy.

'Let's go to my wagon.' He took her hand.

18

Breakfast in the dark, cooking fires around the square, voices quiet, men standing with their wives, holding the small children in farewell. The horses saddled, rifles in the scabbards and blanket rolls behind, four wagons drawn up in the centre of the square with the mules in the traces.

'Pa should be here any minute. It's nearly five o'clock,' said Garry.

'They're all waiting for him,' agreed Sean. He shrugged at the weight of the bandolier strapped over his shoulder.

'Mr Niewehuizen has made me one of the wagon drivers.'

'I know,' said Sean. 'Can you handle it?'

'I think so.'

Jane Petersen came towards them.

'Hello, Jane. Is your brother ready yet?'

'Nearly. He's just saddling up.'

She stopped in front of Sean and shyly held out a scrap of green-and-yellow silk.

'I've made you a cockade for your hat, Sean.'

'Thanks, Jane. Won't you put it on for me?' She pinned up the brim of Sean's hat; he took it back from her and set it at a jaunty angle on his head.

'I look like a general now,' he said and she laughed at him. 'How about a goodbye kiss, Jane?'

'You're terrible,' said little Jane and went away quickly, blushing. Not so little, Sean noticed. There were so many of them you hardly knew where to start.

'Here's Pa,' announced Garry, as Waite Courtney rode into the square.

'Come on,' said Sean and untied his horse. From all around the square, men were leading out their horses.

'See you later,' said Garry and limped off towards one of the waiting mule wagons.

Waite rode at the head of the column. Four troops of fifteen men in double file, four wagons behind them, and then the loose horses driven by black servants.

They moved out across the square, through the litter of the night's festivities, and into the main street. The women watched them in silence, standing motionless with the children gathered around them. These women had seen men ride out before against the tribes; they did not cheer for they too were wise in the ways of death, they had learned that there is no room for glory in the grave.

Anna waved to Sean. He did not see her for his horse was skittish and he was past her before he had it under control. She let her hand drop back to her side and watched him go. He wore the skeepskin coat.

Sean did see the coppery flash and the swiftly-blown kiss from the upstairs window of Pye's store. He saw it because he was looking for it. He forgot his injured pride sufficiently to grin and wave his hat.

Then they were out of the town, and at last even the small boys and dogs that ran beside them fell back and the column trotted out along the road to Zululand.

The sun came up and dried the dew. The dust rose from under the hooves and drifted out at an angle from the road. The column lost its rigidity as men spurred ahead or dropped back to ride with their friends. They rode in groups and straggles, relaxed and cheerfully chatting, as informal as a party out for a day's shooting. Each man had taken to the field in the clothing he considered most suitable. Steff Erasmus wore his church suit, but he was the most formally attired of the group. They had only one standard item of uniform among them: this was the green-and-yellow cockade. However, even here there was scope for individual taste: some wore them on their hats, some on their sleeves and others on their chests. They were farmers, not fighting men, but their rifle scabbards were battered with use, their bandoliers worn with easy familiarity and the wood of their gun butts was polished from the caress of their hands.

It was middle afternoon before they reached the Tugela.

'My God, look at that!' whistled Sean. 'I've never seen so many people in one place in my life before.'

'They say there are four thousand,' said Karl.

'I know there are four thousand.' Sean ran his eyes over the camp. 'But I didn't know four thousand was that many.'

The column was riding down the last slope to Rorke's Drift. The river was muddy brown and wide, rippling over the shallows of the crossing place. The banks were open and grassy with a cluster of stone-walled buildings on the near side. In a quarter-mile radius around the buildings Lord Chelmsford's army was encamped. The tents were laid out in meticulous lines, row upon row with the horses picketed between them. The wagons were marshalled by the drift, five hundred at least, and the whole area swarmed with men.

The Ladyburg Mounted Rifles, in a solid bunch that overflowed the road behind their Colonel, came down to the perimeter of the camp and found their passage blocked by a sergeant in a dress coat and with a fixed bayonet.

'And who be you, may I ask?'

'Colonel Courtney – and a detachment of the Ladyburg Mounted Rifles.'

'What's that? Didn't catch it.'

Waite Courtney stood in his stirrups and turned to face his men.

'Hold on there, gentlemen. We can't all talk at once.'

The hubbub of conversation and comment behind him faded and this time the sergeant heard him.

'Ho! Beg your pardon, sir. I'll call the orderly officer.'

The orderly officer was an aristocrat and a gentleman. He came and looked at them. 'Colonel Courtney?' There was a note of disbelief in his voice.

'Hello,' said Waite with a friendly smile. 'I hope we are not too late for the fun.'

'No, I don't believe you are.' The officer's eyes fastened on Steff Erasmus. Steff lifted his top hat politely. *'More, Meneer.'* The bandoliers of ammunition looked a little out of place slung across his black frockcoat.

The officer tore his eyes away from him. 'You have your own tents, Colonel?'

'Yes, we've got everything we need.'

'I'll get the sergeant here to show you where to make camp.'

'Thank you,' said Waite.

The officer turned to the sergeant. So carried away was he that he took the man by the arm. 'Put them far away. Put them on the other side of the Engineers –' he whispered frantically. 'If the General sees this lot. . . .' He shuddered, but in a genteel fashion.

= 19 =

Garrick first became conscious of the smell. Thinking about it served as a rallying point for his attention and he could start to creep out of the hiding-place in his mind. For Garrick, these returns to reality were always accompanied by a feeling of light-headedness and a heightening of the senses. Colours were vivid, skin sensitive to the touch, tastes and smells sharp and clear.

He lay on a straw mattress. The sun was bright, but he was in shade. He lay on the veranda of the stone-walled hospital above Rorke's Drift. He thought about the smell that had brought him back. It was a blending of corruption and sweat and dung, the smell of ripped bowels and congealing blood.

He recognized it as the smell of death. Then his vision came into focus and be saw the dead. They were piled along the wall of the yard where the cross-fire from the store and the hospital had caught them; they were scattered between the buildings, and the burial squads were busy loading them onto the wagons. They were lying down the slope to the drift, they were in the water and on the far bank. Dead Zulus, with their weapons and shields strewn about them. Hundreds of them, Garrick thought with astonishment: no, thousands of them.

Then he was aware that there were two smells; but both of them were the smells of death. There was the stink of the black, balloon-bellied corpses swelling in the sun and there was the smell from his own body and the bodies of the men about him, the same smell of pain and putrefaction but mixed with the heaviness of disinfectant. Death wearing antiseptic – the way an unclean girl tries to cover her menstrual odour.

Garrick looked at the men around him, They lay in a long row down the veranda, each on his own mattress. Some were dying and many were not but on all of them the bandages were stained with blood and iodine. Garrick looked at his own body. His left arm was strapped across his bare chest and he felt the ache start beating within him, slow and steady as a funeral drum. There were bandages around his head. I'm wounded – again he was astonished. How? But how?

'You've come back to us, Cocky,' cheerful Cockney from beside him. 'We thought you'd gone clean bonkers.'

Garrick turned his head and looked at the speaker; he was a small monkey-faced man in a pair of flannel underpants and a mummy suit of bandages.

'Doc said it was shock. He said you'd come out of it soon enough.' The little man raised his voice, 'Hey, Doc, the hero is completely mentos again.' The doctor came quickly, tired-looking, dark under the eyes, old with overwork.

'You'll do,' he said, having groped and prodded. 'Get some rest. They're sending you back home tomorrow.' He moved away for there were many wounded, but then he stopped and looked back. He smiled briefly at Garrick, 'I doubt it will ease the pain at all but you've been recommended for the Victoria Cross. The General endorsed your citation yesterday. I think you'll get it.' Garrick stared at the doctor as memory come back patchily,

'There was fighting,' Garrick said.

'You're bloody well tooting there was!' the little man beside him guffawed.

'Sean !' said Garrick. 'My, brother! What happened to my brother?' There was silence then and Garrick saw the quick shadow of regret in the doctor's eyes. Garrick struggled into a sitting position.

'And my Pa. What happened to my father?'

'I'm sorry,' said the doctor with simplicity, 'I'm afraid they were both killed.'

Garrick lay on his mattress and looked down at the Drift. They were clearing the corpses out of the shallows now, splashing as they dragged them to the bank. He remembered the splashing as Chelmsford's army had crossed. Sean and his father had been among the scouts who had led the column, three troops of the Ladyburg Mounted Rifles and sixty men of the Natal Police. Chelmsford had used these men who knew the country over which the initial advance was to be made.

Garrick had watched them go with relief. He could hardly believe the good fortune that had granted him a squirting dysentery the day before the ultimatum expired and the army crossed the Tugela.

'The lucky bastards,' protested one of the other sick as they watched them go. Garrick was without envy: he did not want to go to war, he was content to wait here with thirty other sick men and a garrison of sixty more to hold the Drift while Chelmsford took his army into Zululand.

Garrick had watched the scouts fan out from the Drift and disappear into the rolling grassland, and the main body of men and wagons follow them until they too had crawled like a python into the distance and left a well-worn road behind them through the grass.

He remembered the slow slide of days while they waited at the Drift. He remembered grumbling with the others when they were made to fortify the store and the hospital with bags and biscuit tins filled with sand. He remembered the boredom.

Then, his stomach tightening, he remembered the messenger.

'Horseman coming.' Garrick had seen him first. Recovered from his dysentery he was doing sentry duty above the Drift.

'The General's left his toothbrush behind, sent someone back for it,' said his companion. Neither of them stood up. They watched the speck coming across the plain towards the river.

'Coming fast,' said Garrick. 'You'd better go and call the Captain.'

'I suppose so,' agreed the other sentry. He trotted up the slope to the store and Garrick stood up and walked down to the edge of the river. His peg sank deep into the mud.

'Captain says to send him up to the store when he gets here.' Garrick's companion came back and stood beside him.

'Something funny about the way he's riding,' said Garrick, 'he looks tired.'

'He must be drunk. He's falling about in the saddle like it's Saturday night.'

Garrick gasped suddenly, 'He's bleeding, he's wounded.'

The horse plunged into the Drift and the rider fell forward onto its neck; the side of his shirt was shiny black with blood, his face was pale with pain and dust. They caught his horse as it came out of the water and the rider tried to shout but his voice was a croak. 'In the name of God prepare yourselves. The Column's been surrounded and wiped out. They're coming – the whole black howling pack of them. They'll be here before nightfall.'

'My brother,' said Garrick. 'What happened to my brother?'

'Dead,' said the man. 'Dead, they're all dead.' He slid sideways off his horse.

They came, the impis of Zulu in the formation of the bull, the great black bull whose head and loins filled the plain and whose horns circled left and right across the river to surround them. The pull stamped with twenty thousand feet and sang with ten thousand throats until its voice was the sound of the sea on a stormy day. The sunlight reflected brightly from the spear blades as it came singing to the Tugela.

'Look! Those in front are wearing the helmets of the Hussars,' one of the watchers in the hospital exclaimed. 'They've been looting Chelmsford's dead. There's one wearing a dress coat and some are carrying carbines.'

It was hot in the hospital for the roof was corrugated-iron and the windows were blocked with sandbags. The rifle slits let in little air. The men stood at the slits, some in pyjamas, some stripped to the waist and sweating in the heat.

'It's true then, the Column has been massacred.'

'That's enough talking. Stand to your posts and keep your mouths shut.'

The impis of Zulu crossed the Tugela on a front five hundred yards wide. They churned the surface to white with their crossing.

'My God! Oh, my God!' whispered Garrick as he watched them come. 'We haven't got a chance, there are so many of them.'

'Shut up. Damn you,' snapped the sergeant at the Gatling machine-gun beside him and Garry covered his mouth with his hand.

> ' – Grabbed O'Riley by the neck
> Shoved his head in a pail of water
> Rammed that pistol up his –'

sang one of the malaria cases in delirium and somebody else laughed, shrill hysteria in the sound.

'Here they come!'

'Load!'

The metallic clashing of rifle mechanism. 'Hold your fire, men. Fire on command only.'

The voice of the bull changed from a deep sonorous chant to the shrill ululation of the charge – high-pitched frenzy of the blood squeal.

'Steady, men. Steady. Hold it. Hold your fire.'

'Oh, my God!' whispered Garrick softly, watching them come black up the slope. 'Oh, my God! – please don't let me die.'

'Ready!'

The van had reached the wall of the hospital yard. Their plumed head-dresses were the frothy crest of a black wave as they came over the wall.

'Aim!'

Sixty rifles lifted and held, aimed into the press of bodies.

'Fire!'

Thunder, then the strike of bullets into flesh, a sound as though a handful of gravel had been flung into a puddle of mud. The ranks reeled from the blow. The clustered barrels of the Gatling machine-gun jump – jump – jumped as they swung, cutting them down so they fell upon each other, thick along the wall. The stench of burnt black powder was painful to breathe.

'Load!'

The bullet-ravaged ranks were re-forming as those from behind came forward into the gaps.

'Aim!'

They were coming again, solid black and screaming halfway across the yard.

'Fire!'

Garrick sobbed in the shade of the veranda and pressed the fingers of his right hand into his eye sockets to squeeze out the memory.

'What's the trouble, Cocky?' The Cockney rolled painfully onto his side and looked at Garrick.

'Nothing!' said Garrick quickly. 'Nothing!'

'Coming back to you, is it?'

'What happened? I can only remember pieces of it.'

'What happened!' The man echoed his question, 'What didn't happen!'

'The doctor said –' Garrick looked up quickly, 'He said the General had endorsed my citation. That means Chelmsford's alive. My brother and my father – they must be alive as well!'

'No such luck, Cocky. The Doc's taken a fancy to you – you with one leg doing what you did – so he made inquiries about your folk. It's no use.'

'Why?' asked Garrick desperately. 'Surely if Chelmsford's alive they must be too?'

The little man shook his head. 'Chelmsford's made a base camp at a place called Isandhlwana. He left a garrison there with all the wagons and supplies. He took a flying column out to raid, but the Zulus circled around him and attacked the base camp, then they came on here to the Drift. As you know, we held them for two days until Chelmsford's flying column came to help us.'

'My folk – what happened to them?'

'Your father was at the Isandhlwana camp. He didn't escape. Your brother was with Chelmsford's column but he was cut off and killed in one of the skirmishes before the main battle.'

'Sean dead?' Garrick shook his head. 'No, it's not possible. They couldn't have killed him.'

'You'd be surprised how easily they did it,' said the Cockney. 'A few inches of blade in the right place is enough for the best of them.'

'But not Sean – you didn't know him. You couldn't understand.'

'He's dead, Cocky. Him and your Pa and seven hundred others. The wonder is we aren't too.' The man wriggled into a more comfortable position on his mattress. 'The

General made a speech about our defence here. Finest feat of arms in the annals of British courage – or something like that.'

He winked at Garrick. 'Fifteen citations for the old V.C. – you's one of them. I ask you, Cocky, isn't that something? What's your girl friend going to do when you come home with a mucking great gong clanking around on your chest, hey?'

He stared at Garrick and saw the tears oozing in oily lines down his cheeks.

'Come on, Cock. You're a bloody hero.' He looked away from Garrick's grief. 'Do you remember that part – do you remember what you did?'

'No,' Garrick's voice was husky. *Sean. You can't leave me alone. What am I going to do, now that you're gone?*

'I was next to you. I saw it all. I'll tell you about it,' said the Cockney.

As he talked so the events came back and fitted into sequence in Garrick's mind.

'It was on the second day, we'd held off twenty-three charges.'

Twenty-three, was it as many, as that? Garrick had lost count; it might have been but a single surging horror. Even now he could taste the fear in the back of his throat and smell it rancid in his own sweat.

'Then they piled wood against the hospital wall and set fire to it.' Zulus coming across the yard carrying bundles of faggots, falling to the rifles, others picking up the bundles and bringing them closer until they too died and yet others came to take their place. Then flames pale yellow in the sunlight, a dead Zulu lying on the bonfire his face charring, and the smell of him mingled with the smoke.

'We knocked a hole in the back wall and started to move the sick and wounded out through it and across to the store.'

The boy with the assegai through his spine had shrieked like a girl as they lifted him.

'Them bloody savages came again as soon as they saw we were pulling out. They came from that side.' He pointed with his bandaged arm, 'where the chaps in the store couldn't reach them, and there was only you and I and a couple of others at the loopholes – everyone else was carrying the wounded.'

There had been a Zulu with the blue heron feathers of an Induna in his head-dress. He had led the charge. His shield was dried oxhide dappled black and white, and at his wrists and ankles were bunches of war rattles. Garrick had fired at the instant the Zulu half-turned to beckon to his warriors – the bullet sliced across the tensed muscles of his belly and unzipped it like a purse. The Zulu went down on his hands and knees with his entrails bulging out in a pink and purple mass.

'They reached the door of the hospital and we couldn't fire on them from the angle of the windows.'

The wounded Zulu started to crawl towards Garrick, his mouth moving and his eyes fastened on Garrick's face. He still had his assegai in his hand. The other Zulus were beating at the door and one of them ran his spear blade through a crack in the woodwork and lifted the bar. The door was open.

Garrick watched the Zulu crawling towards him through the dust with his pink wet bowels swinging like a pendulum under him. The sweat was running down Garrick's cheeks and dripping off the end of his chin, his lips were trembling. He lifted his rifle and aimed into the Zulu's face. He could not fire.

'That's when you moved, Cocky. I saw the bar lifted out of its brackets and I knew that in the next second there'd be a mob of them in through the door and we'd stand no chance against their spears at close range.'

Garrick let go his rifle and it rattled on the concrete floor. He turned away from the window. He could not watch that crippled, crawling thing. He wanted to run, to hide. That was it – to hide. He felt the fluttering start behind his eyes, and his sight began to grey.

'You were nearest to the door. You did the only thing that could have saved us. Though I know I wouldn't have had the guts to do it.'

The floor was covered with cartridge cases – brass cylinders shiny and treacherous under foot. Garrick stumbled; as he fell he put out his arm.

'Christ,' the little Cockney shuddered, 'to put your arm into the brackets like that – I wouldn't have done it.'

Garrick felt his arm snap as the mob of Zulus threw themselves against the door. He hung there staring at his twisted arm, watching the door tremble and shake as they beat against it. There was no pain and after a while everything was grey and warm and safe.

'We fired through the door until we had cleared them away from the other side. Then we were able to get your arm free, but you were out cold. Been that way ever since.'

Garrick stared out across the river. He wondered if they had buried Sean or left him in the grass for the birds.

Lying on his side Garrick drew his legs up against his chest, his body was curled. Once as a brutal small boy he had cracked the shell of a hermit crab. Its soft fat abdomen was so vulnerable that its vitals showed through the transparent skin. It curled its body into the same defensive attitude.

'I'll reckon you'll get your gong,' said the Cockney.

'Yes,' said Garrick. He didn't want it. He wanted Sean back.

= 20 =

Doctor Van Rooyen gave Ada Courtney his arm as she stepped down from the buggy. In fifty years he had not obtained immunity from other people's sorrow. He had learned only to conceal it: no trace of it in his eyes, or his mouth, or his lined and whiskered face.

'He's well, Ada. They did a good job on his arm: that is, for military surgeons. It will set straight.'

'When did they arrive?' asked Ada.

'About four hours ago. They sent all the Ladyburg wounded back in two wagons.'

Ada nodded, and he looked at her with the professional shield of indifference, hiding the shock he felt at the change in her appearance. Her skin was as dry and lifeless as the petals of a pressed flower, her mouth had set determinedly against her grief and her widow's weeds had doubled her age.

'He's waiting for you inside.' They walked up the steps of the church and the small crowd opened to let them pass. There were subdued greetings for Ada and the usual funereal platitudes. There were other women there wearing black, with swollen eyes.

Ada and the doctor went into the cool gloom of the church. The pews had been pushed against the wall to make room for the mattresses. Women were moving about between them and men lay on them.

'I'm keeping the bad ones here, where I can watch them,' the doctor told her. 'There's Garry.'

Garrick stood up from the bench on which he was sitting. His arm was slung awkwardly across his chest. He limped forward to meet them, his peg tapped loudly on the stone floor.

'Ma, I'm –' he stopped. 'Sean and Pa – '

'I've come to take you home, Garry.' Ada spoke quickly, flinching at the sound of those two names.

'They can't just let them lie out there, they should –'

'Please, Garry. Let's go home,' said Ada. 'We can talk about it later.'

'We are all very proud of Garry,' said the doctor.

'Yes,' said Ada. 'Please, let's go home, Garry.' She could feel it there just below the surface and she held it in: so much sorrow confined in so small a place. She turned back towards the door, she mustn't let them see it. She mustn't cry here in front of them, she must get back to Theunis Kraal.

Willing hands carried Garrick's bags out to the buggy and Ada took the reins. Neither of them spoke again until they crossed the ridge and looked down at the homestead.

'You're the master of Theunis Kraal now, Garry,' said Ada softly and Garrick stirred uneasily on the seat beside her. He didn't want it, he didn't want the medal. He wanted Sean.

21

'I hope you don't mind me coming,' said Anna, 'but I had to talk to you.'

'No. I'm glad you did. Truly I'm glad,' Garrick assured her earnestly. 'It's so good to see you again, Anna. It feels like forever since we left.'

'I know, and so much – so much has happened. My Pa and yours. And – and Sean.' She stopped. 'Oh, Garry, I just can't believe it yet. They've told me and told me but I can't believe it. He was so – so alive.'

'Yes,' said Garrick, 'he was so alive.'

'He talked about dying the night before he left. I hadn't even thought about it until then.' Anna shook her head in disbelief, 'and I never dreamed it could happen to him. Oh, Garry, what am I going to do?'

Garrick turned and looked at Anna. The Anna he loved, Sean's Anna. But Sean was dead. He felt an idea move within him, not yet formed in words, but real enough to cause a sick spasm of conscience. He shied away from it.

'Oh, Garry. What can I do?'

She was asking for help, the appeal was apparent in her voice. Her father killed at Isandhlwana, her elder brothers still with Chelmsford at Tugela, her mother and the three small children to feed. How blind of him not to see it!

'Anna, can I help you? Just tell me.'

'No, Garry. I don't think anyone can.'

'If it's money –' He hesitated discreetly. 'I'm a rich man now. Pa left the whole of Theunis Kraal to Sean and I, and Sean isn't – ' She looked at him without answering.

'I can lend you some to tide you over –' blushed Garrick, 'as much as you need.'

She went on staring at him while her mind adjusted itself. Garrick master of Theunis Kraal, he was rich, twice as rich as Sean would have been. And Sean was dead.

'Please, Anna. Let me help you. I want to, really I do.'

He loved her, it was pathetically obvious – and Sean was dead.

'You will let me, Anna?'

She thought of hunger and bare feet, dresses washed until you could see through them when you held them to the light, petticoats patched and cobbled. And always the fear, the uncertainty you must live with when you are poor. Garry was rich and alive, Sean was dead.

'Please tell me you will.' Garrick leaned forward and took her arm, he gripped it fiercely in his agitation and she looked into his face. You could see the resemblance, she thought, but Sean had strength where here there was softness and uncertainty. The colour was wrong also, pale sand and paler blue instead of brutal black and indigo. It was as though an artist had taken a portrait and with a few subtle strokes had altered its meaning completely so as to make it into an entirely different picture. She did not want to think about his leg.

'It's sweet of you, Garry,' she said, 'but we've got a little in the bank and the plot is free of debt. We've got the horses; we can sell them if we have to.'

'What is it then? Please tell me.'

She knew then what she was going to do. She could not lie to him – it was too late for that. She would have to tell him, but she knew that the truth would not make any difference to him. Well, perhaps a little – but not enough to prevent her getting what she wanted. She wanted to be rich, and she wanted a father for the child she carried within her.

'Garry, I'm going to have a baby.'

Garrick's chin jerked up and his breathing jammed and then started again.

'A baby?'

'Yes, Garrick. I'm pregnant.'

'Whose? Sean's?'

'Yes, Garry. I'm going to have Sean's baby.'

'How do you know, are you sure?'

'I'm sure.'

Garrick pulled himself out of his chair and limped across the veranda. He stopped against the railing and gripped it with his good hand; the other was still in the sling. His back was turned to Anna and he stared out across the lawns of Theunis Kraal to the lightly-forested slope beyond.

Sean's baby. The idea bewildered him. He knew that Sean and Anna did that together. Sean had told him and Garrick had not resented it. He was jealous, but only a little, for Sean had let him share in it by telling him and so some of it had belonged to him also. But a baby. Sean's baby.

Slowly the full implication came to him. Sean's baby would be a living part of his brother, the part that had not been cut down by the Zulu blades. He had not completely lost Sean. Anna – she must have a father for her child, it was unthinkable that she could go another month without marrying. He could have both of them, everything he loved in one package. Sean and Anna. She must marry him, she had no other choice. Triumph surged up within him and he turned to her.

'What will you do, Anna?' He felt sure of her now. 'Sean's dead. What will you do?'

'I don't know.'

'You can't have the baby. It would be a bastard.' He saw her wince at the word. He felt very certain of her.

'I'll have to go away – to Port Natal.' She spoke without expression in her voice. Looking calmly at him, knowing what he would say, 'I'll leave soon,' she said, 'I'll be all right. I'll find some way out.'

Garrick watched her face as she spoke. Her head was small on shoulders wide for a girl, her chin was pointed, her teeth were slightly crooked but white – she was very pretty despite the catlike set of her eyes.

'I love you, Anna,' he said. 'You know that, don't you?'

She nodded slowly and her hair moved darkly on her shoulders. The cat eyes softened contentedly. 'Yes, I know, Garry.'

'Will you marry me?' He said it breathlessly.

'You don't mind? You don't mind about Sean's baby?' she said, knowing he did not.

'I love you, Anna.' He came towards her clumsily and she looked up at his face. She did not want to think about the leg.

'I love you, nothing else matters.' He reached for her and she let him hold her.

'Will you marry me, Anna?' He was trembling.

'Yes.' Her hands were quiescent on his shoulders. He sobbed softly and her expression changed to one of distaste, she made the beginnings of a movement to push him away but stopped herself.

'My darling, you won't regret it. I swear you won't,' he whispered.

'We must do it quickly, Garry.'

'Yes. I'll go into town this afternoon and speak to Padre – '

'No! Not here in Ladyburg,' Anna cut in sharply. 'People will have too much to say. I couldn't stand it.'

'We'll go up to Pietermaritzburg,' Garrick acquiesced.

'When, Garry?'

'As soon as you like.'

'Tomorrow,' she said. 'We'll go tomorrow.'

22

The Cathedral in Pietermaritzburg stands on Church Street. Grey stone with a bell-tower and iron railings between the street and the lawns. Pigeons strut puff-chested on the grass.

Anna and Garrick went up the paved path and into the semi-dark of the Cathedral. The stained glass window had the sun behind it, making the interior glow weirdly with colour. Because they were both nervous they held hands as they stood in the aisle.

'There's no one here,' whispered Garrick.

'There must be,' Anna whispered back. 'Try through that door there.'

'What shall I say?'

'Just tell him we want to get married.'

Garrick hesitated.

'Go on.' Anna still whispered, pushing him gently towards the door of the vestry.

'You come with me,' said Garrick. 'I don't know what to say.'

The priest was a thin man with steel-rimmed spectacles. He looked over the top of them at the nervous pair in the doorway and shut the book on the desk in front of him.

'We want to get married,' Garrick said and blushed crimson.

'Well,' said the priest drily, 'you have the right address. Come in.'

He was surprised at their haste and they argued a little, then he sent Garrick down to the Magistrates' Court for a special licence. He married them, but the ceremony was hollow and unreal. The drone of the priest's voice was almost lost in the immense cavern of the Cathedral as they stood small and awed before him. Two old ladies who came in to pray stayed on gleefully to witness for them, and afterwards they both kissed Anna and the priest shook Garrick's hand. Then they went out again into the sunlight. The pigeons still strutted on the lawn and a mule wagon rattled down Church Street with the coloured driver singing and cracking his whip. It was as though nothing had happened.

'We're married,' said Garrick doubtfully.

'Yes,' agreed Anna, but she sounded as though she didn't believe it either.

They walked back to the hotel side by side. They didn't talk or touch each other. Their luggage had been taken up to their room and the horses had been stabled. Garrick signed the register and the clerk grinned at him.

'I've put you in Number Twelve, sir, it's our honeymoon suite.' One of his eyelids drooped slightly and Garrick stammered in confusion.

After dinner, an excellent dinner, Anna went up to the room and Garrick sat on in the lounge drinking coffee. It was almost an hour later that he mustered the courage to follow her. He crossed the drawing-room of their suite, hesitated at the bedroom door then went in. Anna was in bed. She had pulled the bedclothes up to her chin and she looked at him with her inscrutable cat's eyes.

'I've put your nightshirt in the bathroom, on the table,' she said.

'Thank you,' said Garrick. He stumbled against a chair as he crossed the room. He closed the door behind him, undressed quickly and leaning naked over the basin splashed water onto his face; then he dried and pulled the nightshirt over his head. He went back into the bedroom: Anna lay with her face turned away from him. Her hair was loose on the pillow, shining in the lamplight.

Garrick sat on the edge of the chair. He lifted the hem of his nightshirt above his knee and unfastened the straps of his leg, laid the peg carefully beside the chair and massaged the stump with both hands. It felt stiff. He heard the bed creak softly and he looked up. Anna was watching him, staring at his leg. Hurriedly Garrick pulled down his nightshirt to cover the protruding slightly enlarged end with its folded line of scar-tissue. He stood up, balancing, and then hopped one-legged across to the bed. He was blushing again.

He lifted the edge of the blankets and slipped into the bed and Anna jerked violently away from him.

'Don't touch me,' she said hoarsely.

'Anna. Please don't be scared.'

'I'm pregnant, you mustn't touch me.'

'I won't. I swear I won't.'

She was breathing hard, making no attempt to hide her revulsion.

'Do you want me to sleep in the drawing-room, Anna? I will if you say so.'

'Yes,' she said, 'I want you to.'

He gathered his dressing-gown from the chair and stooping picked up his leg. He hopped to the door and turned back to face her. She was watching him still.

'I'm sorry, Anna, I didn't mean to frighten you.' She did not answer him and he went on.

'I love you. I swear I love you more than anything in the world. I wouldn't hurt you, you know that, don't you? You know I wouldn't hurt you?'

Still she did not answer and he made a small gesture of appeal, the wooden leg clutched in his hand and the tears starting to fill his eyes. 'Anna. I'd kill myself rather than frighten you!'

He went quickly through the door and closed it behind him. Anna scrambled out of the bed and with her nightdress flurrying around her legs she ran across the room to the door and turned the key in the lock.

= 23 =

In the morning Garrick was bewildered to find Anna in a mood of girlish gaiety. She had a green ribbon in her hair and her green frock was faded but pretty. She chattered happily through breakfast and while they were having their coffee she leaned across the table and touched Garrick's hand. 'What shall we do today, Garry?'

Garrick looked surprised, he hadn't thought that far ahead. 'I suppose we'd better catch the afternoon train back to Ladyburg,' he said.

'Oh, Garry,' Anna pouted effectively. 'Don't you love me enough to give me a honeymoon?'

'I suppose –' Garrick hesitated and then 'of course, I didn't think of it.' He grinned excitedly. 'Where can we go?'

'We could take the mail boat down the coast to Capetown,' Anna suggested.

'Yes!' Garrick adopted the idea immediately. 'It'll be fun.'

'But, Garry –' Anna's eagerness faded. 'I only have two old dresses with me.' She touched her clothes. Garrick sobered also while he grappled with this new problem. Then he found the solution.

'We'll buy you some more!'

'Oh, Garry, could we? Could we really?'

'We'll buy you all you can use, more than you can use. Come on, finish your coffee and we'll go into town and see what they have.'

'I'm finished.' Anna stood up from the table ready to go.

— 24 —

They had a stateroom on the *Dunottar Castle* from Port Natal to Capetown. There were other young people aboard. Anna, in her elegant new clothing and sparkling with excitement, formed the centrepiece of a gay little group that played deck games, dined, danced and flirted as the mailboat drove south through the sunny, golden days of early autumn.

At first Garrick was content to stay unobtrusively close to Anna. He was there to hold her coat, fetch a book or carry a rug. He watched her fondly, revelling in her success, hardly jealous when she almost disappeared behind a palisade of attentive young men, not resenting the sofa which formed his uncomfortable bed in the drawing-room of their suite.

Then gradually there came a realization among their travelling companions that Garrick was paying for most of the refreshments and other little expenses that came up each day. They became aware of him and of the fact that he appeared to be the richest of the group. From there it needed only a small adjustment to their thinking to admit Garrick to the circle. The men addressed remarks directly at him and some of the other girls flirted with him openly and sent him on small errands. Garrick was at once overjoyed and appalled by these attentions, for he could not cope with the lightning exchange of banter that flickered around him and left him stammering and blushing. Then Garrick found how easy it really was.

'Have a dram, old chap?'

'No, really. I don't, you know.'

'Nonsense, everybody does. Steward, bring my friend here a whisky.'

'Really, no really I won't.'

And of course Garrick did. It tasted foul and he spilt a little on Anna's evening dress; while he wiped it up with his handkerchief she whispered a barbed reprimand and then laughed gaily at a joke from the moustached gentleman on her right. Garrick shrank miserably back in his chair and forced down the rest of the whisky. Then slowly and exquisitely the glow came upon him, starting deep down inside him and spreading out warmly to the very tips of his fingers.

'Have another one, Mr Courtney?'

'Yes, thanks. I'll have the same again, but I think it's my round.' He had the next drink. They were sitting in deck-chairs on the upper deck in the shelter of the superstructure, there was a moon and the night was warm. Someone was talking about Chelmsford's Zulu campaign.

'You're wrong on that point,' Garrick said clearly. There was a small silence.

'I beg your pardon!' the speaker glanced at him with surprise. Garrick leaned forward easily in his chair and began talking. There was a stiffness at first but he made a witticism and two of the women laughed. Garrick's voice strengthened. He gave a quick and deep-sighted résumé of the causes and effects of the war. One of the men asked a question. It was a sharp one but Garrick saw the essence of it and answered neatly. It was all very clear and he found the words without effort.

'You must have been there,' one of the girls hazarded.

'My husband was at Rorke's Drift,' said Anna quietly, looking at him as though he were a stranger. 'Lord Chelmsford has cited him for the award of the Victoria Cross. We are waiting to hear from London.'

The party was silent again, but with new respect.

'I think it's my round, Mr Courtney. Yours is whisky, isn't it?'

'Thank you.'

The dry musty taste of the whisky was less offensive this time; he sipped it thoughtfully and found that there was a faint sweetness in the dry.

As they went down to their staterooms later that night Garrick put his arm around Anna's waist.

'What fun you were tonight!' she said.

'Only a reflection of your charm, my darling, I am your mirror.' He kissed her cheek and she pulled away, but not violently.

'You're a tease, Garry Courtney.'

Garrick slept on his back on the sofa with a smile on his face and no dreams, but in the morning his skin felt tight and dry and there was a small ache behind his eyes. He went through to the bathroom and cleaned his teeth; it helped a little but the ache behind his eyes was still there. He went back to the drawing-room and rang for the cabin steward.

'Good morning, sir.'

'Can you bring me a whisky and soda?' Garry asked hesitantly.

'Certainly, sir.'

Garry did not put the soda into it but drank it neat, like medicine. Then afterwards miraculously the glow was there again, warming him. He had hardly dared to hope for it.

He went through to Anna's cabin. She was rosy with sleep, her hair a joyous tangle on the pillow.

'Good morning, my darling.' Garrick stooped over her and kissed her, and his hand moved to cover one of her breasts through the silk of her gown.

'Garry, you naughty boy.' She slapped his wrist, but jokingly.

There was another honeymoon couple aboard returning to their farm near Capetown – seventy-five acres of the finest vines on the whole of the Cape Peninsula, the man's own words. Anna and Garrick were forced by sheer persistence to accept their invitation to stay with them.

Peter and Jane Hugo were a delightful pair. Very much in love, rich enough, popular and in demand with Capetown society. With them Anna and Garrick spent an enchanted six weeks.

They went racing at Milnerton.

They swam at Muizenberg in the warm Indian Ocean. They picnicked at Clifton and ate crayfish, fresh caught and grilled over open coals. They rode to hounds with the Cape Hunt and caught two jackals after a wild day's riding over the Hottentots' Holland. They dined at the Fort and Anna danced with the Governor.

They went shopping in the bazaars that were filled with treasures and curiosities from India and the Orient, Whatever Anna wanted she was given. Garry bought himself something as well – a silver flask, beautifully worked and set with cornelians. It fitted into the inside pocket of his coat without showing a bulge. With its help Garrick was able to keep pace with the rest of the company.

Then the time came for them to leave. The last night there were only the four of them for dinner and it was sad with the regret of present parting, but happy with the memory of shared laughter.

Jane Hugo cried a little when she kissed Anna goodnight. Garry and Peter lingered on downstairs until the bottle was finished and then they walked upstairs together and shook hands outside Garry's bedroom. Peter spoke gruffly. 'Sorry to see you two go. We've got used to having you round. I'll wake you early and we can go out for a last early morning ride before the boat leaves.'

Garry changed quietly in the bathroom and went through to the bedroom. His peg made no sound on the heavily carpeted floor. He crossed to his own bed and sat down to unstrap his peg.

'Garry,' Anna whispered.

'Hullo, I thought you were asleep.'

There was a stirring and Anna's hand came out from under the bedclothes, held towards him in invitation.

'I was waiting to say goodnight to you.'

Garry crossed to her bed, suddenly awkward again.

'Sit down for a minute,' said Anna and he perched on the edge of her bed. 'Garry, you don't know how much I've enjoyed these last weeks. They've been the happiest days of my whole life. Thank you so much, my husband.'

She reached up and touched his cheek. She looked small and warm curled up in the bed.

'Kiss me goodnight, Garry.'

He leaned forward to touch her forehead with his lips but she moved quickly and took it full on her mouth.

'You can come in, if you like,' she whispered, her mouth still against his. She opened the bedclothes with one hand.

So Garry came to her when the bed was warm, and the wine still sang a little in her head and she was ready in the peculiar passion of early pregnancy. It should have been so wonderfully good.

Impatient now, ready to lead him, she reached down to touch and then stilled into surprised disbelief. Where there should have been hardness, malc and arrogant, there was slackness and uncertainty.

Anna started to laugh. Not even the shotgun blast had hurt as deeply as that laugh. 'Get out,' she said through the cruel laughter. 'Go to your own bed.'

= 25 =

Anna and Garrick had been married two full months when they came back to Theunis Kraal. Garrick's arm was out of plaster, Peter Hugo's doctor had fixed that for him.

They took the road that by-passed the village and crossed the Baboon Stroom bridge. At the top of the rise Garry pulled the horses to a halt and they looked out across the farm.

'I can't understand why Ma moved into town,' said Garrick. 'She didn't have to do that. There's plenty of room for everybody at Theunis Kraal.'

Anna sat silently and contentedly beside him. She had been relieved when Ada had written to them at Port Natal after they had telegraphed her the news of their marriage. Young as she was Anna was woman enough to recognize the fact that Ada had never liked her. Oh, she was sweet enough when they met, but Anna found those big dark eyes of hers disconcerting. They looked too deep and she knew they found the things she was trying to hide.

'We'll have to go and see her as soon as we can. She must come back to the farm – after all Theunis Kraal is her home too,' Garrick went on. Anna moved slightly in her seat, *let her stay in the house in Ladyburg, let her rot there,* but her voice was mild as she answered, 'Theunis Kraal belongs to you now, Garry, and I'm your wife. Perhaps your stepmother knows what's best.' Anna touched his arm and smiled at him, 'Anyway we'll talk about it some other time. Let's get home now, it's been a long drive and I'm very tired.'

Immediately concerned, Garrick turned to her. 'I'm terribly sorry, my dear. How thoughtless of me.' He touched the horses with the whip and they went down the slope towards the homestead.

The lawns of Theunis Kraal were green and there were cannas in bloom, red and pink and yellow.

It's beautiful, thought Anna, *and it's mine. I'm not poor any more.* She looked at the gabled roof and the heavy yellow wood shutters on the windows as the carriage rolled up the drive.

There was a man standing in the shade of the veranda. Anna and Garrick saw him at the same time. He was tall with shoulders as wide and square as the crosstree of a gallows, he stepped out of the shadow and came down the front steps into the sunlight. He was smiling with white teeth in a brown burnt face; it was the old irresistible smile.

'Sean,' whispered Anna.

= 26 =

Sean really noticed him for the first time when they stopped to water the horses. They had left Chelmsford's Column the previous noon to scout towards the north-east. It was a tiny patrol – four mounted white men and a half-a-dozen Nongaai, the loyal Native troops from Natal.

He took the reins from Sean's hands. 'I will hold your horse while you drink.' His voice had a resonance to it and Sean's interest quickened. He looked at the man's face and liked it immediately. The whites of the eyes had no yellow in them and the nose was more Arabic than negroid. His colour was dark amber and his skin shone with oil.

Sean nodded. There is no word in the Zulu language for 'thank you', just as there are no words for 'I am sorry'.

Sean knelt beside the stream and drank. The water tasted sweet for he was thirsty; when he stood again there were damp patches on his knees and water dripping from his chin.

He looked at the man who was holding his horse. He wore only a small kilt of civet-cat tails: no rattles nor cloak, no head-dress. His shield was black rawhide and he carried two short stabbing spears.

'How are you called?' Sean asked, noticing the breadth of the man's chest and the way his belly muscles stood out like the static ripples on a windswept beach.

'Mbejane.' Rhinoceros.

'For your horn?' The man chuckled with delight, his masculine vanity tickled.

'How are you called, Nkosi?'

'Sean Courtney.'

Mbejane's lips formed the name silently and then he shook his head.

'It is a difficult name.' He never said Sean's name – not once in all the years that were to follow.

'Mount up,' called Steff Erasmus. 'Let's get moving.'

They swung up onto the horses, gathered the reins and loosened the rifles in the scabbards. The Nongaai who had been stretched out resting on the bank stood up.

'Come on,' said Steff. He splashed through the stream. His horse gathered itself and bounded up the far bank and they followed him. They moved in line abreast across the grassland, sitting loose and relaxed in their saddles, the horses trippling smoothly.

At Sean's right stirrup ran the big Zulu, his long extended stride easily pacing Sean's horse. Once in a while Sean dropped his eyes from the horizon and looked down at Mbejane; it was a strangely comforting feeling to have him there.

They camped that night in a shallow valley of grass. There were no cooking fires; they ate biltong for supper, the black strips of dried salt meat, and washed it down with cold water.

'We're wasting our time. There hasn't been a sign of Zulu in two days' riding,' grumbled Bester Klein, one of the troopers.

'I say we should turn back and rejoin the Column, We're getting farther and farther away from the centre of things – we're going to miss the fun when it starts.'

Steff Erasmus wrapped his blanket more closely about his shoulders: the night's first chill was on them.

'Fun, is it?' He spat expertly into the darkness. 'Let them have the fun, if we find the cattle.'

'Don't you mind missing the fighting?'

'Look, you, I've hunted bushmen in the Karroo and the Kalahari, I've fought Xhosas and Fingoes along the Fish river, I went into the mountains after Moshesh and his Basutos. Matabele, Zulu, Bechuana – I've had fun with all of them. Now four or five hundred head of prime cattle will be payment enough for any fun we miss.' Steff lay back and adjusted his saddle behind his head. 'Anyway what makes you think there won't be guards on the herds when we find them. You'll get your fun – I promise you.'

'How do you know they've got the cattle up here?' insisted Sean.

'They're here,' said Steff, 'and we'll find them.' He turned his head towards Sean. 'You've got the first watch, keep your eyes open.' He tilted his top hat forward over his face, groped with his right hand to make sure his rifle lay beside him and then spoke from under the hat, 'Goodnight.' The others settled down into their blankets: fully-dressed, boots on, guns at hand. Sean moved out into the darkness to check the Nongaai pickets.

There was no moon, but the stars were fat and close to earth; they lit the land so that the four grazing horses were dark blobs against the pale grass. Sean circled the camp and found two of his sentries awake and attentive. He had posted Mbejane on the north side and now he went there. Fifty yards in front of him he picked up the shape of the small bush beside which he had left Mbejane. Suddenly Sean smiled and sank down onto his hands and knees, he cradled his rifle across the crooks of his elbows and began his stalk. Moving flat along the ground silently, slowly he closed in on the bush. Ten paces from it he stopped and lifted his head, careful to keep the movement inchingly slow. He stared, trying to find the shape of the Zulu among the scraggy branches and bunches of leaves. The point of a stabbing spear pricked him below the ear in the soft of his neck behind the jaw bone. Sean froze but his eyes rolled sideways and in the starlight he saw Mbejane kneeling over him holding the spear.

'Does the Nkosi seek me?' asked Mbejane solemnly, but there was laughter deep down in his voice. Sean sat up and rubbed the place where the spear had stung him.

'Only a night ape sees in the dark,' Sean protested.

'And only a fresh caught catfish flops on its belly,' chuckled Mbejane,

'You are Zulu,' Sean stated, recognizing the arrogance, although he had known immediately from the man's face and body that he was not one of the bastard Natal tribes who spoke the Zulu language but were no more Zulu than a tabby-cat is a leopard.

'Of Chaka's blood,' agreed Mbejane, reverence in his voice as he said the old king's name.

'And now you carry the spear against Cetewayo, your king?'

'My king?' The laughter was gone from Mbejane's voice. 'My king?' he repeated scornfully.

There was silence and Sean waited. Out in the darkness a jackal barked twice and one of the horses whickered softly.

'There was another who should have been king, but he died with a sharpened stick thrust up into the secret opening of his body, until it pierced his gut and touched his heart. That man was my father,' said Mbejane. He stood up and went back into the shelter of the bush and Sean followed him. They squatted side by side, silent but watchful. The jackal cried again up above the camp and Mbejane's head turned towards the sound.

'Some jackals have two legs,' he whispered thoughtfully. Sean felt the tingle along his forearms.

'Zulus?' he asked. Mbejane shrugged, a small movement in the darkness.

'Even if it is, they will not come for us in the night. In the dawn, yes, but never in the night.' Mbejane shifted the spear in his lap. 'The old one with the tall hat and grey beard understands this. Years have made him wise, that's why he sleeps so sweetly now but mounts up and moves in the darkness before each dawn.'

Sean relaxed slightly. He glanced sideways at Mbejane.

'The old one thinks that some of the herds are hidden near here.'

'Years have made him wise,' repeated Mbejane. 'Tomorrow we will find the land more broken, there are hills and thick thorn bush. The cattle will be hidden among them.'

'Do you think we'll find them?'

'Cattle are difficult to hide from a man who knows where to look.'

'Will there be many guards with the herds?'

'I hope so,' answered Mbejane, his voice a purr. His hand crept to the shaft of his assegai and caressed it. 'I hope there will be very many.'

'You would kill your own people, your brothers, your cousins?' asked Sean.

'I would kill them as they killed my father.' Mbejane's voice was savage now. 'They are not my people. I have no people. I have no brothers – I have nothing.'

Silence settled between them again, but slowly the ugliness of Mbejane's mood evaporated and in its place came a sense of companionship. Each of them felt comforted by the other's presence. They sat on into the night.

27

Mbejane reminded Sean of Tinker working a bird, he had the same half-crouched gait and the same air of complete absorption. The white men sat their horses in silence watching him. The sun was well up already and Sean unbuttoned his sheepskin coat and pulled it off. He strapped it onto the blanket roll behind him.

Mbejane had moved out about fifty yards from them and now he was working slowly back towards them. He stopped and minutely inspected a wet pat of cow dung.

'Hierdie Kaffir verstaan wat hy doen,' opined Steff Erasmus approvingly, but no one else spoke. Bester Klein fidgeted with the hammer of his carbine; his red face was already sweaty in the rising heat.

Mbejane had proved right, they were in hilly country. Not the smoothly rounded hills of Natal but hills with rocky crests, deeply gullied and ravined between. There was thorn forest and euphorbia covering the sides of the hills with a lattice work of reptile grey trunks, and the grass was coarse and tall.

'I could use a drink,' said Frikkie Van Essen and wiped his knuckles across his lips.

'Chee peep, chee peep,' a barbet called stridently in the branches of the kaffir boom tree under which they waited. Sean looked up; the bird was brown and red among the scarlet flowers which covered the tree.

'How many?' asked Steff and Mbejane came to stand at his horse's head.

'Fifty – no more,' he answered.

'When?'

'Yesterday, after the heat of the day they moved slowly down the valley. They were grazing. They cannot be more than half an hour's ride ahead of us.'

Steff nodded. Fifty head only, but there would be more.

'How many men with them?'

Mbejane clucked his tongue disgustedly. 'Two *umfaans.*' He pointed with his spear at a dusty place where the print of a half grown boy's bare foot showed clearly. 'There are no men.'

'Good,' said Steff. 'Follow them.'

'They told us that if we found anything we must go back and report,' protested Bester Klein quickly. 'They said we shouldn't start anything on our own.'

Steff turned in his saddle, 'Are you frightened of two *umfaans*?' he asked coldly.

'I'm not frightened of anything, it's just what they told us.' Klein flushed redder in his already red face.

'I know what they told us, thank you,' said Steff. 'I'm not going to start anything, we're just going to have a look.'

'I know you,' burst out Klein. 'If you see cattle you'll go mad for them. All of you, you're greedy for cattle like some men are for drink. Once you see them you won't stop.' Klein was a railway ganger.

Steff turned away from him. 'Come on, let's go.'

They rode out of the shade of the kaffir boom tree into the sunlight, Klein muttering softly to himself and Mbejane leading them down the valley.

The floor of the valley sloped gradually and on each side of them the ground rose steep and rocky. They travelled quickly with Mbejane and the other Nongaai thrown out as a screen and the horsemen cantering in a line with their stirrups almost touching.

Sean levered open the breech of his rifle and drew out the cartridge. He changed it for another from the bandolier across his chest.

'Fifty head is only ten apiece,' complained Frikkie.

'That's a hundred quid – as much as you earn in six months.' Sean laughed with excitement and Frikkie laughed with him.

'You two keep your mouths shut and your eyes open.' Steff's voice was phlegmatic, but he couldn't stop the excitement from sparkling in his eyes.

'I knew you were going to raid,' sulked Klein. 'I knew it, sure as fate.'

'You shut up also,' said Steff and grinned at Sean.

They rode for ten minutes; then Steff called softly to the Nongaai and the patrol halted. No one spoke and every man stood with his head alert and his ears straining.

'Nothing,' said Steff at last. 'How close are we?'

'Very close,' Mbejane answered. 'We should have heard them from here.'

Mbejane's exquisitely muscled body was shiny with sweat and the pride of his stance set him apart from the other Nongaai. There was a restrained eagerness about him, for the excitement was infectious.

'All right, follow them,' said Steff. Mbejane settled the rawhide shield securely on his shoulder and started forward again.

Twice more they stopped to listen and each time Sean and Frikkie were more restless and impatient.

'Sit still,' snapped Steff. 'How can we hear anything with you moving about?'

Sean opened his mouth, but before he could answer they all heard an ox low mournfully ahead of them among the trees.

'That's it!'

'We've got them!'

'Come on!'

'No, wait!' Steff ordered. 'Sean, take my farlookers and climb up that tree. Tell me what you can see.'

'We're wasting time,' argued Sean. 'We should – '

'We should learn to do as we're damn well told,' said Steff. 'Get up that tree.'

With the binoculars slung around his neck, Sean clambered upwards until he sat high in a crotch of two branches. He reached out and broke off a twig which obscured his vision, then exclaimed immediately, 'There they are, right ahead of us!'

'How many?' Steff called up to him.

'A small herd – two herdboys with them.'

'Are they among the trees?'

'No,' said Sean, 'they're in the open. Looks like a patch of swamp.'

'Make sure there aren't any other Zulus with them.'

'No –' Sean started to answer but Steff cut him short.

'Use the glasses, dammit. They'll be hiding if they're there.'

Sean brought up the glasses and focused them. The cattle were fat and sleek skinned, big horned and bodies dappled black on white. A cloud of white tick-birds hovered over them. The two herdboys were completely naked, youngsters with the thin legs and the disproportionately large genitals of the Africans. Sean turned the glasses slowly back and forth searching the patch of swamp and the surrounding bush. At last he lowered them.

'Only the two herdboys,' he said.

'Come down then,' Steff told him.

The herdboys fled as soon as the patrol rode out into the open. They disappeared among the fever trees on the far side of the swamp.

'Let them go,' laughed Steff. 'The poor little buggers are going to be in enough trouble as it is.'

He spurred his horse forward into the vivid green patch of swamp grass. It was lush: thick and tall enough to reach his saddle.

The others followed him in with the mud squelching and sucking at the hooves of the horses. They could see the backs of the cattle showing above the grass a hundred yards ahead of them. The tick-birds circled squawking.

'Sean, you and Frikkie cut around to the left –' Steff spoke over his shoulder and before he could finish the grass around them was full of Zulus, at least a hundred of them in full war dress.

'Ambush!' yelled Steff. 'Don't try and fight, too many of them. Get out!' and they dragged him off his horse.

Horses panicked in the mud, whinnying as they reared. The bang of Klein's rifle was almost drowned in the triumphant roar of the warriors. Mbejane jumped to catch the bridle of Sean's horse; he dragged its head around.

'Ride, Nkosi, quickly. Do not wait.'

Klein was dead, an assegai in his throat and the blood bursting brightly from the corners of his mouth as he fell backwards.

'Hold on to my stirrup leather.' Sean felt surprisingly calm. A Zulu came at him from the side; Sean held his rifle across his lap and fired with the muzzle almost in the man's face. It cut the top off his head. Sean ejected the cartridge case and reloaded.

'Ride, Nkosi!' Mbejane shouted again. He had made no effort to obey Sean: his shield held high he barged into two of the attackers and knocked them down into the mud. His assegai rose and fell, rose and fell.

'Ngi Dhla,' howled Mbejane. 'I have eaten.' Fighting madness on him, he jumped over the bodies and charged. A man stood to meet him and Mbejane hooked the edge of his shield under his and jerked it aside, exposing the man's left flank to his blade.

'Ngi Dhla,' Mbejane howled again.

He had torn an opening in the ring of attackers and Sean rode for it, his horse churning heavily through the mud. A Zulu caught at his reins and Sean fired with his muzzle touching the man's chest. The Zulu screamed.

'Mbejane,' shouted Sean. 'Take my stirrup!'

Frikkie Van Essen was finished; his horse was down and Zulus swarmed over him with red spears.

Leaning out of the saddle Sean circled Mbejane's waist with his arm and plucked him out of the mud. He struggled wildly but Sean held him. The ground firmed under his horse's hooves, they were moving faster. Another Zulu stood in their way with his assegai ready. With Mbejane kicking indignantly under one arm and his empty rifle in his other hand Sean was helpless to defend himself. He shouted an obscenity at the Zulu as he rode down on him. The Zulu dodged to one side and darted in again. Sean felt the sting of the blade across his shin and then the shock as it went on into his horse's chest. They were through, out of the swamp and into the trees.

Sean's horse carried him another mile before it fell. The assegai had gone in deep. It fell heavily but Sean was able to kick his feet out of the irons and jump clear. He and Mbejane stood looking down at the carcass – both of them were panting.

'Can you run in those boots?' asked Mbejane urgently.

'Yes.' They were light *veldschoen*.

'Those breeches will hold your legs.' Mbejane knelt swiftly and with his assegai cut away the cloth until Sean's legs were bare from the thighs down. He stood up again and listened for the first sounds of pursuit. Nothing.

'Leave your rifle, it is too heavy. Leave your hat and your bandolier.'

'I must take my rifle,' protested Sean.

'Take it then,' Mbejane flashed impatiently. 'Take it and die. If you carry that they'll catch you before noon.'

Sean hesitated a second longer and then he changed his grip, holding the rifle by the barrel like an axe. He swung it against the trunk of the nearest tree. The butt shattered and he threw it from him.

'Now we must go,' said Mbejane.

Sean glanced quickly across at his dead horse, the leather thongs held his sheepskin coat onto the saddle. All Anna's hard work wasted, he thought wryly. Then following Mbejane he started to run.

The first hour was bad; Sean had difficulty matching his step to that of Mbejane. He ran with his body tensed and soon had a stabbing stitch in his side. Mbejane saw his pain and they stopped for a few minutes while Mbejane showed him how to relax it away. Then they went on with Sean running smoothly. Another hour went by and Sean had found his second wind.

'How long will it take us to get back to the main army?' grunted Sean.

'Two days perhaps . . . don't talk,' answered Mbejane.

The land changed slowly about them as they ran. The hills not so steep and jagged, the forest thinned and again they were into the rolling grassland.

'It seems we are not being followed.' It was half an hour since Sean had last spoken.

'Perhaps,' Mbejane was non-committal. 'It is too soon yet to tell.'

They ran on side by side, in step so their feet slapped in unison on the hard-baked earth.

'Christ, I'm thirsty,' said Sean.

'No water,' said Mbejane, 'but we'll stop to rest a while at the top of the next rise.'

They looked back from the crest. Sean's shirt was soaked with sweat and he was breathing deeply but easily.

'No one following us,' Sean's voice was relieved. 'We can slow down a bit now.'

Mbejane did not answer. He also was sweating heavily but the way he moved and held his head showed he was not yet beginning to tire. He carried his shield on his shoulder and the blade of the assegai in his other hand was caked with black, dry blood. He stared out along the way they had come for fully five minutes before he growled angrily and pointed with his assegai.

'There! Close to that clump of trees. Can you see them?'

'Oh, hell!' Sean saw them: about four miles behind, on the edge of the forest where it thinned out, a black pencil line drawn on the brown parchment of grassland. But the line was moving.

'How many of them?' asked Sean.

'Fifty,' hazarded Mbejane. 'Too many.'

'I wish I had brought my rifle,' muttered Sean.

'If you had they would be much closer now – and one gun against fifty –' Mbejane left it unfinished.

'All right, let's get going again,' said Sean.

'We must rest a little longer. This is the last time we can stop before nightfall.'

Their breathing had slowed. Sean took stock of himself: he was aching a little in the legs, but it would be hours yet before he was really tired. He hawked a glob of the thick gummy saliva out of his throat and spat it into the grass. He wanted a drink but knew that would be fatal folly.

'Ah!' exclaimed Mbejane. 'They have seen us.'

'How do you know?' asked Sean.

'Look, they are sending out their chasers.' From the head of the line a trio of specks had detached themselves and were drawing ahead.

'What do you mean?' Sean scratched the side of his nose uneasily. For the first time he was feeling the fear of the hunted – vulnerable, unarmed, with the pack closing in.

'They are sending their best runners ahead to force us beyond our strength. They know that if they push us hard enough – even though they break their own wind while they do it – we will fall easily to the others that follow.'

'Good God,' Sean was now truly alarmed. 'What are we going to do about it?'

'For every trick, there is a trick,' said Mbejane. 'But now we have rested enough, let us go.'

Sean took off down the hill like a startled duiker, but Mbejane pulled him up sharply.

'That is what they want. Run as before.' And once again they fell into the steady lope, swinging long-legged and relaxed.

'They're closer,' said Sean when they reached the top of the next hill. Three specks were now well ahead of the others.

'Yes.' Mbejane's voice was expressionless. They went over the crest and down the other side, the slap-slap-slap of their feet together and their breathing an unaltering rhythm: suck blow, suck blow.

There was a tiny stream in the bottom of the valley, clean water rippling over white sand. Sean jumped it with only a single longing glance and they started up the far slope. They were just short of the crest when behind them they heard a thin distant shout. He and Mbejane looked round. On the top of the hill they had just left, only a half a mile away, were the three Zulu runners, and as Sean watched they plunged down the slope towards him with their tall feather head-dresses bobbing and their leopard-tail kilts swirling about their legs. They had thrown aside their shields, but each man carried an assegai.

'Look at their legs,' exulted Mbejane. Sean saw that they ran with the slack, blundering steps of exhaustion.

'They are finished, they have run too hard.' Mbejane laughed. 'Now we must show them how afraid we are: we must run like the wind, run as though a hundred Tokoloshe* breathe on our necks.'

It was only twenty paces to the crest of the slope and they pelted panic-stricken up and over the top. But the instant they were out of sight Mbejane caught Sean's arm and held him.

'Get down,' he whispered. They sank into the grass and then crawled back on their stomachs until they lay just below the crest.

Mbejane held his assegai pointed forward, his legs were gathered up under him and his lips were drawn back in a half grin.

Sean searched in the grass and found a rock the size of an orange. It fitted neatly into his right hand.

They heard the Zulus coming, their horny bare feet pounding up the hill and then their breathing, hoarse hissing gasps, closer and closer until suddenly they came up over the crest. Their momentum carried them down to where Sean and Mbejane stood up out of the grass to meet them. Their fatigue-grey faces crumbled into expressions of complete disbelief; they had expected to find their quarry half a mile ahead of them. Mbejane killed one with his assegai, the man did not even lift his arms to parry the thrust; the point came out between his shoulders.

Sean hurled the rock into the face of another. It made a sound like a ripe pumpkin dropped on a stone floor; he fell backwards with his assegai spinning from his hand.

The third man turned to run and Mbejane landed heavily on his back, bore him down and then sat astride his chest, pushed his chin back and cut his throat.

Sean looked down at the man he had hit; he had lost his head-dress and his face had changed shape. His jaw hung lopsided, he was still moving feebly.

I have killed three men today, thought Sean, *and it was so easy.*

Without emotion he watched Mbejane come across to his victim. Mbejane stooped over him and the man made a small gasping sound then lay still. Mbejane straightened up and looked at Sean.

'Now they cannot catch us before dark.'

'And only a night ape can see in the dark,' said Sean. Remembering the joke, Mbejane smiled; the smile made his face younger. He picked up a bunch of dry grass and wiped his hands on it.

The night came only just in time to save them. Sean had run all day and at last his body was stiffening in protest; his breathing wheezed painfully and he had no moisture left to sweat with.

'A little longer, just a little longer.' Mbejane whispered encouragement beside him.

The pack was spread out, the stronger runners pressing a scant mile behind them and the others dwindling back into the distance.

* A chimera of Zulu mythology.

'The sun is going; soon you can rest.' Mbejane reached out and touched his shoulder; strangely, Sean drew strength from that brief physical contact. His legs steadied slightly and he stumbled less frequently as they went down the next slope. Swollen and red, the sun lowered itself below the land and the valleys were full of shadow.

'Soon now, very soon.' Mbejane's voice was almost crooning. He looked back: the figures of the nearest Zulu were indistinct. Sean's ankle twisted under him and he fell heavily; he felt the earth graze the skin from his cheek and he lay on his chest with his head down.

'Get up,' Mbejane's voice was desperate. Sean vomited painfully, a cupful of bitter bile.

'Get up,' Mbejane's hands were on him, dragging him to his knees.

'Stand up or die here,' threatened Mbejane. He took a handful of Sean's hair and twisted it mercilessly. Tears of pain ran into Sean's eyes and he swore and lashed out at Mbejane.

'Get up,' goaded Mbejane and Sean heaved to his feet.

'Run,' said Mbejane, half-pushing him and Sean's legs began to move mechanically under him. Mbejane looked back once more. The nearest Zulu was very close but almost merged into the fading twilight. They ran on, Mbejane steadying Sean when he staggered, Sean grunting in his throat with each step, his mouth hanging open, sucking air across a swollen tongue.

Then quickly, in the sudden African transition from day to night, all colour was gone from the land and the darkness shut down in a close circle about them. Mbejane's eyes flicked restlessly back and forth, picking up shapes in the gloom, judging the intensity of the light. Sean reeled unseeing beside him.

'We will try now,' decided Mbejane aloud. He checked Sean's run and turned him right at an acute angle on their original track, now they were heading back towards the hunters at a tangent that would take them close past them but out of sight in the darkness.

They slowed to a walk, Mbejane holding Sean's arm across his shoulders to steady him, carrying his assegai ready in his other hand. Sean walked dully, his head hanging.

They heard the leading pursuers passing fifty paces away in the darkness and a voice called in Zulu, 'Can you see them?'

'*Aibo*!' Negative answered another.

'Spread out, they, may try to turn in the dark.'

'*Yeh-bo*!' Affirmative.

Then the voices were passed and silence and night closed about them once more. Mbejane made Sean keep walking. A little bit of moon came up and gave them light and they kept going with Mbejane gradually working back onto a course towards the south-east. They came to a stream at last with trees along its bank. Sean drank with difficulty, for his throat was swollen and sore. Afterwards they curled together for warmth on the carpet of leaves beneath the trees and they slept.

28

They found Chelmsford's last camp on the following afternoon: the neat lines of black camp fires and the flattened areas where the tents had stood, the stakes which had held the horse pickets and the piles of empty bully-beef tins and five-pound biscuit tins.

'They left two days ago,' said Mbejane.

Sean nodded, not doubting the correctness of this. 'Which way did they go?'

'Back towards the main camp at Isandhlwana.'

Sean looked puzzled.

'I wonder why they did that.'

Mbejane shrugged. 'They went in haste – the horsemen galloped ahead of the infantry.'

'We'll follow them,' said Sean.

The spoor was a wide road for a thousand men had passed along it and the wagons and gun carriages had left deep ruts.

They slept hungry and cold beside the spoor and the next morning there was frost in the low places when they started out.

A little before noon they saw the granite dome of Isandhlwana standing out against the sky and unconsciously they quickened their pace. Isandhlwana, the Hill of the Little Hand. Sean was limping for his boot had rubbed the skin from one heel. His hair was thick and matted with sweat and his face was plastered with dust.

'Even army bully beef is going to taste good,' said Sean in English, and Mbejane did not answer for he did not understand, but he was looking ahead with a vaguely worried frown on his face.

'Nkosi, we have seen no one for two days' march. It comes to me that we should have met patrols from the camp before now.'

'We might have missed them,' said Sean without much interest, but Mbejane shook his head. In silence they went on. The hill was closer now so they could make out the detail of ledge and fissure that covered the dome in a lace-work pattern.

'No smoke from the camp,' said Mbejane. He lifted his eyes and started visibly.

'What is it?' Sean felt the first tingle of alarm.

'N'yoni,' said Mbejane softly and Sean saw them. A dark pall, turning like a wheel slowly, high above the hill of Isandhlwana, still so far off that they could not distinguish the individual birds: only a shadow, a thin dark shadow in the sky. Watching it Sean was suddenly cold in the hot noonday sun. He started to run.

There was movement below them on the plain. The torn canvas of an overturned wagon flapped like a wounded bird, the scurry and scuffle of the jackals and higher up the slope of the kopje the hunch-shouldered trot of a hyena.

'Oh, my God!' whispered Sean. Mbejane leaned on his spear; his face was calm and withdrawn but his eyes moved slowly over the field.

'Are they dead? Are they all dead?' The question required no answer. He could see the dead men in the grass, thick about the wagons and then scattered more thinly back up the slope. They looked very small and inconsequential. Mbejane stood quietly waiting. A big black kolbes vulture planed across their front, the feathers in its wing-tips flated like the fingers of a spread hand. Its legs dropped, touched and it hopped heavily to rest among the dead, a swift transformation from beautiful flight to obscene crouching repose.

It bobbed its head, ruffled its feathers and waddled to dip its beak over a corpse that wore the green Hunting Tartan of the Gordons.

'Where is Chelmsford? Was he caught here also?'

Mbejane shook his head. 'He came too late.'

Mbejane pointed with his spear at the wide spoor that skirted the battlefield and crossed the shoulder of Isandhlwana towards the Tugela. 'He has gone back to the river. He has not stopped even to bury his dead.'

Sean and Mbejane walked down towards the field. On the outskirts they picked their way through the debris of Zulu weapons and shields; there was rust forming on the blades of the assegais. The grass was flattened and stained where the dead had lain, but the Zulu dead were gone – sure sign of victory.

They came to the English lines. Sean gagged when he saw what had been done to them. They lay piled upon each other, faces already black, and each one of them had been disembowelled. The flies crawled in their empty stomach cavities.

'Why do they do that?' he asked. 'Why do they have to hack them up like that?'

He walked on heavily past the wagons. Cases of food and drink had been smashed open and scattered in the grass, clothing and paper and cartridge cases lay strewn around the dead, but the rifles were gone. The smell of putrefaction was so thick that it coated his throat and tongue like castor oil.

'I must find Pa,' Sean spoke quietly in almost a conversational tone. Mbejane walked a dozen paces behind him. They came to the lines where the Volunteers had camped. The tents had been slashed to tatters and trampled into the dust. The horses had been stabbed while still tethered to their picket lines; they were massively bloated. Sean recognized Gypsy, his father's mare. He crossed to her.

'Hello, girl,' he said. The birds had taken her eyes out; she lay on her side, her stomach so swollen that it was as high as Sean's waist. He walked around her. The first of the Ladyburg men lay just beyond. He recognized all fifteen of them although the birds had been at them also. They lay in a rough circle, facing outwards. Then he found a sparse trail of corpses leading up towards the shoulder of the mountain. He followed the attempt that the Volunteers had made to fight their way back towards the Tugela and it was like following a paper chase. Along the trail, thick on each side of it, were the marks where the Zulus had fallen.

'At least twenty of them for every one of us,' whispered Sean, with a tiny flicker of pride. He climbed on up and at the top of the shoulder, close under the sheer rock cliff of Isandhlwana, he found his father.

There were four of them, the last four: Waite Courtney, Tim Hope-Brown, Hans and Nile Erasmus. They lay close together. Waite was on his back with his arms spread open, the birds had taken his face away down to the bone, but they had left his beard and it stirred gently on his chest as the wind touched it. The flies, big metallic green flies, crawled thick as swarming bees in the open pit of his belly.

Sean sat down beside his father. He picked up a discarded felt hat that lay beside him and covered his terribly mutilated face. There was a green-and-yellow silk cockade on the hat, strangely gay in the presence of so much death. The flies buzzed sullenly and some came to settle on Sean's face and lips. He brushed them away.

'You know this man?' asked Mbejane.

'My father,' said Sean, without looking up.

'You too.' Compassion and understanding in his voice, Mbejane turned away and left them alone.

'I have nothing', Mbejane had said. Now Sean also had nothing. There was hollowness: no anger, no sorrow, no ache, no reality even. Staring down at this broken thing, Sean could not make himself believe that this was a man. Meat only; the man had gone.

Later Mbejane came back. He had cut a sheet of canvas from one of the unburned wagons and they wrapped Waite in it. They dug his grave. It was hard work for the soil was thick with rock and shale. They laid Waite in the grave, with his arms still widespread in *rigor mortis* beneath the canvas for Sean could not bring himself to break them. They covered him gently and piled rocks upon the place. They stood together at the head of the grave.

'Well, Pa –' Sean's voice sounded unnatural. He could not make himself believe he was talking to his father.

'Well, Pa –' he started again, mumbling self-consciously. 'I'd like to say thanks for everything you've done for me.' He stopped and cleared his throat. 'I reckon you know I'll look after Ma and the farm as best I can – and Garry also.' His voice trailed away once more and he turned to Mbejane.

'There is nothing to say.' Sean's voice was surprised, hurt almost.

'No,' agreed Mbejane. 'There is nothing to say.'

For a few minutes longer Sean stood struggling to grapple with the enormity of death, trying to grasp the utter finality of it, then he turned away and started walking towards the Tugela. Mbejane walked a little to one side and a pace behind him. *It will be dark before we reach the river,* thought Sean. He was very tired and he limped from his blistered heel.

29

'Not much farther,' said Dennis Petersen.

'No,' Sean grunted. He was irritated at statement of the obvious; when you come out of Mahoba's Kloof and have the Baboon Stroom next to the road on your left hand, then it is five miles to Ladyburg. As Dennis had said: not much farther.

Dennis coughed in the dust. 'That first beer is going to turn to steam in my throat.'

'I think we can ride ahead now.' Sean wiped at his face, smearing the dust. 'Mbejane and the other servants can bring them in the rest of the way.'

'I was going to suggest it.' Dennis was obviously relieved. They had almost a thousand head of cattle crowding the road ahead of them and raising dust for them to breathe. It had been two days' drive from Rorkes Drift where the Commando had disbanded.

'We'll hold them in the sale pens tonight and send them out tomorrow morning – I'll tell Mbejane.'

Sean clapped his heels into his horse and swung across to where the big Zulu trotted at the heels of the herd. A few minutes' talk and then Sean signalled to Dennis. They circled out on each side of the herd and met again on the road ahead of it.

'They've lost a bit of condition,' grumbled Dennis looking back.

'Bound to,' said Sean. 'We've pushed them hard for two days.'

A thousand head of cattle, five men's share of Cetewayo's herds – Dennis and his father, Waite, Sean and Garrick – for even dead men drew a full share.

'How far ahead of the others do you reckon we are?' asked Dennis.

'Dunno,' said Sean. It wasn't important and any answer would be only a guess: pointless question is just as irritating as obvious statement. It suddenly occurred to Sean that but a few months previously a question like that would have started a discussion and argument that might have lasted half an hour. What did that mean? It meant that he had changed. Having answered his own question, Sean grinned sardonically.

'What're you laughing at?' asked Dennis.

'I was just thinking that a lot has changed in the last few months.'

'*Ja,*' said Dennis and then silence except for the broken beat of their hooves. 'It's going to seem funny without Pa,' Dennis said wistfully. Mr Petersen had been at Isandhlwana. 'It's going to seem funny being just Ma, the girls and me on the farm.'

They didn't speak again for a while. They were thinking back across the brief months and the events that had changed their lives.

Neither of them yet twenty years of age, but already head of his family, a holder of land and cattle, initiated into grief and a killer of men. Sean was older now with new lines in his face, and the beard he wore was square and spade-shaped. They had ridden with the Commandos who had burned and plundered to avenge Isandhlwana. At Ulundi they had sat their horses behind the ranks of Chelmsford's infantry in the hot sun, quietly waiting as Cetewayo massed his impis and sent them across open ground to overwhelm the frail square of men. They had waited through the din of the regular, unhurried volleys and watched the great black bull of Zulu tearing itself to shreds against the square. Then at the end the ranks of infantry had opened and they had ridden out, two thousand horsemen strong, to smash for ever the power of the Zulu empire. They had chased and hunted until the darkness had stopped them and they had not kept score of the kill.

'There's the church steeple,' said Dennis.

Sean came back slowly out of the past. They were at Ladyburg.

'Is your stepmother out at Theunis Kraal?' asked Dennis.

'No, she's moved into town – the cottage on Protea Street.'

'I suppose she doesn't want to be in the way now that Anna and Garry are married,' said Dennis.

Sean frowned quickly,

'How do you like old Garry getting Anna?' Dennis chuckled and shook his head. 'I reckon you could have got twenty-to-one odds he didn't have a chance.'

Sean's frown became a scowl. Garry had made him look such a damn fool – Sean hadn't finished with Anna.

'Have you heard from them yet? When are they coming home?'

'The last time we heard was from Pietermaritzburg; they sent a wire to Ma just to say they were married. She got it a couple of days before I arrived home from Isandhlwana. That was two months ago; as far as I know we haven't heard since.'

'I suppose Garry's so firmly settled on the nest they'll have to prise him off with a crowbar.' Dennis chuckled again, lewdly. Sean had a sudden and shockingly vivid mental picture of Garry on top of Anna; her knees were up high, her head was thrown back and her eyes were closed; she was making that little mewing sound.

'Shut up, you dirty bastard,' snarled Sean.

Dennis blinked. 'Sorry, I was only joking.'

'Don't joke about my family, he's my brother.'

'And she was your girl, hey?' murmured Dennis.

'Do you want a punch?'

'Cool down, man, I was joking.'

'I don't like that kind of joke, see?'

'All right. All right. Cool down.'

'It's dirty, that's dirty talk.' Sean was trying desperately to shut out the picture of Anna; she was in wild orgasm, her hands pleading at the small of Garrick's back.

'Jesus, since when have you become a saint?' asked Dennis and, urging his horse into a gallop, drew ahead of Sean; he kept going along the main street towards the hotel. Sean considered calling him back, but finally let him go.

Sean turned right into a shady side street. The cottage was the third house down, Waite had purchased it three years before as an investment. It was a charming little place, set among trees in a small green garden with flowers: thatched, whitewashed and surrounded by a wooden picket fence. Sean hitched his horse at the gate and went up the path.

There were two women in the sitting-room when he pushed the door open. They both stood up, surprise instantly becoming delight as they recognized him. It warmed him inside to see it – it's good to be welcome.

'Oh Sean, we weren't expecting you.' Ada came quickly to him. He kissed her and saw that sorrow had left its marks on her. He felt vaguely guilty that Waite's death had not wrought so obvious a change in him. He held her away at arm's length.

'You're beautiful,' he said. She was thin. Her eyes were too big for her face and the grief was in them like shadows in the forest, but she smiled and laughed at him.

'We thought you'd be back on Friday. I'm so glad you've come earlier.'

Sean looked past Ada.

'Hello, Strawberry Pie.' She was hovering impatiently for his attention.

'Hello, Sean.' She flushed a little with his eyes on her, but she did not drop hers.

'You look older,' she said, hardly noticing the dust that caked his skin, powdered his hair and eyelashes, and reddened his eyes.

'You've just forgotten what I look like,' he said, turning back to Ada.

'No, I'd never do that,' whispered Audrey so softly that neither of them heard her. She felt swollen up inside her chest.

'Sit down, Sean.' Ada led him to the big armchair across from the fireplace. There was a daguerreotype of Waite on the mantel.

'I'll get you a cup of tea.'

'How about a beer, Ma?' Sean sank into the chair.

'Of course – I'll get it.'

'No.' Audrey flew across the room towards the kitchen. 'I'll get it.'

'They're in the pantry, Audrey,' Ada called after her, and then to Sean, 'She's such a sweet child.'

'Look again,' Sean smiled. 'She's no child.'

'I wish Garry –' Ada cut herself short.

'What do you wish?' Sean prompted her. She was quiet for a moment, wishing that Garrick could have found a girl like Audrey instead of –

'Nothing,' she said to Sean and came to sit near him.

'Have you heard from Garry again?' asked Sean.

'No. Not yet, but Mr Pye says he had a cheque come through the bank – cashed in Capetown.'

'Capetown?' Sean raised a dusty eyebrow. 'Our boy's living life to the hilt.'

'Yes,' said Ada, remembering the size of that cheque. 'He is.'

Audrey came back into the room: she had a large bottle and a glass on a tray. She crossed to Sean's chair. Sean touched the bottle; it was cold.

'Quickly, wench,' Sean encouraged her. 'I'm dying of thirst.'

The first glass emptied in three swallows, Audrey poured again and, with the replenished glass in his fist, Sean settled back comfortably in the chair.

'Now,' said Ada, 'tell us all about it.'

In the warmth of their welcome – his muscles aching pleasantly, the glass in his hand – it was good to talk. He had not realized that there was so much to tell. At the first hint of slackening in his flow of speech either Ada or Audrey was ready with a question to keep him going.

'Oh, my goodness,' gasped Audrey at last. 'It's nearly dark outside, I must go.'

'Sean,' Ada stood up. 'Will you see that she gets home safely?'

They walked side by side in the half darkness, under the flamboyants. They walked in silence until Audrey spoke.

'Sean, were you in love with Anna?' She blurted out the question and Sean experienced his standard reaction: quick anger. He opened his mouth to blast her, then checked. It was a nice question. Had he been in love with Anna? He thought about it now for the first time, phrasing the question with care that he might answer it with truth. He felt a sudden rush of relief and he was smiling when he told her.

'No, Strawberry Pie, no, I was never in love with Anna.' The tone of his voice was right, he wasn't lying. She walked on happily beside him.

'Don't bother to come up to the house.' She noticed for the first time his stained and dirty clothing that might embarrass him in front of her parents. She wanted it to be right from the start.

'I'll watch you till you get to the door,' said Sean.

'I suppose you'll be going out to Theunis Kraal tomorrow?' she asked.

'First thing in the morning,' Sean assured her. 'There's a hell of a lot of work to do.'

'But you'll be coming to the store?'

'Yes,' said Sean and the way he looked at her made her blush and hate her redhead's skin which betrayed her so easily. She went quickly up the path and then stopped and looked back.

'Sean, please don't call me Strawberry Pie any more.'

Sean chuckled. 'All right, Audrey, I'll try to remember.'

30

Six weeks had gone since his return from the Zulu Campaign, Sean reflected, six weeks that had passed in a blur of speed. He sipped coffee from a mug the size of a German beer *stein*, sitting in the centre of his bed with his nightshirt hitched up to his waist and his legs crossed in comfortable Buddha fashion. The coffee was hot; he sipped noisily and then exhaled steam from his mouth.

The last six weeks had been full – too full for brooding grief or regret, although in the evenings, when he sat in the study with Waite's memory all about him, the ache was still there.

The days seemed to pass before they had fairly begun. There were three farms now: Theunis Kraal and the other two rented from old man Pye. He had stocked them with the looted cattle and the purchases he had made since his return. The price of prime beef had dropped to a new low, with nearly a hundred thousand cattle brought back from Zululand and Sean could afford to be selective in his buying. He could also afford to wait while the price climbed up again.

Sean swung his legs off the bed and walked across the room to the washstand. He poured water from the jug into the basin and tested it tentatively with one finger. It was so cold it stung. He stood hesitating in his ridiculously feminine nightshirt, with dark chest hairs curling out above the elaborately embroidered front. Then he mustered his courage and plunged his face into the basin; he scooped water with both hands and poured it over the back of his neck, massaged it into his hair with hooked fingers and emerged at last blowing heavily with water dripping down onto his nightshirt. He towelled, stripped off the damp garment and stood naked peering out of the window. It had lightened enough for him to make out the smoky swirl of drizzle and mist beyond the pane.

'A hell of a day,' he grumbled aloud, but his tone was deceptive. He felt excitement for this day; he was fresh and sharp-edged, hungry for breakfast, ready to go for there was work to do.

He dressed, hopping on one leg as he got into his breeches, stuffing in the tails of his shirt and then sitting on the bed to pull on his boots. Now he was thinking about Audrey – he must try and get into town tomorrow to see her.

Sean had decided on matrimony. He had three good reasons. He had found that it was easier to get into the Bank of England's vaults than to get under Audrey's petticoats without marrying her. When Sean wanted something no price was too high to pay.

Living at Theunis Kraal with Garry and Anna, Sean had decided that it would be pleasant to have his own woman to cook for him, mend his clothes and listen to his stories, for Sean was feeling a little left out.

The third consideration, by no means the least significant, was Audrey's connections with the local bank. She was one of the very few weaknesses in old man Pye's armour. He might even weigh in with Mahoba's Kloof Farm as a wedding present, though even the optimist in Sean realized that this hope was extravagant. Pye and his money were not easily parted.

Yes, Sean decided, he would have to find time to get into town and tell Audrey – in Sean's mind it wasn't a question of asking her. Sean brushed his hair, combed his beard, winked at himself in the mirror and went out into the passage. He could smell breakfast cooking and his mouth started to water.

Anna was in the kitchen. Her face was flushed from the heat of the stove.

'What's for breakfast, little sister?'

She turned to him, quickly brushing the hair off her forehead with the back of her hand.

'I'm not your sister,' she said, 'I wish you wouldn't call me that.'

'Where's Garry?' Sean asked as though he had not heard her protest.

'He's not up yet.'

'The poor boy's exhausted, no doubt.' Sean grinned at her and she turned away in confusion. Sean looked at her bottom without desire. Strange that Anna being Garry's wife should kill his appetite for her. Even the memory of what they had done before was vaguely obscene, incestuous.

'You're getting fat,' he said noticing the new heaviness of her body. She ducked her head but did not answer and Sean went on, 'I'll have four eggs, please, and tell Joseph not to dry them out completely.'

Sean went through into the dining-room and Garry came in through the side door at the same moment. His face was still vacant from sleep. Sean got a whiff of his breath; it smelled of stale liquor.

'Good morning, Romeo,' said Sean and Garry grinned sheepishly. His eyes were bloodshot and he hadn't shaved.

'Hello, Sean. How did you sleep?'

'Beautifully, thank you. I take it that you did also.' Sean sat down and spooned porridge from the tureen.

'Have some?' he asked Garry.

'Thanks.' Sean passed him the plate. He noticed how Garry's hand shook. *I'll have to talk to him about letting up on the bottle a trifle.*

'Hell, I'm hungry.' They talked the jerky, disconnected conversation of the breakfast table. Anna came through and joined them. Joseph brought the coffee.

'Have you told Sean yet, Garry?' Anna spoke suddenly, clearly and with decision.

'No.' Garry was taken by surprise, he spluttered his coffee.

'Told me what?' Sean asked. They were silent and Garrick fluttered his hand nervously. This was the moment he had been dreading – what if Sean guessed, what if he knew it was his baby and took them away, Anna and the baby, took them away and left Garry with nothing. Haunted by wild unreasonable fears, Garrick stared fixedly across the table at his brother.

'Tell him, Garry,' commanded Anna.

'Anna's going to have a baby,' he said. He watched Sean's face, saw the surprise change slowly to delight, felt Sean's arm close round his shoulders in a painful hug, almost crushing him.

'That's great,' Sean exulted, 'that's wonderful. We'll have the house full of kids in no time if you keep that up, Garry. I'm proud of you.'

Grinning stupidly with relief Garrick watched Sean hug Anna more gently and kiss her forehead.

'Well done, Anna, make sure it's a boy. We need cheap labour around here.'

He hasn't guessed, thought Garrick, *he doesn't know and it will be mine, No one can take it away from me now.*

That day they worked in the south section. They stayed together, Garry laughing in happy confusion at Sean's banter. It was delightful to have Sean give him so much attention. They finished early; for once Sean was in no mood for work.

'My reproductive brother, every barrel loaded with buck-shot.' Sean leaned across and punched Garry's shoulder. 'Let's knock it off and go into town. We can have a few quick ones to celebrate at the hotel and then go and tell Ada.'

Sean stood up in the stirrup and yelled above the moo and mill of the herd.

'Mbejane, bring those ten sick ones up to the house and don't forget that tomorrow we are going to fetch cattle from the sale pens.'

Mbejane waved in acknowledgement and Sean turned back to Garrick.

'Come on, let's get the hell out of here.'

They rode side by side, globules of moisture covering their oilskins and shining on Sean's beard. It was still cold and the escarpment was hidden in the wet mist.

'It's real brandy-drinking weather,' said Sean and Garrick did not answer. He was frightened again. He didn't want to tell Ada. She would guess. She guessed everything, she would know it was Sean's child. You couldn't lie to her.

The horses' hooves plopped wetly in the mud. They reached the spot where the road forked and climbed over the ridge to Ladyburg.

'Ada's going to love being a grandma,' chuckled Sean, and at that moment his horse stumbled slightly, broke its gait and started favouring its near fore. Sean dismounted, lifted the hoof and saw the splinter driven deep into the frog.

'Damn it to hell,' he swore. He bent his head, gripped the hilt of the splinter with his teeth and drew it out.

'Well, we can't go into Ladyburg now, that leg will be sore for days.' Garry was relieved; it put off the time when he must tell Ada.

'Your horse isn't lame. Off you go, man, give her my love.' Sean looked up at him.

'We can tell her some other time. Let's get back home,' Garry demurred.

'Go on, Garry, it's your baby. Go and tell her.'

Garrick argued until he saw Sean's temper rising, then with a sigh of resignation he went and Sean led his own horse back to Theunis Kraal. Now that he was walking the oilskin was uncomfortably hot and heavy, Sean took it off and slung it over the saddle.

Anna was standing on the *stoep* as he came up to the homestead.

'Where's Garry?' she called.

'Don't worry. He's gone into town to see Ada. He'll be back by supper-time.'

One of the stable boys came to take Sean's horse. They talked together and then Sean stooped to lift the injured hoof. His breeches tightened across his buttocks and enhanced the long moulded taper of his legs. Anna looked at him. He straightened up and his shoulders were wide beneath the damp white linen of his shirt. He smiled at her as he came up the steps of the *stoep*. The rain had made his beard curl and he looked like a mischievous pirate.

'You must take better care of yourself now.' He put his hand on her upper arm to lead her inside. 'You can't stand around in the cold any more.' They went in through the glass doors. Anna looked up at him, the top of her head on a level with his shoulder.

'You're a damn fine woman, Anna, and I'm sure you're going to make a fine baby.' It was a mistake, for as he said it his eyes softened and his face turned down towards her. He let his arm drop around her shoulders.

'Sean!' She said his name as though it were an exclamation of pain. She moved quickly, fiercely within the circle of his arm, her body flattened itself against his and her hands went up to catch in the thick hair at the back of his head. She pulled his face down and her mouth opened warm and wet across his lips, her back arched and thrust her thighs against his legs. She moaned softly as she kissed him. For startled seconds Sean stood imprisoned in her embrace, then he tore his face away.

'Are you mad?' He tried to push her from him, but she fought her way back through his fending hands. She locked her arms around him and pressed her face against his chest.

'I love you. Please, please. I love you. Just let me hold you, that's all. I just want to hold you.' Her voice was muffled by the damp cloth of his shirt. She was shivering.

'Get away from me.' Roughly Sean broke her hold and almost threw her backwards onto the couch beside the fireplace.

'You're Garry's wife now, and you'll soon be the mother of his child. Keep your hot little body for him.' Sean stood back from her with his anger starting to mount.

'But I love you, Sean. Oh, my God, if I could only make you understand how I've suffered, living here with you and not being able to touch you even.'

Sean strode across to where she sat. 'Listen to me.' His voice was harsh, 'I don't want you. I never loved you, but now I could no more touch you than I could go with my own mother.' She could see the revulsion in his face. 'You're Garry's wife; if ever again you look at another man I'll kill you.'

He lifted his hands holding them with the fingers crooked ready. 'I'll kill you with my bare hands.'

His face was close to hers. She could not bear the expression in his eyes: she lashed out at him. He pulled back in time to save his eyes, but her nails gouged bloody lines across his cheek and down the side of his nose. He caught her wrists and held her while a thin trickle of blood dribbled down into his beard. She twisted in his hands, jerking her body from side to side, and she screamed at him.

'You swine, you dirty, dirty swine. Garry's wife, you say. Garry's baby, you say.' She threw her head back and laughed wildly through her screaming. 'Now I'll tell you the truth. What I have within me you gave me. It's yours! Not Garry's!' Sean let go her wrists and backed away from her.

'It can't be,' he whispered, 'you must be lying.' She followed him.

'Don't you remember how you said goodbye to me before you went to war? Don't you remember that night in the wagon? Don't you remember – don't you? Don't you?' She was talking quietly now, using her words to wound him.

'That was months ago. It can't be true,' Sean stammered, still moving away from her.

'Three and a half months,' she told him. 'Your brother's baby will be a little early, don't you think? But lots of people have premature babies –' Her voice droned on steadily, she was shivering uncontrollably now and her face was ghostly pale. Sean could stand it no longer.

'Leave me, leave me alone. I've got to think. I didn't know.' He brushed past her and went out into the passage. She heard the door of Waite's study slam shut and she stood still in the centre of the floor. Gradually her panting came under control and the storm surf of her anger abated to expose the black reefs of hatred beneath. She crossed the floor, went down the passage and into her own bedroom. She stood in front of the mirror and looked at herself.

'I hate him,' her lips formed the words in the mirror. Her face was still pale. 'There's one thing I can take from him. Garry's mine now, not his.'

She pulled the pins from her hair and let them drop onto the floor; her hair fell down her back. She shook it onto her shoulders then lifted her hands and tangled it into confusion. Her teeth closed on her own lips, she bit until she tasted blood.

'Oh, God, I hate him, I hate him,' she whispered through the pain. Her hands came down onto the front of her dress. She tore it open, then in the mirror looked without interest at the round bosses of her nipples that were already darkening with the promise of fruition. She kicked off her shoes.

'I hate him.' She stooped and her hands went up under her skirts into the petticoats. She loosened her pantaloons and stepped out of them; she held them across her chest to tear them, then threw them next to the bed. She swept her arm across the top of her dressing-table: one of the bowls hit the floor and burst with a splash of face-powder and there was the sudden pungent reek of spilled perfume. She crossed to the bed and dropped onto it. She lifted her knees and her petticoats fell back like the petals of a flower: her white legs and lower body were the stamen.

Just before nightfall there was a shy knock on her door.

'What is it?' she asked.

'The Nkosikazi has not told me what I should cook for dinner,' Old Joseph's voice was raised respectfully.

'There will be no dinner tonight. You and all the servants may go.'

'Very well, Nkosikazi.'

Garrick came home in the dark. He had been drinking; she heard him stagger as he crossed the *stoep*, and his voice slur as he called.

'Hallo. Where's everybody? Anna! Anna! I'm back.' Silence for a while as he lit one of the lamps and then the hurried thump, thump of his peg along the passage and his voice again edged with alarm.

'Anna, Anna, where are you?'

He pushed the door open and stood with the lamp in his hand. Anna rolled away from the light, pressing her face into the pillow and hunching her shoulders. She heard him set the lamp down on the dressing-table, felt his hands pulling down her skirts to cover her nakedness, then gently turn her to face him. She looked into his face and saw the uncomprehending horror in it.

'My darling, oh Anna, my darling, what's happened?' He stared at her broken lips and her breasts. Bewildered he turned his head and looked at the bottles on the floor, at her torn pantaloons. His face hardened and came back to her.

'Are you hurt?' She shook her head.

'Who? Tell me who did it.' She turned away from him again, hiding her face.

'My darling, my poor darling. Who was it – one of the servants?'

'No,' her voice stifled with shame.

'Please tell me, Anna. What happened?'

She sat up quickly and threw her arms about him, holding him hard so her lips were near his ear. 'You know, Garry, You know who did it.'

'No, I swear I don't, please tell me.'

Anna drew her breath in deep, held it a second then breathed it out. 'Sean!'

Garrick's body convulsed in her arms, she heard him grunt as though he had been hit. Then he spoke. 'This too. Now this too.'

He loosened her hands from his neck and pushed her gently down onto the pillows. He crossed to the cupboard, opened one of the drawers and took out Waite's service pistol.

He's going to kill Sean, she thought. Garrick went out of the room without looking at her again. She waited with her hands clenched at her sides and her whole body stretched tightly. When the shot came at last it was surprisingly muted and unwarlike. Her body relaxed, her hands opened and she began to cry softly.

= 31 =

Garry limped down the passage. The pistol was heavy and the checkered grip rough in his hand. There was light showing under the study door at the end of the passage. It was unlocked. Garrick went in.

Sean sat with his elbows on the desk and his face in his hands but he looked up as Garrick came in through the door. The scratches had already dried black across his cheek, but the flesh around them was red and inflamed. He looked at the pistol in Garrick's hand.

'She has told you.' There was no question or expression in his voice.

'Yes.'

'I hoped that she wouldn't,' said Sean. 'I wanted her to spare you that at least.'

'Spare me?' Garrick asked. 'What about her? Did you think of her?'

Sean did not answer, instead he shrugged and laid back tiredly in his chair.

'I never realized before what a merciless swine you are,' choked Garrick. 'I have come to kill you.'

'Yes.' Sean watched the pistol come up. Garrick was holding it with both hands, his sandy hair hung forward onto his forehead.

'My poor Garry,' Sean said softly and immediately the pistol started to shake. It sank until Garrick held it, still with both hands between his knees. He crouched over it, blubbering – chewing at his lips to stop himself. Sean started out of his chair to go to him, but Garrick recoiled against the door-jamb.

'Keep away from me,' he yelled, 'don't touch me.' He threw the pistol, the sharp edge of the hammer cut across Sean's forehead, jerking his head back. The pistol glanced off and hit the wall behind him. It fired and the bullet splintered the panelled woodwork.

'We're finished,' Garrick screamed. 'We're finished for ever.' He groped wildly for the door and stumbled out into the passage, through the kitchens into the rain. He fell many times as the grass caught his peg, but each time he scrambled up and kept running. He sobbed with each step in the utter darkness of the night.

At last the growl of the rain-engorged Baboon Stroom blocked his way. He stood on the bank with the drizzle blowing into his face.

'Why me, why always me?' He screamed his agony into the darkness. Then with a rush of relief as strong as the torrent in the river-bed below him he felt the moth flutter its wings behind his eyes. The warmth and the greyness closed about him and he sank down onto his knees in the mud.

= 32 =

Sean took very little with him: his bedroll, a rifle and a spare horse. Twice in the darkness he lost the path to Mbejane's kraal but each time his horse found it again. Mbejane had built his big grass beehive hut well away from the quarters of the other servants, for he was Zulu of royal blood. When at last Sean came to it there were a few minutes of sleepy stirring and muttering within before Mbejane, with a blanket draped around his shoulders and an old paraffin lamp in his hand, came out to Sean's shouts.

'What is it, Nkosi?'

'I am going, Mbejane.'

'Where to?'

'Wherever the roads lead. Will you follow?'

'I will get my spears,' said Mbejane.

Old man Pye was still in his office behind the bank when they reached Ladyburg. He was counting the sovereigns and stacking them in neat golden piles and his hands were as gentle on them as a man's hands on the body of the woman he loves, but he reached quickly for the open drawer at his side as Sean shouldered the door open.

'You don't need that,' said Sean and Pye lifted his hand guiltily off the pistol.

'Good gracious! I didn't recognize you, my boy.'

'How much have I got credited to my account?' Sean cut through the pleasantries.

'This isn't banking hours, you know.'

'Look here, Mr Pye, I'm in a hurry. How much have I got?'

Pye climbed out of his chair and crossed to the big iron safe. Shielding it with his body he tumbled the combination and swung open the door. He brought the ledger across to the desk.

'Carter – Cloete – Courtney,' he muttered as he turned the pages. 'Ah – Ada – Garrick – Sean. Here we are. Twelve hundred and ninety-six pounds eight and eight pence; of course, there are last month's accounts at the store still unpaid.'

'Call it twelve hundred then,' said Sean. 'I want it now and while you are counting it you can give me pen and paper.'

'Help yourself, there on the desk.'

Sean sat at the desk, pushed the piles of gold out of his way, dipped the pen and wrote. When he had finished he looked up at old Pye.

'Witness that, please.'

Pye took the paper and read it through. His face went limp with surprise.

'You're giving your half share of Theunis Kraal and all the cattle to your brother's first born!' he exploded.

'That's right, please witness it.'

'You must be mad,' protested Pye. 'That's a fortune you're giving away. Think what you're doing – think of your future. I had hoped that you and Audrey –' He stopped himself and went on. 'Don't be a fool, man.'

'Please witness it, Mr Pye,' said Sean and, muttering under his breath, Pye signed quickly.

'Thank you.' Sean folded the document, slipped it into an envelope and sealed it. He put it away inside his coat.

'Where's the money?' he asked.

Pye pushed a canvas bag across to him. His expression was one of disgust; he wanted no truck with fools.

'Count it,' he said.

'I'll take your word for it,' said Sean and signed the receipt.

Sean rode out past the sale-pens and up the escarpment along the road to Pietermaritzburg. Mbejane trotted at his stirrup leading the spare horse. They stopped at the top of the escarpment. The wind had blown the clouds open and the starlight came through. They could see the town below them with here and there a lighted window.

I should have said goodbye to Ada, Sean thought. He looked down the valley towards Theunis Kraal. He could see no light. He touched the letter in the inside pocket of his coat.

'I'll post it to Garry from Pietermaritzburg,' he spoke aloud.

'Nkosi?' asked Mbejane.

'I said, "It's a long road, let us begin." '

'Yes,' agreed Mbejane. 'Let us begin.'

TWO

Witwatersrand

= 1 =

They turned north from Pietermaritzburg and climbed steadily up across bleak grassland towards the mountains. On the third day they saw the Drakensberg, jagged and black as the teeth of an ancient shark along the skyline.

It was cold; wrapped in his kaross Mbejane trailed far behind Sean. They had exchanged perhaps two dozen words since they left Pietermaritzburg for Sean had his thoughts and they were evil company. Mbejane was keeping discreetly out of his way. Mbejane felt no resentment, for a man who had just left his home and his cattle was entitled to brood. Mbejane was with sadness himself – he had left a fat woman in his bed to follow Sean.

Mbejane unplugged his small gourd snuff-box, picked a pinch and sniffed it delicately. He looked up at the mountains. The snows upon them were turning pink in the sunset and in a little while now they would make camp, and then again perhaps they would not. It made no difference.

Sean rode on after dark. The road crossed another fold in the veld and they saw the lights in the valley below.

'Dundee', Sean thought without interest. He made no effort to hasten his horse but let it amble down towards the town. Now he could smell the smoke from the coal mine, tarry and thick in the back of his throat. They entered the main street. The town seemed deserted in the cold. Sean did not intend stopping – he would camp on the far side; but when he reached the hotel he hesitated. There was warmth in there and laughter and the sound of men's voices and he was suddenly aware that his fingers were stiff with cold.

'Mbejane, take my horse. Find a place to camp beyond the town and make a fire so I won't miss you in the dark.'

Sean climbed down and walked into the bar. The room was full, miners most of them – he could see the grey coal dust etched into their skins. They looked at him incuriously as he crossed to the counter and ordered a brandy. He drank it slowly, making no attempt to join the loud talk around him.

The drunk was a short man but built like Table Mountain, low, square and solid. He had to stand on tiptoe to put his arm around Sean's neck.

'Have a drink with me, *Boetie.*' His breath smelt sour and old.

'No thanks.' Sean was in no mood for drunks.

'Come on, come on,' the drunk insisted; he staggered and Sean's drink slopped onto the counter.

'Leave me alone.' Sean shrugged the arm away.

'You've got something against me?'

'No. I just feel like drinking alone.'

'You don't like my face, maybe?' The drunk held it close to Sean's. Sean didn't like it.

'Push off, there's a good fellow.'

The drunk slapped the counter.

'Charlie, give this big ape a drink. Make it a double. If he don't drink it, I ram it down his throat.'

Sean ignored the proffered glass. He swallowed what remained in his own and turned for the door. The drunk threw the brandy in his face. The spirit burned his eyes and he hit the man in the stomach. As his head came down Sean hit him again – in the face. The drunk spun sideways, fell and lay bleeding from his nose.

'What you hit him for?' Another miner was helping the drunk into a sitting position.

'It wouldn't cost you nothing to have a drink with him.' Sean felt the hostility in the room; he was the outsider.

'This boy is looking for trouble.'

'He's a tough monkey. We know how to handle tough monkeys.'

'Come on, let's sort this bastard out.'

Sean had hit the man as a reflex action. He was sorry now, but his guilt evaporated as he saw them gathering against him. Gone too was his mood of depression and in its place was a sense of relief. This was what he needed.

There were six of them moving in on him in a pack. Six was a fairly well-rounded number. One of them had a bottle in his hand and Sean started to smile. They were talking loudly, spreading courage and waiting for one of their fellows to start it.

Sean saw movement out of the side of his eye and jumped back to cover it with his hands ready.

'Steady on there,' a very English voice soothed him. 'I have come to offer my services. It seems to me you have adversaries and to spare.' The speaker had stood up from one of the tables behind Sean. He was tall, with a gauntly ravaged face and an immaculate grey suit.

'I want them all,' said Sean.

'Damned unsporting.' The newcomer shook his head. 'I'll buy the three gentlemen on the left if your price is reasonable.'

'Take two as a gift and consider yourself lucky.' Sean grinned at him and the man grinned back. They had almost forgotten the impending action in the pleasure of meeting.

'Very decent of you. May I introduce myself – Dufford Charleywood.' He shifted the light cane into his left hand and extended his right to Sean.

'Sean Courtney.' Sean accepted the hand.

'Are you bastards going to fight or what?' protested one of the miners impatiently.

'We are, dear boy, we are,' said Duff and moved lightly as a dancer towards him, swinging the cane. Thin as it was it made a noise like a well-hit baseball along the man's head.

'Then there were five,' said Duff. He flicked the cane and, weighted with lead, it made a most satisfactory swish. Like a swordsman he lunged into the throat of the second miner. The man lay on the floor and made a strangling noise.

'The rest are yours, Mr Courtney,' said Duff regretfully.

Sean dived in low, spreading his arms to scoop up all four pairs of legs at once. He sat up in the pile of bodies and started punching and kicking.

'Messy, very messy,' murmured Duff disapprovingly. The yelps and thuds gradually petered into silence and Sean stood up. His lip was bleeding and the lapel was torn off his jacket.

'Drink?' asked Duff.

'Brandy, please.' Sean smiled at the elegant figure against the bar. 'I won't refuse another drink this evening.'

They took the glasses to Duff's table, stepping over the bodies as they went.

'Mud in your eye!'

'Down the old red lane!'

Then they studied each other with frank interest, ignoring the clearing up operations being conducted around them.

'You arc travelling?' asked Duff.

'Yes, are you?'

'No such luck. I am in the permanent employ of Dundee Collieries Ltd.'

'You work here?' Sean looked incredulous for Duff was a peacock among pigeons.

'Assistant Engineer,' nodded Duff. 'But not for long; the taste of coal-dust sticks in my craw.'

'May I suggest something to wash it out?'

'A splendid idea,' agreed Duff.

Sean brought the drinks to the table.

'Where are you headed?' asked Duff.

'I was facing north when I started,' shrugged Sean, 'I just kept going that way.'

'Where did you start from?'

'South.' Sean answered abruptly.

'Sorry, I didn't mean to pry.' Duff smiled. 'Yours is brandy, isn't it?'

The barman came round from behind the counter and crossed to their table.

'Hello, Charlie,' Duff greeted him. 'I take it you require compensation for the damage to your fittings and furniture?'

'Don't worry about it, Mr Charleywood. Not often we have a good barney like that. We don't mind the odd table and chair as long as it's worth watching. Have it on the house.'

'That's extremely good of you.'

'That's not what I came across for, Mr Charleywood. I've got something I'd like you to take a look at, you being a mining chap and all. Could you spare a minute, sir?'

'Come on, Sean. Let's see what Charlie's got for us. My guess is it's a beautiful woman.'

'It's not actually, sir,' said Charlie seriously and led the way through into the back room. Charlie reached up and took a lump of rock down from one of the shelves. He held it out to Duff. 'What do you make of that?'

Duff took it and weighed it in his hand, then peered closely at it. It was glassy grey, blotched with white and dark-red and divided by a broad black stripe.

'Some sort of conglomerate.' Duff spoke without enthusiasm. 'What's the mystery?'

'Friend of mine brought it down from Kruger's Republic on the other side of the mountains. He says it's gold bearing. They've made a big strike at a place called Witwatersrand just outside Pretoria. Of course, I don't put much store by these rumours 'cos you hear them all the time: diamonds and gold, gold and diamonds.'

Charlie laughed and wiped his hands on his apron.

'Anyway my friend says the Boers are selling mining licences to them as want to dig for the stuff. Thought I'd just get you to have a look.'

'I'll take this with me, Charlie, and pan it in the morning. Right now my friend and I are drinking.'

= 2 =

Sean opened his eyes the next morning to find the sun burning in through the window above his bed. He closed them again hurriedly and tried to remember where he was. There was a pain in his head that distracted him and a noise. The noise was a regular croaking rattle; it sounded as though someone was dying. Sean opened his eyes and turned his head slowly. Someone was in the bed across the room. Sean groped for a boot and threw it; there was a snort and Duff's head came up. For a second he regarded Sean through eyes as red as a winter sunset and then he subsided gently back into the blankets.

'Keep it down to a bellow,' whispered Sean. 'You are in the presence of grave illness.'

A long time later a servant brought coffee.

'Send word to my office that I am sick,' commanded Duff.

'I have done so.' The servant clearly understood his master. He went on, 'There is one outside who seeks the other Nkosi.' He glanced at Sean. 'He is greatly worried.'

'Mbejane. Tell him to wait,' said Sean.

They drank coffee in silence, sitting on the edge of their beds.

'How did I get here?' asked Sean.

'Laddie, if you don't know, then nobody does.' Duff stood up and crossed the room to find fresh clothing. He was naked and Sean saw that although he was slim as a boy his body was finely muscled.

'My God, what does Charlie put in his liquor?' complained Duff as he picked up his jacket.

He found the lump of rock in the pocket, brought it out and tossed it onto the packing-case that served as a table. He regarded it sourly as he finished dressing, then he went to the great pile of bachelor debris that filled one corner of the room. He scratched around and came out with a steel pestle-and-mortar and a battered black gold pan.

'I feel very old this morning,' he said as he started to crush the rock to powder in the mortar. He poured the powder into the pan, carried it out to the corrugated iron water tank beside the front door and filled the pan from the tap.

Sean followed him and they sat together on the front step. Duff worked the pan, using a practised dip and swing that set the contents spinning like a whirlpool and slopped a little over the front lip with each turn. He filled it again with clean water.

Suddenly Sean felt Duff stiffen beside him. He glanced at his face and saw that his hangover had gone; his lips were shut in a thin line and his bloodshot eyes were fastened on the pan.

Sean looked down and saw the gleam through the water, like the flash of a trout's belly as it turns to take the fly. He felt the excitement prickle up his arms and lift the hair on his neck.

Quickly Duff splashed fresh water into the pan; three more turns and he flicked it out again. They sat still, not speaking, staring at the golden tail curved round the bottom of the pan.

'How much money have you got?' Duff asked without looking up.

'Little over a thousand.'

'As much as that. Excellent! I can raise about five hundred but I'll throw in my mining experience. Equal partners – do you agree?'

'Yes.'

'Then why are we sitting here? I'm going down to the bank. Meet me on the edge of town in half an hour.'

'What about your job?' Sean asked.

'I hate the smell of coal – the hell with my job.'

'What about Charlie?'

'Charlie is a poisoner – the hell with Charlie.'

= 3 =

They camped that night in the mouth of the pass with the mountains standing up before them. They had pushed the pace all that afternoon and the horses were tired – they turned their tails to the wind and cropped at the dry winter grass.

Mbejane built a fire in the shelter of a red stone outcrop and they huddled beside it brewing coffee, trying to keep out of the snow-cold wind, but it came down off the mountains and blew a plume of sparks from the fire. They ate; then Mbejane curled up beside the fire, pulled his kaross over his head and did not move again until morning.

'How far is it to this place?' Sean asked.

'I don't know,' Duff admitted. 'We'll go up through the pass tomorrow – fifty or sixty miles through the mountains – and then we'll be out into the high veld. Perhaps another week's riding after that.'

'Are we chasing rainbows?' Sean poured more coffee into the mugs.

'I'll tell you when we get there.' Duff picked up his mug and cupped his hands around it. 'One thing's certain – that sample was stinking with gold. If there's much of that stuff around somebody's going to get rich.'

'Us, perhaps?'

'I've been on gold stampedes before. The first ones in make the killings. We might find the ground for fifty miles around as thick with claim pegs as quills on a porcupine's back.' Duff sipped noisily at his coffee. 'But we've got money – that's our ace in the hole. If we peg a proposition we've got capital to work it. If we're too late we can buy claims from the brokers. If we can't, well, there're other ways of getting gold than grubbing for it – a store, a saloon, a transport business, take your pick.'

Duff flicked the coffee grounds out of his mug. 'With money in your pocket you're somebody; without it anyone can kick you in the teeth.' He took a long black cheroot out of his top pocket and offered it to Sean. Sean shook his head and Duff bit the tip from the cheroot and spat it into the fire. He picked up a burning twig and lit it, sucking with content.

'Where did you learn mining, Duff?'

'Canada.' The wind whipped the smoke away from his mouth as Duff exhaled.

'You've been around?'

'I have, laddie. It's too damn cold to sleep; we'll talk instead. For a guinea I'll tell you the story of my life.'

'Tell me first, I'll see if it's worth it!' Sean pulled the blanket up around his shoulders and waited.

'Your credit is good,' agreed Duff. He paused dramatically. 'I was born thirty-one years ago, fourth and youngest son to the sixteenth Baron Roxby – that is, not counting the others who never made it to puberty.'

'Blue blood,' said Sean.

'Of course, just look at my nose. But please don't interrupt. Very early in the game my father, the sixteenth Baron, dispelled with a horsewhip any natural affection we may have owed him. Like Henry the Eighth he preferred children in the abstract. We kept out of his way and that suited everybody admirably. A sort of armed truce.

'Dear father had two great passions in life: horses and women. During his sixty-two glorious years he acquired a fine collection of both. My fifteen-year-old cousin, a comely wench as I recall, was his last and unattained ambition. He took her riding every day and fingered her most outrageously as he helped her in and out of the saddle. She told me about it with giggles.

'However father's horse, a commendably moral creature, cut short the pursuit by kicking father on the head, presumably in the middle of one of these touching scenes. Poor father was never the same again. In fact so much was he altered by this experience that two days later, to the doleful clangour of bells and a collective sigh of relief from his sons and his neighbours who owned daughters, they buried him.'

Dufford leaned forward and prodded the fire.

'It was all very sad. I or any of my brothers could have told father that not only was my cousin comely but she had the family sporting instincts developed to a remarkable degree. After all who should know better than we? We were her cousins and you know how cousins will be cousins. Anyway father never found out and to this day I feel guilty – I should have told him. He would have died happier . . . Do I bore you?'

'No, go on. I've had half a guinea's worth already,' Sean laughed.

'Father's untimely decease made no miraculous changes in my life. The seventeenth Baron, brother Tom, once he had the title was every bit as tight-fisted and unpleasant as father had been. There I was at nineteen on an allowance too small to enable me to pursue the family hobbies, gathering mould in a grim old castle forty miles from London, with the development of my sensitive soul being inhibited by the undiluted company of my barbaric brothers.

'I left with three months' advance allowance clutched in my sweaty palm and the farewells of my brothers ringing in my ears. The most sentimental of these was "don't bother to write".

'Everybody was going to Canada: it seemed like a good idea so I went too. I made money and spent it. I made women and spent them also, but the cold got to me in the end.'

Duff's cheroot had died; he re-lit it and looked at Sean.

'It was so cold you couldn't urinate without getting frostbite on your equipment, so I began to think of lands tropical, of white beaches and sun, of exotic fruits and even more exotic maidens. The peculiar circumstances that finally decided me to leave are painful to recall and we will not dwell upon them. I left, to say the least, under a cloud. So here you see me freezing slowly to death, with a bearded ruffian for company and not an exotic maiden within a day's ride.'

'A stirring tale – well told,' applauded Sean.

'One story deserves another – let's hear your tale of woe.'

Sean's smile slid off his face. 'Born and bred here in Natal. Left home a week or so ago, also in painful circumstances.'

'A woman?' asked Duff with deep compassion.

'A woman,' agreed Sean.

'The sweet bitches,' sighed Duff. 'How I love them.'

= 4 =

The pass ran like a twisted gut through the Drakensberg. The mountains stood up sheer and black on each side of them, so they rode in shadow and saw the sun only for a few hours in the middle of the day. Then the mountains dropped away and they were out into the open.

Open was the word for the high veld. It stretched away flat and empty, grass and brown grass dwindling to a distant meeting with the pale empty sky. But the loneliness could not blunt the edge of their excitement: each mile covered, each successive camp along the ribbon road ground it sharper until at last they saw the name in writing for the first time. Forlorn as a scarecrow in a ploughed land the signpost pointed right and said, 'Pretoria', pointed left and said, 'Witwatersrand'.

'The Ridge of White Waters,' whispered Sean. It had a ring to it that name – a ring like a hundred millions in gold.

'We're not the first,' muttered Duff. The left-hand fork of the road was deeply scored by the passage of many wagons.

'No time to worry about that.' Sean had the gold sickness on him now. 'There's a little speed left in these mokes – let's use it.'

It came up on the horizon as a low line above the emptiness, a ridge of hills like a hundred others they had crossed. They went up it and from the top looked down. Two ridges ran side by side, north and south, four miles or so apart. In the shallow valley between they could see the flash of the sun off the swamp pools that gave the hills their name.

'Look at them,' groaned Sean.

The tents and wagons were scattered along the length of the valley and in between them the prospect trenches were raw wounds through the grass. The trenches were concentrated along a line down the centre of the valley.

'That's the strike of the reef,' said Duff, 'and we're too late – it's all pegged!'

'How do you know?' protested Sean.

'Use your eyes, laddie. It's all gone.'

'There might be some they've overlooked.'

'These boys overlook nothing. Let's go down and I'll show you.' Duff prodded his horse and they started down. He spoke over his shoulder to Sean. 'Look up there near that stream – they aren't wasting time. They've got a mill going already. It's a four-stamp rig by the looks of it.'

They rode into one of the larger encampments of tents and wagons; there were women at work around the fires and the smell of food brought saliva jetting from under Sean's tongue. There were men also, sitting among the wagons waiting for their suppers.

'I'm going to ask some of these characters what's going on here,' said Sean. He climbed down off his horse and tossed the reins to Mbejane. Duff watched him with a wry grin as he tried in succession to engage three different men in conversation. Each time Sean's victim avoided his eyes, mumbled vaguely and withdrew. Sean finally gave up and came back to the horses.

'What's wrong with me,' he asked plaintively. 'Have I got a contagious clap?'

Duff chuckled. 'They've got gold sickness,' he said. 'You're a potential rival. You could die of thirst and not one of them would spit on you, lest it gave you strength to crawl out and peg something they hadn't noticed.'

He sobered. 'We're wasting time. There's an hour left before dark, let's go and have a look for ourselves.'

They trotted out towards the area of mauled earth. Men were working pick and shovel in the trenches, some of them lean and tough-looking with a dozen natives working beside them; others fat from an office stool, sweating and gritting teeth against the pain of blistered palms, their faces and arms burnt angry red by the sun. All of them greeted Sean and Duff with the same suspicious hostility.

They rode slowly towards the north and every hundred yards with sickening regularity they came across a claim peg with a cairn of stones around its foot and the scrap of canvas nailed to it. Printed in crude capitals on the canvas was the owner's name and his licence number.

Many of the claims were as yet untouched and on these Duff dismounted and searched in the grass, picking up pieces of rock and peering at them before discarding them again. Then once more they moved on with sinking spirits and increasing exhaustion. They camped after dark on the open windy ridge and while the coffee brewed they talked.

'We're too late.' Sean scowled into the fire.

'We've got money, laddie, just remember that. Most of these gentlemen are broke – they are living on hope, not beef and potatoes. Look at their faces and you'll see despair starting to show. It takes capital to work reef gold: you need machinery and money for wages, you have to pipe in water and pile rock, you need wagons and time.'

'Money's no good without a claim to work,' brooded Sean.

'Stay with me, laddie. Have you noticed how many of these claims haven't been touched yet? They belong to speculators and my guess is that they are for sale. In the next few weeks you'll see the men sorted out from the boys –'

'I feel like packing up. This isn't what I expected.'

'You're tired. Sleep well tonight and tomorrow we'll see how far this reef runs – then we'll start some scheming.'

Duff lit one of his cheroots and sucked on it: in the firelight his face was as gaunt as a Red Indian's. They sat on in silence for a while, then Sean spoke.

'What's that noise?' It was a dull tom-tom beat in the darkness.

'You'll get used to that if you stay around here much longer,' said Duff. 'It's the stamps on that mill we saw from the high ground. It's a mile or so farther up the valley; we'll pass it in the morning.'

They were on the move again before the sun was up and they came to the mill in the morning's uncertain light. The mill crouched black and ugly on the smooth curve of the ridge, defiant as a quixotic monster. Its jaws thumped sullenly as it chewed the rock; it snorted steam and screeched metallically.

'I didn't realize it was so big,' said Sean.

'It's big all right,' agreed Duff, 'and they cost money, they don't give them away. Not many men around here can afford a set-up like that.'

There were men moving around the mill, tending its needs, feeding it rock and fussing about the copper tables over which its gold-laden faeces poured. One of the men came forward to offer them the usual hospitality. 'This is private ground. We don't want sightseers around here – keep on going.'

He was a dapper little man with a round brown face and a derby hat pulled down to his ears. His moustache bristled like the whiskers of a fox terrier.

'Listen, Francois, you miserable bloody earthworm, if you talk to me like that I'll push your face around the back of your head,' Duff told him, and the dapper one blinked uncertainly and came closer, peering up at them.

'Who are you? Do I know you?'

Duff pushed his hat back so the man could see his face.

'Duff!' crowed the little man delightedly. 'It's old Duff.' He bounced forward to take Duff's hand as he dismounted. Sean watched the orgy of reunion with amusement. It lasted until Duff managed to bring it under control and lead the little Afrikander across to make the introduction.

'Sean, this is Francois du Toit. He's an old friend of mine from the Kimberley diamond fields.'

Francois greeted Sean and then relapsed once more into the excited chorus of '*Gott,* it's good to see you old Duff.' He pounded Duff's back despite the nimble footwork that Duff was using to spoil his aim. Another few minutes of this passed before Francois composed himself to make his first coherent statement.

'Listen, old Duff, I'm just in the middle of cleaning the amalgam tables. You and your friend go down to my tent. I'll be with you in half an hour, tell my servant to make you some breakfast. I won't be long, man. *Gott,* man, it's good to see you.'

'An old lover of yours?' asked Sean when they were alone.

Duff laughed. 'We were on the diamond fields together. I did him a favour once – pulled him out of a caving drive when the rock fall had broken his legs. He's a good little guy and meeting him here is the proverbial answer to a prayer. What he can't tell us about this goldfield no one else can.'

Francois came bustling into the tent well under the promised half hour and during breakfast Sean was an outsider in a conversation where every exchange began, 'Do you remember –? or 'What happened to old so and so?'

Then, when the plates were empty and the coffee mugs filled, Duff asked, 'So, what are you doing here, Franz? Is this your own outfit?'

'No, I'm still with the Company.'

'Not that whoreson Hradsky?' Duff registered mock alarm. 'Tha – tha that's ta – ta – terrible,' he imitated a stutter.

'Cut it out, Duff.' Francois looked nervous. 'Don't do that, you want me to lose my job?'

Duff turned to Sean with an explanation. 'Norman Hradsky and God are equals, but in this part of the world God takes his orders from Hradsky.'

'Cut it out, Duff.' Francois was deeply shocked but Duff went on imperturbably.

'The organization through which Hradsky exercises his divine powers is referred to with reverently bated breath as "The Company". In actual fact its full and resounding title is The South African Mining and Lands Company. Do you get the picture?'

Sean nodded smiling and Duff added as an afterthought, 'Hradsky is a bastard and he stutters.'

It was too much for Francois. He leaned across and caught Duff's arm. 'Please, man. My servant understands English, cut it out, Duff.'

'So the Company has started on these fields, hey? Well, well, it must be pretty big,' mused Duff and Francois followed with relief onto safer ground.

'It is! You just wait and see, it's going to make the diamond fields look like a church bazaar!'

'Tell me about it,' said Duff.

'They call it the Rotten Reef or the Banket or the Heidelberg Reef – but in fact there are three reefs, not one. They run side by side like layers in a sandwich cake.'

'All three have pay gold?' Duff shot the question and Francois shook his head. There was a light in his eyes; he was happy talking gold and mining.

'No – you can forget about the outer reef, just traces there. Then there's the Main Reef. That's a bit better, it's as much as six feet thick in places and giving good values, but it's patchy.'

Francois leaned eagerly across the table; in his excitement his thick Afrikaans accent was very noticeable.

'The bottom reef is the winner, we call it the Leader Reef. It's only a few inches thick and some places it fades out altogether, but it's rich. There's gold in it like plums in a pudding. It's rich, Duff, I'm telling you that you won't believe it until you see it!'

'I'll believe you,' said Duff. 'Now tell me where I can get some of this Leader Reef for myself.'

Francois sobered instantly, a shutter dropped over his eyes and hid the light that had shone there a moment before.

'It's gone. It's all gone,' he said defensively. 'It's all been pegged, you've come too late.'

'Well, that's that,' said Duff and a big silence settled on the gathering. Francois fidgeted on his stool, chewing at the ends of his moustache and scowling into his mug. Duff and Sean waited quietly; it was obvious that Francois was wrestling with himself, two loyalties tearing him down the middle. Once he opened his mouth and then closed it again; he blew on his coffee to cool it and the heat came off it in steam.

'Have you got any money?' He fired the question with startling violence.

'Yes,' said Duff.

'Mr Hradsky has gone down to Capetown to raise money. He has a list of a hundred and forty claims that he will buy when he gets back.' Francois paused guiltily. 'I'm only telling you this because of what I owe you.'

'Yes, I know.' Duff spoke softly. Francois took an audible breath and went on.

'On the top of Mr Hradsky's list is a block of claims that belongs to a woman. She is willing to sell and they are the most likely-looking propositions on the whole field.'

'Yes?' Duff encouraged him.

'This woman has started an eating-house about two miles from here on the banks of the Natal Spruit. Her name is Mrs Rautenbach, she serves good food. You could go and have a meal there.'

'Thanks, Francois.'

'I owed it to you,' Francois said gruffly, then his mood changed quickly and he chuckled. 'You'll like her, Duff, she's a lot of woman.'

Sean and Duff went to eat lunch at Mrs Rautenbach's. It was an unpainted corrugated-iron building on a wooden frame and the sign above the veranda said in letters of red and gold 'Candy's Hotel. High-class cuisine. Free toilet facilities. No drunks or horses admitted. Proprietor Mrs Candella Rautenbach.'

They washed off the dust in the enamel basin which stood on the veranda, dried themselves on the free towel and combed in the free mirror on the wall.

'How do I look?' asked Duff.

'Ravishing,' said Sean, 'but you don't smell so good. When did you last bath?'

They went into the dining-room and found it almost full, but there was an empty table against the far wall. The room was hot and thick with pipe smoke and the smell of cabbage. Dusty, bearded men laughed and shouted or ate silently and hungrily. They crossed the room to the table and a coloured waitress came to them.

'Yes?' she asked. Her dress was damp at the armpits.

'May we have the menu?'

The girl looked at Duff with faint amusement. 'Today we got steak and mashed potatoes with pudding afterwards.'

'We'll have it,' Duff agreed.

'You sure as hell won't get nothing else,' the girl assured him and trotted back to the kitchen.

'The service is good,' Duff enthused. 'We can only hope that the food and the proprietress are of the same high standard.'

The meat was tough but well flavoured and the coffee was strong and sweet. They ate with appreciation until Sean who was facing the kitchen stopped his fork on its way to his mouth. A hush was on the room.

'Here she is,' he said.

Candy Rautenbach was a tall and bright, shiny blonde and her skin was Nordic flawlessness as yet unspoiled by the sun. She filled the front of her blouse and the back of her skirt with a pleasant abundance. She was well aware of and yet not disconcerted by the fact that every eye in the room was on one of those areas. She carried a ladle which she twitched threateningly at the first hand that reached out to pinch her rump, the hand withdrew and Candy smiled sweetly and moved on among the tables. She stopped occasionally to chat with her customers and it was clear that many of these lonely men came here not only to eat. They watched her avidly, grinning with pleasure when she spoke to them. She reached their table and Sean and Duff stood up. Candy blinked with surprise.

'Sit down, please.' The small courtesy had touched her. 'You are new here?'

'We got in yesterday,' Duff smiled at her. 'And the way you cook a steak makes me feel as though I were home again.'

'Where are you from?' Candy looked at the two of them with perhaps just a shade more than professional interest.

'We've come up from Natal to have a look around. This is Mr Courtney – he is interested in new investments and he thought that these goldfields might provide an outlet for some of his capital.'

Sean just managed to stop his jaw dropping open and then quickly assumed the slightly superior air of a big financier as Duff went on.

'My name is Charleywood. I am Mr Courtney's mining adviser.'

'Pleased to meet you. I am Candy Rautenbach.' She was impressed.

'Won't you join us for a few minutes, Mrs Rautenbach?' Duff drew back a chair for her and Candy hesitated.

'I have to check up in the kitchen – perhaps later.'

'Do you always lie so smoothly?' Sean spoke with admiration when Candy had gone.

'I spoke no untruths,' Duff defended himself.

'No, but the way you tell the truth! How the hell am I going to play up to the role you have created for me?'

'You'll learn to live with it, don't worry. Just look wise and keep your mouth shut,' Duff advised. 'What do you think of her anyway?'

'Toothsome,' said Sean.

'Decidedly palatable,' agreed Duff.

When Candy came back Duff kept the conversation light and general for a while, but when Candy started asking some sharp questions it was immediately apparent that her knowledge of geology and mining was well above average and Duff remarked on it.

'Yes, my husband was in the game. I picked it up from him.' She reached into one of the pockets of her blue and white checked skirt and brought out a small handful of rock samples. She put them down in front of Duff. 'Can you name those?' she asked. It was the direct test, she was asking him to prove himself.

'Kimberlite. Serpentine. Feldspar.' Duff reeled them off and Candy relaxed visibly.

'As it happens I have a number of claims pegged along the Heidelberg Reef. Perhaps Mr Courtney would care to have a look at them. Actually, I am negotiating at the moment with The South African Mining and Lands Company who are very interested.'

Sean made his solitary but valuable contribution to the conversation. 'Ah yes,' he nodded sagely. 'Good old Norman.'

Candy was shaken – not many men used Hradsky's Christian name. 'Will tomorrow morning be convenient?' she asked.

5

That afternoon they bought a tent from a disillusioned hopeful who had thrown up his job on the Natal Railways to make the pilgrimage to Witwatersrand and now needed money to get home. They pitched it near the Hotel and went down to the Natal Spruit to take a long overdue bath. That night they held a mild celebration on the half bottle of brandy that Duff produced from his saddlebag and the next morning Candy took them out to the claims. She had twenty of them pegged right along the Banket. She led them to a spot where the reef outcropped.

'I'll leave you two to look around. If you're interested we can talk about it when you come to the Hotel. I've got to get back now, there'll be hungry mouths to feed.'

Duff escorted Candy to her horse, giving her his arm across the rough ground and helping her into the saddle in a manner he must have learned from his father. He watched her ride away then came back to Sean. He was elated.

'Tread lightly, Mr Courtney, walk with reverence for beneath your feet lies our fortune.'

They went over the ground, Sean like a friendly bloodhound and Duff cruising with the restless circling of a tiger shark. They inspected the claim notices, paced out the boundaries and filled their pockets with chips of rock, then they rode back to their tent and Duff brought out his pestle, mortar and pan. They took them down to the bank of the Natal Spruit and all afternoon crushed the rock and worked the pan. When they had tested the last sample Duff gave his judgement.

'Well, there's gold – and I'd say it's payable gold. It's not nearly as rich as the one we panned at Dundee but that must have been a selected piece of the Leader Reef!' He paused and looked seriously at Sean. 'I think it's worth a try. If the Leader Reef is there we'll find it and in the meantime we won't lose money by working the main reef.'

Sean picked up a pebble and tossed it into the stream in front of him. He was learning for the first time the alternate thrill and depression of gold sickness when one minute you rode the lightning and the next you dropped abruptly into the depths. The yellow tails in the pan had looked pathetically thin and undernourished to him.

'Supposing you're right and supposing we talk Candy into selling her claims, how do we go about it? That four-stamp mill looked a devilishly complicated and expensive bit of machinery to me, not the kind of thing you can buy over the counter in every general dealer's store.'

Duff punched his shoulder and smiled lopsidedly at him. 'You've got your Uncle Duff looking after you. Candy will sell her claims – she trembles when I touch her, a day or two more and she'll be eating out of my hand. As for the mill . . . When I came out to this country I fell in with a rich Cape farmer whose lifelong ambition had been to have his own gold mine. He selected a ridge which in his undisputed wisdom as a grower of grapes he considered to be an ideal place for his mine. He hired me to run it for him, purchased a mill of the latest and most expensive vintage and prepared himself to flood the market with gold. After six months when we had processed vast quantities of assorted quartz, schist and earth and recovered sufficient gold to fit into a mouse's ear without touching the sides, my patron's enthusiasm was somewhat dampened and he dispensed with my invaluable services and closed the circus down. I left for the diamond fields and as far as I know the machinery is still lying there waiting for the first buyer with a couple of hundred pounds to come and pick it up.' Duff stood up and they walked back towards the tent. 'However, first things first. Do you agree that I should continue the negotiations with Mrs Rautenbach?'

'I suppose so.' Sean was feeling more cheerful again. 'But are you sure your interest in Mrs Rautenbach is strictly line of duty?'

Duff was shocked. 'Don't think for a minute that my intentions are anything but to further the interests of our partnership. You can't believe that my animal appetite plays any part in what I intend doing?'

'No, of course not,' Sean assured him. 'I hope you can force yourself to go through with it.'

Duff laughed. 'While we are on the subject I think this is as good a time as any for you to develop a stomach ailment and retire to your lonely bed. From now on until we've got the agreement signed your boyish charm will be of no great value in the proceedings. I'll tell Candy that you've given me authority to act on your behalf.'

Duff combed his curls, put on the clothes that Mbejane had washed for him and disappeared in the direction of Candy's Hotel. Time passed slowly for Sean; he sat and chatted with Mbejane, drank a little coffee and when the sun went down retired to his tent. He read one of Duff's books by the light of the hurricane lamp but could not concentrate on it; his mind kept straying to thoughts of blonde hair. When someone scratched on the canvas door he leapt up with a confused hope that Candy had decided to come and deal with him direct. It was the coloured girl from the Hotel, her crinkly black hair at odds with what he had been thinking.

'Madame says she's sorry to hear about your sickness and to tell you to have two spoons of this,' she told him and offered Sean the bottle of castor oil.

'Tell your mistress, thank you very much.'

Sean accepted the medicine and started to close the tent flap again.

'Madame told me to stay and make sure that you took two full spoons – I have to take the bottle back and show her how much you've had.'

Sean's stomach cringed. He looked at the coloured girl standing resolute in the doorway, determined to carry out her instructions. He thought of poor Duff doing his duty like a man – he could do no less. He swallowed down the thick clinging oil with his eyes closed then went back to his book. He slept uneasily starting up occasionally to look at the empty bed across the tent. The medicine drove him out into the cold at half past two in the morning. Mbejane was curled up next to the fire and Sean scowled at him. His regular contented snoring seemed a calculated mockery. A jackal yelped miserably up on the ridge, expressing Sean's feelings exactly, and the night wind fanned his bare buttocks.

Duff came home in the dawning. Sean was wide awake.

'Well, what happened?' he demanded.

Duff yawned. 'At one stage I began to doubt whether I was man enough. However, it worked out to the satisfaction of all concerned. What a woman!' He pulled off his shirt and Sean saw the scratches across his back.

'Did she give you any castor oil?' Sean asked bitterly.

'I'm sorry about that.' Duff smiled at him sympathetically. 'I tried to dissuade her – truly I did. She's a very motherly person. Most concerned about your stomach.'

'You still haven't answered my question. Did you make any progress with the claims?'

'Oh that –' Duff pulled the blankets up under his chin. 'We disposed of that early on in the proceedings. She'll take a down payment of ten pounds each on them and give us an option to buy the lot at any time during the next two years for ten thousand. We arranged that over dinner. The rest of the time was devoted, in a manner of speaking, to shaking hands over the deal. Tomorrow afternoon – or rather this afternoon – you and I'll ride across to Pretoria and get a lawyer to write up an agreement for her to sign. But right now I need some sleep. Wake me at lunch time. Goodnight, laddie.'

Duff and Sean brought the agreement back from Pretoria the following evening. It was an impressive four-page document full of 'in so much as' and 'party of the first part.' Candy led them to her bedroom and they sat around anxiously while she read it through twice.

She looked up at last and said, 'That seems all right – but there is just one other thing.' Sean's heart sank and even Duff's smile was strained. It had all been too easy so far.

Candy hesitated and Sean saw with faint surprise that she was blushing. It was a pleasant thing to see the peach of her cheeks turning to ripe apple and they watched it with interest, their tension lessening perceptibly. 'I want the mine named after me.'

They nearly shouted with relief.

'An excellent idea! How about the Rautenbach Reef Mine?'

Candy shook her head. 'I'd rather not be reminded of him – we'll leave him out of it.'

'Very well – let's call it the Candy Deep. A little premature, I suppose, as we are still at ground level, but pessimism never pays,' suggested Duff.

'Yes, that's lovely,' Candy enthused, flushing again but this time with pleasure. She scrawled her name across the bottom of the document while Sean fired out the cork of the champagne which Duff had bought in Pretoria. They clinked glasses and Duff gave the toast 'To Candy and the Candy Deep – may one grow sweeter and the other deeper with each passing day.'

6

'We'll need labour, about ten natives to start with. That'll be your problem,' Duff told Sean. It was the following morning and they were eating breakfast in front of the tent. Sean nodded but didn't try to answer until he had swallowed his mouthful of bacon.

'I'll get Mbejane onto that right away. He'll be able to get us Zulus, even if he has to drive them here with a spear at their backs.'

'Good – in the meantime you and I'll ride back to Pretoria again to buy the basic equipment. Picks, shovels, dynamite and the like.' Duff wiped his mouth and filled his coffee cup. 'I'll show you how to start moving the overburden and stacking the ore in a dump. We'll pick a site for the mill and then I'll leave you to get on with it while I head south for the Cape to see my farmer friend. God and the weather permitting ours will be the second mill working on these fields.'

They brought their purchases back from Pretoria in a small ox wagon. Mbejane had done his work well. There were a dozen Zulus lined up for Sean's approval next to the tent with Mbejane standing guard over them like a cheerful sheepdog. Sean walked down the line stopping to ask each man his name and joke with him in his own language. He came to the last in the line. 'How are you called?'

'My name is Hlubi, Nkosi.'

Sean pointed at the man's well-rounded paunch bulging out above his loincloth.

'If you come to work for me, we'll soon have you delivered of your child.'

They burst out in delighted laughter and Sean smiled at them affectionately: proud simple people, tall and big-muscled, completely defenceless against a well-timed jest. Through his mind flashed the picture of a hill in Zululand, a battlefield below it and the flies crawling in the pit of an empty stomach. He shut the picture out quickly and shouted above their laughter.

'So be it then – sixpence a day and all the food you can eat. Will you sign on to work for me?'

They chorused their assent and climbed up onto the back of the wagon. Sean and Duff took them out to the Candy Deep and they laughed and chattered like children going on a picnic.

It took another week for Duff to instruct Sean in the use of dynamite, to explain how he wanted the first trenches dug and to mark out the site for the mill and the dump. They moved the tent up to the mine and worked twelve hours every day. At night they rode down to Candy's Hotel to eat a full meal and then Sean rode home alone. He was so tired by evening that he hardly envied Duff the comfort of Candy's bedroom; instead he found himself admiring Duff's stamina. Each morning he looked for signs of fatigue in his partner but, although his face was lean and gaunt as ever, his eyes were just as clear and his lopsided smile just as cheerful.

'How you do it beats me,' Sean told him the day they finished marking out the mill site.

Duff winked at him. 'Years of practice, laddie, but between you and me the ride down to the Cape will be a welcome rest.'

'When are you going?' Sean asked.

'Quite frankly I think that every day I stay on here increases the risk of someone else getting in before us. Mining machinery is going to be at a premium from now on. You have got things well in hand now . . . What do you say?'

'I was starting to think along the same lines,' Sean agreed. They walked back to the tent and sat down in the camp chairs, from where they could look down the length of the valley. The week before about two dozen wagons had been outspanned around Candy's Hotel, but now there were at least two hundred and from where they sat they could count another eight or nine encampments, some even larger than the one around Candy's place. Wood and iron buildings were beginning to replace the canvas tents and the whole veld was criss-crossed with rough roads along which mounted men and wagons moved without apparent purpose.

The restless movement, the dust clouds raised by the passage of men and beasts, and the occasional deep crump, crump of dynamite firing in the workings along the Banket – all heightened the air of excitement, of almost breathless expectancy that hung over the whole goldfield.

'I'll leave at first light tomorrow,' Duff decided. 'Ten days' riding to the railhead at Colesberg and another four days by train will get me there. With luck I'll be back in under two months.' He wriggled round in his chair and looked directly at Sean. 'After paying Candy her two hundred pounds and with what I spent in Pretoria I've only got about a hundred and fifty left. Once I get to Paarl I'll have to pay out three or four hundred for the mill, then I'll need to hire twenty or thirty wagons to bring it up here – say eight hundred pounds altogether to be on the safe side.'

Sean looked at him. He had known this man a few short weeks. Eight hundred was the average man's earnings for three years. Africa was a big land, a man could disappear easily. Sean loosened his belt and dropped it onto the table; he unbuttoned the money pouch.

'Give me a hand to count it out,' he told Duff.

'Thanks,' said Duff and he was not talking about the money. With trust asked for so simply and given so spontaneously the last reservations in their friendship shrivelled and died.

= 7 =

When Duff had gone Sean drove himself and his men without mercy. They stripped the overburden off the Reef and exposed it across the whole length of the Candy claims, then they broke it up and started stacking it next to the mill site. The dump grew bigger with every twelve-hour day worked. There was still no trace of the Leader Reef but Sean found little time to worry about that. At night he climbed into bed and slept away his fatigue until another morning called him back to the workings. On Sundays he rode across to Francois's tent and they talked mining and medicines. Francois had an enormous chest of patent medicines and a book titled *The Home Physician*. His health was his hobby and he was treating himself for three major ailments simultaneously. Although he was occasionally unfaithful, his true love was sugar diabetes. The page in *The Home Physician* which covered this subject was limp and grubby from the touch of his fingers. He could recite the symptoms from memory and he had all of them. His other favourite was tuberculosis of the bone; this moved around his body with alarming rapidity taking only a week to leave his hip and reach his wrist. Despite his failing health, however, he was an expert on mining and Sean picked his brain shamelessly. Francois's sugar diabetes did not prevent him from sharing a bottle of brandy with Sean on Sunday evenings. Sean kept away from Candy's Hotel – that shiny blonde hair and peach skin would have been too much temptation. He couldn't trust himself not to wreck his new friendship with Duff by another importunate affair, so instead he sweated away his energy in the trenches of the Candy Deep.

Every morning he set his Zulus a task for the day, always just a little more than the day before. They sang as they worked and it was very seldom that the task was not complete by nightfall. The days blurred into each other and turned to weeks which quadrupled like breeding amoebae and became months. Sean began to imagine Duff giving the Capetown girls a whirl with his eight hundred pounds. One evening he rode south for miles along the Cape road, stopping to question every traveller he met and when he finally gave up and returned to the goldfields he went straight to one of the canteens to look for a fight. He found a big, yellow-haired German miner to oblige him. They went outside and for an hour they battered each other beneath a crisp Transvaal night sky surrounded by a ring of delighted spectators. Then he and the German went back into the canteen, shook each other's bleeding hands, drank a vow of friendship together and Sean returned to the Candy Deep with his devil exorcized for the time being.

The next afternoon Sean was working near the north boundary of the claims; at this point they had burrowed down about fifteen feet to keep contact with the reef. Sean had just finished marking the shot holes for the next blast and the Zulus were standing around him taking snuff and spitting on their hands before attacking the rock once more.

'Mush, you shag-eared villains. What's going on here, a trade union meeting?' The familiar voice came from above their heads, Duff was looking down at them. Sean scrambled straight up the side of the trench and seized him in a bear hug. Duff was thinner, his jowls covered with a pale stubble and his curly hair white with dust. When the fury of greeting had subsided a little Sean demanded, 'Well, where's the present you went to fetch me?'

Duff laughed, 'Not far behind, all twenty-five wagons full of it.'

'You got it then?' Sean roared.

'You're damn right I did! Come with me and I'll show you.'

Duff's convoy was strung out four miles across the veld, most of the wagons double-teamed against the enormous weight of the machinery. Duff pointed to a rust-streaked cylinder that completely filled one of the leading wagons.

'That is my particular cross, seven tons of the most spiteful, stubborn and evil boiler in the world. If it's broken the wagon axle once it's broken it a dozen times since we left Colesberg, not to mention the two occasions on which it capsized itself – once right in the middle of a river.'

They rode along the line of wagons.

'Good God! I didn't realize there'd be so much.' Sean shook his head dubiously. 'Are you sure you know how it all fits together?'

'Leave it to your Uncle Duff. Of course, it's going to need a bit of work done on it, after all it's been lying out in the open for a couple of years. Some of it was rusted up solid, but the judicious use of grease, new paint and the Charleywood brain will see the Candy Deep plant breaking rock and spitting out gold within a month.' Duff broke off and waved to a horseman coming towards them. 'This is the transport contractor. Frikkie Malan – Mr Courtney, my partner.'

The contractor pulled up next to them and acknowledged the introduction. He wiped the dust off his face with the sleeve of his shirt.

'*Gott,* man, Mr Charleywood, I don't mind telling you that this is the hardest money I've ever worked for. Nothing personal – but I'll be *vragtig* glad to see the last of this load.'

8

Duff was wrong; it took much longer than a month. The rust had eaten deep into parts of the machinery and each bolt they twisted open was red with the scaly cancer. They worked the usual twelve-hour day chipping and scraping, filing and greasing, knuckles knocked raw against steel and palms wet and red where the blisters had burst. Then one day suddenly and miraculously they were finished. Along the ridge of the Candy Deep, neat and sweet smelling in its new paint, thick with yellow grease and waiting only to be fitted together, lay the dismembered mill.

'How long has it taken us so far?' Duff asked.

'It seems like a hundred years.'

'Is that all?' Duff feigned surprise. 'Then I declare a holiday – two day's of meditation.'

'You meditate, brother – I'm going to do some carousing.'

'That's an excellent alternative – let's go!'

They started at Candy's place but she threw them out after the third fight so they moved on. There were a dozen places to drink at and they tried them all. Others were celebrating, because the day before old Kruger, the President of the Republic, had given official recognition to the goldfields. This had the sole effect of diverting the payments for mining licences from the pockets of the farmers who owned the land into the Government coffers. No one worried about that, except possibly the farmers. Rather it was an excuse for a party. The canteens were packed with swearing, sweating men. Duff and Sean drank with them.

The Crown and Anchor boards were doing a steady business in every bar and the men who crowded around them were the new population of the goldfields. Diggers bare to the waist and caked with dirt, salesmen with loud clothes and louder voices selling everything from dynamite to dysentery cure, an evangelist peddling salvation, gamblers mining pockets, gentlemen trying to keep the tobacco juice off their boots, boys new-flown from home and wishing themselves back, Boers bearded and drab-suited, drinking little but watching with inscrutable eyes the invaders of their land. Then there were the others, the clerks and farmers, the rogues and contractors listening greedily to the talk of gold.

The coloured girl, Martha, came to find Sean and Duff on the afternoon of the second day. They were in a mud-brick and thatch hut called The Tavern of the Bright Angels. Duff was doing a solo exhibition of the Dashing White Sergeant partnered by a chair; Sean and the fifty or so other customers were beating the rhythm on the bar counter with glasses and empty bottles.

Martha skittered across to Sean, slapping at the hands that tried to dive up her skirts and squealing sharply every time her bottom was pinched. She arrived at Sean's side flushed and breathless.

'Madame says you must come quickly – there's big trouble,' she gasped and started to run the gauntlet back to the door. Someone flipped up her dress behind and a concerted masculine roar approved the fact that she wore nothing under the petticoats.

Duff was so engrossed in his dancing that Sean had to carry him bodily out of the bar and dip his head in the horse trough outside before he could gain his attention.

'What the hell did you do that for?' spluttered Duff and swung a round-arm punch at Sean's head. Sean ducked under it and caught him about the body to save him falling on his back.

'Candy wants us – she says there's big trouble.'

Duff thought about that for a few seconds, frowning with concentration, then he threw back his head and sang to the tune of 'London's Burning',

'Candy wants us – Candy wants us
We don't want Candy, we want brandy.'

He broke out of Sean's grip and headed back for the bar. Sean caught him again and pointed him in the direction of the Hotel. Candy was in her bedroom. She looked at the two of them as they swayed arm-in-arm in the doorway.

'Did you enjoy your debauch?' she asked sweetly. Duff mumbled and tried to straighten his coat. Sean tried to steady him as his feet danced an involuntary sideways jig.

'What happened to your eye?' she asked Sean and he fingered it tenderly; it was puffed and blue. Candy didn't wait for an answer but went on, still sweetly:

'Well, if you two beauties want to own a mine by tomorrow you'd better sober up.'

They stared at her and Sean spoke deliberately but nevertheless indistinctly.

'Why, what's the matter?'

'They're going to jump the claims, that's the matter. This new proclamation of a State goldfield has given the drifters the excuse they've been waiting for. About a hundred of them have formed a syndicate. They claim that the old titles aren't legal any more; they are going to pull out the pegs and put in their own.'

Duff walked without a stagger across to the washbasin beside Candy's bed; he splashed his face, towelled it vigorously then stooped and kissed her. 'Thanks, my sweet.'

'Duff, please be careful,' Candy called after them.

'Let's see if we can't hire a few mercenaries,' Sean suggested.

'Good idea, we'll try and find a few sober characters – there should be some in Candy's dining-room.'

They made a short detour on their way back to the mine and stopped at Francois's tent; it was dark by then and Francois came out in a freshly ironed nightshirt. He raised an eyebrow when he saw the five heavily armed men with Sean and Duff.

'You going hunting?' he asked.

Duff told him quickly and Francois was hopping with agitation before he had finished.

'Steal my claims, the thunders, the stinking thunders!' He rushed into his tent and came out again with a double-barrelled shotgun.

'We'll see, man, we'll see how they look full of buckshot.'

'Francois, listen to me,' Sean shouted him down. 'We don't know which claims they'll go to first. Get your men ready and if you hear shooting our way come and give us a hand – we'll do the same for you.'

'*Ja, ja,* we'll come all right – the dirty thunders.' His nightshirt flapping around his legs Francois trotted off to call his men.

'Mbejane and the other Zulus were cooking dinner, squatting round the three-legged pot. Sean rode up to them.

'Get your spears,' he told them. They ran for their huts and almost immediately came crowding back.

'Nkosi, where's the fight?' they pleaded, food forgotten.

'Come on, I'll show you.'

They placed the hired gunmen amongst the mill machinery from where they could cover the track which led up to the mine. The Zulus they hid in one of the prospect trenches. If it developed into a hand-to-hand fight the syndicate was in for a surprise. Duff and Sean walked a little way down the slope to make sure their defenders were all concealed.

'How much dynamite have we got?' Sean asked thoughtfully. Duff stared at him a second, then he grinned.

'Sufficient, I'd say. You're full of bright ideas this evening.' He led the way back to the shed which they used as a storeroom.

In the middle of the track a few hundred yards down the slope they buried a full case of explosive and placed an old tin can on top of it to mark the spot. They went back to the shed and spent an hour making grenades out of bundles of dynamite sticks, each with a detonator and a very short fuse. Then they settled down huddled into their sheepskin coats, rifles in their laps and waited.

They could see the lights of the encampments straggled down the valley and hear an occasional faint burst of singing from the canteens, but the moonlit road up to the mine remained deserted. Sean and Duff sat side by side with their backs against the newly painted boiler.

'How did Candy find out about this, I wonder?' Sean asked.

'She knows everything. That hotel of hers is the centre of this goldfield and she keeps her ears open.'

They relapsed into silence again while Sean formed his next question.

'She's quite a girl – our Candy.'

'Yes,' agreed Duff.

'Are you going to marry her, Duff ?'

'Good God!' Duff straightened up as though someone had stuck a knife into him. 'You going mad, laddie, or else that was a joke in the worst possible taste.'

'She dotes on you and from what I've seen you're fairly well disposed towards her.' Sean was relieved at Duff's quick rejection of the idea. He was jealous, but not of the woman.

'Yes, we've got a common interest, that I won't deny – but marriage!' Duff shivered slightly, not altogether from the cold. 'Only a fool makes the same mistake twice.'

Sean turned to him with surprise. 'You've been married before?' he asked.

'With a vengeance. She was half Spanish and the rest Norwegian, a smoking bubbly mixture of cold fire and hot ice.' Duff's voice went dreamy. 'The memory has cooled sufficiently for me to think of it with a tinge of regret.'

'What happened?'

'I left her.'

'Why?'

'We only did two things well together and one of them was fight. If I close my eyes I can still see the way she used to pout with those lovely lips and bring them close to my ear before she hissed out a particularly foul word, then – hey ho! back to bed for the reconciliation.'

'Perhaps you made the wrong choice. You look around, you'll see millions of happily, married people.'

'Name me one,' challenged Duff and the silence lengthened as Sean thought.

Then Duff went on, 'There's only one good reason for marriage, and that's children.'

'And companionship – that's another good reason.'

'Companionship from a woman?' Duff cut in incredulously. 'Like perfume from garlic. They're incapable of it. I suppose it's the training they get from their mothers, who are after all women themselves, but how can you be friends with someone who suspicions every little move you make, who takes your every action and weighs it on the balance of he loves me, he loves me not?' Duff shook his head unhappily. 'How long can a friendship last when it needs an hourly declaration of love to nourish it? The catechism of matrimony, "Do you love me, darling?" "Yes, darling, of course I do, my sweet." It's got to sound convincing every time otherwise tears.'

Sean chuckled.

'All right, it's funny – it's hilarious until you have to live with it,' Duff mourned. Have you ever tried to talk to a woman about anything other than love? The same things that interest you leave them cold. It comes as a shock the first time you try talking sense to them and suddenly you realize that their attention is not with you – they get a slightly fixed look in their eyes and you know they are thinking about that new dress or whether to invite Mrs Van der Hum to the party, so you stop talking and that's another mistake. That's a sign; marriage is full of signs that only a wife can read.'

'I hold no brief for matrimony, Duff, but aren't you being a little unfair, judging everything by your own unfortunate experience?'

'Select any woman, slap a ring on her third finger and she becomes a wife. First she takes you into her warm, soft body, which is pleasant, and then she tries to take you into her warm, soft mind, which is not so pleasant. She does not share, she possesses – she clings and she smothers. The relation of man to woman is uninteresting in that it conforms to an inescapable pattern, nature has made it so for the very good reason that it requires us to reproduce; but in order to obtain that result every love, Romeo and Juliet, Bonaparte and Josephine not excepted, must lead up to the co-performance of a simple biological function. It's such a small thing – such a short-lived, trivial little experience. Apart from that man and woman think differently, feel differently and are interested in different things. Would you call that companionship?'

'No, but is that a true picture? Is that all there is between them?' Sean asked.

'You'll find out one day. Nature in her preoccupation with reproduction has planted in the mind of man a barricade; it has sealed him off from the advice and experience of his fellowmen, inoculated him against it. When your time comes you'll go to the gallows with a song on your lips.'

'You frighten me.'

'It's the sameness of it all that depresses me – the goddamn monotony of it.' Duff shifted his seat restlessly then settled back against the boiler. The interesting relationships are those in which sex the leveller takes no hand – brothers, enemies, master and servant, father and son, man and man.'

'Homosexuals?'

'No, that's merely sex out of step and you're back to the original trouble. When a man takes a friend he does it not from an uncontrollable compulsion but in his own free choice. Every friendship is different, ends differently or goes on for ever. No chains bind it, no ritual or written contract. There is no question of forsaking all others, no obligation to talk about it – mouth it up and gloat on it the whole time.' Duff stood up stiffly. 'It's one of the good things in life. How late is it?'

Sean pulled out his watch and tilted its face to catch the moonlight. 'After midnight – it doesn't look as if they're coming.'

'They'll come – there's gold here, another uncontrollable compulsion. They'll come. The question is when.'

The lights along the valley faded out one by one, the deep singsong voices of the Zulus in the prospect trench stilled and a small cold wind came up and moved the grass along the ridge of the Candy Deep. Sitting together, sometimes drowsing, sometimes talking quietly, they waited the night away. The sky paled, then pinked prettily. A dog barked over near Hospital Hill and another joined it. Sean stood up and stretched, he glanced down the valley towards Ferrieras Camp and saw them. A black moving blot of horsemen, overflowing the road, lifting no dust from the dew-damp earth, spreading out to cross the Natal Spruit then bunching together on the near bank before coming on.

'Mr Charleywood, we have company.'

Duff jumped up.

'They might miss us and go onto the Jack and Whistle first.'

'We'll see which road they take when they come to the fork. In the meantime let's get ready. Mbejane,' shouted Sean and the black head popped out of the trench.

'Nkosi?'

'Are you awake? They are coming.'

The blackness parted in a white smile. 'We are awake.'

'Then get down and stay down until I give the word.'

The five mercenaries were lying belly down in the grass, each with a newly-opened packet of cartridges at his elbow. Sean hurried back to Duff and they crouched behind the boiler.

'The tin can shows up clearly from here. Do you think you can hit it?'

'With my eyes closed,' said Sean.

The horsemen reached the fork and turned without hesitation towards the Candy Deep, quickening their paces as they came up the ridge. Sean rested his rifle across the top of the boiler and picked up the speck of silver in his sights.

'What's the legal position, Duff?' he asked out of the corner of his mouth.

'They've just crossed our boundary – they are now officially trespassers,' Duff pronounced solemnly.

One of the leading horses kicked over the tin can and Sean fired at the spot on which it had stood. The shot was indecently loud in the quiet morning and every head in the syndicate lifted with alarm towards the ridge, then the ground beneath them jumped up in a brown cloud to meet the sky. When the dust cleared there was a struggling tangle of downed horses and men. The screams carried clearly up to the crest of the ridge.

'My God,' breathed Sean, appalled at the destruction.

'Shall we let them have it, boss?' called one of the hired men.

'No,' Duff answered him quickly. 'They've had enough.'

The flight started, riderless horses, mounted men and others on foot were scattering back down the valley. Sean was relieved to see that they left only half a dozen men and a few horses lying in the road.

'Well, that's the easiest fiver you've ever earned,' Duff told one of the mercenaries. 'I think you can go home now and have some breakfast.'

'Wait, Duff.' Sean pointed. The survivors of the explosion had reached the road junction again and there they were being stopped by two men on horseback.

'Those two are trying to rally them.'

'Let's change their minds, they're still within rifle range.'

'They are not on our property any more,' disagreed Sean. 'Do you want to wear a rope?'

They watched while those of the syndicate who had had enough fighting for one day disappeared down the road to the camps and the rest coagulated into a solid mass at the crossroad.

'We should have shot them up properly while we had the chance,' grumbled one of the mercenaries uneasily. 'Now they'll come back – look at that bastard talking to them like a Dutch uncle.'

They left their horses and spread out, then they started moving cautiously back up the slope. They hesitated just below the line of boundary pegs then ran forward, tearing up the pegs as they came.

'All together, gentlemen, if you please,' called Duff politely and the seven rifles fired. The range was long and the thirty or so attackers ran doubled up and dodging. The bullets had little effect at first, but as the distance shortened men started falling. There was a shallow donga running diagonally down the slope and as each of the attackers reached it he jumped down into it and from its safety started a heated reply to the fire of Sean's men. Bullets spanged off the machinery, leaving bright scars where they struck.

Mbejane's Zulus were adding their voices to the confusion.

'Let us go down to them now, Nkosi.'

'They are close – let us go.'

'Quiet down, you madmen, you'd not go a hundred paces against those rifles,' Sean snarled impatiently.

'Sean, cover me,' whispered Duff. 'I'm going to sneak round the back of the ridge, rush them from the side and lob a few sticks of dynamite into that donga.'

Sean caught his arm, his fingers dug into it so that Duff winced.

'You take one step and I'll break a rifle butt over your head – you're as bad as those Blacks. Now keep shooting and let me think.' Sean peered over the top of the boiler but ducked again as a bullet rang loudly against it, inches from his ear. He stared at the new paint in front of his nose, put his shoulder against it; the boiler rocked slightly. He looked up and Duff was watching him.

'We'll walk down together and lob that dynamite,' Sean told him. 'Mbejane and his bloodthirsty heathens will roll the boiler in front of us. These other gentlemen will cover us, we'll do this thing in style.'

Sean called the Zulus out of the trench and explained to them. They chorused their approval of the scheme and jostled each other to find a place to push against the boiler. Sean and Duff filled the front of their shirts with the dynamite grenades and lit a short length of tarred rope each.

Sean nodded to Mbejane.

'Where are the children of Zulu?' sang Mbejane, shrilling his voice in the ancient rhetorical question.

'Here,' answered his warriors braced ready against the boiler.

'Where are the spears of Zulu?'

'Here.'

'How bright are the spears of Zulu?'

'Brighter than the Sun.'

'How hungry are the spears of Zulu?'

'Hungrier than the locust.'

'Then let us take them to the feeding.'

'Yeh-bo.' Explosive assent and the boiler revolved slowly to the thrust of black shoulders.

'Yeh-bo.' Another reluctant revolution.

'Yeh-bo.' It moved more readily.

'Yeh-bo.' Gravity caught it. Ponderously it bumped down the slope and they ran behind

it. The fire from the donga doubled its volume, rattling like hail against the huge metal cylinder. The singing of the Zulus changed its tone also; the deep-voiced chanting quickened, climbed excitedly, and became the blood trill. That insane, horrible squealing made Sean's skin crawl, tickled his spine with the ghost fingers of memory, but it inflamed him also. His mouth opened and he squealed with them. He touched the first grenade with the burning rope then flung it in a high spluttering sparking arc. It burst in the air above the donga. He threw again. Crump, crump. Duff was using his explosive as well. The boiler crashed over the lip of the donga and came to rest in a cloud of dust; the Zulus followed it in, spreading out, still shrieking, and now their assegais were busy. The white men broke, clawed frantically out of the ravine and fled, the Zulus hacking at them as they ran.

When Francois arrived with fifty armed diggers following him the fight was over.

'Take your boys down to the camps. Comb them out carefully. We want every one of those that got away,' Duff told him. 'It's about time we had a little law and order on this field.'

'How will we pick out the ones that were in on it?' asked Francois.

'By their white faces and the sweat on their shirts you will know them,' Duff answered.

Francois and his men went, leaving Sean and Duff to clean up the battlefield. It was a messy job – the stabbing spears had made it so. They destroyed those horses that the blast had left still half alive and they gleaned more than a dozen corpses from the donga and the slope below it. Two of them were Zulus. The wounded, and there were many, they packed into a wagon and took them down to Candy's Hotel.

It was early afternoon by the time they arrived. They threaded the wagon through the crowd and stopped it in front of the Hotel. It seemed the entire population of the goldfield was there, packed around the small open space in which Francois was holding his prisoners.

Francois was almost hysterical with excitement. He was sweeping the shotgun around in dangerous circles as he harangued the crowd. Then he darted back to prod one of the prisoners with the twin muzzles.

'You thunders,' he screamed. 'Steal our claims – hey – steal our claims.'

At that moment he caught sight of Duff and Sean bringing the wagon through the press.

'Duff, Duff. We got them. We got the whole lot of them.' The crowd backed respectfully away from the menace of that circling shotgun and Sean flinched as it pointed directly at him for a second.

'So I see, Francois,' Duff assured him. 'In fact, I have seldom seen anyone more completely had.'

Francois's prisoners were swathed in ropes; they could move only their heads and as additional security a digger with a loaded rifle stood over each of them. Duff climbed down off the wagon.

'Don't you think you should slacken those ropes a little?' Duff asked dubiously.

'And have them escape?' Francois was indignant.

'Do you think they'd get very far?'

'No, I don't suppose so.'

'Well, another half hour and they'll all have gangrene – look at that one's hand already, a beautiful shade of blue.'

Reluctantly Francois conceded and told his men to untie them.

Duff pushed his way through the crowd and climbed the steps of the Hotel. From there he held up his hands for silence.

'There have been a lot of men killed today – we don't want it to happen again. One way we can prevent it is to make sure that this lot get what they deserve.' Cheers were led by Francois.

'But we must do it properly. I suggest we elect a committee to deal with this affair and with any other problems that crop up on these fields. Say ten members and a chairman.'

More cheers.

'Call it the Diggers' Committee,' shouted someone and the crowd took up the name enthusiastically.

'All right, the Diggers' Committee it is. Now we want a chairman, any suggestions?'

'Mr Charleywood,' shouted Francois.

'Yes, Duff – he'll do.'

'Yes, Duff Charleywood.'

'Any other suggestions?'

'No,' roared the crowd.

'Thank you, gentlemen.' Duff smiled at them. 'I am sensible of the honour. Now, ten members.'

'Jock and Trevor Heyns.'

'Karl Lochtkamper.'

'Francois du Toit.'

'Sean Courtney.'

There were fifty nominations. Duff baulked at counting votes so the committee was elected by applause. He called the names one at a time and judged the strength of the response to each. Sean and Francois were among those elected. Chairs and a table were brought out onto the veranda and Duff took his seat. With a water-jug he hammered for silence, declared the first session of the Diggers' Committee open and then immediately fined three members of the crowd ten pounds each for discharging firearms during a meeting – gross contempt of Committee. The fines were paid and a proper air of solemnity achieved.

'I'll ask Mr Courtney to open the case for the prosecution.'

Sean stood up and gave a brief description of the morning's battle, ending, 'You were there, Your Honour, so you know all about it anyway.'

'So I was,' agreed Duff. 'Thank you, Mr Courtney. I think that was a very fair picture you presented. Now,' he looked at the prisoners, 'who speaks for you?'

There was a minute of shuffling and whispering, then one of them was pushed forward. He pulled off his hat and blushed purple.

'Your Worship,' he began, then stopped, wriggling with embarrassment.

'Your worship.'

'You've said that already.'

'I don't rightly know where to begin, Mr Charleywood – I mean Your Honour, sir.'

Duff looked at the prisoners again.

'Perhaps you'd like to reconsider your choice.'

Their first champion was withdrawn in disgrace and a fresh one sent forward to face the Committee. He had more fire.

'You bastards got no right to do this to us,' he started and Duff promptly fined him ten pounds. His next attempt was more polite.

'Your Honour, you can't do this to us. We had our rights, you know, that new proclamation and all, I mean, them old titles wasn't legal no more now, was they? We just came along as peaceful as you please, the old titles not being legal, we got a right to do what we done. Then you bastards, I mean Your Honour, dynamited us and like we had a right to protect ourselves, I mean after all, didn't we, sir?'

'A brilliant defence most ably conducted. Your fellows should be grateful to you,' Duff complimented him, then turned to his Committee. 'Well now, how say you merry gentlemen. Guilty or not guilty?'

'Guilty.' They spoke together and Francois added for emphasis, 'the dirty thunders.'

'We will now consider sentence.'

'String them up,' shouted someone and instantly the mood changed. The mob growled: an ugly sound.

'I'm a carpenter, I'll whip you up a handsome set of gallows in no time at all.'

'Don't waste good wood on them. Use a tree.'

'Get the ropes.'

'String them up.'

The crowd surged in, lynch mad. Sean snatched Francois's shotgun and jumped up onto the table.

'So help me God, I'll shoot the first one of you that touches them before this court says so.' They checked and Sean pressed his advantage. 'At this range I can't miss. Come on, try me – there's two loads of buckshot in here. Someone will get cut in half.' They fell back still muttering.

'Perhaps you've forgotten, but there's a police force in this country and there's a law against killing. Hang them today and it'll be your turn tomorrow.'

'You're right, Mr Courtney, it'll be cruel heartless murder. That it will,' wailed the spokesman.

'Shut up, you bloody fool,' Duff snarled at him and someone in the crowd laughed. The laughter caught on and Duff sighed silently with relief. That had been very close.

'Give them the old tar and feathers.'

Duff grinned. 'Now you're talking sense. Who's got a few barrels of tar for sale?' He looked round. 'What, no offers? Then we'll have to think of something else.'

'I've got ten drums of red paint – thirty shillings each, good imported brand.' Duff recognized the speaker as a trader who had opened a general dealer's store down at Ferrieras Camp.

'Mr Tarry suggests paint. What about it?'

'No, it comes off too easily – that's no good.'

'I'll let you have it cheap – twenty-five shillings a drum.'

'No – stick your ruddy paint,' the crowd booed him.

'Give them a twist on Satan's Roulette Wheel,' shouted another voice, and the crowd clamoured agreement.

'That's it – give them the wheel.'

'Round and round and round she goes – where she stops nobody knows,' roared a black-bearded digger from the roof of the shanty across the road. The crowd howled.

Sean watched Duff's expression – the smile had gone. He was weighing it up. If he stopped them again they might lose all patience and risk the shotgun. He couldn't chance it.

'All right. If that's what you want.' He faced the terrified cluster of prisoners. 'The sentence of this court is that you play roulette with the devil for one hour and that you then leave this goldfield – if we catch you back here again you'll get another hour of it. The wounded are excused the first half of the sentence. I think they've had enough. Mr du Toit will supervise the punishment.'

'We'd prefer the paint, Mr Charleywood,' pleaded the spokesman again.

'I bet you would,' said Duff softly, but the crowd was carrying them away already, out towards the open veld beyond the Hotel. Most of them had staked claims of their own and they didn't like claim jumpers. Sean climbed down off the table.

'Let's go and have a drink,' Duff said to him.

'Aren't you going to watch?' asked Sean.

'I've seen it done once before down in the Cape. That was enough.'

'What do they do?'

'Go and have a look, I'll be waiting for you at the Bright Angels. I'll be surprised if you stay the full hour.'

By the time Sean joined the crowd most of the wagons had been gathered from the camps and drawn up in a line. Men swarmed round them fitting jacks under the axles to lift the big back wheels clear of the ground. Then the prisoners were hustled forward – one to each wheel. Eager hands lifted them and held them while their wrists and ankles were lashed to the rim of the wheel with the hub in the middle of their backs and their arms and legs spread-eagled like stranded starfish. Francois hurried along the line checking the ropes and placing four diggers at each wheel, two to start it and another two to take over when those were tired. He reached the end, came back to the centre again, pulled his watch from his pocket, checked the time, then shouted.

'All right – turn them, *kerels.*'

The wheels started moving, slowly at first then faster as they built up momentum. The bodies strapped to them blurred with the speed.

'Round and round and round she goes – round and round and round she goes,' chanted the crowd gleefully.

Within minutes there was a burst of laughter from the end of the line of wagons. Someone had started vomiting, it sprayed from him like yellow sparks from a catherine wheel. Then another and another joined in, Sean could hear them retching and gasping as the centrifugal force flung the vomit up against the back of their throats and out of their noses. He waited a few more minutes but when their bowels started to empty he turned away gagging and headed for the Bright Angel.

'Did you enjoy it?' asked Duff.

'Give me a brandy,' answered Sean.

9

With the Diggers' Committee dispensing rough justice a semblance of order came to the camps. President Kruger wanted no part in policing the nest of ruffians and cut-throats which was growing up just outside his Capital and he contented himself with placing his spies among them and leaving them to work out their own salvation. After all, the field was far from proved and the chances were that in another year the veld would again be as deserted as it had been nine months before. He could afford to wait; in the meantime the Diggers' Committee had his tacit sanction.

While the ants worked, cutting down into the reef with pick and with dynamite, the grasshoppers waited in the bars and shanties. So far only the Jack and Whistle mill was turning out gold, and only Hradsky and Francois du Toit knew how much gold was coming out of it. Hradsky was still in Capetown crusading for capital and Francois spoke to no one, not even to Duff, about the mill's productivity.

The rumours flew like sand in a whirlwind. One day it seemed that the reef had pinched out fifty feet below the surface, and the next the canteens buzzed with the news that the Heyns brothers had gone down a hundred feet and were pulling out nuggets the size of musket balls. Nobody knew but everybody was prepared to guess.

Up at the Candy Deep, Duff and Sean worked on relentlessly. The mill took shape on its concrete platform, its jaws open for the first bite at the rock. The boiler was swung up onto its cradle by twenty sweating, singing Zulus. The copper tables were fitted up ready to be smeared with quicksilver. There was no time to worry about the reef nor the dwindling store of money in Sean's cash belt. They worked and they slept – there was nothing else. Duff took to sharing Sean's tent up on the ridge and Candy had her featherbed to herself again.

On the twentieth of November they fired the boiler for the first time. Tired and horny-handed, their bodies lean and tempered hard with toil, they stood together and watched the needle creek up round the pressure gauge until it touched the red line at the top.

Duff grunted. 'Well, at least we've got power now.' Then he punched Sean's shoulder 'What the hell are you standing here for – do you think this is a Sunday School picnic? There's work to do, laddie.'

On the second of December they fed the mill its first meal and watched the powdered rock flow across the amalgam tables. Sean threw his arm round Duff's neck in an affectionate half-Nelson, Duff hit him in the stomach and pulled his hat down over his eyes, they drank a glass of brandy each at supper and laughed a little but that was all. They were too tired to celebrate. From now on one of them must be in constant attendance on that iron monster. Duff took the first night shift and when Sean went up to the mill next morning he found him weaving on his feet, his eyes sunk deep in dark sockets.

'By my reckoning we've run ten tons of rock through her. Time to clean the tables and see just how much gold we've picked up.'

'You go and get some sleep,' said Sean and Duff ignored him.

'Mbejane, bring a couple of your savages here, we're going to change the tables.'

'Listen, Duff, it can wait an hour or two. Go and get your head down.'

'Please stop drivelling – you're as bad as a wife.'

Sean shrugged. 'Have it your own way, show me how you do it then.'

They switched the flow of powdered rock onto the second table that was standing ready; then with a broad bladed spatula Duff scraped the mercury off the copper top of the first table, collecting it in a ball the size of a coconut.

'The mercury picks up the tiny particles of gold,' he explained to Sean as he worked, 'and lets the grains of rock wash across the table and fall off into the dump. Of course it doesn't collect it all, some of it goes to waste.'

'How do you get the gold out again?'

'You put the whole lot in a retort and boil off the mercury – the gold stays behind.'

'Hell of a waste of mercury, isn't it?'

'No, you catch it as it condenses and use it again. Come on, I'll show you.'

Duff carried the ball of amalgam down to the shed, placed it in the retort and lit the blow-lamp. With the heat on it the ball dissolved and started to bubble. Silently they stared at it. The level in the retort fell.

'Where's the gold?' Sean asked at last.

'Oh, shut up,' Duff snapped impatiently, and then, repentant, 'Sorry, laddie, I feel a bit jaded this morning.'

The last of the mercury steamed off and there it was, glowing bright, molten yellow. A drop of gold the size of a pea. Duff shut off the blow-lamp and neither of them spoke for a while. Then Sean asked, 'Is that all?'

'That, my friend, is all,' agreed Duff wearily. 'What do you want to do with it – fill a tooth?'

He turned towards the door with a droop to his whole body.

'Keep the mill running, we might as well go down with our colours flying.'

= 10 =

It was a miserable Christmas dinner. They ate it at Candy's Hotel. They had credit there. She gave Duff a gold signet ring and Sean a box of cigars. Sean had never smoked before but now the sting of it in his lungs gave him a certain masochistic pleasure. The dining-room roared with men's voices and cutlery clatter, the air was thick with the smell of food and tobacco smoke while in one corner – marooned on a little island of gloom – sat Sean, Duff and Candy.

Once Sean lifted his glass at Duff and spoke like an undertaker's clerk. 'Happy Christmas.'

Duff's lips twitched back in a dead man's grin. 'And the same to you.'

They drank. Then Duff roused himself to speak. 'Tell me again – how much have we got left? I like to hear you say it; you have a beautiful voice, you should have played Shakespeare.'

'Three pounds and sixteen shillings.'

'Yes, yes, you got it just right that time – three pounds and sixteen shillings – now to really make me feel Christmassy, tell me how much we owe.'

'Have another drink,' Sean changed the subject.

'Yes, I think I will, thank you,'

'Oh please, you two, let's just forget about it for today,' pleaded Candy. 'I planned for it to be such a nice party – look, there's Francois! Hey, Francois – over here!'

The dapper du Toit bustled across to their table.

'Happy Christmas, kerels, let me buy you a drink.'

'It's nice to see you.' Candy gave him a kiss. 'How are you? You're looking fine.'

Francois sobered instantly. 'It's funny you should say that, Candy. As a matter of fact I'm a bit worried.' He tapped his chest and sank down into an empty chair. 'My heart, you know, I've been waiting for it to happen, and then yesterday I was up at the mill, just standing there, you understand, when suddenly it was as though a vice was squeezing my chest. I couldn't breathe – well, not very well anyway. Naturally I hurried back to my tent and looked it up. Page eighty-three. Under "Diseases of the Heart".' He shook his head sadly. 'It's very worrying. You know I wasn't a well man before, but now this.'

'Oh, no,' wailed Candy. 'I can't stand it – not you too.'

'I'm sorry, have I said something wrong?'

'Just in keeping with the festive spirit at this table.' She pointed at Duff and Sean. 'Look at their happy faces – if you'll excuse me I'm going to check up in the kitchen.' She went.

'What's wrong, old Duff ?'

Duff flashed his death's head grin across the table at Sean.

'The man wants to know what's wrong – tell him.'

'Three pounds sixteen shillings,' said Sean and Francois looked puzzled.

'I don't understand.'

'He means we're broke – flat broke.'

'*Gott*, I'm sorry to hear that, Duff, I thought you were going good. I've heard the mill running all this month, I thought you'd be rich by now.'

'The mill's been running all right and we've recovered enough gold to block a flea's backside.'

'But why, man? You are working the Leader Reef, aren't you?'

'I'm beginning to think this Leader Reef of yours is a bedtime story.'

Francois peered into his glass thoughtfully.

'How deep are you?'

'We've got one incline shaft down about fifty feet.'

'No sign of the Leader?' Duff shook his head and Francois went on.

'You know when I first spoke to you a lot of what I said was just guessing.'

Duff nodded.

'Well, I know a bit more about it now. What I am going to tell you is for you alone – I'll lose my job if it gets out, you understand?'

Duff nodded again.

'So far the Leader Reef has only been found at two places. We've got it on the Jack and Whistle and I know the Heyns brothers have struck it on the Cousin Jock Mine. Let me draw it for you.' He picked up a knife and drew in the gravy on the bottom of Sean's plate. 'This is the Main Reef running fairly straight. Here I am, here is the Cousin Jock and here you are in between us. Both of us have found the Leader and you haven't. My guess is it's there all right – you just don't know where to look.

'At the far end of the Jack and Whistle claims the Main Reef and the Leader are running side by side two feet apart but by the time they reach the boundary nearest to the Candy

Deep they've opened up to seventy feet apart. Now on the boundary of the Cousin Jock they're back to fifty feet apart. To me it seems that the two reefs form the shape of a long bow, like this.' He drew it in. 'The Main Reef is the string and the Leader Reef is the wood. I'm telling you, Duff, if you cut a trench at right-angles to the Main Reef you'll find it – and when you do you can buy me a drink.'

They listened gravely and when Francois finished Duff leaned back in his chair. 'If we'd known this a month ago! Now how are we going to raise the money to cut this new trench and still keep the mill running?'

'We could sell some of our equipment,' suggested Sean.

'We need it, every scrap of it, and besides if we sold one spade the creditors would be on us like a pack of wolves, howling for their money.'

'I'd make you a loan if I had it – but with what Mr Hradsky pays me –' Francois shrugged. 'You'll need about two hundred pounds. I haven't got it.'

Candy came back to the table in time to hear Francois's last remark.

'What's this all about?'

'Can I tell her, Francois?'

'If you think it will do any good.'

Candy listened, then thought for a moment. 'Well, I've just bought ten plots of ground in Johannesburg, this new Government village down the valley, so I'm short myself. But I could let you have fifty pounds if that would help.'

'I've never borrowed money from a lady before – it'll be a new experience. Candy, I love you.'

'I wish you meant that,' said Candy, but luckily for Duff his hearing failed him completely just as Candy spoke. He went on hurriedly.

'We'll need another hundred and fifty or so – let's hear your suggestions, gentlemen.'

There was a long silence, then Duff started to smile and he was looking at Sean.

'Don't tell me, let me guess,' Sean forestalled him. 'You're going to put me out to stud?'

'Close – but not quite right. How are you feeling, laddie?'

'Thank you, I'm all right.'

'Strong?'

'Yes.'

'Brave?'

'Come on, Duff, let's have it. I don't like that look in your eye.'

Duff pulled a notebook out of his pocket and wrote in it with a stump of pencil. Then he tore out the page and handed it to Sean. 'We'll have posters like this put up in every canteen on the goldfields.'

Sean read it:

> ON NEW YEAR'S DAY MR SEAN COURTNEY HEAVYWEIGHT CHAMPION OF THE TRANSVAAL REPUBLIC WILL STAND TO MEET ALL COMERS IN FRONT OF CANDY'S HOTEL FOR A PURSE OF FIFTY POUNDS ASIDE.
> Spectators' Fee, 2s. All Welcome.

Candy was reading it over his shoulder. She squeaked.

'That's wonderful. I'll have to hire extra waiters to serve drinks and I'll run a buffet luncheon. I suppose I could charge two shillings a head?'

'I'll fix the posters,' Francois was not to be outdone, 'and I'll send a couple of my chaps down to put up a ring.'

'We'll close the mill down until New Year – Sean will have to get a lot of rest. We'll put him on light training only. No drinking, of course, and plenty of sleep,' said Duff.

'It's all arranged then, is it?' asked Sean. 'All I've got to do is go in there and get beaten to a pulp?'

'We're doing this for you, laddie, so that you can be rich and famous.'

'Thank you, thank you very much.'

'You like to fight, don't you?'

'When I'm in the mood.'

'Don't worry, I'll think up some dirty names to call you – get you worked up in no time.'

= 11 =

'How are you feeling?' Duff asked for the sixth time that morning.

'No change since five minutes ago,' Sean reassured him.

Duff pulled out his watch, stared at it, held it to his ear and looked surprised that it was still ticking.

'We've got the challengers lined up on the veranda. I've told Candy to serve them free drinks – as much as they want. Every minute we can wait here gives them a little longer to take on a load of alcohol. Francois is collecting the gate money in my valise; as you win each bout the stakes will go into it as well. I've got Mbejane stationed at the mouth of the alley beside the Hotel. If there's a riot one of us will throw the bag to him and he'll head for the long grass.'

Sean was stretched out on Candy's bed with his hands behind his head. He laughed. 'I can find no fault with your planning. Now for pity's sake calm down, man. You're making me nervous.'

The door burst open and Duff leapt out of his chair at the crash. It was Francois, he stood in the doorway holding his chest.

'My heart,' he panted. 'This is doing my heart no good.'

'What's happening outside?' Duff demanded.

'We've collected over fifty pounds gate money already. There's a mob up on the roof that haven't paid, but every time I go near them they throw bottles at me.'

Francois cocked his head on one side. 'Listen to them.' The noise of the crowd was barely softened by the flimsy walls of the Hotel. 'They won't wait much longer – you'd better come out before they start looking for you.'

Sean stood up. 'I'm ready.'

Francois hesitated.

'Duff, you remember Fernandes, that Portuguese from Kimberley?'

'Oh no!' Duff anticipated him. 'Don't tell me he's here.'

Francois nodded. 'I didn't want to alarm you but some of the local boys clubbed in and telegraphed south for him. He arrived on the express coach half an hour ago. I had hoped he wasn't going to make it in time, but –' He shrugged.

Duff looked at Sean sadly.

'Bad luck, laddie.'

Francois tried to soften the blow. 'I told him it was first come first served. He's sixth in the line so Sean will be able to make a couple of hundred quid anyway – then we can always say he's had enough and close the contest.'

Sean was listening with interest. 'This Fernandes is dangerous?'

'They were thinking of him when they invented that word,' Duff told him.

'Let's go and have a look at him.'

Sean led the way out of Candy's room and down the passage.

'Did you get hold of a scale to weigh them with?' Duff asked Francois as they hurried after Sean.

'No, there's not one on the fields that goes over a hundred and fifty pounds – but I have Gideon Barnard outside.'

'How does that help us?'

'He's a cattle dealer – all his life he's been judging animals on the hoof. He'll give us the weights to within a few pounds.'

Duff chuckled. 'That'll have to do then. Besides I doubt we'll be claiming any world titles.'

Then they were out on the veranda blinking in the brightness of the sun and the thunder of the crowd.

'Which is the Portuguese?' whispered Sean – he needn't have asked. The man stood out like a gorilla in a cage of monkeys. A shaggy coating of hair began on his shoulders and continued down his back and chest, completely hiding his nipples and exaggerating the bulge of his enormous belly.

The crowd opened a path for Sean and Duff and they walked along it to the ring. Hands slapped Sean's back but the well-wishes were drowned in the churning sea of sound. Jock Heyns was the referee – he helped Sean through the ropes and ran his hands over his pockets.

'Just checking,' he apologized. 'We don't want any scrap iron in the ring.' Then he beckoned to a tall, brown-faced fellow who was leaning on the ropes chewing tobacco.

'This is Mr Barnard our weighing steward. Well, what do you say, Gideon?'

The steward hosed a little juice from the side of his mouth.

'Two hundred and ten.'

'Thank you.' Jock held up his hands and after a few minutes was rewarded with a comparative silence.

'Ladies and Gentlemen.'

'Who you talking to, Guvnor?'

'We are privileged to have with us today – Mr Sean Courtney.'

'Wake up, *Boet,* he's been with us for months.'

'The heavyweight champion of the Republic.'

'Why not make it the world, cock, he's got just as much right to that title.'

'Who will fight six bouts –'

'If it lasts that long.'

'– for his title and a purse of fifty pounds each.'

Sustained cheering.

'The first challenger – at two hundred and ten pounds – Mr Anthony –'

'Hold on,' Sean shouted, 'who says he's first?'

Jock Heyns bad taken a deep breath to bellow the name, he let it escape with a hiss. 'It was arranged by Mr du Toit.'

'If I fight them, then I pick them – I want the Port . . .'

Duff's hand whipped over Sean's mouth and his whisper was desperate. 'Don't be a bloody fool – take the easy ones first. Use your head – we aren't doing this for fun, we're trying to finance a mine, remember?'

Sean clawed Duff's hand off his mouth. 'I want the Portuguese,' he shouted.

'He's joking,' Duff assured the crowd, then turned on Sean fiercely. 'Are you mad? That dago's a man-eater, we're fifty pounds poorer before you start.'

'I want the Portuguese,' repeated Sean with all the logic of a small boy picking the most expensive toy in the shop.

'Let him have the dago,' shouted the gentlemen on the hotel roof and Jock Heyns eyed them nervously; it was clear that they were about to add a few more bottles to the argument.

'All right,' he agreed hastily. 'The first challenger, at –' he glanced at Barnard and repeated after him, 'two hundred and fifty-five pounds – Mr Felezardo da Silva Fernandes.'

In a storm of hoots and applause the Portuguese waddled down off the veranda and into the ring. Sean had seen Candy at the dining-room window and he waved to her. She blew him a two-handed kiss and at that instant Trevor Heyns, the timekeeper, hit the bucket which served as a gong and Sean heard Duff's warning shout. Instinctively he started to duck. There was a flash of lightning inside his skull and he found himself sitting in amongst the legs of the first line of spectators.

'The bastard King hit me,' Sean complained loudly. He shook his head and was surprised to find it still attached to his body. Someone poured a glass of beer over him and it steadied him. He felt his anger flaming up through his body.

'Six,' counted Jock Heyns.

The Portuguese was standing at the ropes. 'Come back, Leetle Sheet, I haf some more for you, not half.'

Sean's anger jumped in his throat.

'Seven, eight.'

Sean gathered his legs under him.

'I kiss your mother.' Fernandes puckered his lips and smacked them. 'I love your sister, like this.' He demonstrated graphically.

Sean charged. With the full weight of his run behind it, his fist thudded into the Portuguese's mouth, then the ropes caught Sean and catapulted him back into the crowd once more.

'You weren't even in the ring, how could you hit him?' protested one of the spectators who had broken Sean's fall. He had money on Fernandes.

'Like this!' Sean demonstrated. The man sat down heavily and had nothing further to say. Sean hurdled the ropes. Jock Heyns was halfway through his second count when Sean interrupted him by lifting the reclining Portuguese to his feet, using the tangled bush of his hair as a handle. He balanced the man on his unsteady legs and hit him again.

'One, two, three . . .' resignedly Jock Heyns began his third count, this time he managed to reach ten.

There was a howl of protest from the crowd and Jock Heyns struggled to make himself heard above it.

'Does anyone want to lodge a formal objection?'

It seemed that there were those who did.

'Very well, please step into the ring. I can't accept shouted comments.' Jock's attitude was understandable – he stood to lose a considerable sum if his decision were reversed. But Sean was patrolling the ropes as hungrily as a lion at feeding time. Jock waited a decent interval, then held up Sean's right arm.

'The winner – ten minutes for refreshments before the next bout. Will the keepers please come and fetch their property.' He gestured towards the Portuguese.

'Nice going, laddie, unorthodox perhaps but beautiful to watch.' Duff took Sean's arm and led him to a chair on the veranda.

'Three more to go, then we can call it a day.' He handed Sean a glass.

'What's this?'

'Orange juice.'

'I'd prefer something a little stronger.'

'Later, laddie.'

Duff collected the Portuguese purse and dropped it into the valise while that gentleman was being carried from the ring by his straining sponsors and laid to rest at the far end of the veranda.

Mr Anthony Blair was next. His heart was not in the encounter. He moved prettily enough on his feet but always in the direction best calculated to keep him out of reach of Sean's fists.

'The boy's a natural long-distance champ.'

'Watch it, Courtney, he'll run you to death.'

'Last lap, Blair, once more round the ring and you've done five miles.'

The chase ended when Sean, now sweating gently, herded him in a corner and there dispatched him.

The third challenger had by this time developed a pain in his chest.

'It hurts like you wouldn't believe it,' he announced through gritted teeth.

'Does it sort of gurgle in your lungs as you breathe?' asked Francois.

'Yes, that's it – gurgles like you wouldn't believe it.'

'Pleurisy,' diagnosed du Toit with more than a trace of envy in his voice.

'Is that bad?' the man asked anxiously.

'Yes it is. Page one hundred and sixteen. The treatment is –'

'Then I won't be able to fight, Hell, that's bad luck,' the invalid complained cheerfully.

'It's exceptionally bad luck,' agreed Duff. 'It means you'll have to forfeit your purse money.'

'You wouldn't take advantage of a sick man?'

'Try me,' Duff suggested pleasantly.

The fourth contestant was a German. Big, blond and happy-faced. He stumbled three or four times on his way to the ring, tripped over the ropes and crawled to his corner on hands and knees; once there he was able to regain his feet with a little help from the ring post. Jock went close to him to smell his breath and before he could dodge, the German caught him in a bear hug and led him into the opening steps of a waltz. The crowd loved it ind there were no objections when at the end of the dance Jock declared Sean the winner on a technical knockout. More correctly the decision should have gone to Candy who had provided the free drinks.

'We can close down the circus now if you want to, laddie,' Duff told Sean. 'You've made enough to keep the Candy Deep afloat for another couple of months.'

'I haven't had a single good fight out of the lot of them. But I like the looks of this last one. The others were for business; this one I'll have just for the hell of it.'

'You've been magnificent – now you deserve a little fun,' agreed Duff.

'Mr Timothy Curtis. Heavyweight champion of Georgia, U.S.A.' Jock introduced him.

Gideon Barnard put his weight at two hundred and ten pounds, the same as Sean's. Sean shook his hand and from the touch of it knew he was not going to be disappointed.

'Glad to know you.' The American's voice was as soft as his grip was hard.

'Your servant, sir,' said Sean and hit the air where the man's head had been an instant before. He grunted as a fist slogged into his chest under his raised right arm and backed away warily. A soft sigh blew through the crowd and they settled down contentedly. This was what they had come to see.

The red wine was served early; it flew in tiny drops every time a punch was thrown or received. The fight flowed smoothly around the square of trampled grass. The sound of bone on flesh was followed immediately by the growl of the crowd and the seconds between were filled with the hoarse breathing of the two men and the slither, slither of their feet.

'Yaaaa!' Through the tense half silence ripped a roar like that of a mortally wounded foghorn. Sean and the American jumped apart startled, and turned with everyone else to face Candy's Hotel. Fernandes was with them again; his mountain-wide hairiness seemed to fill the whole veranda. He picked up one of Candy's best tables and holding it across his chest tore off two of its legs as though they were the wings of a roasted chicken.

'Francois, the bag!' shouted Sean. Francois snatched it up and threw it high over the heads of the crowd. Sean held his breath as he followed its slow trajectory, then he blew out again with relief as he saw Mbejane field the pass and vanish around the corner of the Hotel.

'Yaaaa!' Fernandes gave tongue again. With a table leg in each hand he charged the crowd that stood between him and Sean; it scattered before him.

'Do you mind if we finish this some other time?' Sean asked the American.

'Of course not. Any time at all. I was just about to leave myself.'

Duff reached through the ropes and caught Sean's arm.

'There's someone looking for you – or had you noticed?'

'It might just be his way of showing friendliness.'

'I wouldn't bet on it – are you coming?'

Fernandes rumbled to a halt, braced himself and threw. The table leg whirred like a rising pheasant an inch over Sean's head, ruffling his hair with the wind of its passage.

'Lead on, Duff.' Sean was uncomfortably conscious of the fact that Fernandes was again in motion towards him, still armed with a long oak, and that three very thin ropes were all that stood between them. The speed that Sean and Duff turned on then made Mr Blair's earlier exhibition seem like that of a man with both legs in plaster, Fernandes, carrying top weight as he was, never looked like catching them.

Francois came up to the Candy Deep just after midday with the news that the Portuguese, after beating three of his sponsors into insensibility, had left on the noon coach back to Kimberley.

Duff uncocked his rifle. 'Thanks, Franz, we were waiting lunch for him. I thought he might call on us.'

'Have you counted the takings?'

'Yes, your commission is in that paper bag on the table.'

'Thanks, man, let's go down and celebrate.'

'You go and have one for us.'

'Hey, Duff, you promised –' Sean started.

'I said later – in three or four weeks' time. Now we've got a little work to do, like digging a trench fifty feet deep and three hundred yards long.'

'We could start first thing tomorrow.'

'You want to be rich, don't you?' asked Duff.

'Sure, but –'

'You want nice things, like English suits, French champagne and –'

'Yes, but –'

'Well, stop arguing, get off your fat arse and come with me.'

= 12 =

The Chinese use firecrackers to keep the demons away. Duff and Sean applied the same principle. They kept the mill running; as long as its clunking carried across the valley to the ears of their creditors all was well. Everyone accepted the fact that they were working a payable reef and left them alone, but the money they fed into the front of the mill had halved its value by the time it came out of the other side in those pathetic little yellow pellets.

In the meantime they cut their trench, tearing into the earth in a race against Settlement Day. They fired dynamite and as the last stones dropped back out of the sky they were in again, coughing with the fumes, to clear the loosened rock and start drilling the next set of holes. It was summer, the days were long, and while it was light they worked. Some evenings they lit the last fuses by lantern light.

Sand fell through the hour-glass faster than they had bargained for, the money dribbled away and on the fifteenth of February Duff shaved himself, changed his shirt and went to see Candy about another loan. Sean watched him walk away down the slope. They had sold the horses a week before, and he said a small prayer – the first for many years.

Duff came back in the late morning. He stood on the edge of the trench and watched Sean tamping in the charges for the next cut. Sean's back was shiny with sweat; each individual muscle standing out in relief, swelling and subsiding as he moved.

'That's the stuff, laddie, keep at it.'

Sean looked up with dust-reddened eyes. 'How much?' he asked.

'Another fifty, and this is the last – or so she threatens.'

Sean's eyes fastened on the package Duff held under his arm.

'What's that?'

He could see the stains seeping through the brown paper and the saliva flooded out from under his tongue.

'Prime beef chops – no mealie meal porridge for lunch today.' Duff grinned at him.

'Meat.' Sean caressed the word. 'Underdone – bleeding a little as you bite it, a trace of garlic, just enough salt.'

'And you beside me, singing in the wilderness,' agreed Duff. 'Cut out the poetry, light those fuses and let's go and eat.'

An hour later they walked side by side along the bottom of their trench, Mbejane and his Zulus crowding behind them. Sean belched. 'Ah, pleasant memory, I'll never be able to look another plate of mealie meal in the face again.'

They reached the end, where the freshly broken earth and rock lay piled. Sean felt the thrill start in his hands, tingle up his arms and squeeze his lungs. Then Duff's fingers were biting into his shoulder; he could feel them trembling.

It looked like a snake, a fat grey python crawling down one wall of the trench, disappearing under the heap of new rubble and out the other side.

Duff moved first, he knelt and picked up a piece of the reef, a big grey mottled lump of it and he kissed it.

'It must be it, hey, Duff? It must be the Leader?'

'It's the end of the rainbow.'

'No more mealie meal,' Sean said softly and Duff laughed. Then Sean laughed. Wildly, crazily, together they howled their triumph.

13

'Let me hold it again,' said Sean.

Duff passed it across to him.

'Hell, it's heavy.'

'There's nothing heavier,' agreed Duff.

'Must be all of fifty pounds.'

Sean held the bar in two hands, it was the size of a cigar box. 'More!'

'We've retrieved all our losses in two days' working.'

'And some to spare, I'd say.'

Sean placed the gold bar on the table between them. It shone with little yellow smiles in the lantern light and Duff leaned forward and stroked it; its surface felt knobbly from the rough casting.

'I can't keep my hands off it,' he confessed sheepishly.

'I can't either!' Sean reached out to touch it. 'We'll be able to pay Candy out for the claims in another week or two.'

Duff started. 'What did you say?'

'I said we'd be able to pay Candy out.'

'I thought I wasn't hearing things.' Duff patted his arm indulgently. 'Listen to me, laddie, I'll try and put it simply. How long have we got the option on these claims for?'

'Three years.'

'Correct – now the next question. How many people on these fields have any money?'

Sean looked mystified. 'Well, we have now and – and . . .'

'No one else, that is until Hradsky gets back,' Duff finished for him.

'What about the Heyns brothers? They've cut open the Leader Reef.'

'Certainly, but it won't do them any good, not until their machinery arrives from England.'

'Go on!' Sean wasn't quite sure where Duff was leading.

'Instead of paying Candy out now we are going to use this' – he patted the gold bar – 'and all its little brothers to buy up every likely claim we can lay, our hands on. For a start there are Doc Sutherland's claims between us and the Jack and Whistle. Then we are going to order a couple of big ten-stamp mills and when those are spilling out gold we'll use it to buy land, finance brick works, engineering shops, transport companies and the rest. I've told you before there are more ways of making gold than digging for it.'

Sean was staring at him silently.

'Have you got a head for heights?' asked Duff.

Sean nodded.

'You're going to need it, because we are going up where the eagles fly – you are about to be a party to the biggest financial killing this country has ever seen.'

Sean lit one of Candy's cigars; his hand was a little unsteady.

'Don't you think it would be best to – well – not try and go too quickly. Hell, Duff, we've only been working the Leader for two days –'

'And we've made a thousand pounds,' Duff interrupted him. 'Listen to me, Sean, all my life I've been waiting for an opportunity like this. We're the first in on this field, it's as wide open as the legs of a whore. We're going to go in and take it.'

The next morning Duff had the good fortune to find Doc Sutherland early enough to talk business with him, before be began the day's drinking. Another hour would have been too late. As it was Doc knocked over his glass and fell out of his chair before he finally signed away twenty-five claims to Sean and Duff. The ink was hardly dry on the agreement before Duff was riding down to Ferrieras Camp to look for Ted Reynecke who held the claims on the other side of the Cousin Jock. Up on the Candy Deep Sean nursed the mill and bit his nails. Within seven days Duff had bought over one hundred claims and committed them to forty thousand pounds in debts.

'Duff, you're going mad.' Sean pleaded with him. 'We'll lose everything again.'

'How much have we pulled out of the Candy Deep so far?'

'Four thousand.'

'Ten per cent of what we owe in ten days – and with a miserable little four-stamp mill at that. Hold on to your hat, laddie, tomorrow I'm going to sign up for the forty claims on the other side of the Jack and Whistle. I would have had them today but that damned Greek is holding out for a thousand pounds apiece. I'll have to give it to him, I suppose.'

Sean clutched his temples.

'Duff – please, man, we're in over our necks already.'

'Stand back, laddie, and watch the wizard work.'

'I'm going to bed – I suppose I'll have to take your shift again in the morning if you're determined to spend tomorrow ruining us.'

'That's not necessary, I've hired that Yankee – Curtis. You know, your sparring partner. It turns out he's a miner and he's willing to work for thirty a month. So you can come to town with me and watch me make you rich. I'm meeting the Greek at Candy's Hotel at nine o'clock.'

14

At nine o'clock Duff was talking and Sean sat silently on the edge of his chair; at ten the Greek had still not put in an appearance, Duff was moody and Sean was garrulous with relief. At eleven Sean wanted to go back to the mine.

'It's an omen, Duff, God looked down and he saw us sitting here all ready to make a terrible mistake. "No," he said, "I can't let them do it – I'll have the Greek break a leg – I can't let it happen to such nice boys." '

'Why don't you go and join a Trappist monastery?' Duff checked his watch. 'Come on, let's go!'

'Yes, sir!' Sean stood up with alacrity. 'We'll get back in plenty of time to clean the tables before lunch.'

'We're not going home, we're going to look for the Greek.'

'Now listen, Duff.'

'I'll listen later – come on.'

They rode across to the Bright Angels, left the horses outside and walked in together. It was dark in the canteen after the sunshine outside, but even in the gloom a group at one of the tables caught their attention immediately. The Greek sat with his back to them; the line of his parting seemed to be drawn with white chalk and a ruler through the oily black waves of his hair. Sean's eyes switched from him to the two men that sat across the table from him. Jews, there was no mistaking it, but there any similarity ended. The younger one was thin with smooth olive skin drawn tight across the bold bones of his cheeks; his lips were very red and his eyes, fringed with girl's lashes, were toffee-brown and melting. In the chair beside him was a man with a body that had been shaped in wax then held near a hot flame. Shoulders rounded to the verge of deformity drooped down over a pear-shaped body; with difficulty they supported the great Taj Mahal domed head. His hair was styled in the fashion of Friar Tuck, thick only around the ears. But the eyes – the flickering yellow eyes – there was nothing comical about them.

'Hradsky,' hissed Duff, then his expression changed. He smiled as he walked across to the table.

'Hello, Nikky, I thought we had an appointment.'

The Greek twisted quickly in his chair.

'Mr Charleywood, I'm sorry, I was held up.'

'So I see, the woods are full of highwaymen.'

Sean saw the flush start to come up out of Hradsky's collar then sink back again.

'Have you sold?' Duff asked.

The Greek nodded nervously.

'I'm sorry, Mr Charleywood, but Mr Hradsky paid my price and no haggling – cash money, too!'

Duff let his eyes wander across the table.

'Hello, Norman. How's your daughter?'

This time the flush escaped from Hradsky's shirt and flooded over his face. He opened his mouth, his tongue clucked twice, then he closed it again.

Duff smiled, he looked at the younger Jew. 'Say it for him, Max.'

The toffee eyes dropped to the table top. 'Mr Hradsky's daughter is very well.'

'I believe she married soon after my involuntary departure from Kimberley.'

'That is correct.'

'Wise move, Norman, much wiser than having your bully boys run me out of town. That wasn't very nice of you.'

No one spoke.

'We must get together some time and have a chat about old times. Until then, fa – fa – fare ye we – we – well.'

On the way back to the mine Sean asked, 'He's got a daughter? If she looks like him you were lucky to escape.'

'She didn't – she was like a bunch of ripe grapes with the bloom on them.'

'I can hardly credit it.'

'Neither could I. The only conclusion I could reach was that Max did that job for him as well.'

'What's the story about Max?'

'He's the Court Jester. Rumour has it that after Hradsky has finished hanging it out, Max shakes it for him.'

Sean laughed and Duff went on, 'But don't underestimate Hradsky. His stutter is his only weakness and with Max to talk for him he's overcome that. Beneath that monumental skull is a brain as quick and merciless as a guillotine. Now that he's arrived on this goldfield there's going to be some action; we'll have to gallop to keep up with him.'

Sean thought for a few seconds, then, 'Talking about action, Duff, now that we've lost the Greek's claims and won't have to use all our ready money satisfying him, let's give some thought to ordering new machinery to work the claims we have got.'

Duff grinned at him.

'I sent a telegram to London last week. There'll be a pair of brand new ten-stamp mills on the water to us before the end of the month.'

'Good God, why didn't you tell me?'

'You were worried enough as it was – I didn't want to break your heart.'

Sean opened his mouth to blast Duff out of the saddle, Duff winked at him before he could talk and Sean's lips trembled. He felt the laughter in his throat, he tried to stop it but it swamped him.

'How much is it going to cost us?' he howled through his mirth.

'If you ask that question once more, I'll strangle you,' Duff laughed back at him. 'Rest content in the knowledge that if we're going to have enough to honour the bills of lading when those mills arrive at Port Natal, we'll have to run a mountain of Leader Reef through our little rig during the next few weeks.'

'What about the payments on the new claims?'

'That's my department – I'll worry about that.'

And so their partnership crystallized; their relationship was established over the weeks that followed. Duff with his magic tongue and his charming, lopsided grin was the one who negotiated, who poured the oil on the storm waters churned up by impatient creditors. He was the storehouse of mining knowledge which Sean tapped daily, he was the conceiver of schemes, some wild, others brilliant. But his fleeting nervous energy was not designed to bring them to fruition. He lost interest quickly and it was Sean who finally rejected the least likely Charleywood brain children and adopted the others that were more deserving; once he had made himself stepfather to them he reared them as though they were his own. Duff was the theorist, Sean the practician. Sean could see why Duff had never found success before, but at the same time he recognized that without him he would be helpless. He watched with profound admiration the way that Duff used the barely sufficient flow of gold from the Candy Deep to keep the mill running, pay the tradesmen, meet the claim monies as they fell due and still save enough for the new machinery. He was a man juggling with live coals: hold one too long and it burns, let one fall and all fall. And Duff, deep-down-uncertain Duff, had a wall to put his back against. His speech never showed it but his eyes did when he looked at Sean. Sometimes he felt small next to Sean's big body and bigger determination, but it was a good feeling: like being on a friendly mountain.

They put up new buildings around the mill: storerooms, a smelting house and cabins for Sean and Curtis. Duff was sleeping at the Hotel again. The location for the Natives sprawled haphazard down the back slope of the ridge, retreating a little each week as the white mountain of the mine dump grew and pushed it back. The whole valley was changing. Hradsky's new mills arrived and stood up along the ridge, tall and proud until their own dumps dwarfed them. Johannesburg, at first a mere pattern of surveyors' pegs, sucked the scattered encampments onto her grassy chequerboard and arranged them in a semblance of order along her streets.

The Diggers' Committee, its members tired of having to scrape their boots every time they went indoors, decreed public latrines be erected. Then, flushed with their own audacity, they built a bridge across the Natal Spruit, purchased a water cart to lay the dust on the streets of Johannesburg and passed a law prohibiting burials within half a mile of the city centre. Sean and Duff as members of the Committee felt it their duty to demonstrate their faith in the goldfield, so they bought twenty-five plots of ground in Johannesburg, five pounds each to be paid within six months. Candy recruited all her customers and in one weekend of frantic effort they razed her Hotel to the ground, packed every plank and sheet of iron onto their wagons, carried it a mile down the valley and re-erected it on her own land in the centre of the township. During the party she gave them on that Sunday night they nearly succeeded in dismantling it for the second time. Each day the roads from Natal and the Cape fed more wagons, more men into the Witwatersrand goldfield. Duff's suggestion that the Diggers' Committee levy a guinea a head from all newcomers to help finance the public works was reluctantly rejected, the general feeling being that if it led to civil rebellion there were more newcomers than Committee members and no one fancied being on the losing side.

One morning, when he came out to the mine, Duff brought a telegram with him. He handed it to Sean without comment. Sean read it. The machinery had arrived.

'Good God, it's three weeks early.'

'They must have had a downhill sea, or a following wind or whatever it is that makes ships go faster,' muttered Duff.

'Have we got enough to pay the bill?' asked Sean.

'No.'

'What are we going to do?'

'I'll go and see the little man at the bank.'

'He'll throw you out in the street.'

'I'll get him to give us a loan on the claims.'

'How the hell are you going to do that – we haven't paid for them yet.'

'That's what you call financial genius. I'll simply point out to him that they're worth five times what we bought them for.' Duff grinned. 'Can you and Curtis carry on here without me for today while I go and arrange it?'

'You arrange it and I'll happily give you a month's holiday.'

When Duff came back that afternoon he carried a paper with him. It had a red wax seal in the bottom corner, across the top it said 'Letter of Credit' and in the middle, standing out boldly from the mass of small print, was a figure that ended in an impressive string of noughts.

'You're a bloody marvel,' said Sean.

'Yes, I am rather, aren't I?' agreed Duff.

= 15 =

The Heyns brothers' machinery was on the same ship. Jock and Duff rode down to Port Natal together, hired a hundred wagons and brought it all back in one load.

'I'll tell you what I'll do with you, Jock, I'll wager you that we get our mills producing before you do. Loser pays for the transport on the whole shipment,' Duff challenged him when they reached Johannesburg where, in Candy's new bar-room, they were washing the dust out of their throats.

'You're on!'

'I'll go further, I'll put up a side bet of five hundred.'

Sean prodded Duff in the ribs.

'Gently, Duffy – we can't afford it.' But Jock had already snapped up the bet.

'What do you mean we can't afford it?' whispered Duff. 'We've got nearly fifteen hundred pounds left on the letter of credit.'

Sean shook his head. 'No, we haven't.'

Duff pulled the paper from his inside pocket and tapped Sean's nose with it. 'There – read for yourself.'

Sean took it out of Duff's hand.

'Thanks, old chap, I'll go and pay the man now.'

'What man?'

'The man with the wagons.'

'What wagons?'

'The wagons that you and Jock hired in Port Natal. I've bought them.'

'The hell you say!'

'It was your idea to start a transport business. Just as soon as they've offloaded they'll be on their way again to pick up a shipment of coal from Dundee.'

Duff grinned at him. 'Don't you ever forget an idea? All right, laddie, off you go – we'll just have to win the bet, that's all.'

One of the mills they placed on the Candy Deep, the other on the new claims beyond the Cousin Jock Mine. They hired two gangs from among the unemployed in Johannesburg. Curtis supervised one of them and Sean the other, while Duff darted back and forth keeping an eye on both. Each time he passed the Cousin Jock he spent a few minutes checking Trevor and Jock's progress.

'They've got the edge on us, Sean; their boilers are up and holding pressure already,' he reported fretfully, but the next day he was smiling again.

'They didn't mix enough cement in the platform – it started to crumble as soon as they put the crusher on it. They'll have to cast it again. That set them back three or four days.'

The betting down in the canteens fluctuated sharply with each change of fortune. Francois came up to the Candy Deep one Saturday afternoon. He watched them work, made a suggestion or two, then remarked, 'They're giving three-to-one against you at the Bright Angels; they, reckon the Heynses will be finished by next weekend.'

'Go down and put another five hundred pounds on for me,' Duff told him, and Sean shook his head despairingly.

'Don't worry, laddie, we can't lose – that amateur mining engineer, Jock Heyns, has assembled his crusher jaws all arse-about-face. I only noticed it this morning – he's in for a surprise when he tries to start up. He'll have to strip the whole damn rig.'

Duff was right – they brought both their mills into production a comfortable fifteen hours before the Heyns brothers. Jock rode over to see them with his jaw on his chest. 'Congratulations.'

'Thanks, Jock, did you bring your cheque book?'

'That's what I came to talk about. Can you give me a little time?'

'Your credit's good,' Sean assured him, 'come and have a drink and let me sell you some coal.'

'Ah, yes, I heard your wagons arrived back this morning. What price are you charging?'

'Fifteen pounds a hundredweight.'

'Good God. You bloody bandit, I bet it cost you less than five shillings a hundredweight.'

'A man's entitled to a reasonable profit,' protested Sean.

It had been a long hard pull up to the top of the hill but Sean and Duff had arrived at last and from there it was downhill all the way. The money poured in.

The geological freak that had bowed the Leader Reef away from the Main across the Candy Deep claims had, at the same time, enriched it – injected it full of the metal. Francois was there one evening when they put the ball of amalgam into the retort. His eyes bulged as the mercury boiled away; he stared at the gold the way a man watches a naked woman.

'*Gott!* I'm going to have to call you two thunders "Mister" from now on.'

'Have you ever seen richer reef, Francois?' Duff gloated.

Francois shook his head slowly. 'You know my theory about the reef being the bed of an old lake – well this bears it out. The kink in your reef must have been a deep trench along the bottom of the lake. It would have acted as a natural gold trap. Hell, man, what luck. With your eyes closed you have picked the plum out of the pudding. The Jack and Whistle is half as rich as this.'

Their overdraft at the bank dropped like a barometer in a hurricane; the tradesmen started greeting them with a smile; they gave Doc Sutherland a cheque which would have kept even him in whisky for a hundred years. Candy kissed them both when they paid her out in full, plus interest at seven per cent. Then she built herself a new Hotel, double storied, with a crystal chandelier in the dining-room and a magnificent bedroom suite on the second floor done out in maroon and gold. Duff and Sean rented it immediately but with the express understanding that if ever the Queen visited Johannesburg they would allow her to use it. In anticipation Candy called it the Victoria Rooms.

Francois, with a little persuasion, agreed to take over the running of the Candy Deep. He moved his possessions, one chest of clothes and four chests of patent medicines, across from the Jack and Whistle. Timothy Curtis was the manager of the mill on the new claims; they named it the Little Sister Mine. Although not nearly as rich as the Candy Deep it was producing a sweet fortune each month, for Curtis worked as well as he fought.

By the end of August Sean and Duff had no more creditors: the claims were theirs, the mills were theirs and they had money to invest.

'We need an office of our own here in town. We can't run this show from our bedrooms' complained Sean.

'You're right,' agreed Duff, 'we'll build on that corner plot nearest the market square.' The plan was for a modest little four-room building, but it finally expanded to two stories, stinkwood floors, oak panelling and twenty rooms. What they couldn't use they rented.

'The price of land has trebled in three months,' said Sean, 'and it's still moving.'

'You're right – now's the time to buy,' Duff agreed. 'You're starting to think along the right lines.'

'It was your idea.'

'Was it?' Duff looked surprised.

'Don't you remember your "up where the eagles fly" speech?'

'Don't you forget anything?' asked Duff.

They bought land: one thousand acres at Orange Grove and another thousand around Hospital Hill. Their transport wagons, now almost four hundred strong, plied in daily from Port Natal and Lourenço Marques. Their brickfields worked twenty-four hours a day, seven days a week, to try to meet the demand for building materials.

It took Sean almost a week to dissuade Duff from building an Opera House but he succeeded and instead they joined most of the other members of the Diggers' Committee in financing a different type of pleasure palace. At Duff's suggestion they called it the Opera House. They recruited the performers not from the great companies of Europe but from the dock areas of Capetown and Port Natal and chose as the conductor a Frenchwoman of vast experience named Blue Bessie after the colour of her hair. The Opera House provided entertainment on two levels. For the members of the Committee and the other emergent rich there was a discreet side entrance, a lavishly furnished lounge where one could buy the finest champagne and discuss the prices on the Kimberley Stock Exchange, and beyond the lounge were a series of tastefully decorated retiring-rooms. For the workers there was a bare corridor to queue in, no choice for your money and a five-minute time limit. In one month the Opera House produced more gold than the Jack and Whistle mine.

By December there were millionaires in Johannesburg: Hradsky, the Heyns brothers, Karl Lochtkamper, Duff Charleywood, Sean Courtney and a dozen others. They owned the mines, the land, the buildings and the city: the aristocracy of the Witwatersrand, knighted with money and crowned with gold.

A week before Christmas, Hradsky, their unacknowledged but undoubted king, called them all to a meeting in one of the private lounges of Candy's Hotel.

'Who the hell does he think he is,' complained Jock Heyns, 'ordering us round like a bunch of kaffirs.'

'*Verdammt Juden!*' agreed Lochtkamper.

But they went, every last man of them, for whatever Hradsky did had the smell of money about it and they could no more resist it than a dog can resist the smell of a bitch in season.

Duff and Sean were the last to arrive and the room was already hazed with cigar smoke and tense with expectation. Hradsky sagged in one of the polished leather armchairs with Max sitting quietly beside him; his eyes flickered when Duff walked in but his expression never changed. When Duff and Sean had found chairs Max stood up. 'Gentlemen, Mr Hradsky has invited you here to consider a proposition.'

They leaned forward slightly in their chairs and there was a glitter in their eyes like hounds close upon the fox.

'From time to time it is necessary for men in your position to find capital to finance further ventures and to consolidate past gains; on the other hand those of us who have money lying idle will be seeking avenues for investment.' Max cleared his throat and looked at them with his sad brown eyes.

'Up to the present there has been no meeting-place for these mutual needs such as exists in the other centres of the financial world. Our nearest approach to it is the Stock Exchange at Kimberley which, I'm sure you will agree, is too far removed to be of practical use to us here at Johannesburg. Mr Hradsky has invited you here to consider the possibility of forming our own Exchange and, if you accept the idea, to elect a chairman and governing body.'

Max sat down and in the silence that followed they took up the idea, each one fitting it into his scheme of thinking, testing it with the question 'How will I benefit?'.

'*Ja*, it's dom fine idea.' Lochtkamper spoke first.

'Yes, it's what we need.'

'Count me in.'

While they schemed and bargained, setting the fees, the place and the rules, Sean, watched their faces. The faces of bitter men, happy men, quiet ones and big bull-roarers but all with one common feature – that greedy glitter in the eyes. It was midnight before they finished.

Max stood up again.

'Gentlemen, Mr Hradsky would like you to join him in a glass of champagne to celebrate the formation of our new enterprise.'

'This I can't believe; the last time he paid for drinks was back in 'sixty,' declared Duff. 'Quickly somebody – find a waiter before he changes his mind.'

Hradsky hooded his eyes to hide the hatred in them.

16

With its own Stock Exchange and bordel Johannesburg became a city. Even Kruger recognized it; he deposed the Diggers' Committee and sent in his own police force, sold monopolies for essential mining supplies to members of his family and Government, and set about revising his tax laws with special attention to mining profits. Despite Kruger's efforts to behead the gold-laying goose, the city grew, overflowed the original Government plots and spread brawling and blustering out into the surrounding veld.

Sean and Duff grew with it. Their way of life changed swiftly; their visits to the mines fell to a weekly inspection and they left it to their hired men. A steady river of gold poured down from the ridge to their offices on Eloff Street, for the men they hired were the best that money could find.

Their horizons closed in to encompass only the two panelled offices, the Victoria Rooms and the Exchange. Yet within that world Sean found a thrill that he had never dreamed existed. He had been oblivious to it during the first feverish months; he had been so absorbed in laying the foundations that he could spare no energy for enjoying or even noticing it.

Then one day he felt the first voluptuous tickle of it. He had sent to the bank for a land title document he needed, expecting it to be delivered by a junior clerk – but instead the sub-manager and a senior clerk filed respectfully into his office. It was an exquisite physical shock and it gave him a new awareness. He noticed the way men looked at him as he passed them on the street. He realized suddenly that over fifteen hundred human beings depended on him for their livelihood.

There was satisfaction in the way a path cleared for him and Duff as they crossed the floor of the Exchange each morning to take their places in the reserved leather armchairs of the members' lounge. When Duff and he leaned together and talked quietly before the trading began, even the other big fish watched them. Hradsky with his fierce eyes hooded by sleepy lids, Jock and Trevor Heyns, Karl Lochtkamper – any of them would have given a day's production from their mines to overhear those conversations.

'Buy!' said Sean.

'Buy! Buy! Buy!' clamoured the pack and the prices jumped as they hit them, then slumped back as they sucked their money away and put it to work elsewhere.

Then one March morning in 1886 the thrill became so acute it was almost an orgasm. Max left the chair at Norman Hradsky's side and crossed the lounge towards them. He stopped in front of them, lifted his sad eyes off the patterned carpet and almost apologetically proffered a loose sheaf of papers.

'Good morning, Mr Courtney. Good morning, Mr Charleywood. Mr Hradsky has asked me to bring this new share issue to your attention. Perhaps you would be interested in these reports, which are, of course, confidential, but he feels they are worthy of your support.'

You have power when you can force a man who hates you to ask for your favours. After the first advance by Hradsky they worked together often. Hradsky never acknowledged their existence by word or look. Each morning Duff called a cheerful greeting across the full width of the lounge, 'Hello, chatterbox,' or 'Sing for us, Norman.'

Hradsky's eyes would flicker and he would sag a little lower into his chair, but before the bell started the day's trading Max would stand up and come across to them, leaving his master staring into the empty fireplace. A few soft sentences exchanged and Max would walk back to Hradsky's side.

Their combined fortunes were irresistible: in one wild morning's trading alone they added another fifty thousand to their store of pounds.

An untaught boy handles his first rifle like a toy. Sean was twenty-two. The power he held was a more deadly weapon than any rifle, and much sweeter, more satisfying to use. It was a game at first with the Witwatersrand as a chessboard, men and gold for pieces. A word or a signature on a slip of paper would set the gold jingling and the men scampering. The consequences were remote and all that mattered was the score, the score chalked up in black figures on a bank statement. Then in that same March he was made to realize that a man wiped off the board could not be laid back in the box with as much compassion as a carved wooden knight.

Karl Lochtkamper, the German with a big laugh and a happy face, laid himself open. He needed money to develop a new property on the east end of the Rand; he borrowed and signed short-term notes on his loans, certain that he could extend them if necessary. He borrowed secretly from men he thought he could trust. He was vulnerable and the sharks smelt him out.

'Where is Lochtkamper getting his money?' asked Max.

'Do you know?' asked Sean.

'No, but I can guess.'

Then the next day Max came back to them again.

'He has eight notes out. Here is the list,' he whispered sadly. 'Mr Hradsky will buy the ones that have a cross against them. Can you handle the rest?'

'Yes,' said Sean.

They closed on Karl on the last day of the quarter; they called the loans and gave him twenty-four hours to meet them. Karl went to each of the three banks in turn.

'I'm sorry, Mr Lochtkamper, we have loaned over our budget for this quarter.'

'Mr Hradsky is holding your notes – I'm sorry.'

'I'm sorry, Mr Lochtkamper, Mr Charleywood is one of our directors.'

Karl Lochtkamper rode back to the Exchange. He walked across the floor and into the lounge for the last time. He stood in the centre of the big room, his face grey, his voice bitter and broken.

'Let Jesus have this much mercy on you when your time comes. Friends! My friends! Sean, how many times haf we drunk together? And you, Duff, was it yesterday you shook my hand?'

Then he went back across the floor, out through the doors. His suite in the Great North Hotel wasn't fifty yards from the Exchange. In the members' lounge they heard the pistol shot quite clearly.

That night Duff and Sean got drunk together in the Victoria rooms.

'Why did he have to do it? Why did he have to kill himself?'

'He didn't,' answered Duff. 'He was a quitter.'

'If I'd known he was going to do that – my God, if only I'd known.'

'Damn it, man, he took a chance and lost – it's not our fault. He would have done the same to us.'

'I don't like this – it's dirty. Let's get out, Duff.'

'Someone gets knocked down in the rush and you want to cry "enough!" '

'It's different now somehow, it wasn't like this at the start.'

'Yes, and it'll be different in the morning. Come on, laddie, I know what you need.'

'Where are we going?'

'To the Opera House.'

'What will Candy say?'

'Candy doesn't have to know.'

Duff was right; it was different in the morning. There was the usual hurly-burly of work at the office and some tense action at the Exchange. He thought about Karl only once during the day and somehow it didn't seem to matter so much. They sent him a nice wreath.

He had faced the reality of the game he was playing. He had considered the alternative which was to get out with the fortune he had already made; but to do that would mean giving up the power he held. The addiction was already seated too deeply, he could not deny it. So his subconscious opened, sucked in his conscience and swallowed it deep down into its gut. He could feel it struggling there sometimes, but the longer it stayed swallowed the more feeble those struggles became. Duff comforted him: Duff's words were like a gastric juice that helped to digest that lump in the gut and he had not yet learned that what Duff said and what Duff did were not necessarily what Duff believed.

Play the game without mercy, play to win.

= 17 =

Duff stood with his back to the fireplace in Sean's office smoking a cheroot while they waited for the carriage to take them up to the Exchange. The fire behind him silhouetted his slimly tapered legs with the calves encased in polished black leather. He still wore his top coat, for the winter morning was cold. It fell open at his throat to show a diamond that sparkled and glowed in his cravat.

'. . . you get used to a woman somehow,' he was saying. 'I've known Candy four years now and yet it seems I've been with her all my life.'

'She's a fine girl,' Sean agreed absently as he dipped his pen and scribbled his signature on the document in front of him.

'I'm thirty-five now,' Duff went on. 'If I'm ever to have a son of my own . . .'

Sean laid down the pen deliberately and looked up at him; he was starting to grin.

'The man said to me once "They take you into their soft little minds" and again he said "They don't share, they possess". Is this a new tune I hear?'

Duff shifted uneasily from one foot to the other.

'Things change,' he defended himself. 'I'm thirty-five . . .'

'You're repeating yourself,' Sean accused and Duff smiled weakly.

'Well, the truth is . . .'

He never finished the sentence; hooves beat urgently in the street outside and both their faces swung in the direction of the window.

'Big hurry!' said Sean coming quickly to his feet. 'Big trouble!' He crossed to the window. 'It's Curtis, and by his face it's not good news he brings.'

There were voices outside the door raised in agitation and the quick rush of feet, then Timothy Curtis burst into the room without knocking. He wore a miner's overall and splattered gumboots. 'We've hit a mud rush on the ninth level.'

'How bad?' Duff snapped.

'Bad enough – it's flooded right back to number eight.'

'Jesus, that will take two months at least to clear,' Sean exclaimed. 'Does anyone else in town know – have you told anyone?'

'I came straight here – Cronje and five men were up at the face when it blew.'

'Get back there immediately,' ordered Sean, 'but ride quietly, we don't want the whole world to know there's trouble. Don't let a soul off the property. We must have time to sell out.'

'Yes, Mr Courtney.' Curtis hesitated. 'Cronje and five others were hit by the rush. Shall I send word to their wives?'

'Can't you understand English? I don't want a whisper of this to get out before ten o'clock. We've got to have time.'

'But, Mr Courtney – ' Curtis was appalled. He stood staring at Sean and Sean felt the sick little stirring of guilt. Six men drowned in treacle-thick mud . . . He made an irresolute gesture with his hands.

'We can't –' He stopped and Duff cut in.

'They're dead now, and they'll be just as dead when we tell their wives at ten o'clock. Get going, Curtis.'

They sold their shares in the Little Sister within an hour of the start of trading and a week later they bought them back at half the price. Two months later the Little Sister was back on full production again.

= 18 =

They split their land at Orange Grove into plots and sold them, all but a hundred acres and on that they started building a house. Into the designing of it they poured their combined energy and imagination. With money Duff seduced the horticulturist of the Capetown Botanical Gardens and brought him up by express coach. They showed him the land.

'Make me a garden,' said Duff.

'The whole hundred acres?'

'Yes.'

'It'll cost a pretty penny.'

'That is no problem.'

The carpets came from Persia, the wood from the Knysna forests and the marble from Italy. On the gates at the entrance to the main drive they engraved the words 'At Xanadu did Kublai Khan a stately pleasure dome decree'. As the gardener had predicted, it all cost a pretty penny. Each afternoon when the Exchange closed they would drive up together and watch the builders at work. One day Candy came with them and they showed it off to her like two small boys.

'This will be the ballroom.' Sean bowed to her. 'May I have the pleasure of this dance?'

'Thank you, sir.' She curtsied, then swept away on his arm across the unsanded boards.

'This will be the staircase,' Duff told her, 'marble – black and white marble – and there on the main landing in a glass case will be Hradsky's head, beautifully mounted with an apple in his mouth.'

They climbed laughing up the rough concrete ramp.

'This is Sean's room – the bed is being made of oak, thick oak to withstand punishment.' They trooped with linked arms down the passage.

'And this is my room – I was thinking of a solid gold bath but the builder says it's too heavy and Sean says it's too vulgar. Look at that view; from here you can see out across the whole valley. I could lie in bed in the mornings and read the prices on the Exchange floor with a telescope.'

'It's lovely,' Candy said dreamily.

'You like it?'

'Oh, yes.'

'It could be your room too.'

Candy started to blush and then her face tightened with annoyance. 'He was right – you are vulgar.'

She started for the door and Sean fumbled for his cigars to cover his embarrassment. With two quick steps Duff caught her and turned her to face him. 'You sweet idiot, that was a proposal.'

'Let me go.' Near to tears she twisted in his hands. 'I don't think you're funny.'

'Candy – I'm serious. Will you marry me?'

The cigar dropped out of Sean's mouth but he caught it before it hit the ground. Candy was standing very still, her eyes fastened on Duff's face.

'Yes or no – will you marry me?'

She nodded once slowly and then twice very fast.

Duff looked at Sean over his shoulder. 'Leave us, laddie.'

On the way back to town Candy had regained her voice. She chattered happily and Duff answered her with his lopsided grin. Sean hunched morosely in one corner of the carriage. His cigar was burning unevenly and he threw it out of the window.

'You'll let me keep the Victoria rooms, I hope, Candy.'

There was a silence.

'What do you mean?' asked Duff.

'Two's company,' Sean answered.

'Oh, no,' Candy exclaimed.

'It's your house as well.' Duff spoke sharply,

'I give it to you – a wedding present.'

'Oh, shut up,' Duff grinned, 'it's big enough for all of us.'

Candy crossed quickly to Sean's seat and put her hand on his shoulder.

'Please – we've been together a long time. We'd be lonely without you.'

Sean grunted.

'Please!'

'He'll come,' said Duff.

'Please.'

'Oh, well –' Sean frowned ungraciously.

= 19 =

They went racing at Milnerton. Candy with a hat full of ostrich feathers, Sean and Duff with pearl grey toppers and gold heads on their canes.

'You can pay for your wedding gown by putting fifty guineas on Trade Wind! She can't lose –' Duff told Candy.

'What about Mr Hradsky's new filly? I've heard she's a good bet,' Candy asked and Duff frowned.

'You want to go over to the enemy?'

'I thought you and Hradsky were almost partners.' Candy twirled her parasol. 'From the rumours I've heard you work with him all the time.'

Mbejane slowed the carriage as they ran into the crush of pedestrians and coaches outside the Turf Club gates.

'Well you've heard wrong both times. His Sun Dancer will never hold Trade Wind over the distance, she's bred too light in the legs. Frenchified with Huguenot blood; she'll fade within the mile. And as far as Hradsky being our partner, we throw him an occasional bone. Isn't that right, Sean?'

Sean was watching Mbejane's back. The Zulu, in loin clothes only and his spears laid carefully on the boards at his feet, was handling the horses with an easy familiarity. They cocked their ears back to catch his voice, deep and soft, as he talked to them.

'Isn't that right, Sean?' Duff repeated.

'Of course,' agreed Sean vaguely. 'You know – I think I'll get Mbejane a livery. He looks out of place in those skins.'

'Well, some of the other horses from the same stud were stayers. Sun Honey won the Cape Derby twice and Eclipse showed up the English stock in the Metropolitan Handicap last year,' Candy argued.

'Huh,' Duff smiled his superiority, 'well, you can take my word for it that Trade Wind will walk the main race today and he'll be back in his stable before Sun Dancer sees the finishing post.'

'Maroon and gold – the same as our racing colours,' Sean muttered thoughtfully. 'That would go very well with his black skin, perhaps a turban with an ostrich feather in it.'

'What the hell are you talking about?' complained Duff.

'Mbejane's livery.'

They left the carriage in the reserved area and went through to the members' grandstand, Candy sailing prettily between her escorts.

'Well, Duff, we've got the nicest looking woman here today.'

'Thank you.' Candy smiled up at Sean.

'Is that why you keep trying to look down the front of her dress?' challenged Duff.

'You filthy-minded beast.' Sean was shocked.

'Don't deny, it,' Candy teased, 'but I find it very flattering – you're welcome.'

They moved through the throng of butterfly-coloured dresses and stiffly-suited men. A ripple of greetings moved with them.

'Morning, Mr Courtney.' The accent was on the 'Mister'. 'How's your Trade Wind for the big race?'

'Put your pants on him.'

'Hello, Duff, congratulations on your engagement.'

'Thanks, Jock, it's time you took the plunge as well.'

They were rich, they were young, they were handsome and all the world admired them. Sean felt good, with a pretty girl on his arm and a friend walking beside him.

'There's Hradsky – let's go across and engage in a little hog-baiting,' Duff suggested.

'Why do you hate him so much?' Candy asked softly.

'Look at him and answer your own question. Have you ever seen anything more pompous, joyless and unlovable?'

'Oh, leave him alone, Duff, don't spoil the day. Let's go down to the paddock.'

'Come on!' Duff steered them across to where Hradsky and Max were standing alone by the rail of the track.

'Salome, Norman, and peace to you also, Maximilian.'

Hradsky nodded and Max murmured sadly; his lashes touched his cheeks as he blinked.

'I noticed you two chatting away and thought I would come across and listen to your stimulating repartee.'

He received no answer and went on. 'I saw your new filly exercising on the practice track yesterday evening and I said to myself, Norman's got a girl friend – that's what it is – he's bought a hack for his lady. But now they tell me you are going to race her. Oh, Norman, I wish you'd consult me before you do these silly things. You're an impetuous little devil at times.'

'Mr Hradsky is confident that Sun Dancer will make a reasonable showing today,' Max murmured.

'I was about to offer you a side bet, but being a naturally kind-hearted person, I feel it would be taking an unfair advantage.'

A small crowd had gathered round them listening with anticipation. Candy tugged gently at Duff's elbow trying to lead him away.

'I thought five hundred guineas would be acceptable to Norman.' Duff shrugged. 'But let's forget it.'

Hradsky made a fierce little sign with his hands and Max interpreted smoothly. 'Mr Hradsky suggests a thousand.'

'Rash, Norman, extremely rash.' Duff sighed. 'But I suppose I must accommodate you.'

They walked down to the refreshment pavilion. Candy was quiet awhile, then she said, 'An enemy like Mr Hradsky is a luxury that even you two gods can't afford. Why don't you leave him alone?'

'It's a hobby of Duff's,' explained Sean as they found seats at one of the tables. 'Waiter – bring us a bottle of Pol Roger.'

Before the big race they went down to the paddock. A steward opened the wicket gate for them and they passed into the ring of circling horses. A gnome in silk of maroon and gold came to meet them and touched his cap then stood awkwardly, fingering his whip.

'He looks good this morning, sir.' The little man nodded at Trade Wind. There was a dark patch of sweat on the horse's shoulder and he mouthed the snaffle, lifting his feet delicately. Once he snorted and rolled his eyes in mock terror.

'He's got an edge on him, sir, eager kind of – if you follow me.'

'I want you to win, Harry,' said Duff.

'So do I, sir, I'll do my best.'

'There's a thousand guineas for you if you do.'

'A thousand –' the jockey repeated on an outgoing breath.

Duff looked across to where Hradsky and Max were standing talking to their trainer. He caught Hradsky's eye, glanced significantly at Hradsky's honey-coloured filly and shook his head sympathetically.

'Win for me, Harry,' he said softly.

'That I will, sir!'

The groom led the big stallion across to them and Sean flicked the jockey up into the saddle.

'Good luck.'

Harry settled his cap and gathered up the reins; he winked at Sean, his hobgoblin face wrinkling in a grin.

'There's no better luck than a thousand guineas, sir, if you follow me.'

'Come on.' Duff caught Candy's arm. 'Let's get a place at the rail.'

They hustled her out of the paddock and across the members' enclosure. The rail was crowded but a place opened for them respectfully and no one jostled them.

'I can't understand you two,' Candy laughed breathlessly. 'You make an extravagant bet, then you fix it so you can get nothing even if you win.'

'Money's not the problem,' Duff assured her.

'He won that much from me at Klabejas last night,' Sean commented. 'If Trade Wind beats the filly his prize will be the look on Hradsky's face – the loss of a thousand guineas will hurt him like a kick between the legs.'

The horses came parading past, stepping high next to the grooms who held them, then they turned free and cantered back, dancing sideways, throwing their heads, shining in the sunlight like the bright silk upon their backs. They moved away round the curve of the track.

The crowd rustled with excitement, a bookmaker's voice carried over the buzz.

'Twenty-to-one bar two. Sun Dancer at fives. Trade Wind even money.'

Duff showed his teeth as he smiled. 'That's right, you tell the people.'

Candy twisted her gloves nervously and looked up at Sean.

'You there in the grandstand – can you see what they're doing?'

'They're in line now, moving up together – it looks as though they'll get away first time,' Sean told her without taking his binoculars from his eyes. 'Yes, there they go – they're away!'

'Tell me, tell me,' commanded Candy, pounding Sean's shoulder.

'Harry's showing in front already – can you see the filly, Duff?'

'I saw a flash of green in the pack – yes, there she is lying sixth or seventh.'

'What horse is that next to Trade Wind?'

'That's Hamilton's gelding, don't worry about him, he won't last to the turn.'

The frieze of horses, their heads going like hammers and the dust lifting pale and thin behind them, were framed by the guide rail and the white mine dumps beyond them. Like a string of dark beads they moved up the back stretch and then bunched in the straight.

'Trade Wind's still there – I think he's making ground – the gelding's finished and no sign of the filly yet.'

'Yes! There she is, Duff, wide on the outside. She's moving up.'

'Come on, my darling –' Duff half whispered. 'Let's see you foot it now.'

'She's clear of the pack – she's coming up, Duff, she's coming up fast,' Sean warned.

'Come on, Trade Wind, hold her off,' Duff pleaded. 'Keep her there, boy.'

The pounding of the hooves reached them now, a sound like distant surf, but rising sharply. The colours showed, emerald green above a honey skin and maroon and gold leading on the bay.

'Trade Wind – come on Trade Wind,' shrieked Candy. Her hat flopped over her eyes as she hopped; she ripped it off impatiently and her hair tumbled to her shoulders.

'She's catching him, Duff!'

'Give him the whip, Harry, for Christ's sake – the whip, man.'

The hoof beats crescendoed, thundered up to them, then passed. The filly's nose was at Harry's boot, creeping steadily forward, now level with Trade Wind's heaving shoulder.

'The whip, God damn you,' screamed Duff, 'give him the whip.'

Harry's right arm moved, fast as a mamba – crack, crack; they heard the whip above the howling crowd, above the drumming of hooves and the bay jumped at its sting. Like a pair in harness the two horses swept over the finishing line.

'Who won?' Candy asked as though she were in pain.

'I couldn't see, damn it,' Duff answered.

'Nor could I –' Sean took out his handkerchief and wiped his forehead. 'That didn't do my heart any good – as Francois would say. Have a cigar, Duff.'

'Thanks – I need one.'

Everyone in the crowd was turned to face the board above the judges' box and an uneasy silence held them.

'Why do they take such a long time to make up their minds?' complained Candy. 'I'm so upset that I can only last a minute before I visit the Ladies' Room.'

'The numbers are going up,' shouted Sean.

'Who is it?' Candy jumped to try and see over the heads of the crowd then stopped hurriedly with an expression of alarm on her face.

'Number Sixteen,' bellowed Duff and Sean together, 'it's Trade Wind!'

Sean punched Duff in the chest and Duff leaned over and snapped Sean's cigar in half. Then they caught Candy between them and hugged her. She let out a careful shriek and fought her way out of their arms. 'Excuse me,' she said and fled.

'Let me buy you a drink.' Sean lit the mutilated stump of his cigar.

'No, it's my honour, I insist.' Duff took his arm and they walked with big satisfied grins towards the pavilion. Hradsky was sitting at one of the tables with Max. Duff walked up behind him, lifted his top hat off his head with one hand and with the other ruffled Hradsky's few remaining hairs.

'Never mind, Norman, you can't win all the time.'

Hradsky turned slowly. He retrieved his hat and smoothed back his hair, his eyes glittered yellow.

'He's going to talk,' whispered Duff excitedly.

'I agree with you, Mr Charleywood, you can't win all the time,' said Norman Hradsky. It came out quite clearly with only a small catch on the 'c's' – they were always difficult letters for him. He stood up, put his hat back on his head and walked away.

'I will have a cheque delivered to your office early on Monday morning,' Max told them quietly without taking his eyes off the table. Then he stood up and followed Hradsky.

= 20 =

Sean came through from the bathroom, his beard in wild disorder and a bath-towel round his waist.

'The famous Duke of York
He had ten thousand men
He marched them up to the top of the hill
And he marched them down again.'

He sang as he poured bay rum from a cut-glass bottle into his cupped hands and rubbed it into his hair. Duff sat in one of the gilt chairs watching him. Sean combed his hair carefully then smiled at himself in the mirror.

'You magnificent creature,' Sean told his reflection.

'You're getting fat,' Duff grunted.

Sean looked hurt. 'It's muscle.'

'You've got a backside on you like a hippopotamus.'

Sean removed his towel and turned his back to the mirror; he surveyed it over his shoulder.

'I need a heavy hammer to drive a long nail,' he protested.

'Oh, no,' groaned Duff. 'Your wit at this time of the morning is like pork for breakfast, heavy on the stomach.'

Sean took a silk shirt out of his drawer, held it like a toreador's cape, made two passes and swirled it onto his back with a half veronica.

'Olé!' applauded Duff wryly. Sean pulled on his trousers and sat to fit his boots.

'You're in a nice mood this morning,' he told Duff.

'I've just come through an emotional hurricane!'

'What's the trouble?'

'Candy wants a church wedding.'

'Is that bad?'

'Well, it's not good.'

'Why?'

'Is your memory so short?'

'Oh, you mean your other wife.'

'That's right, my other wife.'

'Have you told Candy about her?'

'Good God, no.' Duff looked horrified.

'Yes, I see your problem – what about Candy's husband? Doesn't that even the score between you?'

'No, he has gone to his reward.'

'Well, that's convenient. Does anyone else know you're married already?' Duff shook his head.

'What about Francois?'

'No, I never told him.'

'Well, what's your problem – take her down to the church and marry her.'

Duff looked uncomfortable.

'I don't mind marrying a second time in a magistrate's court, it would only be a couple of old Dutchmen I'd be cheating, but to go into a church –' Duff shook his head.

'I'd be the only one who'd know,' said Sean.

'You and the headman.'

'Duff,' Sean beamed at him. 'Duff, my boy, you have scruples – this is amazing!'

Duff squirmed a little in his chair.

'Let me think.' Sean held his forehead dramatically. 'Yes, yes, it's coming to me – that's it.'

'Come on, tell me.' Duff sat on the edge of his chair.

'Go to Candy and tell her it's all fixed, not only are you prepared to marry her in a church but you're even going to build your own church.'

'That's wonderful,' Duff murmured sarcastically, 'that's the way out of my difficulties all right.'

'Let me finish.' Sean started filling his silver cigar case. 'You also tell her that you want a civil ceremony as well – I believe that's what royalty do. Tell her that, it should win her over.'

'I still don't follow you.'

'Then you build your own chapel up at Xanadu – we can find a distinguished-looking character, dress him up in a dog collar and teach him the right words. That keeps Candy happy. Immediately after the service the priest takes the coach for Capetown. You take Candy down to the magistrate's office and that keeps you happy.'

Duff looked stunned then slowly his face broke into a great happy smile. 'Genius – pure inspired genius.'

Sean buttoned his waistcoat. 'Think nothing of it. And now if you'll excuse me I'll go and do some work – one of us has to make sufficient to allow you to indulge these strange fancies of yours.'

Sean shrugged on his coat, picked up his cane and swung it. The gold head gave it a balance like a hand-made shotgun. The silk next to his skin and the halo of bay rum round his head made him feel good.

He went down the stairs. Mbejane had the carriage waiting for him in the Hotel yard. The body tilted slightly at Sean's weight and the leather upholstery welcomed him with a yeilding softness. He lit his first cigar of the day and Mbejane smiled at him.

'I see you, Nkosi.'

'I see you also, Mbejane, what is that lump on the side of your head?'

'Nkosi, I was a little drunk, otherwise that ape of Basuto would never have touched me with his fighting stick.'

Mbejane rolled the carriage smoothly out of the yard and into the street.

'What were you fighting about?'

Mbejane shrugged. 'Must a man have a reason to fight?'

'It is usual.'

'It is in my memory that there was a woman,' said Mbejane.

'That is also usual – who won this fight?'

'The man bled a little, his friends took him away. The woman, when I left, was smiling in her sleep.'

Sean laughed, then ran his eyes over the undulating plain of Mbejane's bare back. It was definitely not in keeping. He hoped his secretary had remembered to speak to the tailor. They pulled up in front of his offices. One of his clerks hurried down off the veranda and opened the door of the carriage.

'Good morning, Mr Courtney.'

Sean went up the stairs with his clerk running ahead of him like a hunting dog.

'Good morning, Mr Courtney,' another polite chorus from the row of desks in the main office. Sean waved his cane at them and went through into his own office. His portrait leered at him from above the fireplace and he winked at it.

'What have we this morning, Johnson?'

'These requisitions, sir, and the pay cheques, sir, and development reports from the engineers, sir, and . . .'

Johnson was a greasy-haired little man in a greasy-looking alpaca coat; with each 'sir' he made a greasy little bow. He was efficient so Sean hired him, but that didn't mean he liked him.

'You got a stomach ache, Johnson?'

'No, sir.'

'Well, for God's sake, stand up straight, man.'

Johnson shot to attention.

'Now let's have them one at a time.'

Sean dropped into his chair. At this time of the day came the grind. He hated the paper work and so he tackled it with grim concentration, making random checks on the long rows of figures, trying to associate names with faces and querying requisitions that appeared exorbitant until finally he wrote his signature between the last of Johnson's carefully pencilled crosses and threw his pen onto the desk.

'What else is there?'

'Meeting with Mr Maxwell from the Bank at twelve-thirty, sir.'

'And then?'

'The agent for Brooke Bros. at one, and immediately after that Mr MacDougal, sir, then you're expected up at the Candy Deep mine.'

'Thank you, Johnson, I'll be at the Exchange as usual this morning if anything out of the ordinary comes up.'

'Very good, Mr Courtney. Just one other thing.' Johnson pointed at the brown paper parcel on the couch across the room. 'From your tailor.'

'Ah!' Sean smiled. 'Send my servant in here.' He walked across and opened the parcel. Within a few minutes Mbejane filled the doorway.

'Nkosi?'

'Mbejane – your new uniform.' Sean pointed at the clothes laid out on the couch. Mbejane's eyes switched to the gold and maroon finery, his expression suddenly dead.

'Put it on – come on, let's see how you look.'

Mbejane crossed to the couch and picked up the jacket. 'These are for me?'

'Yes, come on, put it on.' Sean laughed.

Mbejane hesitated, then slowly he loosened his loin cloth and let it drop. Sean watched him impatiently as he buttoned on the jacket and pantaloons, then he walked in a critical circle around the Zulu.

'Not bad,' he muttered, and then in Zulu, 'Is it not beautiful?'

Mbejane wriggled his shoulders against the unfamiliar feel of the cloth and said nothing.

'Well, Mbejane, do you like it?'

'When I was a child I went with my father to trade cattle at Port Natal. There was a man who went about the town with a monkey on a chair, the monkey danced and the people laughed and threw money to it. That monkey had such a suit as this. Nkosi, I do not think he was a very happy monkey.'

The smile slipped off Sean's face. 'You would rather wear your skins?'

'What I wear is the dress of a warrior of Zululand.'

There was still no expression on Mbejane's face. Sean opened his mouth to argue with him but before he could speak he lost his temper.

'You'll wear that uniform,' he shouted. 'You'll wear what I tell you to wear and you'll do it with a smile, do you hear me?'

'Nkosi, I hear you.' Mbejane picked up his loin cloth of leopard tails and left the office. When Sean went out to the carriage Mbejane was sitting on the driver's seat in his new livery. All the way to the Exchange his back was stiff with protest and neither of them spoke. Sean glared at the doorman of the Exchange, drank four brandies during the morning, rode back to his office again at noon scowling at Mbejane's still protesting back, shouted at Johnson, snapped at the bank manager, routed the representative from Brooke Bros. and drove out to the Candy Deep in a high old rage. But Mbejane's silence was impenetrable and Sean couldn't re-open the argument without sacrifice of pride. He burst into the new administrative building of the Candy Deep and threw the staff into confusion.

'Where's Mr du Toit?' he roared.

'He's down the Number Three shaft, Mr Courtney.'

'What the hell is he doing down there? He's supposed to be waiting for me here.'

'He didn't expect you for another hour, sir.'

'Well, get me some overalls and a mining helmet, don't just stand there.'

He clapped the tin hat on his head and stamped his heavy gumboots across to the Number Three shaft. The skip dropped him smoothly five hundred feet into the earth and he climbed out at the tenth level.

'Where's Mr du Toit?' he demanded of the shift boss at the lift station.

'He's up at the face, sir.'

The floor of the drive was rough and muddy; his gumboots squelched as he set off down the tunnel. His carbide lamp lit the uneven rock walls with a flat white light and he felt himself starting to sweat. Two natives pushing a cocopan back along the railway lines forced him to flatten himself against one wall to allow them to pass and while he waited he felt inside his overalls for his cigar case. As he pulled it out it slipped from his hand and plunked into the mud. The cocopan was gone by that time so he stooped to pick up the case. His ear came within an inch of the wall and a puzzled expression replaced his frown of annoyance. The rock was squeaking. He laid his ear against it. It sounded like someone grinding his teeth. He listened to it for a while trying to guess the cause; it wasn't the echo of shovels or drills, it wasn't water. He walked another thirty yards or so down the drive and listened again. Not so loud here but now the grinding noise was punctuated with an occasional metallic snap like the breaking of a knife blade. Strange, very strange; he had never heard anything like it before. He walked on down the drive, his bad mood lost in his preoccupation with this new problem. Before be reached the face he met Francois.

'Hello, Mr Courtney.' Sean had long since given up trying to stop Francois calling him that. '*Gott,* I'm sorry I wasn't there to meet you. I thought you were coming at three.'

'That's all right, Francois, how are you?'

'My rheumatism's been giving me blazes, Mr Courtney, but otherwise I'm all right. How's Mr Charleywood?'

'He's fine.' Sean couldn't restrain his curiosity any longer. 'Tell me something, Franz, just now I put my ear against the wall of the drive and I heard an odd noise, I couldn't make out what it was.'

'What kind of noise?'

'A sort of grinding, like – like . . .' Sean searched for words to describe it, 'like two pieces of glass being rubbed together.'

Francois's eyes flew wide open and then began to bulge, the colour of his face changed to grey and he caught Sean's arm.

'Where?'

'Back along the drive.'

The breath jammed in Francois's throat and he struggled to speak through it, shaking Sean's arm desperately.

'Cave-in!' he croaked. 'Cave-in, man!'

He started to run but Sean grabbed him. Francois struggled wildly.

'Francois, how many men up at the face?'

'Cave-in.' Francois's voice was now hysterically shrill. 'Cave-in.' He broke Sean's grip and raced away towards the lift station, the mud flying from his gumboots. His terror infected Sean and he ran a dozen paces after Francois before he stopped himself. For precious seconds he wavered with fear slithering round like a reptile in his stomach; go back to call the others and perhaps die with them or follow Francois and live. Then the fear in his belly found a mate, a thing just as slimy and cold; its name was shame, and shame it was that drove him back towards the face. There were five blacks and a white man there, bare-chested and shiny with sweat in the heat. Sean shouted those two words at them and they reacted the way bathers do when someone on the beach shouts 'shark'. The same moment of paralysed horror, then the panic. They came stampeding back along the tunnel. Sean ran with them, the mud sucked at his heavy boots and his legs were weak with easy living and riding in carriages. One by one the others passed him.

'Wait for me,' he wanted to scream. 'Wait for me.' He slipped on the greasy footing, scraping his shoulder on the rough wall as he fell, and dragged himself up again, mud plastered in his beard, the blood humming in his ears. Alone now he blundered on down the tunnel. With a crack like a rifle shot one of the thick shoring timbers broke under the pressure of the moving rock and dust smoked from the roof of the tunnel in front of him. He staggered on and all around him the earth was talking, groaning, protesting, with little muffled shrieks. The timbers joined in again, crackling and snapping, and as slowly as a theatre curtain the rock sagged down from above him. The tunnel was thick with dust that smothered the beam of his lamp and rasped his throat. He knew then that he wasn't going to make it but he ran on with the loose rock starting to fall about him. A lump hit his mining helmet and jarred him so that he nearly fell. Blinded by the swirling dust fog he crashed at full run into the abandoned cocopan that blocked the tunnel, he sprawled over the metal body of the trolley with his thighs bruised from the collision.

'Now I'm finished,' he thought, but instinctively he pulled himself up and started to grope his way around the cocopan to continue his flight. With a roar the tunnel in front of him collapsed. He dropped on his knees and crawled between the wheels of the cocopan, wriggling under the sturdy steel body just an instant before the roof above him collapsed also. The noise of the fall around him seemed to last for ever, but then it was over and the rustling and grating of the rock as it settled down was almost silence in comparison. His lamp was lost and the darkness pressed as heavily on him as the earth squeezed down on his tiny shelter. The air was solid with dust and he coughed; he coughed until his chest ached and he tasted salty blood in his mouth. There was hardly room to move, the steel body of the trolley was six inches above him, but he struggled until he managed to open the front of his overalls and tear a piece off the tail of his shirt. He held the silk like a surgical mask across his mouth and nose. It strained the dust out of the air so he could breathe. The dust settled; his coughing slowed and finally stopped. He felt surprise that he was still alive and cautiously he started exploring. He tried to straighten out his legs but his feet touched rock. He felt with his hands, six inches of head room and perhaps twelve inches on either side, warm mud underneath him and rock and steel all around. He took off his helmet and used it as a pillow. He was in a steel coffin buried five hundred feet deep, He felt the first flutter of panic. 'Keep your mind busy, think of something, think of anything but the rock around you, count your assets,' he told himself. He started to search his pockets, moving with difficulty in the cramped space.

'One silver cigar case with two Havanas.' He laid it down next to him.

'One box of matches, wet.' He placed it on top of the case.

'One pocket watch.'

'One handkerchief, Irish linen, monogrammed.'

'One comb, tortoiseshell – a man is judged by his appearance.' He started to comb his beard but found immediately that though this occupied his hands it left his mind free. He put the comb down next to his matches.

'Twenty-five pounds in gold sovereigns –' He counted them carefully, 'yes, twenty-five. I shall order a bottle of good champagne.' The dust was chalky in his mouth so he went on hurriedly, 'and a Malay girl from the Opera. No, why be mean – ten Malay girls. I'll have them dance for me, that'll pass the time. I'll promise them a sovereign each to bolster their enthusiasm.'

He continued the search, but there was nothing else. 'Gumboots, socks, well-cut trousers, shirt torn I'm afraid, overalls, a tin hat, and that's all.'

With his possessions laid out carefully beside him and his cell explored he had to start thinking. First he thought about his thirst. The mud in which he lay was too thick to yield water. He tried straining it through his shirt without success, and then he thought about air. It seemed quite fresh and he decided that sufficient was filtering in from the loosely packed rock around him to keep him alive.

To keep him alive – alive until the thirst killed. Until he died curled up like a foetus in the warm womb of the earth. He laughed, a worm in a dark warm womb. He laughed again and recognized it as the beginnings of panic, he thrust his fist into his mouth to stop himself, biting down hard on his knuckles. It was very quiet, the rock had stopped moving.

'How long will it take? Tell me, Doctor. How long have I got?'

'Well, you are sweating. You'll lose moisture quite rapidly. I'd say about four days,' he answered himself.

'What about hunger, Doctor?'

'Oh, no, don't worry about that, you'll be hungry, of course, but the thirst will kill you.'

'And typhoid, or is it typhus, I can never remember. What about that, Doctor?'

'If there were dead men trapped in here with you there'd be a good chance, but you're alone, you know.'

'Do you think I'll go mad, Doctor, not immediately, of course, but in a few days?'

'Yes, you'll go mad.'

'I've never been mad before, not that I know of anyway, but I think it will help to go mad now, don't you?'

'If you mean, will it make it easier, well, I don't know.'

'Ah! now you're being obscure – but I follow you. You mean in that sleep of madness what dreams will come? You mean, will madness be more real than reality? You mean, will dying mad be worse than dying thirsty? But then I may beat the madness. This cocopan might buckle under the strain, after all there must be thousands of tons of rock bearing down on it. That's quite clever, you know, Doctor; as a medical man you should appreciate it. Mother Earth was saved but, alas, the child was stillborn, she bore down too hard.' Sean had spoken aloud, and now he felt foolish. He picked up a piece of stone and tapped the cocopan with it.

'It sounds firm enough. A most pleasing noise, really.' He beat harder on the metal body – one, two, three, one, two, three – then dropped the stone. Soft as an echo, distant as the moon, he heard his taps repeated. His whole body stiffened at the sound, and he started to shiver with excitement. He snatched up the stone: three times he rapped, and three times the answer came back to him.

'They heard me, sweet merciful Christ, they heard me.' He laughed breathlessly. 'Dear Mother Earth, don't bear down, please don't bear down. Just be patient. Wait a few days and by Caesarian they'll take this child out of your womb.'

Mbejane waited until Sean disappeared down the Number Three shaft before he took off his new jacket. He folded it carefully on the driver's seat next to him. He sat and enjoyed the feel of the sun on his skin for a while, then he climbed off the carriage and went to the horses. He took them one at a time to the trough for water then returned them to their harnesses, buckling them in loosely. He picked up his spears from the footboard and moved across to a patch of short grass next to the administrative building. He sat down and went to work on the blade, humming softly to himself as he honed. At last he ran an expert thumb along each edge, grunted, shaved a few hairs off his forearm, smiled contentedly and laid his spears beside him in the grass. He lay back and the sun warmed him to sleep.

The shouting woke him. He sat up and automatically checked the height of the sun. He had slept an hour or more. Duff was shouting and Francois, mud-splattered and frightened-looking, was answering him. They were standing together in front of the administrative building. Duff's horse was sweating. Mbejane stood up and went across to them; he listened closely, trying to understand their staccato voices. They went too fast for him, but something was wrong, that much he knew.

'It's caved in almost to the Number Ten lift station,' Francois said.

'You left him in there,' accused Duff.

'I thought he was following me, but he turned back.'

'What for – why did he turn back?'

'To call the others –'

'Have you started clearing the drive?'

'No, I was waiting for you.'

'You stupid bloody idiot, he might be alive in there . . . every minute is vital.'

'But he hasn't a chance, Mr Charleywood, he must be dead.'

'Shut up, damn you.'

Duff swung away from him and started running towards the shaft. There was a crowd gathered beneath the high steel structure of the head gear, and suddenly Mbejane knew it was Sean. He caught up with Duff before he reached the shaft.

'Is it the Nkosi?'

'Yes.'

'What has happened?'

'The rock has fallen on him.'

Mbejane pushed his way into the skip next to Duff and neither of them spoke again until they reached the tenth level. They went down the drive, only a short way before they reached the end. There were men there with crowbars and shovels standing undecided, waiting for orders, and Mbejane shouldered a path through them. He and Duff stood together in front of the new wall of broken rock that sealed the tunnel, and the silence went on and on. Then Duff turned on the white shift-boss.

'Were you at the face?'

'Yes.'

'He went back to call you, didn't he?'

'Yes.'

'And you left him there?'

The man couldn't look at Duff.

'I thought he was following us,' he muttered.

'You thought only of your own miserable skin,' Duff told him, 'you filthy little coward, you slimy yellow bastard, you . . .'

Mbejane caught Duff's arm and Duff stopped his tirade. They all heard it then – clink, clink, clink.

'It's him – it must be him,' whispered Duff, 'he's alive!' He snatched a crowbar from one of the natives and knocked against the side of the tunnel. They waited, their breathing the only sound, until the answer came back to them louder and sharper than before. Mbejane took the crowbar out of Duff's hands. He thrust it into a crack in the rock jam and his back muscles bunched as he heaved. The bar bent like a liquorice stick, he threw it away and went at the stone with his bare hands.

'You!' Duff snapped at the shift-boss. 'We'll need timber to shore up as we clear the fall – get it.' He turned to the natives. 'Four of you working on the face at one time – the rest of you carry the stone away as we loosen it.'

'Do you want any dynamite?' asked the shift-boss.

'And bring the rock down a second time? Use your brains, man. Go and get that timber and call Mr du Toit while you're at the surface.'

In four hours they cleared fifteen feet of tunnel, breaking the larger slabs of stone with sledge hammers and prising the pieces out of the jam. Duff's body ached and his hands were raw. He had to rest. He walked slowly back to the lift station and there he found blankets and a huge dish of soup.

'Where did this come from?'

'Candy's Hotel, sir. Half Johannesburg is waiting at the head of the shaft.'

Duff huddled into a blanket and drank a little of the soup. 'Where's du Toit?'

'I couldn't find him, sir.'

Up at the face Mbejane worked on. The first four natives came back to rest and fresh men took their place. Mbejane led them, grunting an order occasionally but otherwise reserving his strength for the assault on the rock. For an hour Duff rested and when he returned to the head of the tunnel Mbejane was still there. Duff watched him curl his arms round a piece of stone the size of a beer keg, brace his legs and tear the stone out of the jam. Earth and loose rock followed it burying Mbejane's legs to the knees and Duff jumped forward to help him.

Another two hours and Duff had to rest again. This time he led Mbejane back with him, gave him a blanket and made him drink a little soup. They sat next to each other with their backs against the wall of the tunnel and blankets over their shoulders. The shift-boss came to Duff.

'Mrs Rautenbach sent this down for you, sir.'

It was a half-bottle of brandy.

'Tell her, thank you.' Duff pulled the cork with his teeth and swallowed twice. It brought the tears into his eyes – he offered the bottle to Mbejane.

'It is not fitting,' Mbejane demurred.

'Drink.'

Mbejane drank, wiped the mouth of the bottle carefully on his blanket and handed it back. Duff took another swallow and offered it again but Mbejane shook his head.

'A little of that is strength, too much is weakness. There is work to do now.'

Duff corked the bottle.

'How long before we reach him?' asked Mbejane.

'Another day, maybe two.'

'A man can die in two days,' mused the Zulu.

'Not one with a body like a bull and a temper like a devil,' Duff assured him. Mbejane smiled and Duff went on groping for his words in Zulu.

'You love him, Mbejane?'

'Love is a woman's word.'

Mbejane inspected one of his thumbs; the nail was torn loose, standing up like a tombstone; he took it between his teeth, pulled it off and spat it onto the floor of the drive. Duff shuddered as he watched.

'Those baboons will not work unless they are driven.' Mbejane stood up. 'Are you rested?'

'Yes,' lied Duff, and they went back to the face.

Sean lay in the mud with his head on the hard pillow of the helmet. The darkness was as solid as the rock around him. He tried to imagine where the one ended and the other began – by doing that he could stop himself feeling his thirst so strongly. He could hear the ring of hammer on stone and the rattle of rock falling free but it never seemed to come any closer. The whole side of his body was stiff and sore but he could not turn over, his knees caught on the cocopan every time he tried and the air in his little cave was starting to taste stale – his head ached. He moved again, restlessly, and his hand brushed the small pile of sovereigns. He struck at them, scattering them into the mud. They were the bait that had led him into this trap. Now he would give them, and all the millions of others, for just the feel of the wind in his beard and the sun in his face. The darkness clung to him, thick and cloying as black treacle; it seemed to fill his nose, his throat and eyes, smothering him. He groped and found the matchbox. For a few seconds of light he would burn up most of the precious oxygen in his cave and call it fair exchange – but the box was sodden. He struck match after match but the wet heads crumbled without a spark and he threw them away and clenched his eyelids to keep the darkness out. Bright colours formed in front of his closed eyes, moving and rearranging themselves until suddenly and very clearly they formed a picture of Garrick's face. He hadn't thought about his family for months, he had been too busy reaping the golden harvest, but now memories crowded back. There were so many things he had forgotten. Everything else had become unimportant when compared with power and gold – even lives, men's lives, had meant nothing. But now it was his own life, teetering on the edge of the black cliff.

The sound of the sledge-hammers broke into his thoughts again. There were men on the other side of the blocked tunnel trying to save him, working their way into the treacherous rock pile which might collapse again at any minute. People were more valuable than the poisonous metal, the little gold discs that lay smugly beside him in the mud while men struggled to save him.

He thought of Garry, crippled by his careless shotgun, father to the bastard he had sired, of Ada whom he had left without a word of goodbye, of Karl Lochtkamper with the pistol in his hand and half his head splattered across the floor of his bedroom, of other nameless men dead or broken because of him.

Sean ran his tongue across his lips and listened to the hammers; he was certain they were nearer now.

'If I get out of here, it'll be different. I swear it.'

Mbejane rested for four hours in the next thirty-six. Duff watched the flesh melt off him in sweat. He was killing himself. Duff was worn out; he could no longer work with his hands but he was directing the teams who were shoring up the reclaimed tunnel. By the second evening they had cleared a hundred feet of the drive. Duff paced it out and when he reached the face he spoke to Mbejane.

'How long since you last signalled to him?'

Mbejane stepped back with a sledge-hammer in his tattered hands; its shaft was sticky and brown with blood.

'An hour ago and even then it sounded as though there were but the length of a spear between us.'

Duff took a crowbar from one of the other natives and tapped the rock. The answer came immediately.

'He's hitting something made of iron,' Duff said. 'It sounds as though he's only a few feet away. Mbejane, let these other men take over. If you wish you can stay and watch but you must rest again now.'

For answer Mbejane lifted the hammer and swung it against the face. The rock he hit cracked and two of the natives stepped up and levered it loose with their crowbars. At the back of the hole it left in the wall they could see the corner of the cocopan. Everyone stared at it, then Duff shouted.

'Sean, Sean, can you hear me?'

'Stop talking and get me out of here.' Sean's voice was hoarse with thirst and dust, and muffled by the rock.

'He's under the cocopan.'

'It's him.'

'Nkosi, are you all right?'

'We've found him.'

The shouts were picked up by the men working behind them in the drive and passed back to those waiting at the lift station.

'They've found him – he's all right – they've found him.'

Duff and Mbejane jumped forward together, their exhaustion completely forgotten. They cleared the last few lumps of rock and with their shoulders touching knelt and peered under the cocopan.

'Nkosi, I see you.'

'I see you also, Mbejane, what took you so long?'

'Nkosi, there were a few small stones in the way.'

Mbejane reached under the cocopan and with his hands under Sean's armpits pulled him out.

'What a hell of a place you chose to go to ground in, laddie. How are you feeling?'

'Give me some water and I'll be all right.'

'Water – bring water,' shouted Duff.

Sean gulped it, trying to drink the whole mug in one mouthful. He coughed and it shot out of his nose.

'Easy, laddie, easy.' Duff thumped his back. Sean drank the next mugful more slowly and finished panting from the effort.

'That was good.'

'Come on, we've got a doctor waiting up on top.' Duff draped a blanket over his shoulders. Mbejane picked Sean up across his chest.

'Put me down, damn you, I haven't forgotten how to walk.'

Mbejane set him down gently, but his legs buckled like those of a man just out of bed from a long illness and he clutched at Mbejane's arm. Mbejane picked him up again and carried him down to the lift station. They rode up in the skip into the open.

'The moon's shining. And the stars – my God, they're beautiful.' There was wonder in Sean's voice; he sucked the night air into his lungs but it was too rich for him and he started coughing again. There were people waiting at the head of the shaft and they crowded round them as they stepped out of the skip.

'How is he?'

'Are you all right, Sean?'

'Doc Symmonds is waiting in the office.'

'Quickly, Mbejane,' said Duff, 'get him out of the cold.'

One on either side of him they hurried Sean across to the administrative building and laid him on the couch in Francois's office. Symmonds checked him over, looked down his throat and felt his pulse.

'Have you got a closed carriage here?'

'Yes,' Duff answered.

'Well, wrap him up warmly and get him home to bed. With the dust and bad air he's been breathing there's serious danger of pneumonia. I'll come down with you and give him a sedative.'

'I won't need one, Doc,' Sean grinned at him.

'I think I know what's best for you, Mr Courtney.' Doctor Symmonds was a young man. He was the fashionable doctor among the rich of Johannesburg and he took it very seriously.

'Now if you please, we'll get you to your hotel.' He started to pack his instruments back into his valise.

'You're the doctor,' Sean agreed, 'but before we go will you have a look at my servant's hands, they're in a hell of a mess. There's hardly any meat left on them.'

Doctor Symmonds did not look up from what he was doing. 'I have no Kaffir practice, Mr Courtney, I'm sure you'll find some other doctor to attend to him when we get back to town.'

Sean sat up slowly, he let the blankets slip off his shoulders. He walked across to Doctor Symmonds and held him by the throat against the wall. The doctor had a fine pair of waxed moustaches and Sean took one of them between the thumb and forefinger of his free hand: he plucked it out like feathers from the carcass of a dead fowl and Doctor Symmonds squealed.

'Starting now, Doctor, you have a Kaffir practice,' Sean told him. He pulled the handkerchief out of Symmonds' top pocket and dabbed at the little drops of blood on the doctor's bare upper lip.

'Be a good fellow – see to my servant.'

= 21 =

When Sean woke the next morning the hands of the grandfather clock across the bedroom pointed at the top of their dial. Candy was in the room opening the curtains and with her were two waiters, each with a loaded tray.

'Good morning, how is our hero this morning?' The waiters put down their trays and went out as she came across to Sean's bed.

Sean blinked the sleep out of his eyes. 'My throat feels as though I've just finished a meal of broken glass.'

'That's the dust,' Candy told him and laid her hands on his forehead. Sean's hand sneaked round behind her and she squeaked as he pinched her. Standing well away from the bed she rubbed her bottom and made a face at him.

'There's nothing wrong with you!'

'Good, then I'll get up.' Sean started to pull back the bedclothes.

'Not until the doctor's had a look at you, you won't.'

'Candy, if that bastard puts one foot in this room I'll punch him so hard in the mouth his teeth will march out of his backside like soldiers.'

Candy turned to the breakfast trays to cover her smile. 'That's no way to talk in front of a lady. But don't worry, it isn't Symmonds.'

'Where's Duff?' Sean asked.

'He's having a bath, then he's coming to eat breakfast with you.'

'I'll wait for him, but give me a cup of coffee in the meantime, there's a sweetheart.'

She brought the coffee to him. 'Your savage has been camping on my trail all morning, he wants to see you. I've just about had to put an armed guard on this room to keep him out.'

Sean laughed. 'Will you send him in, Candy?'

She went to the door and stopped with a hand on the latch.

'It's nice to have you back, Sean, don't do anything silly like that again, will you?'

'That's a promise,' Sean assured her.

Mbejane came quickly and stood in the doorway. 'Nkosi, is it well with you?'

Sean looked at the iodine-stained bandages on his hands and the maroon and gold livery without answering. Then he rolled on his back and stared at the ceiling. 'I sent for my servant and instead there comes a monkey on a chain.'

Mbejane stood still, his face expressionless but for the hurt in his eyes.

'Go – find my servant. You will know him by his dress which is that of a warrior of Zululand.'

It took a few seconds for the laughter to start rolling around in Mbejane's belly; it shook his shoulders and creased the corners of his mouth. He closed the door very softly behind him and when he came back in his loin cloth Sean grinned at him.

'Ah! I see you, Mbejane.'

'And I see you also.'

He stood by the bed and they talked. They spoke little of the cave-in and not at all of Mbejane's part in the rescue. Between them it was understood, words could only damage it. Perhaps they would talk of it later, but not now.

'Tomorrow, will you need the carriage?' Mbejane asked at last.

'Yes – go now. Eat and sleep.' Sean reached out and touched Mbejane's arm. Just that small physical contact – that almost guilty touching – and Mbejane left him.

Then Duff came in in a silk dressing-gown and they ate eggs and steak from the trays and Duff sent down for a bottle of wine just to rinse the dust out of their throats once more.

'They tell me Francois is still down at the Bright Angels – he's been on the drunk ever since he got out of that shaft. When he sobers up he can come to the office and collect his pay packet.'

Sean sat up. 'You're going to fire him?'

'I'm going to fire him so high he'll only touch ground when he reaches Capetown.'

'What the hell for?' demanded Sean.

'What for?' Duff echoed. 'What for? For running – that's what for.'

'Duff, he was in a cave-in at Kimberley, wasn't he?'

'Yes.'

'Broke his legs, didn't you say?'

'Yes.'

'Shall I tell you something? If it were to happen to me a second time I'd run as well.'

Duff filled his wine glass without answering.

'Send down to the Bright Angels, tell him alcohol is bad for the liver – that should sober him – tell him unless he's back at work by tomorrow morning we'll dock it off his pay,' Sean said. Duff looked at him with a puzzled expression. 'What is this?'

'I had some time to think while I was down in that hole. I decided that to get to the top you don't have to stamp on everyone you meet.'

'Ah, I understand.' Duff gave his lopsided grin. 'A good resolution – New Year in August. Well, that's all right, you had me worried there, I thought a rock had fallen on your head. I also make good resolutions.'

'Duff, I don't want Francois fired.'

'All right, all right – he stays on. If you like we can open a soup kitchen at the office and turn Xanadu into a home for the aged.'

'Oh, go and burst. I just don't think it's necessary to fire Francois, that's all.'

'Who's arguing? I agreed with you, didn't I? I have deep respect for good resolutions. I make them all the time.'

Duff pulled his chair up to the bed, 'Quite by chance I happen to have a pack of cards with me.' He took them out of his dressing-gown pocket. 'Would you care for a game of Klabejas?'

Sean lost fifty pounds before he was saved by the arrival of the new doctor. The doctor tapped his chest and tut-tutted, looked down his throat and tut-tutted, wrote out a prescription and confined him to bed for the rest of the day. He was just leaving when Jock and Trevor Heyns arrived. Jock had a bunch of flowers which he presented to Sean in an embarrassed fashion.

Then the room began to fill in earnest: the rest of the crowd from the Exchange arrived, someone had brought a case of champagne, a poker game started in one corner and a political meeting in another.

'Who does this Kruger think he is, anyway – God or something? You know what he said last time we went to see him about getting the vote, he said "Protest, protest – I have the guns and you have not! " '

'Three Kings wins – you *are* holding cards!'

' – you wait and see. Consolidated Wits. will hit thirty shillings by the end of the month.'

' – and the taxes – they're putting another twenty per cent on dynamite.'

' – a new piece at the Opera, Jock's got a season ticket on her – no one else has had a look in yet.'

'All right, you two – stop that. If you want to fight go outside – this is a sick room.'

'This bottle's empty – break open a new one, Duff.'

Sean lost another hundred to Duff and then a little after five Candy came in. She was horrified. 'Out, all of you, out!'

The room emptied as quickly as it had filled and Candy wandered around picking up cigar butts and empty glasses.

'The vandals! Someone's burnt a hole in the carpet and look at this – champagne spilt all over the table.'

Duff coughed and started pouring himself another drink.

'Don't you think you've had enough of that, Dufford?'

Duff put down his glass. 'And it's time you went and changed for dinner.' Duff winked sheepishly at Sean, but he went.

Duff and Candy came back to his room after supper and had a liqueur with him.

'Now to sleep,' Candy commanded and went across to draw the curtains.

'It's still early,' protested Duff with no effect. Candy blew the lamp out.

Sean was not tired, he had lain in bed all day and now his brain was overactive. He lit a cigar and smoked, listening to the street noises below his window and it was past midnight before he finally drifted off. When he woke, he woke screaming, for the darkness was on him again and the blankets pressed down on him suffocating him. He fought them off and stumbled blindly across the room. He had to have air and light. He ran into the thick velvet curtains and they closed around his face; he tore himself free and hit the french windows with his shoulder; they burst open and he was out on the balcony, out in the cold air with the moon fat and yellow in the sky above him. His gasping slowed until he was breathing normally again. He went back inside and lit the lamp, then he went through to Duff's empty bedroom. There was a copy of *Twelfth Night* on the bedside table and he took it back to his own room. He sat with the lamp at his elbow and forced his eyes to follow the printed words even though they made no sense. He read until the dawn showed grey through the open windows, then he put down the book. He shaved, dressed and went down the back stairs into the hotel yard. He found Mbejane in the stables.

'Put a saddle on the grey.'

'Where are you going, Nkosi?'

'To kill a devil.'

'Then I will come with you.'

'No, I will be back before midday.'

He rode up to the Candy Deep and tied his horse outside the administration buildings. There was a sleepy clerk in the front offices.

'Good morning, Mr Courtney. Can I help you?'

'Yes. Get me overalls and a helmet.'

Sean went to the Number Three shaft. There was a frost on the ground that crunched as he walked on it and the sun had just cleared the eastern ridge of the Witwatersrand. Sean stopped at the hoist shed and spoke to the driver.

'Has the new shift gone on yet?'

'Half an hour ago, sir.' The man was obviously surprised to see him. 'The night shift finished blasting at five o'clock.'

'Good – drop me down to the fourteenth level.'

'The fourteenth is abandoned now, Mr Courtney, there's no one working there.'

'Yes, I know.'

Sean walked across to the head of the shaft. He lit his carbide lamp and while he waited for the skip he looked out across the valley. The air was clear and the sun threw long shadows. Everything stood out in sharp relief. He had not been up this early in the morning for many months and he had almost forgotten how fresh and delicately coloured a new day was. The skip stopped in front of him. He took a deep breath and stepped into it. When he reached the fourteenth level he got out and pushed the recall signal for the skip and he was alone in the earth again. He walked up the tunnel and the echo of his footsteps went with him. He was sweating and a muscle in his cheek started to jerk;

he reached the face and set the carbide lamp down on a ledge of rock. He checked to make sure his matches were in his pocket, then he blew out the lamp. The darkness came squeezing down on him. The first half hour was the worst. Twice he had the matches in his hand ready to strike but he stopped himself. The sweat formed cold wet patches under his arms and the darkness filled his open mouth and choked him. He had to fight for each lungful of air, suck in, hold it, breathe out. First he regulated his breathing and then slowly, slowly his mind came under control and he knew he had won. He waited another ten minutes breathing easily and sitting relaxed with his back against the side of the tunnel, then he lit the lamp. He was smiling as he went back to the lift station and signalled for the skip. When he reached the surface he stepped out and lit a cigar; he flicked the match into the square black opening of the shaft.

'So much for you, little hole.'

He walked back towards the administration building. What he could not know was that the Number Three shaft of the Candy Deep was to take something from him just as valuable as his courage and that, next time, what it took it would not give back. But that was many years ahead.

= 22 =

By October Xanadu was nearly finished. The three of them drove out to it as usual one Saturday afternoon.

'The builder is only six months behind schedule – now he says he'll be finished by Christmas and I haven't found the courage yet to ask him which Christmas,' Sean remarked.

'It's all the alterations Candy has thought up,' Duff said. 'She's got the poor man so confused he doesn't know whether he's a boy or a girl.'

'Well, if you'd consulted me in the first place it would have saved a lot of trouble,' Candy told them.

The carriage turned in through the marble gates and they looked around them. Already the lawns were smooth and green and the jacaranda trees lining the drive were shoulder high.

'I think it's going to live up to its name – that gardener's doing a good job,' Sean spoke with satisfaction.

'Don't you call him a gardener to his face or we'll have a strike on our hands. He's a horticulturist,' Duff smiled across at him.

'Talking about names,' Candy interrupted, 'don't you think Xanadu is – well, a bit outlandish?'

'No, I do not,' Sean said. 'I picked it myself. I think it's a damn good name.'

'It's not dignified – why don't we call it Fair Oaks?'

'Firstly, because there isn't an oak tree within fifty miles and secondly because it's already called Xanadu.'

'Don't get cross, it was just a suggestion.'

The builder met them at the top of the drive and they began the tour of the house.

That took an hour, then they left the builder and went out into the garden. They found the gardener with a gang of natives near the north boundary.

'How's it going, Joubert?' Duff greeted him.

'Not bad, Mr Charleywood, but it takes time you know.'

'You've done a damn fine job so far.'

'It's kind of you to say so, sir.'

'When are you going to start laying out my maze?'

The gardener looked surprised; he glanced at Candy, opened his mouth, closed it again and looked once more at Candy.

'Oh, I told Joubert not to worry about the maze.'

'Why did you do that? I wanted a maze – ever since I visited Hampton Court as a child I've wanted my own maze.'

'They're silly things,' Candy told him. 'They just take up a lot of space and they're not even nice to look at.'

Sean thought Duff was going to argue, but he didn't. They talked to the gardener a little longer, then they walked back across the lawns in front of the house towards the chapel.

'Dufford, I've left my parasol in the carriage, would you mind getting it for me?' Candy asked.

When Duff was gone Candy took Sean's arm.

'It's going to be a lovely home. We're going to be very happy here.'

'Have you two decided on a date yet?' Sean asked.

'We want the house finished first so we can move straight in. I think we'll make it some time in February next year.'

They reached the chapel and stopped in front of it.

'It's a sweet little church.' Candy spoke dreamily. 'And such a nice idea of Dufford's – a special church of our own.'

Sean shuffled uncomfortably. 'Yes,' he agreed, 'it's a very romantic idea.' He glanced over his shoulder and saw Duff coming back with the parasol.

'Candy – it's none of my business. I don't know anything about marriage, but I know about training horses – you break them to the halter before you put the saddle on their backs.'

'I don't follow you.' Candy looked puzzled. 'What are you trying to say?'

'Nothing – just forget it. Here comes Duff.'

When they got back to the hotel there was a note at the reception desk for Sean. They went through into the main lounge and Candy went off to check the menu for dinner. Sean opened the envelope and read the note:

> 'I should like to meet you and Mr Charleywood to discuss a matter of some importance. I will be at my hotel after dinner this evening and hope that it will be convenient for you to call on me then. N. Hradsky.'

Sean passed the note across to Duff.

'What do you suppose he wants?'

'He has heard of your deadly skill as a Klabejas player. He wants to take lessons,' Duff answered.

'Shall we go?'

'Of course. You know I can't resist Norman's exhilarating company.'

It was a superb dinner. The crayfish, packed in ice, had come up from Capetown by express coach.

'Candy – Sean and I are going across to see Hradsky. We might be back a little late,' Duff told her when they were finished.

'As long as it's Hradsky,' Candy smiled at him. 'Don't get lost – I have my spies at the Opera House you know.'

'Shall we take the carriage?' Duff asked Sean, and Sean noticed that he hadn't laughed at Candy's joke.

'It's only two blocks, we might as well walk.'

They walked in silence. Sean felt his dinner settling down comfortably inside him, he belched softly and took another puff from his cigar. When they had almost reached the Grand National Hotel Duff spoke.

'Sean. . .' He stopped.

'Yes?' Sean prompted him.

'About Candy. . .' He stopped again.

'She's a fine girl,' Sean prompted again.

'Yes, she's a fine girl.'

'Is that all you wanted to say?'

'Well – oh! never mind. Let's go and see what Saul and David want.'

Max met them at the door of Hradsky's suite.

'Good evening, gentlemen, I am so pleased you could come.'

'Hello, Max.' Duff went past him to where Hradsky was standing in front of the fireplace.

'Norman, my dear fellow, how are you?'

Hradsky nodded an acknowledgement and Duff took hold of the lapels of Hradsky's coat and adjusted them carefully; then he picked an imaginary piece of fluff off his shoulder.

'You have a way with clothes, Norman. Don't you agree that Norman has a way with clothes, Sean? I know of no one else who can put on a twenty-guinea suit and make it look like a half-filled bag of oranges.' He patted Hradsky's arm affectionately. 'Yes, thank you – I will have a drink.' He went across to the liquor cabinet and poured one for himself. 'Now, what can you gentlemen do for me?'

Max glanced at Hradsky and Hradsky nodded.

'I will come to the point immediately,' said Max. 'Our two groups of companies are the largest on the Witwatersrand.'

Duff put his glass back on top of the cabinet and dropped his grin. Sean sat down in one of the armchairs, his expression also serious; both of them could guess what was coming.

'In the past,' continued Max, 'we have worked together on numerous occasions and we have both benefited from it. The next logical step, of course, is to combine our strength, pool our resources and go on together to new greatness.'

'I take it that you are proposing a merger?'

'Precisely, Mr Courtney, a merger of these two vast financial ventures.'

Sean leaned back in his chair and started to whistle softly. Duff picked up his glass again and took a sip.

'Well, gentlemen, what are your feelings on the subject?' asked Max.

'Have you got a proposal worked out, Max, something definite for us to think about?'

'Yes, Mr Courtney, I have.' Max went to the stinkwood desk which filled one corner of the room and picked up a sheaf of papers. He carried it across to Sean. Sean scanned through it.

'You've done quite a bit of work here, Max. It's going to take us a day or two to work out exactly what you are offering.'

'I appreciate that, Mr Courtney. Take as long as you wish. We have worked for a month to draw up that scheme and I hope our labours have not been in vain. I think you will find our offer very generous.'

Sean stood up.

'We'll contact you again in the next few days, Max. Shall we go, Duff?'

Duff finished his drink.

'Goodnight, Max, look after Norman. He's very precious to us, you know.'

They went to their building on Eloff Street. Sean let them in through one of the side doors, lit the lamps in his office and Duff pulled up an extra chair to the desk. By two o'clock the following morning they understood the essentials of Hradsky's offer. Sean stood up and went to open one of the windows, for the room was thick with cigar smoke. He came back and flopped onto the couch, arranged a cushion behind his head and looked at Duff.

'Let's hear what you've got to say.'

Duff tapped his teeth with a pencil while he arranged his words.

'Let's decide first if we want to join with him.'

'If he makes it worth our while, we do,' Sean answered.

'I agree with you – but only if he makes it worth our while.' Duff laid back in his chair. 'Now the next point. Tell me, laddie, what is the first thing that strikes you about this scheme of Norman's?'

'We get nice-sounding titles and fat cash payments and Hradsky gets control,' Sean answered.

'You have laid your finger on the heart of it – Norman wants control. More than money, Norman wants control, so that he can sit at the top of the pile, look down on everyone else and say, "All right, you bastards, what if I do stutter?" '

Duff stood up, he walked round the desk and stopped in front of Sean's couch.

'Now for my next question. Do we give him control?'

'If he pays our price, then we give him control,' Sean answered. Duff turned away and went across to the open window.

'You know I rather like the feeling of being top man myself,' he said thoughtfully.

'Listen, Duff, we came here to make money. If we go in with Hradsky we'll make more,' Sean said.

'Laddie, we've got so much now that we could fill this room waist deep in sovereigns. We've got more than we'll ever be able to spend and I like being top man.'

'Hradsky's more powerful than we are – let's face up to that. He's got his diamond interests as well, so you're not top man even now. If we join him you still won't be top man but you'll be a damn sight richer.'

'Unassailable logic,' Duff nodded. 'I agree with you then. Hradsky gets control but he pays for it; we'll put him through the wringer until he's dry.'

Sean swung his legs off the couch. 'Agreed – now let's take this scheme of his by the throat, tear it to pieces and build it up again to suit ourselves.'

Duff looked at his watch. 'It's after two o'clock. We'll leave it now and start on it when we're fresh in the morning.'

They had their lunch brought down to the office the next day, and ate it at the desk. Johnson, who had been sent up to the Stock Exchange with instructions to keep an eye on prices and call them immediately anything out of the ordinary happened, reported back after high change.

'It's been as quiet as a graveyard all day, sir, there's all sorts of rumours flying about. Seems someone saw the lights burning in this office at two o'clock this morning. Then when you didn't come to the Exchange but sent me instead – well, I can tell you, sir, there were a lot of questions asked.' Johnson hesitated, then his curiosity got the better of him.

'Can I help you at all, sir?' He started sidling across towards the desk.

'I think we can manage on our own, Johnson. Shut the door as you go out, please.'

At half-past seven they decided it was enough for one day and they went back to the hotel. As they walked into the lobby Sean saw Trevor Heyns disappear into the lounge and heard his voice.

'Here they are!'

Almost immediately Trevor appeared again with his brother.

'Hello, boys,' Jock appeared surprised to see them. 'What are you doing here?'

'We live here,' said Duff.

'Oh, yes, of course. Well, come and have a drink with us.' Jock smiled expansively.

'And then you can pump us and find out what we've been doing all day,' Duff suggested.

Jock looked embarrassed. 'I don't know what you mean, I just thought we'd have a drink together, that's all.'

'Thanks all the same, Jock, we've had a hard day. I think we'll just go on up to bed,' Duff said. They were halfway across the lobby before Duff turned back to where the two brothers were standing.

'I'll tell you boys something,' he said in a stage whisper. 'This is really big – it's so big it takes a while for the mind to grasp it. When you two realize that it's been right there under your noses all the time, you're going to kick yourselves.'

They left the Heyns brothers in the lobby staring after them and went up the stairs.

'That wasn't very kind,' Sean laughed. 'They won't sleep for a week.'

= 23 =

When neither Sean nor Duff put in an appearance at the Exchange the next morning, the rumours surged round the members' lounge and the prices started running amok. Reliable information that Sean and Duff had struck a rich new goldfield across the vaal sent the prices up like rocketing snipe; then twenty minutes later the denial came in and clipped fifteen shillings a share off the Courtney–Charleywood stock. Johnson ran backwards and forwards between the office and the Exchange all morning. By eleven he was so tired he could hardly talk.

'Don't worry any more, Johnson,' Sean told him. 'Here's a sovereign – go down to the Grand National and buy yourself a drink, you've had a hard morning.'

One of Jock Heyns's men, who had been detailed off to watch the Courtney–Charleywood offices, followed Johnson down to the Grand National and heard him place his order with the barman. He raced back to the Exchange and reported to Jock.

'Their head clerk has just gone and ordered himself a bottle of French champagne,' he panted.

'Good God!' Jock nearly jumped out of his chair and beside him Trevor signalled frantically for his clerk.

'Buy,' he whispered in the man's ear. 'Buy every scrap of their script you can lay your hands on.'

Across the lounge Hradsky settled down a little further in his chair; he clasped his hands contentedly over the front of his stomach and he very nearly smiled.

By midnight Sean and Duff had completed their counter-proposal to Hradsky's offer.

'How do you think Norman will react to it?' asked Sean.

'I hope his heart is strong enough to stand the shock,' Duff grinned. 'The only reason that his jaw won't hit the floor is that his great gut will be in the way.'

'Shall we go down to his hotel now and show him?' suggested Sean.

'Laddie, laddie.' Duff shook his head sorrowfully. 'After all the time I've spent on your education, and you still haven't learned.'

'What do we do then?'

'We send for him, laddie, we make him come to us. We play him on the home ground.'

'How does that help?' Sean asked.

'It gives us an advantage immediately – it makes him remember that he's the one doing the asking.'

Hradsky came down to their office at ten o'clock the next morning; he came in state driven behind a four-in-hand and attended by Max and two secretaries. Johnson met them at the front door and ushered them into Sean's office.

'Norman, dear old Norman, I'm delighted to see you,' Duff greeted him and, fully aware of the fact that Hradsky never smoked, Duff thrust a cheroot between his lips. When everyone was seated Sean opened the meeting.

'Gentlemen, we have spent some time examining your proposition and in the main we find it just, fair and equitable.'

'Hear, hear,' Duff agreed politely.

'At the outset I want to make it quite clear,' Sean went on, 'that Mr Charleywood and myself feel strongly that the union of our two ventures is desirable – nay! essential. If you will forgive the quotation, *"ex unitate vires"*.'

'Hear, hear – hear, hear.' Duff lit his cigar.

'As I was saying, we have examined your proposition and we accept it readily and happily, with the exception of a few minor details which we have listed.' Sean picked up the thick pile of paper. 'Perhaps you would care to glance through it and then we can proceed to the drawing-up of a formal agreement.'

Max accepted the sheaf gingerly. 'If you want privacy, Mr Charleywood's office which adjoins this room is at your disposal.'

Hradsky took his band next door and an hour later when he led them back again they looked like a party of pallbearers. Max was on the verge of tears, he cleared the lump from his throat.

'I think we should examine each item separately,' he said sadly, and three days later they shook hands on the deal.

Duff poured the drinks and gave each man a glass. 'To the new company, Central Rand Consolidated. It has been a long confinement, gentlemen, but I think we have given birth to a child of which we can be proud.'

Hradsky had control, but it had cost him dearly.

Central Rand Consolidated had its christening party on the main floor of the Johannesburg Stock Exchange; ten per cent of the shares were put out for sale to the public. Before the day's dealings began the crowd had overflowed the Stock Exchange building and jammed in the street for a block in each direction. The President of the Exchange read the prospectus of Central Rand Consolidated; in the cathedral hush his every word carried clearly to the members' lounge. The bell rang and still the hush persisted. Hradsky's authorized clerk broke the silence timidly. 'I sell C.R.C.'s.'

It was nearly a massacre; two hundred men were trying to buy shares from him simultaneously. First his jacket and then his shirt disintegrated beneath the clutching hands; he lost his spectacles, crushed to powdered glass beneath the trampling feet. Ten minutes later he managed to fight his way out of the crowd and report to his masters, 'I was able to sell them, gentlemen.'

Sean and Duff laughed. They had reason to laugh, for in those ten minutes their thirty per cent holding in C.R.C. had appreciated in value by half a million pounds.

= 24 =

That year Christmas dinner at Candy's Hotel was considerably better than it had been five years previously. Seventy-five people sat down to it at one table and by three o'clock, when it ended, only half of them were able to stand up. Sean used the banisters to get up the stairs and at the top he told Candy and Duff solemnly, 'I love you – I love you both desperately – but now I must sleep.' He left them and set off down the corridor bouncing against the walls like a trick billiard shot until he ricocheted through the door into his suite.

'You'd better make sure he's all right, Dufford.'

'A case of the blind drunk leading the blind drunk,' said Duff indistinctly, and also employing the wall to wall route followed Sean down the corridor. Sean was sitting on the edge of his bed wrestling with one of his boots.

'What you trying to do, laddie, break your ankle?'

Sean looked up and smiled beatifically. 'Come in, come in – all four of you. Have a drink.'

'Thanks, I brought my own.'

Duff closed the door behind him like a conspirator and produced a bottle from under his coat, 'She didn't see me – she didn't know her little Dufford had a big beautiful bottle in his inside pocket.'

'Would you mind helping me with this damn boot?' Sean asked.

'That's a very good question,' said Duff seriously as he set a course across the room for one of the armchairs. 'I'm glad you asked it.' He reached the chair and dropped into it. 'The answer, of course, is, Yes! I would mind.'

Sean let his foot drop and lay back on the bed.

'Laddie, I want to talk to you,' Duff said.

'Talk's free – help yourself.'

'Sean, what do you think of Candy?'

'Lovely pair of titties,' Sean opined.

'Sure, but a man cannot live by titties alone.'

'No, but I suppose she's also got the other basic equipment,' Sean said drowsily.

'Laddie, I'm being serious now – I want your help. Do you think I am doing the right thing – this marriage business, I mean.'

'Don't know much about marriage.' Sean rolled over on his face.

'She's calling me Dufford already – did you notice that, laddie? That's an omen, that's an omen of the most frightful portent. Did you notice, hey?' Duff waited a second for an answer which he didn't receive. 'That's what the other one used to call me. "Dufford," she'd say – I can hear it now – "Dufford, you're a pig".'

Duff looked hard at the bed. 'Are you still with me?'

No answer.

'Sean, laddie, I need your help.'

Sean snored softly.

'Oh, you drunken oaf,' said Duff miserably.

= 25 =

Xanadu was finished by the end of January and the wedding was set for the twentieth of February. Duff sent the Commandant and the entire police force of Johannesburg an invitation: in return they put a twenty-four hour a day guard on the ballroom of Xanadu where the wedding gifts were laid out on long trestle tables. Sean drove up with Duff and Candy on the afternoon of the tenth, as Duff put it, to make the latest count of the booty. Sean gave the constable on duty a cigar and then they went through into the ballroom.

'Look, oh look,' squealed Candy. 'There's a whole lot of new presents!'

'This one's from Jock and Trevor,' Sean read the card.

'Open quickly, please, Dufford, let's see what they've given us.'

Duff prised the lid off the case and Sean whistled softly,

'A solid gold dinner service,' gasped Candy. She picked up one of the plates and hugged it to her chest, 'Oh, I just don't know what to say.'

Sean examined the other boxes. 'Hey, Duff, this one will make you specially happy – "Best wishes, N. Hradsky".'

'This I must see,' said Duff with the first enthusiasm he had shown in a month. He unwrapped the parcel.

'A dozen of them!' Duff hooted gleefully. 'Norman, you priceless little Israelite, a whole dozen dish towels.'

'It's the thought that counts,' laughed Sean.

'Dear old Norman, how it must have hurt him to shell out for them! I'll have him autograph them and I'll frame them and hang them in the front hall.'

They left Candy to arrange the presents and they went out into the garden.

'Have you got this mock priest organized?' asked Duff.

'Yes, he's at a hotel in Pretoria. He's in training now – he'll be able to rattle through the service like an old hand when the time comes.'

'You don't think that faking it is just as bad as doing it properly?' asked Duff dubiously.

'It's a hell of a time to think of that now,' said Sean.

'Yes, I suppose it is.'

'Where are you going for the honeymoon?' Sean asked.

'We'll coach down to Capetown and take the mail boat to London, then a month or so on the Continent. Be back here about June.'

'You should have a good time.'

'Why don't you get married as well?'

'What for?' Sean looked surprised.

'Well, don't you feel as though you're letting the old firm down a bit – me going into this alone?'

'No,' said Sean. 'Anyway, who is there to marry?'

'What about that lass you brought to the races last Saturday; she's a lovely piece of work.'

Sean raised an eyebrow. 'Did you hear her giggle?'

'Yes, I did,' admitted Duff. 'You couldn't very well miss it.'

'Can you imagine that giggle coming at you across the breakfast table?' Sean asked.

Duff shuddered. 'Yes, I see your point. But as soon as we get back I'll have Candy start picking you out a suitable female.'

'I've got a better idea, you let Candy run your life and I'll run my own.'

'That, laddie, is what I'm very much afraid is going to happen.'

Hradsky reluctantly agreed that the activities of the group – the mines, the workshops, the transport companies, all of them – should be suspended on the twentieth to allow their employees to attend Duff's nuptials. This meant that half the businesses on the Witwatersrand would shut down for the day. Consequently, most of the independent companies decided to close as well. On the eighteenth the wagons carrying the food and liquor started caravanning up the hill to Xanadu. Sean in a burst of benevolence that night invited the entire company from the Opera House to the wedding. He remembered it vaguely the next morning and went down to cancel the invitation but Blue Bessie told him that most of the girls had already gone into town to buy new dresses.

'The hell with it then – let them come. I just hope Candy doesn't guess who they are, that's all.'

On the night of the nineteenth Candy gave them the use of the dining-room and all the downstairs lounges of the Hotel for Duff's bachelor party. Francois arrived with a masterpiece made up in the mine workshops – an enormous ball and chain. This was formally locked onto Duff's leg and the party began.

Afterwards there was a school of thought that maintained that the building contractor commissioned to repair the damage to the Hotel was a bandit and that the bill for just under a thousand pounds that he presented was nothing short of robbery. However, none of them could deny that the Bok-Bok game in the dining-room, played by a hundred men, had done a certain amount of damage to the furniture and fittings; nor that the chandelier had not been able to support Mr Courtney's weight and on the third swing had come adrift from the ceiling and knocked a moderately large hole through the floor. Neither did anyone dispute the fact that after Jock Heyns had tried unsuccessfully for half an hour to shoot a glass off the top of his brother's head with champagne corks, the resulting ankle-deep lake of wine in the one lounge made it necessary for the floor to be relaid. Nevertheless they felt that a thousand was a little bit steep. On one point, however, everyone agreed – it was a memorable party.

At the beginning Sean was worried that Duff's heart wasn't in it for Duff stood by the bar with the metal ball under one arm listening to the lewd comment, with a lopsided grin fixed on his face. After seven or eight drinks Sean stopped worrying about him and went off to have his way with the chandelier. At midnight Duff talked Francois into releasing him from his chains and he slipped out of the room. No one – least of all Sean – noticed him go.

Sean could never remember how he got up to bed that night but next morning he was tactfully awakened by a waiter with a coffee tray and a note.

'What time is it?' asked Sean as he unfolded the note.

'Eight o'clock, baas.'

'No need to shout,' muttered Sean. His eyes focused with difficulty for the pain in his head was pushing them out of their sockets.

'Dear Best Man,

This serves as a reminder that you and Duff have an appointment at eleven o'clock. I am relying on you to get him there, whole or in pieces. Love Candy.'

The brandy fumes in the back of his throat tasted like chloroform, he washed them out with coffee and lit a cigar which started him coughing, and every cough nearly took the top off his head. He stubbed out the cigar and went to the bathroom. Half an hour later he felt strong enough to wake Duff. He went across the sitting-room and pushed open Duff's door; the curtains in the room were still drawn. He pulled them open and was nearly blinded by the sunlight that poured in through them. He turned to the bed and frowned with surprise. He walked slowly across and sat on the edge of it.

'He must have slept in Candy's room,' Sean muttered as he looked at the unused pillows and neatly tucked blankets. It took a few seconds for him to find the fault in his reasoning.

'Then why did she write that note?' He stood up, feeling the first twinge of alarm. A picture of Duff, drunk and helpless lying out in the yard or knocked over the head by one of the busy Johannesburg footpads came very clearly to mind. He ran across the bedroom and into the sitting-room. Halfway to the door he saw the envelope propped up on the mantelpiece and he took it down.

'What is this, a meeting of the authors' guild?' he muttered. 'The place is thick with letters.'

'The paper crackled as he opened it and he recognized Duff's back sloping hand.

'The first the worst, the second the same. I'm not going through with it. You're the best man so make my excuses to all the nice people. I'll be back when the dust has settled a little. D.'

Sean sat down in one of the armchairs, he read through it twice more. Then he exploded.

'Damn you, Charleywood – "make my excuses". You craven bastard. Walk out and leave me to sweep up the mess.'

He rushed across the room with his dressing-gown flapping furiously round his legs. 'You'll make your own damned excuses – even if I have to drag you back on the end of a rope.'

Sean ran down the back stairs. Mbejane was in the stable yard talking to three of the grooms.

'Where is Nkosi Duff?' Sean roared.

They stared at him blankly.

'Where is he?' Sean's beard bristled.

'The baas took a horse and went for a ride,' answered one of the grooms nervously.

'When?' bellowed Sean.

'In the night – perhaps seven, eight hours ago. He should be back soon.'

Sean stared at the groom, breathing heavily. 'Which way did he go?'

'Baas, he did not say.'

Eight hours ago – he could be fifty miles away by now. Sean turned and went back to his room. He threw himself on the bed and poured another cup of coffee.

'This is going to break her up badly –' He imagined the tears and the chaos of undisciplined grief.

'Oh, hell – damn you to hell, Charleywood.' He sipped the coffee and thought about going as well – taking a horse and getting as far away as possible. 'It's no mess of my making – I want no part of it.' He finished the coffee and started dressing. He looked in the mirror to comb his hair and saw Candy standing alone in the chapel, waiting while the silence turned to murmuring and then to laughter.

'Charleywood, you pig,' Sean scowled. 'I can't let her go up there – it'll be bad enough without that. I'll have to tell her.'

He picked up his watch from the dressing-table, it was past nine.

'Damn you, Charleywood.'

He went down the passage and stopped outside Candy's door. He could hear women's voices inside and he knocked before he went in. There were two of Candy's friends and the coloured girl Martha. They stared at him.

'Where's Candy?'

'In the bedroom – but you mustn't go in. It's bad luck.'

'It's the worst bloody luck in the world,' agreed Sean. He knocked on the bedroom door.

'Who is it?'

'Sean.'

'You can't come in – what do you want?'

'Are you decent?'

'Yes, but you mustn't come in.'

He opened the door and looked in on a confusion of squealing females.

'Get out of here' – he said harshly – 'I have to speak to Candy alone.'

They fled and Sean closed the door behind them. Candy was in a dressing-gown. Her face was quick with anticipation; her hair was pulled back and hung shiny and soft. She was beautiful, Sean realized. He looked at the frothy pile of her wedding-dress on the bed.

'Candy, bad news – I'm afraid. Can you take it?' He spoke almost roughly – hating it, hating every second of it.

He saw the bloom on her face wither until her expression was dead – blank and dead as a statue.

'He's gone,' said Sean. 'He's run out on you.'

Candy picked up a brush from her dressing-table and started stroking it listlessly through her hair. It was very quiet in the room.

'I'm sorry, Candy.'

She nodded without looking at him; instead she was looking down the lonely corridor of the future. It was worse than tears would have been, that silent acceptance. Sean scratched the side of his nose – hating it.

'I'm sorry – I wish I could do something about it.' He turned to the door.

'Sean, thank you for coming and telling me.' There was no emotion in her voice; like her face it was dead.

'That's all right,' Sean said gruffly.

He rode up to Xanadu. There were people clustered about the marquees on the lawn; by the quality of their laughter he could tell they were drinking already. The sun was bright and as yet not too hot, the band was playing from the wide veranda of the mansion, the women's dresses were gay against the green of the lawns. 'Gala day' fluttered the flags above the tents. 'Gala day' shouted the laughter.

Sean rode up the drive, lifting his hand in brief acknowledgement of the greetings that were shouted to him. From the vantage point of his horse's back he spotted Francois and Martin Curtis, glasses in hand, standing near the house talking to two of the Opera girls. He gave his horse to one of the native grooms and strode across towards them.

'Hello, boss,' called Curtis. 'Why so glum – you're not the one getting married.' They all laughed.

'Francois, Martin, come with me please.'

'What's the trouble, Mr Courtney?' Francois asked as he led them aside.

'The party's over,' Sean said grimly. 'There'll be no wedding.'

They gaped at him.

'Go around and tell everybody. Tell them they'll get their presents back.'

He turned to leave them.

'What's happened, boss?' Curtis asked.

'Just tell them that Candy and Duff changed their minds.'

'Do you want us to send them home?'

Sean hesitated. 'Oh, the hell with it – let them stay – let them all get sick drunk. Just tell them there'll be no wedding.'

He went up to the house. He found the pseudo-priest waiting nervously in the downstairs study. The man's adam's apple had been rubbed raw by the starch-stiff dog collar.

'We won't need you,' Sean told him.

He took out his cheque book, sat down at the desk and filled in a cheque form.

'That's for your trouble. Now get out of town.'

'Thank you, Mr Courtney, thank you very much.' The man looked mightily relieved; he started for the door.

'My friend,' Sean stopped him. 'If you ever breathe a word about what we planned to do today, I'll kill you. Do I make myself clear?'

Sean went through to the ballroom, he slipped a small stack of sovereigns into the constable's hand.

'Get all these people out of here.' He gestured with his head at the crowds that were wandering among the tables looking at the gifts. 'Then lock the doors.'

He found the chef in the kitchen. 'Take all this food outside – give it to them now. Then lock up the kitchens.'

He went round the house closing the doors and drawing the curtains. When he walked into the study there was a couple on the big leather couch and the man's hand was under the girl's skirts; she was giggling.

'This isn't a whore house,' Sean shouted at them and they left hurriedly. He sank into one of the chairs. He could hear the voices and the laughter from outside on the lawn, the band was playing a Strauss waltz. It irritated him and he scowled at the marble fireplace. His head was aching again and the skin of his face felt dry and tight from the night's debauch.

'What a mess – what a bloody mess,' he said aloud. After an hour he went out and found his horse. He rode out along the Pretoria Road until he had passed the last houses, then he turned off into the veld. He cantered into the sea of grass with his hat pushed back on his head so the sun and the wind could find his face. He sat relaxed and loose in the saddle and let his horse pick its own way. In the late afternoon he came back to Johannesburg and left his horse with Mbejane in the stableyard. He felt better; the exercise and the fresh air had cleared his head and helped him to see things in truer perspective. He ran himself a deep hot bath, climbed into it and while he soaked the last of his anger at Duff smoothed out. He had control of himself again. He got out of the bath and towelled, then he slipped on his gown and went through to the bedroom. Candy was sitting on his bed.

'Hello, Sean.' She smiled at him, a brittle smile. Her hair was a little tangled now, her face was pale and unrouged. She had not changed from the dressing-gown he had seen her in that morning.

'Hello, Candy.' He picked up the cut-glass bottle of bay rum and rubbed some into his hair and beard.

'You don't mind me coming to see you, do you?'

'No, of course not.' He started combing his hair. 'I was about to come and see you myself.'

She drew her legs up under her in the double-jointed manner of women that is impossible for a man to copy.

'Can I have a drink, please?'

'I'm sorry – I thought you never touched the stuff.'

'Oh, today is special.' She laughed too gaily. 'It's my wedding day, you know.'

He poured the brandy without looking at her. He hated this suffering and he felt his anger at Duff coming back strongly. Candy took the drink and sipped it. She pulled a face. 'It tastes awful.'

'It'll do you good.'

'To the bride,' she said and drank it down quickly.

'Another one?' asked Sean.

'No thanks.' She stood up and went across to the window. 'It's getting dark now – I hate the darkness. Darkness distorts things so; what is bad in the daylight is unbearable at night.'

'I'm sorry, Candy, I wish I could help you.'

She whirled and came to him, her arms circled tight round his neck and her face pale and frightened pressed to his chest.

'Oh, Sean, please hold me – I'm so afraid.'

He held her awkwardly.

'I don't want to think about it. Not now, not now in the darkness,' she whispered. 'Please help me. Please help me not to think about it.'

'I'll stay with you. Don't get yourself upset. Come and sit down. I'll get you another drink.'

'No, no,' she clung to him desperately. 'I don't want to be alone. I don't want to think. Please help me.'

'I can't help you – I'll stay with you but that's all I can do.' Anger and pity mixed together in Sean like charcoal and saltpetre; his fingers tightened hard on her shoulders, digging into the flesh until they met bone.

'Yes, hurt me. That way I'll forget for a while. Take me to the bed and hurt me, Sean, hurt me deep.'

Sean caught his breath. 'You don't know what you're saying, that's crazy talk.'

'It's what I want – to forget for a little. Please, Sean, please.'

'I can't do that, Candy, Duff's my friend.'

'He's finished with me and I with him. I'm your friend too. Oh, God, I'm so alone. Don't you leave me too. Help me, Sean, please help me.'

Sean felt his anger slide down from his chest and flare up, cobra-headed, from his thighs. She felt it also.

'Yes, oh please, yes.'

He picked her up and carried her to the bed. He stood over her while he tore off his gown. She moved on the bed shedding her clothing and spreading herself to meet him, to take him in and let him fill the emptiness. He covered her quickly bayoneting through the soft veil and into the warmth of her body. There was no desire in it, it was cruel and hard drawn out to the frontiers of endurance. For him an expression of anger and pity; for her an act of renunciation. Once was not enough. Again and yet again he took her, until there were brown smudges on the bedclothes from his bleeding back, until her body ached and they lay entwined, wet and tired from the fury of it. In the quiescence of after-passion Sean spoke softly. 'It didn't help, did it?'

'Yes, it did.' Physical exhaustion had weakened the barriers that held back her grief. Still holding onto him, she started to cry.

A street lamp outside the room threw a silver square of light on the ceiling. Sean laid on his back and watched it, listening to Candy's sobs. He recognized the moment they reached their climax and followed their decline into silence. They slept then and later before the day woke together as if by arrangement.

'You are the only one who can help him now,' Candy said.

'Help him do what?' asked Sean.

'Find what he is looking for. Peace, himself – whatever you want to call it. He's lost, you know, Sean. He's lost and lonely, almost as lonely as I am. I could have helped him, I'm sure I could.'

'Duff lost?' Sean asked cynically. 'You must be mad!'

'Don't be so blind, Sean, don't be misled by the big talk and the grand manner. Look at the other things.'

'Like what?' asked Sean.

She didn't answer for a while. 'He hated his father, you know.'

'I guessed as much from the little he told me.'

'The way he revolts at any discipline. His attitude to Hradsky, to women, to life. Think about it, Sean, and then tell me if he acts like a happy man.'

'Hradsky did him a disservice once – he just doesn't like him,' Sean defended Duff.

'Oh, no – it's much deeper than that. In a way Hradsky is an image of his father. He's so broken up inside, Sean, that's why he clings to you. You can help him.'

Sean laughed outright. 'Candy, my dear, we like each other that's all, there are no deep and dark motives in our friendship. Don't you start getting jealous of me now.'

Candy sat up and the blankets slipped down to her waist. She leaned towards Sean and her breasts swung forward, heavy, round and silver-white in the half light.

'There's a strength in you, Sean, a kind of solid sureness in you that you haven't discovered yet. Duff has recognized it and so will other unhappy people. He needs you, he needs you very badly. Look after him for me, help him to find what he seeks.'

'Nonsense, Candy,' Sean muttered with embarrassment.

'Promise me you'll help him.'

'It's time you went back to your room,' Sean told her. 'People will start talking.'

'Promise me, Sean.'

'All right, I promise.'

Candy slipped out of the bed. She dressed quickly. 'Thank you, Sean, goodnight.'

= 26 =

For Sean, Johannesburg was poorer without Duff: the streets were not so busy, the Rand Club was drearier and the thrills at the Stock Exchange not so intense. However, there was work to do; his share and Duff's as well.

It was late every evening when the conferences with Hradsky and Max ended and he went back to the Hotel. In the reaction from the day's tension, when his brain was numb and his eyes burned, there was little energy to spare for regret. Yet he was lonely. He went to the Opera House and drank champagne with the crowd there. One of the girls did the Can-Can on the big table in the centre of the room and when she stopped in front of Sean and Trevor Heyns, with her forehead touching her knees and her petticoats hanging forward over her shoulders, Sean let Trevor whip her pants down – a week before he would have punched Trevor in the nose rather than concede the honour. It wasn't so much fun any more. He went home early.

The following Saturday noon Curtis and Francois came into the office for the weekly progress meeting. When they had finished and Hradsky had left, Sean suggested, 'Come along with me, we'll go and have a pot or twelve at the Grand National Bar, baptize the weekend so to speak.'

Curtis and Francois fidgeted in their chairs.

'We had arranged to meet some of the other boys down at the Bright Angels, boss.'

'That's fine, I'll come along with you,' said Sean eagerly, the prospect of being with ordinary men again was suddenly very attractive to him. He felt sickened of the company of those who shook his hand and smiled at him while they waited for a chance to wipe him off the board. It would be good to go along with these two and talk mining and not stocks and shares, to laugh with men who didn't give a damn if C.R.C.'s hit sixty shillings on Monday. He'd get a little drunk with Francois and Curtis; later on perhaps he'd have a fight – an honest, snorting, stand-up fight. God, yes, it would be good to be with men who were clean inside – even if there was dirt under their nails and the armpits of their shirts were stained with sweat.

Curtis glanced quickly at Francois. 'There'll be just a crowd of roughnecks down there, boss, all the diggers come in on a Saturday.'

'That's fine,' said Sean. 'Let's go.'

He stood up and buttoned his dove-grey coat; the lapels were edged in black watered silk and matched the black pearl pin in his tie. He picked up his cane from the desk.

'Come on – let's get moving.'

They ran into the noise from the Bright Angels a block before they reached the building. Sean grinned and quickened his step like an old gun dog with the scent of the bird in its nostrils again. Francois and Curtis hurried along on either side of him. There was a big digger standing on the bar counter. Sean recognized him as one of his men from the Little Sister Mine; the man's body was tilted back to balance the weight of the demijohn he held to his lips and his throat jerked regularly as he swallowed. The crowd around his feet were chanting:

'Drink it, down, down, down, down, down.'

The digger finished, he threw the bottle against the far wall and belched like an air-locked geyser. He bowed to acknowledge the applause and then he caught sight of Sean standing in the doorway. He wiped his mouth guiltily with the back of his hand and jumped down off the counter. The other men in the crowd turned and saw Sean and the noise tapered off. They spread out along the bar in silence. Sean led Francois and Curtis into the room. He placed a pile of sovereigns on the counter.

'Set them up, barman, take the orders. Today is Saturday and it's time to tie the dog loose.'

'Cheers, Mr Courtney.'

'Good luck, sir.'

'*Gezondheid,* Mr Courtney.'

Their voices were subdued with respect.

'Drink up, man, there's plenty more where that came from.' Sean stood with Francois and Curtis at the bar. They laughed at his jokes. His voice was loud with good fellowship and his face flushed with happiness. He bought more drinks. After a while his bladder started making its presence felt and he went through the back door into the washrooms. There were men talking in there; he stopped before he rounded the edge of the screen into the room. ' . . . what's he want to come here for, hey? This isn't the mucking Rand Club.'

'Shh! He'll hear you, man, do you want to lose your job?'

'I don't give a damn. Who does he think he is – "Drink up, boys, there's plenty more where that came from – I'm the boss, boys, do as you're told, boys, kiss my arse, boys." ' Sean stood paralysed.

'Pipe down, Frank, he'll go just now.'

'The sooner the better, say I, the big dandy bastard with his ten-guinea boots and gold cane. Let him go back where he belongs.'

'You're drunk, man, don't talk so loud.'

'Sure I'm drunk, drunk enough to go in there and tell him to his face. . .'

Sean backed out through the door and walked slowly across the bar to Francois and Curtis.

'I hope you'll excuse me; I've just remembered there's something I've got to do this afternoon.'

'That's too bad, boss.' Curtis looked relieved. 'Perhaps some other time, hey?'

'Yes, perhaps some other time.'

They were pleased to see him when he went up to the Rand Club. Three men nearly fought one another to buy him a drink.

27

He had dinner with Candy that night and over the liqueurs he told her about it. She listened without interruption until he finished.

'They didn't want me there, I don't see what I've done to them that they should dislike me that way.'

'And it worries you?' she asked.

'Yes, it worries me. I've never had people feel like that towards me before.'

'I'm glad it worries you.' She smiled gently at him. 'One day you're going to grow into quite a nice person.'

'But why do they hate me?' Sean followed his original line of thought.

'They're jealous of you – you say this man said, "ten-guinea boots and gold cane" – that is what's behind it. You're different from them now, you're rich. You can't expect them to accept that.'

'But I've never done anything to them,' he protested.

'You don't have to. One thing I've found in this life – for everything you get you have to pay a price. This is part of the payment you have to make for success.'

'Hell, I wish Duff was here,' said Sean.

'Then Duff would explain to you that it doesn't matter, wouldn't he?' said Candy. ' "Who gives a damn for them, laddie, the unwashed herd? We can do without them," ' she mimicked. Sean scratched the side of his nose and looked down at the table.

'Please, Sean, don't ever let Duff teach you that people don't matter. He doesn't believe it himself – but he's so convincing. People are important. They are more important than gold or places or – or anything.'

Sean looked up at her. 'I realized that once; when I was trapped in the Candy Deep. I saw it very clearly then in the darkness and the mud. I made a resolution.' He grinned sheepishly. 'I told myself I'd never hurt anyone again if I could help it. I really meant it, Candy. I felt it so strongly at the time – but, but . . .'

'Yes, I think I understand. That's a big resolution to make and a much bigger one to keep. I don't think any single experience is enough to change a person's way of thinking. It's like building a wall brick by brick. You add to it a little at a time until at last it's finished. I've told you before, Sean, that you have a strength in you. I think one day you'll finish building your wall – and when you do, it will have no weak spots.'

= 28 =

The next Tuesday Sean rode up to Xanadu for the first time since Duff had left. Johnson and four of the clerks from the office were at work in the ballroom, packing and labelling the presents.

'Nearly finished, Johnson?'

'Just about, Mr Courtney, I'll send a couple of wagons up tomorrow morning to fetch this lot.'

'Yes, do that. I don't want them lying around here any longer.'

He went up the marble staircase and stood on the top landing. The house had a dead feeling to it: new and sterile, it was waiting for people to come into it and bring it to life. He went down the corridor, stopping to look at the paintings that Candy had chosen. They were oils in soft pastels, woman's colours.

'We can do without these – I'll get some with fire in them, scarlets and blacks and bright blues.'

He pushed open the door to his own bedroom. This was better: vivid Persian rugs on the floor, walls panelled in dark satiny wood and a bed like a polo field. He lay on the bed and looked up at the scrolled ornate plaster ceiling.

'I wish Duff were back – we can do some real living in this house.' He went downstairs again.

Johnson was waiting at the foot of the stairs. 'All finished, sir.'

'Good man! Off you go, then.'

He went through into the study and walked across to the gun rack. He took down a Purdey shotgun, carried it to the french windows and looked at it in the light. His nostrils flared a little at the nostalgic smell of gun oil. He brought the gun up to his shoulder, felt the true exciting balance of it and enjoyed it. He swung the barrels in an arc across the room, following the flight of an imaginary bird, and suddenly Duff's face was in his sights. Sean was taken so by surprise that he stood with the gun trained at Duff's head.

'Don't shoot, I'll come quietly,' said Duff solemnly.

Sean lowered the shotgun and carried it back to the rack.

'Hello.'

'Hello,' Duff answered, still standing in the doorway. Sean made a pretence of fitting the gun into the rack with his back to Duff.

'How are you, laddie?'

'Fine! Fine!'

'How's everybody else?'

'To whom do you refer, in particular?' Sean asked.

'Candy, for one.'

Sean considered the question. 'Well, you could have damaged her more by feeding her into a stamp mill.'

'Bad, hey?'

'Bad,' agreed Sean.

They stood in silence for a while.

'I take it that you are not very well disposed towards me either,' Duff said at last.

Sean shrugged his shoulders and moved across to the fireplace.

'Dufford, you're a pig,' he said conversationally.

Duff winced. 'Well, it was nice knowing you, laddie. I suppose from here on our paths diverge?'

'Don't drivel, Duff, you're wasting time. Pour the drinks and then you can tell me what it feels like being a pig. Also I want to discuss with you those paintings Candy has plastered along the upstairs corridor. I don't know whether to give them away or burn them.'

Duff straightened up from leaning against the door jamb; he tried to stop the relief showing on his face but Sean went on quickly, 'Before we close the lid on the subject and bury it, I want to tell you this. I don't like what you did. I can see why you did it, but I don't like it. That's my piece said. Have you got anything to add to it?'

'No,' said Duff.

'All right then. I think you'll find a bottle of Courvoisier right at the back of the cabinet behind the whisky decanter.'

Sean went down to Candy's Hotel that evening and found Candy in her office.

'He's back, Candy.'

'Oh!' Candy caught her breath. 'How is he, Sean?'

'A little chastened, but not much.'

'I didn't mean that – I meant is he well?'

'The same as ever. He had the grace to ask how you were,' said Sean.

'What did you tell him?' asked Candy.

Sean shrugged and sat down in the chair next to her desk. He looked at the tall stacks of sovereigns that Candy was counting.

'Is that last night's bar takings?' he asked, avoiding her question.

'Yes,' she answered absently.

'You're rich – will you marry me?' he smiled.

Candy stood up and walked across to the window.

'I suppose you two will be moving up to Xanadu now,' she said. Sean grunted and she went on quickly. 'The Heyns brothers will take over the Victoria rooms – they've spoken to me about it already, so don't worry about that. You'll have fun up there, it will be marvellous for you. I bet you'll have parties every night and crowds of people. I don't mind, I've gotten used to the idea now.'

Sean stood up and went to her, he took her gently by the elbow and turned her to face him. He gave her the silk handkerchief out of his top pocket to blow her nose.

'Do you want to see him again, Candy?'

She shook her head, not trusting her voice.

'I'll look after him like I promised.' He gave her a hug and turned to go.

'Sean,' she called after him. He looked back. 'You'll come to see me sometimes. We could have dinner and talk a little. You'll still be my friend, won't you?'

'Of course, Candy, of course, my dear.'

She smiled damply. 'If you pack your things and Duff's I'll have them sent up to Xanadu for you.'

29

Sean looked across the boardroom table at Duff, seeking his support. Duff blew a thick ring of cigar smoke. It spun and expanded like a ripple in a pond before it hit the table top and disintegrated. Duff wasn't going to back him up, Sean realized bitterly. They had argued half the previous night. He had hoped that Duff might still change his mind. Now he knew he wouldn't. He made one last appeal.

'They have asked for a ten per cent wage increase. I believe they need it – prices have soared in this town, but wages have remained the same. These men have wives and children, gentlemen, can't we take that into account?'

Duff blew another smoke ring and Hradsky pulled his watch from his pocket and looked at it pointedly. Max coughed and interrupted. 'I think we've been over that before, Mr Courtney. Could we put it to the vote now?'

Sean watched Hradsky's hand go up against him. He didn't want to look at Duff. He didn't want to see him vote with Hradsky, but he forced himself to turn his head. Duff's hands were on the table in front of him. He blew another smoke ring and watched it hit the table top.

'Those in favour of the motion?' asked Max, and Duff and Sean raised their right hands together. Sean realized then how much it would have meant if Duff had voted against him. Duff winked at him and he couldn't help grinning.

'That is thirty votes for, and sixty against,' declared Max. 'Therefore Mr Courtney's motion falls to the ground. I will inform the Mineworkers' Union of the decision. Now is there any other business before we close the meeting?'

Sean walked with Duff back to his own office.

'The only reason I supported you was because I knew Hradsky would win anyway,' said Duff pleasantly. Sean snorted.

'He's right, of course,' Duff went on unperturbed as he held open the door to Sean's office. 'A ten per cent wage increase would jump the group working costs up ten thousand a month.'

Sean kicked the door closed behind them and didn't answer.

'For God's sake, Sean, don't carry this goodwill-towards-men attitude to absurdity.

Hradsky's right – Kruger is likely to slap another one of his taxes on us at any moment and we've got to finance all that new development on the East Rand. We can't let production costs creep up now.'

'All right,' gruffed Sean. 'It's all settled. I just hope we don't have a strike on our hands.'

'There are ways of dealing with strikes. Hradsky has got the police on our side and we can have a couple of hundred men up from Kimberley in no time at all,' Duff told him.

'Damn it, Duff, it's wrong. You know it's wrong. That grotesque Buddha with the little eyes knows it's wrong. But what can I do? Damn it, what can I do?' Sean exploded. 'I feel so bloody helpless.'

'Well, you're the one who wanted to give him control.' Duff laughed at him. 'Stop trying to change the world and let's go home.'

Max was waiting for them in the outer office. He looked nervous. 'Excuse me, gentlemen, could I have a word with you?'

'Who's talking,' Sean asked abruptly, 'you or Hradsky?'

'It's a private matter, Mr Courtney.' Max dropped his voice.

'Can't it wait until tomorrow?' Sean pushed past him and kept going for the door.

'Please, Mr Courtney, it's of the utmost importance.'

Max plucked desperately at Sean's arm.

'What is it, Max?' Duff asked.

'I have to speak to you alone,' Max dropped his voice again and glanced unhappily at the street door.

'Well, speak then,' Duff encouraged him. 'We're alone now.'

'Not here. Can you meet me later?'

Duff raised an eyebrow. 'What is this, Maximilian, don't tell me you are selling dirty pictures.'

'Mr Hradsky is waiting for me at the hotel. I told him I was coming to find some papers, he'll get suspicious if I don't go back immediately.' Max was nearly in tears; his Adam's apple played hide-and-seek behind his high collar, bobbing out and disappearing again. Duff was suddenly very interested in what Max had to say.

'You don't want Norman to know about this?' he asked.

'My goodness, no.' Max came closer to tears.

'When do you want to meet us?'

'Tonight, after ten o'clock when Mr Hradsky has retired.'

'Where?' asked Duff.

'There's a side road round the east end of the Little Sister Mine dump. It's not used any more.'

'I know it,' said Duff. 'We'll ride along there about half past ten.'

'Thank you, Mr Charleywood, you won't regret it.' Max scampered for the door and disappeared.

Duff adjusted his beaver at the correct angle, then he prodded Sean in the belly with the point of his cane.

'Smell it – suck it in.' Duff sniffed appreciatively and Sean did the same.

'I don't smell a thing,' Sean declared.

'The air is thick with it,' Duff told him. 'The sweet smell of treachery.'

They left Xanadu just after half past nine. Duff insisted on wearing a black opera cloak.

'Atmosphere is vital, laddie, you can't go to a rendezvous like this dressed in dirty khaki pants and *veldschoen.* It would ruin the whole thing.'

'Well, I'm damned if I'm going to get into fancy dress. This is a very good suit. It will have to do.'

'Can't I persuade you to wear a pistol in your belt?' asked Duff wistfully.

'No,' laughed Sean.

'No?' Duff shook his head. 'You're a barbarian, laddie. No taste, that's your trouble.'

They avoided the main streets on their way through Johannesburg and met the Cape road half a mile beyond the town. There was only a minute slice of moon left in the dark bowl of the sky. The stars, however, were big and by their light the white mine dumps, each the size of a large hill, stood out like pustules on the earth's face.

Despite himself, Sean felt a little breathless with excitement – Duff's zest was always infectious. They cantered with their stirrups almost touching, Duff's cloak billowing out behind him and the breeze of their passage fanning the tip of Sean's cigar to a fierce red spark.

'Slow down, Duff, the turning's just about here somewhere. It's overgrown, we'll miss it.'

They reined to a walk.

'What's the time?' asked Duff.

Sean drew on his cigar and held his watch close to the glow. 'A quarter after ten. We're early.'

'My bet is Maximilian will be there before us – here's the road.' Duff turned his horse onto it and Sean followed him. The Little Sister Mine dump rose up next to them, steep and white in the starlight. They skirted it but its bulk threw a shadow over them. Duff's horse snorted and shied and Sean gripped with his knees as his own horse danced sideways. Max had stepped out from a scraggy cluster of bushes next to the road.

'Well met by moonlight, Maximilian,' Duff greeted him.

'Please bring your horses off the road, gentlemen.' Max was still showing signs of the afternoon's agitation. They tied their horses next to Max's among the bushes and walked across to join him.

'Well, Max, what's new? How are the folks?' Duff asked.

'Before we go any further in this matter, I want you gentlemen to give me your word of honour that, whether anything comes of it or not, you will never say a word to anybody of what I tell you tonight.' Max was very pale, Sean thought, or perhaps it was just the starlight.

'I agree to that,' said Sean.

'Cross my heart,' said Duff.

Max opened the front of his coat and brought out a long envelope. 'I think if I show you these first it will make it easier to explain my proposition.'

Sean took the envelope from him. 'What are they, Max?'

'The latest statements from all four banks at which Mr Hradsky deals.'

'Matches, Sean, give us a light, laddie,' said Duff eagerly.

'I have a lantern with me,' Max said and he squatted down to light it. Sean and Duff squatted with him and spread the bank statements in the circle of yellow light. They examined them in silence until at last Sean rocked back on his heels and lit another cigar.

'Well, I am glad I don't owe that much money,' Sean announced. Sean folded up the sheets and put them back in the envelope. He slapped the envelope into the palm of his free hand and started chuckling. Max reached across, took it from him and placed it carefully back inside his coat.

'All right, Max, spell it out for us,' said Sean. Max leaned forward and blew out the lantern. What he had to say was easier said in darkness.

'The large cash payment that Mr Hradsky had to make to you gentlemen and the limitation of output from his diamond mines in terms of the new cartel agreements in the diamond industry have forced him to borrow heavily on all his banks.' Max stopped and cleared his throat. 'The extent of this borrowing you have seen. Of course, the banks demanded security for the loans and Mr Hradsky has given them his entire holding of C.R.C. shares. The banks have set a limit on the shares of thirty-five shillings each. As you know C.R.C.'s are currently quoted at ninety shillings, which leaves a wide margin of safety. However, if the shares were to suffer a setback and fall in price to thirty-five shillings the banks would sell. They would dump every single share that Mr Hradsky owns in C.R.C.'s onto the market.'

'Go on, Max,' said Duff. 'I'm beginning to like the sound of your voice.'

'It occurred to me that if Mr Hradsky were temporarily absent from Johannesburg – say if he went on a trip to England to buy new machinery or something of that nature – it would be possible for you gentlemen to force the price of C.R.C.'s down to thirty-five shillings. Done correctly it would only take three or four days to accomplish. You could sell short and start rumours that the Leader Reef had pinched out at depth. Mr Hradsky would not be here to defend his interests and as soon as C.R.C.'s hit thirty-five shillings the banks would off-load his shares. The price would crash and you, with ready cash available, would be in a position to buy up C.R.C. shares at a fraction of their actual value. There is no reason why you shouldn't gain control of the group and make a couple of million to boot.'

There was another silence. It lasted a long time before Sean asked, 'What do you get out of it, Max?'

'Your cheque for one hundred thousand pounds, Mr Courtney.'

'Wages are going up,' remarked Sean. 'I thought the standard pay for this type of work was thirty pieces of silver. The rate, I believe, was set by a countryman of yours.'

'Shut up,' snapped Duff, then more pleasantly to Max, 'Mr Courtney likes his little jokes. Tell me, Max, is that all you want – just the money? I'll be frank with you – it doesn't ring true. You must be a moderately rich man as it is.'

Max stood up quickly and started towards the horses. He hadn't reached them before he swung around. His face was in darkness but his voice was naked as he screamed at them.

'Do you think I don't know what they call me – "The Court Jester", "Hradsky's tongue", "Lick-arse". Do you think I like it? Do you think I enjoy crawling to him every minute of every day? I want to be free again. I want to be a man again.' His voice choked off and his hands came up and covered his face. He was sobbing. Sean couldn't watch him and even Duff looked down at the ground in embarrassment. When Max spoke again it was in his usual soft and sad voice.

'Mr Courtney, if you wear your yellow waistcoat to the office tomorrow, I will take it as a sign that you intend to follow my suggestion and that my terms are acceptable to you. I will then make the necessary arrangements to ensure Mr Hradsky's absence from the country.' He untied his horse, mounted and rode away down the track towards the Cape Road. Neither Sean nor Duff moved to stand up. They listened to the hoof-beats of Max's horse fade into the darkness, before Duff spoke. 'Those bank statements were genuine – I had a good look at the seals.'

'And even more genuine was Max's emotion.' Sean flicked his cigar away into the bushes. 'No one could act that well. It made me feel quite sick listening to him. Hell, how can a man so cold-bloodedly betray his trust?'

'Laddie, let's not turn this into a discussion of Max's morals. Let's concern ourselves with the facts. Norman has been delivered into our hands, neatly trussed, spiced with garlic and with a sprig of parsley behind each ear. I say let's cook him and eat him.'

Sean smiled at him. 'Give me a few good reasons. I want you to convince me. The way I feel towards him after that meeting this afternoon, I shouldn't be surprised if I convince easily.'

'One,' Duff held up a finger. 'Norman deserves it.'

Sean nodded.

'Two,' another of Duff's fingers came up. 'If we gain control we can run things the way we want. You can indulge your good resolution and give everybody a pay rise and I'll be top man again.'

'Yes!' Sean tugged at his moustache thoughtfully.

'Three. We came here to make money, we'll never get another opportunity like this. And my last reason, but the most potent – you look so beautiful in that yellow waistcoat, laddie, I wouldn't miss seeing you in it tomorrow morning, not for a thousand C.R.C. shares.'

'It is rather natty,' admitted Sean. 'But listen, Duff, I don't want another Lochtkamper business. Messy, you know.'

Duff stood up.

'Norman's a big boy, he wouldn't do that. Anyway, he'll still be rich – he's got his diamond mines. We'll only be relieving him of his responsibilities on the Witwatersrand.'

They walked across to the horses. Sean had his foot in the stirrup when he stiffened and exclaimed, 'My God, I can't do it. It's all off.'

'Why?' Duff was alarmed.

'I spilt gravy on that waistcoat – I can't possibly wear it tomorrow. My tailor would murder me.'

— 30 —

There was no problem in arranging for Hradsky's absence – someone had to go to London. There was machinery to buy for the new areas on the East Rand and they had to select two engineers from the hundred or so applicants waiting in England. Not ungraciously, Hradsky allowed himself to be elected for the job.

'We'll give him a farewell party,' Duff suggested to Sean during dinner that night. 'Well, not really a farewell party – but a wake.'

Sean started whistling the 'Dead March' and Duff tapped it out on the table with the handle of his knife.

'We'll have it at Candy's Hot –' Duff cut himself short. 'We'll have it here. We'll really lay it on for poor old Norman so afterwards he'll be able to say, "the bastards may have cleaned me out, but they certainly gave me a grand party".'

'He doesn't like parties,' said Sean.

'That's an excellent reason why we should give him one,' agreed Duff.

A week later when Hradsky and Max left on the morning coach for Port Natal there were fifty members of the Johannesburg Stock Exchange still in full evening dress from the night's party to wave him goodbye. Duff made a touching, if somewhat slurred, little speech and presented Hradsky with a bouquet of roses. Nervous of the crowd that milled about them, the horses bolted when the driver cracked his whip and Max and Hradsky were thrown together in an undignified heap on the rear seat of the coach. The crowd cheered them out of sight. With an arm around his shoulder Sean led Duff across the street to the office and deposited him in one of the deep leather armchairs.

'Are you sober enough to talk sense?' Sean asked dubiously.

'Sure. Always at your service as the lady said to the customer.'

'I managed to have a word with Max last night,' Sean told him. 'He will send us a telegram from Port Natal when he and Hradsky are safely on the mailboat. We won't start anything until we receive it.'

'Very wise – you're the wisest chap I know,' Duff grinned happily.

'You'd better go to bed,' Sean told him.

'Too far,' said Duff. 'I'll sleep here.'

It was another ten days before Max's telegram arrived. Sean and Duff were eating lunch in the Rand Club when it was delivered to their table. Sean slit open the envelope and read the message to Duff.

'Sailing four o'clock this afternoon. Good luck. Max.'

'I'll drink to that,' Duff lifted his wine glass.

'Tomorrow,' said Sean, 'I'll go up to the Candy Deep and tell Francois to pull all the men out of the bottom levels of the mine. No one's to be allowed in.'

'Put a guard at the fourteenth level,' suggested Duff. 'That'll make it more impressive.'

'Good idea,' agreed Sean. He looked up as someone passed their table and suddenly he started to smile. 'Duff, do you know who that is?'

'Who are you talking about?' Duff looked bewildered.

'That chap who's just gone out into the lounge – there he is, going into the lavatories.'

'Isn't that Elliott, the newspaper fellow?'

'Editor of the *Rand Mail,*' nodded Sean. 'Come with me, Duff.'

'Where are we going?'

'To get a bit of cheap publicity.'

Duff followed Sean out of the dining-room, across the lounge and into the men's lavatories. The door of one of the closets was closed and as they walked in someone farted softly behind it. Sean winked at Duff and went across to the urinal. As he addressed himself to it he said, 'Well, all we can hope for now, Duff, is that Norman will be able to work a miracle in England. Otherwise – ' He shrugged his shoulder. Duff picked up his cue.

'We're taking a hell of a chance relying on that. I still say we should sell out now.

C.R.C.'s were at ninety-one shillings this morning so it's obvious that the story hasn't leaked out yet. But when it does you won't be able to give the bloody shares away. I say we should get out while the going's good.'

'No,' Sean disagreed. 'Let's wait until we hear from Norman. It's taking a bit of a chance, I know, but we have a responsibility to the men working for us.' Sean took Duff's arm and led him out of the lavatory again; at the door he added the cherry to the top of the pie. 'If and when C.R.C. collapses there are going to be thousands of men out of work – do you realize that?'

Sean closed the door behind them and they grinned delightedly at each other.

'You're a genius, laddie,' whispered Duff.

'I'm happy to say I agree with you,' Sean whispered back.

The next morning Sean woke with the knowledge that something exciting was going to happen that day. He lay and savoured the feeling before he sent his mind out to hunt for the reason. Then he sat up suddenly and reached for the newspaper that lay folded on the coffee tray beside his bed. He shook it open and found what he was looking for on the front page, big headlines: *Is all well with the Central Rand Consolidated? Norman Hradsky's mystery journey*. The story itself was a masterpiece of journalistic evasion. Seldom had Sean seen anyone write so fluently or convincingly on a subject about which he knew nothing. 'It is suggested', 'Usually reliable sources report' and 'There is reason to believe' – all the old phrases of no significance. Sean groped for his slippers and padded down the corridor to Duff's room.

Duff had all the blankets and most of the bed; the girl was curled up like a pink anchovy on the outskirts. Duff was snoring and the girl whimpered a little in her sleep. Sean tickled Duff's lips with the tassel of his dressing-gown cord, Duff's nose twitched and his snores gurgled into silence. The girl sat up and looked at Sean with eyes wide but vacant from sleep.

'Quickly, run,' Sean shouted at her, 'the rebels are coming.'

She leapt straight into the air and landed three feet from the bed quivering with panic. Sean ran a critical eye over her. A pretty filly, he decided, and made a mental note to take her for a trot just as soon as Duff put her out to grass.

'All right,' he reassured her, 'they've gone away now.'

She became aware of her nakedness and Sean's frank appraisal of it. She tried to cover it with hands too small for the task. Sean picked up Duff's gown from the foot of the bed and handed it to her.

'Go and have a bath or something, sweetheart, I want to talk to Mr Charleywood.'

With the gown on she recovered her composure and told him severely, 'I didn't have any clothes on, Mr Courtney.'

'I would never have guessed,' said Sean politely.

'It's not nice.'

'You are too modest – I thought it was better than average. Off you go now, there's a good girl.' With a saucy flick of her head she disappeared into the bathroom and Sean transferred his attention to Duff. Duff had held grimly onto the threads of sleep throughout the exchange but he let go when Sean whacked him across the backside with the folded newspaper. Like a tortoise coming out of its shell his head emerged from the blankets. Sean handed him the paper and sat down on the edge of the bed. He watched Duff's face crease into laughter lines before he spoke.

'You better get down to the Editor's office and shout at him a little – just to confirm his suspicions. I'll go up to the Candy Deep and close all the bottom levels. I'll meet you back at the Exchange at opening time and don't forget to clean that grin off your face before you show it round town. Try and look haggard, it shouldn't be difficult for you.'

When Sean arrived at the Stock Exchange building the crowd had filled the street outside. Mbejane eased the landau into it and it opened to give them a passage. Sean scowled straight ahead and ignored the questions which were shouted at him from all around. Mbejane stopped the carriage outside the main entrance and four police constables held back the mob while Sean hurried across the pavement and through the double doors. Duff was there ahead of him, the centre of a turbulent circle of members and brokers. He saw Sean and waved frantically over the heads of his inquisitors. That was sufficient to switch their attention from Duff to Sean and they flocked to him, ringing him in with anxious angry faces. Sean's hat was knocked forward over his eyes and a button popped off his coat as one of them caught hold of his lapels.

'Is it true?' the man shouted, spittle flying from his lips into Sean's face. 'We've got a right to know if it's true.'

Sean swung his cane in a full overarm stroke onto the man's head and sent him tottering backwards into the arms of those behind him.

'Back, you bastards,' he roared at them using both the point and the edge of his cane to beat them away, scattering them across the floor until he stood alone, glowering at them with the cane still twitching restlessly in his hand.

'I'll make a statement later on. Until then, behave yourselves.' He adjusted his hat, picked the loose thread where the button had been from his coat and stalked across to join Duff. He could see Duff's grin starting to lift the corner of his mouth and he cautioned him silently with his eyes. Grim-faced they walked through into the members' lounge.

'How's it going your end?' Duff kept his voice low.

'Couldn't be better.' Sean contrived a worried expression. 'I've got an armed guard on the fourteenth level. When this bunch hear about that, they'll really start frothing at the mouth.'

'When you make your statement, let it ring with obvious false confidence,' Duff instructed. 'If it goes on like this we'll have the shares down to thirty-five shillings within an hour of opening.'

Five minutes before opening time Sean stood in the President's box and made his address to his fellow members, Duff listened to him with mounting admiration. Sean's hearty reassurances and verbal side-stepping were enough to strike despair into the souls of the most hardened optimists. Sean finished his speech and climbed down from the box amid a gloomy lack of applause. The bell rang and the brokers stood singly or in small disconsolate groups about the floor. The first tentative offer was made. 'I sell C.R.C.'

But there was no rush to buy. Ten minutes later there was a sale recorded at eighty-five shillings, six shillings lower than the previous day's closing price. Duff leaned across to Sean. 'We'll have to start selling some of our own shares to get things moving, otherwise everybody's going to keep sitting on the fence.'

'That's all right,' Sean nodded, 'we'll buy them back later at a quarter of the price. But wait until the news about the Candy Deep gets out.'

It was just before ten o'clock when that happened. The reaction was sharp. In one quick burst of selling C.R.C.'s dropped to sixty shillings. But there they hung, fluctuating nervously in the chaos of hope and doubt.

'We'll have to sell now,' whispered Duff, 'they are short of script. We'll have to give it to them otherwise the price will stick here.'

Sean felt his hands trembling and he clenched them in his pockets. Duff was showing signs of the strain as well, there was a nerve jumping in his cheek and his eyes had receded into their sockets a little. This was a game with high stakes.

'Don't overdo it – sell thirty thousand.'

The price of C.R.C.'s sagged under the weight but levelled out at forty-five shillings. There was still another hour until high change and Sean's whole body was screwed up tight with tension. He felt the cold patches of sweat under his arms.

'Sell another thirty thousand,' he ordered his clerk and even to himself his voice sounded wheezy. He stubbed out his cigar in the copper ashtray next to his chair; it was already half full of butts. It was no longer necessary for either of them to act worried. This time the price stuck at forty shillings and the sale of sixty thousand more of their shares failed to move it down more than a few shillings.

'Someone's buying up,' muttered Sean uneasily.

'It looks like it,' agreed Duff. 'I'll lay odds it's that bloody Greek Efthyvoulos. It looks as if we'll have to sell enough to glut him before they'll drop any further.'

By high change Duff and Sean had sold three-quarters of their holdings in C.R.C.'s and the price still stood stubbornly at thirty-seven and sixpence. So tantalizingly close to the magic figure that would release a flood of Hradsky's shares onto the unprepared market, but now they were nearing the stage when they would no longer have any shares with which to force the price down that last two and sixpence.

The market closed and left Duff and Sean sitting limply in their armchairs, shaken and tired as prizefighters at the end of the fifteenth round. Slowly the lounge emptied but still they sat on. Sean leaned across and put his hand on Duff's shoulder. 'It's going to be all right,' he said. 'Tomorrow it will be all right.'

They looked at each other and they exchanged strength, each of them drawing it from the other until they were both smiling. Sean stood up. 'Come on, let's go home.'

Sean went to bed early and alone. Although he felt drained of energy, sleep was a long time coming to him and when it did it was full of confused dreams and punctuated with sharp jerks back into wakefulness. It was almost a relief to see the dawn define the windows as grey squares and to be released from his unrewarding rest. At breakfast he drank a cup of coffee and found that his stomach was unable to accept the plateful of steak and eggs that was offered it for it was already screwing up tight in anticipation of the day ahead. Duff was edgy and tired-looking as well; they spoke only a little during the meal and not at all in the carriage when Mbejane drove them down to the Exchange.

The crowd was outside the Stock Exchange again. They forced their way through it and into the building; they took their seats in the lounge and Sean looked round at the faces of his fellow members. In each of them were the marks of worry, the same darkness round the eyes and the jerkiness in movement. He watched Jock Heyns yawn extravagantly and had to do the same; he lifted his hand to cover his mouth and found it was trembling again. He laid the hand on the arm of his chair and kept it still. Across the lounge Bonzo Barnes caught Sean's eye and looked away quickly, then he also gaped into a cavernous yawn. It was the tension. In the years ahead Sean would see men yawn like that while they waited for the dawn to send them against the Boer guns. Duff leaned across to him and broke his line of thought.

'As soon as the trading starts, we'll sell. Try and panic them. Do you agree?'

'Sudden death,' Sean nodded. He couldn't face another morning of that mental agony. 'Couldn't we offer shares at thirty-two shillings and sixpence and get it over with?' he asked.

Duff grinned at him. 'We can't do that, it's too obvious – we'll just have to go on offering to sell at best and let the price fall on its own.'

'I suppose you're right – but we'll play our high cards now and dump the rest of our shares as soon as the market opens. I don't see how the price can possibly hold after that.'

Duff nodded. He beckoned to their authorized clerk who was waiting patiently at the door of the lounge and when the man came up to them he told him, 'Sell one hundred thousand C.R.C.'s at best.'

The clerk blinked but he jotted the order down on his pad and went out onto the main floor where the other brokers were gathering. It was a few minutes from the bell.

'What if it doesn't work?' Sean asked. The tightness in his belly was nauseating him.

'It must work – it's got to work,' Duff whispered as much to himself as to Sean. He was twisting his fingers round the head of his cane and chewing against clenched teeth. They sat and waited for the bell and when it rang Sean jumped then reached sheepishly for his cigar case. He heard their clerk's voice, raised sharply, 'I sell C.R.C.'s,' and then the confused mumble of voices as the trading started. Through the lounge door he saw the recorder chalk up the first sale. 'Thirty-seven shillings.'

He drew hard on his cigar and lay back in his chair forcing himself to relax, ignoring the restless tapping of Duff's fingers on the arm of the chair next to him. The recorder wiped out the figures and wrote again. 'Thirty-six shillings.'

Sean blew out cigar smoke in a long jet. 'It's moving,' he whispered and Duff's hand clenched on the arm of the chair, his knuckles paling from the pressure of his grip.

'Thirty-five.' The elusive number at last. Sean heard Duff sigh next to him and his voice, 'Now! watch it go, laddie, now the banks will come on. Get ready, laddie, get ready now.'

'Thirty-four and six,' wrote the recorder.

'They must come in now,' said Duff again. 'Get ready to get rich, laddie.'

Their clerk was coming back across the floor and into the lounge. He stopped in front of their chairs. 'I managed to sell them, sir.'

Sean straightened up quickly. 'So soon?' he asked.

'Yes, sir, three big sales and I got rid of them all. I'm afraid the last was only at thirty-four and sixpence.'

Sean stared back at the board. The figure was still at thirty-four and sixpence.

'Duff, something's going on here. Why haven't the banks come in yet?'

'We'll force them to off-load.' Duff's voice was unnaturally hoarse. 'We'll force the bastards.' He pulled himself half out of his chair and snarled at the clerk.

'Sell another one hundred thousand at thirty shillings.' The man's face went slack with surprise. 'Hurry, man, do you hear me? What are you waiting for?' The clerk backed away from Duff, then he turned and scurried out of the lounge.

'Duff, for God's sake.' Sean grabbed his arm. 'Have you gone mad?'

'We'll force them,' muttered Duff. 'They'll have to sell.'

'We haven't got another hundred thousand shares.' Sean jumped up. 'I'm going to stop him.' He ran across the lounge but before he reached the door he saw the sale being chalked up on the board at thirty shillings. He pushed his way across the crowded floor until he reached his clerk. 'Don't sell any more,' he whispered.

The man looked surprised. 'I've sold them already, sir.'

'The whole hundred thousand?' There was horrified disbelief in Sean's voice.

'Yes, sir, someone took the lot in one batch.'

Sean walked back across the floor in a daze. He sank into the chair beside Duff.

'They're sold already.' He spoke as though he didn't believe himself.

'We'll force them, we'll force them to sell,' muttered Duff again and Sean turned to him with alarm. Duff was sweating in little dewdrops across his forehead and his eyes were very bright.

'Duff, for God's sake,' Sean whispered to him, 'steady, man.' Sean knew that they were watched by everybody in the lounge. The watching faces seemed as large as those seen through a telescope and the buzz of their voices echoed strangely in his ears. Sean felt confused: everything seemed to be in slow motion like a bad dream. He looked through into the trading floor and saw the crude number thirty still chalked accusingly against C.R.C. Where were the banks? Why weren't they selling?

'We'll force them, we'll force the bastards,' Duff said again. Sean tried to answer him but the words wouldn't come. He looked back across the trading floor and now he knew it was a bad dream for Hradsky and Max were there, walking across the floor towards the members' lounge. Men were crowding around them and Hradsky was smiling and holding up his hands as if to fend off their questions. They came through into the lounge and Hradsky went to his chair by the fireplace. He lowered himself into it with his shoulders sagging forward and his waistcoat wrinkled tightly around the full bag of his belly. He was still smiling and Sean thought that his smile was one of the most unnerving things he had ever seen. He watched it with flesh-crawling fascination and beside him Duff was just as still and stricken. Max spoke quickly to Hradsky and then he stood up and walked across to Sean and Duff. He stopped in front of them.

'The clerk informs us that you have contracted to sell to Mr Hradsky five hundred thousand shares in C.R.C.'s at an average price of thirty-six shillings.' Max's lashes drooped sadly onto his cheeks. 'The total issue of C.R.C.'s, as you know, is one million shares. During the last two days Mr Hradsky was able to purchase another seventy-five thousand shares apart from the ones you sold to him. This makes his total holdings of C.R.C.'s almost six hundred thousand shares. It seems therefore that you have sold shares that don't exist. Mr Hradsky foresees that you will have some difficulty in fulfilling your contract.'

Sean and Duff went on staring at him. He turned to leave them and Duff blurted out. 'But the banks – why didn't the banks sell?'

Max smiled a mournful little smile. 'The day he reached Port Natal Mr Hradsky transferred sufficient funds from his accounts there to liquidate his overdrafts in Johannesburg. He sent you that telegram and returned here immediately. We only arrived an hour ago.'

'But – but, you lied to us. You tricked us!'

Max inclined his head. 'Mr Charleywood, I will not discuss honesty with a man who does not understand the meaning of the word.' He went back to Hradsky's side. Everyone in the lounge had heard him and while Duff and Sean went on sitting amongst the ruins of their fortune the struggle to buy C.R.C. shares started on the main floor. In five minutes the price was over ninety shillings and still climbing. When it reached one hundred shillings, Sean touched Duff's arm.

'Let's go.' They stood up together and started for the door of the members' lounge. As they passed Hradsky's chair he spoke.

'Yes, Mr Charleywood, you can't win all the time.' It came out quite clearly with only a slight catch on the 'c's' – they were always difficult letters for Norman Hradsky.

Duff stopped, he turned to face Hradsky, his mouth open as he struggled to find a reply. His lips moved, groping, groping for words – but there were none. His shoulders drooped, he shook his head and turned away. He stumbled once at the edge of the floor. Sean held his arm and guided him through the excited jabber of brokers. No one took any notice of the two of them. They were bumped and jostled before they were through the crush and out onto the pavement. Sean signalled Mbejane to bring the carriage. They climbed into it and Mbejane drove them up to Xanadu.

They went through into the drawing-room.

'Get me a drink, please, Sean.' Duff's face was grey and crumpled-looking. Sean poured two tumblers half full of brandy and carried one across to Duff. Duff drank and then sat staring into the empty glass.

'I'm sorry – I lost my head. I thought we'd be able to buy those shares for dirt, when the banks started selling.'

'It doesn't matter,' Sean's voice was tired. 'We were smashed before that happened. Christ! What a well-laid trap it was!'

'We couldn't have known. It was so damn cunning, we couldn't have guessed, could we, Sean?' Duff was trying to excuse himself.

Sean kicked off his boots and loosened his collar. 'That night up at the mine dump – I would have staked my life Max wasn't lying.' He lay back in the chair and stirred his brandy with a circular movement of his hand, 'Christ, how they must have laughed to see us stampede into the pitfall!'

'But we aren't finished, Sean, we aren't completely finished, are we?' Duff was pleading with him, begging for a peg to hang his hope on. 'We'll come out of this all right, you know we will, don't you? We'll save enough out of the wreckage to start again. We'll build it all up again, won't we, Sean?'

'Sure,' Sean laughed brutally. 'You can get a job down at the Bright Angels cleaning out the spittoons and I'll get one at the Opera House playing the piano.'

'But – but – there'll be something left. A couple of thousand even. We could sell this house.'

'Don't dream, Duff, this house belongs to Hradsky. Everything belongs to him.' Sean flicked the brandy that was left in his glass into his mouth and swallowed it. He stood up quickly and went across to the liquor cabinet. 'I'll explain it to you. We owe Hradsky a hundred thousand shares that don't exist. The only way we can deliver them is to buy them from him first and he can set his own price on them. We're finished, Duff, do you know what that means? Smashed! Broken!' Sean poured brandy into his glass, slopping a little on the sideboard. 'Have another drink on Hradsky, it's his brandy now.' Sean swept his arm round the room, pointing at the rich furniture and heavy curtains. 'Take a last look at this lot. Tomorrow the Sheriff will be here to attach it; then through the due processes of the law it will be handed to its rightful owner – Mr Norman Hradsky.' Sean started back towards his chair and then he stopped.

'The due processes of the law,' he repeated softly. 'I wonder – it might just work.'

Duff sat up eagerly in his chair. 'You've got an idea?'

Sean nodded. 'Well, half an idea anyway. Listen, Duff, if I can save a couple of thousand out of this do you agree that we get out of here?'

'Where to – where will we go?'

'We were facing north when we started. It's as good a direction as any. They say there's gold and ivory beyond the Limpopo for those who want it.'

'But, why can't we stay here?' We could play the stock market.' Duff looked uncertain, almost afraid.

'Damn it, Duff, we're finished here. It's a different story playing the market when you are paying the fiddler and calling the tune, but with a mere thousand or so we'd be among the dogs fighting for the scraps under Hradsky's table. Let's get out and start again. We'll go north, hunt ivory and prospect for a new reef. We'll take a couple of wagons and find another fortune. I bet you've forgotten how it feels to sit on a horse and handle a rifle, to have the wind in your face and not a whore or a stockbroker within five hundred miles.'

'But it means leaving everything we've worked for,' Duff groaned.

'Sweet merciful heavens, man, are you blind or just plain stupid?' Sean stormed at him. 'You don't own anything, so how the hell can you leave something you haven't got? I'm going down to see Hradsky and try to make a deal with him. Are you coming?'

Duff looked at him without seeing him, his lips were trembling and he was shaking his head. At last he was realizing the position they were in and the impact of it had dazed him. The higher you ride the further there is to fall.

'All right,' said Sean. 'Wait for me here.'

Hradsky's suite was full of talking, laughing men. Sean recognized most of them as the courtiers who used to cluster round the throne on which he and Duff had sat. The King is dead, long live the King! They saw him standing in the doorway and the laughter and loud voices fizzled out. He saw Max take two quick steps to the stinkwood desk in the corner, pull open the top drawer and drop his hand into it. He stood like that watching Sean. One by one the courtiers picked up their hats and canes and hurried out of the room. Some of them mumbled embarrassed greetings as they brushed passed Sean. Then there were only the three of them left: Sean standing quietly in the doorway, Max behind the desk with his hand on the pistol and Hradsky in the chair by the fireplace watching through yellow, half-hooded eyes.

'Aren't you going to invite me in, Max?' Sean asked and Max glanced quickly at Hradsky, saw his barely perceptible nod and looked back at Sean. 'Come in, please, Mr Courtney.'

Sean pushed the door shut behind him. 'You won't need the gun, Max, the game is over.'

'And the score is in our favour, is it not, Mr Courtney?'

Sean nodded. 'Yes, you've won. We are prepared to make over to you all the C.R.C. shares we hold.'

Max shook his head unhappily. 'I'm afraid it's not quite as easy as that. You have undertaken to sell us a certain number of shares and we must insist upon delivery in full.'

'Just where do you suggest we get them?' Sean asked.

'You could buy them on the Stock Exchange.'

'From you?'

Max shrugged but made no reply.

'So you are going to twist the knife, are you?'

'You put it very poetically, Mr Courtney,' agreed Max.

'Have you considered the consequences of forcing us into bankruptcy?'

'I will admit freely that the consequences to you do not concern us.'

Sean smiled. 'That was not very nice, Max, but I was talking about it from your point of view. Sequestration orders, creditors' meetings – you can rest assured that the liquidator appointed will be a member of the *Volksraad* or a relative of one. There will be court actions and counter actions, enforced sale of the shares in the estate and costs to pay. A liquidator with any sense at all could string it out for three or four years, all the time drawing a handsome commission. Have you thought about that, Max?'

The narrowing of Max's eyes showed that he hadn't. He looked at Hradsky with a trace of helplessness in his face, and Sean took a little comfort from that look.

'Now what I suggest is this – you let us draw ten thousand, take our horses and personal belongings. We in exchange will give you the rest. Shares, bank accounts, property, everything. You cannot possibly get more out of it if you force us into bankruptcy.'

Hradsky gave Max a message in their private facial code and Max interpreted it to Sean.

'Would you mind waiting outside, please, while we discuss this offer of yours.'

'I'll go down and have a drink in the bar,' said Sean. He pulled his watch from his waistcoat pocket and checked the time. 'Will twenty minutes be enough?'

'Ample, thank you, Mr Courtney.'

Sean had his drink by himself although the bar was nowhere near empty. This was not an arrangement of his own choosing, but he was flying the fever flag of failure and so he had to take an isolation berth at one end of the bar while all the other ships steered wide of him. No one looked in his direction and the conversation that went on round him was carefully arranged so as to exclude him. While he waited out the twenty minutes he amused himself by imagining the reactions of these his friends if he were to ask them for a loan. This helped to take the sting out of their snubs but still he felt it rankling. He looked at his watch again. The twenty minutes were up. Sean walked back along the counter towards the door. Jock and Trevor Heyns saw him coming, they turned away abruptly and immediately became absorbed in staring at the bottle-lined shelves behind the bar counter. Sean stopped level with Jock and cleared his throat deferentially. 'Jock, could you spare a minute?'

Jock turned slowly. 'Ah, Sean. Yes, what is it?'

'Duff and I are leaving the Rand. I have something for you, just something to remember us by. I know Duff would want you to have it too.'

Jock reddened with embarrassment. 'That's not necessary,' he said and started to turn back to his drink.

'Please, Jock.'

'Oh, all right,' Jock's voice was irritable. 'What is it?'

'This,' Sean said and stepped forward, moving his weight behind the fist. Jock's large and whisky-flushed nose was a target to dream about. It was not one of Sean's best punches, he was out of training, but it was good enough to send Jock in a spectacular back-somersault over the counter. Dreamily Sean picked up Jock's glass and emptied it over Trevor's head.

'Next time you meet me smile and say "Hello",' he told Trevor. 'Until then – stay out of mischief.'

He went up the stairs to Hradsky's suite in much better spirits. They were waiting for him.

'Give me the word, Max,' Sean could even grin at him.

'Mr Hradsky has very generously –'

'How much?' Sean cut him short.

'Mr Hradsky will allow you to take fifteen hundred and your personal effects. As part of the agreement you will give an undertaking not to embark on any business venture on the Witwatersrand for a period of three years.'

'That will be too soon,' said Sean. 'Make it two thousand and you've got a deal.'

'The offer is not open to discussion.'

Sean could see they meant it. They didn't have to bargain; it was a statement.

'All right, I accept.'

'Mr Hradsky has sent for his lawyer to draw up the agreement. Would you mind waiting, Mr Courtney?'

'Not at all, Max, you forget I am a gentleman of leisure now.'

31

Sean found Duff still sitting in the chair where he had left him in the drawing-room of Xanadu. The bottle clutched in his hand was empty and he was unconscious. He had spilt brandy down the front of his waistcoat and three of the buttons were undone. Huddled in the big chair, his body seemed to have shrunk and the curly hair hanging onto his forehead softened the gaunt lines of his face. Sean loosened his fingers from the neck of the bottle and Duff moved restlessly, muttering and twisting his head.

'Bedtime for small boys,' said Sean. He lifted him out of the chair and hung him over one shoulder.

Duff sicked up copiously.

'That's the way, show Hradsky what you think of his bloody carpet,' Sean encouraged him. 'Give him another one for luck, but not on my boots.'

Duff did as he was bid and, chuckling, Sean carried him up the stairs. At the top he stopped and with Duff still bundled over one shoulder tried to analyse his own feelings. Damn it, he felt happy. It was ridiculous to feel so happy in the midst of disaster. He went on down the passage still wondering at himself and into Duff's room. He dropped Duff on the bed and stripped his clothes off, then he rolled him under the blankets. He brought the enamel wash basin from the bathroom and placed it next to the bed.

'You may need this – sleep well. There's a long ride ahead of us tomorrow.'

He stopped again at the top of the stairs and looked down their marble slope into the splendour of the lobby. He was leaving all of it and that was nothing to feel happy about. He laughed aloud. Perhaps it was because he had faced complete annihilation and at the last instant had changed it into something less; by avoiding the worst he had made defeat into a victory. A pathetic little victory to be sure, but at least they were no worse off now than they had been when they had arrived on the Rand. Was that the reason? Sean thought about it and found that it wasn't the whole truth. There was also a feeling of release. That was another part of it. To go on his way: north to a new land. He felt the tingle of anticipation.

'Not a whore or a stockbroker within five hundred miles,' he said aloud and grinned. He gave up trying to find words for his feeling. Emotion was so damned elusive: as soon as you cornered it, it changed its shape and the net of words which you had ready to throw over it was no longer suitable. He let it go free to range through his body, accepting and enjoying it. He ran down the stairs, out through the kitchens and into the stable yard.

'Mbejane!' he shouted, 'where the hell are you?'

The clatter of a stool overturning in the servants' quarters and the door of one of the rooms burst open.

'Nkosi – what is it?' The urgency of Sean's voice had alarmed Mbejane.

'Which are the six best horses we have?'

Mbejane named them, making no attempt to hide his curiosity.

'Are they all salted against the Nagana?'*

'All of them, Nkosi.'

'Good – have them ready before tomorrow's light. Two with saddles, the others to carry the packs.'

Mbejane turned on his smile. 'Could it be we are going hunting, Nkosi?'

'It could easily be,' Sean agreed.

'How long will we be gone, Nkosi?'

'How long is for ever? Take leave of all your women, bring your kaross and your spears and we will see where the road leads.'

Sean went back to his bedroom. It took him half an hour to pack. The pile of discarded clothing in the centre of the room grew steadily and what he kept made only half a horseload. He crammed it into two leather valises. He found his sheepskin coat in the back of one of the closets and threw it over a chair with his leather breeches and slouch hat, ready to wear in the morning. He went down to the study and made his selection from the gun rack, ignoring the fancy doubles and obscure calibres. He took down a pair of shotguns and four Mannlichers.

Then he went to tell Candy goodbye. She was in her suite but she opened quickly to his knock.

'Have you heard?' he asked her.

'Yes, the whole town knows. Oh! Sean, I'm so sorry – please come in.' She held the door open for him. 'How is Duff?'

'He'll be all right – right now he's both drunk and asleep.'

* Sleeping sickness. Salting involved deliberate exposure to the sting of the tsetse fly. Animals that recovered were then immune.

'I'll go to him,' she said quickly. 'He'll need me now.'

For answer Sean raised an eyebrow and looked at her until she dropped her eyes.

'No, you're right, I suppose. Perhaps later, when he's got over the first shock.' She looked up at Sean and smiled. 'I suppose you need a drink. It must have been hell for you as well.' She went across to the cabinet. She had on a blue gown and it clung to the womanish thrust of her hips and did not go high enough to cover the cleft of her breasts. Sean watched her pour his drink and bring it to him. She was lovely, he thought.

'Till we meet again, Candy,' Sean lifted his glass.

Her eyes went wide and very blue. 'I don't understand. Why do you say that?'

'We're going, Candy, first thing tomorrow.'

'No, Sean – you're joking.' But she knew he wasn't. There wasn't much to say after that. He finished his drink and they talked for a while, then he kissed her.

'Be happy, please,' he ordered her.

'I'll try. Come back one day soon.'

'Only if you promise to marry me,' he smiled at her and she caught hold of his beard and tugged his head from side to side.

'Get away with you – before I hold you to that.' He left her then because he knew she was going to weep and he didn't want to watch it.

The next morning Duff packed his gear under Sean's direction. He followed each instruction with a dazed obedience, answering when Sean spoke but otherwise withdrawn in a protective shell of silence. When he had finished Sean made him pick up his bags and marched him down to where the horses waited in the chill gloom of not-yet day. With the horses were men, four shapes in the darkness. Sean hesitated before going out into the yard.

'Mbejane,' he called. 'Who are these with you?'

They came forward into the light that poured through the doorway and Sean chuckled.

'Hlubi, of the noble belly! Nonga! And is it you, Kandhla?' Men who had worked beside him in the trenches of the Candy Deep, had plied the spades that had uncovered his fortune, had plied the spears that protected it from the first predators. Happy at his recognition of them, for it had been many years, they crowded forward smiling as widely and whitely as only a Zulu can.

'What brings you three rogues together so early in the day?' Sean asked, and Hlubi answered for them.

'Nkosi, we heard talk of a trek and our feet burned, we heard talk of hunting and we could not sleep.'

'There is no money for wages,' Sean spoke gruffly to cover the sudden rush of affection he felt for them.

'We made no talk of wages,' Hlubi answered with dignity. Sean nodded, it was the reply he had expected. He cleared his throat and went on.

'You would come with me when you know that I have the Tagathi on me?' He used the Zulu word for witchcraft. 'You would follow me knowing that behind me I leave a spoor of dead men and sorrow?'

'Nkosi,' Hlubi was grave as he answered. 'Something always dies when the lion feeds – and yet there is meat for those that follow him.'

'I hear the chatter of old women at a beer drink,' Mbejane observed drily. 'There is no more to say and the horses grow restless.'

They rode down the driveway of Xanadu between the jacaranda trees and the smooth wide lawns. Behind them the mansion was grey and unlighted in the half darkness. They took the Pretoria road, climbed to the ridge and checked their horses at the crest. Sean and Duff looked back across the valley. The valley was filled with early morning mist, and the mine headgears probed up out of it. They watched the mists turn to gold as the low sun touched them and a mine hooter howled dismally.

'Couldn't we stay for just a week longer – perhaps we could work something out?' Duff asked softly.

Sean sat silently staring at the golden mist. It was beautiful. It hid the scarred earth and it hid the mills – it was a most appropriate cloak for that evil, greedy city. Sean turned his horse away towards Pretoria and slapped the loose end of his reins across its neck.

THREE

The Wilderness

= 1 =

They stayed five days in Pretoria, just long enough to buy the wagons and commission them, and when they left on the morning of the sixth day they went north on the Hunters Road. The wagons moved in column urged on by the Zulus and a dozen new servants that Sean had hired. They were followed by a mixed bag of black and white urchins and stray dogs; men called good luck after them and women waved from the verandas of the houses which lined the road. Then the town was behind them and they were out into the veld with only a dozen of the more adventurous mongrels still following them.

They made fifteen miles the first day and when they camped that night beside the ford of a small stream, Sean's back and legs ached from his first full day in the saddle in over five years. They drank a little brandy and ate steaks grilled over wood embers, then they let the fire die and sat and looked at the night. The sky was a curtain at which a barrel of grape-shot had been fired, riddling it with the holes through which the stars shone. The voices of the servants made a hive murmur as a background to the wailing of a jackal in the darkness beyond the firelight. They went to their living wagon early and for Sean the feel of rough blankets instead of silk sheets and the hardness of a straw mattress were not sufficient to keep him long from sleep.

From an early start the following morning they put another twenty miles behind them before outspan that night and twenty more the next day. The push and urgent drive were habits Sean had acquired on the Rand when every minute was vital and the loss of a day was a disaster. They were habits that stuck, and he pushed the caravan northward as impatiently as he would have chivvied the men on the Candy Deep who were cutting a drive to intersect the Reef. Then one morning, when they were inspanning the oxen at the usual hour of dawn, Mbejane asked him, 'Do we go to meet someone, Nkosi?'

'No. Why do you ask?'

'When a man moves fast there is usually a reason. I was seeking the reason for our haste.'

'The reason is –' Sean stopped. He looked around him quickly as if to find it, then he cleared his throat and scratched the side of his nose, '– outspan an hour before high sun,' he finished abruptly and went to his horse. He and Duff rode out a mile or two ahead of the wagons that day, then instead of keeping to the track or hurrying back to chase up the caravan Sean suggested, 'Let's ride across to that kopje over there. We'll leave the horses at the bottom and climb up to the top.'

'What for?' asked Duff.

'For the hell of it – come on.'

They hobbled the horses and set off up the steep side of the kopje, picking their way over the tumbled boulders and through the tangle of tree trunks. They were sweating and blowing hard when they came out on the summit and found a place with shade and a flat rock ledge on which to sit. Sean gave Duff a cheroot and they smoked and looked out across the land that was spread like a map below them.

Here the grasslands of the high veld were starting to blend into the forests and hilly country of the bushveld. There were vleis open as wheatfields, ending suddenly against a hill or bounded by haphazard plantations of tall trees. From the height at which they sat they could trace the courses of underground rivers by the dark green and superior height of the trees that grew above them. Everything else was the colour of Africa – brown, a thousand different shades of brown. Pale brown grass on red brown soil, with twisted, chocolate-brown tree trunks reaching up to the moving masses of brown leaves at their tips. Flickering indefinite brown were the herds of springbok that fed amongst the trees and on the slopes of the bare bulging brown hills, and the brown land reached away vast and unhurried into immeasurable distance, unmarred by the scratchings of man: tranquil and dignified in its immensity.

'It makes me feel small, but sort of safe – as though no one will notice me here,' said Duff, then laughed self-consciously.

'I know what you mean,' Sean answered him. He saw that for the first time since they had left the Rand the strain was gone from Duff's face. They smiled at each other and leaned back against the rock face behind them. They watched their wagons, far below them, coil into the tight circle of the laager and the cattle turned free move out to graze. The sun sank and the shadows stretched out longer and longer across the land. At last they went down the hill and found their horses. That night they stayed later than usual next to the fire and though they talked little there was the old feeling between them again. They had discovered a new reef that was rich with the precious elements of space and time. Out here there was more of those two treasures than a man could use in a dozen lifetimes. Space to move, to ride or to fire a rifle; space spread with sunlight and wind, grass and trees, but not filled with them. There was also time. This was where time began: it was a quiet river, moving but not changed by movement; draw on it as much as you would and still it was always full. It was measured by the seasons but not restricted by them, for the summer that was now standing back to let autumn pass was the same summer that had flamed a thousand years before and would flame again a thousand years hence. In the presence of so much space and time all striving was futile.

From then on their lives took their tempo from the leisurely turning of wagon-wheels. Sean's eyes which had been pointing straight ahead along the line of travel now turned aside to look about him. Each morning he and Duff would leave the wagons and wander out into the bush. Sometimes they would spend the day panning for gold in the sands of a stream, another day they would search for the first signs of elephant, but mostly they just rode and talked or lay hidden and watched the herds of game that daily became more numerous. They killed just enough to feed themselves, their servants and the pack of dogs that had followed them when they left Pretoria. They passed the little Boer settlement at Pietersburg and then the Zoutpansberg climbed up over the horizon, its sheer sides dark with rain forest and high rock cliffs. Here under the mountains they spent a week at Louis Trichardt, the most northerly permanent habitation of white men.

In the town they spoke with men who had hunted to the north of the mountains, across the Limpopo. These were taciturn brown-faced Boers with tobacco-stained beards

– big men with the peace of the bush in their eyes. In their courteous, unhurried speech Sean sensed a fierce possessive love of the animals that they hunted and the land through which they moved so freely. They were a different breed from the Natal Afrikanders and those he had met on the Witwatersrand, and he conceived the respect for them that would grow stronger in the years ahead when he would have to fight them.

There was no way through the mountains, they told him, but wagons could pass around them. The western passage skirted the edge of the Kalahari desert and this was bad country where the wagon wheels sank into the sandy soil and the marches between water became successively longer. To the east there was good rich forest land, well watered and stocked with game: low country, hotter the nearer one went to the coast, but the true bushveld where a man could find elephant.

So Sean and Duff turned east and, holding the mountains always in sight at their left hand, they went down into the wilderness.

= 2 =

Within a week's trek they saw elephant sign: trees broken and stripped of their bark. Although it was months old – the trees already dried out – nevertheless Sean felt the thrill of it and that night spent an hour cleaning and oiling his rifles. The forest thickened until the wagons had to weave continually between the trunks of the trees. But there were clearings in the forest – open vleis filled with grass where buffalo grazed like herds of domestic cattle and white tick birds squawked about them. This country was well watered with streams as clear and merry as a Scottish trout stream, but the water was blood-warm and the banks thick with bush. Along the rivers, in the forest and in the open were the herds of game: impala twisting and leaping away at the first approach with their crumpled horns laid back, kudu with big ears and soft eyes, black sable antelope with white bellies and horns curved like a naval cutlass, zebra trotting with the dignity of fat ponies, while about them frolicked their companions, the gnu, waterbuck, nyala, roan antelope and – at last – elephant.

Sean and Mbejane were ranging a mile ahead of the wagons when they found the spoor. It was fresh, so fresh that sap still oozed from the mahoba-hoba tree where the bark had been prised loose with the tip of a tusk and then stripped off. The wood beneath was naked and white.

'Three bulls,' said Mbejane. 'One very big.'

'Wait here,' Sean spun his horse and galloped back to the column. Duff lay on the driver's seat of the first wagon rocking gently to its motion, his hat covering his face and his hands behind his head.

'Elephant! Duff,' Sean yelled. 'Not an hour ahead of us. Get saddled up, man!'

Duff was ready in five minutes. Mbejane was waiting for them; he had already worked the spoor a short distance and picked up the run of it and now he went away on it, They followed him, riding slowly side by side.

'You've hunted elephant before, laddie?' asked Duff.

'Never,' said Sean.

'Good grief!' Duff looked alarmed. 'I thought you were an expert. I think I'll go back and finish my sleep, you can call me when you've had a little more experience.'

'Don't worry,' Sean laughed with excitement. 'I know all about it; I was raised on elephant stories.'

'That sets my heart at ease,' Duff murmured sarcastically and Mbejane glanced over his shoulder at them, not trying to conceal his irritation.

'Nkosi, it is not wise to talk now for we will soon come up with them.'

So they went on in silence: passing a knee-high pile of yellow dung that looked like the contents of a coir mattress, following the oval pad marks in the dust and the trail of torn branches.

It was a good hunt, this first one. The small breeze held steadily into their faces and the spoor ran straight and hot. They closed in, each minute strengthening the certainty of the kill. Sean sat stiff and eager in the saddle with his rifle across his lap, his eyes restlessly moving over the frieze of bush ahead of him. Mbejane stopped suddenly and came back to Sean's stirrup.

'Here they halted for the first time. The sun is hot and they will rest but this place was not to their liking and they have moved on. We will find them soon now.'

'The bush becomes too thick,' Sean grunted; he eyed the untidy tangle of catbush into which the spoor had led them. 'We will leave the horses here with Hlubi and go in on foot.'

'Laddie,' Duff demurred. 'I can run much faster on horseback.'

'Off!' said Sean and nodded to Mbejane to lead. They moved forward again. Sean was sweating and the drops clung heavily to his eyebrows and trickled down his cheeks; he brushed them away. The excitement was an indigestible ball in his stomach and a dryness in his throat.

Duff sauntered casually next to Sean with that small half smile on his face, but there was a quickness in his breathing. Mbejane cautioned them with a gesture of his hand and they stopped. Minutes passed slowly and then Mbejane's hand moved again, pink-palmed eloquence.

'It was nothing,' said the hand. 'Follow me.'

They went on again. There were Mopani flies swarming at the corners of Sean's eyes, drinking the moisture, and he blinked them away. Their buzzing was so loud in his ears that he thought it must carry to their quarry. His every sense was tuned to its limit: hearing magnified, vision sharp and even his sense of smell so clear that he could pick up the taint of dust, the scent of a wild flower and Mbejane's faintly musky body-smell.

Suddenly in front of him Mbejane was still; his hand moved again gently, unmistakably.

'They are here,' said the hand.

Sean and Duff crouched behind him, searching with eyes that could see only brown bush and grey shadows. The tension coarsened their breathing and Duff was no longer smiling. Mbejane's hand came up slowly and pointed at the wall of vegetation in front of them. The seconds strung together like beads on the string of time and still they searched.

An ear flapped lazily and instantly the picture jumped into focus. Bull elephant, big and very close, grey among grey shadow. Sean touched Mbejane's arm. 'I had seen it,' said that touch.

Slowly Mbejane's hand swivelled and pointed again. Another wait, another searching and then a belly rumbled, a great grey belly filled with half-digested leaves. It was a sound so ridiculous in the silence that Sean wanted to laugh – a gurgling sloshy sound – and Sean saw the other bull. It was standing in shadow also, with long yellow ivory and small eyes tight-closed. Sean put his lips to Duff's ear.

'This one is yours,' he whispered. 'Wait until I get into position for the other,' and he began moving out to the side, each step exposing a little more of the second bull's flank until the shoulder was open to him and he could see the point of the elbow beneath the baggy, wrinkled skin. The angle was right; from here he could reach the heart. He nodded at Duff, brought his rifle up – leaning forward against the recoil, aiming close behind the massive shoulder – and he fired.

The gunfire was shockingly loud in the confined thorn bush; dust flew in a spurt from the bull's shoulder and it staggered from the strike of the bullet. Beyond it the third elephant burst from sleep into flight and Sean's hands moved neatly on his weapon, ejecting and reloading, swinging up and firing again. He saw the bullet hit and he knew it was a mortal wound. The two bulls ran together and the bush opened to them and swallowed them: they were gone, crashing away wounded, trumpeting in pain. Sean ran after them, dodging through the catbush, oblivious to the sting of the thorns that snatched at him as he passed.

'This way, Nkosi,' Mbejane shouted beside him. 'Quickly or we will lose them.' They sprinted after the sounds of flight – a hundred yards, two hundred, panting now and sweating in the heat. Suddenly the catbush ended and in front of them was a wide riverbed with steep banks. The river sand was blindingly white and in the middle was a sluggish trickle of water. One of the bulls was dead, lying in the stream with the blood washing off him in a pale brown stain. The other bull was trying to climb the far bank; it was too steep for him and he slid back wearily. The blood dripped from the tip of his trunk, and he swung his head to look at Sean and Mbejane. His ears cocked back defiantly and he began his charge, blundering towards them through the soft river sand.

Sean watched him come and there was sadness in him as he brought up his rifle, but it was the proud regret that a man feels when he watches hopeless courage. Sean killed with a brain shot, quickly.

They climbed down the bank into the riverbed and went to the elephant; it knelt with its legs folded under it and its tusks driven deep into the sand with the force of its fall. The flies were already clustering at the little red mouths of the bullet wounds. Mbejane touched one of the tusks and then he looked up at Sean.

'It is a good elephant.' He said no more, for this was not the time to talk. Sean leaned his rifle against the bull's shoulder; he felt in his top pocket for a cheroot and stood with it unlit between his teeth. He would kill more elephant, he knew, but always this would be the one he would remember. He stroked his hand over the rough skin and the bristles were stiff and sharp.

'Where is Nkosi Duff?' Sean remembered him suddenly. 'Did he also kill?'

'He did not shoot,' answered Mbejane.

'What!' Sean turned quickly to Mbejane. 'Why not?'

Mbejane sniffed a pinch of snuff and sneezed, then he shrugged his shoulders.

'It is a good elephant,' he said again, looking down at it.

'We must go back and find him.' Sean snatched up his rifle and Mbejane followed him.

They found Duff sitting alone in the catbush with his rifle propped beside him and a water-bottle to his lips. He lowered the bottle as Sean came up and saluted him with it.

'Hail! the conquering hero comes.' There was something in his eyes that Sean could not read.

'Did you miss yours?' Sean asked.

'Yes,' said Duff, 'I missed mine.' He lifted the bottle and drank again. Suddenly and sickeningly Sean was ashamed for him. He dropped his eyes, not wanting to acknowledge Duff's cowardice.

'Let's get back to the wagons,' he said. 'Mbejane can come with packhorses for the tusks.'

They did not ride together on the way home.

= 3 =

It was almost dark when they arrived back at the laager. They gave their horses to one of the servants and washed in the basin that Kandhla had ready for them, then they went to sit by the fire. Sean poured the drinks, fussing over the glasses to avoid looking at Duff. He felt awkward. They'd have to talk about it and he searched his brain for a way to bring it into the open. Duff had shown craven and Sean started to find excuses for him – he may have had a misfire or he may have been unsighted by Sean's shot. At all events Sean determined not to let it stay like this, sour and brooding between them. They'd talk it out then forget it. He carried Duff's glass to him and smiled at him.

'That's right, try and cover it with a grin,' Duff lifted his glass. 'To our big brave hunter. Dammit, laddie, how could you do it?'

Sean stared at Duff. 'What do you mean?'

'You know what I mean, you're so damned guilty you can't even look me in the face. How could you kill those bloody great animals – but even worse how could you *enjoy* doing it?'

Sean subsided weakly into his chair. He couldn't tell which of his emotions was uppermost – relief or surprise. Duff went on quickly.

'I know what you're going to say, I've heard the arguments before – from my dear father. He explained it to me one evening after we'd ridden down a fox. When I say "we", I mean twenty horsemen and forty hounds.'

Sean had not yet rallied from the shock of finding himself in the dock after preparing himself to play the role of prosecutor.

'Don't you like hunting?' he asked incredulously. The way he might have asked, 'don't you like eating?'.

'I'd forgotten what it was like. I was carried away by your exitement, but when you started to kill them it all came back to me.' Duff sipped his brandy and stared into the fire. 'They never had a chance. One minute they were sleeping and the next you were ripping them with bullets the way the hounds ripped that fox. They didn't have a chance.'

'But, Duff, it wasn't meant to be a contest.'

'Yes, I know, my father explained that to me. It's a ritual – a sacred rite to Diana. He should have explained it to the fox as well.'

Sean was getting angry now. 'We came out here to hunt ivory – and that's what I'm doing.'

'Tell me that you killed those elephant only for their teeth, laddie, and I'll call you a liar. You loved it. Christ! You should have seen your face and the face of your damned heathen.'

'All right! I like hunting and the only other man I ever met who didn't was a coward,' Sean shouted at him.

Duff's face paled and he looked up at Sean. 'What are you trying to say?' he whispered. They stared at each other and in the silence Sean had to choose between letting his temper run or keeping Duff's friendship, for the words that would spoil it for ever were crowding into his mouth. He made his hands relax their grip on the arms of his chair.

'I didn't mean that,' he said.

'I hoped you didn't,' Duff's grin came precariously back onto his face. 'Tell me why you like hunting, laddie. I'll try and understand but don't expect me to hunt with you again.'

It was like explaining colour to a blind man, describing the lust of the hunter to someone who was born without it. Duff listened in agonized silence as Sean tried to find the words for the excitement that makes a man's blood sing through his body, that heightens his senses and allows him to lose himself in an emotion as old as the urge to mate. Sean tried to show him how the nobler and more beautiful was the quarry, the stronger was the compulsion to hunt and kill it, that it had no conscious cruelty in it but was rather an expression of love: a fierce possessive love. A devouring love that needed the complete and irrevocable act of death for its consummation. By destroying something, a man could have it always as his own: selfish perhaps, but then instinct knows no ethics. It was all very clear to Sean, so much a part of him that he had never tried to voice it before and now he stumbled over the words, gesticulating in helpless inarticulateness, repeating himself, coming at last to the end and knowing by the look on Duff's face that he had failed to show it to him.

'And you were the gentleman who fought Hradsky for the rights of man,' Duff said softly, 'the one who always talked about not hurting people.'

Sean opened his mouth to protest but Duff went on. 'You get ivory for us and I'll look for gold – each of us to what he is best suited. I'll forgive you your elephants as you forgave me my Candy – still equal partners. Agreed?'

Sean nodded and Duff held up his glass.

'It's empty,' he said. 'Do me a favour, laddie.'

4

There was never any after-taste to their disputes, no rankling of unspoken words or lingering of doubt. What they had in common they enjoyed, where there were differences they accepted them. So when after each hunt the packhorses brought the tusks into the camp there was no trace of censure in Duff's face or voice; there was only the genuine pleasure of having Sean back from the bush. Sometimes it was a good day and Sean would cut the spoor, follow, kill and be back in the laager the same night. But more often, when the herd was moving fast or the ground was hard or he could not kill at the first approach, he would be gone for a week or more. Each time he returned they celebrated, drinking and laughing far into the night, lying late in bed the next morning, playing Klabejas on the floor of the wagon between their cots or reading aloud out of the books that Duff had brought with him from Pretoria. Then a day or two later Sean would be gone again, with his dogs and his gunboys trotting behind him.

This was a different Sean from the one who had whored it up at the Opera House and presided over the panelled offices in Eloff Street. His beard, no longer groomed and shaped by a barber, curled onto his chest. The doughy colour of his face and arms had been turned by the sun to the rich brown of a newly-baked loaf. The seat of his pants that had been stretched to danger point across his rump now hung loosely; his arms were thicker and the soft swell of fat had given way to the flatness and bulge of hard muscle. He walked straighter, moved quicker and laughed more easily.

In Duff the change was less noticeable. He was lean and gaunt-faced as ever, but now there was less of the restlessness in his eyes. His speech and movements were slower and the golden beard he was growing had the strange effect of making him appear younger. Each morning he left the wagons, taking one of the servant's with him, and spent the days wandering in the bush, tapping with his prospecting hammer at the occasional outcrops of rock or squatting beside a stream and spinning the gravel in his pan. Every evening he came back to camp and analysed the bag of rock samples he had collected during the day; then he threw them away, bathed and set out a bottle and two glasses on the table beside the fire. While he ate his supper he listened and waited for the dogs to bark, for the sound of horses in the darkness and Sean's voice. If the night remained silent he put the bottle away and climbed up into his wagon. He was lonely then, not with a deep loneliness but just enough to add relish to Sean's return.

Always they moved east, until gradually the silhouette of the Zoutpansberg softened as the mountains became less steep and began to fade into the tail of the range. Scouting along their edge Sean found a pass and they took the wagons up and over and down into the Limpopo valley beyond. Here the country changed character again; it became flat, the monotony of thorn scrub relieved only by the baobab trees with their great, swollen trunks crowned in a little halo of branches. Water was scarce and Sean rode ahead from each camp to find the next waterhole before they moved. However, the hunting was good for the game was concentrated on the isolated drinking places, and before they were halfway from the mountains to the Limpopo Sean had filled another wagon with ivory.

'We'll be coming back this way, I suppose?' Duff asked.

'I suppose so,' agreed Sean.

'Well then, I don't see any point in carrying a ton of ivory with us. Let's bury it and we can pick it up on our way back.'

Sean looked at him thoughtfully. 'About once in every year you come up with a good idea – we'll do exactly that.'

The next camp was a good one. There was water – an acre of muddy liquid not as heavily salted with elephant urine as some of the previous ones had been; there was shade provided by a grove of wild fig trees and the grazing was of a quality that promised to restore the condition that the oxen had lost since crossing the mountains. They decided to make it a rest camp: bury the ivory, do some repairs and maintenance on the wagons and let the servants and animals fatten up a little. The first task was to dig a hole large enough to contain all the hundred-odd tusks they had accumulated and it was evening on the third day before they finished.

5

Sean and Duff sat together inside the laager and watched the sun go down, bleeding below the land, and after it had gone the clouds were oyster and lilac-coloured in the brief twilight. Kandhla threw wood on the fire and it burnt up fiercely. They ate grilled kudu liver, and thick steaks with a rind of yellow fat on them, and they drank brandy with their coffee. The conversation lagged into contented silence for they were both tired. They sat staring into the fire, too lazy to make the effort required for bed. Sean watched the fire pictures form in the coals, the faces and the phantoms flickering and fading. He saw a tiny temple have its columns pulled out from under it by a fiery Samson and collapse in a shower of sparks – a burning horse changed magically into a dragon of blue flame. He looked away to rest his eyes and when he turned back there was a small black scorpion scuttling out from under the loose bark on one of the logs. It lifted its tail like the arm of a flamenco dancer and the flames that ringed it shone on its glossy body armour. Duff was also watching it, leaning forward with his elbows on his knees.

'Will he sting himself to death before the flames reach him?' he asked softly. 'I have heard that they do.'

'No,' said Sean.

'Why not?'

'Only man has the intelligence to end the inevitable; in all other creatures the instinct of survival is too strong,' Sean answered him, and the scorpion crabbed sideways from the nearest flames and stopped again with its raised sting jerking slightly. 'Besides he's immune to his own poison so he has no choice.'

'He could jump down into the fire and get it over with,' murmured Duff, subdued by the little tragedy.

The scorpion started its last desperate circuit of the closing ring. Its tail drooped and the grip of its claws was unsteady on the rough bark; it was shrivelling with the heat, its legs curling up and its tail subsiding. The flames caressed it with swift yellow hands and smeared its shiny body with the dullness of death. The log tipped sideways and the speck was gone.

'Would you?' asked Sean. 'Would you have jumped?'

Duff sighed softly, 'I don't know,' he said and stood up. 'I'm going to pump out my bilges and crawl into bed.' He walked away and went to stand at the edge of the circle of firelight.

Since they had left Pretoria the small voices of the jackals had yapped discreetly around each outspan – they were so much a part of the African night that they went unnoticed – but now suddenly there was a difference. Only one jackal spoke, and with a voice that stammered shrilly – a sound of pain, a crazy hysterical shrieking that made Sean's skin prickle. He scrambled to his feet and stood staring undecided into the darkness. The jackal was coming towards the camp, coming fast – and suddenly Sean knew what was happening.

'Duff!' he called. 'Come back here! Run, man, run!'

Duff looked back at Sean helplessly, his hands held low in front of him and his water arcing down, curving silver in the firelight from his body to the ground.

'Duff!' Sean's voice was a shout. 'It's a rabid jackal. Run, damn you, run!' The jackal was close now, very close, but at last Duff started to move. He was halfway back to the fire before he tripped. He fell and rolled over and brought his feet up under his body to rise. His head turned to face the darkness from which it would come. Then Sean saw it. It flitted out of the shadows like a grey moth in the bad light and went straight for where Duff knelt. Sean saw him try to cover his face with his hands as the jackal sprang at him. One of the dogs twisted out of Mbejane's hand and brushed past Sean's legs. Sean snatched up a piece of firewood and sprinted after it, but already Duff was on his back, his arms flailing frantically as he tried to push away the terrier-sized animal that was slashing at his face and hands. The dog caught it and dragged it off, worrying it, growling through locked jaws. Sean hit the jackal with the club – breaking its back. He swung again and again, beating its body, into shapelessness before he turned to Duff. Duff was on his feet now. He had unwound the scarf from his neck and was mopping with it at his face but the blood dribbled down his chin and blotched the front of his shirt. His hands were trembling. Sean led him close to the fire, pulled Duff's hands down and examined the bites. His nose was torn and the flesh of one cheek hung open in a flap.

'Sit down!'

Duff obeyed, holding the scarf to his face again. Sean went quickly to the fire: with a stick he raked embers into a pile, then he drew his hunting-knife and thrust the blade into the coals.

'Mbejane,' he called, without taking his eyes off the knife. 'Throw that jackal onto the fire. Put on plenty of wood. Do not touch its body with your hands. When you have done that tie up that dog and keep the others away from it.' Sean turned the knife in the fire. 'Duff, drink as much of that brandy as you can.'

'What are you going to do?'

'You know what I've got to do.'

'He bit my wrist as well.' Duff held up his hand for Sean to see the punctures, black holes from which the blood oozed watery and slow.

'Drink.' Sean pointed at the brandy bottle. For a second they looked at each other and Sean saw the horror moving in Duff's eyes: horror of the hot knife and horror of the germs which had been injected into him. The germs that must be burnt out before they escaped into his blood, to breed and ferment there until they ate into his brain and rode him to a screaming, gibbering death.

'Drink,' said Sean again. Duff took up the bottle and lifted it to his mouth. Sean stooped and pulled the knife out of the fire. He held the blade an inch from the back of his hand. It was not hot enough. He thrust it back into the coals.

'Mbejane, Hlubi, stand on each side of the Nkosi's chair. Be ready to hold him.' Sean loosened his belt, doubled the thick leather and handed it to Duff. 'Bite on this.'

He turned back to the fire and this time when he drew the knife its blade was pale pink. 'Are you ready?'

'The work you are about to do will break the hearts of a million maids.' A last hoarse attempt at humour from Duff.

'Hold him,' said Sean.

Duff gasped at the touch of the knife – a great shuddering gasp – and his back arched, but the two Zulus held him down remorselessly. The edges of the wound blackened and hissed as Sean ran the blade in deeper. The stink of burning brought the vomit into his throat. He clenched his teeth. When he stepped back Duff hung slackly in the Zulus' hands, sweat had soaked his shirt and wet his hair. Sean heated the knife again and cleaned the bites in Duff's wrist while Duff moaned and writhed weakly in the chair. He smeared axle grease over the burns and bandaged the wrist loosely with strips torn from a clean shirt. They lifted Duff into the wagon and laid him on his cot. Sean went out to where Mbejane had tied the dog. He found scratches beneath the hair on its shoulder. They put a sack over its head to stop it biting and Sean cauterized its wounds also.

'Tie it to the far wagon, do not let the other dogs near it, see it has food and water,' he told Mbejane.

Then he went back to Duff. Delirious with pain and brandy Duff did not sleep at all that night and Sean stayed by his cot until the morning.

= 6 =

About fifty yards from the laager under one of the wild fig trees the servants built Duff a hut. The framework was of poles and over it they stretched a tarpaulin. They made a bed for him and brought his mattress and blankets from the wagon. Sean joined four trekchains together, forging new links and hammering them closed. He passed one end of the chain round the base of the fig tree and riveted it back up on itself. Duff sat in the shade of a wagon and watched them work. His hurt hand was in a sling and his face was swollen, the wound crusty-looking and edged in angry red. When he was finished with the chain, Sean walked across to him.

'I'm sorry, Duff, we have to do it.'

'They abolished the slave trade some time ago – just in case you didn't know.' Duff tried to grin with his distorted face. He stood up and followed Sean to the hut. Sean looped the loose end of the chain round Duff's waist. He locked it with a bolt through two of the links then flattened the end of the bolt with a dozen strokes of the hammer.

'That should hold you.'

'An excellent fit,' Duff commended him. 'Now let us inspect my new quarters.'

Sean followed him into the hut. Duff lay down on the bed. He looked very tired and sick.

'How long will it take before we know?' he asked quietly.

Sean shook his head. 'I'm not sure. I think you should stay here at least a month – after that we'll allow you back into society.'

'A month – it's going to be fun. Lying here expecting any minute to start barking like a dog and lifting my leg against the nearest tree.'

Sean didn't laugh. 'I did a thorough job with the knife. It's a thousand to one you'll be all right. This is just a precaution.'

'The odds are attractive – I'll put a fiver on it.' Duff crossed his ankles and stared up at the roof. Sean sat down on the edge of the bed. It was a long time before Duff ended the silence.

'What will it be like, Sean, have you ever seen someone with rabies?'

'No.'

'But you've heard about it, haven't you? Tell me what you've heard about it,' Duff persisted.

'For Chrissake, Duff, you're not going to get it.'

'Tell me, Sean, tell me what you know about it.' Duff sat up and caught hold of Sean's arm.

Sean looked steadily at him for a moment before he answered. 'You saw that jackal, didn't you?'

Duff sank back onto his pillows. 'Oh, my God!' he whispered.

Together they started the long wait. They used another tarpaulin to make an open shelter next to the hut and under it they spent the days that followed.

In the beginning it was very bad. Sean tried to pull Duff out of the black despair into which he had slumped, but Duff sat for hours at a time gazing out into the bush, fingering the scabs on his face and only occasionally smiling at the banquet of choice stories that Sean spread for him. But at last Sean's efforts were rewarded – Duff began to talk. He spoke of things he had never mentioned before and listening to him Sean learned more about him than he had in the previous five years. Sometimes Duff paced up and down in front of Sean's chair with the chain hanging down behind him like a tail; at other times he sat quietly, his voice filled with longing for the mother he had never known.

' – there was a portrait of her in the upper gallery, I used to spend whole afternoons in front of it. It was the kindest face I had ever seen –'

Then it hardened again as he remembered his father, 'that old bastard'.

He talked of his daughter. '– she had a fat chuckle that would break your heart. The snow on her grave made it look like a big sugar-iced cake, she would have liked that –'

At other times his voice was puzzled as he examined some past action of his, angry as he remembered a mistake or a missed opportunity. Then he would break off and grin self-consciously. 'I say, I am talking a lot of drivel.'

The scabs on his face began to dry up and come away, and more often now his old gaiety bubbled to the surface.

On one of the poles that supported the tarpaulin roof he started a calendar, cutting a notch for each day. It became a daily ceremony. He cut each notch with the concentration of a sculptor carving marble and when he had finished he would stand back and count them aloud as if by doing so he could force them to add up to thirty, the number that would allow him to shed his chain.

There were eighteen notches on the pole when the dog went mad. It was in the afternoon. They were playing Klabejas. Sean had just dealt the cards when the dog started screaming from among the wagons. Sean knocked over his chair as he jumped up. He snatched his rifle from where it leant against the wall and ran down to the laager. He disappeared behind the wagon to which the dog was tied and almost immediately Duff heard the shot. In the abrupt and complete stillness that followed, Duff slowly lowered his face into his hands.

It was nearly an hour before Sean came back. He picked up his chair, set it to the table and sat down.

'It's you to call – are you going to take on?' he asked as he picked up his cards. They played with grim intensity, fixing their attention on the cards, but both of them knew that there was a third person at the table now.

'Promise you'll never do that to me,' Duff blurted out at last.

Sean looked up at him. 'That I'll never do what to you?'

'What you did to that dog.'

The dog! The bloody dog. He should never have taken a chance with it, he should have destroyed it that first night,

'Just because the dog got it doesn't mean that you – '

'Swear to me,' Duff interrupted fiercely, 'swear you won't bring the rifle to me.'

'Duff, you don't know what you're asking. Once you've got it – ' Sean stopped; anything he said would make it worse.

'Promise me,' Duff repeated.

'All right, I swear it then.'

7

It was worse now than it had been in the beginning. Duff abandoned his calendar and with it the hope that had been slowly growing stronger. If the days were bad then the nights were hell, for Duff had a dream. It came to him every night – sometimes two or three times. He tried to keep awake after Sean had left, reading by the light of a lantern; or he lay and listened to the night noises, the splash and snort of buffalo drinking down at the waterhole, the liquid half-warble of night birds or the deep drumming of a lion. But in the end he would have to sleep and then he dreamed.

He was on horseback riding across a flat brown plain: no hills, no trees, nothing but lawnlike grass stretching away on all sides to the horizon. His horse threw no shadow – he always looked for a shadow and it worried him that there never was one. Then he would find the pool – clear water, blue and strangely shiny. The pool frightened him but he could not stop himself going to it. He would kneel beside it and look into the water; the reflection of his own face looked up at him – animal-snouted, shaggy-brown with wolf teeth, white and long. He would wake then and the horror of that face would last until morning.

Nearly desperate with his own utter helplessness, Sean tried to help him. Because of the accord they had established over the years and because they were so close to each other, Sean had to suffer with him. He tried to shut himself off from it; sometimes he succeeded for an hour or even half a morning, but then it came back with a stomach-swooping shock. Duff was going to die – Duff was going to die an unspeakable death. Was it a mistake to let someone get too deep inside you, so that you must share his agony in every excruciating detail? Didn't a man have enough of his own that he must share the full measure of another's suffering?

By then the October winds had started, the heralds of the rain: hot winds full of dust, winds that dried the sweat on a man's body before it had time to cool him, thirsty winds that during daylight brought the game to the waterhole in full view of the camp.

Sean had half a case of wine hoarded under his cot. That last evening he cooled four bottles, wrapping them in wet sacking. He took them up to Duff's shelter just before supper and set them on the table. Duff watched him. The scars on his face were almost completely healed now, glassy red marks on his pale skin.

'Chateau Olivier,' said Sean and Duff nodded.

'It's a good wine – most probably travel-sick.'

'Well, if you don't want it, I'll take it away again,' said Sean.

'I'm sorry, laddie,' Duff spoke quickly. 'I didn't mean to be ungrateful. This wine suits my mood tonight. Did you know that wine is a sad drink?'

'Nonsense!' Sean disagreed as he twisted the corkscrew into the first cork. 'Wine is gay.' He poured a little into Duff's glass and Duff picked it up and held it towards the fire so the light shone through it.

'You see only the surface, Sean. A good wine has the elements of tragedy within it. The better the wine the more sad it is.'

Sean snorted. 'Explain yourself,' he invited.

Duff put his glass down on the table again and stared at it. 'How long do you suppose this wine has taken to reach its present perfection?'

'Ten or fifteen years, I suppose,' Sean answered.

Duff nodded. 'And now all that remains is to drink it – the work of years destroyed in an instant. Don't you think that is sad?' Duff asked softly.

'My God, Duff, don't be so damned morbid.'

But Duff wasn't listening to him. 'Wine and mankind have this in common. They can find perfection only in age, in a lifetime of seeking. Yet in the finding they find also their own destruction.'

'So you think that if a man lives long enough he will reach perfection?' Sean challenged him, and Duff answered him still staring at the glass.

'Some grapes grew in the wrong soil, some were diseased before they went to the press and some were spoiled by a careless vintner – not all grapes make good wine.' Duff picked up his glass and tasted from it, then he went on. 'A man takes longer and he must find it not within the quiet confines of the cask but in the cauldron of life; therefore his is the greater tragedy.'

'Yes, but no one can live for ever,' Sean protested.

'So you think that makes it less sad?' Duff shook his head. 'You're wrong, of course. It does not detract from it, it enhances it. If only there were some escape, some way of ensuring that what is good could endure instead of this complete hopelessness.'

Duff lay back in his chair, his face pale and gaunt-looking. 'Even that I could accept, if only they had given me more time.'

'I've had enough of this talk. Let's discuss something else. I don't know what you're worrying about. You're not fit to drink yet, you've got another twenty or thirty years to go,' Sean said gruffly and Duff looked up at him for the first time.

'Have I, Sean?'

Sean couldn't meet his eyes. He knew Duff was going to die. Duff grinned his lopsided grin and looked down again at his glass. Slowly the grin disappeared and he spoke again.

'If only I had more time, I could have done it. I could have found the weak places and fortified them. I could have seen the answers.' His voice rose higher. 'I could have! I know I could have! Oh God, I'm not ready yet. I need more time.' His voice was shrill and his eyes wild and haunted. 'It's too soon – it's too soon!'

Sean couldn't stand it, he jumped up and caught Duff's shoulders and shook him.

'Shut up, God damn you, shut up,' he shouted at him. Duff was panting, his lips were parted and quivering. He touched them with the tips of his fingers as though to stop them.

'I'm sorry, laddie, I didn't mean to let go like that.' Sean dropped his hands from Duff's shoulders.

'Both of us are too damned edgy,' he said. 'It's going to be all right, you wait and see.'

'Yes – it will be all right.' Duff ran his fingers through his hair, combing it back from his eyes. 'Open another bottle, laddie.'

8

That night after Sean had gone to bed, Duff had his dream again. The wine he had drunk slowed him down and prevented him from waking. He was trapped in his fancy, struggling to escape into wakefulness but only reaching the surface before he sank back to dream that dream again.

Sean went up to Duff's shelter the next morning early. Although the night's coolness still lingered under the spreading branches of the wild figs the rising day promised to blow dry and burn hot. The animals could sense it. The trek oxen were clustered among the trees and a small herd of eland was moving from the waterhole. The bull, with his short thick horns and the dark tuft on his forehead, was leading his cows away to find shade. Sean stood in the doorway of the hut and waited while his eyes adjusted themselves to its gloom. Duff was awake.

'Get out of bed or you'll have bed sores to add to your happiness.'

Duff swung his feet off the litter and groaned.

'What did you put in that wine last night?' He massaged his temples gently. 'I've got a hundred hobgoblins doing a Cossack dance around the roof of my skull.'

Sean felt the first twinge of alarm. He put his hand on Duff's shoulder feeling for the heat of fever, but Duff was quite cool. He relaxed.

'Breakfast's ready,' said Sean. Duff played with his porridge and barely tasted the grilled eland liver. He kept screwing his eyes up against the glare of the sun and when they had finished their coffee he pushed back his chair.

'I'm going to take my tender head to bed.'

'All right.' Sean stood up as well. 'We're a bit short of meat. I'll go and see if I can get a buck.'

'No, stay and talk to me,' Duff said quickly. 'We can have a few hands of cards.'

They hadn't played in days and Sean agreed readily. He sat on the end of Duff's bed and within half an hour he had won thirty-two pounds from him.

'You must let me teach you this game sometime,' he gloated.

Petulantly, Duff threw his hand in. 'I don't feel like playing any more.' He pressed his fingers to his closed eyelids. 'I can't concentrate with this headache.'

'Do you want to sleep?' Sean gathered up the cards and put them in their box.

'No. Why don't you read to me?'

Duff picked up a leather-bound copy of *Bleak House* from the table beside the bed and tossed it into Sean's lap.

'Where shall I start?' Sean asked.

'It doesn't matter, I know it almost by heart.' Duff lay back and closed his eyes. 'Start anywhere.'

Sean read aloud. He stumbled on for half an hour with his tongue never quite catching the rhythm of the words. Once or twice he glanced up at Duff, but Duff lay still with a faint sheen of sweat on his face and the scars very noticeable. He was breathing easily. Dickens is a powerful sleeping-draught for a hot morning and Sean's eyelids sagged down and his voice slowed and finally stopped. The book slid off his lap.

The small tinkle of Duff's chain disturbed him; he awoke and looked at the bed. Duff crouched apelike. The madness was a fire in his eyes and his cheeks twitched. A yellowish froth coated his teeth and formed a thin line of scum along his lips.

'Duff – ' Sean said, and Duff lunged at him with fingers hooked and a noise in his throat that was not human nor yet animal. It was a sound that jellied Sean's stomach and took the strength from his legs.

'Don't!' screamed Sean, and the chain caught on one of the posts of the bed, jerking Duff back sprawling onto the bed before he could sink his teeth into Sean's paralysed body.

Sean ran. He ran out of the hut and into the bush. He ran with terror trembling in his legs and choking his breath. He ran with his heart taking its beat from his racing feet and his lungs pumping in disordered panic. A branch ripped across his cheek and the sting of it served to steady him. His feet slowed – he stopped and stood gasping, staring back towards the camp. He waited while his body settled and he forced his terror down until it was only a sickening sensation in his stomach. Then he circled through the thorn bush and approached the laager from the side farthest away from Duff's shelter. The camp was empty, the servants had fled in the same terror that had driven Sean. He remembered that his rifle was still in the hut beside Duff's bed. He slipped into his wagon and quickly opened the case of unused rifles. His hands were unsteady again as he fumbled with the locks, for the chain might have parted and at every second he expected to hear that inhuman sound behind him. He found his bandolier hanging on the end of his cot and he took cartridges from it. He loaded the rifle and cocked it. The weight of steel and wood in his hands gave him comfort. It made him a man again.

He jumped down out of the wagon and with the rifle held ready he went cautiously out of the circle of wagons. The chain had held. Duff stood in the shade of the wild fig plucking at it. He was making a sound like a new-born puppy. His back was turned to Sean and he was naked, his torn clothing scattered about him. Sean walked slowly towards him. He stopped outside the reach of the chain.

'Duff!' Sean called uncertainly. Duff spun and crouched, the froth was thick in his golden beard; he looked at Sean and his teeth bared. Then he charged screaming until the chain caught him and threw him onto his back once more. He scrambled to his feet and fought the chain, his eyes fastened hungrily on Sean. Sean backed away. He brought up the rifle and aimed between Duff's eyes.

Swear to me. Swear to me you won't bring the rifle to me.

Sean's aim wavered. He kept moving backwards. Duff was bleeding now. The steel links had smeared the skin off his hips, but still he pulled against them fighting to get at Sean – and Sean was shackled just as effectively by his promise. He could not end it. He lowered the rifle and watched in impotent pity.

Mbejane came to him at last.

'Come away, Nkosi. If you will not end it, come away. He no longer has need of you. The sight of you inflames him.'

Duff still struggled and screamed against his chain. From his torn waist the blood trickled down and clung in the hair of his legs with the stickiness of molten chocolate. With each jerk of his head the froth sprayed from his mouth and splattered his chest and arms.

Mbejane led Sean back into the laager. The other servants were there and Sean roused himself to give orders.

'I want everyone away from here. Take blankets and food – go camp on the far side of the water. I will send for you when it is over.' He waited until they had gathered their belongings and as they were leaving he called Mbejane back. 'What must I do?' he asked.

'If a horse breaks a leg?' Mbejane answered him with a question.

'I gave him my word,' Sean shook his head desperately, still facing towards the sound of Duff's raving.

'Only a rogue and a brave man can break an oath,' Mbejane answered simply. 'We will wait for you.' He turned and followed the others. When they were gone Sean hid in one of the wagons and through a tear in the canvas he watched Duff. He saw the idiotic shaking of his head, the curious shambling gait as he moved around the circle of the chain. He watched when the pain made him roll on the ground and claw at his head, tearing out tufts of hair and leaving long scratches down his face. He listened to the sounds of insanity: the bewildered bellows of pain, the senseless giggling and that growl, that terrible growl.

A dozen times he sighted along the rifle barrel, holding his aim until the sweat ran into his eyes and blurred them and he had to take the butt from his shoulder and turn away.

Out there on the end of the chain, its exposed flesh reddening in the sun a piece of Sean was dying. Some of his youth, some of his laughter, some of his carefree love of life – so he had to creep back to the hole in the canvas and watch.

The sun reached its peak and started down again and the thing on the chain grew weaker. It fell and was a long time crawling on its hands and knees before it regained its feet again.

An hour before sunset Duff had his first convulsion. He was standing facing Sean's wagon, swinging his head from side to side, his mouth working silently. The convulsion took him and he stiffened; his lips pulled up grinning, showing his teeth, his eyes rolled back and disappeared leaving only the whites, and his body started to bend backwards. That beautiful body, still slim as a boy's with the long moulded legs, bending tighter and tighter until with a brittle crack the spine snapped and he fell. He lay wriggling, moaning softly and his trunk was twisted at an impossible angle from the broken spine.

Sean jumped from the wagon and ran to him: standing over him he shot Duff in the head and turned away. He flung his rifle from him and heard it clatter on the hard earth. He walked back to his wagon and took a blanket off Duff's cot. He came back and wrapped Duff in it, averting his eyes from the mutilated head. He carried him to the shelter and laid him on the bed. The blood soaked through the blanket, spreading on the cloth, like ink spilled on blotting-paper. Sean sank down on the chair beside the bed.

Outside the darkness gathered and became complete. Once in the night a hyena came and snuffled at the blood outside on the earth, then it moved away. There was a pride of lions hunting in the bush beyond the waterhole; they killed two hours before dawn and Sean sat in the darkness and listened to their jubilant roaring.

In the morning, Sean stood up stiffly from his chair and went down to the wagons. Mbejane was waiting beside the fire in the laager.

'Where are the others?' Sean asked.

Mbejane stood up. 'They wait where you sent them. I came alone – knowing you would need me.'

'Yes,' said Sean. 'Get two axes from the wagon.'

They gathered wood, a mountain of dry wood, and packed it around Duff's bed – then Sean put fire to it. Mbejane saddled a horse for Sean and he mounted up and looked down at the Zulu.

'Bring the wagons on to the next waterhole. I will meet you there.'

Sean rode out of the laager. He looked back only once and saw that the breeze had spread the smoke from the pyre in a mile long smudge across the tops of the thorn trees.

9

Like a bag of pus at the root of an infected tooth the guilt and grief rotted in Sean's mind. His guilt was double-edged. He had betrayed Duff's trust, and he had lacked the courage to make the betrayal worthwhile. He had waited too long. He should have done it at the beginning, cleanly and quickly, or he should not have done it at all. He longed with every fibre of his body to be given the chance to do it again, but this time the right way. He would gladly have lived once more through all that horror to clear his conscience and clean the stain from the memory of their friendship.

His grief was a thing of emptiness, an aching void – so immense that he was lost in it. Where before there had been Duff's laughter, his twisted grin and his infectious zest there was now only a grey nothingness. No glimmer of sun penetrated it and there were no solid shapes in it.

The next waterhole was shallow soup in the centre of a flat expanse of dry mud the size of a polo field. The mud was cracked in an irregular chequered pattern forming small brickettes, each the size of a hand. A man could have jumped across the water without wetting his feet. Scattered thickly round its circumference were the droppings of the animals that had drunk there. Back and forth across its surface, changing direction as the wind veered, a few loose feathers sailed. The water was brackish and dirty. It was a bad camp. On the third day Mbejane went to Sean's wagon. Sean lay in his cot. He had not changed his clothes since leaving Duff. His beard was beginning to mat, sticky with sweat for it was hot as an oven under the wagon canvas.

'Nkosi, will you come and look at the water. I do not think we should stay here.'

'What is wrong with it?' Sean asked without interest.

'It is dirty, I think we should go on towards the big river.'

'Do whatever you think is right.' Sean rolled away from him, his face towards the side of the wagon.

So Mbejane took the wagon-train down towards the Limpopo. It was two days later that they found the ribbon of dark green trees that lined the banks. Sean stayed in his cot throughout the trek, jolting over the rough ground, sweating in the heat but oblivious to all discomfort. Mbejane put the wagons into laager on the bank above the riverbed, then he and all the other servants waited for Sean to come to life again. Their talk round the fire at nights was baited with worry and they looked often towards Sean's living wagon, where it stood unlit by lantern, dark as the mood of the man that lay within.

Like a bear coming out of its cave at the end of winter, Sean came out of the wagon at last. His clothes were filthy. The dogs hurried to meet him, crowding round his knees, begging for attention and he did not notice them. Vaguely he answered the greetings of his servants. He wandered down the bank into the river bed.

The summer had shrunk the Limpopo into a sparse line of pools strung out down the centre of the watercourse. The pools were dark olive green. The sand around them was white, glaring snowfield white, and the boulders that choked the barely moving river were black and polished smooth. The banks were steep, half a mile apart and walled in with trees. Sean walked through the sand, sinking to his ankles with each step. He reached the water and sat down at the edge, he dabbled his hand in it and found it warm as blood. In the sand next to him was the long slither mark of a crocodile, and a troop of monkeys were shaking the branches of a tree on the far bank and chattering at him. A pair of Sean's dogs splashed across the narrow neck between two pools and went off to chase the monkeys. They went half-heartedly with their tongues flapping at the corners of their mouths for it was very hot in the whiteness of the riverbed. Sean stared into the green water. It was lonely without Duff; he had only his guilt and his sorrow for company. One of the dogs that had stayed with him touched his cheek with its cold nose. Sean put his arm round its neck and the dog leaned against him. He heard footsteps in the sand behind him, he turned and looked up. It was Mbejane.

'Nkosi, Hlubi has found elephant not an hour's march up stream. He has counted twenty who show good ivory.'

Sean looked back at the water. 'Go away,' he said.

Mbejane squatted down beside him with his elbows on his knees. 'For whom do you mourn?' he asked.

'Go away, Mbejane, leave me alone.'

'Nkosi Duff does not need your sorrow – therefore I think that you mourn for yourself.' Mbejane picked up a pebble and tossed it into the pool.

'When a traveller gets a thorn in his foot,' Mbejane went on softly, 'and he is wise he plucks it out – and he is a fool who leaves it and says "I will keep this thorn to prick me so that I will always remember the road upon which I have travelled." Nkosi, it is better to remember with pleasure than with pain.' Mbejane lobbed another pebble into the pool, then he stood up and walked back to the camp. When Sean followed him ten minutes later he found a saddle on his horse, his rifle in the scabbard and Mbejane and Hlubi waiting with their spears. Kandhla handed him his hat, he held it by the brim, turning it in his hands. Then he clapped it onto his head and swung up onto the horse.

'Lead,' he ordered.

During the next weeks Sean hunted with a single-mindedness that left no time for brooding. His returns to the wagons were short and intermittent; his only reasons for returning at all were to bring in the ivory and change his horse. At the end of one of these brief visits to camp and as Sean was about to mount up for another hunt, even Mbejane complained. 'Nkosi, there are better ways to die than working too hard.'

'You look well enough,' Sean assured him, although Mbejane was now as lean as a greyhound and his skin shone like washed anthracite.

'Perhaps all men look healthy to a man on horseback,' Mbejane suggested and Sean stopped with one foot in the stirrup. He looked at Mbejane thoughtfully, then he lowered his leg again. 'We hunt on foot now, Mbejane, and the first to ask for mercy earns the right to be called "woman" by the other.'

Mbejane grinned; the challenge was to his liking. They crossed the river and found spoor before midday – a small herd of young bulls. They followed it until nightfall and slept huddled together under one blanket, then they went on again next morning. On the third day they lost the spoor in rocky ground and they cast back towards the river. They picked up another herd within ten miles of the wagons, went after them and killed that evening – three fine bulls, not a tusk between them under fifty pounds weight. A night march back to the wagons, four hours' sleep and they were away again. Sean was limping a little now and on the second day out, during one of their infrequent halts, he pulled off his boot. The blister on his heel had burst and his sock was stiff with dried blood. Mbejane looked at him expressionlessly. 'How far are we from the wagons?' asked Sean.

'We can be back before dark, Nkosi.' Mbejane carried Sean's rifle for him on the return. Not once did his mask of solemnity slip. Back in camp Kandhla brought a basin of hot water and set it in front of Sean's chair. While Sean soaked his feet in it his entire following squatted in a circle about him. Every face wore an expression of studied concern and the silence was broken only by the clucking sounds of Bantu sympathy. They were loving every minute of it and Mbejane with the timing of a natural actor was building up the effect, playing to his audience. Sean puffed at a cheroot, scowling to stop himself laughing. Mbejane cleared his throat and spat into the fire. Every eye was on him; they waited breathlessly.

'Nkosi,' said Mbejane, 'I would set fifty head of oxen as your marriage price – if you were my daughter.'

One instant more of silence, then a shout of laughter. Sean laughed with them at first, but after a while when Hlubi had nearly staggered into the fire and Nonga was sobbing loudly on Mbejane's shoulder with tears of mirth streaming down his cheeks, Sean's own laughter stopped. It wasn't *that* funny.

He looked at them sourly – at their wide open pink mouths and their white teeth, at their shaking shoulders and heaving chests and suddenly it came to him very clearly that they were no longer laughing at him. They were laughing for the joy of it. They were laughing because they were alive. A chuckle rattled up Sean's throat and escaped before he could stop it, another one bounced around inside his chest and he lay back in his chair, opened his mouth and let it come. The hell with it, he was alive, too.

In the morning when he climbed out of his wagon and limped across to see what Kandhla was cooking for breakfast, there was a faint excitement in him again, the excitement of a new day. He felt good. Duff's memory was still with him, it always would be, but now it was not a sickening ache. He had plucked out the thorn.

= 10 =

They moved camp three times in November, keeping to the south bank of the river, following it back towards the west. Slowly the wagons which they had emptied of ivory beside the waterhole began to fill again, for the game was concentrated along the river. The rest of the land was dry but now each day there was promise of relief.

The clouds that had been scattered across the sky began to crowd together, gathering into rounded dark-edged masses or rearing proudly into thunderheads. All of nature seemed impressed by their growing importance. In the evenings the sun dressed them in royal purple and during the day the whirlwinds did dervish dances for their entertainment. The rains were coming. Sean had to make a decision, cross the Limpopo and cut himself off from the south when the river flooded, or stay where he was and leave the land beyond undisturbed. It wasn't a difficult decision. They found a place where the banks flattened out a little on both sides of the river. They unloaded the first wagon and double-teamed it; then with everybody shouting encouragement the oxen galloped down the steep slope into the riverbed. The wagon bounced behind them until it hit the sand where it came to a halt, tilted at an abandoned angle, with its wheels sunk axle-deep into the sand.

'Onto the spokes,' shouted Sean. 'They flung themselves on the wheels and strained to keep them turning, but half the oxen were down on their knees, powerless in the loose footing.

'Damn it to hell.' Sean glared at the wagon. 'Outspan the oxen and take them back. Get out the axes.'

It took them three days to lay a bridge of corduroyed branches across the river and another two to get all the wagons and ivory to the far bank. Sean declared a holiday when the last wagon was manhandled into the laager and the whole camp slept late the next morning. The sun was high by the time Sean descended from his wagon. He was still muzzy and a little liverish from lying abed. He yawned wide and stretched like a crucifix. He ran his tongue round his mouth and grimaced at the taste, then he scratched his chest and the hair rasped under his fingers.

'Kandhla, where's the coffee? Don't you care that I am near dead from thirst?'

'Nkosi, the water will boil very soon.'

Sean grunted and walked across to where Mbejane squatted with the other servants by the fire watching Kandhla.

'This is a good camp, Mbejane.' Sean looked up at the roof of leaves above them. It was a place of green shade, cool in the late morning heat. Christmas beetles were squealing in the wide stretched branches.

'There is good grazing for the cattle,' Mbejane agreed; he stretched out his hand towards Sean.

'I found this in the grass – someone else has camped here.' Sean took it from him and examined it, a piece of broken china with a blue fig-leaf pattern. It was a shock to Sean, that little fragment of civilization in the wilderness; he turned it in his fingers and Mbejane went on. 'There are the ashes of an old fire there against the shuma tree and I found the ruts where wagons climbed the bank at the same place as ours.'

'How long ago?'

Mbejane shrugged. 'A year perhaps. Grass has grown in the wagon tracks.'

Sean sat down in his chair, he felt disturbed. He thought about it and grinned as he realized he was jealous; there were strangers here in the land he was coming to regard as his own, those year-old tracks gave him a feeling of being in a crowd. Also there was the opposite feeling, that of longing for the company of his own kind. The sneaking desire to see a white face again. It was strange that he could resent something and yet wish for it simultaneously.

'Kandhla, am I to have coffee now or at supper tonight?'

'Nkosi, it is done.' Kandhla poured a little brown sugar into the mug, stirred it with a stick and handed it to him. Sean held the mug in both hands, blowing to cool it, then sipping and sighing with each mouthful. The talk of his Zulus passed back and forth about the circle and the snuff-boxes followed it, each remark of worth being greeted with a solemn chorus of 'It is true, it is true,' and the taking of snuff. Small arguments jumped up and fell back again into the leisurely stream of conversation. Sean listened to them, occasionally joining in or contributing a story until his stomach told him it was time to eat. Kandhla started to cook, under the critical supervision and with the helpful suggestions of those whom idleness had made garrulous. He had almost succeeded in grilling the carcass of a guinea-fowl to the satisfaction of the entire company, although Mbejane felt that he should have added a pinch more salt, when Nonga sitting across the fire from him jumped to his feet and pointed out towards the north. Sean shaded his eyes and looked.

'For Chrissake,' said Sean.

'Ah! ah! ah!' said his servants.

A white man rode towards them through the trees; he cantered with long stirrups, slouched comfortably, close enough already for Sean to make out the great ginger beard that masked the bottom half of his face. He was a big man; the sleeves of his shirt rolled high around thick arms.

'Hello,' shouted Sean and went eagerly to meet him. The rider reined in at the edge of the laager. He climbed stiffly out of the saddle and grabbed Sean's outstretched hand. Sean felt his finger-bones creak in the grip.

'Hello, man! How goes it?' He spoke in Afrikaans. His voice matched the size of his body and his eyes were on a level with Sean's. They pumped each other's arms mercilessly, laughing, putting sincerity into the usual inanities of greeting.

'Kandhla – get out the brandy bottle,' Sean called over his shoulder, then to the Boer, 'Come in, you're just in time for lunch. We'll have a dram to celebrate. Hell, it's good to see a white man again!'

'You're on your own, then?'

'Yes – come in, man, sit down.'

Sean poured drinks and the Boer took one up.

'What's your name?' he asked.

'Courtney – Sean Courtney.'

'I'm Jan Paulus Leroux – glad to meet you, meneer.'

'Good health, meneer,' Sean answered him and they drank. Jan Paulus wiped his whiskers on the palm of his hand and breathed out heavily, blowing the taste of the brandy back into his mouth.

'That was good,' he said and held out his mug. They talked excitedly, tongues loose from loneliness, trying to say everything and ask all the questions at once – meetings in the bush are always like this. Meanwhile the tide was going out in the bottle and the level dropped quickly.

'Tell me, where are your wagons?' Sean asked.

'An hour or two behind. I came ahead to find the river.'

'How many in your party?' Sean watched his face, talking just for the sound of it.

'Ma and Pa, my little sister and my wife – which reminds me – you had better move your wagons.'

'What?' Sean looked puzzled.

'This is my outspan place,' the Boer explained to him. 'See, there are the marks of my fire – this is my camp.'

The smile went out of Sean's voice. 'Look around you, Boer, there is the whole of Africa. Take your pick – anywhere except where I am sitting.'

'But this is my place.' Jan Paulus flushed a little. 'I always camp at the same place when I return along a spoor.'

The whole temper of their meeting had changed in a few seconds. Jan Paulus stood abruptly and went to his horse. He stooped and tightened the girth, hauling so savagely on the strap that the animal staggered off balance. He flung himself onto its back and looked down at Sean.

'Move your wagons,' he said, 'I camp here tonight.'

'Would you like to bet on that?' Sean asked grimly.

'We'll see!' Jan Paulus flashed back.

'We certainly shall,' agreed Sean.

The Boer wheeled his horse and rode away. Sean watched his back disappear among the trees and only then did he let his anger slip. He rampaged through the laager working himself into a fury, pacing out frustrated circles, stopping now and then to glare out in the direction from which the Boer's wagons would come – but under all the external signs of indignation was his unholy anticipation of a fight. Kandhla brought him food, hurrying along behind him with the plate. Sean waved him away impatiently and continued his pugnacious patrol. At last a trek whip popped in the distance and an ox lowed faintly, to be answered immediately by Sean's cattle. The dogs started barking and Sean crossed to one of the wagons on the north side of the laager and leaned against it with assumed nonchalance. The long line of wagons wound out of the trees towards him. There were bright blobs of colour on the high box seat of the lead wagon. Women's dresses! Ordinarily they would have made Sean's nostrils flare like those of a stud stallion, but now his whole attention was concentrated on the larger of the two outriders. Jan Paulus cantered ahead of his father, and Sean, with his fists clenched into bony hammers at his sides, watched him come. Jan Paulus sat straight in the saddle; he stopped his horse a dozen paces from Sean and shoved his hat onto the back of his head with a thumb as thick and as brown as a fried sausage; he tickled his horse a little with his spurs to make it dance and he asked with mock surprise, 'What, *Rooi Nek,* still here?'

Sean's dogs had rushed forward to meet the other pack and now they milled about in a restrained frenzy of mutual bottom-smelling, stiff-limbed with tension, backs abristle and legs cocking in the formal act of urination.

'Why don't you go and climb a tree? You'll feel more at home there,' Sean suggested mildly.

'Ah! so?' Jan Paulus reared in his stirrups. He kicked loose his right foot, swung it back over his horse's rump to dismount and Sean jumped at him. The horse skittered nervously, throwing the Boer off balance and he clutched at the saddle. Sean reached up, took a double handful of his ginger beard and leaned back on it with all his weight. Jan Paulus came over backwards with his arms windmilling, his foot caught in the stirrup and he hung suspended like a hammock, held at one end to the plunging horse and at the other by his chin to Sean's hands. Sean dug his heels in, revelling in the Boer's bellows.

Galvanized into action by Sean's example, the dogs cut short the ceremony and went at each other in a snarling, snapping shambles; the fur flew like sand in a Kalahari dust-storm.

The stirrup-leather snapped; Sean fell backwards and rolled to his feet just in time to meet Jan Paulus's charge. He smothered the punch that the Boer bowled overarm at him, but the power behind it shocked him; then they were chest to chest and Sean felt his own strength matched. They strained silently with their beards touching and their eyes inches apart. Sean shifted his weight quickly and tried for a fall, but smoothly as a dancer Jan Paulus met and held him. Then it was his turn; he twisted in Sean's arms and Sean sobbed with the effort required to stop him. Oupa Leroux joined in by driving his horse at them, scattering the dogs, his hippo-hide sjambok hissing as he swung it.

'Let it stand! you thunders, give over – hey! Enough, let it stand!'

Sean shouted with pain as the lash cut across his back and at the next stroke Jan Paulus howled as loudly. They let go of each other and massaging their whip-weals retreated before the skinny old white-beard on the horse.

The first of the wagons had come up now and two hundred pounds of woman, all in one package, called out from the box seat, 'Why did you stop them, Oupa?'

'No sense in letting them kill each other.'

'Shame on you – so you must spoil the boys' fun. Don't you remember how you loved to fight? Or are you now so old you forget the pleasures of your youth? Leave them alone!'

Oupa hesitated, swinging the sjambok and looking from Sean to Jan Paulus.

'Come away from there, you old busybody,' his wife ordered him. She was solid as a granite kopje, her blouse packed full of bosom and her bare arms brown and thick as a man's. The wide brim of her bonnet shaded her face but Sean could see it was pink and pudding-shaped, the kind of face that smiles more easily than it frowns. There were two girls on the seat beside her but there was no time to look at them. Oupa had pulled his horse out of the way and Jan Paulus was moving down on him. Sean went up on his toes, crouching a little, preoccupied with the taste he had just had of the other's strength, watching Jan Paulus close in for the main course and not too certain he was going to be able to chew this mouthful.

Jan Paulus tested Sean with a long right-hander but Sean rolled his head with it and the thick pad of his beard cushioned the blow; he hooked Jan Paulus in the ribs under his raised arm and Jan Paulus grunted and circled away.

Forgetting his scruples, Oupa Leroux watched them with rising delight. It was going to be a good fight. They were well matched – both big men, under thirty, quick and smooth on their feet. Both had fought before and that often; you could tell it by the way they felt each other out, turning just out of reach, moving in to offer an opening that a less experienced man might have attempted and regretted, then dropping back.

The fluid, almost leisurely pattern of movement exploded. Jan Paulus jumped in, moving left, changed direction like the recoil of a whip lash and used his right hand again; Sean ducked under it and laid himself open to Jan Paulus's left. He staggered back from its kick, bleeding where it had split the flesh across his cheek-bone, and Jan Paulus followed him eagerly, his hands held ready, searching for the opening. Sean kept clear, instinct moving his feet until the blackness faded inside his head and he felt the strength in his arms again. He saw Jan Paulus following him and he let his legs stay rubbery; he dropped his hands and waited for Jan Paulus to commit himself. Too late Jan Paulus caught the cunning in Sean's eyes and tried to break from the trap, but clenched bone raked his face. He staggered away and now he was bleeding also.

They fought through the wagons with the advantage changing hands a dozen times. They came together and used their heads and their knees, they broke and used their fists again. Then locked chest to chest once more they rolled down the steep bank into the river bed of the Limpopo. They fought in the soft sand and it held their legs, it filled their mouths when they fell and clung like white icing-sugar to their hair and beards. They splashed into one of the pools and they fought in the water, coughing with the agony of it in their lungs, floundering like a pair of bull hippos, their movements slowing down until they knelt facing each other, no longer able to rise, the water running from them and the only sound their gasping for air.

Not sure whether the darkness was actuality or a fantasy of fatigue, for the sun had set by the time they were finished, Sean watched Jan Paulus starting to puke, retching with a tearing noise to bring up a small splash of yellow bile. Sean crawled to the edge of the pool and lay with his face in the sand. There were voices echoing in his ears and the light of a lantern – the light was red – filtered through the blood that had trickled into his eyes. His servants lifted him and he hardly felt them. The light and the voices faded into blackness as he slipped over the edge of consciousness.

The sting of iodine woke him and he struggled to sit up but hands pushed him down.

'Gently, gently, the fight is over.' Sean focused his one eye to find the voice. The pinkness of Ouma Leroux hung over him. Her hands touched his face and the antiseptic stung him again. He exclaimed through puffed lips.

'So! Just like a man,' Ouma chuckled. 'Your head nearly knocked off without a murmur but one touch of medicine and you cry like a baby.'

Sean ran his tongue round inside his mouth; one tooth loose but all the others miraculously present. He started to lift his hand to touch his closed eye but Ouma slapped it down impatiently and went on working over him.

'Glory, what a fight!' She shook her head happily. 'You were good, *kerel,* you were very good.'

Sean looked beyond her and saw the girl. She was standing in shadow, a silhouette against the pale canvas. She was holding a basin. Ouma turned and dipped the cloth in it, washing out the blood before she came back to his face. The wagon rocked under her weight and the lantern that hung from the roof swung, lighting the girl's face from the side. Sean's legs straightened on his cot and he moved his head slightly to see her better.

'Be still, *jong*,' Ouma commanded. Sean looked past her at the girl at the full serene line of her lips and the curve of her cheek. He saw the pile of her hair fluff up in happy disarray and then, suddenly – penitent, slide down behind her neck, curl over her shoulder and hang to her waist in a plait as thick as his wrist.

'Katrina, do you expect me to reach right across to the basin each time? Stand closer, girl.'

She stepped into the light and looked at Sean. Green, laughing, almost bubbling green was the colour of her eyes. Then she dropped them to the basin. Sean stared at her, not wanting to miss the moment when she would look up again.

'My big bear,' Ouma spoke with grudging approval. 'Steal our camp site, fight my son and ogle my daughter. If you go on like this I might have to knock the thunder out of you myself. Glory, but you are a dangerous one! Katrina, you had better go back to our wagons and help Henrietta see to your brother. Leave the basin on the chest there.'

She looked at Sean once more before she left. There were secret shadows in the green – she didn't have to smile with her mouth.

= 11 =

Sean woke to the realization that something was wrong. He started to sit up but the pain checked him: the stiffness of bruised muscle and the catch of half-dried scab. He groaned and the movement hurt his lips. Slowly he swung his legs off the cot and roused himself to take stock of the damage. Dark through the hair of his chest showed a heel imprint of Jan Paulus's boot. Sean prodded round it gently, feeling for the give of a broken rib; then, satisfied with that area, he went on to inspect the raw graze that wrapped round onto his back, holding his left arm high and peering closely at the broken skin. He picked a bit of blanket fluff from the scab. He stood up, only to freeze as a torn muscle in his shoulder knifed him. He started to swear then softly, monotonously, and he kept it up all through the painful business of climbing down out of the wagon.

His entire following watched his descent – even the dogs looked worried. Sean reached the ground and started to shout.

'What the hell –' He stopped hurriedly as he felt his lip crack open again and start to bleed.

'What the hell' – he said again, keeping his lips still – 'are you doing standing round like a bunch of women at a beer drink – is there no work here? Hlubi, I thought I sent you out to look for elephant.' Hlubi went. 'Kandhla, where's breakfast? Mbejane, get me a basin of water and my shaving-mirror.' Sean sat in his chair and morosely inspected his face in the mirror.

'If a herd of buffalo had stampeded across it they would have done less damage.'

'Nkosi, it is nothing compared to his face,' Mbejane assured him.

'Is he bad?' Sean looked up.

'I have spoken to one of his servants. He has not left his bed yet and he lies there, growling like a wounded lion in a thicket; but his eyes are as tightly closed as those of a new cub.'

'Tell me more, Mbejane. Say truly, was it a good fight?'

Mbejane squatted down next to Sean's chair. He was silent a moment as he gathered his words.

'When the sky sends its cloud impis against the peaks of the Drakensberg, with thunder and the spears of lightning, it is a thing to thrill a man. When two bull elephants fight unto death there is no braver show in all the veld. Is this not so?'

Sean nodded, his eyes twinkling.

'Nkosi, hear me when I tell you these things were as the play of little children beside this fight.'

Sean listened to the praises. Mbejane was well versed in the oldest art of Zululand and when he had finished he looked at Sean's face. It was happy. Mbejane smiled and took a fold of paper out of his loin cloth. 'A servant from the other camp brought this while you slept.'

Sean read the note. It was written in a big round schoolgirl hand and worded in High Dutch. He liked that writing. It was an invitation to dinner.

'Kandhla, get out my suit and my number one boots.' He picked up the mirror again. There wasn't very much he could do about his face – trim the beard, perhaps, but that was all. He laid the mirror down and looked up stream to where the Leroux wagons were half hidden among the trees.

Mbejane carried a lantern in front of Sean. They walked slowly to enable Sean to limp with dignity. When they reached the other laager, Jan Paulus climbed stiffly out of his chair and nodded an equally stiff greeting. Mbejane had lied – except for a missing tooth there was little to choose between their faces. Oupa slapped Sean's back and pressed a tumbler of brandy into his hand. He was a tall man, but twenty thousand suns had burnt away his flesh and left only stringy muscle, had faded his eyes to a pale green and toughened his skin to the texture of a turkey's neck. His beard was yellowish-white with still a touch of ginger round the mouth. He asked Sean three questions without giving him time to answer the first, then he led him to a chair.

Oupa talked, Sean listened and Jan Paulus sulked. Oupa talked of cattle and hunting and the land to the north. After a few minutes Sean realized that he was not expected to take part in the conversation: his few tentative efforts were crushed under Oupa's verbal avalanche. So Sean listened half to him and half to the whisper of women's voices from the cooking fires behind the laager. Once he heard her laugh. He knew it was her for it was the rich sound of the thing that he had seen in her eyes. At last the women's business with food and pots was finished and Ouma led the girls to where the men sat. Sean stood up and saw that Katrina was tall, with shoulders like a boy. As she walked towards him the movement pressed her skirt against her legs – they were long but her feet were small. Her hair was red-black and tied behind her head in an enormous bun.

'Ah, my battling bear,' Ouma took Sean's arm, 'let me present my daughter-in-law, Henrietta – here is the man that nearly killed your husband.' Jan Paulus snorted from his chair and Ouma laughed, her bosom wobbling merrily. Henrietta was a small dark-eyed girl. *She doesn't like me,* Sean guessed instantly. He bowed slightly and took her hand. She pulled it away.

'This is my youngest daughter, Katrina. You met her last night.'

She does like me. Her fingers were long and square-tipped in his. Sean risked his lips with a smile.

'Without her ministrations I might have bled to death,' he said. She smiled straight back at him but not with her mouth.

'You wear your wounds well, maneer, the blue eye has an air of distinction.'

'That will be enough from you, girl,' Oupa spoke sharply. 'Go and sit by your mother.' He turned to Sean. 'I was telling you about this horse – I said to the fellow, "He's not worth five pounds let alone fifteen, look at those hocks, thin as sticks." So he says to me, trying to get me away, you follow, he says, "Come and look at the saddle." But I can see he's worried –'

The thin cotton of the girl's blouse could hardly contain the impatient push of her breasts, Sean thought that he had never seen anything so wonderful.

There was a trestle-table next to the cooking fire; they went to it at last. Oupa said grace. Sean watched him through his lashes. Oupa's beard waggled as he spoke and at one point he thumped the table to emphasize the point he was making to the Almighty. His 'amen' had such an impressive resonance that Sean had to make an effort to stop himself applauding and Oupa fell back spent.

'Amen,' said Ouma and ladled stew from a pot the size of a bucket. Henrietta added pumpkin fritters and Katrina stacked slices of fresh mealie bread on each plate. A silence fell on the table, spoiled only by the clank of metal on china and the sound of Oupa breathing through his nose.

'Mevrouw Leroux, I have waited a long time to taste food like this again.' Sean mopped up the last bit of gravy with a piece of mealie bread. Ouma beamed.

'There's plenty more, meneer. I love to see a man eat. Oupa used to be a great trencherman. My father made him take me away for he could not afford to feed him every time he came courting.' She took Sean's plate and filled it. 'You look to me like a man who can eat.'

'I think I'll hold my own in most company,' Sean agreed.

'So?' Jan Paulus spoke for the first time. He passed his plate to Ouma. 'Fill it up, please, Mother, tonight I am hungry.'

Sean's eyes narrowed, he waited until Jan Paulus had his plate back in front of him, then he took up his fork deliberately. Jan Paulus did the same.

'Glory,' said Ouma happily. 'Here we go again. Oupa, you may have to go out and shoot a couple of buffalo before dinner is finished tonight.'

'I will bet one sovereign on Jan Paulus,' Oupa challenged his wife. 'He is like an army of termites. I swear that if there was nothing else he'd eat the canvas off the wagons.'

'All right,' agreed Ouma. 'I've never seen the Bear eat before, but it seems to me he has plenty of room to put it.'

'Your woollen shawl against my green bonnet that Jan Paulus gives up first,' Katrina whispered to her sister-in-law.

'When Jannie has finished the stew he'll eat the Englishman,' Henrietta giggled. 'But it's a pretty bonnet – I'll take the wager.'

Plateful for plateful, Ouma measuring out each ladle with scrupulous fairness, they ate against each other. The talk round the table dwindled and halted.

'More?' asked Ouma each time the plates were clean, and each time they looked at each other and nodded. At last the ladle scraped the bottom of the pot.

'That's the end of it, my children, we will have to call it another draw.'

The silence went on after she had spoken. Sean and Jan Paulus sat very still looking at their respective plates. Jan Paulus hiccupped, his expression changed. He stood up and went into the darkness.

'Ah! listen! listen!' crowed Ouma. They waited and then she exploded into laughter. 'The ungrateful wretch, is that what he thinks of my food? Where's your sovereign, Oupa?'

'Wait, you greedy old woman, the game's not finished yet.' He turned and stared at Sean. 'To me it looks as though your horse is nearly blown.'

Sean closed his eyes. The sounds of Jan Paulus's distress came to him very clearly.

'Thank you for a – ' He didn't have time to finish. He wanted to get far away so the girl couldn't hear him.

= 12 =

The following morning during breakfast Sean thought about his next move. He would write an invitation to dinner and then he would deliver it himself. They would have to ask him to stay for coffee and then, if he waited, there would be a chance. Even Oupa would have to stop talking sometime and Ouma might relax her vigilance. He was sure there'd be a chance to talk to the girl. He didn't know what he would say to her but he'd worry about that when the time came. He climbed into the wagon and found pencil and paper in his chest. He went back to the table and spread the paper in front of him. He chewed the end of the pencil and stared out into the bush. Something moved against the trees. Sean put the pencil down and stood up. The dogs barked then stopped as they recognized Hlubi. He was coming at a trot – he was coming with news. Sean waited for him.

'A big herd, Nkosi, with many showing ivory. I saw them drink at the river and then go back into the bush, feeding quietly.'

'When?' asked Sean to gain time. He was searching for a plausible excuse to stay in camp – it would have to be good to satisfy Mbejane who was already saddling one of the horses.

'Before the sun this morning,' answered Hlubi and Sean was trying to remember which was his sore shoulder – he couldn't hunt with a sore shoulder. Mbejane led the horse into the laager. Sean scratched the side of his nose and coughed.

'The tracker from the other camp follows close behind me, Nkosi, he too has seen the herd and brings the news to his master. But I, being as swift as a springbok when I run, have outdistanced him,' Hlubi ended modestly.

'Is that so?' For Sean it changed the whole problem, he couldn't leave the herd to that red-headed Dutchman. He ran across to the wagon and snatched his bandolier from the foot of the cot. His rifle was already in the scabbard.

'Are you tired, Hlubi?' Sean buckled the heavy ammunition belt across his chest. The sweat had run in oily streaks down the Zulu's body; his breathing was deep and quick.

'No, Nkosi.'

'Well, then, lead us to these elephant of yours, my fleet-footed springbok.' Sean swung up onto his horse. He looked over his shoulder at the other camp. She would still be there when he came back.

Sean was limited to the speed of Hlubi's feet while the two Leroux had only to gallop along the easy spoor left by Sean's party and they caught up with him before he had gone two miles.

'Good morning to you,' Oupa greeted him as he drew level and pulled his horse in to a trot. 'Out for a morning's ride, I see.'

Sean made the best of it with a grin. 'If we are all to hunt then we must hunt together. Do you agree?'

'Of course, meneer.'

'And we must share the bag equally, one third to each man.'

'That is always the way.' Oupa nodded.

'Do you agree?' Sean turned in his saddle towards Jan Paulus. Jan Paulus grunted. He showed little inclination to open his mouth since he had lost his tooth.

They found the spoor within an hour. The herd had wrecked a road through the thick bush along the river. They had stripped the bark from the saplings and left them naked and bleeding. They had knocked down bigger trees to reach the tender top leaves and they had dropped their great piles of dung in the grass.

'We need no trackers to follow this.' Jan Paulus had the first excitement on him. Sean looked at him and wondered how many elephant had died in front of his rifle. A thousand perhaps, and yet the excitement was on him again now.

'Tell your servants to follow us. We'll go ahead. We'll catch them within an hour.' He smiled at Sean, gap-toothed, and Sean felt the excitement lift the hair on his own forearms. He smiled back.

They cantered in a rough line abreast, slack-reined to let the horses pick their own way among the fallen trees. The river bush thinned out as they moved north and soon they were into parkland. The grass brushed their stirrups and the ground beneath it was firm and smooth.

They rode without talking, leaning forward in their saddles, looking ahead. The rhythmic beat of hooves was a war drum. Sean ran his fingers along the row of bullets strapped across his chest, then he drew his rifle, checked the load and thrust it back into its scabbard.

'There!' said Oupa and Sean saw the herd. It was massed among a grove of fever trees a quarter of a mile ahead.

'Name of a name,' Paulus whistled. 'There must be two hundred at least.'

Sean heard the first pig-squeal of alarm, saw ears fan out and trunks lift. Then the herd bunched together and ran with their backs humped, a thin screen of dust trailing behind them.

'Paulus take the right flank. You, meneer, in the middle and I'll ride left,' shouted Oupa.

Sean jammed his hat down over his ears and his horse jumped under him as he hit it with his heels. Like a thrown trident the three horsemen hurled themselves at the herd. Sean rode into the dust. He picked an old cow elephant from the moving mountain range in front of him and pressed his horse so close upon her that he could see the bristles in her tail tuft and the erosion of her skin, wrinkled as an old man's scrotum. He touched his hand to his horse's neck and it plunged – from full gallop to standstill in half a dozen strides. Sean threw his feet free of the stirrups and hit the ground, loose-kneed to ride the shock. The cow's spine was a line of lumps beneath the grey skin – Sean broke it with his first bullet and she dropped, sliding on her hindquarters like a dog with worms. His horse started to run again before he was properly in the saddle and everything became movement and noise, dust and the smell of burnt powder. Chase them, coughing in the dust. Close with them. Off the horse and shoot. Wet blood on grey skin. Slam, slam of the rifle – its barrel hot, recoiling savagely. Sweat in the eyes, stinging. Ride. Shoot again. Two more down, screaming, anchored by paralysed legs. Blood-red as a flag. Load, cramming cartridges into the rifle. Ride. Chase them, shoot again and again. The bullets striking on flesh with a hollow sound, then up and ride again. Ride – until the horse could no longer keep up with them and he had to let them go. He stood holding his horse's head, the dust and the thirst closed his throat. He could not swallow. His hands trembled in reaction. His shoulder was aching again. He untied his silk scarf, wiped his face with it and blew the mud out of his nose, then he drank from his water-bottle. The water tasted sweet.

The hunt had led from parkland into mopani bush. It was very thick, shiny green leaves hanging to the ground and pressing close around him. The air was still and warm to breathe. He turned back along the line of the chase. He found them by their squealing. When they saw him they tried to charge, dragging themselves towards him – using the front legs only and groping with their trunks. They sagged into stillness after the head shot. This was the bad part. Sean worked quickly. He could hear the other rifles in the mopani forest around him and when he came to one of the long clearings among the trees he saw Jan Paulus walking towards him, leading his horse.

'How many?' called Sean.

'*Gott*, man, I didn't count. What a killing, hey? Have you got a drink for me? I dropped my water-bottle somewhere.'

Jan Paulus's rifle was in its saddle scabbard. The reins were slung over his shoulder and his horse followed him with its head drooping from exhaustion. The clearing was walled in with the dense mopani trees and a wounded elephant broke into the open. It was lung shot – the side of its chest painted with froth – and when it squealed the blood sprayed in a pink spout from the end of its trunk. It went for Jan Paulus, streaming the black battle ensigns of its ears. His horse reared, the reins snapped, it turned free and galloped away, leaving him full in the path of the charge. Sean went up onto his horse's back without touching stirrups. His horse threw its head, dancing in a tight circle, but he dragged it around and drove it to intercept the charge.

'Don't run, for God's sake, don't run!' he shouted as he cleared his rifle from the scabbard. Jan Paulus heard him. He stood with his hands at his sides, his feet apart and his body braced. The elephant heard Sean shout also and it swung its head and Sean saw the first hesitation in its run. He fired, not trying to pick his shot, hoping only to hurt it, to bring it away from Jan Paulus. The bullet slapped into it with the sound of a wet towel flicked against a wall. The elephant turned, clumsy with the weakness of its shattered lungs. Sean gathered his horse beneath him and wheeled it away and the elephant followed him.

Sean fumbled as he reloaded, his hands were slippery with sweat. One of the brass shells slipped through his fingers, tapped against his knee and dropped into the grass under his horse's hooves. The elephant gained on him. He loosened his bed-roll from the saddle and let it fall – they would sometimes stop to savage even a fallen hat, but not this one. He turned in the saddle and fired into it. It squealed again so close upon him that the blown blood splattered into his face. His horse was almost finished; he could feel its legs flopping with every stride and they were nearly at the end of the clearing racing towards the solid wall of green mopani. He pushed another round into the breech of his rifle and swung his body across the saddle. He slid down until his feet touched the ground and he was running next to his horse. He let go and was flung forward, but he fought to keep his balance, his body jarring with the force of his run. Then, still on his feet, he turned for his first steady shot. The elephant was coming in fast, almost on top of him, hanging over him like a cliff. Its trunk coiled on its chest and the curves of its ivory were lifted high.

It's too close, much too close, I can't hit the brain from here.

He aimed at the hollow in its forehead just above the level of its eyes. He fired and the elephant's legs folded up; its brain burst like an overripe tomato within the bone castle of its skull.

Sean tried to jump aside as the massive body came skidding down upon him, but one of its legs hit him and threw him face down into the grass. He lay there. He felt sick, for his stomach was still full of warm oily fear.

After a while he sat up and looked at the elephant. One of its tusks had snapped off flush with the lip. Jan Paulus came, panting from his run. He stopped next to the elephant and touched the wound in its forehead, then he wiped his fingers on his shirt.

'Are you all right, man?'

He took Sean's arm and helped him to his feet; then he picked up Sean's hat and dusted it carefully before handing it to him.

13

In the three-sided shelter formed by the belly and out-thrust legs of one of the dead elephants they made their camp that night. They drank coffee together and Sean sat between the two Leroux with his back against the rough skin of the elephant's belly. The silhouettes of the tree against the night sky were deformed by the shapes of the vultures that clustered in them and the darkness was ugly with the giggling of hyena. They had set a feast for the scavengers. They spoke little for they were tired, but Sean could feel the gratitude of the men who sat beside him and before they rolled into their blankets Jan Paulus said gruffly, 'Thank you, *kerel*.'

'You might be able to do the same for me one day.'

'I hope so, *ja!* I hope so.'

In the morning Oupa said, 'It's going to take us three or four days to cut out all this ivory.' He looked up at the sky. 'I don't like these clouds. One of us had better ride back to camp to fetch more men and wagons to carry the ivory.'

'I'll go.' Sean stood up quickly.

'I was thinking of going myself.' But Sean was already calling to Mbejane to saddle his horse and Oupa couldn't really argue with him, not after yesterday.

'Tell Ouma to take the wagons across the river,' he acquiesced. 'We don't want to be caught on this side when the river floods. Perhaps you wouldn't mind helping her.'

'No,' Sean assured him. 'I don't mind at all.'

His horse was still tired from the previous day's hunt and it was three hours before he reached the river.

He tied his horse on the bank and went down to one of the pools. He stripped off his clothes and lowered himself into the water. He scrubbed himself with handfuls of the coarse sand and when he waded out of the pool and dried on his shirt his skin was tingling. He rode along the bank and the temptation to gallop his horse was almost unbearable. He laughed to himself a little.

'The field's almost clear, though I wouldn't put it past that suspicious old Dutchman to follow me.'

He laughed again and thought about the colour of her eyes, green as *crème-de-menthe* in a crystal glass, and the shape of her bosom. The muscles in his legs tightened and the horse lengthened its stride in response to the pressure of his knees. 'All right, run then,' Sean encouraged it, 'I don't insist on it, but I would be grateful.'

He went to his own wagons first and changed his sweaty shirt for a fresh one, his leather breeches for clean calico and his scuffed boots for soft polished leather. He scrubbed his teeth with salt and dragged a comb through his hair and beard. He saw in the mirror that the battle damage to his face was fading and he winked at his image. 'How can she resist you?' He gave his moustache one more twirl, climbed out of the wagon and was immediately aware of a most uncomfortable feeling in his stomach. He walked towards the Leroux laager thinking about it, and he recognized it as the same feeling he used to have when Waite Courtney called him to the study to do penance for his boyhood sins.

'That's odd,' he muttered. 'Why should I feel like that?' His confidence faded and he stopped. 'I wonder if my breath smells – I think I'd better go back and get some cloves.' He turned with relief, knew it as cowardice and stopped again. 'Get a grip on yourself. She's only a girl, an uneducated little Dutch girl. You've had fifty finer women.'

'Name me two,' he shot back at himself.

'Well, there was – Oh! for Chrissake, come on.' Resolutely he set off for the Leroux' laager again.

She was sitting in the sun within the circle of wagons. She was leaning forward on the stool and her newly-washed hair fell thickly over her face almost to the ground. With each stroke of the brush it leapt like a live thing and the sun sparkled the red lights in it. Sean wanted to touch it – he wanted to twist fistfuls of it round his hands and he wanted to smell it, it would smell warm and slightly milky like a puppy's fur. He stepped softly towards her but before he reached her she took the shiny mass with both hands and threw it back over her shoulders – a startled flash of green eyes, one despairing wail, 'Oh, no! not with my hair like this.' A swirl of skirts that sent the stool flying and she was gone into her wagon. Sean scratched the side of his nose and stood awkwardly.

'Why are you back so soon, meneer?' she called through the canvas. 'Where are the others? Is everything all right?'

'Yes, they're both fine. I left them and came to fetch wagons to carry the ivory.'

'Oh, that's good.' Sean tried to interpret the inflection of her voice: was it good that they were fine, or good that he had left them? So far the indications were favourable; her confusion at seeing him boded well.

'What's wrong?' Ouma bellowed from one of the other wagons. 'It's not Oupa, don't tell me something has happened to him?' The wagon rocked wildly and her pink face, puckered with sleep, popped out of the opening. Sean's reassurances were smothered by her voice.

'Oh, I knew this would happen. I had a feeling. I shouldn't have let him go.'

'Paulus, oh, Jan Paulus – I must go to him. Where is he?'

Henrietta came running from the cooking fire behind the wagons and then the dogs started barking and the servants added their chatter to the confusion. Sean tried to shout them all down and watch Katrina emerging from her wagon at the same time. She had disciplined her hair now – it had a green ribbon in it and hung down her back. She was laughing and she helped him to quieten Ouma and Henrietta.

They brought him coffee, then they sat round him and listened to the story of the hunt. Sean went into detail on the rescue of Jan Paulus and was rewarded by a softening of the dislike in Henrietta's eyes. By the time Sean had finished talking it was too late to start moving the wagons across the river. So he talked some more, it was most agreeable to have three women as an attentive audience, and then they ate supper.

With ostentatious tact Ouma and Henrietta retired early to their respective living wagons and left Sean and Katrina sitting by the fire. At carefully-spaced intervals there was a stage cough from Ouma's wagon, a reminder that they were not entirely alone. Sean lit a cheroot and frowned into the fire searching desperately for something intelligent to say, but all his brain could dredge up was, 'Thank God, Oupa isn't here.' He sneaked a glance at Katrina: she was staring into the fire as well and she was blushing. Instantly Sean felt his own cheeks starting to heat up. He opened his mouth to talk and made a squawking noise. He shut it again.

'We can speak in English if you like, meneer.'

'You speak English?' Sean's surprise brought his voice back.

'I practise every night – I read aloud out of my books.'

Sean grinned at her delightedly – it was suddenly very important that she could speak his language. The dam, holding back all the questions that there were to ask and all the things there were to say, burst and the words came pouring out over each other. Katrina fluttered her hands when she couldn't find the word she wanted and then lapsed back into Afrikaans. They killed the short taut silences with a simultaneous rush of words, then laughed together in confusion. They sat on the edges of their chairs and watched each other's faces as they talked. The moon came up, a red rain moon, and the fire faded into a puddle of ashes.

'Katrina, it's long past the time decent people were asleep. I'm sure Meneer Courtney is tired.'

They dropped their voices to a whisper, drawing out the last minutes.

'In just one minute, girl, I'm coming out to fetch you to bed.'

They walked to her wagon and with each step her skirts brushed against his leg. She stopped with one hand on the wagon step. She wasn't as tall as he'd imagined, the top of her head came to his chin. The seconds slid by as he hesitated, reluctant to touch, strangely frightened to test the delicate thread they had spun together lest he destroy it before it became strong. Slowly he swayed towards her and something surged up inside him as he saw her chin lift slightly and the lashes fall over her eyes.

'Goodnight, Meneer Courtney.' Ouma's voice again, loud and with an edge to it. Sean started guiltily.

'Goodnight, mevrouw.'

Katrina touched his arm just above the elbow, her fingers were warm.

'Goodnight, meneer, I shall see you in the morning.'

She rustled up the steps and slipped through the opening of the canvas. Sean scowled at Ouma's wagon.

'Thanks very much – and if there is ever anything I can do for you, please don't hesitate to ask.'

= 14 =

They started moving the wagons early next morning. There was no time to talk to Katrina in the bustle of inspanning and working the wagons across the corduroy bridge. Sean spent most of the morning in the riverbed and the white sand bounced the heat up at him. He threw off his shirt and sweated like a wrestler. He trotted beside Katrina's wagon when they ran it through the riverbed. She looked once at his naked chest and arms; her cheeks darkened in the shadow of her bonnet and she dropped her eyes and didn't look at him again. With only the two wagons that were going back to fetch the ivory still on the north bank and the rest safely across, Sean could relax. He washed in one of the pools, put on his shirt and went across to the south bank looking forward to a long afternoon of Katrina's company.

Ouma met him. 'Thank you, my bear, the girls have made you a parcel of cold meat and a bottle of coffee to eat on your way.' Sean's face went slack. He had forgotten all about that stinking ivory; as far as he was concerned Oupa and Paulus could keep the lot of it.

'Don't worry about us any more now, maneer. I know how it is with a man who is a man. When there's work to do everything else comes after.'

Katrina put the food in his hands. Sean looked for a sign from her. One sign and he'd defy even Ouma.

'Don't be too long,' she whispered. The thought that he might shirk work had obviously not even occurred to her. Sean was glad he hadn't suggested it.

It was a long ride back to the elephant.

'You've taken your time, haven't you?' Oupa greeted him with sour suspicion. 'You'd better get to work if you don't want to lose some of your share.'

Taking out the tusks was a delicate task: a slip of the axe would scar the ivory and halve its value. They worked in the heat with a blue haze of flies around their faces, settling on their lips and crawling into their nostrils and eyes. The carcases had started to rot and the gases ballooned their bellies and escaped in posthumous belches. They sweated as they worked and the blood caked their arms to the elbows, but each hour the wagons filled higher until on the third day they loaded the last tusk. Sean reckoned his share at twelve hundred pounds, the equivalent of a satisfactory day on the Stock Exchange.

He was in a good mood on the morning that they started back to the camp, but it deteriorated as the day wore on and they struggled with the heavily-loaded wagons. The rain seemed to have made up its mind at last and now the sky's belly hung down as heavily as that of a pregnant sow. The clouds trapped the heat beneath them and the men panted and the oxen complained mournfully. At mid-afternoon they heard the first far thunder.

'It will be on us before we pass the river,' fretted Oupa. 'See if you can't get some pace out of those oxen.'

They reached Sean's camp an hour after dark and threw his share of the ivory out of the wagons almost without stopping; then they went down to the river and across the bridge to the south bank.

'My mother will have food ready,' Jan Paulus called back to Sean. 'When you have washed come across and eat with us.'

Sean had supper with the Leroux, but his attempts to get Katrina by herself were neatly countered by Oupa whose suspicions were now confirmed. The old man played his trump card immediately after supper and ordered Katrina to bed. Sean could only shrug helplessly in reply to Katrina's appealing little glance. When she had gone Sean went back to his own camp. He was dizzy, with fatigue and he fell onto his cot without bothering to undress.

The rains opened their annual offensive with a midnight broadside of thunder. It startled Sean to his feet before he was awake. He pulled open the front of the wagon and heard the wind coming.

'Mbejane, get the cattle into the laager. Make sure all the canvas is secure.'

'It is done already, Nkosi, I have lashed the wagons together so the oxen cannot stampede and I have –' Then the wind whipped his voice away.

It came out of the east and it frightened the trees so they thrashed their branches in panic; it drummed on the wagon canvas and filled the air with dust and dry leaves. The oxen turned restlessly within the laager. Then came the rain: stinging like hail, drowning the wind and turning the air to water. It swamped the sloping ground that could not drain it fast enough, it blinded and it deafened. Sean went back to his cot and listened to its fury. It made him feel drowsy. He pulled the blankets up to his chin and slept.

In the morning he found his oilskins in the chest at the foot of his cot. They crackled as he pulled them on. He climbed out of the wagon. The cattle had churned the inside of the laager to calf-deep mud and there was no chance of a fire for breakfast. Although the rain was still falling the noise was out of proportion to its strength. Sean paused in his inspection of the camp; he thought about it and suddenly he knew that it was the flood voice of the Limpopo that he heard. Sliding in the mud, he ran out of the laager and stood on the bank of the river. He stared at the mad water. It was so thick with mud it looked solid and it raced so fast it appeared to be standing still. It humped up over piles of submerged rock, gullied through the deeps and hissed in static waves through the shallows. The branches and tree trunks in it whisked past so swiftly that they did little to dispel the illusion that the river was frozen in this brown convulsion.

Reluctantly Sean lifted his eyes to the far bank. The Leroux' wagons were gone.

'Katrina,' he said with the sadness of the might-have-been, then again, 'Katrina,' with the sense of his loss melting in the flame of his anger; and he knew that his wanting was not just the itch that is easily scratched and forgotten, but that it was the true ache, the one that gets into your hands and your head and your heart as well as your loins. He couldn't let her go. He ran back to his wagon and threw his clothes onto the cot.

'I'll marry her,' he said and the words startled him. He stood naked, with an awed expression on his face.

'I'll marry her,' he said again; it was an original thought and it frightened him a little. He took a pair of shorts out of his chest and put his legs into them; he pulled them up and buttoned the fly.

'I'll marry her!' He grinned at his own daring. 'I'm damned if I won't!' He buckled his belt on and tied a pair of *veldschoen* to it by their laces. He jumped down into the mud. The rain was cold on his bare back and he shivered briefly. Then he saw Mbejane coming out of one of the other wagons and he ran.

'Nkosi, Nkosi, what are you doing?' Sean put his head down and ran faster with Mbejane chasing him out onto the bank of the river.

'It's madness . . . let us talk about it first,' Mbejane shouted. 'Please, Nkosi, please.' Sean slipped in the mud and slithered down the bank. Mbejane jumped down after and caught him at the edge of the water, but the mud had coated Sean's body like grease and Mbejane couldn't hold him. Sean twisted out of his hands and sprang far out. He hit the water flat and swam on his back trying to avoid the undertow. The river swept him away. A wave slapped into his mouth and he doubled up to cough; immediately the river caught him by the heels and pulled him under the surface. It let him go again, just long enough to snatch air then it stirred him in a whirlpool and sucked him under once more. He came up beating at the water with his arms, then it tumbled him over a cascade and he knew by the pain in his chest that he was drowning. He swooped down a chute of swift water between rocks and it didn't matter anymore. He was too tired. Something scraped against his chest and he put out his hand to protect himself; his fingers closed round a branch and his head lifted out of the water. He drank air and then he was clinging to the branch, still alive and wanting to live. He started kicking, edging across the current, riding the river with his arms around the log.

One of the eddies beneath the south bank swung the log in, under the branches of a tree. He reached up, caught them and dragged himself out. He knelt in the mud and water came gushing up out of him, half through his mouth and half through his nose. He had lost his *veldschoen*. He belched painfully and looked at the river. How fast was it moving, how long had he been in the water? He must be fifteen miles below the wagons. He wiped his face with his hand. It was still raining. He stood shakily and faced upstream.

It took him three hours to reach the spot opposite his wagons. Mbejane and the others waved in wild relief when they saw him, but their shouts could not carry across the river. Sean was cold now and his feet were sore. The tracks of the Leroux wagons were dissolving in the rain. He followed them and at last the pain in his feet healed as he saw the flash of canvas in the rain mist ahead of him.

'Name of a name,' shouted Jan Paulus. 'How did you cross the river?'

'I flew, how else?' said Sean. 'Where's Katrina?'

Paulus started to laugh, leaning back in the saddle. 'So that's it then, you haven't come all this way to say goodbye to me.'

Sean flushed. 'All right, laughing boy. That's enough merriment for today . . . Where is she?'

Oupa came galloping back towards them. He asked his first question when he was fifty yards away and his fifth as he arrived. From experience Sean knew there was no point in trying to answer them. He looked beyond the two Leroux and saw her coming. She was running back from the lead wagon, her bonnet hanging from its ribbon around her throat and her hair bouncing loosely with each step. She held her skirts out of the mud, her cheeks flushed darker than the brown of her face and her eyes were very green. Sean ducked under the neck of Oupa's horse and went wet, muddy and eager to meet her.

Then the shyness stopped them and they stood paces apart. 'Katrina, will you marry me?'

She went pale. She stared at him then turned away, she was crying and Sean felt the bottom drop out of his stomach.

'No,' shouted Oupa furiously. 'She won't marry you. Leave her alone, you big baboon. You've made her cry. Get out of here. She's only a baby. Get out of here.' He forced his horse between them.

'You hold your mouth, you old busybody.' Ouma came panting back to join the discussion. 'What do you know about it anyway? Just because she's crying doesn't mean she doesn't want him.'

'I thought he was going to let me go,' sobbed Katrina, 'I thought he didn't care.'

Sean whooped and tried to dodge around Oupa's horse.

'You leave her alone,' shouted Oupa desperately, manoeuvring his horse to cut Sean off. 'You made her cry. I tell you she's crying.'

Katrina was undoubtedly crying. She was also trying to get around Oupa's horse.

'Vat haar,' shouted Jan Paulus. 'Get her, man, go and get her!'

Ouma caught the horse by the reins and dragged it away: she was a powerful woman. Sean and Katrina collided and held tight.

'Hey, that's it, man,' Jan Paulus jumped off his horse and pounded Sean's back from behind. Unable to protect himself Sean was driven forward a pace with each blow.

Much later Oupa muttered sulkily. 'She can have two wagons for her dowry.'

'Three!' said Katrina.

'Four!'said Ouma.

'Very well, four. Take your hands off him, girl. Haven't you any shame?' Hastily Katrina dropped her arm from Sean's waist. Sean had borrowed a suit of clothing from Paulus and they were all standing round the fire. It had stopped raining but the low clouds were prematurely bringing on the night.

'And four of the horses,' Ouma prompted her husband.

'Do you want to beggar me, woman?'

'Four horses,' repeated Ouma.

'All right, all right . . . four horses.' Oupa looked at Katrina, his eyes were stricken. 'She's only a baby, man, she's only fifteen years.'

'Sixteen,' said Ouma.

'Nearly seventeen,' said Katrina, 'and anyway you've promised, Pa, you can't go back on your word now.'

Oupa sighed; then he looked at Sean and his face hardened.

'Paulus, get the Bible out of my wagon. This big baboon is going to swear an oath.'

Jan Paulus put the Bible on the tailboard of the wagon. It was thick and the cover was of black leather, dull with use.

'Come here,' Oupa said to Sean. 'Put your hand on the book . . . don't look at me. Look up, man, look up. Now say after me, "I do most solemnly swear to look after this woman" – don't gobble, speak slower – "until I can find a priest to say the proper words. Should I fail in this then I ask you, God, to blast me with lightning, sting me with serpents, burn me in eternal fire –" ' Oupa completed the list of atrocities, then he grunted with satisfaction and tucked the Bible under his arm. 'He won't have a chance to do all that to you . . . I'll get you first.'

Sean shared Jan Paulus's wagon that night; he wasn't in a mood for sleep and anyway Jan Paulus snored. It was raining again in the morning, depressing weather for farewells. Jan Paulus laughed, Henrietta cried and Ouma did both. Oupa kissed his daughter.

'Be a woman like your mother,' he said, then he scowled at Sean.

'Remember, just you remember!'

Sean and Katrina stood together and watched the trees and the curtain of rain hide the wagon train. Sean held Katrina's hand. He could feel the sadness on her; he put his arm round her and her dress was damp and cold. The last wagon disappeared and they were alone in a land as vast as solitude. Katrina shivered and looked up at the man beside her. He was so big and overpoweringly male; he was a stranger. Suddenly she was frightened. She wanted to hear her mother's laugh and see her brother and father riding ahead of her wagon, the way it had always been.

'Oh, please, I want . . .' she pulled out from his arm. She never finished that sentence, for she looked at his mouth and his lips were full and burnt dark by the sun – they were smiling. Then she looked at his eyes and her panic smoothed away. With those eyes watching over her she was never to feel frightened again, not until the very end and that was a long time away. Going into his love was like going into a castle, a thick-walled place. A safe place where no one else could enter. The first feeling of it was so strong that she could only stand quietly and let the warmth wrap her.

15

That evening they outspanned Katrina's wagons back at the south bank of the river. It was still raining. Sean's servants waved and signalled to them, but the brown water bellowed down between them cutting off all sound and hope of passage. Katrina looked at the water. 'Did you really swim that, meneer?'

'So fast that I hardly got wet.'

'Thank you,' she said.

Despite the rain and smoky fire Katrina served up a meal as good as one of Ouma's. They ate it in the shelter of the tarpaulin beside her wagon. The wind guttered the hurricane lamp, flogged the canvas and blew a fine haze of rain in on them. It was so uncomfortable that when Sean suggested that they go into the wagon Katrina barely hesitated before agreeing. She sat on the edge of her cot and Sean sat on the chest opposite her. From an awkward start their conversation was soon running as fast as the river outside the wagon.

'My hair is still wet,' Katrina exclaimed at last. 'Do you mind if I dry it while we talk?'

'Of course not.'

'Then let me get my towel out of the chest.'

They stood up at the same time. There was very little space in the wagon. They touched. They were on the cot. The movement of his mouth on hers, the warm taste of it, the strong pleading of his fingers at the nape of her neck and along her spine – all these things were strangely confusing. She responded slowly at first, then faster with bewildered movements of her own body and little graspings at his arms and shoulders. She did not understand and she did not care. The confusion spread through her whole body and she could not stop it, she did not want to. She reached up and her fingers went into his hair. She pulled his face down on hers. His teeth crushed her lips – sweet, exciting pain. His hand came round from her back and enclosed a fat round breast. Through the thin cotton he found the erectness of her nipple and rolled it gently between his fingers. She reacted like a filly feeling the whip for the first time. One instant she lay under the shock of his touch and then her convulsive heave caught him by surprise. He went backwards off the cot and his head cracked against the wooden chest. He sat on the floor and stared up at her, too surprised even to rub the lump on his head. Her face was flushed and she pushed the hair back from her forehead with both hands. She was shaking her head wildly in her effort to speak through her gasping. 'You must go now, meneer – the servants have made a bed for you in one of the other wagons.'

Sean scrambled to his feet. 'But, I thought . . . surely we are . . . well, I mean.'

'Keep away from me,' she warned anxiously. 'If you touch me again tonight, I'll . . . I'll bite you.'

'But, Katrina, please, I can't sleep in the other wagon.' The thought appalled him.

'I'll cook your food, mend your clothes . . . everything! But until you find a priest . . .' She didn't go on, but Sean got the idea. He started to argue. It was his introduction to Boer immovability and at last he went to find his own bed. One of Katrina's dogs was there before him – a three-quarters-grown brindle hound. Sean's attempts to persuade it to leave were as ill-fated as had been his previous arguments with its mistress. They shared the bed. During the night a difference of opinion arose between them as to what constituted a half-share of the blankets. From it the dog earned its name – Thief.

= 16 =

Sean determined to show Katrina just how strongly he resented her attitude. He would be polite but distant. Five minutes after they had sat down to breakfast the next morning this demonstration of disapproval had deteriorated to the stage where he was unable to take his eyes off her face and he was talking so much that breakfast lasted an hour.

The rain held steady for three more days and then it stopped. The sun came back, as welcome as an old friend, but it was another ten days before the river regained its sanity. Time, rain or river meant very little to the two of them. They wandered out into the bush together to pick mushrooms; they sat in camp and when Katrina was working Sean followed her around. Then, of course, they talked. She listened to him. She laughed at the right places and gasped with wonder when she was meant to. She was a good listener. As for Sean, if she had repeated the same word over and over the sound of her voice alone would have held him entranced. The evenings were difficult. Sean would start getting restless and make excuses to touch her. She wanted him to, but she was frightened of the confusion that had so nearly trapped her the first night. So she drew up a set of rules and put them to him. 'Do you promise not to do anything more than kiss me?'

'Not unless you say I can,' Sean agreed readily.

'No.' She saw the catch in that.

'You mean, I must never do anything but kiss you even if you say I can?'

She started to blush. 'If I say so in the daytime, that's different . . . but anything I say at night doesn't count, and if you break your promise I'll never let you touch me again.'

Katrina's rules stood unchanged by the time the river had dropped enough for the wagons to be taken across to the north bank. The rains were resting, gathering their strength, but soon they would set in once more. The river was full but no longer murderous. Now was the time to cross. Sean took the oxen across first, swimming them in a herd. Holding on to one of their tails he had a Nantucket sleigh-ride across the river and when he reached the north bank there was a joyous welcome awaiting him.

They took six thick coils of unused rope from the stores wagon and joined them together. With the end of the rope round his waist Sean made one of his horses tow him back across the river, Mbejane paying out the line to him as he went. Then Sean supervised Katrina's servants as they emptied all the water barrels and lashed them to the sides of the first wagon to serve as floats. They ran the wagon into the water, tied on the rope and adjusted the barrels so that the wagon floated level. Sean signalled to Mbejane and waited until he had made the other end of the rope fast to a tree on the north bank. Then they pushed the wagon into the current and watched anxiously as it swung across the river like a pendulum, the current driving it but the tree anchoring it. It hit the north bank a distance the exact width of the river downstream of the tree, and Sean's party cheered as Mbejane and the other servants ran down the bank to retrieve it. Mbejane had a team of oxen standing ready and they dragged it out. Sean's horse towed him across the river again to fetch the rope.

Sean, Katrina and all her servants rode across on the last wagon. Sean stood behind Katrina with his arms round her waist, ostensibly to steady her, and the servants shouted and chattered like children on a picnic.

The water piled up brown against the side of the wagon, tilting it and making it roll, and with an exhilarating swoop they shot across the river and crashed into the far bank. The impact tumbled them overboard, throwing them into the knee-deep water beside the bank. They scrambled ashore. The water streamed out of Katrina's dress, her hair melted wetly over her face; she had mud on one cheek and she was gasping with laughter. Her sodden petticoats clung to her legs, tripping her, and Sean picked her up and carried her to his own laager. His servants shouted loud encouragement after him and Katrina shrieked genteelly to be put down, but held tight round his neck with both arms.

17

Now that the rains had changed every irregularity in the land into a waterhole and sowed new green grass where before had been dust and dry earth, the game scattered away from the river. Every few days Sean's trackers came into camp to report that there were no elephant. Sean condoled with them and sent them out again. He was well satisfied; there was a new quarry now, more elusive and therefore more satisfying than an old bull elephant with a hundred and fifty pounds of ivory on each side of his face. Yet to call Katrina his quarry was a lie. She was much more than that.

She was a new world – a place of endless mysteries and unexpected delights, an enchanting mixture of woman and child. She supervised the domestic routine with deceptive lack of fuss. With her there, suddenly his clothes were clean and had their full complement of buttons; the stew of boots and books and unwashed socks in his wagon vanished. There were fresh bread and fruit preserves on the table; Kandhla's eternal grilled steaks gave way to a variety of dishes. Each day she showed a new accomplishment. She could ride astride, though Sean had to turn his back when she mounted and dismounted. She cut Sean's hair and made as good a job of it as his barber in Johannesburg. She had a medicine chest in her wagon from which she produced remedies for every ailing man or beast in the company. She handled a rifle like a man and could strip and clean Sean's Mannlicher. She helped him load cartridges, measuring the charges with a practised eye. She could discuss birth and procreation with a clinical objectivity and a minute later blush all over when he looked at her that way. She was as stubborn as a mule, haughty when it suited her, serene and inscrutable at times and at others a little girl. She would push a handful of grass down the back of his shirt and run for him to chase her, giggle for minutes at a secret thought, play long imaginative games in which the dogs were her children and she talked to them and answered for them. Sometimes she was so naive that Sean thought she was joking until he remembered how young she was. She could drive him from happiness to spitting anger and back again within the space of an hour. But, once he had won her confidence and she knew that he would play to the rules, she responded to his caresses with a violence that startled them both. Sean was completely absorbed in her. She was the most wonderful thing he had ever found and, best of all, he could talk to her. He told her about Duff. She saw the extra cot in his wagon and found clothing that was obviously too small for him. She asked about it and he told her all of it and she understood.

The days became weeks. The cattle grew fat, their skins sleek and tight. Katrina planted a small vegetable garden and reaped a crop from it. Christmas came and Katrina baked a cake. Sean gave her a kaross of monkey skins that Mbejane had worked on in secret. Katrina gave Sean hand-sewn shirts, each with his initials embroidered on the top pocket, and she relaxed the rules a fraction.

Then when the new year had begun and Sean hadn't killed an elephant in six weeks, Mbejane headed a deputation from the gunboys. The question he had to ask, though tactfully disguised, was simply, 'Did we come here to hunt, or what?'

They broke camp and moved north again and the strain was showing on Sean at last. He tried to sweat it out by long days of hunting but this didn't help for conditions were so bad that they added to his irritability. The grass in most places was higher than a mounted man's head, its sharp edges cut as he passed through it. But the grass seeds were the worst: half an inch long and barbed like an arrow they worked their way quickly through clothing and into the skin. In the humid heat the small wounds they made festered within hours. Then there were the flies. Hippo-flies, greenheaded flies, sand-flies all with one thing in common – they stung. The soft skin behind the ears was their favourite place. They'd creep upon him, settle so lightly he wouldn't feel it – then, ping with the red-hot needle. Always wet, sometimes with sweat, other times with rain, Sean would close with a herd of elephant. He would hear them moving in the long grass around him and see the white canopy of egrets fluttering over them, but it was seldom he could get a shot at them. If he did he had to stand in the centre of a storm of blundering bodies. Often they would be following a herd, almost upon them, when Sean would lose interest and they'd all go back to camp. He couldn't keep away.

He was miserable, his servants were miserable, and Katrina was happy as a bird at daybreak. She had a man, she was mistress of a household which she ran with confidence and, because her senses were not yet as seasoned as Sean's, she was physically content. Even with Sean's strict adherence to the rules, their evenings in her wagon would end for her with a sigh and a shudder and she would go dreamy-eyed to bed and leave Sean with a burning devil inside of him. The only person Sean could complain to was Thief. He would lie with his snout buried in Sean's armpit, with at least his share of the blankets over him, and listen quietly.

The Zulus could see what the trouble was but they didn't understand it. They didn't discuss it, of course, but if one of them spread his hands expressively or coughed in a certain way the others knew what he meant. Mbejane came closest to actually putting it into words. Sean had just thrown a tantrum. It was a matter of a lost axe and who was responsible. Sean lined them up and expressed doubts as to their ancestry, present worth and future prospects, then he stormed off to his wagon. There was a long silence and Hlubi offered his snuff-box to Mbejane.

Mbejane took a pinch and said, 'It's a stupid stallion that doesn't know how to kick down a fence.'

'It is true, it is true,' they agreed, and there the matter rested.

= 18 =

A week later they reached the Sabi river. The mountains on the far side were blue-grey with distance and the river was full – brown and full.

The next morning was fresh and cool from the night's rain. The camp smelt of wood-smoke, cattle and wild mimosa. From one of the ostrich eggs that Mbejane had found the day before, Katrina made an omelette the size of a soup-plate. It was flavoured with nutmeg and chunks of mushroom, yellow and rich. Afterwards there were scones and wild honey, coffee and a cheroot for Sean.

'Are you going out today?' Katrina asked.

'Uh huh.'

'Oh!'

'Don't you want me to?'

'You haven't stayed in camp for a week.'

'Don't you want me to go?'

She stood up quickly and started clearing the table. 'Anyway you won't find any elephant . . . you haven't found anything for ages.'

'Do you want me to stay?'

'It's such a lovely day.' She signed to Kandhla to take the plates away.

'If you want me to stay, ask me properly.'

'We could look for mushrooms.'

'Say it,' said Sean.

'All right then, please!'

'Mbejane! Take the saddle off that horse, I won't be using him.'

Katrina laughed. She ran to her wagon, skirts swirling around her legs, calling to the dogs. She came back with her bonnet on and a basket in her hand. The dogs crowded round them, jumping up and barking.

'Go on . . . seek up then,' Sean told them and they raced ahead, circling back barking, chasing one another. Sean and Katrina walked holding hands. The brim of Katrina's bonnet kept her face in shadow, but even then her eyes when she looked at him were bright green. They picked the new mushrooms, round and hard, brown and slightly sticky on top, fluted underneath delicately as a lady's fan. In an hour they had filled the basket and they stopped under a marula tree. Sean lay on his back. Katrina broke off a blade of grass and tickled his face with it until he caught her wrist and pulled her down onto his chest. The dogs watched them, sitting around them in a circle, their tongues hanging out pink and wet.

'There's a place in the Cape, just outside Paarl. The mountains stand over it and there's a river . . . the water's very clear, you can see the fish lying on the bottom,' said Katrina. Her ear was against his chest and she was listening to his heart. 'Will you buy me a farm there one day?'

'Yes,' said Sean.

'We'll build a house with a wide veranda and on Sundays we'll drive to church with the girls and the little ones in the back and the bigger boys riding next to the buggy.'

'How many will there be?' asked Sean. He lifted the side of her bonnet and looked at her ear. It was a very pretty ear, in the sunlight he could see the fine fur on the lobe.

'Oh lots . . . boys mostly, but a few girls.'

'Ten?' suggested Sean.

'More than that.'

'Fifteen?'

'Yes, fifteen.'

They lay and thought about it. To Sean it seemed a fairly well-rounded number.

'And I'll keep chickens, I want lots of chickens.'

'All right,' said Sean.

'You don't mind?'

'Should I?'

'Some people mind chickens, some people don't like them at all,' said Katrina. 'I'm glad you don't mind them. I've always wanted them.'

Stealthily Sean advanced his mouth towards her ear but she felt him move and sat up.

'What are you doing?'

'This,' said Sean and his arm shot out.

'No, Sean, they're watching us.' She waved her hand at the dogs.

'They'll understand,' said Sean and then they were both quiet for a long time.

The dogs burst out together in full hunting chorus. Katrina sat up and Sean turned his head and saw the leopard. It stood fifty yards away on the edge of the thick bush along the river bank watching them, poised elegantly in tights of black and gold, long and small-bellied. It moved then, blurring with speed, touching the ground as lightly as a swallow touches the water when it drinks in flight. The dogs went after it in a pack, Thief leading them, his voice cracking with excitement.

'Back, come back,' shouted Sean. 'Leave it, damn you, come back.'

'Stop them, Sean, go after them. We'll lose them all.'

'Wait here,' Sean told her.

He ran after the sound of the pack. Not shouting, saving his wind. He knew what would happen and he listened for it. He heard the tone of the hunt change – sharper now. Sean stopped and stood panting, peering ahead. The dogs were not moving. The sound of their barking was steady in volume.

'The swine has stopped; he's going to take them.'

He started running again and almost immediately heard the first dog scream. He kept running. He found the dog lying where the leopard had flung it – the old bitch with white ears, her stomach was stripped out. Sean went on. The tan ridgeback next, disembowelled, still alive and crawling to meet him. He ran on; always the hunt was out of sight ahead of him but he kept after it. He no longer stopped to help the dogs that had been mauled. Most of them were dead before he reached them. The saliva thickened in his mouth, his heart jumped against his ribs and he reeled as he ran.

Suddenly he was in the open and the hunt was spread out before him. There were three dogs left. One of them was Thief. They were circling the leopard, belling him, darting in at his back legs, snapping, then jumping back as the leopard spun snarling. The grass was short and green in the clearing. The sun was directly overhead: it threw no shadow, it lit everything with a flat, even light. Sean tried to shout but his throat wouldn't let the sound out. The leopard dropped onto its back and lay with the sprawled grace of a sleeping cat, its legs open and its belly exposed. The dogs hung back, hesitating. Sean shouted again but his voice still would not carry. That creamy yellow belly, soft and fluffy, was too much temptation. One of the dogs went for it, dipping its head, its mouth open. The leopard closed on it like a spring trap. It caught and held the dog with its front paws and its back legs worked quickly. The dog yammered at the swift surgeon strokes and then it was thrown aside, its bowels hanging out. The leopard relaxed again to show the yellow bait of its belly. Sean was close now and this time the two dogs heard his shout. The leopard heard it also. It flashed to its feet and tried to break, but the instant it turned Thief was at it, slashing at its back legs forcing it to swing and crouch.

'Here, boy, leave him! Here, Thief, come here!'

Thief took Sean's shout as encouragement. He danced just out of reach of the flicking paws, shrilly taunting the leopard. The hunt was finely balanced now. Sean knew if he could get the dogs to slacken their attack the leopard would run. He went forward a pace, stooped to pick up a stone to throw at Thief and his movement tipped the balance. When he straightened up the leopard was watching him and he felt the eel of fear move in his stomach. It was going to come for him. He knew it by the way its ears flattened against its head and its shoulders bunched like loaded springs. Sean dropped the stone and reached for the knife on his belt.

The leopard's lips peeled back. Its teeth were yellow, its head with the ears flattened was like a snake's. It came fast and low against the ground, brushing the dogs aside. Its run was long-reaching, smoothly beautiful. It snaked towards him, fast over the short grass. It came into the air, lifting high, very fast and very smoothly. Sean felt the shock and the pain together. The shock threw him backwards and the pain sucked the breath from his lungs. Its claws hooked into his chest, he felt them scrape his ribs. He held its mouth from his face, his forearm against its throat and he smelt the overripe grave smell of its breath. They rolled together in the grass, its front claws still holding in the flesh of his chest, and he felt its back legs coming up to rake his stomach. He twisted desperately to keep clear of them, using his knife at the same time, slipping the blade into its back. The leopard screamed, its back legs came up again; he felt the claws go into his hip and tear down his thigh. The pain was deep and strong and he knew he was badly hurt. The legs came up again. This time they would kill him.

Thief locked his teeth in the leopard's leg before the claws could catch in Sean's flesh, he dragged back, digging in with his front feet, holding the leopard stretched out across Sean's body. Sean's vision was dissolving into blackness and bright lights. He pushed the knife into the leopard's back, close to the spine and pulled it down between the ribs the way a butcher cuts a chop. The leopard screamed again with its body shuddering and its claws curling in Sean's flesh. Sean cut again, deep and long – and again, then again. Tearing at it, mad with the pain, its blood gushed out and mixed with his and he rolled away from it. The dogs were worrying it, growling. It was dead. Sean let the knife slip out of his hand and touched the tears in his leg. The blood was dark red, pouring with the thickness of treacle, much blood. He was looking down a funnel of darkness. The leg was far away, not his – not his leg.

'Garry,' he whispered. 'Garry, oh God! I'm sorry. I slipped, I didn't mean it, I slipped.' The funnel closed and there was no leg – only darkness. Time was a liquid thing, all the world was liquid, moving in darkness. The sun was dark and only the pain was steady, steady as a rock in the dark moving sea. He saw Katrina's face indistinct in the darkness. He tried to tell her how sorry he was. He tried to tell her it was an accident, but the pain stopped him. She was crying. He knew she would understand so he went back into the dark sea. Then the surface of the sea boiled and he choked in the heat, but always the pain was there like a rock to hold onto. The steam from the sea coiled up around him and it hardened into the shape of a woman and he thought it was Katrina, then he saw its head was a leopard's head and its breath stank like the rotting of a gangrenous leg.

'I don't want you – I know who you are,' he shouted at it. 'I don't want you. It's not my child,' and the thing broke into steam, twisting grey steam, and came back gibbering at him on a chain that tinkled, frothing yellow from the grey misty mouth, and terror came with it. He twisted and covered his face, holding onto the pain for the pain was real and steady.

Then after a thousand years the sea froze and he walked on it and the white ice stretched away wherever he looked. It was cold and lonely on the ice. There was a small wind, a cold small wind, the wind whispered across the ice and its whispering was a sad sound, and Sean held his pain, hugging it close to him for he was lonely and only the pain was real. Then there were other figures moving around him on the ice, dark figures all hurrying one way, crowding him, pushing him along with them and he lost his pain, lost it in the desperate hurrying press. And though they had no faces, some of the figures wept and others laughed and they hurried forward until they came to the place where the crevasse split across the ice in front of them. The crevasse was wide and deep and its sides were white, then pale-green shading to blue and at last to infinite blackness, and some of the figures threw themselves joyfully into it singing as they fell. Others clung to edges, their formless faces full of fear, and still others stepped off into the void, tiredly, like travellers at the end of a long journey. When Sean saw the crevasse he began to fight, throwing himself back against the crowd that bore him forward, carrying him to the edge of the pit, and his feet slid over the edge. He clawed with his fingers at the slippery edge of the ice. He fought and he shouted as he fought for the dark drop sucked at his legs. Then he lay quietly and the crevasse had closed and he was alone. He was tired – wasted and terribly tired. He closed his eyes and the pain carne back to him, throbbing softly in his leg.

He opened his eyes and he saw Katrina's face. She was pale and her eyes were big and heavily underscored in blue. He tried to lift his hand to touch her face but he couldn't move.

'Katrina,' he said. He saw her eyes go green with surprise and happiness.

'You've come back. Oh, thank God. You've come back.'

Sean rolled his head and looked at the canvas of the wagon tent.

'How long?' he asked. His voice was a whisper.

'Five days . . . Don't talk – please, don't talk.'

Sean closed his eyes. He was very tired so he slept.

= 19 =

Katrina washed him when he woke. Mbejane helped her lift and turn him, his big pink-palmed hands very gentle as he handled the leg. They washed the smell of fever off him and changed the dressings. Sean watched Katrina as she worked and every time she looked up they smiled at each other. Once he used a little of his strength to ask Mbejane, 'Where were you when I needed you?'

'I slept in the sun, Nkosi, like an old woman,' Mbejane half-laughed, half-apologized. Katrina brought him food and when he smelt it he was hungry. He ate it all and then he slept again.

Mbejane built a shelter with open sides and a roof of thatch. He sited it in the shade on the bank of the Sabi. Then he made a bed of poles and laced leather thongs. They carried Sean from the wagon, Katrina fussing around them until they had laid him in the shelter. Katrina went back to the wagon for pillows and when she returned she found Thief and Sean settling down comfortably.

'Sean, get that monster out of there – those blankets have just been washed.'

Thief flattened his body and hid his head in Sean's armpit.

'It's all right, he's quite clean,' Sean protected him.

'He smells.'

'He does not.' Sean sniffed at Thief. 'Well, not much anyway.'

'You two!' She put the pillows under Sean's head and went round to his leg. 'How does it feel?'

'It's fine,' said Sean. Thief inched himself up the bed until he reached the pillows.

In the slow slide of days Sean's body healed and the well of his strength filled. The moving air under the shelter dried the scabs off his chest and leg, but there would be scars. In the mornings, after breakfast, Sean held court from his couch. Katrina sat on the end of the bed and his servants squatted around him. First they talked over domestic matters – the health of the oxen, mentioning them by name, discussing their eyes, hooves and stomachs. There was a tear in the canvas of one wagon. The single remaining bitch was in season – was Thief man enough for the job yet? There was meat to kill – perhaps the Nkosikaze would take the rifle later today. Hlubi had caught four barbel of medium size in his fish trap, and here the talk turned to the bush around them. A lion had killed a buffalo below the first bend in the river – there you could see the vultures. During the night a herd of cow elephant had drunk a mile upstream. Each item was considered by the meeting. Everyone felt free to comment or argue against any view which conflicted with his own. When everything had been said Sean gave them their tasks for the day and sent them away. Then he and Katrina could be alone.

From the shelter they could see the full sweep of the river, with the crocodiles lying on the white sandbars and the kingfishers plopping into the shallows. They sat close to each other and they talked of the farm they would have. Sean would grow grapes and breed horses and Katrina would keep chickens. By the next rainy season they would have filled all the wagons; one more trip after that and they would have enough to buy the farm.

Katrina kept him in bed long after he was strong enough to leave it. She mothered him and he loved it. Shamelessly, in the fashion of the male, he accepted her attentions and even exaggerated his injuries a little. Finally but reluctantly Katrina let him up. He stayed in camp a week more, until his legs stopped wobbling, then one evening he took his rifle and went with Mbejane to shoot fresh meat. They went slowly, Sean favouring his leg, and he shot a young eland not far from the laager. Sean sat against a msasa tree and smoked a cheroot while Mbejane went back to fetch servants to carry the meat. Sean watched them butcher the carcass; there were slabs of white fat on the meat. They slung it on poles and carried it between them, two men to a pole, and when they got back to camp Sean found Katrina in one of her inscrutable moods. When he talked to her at supper she answered him from far away and afterwards by the fire she sat detached from him. She was very lovely and Sean was puzzled and a little resentful. At last he stood up.

'It's time for bed – I'll see you to your wagon.'

'You go. I'll sit a little longer.'

Sean hesitated. 'Is there something wrong? Have I done something wrong?'

'No,' she said quickly. 'No. I'm all right. You go to bed.'

He kissed her cheek. 'If you need me I'll be close. Goodnight, sleep sweet.'

He straightened up. 'Come on, Thief,' he said. 'Time for bed.'

'Leave Thief with me, please.' Katrina caught the skin at the back of the dog's neck and restrained him.

'Why?'

'I just feel like company.'

'Then I'll stay as well,' Sean moved to sit down again.

'No, you go to bed.' She sounded desperate and Sean looked hard at her.

'Are you sure you're all right?'

'Yes, please go.'

He went to his wagon and looked back at her. She was sitting very straight, holding the dog. He climbed into the wagon. The lamp was lit and he stopped in surprise when he saw his cot. There were sheets on it, not just the rough blankets. He ran his hand over the smooth fabric; it was crisp from new ironing. He sat on the cot and pulled off his boots. He undid his shirt and threw it onto the chest, then he lay back and looked up at the lamp.

'There's something bloody funny going on here,' he said.

'Sean' – her voice just outside the wagon. Sean jumped up and opened the flap. 'Can I come in?'

'Yes, of course.' He gave her his hand and lifted her into the wagon. He looked at her face. She was frightened.

'There *is* something wrong,' he said.

'No, don't touch me. There's something I've got to tell you. Sit down on the cot.'

Sean watched her face. He was worried.

'I thought I loved you when I came away with you. I thought we had for ever to be together.' She swallowed painfully. 'Then I found you there in the grass – torn and dead. Before our life together had begun you were dead.'

Sean saw the pain come back into her eyes; she was living it again. He put out his hand to her but she held his wrist.

'No, wait . . . please let me finish. I have to explain to you. It's very important.'

Sean dropped his hand and she went on speaking quickly.

'You were dead and I, too, was dying inside. I felt empty. There was nothing left. Nothing . . . just the hollowness inside and the dry dead feeling on the outside. I touched your face and you looked at me. I prayed then, Sean, and I prayed through the days when you fought the rotting of your body.'

She knelt in front of him and held him around the waist.

'Now we are alive and together again, but I know that it cannot be for ever. A day more, a year, if we are lucky, twenty. But not for ever. I see how small I have been to us. I want to be your wife.'

He bent to her quickly but she pulled away and stood up. She slipped the buttons and her clothing fell away. She loosed her hair and let it drop shiny bright down the whiteness of her body.

'Look at me, Sean, I want you to look at me. This and my love I can give you . . . is it enough?'

There was smoothness, hollow and swell, hair like black fire and soft light on soft skin. He saw the flush from her cheeks spread onto her breasts until they glowed, pink and shy but proud in their perfection. He looked no further. He took her to him and covered her nakedness with his big body. She was trembling and he put her between the sheets and gentled her with his voice until the trembling stopped and she lay with her face pressed up under his beard into his neck.

'Show me how . . . I want to give everything to you. Please show me how,' she whispered.

So they married each other and their marriage was a co-mingling of many things. There was the softness of the wind in it and wanting, the way the baked earth wants the rain. There was pain sharp and swift, movement like running horses, sound low as voices in the night but glad as a greeting, joy climbing on eagles' wings, the triumphant surge and burst of wild water on a rock shore and then there was stillness and warmth within and the snuggling of drowsy puppies, and sleep. Yet it did not end in the sleep, it went on to another seeking and finding, another union and a stranger mystery in the secret depths of her body.

= 20 =

In the morning she brought her Bible to him.

'Hey, hey,' protested Sean, 'I've already sworn one oath.' Katrina laughed at him, the memory of the night still warm and happy inside her. She opened the book at its fly leaf.

'You've got to write your name in it . . . here, next to mine.'

She watched him, standing next to his chair with her hip touching his shoulder.

'And your date of birth,' she said.

Sean wrote: 'Ninth Jan. 1862.' Then he said: 'What's this "date of death" . . . do you want me to fill that in as well?'

'Don't talk like that,' she said quickly and touched the wooden table.

Sean was sorry he'd said it. He tried to cover up. 'There's only space for six children.'

'We can write the others in the margin. That's what Ma did . . . hers even go over onto the first page of Genesis. Do you think we'll get that far, Sean?'

Sean smiled at her. 'The way I feel now we should reach the New Testament without much trouble.'

They had made a good start. By June the rains were over and Katrina walked with her shoulders back to balance her load. There was a good feeling in the camp. Katrina was more woman than child now. She was big and radiant, pleased with the awe her condition inspired in Sean. She sang to herself often and sometimes in the night she would let him share in it. She would let him pull the nightdress back from the mound of her stomach and lay his ear against the tight-stretched, blue-veined skin. He listened to the suck and gurgle and felt the movement against his cheek. When he sat up his eyes would be full of the wonder of it and she would smile proudly at him and take his head on her shoulder and they would lie together quietly. In the daytime things were right as well. Sean laughed with the servants and hunted without the intensity of before.

They moved north along the Sabi river. Sometimes they camped for a month at one place. The game came back to the rivers as the veld dried out and once more the ivory started piling up in the wagons.

One afternoon in September Sean and Katrina left the camp and walked along the bank. The land was brown again and smelt of dry grass. The river was pools and white sand.

'Hell, it's hot.' Sean took off his hat and wiped the sweat off his forehead. 'You must be cooking under all those clothes.'

'No, I'm all right.' Katrina was holding his arm.

'Let's have a swim.'

'You mean with no clothes on?' Katrina looked shocked.

'Yes, why not?'

'It's rude.'

'Come on.' He took her down the bank protesting every step and at a place where boulders screened the water he prised her out of her dress. She was laughing and gasping and blushing all at the same time. He carried her into the pool and she sat down thankfully with the water up to her chin.

'How's that feel?' Sean asked.

She let her hair down and it floated out round her, she wriggled her toes in the sand and her stomach showed through the water like the back of a white whale.

'It's nice,' she admitted. 'It feels like silk underwear against my skin.'

Sean stood over her with only his hat on. She looked at him.

'Sit down,' she said uncomfortably and looked away from him.

'Why?' he asked.

'You know why . . . you're rude, that's why.'

Sean sat down beside her.

'You should be used to me by now.'

'Well, I'm not.'

Sean put his arm round her under the water.

'You're lovely,' he said. 'You're my fancy.'

She let him kiss her ear.

'What's it going to be?' He touched the ripe swelling. 'Boy or girl?' This was currently the favourite topic of conversation.

'Boy.' She was very definite.

'What shall we call him?'

'Well, if you don't find a *predikant* soon we'll have to call him the name you're always giving to the servants.'

Sean stared at her. 'What do you mean?'

'You know what you call them when you're cross.'

'Bastard,' said Sean, then really concerned, 'Hell, I hadn't thought of that! We'll have to find a priest. No child of mine will be a bastard. We'll have to go back to Louis Trichardt.'

'You've got about a month,' Katrina warned him.

'My God, we'll never make it. We've left it too late.' Sean's face was ghastly. 'Wait, I've got it. There are Portuguese settlements across the mountains on the coast.'

'Oh, Sean, but they're Roman Catholics.'

'They all work for the same boss.'

'How long will it take to cross the mountains?' Katrina asked doubtfully.

'I don't know. Perhaps two weeks to reach the coast on horseback.'

'On horseback?' Katrina looked still more doubtfully.

'Oh hell . . . you can't ride!' Sean scratched the side of his nose. 'I'll have to go and fetch one. Will you stay on your own? I'll leave Mbejane to look after you.'

'Yes, I'll be all right.'

'I won't go if you don't want me to. It's not that important.'

'It is important, you know it is. I'll be all right, truly I will.'

Before he left the next morning Sean took Mbejane aside. 'You know why you're not coming with me, don't you?'

Mbejane nodded, but Sean answered his own question. 'Because there is more important work for you to do here.'

'At night,' said Mbejane, 'I will sleep beneath the Nkosikazi's wagon.'

'You'll sleep?' asked Sean threateningly.

'Only once in a while and then very lightly,' Mbejane grinned.

'That's better,' said Sean.

= 21 =

Sean said goodbye to Katrina. There were no tears, she understood necessity and helped him to a quiet acceptance of it. They stood a long while beside their wagon, holding each other, their lips almost touching as they whispered together and then Sean called for his horse. Hlubi followed him leading the packhorse when he crossed the Sabi and when Sean reached the far bank he turned and looked back. Katrina was still standing by their wagon and behind her hovered Mbejane. In her bonnet and green dress she looked very young. Sean waved his hat over his head and then set off towards the mountains.

The forests dwindled into grassland as they climbed and each night was colder than the last. Then, in its turn the grassland conceded to the sheer bluffs and misty gorges of the mountain back. Sean and Hlubi struggled upwards, following the game trails, losing them, turning back from impassable cliffs, scouting for a pass, leading the horses over the steep pitches and at night sitting close to the fire and listening to the baboons barking in the kranses around them. Then suddenly, in the middle of a morning that was bright as a cut diamond, they were at the top. To the west the land lay spread out like a map and the distance they had travelled in a week was pathetically small. By straining his eyes and his imagination Sean could make out the dark-green belt of the Sabi watercourse. To the cast the land merged with a blueness that was not the sky and for a while he failed to recognize it. Then – 'the sea,' he shouted and Hlubi laughed with him for it was a godlike feeling to stand above the world. They found an easier route down the eastern slopes and followed it onto the coastal plain. At the bottom of the mountains they came to a native village. To see cultivated lands and human dwellings again was a small shock to Sean. He had come to accept the fact that he and his retinue were the only people left on earth.

The entire population of the village fled when they saw him. Mothers snatched up a child in each hand and ran as fast as their menfolk – memories of the slave-traders still persisted in this part of Africa. Within two minutes of his arrival Sean again had the feeling that he was the only person left on earth. With the contempt of the Zulu for every other tribe in Africa, Hlubi shook his head sadly.

'Monkeys,' he said.

They dismounted and tied their horses under the big tree that was the centre of the village. They sat in the shade and waited. The huts were grass beehives, their roofs blackened with smoke, and a few chickens picked and scratched at the bare earth between them. Half an hour later Sean saw a black face watching him from the edge of the bush and he ignored it. Slowly the face emerged, followed closely by a reluctant body. With a twig, Sean went on drawing patterns in the dust between his feet. Out of the corner of his eye he watched the hesitant approach. It was an old man with stork thin legs and one eye glazed into a white jelly by tropical ophthalmia. Sean concluded that his fellows had picked him to act as ambassador on the grounds that of all their number he would be the least loss.

Sean looked up and gave him a radiant smile. The old man froze and then his lips twitched into a sickly grin of relief. Sean stood up, dusted his hands on the sides of his breeches and went to shake the old man's hand. Immediately the bush around them swarmed with people, they poured back into the village jabbering and laughing: they crowded round Sean and felt his clothing, peered into his face and exclaimed delightedly. It was obvious that most of them had never seen a white man before. Sean was trying to shake off One-Eye, who still had a possessive hold on Sean's right hand, and Hlubi leaned disdainfully against the tree, taking no part in the welcome. One-Eye ended the confusion by screeching at them in a voice rusty with age. The courage he had displayed earlier now earned its reward. At his command a dozen of the younger women scampered off and came back with a carved wooden stool and six earthenware pots of native beer. By the hand, on which he had not for an instant relaxed his grip, One-Eye led Sean to the stool and made him sit; the rest of the villagers squatted in a circle round him and one of the girls brought the biggest beer-pot to Sean. The beer was yellow and it bubbled sullenly. Sean's stomach shied at the sight of it. He glanced at One-Eye who was watching him anxiously, he lifted the pot and sipped. Then he smiled with surprise; it was creamy and pleasantly tart.

'Good,' he said.

'Goot,' chorused the villagers.

'Your health,' said Sean.

' 'ealt,' said the village as one man, and Sean drank deep. One of the girls took another beer-pot to Hlubi. She knelt in front of him and shyly offered it. She had a plaited-grass string around her waist from which a small kilt hung down in front, but her stern was completely exposed and her bosoms were the size and shape of ripe melons. Hlubi looked at them until the girl hung her head, then he lifted the beer-pot.

Sean wanted a guide to the nearest Portuguese settlement. He looked at One-Eye and said, 'Town? Portagee?'

One-Eye was almost overcome by Sean's attention. He grabbed Sean's hand again before he could pull it away and shook it vigorously.

'Stop that, you bloody fool,' said Sean irritably and One-Eye grinned and nodded, then without releasing Sean's hand he began an impassioned speech to the other villagers. Sean meanwhile was searching his memory for the name of one of the Portuguese ports on this coast.

'Nova Sofala,' he shouted as he got it.

One-Eye broke off his speech abruptly and stared at Sean.

'Nova Sofala,' said Sean again pointing vaguely towards the east and One-Eye showed his gums in his biggest grin yet.

'Nova Sofala,' he agreed pointing with authority and then it was only a matter of minutes before it was understood between them that he would act as guide. Hlubi saddled the horses, One-Eye fetched a grass sleeping mat and a battle-axe from one of the huts. Sean mounted and looked at Hlubi to do the same but Hlubi was acting strangely.

'Yes?' Sean asked with resignation. 'What is it?'

'Nkosi.' Hlubi was looking at the branches of the tree above them. 'The Old One could lead the packhorse.'

'You can take it in turns,' said Sean.

Hlubi coughed and transferred his eyes to the fingernails of his left hand.

'Nkosi, is it possible that you will return to this village on the way back from the sea?'

'Yes, of course,' said Sean, 'we'll have to leave the Old One here. Why do you ask?'

'I have a thorn in my foot, Nkosi, it gives me pain. If you do not require me I will wait here for you. Perhaps the thorn wound will have healed by then.' Hlubi looked up at the tree again and shuffled his feet with embarrassment. Sean had not noticed him limping and he was puzzled as to why Hlubi should start malingering now. Then Hlubi could not stop himself from glancing at where the girl stood in the circle of villagers. Her kilt was very small and from the sides gave her no cover at all. Understanding came to Sean and he chuckled.

'The thorn you have is painful, but it's not in your foot.' Hlubi shuffled his feet again. 'You said they were monkeys . . . have you changed your mind?' Sean asked.

'Nkosi, they are indeed monkeys,' Hlubi sighed. 'But very friendly monkeys.'

'Stay then . . . but do not weaken yourself too much. We have mountains to cross on the way home.'

= 22 =

One-Eye led the packhorse – this made him very proud. Through tall grass, mangrove swamp and thick hot jungle, then through white coral sand and the curving stems of palm trees, they came at last to the sea. Nova Sofala was a fort with brass cannon and thick walls. The sea beyond it was muddy brown from the estuary that flowed into it.

The sentry at the gates said, *'Madre de Dio'* when he saw Sean, and took him to the Commandant. The Commandant was a small man with fever-yellowed face and a tired, sweat-darkened tunic. The Commandant said, *'Madre de Dio,'* and shot his chair back from his desk. It took some time for him to realize that contrary to appearance this dirty, bearded giant was not dangerous. The Commandant could speak English and Sean laid his problem before him.

For a certainty he could be of assistance. There were three Jesuit missionaries in the fort, freshly arrived from Portugal and eager for employment. Sean could take his pick but first he must bath, eat dinner with the Commandant and help him sample the wines that had arrived on the same boat as the missionaries. Sean thought that was a good idea.

At dinner he met the missionaries. They were young men, pink-faced still, for Africa had not yet had a chance to mark them. All three of them were willing to go with him and Sean selected the youngest – not for his appearance but rather for his name. 'Father Alphonso' had a heroic ring to it. The Jesuits went early to bed and left the Commandant, the four junior officers and Sean to the port. They drank toasts to Queen Victoria and her family and to the King of Portugal and his family. This made them thirsty so they drank to absent friends, then to each other. The Commandant and Sean swore a mutual oath of friendship and loyalty and this made the Commandant very sad, he cried and Sean patted his shoulder and offered to dance the Dashing White Sergeant for him, The Commandant said that he would esteem it as a very great honour and furthermore he would be delighted. He himself did not know this dance but perhaps Sean would instruct him. They danced on the table. The Commandant was doing very well until in his enthusiasm he misjudged the size of the table. Sean helped the junior officers put him to bed and in the morning Sean, Father Alphonso and One-Eye started back towards the mountains.

Sean was impatient of any delay now; he wanted to get back to Katrina. Father Alphonso's English was on a par with Sean's Portuguese. This made conversation difficult, so Alphonso solved the problem by doing all the talking. At first Sean listened but when he decided that the good father was trying to convert him he no longer bothered. Alphonso did not seem put out – he just went on talking and clinging to the horse with both hands while his cassock flapped about his legs and his face sweated in the shade of his wide-brimmed hat. One-Eye followed them like an ancient stork.

It took them two days back to One-Eye's village and their entry was a triumphal procession. Father Alphonso's face lit up when he saw so many prospective converts. Sean could see him mentally rubbing his hands together, and he decided to keep going before Alphonso forgot the main object of the expedition. He gave One-Eye a hunting-knife in payment for his services. One-Eye sat down under the big tree in the centre of the village, his own thin legs no longer able to support his weight and the knife clutched to his chest.

'Hlubi, you've had enough of that . . . come on now!' Sean had not dismounted and was restlessly waiting for Hlubi to say his farewells to three of the village girls. Hlubi had displayed traditional Zulu taste – all three of them were big-breasted, big-bottomed and young. They were also crying.

'Come on, Hlubi . . . what's the trouble?'

'Nkosi, they believe that I have taken them for my wives.'

'What made them think that?'

'Nkosi, I do not know.' Hlubi broke the armhold that the plumpest and youngest had around his neck, he snatched up his spears and fled. Sean and Alphonso galloped after him. The villagers shouted farewells and Sean looked back and saw One-Eye still sitting at the base of the big tree.

The pace which Sean set was at last telling on Alphonso. His verbal spring-tides slackened and he showed a measure of reluctance to let his backside touch the saddle; he rode crouched forward on his horse's neck with his buttocks in the air. They crossed the mountains and went down the other side; the ground levelled out into the Sabi Valley and they rode into the forest. On the ninth day out from Nova Sofala they reached the Sabi river. It was late afternoon. Flocks of guinea-fowl were drinking in the riverbed, they went up in a blue haze of whirling wings as Sean led his party down the bank. While the horses watered Sean spoke with Hlubi.

'Do you recognize this part of the river?'

'Yes, Nkosi, we are two hours' march upstream from the wagons . . . we held too far to the north coming through the forest.'

Sean looked at the sun, it was on the tree-tops.

'Half an hour's light left . . . and there's no moon tonight.'

'We could wait until morning,' Hlubi suggested hopefully. Sean ignored him and motioned to Alphonso to mount up. Alphonso was prepared to debate the advisability of moving on. Sean took a handful of his cassock and helped him into the saddle.

= 23 =

In the darkness the lantern burning in Katrina's wagon glowed through the canvas and guided them the last half mile into camp. Thief bayed them welcome and Mbejane ran out at the head of the other servants to take Sean's horse. His voice was loud with worry and relief.

'Nkosi, there is little time . . . it has begun.'

Sean jumped off his horse and ran to the wagon. He tore open the canvas flap.

'Sean.' She sat up. Her eyes were very green in the lantern light, but they were dark-ringed. 'Thank God, you've come.'

Sean knelt beside her cot and held her. He said certain things to her and she clung to him and moved her lips across his face. The world receded and left one wagon standing in darkness, lit by a single lamp and the love of two people.

Suddenly she stiffened in his arms and gasped. Sean held her, his face suddenly helpless and his big hands timid and uncertain on her shoulders.

'What can I do, my fancy? How can I help you?'

Her body relaxed slowly and she whispered, 'Did you find a priest?'

'The priest!' Sean had forgotten about him. Still holding onto her he turned his head and bellowed, 'Alphonso . . . Alphonso. Hurry, man.'

Father Alphonso's face in the opening of the wagon was pale with fatigue and grimy with dust.

'Marry us,' said Sean. 'Quickly, man, che-cha, chop-chop . . . you savvy?'

Alphonso climbed into the wagon. The skirts of his cassock were torn and his knees were white and bony through the holes. He stood over them and opened his book. 'Ring?' he asked in Portuguese.

'I do,' said Sean.

'No! No! Ring?' Alphonso held up a finger and made an encircling gesture. 'Ring?'

'I think he wants a wedding ring,' whispered Katrina.

'Oh, my God,' said Sean. 'I'd forgotten about that.' He looked round desperately. 'What can we use? Haven't you got one in your chest or something?'

Katrina shook her head, opened her lips to answer but closed them again as another pain took her. Sean held her while it lasted and when she relaxed he looked up angrily at Alphonso.

'Marry us . . . damn you. Don't you see there's no time for all the trimmings?'

'Ring?' said Alphonso again. He looked very unhappy.

'All right, I'll get you a ring.' Sean leapt out of the wagon and shouted at Mbejane. 'Bring my rifle, quickly.'

If Sean wanted to shoot the Portuguese that was his business and Mbejane's duty was to help him. He brought Sean the rifle. Sean found a gold sovereign in the pouch on his belt, he threw it on the ground and held the muzzle of the rifle on it. The bullet punched a ragged hole through it. He tossed the rifle back to Mbejane, picked up the small gold circle and scrambled back into the wagon.

Three times during the service the pains made Katrina gasp and each time Sean held her tight and Alphonso increased the speed of his delivery. Sean put the punctured sovereign on Katrina's finger and kissed her. Alphonso gabbled out the last line of Latin and Katrina said, 'Oh, Sean, it's coming.'

'Get out,' Sean told Alphonso and made an expressive gesture towards the door – thankfully Alphonso went.

It did not take long then, but to Sean it was an eternity – like that time when they had taken Garrick's leg. Then in a slippery rush it was finished. Katrina lay very quiet and pale, while on the cot below her, still linked to her, purple-blotched and bloody lay the child that they had made.

'It's dead,' croaked Sean. He was sweating and he had backed away against the far wall of the wagon.

'No,' Katrina struggled up fiercely. 'No, it's not . . . Sean, you must help me.'

She told him what to do and at last the child cried.

'It's a boy,' said Katrina softly. 'Oh, Sean . . . it's a boy.' She was more beautiful than he had ever seen her before; pale and tired and beautiful.

= 24 =

Sean's protests were in vain – Katrina left her bed the next morning and squeezed into one of her old dresses. Sean hovered between her and the child on the cot.

'I'm still so *fat,*' she lamented.

'Fancy, please stay in bed another day or two.'

She pulled a face at him and went on struggling with the lacing of her bodice.

'Who's going to look after the baby?'

'I will!' said Sean earnestly. 'You can tell me what to do.'

Arguing with Katrina was like trying to pick up quicksilver with your fingers, not worth the effort. She finished dressing and took up the child.

'You can help me down the steps.' She smiled at him. Sean and Alphonso set a chair for her in the shade of one of the big shuma trees and the servants came to see the child. Katrina held him in her lap and Sean stood over them in uncertain possession. For Sean it seemed unreal yet . . . too much for his mind to digest in so short a time. He grinned dazedly at the steady stream of comment from his servants and his arm was limp when Alphonso shook his hand for the twentieth time that morning.

'Hold your child . . . Nkosi. Let us see you with him on your arm,' called Mbejane and the other Zulus took up the cry. Sean's expression changed slowly to one of apprehension.

'Pick him up, Nkosi.'

Katrina proffered the bundle and a hunted look came into Sean's eyes.

'Have no fear, Nkosi, he has no teeth, he cannot harm you,' Hlubi encouraged him. Sean held his first-born awkwardly and assumed the hunchbacked posture of the new father. The Zulus cheered him and slowly Sean's face relaxed and his smile was a glow of pride.

'Mbejane, is he not beautiful?'

'As beautiful as his father,' Mbejane agreed.

'Your words are a blade with two edges,' laughed Sean. He looked at the child closely. It wore a cap of dark hair, its nose was flat as a bulldog's, its eyes were milky-grey and its legs were long, skinny and red,

'How will you name him?' asked Hlubi. Sean looked at Katrina.

'Tell them,' he said.

'He shall be called Dirk,' she said in Zulu.

'What is the meaning?' asked Hlubi, and Sean answered him.

'It means a dagger . . . a sharp knife.'

There was immediate nodded approval from all the servants. Hiubi produced his snuff-box and passed it among them and Mbejane took a pinch.

'That,' he said, 'is a good name.'

= 25 =

Paternity, the subtle alchemist, transformed Sean's attitude to life within twelve hours. Never before had anything been so utterly dependent upon him, so completely vulnerable. That first evening in their wagon he watched Katrina sitting cross-legged on her cot, stooping forward over the child to give it her breast. Her hair hung in a soft wing across one cheek, her face was fuller, more matronly and the child in her lap fed with a red face and small wheezings. She looked up at him and smiled and the child tugged her breast with its tiny fists and hunting mouth.

Sean crossed to the cot, sat beside them and put his arm around them. Katrina rubbed her cheek against his chest and her hair smelt warm and clean. The boy went on feeding noisily. Sean felt vaguely excited as though he were on the threshold of a new adventure.

A week later, when the first rain clouds built up in the sky, Sean took the wagons across the Sabi and onto the slopes of the mountains to escape the heat of the plains. There was a valley he had noticed when he and Hlubi had made their journey to the coast. The valley bottom was covered with short sweet grass and cedar trees grew along a stream of clean water. Sean took them to this place.

Here they would wait out the rainy season and when it was finished and the baby was strong enough to travel they could take the ivory south and sell it in Pretoria. It was a happy camp. The oxen spread out along the valley, filling it with movement and the contented sound of their lowing; there was laughter among the wagons and at night when the mist slumped down off the mountains the camp fire was bright and friendly. Father Alphonso stayed with them for nearly two weeks. He was a pleasant young man and although he and Sean never understood what the other was saying yet they managed well enough with sign language. He left at last with Hlubi and one of the other servants to escort him back over the mountains, but before he did he managed to embarrass Sean by kissing him goodbye. Sean and Katrina were sorry to see him go. They had grown to like him and Katrina had almost forgiven him his religion.

The rains came with the usual flourish and fury. Weeks drifted into months. Happy months, with life centring around Dirk's cot. Mbejane had made the cot for him out of cedarwood and one of Katrina's chests produced the sheets and blankets for it. The child grew quickly: each day he seemed to occupy more of his cot, his legs filled out, his skin lost its blotchy-purple look and his eyes were no longer a vague milky-blue. There was green in them now – they would be the same colour as his mother's.

To fill the long lazy days Sean started to build a cabin beside the stream. The servants joined in and from a modest first plan it grew into a thing of sturdy plastered walls and neatly thatched roof with a stone fireplace at one end. When it was finished Sean and Katrina moved into it. After their wagon with its thin canvas walls, the cabin gave a feeling of permanence to their love. One night, when the rain hissed down in darkness outside and the wind whined at the door like a dog wanting to be let in, they spread a mattress in front of the fireplace and there in the moving firelight they started another baby.

Christmas came, and after it the New Year. The rains stuttered and stopped and still they stayed on in their valley. Then at last they had to go, for their supplies of basic stores – powder, salt, medicines, cloth – were nearly finished. They loaded the wagons, inspanned and left in the early morning. As the line of wagons wound down the valley towards the plains Katrina sat on the box-seat of the lead wagon holding Dirk on her lap and Sean rode beside her. She looked back – the roof of their cabin showed brown through the branches of the cedar trees. It seemed forlorn and lonely.

'We must come back one day, we've been so happy here,' she said softly. Sean leaned out of the saddle towards her and touched her arm.

'Happiness isn't a place, my fancy, we aren't leaving it here, we're taking it with us.'

She smiled at him. The second baby was starting to show already.

= 26 =

They reached the Limpopo river at the end of July and found a place to cross. It took three days to unload the wagons, work them through the soft sand and then carry the ivory and stores across. They finished in the late afternoon of the third day and by then everyone was exhausted. They ate an early supper and an hour after sunset the Zulus were rolled in their blankets, and Sean and Katrina were sleeping arms-around and head-on-chest in the wagon. In the morning Katrina was quiet and a little pale. Sean didn't notice it until she told him that she felt tired and was going to lie down – immediately he was all attentive. He helped her into the wagon and settled the pillows under her head.

'Are you sure you're all right?' he kept asking.

'Yes . . . it's nothing, I'm just a bit tired. I'll be all right,' she assured him. She appreciated his concern but was relieved when finally he went to see to the business of reloading the wagons for Sean's ministrations were always a little clumsy. She wanted to be left alone, she felt tired and cold.

By midday the wagons were loaded to Sean's satisfaction. He went to Katrina's wagon, lifted the canvas and peeped in. He expected her to be asleep. She was lying on the cot with her eyes open and two of the thick grey blankets wrapped around her. Her face was as pale as a two-day corpse. Sean felt the first leap of alarm, he scrambled into the wagon.

'My dear, you look ghastly. Are you sick?' He put his hand on her shoulder and she was shivering. She didn't answer him, instead her eyes moved from his face to the floor near the foot of the bed and Sean's eyes followed hers. Katrina's luxury was her chamber-pot; it was a massive china thing with red roses hand-painted on it. She loved it dearly and Sean used to tease her when she was perched on top of it. Now the pot stood near the foot of the bed and when Sean saw what was in it his breathing stopped. It was half full of a liquid the colour of milk stout. 'Oh, my God,' he whispered. He went on staring at it, standing very still while a gruesome snatch of doggerel he remembered hearing sung in the canteens of the Witwatersrand began trotting through his brain like an undertaker's hack.

Black as the Angel,
Black as disgrace
When the fever waters flow
They're as black as the ace.

Roll him in a blanket
Feed him on quinine
But all of us we know
It's the end of the line.

Black as the Angel
Black as disgrace
Soon we'll lay him down below
And chuck dirt in his face.

He raised his head and looked steadily at her, searching for the signs of fear. But just as steadily she looked back at him.

'Sean, it's blackwater.'

'Yes . . . I know,' Sean said, for there was nothing to be gained by denial, no room for extravagant hope. It was blackwater fever: malaria in its most malignant form, attacking the kidneys and turning them to fragile sacks of black blood that the slightest movement could rupture. Sean knelt by her cot. 'You must lie very still.' He touched her forehead lightly with the tips of his fingers and felt the heat of her skin.

'Yes,' she answered him, but already the expression in her eyes was blurring and she made the first restless movement of delirium. Sean put his arm across her chest to hold her from struggling.

By nightfall Katrina was deep in the nightmare of malaria. She laughed, she screamed in senseless terror, she shook her head and fought him when he tried to make her drink.

But she had to drink, it was her one chance, to flush out her kidneys that she might live. Sean held her head and forced her.

Dirk started crying, hungry and frightened by the sight of his mother.

'Mbejane!' shouted Sean, his voice pitched high with desperation. Mbejane had waited all afternoon at the entrance of the wagon.

'Nkosi, what can I do?'

'The child . . . can you care for him?'

Mbejane picked up the cot with Dirk still in it. 'Do not worry about him again. I will take him to the other wagon.'

Sean turned his whole attention back to Katrina. The fever built up steadily within her. Her body was a furnace, her skin was dry and with every hour she was wilder and her movements more difficult to control.

An hour after dark Kandhla came to the wagon with a pot of steaming liquid and a cup. Sean's nose wrinkled as he caught the smell of it.

'What the hell is that?'

'I have stewed the bark from a maiden's breast tree . . . the Nkosikazi must drink it.'

It had the same musty smell as boiling hops and Sean hesitated. He knew the tree. It grew on high ground, it had a diseased-looking lumpy bark and each lump was the size and shape of a breast surmounted by a thorn.

'Where did you get it? I have seen none of these trees near the river.' Sean was marking time while he decided whether to make Katrina drink the brew. He knew these Zulu remedies, what they didn't kill they sometimes cured.

'Hlubi went back to the hills where we camped four days ago . . . he brought the bark into the camp an hour ago.'

A thirty-mile round journey in something under six hours – even in his distress Sean could smile.

'Tell Hlubi the Nkosikazi will drink his medicine.'

Kandhla held her head and Sean forced the evil-smelling liquid between her lips – he made her finish the whole potful. The juice of the bark seemed to relieve the congestion of her kidneys; four times before morning she passed frothy black water. Each time Sean held her gently, cushioning her body from any movement that might have killed her. Gradually her delirium became coma; she lay huddled and still in the cot, shaken only by the brief fits of shivering. When the morning sun hit the wagon canvas and lit the interior, Sean saw her face, and he knew that she was dying. Her skin was an opaque yellowish white, her hair had lost its glow and was lifeless as dry grass. Kandhla brought another pot of the medicine and they fed it to her. When the pot was empty Kandhla said, 'Nkosi, let me lay a mattress on the floor beside the Nkosikazi's bed. You must sleep and I will stay here with you and wake you if the Nkosikazi stirs.'

Sean looked at him with haunted eyes. 'There will be time to sleep later, my friend.' He looked down at Katrina and went on softly. 'Perhaps, very soon there will be time.'

Suddenly Katrina's body stiffened and Sean dropped on his knees beside her cot. Kandhla hovered anxiously behind him. It took Sean a while to understand what was happening and then he looked up at Kandhla.

'Go! go quickly!' he said and the suffering in his voice sent Kandhla stumbling blindly from the wagon. Sean's second son was born that morning and while Kandhla watched over Katrina Sean wrapped the child in a blanket, took him into the veld and buried him.

Then he went back to Katrina and stayed with her while days and nights blended together into a hopeless muddle of grief. As near as Katrina was to death, that near was Sean to insanity. He never moved out of the wagon, he squatted on the mattress next to her cot, wiping the perspiration from her face, holding a cup to her lips or just sitting and watching her. He had lost his child and before his eyes Katrina was turning into a wasted yellow skeleton. Dirk saved him. Mbejane brought the boy to him and he romped on the mattress, crawling into Sean's lap and pulling his beard. It was the one small glimmer of light in the darkness.

= 27 =

Katrina survived. She came back slowly from the motionless coma that precedes death and with her hesitant return Sean's despair changed to hope and then to a wonderful relief. Her water was no longer black but dark pink and thick with sediment. She was aware of him now and, although she was so weak that she could not lift her head off the pillow, her eyes followed him as he moved about the wagon. It was another week before she learned about the baby. She asked him, her voice a tired whisper, and Sean told her with all the gentleness of which he was capable. She did not have the strength for any great show of emotion; she laid quietly staring up at the canvas above her head and her tears slid down across her yellow cheeks.

The damage that the fever had done to her body was hardly credible. Her limbs were so thin that Sean could completely encircle her thigh with one hand. Her skin hung in loose yellow folds from her face and body and pink blood still stained her water. This was not all: the fever had sucked all the strength from her mind. She had nothing left to resist the sorrow of her baby's death, and the sorrow encased her in a shell through which neither Sean nor Dirk could reach her. Sean struggled to bring her back to life, to repair the terrible damage to her mind and body. Every minute of his time he employed in her service.

He and the servants scoured the veld for thirty miles around the laager to find delicacies to tempt her appetite, wild fruits, honey, giraffe marrows, the flesh of a dozen animals: kabobs of elephant heart and duiker liver, roasted iguana lizard as white and tender as a plump pullet, golden fillets of the yellow-mouthed bream from the river. Katrina picked at them listlessly then turned away and lay staring at the canvas wall of the cot.

Sean sat beside her and talked about the farm they would buy, trying vainly to draw her into a discussion of the house they would build. He read to her from Duff's books and the only reaction he received was a small quivering of her lips when he read the words 'death' or 'child'. He talked about the days on the Witwatersrand, searching his mind for stories that might amuse her. He brought Dirk to her and let him play about the wagon. Dirk was walking now, his dark hair had started to curl and his eyes were green. Dirk, however, could not be too long confined in the wagon. There was too much to do, too much to explore. Before long he would stagger to the entrance and issue the imperial summons: 'Bejaan! Bejaan!'

Almost immediately Mbejane's head would appear in the opening and he would glance at Sean for permission.

'All right, take him out then . . . but tell Kandhla not to stuff him full of food.'

Quickly, before Sean changed his mind, Mbejane would lift Dirk down and lead him away. Dirk had nearly two dozen Zulus to spoil him. They competed hotly for his affections, no effort was too much – dignified Mbejane down on his hands and knees being ridden mercilessly in and out among the wagons, Hlubi scratching himself under the arms and gibbering insanely in his celebrated imitation of a baboon while Dirk squealed with delight, fat Kandhla raiding Katrina's store of fruit preserves to make sure Dirk was properly fed and the others keeping in the background, anxious to join the worship but fearful of incurring the jealousy of Mbejane and Hlubi. Sean knew what was happening but he was powerless to prevent it. His time was completely devoted to Katrina.

For the first time in his life Sean was giving more than just a superficial part of himself to another human being. It was not an isolated sacrifice: it went on throughout the months it took for Katrina to regain sufficient of her strength to enable her to sit up in bed without assistance; it continued through the months that she needed before Sean judged it safe to resume the trek towards the south. They built a litter for her – Sean would not risk the jarring of the wagon – and the first day's trek lasted two hours. Four of the servants carried the litter and Katrina lay in it, protected from the sun by a strip of canvas spread above her head. Despite the gentleness with which the Zulus handled her, at the end of the two hours Katrina was exhausted. Her back ached and she was sweating in small beads from her yellow skin. The next week they travelled two hours daily and then gradually increased the time until they were making a full day's journey.

They were halfway to the Magaliesberg, camped at a muddy waterhole in the thorn flats, when Mbejane came to Sean.

'There is still one wagon empty of ivory, Nkosi.'

'The others are full,' Sean pointed out.

'Four hours' march from this place there is enough ivory buried to fill those wagons.'

Sean's mouth twisted with pain. He looked away towards the south-east and he spoke softly. 'Mbejane, I am still a young man and yet already I have stored up enough ugly memories to make my old age sad. Would you have me steal from a friend not only his life but his share of ivory also?'

Mbejane shook his head. 'I asked, that is all.'

'And I have answered, Mbejane. It is his . . . let it lie.'

— 28 —

They crossed the Magaliesberg and turned west along the mountain range. Then, two months after they had left the Limpopo river, they reached the Boer settlement at Louis Trichardt. Sean left Mbejane to outspan the wagons on the open square in front of the church and he went to search for a doctor. There was only one in the district, Sean found him in his surgery above the general dealer's store and took him to the wagons. Sean carried his bag for him and the doctor, a greybeard and unused to such hardships, trotted to keep up with Sean. He was panting and pouring sweat by the time they arrived. Sean waited outside while the doctor completed his examination and when he finally made his descent from the wagon Sean fell on him impatiently. 'What do you think, man?'

'I think, meneer, that you should give hourly thanks to your Maker.' The doctor shook his head in amazement. 'It seems hardly possible that your wife could have survived both the fever and the loss of the child.'

'She is safe then, there's no chance of a relapse?' Sean asked.

'She is safe now . . . but she is still a very sick woman. It may take a year before her body is fully mended. There is no medicine I can give you. She must be kept quiet, feed her well and wait for time to cure her.' The doctor hesitated. 'There is other damage –' he tapped his forehead with his forefinger. 'Grief is a terrible destroyer. She will need love and gentleness and after another six months she will need a baby to fill the emptiness left by the one she lost. Give her those three things, meneer, but most of all give her love.' The doctor hauled his watch from his waistcoat and looked at it. 'Time! there is so little time. I must go, there are others who need me.' He held out his hand to Sean. 'Go with God, meneer.'

Sean shook his hand. 'How much do I owe you?'

The doctor smiled, he had a brown face and his eyes were pale blue; when he smiled he looked like a boy. 'I make no charge for words. I wish I could have done more.' He hurried away across the square and when he walked you could see that his smile lied, he was an old man.

'Mbejane,' said Sean. 'Get a big tusk out of the wagon and take it to the doctor's room above the store.'

Katrina and Sean went to the morning service in the church next day. Katrina could not stand through the hymns. She sat quietly in her pew, watching the altar, her lips forming the words of the hymn and her eyes full of her sorrow.

They stayed on for three more days in Louis Trichardt and they were made welcome. Men came to drink coffee with them and see the ivory and the women brought them eggs and fresh vegetables, but Sean was anxious to move south. So on the third day they started the last stage of their trek.

Katrina regained her strength rapidly now. She took over the management of Dirk from the servants, to their ill-concealed disappointment, and soon she left her litter and rode on the box seat of the lead wagon again. Her body filled out and there was colour showing once more through the yellow skin of her cheeks. Despite the improvement to her body the depression of her mind still persisted and there was nothing that Sean could do to lift it.

A month before the Christmas of 1895 Sean's wagon train climbed the low range of hills above the city and they looked down into Pretoria. The jacaranda trees that filled every garden were in bloom – masses of purple – and the busy streets spoke well of the prosperity of the Transvaal Republic. Sean outspanned on the outskirts of the city, simply pulling the wagons off the road and camping beside it, and once the camp was established and Sean had made certain that Katrina no longer needed his help he put on his one good suit and called for his horse. His suit had been cut to the fashion of four years previously and had been made to encompass the belly he had acquired on the Witwatersrand. Now it hung loosely down his body but bunched tightly around his thickened arms. His face was burnt black by the sun and his beard bushed down onto his chest and concealed the fact that the stiff collar of his shirt could no longer close around his neck. His boots were scuffed almost through the uppers, there was not a suspicion of polish on them and they had completely lost their shape. Sweat had soaked through his hat around the level of the band and left dark greasy marks; the brim drooped down over his eyes so he had to wear it pushed onto the back of his head. There was, therefore, some excuse for the curious glances that followed him that afternoon as he rode down Church Street with a great muscular savage trotting at his one stirrup and an overgrown brindle hound at the other. They pushed their way between the wagons that cluttered the wide street; they passed the Raadsaal of the Republican Parliament, passed the houses standing back from the road in their spacious purple and green gardens and came at last to the business area of the city that crowded round the railway station. Sean and Duff had bought their supplies at a certain general dealer's stores and now Sean went back to it. It was hardly changed – the signboard in front had faded a little but still declared that I. Goldberg, Importer & Exporter, Dealer in Mining Machinery, Merchant & Wholesaler, was prepared to consider the purchase of gold, precious stone, hides and skins, ivory and other natural produce. Sean swung down from the saddle and tossed his reins to Mbejane. 'Unsaddle, Mbejane. This may take time.'

Sean stepped up onto the sidewalk, lifted his hat to two passing ladies and went through into the building where Mr Goldberg conducted his diverse activities. One of the assistants hurried to meet him, but Sean shook his head and the man went back behind the counter. He had seen Mr Goldberg with two customers at the far end of the store. He was content to wait. He browsed around among the loaded shelves of merchandise, feeling the quality of a shirt, sniffing at a box of cigars, examining an axe, lifting a rifle down off the rack and sighting at a spot on the wall, until Mr Goldberg bowed his customers through the door and turned to Sean. Mr Goldberg was short and fat. His hair was cropped short and his neck bulged over the top of his collar. He looked at Sean and his eyes were expressionless while he rifled through the index cards of his memory for the name. Then he beamed like a brilliant burst of sunlight. 'Mr Courtney, isn't it?'

Sean grinned. 'That's right. How are you, Izzy?' They shook hands. 'How's business?'

Mr Goldberg's face fell. 'Terrible, terrible, Mr Courtney. I'm a worried man.'

'You look well enough on it,' Sean prodded his stomach. 'You've put on weight.'

'You can joke, Mr Courtney, but I'm telling you it's terrible. Taxes and worry, taxes and worry.' Mr Goldberg sighed, 'and now there's talk of war.'

'What's this?' Sean frowned.

'War, Mr Courtney, war between Britain and the Republic.'

Sean's frown dissolved and he laughed. 'Nonsense, man, not even Kruger could be such a bloody fool! Get me a cup of coffee and a cigar and we'll go through to your office and talk business.'

Mr Goldberg's face went blank and his eyelids drooped almost sleepily.

'Business, Mr Courtney?'

'That's right, Izzy, this time I'm selling and you're buying.'

'What are you selling, Mr Courtney?'

'Ivory!'

'Ivory?'

'Twelve wagon loads of it.'

Mr Goldberg sighed sadly. 'Ivory's no good now, the bottom's fallen out of it. You can hardly give it away.' It was very well done; if Sean had not been told the ruling prices two days before he might have been convinced.

'I'm sorry to hear that,' he said. 'If you're not interested, I'll see if I can find someone else.'

'Come along to my office anyway,' said Mr Goldberg. 'We can talk about it. Talk costs nothing.'

Two days later they were still talking about it. Sean had fetched his wagons and had off-loaded the ivory in the back yard of the store. Mr Goldberg had personally weighed each tusk and written the weights down on a sheet of paper. He and Sean had added the columns of figures and agreed on the total. Now they were in the last stages of agreeing the price.

'Come on, Izzy, we've wasted two days already. That's a fair price and you know it . . . let's get it over with,' Sean growled.

'I'll lose money on this,' protested Mr Goldberg. 'I've got to make a living, every man's got to live.'

'Come on,' Sean held out his right hand. 'Let's call it a deal.'

Mr Goldberg hesitated a second longer, then he put his pudgy hand in Sean's fist and they grinned at each other, both well satisfied. One of Mr Goldberg's assistants counted out the sovereigns, stacking them in piles of fifty along the counter, then Sean and Mr Goldberg checked them and agreed once more. Sean filled two canvas bags with the gold, slapped Mr Goldberg's back, helped himself to another cigar and headed heavily laden for the bank.

'When are you going into the veld again?' Mr Goldberg called after him.

'Soon!' said Sean.

'Don't forget to get your supplies here.'

'I'll be back,' Sean assured him.

Mbejane carried one of the bags and Sean the other. Sean was smiling and streamers of cigar smoke swirled back from his head as he strode along the sidewalk. There's something in the weight of a sack of gold that makes the man who holds it stand eight feet tall.

That night as they lay together in the darkness of the wagon Katrina asked him.

'Have we enough money to buy the farm yet, Sean?'

'Yes,' said Sean. 'We've got enough for the finest farm in the whole Cape peninsular . . . and, after one more trip, we'll have enough to build the house and the barns, buy the cattle, lay out the vineyard and still have some left over.'

Katrina was silent for a moment then, 'So we are going back into the bushveld again?'

'One more trip,' said Sean. 'Another two years and then we'll go down to the Cape.' He gave her a hug. 'You don't mind, do you?'

'No,' she said. 'I think I'd like that. When will we leave?'

'Not just yet awhile,' Sean laughed. 'First we're going to have some fun.' He hugged her again, her body was still painfully thin; he could feel the bones of her hips pressed against him.

'Some pretty clothes for you, my fancy, and a suit for me that doesn't look like a fancy dress. Then we'll go out and see what this burg has to offer in the way of entertainment –' He stopped as the idea swelled up in his mind. 'Damn it! I know what we'll do. We'll hire a carriage and go across to Jo'burg. We'll take a suite at the Grand National Hotel and do some living. Bath in a china bath, sleep in a real bed; you can have your hair prettied-up and I'll have my beard trimmed by a barber. We'll eat crayfish and penguin eggs . . . I can't remember when I last tasted pork or mutton . . . we'll wash it down with the old bubbling wine and waltz to a good band –' Sean raced on and when he stopped for breath Katrina asked softly, 'Isn't the waltz a very sinful dance, Sean?'

Sean smiled in the darkness. 'It certainly is!'

'I'd like to be sinful just once . . . not too much, just a little with you to see what it's like.'

'We will be' – said Sean – 'as wicked as hell.'

29

The next day Sean took Katrina to the most exclusive ladies' shop in Pretoria. He chose the material of half a dozen dresses. One of them was to be a ball gown in canary-yellow silk. It was extravagance and he knew it, but he didn't care once he saw the flash of guilty delight in Katrina's cheeks and the old green sparkle in her eyes. For the first time since the fever she was living again. He spilled out his sovereigns with thankful abandon. The sales girls were delighted with him, they crowded round him with trays of feminine accessories.

'A dozen of those,' said Sean and, 'yes, those will do.' Then a flash of green on the racks across the room caught his eye – it was Katrina's green.

'What's that?' He pointed and two sales girls nearly knocked each other down in the rush to get it for him. The winner carried the shawl back to him and Sean took it and placed it around Katrina's shoulders. It was a beautiful thing.

'We'll take it,' said Sean and Katrina's lips quivered – then suddenly she was crying, sobbing brokenly. The excitement had been too much. There was immediate consternation among the shop assistants, they flapped around Sean like hens at feeding time while he picked Katrina up and carried her out to the hired carriage. At the door he paused and spoke over his shoulder.

'I want those dresses finished by tomorrow evening. Can you do it?'

'They'll be ready, Mr Courtney, even if my girls have to work all night on them.'

He took Katrina back to the wagons and laid her on her cot.

'Please forgive me, Sean, I've never done that in my life before.'

'It's all right, my fancy, I understand. Now you just go to sleep.'

The following day Katrina stayed at the camp resting, while Sean went to see Mr Goldberg again and buy from him the stores they would need for the next expedition. It took another day to load the wagons and by then Katrina seemed well enough to make the trip to Johannesburg.

They left in the early afternoon. Mbejane driving, Sean and Katrina sitting close together on the back seat holding hands under the travelling rug and Dirk bouncing round the interior of the carriage, pausing now and then to flatten his face against a window and keeping up a flow of comment in the peculiar mixture of English, Dutch and Zulu that Sean called Dirkese. They reached Johannesburg long before Sean expected to. In four years the town had doubled its size and had spread out into the veld to meet them. They followed the main road through the new areas and came to the centre. There were changes here as well but it was, in the main, the way he remembered it. They threaded their way through the babble of Eloff Street, and around them, mingling with the crowds on the sidewalks, were the ghosts of the past. He heard Duff laugh and twisted quickly in his seat to place the sound; a dandy in a boater hat with gold fillings in his teeth laughed again from a passing carriage and Sean heard that it was not Duff's laugh. Very close, but not the same. All of it was like that – similar but subtly changed, nostalgic but sad with the knowledge of loss. The past was lost – and he knew then that you can never go back. Nothing is the same, for reality can exist at one time only and in one place only. Then it dies and you have lost it and you must go on to find it at another time and in another place.

They took a suite at the Grand National, with a sitting-room and two bedrooms, a private bathroom and a balcony that looked out over the street – over the rooftops to where the headgears and white dumps stood along the ridge. Katrina was exhausted. They had supper sent up to the room early and when they had eaten Katrina went to bed and Sean went down alone to drink a nightcap at the bar. The bar-room was crowded. Sean found a seat in the corner and sat silently in the jabber of conversation. In it, but no longer a part of it.

They had changed the picture above the bar – it used to be a hunting print; but now it was a red-coated general, impressively splattered with blood, taking leave of his staff in the middle of a battlefield. The staff looked bored. Sean let his eyes wander on along the dark panelled walls. He remembered – there was so much to remember! Suddenly he blinked. Near the side door was a star-shaped crack in the wooden panelling. Sean started to grin and put down his glass and massaged the knuckles of his right hand. If Oakie Henderson hadn't ducked under that punch it would have taken his head off.

Sean signalled to the barman. 'Another brandy, please.' While the man was pouring, Sean asked, 'What happened to that panel near the door?'

The man glanced up and then back at the bottle. 'Some fellow put his fist through it in the old days. Boss left it like that, sort of souvenir, you know.'

'He must have been quite a fellow . . . that wood's an inch thick. Who was he?' Sean asked expectantly.

The man shrugged. 'One of the drifters. They come and they go. Make a few pounds, piss it against the wall and then go back where they came from.' He looked at Sean with bored eyes. 'That'll be half a dollar, mate.' Sean drank the brandy slowly, turning the glass in his hands between sips and watching the liquor cling to its sides like thin oil. By a cracked panel in a bar-room they shall remember you.

And now I shall go to bed, he decided, this is no longer my world. My world is upstairs sleeping – I hope! He smiled a little to himself and finished the brandy in his glass.

'Sean' – a voice at his ear and a hand on his shoulder as he turned to leave. 'My God, Sean, is it really you?'

Sean stared at the man beside him. He did not recognize the neatly clipped beard and the big sun-burned nose with the skin peeling off the tip, but suddenly he knew the eyes.

'Dennis, you old rogue. Dennis Petersen from Ladyburg. That's right isn't it?'

'You didn't recognize me!' laughed Dennis. 'So much for our friendship – you disappear without a word and ten years later you don't even know me!'

Now they were both laughing.

'I thought they would have hanged you long ago –' Sean defended himself. 'What on earth are you doing in Johannesburg?'

'Selling beef – I'm on the committee of the Beef Growers' Association.' There was pride in Dennis's voice. 'I have been up here negotiating the renewal of our contracts.'

'When are you going back?'

'My train leaves in an hour.'

'Well, there's time for a drink before you go – what will it be?'

'I'll have a small brandy, thanks.'

Sean ordered the drinks and they took them up and stood, suddenly awkward in the awareness that ten years were between their once complete accord.

'So, what have you been doing with yourself?' Dennis ended the pause.

'This and that, you know – a bit of mining, just come back from the bushveld. Nothing very exciting.'

'Well, it's good to see you again anyway. Your health.'

'And yours,' said Sean, and then suddenly he realized that here was news of his family – news he had been without for many years.

'How's everyone at Ladyburg – your sisters?'

'Both married – so am I, with four sons,' and the pride was in Dennis's voice again.

'Anyone I know?' asked Sean.

'Audrey – you know old Pye's daughter.'

'No!' Sean ripped out the word, and then quickly, 'That's wonderful, Dennis. I'm pleased for you – she was a lovely girl.'

'The best,' agreed Dennis complacently. He had the sleek well-fed, well-cared for look of a married man, fatter in the face and his stomach starting to show. I wonder if I have it yet, Sean thought. 'Of course, old man Pye's dead now – that's one creditor he couldn't buy off. Ronnie's taken over the bank and the store.'

'The bat-eared bush rat,' said Sean and knew immediately that he had said the wrong thing. Dennis frowned slightly. 'He's family now, Sean. A very decent chap really – and a clever business man.'

'I'm sorry, I was joking. How's my mother?' Sean changed the subject by asking the question that had been in the forefront of his mind and he had picked the right topic. Dennis's expression softened immediately – you could see the warmth in his eyes.

'The same as ever. She's got a dress shop now, next door to Ronnie's store. It's a gold mine – no one would think of buying anywhere else but at Aunt Ada's. She's godmother to my two eldest, I guess she's godmother to half the kids in the district,' and then his expression hardened again, 'The least you could have done was write to her sometime, Sean. You can't imagine the pain you have caused her.'

'There were circumstances.' Sean dropped his eyes to his glass.

'That's no excuse – you have a duty which you neglected. There is no excuse for it.'

You little man, Sean lifted his head and looked at him without trying to disguise his annoyance. You pompous, preaching little man peering out at the world one-eyed through the keyhole of your own self-importance. Dennis had not noticed Sean's reaction and he continued. 'That's a lesson a man must learn before he grows up – we all have our responsibilities and our duties. A man grows up when he faces those duties, when he accepts the burdens that society places on him. Take my own case: despite the vast amount of work I have on the farms – I now own Mahoba's Kloof as well – and despite the demands made on me by my family, yet I have time to represent the district on the committee of the Beef Growers' Association, I am a member of the Church Council and the village management board, and I have every reason to believe that next month I will be asked to accept the office of mayor.' Then he looked steadily at Sean, 'What have *you* done with your life so far?'

'I've lived it,' Sean answered, and Dennis looked a little perplexed – then he gathered himself.

'Are you married yet?'

'I was – but I sold her to the Arab slavers up north.'

'You did what?'

'Well,' grinned Sean, 'she was an old wife and the price was good.'

'That's a joke, hey? Ha, ha!' You couldn't fool good old Dennis – Sean laughed out loud. This unbelievable little man!

'Have a drink, Dennis,' he suggested.

'Two is my limit, thanks Sean.' Dennis pulled the gold hunter from his waistcoat pocket and inspected it. 'Time to go – I'm afraid. Nice seeing you again.'

'Wait,' Sean stopped him. 'My brother – how's Garry?'

'Poor old Garry.' Dennis shook his head solemnly.

'What's wrong with him?' Sean's voice was sharp with his sense of dread.

'Nothing – Dennis reassured him quickly. 'Well, I mean nothing more than ever was.'

'Why did you say "poor old Garry" then?'

'I don't really know – except that everybody says it. It's habit, I suppose – he's just one of those people you say *poor old* in front of.'

Sean suppressed his irritation, he wanted to know. He had to know.

'You haven't answered me – how is he?'

Dennis made a significant gesture with his right hand. 'Looking into the bottle quite a bit these days – not that I blame him with that woman he married. You were well out of it there if I may say so, Sean.'

'You may,' Sean acquiesced, 'but is he well? How are things at Theunis Kraal?'

'We all took a bit of a beating with the rindepest* but Garry – well, he lost over half of his herds. Poor old Garry, everything happens to him.'

'My God – fifty per cent!'

'Yes – but, of course, Ronnie helped him out. Gave him a mortgage on the farm to tide him over.'

'Theunis Kraal bonded again,' groaned Sean. 'Oh Garry, Garry.'

'Yes – well,' Dennis coughed uneasily. 'Well, I think I'd better be going. *Totsiens,* Sean.' He held out his hand. 'Shall I tell them I saw you?'

'No,' said Sean quickly. 'Just leave it stand.'

'Very well then.' Dennis hesitated. 'Are you all right, Sean? I mean' – he coughed again – 'are you all right for money?'

Sean felt his unhappiness dissolve a little; this pompous little man was going to offer him a loan. 'That's very good of you, Dennis. But I've got a couple of pounds saved up – enough to eat on for a few days,' he spoke seriously.

* An epidemic cattle disease.

'All right then.' Dennis looked mightily relieved. 'All right then – *totsiens,* Sean,' and he turned and walked quickly out of the bar. As he left the room so he went out of Sean's mind, and Sean was thinking of his brother again.

Then suddenly Sean decided. I will go back to Ladyburg when this next trip is over. The dream farm outside Paarl would not lose anything in being transplanted to Natal – and he suddenly longed to sit in the panelled study at Theunis Kraal again, and to feel the mist come cold down the escarpment in the mornings, and see the spray blowing off the white falls in the wind. He wanted to hear Ada's voice again and to explain to her, knowing she would understand and forgive.

But more, much more it was Garry – poor old Garry. I must go back to him – ten years is a long time and he will have lost the bitterness. I must go back to him – for his sake and for Theunis Kraal. With the decision made, Sean finished his drink and went up the stairs to his suite.

Katrina was breathing softly in her sleep, the dark mass of her hair spread out on the pillow. While he undressed he watched her and slowly the melancholy dissolved. Gently he pulled back the blankets on his side of the bed and just then Dirk whimpered from the next room. Sean went through to him. 'All right, what's the trouble?'

Dirk blinked owlishly and searched for an excuse, then the relief flooded into his face and he produced the one that creaked with age. 'I want a drink a water.'

The delay while Sean went through to the bathroom gave Dirk an opportunity to rally his forces and when Sean came back he opened the offensive in earnest.

'Tell me a story, Daddy.' He was sitting up now, bright-eyed.

'I'll tell you a story about Jack and a Nory –' said Sean.

'Not that one –' protested Dirk. The saga of Jack and his brother lasted five seconds and Dirk knew it. Sean sat down on the edge of the bed and held the glass for him.

'How about this one? There once was a king who had everything in the world . . . but when he lost it he found out that he had never had anything and that he now had more than he ever had before.'

Dirk looked stunned.

'That's not a very good one,' he gave his opinion at last.

'No,' said Sean. 'It isn't . . . is it? But I think we should be charitable and admit that it's not too bad for this time of night.'

30

Sean woke feeling happy. Katrina was sitting up in bed filling cups from a pewter coffee pot and Dirk was hammering at the door to be let in. Katrina smiled at him. 'Good morning, meneer.'

Sean sat up and kissed her. 'How did you sleep, fancy?'

'Well, thank you,' but there were dark rings under her eyes. Sean went across to the bedroom door.

'Prepare to receive cavalry,' he said and swung it open. Dirk's charge carried him onto the bed and Sean dived after him. When two men are evenly matched, weight will usually decide and within seconds Dirk had straddled Sean's chest, pinning him helplessly and Sean was pleading for quarter.

After breakfast Mbejane brought the carriage round to the front of the hotel. When the three of them were settled in it, Sean opened the small window behind the driver's seat and told Mbejane, 'To the office first. Then we have to be at the Exchange by ten o'clock.'

Mbejane grinned at him. 'Yes, Nkosi, then lunch at the Big House.' Mbejane had never been able to master the word Xanadu.

They went to all the old places. Sean and Mbejane laughing and reminiscing at each other through the window. There was a panic at the Exchange, crowds on the pavement outside. The offices on Eloff Street had been refaced and a brass plate beside the front door carried the roll of the subsidiaries of Central Rand Consolidated. Mbejane stopped the carriage outside and Sean boasted to Katrina. She sat silently and listened to him, suddenly feeling inadequate for a man who had done so much. She misinterpreted Sean's enthusiasm and thought he regretted the past and wished he were back.

'Mbejane, take us up to the Candy Deep,' Sean called at last. 'Let's see what's happening there.'

The last five hundred yards of the road was overgrown and pitted with disuse. The administration block had been demolished and grass grew thick over the foundations. There were new buildings and headgears half a mile farther along the ridge, but here the reef had been worked out and abandoned. Mbejane pulled up the horses in the circular drive in front of where the offices had stood. He jumped down and held their heads while Sean helped Katrina out of the carriage. Sean lifted Dirk and sat him on his shoulder and they picked their way through the waist-high grass and piles of bricks and rubbish towards the Candy Deep Number Three Shaft.

The bare white concrete blocks that had held the machinery formed a neat geometrical pattern in the grass. Beyond them reared the white mine dump; some mineral in the powdered rock had leaked out in long yellow stains down its sides. Duff had once had the mineral identified. It was of little commercial value, used occasionally in the ceramics industry. Sean had forgotten the name of it; it sounded like the name of a star – Uranus perhaps.

They came to the shaft. The edges of it had crumbled and the grass hung into it, the way an unkempt moustache hangs into an old man's mouth. The headgear was gone and only a rusty barbed-wire fence ringed the shaft. Sean bent his knees: keeping his back straight for Dirk still sat on his shoulder, he picked up a lump of rock the size of a man's fist and tossed it over the fence. They stood quietly and listened to it clatter against the sides as it fell. It fell for a long time and when at last it hit the bottom the echo rang faintly up from a thousand feet below.

'Throw more!' commanded Dirk, but Katrina stopped him.

'No, Sean, let's go. It's an evil place.' She shuddered slightly. 'It looks like a grave.'

'It very nearly was,' said Sean softly, remembering the darkness and the rock pressing down upon him.

'Let's go,' she said again, and they went back to where Mbejane waited with the carriage.

Sean was gay at lunch, he drank a small bottle of wine, but Katrina was tired and more miserable than she had been since they left Louis Trichardt. She had begun to realize the type of life he had led before she met him and she was frightened that now he wanted to return to it. She had only known the bush and the life of the Trek-Boer, she knew she could never learn to live like this. She watched as he laughed and joked during the meal, she watched the easy assurance with which he commanded the white head waiter, the way he picked his way through the maze of cutlery that was spread out on the table before them and at last she could hold it in no longer.

'Let's go away, let's go back into the bush.'

Sean stopped with a loaded fork halfway to his mouth. 'What?'

'Please, Sean, the sooner we go the sooner we'll be able to buy the farm.'

Sean chuckled. 'A day or two more won't make any difference. We're starting to have fun. Tonight I'll take you dancing – we were going to be sinful, remember?'

'Who will look after Dirk?' she asked weakly.

'Mbejane will –' Sean looked at her closely. 'You have a good sleep this afternoon and tonight we'll go out and tie the dog loose.' He grinned at the memories that expression invoked.

When Katrina woke from her rest that evening she found the other part of the reason for her depression. For the first time since the baby her periodic bleeding had started again, the tides of her body and mind were at their lowest ebb. She said nothing to Sean, but bathed and put on the yellow gown. She brushed her hair furiously, dragging the brush through it until her scalp tingled, but still it hung dull and lifeless – as dull as the eyes that looked back at her out of the yellow face in the mirror.

Sean came up behind her and leaned over her to kiss her cheek. 'You look,' said he, 'like a stack of gold bars five-and-a-half feet high.' But he realized that the yellow gown had been a mistake: it matched too closely the fever colour of her skin. Mbejane was waiting in the sitting-room when they went through.

'It may be late before we return,' Sean told him.

'That is of no account, Nkosi,' Mbejane's face was as impassive as ever, but Sean caught a sparkle of anticipation in his eyes and realized that Mbejane could hardly wait to get Dirk to himself.

'You are not to go into his room,' Sean warned.

'What if he cries, Nkosi?'

'He won't . . . but if he does see what he wants, give it to him then leave him to sleep.'

Mbejane's face registered his protest.

'I'm warning you, Mbejane, if I come home at midnight and find him riding you round the room I'll have both your hides for a kaross.'

'His sleep shall be unspoiled, Nkosi,' lied Mbejane.

In the hotel lobby Sean spoke to the receptionist. 'Where can we find the best food in this town?' he asked.

'Two blocks down, sir, the Golden Guinea. You can't miss it.'

'It sounds like a gin palace,' Sean was dubious.

'I assure you, sir, that you'll have no complaint when you get there. Everyone goes there. Mr Rhodes dines there when he's in town, Mr Barnato, Mr Hradsky –'

'Dick Turpin, Cesare Borgia, Benedict Arnold,' Sean continued for him. 'All right, you have convinced me. I'll take a chance on having my throat cut.'

Sean went out through the front entrance with Katrina on his arm. The splendour of the Golden Guinea subdued even Sean a little. A waiter with a uniform like a major-general's led them down a marble staircase, across the wide meadow of carpet between the group of elegant men and women to a table that even in the soft light dazzled with its bright silver and snowy linen. Chandeliers of crystal hung from the vaulted ceiling, the band was good, and the air was rich with the fragrance of perfume and expensive cigars.

Katrina stared helplessly at the menu until Sean came to her rescue and ordered the meal in a French accent that impressed her but not the waiter. The wine came and with it Sean's high spirits returned. Katrina sat quietly opposite him and listened. She tried to think of something witty to answer him with; in their wagon or alone in the veld they could talk for hours at a time but here she was dumb.

'Shall we dance?' Sean leaned across the table and squeezed her hand. She shook her head.

'Sean, I couldn't. Not with all these people watching. I'd only make a fool of myself.'

'Come on, I'll show you how . . . it's easy.'

'No, I couldn't, truly I couldn't.'

And to himself Sean had to admit that the dance floor of the Golden Guinea on a Saturday night was not the best place for a waltz lesson. The waiter brought the food, great steaming dishes of it. Sean addressed himself to it and the one-sided conversation wilted. Katrina watched him, picking at the too rich food herself, acutely conscious of the laughter and voices around them, feeling out of place and desperately miserable.

'Come on, Katrina,' Sean smiled at her. 'You've hardly touched your glass. Be a devil and get a little of that in you to warm you up.'

Obediently she sipped the champagne. She didn't like the taste. Sean finished the last of his crayfish thermidor and leaning back in his chair glowing with wine and good food said, 'Man . . . I only pray the chef can keep the rest of the meal up to that standard.' He belched softly behind his fingers and ran his eyes contentedly round the room. 'Duff used to say that a well-cooked crayfish was proof that –'

Sean stopped abruptly. He was staring at the head of the marble staircase – a party of three had appeared there. Two men in evening dress hovering attentively on each side of a woman. The woman was Candy Rautenbach. Candy with her blonde hair piled on top of her head. Candy with diamonds in her ears and at her throat, her bosom overflowing her gown as white as the frothy head on a beer tankard. Candy with bright blue eyes above a red mouth, Candy poised and lovely. Laughing, she glanced towards him and her eyes met his across the room. She stared in open disbelief, the laughter frozen on her lips, then suddenly her poise was gone and she was running down the stairs towards him, holding her skirts up to her knees, her escorts cantering after her in alarm, waiters scattering out of her path and every head in the room turning to watch her. Sean pushed back his chair, stood up to meet her and Candy reached him and jumped up to throw her arms around his neck. There was a long incoherent exchange of greetings and at last Sean prised her loose from his neck and turned her to face Katrina. Candy was flushed and panting with excitement; with every breath her bosom threatened to spring out of her bodice, and she was still holding on to Sean's arm.

'Candy, I want you to meet my wife, Katrina. My dear, this is Candy Rautenbach.'

'How do you do.' Katrina smiled uncertainly and Candy said the wrong thing.

'Sean, you're joking! You married?'

Katrina's smile faded. Candy noticed the change and went on quickly, 'But I must applaud your choice. I am so pleased to meet you, Katrina. We must get together sometime and I'll tell you all about Sean's terrible past.'

Candy was still holding Sean's arm and Katrina was watching her hand – the long tapered fingers against the dark cloth of Sean's suit. Sean saw the direction of Katrina's eyes and tried tactfully to disengage himself but Candy held on. 'Sean, these are my two current beaux.' They were standing to heel behind her like well-trained gundogs. 'They are both so nice I can't make up my mind about them. Harry Lategaan and Derek Goodman. Boys, this is Sean Courtney. You've heard lots about him.'

They shook hands all round.

'Do you mind if we join you?' asked Derek Goodman.

'I'd be upset if you didn't!' said Sean. The men spread out to find chairs while Candy and Katrina studied each other. 'Is this your first visit to Johannesburg, Mrs Courtney?' Candy smiled sweetly. *I wonder where Sean found her, she's thin as a stick and that complexion! – that accent! he could have done better for himself – he could have had his pick.*

'Yes, we won't be here very long though.' *She's a harlot. She must be – her breasts half-naked and the paint on her face and they way she touches Sean. She must have been his mistress. If she touches him again I'll – I'll kill her.*

Sean came back to the table carrying a chair and set it down for Candy. 'Candy's one of my old friends, my dear, I'm sure you two will like each other.'

'I'm sure we will,' said Candy but Katrina didn't answer and Candy turned back to him. 'Sean, how wonderful it is to see you again. You look so well . . . as sunburnt and handsome as the first time I met you. Do you remember that day you and Duff came to eat at the Hotel?'

A shadow fell across Sean's face at the mention of Duff's name. 'Yes, I remember.' He looked round and snapped his fingers for the waiter. 'Let's have some more champagne.'

'I'll get it,' Candy's escorts cut in simultaneously and then started wrangling good-naturedly as to whose turn it was.

'Is Duff with you tonight, Sean?' Candy asked.

'Candy, didn't Derek get the drinks last time? It's my turn now.' Harry sought her support. Candy ignored them and looked at Sean for a reply but he turned and went round the table to the seat beside Katrina.

'I say, old girl, can I have the first dance?' asked Derek.

'I'll spin you for it, Derek, winner pays but gets first dance,' Harry suggested.

'You're on.'

'Sean, I said is Duff here tonight?' Candy looked at him across the table,

'No, he's not. Listen, you two, how about letting me in on this.' Sean avoided her eyes and joined in the haggle with Harry and Derek. Candy bit her lip – she wanted to press Sean further. She wanted to know about Duff – then suddenly she turned on her smile again. She wasn't going to plead with him.

'What is this?' She tapped Harry's shoulder with her fan. 'Am I going to be the prize in a game of chance? Derek will pay for the wine and Sean gets first dance.'

'I say old girl, that's a bit rough, you know.' But Candy was already standing up.

'Come on, Sean, let's see if you can still tread a stately measure.'

Sean glanced at Katrina. 'You don't mind, do you . . . just one dance?'

Katrina shook her head.

I hate her. She's a harlot. Katrina had never in her life spoken the word out loud, she had seen it only in her Bible, but now it gave her a fierce pleasure to think it. She watched Sean and Candy walk arm-in-arm to the dance floor.

'Would you care to dance, Mrs Courtney?' said Derek. Katrina shook her head again without looking at him. She was staring at Sean and Candy. She saw Sean take her in his arms and a cold lump settled in her stomach. Candy was looking up into Sean's face, laughing at him, her arm on his shoulder, her hand in his.

She's a harlot. Katrina felt her tears very near the surface and thinking that word held them back. Sean swirled Candy into a turn – Katrina stiffened in her chair, her hands clenching in her lap – their legs were touching, she saw Candy arch her back slightly and press her thighs against Sean. Katrina felt as though she were suffocating, jealousy had spread up cold and tight through her chest.

I could go and pull him away, she thought. *I could stop him doing that, He has no right. It's as though the two of them are doing – doing it together. I know they have before, I know it now – Oh God, make them stop it. Please make them stop.*

At last Sean and Candy came back to the table. They were laughing together and when he reached her chair Sean dropped his hand on Katrina's shoulder, She moved away from it but Sean seemed not to notice. Everybody was having a good time. Everybody except Katrina. Harry and Derek were jostling for position. Sean's big laugh kept booming out and Candy was sparkling like the diamonds she wore. Every few minutes Sean turned to Katrina and tried to draw her into the conversation but Katrina stubbornly refused to be drawn. She sat there hating them all. Hating even Sean – for the first time she was unsure of him, jealous and frightened for him. She stared down at her hands on the tablecloth in front of her and saw how bony they were, chapped and reddened by the sun and wind, ugly compared to Candy's. She pulled them quickly into her lap and leaned across towards Sean. 'Please, I want to go back to the hotel. I don't feel well.'

Sean stopped in the middle of a story and looked at her with a mixture of concern and dismay. He didn't want to leave and yet he knew she was still sick. He hesitated one second and then he said, 'Of course, my fancy, I'm sorry. I didn't realize –' He turned to the others. 'We'll have to be going . . . my wife's not too strong . . . she's just had one hell of a go of blackwater.'

'Oh, Sean, must you?' Candy couldn't hide her disappointment. 'There's still so much to talk about.'

'I'm afraid so. We'll get together another night.'

'Yes,' agreed Katrina quickly, 'next time we come to Johannesburg we'll see you.'

'Oh, I don't know . . . perhaps before we go,' Sean demurred. 'Some night next week. How about Monday?'

Before Candy could answer Katrina interrupted. 'Please, Sean, can we go now. I'm very tired.' She started towards the stairs but looked back to see Candy jump up and take Sean's arm, hold her lips close to his ear and whisper a question. Sean answered her tersely and Candy turned back to the table and sat down. When they were out on the street Katrina asked, 'What did she say to you?'

'She just said goodbye,' muttered Sean and Katrina knew he was lying. They didn't talk again on the way back to the hotel. Katrina was preoccupied with her jealousy and Sean was thinking about what Candy had asked and what he had answered.

'Sean, where's Duff? You must tell me.'

'He's dead, Candy.'

The second before she turned back to the table Sean had seen her eyes.

= 31 =

Sean woke with a headache and Dirk's jumping on his chest did not help to ease it at all. Sean had to bribe him off with the promise of sweets. Dirk, sensing his advantage, raised his price to a packet of bull's eyes and two lollipops, the kind with red stripes, before he allowed Katrina to lead him away to the bathroom. Sean sighed and settled back under the blankets. The pain moved up and crouched just behind his eyes. He could taste stale champagne on his own breath and his skin smelt of cigar smoke. He drowsed back in half sleep and the ache faded a little.

'Sean, it's Sunday you know. Are you coming to church with us?' Katrina asked coldly from the bedroom door. Sean squeezed his eyelids tighter closed.

'Sean!' No answer.

'Sean!' He opened one eye.

'Are you going to get up?'

'I don't feel very well,' he croaked. 'I think I have a touch of malaria.'

'Are you coming?' Katrina demanded remorselessly. Her feelings towards him had not softened during the night.

'I don't feel up to it this morning, truly I don't. I'm sure the Good Lord will understand.'

'Thou shalt not take the Lord's name in vain,' Katrina warned him with ice in her voice.

'I'm sorry.' Sean pulled the blankets up to his chin defensively. 'But truly, fancy, I can't get up for another couple of hours. My head would burst.'

Katrina turned back into the sitting-room and Sean heard her speak to Dirk in a voice purposely pitched to reach him.

'Your father's not coming with us. We will have to go down to breakfast by ourselves. Then we will have to go to church on our own.'

'But,' Dirk pointed out, 'he's going to buy me a packet of bull's eyes and *two* lollipops with red stripes.' In Dirk's opinion that levelled the score. Sean heard the door of the suite close and Dirk's voice receded down the passage. Sean relaxed slowly and waited for the ache behind his eyes to diminish. After a while he became aware of the coffee tray on the table beside the bed and he weighed the additional pain that the effort of sitting up would involve against the beneficial effect of a large cup of coffee. It was a difficult decision but in the end he carefully raised his body to a sitting position and poured a cupful. There was a small jug of fresh cream on the tray, he took it in his right hand and was just about to add a little to the cup when there was a knock on the sitting-room door.

'Come in!' called Sean. He supposed it was the waiter coming to collect the tray. Sean searched his mind for a really scathing remark to send him on his way. He heard the sitting-room door open.

'Who is it?' he asked. There were quick footsteps and then Sean started so violently that the cream slopped out of the jug onto his sheets and his new nightshirt.

'Good God, Candy, you shouldn't have come here.' Sean was in a frenzy of agitation.

He put the jug back on the tray with nervous haste and wiped ineffectually at the mess on his nightshirt with his hands. 'If my wife . . . Did anyone see you? You mustn't stay. If Katrina knows you've been here she'll . . . well I mean, she won't understand.'

Candy's eyes were puffy and rimmed with red. She looked as though she hadn't slept. 'It's all right, Sean, I waited across the street until I saw your wife leave. One of my servants followed her, she went to the Dutch church on Commissioner Street and there the service lasts about fifty years.' She came into the room and sat down on the edge of his bed.

'I had to talk to you alone. I couldn't let you go without knowing about Duff. I want you to tell me about it . . . everything about it. I promise not to cry, I know how you hate it.'

'Candy, let's not torture ourselves with it. He's dead. Let's remember him alive.' Sean had forgotten his headache for its place had been taken by pity for her and worry at the position in which she had placed him.

'Tell me, please. I must know. I'd never rest again if I didn't,' she said quietly.

'Candy, don't you see that it doesn't matter? The way in which he went is not important. All that you need to know is he's gone.' Sean's voice faded but went on softly, almost to himself, 'He's gone, that is the only thing that matters, he's gone and left us richer for knowing him and a little poorer for having lost him.'

'Tell me,' she said again and they looked at each other, their emotions locked behind expressionless faces. Then Sean told her, his words limping at first, then faster and stronger as the horror of it came back to him. When he had finished she said nothing. She sat on the edge of the bed staring down at the patterned carpet. Sean moved closer to her and put his arm around her.

'There is nothing we can do. That's the thing about death, there is nothing you can do to make it change its mind.'

She leaned against him, against the comfort of his big body and they sat silently until suddenly Candy pulled away from him and smiled her gay brittle smile.

'And now tell me about you. Are you happy? Was that your son with Katrina? He's a lovely child.'

With relief Sean followed her away from the memory of Duff. They talked about each other, filling in the blanks from the time they had last met until suddenly Sean returned to reality.

'Good God, Candy, we've been talking for ages. Katrina will be back at any moment. You had better run.'

At the door she turned, buried her fingers in his beard and tugged his head from side to side. 'If she ever throws you out, you magnificent brute, here's somebody who'll have a place for you.'

She stood up on her toes and kissed him. 'Be happy,' she commanded and the door closed softly behind her.

Sean rubbed his chin, then he pulled off his nightshirt, screwed it into a ball, tossed it through the open door of the bedroom and went to the bathroom. He was towelling himself and whistling the waltz that the band had played the night before, sweating a little in the steamy warmth of the bathroom when he heard the front door open. 'Is that you, Fancy?'

'Daddy! Daddy! Mummy got sweets for me.' Dirk hammered on the bathroom door, and Sean wrapped the towel round his waist before opening it.

'Look! Look at all my sweets,' gloated Dirk. 'Do you want one, Pa?'

'Thank you, Dirk,' Sean put one of the huge striped humbugs in his mouth, moved it to one side and spoke around it.

'Where's your Mummy?'

'There.' Dirk pointed at the bedroom. He closed the sweet packet carefully. 'I'll keep some for Bejaan,' he announced.

'He'll like that,' Sean said and went across to the bedroom. Katrina lay on the bed; as soon as he saw her he knew something was desperately wrong. She lay staring up at the ceiling, her eyes unseeing, her face as yellow and set as that of a corpse. Two quick strides carried him to her. He touched her cheek with his fingers and the sense of dread settled on him again, heavily, darkly.

'Katrina?' There was no response. She lay still without a flicker of life in her eyes. Sean swung round and ran out of the suite, down the corridor to the head of the stairs. There were people in the lobby below him and he yelled over their heads to the clerk behind the desk.

'Get a doctor, man, as fast as you can . . . my wife's dying.'

The man stared up at him blankly. He had a neck too thin for his high stiff collar and his black hair was parted down the centre and polished with grease.

'Hurry, you stupid bastard, get moving,' roared Sean. Everybody in the lobby was looking at him. He still wore only a small towel around his waist and, heavy with water, his hair hung down over his forehead.

'Move, man! Move!' Sean was dancing with impatience. There was a heavy stone vase on the banister at Sean's side, he picked it up threateningly and the clerk jerked out of his trance and scuttled for the front door. Sean ran back to the suite.

Dirk was standing by Katrina's bed, his face distorted by the humbug it contained and his eyes large with curiosity. Sean snatched him up, carried him through to the other bedroom and locked the door on his outraged howls. Dirk was unused to being handled in that manner. Sean went back to Katrina and knelt beside her bed. He was still kneeling there when the doctor arrived. Tersely Sean explained about the blackwater, and the doctor listened then sent him to wait in the sitting-room. It was a long wait before the doctor came through to him and Sean sensed that behind his professional poker face the man was puzzled.

'Is it a relapse?' Sean demanded.

'No, I don't think so. I've given her a sedative.'

'What's wrong with her? What is it?' Sean pursued him and the doctor hedged.

'Has your wife had some sort of shock . . . some bad news, something that could have alarmed her? Has she been under nervous strain?'

'No . . . she's just come back from church. Why? What's wrong?' Sean caught the doctor's lapels and shook him in his agitation.

'It appears to be some sort of paralytic hysteria. I've given her laudanum. She'll sleep now and I'll come back to see her this evening.'

The doctor was trying to loosen Sean's hands from his jacket. Sean let him go and pushed past him to the bedroom.

The doctor called again just before dark, Sean had undressed Katrina and put her into the bed, but apart from that she had not moved. Her breathing was shallow and fast despite the drug she had been given. The doctor was baffled.

'I can't understand it, Mr Courtney. There is nothing I can find wrong with her apart from her general run-down condition. I think we'll just have to wait and see, I don't want to give her any more drugs.'

Sean knew the man could be of no more help to him and he hardly noticed when he left with a promise to come again in the morning. Mbejane gave Dirk his bath, fed him and put him to bed and then he slipped quietly out of the suite and left Sean alone with Katrina. The afternoon of worry had tired Sean. He left the gas burning in the sitting-room and stretched out on his own bed. After a while he slept.

When the rhythm of his breathing changed Katrina looked across at him. Sean lay fully clothed on top of his blankets, one thickly-muscled arm thrown above his head and his tension betrayed by the twitching of his lips and the frown that puckered his face. Katrina stood up and moved across to stand over him, lonely as she had never been in the solitude of the bush, hurt beyond the limits of physical pain and with everything that she believed in destroyed in those few minutes that it had taken for her to discover the truth.

She looked down at Sean and with surprise realized that she still loved him, but now the security that she had found with him was gone. The walls of her castle had proved paper. She had felt the first cold draughts blowing in through them as she watched him reliving his past and regretting it. She had felt the walls tremble and the wind howl stronger outside when he danced with that woman – then, they had collapsed into ruin around her. Standing in the half-darkened room, watching the man she trusted so completely and who just as completely had betrayed her, she went carefully over the ground again to make sure there was no mistake.

That morning, she and Dirk had stopped at the sweet shop on the way back from church. It was almost opposite the hotel. It had taken Dirk a long time to select his tuppenny worth. The profusion of wares on display unmanned him and reduced him to a state of dithering indecision. Finally, with the assistance of the proprietor and a little prompting from Katrina his purchases were made and packed into a brown paper bag. They were just about to go when Katrina looked out through the large front window of the shop and saw Candy Rautenbach leaving the hotel. She came quickly down the front steps, glanced about her, crossed the street to a waiting carriage and her coachman whisked her away. Katrina had stopped the instant she caught sight of her. A pang of last night's jealousy returned, for Candy looked very lovely even in the morning sunlight. It was not until Candy's carriage disappeared that Katrina began to question her presence at their hotel at eleven o'clock on a Sunday morning. Her jealousy was a bayonet thrust up under her ribs: it made her catch her breath. Vividly she remembered Candy's whispered question as they left the Golden Guinea the previous night. She remembered the way Sean had answered and the way he had lied about it afterwards. Sean knew that Katrina would go to church that morning. How simple it all was! Sean had arranged to meet her, he had refused to accompany Katrina and while Katrina was out of the way that harlot had gone to him.

'Mummy, you're hurting me.' Unconsciously she had tightened her grip on Dirk's hand. She hurried out of the shop, dragging Dirk with her. She almost ran across the hotel lobby, up the stairs and along the passage. The door was closed. She opened it and the smell of Candy's perfume met her. Her nostrils flared at it. There was no mistaking it, she remembered it from the previous evening – the smell of fresh violets. She heard Sean call from the bathroom, Dirk ran across the room and hammered on the door.

'Daddy! Daddy! Mummy got sweets for me.'

She put her Bible down on top of the writing desk and moved across the thick carpet with the smell of violets all around her. She stood in the doorway of the bedroom. Sean's nightshirt lay on the floor, there were still damp stains on it. She felt her legs begin to tremble. She looked up and saw the stains on the bed, grey on the white sheets. She felt giddy, her cheeks burned; she only just managed to reach her own bed.

= 32 =

She knew there was no mistake. Sean had taken that woman in such a casually blatant manner – in their own bedroom, almost before her eyes, that his rejection of her could hardly have been more final if he had slapped her face and thrown her into the street. Weakened by fever, depressed by the loss of her child and the phase of her cycle, she had not the resilience to fight against it. She had loved him but she had proved insufficient for him. She could not stay with him: the stubborn pride of her race would not allow it. There was only one alternative.

Timidly she bent over him and as she kissed him she smelt the warm man-smell of his body and felt his beard brush her cheek. Her determination wavered; she wanted to throw herself across his chest, lock her arms around his neck and plead with him. She wanted to ask for another chance. If he could tell her how she had failed him she could try to change, if only he could show her what she had done wrong. Perhaps if they went back into the bush again – She dragged herself away from his bed. She pressed her knuckles hard against her lips. It was no use. He had decided and even if she begged him to take her back there would always be this thing between them. She had lived in a castle and she would not change it now for a mud hut. Driven by the trek whip of her pride she moved quickly across to the wardrobe. She put on a coat and buttoned it – it reached to her ankles and covered her nightdress; she spread the green shawl over her head, winding the loose end around her throat. Once more she looked across at Sean. He slept with his big body sprawled and the frown still on his face.

In the sitting-room she stopped beside the writing desk. Her Bible lay where she had left it. She opened the front cover, dipped the pen and wrote. She closed the book and went to the door. There she hesitated once more and looked back at Dirk's bedroom. She could not trust herself to see him again. She lifted an end of the shawl to cover her mouth, then she went out into the passage and closed the door softly behind her.

33

Sean was surprised to find himself fully dressed and lying on top of his bed when he woke next morning. It was still half dark outside the hotel windows and the room was cold. He propped himself up on one elbow and rubbed at his eyes with the back of a clenched fist. Then he remembered and he swung his legs off the bed and looked at Katrina's bed. The blankets were thrown back and it was empty. Sean's first feeling was relief, she had recovered enough to get up on her own. He went through to the bathroom, stumbling a little from the stiffness of uneasy sleep. He tapped on the closed door.

'Katrina?' he questioned and then again louder. 'Katrina, are you in there?'

The handle turned when he tried it and the door swung open without resistance. He blinked at the empty room, white tiles reflecting the uncertain light, a towel thrown across a chair where he had left it. He felt the first twinge of alarm. Dirk's room – the door was still locked, the key on the outside. He flung it open. Dirk sat up in bed, his face flushed, his curls standing up like the leaves of a sisal bush. Sean ran out into the passage, along it and looked down into the lobby. There was a light burning behind the reception desk. The clerk slept with his head on his arms, sitting forward on his chair snoring, Sean went down the stairs three at a time. He shook the clerk.

'Has anybody been out through here during the night?' Sean demanded.

'I . . . I don't know.'

'Is that door locked?' Sean pointed at the front door.

'No, sir, there's a night latch on it. You can get out but not in.'

Sean ran out onto the pavement. Which way, which way to search for her? Which way had she gone? Back to Pretoria to the wagons? Sean thought not. She would need transport and she had no money to hire it. Why should she leave without waking him, leave Dirk, leave her clothing and disappear into the night. She must have been unbalanced by the drugs the doctor had given her. Perhaps there was something in his theory that she had suffered a shock, perhaps she was wandering in her nightdress through the streets with no memory, perhaps – Sean stood in the cold grey Transvaal morning, the city starting to murmur into wakefulness around him, the questions crowding into his head and finding there no answers with which to mate.

He turned and ran back through the hotel, out of the rear door into the stable yard.

'Mbejane,' he shouted, 'Mbejane, where the hell are you?'

Mbejane appeared quickly from the stall where he was currying one of the hired horses.

'Nkosi.'

'Have you seen the Nkosikazi?'

Mbejane's face creased into a puzzled frown. 'Yesterday –' 'No, man,' shouted Sean. 'Today, last night . . . have you seen her?'

Mbejane's expression was sufficient reply.

Sean brushed impatiently past him and ran into the stable. He snatched a saddle off the rack and threw it onto the back of the nearest horse. While he clinched the girth and forced a bit between its teeth he spoke to Mbejane.

'The Nkosikazi is sick. She has left during the night. It is possible that she walks as one who still sleeps. Go quickly among your friends and tell them to search for her, tell them that there's ten pounds in gold for the one who finds her. Then come back here and care for Dirk until I return.'

Sean led the horse from the stable and Mbejane hurried off to spread the word. Sean knew that within minutes half the Zulus in Johannesburg would be looking for Katrina – tribal loyalty and ten pounds in gold were strong incentives. He swung up onto the horse and galloped out of the yard. He tried the Pretoria road first. Three miles out of town a native herd boy grazing sheep beside the road convinced him that Katrina hid not passed that way. He turned back. He paid a visit to the police station at Marshal Square. The Kommandant remembered him from the old days; Sean could rely on his co-operation. Sean left him and rode fast through the streets that were starting to fill with the bustle of a working day. He hitched his horse outside the hotel and took the front steps three at a time. The clerk had no news for him. He ran up the stairs and along the passage to his suite. Mbejane was feeding Dirk his breakfast. Dirk beamed at Sean through a faceful of egg and spread his arms to be picked up but Sean had no time for him.

'Has she come back?'

Mbejane shook his head. 'They will find her, Nkosi. Fifty men are searching for her now.'

'Stay with the child,' said Sean and went down to his horse. He stood beside it ready to mount but not knowing which way to go. 'Where the hell has she got to?' he demanded aloud. In her night clothes with no money, where the hell had she gone?

He mounted and rode with aimless urgency through the streets, searching the faces of the people along the sidewalks, turning down the sanitary lanes and peering into back-yards and vacant plots. By midday he had tired his horse and worked himself into a ferment of worry and bad temper. He had searched every street in Johannesburg, made a nuisance of himself at the police station and sworn at the hotel clerk, but there was still no sign of Katrina. He was riding down Jeppe Street for the fifth time when the imposing double-storey of Candy's Hotel registered through his preoccupation.

'Candy,' he whispered. 'She can help.'

He found her in her office among Persian rugs and gilt furniture, walls covered with pink and blue patterned wallpaper, a mirrored ceiling hung with six crystal waterfalls of chandeliers and a desk with an Indian mosaic top. Sean pushed aside the little man in the black alpaca coat who tried to stop him entering and burst into the room. Candy looked up and her small frown of annoyance smoothed as she saw who it was.

'Sean . . . oh, how nice to see you.' She came round from behind the desk, the bell tent of her skirts covering the movement of her legs so she seemed to float. Her skin was smooth white and her eyes were happy blue. She held out her hand to him, but hesitated as she saw his face. 'What is it, Sean?'

He told her in a rush and she listened and when he had finished she rang the bell on her desk.

'There's brandy in the cabinet by the fireplace,' she said, 'I expect you are in need of one.'

The little man in the alpaca coat came quickly to the bell. Sean poured himself a large brandy and listened to Candy giving orders.

'Check the railway station. Telegraph the coach stages on each of the main roads. Send someone up to the hospital. Check the registers of every hotel and boarding-house in town.'

'Very well, madame.' The little man bobbed his head as he acknowledged each instruction and then he was gone.

Candy turned back to Sean.

'You can pour a drink for me also and then sit down and simmer down. You're behaving just the way she wanted you to.'

'What do you mean?' demanded Sean.

'You are being given a little bit of wifely discipline, my dear. Surely you have been married long enough to recognize that?'

Sean carried the glass across to her and Candy patted the sofa next to her.

'Sit down,' she said. 'We'll find your little Cinderella for you.'

'What do you mean . . . wifely discipline?' he demanded again.

'Punishment for bad behaviour. You may have eaten with your mouth open, answered back, taken more than your share of the blankets, not said good morning with the right inflection or committed one of the other mortal sins of matrimony, but –' Candy sipped her drink and gasped slightly, 'I see that time has not given you a lighter hand with the brandy bottle. One Courtney tot always did equal an imperial gallon . . . but, as I was saying, my guess is that little Katy is having an acute attack of jealousy. Probably her first, seeing that the two of you have spent your whole married life out in the deep sticks and she has never had an opportunity of watching the Courtney charm work on any other female before.'

'Nonsense,' said Sean. 'Who's she got to be jealous of?'

'Me,' said Candy. 'Every time she looked at me the other night I felt as though I'd been hit in the chest with an axe.' Candy touched her magnificent bosom with her fingertips, skilfully drawing Sean's attention to it. Sean looked at it. It was deeply cleft and smelt of fresh violets. He shifted restlessly and looked away.

'Nonsense,' he said again. 'We're just old friends, almost like –' he hesitated.

'I hope, my dear, that you weren't going to say "brother and sister" . . . I'll not be party to any incestuous relationship . . . or had you forgotten about that?'

Sean had not forgotten. Every detail of it was still clear. He blushed and stood up.

'I'd better be going,' he said. 'I'm going to keep looking for her. Thanks for your help, Candy, and for the drink.'

'Whatever I have is yours, m'sieur,' she murmured, lifting an eyebrow at him, enjoying the way he blushed. 'I'll let you know as soon as we hear anything.'

The assurance that Candy had given him wore thinner as the afternoon went by with no news of Katrina. By nightfall Sean was again wild with worry, it had completely swamped his bad temper and even anaesthetized his fatigue. One by one Mbejane's tribesmen came in to report a blank score, one by one the avenues Candy's men were exploring proved empty, and long before midnight Sean was the only hunter left. He rode hunched in the saddle, a lantern in his hand, riding the ground that had already been covered a dozen times, visiting the mining camps along the ridge, stopping to question late travellers he met along the network of roads between the mines. But the answer was always the same. Some thought he was joking: they laughed until they saw that his face was haunted and dark-eyed in the lantern light, then they stopped laughing and moved hurriedly on. Others had heard about the missing woman; they started to question him, but as soon as Sean realized they could not help him, he pushed past them and went on searching. At dawn he was back at the hotel. Mbejane was waiting for him.

'Nkosi, I have had food ready for you since last night. Eat now and sleep a little. I will send the men out to search again today, they will find her.'

'Tell them, I will give one hundred pounds to the one who finds her.' Sean passed his hand wearily across his face. 'Tell them to hunt the open veld beyond the ridges, she may not have followed a road.'

'I will tell them . . . but now you must eat.'

Sean blinked his eyes, they were red-veined and each had a little lump of yellow mucus in the corner.

'Dirk?' he asked.

'He is well, Nkosi, I have stayed with him all the while.'

Mbejane took Sean firmly by the arm. 'There is food ready. You must eat.'

'Saddle me another horse,' said Sean. 'I will eat while you do it.'

Without sleep, unsteady in the saddle as the day wore on, Sean widened the circle of his search until he was out into the treeless veld and the mine headgears were small spidery triangles on the horizon.

A dozen times he met Zulus from the city, big black men in loin cloths, moving at their businesslike trot, hunting the ground like hounds. There was a concealed sympathy behind their greetings.

'Mbejane has told us, Nkosi. We will find her.' And Sean left them and rode on alone, more alone than he had ever been in his life before. After dark he rode back into Johannesburg, the faint flutter of hope inside him stilled as he limped stiffly into the gas-lit lobby, of the hotel and saw the pity in the reception clerk's face.

'No word, I'm afraid, Mr Courtney.'

Sean nodded. 'Thanks anyway. Is my son all right?'

'Your servant has taken good care of him, sir. I sent dinner up to him an hour ago.'

The stairs seemed endless as he climbed them. By God, he was tired – sick-tired and sick with worry. He pushed open the door of his suite and Candy stood up from a chair across the room. The hope flared up in him again.'

'Have you –' he started eagerly.

'No,' she said quickly. 'No, Sean, I'm sorry.' He flopped into one of the chairs and Candy poured a drink for him from a decanter that was waiting on the writing desk. He smiled his thanks and took a big gulp at the glass. Candy lifted his legs one at a time and pulled off his boots, ignoring his faint protest. Then she took up her own glass and went to sit across the room from him.

'I'm sorry I joked yesterday,' she apologized softly. 'I don't think I realized how much you love her.' She lifted her glass to him. 'Here's a speedy end to the search.'

Sean drank again, half a glass at a swallow.

'You do love her, don't you?' Candy asked.

Sean answered her sharply. 'She's my wife.'

'But it's not only that,' Candy went on recklessly, knowing his anger was just below the surface of his fatigue.

'Yes, I love her. I'm just learning how much, I love her as I'll never be able to love again.' He drained his glass and stared at it, his face grey under the brown and his eyes dark with unhappiness. 'Love,' he said. 'Love,' mouthing the word, weighing it. 'They've dirtied that word . . . they sell love at the Opera House . . . they have used that word so much that now when I want to say "I love Katrina" it doesn't sound what I mean.' Sean hurled the glass against the far wall, it shattered with a crack and a tingle and Dirk stirred in the bedroom. Sean dropped his voice to a fierce whisper. 'I love her so it screws my gut, I love her so that to think of losing her now is like thinking of dying.'

He clenched his fists and leaned forward in his chair. 'I'll not lose her now, by Christ, I'll find her and when I do I'll tell her this. I'll tell her just like I'm telling you.' He stopped and frowned. 'I don't think I've ever said to her "I love you." I've never liked using that word. I've said "Marry me" and "You're my fancy," but I've never said it straight before.'

'Perhaps that's part of the reason she ran away, Sean, perhaps because you never said it she thought you never felt it.' Candy was watching him with a strange expression – pity and understanding and a little yearning.

'I'll find her,' said Sean, 'and this time I'll tell her . . . if it's not too late.'

'You'll find her and it won't be too late. The earth can't have swallowed her, and she'll be glad to hear you say it.' Candy stood up. 'You must rest now, you have a hard day ahead of you.'

Sean slept fully dressed in the chair in the sitting-room. He slept brokenly, his mind struggling and kicking him back to half wakefulness every few minutes. Candy had turned the gas low before she left and its light fell in a soft pool onto the writing desk beneath it. Katrina's Bible lay where she had left it and each time Sean started awake the fat, leather-covered book caught his eye. Some time before dawn he woke for the last time and knew he could not sleep again.

He stood up and his body still ached and his eyes felt gritty. He moved across to the gas lamp and turned it up high, he let his hand drop from the lamp onto the Bible. Its leather was cool and softly polished beneath his fingers. He opened the front cover and caught his breath with a hiss.

Beneath Katrina's name, in her carefully rounded writing, the ink still freshly blue, *she had filled in the date of death.*

The page magnified slowly in front of his eyes until it filled the whole field of his vision. There was a rushing sound in his ears, the sound of a river in flood, but above it he heard voices, different voices.

'Let's go, Sean, it looks like a grave.'

'But more than anything she needs love.'

'The earth can't have swallowed her.'

And his own voice, 'If it's not too late, if it's not too late.'

The morning light was gathering strength as he reached the ruins of the old Candy Deep office block. He left his horse and ran through the grass towards the mine dump. The wind was small and cold; it moved the tops of the grass and went on to where Katrina's green shawl was caught on the barbed wire fence that ringed the shaft. In the wind the shawl flapped its wings like a big green bird of prey.

Sean reached the fence and looked down into the mouth of the shaft. At one place the grass had been torn away from the edge as though someone had snatched at it as they fell.

Sean loosed the shawl from the spikes of the barbed wire, he balled the heavy material in his fists, then he held it out over the shaft and let it drop. It spread out as it floated down into the blackness, and it was the bright green of Katrina's eyes.

'Why?' whispered Sean. 'Why have you done this to us, my fancy?' He turned away and walked back to his horse, stumbling carelessly in the rough footing.

Mbejane was waiting for him in the hotel suite.

'Get the carriage,' Sean told him.

'The Nkosikazi –?'

'Get the carriage,' Sean repeated.

Sean carried Dirk downstairs. He paid his bill at the reception desk and went out to where Mbejane had the carriage ready. He climbed up into it and held Dirk on his lap.

'Drive back to Pretoria,' Sean said.

'Where's Mummy?' Dirk demanded.

'She's not coming with us.'

'Are we going alone?' Dirk insisted and Sean nodded wearily.

'Yes, Dirk, we are going alone.'

'Is Mummy coming just now?'

'No, Dirk. No, she's not.'

It was finished, Sean thought. It was all over – all the dreams and the laughter and the love. He was too numbed to feel the pain yet – it would come later.

'Why are you squeezing me so hard, Daddy?'

Sean slackened his grip and looked down at the child on his lap. It was not finished, he realized; it was only a new beginning.

But first I must have time for this to heal: time – and a quiet place to lie up with this wound. The wagons are waiting and I must go back into the wilderness.

Perhaps after another year I will have healed sufficiently to start again, to go back to Ladyburg with my son, back to Ladyburg, and to Ada and to Garry – he thought. Then suddenly and sickeningly he felt the pain again, and the deep raw ache of it frightened him. *Please God,* prayed Sean who had never prayed before, *please God give me the strength to endure it.*

'Are you going to cry, Daddy? You look like you're going to cry.' Dirk was watching Sean's face with solemn curiosity. Sean pulled the child's head gently against his shoulder and held it there.

If tears could pay both our debts, thought Sean, if with my tears I could buy for you an indulgence from all pain, if by weeping now I could do all your weeping for you – then I would cry until my eyes were washed away.

'No, Dirk,' he answered. 'I am not going to cry – crying never helps very much.'

And Mbejane took them to where the wagons waited at Pretoria.

THE DARK OF THE SUN

= 1 =

'I don't like the idea,' announced Wally Hendry, and belched. He moved his tongue round his mouth getting the taste of it before he went on. 'I think the whole idea stinks like a ten-day corpse.' He lay sprawled on one of the beds with a glass balanced on his naked chest and he was sweating heavily in the Congo heat.

'Unfortunately your opinion doesn't alter the fact that we are going.' Bruce Curry went on laying out his shaving tackle without looking up.

'You should-a told them to keep it, told them we were staying here in Elisabethville – why didn't you tell them that, hey?' Hendry picked up his glass and swallowed the contents.

'Because they pay me not to argue.' Bruce spoke without interest and looked at himself in the fly-spotted mirror above the wash-basin. The face that looked back was sun-darkened with a cap of close-cropped black hair; soft hair that would be unruly and inclined to curl if it were longer. Black eyebrows slanting upwards at the corners, green eyes with a heavy fringe of lashes and a mouth which could smile as readily as it could sulk. Bruce regarded his good looks without pleasure. It was a long time since he had felt that emotion, a long time since his mouth had either smiled or sulked. He did not feel the old tolerant affection for his nose, the large slightly hooked nose that rescued his face from prettiness and gave him the air of a genteel pirate.

'Jesus!' growled Wally Hendry from the bed. 'I've had just about a gutsful of this nigger army. I don't mind fighting – but I don't fancy going hundreds of miles out into the bush to play nursemaid to a bunch of bloody refugees.'

'It's a hell of a life,' agreed Bruce absently and spread shaving-soap on his face. The lather was very white against his tan. Under a skin that glowed so healthily that it appeared to have been freshly oiled, the muscles of his shoulders and chest changed shape as he moved. He was in good condition, fitter than he had been for many years, but this fact gave him no more pleasure than had his face.

'Get me another drink, André.' Wally Hendry thrust his empty glass into the hand of the man who sat on the edge of the bed.

The Belgian stood up and went across to the table obediently.

'More whisky and less beer in this one,' Wally instructed, turned once more to Bruce and belched again. 'That's what I think of the idea.'

As André poured Scotch whisky into the glass and filled it with beer Wally hitched around the pistol in its webbing holster until it hung between his legs.

'When are we leaving?' he asked.

'There'll be an engine and five coaches at the goods yard first thing tomorrow morning. We'll load up and get going as soon as possible.' Bruce started to shave, drawing the razor down from temple to chin and leaving the skin smooth and brown behind it.

'After three months of fighting a bunch of greasy little Gurkhas I was looking forward to a bit of fun – I haven't even had a pretty in all that time – now the second day after the ceasefire and they ship us out again.'

'C'est la guerre,' muttered Bruce, his face twisted in the act of shaving.

'What's that mean?' demanded Wally suspiciously.

'That's war,' Bruce translated.

'Talk English, Bucko.'

It was the measure of Wally Hendry that after six months in the Belgian Congo he could neither speak nor understand a single word of French.

There was silence again, broken only by the scraping of Bruce's razor and the small metallic sound as the fourth man in the hotel room stripped and cleaned his FN rifle.

'Have a drink, Haig,' Wally invited him.

'No, thanks.' Michael Haig glanced up, not trying to conceal his distaste as he looked at Wally.

'You're another snotty bastard – don't want to drink with me, hey? Even the high-class Captain Curry is drinking with me. What makes you so goddam special?'

'You know that I don't drink.' Haig turned his attention back to his weapon, handling it with easy familiarity. For all of them the ugly automatic rifles had become an extension of their own bodies. Even while shaving Bruce had only to drop his hand to reach the rifle propped against the wall, and the two men on the bed had theirs on the floor beside them.

'You don't drink!' chuckled Wally. 'Then how did you get that complexion, Bucko? How come your nose looks like a ripe plum?'

Haig's mouth tightened and the hands on his rifle stilled.

'Cut it out, Wally,' said Bruce without heat.

'Haig don't drink,' crowed Wally, and dug the little Belgian in the ribs with his thumb, 'get that, André! He's a tea-bloody-total! My old man was a teetotal also; sometimes for two, three months at a time he was teetotal, and then he'd come home one night and sock the old lady in the clock so you could hear her teeth rattle from across the street.'

His laughter choked him and he had to wait for it to clear before he went on.

'My bet is that you're that kind of teetotal, Haig. One drink and you wake up ten days later; that's it, isn't it? One drink and – pow! – the old girl gets it in the chops and the kids don't eat for a couple of weeks.'

Haig laid the rifle down carefully on the bed and looked at Wally with his jaws clenched, but Wally had not noticed. He went on happily.

'André, take the whisky bottle and hold it under Old Teetotal Haig's nose. Let's watch him slobber at the mouth and his eyes stand out like a pair of dog's balls.'

Haig stood up. Twice the age of Wally – a man in his middle fifties, with grey in his hair and the refinement of his features not completely obliterated by the marks that life had left upon them. He had arms like a boxer and a powerful set to his shoulders. 'It's about time you learned a few manners, Hendry. Get on your feet.'

'You wanta dance or something? I don't waltz – ask André. He'll dance with you – won't you, André?'

Haig was balanced on the balls of his feet, his hands closed and raised slightly. Bruce Curry placed his razor on the shelf above the basin, and moved quietly round the table with soap still on his face to take up a position from which he could intervene. There he waited, watching the two men.

'Get up, you filthy guttersnipe.'

'Hey, André, get that. He talks pretty, hey? He talks real pretty.'

'I'm going to smash that ugly face of yours right into the middle of the place where your brain should have been.'

'Jokes! This boy is a natural comic.' Wally laughed, but there was something wrong with the sound of it. Bruce knew then that Wally was not going to fight. Big arms and swollen chest covered with ginger hair, belly flat and hard-looking, thick-necked below the wide flat-featured face with its little Mongolian eyes; but Wally wasn't going to fight. Bruce was puzzled: he remembered the night at the road bridge and he knew that Hendry was no coward, and yet now he was not going to take up Haig's challenge.

Mike Haig moved towards the bed.

'Leave him, Mike.' André spoke for the first time, his voice soft as a girl's. 'He was only joking. He didn't mean it.'

'Hendry, don't think I'm too much of a gentleman to hit you because you're on your back. Don't make that mistake.'

'Big deal,' muttered Wally. 'This boy's not only a comic, he's a bloody hero also.'

Haig stood over him and lifted his right hand with the fist, bunched like a hammer, aimed at Wally's face.

'Haig!' Bruce hadn't raised his voice but its tone checked the older man.

'That's enough,' said Bruce.

'But this filthy little —'

'Yes, I know,' said Bruce. 'Leave him!' With his fist still up Mike Haig hesitated, and there was no movement in the room. Above them the corrugated iron roof popped loudly as it expanded in the heat of the Congo midday, and the only other sound was Haig's breathing. He was panting and his face was congested with blood.

'Please, Mike,' whispered André. 'He didn't mean it.'

Slowly Haig's anger changed to disgust and he dropped his hand, turned away and picked up his rifle from the other bed.

'I can't stand the smell in this room another minute. I'll wait for you in the truck downstairs, Bruce.'

'I won't be long,' agreed Bruce as Mike went to the door.

'Don't push your luck, Haig,' Wally called after him. 'Next time you won't get off so easily.'

In the doorway Mike Haig swung quickly, but, with a hand on his shoulder, Bruce turned him again.

'Forget it, Mike,' he said, and closed the door after him.

'He's just bloody lucky that he's an old man,' growled Wally. 'Otherwise I'd have fixed him good.'

'Sure,' said Bruce. 'It was decent of you to let him go.' The soap had dried on his face and he wet his brush to lather again.

'Yeah, I couldn't hit an old bloke like that, could I?'

'No.' Bruce smiled a little. 'But don't worry, you frightened the hell out of him. He won't try it again.'

'He'd better not!' warned Hendry. 'Next time I'll kill the old bugger.'

No, you won't, thought Bruce, you'll back down again as you have just done, as you've done a dozen times before. Mike and I are the only ones who can make you do it; in the same way as an animal will growl at its trainer but cringe away when he cracks the whip. He began shaving again.

The heat in the room was unpleasant to breathe; it drew the perspiration out of them and the smell of their bodies blended sourly with stale cigarette smoke and liquor fumes.

'Where are you and Mike going?' André ended the long silence.

'We're going to see if we can draw the supplies for this trip. If we have any luck we'll take them down to the goods yard and have Ruffy put an armed guard on them overnight,' Bruce answered him, leaning over the basin and splashing water up into his face.

'How long will we be away?'

Bruce shrugged. 'A week – ten days'. He sat on his bed and pulled on one of his jungle boots. 'That is, if we don't have any trouble.'

'Trouble, Bruce?' asked André.

'From Msapa Junction we'll have to go two hundred miles through country crawling with Baluba.'

'But we'll be in a train,' protested André. 'They've only got bows and arrows, they can't touch us.'

'André, there are seven rivers to cross – one big one – and bridges are easily destroyed. Rails can be torn up.' Bruce began to lace the boot. 'I don't think it's going to be a Sunday school picnic.'

'Christ. I think the whole thing stinks,' repeated Wally moodily. 'Why are we going anyway?'

'Because,' Bruce began patiently, 'for the last three months the entire population of Port Reprieve has been cut off from the rest of the world. There are women and children with them. They are fast running out of food and the other necessities of life.' Bruce paused to light a cigarette, and then went on talking as he exhaled. 'All around them the Baluba tribe is in open revolt, burning, raping and killing indiscriminately. As yet they haven't attacked the town but it won't be very long until they do. Added to which there are rumours that rebel groups of Central Congolese troops and of our own forces have formed themselves into bands of heavily-armed *shufta*. They also are running amok through the northern part of the territory. Nobody knows for certain what is happening out there, but whatever it is you can be sure it's not very pretty. We are going to fetch those people in to safety.'

'Why don't the U.N. people send out a plane?' asked André.

'No landing field.'

'Helicopters?'

'Out of range.'

'For my money the bastards can stay there,' grunted Wally. 'If the Balubas fancy a little man steak, who are we to do them out of a meal? Every man's entitled to eat and as long as it's not me they're eating, more power to their teeth, say I.' He placed his foot against André's back and straightened his leg suddenly, throwing the Belgian off the bed on to his knees.

'Go and get me a pretty.'

'There aren't any, Wally. I'll get you another drink.' André scrambled to his feet and reached for Wally's empty glass, but Wally's hand dropped on to his wrist.

'I said *pretty*, André, not *drink*.'

'I don't know where to find them, Wally.' André's voice was desperate. 'I don't know what to say to them even.'

'You're being stupid, Bucko. I might have to break your arm.' Wally twisted the wrist slowly. 'You know as well as I do that the bar downstairs is full of them. You know that, don't you?'

'But what do I say to them?' André's face was contorted with the pain of his twisted wrist.

'Oh, for Christ's sake, you stupid bloody frog-eater – just go down and flash a banknote. You don't have to say a dicky bird.'

'You're hurting me, Wally.'

'No? You're kidding!' Wally smiled at him, twisting harder, his slitty eyes smoky from the liquor, and Bruce could see he was enjoying it. 'Are you going, Bucko? Make up your mind – get me a pretty or get yourself a broken arm.'

'All right, if that's what you want. I'll go. Please leave me, I'll go,' mumbled André.

'That's what I want.' Wally released him, and he straightened up massaging his wrist.

'See that she's clean and not too old. You hear me?'

'Yes, Wally. I'll get one.' André went to the door and Bruce noticed his expression. It was stricken beyond the pain of a bruised wrist. What lovely creatures they are, thought Bruce, and I am one of them and yet apart from them. I am the watcher, stirred by them as much as I would be by a bad play. André went out.

'Another drink, Bucko?' said Wally expansively. 'I'll even pour you one.'

'Thanks,' said Bruce, and started on the other boot. Wally brought the glass to him and he tasted it. It was strong, and the mustiness of the whisky was ill-matched with the sweetness of the beer, but he drank it.

'You and I,' said Wally, 'we're the shrewd ones. We drink 'cause we want to, not 'cause we have to. We live like we want to live, not like other people think we should. You and I got a lot in common, Bruce. We should be friends, you and I. I mean us being so much alike.' The drink was working in him now, blurring his speech a little.

'Of course we are friends – I count you as one of my very dearest, Wally.' Bruce spoke solemnly, no trace of sarcasm showing.

'No kidding?' Wally asked earnestly. 'How's that, hey? Christ, I always thought you didn't like me. Christ, you never can tell, isn't that right? You just never can tell,' shaking his head in wonder, suddenly sentimental with the whisky. 'That's really true? You like me. Yeah, we could be buddies. How's that, Bruce? Every guy needs a buddy. Every guy needs a back stop.'

'Sure,' said Bruce. 'We're buddies. How's that, hey?'

'That's on, Bucko!' agreed Wally with deep feeling, *and I feel nothing,* thought Bruce, *no disgust, no pity – nothing. That way you are secure; they cannot disappoint you, they cannot disgust you, they cannot sicken you, they cannot smash you up again.*

They both looked up as André ushered the girl into the room. She had a sexy little pug face, painted lips – ruby on amber.

'Well done, André,' applauded Wally, looking at the girl's body. She wore high heels and a short pink dress that flared into a skirt from her waist but did not cover her knees.

'Come here, cookie.' Wally held out his hand to her and she crossed the room without hesitation, smiling a bright professional smile. Wally drew her down beside him on to the bed.

André went on standing in the doorway. Bruce got up and shrugged into his camouflage battle-jacket, buckled on his webbing belt and adjusted the holstered pistol until it hung comfortably on his outer thigh.

'Are you going?' Wally was feeding the girl from his glass.

'Yes.' Bruce put his slouch hat on his head; the red, green and white Katangese sideflash gave him an air of artificial gaiety.

'Stay a little – come on, Bruce.'

'Mike is waiting for me.' Bruce picked up his rifle.

'Muck him. Stay a little, we'll have some fun.'

'No, thanks.' Bruce went to the door.

'Hey, Bruce. Take a look at this.' Wally tipped the girl backwards over the bed, he pinned her with one arm across her chest while she struggled playfully and with the other hand he swept her skirt up above her waist.

'Take a good look at this and tell me you still want to go!'

The girl was naked under the skirt, her lower body shaven so that her plump little sex pouted sulkily.

'Come on, Bruce,' laughed Wally. 'You first. Don't say I'm not your buddy.'

Bruce glanced at the girl, her legs scissored and her body wriggled as she fought with Wally. She was giggling.

'Mike and I will be back before curfew. I want this woman out of here by then,' said Bruce.

There is no desire, he thought as he looked at her, *that is all finished.* He opened the door.

'Curry!' shouted Wally. 'You're a bloody nut also. Christ, I thought you were a man. Jesus Christ! You're as bad as the others. André, the doll boy. Haig, the rummy. What's with you, Bucko? It's women with you, isn't it? You're a bloody nut-case also!'

Bruce closed the door and stood alone in the passage. The taunt had gone through a chink in his armour and he clamped his mind down on the sting of it, smothering it.

It's all over. She can't hurt me any more. He thought with determination, remembering her, the woman, not the one in the room he had just left but the other one who had been his wife.

'The bitch,' he whispered, and then quickly, almost guiltily, 'I do not hate her. There is no hatred and there is no desire.'

= 2 =

The lobby of the Hotel Grand Leopold II was crowded. There were gendarmes carrying their weapons ostentatiously, talking loudly, lolling against walls and over the bar; women with them, varying in colour from black through to pastel brown, some already drunk; a few Belgians still with the stunned disbelieving eyes of the refugee, one of the women crying as she rocked her child on her lap; other white men in civilian clothes but with the alertness about them and the quick restless eyes of the adventurer, talking quietly with Africans in business suits; a group of journalists at one table in damp shirtsleeves, waiting and watching with the patience of vultures. And everybody sweated in the heat.

Two South African charter pilots hailed Bruce from across the room.

'Hi, Bruce. How about a snort?'

'Dave. Carl.' Bruce waved. 'Big hurry now – tonight perhaps.'

'We're flying out this afternoon.' Carl Engelbrecht shook his head. 'Back next week.'

'We'll make it then,' Bruce agreed, and went out of the front door into the Avenue du

Kasai. As he stopped on the sidewalk the white-washed buildings bounced the glare into his face. The naked heat made him wince and he felt fresh sweat start out of his body beneath his battle-suit. He took the dark glasses from his top pocket and put them on as he crossed the street to the Chev three-tonner in which Mike Haig waited.

'I'll drive, Mike.'

'Okay.' Mike slid across the seat and Bruce stepped up into the cab. He started the truck north down the Avenue du Kasai.

'Sorry about that scene, Bruce.'

'No harm done.'

'I shouldn't have lost my temper like that.'

Bruce did not answer, he was looking at the deserted buildings on either side. Most of them had been looted and all of them were pock-marked with shrapnel from the mortar bursts. At intervals along the sidewalk were parked the burnt out bodies of automobiles looking like the carapaces of long-dead beetles.

'I shouldn't have let him get through to me, and yet the truth hurts like hell.'

Bruce was silent but he trod down harder on the accelerator and the truck picked up speed. *I don't want to hear,* he thought, *I am not your confessor – I just don't want to hear.* He turned into the Avenue l'Etoile, headed towards the zoo.

'He was right, he had me measured to the inch,' persisted Mike.

'We've all got our troubles, otherwise we wouldn't be here.' And then, to change Mike's mood, 'We few, we happy few. We band of brothers.'

Mike grinned and his face was suddenly boyish. 'At least we have the distinction of following the second oldest profession – we, the mercenaries.'

'The oldest profession is better paid and much more fun,' said Bruce and swung the truck into the driveway of a double-storeyed residence, parked outside the front door and switched off the engine.

Not long ago the house had been the home of the chief accountant of Union Minière du Haut, now it was the billet of 'D' section, Special Striker Force, commanded by Captain Bruce Curry.

Half a dozen of his black gendarmes were sitting on the low wall of the verandah, and as Bruce came up the front steps they shouted the greeting that had become traditional since the United Nations intervention.

'U.N. – Merde!'

'Ah!' Bruce grinned at them in the sense of companionship that had grown up between them in the past months. 'The cream of the Army of Katanga!'

He offered his cigarettes around and stood chatting idly for a few minutes before asking, 'Where's Sergeant Major?' One of the gendarmes jerked a thumb at the glass doors that led into the lounge and Bruce went through with Mike behind him.

Equipment was piled haphazardly on the expensive furniture, the stone fireplace was half filled with empty bottles, a gendarme lay snoring on the Persian carpet, one of the oil paintings on the wall had been ripped by a bayonet and the frame hung askew, the imbuia-wood coffee table tilted drunkenly towards its broken leg, and the whole lounge smelled of men and cheap tobacco.

'Hello, Ruffy,' said Bruce.

'Just in time, boss.' Sergeant Major Ruffararo grinned delightedly from the armchair which he was overflowing. 'These goddam Arabs have run fresh out of folding stuff.'

He gestured at the gendarmes that crowded about the table in front of him. 'Arab' was Ruffy's word of censure or contempt, and bore no relation to a man's nationality.

Ruffy's accent was always a shock to Bruce. You never expected to hear pure Americanese come rumbling out of that huge black frame. But three years previously Ruffy had returned from a scholarship tour of the United States with a command of the idiom, a diploma in land husbandry, a prodigious thirst for bottled beer (preferably Schlitz, but any other was acceptable) and a raving dose of the Old Joe.

The memory of this last, which had been a farewell gift from a high yellow sophomore of U.C.L.A., returned most painfully to Ruffararo when he was in his cups; so painfully that it could be assuaged only by throwing the nearest citizen of the United States.

Fortunately, it was only on rare occasions that an American and the necessary five or six gallons of beer were assembled in the same vicinity so that Ruffy's latent race antipathy could find expression. A throwing by Ruffy was an unforgettable experience, both for the victim and the spectators. Bruce vividly recalled that night at the Hotel Lido when he had been a witness at one of Ruffy's most spectacular throwings.

The victims, three of them, were journalists representing publications of repute. As the evening wore on they talked louder; an American accent has a carry like a well-hit golf ball and Ruffy recognized it from across the terrace. He became silent, and in his silence drank the last gallon which was necessary to tip the balance. He wiped the froth from his upper lip and stood up with his eyes fastened on the party of Americans.

'Ruffy, hold it. Hey!' – Bruce might not have spoken. Ruffy started across the terrace. They saw him coming and fell into an uneasy silence.

The first was in the nature of a practice throw; besides, the man was not aerodynamically constructed and his stomach had too much wind resistance. A middling distance of twenty feet.

'Ruffy, leave them!' shouted Bruce.

On the next throw Ruffy was getting warmed up, but he put excessive loft into it. Thirty feet; the journalist cleared the terrace and landed on the lawn below with his empty glass still clutched in his hand.

'Run, you fool!' Bruce warned the third victim, but he was paralysed.

And this was Ruffy's best ever, he took a good grip – neck and seat of the pants – and put his whole weight into it. Ruffy must have known that he had executed the perfect throw, for his shout of 'Gonorrhoea!' as he launched his man had a ring of triumph to it.

Afterwards, when Bruce had soothed the three Americans, and they had recovered sufficiently to appreciate the fact that they were privileged by being party to a record throwing session, they all paced out the distances. The three journalists developed an almost proprietary affection for Ruffy and spent the rest of the evening buying him beers and boasting to every newcomer in the bar. One of them, he who had been thrown last and farthest, wanted to do an article on Ruffy – with pictures. Towards the end of the evening he was talking wildly of whipping up sufficient enthusiasm to have a man-throwing event included in the Olympic Games.

Ruffy accepted both their praise and their beer with modest gratitude; and when the third American offered to let Ruffy throw him again, he declined the offer on the grounds that he never threw the same man twice. All in all, it had been a memorable evening.

Apart from these occasional lapses, Ruffy had a more powerful body and happier mind than any man Bruce had ever known, and Bruce could not help liking him. He could not prevent himself smiling as he tried to reject Ruffy's invitation to play cards.

'We've got work to do now, Ruffy. Some other time.'

'Sit down, boss,' Ruffy repeated, and Bruce grimaced resignedly and took the chair opposite him.

'How much you going to bet?' Ruffy leaned forward.

'Un mille.' Bruce laid a thousand-franc note on the table; 'when that's gone, then we go.'

'No hurry,' Ruffy soothed him. 'We got all day.' He dealt the three cards face down. 'The old Christian monarch is in there somewhere; all you got to do is find him and it's the easiest mille you ever made.'

'In the middle,' whispered the gendarme standing beside Bruce's chair. 'That's him in the middle.'

'Take no notice of that mad Arab – he's lost five mille already this morning,' Ruffy advised.

Bruce turned over the right-hand card.

'Mis-luck,' crowed Ruffy. 'You got yourself the queen of hearts.' He picked up the banknote and stuffed it into his breast pocket. 'She'll see you wrong every time, that sweet-faced little bitch.' Grinning, he turned over the middle card to expose the Jack of spades with his sly eyes and curly little moustache. 'She's been shacked up there with the Jack right under the ole King's nose.' He turned the king face up. 'Look you at that dozy old guy – he's not even facing in the right direction.'

Bruce stared at the three cards and he felt that sickness in his stomach again. The whole story was there; even the man's name was right, but the Jack should have worn a beard and driven a red Jaguar and his queen of hearts never had such innocent eyes. Bruce spoke abruptly. 'That's it, Ruffy. I want you and ten men to come with me.'

'Where we going?'

'Down to Ordinance – we're drawing special supplies.'

Ruffy nodded and buttoned the playing cards into his top pocket while he selected the gendarmes to accompany them; then he asked Bruce. 'We might need some oil; what you think, boss?'

Bruce hesitated; they had only two cases of whisky left of the dozen they had looted in August. The purchasing power of a bottle of genuine Scotch was enormous and Bruce was loath to use them except in extraordinary circumstances. But now he realized that his chances of getting the supplies he needed were remote, unless he took along a substantial bribe for the quartermaster.

'Okay, Ruffy. Bring a case.'

Ruffy came up out of the chair and clapped his steel helmet on his head. The chin straps hung down on each side of his round black face.

'A full case?' He grinned at Bruce. 'You want to buy a battleship?'

'Almost,' agreed Bruce; 'go and get it.'

Ruffy disappeared into the back area of the house and returned almost immediately with a case of Grant's Standfast under one arm and half a dozen bottles of Simba beer held by their necks between the fingers of his other hand.

'We might get thirsty,' he explained.

The gendarmes climbed back into the back of the truck with a clatter of weapons and shouted cheerful abuse at their fellows on the verandah. Bruce, Mike and Ruffy crowded into the cab and Ruffy set the whisky on the floor and placed two large booted feet upon it.

'What's this all about, boss?' he asked as Bruce trundled the truck down the drive and turned into the Avenue l'Etoile. Bruce told him and when he had finished Ruffy grunted noncommittally and opened a bottle of beer with his big white chisel-blade teeth; the gas hissed softly and a little froth ran down the bottle and dripped onto his lap.

'My boys aren't going to like it,' he commented as he offered the open bottle to Mike Haig. Mike shook his head and Ruffy passed the bottle to Bruce.

Ruffy opened a bottle for himself and spoke again. 'They going to hate it like hell.' He shook his head. 'And there'll be even bigger trouble when we get to Port Reprieve and pick up the diamonds.'

Bruce glanced sideways at him, startled. 'What diamonds?'

'From the dredgers,' said Ruffy. 'You don't think they're sending us all that way just to bring in these other guys. They're worried about the diamonds, that's for sure!'

Suddenly, for Bruce, much which had puzzled him was explained. A half-forgotten conversation that he had held earlier in the year with an engineer from Union Minière jumped back into his memory. They had discussed the three diamond dredgers that worked the gravel from the bed of the Lufira swamps. The boats were based on Port Reprieve and clearly they would have returned there at the beginning of the emergency; they must still be there with three or four months' recovery of diamonds on board. Something like half a million sterling in uncut stones. That was the reason why the Katangese Government placed such priority on this expedition, the reason why such a powerful force was being used, the reason why no approaches had been made to the U.N. authorities to conduct the rescue.

Bruce smiled sardonically as he remembered the humanitarian arguments that had been given to him by the Minister of the Interior.

'It is our duty, Captain Curry. We cannot leave these people to the not-so-tender mercy of the tribesmen. It is our duty as civilized human beings.'

There were others cut off in remote mission stations and government outposts throughout southern Kasai and Katanga; nothing had been heard of them for months, but their welfare was secondary to that of the settlement at Port Reprieve.

Bruce lifted the bottle to his lips again, steering with one hand and squinting ahead through the windscreen as he drank. All right, we'll fetch them in and afterwards an ammunition box will be loaded on to a chartered aircraft, and later still there will be another deposit to a numbered account in Zurich. Why should I worry? They're paying me for it.

'I don't think we should mention the diamonds to my boys.' Ruffy spoke sadly. 'I don't think it would be a good idea at all.'

Bruce slowed the truck as they ran into the industrial area beyond the railway line. He watched the buildings as they passed, until he recognized the one he wanted and swung off the road to stop in front of the gate. He blew a blast on the hooter and a gendarme came out and inspected his pass minutely. Satisfied, he shouted out to someone beyond the gate and it swung open. Bruce drove the truck through into the yard and switched off the engine.

There were half a dozen other trucks parked in the yard, all emblazoned with the

Katangese shield and surrounded by gendarmes in uniforms patchy with sweat. A white lieutenant leaned from the cab of one of the trucks and shouted.

'Ciao, Bruce!'

'How things, Sergio?' Bruce answered him.

'Crazy! Crazy!' Bruce smiled. For the Italian everything was crazy. Bruce remembered that in July, during the fighting at the road bridge, he had bent him over the bonnet of a Landrover and with a bayonet dug a piece of schrapnel out of his hairy buttocks – that had also been crazy.

'See you around,' Bruce dismissed him and led Mike and Ruffy across the yard to the warehouse. There was a sign on the large double doors *Dépôt Ordinance – Armée du Katanga* and beyond them at a desk in a glass cubicle sat a major with a pair of Gandhi-type steel-rimmed spectacles perched on a face like that of a jovial black toad. He looked up at Bruce.

'Non,' he said with finality. 'Non, non.' Bruce produced his requisition form and laid it before him. The major brushed it aside contemptuously.

'We have not got these items, we are destitute. I cannot do it. No! I cannot do it. There are priorities. There are circumstances to consider. No, I am sorry.' He snatched a sheaf of papers from the side of his desk and turned his whole attention to them, ignoring Bruce.

'This requisition is signed by Monsieur le Président,' Bruce pointed out mildly, and the major laid down his papers and came round from behind the desk. He stood close to Bruce with the top of his head on a level with Bruce's chin.

'Had it been signed by the Almighty himself, it would be of no use. I am sorry, I am truly sorry.'

Bruce lifted his eyes and for a second allowed them to wander over the mountains of stores which packed the interior of the warehouse. From where he stood he could identify at least twenty items that he needed. The major noticed the gesture and his French became so excited that Bruce could only make out the repeated use of the word 'Non'. He glanced significantly at Ruffy and the sergeant major stepped forward and placed an arm soothingly about the major's shoulders; then very gently he led him, still protesting, out into the yard and across to the truck. He opened the door of the cab and the major saw the case of whisky.

A few minutes later, after Ruffy had prised open the lid with his bayonet and allowed the major to inspect the seals on the caps, they returned to the office with Ruffy carrying the case.

'Captain,' said the major as he picked up the requisition from the desk. 'I see now that I was mistaken. This is indeed signed by Monsieur le Président. It is my duty to afford you the most urgent priority.'

Bruce murmured his thanks and the major beamed at him. 'I will give you men to help you.'

'You are too kind. It would disrupt your routine. I have my own men.'

'Excellent,' agreed the major and waved a podgy hand around the warehouse. 'Take what you need.'

= 3 =

Again Bruce glanced at his wristwatch. It was still twenty minutes before the curfew ended at 06.00 hours. Until then he must fret away the time watching Wally Hendry finishing his breakfast. This was a spectacle without much appeal, for Hendry was a methodical but untidy eater.

'Why don't you keep your mouth closed?' snapped Bruce irritably, unable to stand it any longer.

'Do I ask you your business?' Hendry looked up from his plate. His jowels were covered with a ginger stubble of beard, and his eyes were inflamed and puffy from the previous evening's debauchery. Bruce looked away from him and checked his watch again.

The suicidal temptation to ignore the curfew and set off immediately for the railway station was very strong. It required an effort to resist it. The least he could expect if he followed that course was an arrest by one of the patrols and a delay of twelve hours while he cleared himself; the worst thing would be a shooting incident.

He poured himself another cup of coffee and sipped it slowly. Impatience has always been one of my weaknesses, he reflected; nearly every mistake I have ever made stems from that cause. But I have improved a little over the years – at twenty I wanted to live my whole life in a week. Now I'll settle for a year.

He finished his coffee and checked the time again. Five minutes before six, he could risk it now. It would take almost that long to get out to the truck.

'If you are ready, gentlemen.' He pushed back his chair and picked up his pack, slung it over his shoulder and led the way out.

Ruffy was waiting for them, sitting on a pile of stones in one of the corrugated iron goods sheds. His men squatted round a dozen small fires on the concrete floor cooking breakfast.

'Where's the train?'

'That's a good question, boss,' Ruffy congratulated him, and Bruce groaned.

'It should have been here long ago,' Bruce protested, and Ruffy shrugged.

'*Should have been* is a lot different from *is*.'

'Goddammit! We've still got to load up. We'll be lucky if we get away before noon,' snapped Bruce. 'I'll go up to the station master.'

'You'd better take him a present, boss. We've still got a case left.'

'No, hell!' Bruce growled. 'Come with me, Mike.'

With Mike beside him they crossed the tracks to the main platform and clambered up on to it. At the far end a group of railway officials stood chatting and Bruce fell upon them furiously.

Two hours later Bruce stood beside the coloured engine driver on the footplate and they puffed slowly down towards the goods yard.

The driver was a roly-poly little man with a skin too dark for mere sunburn and a set of teeth with bright red plastic gums.

'Monsieur, you do not wish to proceed to Port Reprieve?' he asked anxiously.

'Yes.'

'There is no way of telling the condition of the permanent way. No traffic has used it these last four months.'

'I know. You'll have to proceed with caution.'

'There is a United Nations barrier across the lines near the old aerodrome,' protested the man.

'We have a pass.' Bruce smiled to soothe him; his bad temper was abating now that he had his transport. 'Stop next to the first shed.'

With a hiss of steam brakes the train pulled up beside the concrete platform and Bruce jumped down.

'All right, Ruffy,' he shouted. 'Let's get cracking.'

Bruce had placed the three steel-sided open trucks in the van, for they were the easiest to defend. From behind the breast-high sides the Bren guns could sweep ahead and on both flanks. Then followed the two passenger coaches, to be used as store rooms and officer's quarters; also for accommodation of the refugees on the return journey. Finally, the locomotive in the rear, where it would be least vulnerable and would not spew smoke and soot back over the train.

The stores were loaded into four of the compartments, the windows shuttered and the doors locked. Then Bruce set about laying out his defences. In a low circle of sandbags on the roof of the leading coach he sited one of the Brens and made his own post. From here he could look down over the open trucks, back at the locomotive, and also command an excellent view of the surrounding country.

The other Brens he placed in the leading truck and put Hendry in command there. He had obtained from the major at Ordinance three of the new walkie-talkie sets; one he gave to the engine driver, another to Hendry up front, and the third he retained in his emplacement; and his system of communication was satisfactory.

It was almost twelve o'clock before these preparations were complete and Bruce turned to Ruffy who sat on the sandbags beside him.

'All set?'

'All set, boss.'

'How many missing?' Bruce had learned from experience never to expect his entire command to be in any one place at any one time.

'Eight, boss.'

'That's three more than yesterday; leaves us only fifty-two men. Do you think they've taken off into the bush also?' Five of his men had deserted with their weapons on the day of the cease-fire. Obviously they had gone out into the bush to join one of the bands of *shufta* that were already playing havoc along the main roads: ambushing all unprotected traffic, beating up lucky travellers and murdering those less fortunate, raping when they had the opportunity, and generally enjoying themselves.

'No, boss. I don't think so, those three are good boys. They'll be down in the cité indigène having themselves some fun; guess they just forgot the time.' Ruffy shook his head. 'Take us about half an hour to find them; all we do is go down and visit all the knock-shops. You want to try?'

'No, we haven't time to mess around if we are going to make Msapa Junction before dark. We'll pick them up again when we get back.' Was there ever an army since the Boer War that treated desertion so lightly, Bruce wondered.

He turned to the radio set beside him and depressed the transmit button.

'Driver.'

'Oui, monsieur.'

'Proceed – very slowly until we approach the United Nations barrier. Stop well this side of it.'

'Oui, monsieur.'

They rolled out of the goods yard, clicking over the points; leaving the industrial quarter on their right with the Katangese guard posts on the Avenue du Cimetière intersection; out through the suburbs until ahead of them Bruce saw the U.N. positions and he felt the first stirring of anxiety. The pass he carried in the breast pocket of his jacket was signed by General Rhee Singh, but before in this war the orders of an Indian general had not been passed by a Sudanese captain to an Irish sergeant. The reception that awaited them could be exciting.

'I hope they know about us.' Mike Haig lit his cigarette with a show of nonchalance, but he peered over it anxiously at the piles of fresh earth on each side of the tracks that marked the position of emplacements.

'These boys have got bazookas, and they're Irish Arabs,' muttered Ruffy. 'I reckon it's the maddest kind of Arabs there is – Irish. How would you like a bazooka bomb up your throat, boss?'

'No, thanks, Ruffy,' Bruce declined, and pressed the button of the radio.

'Hendry!'

In the leading truck Wally Hendry picked up his set and, holding it against his chest, looked back at Bruce.

'Curry?'

'Tell your gunners to stand away from the Brens, and the rest of them to lay down their rifles.'

'Right.'

Bruce watched him relaying the order, pushing them back, moving among the gendarmes who crowded the forward trucks. Bruce could sense the air of tension that had fallen over the whole train, watched as his gendarmes reluctantly laid down their weapons and stood empty-handed staring sullenly ahead at the U.N. barrier.

'Driver!' Bruce spoke again into the radio. 'Slow down. Stop fifty metres this side of the barrier. But if there is any shooting open the throttle and take us straight through.'

'Oui, monsieur.'

Ahead of them there was no sign of a reception committee, only the hostile barrier of poles and petrol drums across the line.

Bruce stood upon the roof and lifted his arms above his head in a gesture of neutrality. It was a mistake; the movement changed the passive mood of the gendarmes in the trucks below him. One of them lifted his arms also, but his fists were clenched.

'U.N. – merde!' he shouted, and immediately the cry was taken up.

'U.N. – merde! U.N. – merde!' They chanted the war cry – laughing at first, but then no longer laughing, their voices rising sharply.

'Shut up, damn you,' Bruce roared and swung his open hand against the head of the gendarme beside him, but the man hardly noticed it. His eyes were glazing with the infectious hysteria to which the African is so susceptible; he had snatched up his rifle and was holding it across his chest; already his body was beginning to jerk convulsively as he chanted.

Bruce hooked his fingers under the rim of the man's steel helmet and yanked it forward over his eyes so the back of his neck was exposed; he chopped him with a judo blow and the gendarme slumped forward over the sandbags, his rifle slipping from his hands.

Bruce looked up desperately; in the trucks below him the hysteria was spreading.

'Stop them – Hendry, de Surrier! Stop them for God's sake.' But his voice was lost in the chanting.

A gendarme snatched up his rifle from where it lay at his feet; Bruce saw him elbow his way towards the side of the truck to begin firing; he was working the slide to lever a round into the breech.

'Mwembe!' Bruce shouted the gendarme's name, but his voice could not penetrate the uproar.

In two seconds the whole situation would dissolve into a pandemonium of tracer and bazooka fire.

Poised on the forward edge of the roof, Bruce checked for an instant to judge the distance, and then he jumped. He landed squarely on the gendarme's shoulders, his weight throwing the man forward so his face hit the steel edge of the truck, and they went down together on to the floor.

The gendarme's finger was resting on the trigger and the rifle fired as it spun from his hands. A complete hush followed the roar of the rifle and in it Bruce scrambled to his feet, drawing his pistol from the canvas holster on his hip.

'All right,' he panted, menacing the men around him. 'Come on, give me a chance to use this!' He picked out one of his sergeants and held his eyes. 'You! I'm waiting for you – start shooting!'

At the sight of the revolver the man relaxed slowly and the madness faded from his face. He dropped his eyes and shuffled awkwardly.

Bruce glanced up at Ruffy and Haig on the roof, and raised his voice.

'Watch them. Shoot the first one who starts it again.'

'Okay, boss.' Ruffy thrust forward the automatic rifle in his hands. 'Who's it going to be?' he asked cheerfully, looking down at them. But the mood had changed. Their attitudes of defiance gave way to sheepish embarrassment and a small buzz of conversation filled the silence.

'Mike,' Bruce yelled, urgent again. 'Call the driver, he's trying to take us through!'

The noise of their passage had risen, the driver accelerating at the sound of the shot, and now they were racing down towards the U.N. barrier.

Mike Haig grabbed the set, shouted an order into it, and immediately the brakes swooshed and the train jolted to a halt not a hundred yards short of the barrier.

Slowly Bruce clambered back on to the roof of the coach.

'Close?' asked Mike.

'My God!' Bruce shook his head, and lit a cigarette with slightly unsteady hands. 'Another fifty yards –!' Then he turned and stared coldly down at his gendarmes.

'Canaille! Next time you try to commit suicide don't take me with you.' The gendarme he had knocked down was now sitting up, fingering the ugly black swelling above his eye. 'My friend,' Bruce turned on him, 'later I will have something for your further discomfort!' Then to the other man in the emplacement beside him who was massaging his neck, 'And for you also! Take their names, Sergeant Major.'

'Sir!' growled Ruffy.

'Mike.' Bruce's voice changed, soft again. 'I'm going ahead to toss the blarney with our friends behind the bazookas. When I give you the signal bring the train through.'

'You don't want me to come with you?' asked Mike.

'No, stay here.' Bruce picked up his rifle, slung it over his shoulder, dropped down the ladder on to the path beside the tracks, and walked forward with the gravel crunching beneath his boots.

An auspicious beginning to the expedition, he decided grimly, tragedy averted by the wink of an eye before they had even passed the outskirts of the city.

At least the Mickies hadn't added a few bazooka bombs to the altercation. Bruce peered ahead, and could make out the shape of helmets behind the earthworks.

Without the breeze of the train's passage it was hot again, and Bruce felt himself starting to sweat.

'Stay where you are, Mister.' A deep brogue from the emplacement nearest the tracks; Bruce stopped, standing on the wooden crossties in the sun. Now he could see the faces of the men beneath the helmets: unfriendly, not smiling.

'What was the shooting for?' the voice questioned.

'We had an accident.'

'Don't have any more or we might have one also.'

'I'd not be wanting that, Paddy.' Bruce smiled thinly, and the Irishman's voice had an edge to it as he went on. 'What's your mission?'

'I have a pass, do you want to see it?' Bruce took the folded sheet of paper from his breast pocket.

'What's your mission?' repeated the Irishman.

'Proceed to Port Reprieve and relieve the town.'

'We know about you.' The Irishman nodded. 'Let me see the pass.'

Bruce left the tracks, climbed the earth wall and handed the pink slip to the Irishman. He wore the three pips of a captain, and he glanced briefly at the pass before speaking to the man beside him.

'Very well, Sergeant, you can be clearing the barrier now.'

'I'll call the train through?' Bruce asked, and the captain nodded again.

'But make sure there are no more accidents – we don't like hired killers.'

'Sure and begorrah now, Paddy, it's not your war you're a-fighting either,' snapped Bruce and abruptly turned his back on the man, jumped down on to the tracks and waved to Mike Haig on the roof of the coach.

The Irish sergeant and his party had cleared the tracks and while the train rumbled slowly down to him Bruce struggled to control his irritation – the Irish captain's taunt had reached him. Hired killer, and of course that was what he was. Could a man sink any lower?

As the coach drew level with where he stood, Bruce caught the hand rail and swung himself aboard, waved an ironical farewell to the Irish captain and climbed up on to the roof.

'No trouble?' asked Mike.

'A bit of lip, delivered in music-hall brogue,' Bruce answered, 'but nothing serious.' He picked up the radio set.

'Driver.'

'Monsieur?'

'Do not forget my instructions.'

'I will not exceed forty kilometres the hour, and I shall at all times be prepared for an emergency stop.'

'Good!' Bruce switched off the set and sat down on the sandbags between Ruffy and Mike.

Well, he thought, here we go at last. Six hours run to Msapa Junction. That should be easy. And then – God knows, God alone knows.

The tracks curved, and Bruce looked back to see the last white-washed buildings of Elisabethville disappear among the trees. They were out into the open savannah forest.

Behind them the black smoke from the loco rolled sideways into the trees; beneath them the crossties clattered in strict rhythm, and ahead the line ran arrow straight for miles, dwindling with perspective until it merged into the olive-green mass of the forest.

Bruce lifted his eyes. Half the sky was clear and tropical blue, but in the north it was bruised with cloud, and beneath the cloud grey rain drifted down to meet the earth. The sunlight through the rain spun a rainbow, and the cloud shadow moved across the land as slowly and as darkly as a herd of grazing buffalo.

He loosened the chin strap of his helmet and laid his rifle on the roof beside him.

'You'd like a beer, boss?'

'Have you any?'

'Sure.' Ruffy called to one of the gendarmes and the man climbed down into the coach and came back with half a dozen bottles. Ruffy opened two with his teeth. Each time half the contents frothed out and splattered back along the wooden side of the coach.

'This beer's as wild as an angry woman,' he grunted as he passed a bottle to Bruce.

'It's wet anyway.' Bruce tasted it, warm and gassy and too sweet.

'Here's how!' said Ruffy.

Bruce looked down into the open trucks at the gendarmes who were settling in for the journey. Apart from the gunners at the Brens, they were lying or squatting in attitudes of complete relaxation and most of them had stripped down to their underwear. One skinny little fellow was already asleep on his back with his helmet as a pillow and the tropical sun beating full into his face.

Bruce finished his beer and threw the bottle overboard. Ruffy opened another and placed it in his hand without comment.

'Why we going so slowly, boss?'

'I told the driver to keep the speed down – give us a chance to stop if the tracks have been torn up.'

'Yeah. Them Balubas might have done that – they're mad Arabs all of them.'

The warm beer drunk in the sun was having a soothing effect on Bruce. He felt at peace, now, withdrawn from the need to make decisions, to participate in the life around him.

'Listen to that train-talk,' said Ruffy, and Bruce focused his hearing on the clickety-clack of the crossties.

'Yes, I know. You can make it say anything you want it to,' agreed Bruce.

'And it can sing,' Ruffy went on. 'It's got real music in it, like this.' He inflated the great barrel of his chest, lifted his head and let it come.

His voice was deep but with a resonance that caught the attention of the men in the open trucks below them. Those who had been sprawled in the amorphous shapes of sleep stirred and sat up. Another voice joined in humming the tune, hesitantly at first, then more confidently; then others took it up, the words were unimportant, it was the rhythm that they could not resist. They had sung together many times before and like a well-trained choir each voice found its place, the star performers leading, changing the pace, improvising, quickening until the original tune lost its identity and became one of the tribal chants. Bruce recognized it as a planting song. It was one of his favourites and he sat drinking his lukewarm beer and letting the singing wash round him, build up into the chorus like storm waves, then fall back into a tenor solo before rising once more. And the train ran on through the sunlight towards the rain clouds in the north.

Presently André came out of the coach below him and picked his way forward through the men in the trucks until he reached Hendry. The two of them stood together, André's face turned up towards the taller man and deadly earnest as he talked.

'*Doll boy*,' Hendry had called him, and it was an accurate description of the effeminently pretty face with the big toffee eyes; the steel helmet he wore seemed too large for his shoulders to carry.

I wonder how old he is; Bruce watched him laugh suddenly, his face still turned upwards to Hendry; not much over twenty and I have never seen anything less like a hired killer.

'How the hell did anyone like de Surrier get mixed up in this?' His voice echoed the thought, and beside him Mike answered.

'He was working in Elisabethville when it started, and he couldn't return to Belgium. I don't know the reason but I guess it was something personal. When it started his firm closed down. I suppose this was the only employment he could find.'

'That Irishman, the one at the barrier, he called me a hired killer.' Thinking of André's position in the scheme of things had turned Bruce's thoughts back to his own status. 'I hadn't thought about it that way before, but I suppose he's right. That is what we are.'

Mike Haig was silent for a moment, but when he spoke there was a stark quality in his voice.

'Look at these hands!' Involuntarily Bruce glanced down at them, and for the first time noticed that they were narrow with long moulded fingers, possessed of a functional beauty, the hands of an artist.

'Look at them,' Mike repeated, flexing them slightly; 'they were fashioned for a purpose, they were made to hold a scalpel, they were made to save life.' Then he relaxed them and let them drop on to the rifle across his lap, the long delicate fingers incongruous upon the blue metal. 'But look what they hold now!'

Bruce stirred irritably. He had not wanted to provoke another bout of Mike Haig's soul-searching. Damn the old fool – why must he always start this, he knew as well as anyone that in the mercenary army of Katanga there was a taboo upon the past. It did not exist.

'Ruffy,' Bruce snapped, 'aren't you going to feed your boys.'

'Right now, boss.' Ruffy opened another beer and handed it to Bruce. 'Hold that – it will keep your mind off food while I rustle it up.' He lumbered off along the roof of the coach still singing.

'Three years ago, it seems like all eternity,' Mike went on as though Bruce had not interrupted. 'Three years ago I was a surgeon and now this —' The desolation had spread to his eyes, and Bruce felt his pity for the man deep down where he kept it imprisoned with all his other emotions. 'I was good. I was one of the best. Royal College. Harley Street. Guy's.' Mike laughed without humour, with bitterness. 'Can you imagine my being driven in my Rolls to address the College on my advanced technique of cholecystectomy?'

'What happened?' The question was out before he could stop it, and Bruce realized how near to the surface he had let his pity rise. 'No, don't tell me. It's your business. I don't want to know.'

'But I'll tell you, Bruce, I want to. It helps somehow, talking about it.'

At first, thought Bruce, I wanted to talk also, to try and wash the pain away with words.

Mike was silent for a few seconds. Below them the singing rose and fell, and the train ran on through the forest.

'It had taken me ten hard years to get there, but at last I had done it. A fine practice; doing the work I loved with skill, earning the rewards I deserved. A wife that any man would have been proud of, a lovely home, many friends, too many friends perhaps; for success breeds friends the way a dirty kitchen breeds cockroaches.'

Mike pulled out a handkerchief and dried the back of his neck where the wind could not reach.

'Those sort of friends mean parties,' he went on. 'Parties when you've worked all day and you're tired; when you need the lift that you can get so easily from a bottle. You don't know if you have the weakness for the stuff until it's too late; until you have a bottle in the drawer of your desk; until suddenly your practice isn't so good any more.'

Mike twisted the handkerchief around his fingers as he ploughed doggedly on. 'Then you know it suddenly. You know it when your hands dance in the morning and all you want for breakfast is *that*, when you can't wait until lunchtime because you have to operate and that's the only way you can keep your hands steady. But you know it finally and utterly when the knife turns in your hand and the artery starts to spurt and you watch it paralysed – you watch it hosing red over your gown and forming pools on the theatre floor.' Mike's voice dried up then and he tapped a cigarette from his pack and lit it. His shoulders were hunched forward and his eyes were full of shadows of his guilt. Then he straightened up and his voice was stronger.

'You must have read about it. I was headlines for a few days, all the papers. But my name wasn't Haig in those days. I got that name off a label on a bottle in a bar-room.

'Gladys stayed with me, of course, she was that type. We came out to Africa. I had enough saved from the wreck for a down payment on a tobacco farm in the Centenary block outside Salisbury. Two good seasons and I was off the bottle. Gladys was having our first baby, we had both wanted one so badly. It was all coming right again.'

Mike stuffed the handkerchief back in his pocket, and his voice lost its strength again, turned dry and husky.

'Then one day I took the truck into the village and on the way home I stopped at the club. I had been there often before, but this time they threw me out at closing time and when I got back to the farm I had a case of Scotch on the seat beside me.'

Bruce wanted to stop him; he knew what was coming and he didn't want to hear it.

'The first rains started that night and the rivers came down in flood. The telephone lines were knocked out and we were cut off. In the morning —' Mike stopped again and turned to Bruce.

'I suppose it was the shock of seeing me like that again, but in the morning Gladys went into labour. It was her first and she wasn't so young any more. She was still in labour the next day, but by then she was too weak to scream. I remember how peaceful it was without her screaming and pleading with me to help. You see she knew I had all the instruments I needed. She begged me to help. I can remember that; her voice through the fog of whisky. I think I hated her then. I think I remember hating her, it was all so confused, so mixed up with the screaming and the liquor. But at last she was quiet. I don't think I realized she was dead. I was simply glad she was quiet and I could have peace.'

He dropped his eyes from Bruce's face.

'I was too drunk to go to the funeral. Then I met a man in a bar-room, I can't remember how long after it was, I can't even remember where. It must have been on the Copperbelt. He was recruiting for Tshombe's army and I signed up; there didn't seem anything else to do.'

Neither of them spoke again until a gendarme brought food to them, hunks of brown bread spread with tinned butter and filled with bully beef and pickled onions. They ate in silence listening to the singing, and Bruce said at last:

'You needn't have told me.'

'I know.'

'Mike –' Bruce paused.

'Yes?'

'I'm sorry, if that's any comfort.'

'It is,' Mike said. 'It helps to have – not to be completely alone. I like you, Bruce.' He blurted out the last sentence and Bruce recoiled as though Mike had spat in his face.

You fool, he rebuked himself savagely, *you were wide open then. You nearly let one of them in again.*

Remorselessly he crushed down his sympathy, shocked at the effort it required, and when he picked up the radio the gentleness had gone from his eyes.

'Hendry,' he spoke into the set, 'don't talk so much. I put you up front to watch the tracks.'

From the leading truck Wally Hendry looked round and forked two fingers at Bruce in a casual obscenity, but he turned back and faced ahead.

'You'd better go and take over from Hendry,' Bruce told Mike. 'Send him back here.'

Mike Haig stood up and looked down at Bruce.

'What are you afraid of?' his voice softly puzzled.

'I gave you an order, Haig.'

'Yes, I'm on my way.'

= 4 =

The aircraft found them in the late afternoon. It was a Vampire jet of the Indian Air Force and it came from the north.

They heard the soft rumble of it across the sky and then saw it glint like a speck of mica in the sunlight above the storm clouds ahead of them.

'I bet you a thousand francs to a handful of dung that this Bucko don't know about us,' said Hendry with anticipation, watching the jet turn off its course towards them.

'Well, he does now,' said Bruce.

Swiftly he surveyed the rain clouds in front of them. They were close; another ten minutes' run and they would be under them, and once there they were safe from air attack for the belly of the clouds pressed close against the earth and the rain was a thick blue-grey mist that would reduce visibility to a few hundred feet. He switched on the radio.

'Driver, give us all the speed you have – get us into that rain.'

'Oui, monsieur,' came the acknowledgement and almost immediately the puffing of the loco quickened and the clatter of the crossties changed its rhythm.

'Look at him come,' growled Hendry. The jet fell fast against the back-drop of cloud, still in sunlight, still a silver point of light, but growing.

Bruce clicked over the band selector of the radio, searching the ether for the pilot's voice. He tried four wavelengths and each time found only the crackle and drone of static, but with the fifth came the gentle sing-song of Hindustani. Bruce could not understand it, but he could hear that the tone was puzzled. There was a short silence on the radio while the pilot listened to an instruction from the Kamina base which was beyond the power of their small set to receive, then a curt affirmative.

'He's coming in for a closer look,' said Bruce, then raising his voice, 'Everybody under cover – and stay there.' He was not prepared to risk another demonstration of friendship.

The jet came cruising in towards them under half power, yet incredibly fast, leaving the sound of its engine far behind it, sharklike above the forest. Then Bruce could see the pilot's head through the canopy; now he could make out his features. His face was very brown beneath the silver crash helmet and he had a little moustache, the same as the Jack of spades. He was so close that Bruce saw the exact moment that he recognized them as Katangese; his eyes showed white and his mouth puckered as he swore. Beside Bruce the radio relayed the oath with metallic harshness, and then the jet was banking away steeply, its engine howling in full throttle, rising, showing its swollen silver belly and the racks of rockets beneath its wings.

'That frightened seven years' growth out of him,' laughed Hendry. 'You should have let me blast him. He was close enough for me to hit him in the left eyeball.'

'You'll get another chance in a moment,' Bruce assured him grimly. The radio was gabbling with consternation as the jet dwindled back into the sky. Bruce switched quickly to their own channel.

'Driver, can't you get this thing moving?'

'Monsieur, never before has she moved as she does now.'

Once more he switched back to the jet's frequency and listened to the pilot's excited voice. The jet was turning in a wide circle, perhaps fifteen miles away. Bruce glanced at the piled mass of cloud and rain ahead of them; it was moving down to meet them, but with ponderous dignity.

'If he comes back,' Bruce shouted down at his gendarmes, 'we can be sure that it's not just to look at us again. Open fire as soon as he's in range. Give him everything you've got, we must try and spoil his aim.'

Their faces were turned up towards him, subdued by the awful inferiority of the earth-bound to the hunter in the sky. Only André did not look at Bruce; he was staring at the aircraft with his jaws clenching nervously and his eyes too large for his face.

Again there was silence on the radio, and every head turned back to watch the jet.

'Come on, Bucko, come on!' grunted Hendry impatiently. He spat into the palm of his right hand and then wiped it down the front of his jacket. 'Come on, we want you.' With his thumb he flicked the safety catch of his rifle on and off, on and off.

Suddenly the radio spoke again. Two words, obviously acknowledging an order, and one of the words Bruce recognized. He had heard it before in circumstances that has burned it into his memory. The Hindustani word '*Attack!*'

'All right,' he said and stood up. 'He's coming!'

The wind fluttered his shirt against his chest. He settled his helmet firmly and pumped a round into the chamber of his FN.

'Get down into the truck, Hendry,' he ordered.

'I can see better from here.' Hendry was standing beside him, legs planted wide to brace himself against the violent motion of the train.

'As you like,' said Bruce. 'Ruffy, you get under cover.'

'Too damn hot down there in that box,' grinned the huge Negro.

'You're a mad Arab too,' said Bruce.

'Sure, we're all mad Arabs.'

The jet wheeled sharply and stooped towards the forest, levelling, still miles out on their flank.

'This Bucko is a real apprentice. He's going to take us from the side, so we can all shoot at him. If he was half awake he'd give it to us up the bum, hit the loco and make sure that we were all shooting over the top of each other,' gloated Hendry.

Silently, swiftly it closed with them, almost touching the tops of the trees. Then suddenly the cannon fire sparkled lemon-pale on its nose and all around them the air was filled with the sound of a thousand whips. Immediately every gun on the train opened up in reply. The tracers from the Brens chased each other out to meet the plane and the rifles joined their voices in a clamour that drowned the cannon fire.

Bruce aimed carefully, the jet unsteady in his sights from the lurching of the coach; then he pressed the trigger and the rifle juddered against his shoulder. From the corner of his eye he saw the empty cartridge cases spray from the breech in a bright bronze stream, and the stench of cordite stung his nostrils.

The aircraft slewed slightly, flinching from the torrent of fire.

'He's yellow!' howled Hendry. 'The bastard's yellow!'

'Hit him!' roared Ruffy. 'Keep hitting him.'

The jet twisted, lifted its nose so that the fire from its cannons passed harmlessly over their heads. Then its nose dropped again and it fired its rockets, two from under each wing. The gunfire from the train stopped abruptly as everybody ducked for safety; only the three of them on the roof kept shooting.

Shrieking like four demons in harness, leaving parallel lines of white smoke behind them, the rockets came from about four hundred yards out and they covered the distance in the time it takes to draw a deep breath, but the pilot had dropped his nose too sharply and fired too late. The rockets exploded in the embankment of the tracks below them.

The blast threw Bruce over backwards. He fell and rolled, clutching desperately at the smooth roof, but as he went over the edge his fingers caught in the guttering and he hung there. He was dazed with the concussion, the guttering cutting into his fingers, the shoulder-strap of his rifle round his neck strangling him, and the gravel of the embankment rushing past beneath him.

Ruffy reached over, caught him by the front of his jacket and lifted him back like a child.

'You going somewhere, boss?' The great round face was coated with dust from the explosions, but he was grinning happily. Bruce had a confused conviction that it would take at least a case of dynamite to make any impression on that mountain of black flesh.

Kneeling on the roof Bruce tried to rally himself. He saw that the wooden side of the coach nearest the explosions was splintered and torn and the roof was covered with earth and pebbles. Hendry was sitting beside him, shaking his head slowly from side to side; a small trickle of blood ran down from a scratch on his cheek and dripped from his chin. In the open trucks the men stood or sat with stunned expressions on their faces, but the train still raced on towards the rain storm and the dust of the explosions hung in a dense brown cloud above the forest far behind them.

Bruce scrambled to his feet, searched frantically for the aircraft and found its tiny shape far off above the mass of cloud.

The radio was undamaged, protected by the sandbags from the blast. Bruce reached for it and pressed the transmit button.

'Driver, are you all right?'

'Monsieur, I am greatly perturbed. Is there –'

'Not you alone,' Bruce assured him. 'Keep this train going.'

'Oui, monsieur.'

Then he switched to the aircraft's frequency. Although his ears were singing shrilly from the explosions, he could hear that the voice of the pilot had changed its tone. There was a slowness in it, a breathless catch on some of the words. He's frightened or he's hurt, thought Bruce, but he still has time to make another pass at us before we reach the storm front.

His mind was clearing fast now, and he became aware of the complete lack of readiness in his men.

'Ruffy!' he shouted. 'Get them on their feet. Get them ready. That plane will be back any second now.'

Ruffy jumped down into the truck and Bruce heard his palm slap against flesh as he began to bully them into activity. Bruce followed him down, then climbed over into the second truck and began the same process there.

'Haig, give me a hand, help me get the lead out of them.'

Further removed from the shock of the explosion, the men in this truck reacted readily and crowded to the side, starting to reload, checking their weapons, swearing, faces losing the dull dazed expressions.

Bruce turned and shouted back, 'Ruffy, are any of your lot hurt?'

'Couple of scratches, nothing bad.'

On the roof of the coach Hendry was standing again, watching the aircraft, blood on his face and his rifle in his hands.

'Where's André?' Bruce asked Haig as they met in the middle of the truck.

'Up front. I think he's been hit.'

Bruce went forward and found André doubled up, crouching in a corner of the truck, his rifle lying beside him and both hands covering his face. His shoulders heaved as though he were in pain.

Eyes, thought Bruce, he's been hit in the eyes. He reached him and stooped over him, pulling his hands from his face, expecting to see blood.

André was crying, his cheeks wet with tears and his eyelashes gummed together. For a second Bruce stared at him and then he caught the front of his jacket and pulled him to his feet. He picked up André's rifle and the barrel was cold, not a single shot had been fired out of it. He dragged the Belgian to the side and thrust the rifle into his hands.

'De Surrier,' he snarled, 'I'm going to be standing beside you. If you do that again I'll shoot you. Do you understand?'

'I'm sorry, Bruce.' André's lips were swollen where he had bitten them; his face was smeared with tears and slack with fear. 'I'm sorry. I couldn't help it.'

Bruce ignored him and turned his attention back to the aircraft. It was turning in for its next run.

He's going to come from the side again, Bruce thought; this time he'll get us. He can't miss twice in a row.

In silence once more they watched the jet slide down the valley between two vast white mountains of cloud and level off above the forest. Small and dainty and deadly it raced in towards them.

One of the Bren guns opened up, rattling raucously, sending out tracers like bright beads on a string.

'Too soon,' muttered Bruce. 'Much too soon; he must be all of a mile out of range.'

But the effect was instantaneous. The jet swerved, almost hit the tree tops and then over-corrected, losing its line of approach.

A howl of derision went up from the train and was immediately lost in the roar as every gun opened fire. The jet loosed its remaining rockets, blindly, hopelessly, without a chance of a hit. Then it climbed steeply, turning away into the cloud ahead of them. The sound of its engines receded, was muted by the cloud and then was gone.

Ruffy was performing a dance of triumph, waving his rifle over his head. Hendry on the roof was shouting abuse at the clouds into which the jet had vanished, one of the Brens was still firing short ecstatic bursts, someone else was chanting the Katangese war cry and others were taking it up. And then the driver in the locomotive came in with his whistle, spurting steam with each shriek.

Bruce slung his rifle over his shoulder, pushed his helmet on to the back of his head, took out a cigarette and lit it, then stood watching them sing and laugh and chatter with the relief from danger.

Next to him André leaned out and vomited over the side; a little of it came out of his nose and dribbled down the front of his battle-jacket. He wiped his mouth with the back of his hand.

'I'm sorry, Bruce. I'm sorry, truly I'm sorry,' he whispered.

And they were under the cloud, its coolness slumped over them like air from an open refrigerator. The first heavy drops stung Bruce's cheek and then rolled down heavily washing away the smell of cordite, melting the dust from Ruffy's face until it shone again like washed coal.

Bruce felt his jacket cling wetly to his back.

'Ruffy, two men at each Bren. The rest of them can get back into the covered coaches.

We'll relieve every hour.' He reversed his rifle so the muzzle pointed downwards. 'De Surrier, you can go, and you as well, Hendry.'

'I'll stay with you, Bruce.'

'All right then.'

The gendarmes clambered back into the covered coaches still laughing and chattering, and Ruffy came forward with a groundsheet and handed it to Bruce.

'The radios are all covered. If you don't need me, boss, I got some business with one of those Arabs in the coach. He's got near twenty thousand francs on him; so I'd better go and give him a couple of tricks with the cards.'

'One of these days I'm going to explain your Christian monarchs to the boys. Show them that the odds are three to one against them,' Bruce threatened.

'I wouldn't do that, boss,' Ruffy advised seriously. 'All that money isn't good for them, just gets them into trouble.'

'Off you go then. I'll call you later,' said Bruce. 'Tell them I said "well done", I'm proud of them.'

'Yeah. I'll tell them,' promised Ruffy.

Bruce lifted the tarpaulin that covered the set.

'Driver, desist before you burst the boiler!'

The abandoned flight of the train steadied to a more sedate pace, and Bruce tilted his helmet over his eyes and pulled the groundsheet up around his mouth before he leaned out over the side of the truck to inspect the rocket damage.

'All the windows blown out on this side and the woodwork torn a little,' he muttered. 'But a lucky escape all the same.'

'What a miserable comic-opera war this is,' grunted Mike Haig. 'That pilot had the right idea: why risk your life when it's none of your business.'

'He was wounded,' Bruce guessed. 'I think we hit him on his first run.'

Then they were silent, with the rain driving into their faces, slitting their eyes to peer ahead along the tracks. The men at the Brens huddled into their brown and green camouflage groundsheets, all their jubilation of ten minutes earlier completely gone. They are like cats, thought Bruce as he noticed their dejection, they can't stand being wet.

'It's half past five already.' Mike spoke at last. 'Do you think we'll make Msapa Junction before nightfall?'

'With this weather it will be dark by six.' Bruce looked up at the low cloud that was prematurely bringing on the night. 'I'm not going to risk travelling in the dark. This is the edge of Baluba country and we can't use the headlights of the loco.'

'You going to stop then?'

Bruce nodded. What a stupid bloody question, he thought irritably. Then he recognized his irritation as reaction from the danger they had just experienced, and he spoke to make amends.

'We can't be far now – if we start again at first light we'll reach Msapa before sun-up.'

'My God, it's cold,' complained Mike and he shivered briefly.

'Either too hot or too cold,' Bruce agreed; he knew that it was also reaction that was making him garrulous. But he did not attempt to stop himself. 'That's one of the things about this happy little planet of ours: nothing is in moderation. Too hot or too cold, either you are hungry or you've overeaten, you are in love or you hate the world –'

'Like you?' asked Mike.

'Dammit, Mike, you're as bad as a woman. Can't you conduct an objective discussion without introducing personalities?' Bruce demanded. He could feel his temper rising to the surface, he was cold and edgy, and he wanted a smoke.

'Objective theories must have subjective application to prove their worth,' Mike pointed out. There was just a trace of an amused smile on his broad ravaged old face.

'Let's forget it then. I don't want to talk personalities,' snapped Bruce; then immediately went on to do so. 'Humanity sickens me if I think about it too much. De Surrier puking his heart out with fear, that animal Hendry, you trying to keep off the liquor, Joan –' He stopped himself abruptly.

'Who is Joan?'

'Do I ask you your business?' Bruce flashed the standard reply to all personal questions in the mercenary army of Katanga.

'No. But I'm asking you yours – who is Joan?'

All right. I'll tell him. If he wants to know, I'll tell him. Anger had made Bruce reckless.

'Joan was the bitch I married.'

'So, that's it then!'

'Yes – that's it! Now you know. So you can leave me alone.'

'Kids?'

'Two – a boy and a girl.' The anger was gone from Bruce's voice, and the raw naked pain was back for an instant. Then he rallied and his voice was neutral once more.

'And none of it matters a damn. As far as I'm concerned the whole human race – all of it – can go and lose itself. I don't want any part of it.'

'How old are you, Bruce?'

'Leave me alone, damn you!'

'How old are you?'

'I'm thirty.'

'You talk like a teenager.'

'And I feel like an old, old man.'

The amusement was no longer on Mike's face as he asked.

'What did you do before this?'

'I slept and breathed and ate – and got trodden on.'

'What did you do for a living?'

'Law.'

'Were you successful?'

'How do you measure success? If you mean, did I make money, the answer is yes.'

I made enough to pay off the house and the car, he thought bitterly, and to contest custody of my children, and finally to meet the divorce settlement. I had enough for that, but, of course, I had to sell my partnership.

'Then you'll be all right,' Mike told him. 'If you've succeeded once you'll be able to do it again when you've recovered from the shock; when you've rearranged your life and taken other people into it to make you strong again.'

'I'm strong now, Haig. I'm strong *because* there is no one in my life. That's the only way you can be secure, on your own. Completely free and on your own.'

'Strong!' Anger flared in Mike's voice for the first time. 'On your own you're *nothing*, Curry. On your own you're so weak I could piss on you and wash you away!' Then the anger evaporated and Mike went on softly, 'But you'll find out – you're one of the lucky ones. You attract people to you. You don't have to be alone.'

'Well, that's the way I'm going to be from now on.'

'We'll see,' murmured Mike.

'Yes, we'll see,' Bruce agreed, and lifted the tarpaulin over the radio.

'Driver, we are going to halt for the night. It's too dark to proceed with safety.'

5

Brazzaville Radio came through weakly on the set and the static was bad, for outside the rain still fell and thunder rolled around the sky like an unsecured cargo at sea.

'– Our Elisabethville correspondent reports that elements of the Kantangese Army in the South Kasai province today violated the cease-fire agreement by firing upon a low-flying aircraft of the United Nations command. The aircraft, a Vampire jet fighter of the Indian Air Force, returned safely to its base at Kamina airfield. The pilot, however, was wounded by small arms fire. His condition is satisfactory.

'The United Nations Commander in Katanga, General Rhee, has lodged a strong protest with the Kantangese government – ' The announcer's voice was overlaid by the electric crackle of static.

'We winged him!' rejoiced Wally Hendry. The scab on his cheek had dried black, with angry red edges.

'Shut up,' snapped Bruce, 'we're trying to hear what's happening.'

'You can't hear a bloody thing now. André, there's a bottle in my pack. Get it! I'm going to drink to that coolie with a bullet up his –'

Then the radio cleared and the announcer's voice came through loudly.

'- at Senwati Mission fifty miles from the river harbour of Port Reprieve. A spokesman for the Central Congolese Government denied that the Congolese troops were operating in this area, and it is feared that a large body of armed bandits is taking advantage of the unsettled conditions to – ' Again the static drowned it out.

'Damn this set,' muttered Bruce as he tried to tune it.

'– stated today that the removal of missile equipment from the Russian bases in Cuba had been confirmed by aerial reconnaissance –'

'That's all that we are interested in.' Bruce switched off the radio. 'What a shambles! Ruffy, where is Senwati Mission?'

'Top end of the swamp, near the Rhodesian border.'

'Fifty miles from Port Reprieve,' muttered Bruce, not attempting to conceal his anxiety.

'It's more than that by road, boss, more like a hundred.'

'That should take them three or four days in this weather, with time off for looting along the way,' Bruce calculated. 'It will be cutting it fairly fine. We must get through to Port Reprieve by tomorrow evening and pull out again at dawn the next day.'

'Why not keep going tonight?' Hendry removed the bottle from his lips to ask. 'Better than sitting here being eaten by mosquitoes.'

'We'll stay,' Bruce answered. 'It won't do anybody much good to derail this lot in the dark.' He turned back to Ruffy. 'Three-hour watches tonight. Sergeant Major. Lieutenant

Haig will take the first, then Lieutenant Hendry, then Lieutenant de Surrier, and I'll do the dawn spell.'

'Okay, boss. I'd better make sure my boys aren't sleeping.'

He left the compartment and the broken glass from the corridor windows crunched under his boots.

'I'll be on my way also.' Mike stood up and pulled the ground sheet over his shoulders.

'Don't waste the batteries of the searchlights, Mike. Sweep every ten minutes or so.'

'Okay, Bruce.' Mike looked across at Hendry. 'I'll call you at nine o'clock.'

'Jolly good show, old fruit.' Wally exaggerated Mike's accent. 'Good hunting, what!' and then as Mike left the compartment, 'Silly old bugger, why does he have to talk like that?'

No one answered him, and he pulled up his shirt behind.

'André, what's this on my back?'

'It's a pimple.'

'Well, squeeze it then.'

Bruce woke in the night, sweating, with the mosquitoes whining about his face. Outside it was still raining and occasionally the reflected light from the searchlight on the roof of the coach lit the interior dimly.

On one of the bottom bunks Mike Haig lay on his back. His face was shining with sweat and he rolled his head from side to side on the pillow. He was grinding his teeth – a sound to which Bruce had become accustomed, and he preferred it to Hendry's snores.

'You poor old bugger,' whispered Bruce.

From the bunk opposite, André de Surrier whimpered. In sleep he looked like a child with dark soft hair falling over his forehead.

= 6 =

The rain petered out in the dawn and the sun was hot before it cleared the horizon. It lifted a warm mist from the dripping forest. As they ran north the forest thickened, the trees grew closer together and the undergrowth beneath them was coarser than it had been around Elisabethville.

Through the warm-misty dawn Bruce saw the water tower at Msapa Junction rising like a lighthouse above the forest, its silver paint streaked with brown rust. Then they came round the last curve in the tracks and the little settlement huddled before them.

It was small, half a dozen buildings in all, and there was about it the desolate aspect of human habitation reverting to jungle.

Beside the tracks stood the water tower and the raised concrete coal bins. Then the station buildings of wood and iron, with the large sign above the verandah:

'MSAPA JUNCTION. Elevation 963m.'

An avenue of casia flora trees with very dark green foliage and orange flowers; and beyond that, on the edge of the forest, a row of cottages.

One of the cottages had been burned, its ruins were fire blackened and tumbled; and the gardens had lost all sense of discipline with three month's neglect.

'Driver, stop beside the water tower. You have fifteen minutes to fill your boiler.'

'Thank you, monsieur.'

With a heavy sigh of steam the loco pulled up beside the tower.

'Haig, take four men and go back to give the driver a hand.'

'Okay, Bruce.'

Bruce turned once more to the radio.

'Hendry.'

'Hello there.'

'Get a patrol together, six men, and search those cottages. Then take a look at the edge of the bush, we don't want any unexpected visitors.'

Wally Hendry waved an acknowledgement from the leading truck, and Bruce went on:

'Put de Surrier on.' He watched Hendry pass the set to André. 'De Surrier, you are in charge of the leading trucks in Hendry's absence. Keep Hendry covered, but watch the bush behind you also. They could come from there.'

Bruce switched off the set and turned to Ruffy. 'Stay up here on the roof, Ruffy. I'm going to chase them up with the watering. If you see anything, don't write me a postcard, start pooping off.'

Ruffy nodded. 'Have some breakfast to take with you.' He proffered an open bottle of beer.

'Better than bacon and eggs.' Bruce accepted the bottle and climbed down on to the platform. Sipping the beer he walked back along the train and looked up at Mike and the engine driver in the tower.

'Is it empty?' he called up at them.

'Half full, enough for a bath if you want one,' answered Mike.

'Don't tempt me.' The idea was suddenly very attractive, for he could smell his own stale body odour and his eyelids were itchy and swollen from mosquito bites. 'My kingdom for a bath.' He ran his fingers over his jowls and they rasped over stiff beard.

He watched them swing the canvas hose out over the loco. The chubby little engine driver clambered up and sat astride the boiler as he fitted the hose.

A shout behind him made Bruce turn quickly, and he saw Hendry's patrol coming back from the cottages. They were dragging two small prisoners with them.

'Hiding in the first cottage,' shouted Hendry. 'They tried to leg it into the bush.' He prodded one of them with his bayonet. The child cried out and twisted in the hands of the gendarme who held her.

'Enough of that.' Bruce stopped him from using the bayonet again and went to meet them. He looked at the two children.

The girl was close to puberty with breasts like insect bites just starting to show, thin-legged with enlarged knee-caps out of proportion to her thighs and calves. She wore only a dirty piece of trade cloth drawn up between her legs and secured around her waist by a length of bark string, and the tribal tattoo marks across her chest and cheeks and forehead stood proud in ridges of scar tissue.

'Ruffy.' Bruce called him down from the coach. 'Can you speak to them?'

Ruffy picked up the boy and held him on his hip. He was younger than the girl –

seven, perhaps eight years old. Very dark skinned and completely naked, as naked as the terror on his face.

Ruffy grunted sharply and the gendarme released the girl. She stood trembling, making no attempt to escape.

Then in a soothing rumble Ruffy began talking to the boy on his hip; he smiled as he spoke and stroked the child's head. Slowly a little of the fear melted and the boy answered in a piping treble that Bruce could not understand.

'What does he say?' urged Bruce.

'He thinks we're going to eat them,' laughed Ruffy. 'Not enough here for a decent breakfast.' He patted the skinny little arm, grey with crushed filth, then he gave an order to one of the gendarmes. The man disappeared into the coach and came back with a handful of chocolate bars. Still talking, Ruffy peeled one of them and placed it in the boy's mouth. The child's eyes widened appreciatively at the taste and he chewed quickly, his eyes on Ruffy's face, his answers now muffled with chocolate.

At last Ruffy turned to Bruce.

'No trouble here, boss. They come from a small village about an hour's walk away. Just five or six families, and no war party. These kids sneaked across to have a look at the houses, pinch what they could perhaps, but that's all.'

'How many men at this village?' asked Bruce, and Ruffy turned back to the boy. In reply to the question he held up the fingers of both hands, without interrupting the chewing.

'Does he know if the line is clear through to Port Reprieve? Have they burnt the bridges or torn up the tracks?' Both children were dumb to this question. The boy swallowed the last of his chocolate and looked hungrily at Ruffy, who filled his mouth again.

'Jesus,' muttered Hendry with deep disgust. 'Is this a crèche or something. Let's all play ring around the roses.'

'Shut up,' snapped Bruce, and then to Ruffy, 'Have they seen any soldiers?'

Two heads shaken in solemn unison.

'Have they seen any war parties of their own people?'

Again solemn negative.

'All right, give them the rest of the chocolate,' instructed Bruce. That was all he could get out of them, and time was wasting. He glanced back at the tower and saw that Haig and the engine driver had finished watering. For a further second he studied the boy. His own son would be about the same age now; it was twelve months since – Bruce stopped himself hurriedly. That way lay madness.

'Hendry, take them back to the edge of the bush and turn them loose. Hurry up. We've wasted long enough.'

'You're telling me!' grunted Hendry and beckoned to the two children. With Hendry leading and a gendarme on each side they trotted away obediently and disappeared behind the station building.

'Driver, are your preparations complete?'

'Yes, monsieur, we are ready to depart.'

'Shovel all the coal in, we've gotta keep her rolling.' Bruce smiled at him, he liked the little man and their stilted exchanges gave him pleasure.

'Pardon, monsieur.'

'It was an imbecility, a joke – forgive me.'

'Ah, a joke!' The roly-poly stomach wobbled merrily.

'Okay, Mike,' Bruce shouted, 'get your men aboard. We are –'

A burst of automatic gunfire cut his voice short. It came from behind the station buildings, and it battered into the heat-muted morning with such startling violence that for an instant Bruce stood paralysed.

'Haig,' he yelled, 'get up front and take over from de Surrier.' That was the weak point, and Mike's party ran down the train.

'You men.' Bruce stopped the six gendarmes. 'Come with me.' They fell in behind him, and with a quick glance Bruce assured himself that the train was safe. All along its length rifle barrels were poking out protectively, while on the roof Ruffy was dragging the Bren round to cover the flank. A charge by even a thousand Baluba must fail before the fire power that was ready now to receive it.

'Come on,' said Bruce and ran, with the gendarmes behind him, to the sheltering wall of the station building. There had been no shot fired since that initial burst, which could mean either that it was a false alarm or that Hendry's party had been overwhelmed by the first rush.

The door of the station master's office was locked. Bruce kicked and it crashed open with the weight of his booted foot behind it.

I've always wanted to do that, he thought happily in his excitement, ever since I saw Gable do it in *San Francisco*.

'You four – inside! Cover us from the windows.' They crowded into the room with their rifles held ready. Through the open door Bruce saw the telegraph equipment on the table by the far wall; it was clattering metallically from traffic on the Elisabethville-Jadotville line. Why is it that under the stimulus of excitement my mind always registers irrelevances? Which thought is another irrelevancy, he decided.

'Come on, you two, stay with me.' He led them down the outside wall, keeping in close to its sheltering bulk, pausing at the corner to check the load of his rifle and slip the selector on to rapid fire.

A further moment he hesitated. What will I find around this corner? A hundred naked savages crowded round the mutilated bodies of Hendry and his gendarmes, or . . . ?

Crouching, ready to jump back behind the wall, rifle held at high port across his chest, every muscle and nerve of his body cocked like a hair-trigger, Bruce stepped sideways into the open.

Hendry and the two gendarmes stood in the dusty road beyond the first cottage. They were relaxed, talking together, Hendry reloading his rifle, cramming the magazine with big red hands on which the gingery hair caught the sunlight. A cigarette dangled from his lower lip and he laughed suddenly, throwing his head back as he did so and the cigarette ash dropped down his jacket front. Bruce noticed the long dark sweat stain across his shoulders.

The two children lay in the road fifty yards farther on.

Bruce was suddenly cold, it came from inside, a cramping coldness of the guts and chest. Slowly he straightened up and began to walk towards the children. His feet fell silently in the powder dust and the only sound was his own breathing, hoarse, as though a wounded beast followed close behind him. He walked past Hendry and the two gendarmes without looking at them; but they stopped talking, watching him uneasily.

He reached the girl first and went down on one knee beside her, laying his rifle aside and turning her gently on to her back.

'This isn't true,' he whispered. 'This can't be true.'

The bullet had taken half her chest out with it, a hole the size of a coffee cup, with the blood still moving in it, but slowly, oozing, welling up into it with the viscosity of new honey.

Bruce moved across to the boy; he felt an almost dreamlike sense of unreality.

'No, this isn't true.' He spoke louder, trying to undo it with words.

Three bullets had hit the boy; one had torn his arm loose at the shoulder and the sharp white end of the bone pointed accusingly out of the wound. The other bullets had severed his trunk almost in two.

It came from far away, like the rising roar of a train along a tunnel. Bruce could feel his whole being shaken by the strength of it, he shut his eyes and listened to the roaring in his head, and with his eyes tight closed his vision was filled with the colour of blood.

'Hold on!' a tiny voice screamed in his roaring head. 'Don't let go, fight it. Fight it as you've fought before.'

And he clung like a flood victim to the straw of his sanity while the great roaring was all around him. Then the roar was muted, rumbling away, gone past, a whisper, now nothing.

The coldness came back to him, a coldness more vast than the flood had been.

He opened his eyes and breathed again, stood up and walked back to where Hendry stood with the two gendarmes.

'Corporal,' Bruce addressed one of the men beside Hendry; and with a shock he heard that his own voice was calm, without any trace of the fury that had so nearly carried him away on its flood.

'Corporal, go back to the train. Tell Lieutenant Haig and Sergeant Major Ruffararo that I want them here.'

Thankfully the man went, and Bruce spoke to Wally Hendry in the same dispassionate tone.

'I told you to turn them loose,' he said.

'So they could run home and call the whole pack down on us – is that what you wanted, Bucko?' Hendry had recovered now, he was defiant, grinning.

'So instead you murdered them?'

'Murdered! You crazy or something, Bruce? They're Balubes, aren't they? Bloody man-eating Balubes!' shouted Hendry angrily, no longer grinning. 'What's wrong with you, man? This is war, Bucko, war. C'est la guerre, like the man said, c'est la guerre!' Then suddenly his voice moderated again. 'Let's forget it. I did what was right, now let's forget it; what's two more bloody Balubes after all the killing that's been going on. Let's forget it.'

Bruce did not answer, he lit a cigarette and looked beyond Hendry for the others to come.

'How's that, Bruce? You willing we just forget it?' persisted Hendry.

'On the contrary, Hendry, I make you a sacred oath, and I call upon God to witness it.' Bruce was not looking at him, he couldn't trust himself to look at Hendry without killing him. 'This is my promise to you: I will have you hanged for this, not shot, hanged on good hemp rope. I have sent for Haig and Ruffararo so we'll have plenty of witnesses.

The first thing I do once we get back to Elisabethville will be to turn you over to the proper authorities.'

'You don't mean that!'

'I have never meant anything so serious in my life.'

'Jesus, Bruce —!'

Then Haig and Ruffy came; they came running until they saw, and they stopped suddenly and stood uncertainly in the bright sun, looking from Bruce to the two frail little corpses lying in the road.

'What happened?' asked Mike.

'Hendry shot them,' answered Bruce.

'What for?'

'Only he knows.'

'You mean he – he just killed them, just shot them down?'

'Yes.'

'My God,' said Mike, and then again, his voice dull with shock, 'my God.'

'Go and look at them, Haig. I want you to look closely so you remember.'

Haig walked across to the children.

'You too, Ruffy. You'll be a witness at the trial.'

Mike Haig and Ruffy walked side by side to where the children lay, and stood staring down at them. Hendry shuffled his feet in the dust awkwardly and then went on loading the magazine of his rifle.

'Oh, for Chrissake!' he blustered. 'What's all the fuss. They're just a couple of Balubes.'

Wheeling slowly to face him Mike Haig's face was a yellowish colour with only his cheeks and his nose still flushed with the tiny burst of veins beneath the surface of the skin, but there was no colour in his lips. Each breath he drew sobbed in his throat. He started back towards Hendry, still breathing that way, and his mouth was working as he tried to force it to speak. As he came on he unslung the rifle from his shoulder.

'Haig!' said Bruce sharply.

'This time – you – you bloody – this is the last —' mouthed Haig.

'Watch it, Bucko!' Hendry warned him. He stepped back, clumsily trying to fit the loaded magazine on to his rifle.

Mike Haig dropped the point of his bayonet to the level of Hendry's stomach.

'Haig!' shouted Bruce, and Haig charged surprisingly fast for a man of his age, leaning forward, leading with the bayonet at Hendry's stomach, the incoherent mouthings reaching their climax in a formless bellow.

'Come on, then!' Hendry answered him and stepped forward. As they came together Hendry swept the bayonet to one side with the butt of his own rifle. The point went under his armpit and they collided chest to chest, staggering as Haig's weight carried them backwards. Hendry dropped his rifle and locked both arms round Haig's neck, forcing his head back so that his face was tilted up at the right angle.

'Look out, Mike, he's going to butt!' Bruce had recognized the move, but his warning came too late. Hendry's head jerked forward and Mike gasped as the front of Hendry's steel helmet caught him across the bridge of his nose. The rifle slipped from Mike's grip and fell into the road, he lifted his hands and covered his face with spread fingers and the redness oozed out between them.

Again Hendry's head jerked forward like a hammer and again Mike gasped as the steel smashed into his face and fingers.

'Knee him, Mike!' Bruce yelled as he tried to take up a position from which to intervene, but they were staggering in a circle, turning like a wheel and Bruce could not get in.

Hendry's legs were braced apart as he drew his head back to strike again, and Mike's knee went up between them, all the way up with power into the fork of Hendry's crotch.

Breaking from the clinch, his mouth open in a silent scream of agony, Hendry doubled up with both hands holding his lower stomach, and sagged slowly on to his knees in the dust.

Dazed, with blood running into his mouth, Mike fumbled with the canvas flap of his holster.

'I'll kill you, you murdering swine.'

The pistol came out into his right hand; short-barrelled, blue and ugly.

Bruce stepped up behind him, his thumb found the nerve centre below the elbow and as he dug in the pistol dropped from Mike's paralysed hand and dangled on its lanyard against his knee.

'Ruffy, stop him,' Bruce shouted, for Hendry was clawing painfully at the rifle that lay in the dust beside him.

'Got it, boss!' Ruffy stooped quickly over the crawling body at his feet, in one swift movement opened the flap of the holster, drew the revolver and the lanyard snapped like cotton as he jerked on it.

They stood like that: Bruce holding Haig from behind, and Hendry crouched at Ruffy's feet. The only sound for several seconds was the hoarse rasping of breath.

Bruce felt Mike relaxing in his grip as the madness left him; he unclipped his pistol from his lanyard and let it drop.

'Leave me, Bruce. I'm all right now.'

'Are you sure? I don't want to shoot you.'

'No, I'm all right.'

'If you start it again, I'll have to shoot you. Do you understand?'

'Yes, I'll be all right now. I lost my senses for a moment.'

'You certainly did,' Bruce agreed, and released him.

They formed a circle round the kneeling Hendry, and Bruce spoke.

'If either you or Haig start it again you'll answer to me, do you hear me?'

Hendry looked up, his small eyes slitted with pain. He did not answer.

'Do you hear me?' Bruce repeated the question and Hendry nodded.

'Good! From now on, Hendry, you are under open arrest. I can't spare men to guard you, and you're welcome to escape if you'd like to try. The local gentry would certainly entertain you most handsomely, they'd probably arrange a special banquet in your honour.'

Hendry's lips drew back in a snarl that exposed teeth with green slimy stains on them.

'But remember my promise, Hendry, as soon as we get back to –'

'Wally, Wally, are you hurt?' André came running from the direction of the station. He knelt beside Hendry.

'Get away, leave me alone.' Hendry struck out at him impatiently and André recoiled.

'De Surrier, who gave you permission to leave your post? Get back to the train.'

André looked up uncertainly, and then back to Hendry.

'De Surrier, you heard me. Get going. And you also, Haig.'

He watched them disappear behind the station building before he glanced once more at the two children. There was a smear of blood and melted chocolate across the boy's cheek and his eyes were wide open in an expression of surprise. Already the flies were settling, crawling delightedly over the two small corpses.

'Ruffy, get spades. Bury them under those trees.' He pointed at the avenue of casia flora. 'But do it quickly.' He spoke brusquely so that how he felt would not show in his voice.

'Okay, boss. I'll fix it.'

'Come on, Hendry,' Bruce snapped, and Wally Hendry heaved to his feet and followed him meekly back to the train.

7

Slowly from Msapa Junction they travelled northwards through the forest. Each tree seemed to have been cast from the same mould, tall and graceful in itself, but when multiplied countless million times the effect was that of numbing monotony. Above them was a lane of open sky with the clouds scattered, but slowly regrouping for the next assault, and the forest shut in the moist heat so they sweated even in the wind of the train's movement.

'How is your face?' asked Bruce and Mike Haig touched the parallel swellings across his forehead where the skin was broken and discoloured.

'It will do,' he decided; then he lifted his eyes and looked across the open trucks at Wally Hendry. 'You shouldn't have stopped me, Bruce.'

Bruce did not answer, but he also watched Hendry as he leaned uncomfortably against the side of the leading truck, obviously favouring his injuries, his face turned half away from them, talking to André.

'You should have let me kill him,' Mike went on. 'A man who can shoot down two small children in cold blood and then laugh about it afterwards —!' Mike left the rest unsaid, but his hands were opening and closing in his lap.

'It's none of your business,' said Bruce, sensitive to the implied rebuke. 'What are you? One of God's avenging angels?'

'None of my business, you say?' Mike turned quickly to face Bruce. 'My God, what kind of man are you? I hope for your sake you don't mean that!'

'I'll tell you in words of one syllable what kind of man I am, Haig,' Bruce answered flatly. 'I'm the kind that minds my own bloody business, that lets other people lead their own lives. I am ready to take reasonable measures to prevent others flouting the code which society has drawn up for us, but that's all. Hendry has committed murder; this I agree is a bad thing, and when we get back to Elisabethville I will bring it to the attention of the people whose business it is. But I am not going to wave banners and quote from the Bible and froth at the mouth.'

'That's all?'

'That's all.'

'You don't feel sorry for those two kids?'

'Yes I do. But pity doesn't heal bullet wounds; all it does is distress me. So I switch off the pity – they can't use it.'

'You don't feel anger or disgust or horror at Hendry.'

'The same thing applies,' explained Bruce, starting to lose patience again. 'I could work up a sweat about it if I let myself loose on an emotional orgy, as you are doing.'

'So instead you treat something as evil as Hendry with an indifferent tolerance?' asked Mike.

'Jesus Christ!' grated Bruce. 'What the hell do you want me to do?'

'I want you to stop playing dead. I want you to be able to recognize evil and to destroy it.' Mike was starting to lose his temper also; his nerves were taut.

'That's great! Do you know where I can buy a secondhand crusader outfit and a white horse, then single-handed I will ride out to wage war on cruelty and ignorance, lust and greed and hatred and poverty –'

'That's not what I –' Mike tried to interrupt, but Bruce overrode him, his handsome face flushed darkly with anger and the sun. 'You want me to destroy evil wherever I find it. You old fool, don't you know that it has a hundred heads and that for each one you cut off another hundred grow in its place? Don't you know that it's in you also, so to destroy it you have to destroy yourself?'

'You're a coward, Curry! The first time you burn a finger you run away and build yourself an asbestos shelter –'

'I don't like being called names, Haig. Put a leash on your tongue.'

Mike paused and his expression changed, softening into a grin.

'I'm sorry, Bruce. I was just trying to teach you –'

'Thank you,' scoffed Bruce, his voice still harsh; he had not been placated by the apology. 'You are going to teach me, thanks very much! But what are you going to teach me, Haig? What are you qualified to teach? "How to find success and happiness" by Laughing Lad Haig who worked his way down to a lieutenancy in the black army of Katanga – how's that as a title for your lecture, or do you prefer something more technical like: "The applications of alcohol to spiritual research –" '

'All right, Bruce. Drop it, I'll shut up,' and Bruce saw how deeply he had wounded Mike. He regretted it then, he would have liked to unsay it. But that's one thing you can never do.

Beside him Mike Haig was suddenly much older and more tired looking, the pouched wrinkles below his eyes seemed to have deepened in the last few seconds, and a little more of the twinkle had gone from his eyes. His short laughter had a bitter humourless ring to it.

'When you put it that way it's really quite funny.'

'I punched a little low,' admitted Bruce, and then, 'perhaps I should let you shoot Hendry. A waste of ammunition really, but seeing that you want to so badly,' Bruce drew his pistol and offered it to Mike butt first, 'use mine.' He grinned disarmingly at Mike and his grin was almost impossible to resist; Mike started to laugh. It wasn't a very good joke, but somehow it caught fire between them and suddenly they were laughing together.

Mike Haig's battered features spread like warm butter and twenty years dropped from his face. Bruce leaned back against the sandbags with his mouth wide open, the pistol still in his hand and his long lean body throbbing uncontrollably with laughter.

There was something feverish in it, as though they were trying with laughter to gargle away the taste of blood and hatred. It was the laughter of despair.

Below them the men in the trucks turned to watch them, puzzled at first, and then beginning to chuckle in sympathy, not recognizing the sickness of that sound.

'Hey, boss,' called Ruffy. 'First time I ever seen you laugh like you meant it.'

And the epidemic spread, everyone was laughing, even André de Surrier was smiling.

Only Wally Hendry was untouched by it, silent and sullen, watching them with small expressionless eyes.

They came to the bridge over the Cheke in the middle afternoon. Both the road and the railway crossed it side by side, but after this brief meeting they diverged and the road twisted away to the left. The river was padded on each bank by dense dark green bush; three hundred yards thick, a matted tangle of thorn and tree fern with the big trees growing up through it and bursting into flower as they reached the sunlight.

'Good place for an ambush,' muttered Mike Haig, eyeing the solid green walls of vegetation on each side of the lines.

'Charming, isn't it,' agreed Bruce, and by the uneasy air of alertness that had settled on his gendarmes it was clear that they agreed with him.

The train nosed its way carefully into the river bush like a steel snake along a rabbit run, and they came to the river. Bruce switched on the set.

'Driver, stop this side of the bridge. I wish to inspect it before entrusting our precious cargo to it.'

'Oui, monsieur.'

The Cheke river at this point was fifty yards wide, deep, quick-flowing and angry with flood water which had almost covered the white sand beaches along each bank. Its bottle-green colour was smoked with mud and there were whirlpools round the stone columns of the bridge.

'Looks all right,' Haig gave his opinion. 'How far are we from Port Reprieve now?'

Bruce spread his field map on the roof of the coach between his legs and found the brackets that straddled the convoluted ribbon of the river.

'Here we are.' He touched it and then ran his finger along the stitched line of the railway until it reached the red circle that marked Port Reprieve. 'About thirty miles to go, another hour's run. We'll be there before dark.'

'Those are the Lufira hills.' Mike Haig pointed to the blue smudge that only just showed above the forest ahead of them.

'We'll be able to see the town from the top,' agreed Bruce. 'The river runs parallel to them on the other side, and the swamp is off to the right, the swamp is the source of the river.'

He rolled the map and passed it back to Ruffy who slid it into the plastic map case.

'Ruffy, Lieutenant Haig and I are going ahead to have a look at the bridge. Keep an eye on the bush.'

'Okay, boss. You want a beer to take with you?'

'Thanks.' Bruce was thirsty and he emptied half the bottle before climbing down to join Mike on the gravel embankment. Rifles unslung, watching the bush on each side uneasily, they hurried forward and with relief reached the bridge and went out into the centre of it.

'Seems solid enough,' commented Mike. 'No one has tampered with it.'

'It's wood.' Bruce stamped on the heavy wild mahogany timbers. They were three feet thick and stained with a dark chemical to inhibit rotting.

'So, it's wood?' enquired Mike.

'Wood burns,' explained Bruce. 'It would be easy to burn it down.' He leaned his elbows on the guard rail, drained the beer bottle and dropped it to the surface of the river twenty feet below. There was a thoughtful expression on his face.

'Very probably there are Baluba in the bush' – he pointed at the banks – 'watching us at this moment. They might get the same idea. I wonder if I should leave a guard here?'

Mike leaned on the rail beside him and they both stared out to where the river took a bend two hundred yards downstream; in the crook of the bend grew a tree twice as tall as any of its neighbours. The trunk was straight and covered with smooth silvery bark and its foliage piled to a high green steeple against the clouds. It was the natural point of focus for their eyes as they weighed the problem.

'I wonder what kind of tree that is. I've never seen one like it before.' Bruce was momentarily diverted by the grandeur of it. 'It looks like a giant blue gum.'

'It's quite a sight,' Mike concurred. 'I'd like to go down and have a closer –'

Then suddenly he stiffened and there was an edge of alarm in his voice as he pointed. 'Bruce, there! What's that in the lower branches.'

'Where?'

'Just above the first fork, on the left –' Mike was pointing and suddenly Bruce saw it. For a second he thought it was a leopard, then he realized it was too dark and long.

'It's a man,' exclaimed Mike.

'Baluba,' snapped Bruce; he could see the shape now and the sheen of naked black flesh, the kilt of animal tails and the headdress of feathers. A long bow stood up behind the man's shoulder as he balanced on the branch and steadied himself with one hand against the trunk. He was watching them.

Bruce glanced round at the train. Hendry had noticed their agitation and, following the direction of Mike's raised arm, he had spotted the Baluba. Bruce realized what Hendry was going to do and he opened his mouth to shout, but before he could do so Hendry had snatched his rifle off his shoulder, swung it up and fired a long, rushing, hammering burst.

'The trigger-happy idiot,' snarled Bruce and looked back at the tree. Slabs of white bark were flying from the trunk and the bullets reaped leaves that fluttered down like crippled insects, but the Baluba had disappeared.

The gunfire ceased abruptly and in its place Hendry was shouting with hoarse excitement.

'I got him, I got the bastard.'

'Hendry!' Bruce's voice was also hoarse, but with anger, ' – Who ordered you to fire?'

'He was a bloody Baluba, a mucking big bloody Baluba. Didn't you see him, hey? Didn't you see him, man?'

'Come here, Hendry.'

'I got the bastard,' rejoiced Hendry.

'Are you deaf? Come here!'

While Hendry climbed down from the truck and came towards them Bruce asked Haig: 'Did he hit him?'

'I'm not sure. I don't think so, I think he jumped. If he had been hit he'd have been thrown backwards, you know how it knocks them over.'

'Yes,' said Bruce, 'I know.' A .300 bullet from an FN struck with a force of well over a ton. When you hit a man there was no doubt about it. All right, so the Baluba was still in there.

Hendry came up, swaggering, laughing with excitement.

'So you killed, hey?' Bruce asked.

'Stone dead, stone bloody dead!'

'Can you see him?'

'No, he's down in the bush.'

'Do you want to go and have a look at him, Hendry? Do you want to go and get his ears?'

Ears are the best trophy you can take from a man, not as good as the skin of a black-maned lion or the great bossed horns of a buffalo, but better then the scalp. The woolly cap of an African scalp is a drab thing, messy to take and difficult to cure. You have to salt it and stretch it inside out over a helmet; even then it smells badly. Ears are much less trouble and Hendry was an avid collector. He was not the only one in the army of Katanga; the taking of ears was common practice.

'Yeah, I want them.' Hendry detached the bayonet from the muzzle of his rifle. 'I'll nip down and get them.'

'You can't let anyone go in there, Bruce. Not even him,' protested Haig quietly.

'Why not? He deserves it, he worked hard for it.'

'Only take a minute.' Hendry ran his thumb along the bayonet to test the edge. My God! He really means it, thought Bruce; he'd go into that tangled stuff for a pair of ears – he's not brave, he's just stupendously lacking in imagination.

'Wait for me, Bruce, it won't take long.' Hendry started back.

'You're not serious, Bruce?' Mike asked.

'No,' agreed Bruce, 'I'm not serious,' and his voice was cold and hard as he caught hold of Hendry's shoulder and stopped him.

'Listen to me! You have no more chances – that was it. I'm waiting for you now, Hendry. Just once more, that's all. Just once more.'

Hendry's face turned sullen again.

'Don't push me, Bucko.'

'Get back to the train and bring it across,' said Bruce contemptuously and turned to Haig.

'Now we'll have to leave a guard here. They know we've gone across and they'll burn it for a certainty, especially after that little fiasco.'

'Who are you going to leave?'

'Ten men, say, under a sergeant. We'll be back by nightfall or tomorrow morning at the latest. They should be safe enough. I doubt there is a big war party here, a few strays perhaps, but the main force will be closer to the town.'

'I hope you're right.'

'So do I,' said Bruce absently, his mind busy with the problem of defending the bridge. 'We'll strip all the sandbags off the coaches and build an emplacement here in the middle of the roadway, leave two of the battery-operated searchlights and a case of flares with them, one of the Brens and a couple of cases of grenades. Food and water for a week. No, they'll be all right.'

The train was rolling down slowly towards them – and a single arrow rose from the edge of the jungle. Slowly it rose, curving in flight and falling towards the train, dropping faster now, silently into the mass of men in the leading truck.

So Hendry had missed and the Baluba had come up stream through the thick bush to launch his arrow in retaliation. Bruce sprang to the guard rail and, using it as a rest for his rifle, opened up in short bursts, searching the green mass and seeing it tremble with his bullets. Haig was shooting also, hunting the area from which the arrow had come.

The train was up to them now and Bruce slung his rifle over his shoulder and scrambled up the side of the truck. He pushed his way to the radio set.

'Driver, stop the covered coaches in the middle of the bridge,' he snapped, and then he switched it off and looked for Ruffy.

'Sergeant Major, get all those sandbags off the roof into the roadway.' While they worked, the gendarmes would be protected from further arrows by the body of the train.

'Okay, boss.'

'Kanaki.' Bruce picked his most reliable sergeant. 'I am leaving you here with ten men to hold the bridge for us. Take one of the Brens, and two of the lights – ' Quickly Bruce issued his orders and then he had time to ask André:

'What happened to that arrow? Was anyone hit?'

'No, missed by a few inches. Here it is.'

'That was a bit of luck.' Bruce took the arrow from André and inspected it quickly. A light reed, crudely fletched with green leaves and with the iron head bound into it with a strip of rawhide. It looked fragile and ineffectual, but the barbs of the head were smeared thickly with a dark paste that had dried like toffee.

'Pleasant,' murmured Bruce, and then he shuddered slightly. He could imagine it embedded in his body with the poison purple-staining the flesh beneath the skin. He had heard that it was not a comfortable death, and the iron-tipped reed was suddenly malignant and repulsive. He snapped it in half and threw it out over the side of the bridge before he jumped down from the truck to supervise the building of the guard post.

'Not enough sandbags, boss.'

'Take the mattresses off all the bunks, Ruffy.' Bruce solved that quickly. The leather-covered coir pallets would stop an arrow with ease.

Fifteen minutes later the post was completed, a shoulder-high ring of sandbags and mattresses large enough to accommodate ten men and their equipment, with embrasures sited to command both ends of the bridge.

'We'll be back early tomorrow, Kanaki. Let none of your men leave this post for any purpose; the gaps between the timbers are sufficient for purposes of sanitation.'

'We shall enjoy enviable comfort, Captain. But we will lack that which soothes.' Kanaki grinned meaningly at Bruce.

'Ruffy, leave them a case of beer.'

'A whole case?' Ruffy made no attempt to hide his shocked disapproval of such a prodigal order.

'Is my credit not good?'

'You credit is okay, boss,' and then he changed to French to make his protest formal. 'My concern is the replacement of such a valuable commodity.'

'You're wasting time, Ruffy!'

8

From the bridge it was thirty miles to Port Reprieve. They met the road again six miles outside the town; it crossed under them and disappeared into the forest again to circle out round the high ground taking the easier route into Port Reprieve. But the railroad climbed up the hills in a series of traverses and came out at the top six hundred feet above the town. On the stony slopes the forest found meagre purchase and the vegetation was sparser; it did not obscure the view.

Standing on the roof Bruce looked out across the Lufira swamps to the north, a vastness of poisonous green swamp grass and open water, disappearing into the blue heat haze without any sign of ending. From its southern extremity it was drained by the Lufira river. The river was half a mile wide, deep olive-green, ruffled darker by eddies of wind across its surface, fenced into the very edge of the water by a solid barrier of dense river bush. In the angle formed by the swamp and the river was a headland which protected the natural harbour of Port Reprieve. The town was on a spit of land, the harbour on one side and a smaller swamp on the other. The road came round the right-hand side of the hills, crossed a causeway over the swamp and entered the single street of the town from the far side.

There were three large buildings in the centre of the town opposite the railway yard, their iron roofs bright beacons in the sunlight; and clustered round them were perhaps fifty smaller thatched dwellings.

Down on the edge of the harbour was a long shed, obviously a workshop, and two jetties ran into the water. The diamond dredgers were moored alongside; three of them, ungainly black hulks with high superstructures and blunt ends.

It was a place of heat and fever and swamp smells, an ugly little village by a green reptile river.

'Nice place to retire,' Mike Haig grunted.

'Or open a health resort,' said Bruce.

Beyond the causeway, on the main headland, there was another cluster of buildings, just the tops were showing above the forest. Among them rose the copper-clad spire of a church.

'Mission station,' guessed Bruce.

'St Augustine's,' agreed Ruffy. 'My first wife's little brudder got himself educated there. He's an attaché to the ministry of something or other in Elisabethville now, doing damn good for himself.' Boasting a little.

'Bully for him,' said Bruce.

The train had started angling down the hills towards the town.

'Well, I reckon we've made it, boss.'

'I reckon also; all we have to do is get back again.'

'Yessir, I reckon that's all.'

And they ran into the town.

There were more than forty people in the crowd that lined the platform to welcome them.

We'll have a heavy load on the way home, thought Bruce as he ran his eye over them. He saw the bright spots of women's dresses in the throng. Bruce counted four of them. That's another complication; one day I hope I find something in this life that turns out exactly as expected, something that will run smoothly and evenly through to its right and logical conclusion. Some hope, he decided, some bloody hope.

The joy and relief of the men and women on the platform was pathetically apparent in their greetings. Most of the women were crying and the men ran beside the train like small boys as it slid in along the raised concrete platform. All of them were of mixed blood, Bruce noted. They varied in colour from creamy yellow to charcoal. The Belgians had certainly left much to be remembered by.

Standing back from the throng, a little aloof from the general jollification, was a half-blooded Belgian. There was an air of authority about him that was unmistakable. On one side of him stood a large bosomy woman of his own advanced age, darker skinned than he was; but Bruce saw immediately that she was his wife. At his other hand stood a figure dressed in a white open-necked shirt and blue jeans that Bruce at first thought was a boy, until the head turned and he saw the long plume of dark hair that hung down her back, and the unmanly double pressure beneath the white shirt.

The train stopped and Bruce jumped down on to the platform and laughingly pushed his way through the crowds towards the Belgian. Despite a year in the Congo, Bruce had not grown accustomed to being kissed by someone who had not shaved for two or three days and who smelled strongly of garlic and cheap tobacco. This atrocity was committed upon him a dozen times or more before he arrived before the Belgian.

'The Good Lord bless you for coming to our aid, Monsieur Captain.' The Belgian recognized the twin bars on the front of Bruce's helmet and held out his hand. Bruce had expected another kiss, so he accepted the handshake with relief.

'I am only glad that we are in time,' he answered.

'May I introduce myself – Martin Boussier, district manager of Union Minière Corporation, and this is my wife, Madame Boussier.' He was a tall man, but unlike his wife, sparsely fleshed. His hair was completely silver and his skin folded, toughened and browned by a life under the equatorial sun. Bruce took an instant liking to him. Madame Boussier pressed her bulk against Bruce and kissed him heartily. Her moustache was too soft to cause him discomfort and she smelled of toilet soap, which was a distinct improvement, decided Bruce.

'May I also present Madame Cartier,' and for the first time Bruce looked squarely at the girl. A number of things registered in his mind simultaneously: the paleness of her skin which was not unhealthy but had an opaque coolness which he wanted to touch, the size of her eyes which seemed to fill half her face, the unconscious provocation of her lips, and the use of the word *Madame* before her name.

'Captain Curry – of the Katanga Army,' said Bruce. She's too young to be married, can't be more than seventeen. She's still got that little girl freshness about her and I bet she smells like an unweaned puppy.

'Thank you for coming, monsieur.' She had a throatiness in her voice as though she were just about to laugh or to make love, and Bruce added three years to his estimate of her age. That was not a little girl's voice, nor were those little girl's legs in the jeans, and little girls had less under their shirt fronts.

His eyes came back to her face and he saw that there was colour in her cheeks now and sparks of annoyance in her eyes.

My God, he thought, I'm ogling her like a matelot on shore leave. He hurriedly transferred his attention back to Boussier, but his throat felt constricted as he asked:

'How many are you?'

'There are forty-two of us, of which five are women and two are children.'

Bruce nodded, it was what he had expected. The women could ride in one of the covered coaches. He turned and surveyed the railway yard.

'Is there a turn-table on which we can revolve the locomotive?' he asked Boussier.

'No, Captain.'

They would have to reverse all the way back to Msapa Junction, another complication. It would be more difficult to keep a watch on the tracks ahead, and it would mean a sooty and uncomfortable journey.

'What precautions have you taken against attack, monsieur?'

'They are inadequate, Captain,' Boussier admitted. 'I have not sufficient men to defend the town – most of the population left before the emergency. Instead I have posted sentries on all the approaches and I have fortified the hotel to the best of my ability. It was there we intended to stand in the event of attack.'

Bruce nodded again and glanced up at the sun. It was already reddening as it dropped towards the horizon, perhaps another hour or two of daylight.

'Monsieur, it is too late to entrain all your people and leave before nightfall. I intend to load their possessions this evening. We will stay overnight and leave in the early morning.'

'We are all anxious to be away from this place; we have twice seen large parties of Baluba on the edge of the jungle.'

'I understand,' said Bruce. 'But the dangers of travelling by night exceed those of waiting another twelve hours.'

'The decision is yours,' Boussier agreed. 'What do you wish us to do now.'

'Please see to the embarkation of your people. I regret that only the most essential possessions may be entertained. We will be almost a hundred persons.'

'I shall see to that myself,' Boussier assured him, 'and then?'

'Is that the hotel?' Bruce pointed across the street at one of the large double-storeyed buildings. It was only two hundred yards from where they stood.

'Yes, Captain.'

'Good,' said Bruce. 'It is close enough. Your people can spend the night there in more comfort than aboard the train.'

He looked at the girl again; she was watching him with a small smile on her face. It was a smile of almost maternal amusement, as though she were watching a little boy playing at soldiers. Now it was Bruce's turn to feel annoyed. He was suddenly embarrassed by his uniform and epaulettes, by the pistol at his hip, the automatic rifle across his shoulder and the heavy helmet on his head.

'I will require someone who is familiar with the area to accompany me, I want to inspect your defences,' he said to Boussier.

'Madame Cartier could show you,' suggested Boussier's wife artlessly. I wonder if she noticed our little exchange, thought Bruce. Of course she did. All women have a most sensitive nose for that sort of thing.

'Will you go with the captain, Shermaine?' asked Madame Boussier.

'As the captain wishes.' She was still smiling.

'That is settled then,' said Bruce gruffly. 'I will meet you at the hotel in ten minutes, after I have made arrangements here.' He turned back to Boussier. 'You may proceed with the embarkation, monsieur.' Bruce left them and went back to the train.

'Hendry,' he shouted, 'you and de Surrier will stay on board. We are not leaving until the morning but these people are going to load their stuff now. In the meantime rig the searchlights to sweep both sides of the track and make sure the Brens are properly sited.'

Hendry grunted an acknowledgement without looking at Bruce.

'Mike, take ten men with you and go to the hotel. I want you there in case of trouble during the night.'

'Okay, Bruce.'

'Ruffy.'

'Sa!'

'Take a gang and help the driver refuel.'

'Okay, boss. Hey, boss!'

'Yes.' Bruce turned to him.

'When you go to the hotel, have a look-see maybe they got some beer up there. We're just about fresh out.'

'I'll keep it in mind.'

'Thanks, boss.' Ruffy looked relieved. 'I'd hate like hell to die of thirst in this hole.'

The townsfolk were streaming back towards the hotel. The girl Shermaine walked with the Boussiers, and Bruce heard Hendry's voice above him.

'Jesus, look what that pretty has got in her pants. What ever it is, one thing is sure: it's round and it's in two pieces, and those pieces move like they don't belong to each other.'

'You haven't any work to do Hendry?' Bruce asked harshly.

'What's wrong, Curry,' Hendry jeered down at him. 'You got plans yourself. Is that it, Bucko?'

'She's married,' said Bruce, and immediately was surprised that he had said it.

'Sure,' laughed Hendry. 'All the best ones are married; that don't mean a thing, not a bloody thing.'

'Get on with your work,' snapped Bruce, and then to Haig, 'Are you ready? Come with me then.'

= 9 =

When they reached the hotel Boussier was waiting for them on the open verandah. He led Bruce aside and spoke quietly.

'Monsieur, I don't wish to be an alarmist but I have received some most disturbing news. There are brigands armed with modern weapons raiding down from the north.

The last reports state that they had sacked Senwati Mission about three hundred kilometres north of here.'

'Yes,' Bruce nodded, 'I know about them. We heard on the radio.'

'Then you will have realized that they can be expected to arrive here very soon.'

'I don't see them arriving before tomorrow afternoon; by then we should be well on our way to Msapa Junction.'

'I hope you are right, Monsieur. The atrocities committed by this General Moses at Senwati are beyond the conception of any normal mind. He appears to bear an almost pathological hatred for all people of European descent.' Boussier hesitated before going on. 'There were a dozen white nuns at Senwati. I have heard that they —'

'Yes,' Bruce interrupted him quickly; he did not want to listen to it. 'I can imagine. Try and prevent these stories circulating amongst your people. I don't want to have them panic.'

'Of course,' Boussier nodded.

'Do you know what force this General Moses commands?'

'It is not more than a hundred men but, as I have said, they are all armed with modern weapons. I have even heard that they have with them a cannon of some description, though I think this unlikely. They are travelling in a convoy of stolen vehicles and at Senwati they captured a gasoline tanker belonging to the commercial oil companies.'

'I see,' mused Bruce. 'But it doesn't alter my decision to remain here overnight. However, we must leave at first light tomorrow.'

'As you wish, Captain.'

'Now, monsieur,' Bruce changed the subject, 'I require some form of transport. Is that car in running order?' He pointed at a pale green Ford Ranchero station wagon parked beside the verandah wall.

'It is. It belongs to my company.' Boussier took a key ring from his pocket and handed it to Bruce. 'Here are the keys. The tank is full of gasoline.'

'Good,' said Bruce. 'Now if we can find Madame Cartier —'

She was waiting in the hotel lounge and she stood up as Bruce and Boussier came in.

'Are you ready, madame?'

'I await your pleasure,' she answered, and Bruce looked at her sharply. Just a trace of a twinkle in her dark blue eyes suggested that she was aware of the double meaning.

They walked out to the Ford and Bruce opened the door for her.

'You are gracious, monsieur.' She thanked him and slid into the seat. Bruce went round to the driver's side and climbed in beside her.

'It's nearly dark,' he said.

'Turn right on to the Msapa Junction road, there is one post there.'

Bruce drove out along the dirt road through the town until they came to the last house before the causeway. 'Here,' said the girl and Bruce stopped the car. There were two men there, both armed with sporting rifles. Bruce spoke to them. They had seen no sign of Baluba, but they were both very nervous. Bruce made a decision.

'I want you to go back to the hotel. The Baluba will have seen the train arrive; they won't attack in force, we'll be safe tonight. But they may try and cut a few throats if we leave you out here.'

The two half-breeds gathered together their belongings and set off towards the centre of town, obviously with lighter hearts.

'Where are the others?' Bruce asked the girl.

'The next post is at the pumping station down by the river, there are three men there.'

Bruce followed her directions. Once or twice as he drove he glanced surreptitiously at her. She sat in her corner of the seat with her legs drawn up sideways under her. She sat very still, Bruce noticed. I like a woman who doesn't fidget; it's soothing. Then she smiled; this one isn't soothing. She is as disturbing as hell! She turned suddenly and caught him looking again, but this time she smiled.

'You are English, aren't you, Captain?'

'No, I am a Rhodesian,' Bruce answered.

'It's the same,' said the girl. 'You speak French so very badly that you had to be English.'

Bruce laughed. 'Perhaps your English is better than my French,' he challenged her.

'It couldn't be much worse,' she answered him in his own language. 'You are different when you laugh, not so grim, not so heroic. Take the next road to your right.'

Bruce turned the Ford down towards the harbour.

'You are very frank,' he said. 'Also your English is excellent.'

'Do you smoke?' she asked, and when he nodded she lit two cigarettes and passed one to him.

'You are also very young to smoke, and very young to be married.'

She stopped smiling and swung her legs off the seat.

'Here is the pumping station,' she said.

'I beg your pardon. I shouldn't have said that.'

'It's of no importance.'

'It was an impertinence,' Bruce demurred.

'It doesn't matter.'

Bruce stopped the car and opened his door. He walked out on to the wooden jetty towards the pump house, and the boards rang dully under his boots. There was a mist coming up out of the reeds round the harbour and the frogs were piping in fifty different keys. He spoke to the men in the single room of the pump station.

'You can get back to the hotel by dark if you hurry.'

'Oui, monsieur,' they agreed. Bruce watched them set off up the road before they went to the car. He spun the starter motor and above the noise of it the girl asked:

'What is your given name, Captain Curry?'

'Bruce.'

She repeated it, pronouncing it 'Bruise,' and then asked:

'Why are you a soldier?'

'For many reasons.' His tone was flippant.

'You do not look like a soldier, for all your badges and your guns, for all the grimness and the frequent giving of orders.'

'Perhaps I am not a very good soldier.' He smiled at her.

'You are very efficient and very grim except when you laugh. But I am glad you do not look like one,' she said.

'Where is the next post?'

'On the railway line. There are two men there. Turn to your right again at the top, Bruce.'

'You are also very efficient, Shermaine.' They were silent again, having used each other's names. Bruce could feel it between them, a good feeling, warm like new bread. But what of her husband, he thought, I wonder where he is, and what he is like. Why isn't he here with her?

'He is dead,' she said quietly. 'He died four months ago of malaria.'

With the shock of it, Shermaine answering his unspoken question and also the answer itself, Bruce could say nothing for the moment, then:

'I'm sorry.'

'There is the post,' she said, 'in the cottage with the thatched roof.'

Bruce stopped the car and switched off the engine. In the silence she spoke again.

'He was a good man, so very gentle. I only knew him for a few months but he was a good man.'

She looked very small sitting beside him in the gathering dark with the sadness on her, and Bruce felt a great wave of tenderness wash over him. He wanted to put his arm round her and hold her, to shield her from the sadness. He searched for the words, but before he found them, she roused herself and spoke in a matter-of-fact tone.

'We must hurry, it's dark already.'

At the hotel the lounge was filled with Boussier's employees; Haig had mounted a Bren in one of the upstairs windows to cover the main street and posted two men in the kitchens to cover the back. The civilians were in little groups, talking quietly, and their expressions of complete doglike trust as they looked at Bruce disconcerted him.

'Everything under control, Mike?' he asked brusquely.

'Yes, Bruce. We should be able to hold this building against a sneak attack. De Surrier and Hendry, down at the station yard, shouldn't have any trouble either.'

'Have these people,' Bruce pointed at the civilians, 'loaded their luggage?'

'Yes, it's all aboard. I have told Ruffy to issue them with food from our stores.'

'Good.' Bruce felt relief; no further complications so far.

'Where is old man Boussier?'

'He is across at his office.'

'I'm going to have a chat with him.'

Unbidden, Shermaine fell in beside Bruce as he walked out into the street, but he liked having her there.

Boussier looked up as Bruce and Shermaine walked into his office. The merciless glare of the petromax lamp accentuated the lines at the corners of his eyes and mouth, and showed up the streaks of pink scalp beneath his neatly combed hair.

'Martin, you are not still working!' exclaimed Shermaine, and he smiled at her, the calm smile of his years.

'Not really, my dear, just tidying up a few things. Please be seated, Captain.'

He came round and cleared a pile of heavy leather-bound ledgers off the chair and packed them into a wooden case on the floor, went back to his own chair, opened a drawer in the desk, brought out a box of cheroots and offered one to Bruce.

'I cannot tell you how relieved I am that you are here, Captain. These last few months have been very trying. The doubt. The anxiety.' He struck a match and held it out to Bruce who leaned forward across the desk and lit his cheroot. 'But now it is all at an end; I feel as though a great weight has been lifted from my shoulders.' Then his voice sharpened. 'But you were not too soon. I have heard within the last hour that this General

Moses and his column have left Senwati and are on the road south, only two hundred kilometres north of here. They will arrive tomorrow at their present rate of advance.'

'Where did you hear this?' Bruce demanded.

'From one of my men, and do not ask me how he knows. There is a system of communication in this country which even after all these years I do not understand. Perhaps it is the drums, I heard them this evening, I do not know. However, their information is usually reliable.'

'I had not placed them so close,' muttered Bruce. 'Had I known this I might have risked travelling tonight, at least as far as the bridge.'

'I think your decision to stay over the night was correct. General Moses will not travel during darkness – none of his men would risk that – and the condition of the road from Senwati after three months neglect is such that he will need ten or twelve hours to cover the distance.'

'I hope you're right.' Bruce was worried. 'I'm not sure that we shouldn't pull out now.'

'That involves a risk also, Captain,' Boussier pointed out. 'We know there are tribesmen in close proximity to the town. They have been seen. They must be aware of your arrival, and might easily have wrecked the lines to prevent our departure. I think your original decision is still good.'

'I know.' Bruce was hunched forward in his chair, frowning, sucking on the cheroot. At last he sat back and the frown evaporated. 'I can't risk it. I'll place a guard on the causeway, and if this Moses gentleman arrives we can hold him there long enough to embark your people.'

'That is probably the best course,' agreed Boussier. He paused, glanced towards the open windows and lowered his voice. 'There is another point, Captain, which I wish to bring to your attention.'

'Yes?'

'As you know, the activity of my company in Port Reprieve is centred on the recovery of diamonds from the Lufira swamps.'

Bruce nodded.

'I have in my safe' – Boussier jerked his thumb at the heavy steel door built into the wall behind his desk – 'nine and a half thousand carats of gem-quality diamonds and some twenty-six thousand carats of industrial diamonds.'

'I had expected that.' Bruce kept his tone non-committal.

'It may be as well if we could agree on the disposition and handling of these stones.'

'How are they packaged?' asked Bruce.

'A single wooden case.'

'Of what size and weight?'

'I will show you.'

Boussier went to the safe, turned his back to them and they heard the tumblers whirr and click. While he waited Bruce realized suddenly that Shermaine had not spoken since her initial greeting to Boussier. He glanced at her now and she smiled at him. I like a woman who knows when to keep her mouth shut.

Boussier swung the door of the safe open and carried a small wooden case across to the desk.

'There,' he said.

Bruce examined it. Eighteen inches long, nine deep and twelve wide. He lifted it experimentally.

'About twenty pounds weight,' he decided. 'The lid is sealed.'

'Yes,' agreed Boussier, touching the four wax imprints.

'Good,' Bruce nodded. 'I don't want to draw unnecessary attention to it by placing a guard upon it.'

'No, I agree.'

Bruce studied the case a few seconds longer and then he asked:

'What is the value of these stones?'

Boussier shrugged. 'Possibly five hundred million francs.' And Bruce was impressed; half a million sterling. Worth stealing, worth killing for.

'I suggest, monsieur, that you secrete this case in your luggage. In your blankets, say. I doubt there will be any danger of theft until we reach Msapa Junction. A thief will have no avenue of escape. Once we reach Msapa Junction I will make other arrangements for its safety.'

'Very well, Captain.'

Bruce stood up and glanced at his watch. 'Seven o'clock, as near as dammit. I will leave you and see to the guard on the causeway. Please make sure that your people are ready to entrain before dawn tomorrow morning.'

'Of course.'

Bruce looked at Shermaine and she stood up quickly. Bruce held the door open for her and was just about to follow her when a thought struck him.

'That mission station – St Augustine's, is it? I suppose it's deserted now?'

'No, it's not.' Boussier looked a little shamefaced. 'Father Ignatius is still there, and of course the patients at the hospital.'

'Thanks for telling me.' Bruce was bitter.

'I'm sorry, Captain. It slipped my mind, there are so many things to think of.'

'Do you know the road out to the mission?' he snapped at Shermaine. *She* should have told him.

'Yes, Bruce.'

'Well, perhaps you'd be good enough to direct me.'

'Of course.' She also looked guilty.

Bruce slammed the door of Boussier's office and strode off towards the hotel with Shermaine trotting to keep pace with him. You can't rely on anyone, he thought, not anybody!

And then he saw Ruffy coming up from the station, looking like a big bear in the dusk. With a few exceptions, Bruce corrected himself.

'Sergeant Major.'

'Hello, boss.'

'This General Moses is closer to us than we reckoned. He's reported two hundred kilometres north of here on the Senwati road.'

Ruffy whistled through his teeth. 'Are you going to take off now, Boss?'

'No, I want a machine-gun post on this end of the causeway. If they come we can hold them there long enough to get away. I want you to take command.'

'I'll see to it now.'

'I'm going out to the mission – there's a white priest there. Lieutenant Haig is in command while I'm away.'

'Okay, boss.'

= 10 =

'I'm sorry, Bruce. I should have told you.' Shermaine sat small and repentant at her end of the Ranchero.

'Don't worry about it,' said Bruce, not meaning it.

'We have tried to make Father Ignatius come in to town. Martin has spoken to him many times, but he refuses to move.'

Bruce did not answer. He took the car down on to the causeway, driving carefully. There were shreds of mist lifting out of the swamp and drifting across the concrete ramp. Small insects, bright as tracer in the headlights, zoomed in to squash against the windscreen. The froggy chorus from the swamp honked and clinked and boomed deafeningly.

'I have apologized,' she murmured.

'Yes, I heard you,' said Bruce. 'You don't have to do it again.'

She was silent, and then:

'Are you always so bad-tempered?' she asked in English.

'*Always*,' snapped Bruce, 'is one of the words which should be eliminated from the language.'

'Since it has not been, I will continue to use it. You haven't answered my question: are you always so bad tempered?'

'I just don't like balls-ups.'

'What is *balls-up*, please?'

'What has just happened: a mistake, a situation precipitated by inefficiency, or by somebody not using his head.'

'You never make balls-up, Bruce?'

'It is not a polite expression, Shermaine. Young ladies of refinement do not use it.' Bruce changed into French.

'You never make mistakes?' she corrected herself. Bruce did not answer. That's quite funny, he thought – never make mistakes! Bruce Curry, the original balls-up.

Shermaine held one hand across her middle and sat up straight.

'Bonaparte,' she said. 'Cold, silent, efficient.'

'I didn't say that –' Bruce started to defend himself. Then in the glow from the dash light he saw her impish expression and he could not stop himself; he had to grin.

'All right, I'm acting like a child.'

'You would like a cigarette?' she asked.

'Yes, please.'

She lit it and passed it to him.

'You do not like – ' she hesitated, 'mistakes. Is there anything you do like?'

'Many things,' said Bruce.

'Tell me some.'

They bumped off the end of the causeway and Bruce accelerated up the far bank.

'I like being on a mountain when the wind blows, and the taste of the sea. I like Sinatra, crayfish thermidor, the weight and balance of a Purdey Royal, and the sound of a little girl's laughter. I like the first draw of a cigarette lit from a wood fire, the scent of jasmine, the feel of silk; I also enjoy sleeping late in the morning, and the thrill of forking a queen with my knight. Shadows on the floor of a forest please me. And, of course, money. But especially I like women who do not ask too many questions.'

'Is that all?'

'No, but it's a start.'

'And apart from – mistakes, what are the things you do not like.'

'Women who ask too many questions,' and he saw her smile. 'Selfishness except my own, turnip soup, politics, blond pubic hairs, Scotch whisky, classical music and hangovers.'

'I'm sure that is not all.'

'No, not nearly.'

'You are very sensual. All these things are of the senses.'

'Agreed.'

'You do not mention other people. Why?'

'Is this the turn off to the mission?'

'Yes, go slowly, the road is bad. Why do you not mention your relationship to other people?'

'Why do you ask so many questions? Perhaps I'll tell you some day.'

She was silent a while and then softly:

'And what do you want from life – just those things you have spoken of? Is that all you want?'

'No. Not even them. I want nothing, expect nothing; that way I cannot be disappointed.'

Suddenly she was angry. 'You not only act like a child, you talk like one.'

'Another thing I don't like: criticism.'

'You are young. You have brains, good looks –'

'Thank you, that's better.'

'– and you are a fool.'

'That's not so good. But don't fret about it.'

'I won't, don't worry,' she flamed at him. 'You can –' she searched for something devastating. 'You can go jump out of the lake.'

'Don't you mean into?'

'Into, out of, backwards, sideways. I don't care!'

'Good, I'm glad we've got that settled. There's the mission, I can see a light.'

She did not answer but sat in her corner, breathing heavily, drawing so hard on her cigarette that the glowing tip lit the interior of the Ford.

The church was in darkness, but beyond it and to one side was a long low building. Bruce saw a shadow move across one of the windows.

'Is that the hospital?'

'Yes.' Abruptly.

Bruce stopped the Ford beside the small front verandah and switched off the headlights and the ignition.

'Are you coming in?'

'No.'

'I'd like you to present me to Father Ignatius.'

For a moment she did not move, then she threw open her door and marched up the steps of the verandah without looking back at Bruce.

He followed her through the front office, down the passage, past the clinic and small operating theatre, into the ward.

'Ah, Madame Cartier.' Father Ignatius left the bed over which he was stooping and came towards her.

'I heard that the relief train had arrived at Port Reprieve. I thought you would have left by now.'

'Not yet, Father. Tomorrow morning.'

Ignatius was tall, six foot three or four, Bruce estimated, and thin. The sleeve of his brown cassock had been cut short as a concession to the climate and his exposed arms appeared to be all bone, hairless, with the veins blue and prominent. Big bony hands, and big bony feet in brown open sandals.

Like most tall, thin men he was round-shouldered. His face was not one that you would remember, an ordinary face with steel-rimmed spectacles perched on a rather shapeless nose, neither young nor old, nondescript hair without grey in it, but there was about him, that unhurried serenity you often find in a man of God. He turned his attention to Bruce, scrutinizing him gently through his spectacles.

'Good evening, my son.'

'Good evening, Father.' Bruce felt uncomfortable; they always made him feel that way. If only, he wished with envy, I could be as certain of one thing in my life as this man is certain of everything in his.

'Father, this is Captain Curry.' Shermaine's tone was cold, and then suddenly she smiled again. 'He does not care for people, that is why he has come to take you to safety.'

Father Ignatius held out his hand and Bruce found the skin was cool and dry, making him conscious of the moistness of his own.

'That is most thoughtful of you,' he said smiling, sensing the tension between them. 'I don't want to seem ungrateful, but I regret I cannot accept your offer.'

'We have received reports that a column of armed bandits are only two hundred kilometres or so north of here. They will arrive within a day or two. You are in great danger, these people are completely merciless,' Bruce urged him.

'Yes,' Father Ignatius nodded. 'I have also heard, and I am taking the steps I consider necessary. I shall take all my staff and patients into the bush.'

'They'll follow you,' said Bruce.

'I think not.' Ignatius shook his head. 'They will not waste their time. They are after loot, not sick people.'

'They'll burn your mission.'

'If they do, then we shall have to rebuild it when they leave.'

'The bush is crawling with Baluba, you'll end up in the cooking pot.' Bruce tried another approach.

'No.' Ignatius shook his head. 'Nearly every member of the tribe has at one time or another been a patient in this hospital. I have nothing to fear there, they are my friends.'

'Look here, Father. Don't let us argue. My orders are to bring you back to Elisabethville. I must insist.'

'And my orders are to stay here. You do agree that mine come from a higher authority than yours?' Ignatius smiled mildly. Bruce opened his mouth to argue further; then, instead, he laughed.

'No, I won't dispute that. Is there anything you need that I might be able to supply?'

'Medicines?' asked Ignatius.

'Acriflavine, morphia, field dressings, not much I'm afraid.'

'They would help, and food?'

'Yes, I will let you have as much as I can spare,' promised Bruce.

One of the patients, a woman at the end of the ward, screamed so suddenly that Bruce started.

'She will be dead before morning,' Ignatius explained softly. 'There is nothing I can do.'

'What's wrong with her?'

'She has been in labour these past two days; there is some complication.'

'Can't you operate?'

'I am not a doctor, my son. We had one here before the trouble began, but he is here no longer – he has gone back to Elisabethville. No,' his voice seemed to carry helpless regret for all the suffering of mankind, 'No, she will die.'

'Haig!' said Bruce.

'Pardon?'

'Father, you have a theatre here. Is it fully equipped?'

'Yes, I believe so.'

'Anaesthetic?'

'We have chloroform and pentothal.'

'Good,' said Bruce. 'I'll get you a doctor. Come on, Shermaine.'

11

'This heat, this stinking heat!' Wally Hendry mopped at his face with a grubby handkerchief and threw himself down on the green leather bunk. 'You notice how Curry leaves me and you here on the train while he puts Haig up at the hotel and he goes off with that little French bit. It doesn't matter that me and you must cook in this box, long as he and his buddy Haig are all right. You notice that, hey?'

'Somebody's got to stay aboard, Wally,' André said.

'Yeah, but you notice who it is? Always you and me – those high society boys stick together, you've got to give them that, they look after each other.' He transferred his attention back to the open window of the compartment. 'Sun's down already, and still hot enough to boil eggs. I could use a drink.' He unlaced his jungle boots, peeled off his socks and regarded his large white feet with distaste. 'This stinking heat got my athlete's foot going again.'

He separated two of his toes and picked at the loose scaly skin between. 'You got any of that ointment left, André?'

'Yes, I'll get it for you.' André opened the flap of his pack, took out the tube and crossed to Wally's bunk.

'Put it on,' instructed Wally and lay back offering his feet. André took them in his lap as he sat down on the bunk and went to work. Wally lit a cigarette and blew smoke towards the roof, watching it disperse.

'Hell, I could use a drink. A beer with dew on the glass and a head that thick.' He held up four fingers, then he lifted himself on one elbow and studied André as he spread ointment between the long prehensile toes.

'How's it going?'

'Nearly finished, Wally.'

'Is it bad?'

'Not as bad as last time, it hasn't started weeping yet.'

'It itches like you wouldn't believe it,' said Wally.

André did not answer and Wally kicked him in the ribs with the flat of his free foot.

'Did you hear what I said?'

'Yes, you said it itches.'

'Well, answer me when I talk to you. I ain't talking to myself.'

'I'm sorry, Wally.'

Wally grunted and was silent a while, then:

'Do you like me, André?'

'You know I do, Wally.'

'We're friends, aren't we, André?'

'Of course, you know that, Wally.'

An expression of cunning had replaced Wally's boredom.

'You don't mind when I ask you to do things for me, like putting stuff on my feet?'

'I don't mind – it's a pleasure, Wally.'

'It's a pleasure, is it?' There was an edge in Wally's voice now. 'You like doing it?'

André looked up at him apprehensively. 'I don't mind it.' His molten toffee eyes clung to the narrow Mongolian ones in Wally's face.

'You like touching me, André?'

André stopped working with the ointment and nervously wiped his fingers on his towel.

'I said, do you like touching me, André? Do you sometimes wish I'd touch you?'

André tried to stand up, but Wally's right arm shot out and his hand fastened on André's neck, forcing him down on to the bunk.

'Answer me, damn you, do you like it?'

'You're hurting me, Wally,' whispered André.

'Shame, now ain't that a shame!'

Wally was grinning. He shifted his grip to the ridge of muscle above André's collar bone and dug his fingers in until they almost met through the flesh.

'Please, Wally, please,' whimpered André, wriggling face down on the bunk.

'You love it, don't you? Come on, answer me.'

'Yes, all right, yes. Please don't hurt me, Wally.'

'Now, tell me truly, doll boy, have you ever had it before? I mean for real.' Wally put his knee in the small of André's back, bearing down with all his weight.

'No!' shrieked André. 'I haven't. Please, Wally, don't hurt me.'

'You're lying to me, André. Don't do it.'

'All right. I was lying.' André tried to twist his head round, but Wally pushed his face into the bunk.

'Tell me all about it – come on, doll boy.'

'It was only once, in Brussels.'

'Who was this beef bandit?'

'My employer. I worked for him. He had an export agency.'

'Did he throw you out, doll boy? Did he throw you out when he was tired of you?'

'No, you don't understand!' André denied with sudden vehemence. 'You don't understand. He looked after me. I had my own apartment, my own car, everything. He wouldn't have abandoned me if it hadn't been for – for what happened. He couldn't help it, he was true to me. I swear to you – he loved me!'

Wally snorted with laughter, he was enjoying himself now.

'Loved you! Jesus wept!' He threw his head back, for the laughter was almost strangling him, and it was ten seconds before he could ask: 'Then what happened between you and your true blue lover? Why didn't you get married and settle down to raise a family, hey?' At the improbability of his own sense of humour Wally convulsed with laughter once more.

'There was an investigation. The police – ooh! you're hurting me, Wally.'

'Keep talking, mamselle!'

'The police – he had no alternative. He was a man of position, he couldn't afford the scandal. There was no other way out – there never is for us. It's hopeless, there is no happiness.'

'Cut the crap, doll boy. Just give me the story.'

'He arranged employment for me in Elisabethville, gave me money, paid for my air fare, everything. He did everything, he looked after me, he still writes to me.'

'That's beautiful, real true love. You make me want to cry.'

Then Wally's laughter changed its tone, harsher now. 'Well, get this, doll boy, and get it good. I don't like queers!' He dug his fingers in again and André squealed.

'I'll tell you a story. When I was in reform school there was a queer there that tried to touch me up. One day I got him in the shower rooms with a razor, just an ordinary Gillette razor. There were twenty guys singing and shouting in the other cubicles. He screamed just like they were all screaming when the cold water hit them. No one took any notice of him. He wanted to be a woman, so I helped him.' Hendry's voice went hoarse and gloating with the memory. 'Jesus!' he whispered. 'Jesus, the blood!' André was sobbing now, his whole body shaking.

'I won't – please, Wally, I can't help it. It was just that one time. Please leave me.'

'How would you like me to help you, André'

'No,' shrieked André. And Hendry lost interest; he released him, left him lying on the bunk and reached for his socks.

'I'm going to find me a beer.' He laced on his boots and stood up.

'Just you remember,' he said darkly, standing over the boy on the bunk. 'Don't get any ideas with me, Bucko.' He picked up his rifle and went out into the corridor.

Wally found Boussier on the verandah of the hotel talking with a group of his men.

'Where's Captain Curry?' he demanded.

'He has gone out to the mission station.'

'When did he leave?'

'About ten minutes ago.'

'Good,' said Wally. 'Who's got the key to the bar?'

Boussier hesitated.

'The captain has ordered that the bar is to remain locked.'

Wally unslung his rifle.

'Don't give me a hard time, friend.'

'I regret, monsieur, that I must obey the captain's instructions.'

For a minute they stared at each other, and there was no sign of weakening in the older man.

'Have it your way, then,' said Wally and swaggered through the lounge to the bar-room door. He put his foot against the lock and the flimsy mechanism yielded to the pressure. The door flew open and Wally marched across to the counter, laid his rifle on it and reached underneath to the shelves loaded with Simba beer.

The first bottle he emptied without taking it from his lips. He belched luxuriously and reached for the second, hooked the cap off with the opener and inspected the bubble of froth that appeared at its mouth.

'Hendry!' Wally looked up at Mike Haig in the doorway.

'Hello, Mike.' He grinned.

'What do you think you're doing?' Mike demanded.

'What does it look like?' Wally raised the bottle in salutation and then sipped delicately at the froth.

'Bruce has given strict orders that no one is allowed in here.'

'Oh, for Chrissake, Haig. Stop acting like an old woman.'

'Out you get, Hendry. I'm in charge here.'

'Mike,' Wally grinned at him, 'you want me to die of thirst or something?' He leaned his elbows on the counter. 'Give me a couple more minutes. Let me finish my drink.'

Mike Haig glanced behind him into the lounge and saw the interested group of civilians who were craning to see into the bar-room. He closed the door and walked across to stand opposite Hendry.

'Two minutes, Hendry,' he agreed in an unfriendly tone, 'then out with you.'

'You're not a bad guy, Mike. You and I rubbed each other up wrong. I tell you something, I'm sorry about us.'

'Drink up!' said Mike. Without turning Wally reached backwards and took a bottle of Remy Martin cognac off the shelf. He pulled the cork with his teeth, selected a brandy balloon with his free hand and poured a little of the oily amber fluid into it.

'Keep me company, Mike,' he said and slid the glass across the counter towards Haig. First without expression, and then with his face seeming to crumble, Mike Haig stared at the glass. He moistened his lips, again older and tired-looking. With a physical wrench he pulled his eyes away from the glass.

'Damn you, Hendry.' His voice unnaturally low.

'God damn you to hell.' He hit out at the glass, spinning it off the counter to shatter against the far wall.

'Did I do something wrong, Mike?' asked Hendry softly. 'Just offered you a drink, that's all.'

The smell of spilt brandy, sharp, fruity with the warmth of the grape, and Mike moistened his lips again. The saliva jetting from under his tongue, and the deep yearning aching want in his stomach spreading outwards slowly, numbing him.

'Damn you,' he whispered. 'Oh, damn you, damn you,' pleading now as Hendry filled another glass.

'How long has it been, Mike? A year, two years? Try a little, just a mouthful. Remember the lift it gives you. Come on, boy. You're tired, you've worked hard. Just one – there you are. Just have this one with me.'

Mike wiped his mouth with the back of his hand, sweating now across the forehead and on his upper lip, tiny jewels of sweat squeezed out of the skin by the craving of his body.

'Come on, boy.' Wally's voice hoarse with excitement; teasing, wheedling, tempting.

Mike's hand closed round the tumbler, moving of its own volition, lifting it towards lips that were suddenly slack and trembling, his eyes filled with mingled loathing and desire.

'Just this one,' whispered Hendry. 'Just this one.'

Mike gulped it with a sudden savage flick of his arm, one swallow and the glass was empty. He held it with both hands, his head bowed over it.

'I hate you. My God, I hate you.' He spoke to Hendry, and to himself, and to the empty glass.

'That's my boy!' crowed Wally. 'That's the lad! Come on, let me fill you up.'

= 12 =

Bruce went in through the front door of the hotel with Shermaine trying to keep pace with him. There were a dozen or so people in the lobby, and an air of tension amongst them. Boussier was one of them and he came quickly to Bruce.

'I'm sorry, Captain, I could not stop them. That one, that one with the red hair, he was violent. He had his gun and I think he was ready to use it.'

'What are you talking about?' Bruce asked him, but before Boussier could answer there was the bellow of Hendry's laughter from behind the door at the far end of the lobby; the door to the bar-room.

'They are in there,' Boussier told him. 'They have been there for the past hour.'

'Goddam it to hell,' swore Bruce. 'Now of all times. Oh, goddam that bloody animal.'

He almost ran across the room and threw open the double doors. Hendry was standing against the far wall with a tumbler in one hand and his rifle in the other. He was holding the rifle by the pistol grip and waving vague circles in the air with it.

Mike Haig was building a pyramid of glasses on the bar counter. He was just placing the final glass on the pile.

'Hello, Bruce, old cock, old man, old fruit,' he greeted Bruce, and waved in an exaggerated manner. 'Just in time, you can have a couple of shots as well. But Wally's first, he gets first shot. Must abide by the rules, no cheating, strictly democratic affair, everyone has equal rights. Rank doesn't count. That's right, isn't it Wally?' Haig's features had blurred; it was as though he were melting, losing his shape. His lips were loose and flabby, his jowls hung pendulously as an old woman's breasts, and his eyes were moist.

He picked up a glass from beside the pyramid, but this glass was nearly full and a bottle of Remy Martin cognac stood beside it.

'A very fine old brandy, absolutely exquisite.' The last two words didn't come out right, so he repeated them carefully. Then he grinned loosely at Bruce and his eyes weren't quite in focus.

'Get out of the way, Mike,' said Hendry, and raised the rifle one-handed, aiming at the pile of glasses.

'Every time she bucks, she bounces,' hooted Haig, 'and every time she bounces you win a coconut. Let her rip, old fruit.'

'Hendry, stop that,' snapped Bruce.

'Go and get mucked,' answered Hendry and fired. The rifle kicked back over his shoulder and he fell against the wall. The pyramid of glasses exploded in a shower of fragments and the room was filled with the roar of the rifle.

'Give the gentleman a coconut!' crowed Mike.

Bruce crossed the room with three quick strides and pulled the rifle out of Hendry's hand.

'All right, you drunken ape. That's enough.'

'Go and muck yourself,' growled Hendry. He was massaging his wrist; the rifle had twisted it.

'Captain Curry,' said Haig from behind the bar, 'you heard what my friend said. You go and muck yourself sideways to sleep.'

'Shut up, Haig.'

'This time I'll fix you, Curry,' Hendry growled. 'You've been on my back too long – now I'm going to shake you off!'

'Kindly descend from my friend's back, Captain Curry,' chimed in Mike Haig. 'He's not a howdah elephant, he's my blood brother. I will not allow you to persecute him.'

'Come on, Curry. Come on then!' said Wally.

'That's it, Wally. Muck him up.' Haig filled his glass again as he spoke. 'Don't let him ride you.'

'Come on then, Curry.'

'You're drunk,' said Bruce.

'Come on then; don't talk, man. Or do I have to start it?'

'No, you don't have to start it,' Bruce assured him, and lifted the rifle butt-first under his chin, swinging it up hard. Hendry's head jerked and he staggered back against the wall. Bruce looked at his eyes; they were glazed over. That will hold him, he decided; that's taken the fight out of him. He caught Hendry by the shoulder and threw him into one of the chairs. I must get to Haig before he absorbs any more of that liquor, he thought, I can't waste time sending for Ruffy and I can't leave this thing behind me while I work on Haig.

'Shermaine,' he called. She was standing in the doorway and she came to his side. 'Can you use a pistol?'

She nodded. Bruce unclipped his Smith & Wesson from its lanyard and handed it to her.

'Shoot this man if he tries to leave that chair. Stand here where he cannot reach you.'

'Bruce –' she started.

'He is a dangerous animal. Yesterday he murdered two small children and, if you let him, he'll do the same to you. You must keep him here while I get the other one.'

She lifted the pistol, holding it with both hands and her face was even paler than was usual.

'Can you do it?' Bruce asked.

'Now I can,' she said and cocked the action.

'Hear me, Hendry.' Bruce took a handful of his hair and twisted his face up. 'She'll kill you if you leave this chair. Do you understand. She'll shoot you.'

'Muck you and your little French whore, muck you both. I bet that's what you two have been doing all evening in that car – playing "hide the sausage" down by the river side.'

Anger flashed through Bruce so violently that it startled him. He twisted Hendry's hair until he could feel it coming away in his hand. Hendry squirmed with pain.

'Shut that foul mouth – or I'll kill you.'

He meant it, and suddenly Hendry knew he meant it.

'Okay, for Chrissake, okay. Just leave me.'

Bruce loosened his grip and straightened up.

'I'm sorry, Shermaine,' he said.

'That's all right – go to the other one.'

Bruce went to the bar counter, and Haig watched him come.

'What do you want, Bruce? Have a drink.' He was nervous. 'Have a drink, we are all having a little drink. All good clean fun, Bruce. Don't get excited.'

'You're not having any more; in fact, just the opposite,' Bruce told him as he came round the counter. Haig backed away in front of him.

'What are you going to do?'

'I'll show you,' said Bruce and caught him by the wrist, turning him quickly and lifting his arm up between his shoulder-blades.

'Hey, Bruce. Cut it out, you've made me spill my drink.'

'Good,' said Bruce and slapped the empty glass out of his hand. Haig started to struggle. He was still a powerful man but the liquor had weakened him and Bruce lifted his wrist higher, forcing him on to his toes.

'Come along, buddy boy,' instructed Bruce and marched him towards the back door of the bar-room. He reached round Haig with his free hand, turned the key in the lock and opened the door.

'Through here,' he said and pushed Mike into the kitchens. He kicked the door shut behind him and went to the sink, dragging Haig with him.

'All right, Haig, let's have it up,' he said and changed his grip quickly, thrusting Haig's head down over the sink. There was a dishtowel hanging beside it which Bruce screwed into a ball; then he used his thumbs to open Haig's jaws and wedged the towel between his back teeth.

'Let's have all of it.' He probed his finger down into Haig's throat. It came up hot and gushing over his hand, and he fought down his own nausea as he worked. When he had finished he turned on the cold tap and held Haig's head under it, washing his face and his own hand.

'Now, I've got a little job for you, Haig.'

'Leave me alone, damn you,' groaned Haig, his voice indistinct beneath the rushing tap. Bruce pulled him up and held him against the wall.

'There's a woman in childbirth at the mission. She's going to die, Haig. She's going to die if you don't do something about it.'

'No,' whispered Haig. 'No, not that. Not that again.'

'I'm taking you there.'

'No, please not that. I can't – don't you see that I can't.' The little red and purple veins in his nose and cheeks stood out in vivid contrast to his pallor. Bruce hit him open-handed across the face and the water flew in drops from his hair at the shock.

'No,' he mumbled, 'please Bruce, please.'

Bruce hit him twice more, hard. Watching him carefully, and at last he saw the first flickering of anger.

'Damn you, Bruce Curry, damn you to hell.'

'You'll do,' rejoiced Bruce. 'Thank God for that.'

He hustled Haig back through the bar-room. Shermaine still stood over Hendry, holding the pistol.

'Come on, Shermaine. You can leave that thing now. I'll attend to him when we get back.'

As they crossed the lobby Bruce asked Shermaine. 'Can you drive the Ford?'

'Yes.'

'Good,' said Bruce. 'Here are the keys. I'll sit with Haig in the back. Take us out to the mission.'

Haig lost his balance on the front steps of the hotel and nearly fell, but Bruce caught him and half carried him to the car. He pushed him into the back seat and climbed in beside him. Shermaine slid in behind the wheel, started the engine and U-turned neatly across the street.

'You can't force me to do this, Bruce. I can't, I just can't,' Haig pleaded.

'We'll see,' said Bruce.

'You don't know what it's like. You can't know. She'll die on the table.' He held out his hands palms down. 'Look at that, look at them. How can I do it with these?' His hands were trembling violently.

'She's going to die anyway,' said Bruce, his voice hard. 'So you might as well do it for her quickly and get it over with.'

Haig brought his hands up to his mouth and wiped his lips.

'Can I have a drink, Bruce? That'll help. I'll try then, if you give me a drink.'

'No,' said Bruce, and Haig began to swear. The filth poured from his lips and his face twisted with the effort. He cursed Bruce, he cursed himself, and God in a torrent of the most obscene language that Bruce had ever heard. Then suddenly he snatched at the door handle and tried to twist it open. Bruce had been waiting for this and he caught the back of Haig's collar, pulled him backwards across the seat and held him there. Haig's struggles ceased abruptly and he began to sob softly.

Shermaine drove fast; across the causeway, up the slope and into the side road. The headlights cut into the darkness and the wind drummed softly round the car. Haig was still sobbing on the back seat.

Then the lights of the mission were ahead of them through the trees and Shermaine slowed the car, turned in past the church and pulled up next to the hospital block.

Bruce helped Haig out of the car, and while he was doing so the side door of the building opened and Father Ignatius came out with a petromax lantern in his hand. The harsh white glare of the lantern lit them all and threw grotesque shadows behind them. It fell with special cruelty on Haig's face.

'Here's your doctor, Father,' Bruce announced.

Ignatius lifted the lantern and peered through his spectacles at Haig.

'Is he sick?'

'No, Father, said Bruce. 'He's drunk.'

'Drunk? Then he can't operate?'

'Yes, he damn well can!'

Bruce took Haig through the door and along the passage to the little theatre. Ignatius and Shermaine followed them.

'Shermaine, go with Father and help him bring the woman,' Bruce ordered, and they went; then he turned his attention back to Haig.

'Are you so far down there in the slime that you can't understand me?'

'I can't do it, Bruce. It's no good.'

'Then she'll die. But this much is certain: you are going to make the attempt.'

'I've got to have a drink, Bruce.' Haig licked his lips. 'It's burning me up inside, you've got to give me one.'

'Finish the job and I'll give you a whole case.'

'I've got to have one now.'

'No.' Bruce spoke with finality. 'Have a look at what they've got here in the way of instruments. Can you do it with these?' Bruce crossed to the sterilizer and lifted the lid, the steam came up out of it in a cloud. Haig looked in also.

'That's all I need, but there's not enough light in here, and I need a drink.'

'I'll get you more light. Start cleaning up.'

'Bruce, please let me —'

'Shut up,' snarled Bruce. 'There's the basin. Start getting ready.'

Haig crossed to the hand basin; he was more steady on his feet and his features had firmed a little. You poor old bastard, thought Bruce, I hope you can do it. My God, how much I hope you can.

'Get a move on, Haig, we haven't got all night.'

Bruce left the room and went quickly down the passage to the ward. The windows of the theatre were fixed and Haig could escape only into the passage. Bruce knew that he could catch him if he tried to run for it.

He looked into the ward. Shermaine and Ignatius, with the help of an African orderly, had lifted the woman on to the theatre trolley.

'Father, we need more light.'

'I can get you another lantern, that's all.'

'Good, do that then. I'll take the woman through.'

Father Ignatius disappeared with the orderly and Bruce helped Shermaine manoeuvre the trolley down the length of the ward and into the passage. The woman was whimpering with pain, and her face was grey, waxy grey. They only go like that when they are very frightened, or when they are dying.

'She hasn't much longer,' he said.

'I know,' agreed Shermaine. 'We must hurry.'

The woman moved restlessly on the trolley and gabbled a few words; then she sighed so that the great blanket-covered mound of her belly rose and fell, and she started to whimper again.

Haig was still in the theatre. He had stripped off his battle-jacket and, in his vest, he stooped over the basin washing. He did not look round as they wheeled the woman in.

'Get her on the table,' he said, working the soap into suds up to his elbows.

The trolley was of a height with the table and, using the blanket to lift her, it was easy to slide the woman across.

'She's ready, Haig,' said Bruce. Haig dried his arms on a clean towel and turned. He came to the woman and stood over her. She did not know he was there; her eyes were open but unseeing. Haig drew a breath; he was sweating a little across his forehead and the stubble of beard on the lower part of his face was stippled with grey.

He pulled back the blanket. The woman wore a short white jacket, open-fronted, that did not cover her stomach. Her stomach was swollen out, hard-looking, with the navel inverted. Knees raised slightly and the thick peasant's thighs spread wide in the act of labour. As Bruce watched, her whole body arched in another contraction. He saw the stress of the muscles beneath the dark greyish skin as they struggled to expel the trapped foetus.

'Hurry, Mike!' Bruce was appalled by the anguish of birth. I didn't know it was like this; in sorrow thou shalt bring forth children – but this! Through the woman's dry grey swollen lips burst another of those moaning little cries, and Bruce swung towards Mike Haig.

'Hurry, goddam you!'

And Mike Haig began his examination, his hands very pale as they groped over the dark skin. At last he was satisfied and he stood back from the table.

Ignatius and the orderly came in with two more lanterns. Ignatius started to say something, but instantly he sensed the tension in the room and he fell silent. They all watched Mike Haig's face.

His eyes were tight closed, and his face was hard angles and harsh planes in the lantern light. His breathing was shallow and laboured.

I must not push him now, Bruce knew instinctively, I have dragged him to the lip of the precipice and now I must let him go over the edge on his own.

Mike opened his eyes again, and he spoke.

'Caesarian section,' he said, as though he had pronounced his own death sentence. Then his breathing stopped. They waited, and at last the breath came out of him in a sigh.

'I'll do it,' he said.

'Gowns and gloves?' Bruce fired the question at Ignatius.

'In the cupboard.'

'Get them!'

'You'll have to help me, Bruce. And you also Shermaine.'

'Yes, show me.'

Quickly they scrubbed and dressed. Ignatius held the pale green theatre gowns while they dived into them and flapped and struggled through.

'That tray, bring it here,' Mike ordered as he opened the sterilizer. With a pair of long-nosed forceps he lifted the instruments out of the steaming box and laid them on the tray naming each one as he did so.

'Scalpel, retractors, clamps.'

In the meantime the orderly was swabbing the woman's belly with alcohol and arranging the sheets.

Mike filled the syringe with pentothal and held it up to the light. He was an unfamiliar figure now; his face masked, the green skull cap covering his hair, and the flowing gown falling to his ankles. He pressed the plunger and a few drops of the pale fluid dribbled down the needle.

He looked at Bruce, only his haunted eyes showing above the mask.

'Ready?'

'Yes,' Bruce nodded. Mike stooped over the woman, took her arm and sent the needle searching under the soft black skin on the inside of her elbow. The fluid in the syringe was suddenly discoloured with drawn blood as Mike tested for the vein, and then the plunger slid slowly down the glass barrel.

The woman stopped whimpering, the tension went out of her body and her breathing slowed and became deep and unhurried.

'Come here.' Mike ordered Shermaine to the head of the table, and she took up the chloroform mask and soaked the gauze that filled the cone.

'Wait until I tell you.'

She nodded. Christ, what lovely eyes she has, thought Bruce, before he turned back to the job in hand.

'Scalpel,' said Mike from across the table, pointing to it on the tray, and Bruce handed it to him.

Afterwards the details were confused and lacking reality in Bruce's mind.

The wound opening behind the knife, the tight stretched skin parting and the tiny blood vessels starting to squirt.

Pink muscle laced with white; butter-yellow layers of sub-cutaneous fat, and then through to the massed bluish coils of the gut. Human tissue, soft and pulsing, glistening in the flat glare of the petromax.

Clamps and retractors, like silver insects crowding into the wound as though it were a flower.

Mike's hands, inhuman in yellow rubber, moving in the open pit of the belly. Swabbing, cutting, clamping, tying off.

Then the swollen purple bag of the womb, suddenly unzipped by the knife.

And at last, unbelievably, the child curled in a dark grey ball of legs and tiny arms, head too big for its size, and the fat pink snake of the placenta enfolding it.

Lifted out, the infant hung by its heels from Mike's hand like a small grey bat, still joined to its mother.

Scissors snipped and it was free. Mike worked a little longer, and the infant cried.

It cried with minute fury, indignant and alive. From the head of the table Shermaine laughed with spontaneous delight, and clapped her hands like a child at a Punch and Judy show. Suddenly Bruce was laughing also. It was a laugh from long ago, coming out from deep inside him.

'Take it,' said Haig and Shermaine cradled it, wet and feebly wriggling in her arms.

She stood with it while Haig sewed up. Watching her face and the way she stood, Bruce suddenly and unaccountably felt the laughter snag his throat, and he wanted to cry.

Haig closed the womb, stitching the complicated pattern of knots like a skilled seamstress, then the external sutures laid neatly across the fat lips of the wound, and at last the white tape hiding it all. He covered the woman, jerked the mask from his face and looked up at Shermaine.

'You can help me clean it up,' he said, and his voice was strong again and proud. The two of them crossed to the basin.

Bruce threw off his gown and left the room, went down the passage and out into the night. He leaned against the bonnet of the Ford and lit a cigarette.

Tonight I laughed again, he told himself with wonder, and then I nearly cried. And all because of a woman and a child. It is finished now, the pretence. The withdrawal. The big act. There was more than one birth in there tonight. I laughed again, I had the need to laugh again, and the desire to cry. A woman and a child, the whole meaning of life. The abscess had burst, the poison drained, and he was ready to heal.

'Bruce, Bruce, where are you?' She came out through the door; he did not answer her for she had seen the glow of his cigarette and she came to him. Standing close in the darkness.

'Shermaine —' Bruce said, then he stopped himself. He wanted to hold her, just hold her tightly.

'Yes, Bruce.' Her face was a pale round in the darkness, very close to him.

'Shermaine, I want —' said Bruce and stopped again.

'Yes, me too,' she whispered and then, drawing away, 'come, let's go and see what your doctor is doing now.' She took his hand and led him back into the building. Her hand was cool and dry with long tapered fingers in his.

Mike Haig and Father Ignatius were leaning over the cradle that now stood next to the table on which lay the blanket-covered body of the Baluba woman. The woman was breathing softly, and the expression on her face was of deep peace.

'Bruce, come and have a look. It's a beauty,' called Haig.

Still holding hands Bruce and Shermaine crossed to the cradle.

'He'll go all of eight pounds,' announced Haig proudly. Bruce looked at the infant; new born black babies are more handsome than ours – they have not got that half-boiled look.

'Pity he's not a trout,' murmured Bruce. 'That would be a national record.' Haig stared blankly at him for a second, then he threw back his head and laughed; it was a good sound. There was a different quality in Haig now, a new confidence in the way he held his head, a feeling of completeness about him.

'How about that drink I promised you, Mike?' Bruce tested him.

'You have it for me, Bruce, I'll duck this one.' He isn't just saying it either, thought Bruce, as he looked at his face; he really doesn't need it now.

'I'll make it a double as soon as we get back to town.' Bruce glanced at his watch. 'It's past ten, we'd better get going.'

'I'll have to stay until she comes out from the anaesthetic,' demurred Haig. 'You can come back for me in the morning.'

Bruce hesitated. 'All right then. Come on, Shermaine.'

They drove back to Port Reprieve, sitting close together in the intimate darkness of the car. They did not speak until after they had reached the causeway, then Shermaine said:

'He is a good man, your doctor. He is like Paul.'

'Who is Paul?'

'Paul was my husband.'

'Oh.' Bruce was embarrassed. The mention of that name snapped the silken thread of his mood. Shermaine went on, speaking softly and staring down the path of the headlights.

'Paul was of the same age. Old enough to have learned understanding – young men are so cruel.'

'You loved him.' Bruce spoke flatly, trying to keep any trace of jealousy from his voice.

'Love has many shapes,' she answered. Then, 'Yes, I had begun to love him. Very soon I would have loved him enough to –' She stopped.

'To what?' Bruce's voice had gone rough as a wood rasp. *Now it starts,* he thought, *once again I am vulnerable.*

'We were only married four months before he – before the fever.'

'So?' Still harsh, his eyes on the road ahead.

'I want you to know something. I must explain it all to you. It is very important. Will you be patient with me while I tell you?' There was a pleading in her voice that he could not resist and his expression softened.

'Shermaine, you don't have to tell me.'

'I must. I want you to know.' She hesitated a moment, and when she spoke again her voice had steadied. 'I am an orphan, Bruce. Both my Mama and Papa were killed by the Germans, in the bombing. I was only a few months old when it happened, and I do not remember them. I do not remember anything, not one little thing about them; there is not even a photograph.' For a second her voice had gone shaky but again it firmed. 'The nuns took me, and they were my family. But somehow that is different, not really your own. I have never had anything that has truly belonged to me, something of my very own.'

Bruce reached out and took her hand; it lay very still in his grasp. You have now, he thought, you have me for your very own.

'Then when the time came the nuns made the arrangements with Paul Cartier. He was an engineer with Union Minière du Haut here in the Congo, a man of position, a suitable man for one of their girls.

'He flew to Brussels and we were married. I was not unhappy, for although he was old – as old as Doctor Mike – yet he was very gentle and kind, of great understanding. He did not – ' She stopped and turned suddenly to Bruce, gripping his hand with both of hers, leaning towards him with her face serious and pale in the half-darkness, the plume of dark hair falling forward over her shoulder and her voice full of appeal. 'Bruce, do you understand what I am trying to tell you?'

Bruce stopped the car in front of the hotel, deliberately he switched off the ignition and deliberately he spoke.

'Yes, I think so.'

'Thank you,' and she flung the door open and went out of it and up the steps of the hotel with her long jeaned legs flying and her hair bouncing on her back.

Bruce watched her go through the double doors. Then he pressed the lighter on the dashboard and fished a cigarette from his pack. He lit it, exhaled a jet of smoke against the windscreen, and suddenly he was happy. He wanted to laugh again.

He threw the cigarette away only a quarter finished and climbed out of the Ford. He looked at his wrist watch; it was after midnight. My God, I'm tired. Too much has happened today; rebirth is a severe emotional strain. And he laughed out loud, savouring the sensation, letting it come slowly shaking up his throat from his chest.

Boussier was waiting for him in the lounge. He wore a towelling dressing-gown, and the creases of sleep were on his face.

'Are all your preparations complete, monsieur?'

'Yes,' the old man answered. 'The women and the two children are asleep upstairs. Madame Cartier has just gone up.'

'I know,' said Bruce, and Boussier went on, 'As you see, I have all the men here.' He gestured at the sleeping bodies that covered the floor of the lounge and bar-room.

'Good,' said Bruce. 'We'll leave as soon as it's light tomorrow.' He yawned, then rubbed his eyes, massaging them with his finger tips.

'Where is my officer, the one with the red hair?'

'He has gone back to the train, very drunk. We had more trouble with him after you had left.' Boussier hesitated delicately. 'He wanted to go upstairs, to the women.'

'Damn him.' Bruce felt his anger coming again. 'What happened?'

'Your sergeant major, the big one, dissuaded him and took him away.'

'Thank God for Ruffy.'

'I have reserved a place for you to sleep.' Boussier pointed to a comfortable leather armchair. 'You must be exhausted.'

'That is kind of you,' Bruce thanked him. 'But first I must inspect our defences.'

= 13 =

Bruce woke with Shermaine leaning over the chair and tickling his nose. He was fully dressed with his helmet and rifle on the floor beside him and only his boots unlaced.

'You do not snore, Bruce,' she congratulated him, laughing her small husky laugh. 'That is a good thing.'

He struggled up, dopey with sleep.

'What time is it?'

'Nearly five o'clock. I have breakfast for you in the kitchen.'

'Where is Boussier?'

'He is dressing; then he will start moving them down to the train.'

'My mouth tastes as though a goat slept in it.' Bruce moved his tongue across his teeth, feeling the fur on them.

'Then I shall not kiss you good morning, mon capitaine.' She straightened up with the laughter still in her eyes. 'But your toilet requisites are in the kitchen. I sent one of your gendarmes to fetch them from the train. You can wash in the sink.'

Bruce laced up his boots and followed her through into the kitchen, stepping over sleeping bodies on the way.

'There is no hot water,' Shermaine apologized.

'That is the least of my worries.' Bruce crossed to the table and opened his small personal pack, taking out his razor and soap and comb.

'I raided the chicken coop for you,' Shermaine confessed. 'There were only two eggs. How shall I cook them?'

'Soft boiled, one minute.' Bruce stripped off his jacket and shirt, went to the sink and filled it. He sluiced his face and lifted handfuls of water over his head, snorting with pleasure.

Then he propped his shaving mirror above the taps and spread soap on his face. Shermaine came to sit on the draining board beside him and watched with frank interest.

'I will be sorry to see the beard go,' she said. 'It looked like the pelt of an otter, I liked it.'

'Perhaps I will grow it for you one day.' Bruce smiled at her. 'Your eyes are blue, Shermaine.'

'It has taken you a long time to find that out,' she said and pouted dramatically. Her skin was silky and cool-looking, lips pale pink without make-up. Her dark hair, drawn back, emphasized the high cheek bones and the size of her eyes.

'In India "sher" means "tiger",' Bruce told her, watching her from the corner of his eye. Immediately she abandoned the pout and drew her lips up into a snarl. Her teeth were small and very white and only slightly uneven. Her eyes rolled wide and then crossed at an alarming angle. She growled. Taken by surprise, Bruce laughed and nearly cut himself.

'I cannot abide a woman who clowns before breakfast. It ruins my digestion,' he laughed at her.

'Breakfast!' said Shermaine and uncrossed her eyes, jumped off the draining board and ran to the stove.

'Only just in time.' She checked her watch. 'One minute and twenty seconds, will you forgive me?'

'This once only, never again.' Bruce washed the soap off his face, dried and combed his hair and came to the table. She had a chair ready for him.

'How much sugar in your coffee?'

'Three, please.' Bruce chopped the top off his egg, and she brought the mug and placed it in front of him.

'I like making breakfast for you.' Bruce didn't answer her. This was dangerous talk. She sat down opposite him, leaned forward on her elbows with her chin in her hands.

'You eat too fast,' she announced and Bruce raised an eyebrow. 'But at least you keep your mouth closed.'

Bruce started on his second egg.

'How old are you?'

'Thirty,' said Bruce.

'I'm twenty – nearly twenty-one.'

'A ripe old age.'

'What do you do?'

'I'm a soldier,' he answered.

'No, you're not.'

'All right, I'm a lawyer.'

'You must be clever,' she said solemnly.

'A genius, that's why I'm here.'

'Are you married?'

'No – I was. What is this, a formal interrogation?'

'Is she dead?'

'No.' He prevented the hurt from showing in his face, it was easier to do now.

'Oh!' said Shermaine. She picked up the teaspoon and concentrated on stirring his coffee.

'Is she pretty?'

'No – yes, I suppose so.'

'Where is she?' Then quickly, 'I'm sorry it's none of my business.'

Bruce took the coffee from her and drank it. Then he looked at his watch.

'It's nearly five fifteen. I must go out and get Mike Haig.'

Shermaine stood up quickly.

'I'm ready.'

'I know the way – you had better get down to the station.'

'I want to come with you.'

'Why?'

'Just because, that's why.' Searching for a reason. 'I want to see the baby again.'

'You win.' Bruce picked up his pack and they went through into the lounge. Boussier was there, dressed and efficient. His men were nearly ready to move.

'Madame Cartier and I are going out to the mission to fetch the doctor. We will be back in half an hour or so. I want all your people aboard by then.'

'Very well, Captain.'

Bruce called to Ruffy who was standing on the verandah. 'Did you load those supplies for the mission?'

'They're in the back of the Ford, boss.'

'Good. Bring all your sentries in and take them down to the station. Tell the engine driver to get steam up and keep his hand on the throttle. We'll shove off as soon as I get back with Lieutenant Haig.'

'Okay, boss.'

Bruce handed him his pack. 'Take this down for me, Ruffy.' Then his eyes fell on the large heap of cardboard cartons at Ruffy's feet. 'What's that?'

Ruffy looked a little embarrassed. 'Coupla bottles of beer, boss. Thought we might get thirsty going home.'

'Good for you!' grinned Bruce. 'Put them in a safe place and don't drink them all before I get back.'

'I'll save you one or two,' promised Ruffy.

'Come along, tiger girl,' and Bruce led Shermaine out to the Ford. She sat closer to him than the previous day, but with her legs curled up under her, as before. As they crossed the causeway she lit two cigarettes and passed one to him.

'I'll be glad to leave this place,' she said, looking out across the swamp with the mist lifting sluggishly off it in the dawn, hanging in grey shreds from the fluffy tops of the papyrus grass.

'I've hated it here since Paul died. I hate the swamp and the mosquitoes and the jungle all around. I'm glad we're going.'

'Where will you go?' Bruce asked.

'I haven't thought about it. Back to Belgium, I suppose. Anywhere away from the Congo. Away from this heat to a country where you can breathe. Away from the disease and the fear. Somewhere so that I know tomorrow I will not have to run. Where human life has meaning, away from the killing and the burning and the rape.' She drew on her cigarette almost fiercely, staring ahead at the green wall of the forest.

'I was born in Africa,' said Bruce. 'In the time when the judge's gavel was not the butt of an FN rifle, before you registered your vote with a burst of gunfire.' He spoke softly with regret. 'In the time before the hatred. But now I don't know. I haven't thought much about the future either.'

He was silent for a while. They reached the turn-off to the mission and he swung the Ford into it.

'It has all changed so quickly; I hadn't realized how quickly until I came here to the Congo.'

'Are you going to stay here, Bruce? I mean, stay here in the Congo?'

'No,' he said, 'I've had enough. I don't even know what I'm fighting for.'

He threw the butt of his cigarette out of the window.

Ahead of them were the mission buildings.

Bruce parked the car outside the hospital buildings and they sat together quietly.

'There must be some other land,' he whispered, 'and if there is I'll find it.'

He opened the door and stepped out. Shermaine slid across the seat under the wheel and joined him. They walked side by side to the hospital; her hand brushed his and he caught it, held it and felt the pressure of his fingers returned by hers. She was taller than his shoulder, but not much.

Mike Haig and Father Ignatius were together in the women's ward, too engrossed to hear the Ford arrive.

'Good morning, Michael,' called Bruce. 'What's the fancy dress for?'

Mike Haig looked up and grinned. 'Morning, Bruce. Hello, Shermaine.' Then he looked down at the faded brown cassock he wore.

'Borrowed it from Ignatius. A bit long in the leg and tight round the waist, but less out of place in a sick ward than the accoutrements of war.'

'It suits you, Doctor Mike,' said Shermaine.

'Nice to hear someone call me that again.' The smile spread all over Haig's face. 'I suppose you want to see your baby, Shermaine?'

'Is he well?'

'Mother and child both doing fine,' he assured her and led Shermaine down between the row of beds, each with a black woolly head on the pillow and big curious eyes following their progress.

'May I pick him up?'

'He's asleep, Shermaine.'

'Oh, please!'

'I doubt it will kill him. Very well, then.'

'Bruce, come and look. Isn't he a darling?' She held the tiny black body to her chest and the child snuffled, its mouth automatically starting to search. Bruce leaned forward to peer at it.

'Very nice,' he said and turned to Ignatius. 'I have those supplies I promised you. Will you send an orderly to get them out of the car?' Then to Mike Haig, 'You'd better get changed, Mike. We're all ready to leave.'

Not looking at Bruce, fiddling with the stethoscope round his neck, Mike shook his head. 'I don't think I'll be going with you, Bruce.'

Surprised, Bruce faced him.

'What?'

'I think I'll stay on here with Ignatius. He has offered me a job.'

'You must be mad, Mike.'

'Perhaps,' agreed Haig and took the infant from Shermaine, placed it back in the cradle beside its mother and tucked the sheet in round its tiny body, 'and then again, perhaps not.' He straightened up and waved a hand down the rows of occupied beds. 'There's plenty to do here, that you must admit.'

Bruce stared helplessly at him and then appealed to Shermaine.

'Talk him out of it. Perhaps you can make him see the futility of it.'

Shermaine shook her head. 'No, Bruce, I will not.'

'Mike, listen to reason, for God's sake. You can't stay here in this disease-ridden backwater, you can't –'

'I'll walk out to the car with you, Bruce. I know you're in a hurry –'

He led them out through the side door and stood by the driver's window of the Ford while they climbed in. Bruce extended his hand and Mike took it, gripping hard.

'Cheerio, Bruce. Thanks for everything.'

'Cheerio, Mike. I suppose you'll be taking orders and having yourself made into a fully licensed dispenser of salvation?'

'I don't know about that, Bruce. I doubt it. I just want another chance to do the only work I know. I just want a last-minute rally to reduce the formidable score that's been chalked up against me so far.'

'I'll report you "missing, believed killed" – throw your uniform in the river,' said Bruce.

'I'll do that.' Mike stepped back. 'Look after each other, you two.'

'I don't know what you mean,' Shermaine informed him primly, trying not to smile.

'I'm an old dog, not easy to fool,' said Mike. 'Go to it with a will.'

Bruce let out the clutch and the Ford slid forward.

'God speed, my children.' That smile spread all over Mike's face as he waved.

'Au revoir, Doctor Michael.'

'So long, Mike.'

Bruce watched him in the rear-view mirror, tall in his ill-fitting cassock, something proud and worthwhile in his stance. He waved once more and then turned and hurried back into the hospital.

Neither of them spoke until they had almost reached the main road. Shermaine nestled softly against Bruce, smiling to herself, looking ahead down the tree-lined passage of the road.

'He's a good man, Bruce.'

'Light me a cigarette, please, Shermaine.' He didn't want to talk about it. It was one of those things that can only be made grubby by words.

Slowing for the intersection, Bruce dropped her into second gear, automatically glancing to his left to make sure the main road was clear before turning into it.

'Oh my God!' he gasped.

'What is it, Bruce?' Shermaine looked up with alarm from the cigarette she was lighting.

'Look!'

A hundred yards up the road, parked close to the edge of the forest, was a convoy of six large vehicles. The first five were heavy canvas-canopied lorries painted dull military olive, the sixth was a gasoline tanker in bright yellow and red with the Shell Company insignia on the barrel-shaped body. Hitched behind the leading lorry was a squat, rubber-tyred 25-pounder anti-tank gun with its long barrel pointed jauntily skywards. Round the vehicles, dressed in an assortment of uniforms and different styled helmets, were at least sixty men. They were all armed, some with automatic weapons and others with obsolete bolt-action rifles. Most of them were urinating carelessly into the grass that lined the road, while the others were standing in small groups smoking and talking.

'General Moses!' said Shermaine, her voice small with the shock.

'Get down,' ordered Bruce and with his free hand thrust her on to the floor. He rammed the accelerator flat and the Ford roared out into the main road, swerving violently, the back end floating free in the loose dust as he held the wheel over. Correcting the skid, meeting it and straightening out, Bruce glanced at the rear-view mirror. Behind them the men had dissolved into a confused pattern of movement; he heard their shouts high and thin above the racing engine of the Ford. Bruce looked ahead; it was another hundred yards to the bend in the road that would hide them and take them down to the causeway across the swamp.

Shermaine was on her knees pulling herself up to look over the back of the seat.

'Keep on the floor, damn you!' shouted Bruce and pushed her head down roughly.

As he spoke the roadside next to them erupted in a rapid series of leaping dust fountains and he heard the high hysterical beat of machine-gun fire.

The bend in the road rushed towards them, just a few more seconds. Then with a succession of jarring crashes that shook the whole body of the car a burst of fire hit them from behind. The windscreen starred into a sheet of opaque diamond lacework, the dashboard clock exploded powdering Shermaine's hair with particles of glass, two bullets tore through the seat ripping out the stuffing like the entrails of a wounded animal.

'Close your eyes,' shouted Bruce and punched his fist through the windscreen. Slitting his own eyes against the chips of flying glass, he could just see through the hole his fist had made. The corner was right on top of them and he dragged the steering-wheel over, skidding into it, his off-side wheels bumping into the verge, grass and leaves brushing the side of the car.

Then they were through the corner and racing down towards the causeway.

'Are you all right, Shermaine?'

'Yes, are you?' She emerged from under the dashboard, a smear of blood across one cheek where the glass had scratched her, and her eyes bigger than ever with fright.

'I only pray that Boussier and Hendry are ready to pull out. Those bastards won't be five minutes behind us.'

They went across the causeway with the needle of the speedometer touching eighty, up the far side and into the main street of Port Reprieve. Bruce thrust his hand down on the hooter ring, blowing urgent warning blasts.

'Please God, let them be ready,' he muttered. With relief he saw that the street was empty and the hotel seemed deserted. He kept blowing the horn as they roared down towards the station, a great billowing cloud of dust rising behind them. Braking the Ford hard, he turned it in past the station buildings and on to the platform.

Most of Boussier's people were standing next to the train. Boussier himself was beside the last truck with his wife and the small group of women around him. Bruce shouted at them through the open window.

'Get those women into the train, the *shufta* are right behind us, we're leaving immediately.'

Without question or argument old Boussier gathered them together and hurried them up the steel ladder into the truck. Bruce drove down the station platform shouting as he went.

'Get in! For Chrissake, hurry up! They're coming!'

He braked to a standstill next to the cab of the locomotive and shouted up at the bald head of the driver.

'Get going. Don't waste a second. Give her everything she's got. There's a bunch of *shufta* not five minutes behind us.'

The driver's head disappeared into the cab without even the usual polite, 'Oui monsieur.'

'Come on, Shermaine.' Bruce grabbed her hand and dragged her from the car. Together they ran to one of the covered coaches and Bruce pushed her half way up the steel steps.

At that moment the train jerked forward so violently that she lost her grip on the hand rails and tumbled backwards on top of Bruce. He was caught off balance and they fell together in a heap on the dusty platform. Above them the train gathered speed, pulling away. He remembered this nightmare from his childhood, running after a train and never catching it. He had to fight down his panic as he and Shermaine scrambled up, both of them panting, clinging to each other, the coaches clackety-clacking past them, the rhythm of their wheels mounting.

'Run!' he gasped, 'Run!' and with the panic weakening their legs he just managed to catch the hand rail of the second coach. He clung to it, stumbling along beside the train, one arm round Shermaine's waist. Sergeant Major Ruffararo leaned out, took Shermaine by the scruff of her neck and lifted her in like a lost kitten. Then he reached down for Bruce.

'Boss, some day we going to lose you if you go on playing around like that.'

'I'm sorry, Bruce,' she panted, leaning against him.

'No damage done.' He could grin at her. 'Now I want you to get into that compartment and stay there until I tell you to come out. Do you understand?'

'Yes, Bruce.'

'Off you go.' He turned from her to Ruffy. 'Up on to the roof, Sergeant Major! We're going to have fireworks. Those *shufta* have got a field gun with them and we'll be in full view of the town right up to the top of the hills.'

By the time they reached the roof of the train it had pulled out of Port Reprieve and was making its first angling turn up the slope of the hills. The sun was up now, well clear of the horizon, and the mist from the swamp had lifted so that they could see the whole village spread out beneath them.

General Moses's column had crossed the causeway and was into the main street. As Bruce watched, the leading truck swung sharply across the road and stopped. Men boiled out from under the canopy and swarmed over the field gun, unhitching it, manhandling it into position.

'I hope those Arabs haven't had any drill on that piece,' grunted Ruffy.

'We'll soon find out,' Bruce assured him grimly and looked back along the train. In the last truck Boussier stood protectively over the small group of four women and their children, like an old white-haired collie with its sheep. Crouched against the steel side of the truck, André de Surrier and half a dozen gendarmes were swinging and sighting the two Bren guns. In the second truck also the gendarmes were preparing to open fire.

'What are you waiting for?' roared Ruffy. 'Get me that field gun – start shooting.'

They fired a ragged volley, then the Bren guns joined in. With every burst André's helmet slipped forward over his eyes and he had to stop and push it back. Lying on the roof of the leading coach, Wally Hendry was firing short businesslike bursts.

The *shufta* round the field gun scattered, leaving one of their number lying in the road, but there were men behind the armour shield – Bruce could see the tops of their helmets.

Suddenly there was a long gush of white smoke from the barrel, and the shell rushed over the top of the train, with a noise like the wings of a giant pheasant.

'Over!' said Ruffy.

'Under!' to the next shot as it ploughed into the trees below them.

'And the third one right up the throat,' said Bruce. But it hit the rear of the train. They were using armour-piercing projectiles, not high explosive, for there was not the burst of yellow cordite fumes but only the crash and jolt as it struck.

Anxiously Bruce tried to assess the damage. The men and women in the rear trucks looked shaken but unharmed and he started a sigh of relief, which changed quickly to a gasp of horror as he realized what had happened.

'They've hit the coupling,' he said. 'They've sheared the coupling on the last truck.'

Already the gap was widening, as the rear truck started to roll back down the hill, cut off like the tail of a lizard.

'Jump,' screamed Bruce, cupping his hands round his mouth. 'Jump before you gather speed.'

Perhaps they did not hear him, perhaps they were too stunned to obey, but no one moved. The truck rolled back, faster and faster as gravity took it, down the hill towards the village and the waiting army of General Moses.

'What can we do, boss?'

'Nothing,' said Bruce.

The firing round Bruce had petered out into silence as every man, even Wally Hendry, stared down the slope at the receding truck. With a constriction of his throat Bruce saw old Boussier stoop and lift his wife to her feet, hold her close to his side and the two of them looking back at Bruce on the roof of the departing train. Boussier raised his right hand in a gesture of farewell and then he dropped it again and stood very still. Behind him, André de Surrier had left the Bren gun and removed his helmet. He also was looking back at Bruce, but he did not wave.

At intervals the field gun in the village punctuated the stillness with its deep boom and gush of smoke, but Bruce hardly heard it. He was watching the *shufta* running down towards the station yard to welcome the truck. Losing speed it ran into the platform and halted abruptly as it hit the buffers at the end of the line. The *shufta* swarmed over it like little black ants over the body of a beetle and faintly Bruce heard the pop, pop, pop of their rifles, saw the low sun glint on their bayonets. He turned away.

They had almost reached the crest of the hills; he could feel the train increasing speed under him. But he felt no relief, only the prickling at the corners of his eyes and the ache of it trapped in his throat.

'The poor bastards,' growled Ruffy beside him. 'The poor bastards.' And then there was another crashing jolt against the train, another hit from the field gun. This time up forward, on the locomotive. Shriek of escaping steam, the train checking its pace, losing power. But they were over the crest of the hills, the village was out of sight and gradually the train speeded up again as they started down the back slope. But steam spouted out of it, hissing white jets of it, and Bruce knew they had received a mortal wound. He switched on the radio.

'Driver, can you hear me? How bad is it?'

'I cannot see, Captain. There is too much steam. But the pressure on the gauge is dropping swiftly.'

'Use all you can to take us down the hill. It is imperative that we pass the level crossing before we halt. It is absolutely imperative – if we stop this side of the level crossing they will be able to reach us with their lorries.'

'I will try, Captain.'

They rocketed down the hills but as soon as they reached the level ground their speed began to fall off. Peering through the dwindling clouds of steam Bruce saw the pale brown ribbon of road ahead of them, and they were still travelling at a healthy thirty miles an hour as they passed it. When finally the train trickled to a standstill Bruce estimated that they were three or four miles beyond the level crossing, safely walled in by the forest and hidden from the road by three bends.

'I doubt they'll find us here, but if they do they'll have to come down the line from the level crossing to get at us. We'll go back a mile and lay an ambush in the forest on each side of the line,' said Bruce.

'Those Arabs won't be following us, boss. They've got themselves women and a whole barful of liquor. Be two or three days before old General Moses can sober them up enough to move them on.'

'You're probably right, Ruffy. But we'll take no chances. Get that ambush laid and then we'll try and think up some idea for getting home.'

Suddenly a thought occurred to him: Martin Boussier had the diamonds with him. They would not be too pleased about that in Elisabethville.

Almost immediately Bruce was disgusted with himself. The diamonds were by far the least important thing that they had left behind in Port Reprieve.

14

André de Surrier held his steel helmet against his chest the way a man hold his hat at a funeral, the wind blew cool and caressing through his dark sweat-damp hair. His hearing was dulled by the strike of the shell that had cut the truck loose from the rear of the train, he could hear one of the children crying and the crooning, gentling voice of its mother. He stared back up the railway line at the train, saw the great bulk of Ruffy beside Bruce Curry on the roof of the second coach.

'They can't help us now.' Boussier spoke softly. 'There's nothing they can do.' He lifted his hand stiffly in almost a military salute and then dropped it to his side. 'Be brave, ma chère,' he said to his wife. 'Please be brave,' and she clung to him.

André let the helmet drop from his hands. It clanged on to the metal floor of the truck. He wiped the sweat from his face with nervous fluttering hands and then turned slowly to look down at the village.

'I don't want to die,' he whispered. 'Not like this, not now, please not now.' One of his gendarmes laughed, a sound without mirth, and stepped across to the Bren. He pushed André away from it and started firing at the tiny running figures of the men in the station yard.

'No,' shrilled André. 'Don't do that, no, don't antagonize them. They'll kill us if you do that —'

'They'll kill us anyway,' laughed the gendarme and emptied the magazine in one long despairing burst. André started towards him, perhaps to pull him away from the gun, but his resolve did not carry him that far. His hands dropped to his sides, clenching and unclenching. His lips quivered and then opened to spill out his terror.

'No!' he screamed. 'Please, no! No! Oh, God have mercy. Oh, save me, don't let this happen to me, please, God. Oh, my God.'

He stumbled to the side of the truck and clambered on to it. The truck was slowing as it ran into the platform. He could sec men coming with rifles in their hands, shouting as they ran, black men in dirty tattered uniforms, their faces working with excitement, pink shouting mouths, baying like hounds in a pack.

André jumped and the dusty concrete of the platform grazed his cheek and knocked the wind out of him. He crawled to his knees, clutching his stomach and trying to scream. A rifle butt hit him between the shoulder-blades and he collapsed. Above him a voice shouted in French.

'He is white, keep him for the general. Don't kill him.' And again the rifle butt hit him, this time across the side of the head. He lay in the dust, dazed, with the taste of blood in his mouth and watched them drag the others from the truck.

They shot the black gendarmes on the platform, without ceremony, laughing as they competed with each other to use their bayonets on the corpses. The two children died quickly torn from their mothers, held by the feet and swung head first against the steel side of the truck.

Old Boussier tried to prevent them stripping his wife and was bayoneted from behind in anger, and then shot twice with a pistol held to his head as he lay on the platform.

All this happened in the first few minutes before the officers arrived to control them; by that time André and the four women were the only occupants of the truck left alive.

André lay where he had fallen, watching in fascinated skin-crawling horror as they tore the clothing off the women and with a man to each arm and each leg held them down on the platform as though they were calves to be branded, hooting with laughter at their struggling naked bodies, bickering for position, already unbuckling belts, pushing each other, arguing, some of them with fresh blood on their clothing.

But then two men, who by their air of authority and the red sashes across their chests were clearly officers, joined the crowd. One of them fired his pistol in the air to gain their attention and both of them started a harangue that slowly had effect. The women were dragged up and herded off towards the hotel.

One of the officers came across to where André lay, stooped over him and lifted his head by taking a handful of hair.

'Welcome, mon ami. The general will be very pleased to see you. It is a pity that your other white friends have left us, but then, one is better than nothing.'

He pulled André into a sitting position, peered into his face and then spat into his eyes with sudden violence. 'Bring him! The general will talk to him later.'

They tied André to one of the columns on the front verandah of the hotel and left him there. He could have twisted his head and looked through the large windows into the lounge at what they were doing to the women, but he did not. He could hear what was happening; by noon the screams had become groans and sobbing; by mid-afternoon the women were making no sound at all. But the queue of *shufta* was still out of the front door of the lounge. Some of them had been to the head of the line and back to the tail three or four times.

All of them were drunk now. One jovial fellow carried a bottle of Parfait Amour liqueur in one hand and a bottle of Harpers whisky in the other. Every time he came back to join the queue again he stopped in front of André.

'Will you drink with me, little white boy?' he asked. 'Certainly you will,' he answered himself, filled his mouth from one of the bottles and spat it into André's face. Each time it got a big laugh from the others waiting in the line. Occasionally one of the other *shufta* would stop in front of André, unsling his rifle, back away a few paces, sight along the bayonet at André's face and then charge forward, at the last moment twisting the point aside so that it grazed his cheek. Each time André could not suppress his shriek of terror, and the waiting men nearly collapsed with merriment.

Towards evening they started to burn the houses on the outskirts of town. One group, sad with liquor and rape, sat together at the end of the verandah and started to sing. Their deep beautiful voices carrying all the melancholy savagery of Africa, they kept on singing while an argument between two *shufta* developed into a knife fight in the road outside the hotel.

The sweet bass lilt of singing covered the coarse breathing of the two circling, bare-chested knife fighters and the shuffle, shuffle, quick shuffle of their feet in the dust. When finally they locked together for the kill, the singing rose still deep and strong but with a triumphant note to it. One man stepped back with his rigid right arm holding the knife buried deep in the other's belly and as the loser sank down, sliding slowly off the knife, the singing sank with him, plaintive, regretful and lamenting into silence.

They came for André after dark. Four of them less drunk than the others. They led him down the street to the Union Minière offices. General Moses was there, sitting alone at the desk in the front office.

There was nothing sinister about him; he looked like an elderly clerk, a small man with the short woollen cap of hair grizzled to grey above the ears and a pair of horn-rimmed spectacles. On his chest he wore three rows of full-dress medals; each of his fingers was encased in rings to the second joint, diamonds, emeralds and the occasional red glow of a ruby; most of them had been designed for women, but the metal had been cut to enlarge them for his stubby black fingers. The face was almost kindly, except the eyes. There was a blankness of expression in them, the lifeless eyes of a madman. On the desk in front of him was a small wooden case made of unvarnished deal which bore the seal of the Union Minière Company stencilled in black upon its side. The lid was open, and as André came in through the door with his escort General Moses lifted a white canvas bag from the case, loosened the draw string and poured a pile of dark grey industrial diamonds on to the blotter in front of him.

He prodded them thoughtful with his finger, stirring them so they glittered dully in the harsh light of the petromax.

'Was this the only case in the truck?' he asked without looking up.

'Oui, mon général. There was only the one,' answered one of André's escorts.

'You are certain?'

'Qui, mon général. I myself have searched thoroughly.'

General Moses took another of the canvas bags from the case and emptied it on to the blotter. He grunted with disappointment as he saw the drab little stones. He reached for another bag, and another, his anger mounting steadily as each yielded only dirty grey and black industrial diamonds. Soon the pile on the blotter would have filled a pint jug.

'Did you open the case?' he snarled.

'Non, mon général. It was sealed. The seal was not broken, you saw that.'

General Moses grunted again, his dark chocolate face set hard with frustration. Once more he dipped his hand into the wooden case and suddenly he smiled.

'Ah!' he said pleasantly. 'Yes! yes! what is this?' He brought out a cigar box, with the gaudy wrappers still on the cedar wood. A thumb nail prised the lid back and he beamed happily. In a nest of cotton wool, sparkling, breaking the white light of the petromax into all the rainbow colours of the spectrum, were the gem stones. General Moses picked one up and held it between thumb and forefinger.

'Pretty,' he murmured. 'Pretty, so pretty.' He swept the industrial stones to one side and laid the gem in the centre of the blotter. Then one by one he took the others from the cigar box, fondling each and laying it on the blotter, counting them, smiling, once chuckling softly, touching them, arranging them in patterns.

'Pretty,' he kept whispering. 'Bon – forty-one, forty-two. Pretty! My darlings! Forty-three.'

Then suddenly he scooped them up and poured them into one of the canvas bags, tightened the draw string, dropped it into his breast pocket above the medals and buttoned the flap.

He laid his black, bejewelled hands on the desk in front of him and looked up at André.

His eyes were smoky yellow with black centres behind his spectacles. They had an opaque, dreamlike quality.

'Take off his clothes,' he said in a voice that was as expressionless as the eyes.

They stripped André with rough dispatch and General Moses looked at his body.

'So white,' he murmured. 'Why so white?' Suddenly his jaws began chewing nervously and there was a faint shine of sweat on his forehead. He came round from behind the desk, a small man, yet with an intensity about him that doubled his size.

'White like the maggots that feed in the living body of the elephant.' He brought his face close to André's. 'You should be fatter, my maggot, having fed so long and so well. You should be much fatter.'

He touched André's body, running his hands down his flanks in a caress.

'But now it is too late, little white maggot,' he said, and André cringed from his touch and from his voice. 'For the elephant has shaken you from the wound, shaken you out on to the ground, shaken you out beneath his feet – and will you pop when he crushes you?'

His voice was still soft though the sweat oozed in oily lines down his cheeks and the dreaminess of his eyes had been replaced by a burning black brightness.

'We shall see,' he said and drew back. 'We shall see, my maggot,' he repeated, and brought his knee up into André's crotch with a force that jerked his whole frame and flung his shoulders back.

The agony flared through André's lower body, fierce as the touch of heated steel. It clamped in on his stomach, contracting it in a spasm like childbirth, it rippled up across the muscles of his chest into his head and burst beneath the roof of his skull in a whiteness that blinded him.

'Hold him,' commanded General Moses, his voice suddenly shrill. The two guards took André by the elbows and forced him to his knees, so that his genitals and lower belly were easily accessible to the general's boots. They had done this often.

'For the times you gaoled me!' And General Moses swung his booted foot into André's body. The pain blended with the other pain, and it was too strong for André to scream.

'This, for the insults,' and André could feel his testicles crush beneath it. Still it was too strong – he could not use his voice.

'This, for the times I have grovelled.' The pain had passed its zenith, this time he could scream with it. He opened his mouth and filled his empty lungs.

'This, for the times I have hungered.' Now he must scream. Now he must – the pain, oh, sweet Christ, I must, please let me scream.

'This, for your white man's justice.' Why can't I, please let me. Oh, no! No – please. Oh, God, oh, please.

'This, for your prisons and your Kiboko!'

The kicks so fast now, like the beat of an insane drummer, like rain on a tin roof. In his stomach he felt something tear.

'And this, and this, and this.'

The face before him filled the whole field of his vision. The voice and the sound of boot into him filled his ears.

'This, and this, and this.' The voice high-pitched and within him the sudden warm flood of internal bleeding.

The pain was fading now as his body closed it out in defence, and he had not screamed. The leap of elation as he knew it. *This last thing I can do well, I can die now WITHOUT SCREAMING*. He tried to stand up, but they held him down and his legs were not his own, they were on the other side of the great numb warmth of his belly. He lifted his head and looked at the man who was killing him.

'This for the white filth that bore you, and this, and this –'

The blows were not a part of reality, he could feel the shock of them as though he stood close to a man who was cutting down a tree with an axe. And André smiled.

He was still smiling when they let him fall forward to the floor.

'I think he is dead,' said one of the guards. General Moses turned away and walked back to his seat at the desk. He was shaking as though he had run a long way, and his breathing was deep and fast. The jacket of his uniform was soaked with sweat. He sank into the chair and his body seemed to crumple; slowly the brightness faded from his eyes until once more they were filmed over, opaque and dreamy. The two guards squatted down quickly on each side of André's body; they knew it would be a long wait.

Through the open window there came an occasional shout of drunken laughter, and the red flicker and leap of flames.

= 15 =

Bruce stood in the centre of the tracks and searched the floor of the forest critically. At last he could make out the muzzle of the Bren protruding a few inches from the patch of elephant grass. Despite the fact that he knew exactly where to look for it, it had taken him a full two minutes to find it.

'That'll do, Ruffy,' he decided. 'We can't get it much better than that.'

'I reckon not, boss.'

Bruce raised his voice. 'Can you hear me?' There were muffled affirmatives from the bush on each side, and Bruce continued.

'If they come you must let them reach this spot before you open fire. I will mark it for you.' He went to a small shrubbeside the line, broke off a branch and dropped it on the tracks.

'Can you see that?'

Again the affirmatives from the men in ambush. 'You will be relieved before darkness – until then stay where you are.'

The train was hidden beyond a bend in the line, half a mile ahead, and Bruce walked back with Ruffy.

The engine driver was waiting for them, talking with Wally Hendry beside the rear truck.

'Any luck?' Bruce asked him.

'I regret, mon capitaine, that she is irreparably damaged. The boiler is punctured in two places and there is considerable disruption of the copper tubing.'

'Thank you,' Bruce nodded. He was neither surprised nor disappointed. It was precisely what his own judgement had told him after a brief examination of the locomotive.

'Where is Madame Cartier?' he asked Wally.

'*Madame* is preparing the luncheon, *monsir*,' Wally told him with heavy sarcasm. 'Why do you ask, Bucko? Are you feeling randy again so soon, hey? You feel like a slice of veal for lunch, is that it?'

Bruce snuffed out the quick flare of his temper and walked past him. He found Shermaine with four gendarmes in the cab of the locomotive. They had scraped the coals from the furnace into a glowing heap on the steel floor and were chopping potatoes and onions into the five gallon pots.

The gendarmes were all laughing at something Shermaine had said. Her usually pale cheeks were flushed with the heat; there was a sooty smudge on her forehead. She wielded the big knife with professional dexterity. She looked up and saw Bruce, her face lighting instantly and her lips parting.

'We're having a Hungarian goulash for lunch – bully beef, potatoes and onions.'

'As of now I am rating you acting second cook without pay.'

'You are too kind,' and she put her tongue out at him. It was a pink pointed little tongue like a cat's. Bruce felt the old familiar tightening of his legs and the dryness in his throat as he looked at it.

'Shermaine, the locomotive is damaged beyond repair. It is of no further use.' He spoke in English.

'It makes a passable kitchen,' she demurred.

'Be serious.' Bruce's anxiety made him irritable. 'We're stranded here until we think of something.'

'But, Bruce, you are the genius. I have complete faith in you. I'm sure you'll think of some truly beautiful idea.' Her face was solemn but she couldn't keep the banter out of her eyes. 'Why don't you go and ask General Moses to lend you his transportation.'

Bruce's eyes narrowed in thought and the black inverted curves of his eyebrows nearly touched above the bridge of his nose.

'The food better be good or I'll break you to third cook,' he warned, clambered down from the cab to the ground and hurried back along the train.

'Hendry, Sergeant Major, come here, please. I want to discuss something with you.'

They came to join him and he led the way up the ladder into one of the covered coaches. Hendry dropped on to the bunk and placed his feet on the wash basin.

'That was a quick one,' he grinned through the coppery stubble of his beard.

'You're the most uncouth, filthy-mouthed son of a bitch I have ever met, Hendry,' said Bruce coldly. 'When I get you back to Elisabethville I'm going to beat you to pulp before I hand you over to the military authority for murder.'

'My, my,' laughed Hendry. 'Big talker, hey? Curry, big, big talker.'

'Don't make me kill you now – don't do that, please. I still need you.'

'What's with you and that Frenchy, hey? You love it or something? You love it, or you just fancy a bit of that fat little arse? It can't be her titties – she ain't got much there, not even a handful each side.'

Bruce started for him, then changed his mind and swung round to stare out of the window. His voice was strangled when he spoke.

'I'll make a bargain with you, Hendry. Until we get out of this you keep off my back and I'll keep off yours. When we reach Msapa Junction the truce is off. You can do and say whatever you like and, if I don't kill you for it, I'll try my level best to see you hanged for murder.'

'I'm making no bargain with you or nobody, Curry. I play along until it suits me, and I won't give you no warning when it doesn't suit me to play along any more. And let me tell you now, Bucko, I don't need you and I don't need nobody. Not Haig or you, with your fancy too-good-to-kiss-my-arse talk; when the time comes I'm going to trim you down to size – just remember that, Curry. And don't say I didn't warn you.' Hendry was leaning forward, hands on his knees, body braced and his whole face twisting and contorted with the vehemence of his speech.

'Let's make it now, Hendry.' Bruce wheeled away from the window, crouching slightly, his hands stiffening into the flat hard blades of the judo fighter.

Sergeant Major Ruffararo stood up from the opposite bunk with surprising grace and speed for such a big man. He interposed his great body.

'You wanted to tell us something, boss?'

Slowly Bruce straightened out of his crouch, his hands relaxing. Irritably he brushed at the damp lock of dark hair that had fallen on to his forehead, as if to brush Wally Hendry out of his mind with the same movement.

'Yes,' controlling his voice with an effort, 'I wanted to discuss our next move.' He fished the cigarette pack from his top pocket and lit one, sucking the smoke down deep. Then he perched on the lid of the wash basin and studied the ash on the tip of the cigarette. When he spoke again his voice was normal.

'There is no hope of repairing this locomotive, so we have to find alternative transport out of here. Either we can walk two hundred miles back to Msapa Junction with our friends the Baluba ready to dispute our passage, or we can ride back in General Moses's trucks!' He paused to let it sink in.

'You going to pinch those trucks off him?' asked Ruffy. 'That's going to take some doing, boss.'

'No, Ruffy, I don't think we have any chance of getting them out from under his nose. What we will have to do is attack the town and wipe him out.'

'You're bloody crazy,' exclaimed Wally. 'You're raving bloody mad.'

Bruce ignored him. 'I estimate that Moses has about sixty men. With Kanaki and nine men on the bridge, Haig and de Surrier and six others gone, we have thirty-four men left. Correct, Sergeant Major?'

'That's right, boss.'

'Very well,' Bruce nodded. 'We'll have to leave at least ten men here to man that ambush in case Moses sends a patrol after us, or in case of an attack by the Baluba. It's not enough, I know, but we will just have to risk it.'

'Most of these civilians got arms with them, shotguns and sports rifles,' said Ruffy.

'Yes,' agreed Bruce. 'They should be able to look after themselves. So that leaves twenty-four men to carry out the attack, something like three to one.'

'Those *shufta* will be so full of liquor, half of them won't be able to stand up.'

'That's what I am banking on: drunkenness and surprise. We'll hit them and try and finish it before they know what's happened. I don't think they will have realized how badly we were hit; they probably expect us to be a hundred miles away by now.'

'When do you want to leave, boss?'

'We are about twelve miles from Port Reprieve – say, six hours' march in the dark. I want to attack in the early hours of tomorrow morning, but I'd like to be in position around midnight. We'll leave here at six o'clock, just before dark.'

'I'd better go and start sorting the boys out.'

'Okay, Ruffy. Issue an extra hundred rounds to each man and ten grenades. I'll want four extra haversacks of grenades also.' Bruce turned to Hendry and looked at him for the first time. 'Go with the sergeant major, Hendry, and give him a hand.'

'Jesus, this is going to be a ball,' grinned Wally in anticipation. 'With any luck I'll get me a sackful of ears.' He disappeared down the corridor behind Ruffy, and Bruce lay back on the seat and took off his helmet. He closed his eyes and once again he saw Boussier and his wife standing together in the truck as it rolled back down the hill, he saw the huddle of frightened women, and André standing bareheaded staring back at him with big brown gentle eyes. He groaned softly. 'Why is it always the good ones, the harmless, the weak?'

A tap on the door roused him and he sat up quickly.

'Yes?'

'Hello, Bruce.' Shermaine came in with a multiple-decked metal canteen in one hand and two mugs in the other. 'It's lunchtime.'

'Already!' Bruce checked his watch. 'Good Lord, it's after one.'

'Are you hungry?'

'Breakfast was a century ago.'

'Good,' she said, lowered the collapsible table and began serving the food.

'Smells good.'

'I am a chef Cordon Bleu. My bully beef goulash is demanded by the crowned heads of Europe.'

They ate in silence for both of them were hungry. Once they looked at each other and smiled but returned to the food.

'That was good,' sighed Bruce at last.

'Coffee, Bruce?'

'Please.'

As she poured it she asked, 'So, what happens now?'

'Do you mean what happens now we are alone?'

'You are forward, monsieur. I meant how do we get out of here.'

'I am adopting your suggestion: borrowing General Moses's transportation.'

'You make jokes, Bruce!'

'No,' he said, and explained briefly.

'It will be very dangerous, will it not? You may be hurt?'

'Only the good die young.'

'That is why I worry. Please do not get hurt – I am starting to think I would not like that.' Her face was very serious and pale. Bruce crossed quickly and stooped over her, lifting her to her feet.

'Shermaine, I –'

'No, Bruce. Don't talk. Don't say anything.' Her eyes were closed with thick black lashes interlaced, her chin lifted exposing the long smooth swell of her neck. He touched it with his lips and she made a soft noise in her throat so he could feel the skin vibrate. Her body flattened against his and her fingers closed in the hair at the back of his head.

'Oh, Bruce. My Bruce, please do not get hurt. Do not let them hurt you.'

Wanting now, urgently, his mouth hunted upwards and hers came to meet it, willing prey. Her lips were pink and not greased with make-up, they parted to the pressure of his tongue, he felt the tip of her nose cool upon his cheek and his hand moved up her back and closed round the nape of her neck, slender neck with silky down behind her ears.

'Oh, Bruce –' she said into his mouth. His other hand went down on to the proud round, deeply divided thrust of her buttocks, he pulled her lower body against his and she gasped as she felt him – the arrogant maleness through cloth.

'No,' she gasped and tried to pull away, but he held her until she relaxed against him once more. She shook her head, 'Non, non,' but her mouth was open still and her tongue fluttered against his. Down came his hand from her neck and twitched her shirt tails loose from under her belt, then up again along her back, touching the deep lateral depression of her spine so that she shuddered, clinging to him. Stroking velvet skin stretched tight over rubber-hard flesh, finding the outline of her shoulder-blades, tracing them upwards then back to the armpits, silky-haired armpits that maddened him with excitement, quickly past them to her breasts, small breasts with soft tips hardening to his touch.

Now she struggled in earnest, her fists beating on his shoulders and her mouth breaking from his, and he stopped himself, dropped the hand away to encircle her waist. Holding her loosely within his arms.

'That was not good, Bruce. You get naughty very quick.' Her cheeks flamed with colour and her blue eyes had darkened to royal, her lips still wet from his, and her voice was unsteady, as unsteady as his when he answered.

'I'm sorry, Shermaine. I don't know what happened then, I did not mean to frighten you.'

'You are very strong, Bruce. But you do not frighten me, only a little bit. Your eyes frighten me when they look at me but do not see.'

You really made a hash of that one, he rebuked himself. Bruce Curry, the gentle sophisticated lover. Bruce Curry, the heavyweight, catch-as-catch-can, two-fisted rape artist.

He felt shaky, his legs wobbly, and there was something seriously wrong with his breathing.

'You do not wear a brassière,' he said without thinking, and immediately regretted it, but she chuckled, soft and husky.

'Do you think I need to, Bruce?'

'No, I didn't mean that,' he protested quickly, remembering the saucy tilt of that small breast. He was silent then, marshalling his words, trying to control his breathing, fighting down the madness of desire.

She studied his eyes. 'You can see again now – perhaps I will let you kiss me.'

'Please,' he said and she came back to him.

Gently now, Bruce me boy.

The door of the compartment flew back with a crash and they jumped apart. Wally Hendry stood on the threshold.

'Well, well, well.' His shrewd little eyes took it all in. 'That's nice!'

Shermaine was hurriedly tucking in her shirt tail and trying to smooth her hair at the same time.

Wally grinned. 'Nothing like it after a meal, I always say. Gets the digestion going.'

'What do you want?' snapped Bruce.

'There's no doubt what you want,' said Wally. 'Looks like you're getting it too.' He let his eyes travel up from Shermaine's waist, slowly over her body to her face.

Bruce stepped out into the corridor, pushing Hendry back and slammed the door.

'What do you want?' he repeated.

'Ruffy wants you to check his arrangements, but I'll tell him you're busy. We can put the attack off until tomorrow night if you like.'

Bruce scowled at him. 'Tell him I'll be with him in two minutes.'

Wally leaned against the door. 'Okay, I'll tell him.'

'What are you waiting for?'

'Nothing, just nothing,' grinned Wally.

'Well, bugger off then,' snarled Bruce.

'Okay, okay, don't get your knickers in a knot, Bucko.'

He sauntered off down the corridor.

Shermaine was standing where Bruce had left her, but with her eyes bright with tears of anger.

'He is a pig, that one. A filthy, filthy pig.'

'He's not worth worrying about.' Bruce tried to take her in his arms again, but she shrugged him off.

'I hate him. He makes everything seem so cheap, so dirty.'

'Nothing between you and I could be cheap and dirty,' said Bruce, and instantly her fury abated.

'I know, my Bruce. But he can make it seem that way.' They kissed gently.

'I must go. They want me.' For a second she clung to him.

'Be careful. Promise me you'll be careful.'

'I promise,' said Bruce and she let him go.

= 16 =

They left before dark, but the clouds had come up, during the afternoon and now they hung low over the forest, trapping the heat beneath them.

Bruce led, with Ruffy in the middle of the line and Hendry in the rear.

By the time they reached the level crossing the night was on them and it had started to rain, soft fat drops weeping like a woman exhausted with grief, warm rain in the darkness. And the darkness was complete. Once Bruce touched the top of his nose with his open palm, but he could not see his hand.

He used a staff to keep contact with the steel rail that ran beside him, tapping along it like a blind man, and at each step the gravel of the embankment crunched beneath his feet. The hand of the man behind him was on his shoulder, and he could sense the presence of the others that followed him like the body of a serpent, could hear the crunch of their steps and the muted squeak and rattle of their equipment. A man's voice was raised in protest and immediately quenched by Ruffy's deep rumble.

They crossed the road and the gradient changed beneath Bruce's feet so that he had to lean forward against it. They were starting up the Lufira hills.

I will rest them at the top, he thought, and from there we will be able to see the lights of the town.

The rain stopped abruptly, and the quietness after it was surprising. Now he could distinctly hear the breathing of the man behind him above the small sounds of their advance, and in the forest nearby a tree frog clinked as though steel pellets were being dropped into a crystal glass. It was a sound of great purity and beauty.

All Bruce's senses were enhanced to compensate for his lack of sight; his hearing; his sense of smell, so that he could catch the over-sweet perfume of a jungle-flower and the heaviness of decaying wet vegetation; his sense of touch, so that he could feel the raindrops on his face and the texture of his clothing against his body; then the other animal sense of danger told him with sickening, stomach-tripping certainty that there was something ahead of him in the darkness.

He stopped, and the man following him bumped into him throwing him off balance. All along the line there was a ripple of confusion and then silence. They all waited.

Bruce strained his hearing, half crouched with his rifle held ready. There was something there, he could almost feel it.

Please God, let them not have a machine-gun set up here, he thought; they could cut us into a shambles.

He turned cautiously and felt for the head of the man behind him, found it and drew it towards him until his mouth was an inch from the ear.

'Lie down very quietly. Tell the one behind you that he may pass it back.'

Bruce waited poised, listening and trying to see ahead into the utter blackness. He felt a gentle tap on his ankle from the gendarme at his feet. They were all down.

'All right, let's go take a look.' Bruce detached one of the grenades from his webbing belt. He drew the pin and dropped it into the breast pocket of his jacket. Then feeling for the crossties of the rails with each foot he started forward. Ten paces and he stopped again. Then he heard it, the tiny click of two pebbles just ahead of him. His throat closed so he could not breathe and his stomach was very heavy.

I'm right on top of them. My God, if they open up now –

Inch by inch he drew back the hand that held the grenade.

I'll have to lob short and get down fast. Five-second fuse – too long, they'll hear it and start shooting.

His hand was right back, he bent his legs and sank slowly on to his knees.

Here we go, he thought, and at that instant sheet lightning fluttered across the sky and Bruce could see. The hills were outlined black below the pale grey belly of the clouds, and the steel rails glinted in the sudden light. The forest was dark and high at each hand, and – a leopard, a big golden and black leopard, stood facing Bruce. In that brief second they stared at each other and then the night closed down again.

The leopard coughed explosively in the darkness, and Bruce tried desperately to bring his rifle up, but it was in his left hand and his other arm was held back ready to throw.

This time for sure, he thought, this time they lower the boom on you.

It was with a feeling of disbelief that he heard the leopard crash sideways into the undergrowth, and the scrambling rush of its run dwindle into the bush.

He subsided on to his backside, with the primed grenade in his hand, the hysterical laughter of relief coming up into his throat.

'You okay, boss?' Ruffy's voice lifted anxiously.

'It was a leopard,' answered Bruce, and was surprised at the squeakiness of his own voice.

There was a buzz of voices from the gendarmes and a rattle and clatter as they started to stand up. Someone laughed.

'That's enough noise,' snapped Bruce and climbed to his feet; he found the pin in his pocket and fitted it back into the grenade. He groped his way back, picked up the staff from where he had dropped it, and took his position at the head of the column again.

'Let's go,' he said.

His mouth was dry, his breathing too quick and he could feel the heat beneath the skin of his cheeks from the shock of the leopard.

I truly squirted myself full of adrenalin that time, Bruce grinned precariously in the dark, I'm as windy as hell. And before tonight is over I shall find fear again.

They moved on up the incline of the hills, a serpent of twenty-six men, and the tension was in all of them. Bruce could hear it in the footsteps behind him, feel it in the grip of the hand upon his shoulder and catch it in the occasional whiffs of body smell that came forward to him, the smell of nervous sweat like acid on metal.

Ahead of them the clouds that had crouched low upon the hills lifted slowly, and Bruce could see the silhouette of the crests. It was no longer utterly dark for there was a glow on the belly of the clouds now. A faint orange glow of reflected light that grew in strength, then faded and grew again. It puzzled Bruce for a while, and thinking about it gave his nerves a chance to settle. He plodded steadily on watching the fluctuations of the light. The ground tilted more sharply upwards beneath his feet and he leaned forward against it, slogging up the last half mile to the pass between the peaks, and at last came out on the top.

'Good God,' Bruce spoke aloud, for from here he could see the reason for that glow on the clouds. They were burning Fort Reprieve. The flames were well established in the buildings along the wharf, and as Bruce watched one of the roofs collapsed slowly in upon itself in a storm of sparks leaving the walls naked and erect, the wooden sills of the windows burning fiercely. The railway buildings were also on fire, and there was fire in the residential area beyond the Union Minière offices and the hotel. Quickly Bruce looked towards St Augustine's. It was dark, no flames there, no light even, and he felt a small lift of relief.

'Perhaps they have overlooked it, perhaps they're too busy looting,' and as he looked back at Port Reprieve, his mouth hardened. 'The senseless wanton bastards!' His anger started as he watched the meaningless destruction of the town.

'What can they possibly hope to gain by this?' There were new fires nearer the hotel. Bruce turned to the man behind him.

'We will rest here, but there will be no smoking and no talking.'

He heard the order passed back along the line and the careful sounds of equipment being lowered and men settling gratefully down upon the gravel embankment. Bruce unslung the case that contained his binoculars. He focused them on the burning town.

It was bright with the light of fires and through the glasses he could almost discern the features of the men in the streets. They moved in packs, heavily armed and restless. Many carried bottles and already the gait of some of them was unsteady. Bruce tried to estimate their numbers but it was impossible, men kept disappearing into buildings and reappearing, groups met and mingled and dispersed.

He dropped his glasses on to his chest to rest his eyes, and heard movement beside him in the dark. He glanced sideways. It was Ruffy, his bulk exaggerated by the load he carried; his rifle across one shoulder, on the other a full case of ammunition, and round his neck half a dozen haversacks full of grenades.

'Looks like they're having fun, hey, boss?'

'Fifth of November,' agreed Bruce. 'Aren't you going to take a breather?'

'Why not?' Ruffy set down the ammunition case and lowered his great backside on to it. 'Can you see any of those folks we left behind?' he asked.

Bruce lifted the glasses again and searched the area beyond the station buildings. It was darker there but he made out the square shape of the truck standing among the moving shadows.

'The truck's still there,' he murmured, 'but I can't see –'

At that moment the thatched roof of one of the houses exploded upwards in a column of flame, lighting the railway yard, and the truck stood out sharply.

'Yes,' said Bruce, 'I can see them now.' They were littered untidily across the yard, still lying where they had died. Small and fragile, unwanted as broken toys.

'Dead?' asked Ruffy.

'Dead,' confirmed Bruce.

'The women?'

'It's hard to tell.' Bruce strained his eyes. 'I don't think so.'

'No.' Ruffy's voice was soft and very deep. 'They wouldn't waste the women. I'd guess they've got them up at the hotel, taking it in turn to give them the business. Four women only – they won't last till morning. Those bastards down there could shag an elephant to death.' He spat thoughtfully into the gravel at his feet. 'What you going to do, boss?'

Bruce did not answer for a minute; he swung the glasses slowly back across the town. The field gun was still standing where he had last seen it, its barrel pointing accusingly up towards him. The transports were parked before the Union Minière offices; he could see the brilliant yellow and red paint and the Shell sign on the tanker. I hope it's full, Bruce thought, we'll need plenty of gasoline to get us back to Elisabethville.

'Ruffy, you'd better tell your boys to keep their bullets away from that tanker, otherwise it'll be a long walk home.'

'I'll tell them,' grunted Ruffy. 'But you know these mad Arabs – once they start shooting they don't stop till they're out of bullets, and they not too fussy where those bullets go.'

'We'll split into two groups when we get to the bottom of the hilll. You and I will take our lot through the edge of the swamp and cross to the far side of the town. Tell Lieutenant Hendry to come here.' Bruce waited until Wally came forward to join them, and when the three of them crouched together he went on.

'Hendry, I want you to spread your men out at the top of the main street – there in the darkness on this side of the station. Ruffy and I are going to cross the edge of the swamp to the causeway and lay out on the far side. For God's sake keep your boys quiet until Ruffy and I hit them – all we need is for your lot to start pooping off before we are ready and we won't need those lorries, we'll need coffins for the rest of our journey. Do you understand me?'

'Okay, okay, I know what I'm doing,' muttered Wally.

'I hope so,' said Bruce, and then went on. 'We'll hit them at four o'clock tomorrow morning, just before first light. Ruffy and I will go into the town and bomb the hotel – that's where most of them will be sleeping. The grenades should force the survivors into the street and as soon as that happens you can open up – but not before. Wait until you get them in the open. Is that clear?'

'Jesus,' growled Hendry. 'Do you think I'm a bloody fool, do you think I can't understand English?'

'The crossfire from the two groups should wipe most of them out.' Bruce ignored Wally's outburst. 'But we mustn't give the remainder a chance to organize. Hit them hard and as soon as they take cover again you must follow them in – close with them and finish them off. If we can't get it over in five to ten minutes then we are going to be in trouble. They outnumber us three to one, so we have to exploit the element of surprise to the full.'

'Exploit the element of surprise to the full!' mimicked Wally. 'What for all the fancy talk – why not just murder the bastards?'

Bruce grinned lightly in the dark. 'All right, murder the bastards,' he agreed. 'But do it as quickly as bloody possible.' He stood up and inclined the luminous dial of his wrist watch to catch the light. 'It's half past ten now – we'll move down on them. Come with me, Hendry, and we'll sort them into two groups.'

Bruce and Wally moved back along the line and talked to each man in turn.

'You will go with Lieutenant Hendry.'

'You come with me.'

Making sure that the two English-speaking corporals were with Wally, they took ten minutes to divide them into two units and to redistribute the haversacks of grenades. Then they moved on down the slope, still in Indian file.

'This is where we leave you, Hendry,' whispered Bruce. 'Don't go jumping the gun – wait until you hear my grenades.'

'Yeah, okay – I know all about it.'

'Good luck,' said Bruce.

'Your bum in a barrel, Captain Curry,' rejoined Wally and moved away.

'Come on, Ruffy.' Bruce led his men off the embankment down into the swamp. Almost immediately the mud and slime was knee deep and as they worked their way out to the right it rose to their waists and then to their armpits, sucking and gurgling sullenly as they stirred it with their passage, belching little evil-smelling gusts of swamp gas.

The mosquitoes closed round Bruce's face in a cloud so dense that he breathed them into his mouth and had to blink them out of his eyes. Sweat dribbled down from under his helmet and clung heavily in his eyebrows and the matted stems of the papyrus grass dragged at his feet. Their progress was tortuously slow and for fifteen minutes at a time Bruce lost sight of the lights of the village through the wall of papyrus; he steered by the glow of the fires and the occasional column of sparks.

It was an hour before they had half completed their circuit of Port Reprieve. Bruce stopped to rest, still waist deep in swamp ooze and with his arms aching numb from holding his rifle above his head.

'I could use a smoke now, boss,' grunted Ruffy.

'Me too,' answered Bruce, and he wiped his face on the sleeve of his jacket. The mosquito bites on his forehead and round his eyes burnt like fire.

'What a way to make a living,' he whispered.

'You go on living and you'll be one of the lucky ones,' answered Ruffy. 'My guess is there'll be some dying before tomorrow.'

But the fear of death was submerged by physical discomfort. Bruce had almost forgotten that they were going into battle; right now he was more worried that the leeches which had worked their way through the openings in his anklets and were busily boring into his lower legs might find their way up to his crotch. There was a lot to be said in favour of a zip fly, he decided.

'Let's get out of this,' he whispered. 'Come on, Ruffy. Tell your boys to keep it quiet.'

He worked in closer to the shore and the level fell to their knees once more. Progress was more noisy now as their legs broke the surface with each step and the papyrus rustled and brushed against them.

It was almost two o'clock when they reached the causeway. Bruce left his men crouched in the papyrus while he made a stealthy reconnaissance along the side of the concrete bridge, keeping in its shadow, moving doubled up until he came to dry land on the edge of the village. There were no sentries posted and except for the crackle of the flames the town was quiet, sunk into a drunken stupor, satiated. Bruce went back to call his men up.

He spread them in pairs along the outskirts of the village. He had learned very early in this campaign not to let his men act singly; nothing drains an African of courage more than to be on his own, especially in the night when the ghosts are on the walk-about.

To each couple he gave minute instructions.

'When you hear the grenades you shoot at anybody in the streets or at the windows. When the street is empty move in close beside that building there. Use your own grenades on every house and watch out for Lieutenant Hendry's men coming through from the other side. Do you understand?

'It is understood.'

'Shoot carefully. Aim each shot – not like you did at the road bridge, and in the name of God do not hit the gasoline tanker. We need that to get us home.'

Now it was three o'clock, Bruce saw by the luminous figures on his wrist watch. Eight hours since they had left the train, and twenty-two hours since Bruce had last slept. But he was not tired, although his body ached and there was that gritty feeling under his eyelids, yet his mind was clear and bright as a flame.

He lay beside Ruffy under a low bush on the outskirts of Port Reprieve and the night wind drifted the smoke from the burning town down upon them, and Bruce was not tired. For I am going to another rendezvous with fear.

Fear is a woman, he thought, with all the myriad faces and voices of a woman. Because she is a woman and because I am a man I must keep going back to her. Only this time the appointment is one that I cannot avoid, this time I am not deliberately seeking her out.

I know she is evil, I know that after I have possessed her I will feel sick and shaken. I will say, 'That was the last time, never again.'

But just as certainly I know I will go back to her again, hating her, dreading her, but also needing her.

I have gone to find her on a mountain – on Dutoits Kloof Frontal, on Turret Towers, on the Wailing Wall, and the Devil's Tooth.

And she was there, dressed in a flowing robe of rock, a robe that fell sheer two thousand feet to the scree slope below. And she shrieked with the voice of the wind along the exposed face. Then her voice was soft, tinkling like cooling glass in the Berg ice underfoot, whispering like nylon rope running free, grating as the rotten rock moved in my hand.

I have followed her into the Jessie bush on the banks of the Sabi and the Luangwa, and she was there, waiting, wounded, in a robe of buffalo hide with the blood dripping from her mouth. And her smell was the sour-acid smell of my own sweat, and her taste was like rotten tomatoes in the back of my throat.

I have looked for her beyond the reef in the deep water with the demand valve of a scuba repeating my breathing with metallic hoarseness. And she was there with rows of white teeth in the semicircle of her mouth, a tall fin on her back, dressed this time in shagreen, and her touch was cold as the ocean, and her taste was salt and the taint of dying things.

I have looked for her on the highway with my foot pressed to the floorboards and she was there with her cold arm draped round my shoulders, her voice the whine of rubber on tarmac and the throaty hum of the motor.

With Colin Butler at the helm (a man who treated fear not as a lover, but with tolerant contempt as though she were his little sister) I went to find her in a small boat. She was dressed in green with plumes of spray and she wore a necklace of sharp black rock. And her voice was the roar of water breaking on water.

We met in darkness at the road bridge and her eyes glinted like bayonets. But that was an enforced meeting not of my choosing, as tonight will be.

I hate her, he thought, but she is a woman and I am a man.

Bruce lifted his arm and turned his wrist to catch the light of the fires.

'Fifteen minutes to four, Ruffy. Let's go and take a look.'

'That's a good idea, boss.' Ruffy grinned with a show of white teeth in the darkness.

'Are you afraid, Ruffy?' he asked suddenly, wanting to know, for his own heart beat like a war drum and there was no saliva in his mouth.

'Boss, some questions you don't ask a man.' Ruffy rose slowly into a crouch. 'Let's go take a look around.'

So they moved quickly together into the town, along the street, hugging the hedges and the buildings, trying to keep in shadow, their eyes moving everywhere, breathing quick and shallow, nerves screwed up tight until they reached the hotel.

There were no lights in the windows and it seemed deserted until Bruce made out the untidy mass of humanity strewn in sleep upon the front verandah.

'How many there, Ruffy?'

'Dunno – perhaps ten, fifteen.' Ruffy breathed an answer. 'Rest of them will be inside.'

'Where are the women – be careful of them.'

'They're dead long ago, you can believe me.'

'All right then, let's get round the back.' Bruce took a deep breath and then moved quickly across the twenty yards of open firelit street to the corner of the hotel. He stopped in the shadow and felt Ruffy close beside him. 'I want to take a look into the main lounge, my guess is that most of them will be in there,' he whispered.

'There's only four bedrooms,' agreed Ruffy. 'Say the officers upstairs and the rest in the lounge.'

Now Bruce moved quickly round the corner and stumbled over something soft. He felt it move against his foot.

'Ruffy!' he whispered urgently as he teetered off balance. He had trodden on a man, a man sleeping in the dust beside the wall. He could see the firelight on his bare torso and the glint of the bottle clutched in one outflung hand. The man sat up, muttering, and then began to cough, hacking painfully, swearing as he wiped his mouth with his free hand. Bruce regained his balance and swung his rifle up to use the bayonet, but Ruffy was quicker. He put one foot on the man's chest and trod him flat on to his back once more, then standing over him he used his bayoneted rifle the way a gardener uses a spade to lift potatoes, leaning his weight on it suddenly and the blade vanished into the man's throat.

The body stiffened convulsively, legs thrust out straight and arms rigid, there was a puffing of breath from the severed windpipe and then the slow melting relaxation of death. Still with his foot on the chest, Ruffy withdrew the bayonet and stepped over the corpse.

That was very close, thought Bruce, stifling the qualm of horror he felt at the next execution. The man's eyes were fixed open in almost comic surprise, the bottle still in his hand, his chest bare, the front of his trousers unbuttoned and stiff with dried blood – not his blood, guessed Bruce angrily.

They moved on past the kitchens. Bruce looked in and saw that they were empty with the white enamel tiles reflecting the vague light and piles of used plates and pots cluttering the tables and the sink. Then they reached the bar-room and there was a hurricane lamp on the counter diffusing a yellow glow; the stench of liquor poured out through the half-open window, the shelves were bare of bottles and men were asleep upon the counter, men lay curled together upon the floor like a pack of dogs, broken glass and rifles and shattered furniture littered about them. Someone had vomited out of the window leaving a yellow streak down the whitewashed wall.

'Stand here,' breathed Bruce into Ruffy's ear. 'I will go round to the front where I can throw on to the verandah and also into the lounge. Wait until you hear my first grenade blow.'

Ruffy nodded and leaned his rifle against the wall; he took a grenade in each fist and pulled the pins.

Bruce slipped quickly round the corner and along the side wall. He reached the windows of the lounge. They were tightly closed and he peered in over the sill. A little of the light from the lamp in the bar-room came through the open doors and showed up the interior. Here again there were men covering the floor and piled upon the sofas along the far wall. Twenty of them at least, he estimated by the volume of their snoring, and he grinned without humour. My God, what a shambles it is going to be.

Then something at the foot of the stairs caught his eye and the grin on his face became fixed, baring his teeth and narrowing his eyes to slits. It was the mound of nude flesh formed by the bodies of the four women; they had been discarded once they had served their purpose, dragged to one side to clear the floor for sleeping space, lying upon each other in a jumble of naked arms and legs and cascading hair.

No mercy now, thought Bruce with hatred replacing his fear as he looked at the women and saw by the attitudes in which they lay that there was no life left in them. *No mercy now*!

He slung his rifle over his left shoulder and filled his hand with grenades, pulled the pins and moved quickly to the corner so that he could look down the length of the covered verandah. He rolled both grenades down among the sleeping figures, hearing clearly the click of the priming and the metallic rattle against the concrete floor. Quickly he ducked back to the lounge window, snatching two more grenades from his haversack and pulling the pins, he hurled them through the closed windows. The crash of breaking glass blended with the double thunder of the explosions on the verandah.

Someone shouted in the room, a cry of surprise and alarm, then the windows above Bruce blew outwards, showering him with broken glass and the noise half deafening him as he tossed two more grenades through the gaping hole of the window. They were screaming and groaning in the lounge. Ruffy's grenades roared in the bar-room bursting through the double doors, then Bruce's grenades snuffed out the sounds of life in the lounge with violent white flame and thunder. Bruce tossed in two more grenades and ran back to the corner of the verandah unslinging his rifle.

A man with his hands over his eyes and blood streaming through his fingers fell over the low verandah wall and crawled to his knees. Bruce shot him from so close that the shaft of gun flame joined the muzzle of his rifle and the man's chest, punching him over backwards, throwing him spreadeagled on to the earth.

He looked beyond and saw two more in the road, but before he could raise his rifle the fire from his own gendarmes found them, knocking them down amid spurts of dust.

Bruce hurdled the verandah wall. He shouted, a sound without form or meaning. Exulting, unafraid, eager to get into the building, to get amongst them. He stumbled over the dead men on the verandah. A burst of gunfire from down the street rushed past him, so close he could feel the wind on his face. Fire from his own men.

'You stupid bastards!' Shouting without anger, without fear, with only the need to shout, he burst into the lounge through the main doors. It was half dark but he could see through the darkness and the haze of plaster dust.

A man on the stairs, the bloom of gunfire and the sting of the bullet across Bruce's thigh, fire in return, without aiming from the hip, miss and the man gone up and round the head of the stairs, yelling as he ran.

A grenade in Bruce's right hand, throw it high, watch it hit the wall and bounce sideways round the angle of the stairs. The explosion shocking in the confined space and the flash of it lighting the building and outlining the body of the man as it blew him back into the lounge, lifting him clear of the banisters, shredded and broken by the blast, falling heavily into the room below.

Up the stairs three at a time and into the bedroom passage, another man naked and bewildered staggering through a doorway still drunk or half asleep, chop him down with a single shot in the stomach, jump over him and throw a grenade through the glass skylight of the second bedroom, another through the third and kick open the door of the last room in the bellow and flash of the explosions.

A man was waiting for Bruce across the room with a pistol in his hand, and both of them fired simultaneously, the clang of the bullet glancing off the steel of Bruce's helmet, jerking his head back savagely, throwing him sideways against the wall, but he fired again, rapid fire, hitting with every bullet, so that the man seemed to dance, a jerky grotesque twitching jig, pinned against the far wall by the bullets.

On his knees now Bruce was stunned, ears singing like a million mad mosquitoes, hands clumsy and slow on the reload, back on his feet, legs rubbery but the loaded rifle in his hands making a man of him.

Out into the passage, another one right on top of him, a vast dark shape in the darkness – kill him! kill him!

'Don't shoot, boss!'

Ruffy, thank God, Ruffy.

'Are there any more?'

'All finished, boss – you cleaned them out good.'

'How many?' Bruce shouted above the singing in his ears.

'Forty or so. Jesus, what a mess! There's blood all over the place. Those grenades –'

'There must be more.'

'Yes, but not in here, boss. Let's go and give the boys outside a hand.'

They ran back down the passage, down the stairs, and the floor of the lounge was sodden and sticky, dead men everywhere; it smelt like an abattoir – blood and ripped bowels. One still on his hands and knees, creepy-crawling towards the door. Ruffy shot him twice, flattening him.

'Not the front door, boss. Our boys will get you for sure. Go out the window.'

Bruce dived through the window head first, rolled over behind the cover of the verandah wall and came to his knees in one movement. He felt strong and invulnerable. Ruffy was beside him.

'Here come our boys,' said Ruffy, and Bruce could see them coming down the street, running forward in short bursts, stopping to fire, to throw a grenade, then coming again.

'And there are Lieutenant Hendry's lot.' From the opposite direction but with the same dodging, checking run, Bruce could see Wally with them. He was holding his rifle across his hip when he fired, his whole body shaking with the juddering of the gun.

Like a bird rising in front of the beaters one of the *shufta* broke from the cover of the grocery store and ran into the street unarmed, his head down and his arms pumping in time with his legs. Bruce was close enough to see the panic in his face. He seemed to be moving in slow motion, and the flames lit him harshly, throwing a distorted shadow in front of him. When the bullets hit him he stayed on his feet, staggering in a circle, thrashing at the air with his hands as though he were beating off a swarm of bees, the bullets slapping loudly against his body and lifting little puffs of dust from his clothing. Beside Bruce, Ruffy aimed carefully and shot him in the head, ending it.

'There must be more,' protested Bruce. 'Where are they hiding?'

'In the offices, I'd say.'

And Bruce turned his attention quickly to the block of Union Minière offices. The windows were in darkness and as he stared he thought he saw movement. He glanced quickly back at Wally's men and saw that four of them had bunched up close behind Wally as they ran.

'Hendry, watch out!' he shouted with all his strength. 'On your right, from the offices!'

But it was too late, gunfire sparkled in the dark windows and the little group of running men disintegrated.

Bruce and Ruffy fired together, raking the windows, emptying their automatic rifles into them. As he reloaded Bruce glanced back at where Wally's men had been hit. With disbelief he saw that Wally was the only one still on his feet; crossing the road, sprinting through an area of bullet-churned earth towards them, he reached the verandah and fell over the low wall.

'Are you wounded?' Bruce asked.

'Not a touch – those bastards couldn't shoot their way out of a French letter,' Wally shouted defiantly, and his voice carried clearly in the sudden hush. He snatched the empty magazine off the bottom of his rifle, threw it aside and clipped on a fresh one. 'Move over,' he growled, 'let me get a crack at those bastards.' He lifted his rifle and rested the stock on top of the wall, knelt behind it, cuddled the butt into his shoulder and began firing short bursts into the windows of the office block.

'This is what I was afraid of.' Bruce lifted his voice above the clamour of the guns.

'Now we've got a pocket of resistance right in the centre of the town. There must be fifteen or twenty of them in there – it might take us days to winkle them out.' He cast a longing look at the canvas-covered trucks lined up outside the station yard. 'They can cover the lorries from here, and as soon as they guess what we're after, as soon as we try and move them, they'll knock out that tanker and destroy the trucks.'

The firelight flickered on the shiny yellow and red paint of the tanker. It looked so big and vulnerable standing there in the open. It needed just one bullet out of the many hundred that had already been fired to end its charmed existence.

We've got to rush them now, he decided. Beyond the office block the remains of Wally's group had taken cover and were keeping up a heated fire. Bruce's group straggled up to the hotel and found positions at the windows.

'Ruffy.' Bruce caught him by the shoulder. 'We'll take four men with us and go round the back of the offices. From that building there we've got only twenty yards or so of open ground to cover. Once we get up against the wall they won't be able to touch us and we can toss grenades in amongst them.'

'That twenty yards looks like twenty miles from here,' rumbled Ruffy, but picked up his sack of grenades and crawled back from the verandah wall.

'Go and pick four men to come with us,' ordered Bruce.

'Okay, boss. We'll wait for you in the kitchen.'

'Hendry. Listen to me.'

'Yeah. What is it?'

'When I reach that corner over there I'll give you a wave. We'll be ready to go then. I want you to give us all the cover you can – keep their heads down.'

'Okay,' agreed Wally and fired another short burst.

'Try not to hit us when we close in.'

Wally turned to look at Bruce and he grinned wickedly.

'Mistakes happen, you know. I can't promise anything. You'd look real grand in my sights.'

'Don't joke,' said Bruce.

'Who's joking?' grinned Wally and Bruce left him. He found Ruffy and four gendarmes waiting in the kitchen.

'Come on,' he said and led them out across the kitchen yard, down the sanitary lane with the steel doors for the buckets behind the outhouses and the smell of them thick and fetid, round the corner and across the road to the buildings beyond the office block. They stopped there and crowded together, as though to draw courage and comfort from each other. Bruce measured the distance with his eye.

'It's not far,' he announced.

'Depends on how you look at it,' grunted Ruffy.

'There are only two windows opening out on to this side.'

'Two's enough – how many do you want?'

'Remember, Ruffy, you can only die once.'

'Once is enough,' said Ruffy. 'Let's cut out the talking, boss. Too much talk gets you in the guts.'

Bruce moved across to the corner of the building out of the shadows. He waved towards the hotel and imagined that he saw an acknowledgement from the end of the verandah.

'All together,' he said, sucked in a deep breath, held it a second and then launched himself into the open. He felt small now, no longer brave and invulnerable, and his legs moved so slowly that he seemed to be standing still. The black windows gaped at him.

Now, he thought, now you die.

Where, he thought, not in the stomach, please God, not in the stomach.

And his legs moved stiffly under him, carrying him half way across.

Only ten more paces, he thought, one more river, just one more river to Jordan. But not in the stomach, please God, not in my stomach. And his flesh cringed in anticipation, his stomach drawn in hard as he ran.

Suddenly the black windows were brightly lit, bright white oblongs in the dark buildings, and the glass sprayed out of them like untidy spittle from an old man's mouth. Then they were dark again, dark with smoke billowing from them and the memory of the explosion echoing in his ears.

'A grenade!' Bruce was bewildered. 'Someone let off a grenade in there!'

He reached the back door without stopping and it burst open before his rush. He was into the room, shooting, coughing in the fumes, firing wildly at the small movements of dying men.

In the half darkness something long and white lay against the far wall. A body, a white man's naked body. He crossed to it and looked down.

'André,' he said, 'it's André – he threw the grenade.' And he knelt beside him.

= 17 =

Curled naked upon the concrete floor, André was alive but dying as the haemorrhage within him leaked his life away. His mind was alive and he heard the crump, crump of Bruce's grenades, then the gunfire in the street, and the sound of running men. The shouts in the night and then the guns very close, they were in the room in which he lay.

He opened his eyes. There were men at each of the windows, crouched below the sills, and the room was thick with cordite fumes and the clamour of the guns as they fired out into the night.

André was cold, the coldness was all through him. Even his hands drawn up against his chest were cold and heavy. His stomach only was warm, warm and immensely bloated.

It was an effort to think, for his mind also was cold and the noise of the guns confused him.

He watched the men at the windows with a detached disinterest, and slowly his body lost its weight. He seemed to float clear of the floor and look down upon the room from the roof. His eyelids sagged and he dragged them up again, and struggled down towards his own body.

There was suddenly a rushing sound in the room and plaster sprayed from the wall above André's head, filling the air with pale floating dust. One of the men at the windows fell backwards, his weapon ringing loudly on the floor as it dropped from his hands; he flopped over twice and lay still, face down within arm's length of André.

Ponderously André's mind analysed the sights his eyes were recording. Someone was firing on the building from outside. The man beside him was dead and from his head wound the blood spread slowly across the floor towards him. André closed his eyes again, he was very tired and very cold.

There was a lull in the sound of gunfire, one of those freak silences in the midst of battle. And in the lull André heard a voice far off, shouting. He could not hear the words but he recognized the voice and his eyelids flew open. There was an excitement in him, a new force, for it was Wally's voice he had heard.

He moved slightly, clenching his hands and his brain started to sing.

Wally has come back for me – he has come to save me. He rolled his head slowly, painfully, and the blood gurgled in his stomach.

I must help him, I must not let him endanger himself – these men are trying to kill him. I must stop them. I mustn't let them kill Wally.

And then he saw the grenades hanging on the belt of the man that lay beside him. He fastened his eyes on the round polished metal bulbs and he began to pray silently.

'Hail, Mary, full of grace, the Lord is with thee.'

He moved again, straightening his body.

'Blessed art thou among women, and blessed is the fruit of thy womb, Jesus.'

His hand crept out into the pool of blood, and the sound of the guns filled his head so he could not hear himself pray. Walking on its fingers, his hand crawled through the blood as slowly as a fly through a saucer of treacle.

'Blessed is the fruit of thy womb, Jesus. Oh, Jesus. Pray for me now, and at the hour. Full of grace.'

He touched the smooth, deeply segmented steel of the grenade.

'Us sinners – at the day, at the hour. This day – this day our daily bread.'

He fumbled at the clip, fingers stiff and cold.

'Hallowed be thy – Hallowed be thy —'

The clip clicked open and he held the grenade, curling his fingers round it.

'Hail, Mary, full of grace.'

He drew the grenade to him and held it with both hands against his chest. He lifted it to his mouth and took the pin between his teeth.

'Pray for us sinners,' he whispered, and pulled the pin.

'Now and at the hour of our death.'

And he tried to throw it. It rolled from his hand and bumped across the floor. The firing handle flew off and rattled against the wall. General Moses turned from the window and saw it – his lips opened and his spectacles glinted above the rose-pink cave of his mouth. The grenade lay at his feet. Then everything was gone in the flash and roar of the explosion.

Afterwards in the acrid swirl of fumes, in the patter of falling plaster, in the tinkle and crunch of broken glass, in the small scrabbling noises and the murmur and moan of dying men, André was still alive. The body of the man beside him had shielded his head and chest from the full force of the blast.

There was still enough life in him to recognize Bruce Curry's face close to his, though he could not feel the hands that touched him.

'André!' said Bruce. 'It's André – he threw the grenade!'

'Tell him —' whispered André and stopped.

'Yes, André —?' said Bruce.

'I didn't, this day and at the hour. I had to – not this time.' He could feel it going out in him like a candle in a high wind and he tried to cup his hands around it.

'What is it, André. What must I tell him?' Bruce's voice, but so far away.

'Because of him – this time – not of it, I didn't.' He stopped again and gathered all of what was left. His lips quivered as he tried so hard to say it.

'Like a man!' he whispered and the candle went out.

'Yes,' said Bruce softly, holding him. 'This time like a man.'

He lowered André gently until his head touched the floor again; then he stood upright and looked down at the terribly mutilated body. He felt empty inside, a hollowness, the same feeling as after love.

He moved across to the desk near the far wall. Outside the gunfire dwindled like half-hearted applause, flared up again and then ceased. Around him Ruffy and the four gendarmes moved excitedly, inspecting the dead, exclaiming, laughing and awkward embarrassed laughter of men freshly released from mortal danger.

Loosening the chin straps of his helmet with slow steady fingers, Bruce stared across the room at André's body.

'Yes,' he whispered again. 'This time like a man. All the other times are wiped out, the score is levelled.'

His cigarettes were damp from the swamp, but he took one from the centre of the pack and straightened it with calm nerveless fingers. He found his lighter and flicked it open – then, without warning, his hands started to shake. The flame of the lighter fluttered and he had to hold it steady with both hands. There was blood on his hands, new sticky blood. He snapped the lighter closed and breathed in the smoke. It tasted bitter and the saliva flooded into his mouth. He swallowed it down, nausea in his stomach, and his breathing quickened.

It was not like this before, he remembered, even that night at the road bridge when they broke through on the flank and we met them with bayonets in the dark. Before it had no meaning, but now I can feel again. Once more I'm alive.

Suddenly he had to be alone; he stood up.

'Ruffy.'

'Yes, boss?'

'Clean up here. Get blankets from the hotel for de Surrier and the women, also those men down in the station yard' It was someone else speaking; he could hear the voice as though it were a long way off.

'You okay, boss?'

'Yes.'

'Your head?'

Bruce lifted his hand and touched the long dent in his helmet.

'It's nothing,' he said.

'Your leg?'

'Just a touch, get on with it.'

'Okay, boss. What shall we do with these others?'

'Throw them in the river,' said Bruce and walked out into the street. Hendry and his gendarmes were still on the verandah of the hotel, but they had started on the corpses there, using their bayonets like butchers' knives, taking the ears, laughing also the strained nervous laughter.

Bruce crossed the street to the station yard. The dawn was coming, drawing out across the sky like a sheet of steel rolled from the mill, purple and lilac at first, then red as it spread above the forest.

The Ford Ranchero stood on the station platform where he had left it. He opened the door, slid in behind the wheel, and watched the dawn become day.

= 18 =

'Captain, the sergeant major asks you to come. There is something he wants to show you.'

Bruce lifted his head from where it was resting on the steering wheel. He had not heard the gendarme approach.

'I'll come,' he said, picked up his helmet and his rifle from the seat beside him and followed the man back to the office block.

His gendarmes were loading a dead man into one of the trucks, swinging him by his arms and legs.

'Un, deux, trois,' and a shout of laughter as the limp body flew over the tailboard on to the gruesome pile already there.

Sergeant Jacque came out of the office dragging a man by his heels. The head bumped loosely down the steps and there was a wet brown drag mark left on the cement verandah.

'Like pork,' Jacque called cheerily. The corpse was that of a small grey-headed man, skinny, with the marks of spectacles on the bridge of his nose and a double row of decorations on his tunic. Bruce noted that one of them was the purple and white ribbon of the military cross – strange loot for the Congo. Jacque dropped the man's heels, drew his bayonet and stooped over the man. He took one of the ears that lay flat against the grizzled skull, pulled it forward and freed it with a single stroke of the knife. The opened flesh was pink with the dark hole of the eardrum in the centre.

Bruce walked on into the office and his nostrils flared at the abattoir stench.

'Have a look at this lot, boss.' Ruffy stood by the desk.

'Enough to buy you a ranch in Hyde Park,' grinned Hendry beside him. In his hand he held a pencil. Threaded on to it like a kebab were a dozen human ears.

'Yes,' said Bruce as he looked at the pile of industrial and gem diamonds on the blotter. 'I know about those. Better count them, Ruffy, then put them back in the bags.'

'You're not going to turn them in?' protested Hendry. 'Jesus, if we share this lot three ways – you, Ruffy and I – there's enough to make us all rich.'

'Or put us against a wall,' said Bruce grimly. 'What makes you think the gentlemen in Elisabethville don't know about them?' He turned his attention back to Ruffy. 'Count them and pack them. You're in charge of them. Don't lose any.'

Bruce looked across the room at the blanket-wrapped bundle that was André de Surrier.

'Have you detailed a burial squad?'

'Yes, boss. Six of the boys are out back digging.'

'Good,' Bruce nodded. 'Hendry, come with me. We'll go and have a look at the trucks.'

Half an hour later Bruce closed the bonnet of the last vehicle.'This is the only one that won't run. The carburettor's smashed. We'll take the tyres off it for spares.' He wiped his greasy hands on the sides of his trousers. 'Thank God, the tanker is untouched. We've got six hundred gallons there, more than enough for the return trip.'

'You going to take the Ford?' asked Hendry,.

'Yes, it may come in useful.'

'And it will be more comfortable for you and your little French thing.' Heavy sarcasm in Hendry's voice.

'That's right,' Bruce answered evenly. 'Can you drive?'

'What you think? You think I'm a bloody fool?'

'Everyone is always trying to get at you, aren't they? You can't trust anyone, can you?' Bruce asked softly.

'You're so bloody right!' agreed Hendry.

Bruce changed the subject. 'André had a message for you before he died.'

'Old doll boy!'

'He threw that grenade. Did you know that?'

'Yeah. I knew it.'

'Don't you want to hear what he said?'

'Once a queer, always a queer, and the only good queer is a dead queer.'

'All right.' Bruce frowned. 'Get a couple of men to help you. Fill the trucks with gas. We've wasted enough time already.'

They buried their dead in a communal grave, packing them in quickly and covering them just as quickly. Then they stood embarrassed and silent round the mound.

'You going to say anything, boss?' Ruffy asked, and they all looked at Bruce.

'No.' Bruce turned away and started for the trucks.

What the hell can you say, he thought angrily. Death is not someone to make conversation with. All you can say is, 'These were men; weak and strong, evil and good, and a lot in between. But now they're dead – like pork.'

He looked back over his shoulder.

'All right, let's move out.'

The convoy ground slowly over the causeway. Bruce led in the Ford and the air blowing in through the shattered windscreen was too humid and steamy to give relief from the rising heat.

The sun stood high above the forest as they passed the turnoff to the mission.

Bruce looked along it, and he wanted to signal the convoy to continue while he went up to St Augustine's. He wanted to see Mike Haig and Father Ignatius, make sure that they were safe.

Then he put aside the temptation. If there is more horror up there at St Augustine's, if the *shufta* have found them and there are raped women and dead men there, then there is nothing I can do and I don't want to know about it.

It is better to believe that they are safely hidden in the jungle. It is better to believe that out of all this will remain something good.

He led the convoy resolutely past the turn-off and over the hills towards the level crossing.

Suddenly another idea came to him and he thought about it, turning it over with pleasure.

Four men came to Port Reprieve, men without hope, men abandoned by God.

And they learned that it was not too late, perhaps it is never too late.

For one of them found the strength to die like a man, although he had lived his whole life with weakness.

Another rediscovered the self-respect he had lost along the way, and with it the chance to start again.

The third found – he hesitated – yes, the third found love.

And the fourth? Bruce's smile faded as he thought of Wally Hendry. It was a neat little parable, except for Wally Hendry. What had he found? A dozen human ears threaded on a pencil?

= 19 =

'Can't you get up enough steam to move us back to the crossing – only a few miles.'

'I am desolate, m'sieur. She will not hold even a belch, to say nothing of a head of steam.' The engine driver spread his pudgy little hands in a gesture of helplessness. Bruce studied the rent in the boiler. The metal was torn open like the petals of a flower. He knew it had been a forlorn request.

'Very well. Thank you.' He turned to Ruffy. 'We'll have to carry everything back to the convoy. Another day wasted.'

'It's a long walk,' Ruffy agreed. 'Better get started.'

'How much food have we?'

'Not too much. We've been feeding a lot of extra mouths, and we sent a lot out to the mission.'

'How much?'

'About two more days.'

'That should get us to Elisabethville.'

'Boss, you want to carry everything to the lorries? Searchlights, ammunition, blankets – all of it?'

Bruce paused for a moment. 'I think so. We may need it.'

'It's going to take the rest of the day.'

'Yes,' agreed Bruce. Ruffy walked back along the train but Bruce called after him.

'Ruffy!'

'Boss?'

'Don't forget the beer.'

Ruffy's black moon of a face split laterally into a grin.

'You think we should take it?'

'Why not?' Bruce laughed.

'Man, you talked me right into it!'

And the night was almost on them before the last of the equipment had been carried back from the abandoned train to the convoy and loaded into the trucks.

Time is a slippery thing, even more so than wealth. No bank vault can hold it for you, this precious stuff which we spend in such prodigal fashion on the trivialities. By the time we have slept and eaten and moved from one place to the next there is such a small percentage left for the real business of living.

Bruce felt futile resentment as he always did when he thought about it. And if you discount the time spent at an office desk, then how much is there left? Half of one day a week, that's how much the average man lives! That's how far short of our potential is the actuality of existence.

Take it further than that: we are capable of using only a fraction of our physical and mental strength. Only under hypnosis are we able to exert more than a tenth of what is in us. So divide that half of one day a week by ten, and the rest is waste! Sickening waste!

'Ruffy, have you detailed sentries for tonight?' Bruce barked at him.

'Not yet. I was just –'

'Well, do it, and do it quickly.'

Ruffy looked at Bruce in speculation and through his anger Bruce felt a qualm of regret that he had selected that mountain of energy on which to vent his frustration.

'Where the hell is Hendry?' he snapped.

Without speaking Ruffy pointed to a group of men round one of the trucks at the rear of the convoy and Bruce left him.

Suddenly consumed with impatience Bruce fell upon his men. Shouting at them, scattering them to a dozen different tasks. He walked along the convoy making sure that his instructions were being carried out to the letter; checking the siting of the Brens and the searchlights, making sure that the single small cooking fire was screened from Baluba eyes, stopping to watch the refuelling of the trucks and the running maintenance he had ordered. Men avoided catching his eye and bent to their tasks with studied application. There were no raised voices or sounds of laughter in the camp.

Again Bruce had decided against a night journey. The temptation itched within him, but the exhaustion of those gendarmes who had not slept since the previous morning and the danger of travelling in the dark he could not ignore.

'We'll leave as soon as it's light tomorrow,' Bruce told Ruffy.

'Okay, boss,' Ruffy nodded, and then soothingly, 'you're tired. Food's nearly ready, then you get some sleep.'

Bruce glared at him, opening his mouth to snarl a retort, and then closed it again. He turned and strode out of the camp into the forest.

He found a fallen log, sat down and lit a cigarette. It was dark now and there were only a few stars among the rain clouds that blackened the sky. He could hear the faint sounds from the camp but there were no lights – the way he had ordered it.

The fact that his anger had no focal point inflamed it rather than quenched it. It ranged restlessly until at last it found a target – himself.

He recognized the brooding undirected depression that was descending upon him. It was a thing he had not experienced for a long time, nearly two years. Not since the wreck of his marriage and the loss of his children. Not since he had stifled all emotion and trained himself not to participate in the life around him.

But now his barrier was gone, there was no sheltered harbour from the storm surf and he would have to ride it out. Furl all canvas and rig a sea anchor.

The anger was gone now. At least anger had heat but this other thing was cold; icy waves of it broke over him, and he was small and insignificant in the grip of it.

His mind turned to his children and the loneliness howled round him like a winter wind from the south. He closed his eyes and pressed his fingers against the lids. Their faces formed in the eye of his mind.

Christine with pink fat legs under her frilly skirt, and the face of a thoughtful cherub below soft hair cropped like a page boy.

'I love you best of all,' said with much seriousness, holding his face with small hands only a little sticky with ice cream.

Simon, a miniature reproduction of Bruce even to the nose. Scabs on the knees and dirt on the face. No demonstrations of affection from him, but in its place something much better, a companionship far beyond his six years. Long discussions on everything from religion, 'Why didn't Jesus used to shave?' to politics, 'When are you gong to be prime minister, Dad?'

And the loneliness was a tangible thing now, like the coils of a reptile squeezing his chest. Bruce ground out the cigarette beneath his heel and tried to find refuge in his hatred for the woman who had been his wife. The woman who had taken them from him.

But his hatred was a cold thing also, dead ash with a stale taste. For he knew that the blame was not all hers. It was another of his failures; perhaps if I had tried harder, perhaps if I had left some of the cruel things unsaid, perhaps – yes, it might have been, and perhaps and maybe. But it was not. It was over and finished and now I am alone. There is no worse condition; no state beyond loneliness. It is the waste land and the desolation.

Something moved near him in the night, a soft rustle of grass, a presence felt rather than seen. And Bruce stiffened. His right hand closed over his rifle. He brought it up slowly, his eyes straining into the darkness.

The movement again, closer now. A twig popped underfoot. Bruce slowly trained his rifle round to cover it, pressure on the trigger and his thumb on the safety. Stupid to have wandered away from the camp; asking for it, and now he had got it. Baluba tribesmen! He could see the figure now in the dimness of starlight, stealthily moving across his front. How many of them, he wondered. If I hit this one, there could be a dozen others with him. Have to take a chance. One quick burst and then run for it. A hundred yards to the camp, about an even chance. The figure was stationary now, standing listening. Bruce could see the outline of the head – no helmet, can't be one of us. He raised the rifle and pointed it. Too dark to see the sights, but at that range he couldn't miss. Bruce drew his breath softly, filling his lungs, ready to shoot and run.

'Bruce?' Shermaine's voice, frightened, almost a whisper. He threw up the rifle barrel. God, that was close. He had nearly killed her.

'Yes, I'm here.' His own voice was scratchy with the shock of realization.

'Oh, there you are.'

'What the hell are you doing out of the camp?' he demanded furiously as anger replaced his shock.

'I'm sorry, Bruce, I came to see if you were all right. You were gone such a long time.'

'Well, get back to the camp, and don't try any more tricks like that.'

There was a long silence, and then she spoke softly, unable to keep the hurt out of her tone.

'I brought you something to eat. I thought you'd be hungry. I'm sorry if I did wrong.'

She came to him, stooped and placed something on the ground in front of him. Then she turned and was gone.

'Shermaine.' He wanted her back, but the only reply was the fading rustle of the grass and then silence. He was alone again.

He picked up the plate of food.

You fool, he thought. You stupid, ignorant, thoughtless fool. You'll lose her, and you'll have deserved it. You deserve everything you've had, and more.

You never learn, do you, Curry? You never learn that there is a penalty for selfishness and for thoughtlessness.

He looked down at the plate in his hands. Bully beef and sliced onion, bread and cheese.

Yes, I have learned, he answered himself with sudden determination. I will not spoil this, this thing that is between this girl and me. That was the last time; now I am a man I will put away childish things, like temper and self-pity.

He ate the food, suddenly aware of his hunger. He ate quickly, wolfing it. Then he stood up and walked back to the camp.

A sentry challenged him on the perimeter and Bruce answered with alacrity. At night his gendarmes were very quick on the trigger; the challenge was an unusual courtesy.

'It is unwise to go alone into the forest in the darkness,' the sentry reprimanded him.

'Why?' Bruce felt his mood changing. The depression evaporated.

'It is unwise,' repeated the man vaguely.

'The spirits?' Bruce teased him delicately.

'An aunt of my sister's husband disappeared not a short throw of a spear from my hut. There was no trace, no shout, nothing. I was there. It is not a matter for doubt,' said the man with dignity.

'A lion perhaps?' Bruce prodded him.

'If you say so, then it is so. I know what I know. But I say only that there is no wisdom in defying the custom of the land.'

Suddenly touched by the man's concern for him, Bruce dropped a hand on to his shoulder and gripped it in the old expression of affection.

'I will remember. I did it without thinking.'

He walked into the camp. The incident had confirmed something he had vaguely suspected, but in which previously he had felt no interest. The men liked him. A hundred similar indications of this fact he had only half noted, not caring one way or the other. But now it gave him intense pleasure, fully compensating for the loneliness he had just experienced.

He walked past the little group of men round the cooking fire to where the Ford stood at the head of the convoy. Peering through the side window he could make out Shermaine's blanket-wrapped form on the back seat. He tapped on the glass and she sat up and rolled down the window.

'Yes?' she asked coolly.

'Thank you for the food.'

'It is nothing.' The slightest hint of warmth in her voice.

'Shermaine, sometimes I say things I do not mean. You startled me. I nearly shot you.'

'It was my fault. I should not have followed you.'

'I was rude,' he persisted.

'Yes.' She laughed now. That husky little chuckle. 'You were rude but with good reason. We shall forget it.' She placed her hand on his arm. 'You must rest, you haven't slept for two days.'

'Will you ride in the Ford with me tomorrow to show that I am forgiven?'

'Of course,' she nodded.

'Good night, Shermaine.'

'Good night, Bruce,'

No, Bruce decided as he spread his blankets beside the fire, I am not alone. Not any more.

= 20 =

'What about breakfast, boss?'

'They can eat on the road. Give them a tin of bully each – we've wasted enough time on this trip.'

The sky was paling and pinking above the forest. It was light enough to read the dial of his wrist watch. Twenty minutes to five.

'Get them moving, Ruffy. If we make Msapa Junction before dark we can drive through the night. Home for breakfast tomorrow.'

'Now you're talking, boss.' Ruffy clapped his helmet on to his head and went off to rouse the men who lay in the road beside the trucks.

Shermaine was asleep. Bruce leaned into the window of the Ford and studied her face. A wisp of hair lay over her mouth, rising and falling with her breathing. It tickled her nose and in her sleep it twitched like a rabbit.

Bruce felt an almost unbearable pang of tenderness towards her. With one finger he lifted the hair off her face. Then he smiled at himself.

If you can feel like this before breakfast, then you've got it in a bad way, he told himself.

Do you know something, he retorted. I like the feeling.

'Hey, you lazy wench!' He pulled the lobe of her ear. 'Time to wake up.'

It was almost half past five before the convoy got under way. It had taken that long to bully and cajole the sleep out of sixty men and get them into the lorries. This morning Bruce did not find the delay unbearable. He had managed to find time for four hours' sleep during the night. Four hours was not nearly enough to make up for the previous two days.

Now he felt light-headed, a certain unreal quality of gaiety overlaying his exhaustion, a carnival spirit. There was no longer the same urgency, for the road to Elisabethville was clear and not too long. Home for breakfast tomorrow!

'We'll be at the bridge in a little under an hour.' He glanced sideways at Shermaine.

'You've left a guard on it?'

'Ten men,' answered Bruce. 'We'll pick them up almost without stopping, and then the next stop, room 201, Grand Hotel Leopold II, Avenue du Kasai.' He grinned in anticipation. 'A bath so deep it will slop over on to the floor, so hot it will take five minutes to get into it. Clean clothes. A steak that thick, with French salad and a bottle of Liebfraumilch.'

'For breakfast!' protested Shermaine.

'For breakfast,' Bruce agreed happily. He was silent for a while, savouring the idea. The road ahead of him was tiger-striped with the shadows of the trees thrown by the low sun. The air that blew in through the missing windscreen was cool and clean-smelling. He felt good. The responsibility of command lay lightly on his shoulders this morning; a pretty girl beside him, a golden morning, the horror of the last few days half-forgotten – they might have been going on a picnic.

'What are you thinking?' he asked suddenly. She was very quiet beside him.

'I was wondering about the future,' she answered softly. 'There is no one I know in Elisabethville, and I do not wish to stay there.'

'Will you return to Brussels?' he asked. The question was without significance, for Bruce Curry had very definite plans for the immediate future, and these included Shermaine.

'Yes, I think so. There is nowhere else.'

'You have relatives there?'

'An aunt.'

'Are you close?'

Shermaine laughed, but there was bitterness in the husky chuckle. 'Oh, very close. She came to see me once at the orphanage. Once in all those years. She brought me a comic book of a religious nature and told me to clean my teeth and brush my hair a hundred strokes a day.'

'There is no one else?' asked Bruce.

'No.'

'Then why go back?'

'What else is there to do?' she asked. 'Where else is there to go?'

'There's a life to live, and the rest of the world to visit.'

'Is that what you are going to do?'

'That is exactly what I'm going to do, starting with a hot bath.'

Bruce could feel it between them. They both knew it was there, but it was too soon to talk about it. I have only kissed her once, but that was enough. So what will happen? Marriage? His mind shied away from that word with startling violence, then came hesitantly back to examine it. Stalking it as though it were a dangerous beast, ready to take flight again as soon as it showed its teeth.

For some people it is a good thing. It can stiffen the spineless; ease the lonely; give direction to the wanderers; spur those without ambition – and, of course, there was the final unassailable argument in its favour. Children.

But there are some who can only sicken and shrivel in the colourless cell of matrimony. With no space to fly, your wings must weaken with disuse; turned inwards, your eyes become short-sighted; when all your communication with the rest of the world is through the glass windows of the cell, then your contact is limited.

And I already have children. I have a daughter and I have a son.

Bruce turned his eyes from the road and studied the girl beside him. There is no fault I can find. She is beautiful in the delicate, almost fragile way that is so much better and longer-lived than blond hair and big bosoms. She is unspoilt; hardship has long been her travelling companion and from it she has learned kindness and humility.

She is mature, knowing the ways of this world; knowing death and fear, the evilness of men and their goodness. I do not believe she has ever lived in the fairy-tale cocoon that most young girls spin about themselves.

And yet she has not forgotten how to laugh.

Perhaps, he thought, perhaps. But it is too soon to talk about it.

'You are very grim.' Shermaine broke the silence, but the laughter shivered just below the surface of her voice. 'Again you are Bonaparte. And when you are grim your nose is too big and cruel. It is a nose of great brutality and it does not fit the rest of your face. I think that when they had finished you they had only one nose left in stock. "It is too big," they said, "but it is the only nose left, and when he smiles it will not look too bad." So they took a chance and stuck it on anyway.'

'Were you never taught that it is bad manners to poke fun at a man's weakness?' Bruce fingered his nose ruefully.

'Your nose is many things, but not weak. Never weak.' She laughed now and moved a little closer to him.

'You know you can attack me from behind your own perfect nose, and I cannot retaliate.'

'Never trust a man who makes pretty speeches so easily, because he surely makes them to every girl he meets.' She slid an inch further across the seat until they were almost touching. 'You waste your talents, mon Capitaine. I am immune to your charm.'

'In just one minute I will stop this car and –'

'You cannot.' Shermaine jerked her head to indicate the two gendarmes in the seat behind them. 'What would they think, Bonaparte? It would be very bad for discipline.'

'Discipline or no discipline, in jut one minute I will stop this car and spank you soundly before I kiss you.'

'One threat does not frighten me, but because of the other I will leave your poor nose.' She moved away a little and once more Bruce studied her face. Beneath the frank scrutiny she fidgeted and started to blush.

'Do you mind! Were you never taught that it is bad manners to stare?'

So now I am in love again, thought Bruce. This is only the third time, an average of once every ten years or so. It frightens me a little because there is always pain with it. The exquisite pain of loving and the agony of losing.

It starts in the loins and it is very deceptive because you think it is only the old thing, the tightness and tension that any well-rounded stern or cheeky pair of breasts will give you. Scratch it, you think, it's just a small itch. Spread a little of the warm salve on it and it will be gone in no time.

But suddenly it spreads, upwards and downwards, all through you. The pit of your stomach feels hot, then the flutters round the heart. It's dangerous now; once it gets this far it's incurable and you can scratch and scratch but all you do is inflame it.

Then the last stages, when it attacks the brain. No pain there, that's the worst sign. A heightening of the senses; your eyes are sharper, your blood runs too fast, food tastes good, your mouth wants to shout and legs want to run. Then the delusions of grandeur: you are the cleverest, strongest, most masculine male in the universe, and you stand ten feet tall in your socks.

How tall are you now, Curry, he asked himself. About nine feet six and I weigh twenty stone, he answered, and almost laughed aloud.

And how does it end? It ends with words. Words can kill anything. It ends with cold words; words like fire that stick in the structure and take hold and lick it up, blackening and charring it, bringing it down in smoking ruins.

It ends in suspicion of things not done, and in the certainty of things done and remembered. It ends with selfishness and carelessness, and words, always words.

It ends with pain and greyness, and it leaves scar tissue and damage that will never heal.

Or it ends without fuss and fury. It just crumbles and blows away like dust on the wind. But there is still the agony of loss.

Both these endings I know well, for I have loved twice, and now I love again.

Perhaps this time it does not have to be that way. Perhaps this time it will last. Nothing is for ever, he thought. Nothing is for ever, not even life, and perhaps this time if I cherish it and tend it carefully it will last that long, as long as life.

'We are nearly at the bridge,' said Shermaine beside him, and Bruce started. The miles had dropped unseen behind them and now the forest was thickening. It crouched closer to the earth, greener and darker along the river.

Bruce slowed the Ford and the forest became dense bush around them, the road a tunnel through it. They came round one last bend in the track and out of the tunnel of green vegetation into the clearing where the road met the railway line and ran beside it on to the heavy timber platform of the bridge.

Bruce stopped the Ranchero, switched off the engine and they all sat silently, staring out at the solid jungle on the far bank with its screen of creepers and monkey-ropes hanging down, trailing the surface of the deep green swift-flowing river. They stared at the stumps of the bridge thrusting out from each bank towards each other like the arms of parted lovers; at the wide gap between with the timbers still smouldering and the smoke drifting away downstream over the green water.

'It's gone,' said Shermaine. 'It's been burnt.'

'Oh, no,' groaned Bruce. 'Oh, God, no!'

With an effort he pulled his eyes from the charred remains of the bridge and turned them on to the jungle about them, a hundred feet away, ringing them in. Hostile, silent. 'Don't get out of the car,' he snapped as Shermaine reached for the door handle. 'Roll your window up, quickly.'

She obeyed.

'They're waiting in there.' He pointed at the edge of the jungle.

Behind them the first of the convoy came round the bend into the clearing. Bruce jumped from the Ford and ran back towards the leading truck.

'Don't get out, stay inside,' he shouted and ran on down the line, repeating the instruction to each of them as he passed. When he reached Ruffy's cab he jumped on to the running board, jerked the door open, slipped in on to the seat and slammed the door.

'They've burnt the bridge.'

'What's happened to the boys we left to guard it?'

'I don't know but we'll find out. Pull up alongside the others so that I can talk to them.'

Through the half-open window he issued his orders to each of the drivers and within ten minutes all the vehicles had been manoeuvred into the tight defensive circle of the laager, a formation Bruce's ancestors had used a hundred years before.

'Ruffy, get out those tarpaulins and spread them over the top to form a roof. We don't want them dropping arrows in amongst us.'

Ruffy selected half a dozen gendarmes and they went to work, dragging out the heavy folded canvas.

'Hendry, put a couple of men under each truck. Set up the Brens in case they try to rush us.'

In the infectious urgency of defence, Wally did not make his usual retort, but gathered his men. They wriggled on their stomachs under the vehicles, rifles pointed out towards the silent jungle.

'I want the extinguishers here in the middle so we can get them in a hurry. They might use fire again.'

Two gendarmes ran to each of the cabs and unclipped the fire-extinguishers from the dashboards.

'What can I do?' Shermaine was standing beside Bruce.

'Keep quiet and stay out of the way,' said Bruce as he turned and hurried across to help Ruffy's gang with the tarpaulins.

It took them half an hour of desperate endeavour before they completed the fortifications to Bruce's satisfaction.

'That should hold them.' Bruce stood with Ruffy and Hendry in the centre of the laager and surveyed the green canvas roof above them and the closely packed vehicles around them. The Ford was parked beside the tanker, not included in the outer ring for its comparative size would have made it a weak point in the defence.

'It's going to be bloody hot and crowded in here,' grumbled Hendry.

'Yes, I know.' Bruce looked at him. 'Would you like to relieve the congestion by waiting outside?'

'Funny boy, big laugh,' answered Wally.

'What now, boss?' Ruffy put into words the question Bruce had been asking himself.

'You and I will go and take a look at the bridge,' he said.

'You'll look a rare old sight with an arrow sticking out of your jack,' grinned Wally. 'Boy, that's going to kill me!'

'Ruffy, get us half a dozen gas capes each. I doubt their arrows will go through them at a range of a hundred feet, and of course we'll wear helmets.'

'Okay, boss.'

It was like being in a sauna bath beneath the six layers of rubberized canvas. Bruce could feel the sweat squirting from his pores with each pace, and rivulets of it coursing down his back and flanks as he and Ruffy left the laager and walked up the road to the bridge.

Beside him Ruffy's bulk was so enhanced by the gas capes that he reminded Bruce of a prehistoric monster reaching the end of its gestation period.

'Warm enough, Ruffy?' he asked, feeling the need for humour. The ring of jungle made him nervous. Perhaps he had underestimated the carry of a Baluba arrow – despite the light reed shaft, they used iron heads, barbed viciously and ground to a needle point, and poison smeared thickly between the barbs.

'Man, look at me shiver,' grunted Ruffy and the sweat greased down his jowls and dripped from his chin.

Long before they reached the access to the bridge the stench of putrefaction crept out to meet them. In Bruce's mind every smell had its own colour, and this one was green, the same green as the sheen of putrefaction on rotting meat. The stench was heavy so he could almost feel it bearing down on them, choking in his throat and coating his tongue and the roof of his mouth with the oily over-sweetness.

'No doubt what that is!' Ruffy spat, trying to get the taste out of his mouth.

'Where are they?' gagged Bruce, starting to pant from the heat and the effort of breathing the fouled air.

They reached the bank and Bruce's question was answered as they looked down on to the narrow beach.

There were the black remains of a dozen cooking fires along the water's edge, and closer to the high bank were two crude structures of poles. For a moment their purpose puzzled Bruce and then he realized what they were. He had seen those cross-pieces suspended between two uprights often before in hunting camps throughout Africa. They were paunching racks! At intervals along the crosspieces were the bark ropes that had been used to string up the game, heels first, with head and forelegs dangling and belly bulging forward so that at the long abdominal stroke of the knife the viscera would drop out easily.

But the game they had butchered on *these* racks were men, his men. He counted the hanging ropes. There were ten of them, so no one had escaped.

'Cover, me Ruffy. I'm going down to have a look.' It was a penance Bruce was imposing upon himself. They were his men, and he had left them there.

'Okay, boss.'

Bruce clambered down the well-defined path to the beach. Now the smell was almost unbearable and he found the source of it. Between the racks lay a dark shapeless mass. It moved with flies; its surface moved, trembled, crawled with flies. Suddenly, humming, they lifted in a cloud from the pile of human debris, and then settled once more upon it.

A single fly buzzed round Bruce's head and then settled on his hand. Metallic blue body, wings cocked back, it crouched on his skin and gleefully rubbed its front legs together. Bruce's throat and stomach convulsed as he began to retch. He struck at the fly and it darted away.

There were bones scattered round the cooking fires and a skull lay near his feet, split open to yield its contents.

Another spasm took Bruce and this time the vomit came up into his mouth, acid and warm. He swallowed it, turned away and scrambled up the bank to where Ruffy waited. He stood there gasping, suppressing his nausea until at last he could speak.

'All right, that's all I wanted to know,' and he led the way back to the circle of vehicles.

Bruce sat on the bonnet of the Ranchero and sucked hard on his cigarette, trying to get the taste of death from his mouth.

'They probably swam downstream during the night and climbed the supports of the bridge. Kanaki and his boys wouldn't have known anything about it until they came over the sides.' He drew on the cigarette again and trickled the smoke out of his nostrils, fumigating the back of his throat and his nasal passages. 'I should have thought of that. I should have warned Kanaki of that.'

'You mean they ate all ten of them – Jesus!' even Wally Hendry was impressed. 'I'd like to have a look at that beach. It must be quite something.'

'Good!' Bruce's voice was suddenly harsh. 'I'll put you in charge of the burial squad. You can go down there and clean it up before we start work on the bridge.' And Wally did not argue.

'You want me to do it now?' he asked.

'No,' snapped Bruce. 'You and Ruffy are going to take two of the trucks back to Port Reprieve and fetch the materials we need to repair the bridge.'

They both looked at Bruce with rising delight.

'I never thought of that,' said Wally.

'There's plenty of roofing timber in the hotel and the office block,' grinned Ruffy.

'Nails,' said Wally as though he were making a major contribution. 'We'll need nails.'

Bruce cut through their comments. 'It's two o'clock now. You can get back to Port Reprieve by nightfall, collect the material tomorrow morning and return here by the evening. Take those two trucks there – check to see they're full of gas and you'll need about fifteen men. Say, five gendarmes, in case of trouble, and ten of those civilians.'

'That should be enough,' agreed Ruffy.

'Bring a couple of dozen sheets of corrugated iron back with you. We'll use them to make a shield to protect us from arrows while we're working.'

'Yeah, that's a good idea.'

They settled the details, picked men to go back, loaded the trucks, worked them out of the laager, and Bruce watched them disappear down the road towards Port Reprieve. An ache started deep behind his eyes and suddenly he was very tired, drained of energy by too little sleep, by the heat and by the emotional pace of the last four days. He made one last circuit of the laager, checking the defences, chatting for a few minutes with his gendarmes and then he stumbled to the Ford, slid on to the front seat, laid his helmet and rifle aside, lowered his head on to his arms and was instantly asleep.

= 21 =

Shermaine woke him after dark with food unheated from the cans and a bottle of Ruffy's beer.

'I'm sorry, Bruce, we have no fire to cook upon. It is very unappetizing and the beer is warm.'

Bruce sat up and rubbed his eyes. Six hours' sleep had helped; they were less swollen and inflamed. The headache was still there.

'I'm not really hungry, thank you. It's this heat.'

'You must eat, Bruce. Try just a little,' and then she smiled. 'At least you are more gallant after having rested. It is "Thank you" now, instead of "Keep quiet and stay out of the way".'

Ruefully Bruce grimaced. 'You are one of those women with a built-in recording unit;

every word remembered and used in evidence against a man later.' Then he touched her hand. 'I'm sorry.'

'I'm sorry,' she repeated. 'I like your apologies, mon capitaine. They are like the rest of you, completely masculine. There is nothing about you which is not male, sometimes almost overpoweringly so.' Impishly she watched his eyes; he knew she was talking about the little scene on the train that Wally Hendry had interrupted.

'Let's try this food,' he said, and then a little later, 'not bad – you are an excellent cook.'

'This time the credit must go to M. Heinz and his fifty-seven children. But one day I shall make for you one of my tournedos au Prince. It is my special.'

'Speciality,' Bruce corrected her automatically.

The murmur of voices within the laager was punctuated occasionally by a burst of laughter. There was a feeling of relaxation. The canvas roof and the wall of vehicles gave security to them all. Men lay in dark huddles of sleep or talked quietly in small groups.

Bruce scraped the metal plate and filled his mouth with the last of the food.

'Now I must check the defences again.'

'Oh, Bonaparte. It is always duty.' Shermaine sighed with resignation.

'I will not be long.'

'And I'll wait here for you.'

Bruce picked up his rifle and helmet, and was half-way out of the Ford when out in the jungle the drum started.

'Bruce!' whispered Shermaine and clutched his arm. The voices round them froze into a fearful silence, and the drum beat in the night. It had a depth and resonance that you could feel; the warm sluggish air quivered with it. Not fixed in space but filling it, beating monotonously, insistently, like the pulse of all creation.

'Bruce!' whispered Shermaine again; she was trembling and the fingers on his arm dug into his flesh with the strength of terror. It steadied his own leap of fear.

'Baby, baby,' he soothed her, taking her to his chest and holding her there. 'It's only the sound of two pieces of wood being knocked together by a naked savage. They can't touch us here, you now that.'

'Oh, Bruce, it's horrible – it's like bells, funeral bells.'

'That's silly talk.' Bruce held her at arms' length. 'Come with me. Help me calm down these others, they'll be terrified. You'll have to help me.'

And he pulled her gently across the seat out of the Ford, and with one arm round her waist walked her into the centre of the laager.

What will counteract the stupefying influence of the drum, the hypnotic beat of it, he asked himself. Noise, our own noise.

'Joseph, M'pophu –' he shouted cheerfully picking out the two best singers amongst his men. 'I regret the drumming is of a low standard, but the Baluba are monkeys with no understanding of music. Let us show them how a Bambala can sing.'

They stirred; he could feel the tension diminish.

'Come, Joseph –' He filled his lungs and shouted the opening chorus of one of the planting songs, purposely off-key, singing so badly that it must sting them.

Someone laughed, then Joseph's voice hesitantly starting the chorus, gathering strength. M'pophu coming in with the bass to give a solid foundation to the vibrant, sweet-ringing tenor. Half-beat to the drum, hands clapped in the dark; around him Bruce could feel the rhythmic swinging of bodies begin.

Shermaine was no longer trembling; he squeezed her waist and felt her body cling to him.

Now we need light, thought Bruce. A night lamp for my children who fear the darkness and the drum.

With Shermaine beside him he crossed the laager.

'Sergeant Jacque.'

'Captain?'

'You can start sweeping with the searchlights.'

'Oui, Captain.' The answer was less subdued. There were two spare batteries for each light, Bruce knew. Eight hours' life in each, so they would last tonight and tomorrow night.

From each side of the laager the beams leapt out, solid white shafts through the darkness; they played along the edge of the jungle and reflected back, lighting the interior of the laager sufficiently to make out the features of each man. Bruce looked at their faces. They're all right now, he decided, the ghosts have gone away.

'Bravo, Bonaparte,' said Shermaine, and Bruce became aware of the grins on the faces of his men as they saw him embracing her. He was about to drop his arm, then stopped himself. The hell with it, he decided, give them something else to think about. He led her back to the Ford.

'Tired?' he asked.

'A little,' she nodded.

'I'll fold down the seat for you. A blanket over the windows will give you privacy.'

'You'll stay close?' she asked quickly.

'I'll be right outside.' He unbuckled the webbing belt that carried his pistol. 'You'd better wear this from now on.'

Even at its minimum adjustment the belt was too large for her and the pistol hung down almost to her knee.

'The Maid of Orleans.' Bruce revenged himself. She pulled a face at him and crawled into the back of the station wagon.

A long while later she called softly above the singing and the throb of the drum.

'Bruce.'

'Yes?'

'I wanted to make sure you were there. Good night.'

'Good night, Shermaine.'

Bruce lay on a single blanket and sweated. The singing had long ago ceased but the drum went on and on, never faltering, throb-throb-throbbing out of the jungle. The searchlights swept regularly back and forth, at times lighting the laager clearly and at others leaving it in shadow. Bruce could hear around him the soft sounds of sleep, the sawing of breath, a muted cough, a gabbled sentence, the stirring of dreamers.

But Bruce could not sleep. He lay on his back with one hand under his head, smoking, staring up at the canvas. The events of the preceding four days ran through his mind:

snatches of conversation, André dying. Boussier standing with his wife, the bursting of grenades, blood sticky on his hands, the smell of dead, the violence and the horror.

He moved restlessly, flicked away his cigarette and covered his eyes with his hands as though to shut out the memories. But they went on flickering through his mind like the images of a gigantic movie projector, confused now, losing all meaning but retaining the horror.

He remembered the fly upon his arm, grinning at him, rubbing its legs together, gloating, repulsive. He rolled his head from side to side on the blanket.

I'm going mad, he thought, I must stop this.

He sat up quickly hugging his knees to his chest and the memories faded. But now he was sad, and alone. So terribly alone, so lost, so without purpose.

He sat alone on the blanket and he felt himself shrinking, becoming small and frightened.

I'm going to cry, he thought, I can feel it there heavy in my throat. And like a hurt child crawling into its mother's lap, Bruce Curry groped his way over the tailboard of the station wagon to Shermaine.

'Shermaine!' he whispered, blindly, searching for her.

'Bruce, what is it?' She sat up quickly. She had not been sleeping either.

'Where are you?' There was panic in Bruce's voice.

'Here I am – what's the matter?'

And he found her; clumsily he caught her to him.

'Hold me, Shermaine, please hold me.'

'Darling.' She was anxious. 'What is it? Tell me, my darling.'

'Just hold me, Shermaine. Don't talk.' He clung to her, pressing his face into her neck. 'I need you so much – oh, God! How I need you!'

'Bruce.' She understood, and her fingers were at the nape of his neck, stroking, soothing.

'My Bruce,' she said and held him. Instinctively her body began to rock, gentling him as though he were her child.

Slowly his body relaxed, and he sighed against her – a gusty broken sound.

'My Bruce, my Bruce.' She lifted the thin cotton vest that was all she wore and, instinctively in the ageless ritual of comfort, she gave him her breasts. Holding his mouth to them with both her arms clasped around his neck, her head bowed protectively over his, her hair falling forward and covering them both.

With the hard length of his body against hers, with the soft tugging at her bosom, and in the knowledge that she was giving strength to the man she loved, she realized she had never known happiness before this moment. Then his body was no longer quiescent; she felt her own mood change, a new urgency.

'Oh yes, Bruce, yes!' Speaking up into his mouth, his hungry hunting mouth and he above her, no longer child, but full man again.

'So beautiful, so warm.' His voice was strangely husky, she shuddered with the intensity of her own need.

'Quickly, Bruce, oh, Bruce.' His cruel loving hands, seeking, finding.

'Oh, Bruce – quickly,' and she reached up for him with her hips.

'I'll hurt you.'

'No – yes, I want the pain.' She felt the resistance to him within her and cried out impatiently against it.

'Go through!' and then, 'Ah! It burns.'

'I'll stop.'

'No, No!'

'Darling. It's too much.'

'Yes – I can't – oh, Bruce. My heart – you've touched my heart.'

Her clenched fists drumming on his back. And in to press against the taut, reluctantly yielding springiness, away, then back, away, and back to touch the core of all existence, leave it, and come long gliding back to it, nuzzle it, feel it tilt, then come away, then back once more. Welling slowly upwards scalding, no longer to be contained, with pain almost – and gone, and gone, and gone.

'I'm falling. Oh, Bruce! Bruce! Bruce!'

Into the gulf together – gone, all gone. Nothing left, no time, no space, no bottom to the gulf.

Nothing and everything. Complete.

Out in the jungle the drum kept beating.

Afterwards, long afterwards, she slept with her head on his arm and her face against his chest. And he unsleeping listened to her sleep. The sound of it was soft, so gentle breathing soft that you could not hear it unless you listened very carefully – or unless you loved her, he thought.

Yes. I think I love this woman – but I must be certain. In fairness to her and to myself I must be entirely certain, for I cannot live through another time like the last, and because I love her I don't want her to take the terrible wounding of a bad marriage. Better, much better to leave it now, unless it has the strength to endure.

Bruce rolled his head slowly until his face was in her hair, and the girl nuzzled his chest in her sleep.

But it is so hard to tell, he thought. It is so hard to tell at the beginning. It is so easy to confuse pity or loneliness with love, but I cannot afford to do that now. So I must try to think clearly about my marriage to Joan. It will be difficult, but I must try.

Was it like this with Joan in the beginning? It was so long ago, seven years, that I do not know, *he answered truthfully*. All I have left from those days are the pictures of places and the small heaps of words that have struck where the wind and the pain could not blow them away.

A beach with the sea mist coming in across it, a whole tree of driftwood half buried in the sand and bleached white with the salt, a basket of strawberries bought along the road, so that when I kissed her I could taste the sweet tartness of the fruit on her lips.

I remember a tune that we sang together, 'The mission bells told me that I mustn't stay, South of the border, down Mexico way.' I have forgotten most of the words.

And I remember vaguely how her body was, and the shape of her breasts before the children were born.

But that is all I have left from the good times.

The other memories are clear, stinging, whiplash clear. Each ugly word, and the tone in which it was said. The sound of sobbing in the night, the way it dragged itself on for three long grey years after it was mortally wounded, and both of us using all our strength to keep it moving because of the children.

The children! Oh, God, I mustn't think about them now. It hurts too much. Without the children to complicate it, I must think about her for the last time; I must end this woman Joan. So now finally and for all to end this woman who made me cry. I do not hate her for the man with whom she went away. She deserved another try for happiness. But I hate her for my children and for making shabby the love that I could have given Shermaine as a new thing. Also, I pity her for her inability to find the happiness for which she hunts so fiercely. I pity her for her coldness of body and of mind, I pity her for her prettiness that is now almost gone (it goes round her eyes first, cracking like oil paint) and I pity her for her consuming selfishness which will lose her the love of her children.

My children – not hers! My children!

That is all, that is an end to Joan, and now I have Shermaine who is none of the things that Joan was. I also deserve another try.

'Shermaine,' he whispered and turned her head slightly to kiss her. 'Shermaine, wake up.'

She stirred and murmured against him.

'Wake up.' He took the lobe of her ear between his teeth and bit it gently. Her eyes opened.

'Bon matin, madame.' He smiled at her.

'Bon jour, monsieur,' she answered and closed her eyes to press her face once more against his chest.

'Wake up. I have something to tell you.'

'I am awake, but tell me first if I am still dreaming. I have a certainty that this cannot be reality.'

'You are not dreaming.'

She sighed softly, and held him closer.

'Now tell me the other thing.'

'I love you,' he said.

'No. Now I am dreaming.'

'In truth,' he said.

'No, do not wake me. I could not bear to wake now.'

'And you?' he asked.

'You know it –' she answered. 'I do not have to tell you.'

'It is almost morning,' he said. 'There is only a little time.'

'Then I will fill that little time with saying it –' He held her and listened to her whispering it to him.

No, he thought, now I am certain. I could not be that wrong. This is my woman.

= 22 =

The drum stopped with the dawn. And after it the silence was very heavy, and it was no relief.

They had grown accustomed to that broken rhythm and now in some strange way they missed it.

As Bruce moved around the laager he could sense the uneasiness in his men. There was a feeling of dread anticipation on them all. They moved with restraint, as though they did not want to draw attention to themselves. The laughter with which they acknowledged his jokes was nervous, quickly cut off, as though they had laughed in a cathedral. And their eyes kept darting back towards the ring of jungle.

Bruce found himself wishing for an attack. His own nerves were rubbed sensitive by contact with the fear all around him.

If only they would come, he told himself. If only they would show themselves and we could see men not phantoms.

But the jungle was silent. It seemed to wait, it watched them. They could feel the gaze of hidden eyes. Its malignant presence pressed closer as the heat built up.

Bruce walked across the laager to the south side, trying to move casually. He smiled at Sergeant Jacque, squatted beside him and peered from under the truck across open ground at the remains of the bridge.

'Trucks will be back soon,' he said. 'Won't take long to repair that.'

Jacque did not answer. There was a worried frown on his high intelligent forehead and his face was shiny with perspiration.

'It's the waiting, Captain. It softens the stomach.'

'They will be back soon,' repeated Bruce. If this one is worried, and he is the best of them, then the others must be almost in a jelly of dread.

Bruce looked at the face of the man on the other side of Jacque. Its expression shrieked with fear.

If they attack now, God knows how it will turn out. An African can think himself to death, they just lie down and die. They are getting to that stage now; if an attack comes they will either go berserk or curl up and wail with fear. You can never tell.

Be honest with yourself – you're not entirely happy either, are you? No, Bruce agreed, it's the waiting does it.

It came from the edge of the clearing on the far side of the laager. A high-pitched inhuman sound, angry, savage.

Bruce felt his heart trip and he spun round to face it. For a second the whole laager seemed to cringe from it.

It came again. Like a whip across aching nerves. Immediately it was lost in the roar of twenty rifles.

Bruce laughed. Threw his head back and let it come from the belly.

The gunfire stammered into silence and others were laughing also. The men who had fired grinned sheepishly and made a show of reloading.

It was not the first time that Bruce had been startled by the cry of a yellow hornbill. But now he recognized his laughter and the laughter of the men around him, a mild form of hysteria.

'Did you want the feathers for your hat?' someone shouted and the laughter swept round the laager.

The tension relaxed as the banter was tossed back and forth. Bruce stood up and brought his own laughter under control.

No harm done, he decided. For the price of fifty rounds of ammunition, a purchase of an hour's escape from tension. A good bargain.

He walked across to Shermaine. She was smiling also.

'How is the catering section?' He grinned at her. 'What miracle of the culinary art is there for lunch?'

'Bully beef.'

'And onions?'

'No, just bully beef. The onions are finished.'

Bruce stopped smiling.

'How much is left?' he asked.

'One case – enough to last till lunchtime tomorrow.'

It would take at least two days to complete the repairs to the bridge; another day's travel after that.

'Well,' he said, 'we should all have healthy appetites by the time we get home. You'll have to try and spread it out. Half rations from now on.'

He was so engrossed in the study of this new complication that he did not notice the faint hum from the outside the laager.

'Captain,' called Jacques. 'Can you hear it?'

Bruce inclined his head and listened.

'The trucks!' His voice was loud with relief, and instantly there was an excited murmur round the laager.

The waiting was over.

They came growling out of the bush into the clearing. Heavily loaded, timber and sheet-iron protruding backwards from under the canopies, sitting low on their suspensions.

Ruffy leaned from the cab of the leading truck and shouted.

'Hello boss. Where shall we dump?'

'Take it up to the bridge. Hang on a second and I'll come with you.'

Bruce slipped out of the laager and crossed quickly to Ruffy's truck. He could feel his back tingling while he was in the open and he slammed the door behind him with relief.

'I don't relish stopping an arrow,' he said.

'You have any trouble while we were gone?'

'No,' Bruce told him. 'But they're here. They were drumming in the jungle all night.'

'Calling up their buddies,' grunted Ruffy and let out the clutch. 'We'll have some fun before we finish this bridge. Most probably take them a day or two to get brave, but in the end they'll have a go at us.'

'Pull over to the side of the bridge, Ruffy,' Bruce instructed and rolled down his window. 'I'll signal Hendry to pull in beside us. We'll off-load into the space between the two trucks and start building the corrugated iron shield there.'

While Hendry manoeuvred his truck alongside, Bruce forced himself to look down on the carnage of the beach.

'Crocodiles,' he exclaimed with relief. The paunching racks still stood as he had last seen them, but the reeking pile of human remains was gone. The smell and the flies, however, still lingered.

'During the night,' agreed Ruffy as he surveyed the long slither marks in the sand of the beach.

'Thank God for that.'

'Yeah, it wouldn't have made my boys too joyful having to clean up that lot.'

'We'll send someone down to tear out those racks. I don't want to look at them while we work.'

'No, they're not very pretty.' Ruffy ran his eyes over the two sets of gallows.

Bruce climbed down into the space between the trucks.

'Hendry.'

'That's my name.' Wally leaned out of the window.

'Sorry to disappoint you, but the crocs have done the chore for you.'

'I can see. I'm not blind.'

'Very well then. On the assumption that you are neither blind nor paralysed, how about getting your trucks unloaded?'

'Big deal,' muttered Hendry, but he climbed down and began shouting at the men under the canvas canopy.

'Get the lead out there, you lot. Start jumping about!'

'What were the thickest timbers you could find?' Bruce turned to Ruffy.

'Nine by threes, but we got plenty of them.'

'They'll do,' decided Bruce. 'We can lash a dozen of them together for each of the main supports.' Frowning with concentration, Bruce began the task of organizing the repairs.

'Hendry, I want the timber stacked by sizes. Put the sheet-iron over there.' He brushed the flies from his face. 'Ruffy, how many hammers have we got?'

'Ten, boss, and I found a couple of handsaws.'

'Good. What about nails and rope?'

'We got plenty. I got a barrel of six-inch and –'

Preoccupied, Bruce did not notice one of the coloured civilians leave the shelter of the trucks. He walked a dozen paces towards the bridge and stopped. Then unhurriedly he began to unbutton his trousers and Bruce looked up.

'What the hell are you doing?' he shouted and the man started guiltily. He did not understand the English words, but Bruce's tone was sufficiently clear.

'Monsieur,' he explained, 'I wish to –'

'Get back here!' roared Bruce. The man hesitated in confusion and then he began closing his fly.

'Hurry up – you bloody fool.'

Obediently the man hastened the closing of his trousers. Everyone had stopped work and they were all watching him. His face was dark with embarrassment and he fumbled clumsily.

'Leave that.' Bruce was frantic. 'Get back here.'

The first arrow rose lazily out of the undergrowth along the river in a silent parabola. Gathering speed in its descent, hissing softly, it dropped into the ground at the man's feet and stuck up jauntily. A thin reed, fletched with green leaves, it looked harmless as a child's plaything.

'Run,' screamed Bruce. The man stood and stared with detached disbelief at the arrow.

Bruce started forward to fetch him, but Ruffy's huge black hand closed on his arm and he was helpless in its grip. He struck out at Ruffy, struggling to free himself but he could not break that hold.

A swarm of them like locusts on the move, high arching, fluting softly, dropping all around the man as he started to run.

Bruce stopped struggling and watched. He heard the metal heads clanking on the bonnet of the truck, saw them falling wide of the man, some of the frail shafts snapping as they hit the ground.

Then between the shoulders, like a perfectly placed banderilla, one hit him. It flapped against his back as he ran and he twisted his arms behind him, vainly trying to reach it, his face twisted in horror and in pain.

'Hold him down,' shouted Bruce as the coloured man ran into the shelter. Two gendarmes jumped forward, took his arms and forced him face downwards on to the ground.

He was gabbling incoherently with horror as Bruce straddled his back and gripped the shaft. Only half the barbed head had buried itself – a penetration of less than an inch – but when Bruce pulled the shaft it snapped off in his hand leaving the steel twitching in the flesh.

'Knife,' shouted Bruce and someone thrust a bayonet into his hand.

'Watch those barbs, boss. Don't cut yourself on them.'

'Ruffy, get your boys ready to repel them if they rush us,' snapped Bruce and ripped away the shirt. For a moment he stared at the crudely hand-beaten iron arrow-head. The poison coated it thickly, packed in behind the barbs, looking like sticky black toffee.

'He's dead,' said Ruffy from where he leaned over the bonnet of the truck. 'He just ain't stopped breathing yet.'

The man screamed and twisted under Bruce as he made the first incision, cutting in deep beside the arrowhead with the point of the bayonet.

'Hendry, get those pliers out of the took kit.'

'Here they are.'

Bruce gripped the arrow-head with the steel jaws and pulled. The flesh clung to it stubbornly, lifting in a pyramid. Bruce hacked at it with the bayonet, feeling it tear. It was like trying to get the hook out of the rubbery mouth of a cat-fish.

'You're wasting your time, boss!' grunted Ruffy with all the calm African acceptance of violent death. 'This boy's a goner. That's no horse! That's snake juice in him, fresh mixed. He's finished.'

'Are you sure, Ruffy?' Bruce looked up, 'Are you sure it's snake venom?'

'That's what they use. They mix it with kassava meal.'

'Hendry, where's the snake bite outfit?'

'It's in the medicine box back at the camp.'

Bruce tugged once more at the arrow-head and it came away, leaving a deep black hole between the man's shoulder-blades.

'Everybody into the trucks, we've got to get him back. Every second is vital.'

'Look at his eyes,' grunted Ruffy. 'That injection stuff ain't going to help him much.'

The pupils had contracted to the size of match heads and he was shaking uncontrollably as the poison spread through is body.

'Get him into the truck.'

They lifted him into the cab and everybody scrambled aboard. Ruffy started the engine, slammed into reverse and the motor roared as he shot backwards over the intervening thirty yards to the laager.

'Get him out,' instructed Bruce. 'Bring him into the shelter.'

The man was blubbering through slack lips and he had started to sweat. Little rivulets of it coursed down his face and naked upper body. There was hardly any blood from the wound, just a trickle of brownish fluid. The poison must be a coagulant, Bruce decided.

'Bruce, are you all right?' Shermaine ran to meet him.

'Nothing wrong with me.' Bruce remembered to check his tongue this time. 'But one of them has been hit.'

'Can I help you?'

'No, I don't want you to watch.' And he turned from her. 'Hendry, where's that bloody snake bite outfit?' he shouted.

They had dragged the man into the laager and laid him on a blanket in the shade. Bruce went to him and knelt beside him. He took the scarlet tin that Hendry handed him and opened it.

'Ruffy, get those two trucks worked into the circle and make sure your boys are on their toes. With this success they may get brave sooner than you expected.'

Bruce fitted the hypodermic needle on to the syringe as he spoke.

'Hendry, get them to rig some sort of screen round us. You can use blankets.'

With his thumb he snapped the top off the ampoule and filled the syringe with the pale yellow serum.

'Hold him,' he said to the two gendarmes, lifted a pinch of skin close beside the wound and ran the needle under it. The man's skin felt like that of a frog, damp and clammy.

As he expelled the serum Bruce was trying to calculate the time that had elapsed since the arrow had hit. Possibly seven or eight minutes; mamba venom kills in fourteen minutes.

'Roll him over,' he said.

The man's head lolled sideways, his breathing was quick and shallow and the saliva poured from the corners of his mouth, running down his cheeks.

'Get a load of that!' breathed Wally Hendry, and Bruce glanced up at his face. His expression was a glow of deep sensual pleasure and his breathing was as quick and shallow as that of the dying man.

'Go and help Ruffy,' snapped Bruce as his stomach heaved with disgust.

'Not on your Nelly. This I'm not going to miss.'

Bruce had no time to argue. He lifted the skin of the man's stomach and ran the needle in again. There was an explosive spitting sound as the bowels started to vent involuntarily.

'Jesus,' whispered Hendry.

'Get away,' snarled Bruce. 'Can't you let him die without gloating over it?'

Hopelessly he injected again, under the skin of the chest above the heart. As he emptied the syringe the man's body twisted violently in the first seizure and the needle snapped off under the skin.

'There he goes,' whispered Hendry, 'there he goes. Just look at him, man. That's really something.'

Bruce's hands were trembling and slowly a curtain descended across his mind.

'You filthy swine,' he screamed and hit Hendry across the face with his open hand, knocking him back against the side of the gasoline tanker. Then he went for his throat and found it with both hands. The wind pipe was ropey and elastic under his thumbs.

'Is nothing sacred to you, you unclean animal,' he yelled into Hendry's face. 'Can't you let a man die without –'

Then Ruffy was there, effortlessly plucking Bruce's hands from the throat, interposing the bulk of his body, holding them away from each other.

'Let it stand, boss.'

'For that –' gasped Hendry as he massaged his throat. 'For that I'm going to make you pay.'

Bruce turned away, sick and ashamed, to the man on the blanket.

'Cover him up.' His voice was shaky. 'Put him in the back of one of the trucks. We'll bury him tomorrow.'

= 23 =

Before nightfall they had completed the corrugated iron screen. It was a simple four-walled structure with no roof to it. One end of it was detachable and all four walls were pierced at regular intervals with small loopholes for defence.

Long enough to accommodate a dozen men in comfort, high enough to reach above the heads of the tallest, and exactly the width of the bridge, it was not a thing of beauty.

'How you going to move it, boss?' Ruffy eyed the screen dubiously.

'I'll show you. We'll move it back to the camp now, so that in the morning we can commute to work in it.'

Bruce selected twelve men and they crowded through the open end into the shelter, and closed it behind them.

'Okay, Ruffy. Take the trucks away.'

Hendry and Ruffy reversed the two trucks back to the laager, leaving the shelter standing at the head of the bridge like a small Nissen hut. Inside it Bruce stationed his men at intervals along the walls.

'Use the bottom timber of the frame to lift on,' he shouted. 'Are you all ready? All right, lift!'

The shelter swayed and rose six inches above the ground. From the laager they could see only the boots of the men inside.

'All together,' ordered Bruce. 'Walk!'

Rocking and creaking over the uneven ground the structure moved ponderously back towards the laager. Below it the feet moved like those of a caterpillar.

The men in the laager started to cheer, and from inside the shelter they answered with whoops of laughter. It was fun. They were enjoying themselves enormously, completely distracted from the horror of poison arrows and the lurking phantoms in the jungle around them.

They reached the camp and lowered the shelter. Then one at a time the gendarmes slipped across the few feet of open into the safety of the laager to be met with laughter, and back-slapping and mutual congratulation.

'Well, it works, boss,' Ruffy greeted Bruce in the uproar.

'Yes.' Then he lifted his voice. 'That's enough. Quiet down all of you. Get back to your posts.'

The laughter subsided and the confusion became order again. Bruce walked to the centre of the laager and looked about him. There was complete quiet now. They were all watching him. I have read about this so often, he grinned inwardly, the heroic speech to the men on the eve of battle. Let's pray I don't make a hash of it.

'Are you hungry?' he asked loudly in French and received a chorus of hearty affirmatives.

'There is bully beef for dinner.' This time humorous groans.

'And bully beef for breakfast tomorrow,' he paused, 'and then it's finished.'

They were silent now.

'So you are going to be truly hungry by the time we cross this river. The sooner we repair the bridge the sooner you'll get your bellies filled again.'

I might as well rub it in, decided Bruce.

'You all saw what happened to the person who went into the open today, so I don't have to tell you to keep under cover. The sergeant major is making arrangements for sanitation – five-gallon drums. They won't be very comfortable, so you won't be tempted to sit too long.'

They laughed a little at that.

'Remember this. As long as you stay in the laager or the shelter they can't touch you. There is absolutely nothing to fear. They can beat their drums and wait as long as they like, but they can't harm us.'

A murmur of agreement.

'And the sooner we finish the bridge the sooner we will be on our way.'

Bruce looked round the circle of faces and was satisfied with what he saw. The completion of the shelter had given their morale a boost.

'All right, Sergeant Jacque. You can start sweeping with the searchlights as soon as it's dark.'

Bruce finished and went across to join Shermaine beside the Ford. He loosed the straps of his helmet and lifted it off his head. His hair was damp with perspiration and he ran his fingers through it.

'You are tired,' Shermaine said softly, examining the dark hollows under his eyes and the puckered marks of strain at the corners of his mouth.

'No. I'm all right,' he denied, but every muscle in his body ached with fatigue and nervous tension.

'Tonight you must sleep all night,' she ordered him. 'I will make the bed in the back of the car.'

Bruce looked at her quickly. 'With you?' he asked.

'Yes.'

'You do not mind that everyone should know?'

'I am not ashamed of us.' There was a fierceness in her tone.

'I know, but –'

'You said once that nothing between you and I could ever be dirty.'

'No, of course it couldn't be dirty. I just thought –'

'Well then, I love you and from now on we have only one bed between us.' She spoke with finality.

Yesterday she was a virgin, he thought with amazement, and now – well, now it's no holds barred. Once she is roused a woman is more reckless of consequences than any man. They are such wholesale creatures. But she's right, of course. She's my woman and she belongs in my bed. The hell with the rest of the world and what it thinks!

'Make the bed, wench.' He smiled at her tenderly.

Two hours after dark the drum started again. They lay together, holding close, and listened to it. It held no terror now, for they were warm and secure in the afterglow of passion. It was like lying and listening to the impotent fury of a rainstorm on the roof at night.

= 24 =

They went out to the bridge at sunrise, the shelter moving across the open ground like the carapace of a multi-legged metallic turtle. The men chattered and joked loudly inside, still elated by the novelty of it.

'All right, everybody. That's enough talking,' Bruce shouted them down. 'There's work to do now.'

And they began.

Within an hour the sun had turned the metal box into an oven. They stripped to the waist and the sweat dripped from them as they worked. They worked in a frenzy, gripped by a new urgency, oblivious of everything but the rough-sawed timber that drove white splinters into their skin at the touch. They worked in the confined heat, amidst the racket of hammers and in the piney smell of sawdust. The labour fell into its own pattern with only an occasional grunted order from Bruce or Ruffy to direct it.

By midday the four main trusses that would span the gap in the bridge had been made up. Bruce tested their rigidity by propping one at both ends and standing all his men on the middle of it. It gave an inch under their combined weight.

'What do you think, boss?' Ruffy asked without conviction.

'Four of them might just do it. We'll put in king-posts underneath,' Bruce answered.

'Man, I don't know. That tanker weighs plenty.'

'It's no flyweight,' Bruce agreed. 'But we'll have to take the chance. We'll bring the Ford across first, then the trucks and the tanker last.'

Ruffy nodded and wiped his face on his forearm; the muscles below his armpits knotted as he moved and there was no flabbiness in the powerful bulge of his belly above his belt.

'Phew!' He blew his lips out. 'I got the feeling for a beer now. This thirst is really stalking me.'

'You've got some with you?' Bruce asked as he passed his thumbs across his eyebrows and squeezed the moisture from them so it ran down his cheeks.

'Two things I never travel without, my trousers and a stock of the brown and bubbly.' Ruffy picked up the small pack from the corner of the shelter and it clinked coyly. 'You hear that sound, boss?'

'I hear it, and it sounds like music,' grinned Bruce. 'All right, everybody.' He raised his voice. 'Take ten minutes.'

Ruffy opened the bottles and passed them out, issuing one to be shared between three gendarmes. 'These Arabs don't properly appreciate this stuff,' he explained to Bruce. 'It'd just be a waste.'

The liquor was lukewarm and gassy; it merely aggravated Bruce's thirst. He drained the bottle and tossed it out of the shelter.

'All right.' He stood up. 'Let's get these trusses into position.'

'That's the shortest ten minutes I ever lived,' commented Ruffy.

'Your watch is slow,' said Bruce.

Carrying the trusses within it, the shelter lumbered out on to the bridge. There was no laughter now, only laboured breathing and curses.

'Fix the ropes!' commanded Bruce. He tested the knots personally, then looked up at Ruffy and nodded.

'That'll do.'

'Come on, you mad bastards,' Ruffy growled. 'Lift it.'

The first truss rose to the perpendicular and swayed there like a grotesque maypole with the ropes hanging from its top.

'Two men on each rope,' ordered Bruce. 'Let it down gently.' He glanced round to ensure that they were all ready.

'Drop it over the edge, and I'll throw you bastards in after it,' warned Ruffy.

'Lower away!' shouted Bruce.

The truss leaned out over the gap towards the fire-blackened stump of bridge on the far side slowly at first, then faster as gravity took it.

'Hold it, damn you. Hold it!' roared Ruffy with the muscles in his shoulders humped out under the strain. They lay back against the ropes, but the weight of the truss dragged them forward as it fell.

It crashed down across the gap, lifted a cloud of dead wood ash as it struck, and lay there quivering.

'Man, I thought we'd lost that one for sure,' growled Ruffy, then turned savagely on his men.

'You bastards better be sharper with the next one – if you don't want to swim this river.'

They repeated the process with the second truss, and again they could not hold its falling length, but this time they were not so lucky. The end of the truss hit the far side, bounced and slid sideways.

'It's going! Pull, you bastards, pull!' shouted Ruffy.

The truss toppled slowly sideways and over the edge. It hit the river below them with a splash, disappeared under the surface, then bobbed up and floated away downstream until checked by the ropes.

Both Bruce and Ruffy fumed and swore during the lengthy exasperating business of dragging it back against the current and manhandling its awkward bulk back on to the bridge. Half a dozen times it slipped at the crucial moment and splashed back into the river.

Despite his other virtues, Ruffy's vocabulary of cursing words was limited and it added to his frustration that he had to keep repeating himself. Bruce did much better – he remembered things that he had heard and he made up a few.

When finally they had the dripping baulk of timber back on the bridge and were resting, Ruffy turned to Bruce with honest admiration.

'You swear pretty good,' he said. 'Never heard you before, but no doubt about it, you're good! What's that one about the cow again?'

Bruce repeated it for him a little self-consciously.

'You make that up yourself?' asked Ruffy.

'Spur of the moment,' laughed Bruce.

'That's 'bout the dirtiest I ever heard.' Ruffy could not conceal his envy. 'Man, you should write a book.'

'Let's get this bridge finished first,' said Bruce. 'Then I'll think about it.'

Now the truss was almost servile in its efforts to please. It dropped neatly across the gap and lay beside its twin.

'You curse something good enough, and it works every time,' Ruffy announced sagely. 'I think your one about the cow made all the difference, boss.'

With two trusses in position they had broken the back of the project. They carried the shelter out and set it on the trusses, straddling the gap. The third and fourth trusses were dragged into position and secured with ropes and nails before nightfall.

When the shelter waddled wearily back to the laager at dusk, the men within it were exhausted.Their hands were bleeding and bristled with wood splinters, but they were also mightily pleased with themselves.

'Sergeant Jacque, keep one of your searchlights trained on the bridge all night. We don't want our friends to come out and set fire to it again.

'There are only a few hours' life left in each of the batteries.' Jacque kept his voice low.

'Use them one at a time then.' Bruce spoke without hesitation. 'We must have that bridge lit up all night.'

'You think you could spare a beer for each of the boys that worked on the bridge today?'

'A whole one each!' Ruffy was shocked. 'I only got a couple cases left.'

Bruce fixed him with a stern eye and Ruffy grinned.

'Okay, boss. Guess they've earned it.'

Bruce transferred his attention to Wally Hendry who sat on the running-board of one of the trucks cleaning his nails with the point of his bayonet.

'Everything under control here, Hendry?' he asked coolly.

'Sure, what'd you think would happen? We'd have a visit from the archbishop? The sky'd fall in? Your French thing'd have twins or something?' He looked up from his nails at Bruce. 'When are you jokers going to get that bridge finished, instead of wandering around asking damn-fool questions?'

Bruce was too tired to feel annoyed. 'You've got the night watch, Hendry,' he said, 'from now until dawn.'

'Is that right, hey? And you? What're you going to do all night, or does that question make you blush?'

'I'm going to sleep, that's what I'm going to do. I haven't been lolling round camp all day.'

Hendry pegged the bayonet into the earth between his feet and snorted.

'Well, give her a little bit of sleep for me too, Bucko.'

Bruce left him and crossed to the Ford.

'Hello, Bruce. How did it go today? I missed you,' Shermaine greeted him, and her face lit up as she looked at him. It is a good feeling to be loved, and some of Bruce's fatigue lifted.

'About half finished, another day's work.' Then he smiled back at her. 'I won't lie and say I missed you – I've been too damn busy.'

'Your hands!' she said with quick concern and lifted them to examine them. 'They're in a terrible state.'

'Not very pretty, are they?'

'Let me get a needle from my case. I'll get the splinters out.'

From across the laager Wally Hendry caught Bruce's eye and with one hand made a suggestive sign below his waist. Then, at Bruce's frown of anger, he threw back his head and laughed with huge delight.

= 25 =

Bruce's stomach grumbled with hunger as he stood with Ruffy and Hendry beside the cooking fire. In the early morning light he could just make out the dark shape of the bridge at the end of the clearing. That drum was still beating in the jungle, but they hardly noticed it now. It was taken for granted like the mosquitoes. 'The batteries are finished,' grunted Ruffy. The feeble yellow beam of the searchlight reached out tiredly towards the bridge.

'Only just lasted the night,' agreed Bruce.

'Christ, I'm hungry,' complained Hendry. 'What could I do to a couple of fried eggs and a porterhouse steak.'

At the mention of food Bruce's mouth flooded with saliva. He shut his mind against the picture that Wally's words had evoked in his imagination.

'We won't be able to finish the bridge and get the trucks across today,' he said, and Ruffy agreed.

'There's a full day's work left on her, boss.'

'This is what we'll do then,' Bruce went on. 'I'll take the work party out to the bridge. Hendry, you will stay here in the laager and cover us the same as yesterday. And Ruffy, you take one of the trucks and a dozen of your boys. Go back ten miles or so to where the forest is open and they won't be able to creep up on you. Then cut us a mountain of firewood; thick logs that will burn all night. We will set a ring of watch fires round the camp tonight.'

'That makes sense,' Ruffy nodded. 'But what about the bridge?'

'We'll have to put a guard on it,' said Bruce, and the expressions on their faces changed as they thought about this.

'More pork chops for the boys in the bushes,' growled Hendry. 'You won't catch me sitting out on the bridge all night.'

'No one's asking you to,' snapped Bruce. 'All right, Ruffy. Go and fetch the wood, and plenty of it.'

Bruce completed the repairs to the bridge in the late afternoon. The most anxious period was in the middle of the day when he and four men had to leave the shelter and clamber down on to the supports a few feet above the surface of the river to set the king-posts in place. Here they were exposed at random range to arrows from the undergrowth along the banks. But no arrows came and they finished the job and climbed back to safety again with something of a sense of anticlimax.

They nailed the crossties over the trusses and then roped everything into a compact mass.

Bruce stood back and surveyed the fruit of two full days' labour.

'Functional,' he decided, speaking aloud. 'But we certainly aren't going to win any prizes for aesthetic beauty or engineering design.'

He picked up his jacket and thrust his arms into the sleeves; his sweaty upper body was cold now that the sun was almost down.

'Home, gentlemen,' he said, and his gendarmes scattered to their positions inside the shelter.

The metal shelter circled the laager, squatting every twenty or thirty paces like an old woman preparing to relieve herself. When it lifted and moved on it left a log fire behind it. The ring of fires was completed by dark and the shelter returned to the laager.

'Are you ready, Ruffy?' From inside the shelter Bruce called across to where Ruffy waited.

'All set, boss.'

Followed by six heavily armed gendarmes, Ruffy crossed quickly to join Bruce and they set off to begin their all-night vigil on the bridge.

Before midnight it was cold in the corrugated iron shelter, for the wind blew down the river and they were completely exposed to it, and there was no cloud cover to hold the day's warmth against the earth.

The men in the shelter huddled under their gas capes and waited. Bruce and Ruffy leaned together against the corrugated iron wall, their shoulders almost touching, and there was sufficient light from the stars to light the interior of the shelter and allow them to make out the guard rails of the bridge through the open ends.

'Moon will be up in an hour,' murmured Ruffy.

'Only a quarter of it, but it will give us a little more light,' Bruce concurred, and peered down into the black hole between his feet where he had prised up one of the newly laid planks.

'How about taking a shine with the torch?' suggested Ruffy.

'No.' Bruce shook his head, and passed the flashlight into his other hand. 'Not until I hear them.'

'You might not hear them.'

'If they swim downstream and climb up the piles, which is what I expect, then we'll hear them all right. They'll be dripping water all over the place,' said Bruce.

'Kanaki and his boys didn't her them,' Ruffy pointed out.

'Kanaki and his boys weren't listening for it,' said Bruce.

They were silent then for a while. One of the gendarmes started to snore softly and Ruffy shot out a huge booted foot that landed in the small of his back. The man cried out and scrambled to his knees, looking wildly about him.

'You have nice dreams?' Ruffy asked pleasantly.

'I wasn't sleeping,' the man protested. 'I was thinking.'

'Well, don't think so loudly,' Ruffy advised him. 'Sounds though you sawing through the bridge with a cross cut.'

Another half hour dragged itself by like a cripple.

'Fires are burning well,' commented Ruffy, and Bruce turned his head and glanced through the loophole in the corrugated iron behind him at the little garden of orange flame-flowers in the darkness.

'Yes, they should last till morning.'

Silence again, with only the singing of the mosquitoes and the rustle of the river as it flowed by the piles of the bridge. Shermaine has my pistol, Bruce remembered with a small trip in his pulse, I should have taken it back from her. He unclipped the bayonet from the muzzle of his rifle, tested the edge of the blade with his thumb, and slid it into the scabbard on his web-belt. Could easily lose the rifle if we start mixing it in the dark, he decided.

'Christ, I'm hungry,' grunted Ruffy beside him.

'You're too fat,' said Bruce. 'The diet will do you good.' And they waited.

Bruce stared down into the hole in the floorboards. His eyes began weaving fantasies out of the darkness, he could see vague shapes that moved, like things seen below the surface of the sea. His stomach tightened and he fought the impulse to shine his flashlight into the hole. He closed his eyes to rest them. I will count slowly to ten, he decided, and then look again.

Ruffy's hand closed on his upper arm; the pressure of his fingers transmitted alarm like a current of electricity. Bruce's eyelids flew open.

'Listen,' breathed Ruffy.

Bruce heard it. The stealthy drip of water on water below them. Then something bumped the bridge, but so softly that he felt rather than heard the jar.

'Yes,' Bruce whispered back. He reached out and tapped the shoulder of the gendarme beside him and the man's body stiffened at his touch.

With his breath scratching his dry throat, Bruce waited until he was sure the warning had been passed to all his men. Then he shifted the weight of his rifle from across his knees and aimed down into the hole.

He drew in a deep breath and switched on the flashlight. The beam shot down and he looked along it over his rifle barrel.

The square aperture in the floorboards formed a frame for the picture that flashed into his eyes. Black bodies, naked, glossy with wetness, weird patterns of tattoo marks, a face staring up at him, broad sloped forehead above startlingly white eyes and flat nose. The long gleaming blade of a panga. Clusters of humanity clinging to the wooden piles like ticks on the legs of a beast. Legs and arms and shiny trunks merged into a single organism, horrible as some slimy sea-creature.

Bruce fired into it. His rifle shuddered against his shoulder and the long orange spurts from its muzzle gave the picture a new flickering horror. The mass of bodies heaved, and struggled like a pack of rats trapped in a dry well. They dropped splashing into the river, swarmed up the timber piles, twisting and writhing as the bullets hit them, screaming, babbling over the sound of the rifle.

Bruce's weapon clicked empty and he groped for a new magazine. Ruffy and his gendarmes were hanging over the guard rails of the bridge, firing downwards, sweeping the piles below them with long bursts, the flashes lighting their faces and outlining their bodies against the sky.

'They're still coming!' roared Ruffy. 'Don't let them get over the side.'

Out of the hole at Bruce's feet thrust the head and naked upper body of a man. There was a panga in his hand; he slashed at Bruce's legs, his eyes glazed in the beam of the flashlight.

Bruce jumped back and the knife missed his knees by inches. The man wormed his way out of the hole towards Bruce. He was screaming shrilly, a high meaningless sound of fury.

Bruce lunged with the barrel of his empty rifle at the contorted black face. All his weight was behind that thrust and the muzzle went into the Baluba's eye. The foresight and four inches of the barrel disappeared into his head, stopping only when it hit bone. Colourless fluid from the burst eyeball gushed from round the protruding steel.

Tugging and twisting, Bruce tried to free the rifle, but the foresight had buried itself like the barb of a fish hook. The Baluba had dropped his panga and was clinging to the rifle barrel with both hands. He was wailing and rolling on his back upon the floorboards, his head jerking every time Bruce tried to pull the muzzle out of his head.

Beyond him the head and shoulders of another Baluba appeared through the aperture.

Bruce dropped his rifle and gathered up the fallen panga; he jumped over the writhing body of the first Baluba and lifted the heavy knife above his head with both hands.

The man was jammed in the hole, powerless to protect himself. He looked up at Bruce and his mouth fell open.

Two-handed, as though he were chopping wood, Bruce swung his whole body into the stroke. The shock jarred his shoulders and he felt blood splatter his legs. The untempered blade snapped off at the hilt and stayed imbedded in the Baluba's skull.

Panting heavily, Bruce straightened up and looked wildly about him. Baluba were swarming over the guard rail on one side of the bridge. The starlight glinted on their wet skins. One of his gendarmes was lying in a dark huddle, his head twisted back and his rifle still in his hands. Ruffy and the other gendarmes were still firing down over the far side.

'Ruffy!' shouted Bruce. 'Behind you! They're coming over!' and he dropped the handle of the panga and ran towards the body of the gendarme. He needed that rifle.

Before he could reach it the naked body of a Baluba rushed at him. Bruce ducked under the sweep of the panga and grappled with him. They fell locked together, the man's body slippery and sinuous against him, and the smell of him fetid as rancid butter.

Bruce found the pressure point below the elbow of his knife arm and dug in with his thumb. The Baluba yelled and his panga clattered on the floorboards. Bruce wrapped his arm round the man's neck while with his free hand he reached for his bayonet.

The Baluba was clawing for Bruce'e eyes with his fingers, his nails scored the side of Bruce's nose, but Bruce had his bayonet out now. He placed the point against the man's chest and pressed it in. He felt the steel scrape against the bone of a rib and the man redoubled his struggles at the sting of it. Bruce twisted the blade, working it in with his wrist, forcing the man's head backwards with his other arm.

The point of the bayonet scraped over the bone and found the gap between. Like taking a virgin, suddenly the resistance to its entrance was gone and it slid home full length. The Baluba's body jerked mechanically and the bayonet twitched in Bruce's fist.

Bruce did not even wait for the man to die. He pulled the blade out against the sucking reluctance of tissue that clung to it and scrambled to his feet in time to see Ruffy pick another Baluba from his feet and hurl him bodily over the guard rail.

Bruce snatched the rifle from the gendarme's dead hands and stepped to the guard rail. They were coming over the side, those below shouting and pushing at the ones above.

Like shooting a row of sparrows from a fence with a shotgun, thought Bruce grimly, and with one long burst he cleared the rail. Then he leaned out and sprayed the piles below the bridge. The rifle was empty. He reloaded with a magazine from his pocket. But it was all over. They were dropping back into the river, the piles below the bridge were clear of men, their heads bobbed away downstream.

Bruce lowered his rifle and looked about him. Three of his gendarmes were killing the man that Bruce had wounded, standing over him and grunting as they thrust down with their bayonets. The man was still wailing.

Bruce looked away.

One horn of the crescent moon showed above the trees; it had a gauzy halo about it.

Bruce lit a cigarette and behind him those gruesome noises ceased.

'Are you okay, boss?'

'Yes, I'm fine. How about you, Ruffy?'

'I got me a terrible thirst now. Hope nobody trod on my pack.'

About four minutes from the first shot to the last, Bruce guessed. That's the way of war, seven hours of waiting and boredom, then four minutes of frantic endeavour. Not only of war either, he thought. The whole of life is like that.

Then he felt the trembling in his thighs and the first spasm of nausea as the reaction started.

'What's happening?' A shout floated across from the laager. Bruce recognized Hendry's voice. 'Is everything all right?'

'We've beaten them off,' Bruce shouted back. 'Everything under control. You can go to sleep again.'

And now I have got to sit down quickly, he told himself.

Except for the tattoos upon his cheeks and forehead the dead Baluba's features were little different from those of the Bambala and Bakuba men who made up the bulk of Bruce's command.

Bruce played the flashlight over the corpse. The arms and legs were thin but stringy with muscle, and the belly bulged out from years of malnutrition. It was an ugly body, gnarled and crabbed. With distaste Bruce moved the light back to the features. The bone of the skull formed harsh angular planes beneath the skin, the nose was flattened and the thick lips had about them a repellent brutality. They were drawn back slightly to reveal the teeth which had been filed to sharp points like those of a shark.

'This is the last one, boss. I'll toss him overboard.' Ruffy spoke in the darkness beside Bruce.

'Good.'

Ruffy heaved and grunted, the corpse splashed below them and Ruffy wiped his hands on the guard rail, then came to sit beside Bruce.

'Goddam apes.' Ruffy's voice was full of the bitter tribal antagonism of Africa. 'When we get shot of these U.N. people there'll be a bit of sorting out to do. They've got a few things to learn, these bloody Baluba.'

And so it goes, thought Bruce, Jew and Gentile, Catholic and Protestant, black and white, Bambala and Baluba.

He checked the time, another two hours to dawn. His nervous reaction from physical violence had abated now; the hand that held the cigarette no longer trembled.

'They won't come again,' said Ruffy. 'You can get some sleep now if you want. I'll keep an eye open, boss.'

'No, thanks. I'll wait with you.' His nerves had not settled down enough for sleep.

'How's it for a beer?'

'Thanks.'

Bruce sipped the beer and stared out at the watch fires round the laager. They had burned down to puddles of red ash but Bruce knew that Ruffy was right. The Baluba would not attack again that night.

'So how do you like freedom?'

'How's that, boss?' The question puzzled Ruffy and he turned to Bruce questioningly.

'How do you like it now the Belgians have gone?'

'It's pretty good, I reckon.'

'And if Tshombe has to give in to the Central Government?'

'Those mad Arabs!' snarled Ruffy. 'All they want is our copper. They're going to have to get up early in the morning to take it. We're in the saddle here.'

The great jousting tournament of the African continent. I'm in the saddle, try to unhorse me! As in all matters of survival it was not a question of ethics and political doctrine (except to the spectators in Whitehall, Moscow, Washington and Peking). There were big days coming, thought Bruce. My own country, when she blows, is going to make Algiers look like an old ladies' sewing circle.

26

The sun was up, throwing long shadows out into the clearing, and Bruce stood beside the Ford and looked across the bridge at the corrugated iron shelter on the far bank.

He relaxed for a second and let his mind run unhurriedly over his preparations for the crossing. Was there something left undone, some disposition which could make it more secure?

Hendry and a dozen men were in the shelter across the bridge, ready to meet any attack on that side.

Shermaine would take the Ford across first. Then the lorries would follow her. They would cross empty to minimize the danger of the bridge collapsing, or being weakened for the passage of the tanker. After each lorry had crossed, Hendry would shuttle its load and passengers over in the shelter and deposit them under the safety of the canvas canopy.

The last lorry would go over fully loaded. That was regrettable but unavoidable.

Finally Bruce himself would drive the tanker across. Not as an act of heroism, although it was the most dangerous business of the morning, but because he would trust no one else to do it, not even Ruffy. The five hundred gallons of fuel it contained was their safe-conduct home. Bruce had taken the precaution of filling all the gasoline tanks in the convoy in case of accidents, but they would need replenishing before they reached Msapa Junction.

He looked down at Shermaine in the driver's seat of the Ford.

'Keep it in low gear, take her over slowly but steadily.Whatever else you do, don't stop.'

She nodded. She was composed and she smiled at him. Bruce felt a stirring of pride as he looked at her, so small and lovely, but today she was doing man's work. He went on. 'As soon as you are over, I will send one of the trucks after you. Hendry will put six of his men into it and then come back for the others.'

'Oui, Monsieur Bonaparte.'

'You'll pay for that tonight,' he threatened her. 'Off you go.'

Shermaine let out the clutch and the Ford bounced over rough ground to the road, accelerated smoothly out on to the bridge.

Bruce held his breath, but there was only a slight check and sway as it crossed the repaired section.

'Thank God for that,' Bruce let out his breath and watched while Shermaine drew up alongside the shelter.

'Allez,' Bruce shouted at the coloured engine driver who was ready at the wheel of the first truck. The man smiled his cheerful chubby-faced smile, waved, and the truck rolled forward.

Watching anxiously as it went on to the bridge, Bruce saw the new timbers give perceptibly beneath the weight of the truck, and he heard them creak loudly in protest.

'Not so good,' he muttered.

'No –' agreed Ruffy. 'Boss, why don't you let someone else take the tanker over?'

'We've been over that already,' Bruce answered him without turning his head. Across the river Hendry was transferring his men from the shelter to the back of the truck. Then the shelter started its tedious way back towards them.

Bruce fretted impatiently during the four hours that it took to get four trucks across. The long business was the shuttling back and forth of the corrugated iron shelter, at least ten minutes for each trip.

Finally there was only the fifth truck and the tanker left on the north bank. Bruce started the engine of the tanker and put her into auxiliary low, then he blew a single blast on the horn. The driver of the truck ahead of him waved an acknowledgement and pulled forward.

The truck reached the bridge and went out into the middle. It was fully loaded, twenty men aboard. It came to the repaired section and slowed down, almost stopping.

'Go on! Keep it going, damn you,' Bruce shouted in impotent anger. The fool of a driver was forgetting his orders. He crawled forward and the bridge gave alarmingly under the full weight, the high canopied roof rocked crazily, and even above the rumble of his own engine Bruce could hear the protesting groan of the bridge timbers.

'The fool, oh, the bloody fool,' whispered Bruce to himself. Suddenly he felt very much alone and unprotected here on the north bank with the bridge being mutilated by the incompetence of the truck driver. He started the tanker moving.

Ahead of him the other driver had panicked. He was racing his engine, the rear wheels spun viciously, blue smoke of scorched tyres, and one of the floorboards tore loose. Then the truck lurched forward and roared up the south bank.

Bruce hesitated, applying the brakes and bringing the tanker to a standstill on the threshold of the bridge.

He thought quickly. The sensible thing would be to repair the damage to the bridge before chancing it with the weight of the tanker. But that would mean another day's delay. None of them had eaten since the previous morning. Was he justified in gambling against even odds, for that's what they were? A fifty-fifty chance, heads you get across, tails you dump the tanker in the middle of the river.

Then unexpectedly the decision was made for him.

From across the river a Bren gun started firing. Bruce jumped in his seat and looked up. Then a dozen other guns joined in and the tracer flew past the tanker. They were firing across towards him, close on each side of him. Bruce struggled to drag from his uncomprehending brain an explanation of this new development. Suddenly everything was moving too swiftly. Everything was confusion and chaos.

Movement in the rear-view mirror of the tanker caught his eye. He stared at it blankly. Then he twisted quickly in his seat and looked back.

'Christ!' he swore with fright.

From the edge of the jungle on both sides of the clearing Baluba were swarming into the open. Hundreds of them running towards him, the animal-skin kilts swirling about their legs, feather head-dresses fluttering, sun bright on the long blades of their pangas. An arrow rang dully against the metal body of the tanker.

Bruce revved the engine, gripped the wheel hard with both hands and took the tanker out on to the bridge. Above the sound of the guns he could hear the shrill ululation, the excited squealing of two hundred Baluba. It sounded very close, and he snatched a quick look in the mirror. What he saw nearly made him lose his head and give the tanker full throttle. The nearest Baluba, screened from the guns on the south bank by the tanker's bulk, was only ten paces away. So close that Bruce could see the tattoo marks on his face and chest.

With an effort Bruce restrained his right foot from pressing down too hard, and instead he bore down on the repaired section of the bridge at a sedate twenty miles an hour. He tried to close his mind to the squealing behind him and the thunder of gunfire ahead of him.

The front wheels hit the new timbers, and above the other sounds he heard them groan loudly, and felt them sag under him.

The tanker rolled on and the rear wheels brought their weight to bear. The groan of wood became a cracking, rending sound. The tanker slowed as the bridge subsided, its wheels spun without purchase, it tilted sideways, no longer moving forward.

A sharp report, as one of the main trusses broke, and Bruce felt the tanker drop sharply at the rear; its nose pointed upwards and it started to slide back.

'Get out!' his brain shrieked at him. 'Get out, it's falling!' He reached for the door handle beside him, but at that moment the bridge collapsed completely. The tanker rolled off the edge.

Bruce was hurled across the cab with a force that stunned him, his legs wedged under the passenger seat and his arms tangled in the strap of his rifle. The tanker fell free and Bruce felt his stomach swoop up and press against his chest as though he rode a giant roller coaster.

The sickening drop lasted only an instant, and then the tanker hit the river. Immediately the sounds of gunfire and the screaming of Baluba were drowned out as the tanker disappeared below the surface. Through the windscreen Bruce saw now the cool cloudy green of water, as though he looked into the windows of an aquarium. With a gentle rocking motion the tanker sank down through the green water.

'Oh, my God, not this!' He spoke aloud as he struggled up from the floor of the cab. His ears were filled with the hiss and belch of escaping air bubbles; they rose in silver clouds past the windows.

The truck was still sinking, and Bruce felt the pain in his eardrums as the pressure built up inside the cab. He opened his mouth and swallowed convulsively, and his eardrums squeaked as the pressure equalized and the pain abated. Water was squirting in through the floor of the cab and jets of it spurted out of the instrument panel of the dashboard. The cab was flooding.

Bruce twisted the handle of the door beside him and hit it with his shoulder. It would not budge an inch. He flung all his weight against it, anchoring his feet on the dashboard and straining until he felt his eyeballs starting out of their sockets. It was jammed solid by the immense pressure of water on the outside.

'The windscreen,' he shouted aloud. 'Break the windscreen.' He groped for his rifle. The cab had flooded to his waist as he sat in the passenger's seat. He found the rifle and brought it dripping to his shoulder. He touched the muzzle to the windscreen and almost fired. But his good sense warned him.

Clearly he saw the danger of firing. The concussion in the confined cab would burst his eardrums, and the avalanche of broken glass that would be thrown into his face by the water pressure outside would certainly blind and maim him.

He lowered the rifle despondently. He felt his panic being slowly replaced by the cold certainty of defeat. He was trapped fifty feet below the surface of the river. There was no way out.

He thought of turning the rifle on himself, ending the inevitable, but he rejected the idea almost as soon as it had formed. Not that way, never that way!

He flogged his mind, driving it out of the cold lethargic clutch of certain death. There must be something. Think! Damn you, think!

The tanker was till rocking; it had not yet settled into the ooze of the river bottom. How long had he been under? About twenty seconds. Surely it should have hit the bottom long ago.

Unless! Bruce felt hope surge into new life within him. The tank! By God, that was it. The great, almost empty tank behind him! The five-thousand-gallon tank which now contained only four hundred gallons of gasoline – it would have a displacement of nearly eighteen tons! It would float.

As if in confirmation of his hope, he felt his eardrums creak and pop. The pressure was falling! He was rising.

Bruce stared out at green water through the glass. The silver clouds of bubbles no longer streamed upwards; they seemed to hang outside the cab. The tanker had overcome the initial impetus that had driven it far below the surface, and now it was floating upwards at the same rate of ascent as its bubbles.

The dark green of deep water paled slowly to the colour of Chartreuse. And Bruce laughed. It was a gasping hysterical giggle and the sound of it shocked him. He cut it off abruptly.

The tanker bobbed out on to the surface, water streamed from the windscreen and through it Bruce caught a misty distorted glimpse of the south bank.

He twisted the door handle and this time the door burst open readily, water poured into the cab and Bruce floundered out against its rush.

With one quick glance he took in his position. The tanker had floated down twenty yards below the bridge, the guns on the south bank had fallen silent, and he could see no Baluba on the north bank. They must have disappeared back into the jungle.

Bruce plunged into the river and struck out for the south bank. Vaguely he heard the thin high shouts of encouragement from his gendarmes.

Within a dozen strokes he knew he was in difficulties. The drag of his boots and his sodden uniform was enormous. Treading water he tore off his steel helmet and let it sink. Then he tried to struggle out of his battle-jacket. It clung to his arms and chest and he disappeared under the surface four times before he finally got rid of it. He had breathed water into his lungs and his legs were tired and heavy.

The south bank was too far away. He would never make it. Coughing painfully he changed his objective and struck upstream against the current towards the bridge.

He felt himself settling lower in the water; he had to force his arms to lift and fall forward into each stroke.

Something plopped into the water close beside him. He paid no attention to it; suddenly a sense of disinterest had come over him, the first stage of drowning. He mistimed a breath and sucked in more water. The pain of it goaded him into a fresh burst of coughing. He hung in the water, gasping and hacking painfully.

Again something plopped close by, and this time he lifted his head. An arrow floated past him – then they began drooping steadily about him.

Baluba hidden in the thick bush above the beach were shooting at him; a gentle pattering rain of arrows splashed around his head. Bruce started swimming again, clawing his way frantically upstream. He swam until he could no longer lift his arms clear of the surface and the weight of his boots dragged his feet down.

Again he lifted his head. The bridge was close, not thirty feet away, but he knew that those thirty feet were as good as thirty miles. He could not make it.

The arrows that fell about him were no longer a source of terror. He thought of them only with mild irritation.

Why the hell can't they leave me alone? I don't want to play any more. I just want to relax. I'm so tired, so terribly tired.

He stopped moving and felt the water rise up coolly over his mouth and nose.

'Hold on, boss. I'm coming.' The shout penetrated through the grey fog of Bruce's drowning brain. He kicked and his head rose once more above the surface. He looked up at the bridge.

Stark naked, big belly swinging with each pace, thick legs flying, the great dangling bunch of his genitals bouncing merrily, black as a charging hippopotamus, Sergeant Major Ruffararo galloped out along the bridge.

He reached the fallen section and hauled himself up on to the guard rail. The arrows were falling around him, hissing down like angry insects. One glanced off his shoulder without penetrating and Ruffy shrugged at it, then launched himself up and out, falling in an ungainly heap of arms and legs to hit the water with a splash.

'Where the hell are you, boss?'

Bruce croaked a water-strangled reply and Ruffy came ploughing down towards him with clumsy overarm strokes.

He reached Bruce.

'Always playing around,' he grunted. 'Guess some guys never learn!' His fist closed on a handful of Bruce's hair.

Struggling unavailingly Bruce felt his head tucked firmly under Ruffy's arm and he was dragged through the water. Occasionally his face came out long enough to suck a breath but mostly he was under water. Consciousness receded and he felt himself going, going.

His head bumped against something hard but he was too weak to reach out his hand.

'Wake up, boss. You can have a sleep later.' Ruffy's voice bellowed in his ear. He opened his eyes and saw beside him the pile of the bridge.

'Come on. I can't carry you up here.'

Ruffy had worked round the side of the pile, shielding them from arrows, but the current was strong here, tugging at their bodies. Without the strength to prevent it Bruce's head rolled sideways and his face flopped forward into the water.

'Come on, wake up.' With a stinging slap Ruffy's open hand hit Bruce across the cheek. The shock roused him, he coughed and a mixture of water and vomit shot up his throat and out of his mouth and nose. Then he blenched painfully and retched again.

'How's it feel now?' Ruffy demanded.

Bruce lifted a hand from the water and wiped his mouth. He felt much better.

'Okay? Can you make it?'

Bruce nodded.

'Let's go then.'

With Ruffy dragging and pushing him, he worked his way up the pile. Water poured from his clothing as his body emerged, his hair was plastered across his forehead and he could feel each breath gurgle in his lungs.

'Listen boss. When we get to the top we'll be in the open again. There'll be more arrows – not time to sit around and chat. We're going over the rail fast and then run like hell, okay?'

Bruce nodded again. Above him were the floorboards of the bridge. With one hand he reached up and caught an upright of the guard rail, and he hung there without strength to pull himself the rest of the way.

'Hold it there,' grunted Ruffy and wriggled his shiny wet bulk up and over.

The arrows started falling again; one pegged into the wood six inches from Bruce's face and stood there quivering. Slowly Bruce's grip relaxed. I can't hold on, he thought, I'm going.

Then Ruffy's hand closed on his wrist, he felt himself dragged up, his legs dangled. He hung suspended by one arm and the water swirled smoothly past twenty feet below.

Slowly he was drawn upwards, his chest scraped over the guard rail, tearing his shirt, then he tumbled over it into an untidy heap on the bridge.

Vaguely he heard the guns firing on the south bank, the flit and thump of the arrows, and Ruffy's voice.

'Come on, boss. Get up.'

He felt himself being lifted and dragged along. With his legs boneless soft under him, he staggered beside Ruffy. Then there were no more arrows; the timbers of the bridge became solid earth under his feet. Voices and hands on him. He was being lifted, then lowered faced down on to the wooden floor of a truck. The rhythmic pressure on his chest as someone started artificial respiration above him, the warm gush of water up his throat, and Shermaine's voice. He could not understand what she was saying, but just the sound of it was enough to make him realize he was safe. Darkly through the fog he became aware that her voice was the most important sound in his life.

He vomited again.

Hesitantly at first, and then swiftly, Bruce came back from the edge of oblivion.

'That's enough,' he mumbled and rolled out from under Sergeant Jacque who was administering the artificial respiration. The movement started a fresh paroxysm of coughing and he felt Shermaine's hands on his shoulders restraining him.

'Bruce, you must rest.'

'No.' He struggled into a sitting position. 'We've got to get out into the open,' he gasped.

'No hurry, boss. We've left all the Balubes on the other bank. There's a river between us.'

'How do you know?' Bruce challenged him.

'Well –'

'You don't!' Bruce told him flatly. 'There could easily be another few hundred on this side.' He coughed again painfully and then went on. We're leaving in five minutes, get them ready.'

'Okay.' Ruffy turned to leave.

'Ruffy!'

'Boss?' He turned back expectantly.

'Thank you.'

Ruffy grinned self-consciously. "At's all right. I needed a wash anyway.'

'I'll buy you a drink when we get home.'

'I won't forget,' Ruffy warned him, and climbed down out of the truck. Bruce heard him shouting to his boys.

'I thought I'd lost you.' Shermaine's arm was still round his shoulders and Bruce looked at her for the first time.

'My sweet girl, you won't get rid of me that easily,' he assured her. He was feeling much better now.

'Bruce, I want to – I can't explain –' Unable to find the words she leaned forward instead and kissed him, full on the mouth.

When they drew apart, Sergeant Jacque and the two gendarmes with him were grinning delightedly.

'There is nothing wrong with you now, Captain.'

'No, there isn't,' Bruce agreed. 'Make your preparations for departure.'

From the passenger seat of the Ford Bruce took one last look at the bridge.

The repaired section hung like a broken drawbridge into the water. Beyond it on the far bank were scattered a few dead Baluba, like celluloid dolls in the sunlight. Far downstream the gasoline tanker had been washed by the current against the beach. It lay on its side, half-submerged in the shallows and the white Shell insignia showed clearly.

And the river flowed on, green and inscrutable, with the jungle pressing close along its banks.

'Let's get away from here,' said Bruce.

Shermaine started the engine and the convoy of trucks followed them along the track through the belt of thick river bush and into the open forest again.

Bruce looked at his watch. The inside of the glass was dewed with moisture and he lifted it to his ear.

'Damn thing has stopped. What's your time?'

'Twenty minutes to one.'

'Half the day wasted,' Bruce grumbled.

'Will we reach Msapa Junction before dark?'

'No, we won't. For two good reasons. Firstly, it's too far, and secondly, we haven't enough gas.'

'What are you going to do?' Her voice was unruffled, already she had complete faith in him. I wonder how long it will last, he mused cynically. At first you're a god. You have not a single human weakness. They set a standard for you, and the standard is perfection. Then the first time you fall short of it, their whole world blows up.

'We'll think of something,' he assured her.

'I'm sure you will,' she agreed complacently and Bruce grinned. The big joke, of course, was that when she said it he also believed it. Damned if being in love doesn't make you feel one hell of a man.

He changed to English so as to exclude the two gendarmes in the back seat from the conversation.

'You are the best thing that has happened to me in thirty years.'

'Oh, Bruce.' She turned her face towards him and the expression of trusting love in it and the intensity of his own emotion struck Bruce like a physical blow.

I will keep this thing alive, he vowed. I must nourish it with care and protect it from the dangers of selfishness and familiarity.

'Oh, Bruce, I do love you so terribly much. This morning when – when I thought I had lost you, when I saw the tanker go over into the river –' She swallowed and now her eyes were full of tears. 'It was as though the light had gone – it was so dark, so dark and cold without you.'

Absorbed with him so that she had forgotten about the road, Shermaine let the Ford veer and the offside wheels pumped into the rough verge.

'Hey, watch it!' Bruce cautioned her. 'Dearly as I love you also, I have to admit that you're a lousy driver. Let me take her.'

'Do you feel up to it?'

'Yes, pull into the side.'

Slowly, held to the speed of the lumbering vehicles behind them, they drove on through the afternoon. Twice they passed deserted Baluba villages beside the road, the grass huts disintegrating and the small cultivated lands about them thickly overgrown.

'My God, I'm hungry. I've got a headache from it and my belly feels as though it's full of warm water,' complained Bruce.

'Don't think you're the only one. This is the strictest diet I've ever been on, must have lost two kilos! But I always lose in the wrong place, never on my bottom.'

'Good,' Bruce said. 'I like it just the way it is, never shed an ounce there.' He looked over his shoulder at the two gendarmes. 'Are you hungry?' he asked in French.

'Mon Dieu!' exclaimed the fat one. 'I will not be able to sleep tonight, if I must lie on an empty stomach.'

'Perhaps it will not be necessary.' Bruce let his eyes wander off the road into the surrounding bush. The character of the country had changed in the last hundred miles. 'This looks like game country. I've noticed plenty of spoor on the road. Keep your eyes open.'

The trees were tall and widely spaced with grass growing beneath them. Their branches did not interlock so that the sky showed through. At intervals there were open glades filled with green swamp grass and thickets of bamboo and ivory palms.

'We've got another half hour of daylight. We might run into something before then.'

In the rear-view mirror he watched the lumbering column of transports for a moment. They must be almost out of gasoline by now, hardly enough for another half hour's driving. There were compensations however; at least they were in open country now and only eighty miles from Msapa Junction.

He glanced at the petrol gauge – half the tank. The Ranchero still had sufficient to get through even if the trucks were almost dry.

Of course! That was the answer. Find a good camp, leave the convoy, and go on in the Ford to find help. Without the trucks to slow him down he could get through to Msapa Junction in two hours. There was a telegraph in the station office, even if the junction was still deserted.

'We'll stop on the other side of this stream,' said Bruce and slowed the Ford, changed into second gear and let it idle down the steep bank.

The stream was shallow. The water hardly reached the hubcaps as they bumped across the rocky bottom. Bruce gunned the Ford up the far bank into the forest again.

'There!' shouted one of the gendarmes from the back seat and Bruce followed the direction of his arm.

Standing with humped shoulders, close beside the road, bunched together with mournfully drooping horns, heads held low beneath the massive bosses, bodies very big and black, were two old buffalo bulls.

Bruce hit the brakes, skidding the Ranchero to a stop, reaching for his rifle at the same instant. He twisted the door handle, hit the door with his shoulder and tumbled out on to his feet.

With a snort and a toss of their ungainly heads the buffalo started to run.

Bruce picked the leader and aimed for the neck in front of the plunging black shoulder. Leaning forward against the recoil of the rifle he fired and heard the bullet strike with a meaty thump. The bull slowed, breaking his run. The stubby forelegs settled and he slid forward on his nose, rolling as he fell, dust and legs kicking.

Turning smoothly without taking the butt from his shoulder, swinging with the run of the second bull, Bruce fired again, and again the thump of bullet striking.

The buffalo stumbled, giving in the legs, then he steadied and galloped on like a grotesque rocking horse, patches of baldness grey on his flanks, big-bellied, running heavily.

Bruce shifted the bead of the foresight on to his shoulder and fired twice in quick succession, aiming low for the heart, hitting each time, the bull so close he could see the bullet wounds appear on the dark skin.

The gallop broke into a trot, with head swinging low, mouth open, legs beginning to fold. Aiming carefully for the head Bruce fired again. The bull bellowed – a sad lonely sound – and collapsed into the grass.

The lorries had stopped in a line behind the Ford, and now from each of them swarmed black men. Jabbering happily, racing each other, they streamed past Bruce to where the buffalo had fallen in the grass beside the road.

'Nice shooting, boss,' applauded Ruffy. 'I'm going to have me a piece of tripe the size of a blanket.'

'Let's make camp first.' Bruce's ears were still singing with gunfire. 'Get the lorries into a ring.'

'I'll see to it.'

Bruce walked up to the nearest buffalo and watched for a while as a dozen men strained to roll it on to its back and begin butchering it. There were clusters of grape-blue ticks in the folds of skin between the legs and body.

A good head, he noted mechanically, forty inches at least.

'Plenty of meat, Captain. Tonight we eat thick!' grinned one of his gendarmes as he bent over the huge body to begin flensing.

'Plenty,' agreed Bruce and turned back to the Ranchero. In the heat of the kill it was a good feeling: the rifle's kick and your stomach screwed up with excitement. But afterwards you felt a little bit dirtied; sad and guilty as you do after lying with a woman you do not love.

He climbed into the car and Shermaine sat away from him, withdrawn.

'They were so big and ugly – beautiful,' she said softly.

'We needed the meat. I didn't kill them for fun.' But he thought with a little shame, I have killed many others for fun.

'Yes,' she agreed. 'We needed the meat.'

He turned the car off the road and signalled to the truck drivers to pull in behind him.

= 27 =

Later it was all right again. The meat-rich smoke from a dozen cooking fires drifted across the camp. The dark treetops silhouetted against a sky full of stars, the friendly glow of the fires, and laughter, men's voices raised, someone singing, the night noises of the bush – insects and frogs in the nearby stream – a plate piled high with grilled fillets and slabs of liver, a bottle of beer from Ruffy's hoard, the air at last cooler, a small breeze to keep the mosquitoes away, and Shermaine sitting beside him on the blankets.

Ruffy drifted across to them, in one hand a stick loaded with meat from which the juice dripped and in the other hand a bottle held by the throat.

'How's it for another beer, boss?'

'Enough.' Bruce held up his hand. 'I'm full to the back teeth.'

'You're getting old, that's for sure. Me and the boys going to finish them buffalo or burst trying.' He squatted on his great haunches and his tone changed. 'The trucks are flat, boss. Reckon there's not a bucketful of gas in the lot of them.'

'I want you to drain all the tanks, Ruffy, and pour it into the Ford.'

Ruffy nodded and bit a hunk of meat off the end of the stick.

'Then first thing tomorrow morning you and I will go on to Msapa in the Ranchero and leave everyone else here. Lieutenant Hendry will be in charge.'

'You talking about me?' Wally came from one of the fires.

'Yes, I'm going to leave you in charge here while Ruffy and I go on to Msapa Junction to fetch help.' Bruce did not look at Hendry and he had difficulty keeping the loathing out of his voice. 'Ruffy, fetch the map will you?'

They spread it on the earth and huddled round it. Ruffy held the flashlight.

'I'd say we are about here.' Bruce touched the tiny black vein of the road. 'About seventy, eighty miles to Msapa.' He ran his finger along it. 'It will take us about five hours there and back. However, if the telegraph isn't working we might have to go on until we meet a patrol or find some other way of getting a message back to Elisabethville.'

Almost parallel to the road and only two inches from it on the large scale map ran the thick red line that marked the Northern Rhodesian border. Wally Hendry's slitty eyes narrowed even further as he looked at it.

'Why not leave Ruffy here, and I'll go with you.' Hendry looked up at Bruce.

'I want Ruffy with me to translate if we meet any Africans along the way.' Also, thought Bruce, I don't want to be left on the side of the road with a bullet in my head while you drive on to Elisabethville.

'Suits me,' grunted Hendry. He dropped his eyes to the map. About forty miles to the border. A hard day's walk.

Bruce changed to French and spoke swiftly. 'Ruffy, hide the diamonds behind the dashboard of your truck. That way we are certain they will send a rescue party, even if we have to go Elisabethville.'

'Talk English, Bucko,' growled Hendry, but Ruffy nodded and answered, also in French.

'I will leave Sergeant Jacque to guard them.'

'NO!' said Bruce. 'Tell no one.'

'Cut it out!' rasped Hendry. 'Anything you say I want to hear.'

'We'll leave at dawn tomorrow,' Bruce reverted to English.

'May I go with you?' Shermaine spoke for the first time.

'I don't see why not.' Bruce smiled quickly at her, but Ruffy coughed awkwardly.

'Reckon that's not such a good idea, boss.'

'Why?' Bruce turned on him with his temper starting to rise.

'Well, boss,' Ruffy hesitated, and then went on, 'you, me and the lady all shoving off towards Elisabethvile might not look so good to the boys. They might get ideas, think we're not coming back or something.'

Bruce was silent, considering it.

'That's right,' Hendry cut in. 'You might just take it into your head to keep going. Let her stay, sort of guarantee for the rest of us.'

'I don't mind, Bruce. I didn't think about it that way. I'll stay.'

'She'll have forty good boys looking after her, she'll be all right,' Ruffy assured Bruce.

'All right then, that's settled. It won't be for long, Shermaine.'

'I'll go and see about draining the trucks.' Ruffy stood up. 'See you in the morning, boss.'

'I'm going to get some more of that meat.' Wally picked up the map carelessly. 'Try and get some sleep tonight, Curry. Not too much grumble and grunt.'

In his exasperation, Bruce did not notice that Hendry had taken the map.

= 28 =

It rained in the early hours before the dawn and Bruce lay in the back of the Ranchero and listened to it drum on the metal roof. It was a lulling sound and a good feeling to lie warmly listening to the rain with the woman you love in your arms.

He felt her waking against him, the change in her breathing and the first slow movements of her body.

There were buffalo steaks for breakfast, but no coffee. They ate swiftly and then Bruce called across to Ruffy.

'Okay, Ruffy?'

'Let's go, boss.' They climbed into the Ford and Ruffy filled most of the seat beside Bruce. His helmet perched on the back of his head, rifle sticking out through the space where the windscreen should have been, and two large feet planted securely on top of the case of beer on the floor.

Bruce twisted the key and the engine fired. He warmed it at a fast idle and turned to Hendry who leaned against the roof of the Ford and peered through the window.

'We'll be back this afternoon. Don't let anybody wander away from camp.'

'Okay.' Hendry breathed his morning breath full into Bruce's face.

'Keep them busy, otherwise they'll get bored and start fighting.'

Before he answered Hendry let his eyes search the interior of the Ford carefully and then he stood back.

'Okay,' he said again. 'On your way!'

Bruce looked beyond him to where Shermaine sat on the tailboard of a truck and smiled at her.

'Bon voyage!' she called and Bruce let out the clutch. They bumped out on to the road amid a chorus of cheerful farewells from the gendarmes round the cooking fires and Bruce settled down to drive. In the rear-view mirror he watched the camp disappear round the curve in the road. There were puddles of rain water in the road, but above them the clouds had broken up and scattered across the sky.

'How's it for a beer, bos?'

'Instead of coffee?' asked Bruce.

'Nothing like it for the bowels,' grunted Ruffy and reached down to open the case.

Wally Hendry lifted his helmet and scratched his scalp. His short red hair felt stiff and wiry with dried sweat and there was a spot above his right ear that itched. He fingered it tenderly.

The Ranchero disappeared round a bend in the road, the trees screening it abruptly, and the hum of its motor faded.

Okay, so they haven't taken the diamonds with them. I had a bloody good look around. I guessed they'd leave them. The girl knows where they are like as not. Perhaps – no, she'd squeal like a stuck pig if I asked.

Hendry looked sideways at Shermaine; she was staring after the Ranchero.

Silly bitch! Getting all broody now that Curry's giving her the rod. Funny how these educated Johnnies like their women to have small tits – nice piece of arse though. Wouldn't mind a bit of that myself. Jesus, that would really get to Mr High Class Bloody Curry, me giving his pretty the business. Not a chance though. These niggers think he's a God or something. They'd tear me to pieces if I touched her. Forget about it! Let's get the diamonds and take off for the border.

Hendry settled his helmet back on to his head and strolled casually across to the truck that Ruffy had been driving the day before.

Got a map, compass, coupla spare clips of ammo – now all we need is the glass.

He climbed into the cab and opened the cubbyhole.

Bet a pound to a pinch of dung that they've hidden them somewhere in this truck. They're not worried – think they've got me tied up here. Never occurred to them that old Uncle Wally might up and walk away. Thought I'd just sit here and wait for them to come back and fetch me – take me in and hand me over to a bunch of nigger police aching to get their hands on a white man.

Well, I got news for you, Mr Fancy-talking Curry!

He rummaged in the cubbyhole and then slammed it shut.

Okay, they're not there. Let's try under the seats. The border is not guarded, might take me three or four days to get through to Fort Rosebery, but when I do I'll have me a pocket full of diamonds and there's a direct air service out to Ndola and the rest of the world. Then we start living!

There was nothing under the seats except a greasy dust-coated jack and wheel spanner. Hendry turned his attention to the floorboards.

Pity I'll have to leave that bastard Curry. I had plans for him. There's a guy who really gets to me. So goddam cocksure of himself. One of them. Makes you feel you're shit – fancy talk, pretty face, soft hands. Christ, I hate him.

Viciously he tore the rubber mats off the floor and the dust made him cough.

Been to university, makes him think he's something special. The bastard. I should have fixed him long ago – that night at the road bridge I nearly gave it to him in the dark. Nobody would have known, just a mistake. I shoulda done it then. I shoulda done it at Port Reprieve when he ran out across the road to the office block. Big bloody hero. Big lover. Bet he had everything he ever wanted, bet his Daddy gave him all the money he could use. And he looks at you like that, like you crawled out of rotting meat.

Hendry straightened up and gripped the steering wheel, his jaws chewing with the strength of his hatred. He stared out of the windscreen.

Shermaine Cartier walked past the front of the truck. She had a towel and a pink plastic toilet bag in her hand; the pistol swung against her leg as she moved.

Sergeant Jacque stood up from the cooking fire and moved to intercept her. They talked, arguing, then Shermaine touched the pistol at her side and laughed. A worried frown creased Jacque's black face and he shook his head dubiously. Shermaine laughed again, turned from him and set off down the road towards the stream. Her hair, caught carelessly at her neck with a ribbon, hung down her back on to the rose-coloured shirt she wore and the heavy canvas holster emphasized the unconsciously provocative swing of her hips. She went out of sight down the steep bank of the stream.

Wally Hendry chuckled and then licked his lips with the quick-darting tip of his tongue.

'This is going to make it perfect,' he whispered. 'They couldn't have done things to suit me better if they'd spent a week working it out.'

Eagerly he turned back to his search for the diamonds. Leaning forward he thrust his hand up behind the dashboard of the truck and it brushed against the bunch of canvas bags that hung from the mass of concealed wires.

'Come to Uncle Wally.' He jerked them loose and, holding them in his lap, began checking their contents. The third bag he opened contained the gem stones.

'Lovely, lovely grub,' he whispered at the dull glint and sparkle in the depths of the bag. Then he closed the draw string, stuffed the bag into the pocket of his battle-jacket and buttoned the flap. He dropped the bags of industrial diamonds on to the floor and kicked them under the seat, picked up his rifle and stepped down out of the truck.

Three of four gendarmes looked up curiously at him as he passed the cooking fires. Hendry rubbed his stomach and pulled a face.

'Too much meat last night!'

The gendarme who understood English laughed and translated into French. They all laughed and one of them called something in a dialect that Hendry did not understand. They watched him walk away among the trees.

As soon as he was out of sight of the camp Hendry started to run, circling back towards the stream.

'This is going to be a pleasure!' He laughed aloud.

= 29 =

Fifty yards below the drift where the road crossed the stream Shermaine found a shallow pool. There were reeds with fluffy heads around it and a small beach of white river sand, black boulders, polished round and glossy smooth, the water almost blood warm and so clear that she could see a shoal of fingerlings nibbling at the green algae that coated the boulders beneath the surface.

She stood barefooted in the sand and looked around carefully, but the reeds screened her, and she had asked Jacque not to let any of his men come down to the river while she was there.

She undressed, dropped her clothes across one of the black boulders and with a cake of soap in her hand waded out into the pool and lowered herself until she sat with the water up to her neck and the sand pleasantly rough under her naked behind.

She washed her hair first and then lay stretched out with the water moving gently over her, soft as the caress of silk. Growing bold the tiny fish darted in and nibbled at her skin, tickling, so that she gasped and splashed at them.

At last she ducked her head under the surface and, with the water streaming out of her hair into her eyes, she groped her way back to the bank.

As she stooped, still half blinded, for her towel Wally Hendry's hand closed over her mouth and his other arm circled her waist from behind.

'One squeak out of you and I'll wring your bloody neck.' He spoke hoarsely into her ear. She could smell his breath, warm and sour in her face. 'Just pretend I'm old Bruce – then both of us will enjoy it.' And he chuckled.

Sliding quickly over her hip his hand moved downwards and the shock of it galvanized her into frantic struggles. Holding her easily Hendry kept on chuckling.

She opened her mouth suddenly and one of his fingers went in between her teeth. She bit with all her strength and felt the skin break and tasted blood in her mouth.

'You bitch!' Hendry jerked his hand away and she opened her mouth to scream, but the hand swung back, clenched, into the side of her face, knocking her head across. The scream never reached her lips for he hit her again and she felt herself falling.

Stunned by the blows, lying in the sand, she could not believe it was happening, until she felt his weight upon her and his knee forced cruelly between hers.

Then she started to struggle again, trying to twist away from his mouth and the smell of his breath.

'No, no, no.' She repeated it over and over, her eyes shut tightly so she did not have to see that face above her, and her head rolling from side to side in the sand. He was so strong, so immensely powerful.

'No,' she said, and then, 'Ooah!' at the pain, the tearing stinging pain within, and the thrusting heaviness above.

And through the pounding, grunting, thrusting nightmare she could smell him and feel the sweat drip from him and splash into her upturned unprotected face.

It lasted forever, and then suddenly the weight was gone and she opened her eyes.

He stood over her, fumbling with his clothing, and there was a dullness in his expression. He wiped his mouth with the back of his hand and she saw the fingers were trembling. His voice when he spoke was tired and disinterested.

'I've had better.'

Swiftly Shermaine rolled over and reached for the pistol that lay on top of her clothes. Hendry stepped forward with all his weight on her wrist and she felt the bones bend under his boot and she moaned. But through pain she whispered. 'You pig, you filthy pig,' and he hit her again, flat-handed across the face, knocking her on to her back once more.

He picked up the pistol and opened it, spilling the cartridges into the sand, then he unclipped the lanyard and threw the pistol far out into the reed bed.

'Tell Curry I say he can have my share of you,' he said and walked quickly away among the reeds.

The white sand coated her damp body like icing sugar. She sat up slowly holding her wrist, the side of her face inflamed and starting to swell where he had hit her.

She started to cry, shaking silently, and the tears squeezed out between her eyelids and matted her long dark lashes.

= 30 =

Ruffy held up the brown bottle and inspected it ruefully.

'Seems like one mouthful and it's empty.' He threw the bottle out of the side window. It hit a tree and burst with a small pop.

'We can always find our way back by following the empties,' smiled Bruce, once more marvelling at the man's capacity. But there was plenty of storage space. He watched Ruffy's stomach spread on to his lap as he reached down to the beer crate.

'How we doing, boss?'

Bruce glanced at the milometer.

'We've come eighty-seven miles,' and Ruffy nodded.

'Not bad going. Be there pretty soon now.'

They were silent. The wind blew in on to them through the open front. The grass that grew between the tracks brushed the bottom of the chassis with a continuous rushing sound.

'Boss–' Ruffy spoke at last.

'Yes?'

'Lieutenant Hendry – those diamonds. You reckon we did a good thing leaving him there?'

'He's stranded in the middle of the bush. Even if he did find them they wouldn't do him much good.'

'Suppose that's right.' Ruffy lifted the beer bottle to his lips and when he lowered it he went on. 'Mind you, that's one guy you can never be sure of.' He tapped his head with a finger as thick and as black as a blood-sausage. 'Something wrong with him – he's one of the maddest Arabs I've found in a long time of looking.'

Bruce grunted grimly.

'You want to be careful there, boss,' observed Ruffy. 'Any time now he's going to try for you. I've seen it coming. He's working himself up to it. He's a mad Arab.'

'I'll watch him,' said Bruce.

'Yeah, you do that.'

Again they were silent in the steady swish of the wind and the drone of the motor.

'There's a railway.' Ruffy pointed to the blue-gravelled embankment through the trees.

'Nearly there,' said Bruce.

They came out into another open glade and beyond it the water tank of Msapa Junction stuck up above the forest.

'Here we are,' said Ruffy and drained the bottle in his hand.

'Just say a prayer that the telegraph lines are still up and that there's an operator on the Elisabethville end.'

Bruce slowed the Ford past the row of cottages. They were exactly as he remembered them, deserted and forlorn. The corners of his mouth were compressed into a hard angle as he looked at the two small mounds of earth beneath the casia flora trees. Ruffy looked at them also but neither of them spoke.

Bruce stopped the Ford outside the station building and they climbed out stiffly and walked together on to the verandah. The wooden flooring echoed dully under their boots as they made for the door of the office.

Bruce pushed the door open and looked in. The walls were painted a depressing utility green, loose paper was scattered on the floor, the drawers of the single desk hung open, and a thin grey skin of dust coated everything.

'There she is,' said Ruffy and pointed to the brass and varnished wood complexity of the telegraph on a table against the far wall.

'Looks all right,' said Bruce. 'As long as the lines haven't been cut.'

As if to reassure him, the telegraph began to clatter like a typewriter.

'Thank God for that,' sighed Bruce.

They walked across to the table.

'You know how to work this thing?' asked Ruffy.

'Sort of,' Bruce answered and set his rifle against the wall. He was relieved to see a Morse table stuck with adhesive tape to the wall above the apparatus. It was a long time since he had memorized it as a boy scout.

He laid his hand on the transmission key and studied the table. The call sign for Elisabethville was 'EE'.

He tapped it out clumsily and then waited. Almost immediately the set clattered back at him, much too fast to be intelligible and the roll of paper in the repeater was exhausted. Bruce took off his helmet and laboriously spelled out, 'Transmit slower.'

It was a long business with requests for repetition. 'Not understood' was made nearly every second signal, but finally Bruce got the operator to understand that he had an urgent message for Colonel Franklyn of President Tshombe's staff.

'Wait,' came back the laconic signal.

And they waited. They waited an hour, then two.

'That mad bastard's forgotten about us,' grumbled Ruffy and went to the Ford to fetch the beer crate. Bruce fidgeted restlessly on the unpadded chair beside the telegraph table. He reconsidered anxiously all his previous arguments for leaving Wally Hendry in charge of the camp, but once again decided that it was safe. He couldn't do much harm. Unless, unless, Shermaine! No, it was impossible. Not with forty loyal gendarmes to protect her.

He started to think about Shermaine and the future. There was a year's mercenary captain's pay accumulated in the Crédit Banque Suisse at Zurich. He made the conversion from francs to pounds – about two and a half thousand. Two years' operating capital, so they could have a holiday before he started working again. They could take a chalet up in the mountains, there should be good snow this time of the year.

Bruce grinned. Snow that crunched like sugar, and a twelve-inch-thick eiderdown on the bed at night.

Life had purpose and direction again.

'What you're laughing at, boss?' asked Ruffy.

'I was thinking about a bed.'

'Yeah? That's a good thing to think about. You start there, you're born there, you spend most of your life in it, you have plenty of fun in it, and if you're lucky you die there. How's it for a beer?'

The telegraph came to life at Bruce's elbow. He turned to it quickly.

'Curry – Franklyn,' it clattered. Bruce could imagine the wiry, red-faced little man at the other end. Ex-major in the third brigade of the Legion. A prime mover in the O.A.S., with a sizeable price still on his head from the De Gaulle assassination attempt.

'Franklyn – Curry,' Bruce tapped back. 'Train unserviceable. Motorized transport stranded without fuel. Port Reprieve road. Map reference approx –' He read the numbers off the sheet on which he had noted them.

There was a long pause, then:

'Is U.M.C. property in your hands?' The question was delicately phrased.

'Affirmative,' Bruce assured him.

'Await air-drop at your position soonest. Out.'

'Message understood. Out.' Bruce straightened from the telegraph and sighed with relief.

'That's that, Ruffy. They'll drop gas to us from one of the Dakotas. Probably tomorrow morning.' He looked at his wrist watch. 'Twenty to one, let's get back.'

Bruce hummed softly, watching the double tracks ahead of him, guiding the Ford with a light touch on the wheel.

He was contented. It was all over. Tomorrow the fuel would drop from the Dakota under those yellow parachutes. (He must lay out the smudge signals this evening.) And ten hours later they would be back in Elisabethville.

A few words with Carl Engelbrecht would fix seats for Shermaine and himself on one of the outward-bound Daks. Then Switzerland, and the chalet with icicles hanging from the eaves. A long rest while he decided where to start again. Louisiana was under Roman-Dutch Law, or was it Code Napoléon? He might even have to rewrite his bar examinations, but the prospect pleased rather than dismayed him. It was fun again.

'Never seen you so happy,' grunted Ruffy.

'Never had so much cause,' Bruce agreed.

'She's a swell lady. Young still – you can teach her.'

Bruce felt his hackles rise, and then he thought better of it and laughed.

'You going to sign her up, boss?'

'I might.'

Ruffy nodded wisely. 'Man should have plenty wives – I got three. Need a couple more.'

'One I could only just handle.'

'One's difficult. Two's easier. Three, you can relax. Four, they're so busy with each other they don't give you no trouble at all.'

'I might try it.'

'Yeah, you do that.'

And ahead of them through the trees they saw the ring of trucks.

'We're home,' grunted Ruffy, then he stirred uncomfortably in his seat. 'Something going on.'

Men stood in small groups. There was something in their attitude: strain, apprehension. Two men ran up the road to meet them. Bruce could see their mouths working, but could not hear the words.

Dread, heavy and cold, pushed down on the pit of Bruce's gut.

Gabbled, incoherent, Sergeant Jacque was trying to tell him something as he ran beside the Ford.

'Tenente Hendry – the river – the madame – gone.' French words like driftwood in the torrent of dialect.

'Your girl,' translated Ruffy. 'Hendry's done her.'

'Dead?' The question dropped from Bruce's mouth.

'No. He's hurt her. He's – you know!'

'Where's she?'

'They've got her in the back of the truck.'

Bruce climbed heavily out of the car. Now they were silent, grouped together, not looking at him, faces impassive, waiting.

Bruce walked slowly to the truck. He felt cold and numb. His legs moved automatically beneath him. He drew back the canvas and pulled himself up into the interior. It was an effort to move forward, to focus his eyes in the gloom.

Wrapped in a blanket she lay small and still.

'Shermaine.' It stuck in his throat.

'Shermaine,' he said again and knelt beside her. A great livid swelling distorted the side of her face. She did not turn her head to him, but lay staring up at the canvas roof.

He touched her face and the skin was cold, cold as the dread that gripped his stomach. The coldness of it shocked him so he jerked his hand away.

'Shermaine.' This time it was a sob. The eyes, her big haunted eyes, turned unseeing towards him and he felt the lift of escape from the certainty of her death.

'Oh, God,' he cried and took her to him, holding the unresisting frailty of her to his chest. He could feel the slow even thump of her heart beneath his hand. He drew back the blanket and there was no blood.

'Darling, are you hurt? Tell me, are you hurt?' She did not answer. She lay quietly in his arms, not seeing him.

'Shock,' he whispered. 'It's only shock,' and he opened her clothing. With tenderness he examined the smoothly pale body; the skin was clammy and damp, but there was no damage.

He wrapped her again and laid her gently back on to the floor.

He stood and the thing within him changed shape. Cold still, but now burning cold as dry ice.

Ruffy and Jacque were waiting for him beside the tailboard.

'Where is he?' asked Bruce softly.

'He is gone.'

'Where?'

'That way.' Jacque pointed towards the south-east. 'I followed the spoor a short distance.'

Bruce walked to the Ford and picked up his rifle from the floor. He opened the cubbyhole and took two spare clips of ammunition from it.

Ruffy followed him. 'He's got the diamonds, boss.'

'Yes,' said Bruce and checked the load of his rifle. The diamonds were of no importance.

'Are you going after him, boss?'

Bruce did not answer. Instead he looked up at the sky. The sun was half way towards the horizon and there were clouds thickly massed around it.

'Ruffy, stay with her,' he said softly. 'Keep her warm.'

Ruffy nodded.

'Who is the best tracker we've got?'

'Jacque. Worked for a safari outfit before the war as a tracker boy.'

Bruce turned to Jacque. The thing was still icy cold inside him, with tentacles that spread out to every extremity of his body and his mind.

'When did this happen?'

'About an hour after you left,' answered Jacque.

Eight hours start. It was a long lead.

'Take the spoor,' said Bruce softly.

= 31 =

The earth was soft from the night's rain and the spoor deep trodden, the heels had bitten in under Hendry's weight, so they followed fast.

Watching Sergeant Jacque work, Bruce felt his anxiety abating, for although the footprints were so easy to follow in these early stages that it was no test of his ability, yet from the way he moved swiftly along – half-crouched and wholly absorbed, occasionally glancing ahead to pick up the run of the spoor, stooping now and then to touch the earth and determine its texture – Bruce could tell that this man knew his business.

Through the open forest with tufted grass below, holding steadily south by east, Hendry led them straight towards the Rhodesian border. And after the first two hours Bruce knew they had not gained upon him. Hendry was still eight hours ahead, and at the pace he was setting eight hours' start was something like thirty miles in distance.

Bruce looked over his shoulder at the sun where it lay wedged between two vast piles of cumulus nimbus. There in the sky were the two elements which could defeat him.

Time. There were perhaps two more hours of daylight. With the onset of night they would be forced to halt.

Rain. The clouds were swollen and dark blue round the edges. As Bruce watched, the lightning lit them internally, and at a count of ten the thunder grumbled suddenly. If it rained again before morning there would be no spoor to follow.

'We must move faster,' said Bruce.

Sergeant Jacque straightened up and looked at Bruce as though he were a stranger. He had forgotten his existence.

'The earth hardens.' Jacque pointed at the spoor and Bruce saw that in the last half hour the soil had become gritty and compacted. Hendry's heels no longer broke the crust. 'It is unwise to run on such a lean trail.'

Again Bruce looked back at the menace of gathering clouds.

'We must take the chance,' he decided.

'As you wish,' grunted Jacque, and transferred his rifle to his other shoulder, hitched up his belt and settled the steel helmet more firmly on his head.

'Allez!'

They trotted on through the forest towards the south-east. Within a mile Bruce's body had settled into the automatic rhythm of his run, leaving his mind free.

He thought about Wally Hendry, saw again the little eyes and round them the puffy folded skin, and the mouth below, thin and merciless, the obscene ginger stubble of beard. He could almost smell him. His nostrils flared at the memory of the rank redhead's body odour. Unclean, he thought, unclean mind and unclean body.

His hatred of Wally Hendry was a tangible thing. He could feel it sitting heavily at the base of his throat, tingling in his fingertips and giving strength to his legs.

And yet there was something else. Suddenly Bruce grinned: a wolfish baring of his teeth. That tingling in his fingertips was not all hatred, a little of it was excitement.

What a complex thing is a man, he thought. He can never hold one emotion – always there are others to confuse it. Here I am hunting the thing that I most loathe and hate, and I am enjoying it. Completely unrelated to the hatred is the thrill of hunting the most dangerous and cunning game of all, man.

I have always enjoyed the chase, he thought. It has been bred into me, for my blood is that of the men who hunted and fought with Africa as the prize.

The hunting of this man will give me pleasure. If ever a man deserved to die, it is Wally Hendry. I am the plaintiff, the judge and the executioner.

Sergeant Jacque stopped so suddenly that Bruce ran into him and they nearly fell.

'What is it?' panted Bruce, coming back to reality.

'Look!'

The earth ahead of them was churned and broken.

'Zebra,' groaned Bruce, recognizing the round uncloven hoof prints. 'God damn it to hell – of all the filthy luck!'

'A big herd,' Jacque agreed. 'Spread out. Feeding.'

As far ahead as they could see through the forest the herd had wiped out Hendry's tracks.

'We'll have to cast forward.' Bruce's voice was agonized by his impatience. He turned to the nearest tree and hacked at it with his bayonet, blazing it to mark the end of the trail, swearing softly, venting his disappointment on the trunk.

'Only another hour to sunset,' he whispered. 'Please let us pick him up again before dark.'

Sergeant Jacque was already moving forward, following the approximate line of Hendry's travel, trying vainly to recognize a single footprint through the havoc created there by the passage of thousands of hooves. Bruce hurried to join him and then moved out on his flank. They zigzagged slowly ahead, almost meeting on the inward leg of each tack and then separating again to a distance of a hundred yards.

There it was! Bruce dropped to his knees to make sure. Just the outline of the toecap showing from under the spoor of an old zebra stallion. Bruce whistled, a windy sound through his dry lips, and Jacque came quickly. One quick look, then:

'Yes, he is holding more to the right now.' He raised his eyes and squinted ahead, marking a tree which was directly in line with the run of the spoor. They went forward.

'There's the herd.' Bruce pointed at the flicker of a grey body through the trees.

'They've got our wind.'

A zebra snorted and then there was a rumbling, a low blurred drumming of hooves as the herd ran. Through the trees Bruce caught glimpses of the animals on the near side of the herd. Too far off to show the stripes, looking like fat grey ponies as they galloped, ears up, black-maned heads nodding. Then they were gone and the sound of their flight dwindled.

'At least they haven't run along the spoor,' muttered Bruce, and then bitterly: 'Damn them, the stupid little donkeys! They've cost us an hour. A whole priceless hour.'

Desperately searching, wild with haste, they worked back and forth. The sun was below the trees; already the air was cooling in the short African dusk. Another fifteen minutes and it would be dark.

Then abruptly the forest ended and they came out on the edge of a vlei. Open as wheatland, pastured with green waist-high grass, hemmed in by the forest, it stretched ahead of them for nearly two miles. Dotted along it were clumps of ivory palms with each graceful stem ending in an untidy cluster of leaves. Troops of guinea-fowls were scratching and chirruping along the edge of the clearing, and near the far end a herd of buffalo formed a dark mass as they grazed beneath a canopy of white egrets.

In the forest beyond the clearing, rising perhaps three hundred feet out of it, stood a kopje of tumbled granite. The great slabs of rock with their sheer sides and square tops looked like a ruined castle. The low sun struck it and gave the rock an orange warmth.

But Bruce had no time to admire the scene; his eyes were on the earth, searching for the prints of Hendry's jungle boots.

Out on his left Sergeant Jacque whistled sharply and Bruce felt the leap of excitement in his chest. He ran across to the crouching gendarme.

'It has come away.' Jacque pointed at the spoor that was strung ahead of them like beads on a string, skirting the edge of the vlei, each depression filled with shadow and standing out clearly on the sandy grey earth.

'Too late,' groaned Bruce. 'Damn those bloody zebra.' The light was fading so swiftly it seemed as though it were a stage effect.

'Follow it.' Bruce's voice was sharp with helpless frustration. 'Follow it as long as you can.'

It was not a quarter of a mile farther on that Jacque rose out of his crouch and only the white of his teeth showed in the darkness as he spoke.

'We will lose it again if we go on.'

'All right.' Bruce unslung his rifle with weary resignation. He knew that Wally Hendry was at least forty miles ahead of them; more if he kept travelling after dark. The spoor was cold. If this had been an ordinary hunt he would long ago have broken off the chase.

He looked up at the sky. In the north the stars were fat and yellow, but above them and to the south it was black with cloud.

'Don't let it rain,' he whispered. 'Please God, don't let it rain.'

The night was long. Bruce slept once for perhaps two hours and then the strength of his hatred woke him. He lay flat upon his back and stared up at the sky. It was all dark with clouds; only occasionally they opened and let the stars shine briefly through.

'It must not rain. It must not rain.' He repeated it like a prayer, staring up at the dark sky, concentrating upon it as though by the force of his mind he could control the elements.

There were lions hunting in the forest. He heard the male roaring, moving up from the south, and once his two lionesses answered him. They killed a little before dawn and Bruce lay on the hard earth and listened to their jubilation over the kill. Then there was silence as they began to feed.

That I might have success as well, he thought. I do not often ask for favours, Lord, but grant me this one. I ask it not only for myself but for Shermaine and the others.

In his mind he saw again the two children lying where Hendry had shot them. The smear of mingled blood and chocolate across the boy's cheek.

He deserves to die, prayed Bruce, so please don't let it rain.

As long as the night had been, that quickly came the dawn. A grey dawn, gloomy with low cloud.

'Will it go?' Bruce asked for the twentieth time, and this time Jacque looked up from where he knelt beside the spoor.

'We can try now.'

They moved off slowly with Jacque leading, doubled over to peer short-sightedly at the earth and Bruce close behind him, bedevilled by his impatience and anxiety, lifting his head every dozen paces to the dirty grey roof of cloud.

The light strengthened and the circle of their vision opened from six feet to as many yards, to a hundred, so they could make out the tops of the ivory palms, shaggy against the grey cloud.

Jacque broke into a trot and ahead of them was the end of the clearing and the beginning of the forest. Two hundred yards beyond rose the massive pile of the kopje, in the early light looking more than ever like a castle, turreted and sheer. There was something formidable in its outline. It seemed to brood above them and Bruce looked away from it uneasily.

Cold and with enough weight behind it to sting, the first raindrop splashed against Bruce's cheek.

'Oh, no!' he protested, and stopped. Jacque straightened up from the spoor and he too looked at the sky.

'It is finished. In five minutes there will be nothing to follow.'

Another drop hit Bruce's upturned face and he blinked back the tears of anger and frustration that pricked the rims of his eyelids.

Faster now, tapping on his helmet, plopping on to his shoulders and face, the rain fell.

'Quickly,' cried Bruce. 'Follow as long as you can.'

Jacque opened his mouth to speak, but before a word came out he was flung backwards, punched over as though by an invisible fist, his helmet flying from his head as he fell and his rifle clattering on the earth.

Simultaneously Bruce felt the bullet pass him, disrupting the air, so the wind of it flattened his shirt against his chest, cracking viciously in his ears, leaving him dazedly looking down at Sergeant Jacque's body.

It lay with arms thrown wide, the jaw and the side of the head below the ear torn away; white bone and blood bubbling over it. The trunk twitched convulsively and the hands fluttered like trapped birds. Then flat-sounding through the rain he heard the report of the rifle.

The kopje, screamed Bruce's brain, *he's lying in the kopje*!

And Bruce moved, twisting sideways, starting to run.

= 32 =

Wally Hendry lay on his stomach on the flat top of the turret. His body was stiff and chilled from the cold of the night and the rock was harsh under him, but the discomfort hardly penetrated the fringe of his mind. He had built a low parapet with loose flakes of granite, and he had screened the front of it with the thick bushy stems of broom bush.

His rifle was propped on the parapet in front of him and at his elbow were the spare ammunition clips.

He had lain in this ambush for a long time now – since early the preceding afternoon. Now it was dawn and the darkness was drawing back; in a few minutes he would be able to see the whole of the clearing below him.

I coulda been across the river already, he thought, *coulda been fifty miles away*. He did not attempt to analyse the impulse that had made him lie here unmoving for almost twenty hours.

Man, I knew old Curry would have to come. I knew he would only bring one nigger tracker with him. These educated Johnnies got their own rules – man to man stuff, and he chuckled as he remembered the two minute figures that he had seen come out of the forest in the fading light of the previous evening.

The bastard spent the night down there in the clearing. Saw him light a match and have hisself a smoke in the night – well, I hope he enjoyed it, his last.

Wally peered anxiously out into the gradually gathering dawn.

They'll be moving now, coming up the clearing. Must get them before they reach the trees again. Below him the clearing showed as a paleness, a leprous blotch, on the dark forest.

The bastard! Without preliminaries Hendry's hatred returned to him. *This time he don't get to make no fancy speeches. This time he don't get no chance to be hoity-toity.*

The light was stronger now. He could see the clumps of ivory palms against the pale brown grass of the clearing.

'Ha!' Hendry exclaimed.

There they were, like two little ants, dark specks moving up the middle of the clearing. The tip of Hendry's tongue slipped out between his lips and he flattened down behind his rifle.

Man, I've waited for this. Six months now I've thought about this, and when it's finished I'll go down and take his ears. He slipped the safety catch; it made a satisfying mechanical click.

Nigger's leading, that's Curry behind him. Have to wait till they turn, don't want the nigger to get it first. Curry first, then the nigger.

He picked them up in his sights, breathing quicker now, the thrill of it so intense that he had to swallow and it caught in his throat like dry bread.

A raindrop hit the back of his neck. It startled him. He looked up quickly at the sky and saw it coming.

'Goddam it,' he groaned, and looked back at the clearing. Curry and nigger were standing together, a single dark blob in the half-light. There was no chance of separating them. The rain fell faster, and suddenly Hendry was overwhelmed by the old familiar feeling of inferiority; of knowing that everything, even the elements, conspired against him; the knowledge that he could never win, not even this once.

They, God and the rest of the world.

The ones who had given him a drunk for a father.

A squalid cottage for a home and a mother with cancer of the throat.

The ones who had sent him to reform school, had fired him from two dozen jobs, had pushed him, laughed at him, gaoled him twice – They, all of them (and Bruce Curry who was their figurehead), they were going to win again. Not even this once, not even ever.

'Goddam it,' he cursed in hopeless, wordless anger against them all.

'Goddamn it, goddam it to hell,' and he fired at the dark blob in his sights.

— 33 —

As he ran Bruce looked across a hundred yards of open ground to the edge of the forest.

He felt the wind of the next bullet as it cracked past him.

If he uses rapid fire he'll get me even at three hundred yards.

And Bruce jinked his run like a jack-rabbit. The blood roaring in his ears, fear driving his feet.

Then all around him the air burst asunder, buffeting him so he staggered; the vicious whip-whip-whip of bullets filled his head.

I can't make it.

Seventy yards to the shelter of the trees. Seventy yards of open meadow land, and above him the commanding mass of the kopje.

The next burst is for me – it must come, now!

And he flung himself to one side so violently that he nearly fell. Again the air was ripping to tatters close beside him.

I can't last! He must get me!

In his path was an ant-heap, a low pile of clay, a pimple on the open expanse of earth. Bruce dived for it, hitting the ground so hard that the wind was forced from his lungs out through his open mouth.

The next burst of gunfire kicked lumps of clay from the top of the ant-heap, showering Bruce's back.

He lay with his face pressed into the earth, wheezing with the agony of empty lungs, flattening his body behind the tiny heap of clay.

Will it cover me? Is there enough of it?

And the next hail of bullets thumped into the ant-heap, throwing fountains of earth, but leaving Bruce untouched.

'*I'm safe*.' The realization came with a surge that washed away his fear.

But I'm helpless, answered his hatred. *Pinned to the earth for as long as Hendry wants to keep me here.*

The rain fell on his back. Soaking through his jacket, coldly caressing the nape of his neck and dribbling down over his jaws.

He rolled his head sideways, not daring to lift it an inch, and the rain beat on to the side of his face.

The rain! Falling faster. Thickening. Hanging from the clouds like the skirts of a woman's dress.

Curtains of rain. Greying out the edge of the forest, leaving no solid shapes in the mist of falling liquid mother-of-pearl.

Still gasping but with the pain slowly receding, Bruce lifted his head.

The kopje was a vague blue-green shape ahead of him, then it was gone, swallowed by the eddying columns of rain.

Bruce pushed himself up on to his knees and the pain in his chest made him dizzy.

Now! he thought. *Now, before it thins,* and he lumbered clumsily to his feet.

For a moment he stood clutching his chest, sucking for breath in the haze of water-filled air, and then he staggered towards the edge of the forest.

His feet steadied under him, his breathing eased, and he was into the trees.

They closed round him protectively. He leaned against the rough bark of one of them and wiped the rain from his face with the palm of his hand. The strength came back to him and with it his hatred and his excitement.

He unslung the rifle from his shoulder and stood away from the tree with his feet planted wide apart.

'Now, my friend,' he whispered, 'we fight on equal terms.' He pumped a round into the chamber of the FN and moved towards the kopje, stepping daintily, the weight of the rifle in his hands, his mind suddenly sharp and clear, vision enhanced, feeling his strength and the absence of fear like a song within him, a battle hymn.

He made out the loom of the kopje through the dripping rain-heavy trees and he circled out to the right. There is plenty of time, he thought. I can afford to case the joint thoroughly. He completed his circuit of the rock pile.

The kopje, he found, was the shape of a galleon sinking by the head. At one end the high double castles of the poop, from which the main deck canted steeply forward as though the prow were already under water. This slope was scattered with boulders and densely covered with dwarf scrub, an interwoven mass of shoulder-high branches and leaves.

Bruce squatted on his haunches with the rifle in his lap and looked up the ramp at the twin turrets of the kopje. The rain had slackened to a drizzle.

Hendry was on top. Bruce knew he would go to the highest point. Strange how height makes a man feel invulnerable, makes him think he is a god.

And since he had fired upon them he must be in the turret nearest the vlei, which was slightly the higher of the two, its summit crowned by a patch of stunted broom bush.

So now I know exactly where he is and I will wait half an hour. He may become impatient and move; if he does I will get a shot at him from here.

Bruce narrowed his eyes, judging the distance.

'About two hundred yards.'

He adjusted the rear-sight of the FN and then checked the load, felt in the side pocket of his jacket to make sure the two extra clips of ammunition were handy, and settled back comfortably to wait.

'Curry, you sonofabitch, where are you?' Hendry's shout floated down through the drizzling rain and Bruce stiffened. *I was right – he's on top of the left-hand turret.*

'Come on, Bucko. I've been waiting for you since yesterday afternoon.'

Bruce lifted the rifle and sighted experimentally at a dark patch on the wall of the rock. It would be difficult shooting in the rain, the rifle slippery with wet, the fine drizzle clinging to his eyebrows and dewing the sights of the rifle with little beads of moisture.

'Hey, Curry, how's your little French piece of pussy? Man, she's hot, that thing, isn't she?'

Bruce's hands tightened on the rifle.

'Did she tell you how I gave her the old business? Did she tell you how she loved it? You should have heard her panting like a steam engine. I'm telling you, Curry, she just couldn't get enough!'

Bruce felt himself start to tremble. He clenched his jaws, biting down until his teeth ached.

Steady, Bruce my boy, that's what he wants you to do.

The trees dripped steadily in the silence and a gust of wind stirred the scrub on the slope of the kopje. Bruce waited, straining his eyes for the first hint of movement on the left-hand turret.

'You yellow or something, Curry? You scared to come on up here? Is that what it is?'

Bruce shifted his position slightly, ready for a snap shot.

'Okay, Bucko. I can wait, I've got all day. I'll just sit here thinking about how I mucked your little bit of French. I'm telling you it was something to remember. Up and down, in and out, man it was something!'

Bruce came carefully up on to his feet behind the trunk of the tree and once more studied the layout of the kopje.

If I can move up the slope, keeping well over to the side, until I reach the right-hand turret, there's a ledge there that will take me to the top. I'll be twenty or thirty feet from him, and at that range it will all be over in a few seconds.

He drew a deep breath and left the shelter of the tree.

Wally Hendry spotted the movement in the forest below him; it was a flash of brown quickly gone, too fast to get a bead on it.

He wiped the rain off his face and wriggled a foot closer to the edge.

'Come on, Curry. Let's stop buggering about,' he shouted, and cuddled the butt of his rifle into his shoulder. The tip of his tongue kept darting out and touching his lips.

At the foot of the slope he saw a branch move slightly, stirring when there was no wind. He grinned and snuggled his hips down on to the rock. *Here he comes,* he gloated, *he's crawling up, under the scrub.*

'I know you're sitting down there. Okay, Curry, I can wait also.'

Half-way up the slope the top leaves of another bush swayed gently, parting and closing.

'Yes!' whispered Wally, 'Yes!' and he clicked off the safety catch of the rifle. His tongue came out and moved slowly from one corner of his mouth to the other.

I've got him, for sure! There – he'll have to cross that piece of open ground. A couple a yards, that's all. But it'll be enough.

He moved again, wriggling a few inches to one side, settling his aim into the gap between two large grey boulders; he pushed the rate-of-fire selector on to rapid and his forefinger rested lightly on the trigger.

'Hey, Curry, I'm getting bored. If you are not going to come up, how about singing to me or cracking a few jokes?'

Bruce Curry crouched behind a large grey boulder. In front of him were three yards of open ground and then the shelter of another rock. He was almost at the top of the slope and Hendry had not spotted him. Across the patch of open ground was good cover to the foot of the right-hand turret.

It would take him two seconds to cross and the chances were that Hendry would be watching the forest at the foot of the slope.

He gathered himself like a sprinter on the starting blocks.

'Go!' he whispered and dived into the opening, and into a hell storm of bullets. One struck his rifle, tearing it out of his hand with such force that his arm was paralysed to the shoulder, another stung his chest, and then he was across. He lay behind the far boulder, gasping with the shock, and listened to Hendry's voice roaring triumphantly.

'Fooled you, you stupid bastard! Been watching you all the way up from the bottom.'

Bruce held his left arm against his stomach; the use of it was returning as the numbness subsided, but with it came the ache. The top joint of his thumb had caught in the trigger guard and been torn off; now the blood welled out of the stump thickly and slowly, dark blood the colour of apple jelly. With his right hand he groped for his handkerchief.

'Hey, Curry, your rifle's lying there in the open. You might need it in a few minutes. Why don't you go out and fetch it?'

Bruce bound the handkerchief tightly round the stump of his thumb and the bleeding slowed. Then he looked at the rifle where it lay ten feet away. The foresight had been knocked off, and the same bullet that had amputated his thumb had smashed into the breech, buckled the loading handle and the slide. He knew that it was damaged beyond repair.

'Think I'll have me a little target practice,' shouted Hendry from above, and again the was a burst of automatic fire. Bruce's rifle disappeared in a cloud of dust and flying rock fragments and when it cleared the woodwork of the rifle was splintered and torn and there was further damage to the action.

Well, that's that, thought Bruce, *rifle's wrecked, Shermaine has the pistol, and I have only one good hand. This is going to be interesting*.

He unbuttoned the front of his jacket and examined the welt that the bullet had raised across his chest. It looked like a rope burn, painful and red, but not serious. He rebuttoned his jacket.

'Okay, Bruce Baby, the time for games is over. I'm coming down to get you.' Hendry's voice was harsh and loud, filled with confidence.

Bruce rallied under the goading of it. He looked round quickly. *Which way to go? Climb high so he must come up to get at you. Take the right-hand turret, work round the side of it and wait for him on the top*.

In haste now, spurred by the dread of being the hunted, he scrambled to his feet and dodged away up the slope, keeping his head down using the thick screen of rock and vegetation.

He reached the wall of the right-hand turret and followed it round, found the spiral ledge that he had seen from below and went on to it, up along it like a fly on a wall, completely exposed, keeping his back to the cliff of granite, shuffling sideways up the eighteen-inch ledge with the drop below him growing deeper with each step.

Now he was three hundred feet above the forest and could look out across the dark green land to another row of kopjes on the horizon. The rain had ceased but the cloud was unbroken. covering the sky.

The ledge widened, became a platform and Bruce hurried across it round the far shoulder and came to a dead end. The ledge had petered out and there was only the drop below. He had trapped himself on the side of the turret – the summit was unattainable. If Hendry descended to the forest floor and circled the kopje he would find Bruce completely at his mercy, for there was no cover on the narrow ledge. Hendry could have a little more target practice.

Bruce leaned against the rock and struggled to control his breathing. His throat was clogged with the thick saliva of exhaustion and fear. He felt tired and helpless, his thumb throbbed painfully and he lifted it to examine it once more. Despite the tourniquet it was bleeding slowly, a wine-red drop at a time.

Bleeding! Bruce swallowed the thick gluey stuff in his throat and looked back along the way he had come. On the grey rock the bright red splashes stood out clearly. He had laid a blood spoor for Hendry to follow.

All right then, perhaps it is best this way. At least I may be able to come to grips with him. If I wait behind this shoulder until he starts to cross the platform, there's a three hundred foot drop on one side, I may be able to rush him and throw him off,

Bruce leaned against the shoulder of granite, hidden from the platform, and tuned his ears to catch the first sound of Hendry's approach.

The clouds parted in the eastern sector of the sky and the sun shone through, slanting across the side of the kopje.

It will be better to die in the sun, thought Bruce, *a sacrifice to the Sun god thrown from the roof of the temple,* and he grinned without mirth, waiting with patience and with pain.

The minutes fell like drops into the pool of time, slowly measuring out the ration of life that had been allotted to him. The pulse in his ears counted also, and his breath that he drew and held and gently exhaled – how many more would there be?

I should pray, he thought, *but after this morning when I prayed that it should not rain, and the rains came and saved me, I will not presume again to tell the Old Man how to run things. Perhaps he knows best after all.*

Thy will be done, he thought instead, and suddenly his nerves jerked tight as a line hit by a marlin. The sound he had heard was that of cloth brushing against rough rock.

He held his breath and listened, but all he could discern was the pulse in his ears and the wind in the trees of the forest below. The wind was a lonely sound.

Thy will be done, he repeated without breathing, and heard Hendry breathe close behind the shoulder of rock.

He stood away from the wall and waited. Then he saw Hendry's shadow thrown by the early morning sun along the ledge. A great distorted shadow on the grey rock.

Thy will be done. And he went round the shoulder fast, his good hand held like a blade and the weight of his body behind it.

Hendry was three feet away, the rifle at high port across his chest, standing close in against the cliff, the cup-shaped steel helmet pulled low over the slitty eyes and little beads of sweat clinging in the red-gold stubble of his beard. He tried to drop the muzzle of the rifle but Bruce was too close.

Bruce lunged with stiff fingers at his throat and he felt the crackle and give of cartilage. Then his weight carried him on and Hendry sprawled backwards on to the stone platform with Bruce on top of him.

The rifle slithered across the rock and dropped over the edge, and they lay chest to chest with legs locked together in a horrible parody of the love act. But in *this* act we do not procreate, we destroy!

Hendry's face was purple and swollen above his damaged throat, his mouth open as he struggled for air, and his breath smelt old and sour in Bruce's face.

With a twist towards the thumb Bruce freed his right wrist from Hendry's grip and, lifting it like an axe, brought it down across the bridge of Hendry's nose. Twin jets of blood spouted from the nostrils and gushed into his open mouth.

With a wet strangling sound in his throat Hendry's body arched violently upwards and Bruce was thrown back against the side of the cliff with such force that for a second he lay there.

Wally was on his knees, facing Bruce, his eyes glazed and sightless, and the strangling rattling sound spraying from his throat in a pink cloud of blood. With both hands he was fumbling his pistol out of its canvas holster.

Bruce drew his knees up on to his chest, then straightened his legs in a mule kick. His feet landed together in the centre of Hendry's stomach, throwing him backwards off the platform. Hendry made that strangled bellow all the way to the bottom, but at the end it was cut off abruptly, and afterwards there was only the sound of the wind in the forest below.

For a long time, drained of strength and the power to think, Bruce sat on the ledge with his back against the rock.

Above him the clouds had rolled aside and half the sky was blue. He looked out across the land and the forest was lush and clean from the rain. *And I am still alive*. The realization warmed Bruce's mind as comfortably as the early sun was warming his body. He wanted to shout it out across the forest. *I am still alive!*

At last he stood up, crossed to the edge of the cliff and looked down at the tiny crumpled figure on the rocks below. Then he turned away and dragged his beaten body down the side of the turret.

It took him twenty minutes to find Wally Hendry in the chaos of broken rock and scrub below the turret. He lay on his side with his legs drawn up as though he slept. Bruce knelt beside him and drew his pistol from the olive-green canvas holster; then he unbuttoned the flap of Hendry's bulging breast pocket and took out the white canvas bag.

He stood up, opened the mouth of the bag and stirred the diamonds with is forefinger. Satisfied, he jerked the draw string closed and dropped them into his own pocket.

In death he is even more repulsive than he was alive, thought Bruce without regret as he looked down at the corpse.

The flies were crawling into the bloody nostrils and clustering round the eyes.

Then he spoke aloud.

'So Mike Haig was right and I was wrong – you can destroy it.'

Without looking back he walked away. The tiredness left him.

= 34 =

Carl Engelbrecht came through the doorway from the cockpit into the main cabin of the Dakota.

'Are you two happy?' he asked above the deep drone of the engines, and then grinning with his big brown face, 'I can see you are!'

Bruce grinned back at him and tightened his arm around Shermaine's shoulders.

'Go away! Can't you see we're busy?'

'You've got lots of cheek for a hitch-hiker – bloody good mind to make you get out and walk,' he grumbled as he sat down beside them on the bench that ran the full length of the fuselage. 'I've brought you some coffee and sandwiches.'

'Good. Good. I'm starving.' Shermaine sat up and reached for the thermos flask and the greaseproof paper packet. The bruise on her cheek had faded to a shadow with yellow edges – it was almost ten days old. With his mouth full of chicken sandwich Bruce kicked one of the wooden cases that were roped securely to the floor of the aircraft.

'What have you got in these, Carl?'

'Dunno,' said Carl and poured coffee into the three plastic mugs. 'In this game you don't ask questions. You fly out, take your money, and let it go.' He drained his mug and stood up. 'Well, I'll leave you two alone now. We'll be in Nairobi in a couple of hours, so you can sleep or something!' He winked. 'You'll have to stay aboard while we refuel. But we'll be airborne again in an hour or so, and the day after tomorrow, God and the weather permitting, we'll set you down in Zurich.'

'Thanks, old cock.'

'Think nothing of it – all in the day's work.'

He went forward and disappeared into the cockpit, closing the door behind him.

Shermaine turned back to Bruce, studied him for a moment and then laughed.

'You look so different – now you look like a lawyer!'

Self-consciously Bruce tightened the knot of his Old Michaelhouse tie.

'I must admit it feels strange to wear a suit and tie again.' He looked down at the well-cut blue suit – the only one he had left – and then up again at Shermaine.

'And in a dress I hardly recognize you either.' She was wearing a lime-green cotton frock, cool and crisp looking, white high-heel shoes and just a little make-up to cover the bruise. A damn fine woman, Bruce decided with pleasure.

'How does your thumb feel?' she asked, and Bruce held up the stump with its neat little turban of adhesive tape.

'I had almost forgotten about it.'

Suddenly Shermaine's expression changed, and she pointed excitedly out of the perspex window behind Bruce's shoulder.

'Look, there's the sea!' It lay far below them, shaded from blue to pale green in the shallows, with a round of white beach and the wave formation moving across it like ripples on a pond.

'That's Lake Tanganyika.' Bruce laughed. 'We've left the Congo behind.'

'Forever?' she asked.

'Forever!' he assured her.

The aircraft banked slightly, throwing them closer together, as Carl picked out his landmarks and altered course towards the north-east.

Four thousand feet below them the dark insect that was their shadow flitted and hopped across the surface of the water.

HUNGRY AS THE SEA

This book is for my wife Danielle

Nicholas Berg stepped out of the taxi on to the floodlit dock and paused to look up at the *Warlock*. At this state of the tide she rode high against the stone quay, so that even though the cranes towered above her, they did not dwarf her.

Despite the exhaustion that fogged his mind and cramped his muscles until they ached, Nicholas felt a stir of the old pride, the old sense of value achieved, as he looked at her. She looked like a warship, sleek and deadly, with the high flared bows and good lines that combined to make her safe in any seaway.

The superstructure was moulded steel and glittering armoured glass, behind which her lights burned in carnival array. The wings of her navigation bridge swept back elegantly and were covered to protect the men who must work her in the cruellest weather and most murderous seas.

Overlooking the wide stern deck was the second navigation bridge, from which a skilled seaman could operate the great winches and drums of cable, could catch and control the hawser on the hydraulically operated rising fairleads, could baby a wallowing oil rig or a mortally wounded liner in a gale or a silky calm.

Against the night sky high above it all, the twin towers replaced the squat single funnel of the old-fashioned salvage tugs – and the illusion of a man-of-war was heightened by the fire cannons on the upper platforms from which the *Warlock* could throw fifteen hundred tons of sea water an hour on to a burning vessel. From the towers themselves could be swung the boarding ladders over which men could be sent aboard a hulk, and between them was painted the small circular target that marked the miniature heliport. The whole of it, hull and upper decks, was fireproofed so she could survive in the inferno of burning petroleum from a holed tanker or the flaming chemical from a bulk carrier.

Nicholas Berg felt a little of the despondency and spiritual exhaustion slough away, although his body still ached and his legs carried him stiffly, like those of an old man, as he started towards the gangplank.

'The hell with them all,' he thought. 'I built her and she is strong and good.'

Although it was an hour before midnight, the crew of the *Warlock* watched him from every vantage point they could find; even the oilers had come up from the engine room when the word reached them, and now loafed unobtrusively on the stern working deck.

David Allen, the First Officer, had placed a hand at the main harbour gates with a photograph of Nicholas Berg and a five-cent piece for the telephone call box beside the gate, and the whole ship was alerted now.

David Allen stood with the Chief Engineer in the glassed wing of the main navigation bridge and they watched the solitary figure pick his way across the shadowy dock, carrying his own case.

'So that's him,' David's voice was husky with awe and respect. He looked like a schoolboy under his shaggy bush of sun-bleached hair.

'He's a bloody film star,' Vinny Baker, the Chief Engineer, hitched up his sagging trousers with both elbows, and his spectacles slid down the long thin nose, as he snorted. 'A bloody film star,' he repeated the term with utmost scorn.

'He was first to Jules Levoisin,' David pointed out, and again the note of awe as he intoned that name, 'and he is a tug man from way back.'

'That was fifteen years ago.' Vinny Baker released his elbow grip on his trousers and pushed his spectacles up on to the bridge of his nose. Immediately his trousers began their slow but inexorable slide deckwards. 'Since then he's become a bloody glamour boy – and an owner.'

'Yes,' David Allen agreed, and his baby face crumpled a little at the thought of those two legendary animals, master and owner, combined in one monster. A monster which was on the point of mounting his gangway to the deck of *Warlock*.

'You'd better go down and kiss him on the soft spot,' Vinny grunted comfortably, and drifted away. Two decks down was the sanctuary of his control room where neither masters nor owners could touch him. He was going there now.

David Allen was breathless and flushed when he reached the entry port. The new Master was halfway up the gangway, and he lifted his head and looked steadily at the mate as he stepped aboard.

Though he was only a little above average, Nicholas Berg gave the impression of towering height, and the shoulders beneath the blue cashmere of his jacket were wide and powerful. He wore no hat and his hair was very dark, very thick and brushed back from a wide unlined forehead. The head was big-nosed and gaunt-boned, with a heavy jaw, blue now with new beard, and the eyes were set deep in the cages of their bony sockets, underlined with dark plum-coloured smears, as though they were bruised.

But what shocked David Allen was the man's pallor. His face was drained, as though he had been bled from the jugular. It was the pallor of mortal illness or of exhaustion close to death itself, and it was emphasized by the dark eye-sockets. This was not what David had expected of the legendary Golden Prince of Christy Marine. It was not the face he had seen so often pictured in newspapers and magazines around the world. Surprise made him mute and the man stopped and looked down at him.

'Allen?' asked Nicholas Berg quietly. His voice was low and level, without accent, but with a surprising timbre and resonance.

'Yes, sir. Welcome aboard, sir.'

When Nicholas Berg smiled, the edges of sickness and exhaustion smoothed away at his brow and at the corners of his mouth. His hand was smooth and cool, but his grip was firm enough to make David blink.

'I'll show you your quarters, sir.' David took the Louis Vuitton suitcase from his grip.

'I know the way,' said Nick Berg. 'I designed her.'

He stood in the centre of the Master's day cabin, and felt the deck tilt under his feet, although the *Warlock* was fast to the stone dock, and the muscles in his thighs trembled.

'The funeral went off all right?' Nick asked.

'He was cremated, sir,' David said. 'That's the way he wanted it. I have made the arrangements for the ashes to be sent home to Mary. Mary is his wife, sir,' he explained quickly.

'Yes,' said Nick Berg. 'I know. I saw her before I left London. Mac and I were shipmates once.'

'He told me. He used to boast about that.'

'Have you cleared all his gear?' Nick asked, and glanced around the Master's suite.

'Yes sir, we've packed it all up. There is nothing of his left in here.'

'He was a good man.' Nick swayed again on his feet and looked longingly at the day couch, but instead he crossed to the port and looked out on to the dock. 'How did it happen?'

'My report –'

'Tell me!' said Nicholas Berg, and his voice cracked like a whip.

'The main tow-cable parted, sir. He was on the afterdeck. It took his head off like a bullwhip.'

Nick stood quietly for a moment, thinking about that terse description of tragedy. He had seen a tow part under stress once before. That time it had killed three men.

'All right.' Nick hesitated a moment, the exhaustion had slowed and softened him so that for a moment he was on the point of explaining why he had come to take command of *Warlock* himself, rather than sending another hired man to replace Mac.

It might help to have somebody to talk to now, when he was right down on his knees, beaten and broken and tired to the very depths of his soul. He swayed again, then caught himself and forced aside the temptation. He had never whined for sympathy in his life before.

'All right,' he repeated. 'Please give my apologies to your officers. I have not had much sleep in the last two weeks, and the flight out from Heathrow was murder, as always. I'll meet them in the morning. Ask the cook to send a tray with my dinner.'

The cook was a huge man who moved like a dancer in a snowy apron and a theatrical chef's cap. Nick Berg stared at him as he placed the tray on the table at his elbow. The cook wore his hair in a shiny carefully coiffured bob that fell to his right shoulder, but was drawn back from the left cheek to display a small diamond earring in the pierced lobe of that ear.

He lifted the cloth off the tray with a hand as hairy as that of a bull gorilla, but his voice was as lyrical as a girl's, and his eyelashes curled soft and dark on to his cheek.

'There's a lovely bowl of soup, and a *pot-au-feu*. It's one of my little special things. You will adore it,' he said, and stepped back. He surveyed Nick Berg with those huge hands on his hips. 'But I took one look at you as you came aboard and I just knew what you really needed.' With a magician's flourish, he produced a half-bottle of Pinch Haig from the deep pocket of his apron. 'Take a nip of that with your dinner, and then straight into bed with you, you poor dear.'

No man had ever called Nicholas Berg 'dear' before, but his tongue was too thick and slow for the retort. He stared after the cook as he disappeared with a sweep of his white apron and the twinkle of the diamond, and then he grinned weakly and shook his head, weighing the bottle in his hand.

'Damned if I don't need it,' he muttered, and went to find a glass. He poured it half full, and sipped as he came back to the couch and lifted the lid of the soup pot. The steaming aroma made the little saliva glands under his tongue spurt.

The hot food and whisky in his belly taxed his last reserves, and Nicholas Berg kicked off his shoes as he staggered into his night cabin.

He awoke with the anger on him. He had not been angry in two weeks which was a measure of his despondency.

But when he shaved, the mirrored face was that of a stranger still, too pale and gaunt and set. The lines that framed his mouth were too deeply chiselled, and the early sunlight through the port caught the dark hair at his temple and he saw the frosty glitter there and leaned closer to the mirror. It was the first time he had noticed the flash of silver hair – perhaps he had never looked hard enough, or perhaps it was something new.

'Forty,' he thought. 'I'll be forty years old next June.'

He had always believed that if a man never caught the big one before he was forty, he was doomed never to do so. So what were the rules for the man who caught the big wave before he was thirty, and rode it fast and hard and high, then lost it again before he was forty and was washed out into the trough of boiling white water. Was he doomed also? Nick stared at himself in the mirror and felt the anger in him change its form, becoming directed and functional.

He stepped into the shower, and let the needles of hot water sting his chest. Through the tiredness and disillusion, he was aware, for the first time in weeks, of the underlying strength which he had begun to doubt was still there. He felt it rising to the surface in him, and he thought again of what an extraordinary sea creature he was, how it needed only a deck under him and the smell of the sea in his throat.

He stepped from the shower and dried quickly. This was the right place to be now. This was the place to recuperate – and he realized that his decision not to replace Mac with a hired skipper had been a gut decision. He needed to be here himself.

Always he had known that if you wanted to ride the big wave, you must first be at the place where it begins to peak. It's an instinctive thing, a man just knows where that place is. Nick Berg knew deep in his being that this was the place now, and, with his rising strength, he felt the old excitement, the old 'I'll show the bastards who is beaten' excitement, and he dressed swiftly and went up the Master's private companionway to the upper deck.

Immediately, the wind flew at him and flicked his dark wet hair into his face. It was force five from the south-east, and it came boiling over the great flat-topped mountain which crouched above the city and harbour. Nick looked up at it and saw the thick white cloud they called the 'table cloth' spilling off the heights, and swirling along the grey rock cliffs.

'The Cape of Storms,' he murmured. Even the water in the protected dock leaped and peaked into white crests which blew away like wisps of smoke.

The tip of Africa thrust southwards into one of the most treacherous seas on all the globe. Here two oceans swept turbulently together off the rocky cliffs of Cape Point, and then roiled over the shallows of the Agulhas bank.

Here wind opposed current in eternal conflict. This was the breeding ground of the freak wave, the one that mariners called the 'hundred-year wave', because statistically that was how often it should occur.

But off the Agulhas bank, it was always lurking, waiting only for the right combination of wind and current, waiting for the inphase wave sequence to send its crest rearing a hundred feet high and steep as those grey rock cliffs of Table Mountain itself.

Nick had read the accounts of seamen who had survived that wave, and, at a loss for words, they had written only of a great hole in the sea into which a ship fell helplessly. When the hole closed, the force of breaking water would bury her completely. Perhaps the *Waratah Castle* was one which had fallen into that trough. Nobody would ever know – a great ship of 9,000 tons burden, she and her crew of 211 had disappeared without trace in these seas.

Yet here was one of the busiest sea lanes on the globe, as a procession of giant tankers ploughed ponderously around that rocky Cape on their endless shuttle between the Western world and the oil Gulf of Persia. Despite their bulk, those supertankers were perhaps some of the most vulnerable vehicles yet designed by man.

Now Nick turned and looked across the wind-ripped waters of Duncan Dock at one of them. He could read her name on the stern that rose like a five-storied apartment block. She was owned by Shell Oil, 250,000 dead weight tons, and, out of ballast, she showed much of her rust-red bottom. She was in for repairs, while out in the roadstead of Table Bay, two other monsters waited patiently for their turn in the hospital dock.

So big and ponderous and vulnerable – and valuable. Nick licked his lips involuntarily – hull and cargo together, she was thirty million dollars, piled up like a mountain.

That was why he had stationed the *Warlock* here at Cape Town on the southernmost tip of Africa. He felt the strength and excitement surging upwards in him.

All right, so he had lost his wave. He was no longer cresting and racing. He was down and smothered in white water. But he could feel his head breaking the surface, and he was still on the break-line. He knew there was another big wave racing down on him. It was just beginning to peak and he knew he still had the strength to catch her, to get up high and race again.

'I did it once – I'll damned well do it again,' he said aloud, and went down for breakfast.

He stepped into the saloon, and for a long moment nobody realized he was there. There was an excited buzz of comment and speculation that absorbed them all.

The Chief Engineer had an old copy of *Lloyd's List* folded at the front page and held above a plate of eggs as he read aloud. Nicholas wondered where he had found the ancient copy.

His spectacles had slid right to the end of his nose, so he had to tilt his head far backwards to see through them, and his Australian accent twanged like a guitar.

'In a joint statement issued by the new Chairman and incoming members of the Board, a tribute was paid to the fifteen years of loyal service that Mr Nicholas Berg had given to Christy Marine.'

The five officers listened avidly, ignoring their breakfasts, until David Allen glanced up at the figure in the doorway.

'Captain, sir,' he shouted, and leapt to his feet, while with the other hand, he snatched the newspaper out of Vinny Baker's hands and bundled it under the table.

'Sir, may I present the officers of *Warlock*.'

Shuffling, embarrassed, the younger officers shook hands hurriedly and then applied themselves silently to their congealing breakfasts with a total dedication that precluded any conversation, while Nick Berg took the Master's seat at the head of the long table in the heavy silence and David Allen sat down again on the crumpled sheets of newsprint.

The steward offered the menu to the new Captain, and returned almost immediately with a dish of stewed fruit.

'I ordered a boiled egg,' said Nick mildly, and an apparition in snowy white appeared from the galley, with the chef's cap at a jaunty angle.

'The sailor's curse is constipation, Skipper. I look after my officers – that fruit is delicious and good for you. I'm doing you your eggs now, dear, but eat your fruit first.' And the diamond twinkled again as he vanished.

Nick stared after him in the appalled silence.

'Fantastic cook,' blurted David Allen, his fair skin flushed pinkly and the *Lloyd's List* rustled under his backside. 'Could get a job on any passenger liner, could Angel.'

'If he ever left the *Warlock*, half the crew would go with him,' growled the Chief Engineer darkly, and hauled at his pants with elbows below the level of the table. 'And I'd be one of them.'

Nick Berg turned his head politely to follow the conversation.

'He's almost a doctor,' David Allen went on, addressing the Chief Engineer.

'Five years at Edinburgh Medical School,' agreed the Chief solemnly.

'Do you remember how he set the Second's leg? Terribly useful to have a doctor aboard.'

Nick picked up his spoon, and tentatively lifted a little of the fruit to his mouth. Every officer watched him intently as he chewed. Nick took another spoonful.

'You should taste his jams, sir,' David Allen addressed Nick directly at last. 'Absolutely Cordon Bleu stuff.'

'Thank you, gentlemen, for the advice,' said Nick. The smile did not touch his mouth, but crinkled his eyes slightly. 'But would somebody convey a private message to Angel that if he ever calls me "dear" again I'll beat that ridiculous cap down about his ears.'

In the relieved laughter that followed, Nick turned to David Allen and sent colour flying to his cheeks again by asking, 'You seem to have finished with that old copy of the *List*, Number One. Do you mind if I glance at it again?'

Reluctantly, David lifted himself and produced the newspaper, and there was another tense silence as Nick Berg rearranged the rumpled sheets and studied the old headlines without any apparent emotion.

THE GOLDEN PRINCE OF CHRISTY MARINE DEPOSED

Nicholas hated that name, it had been old Arthur Christy's quirk to name all of his vessels with the prefix 'Golden' and twelve years ago, when Nick had rocketed to head of operations at Christy Marine, some wag had stuck that label on him.

ALEXANDER TO HEAD THE CHRISTY BOARD OF DIRECTORS

Nicholas was surprised by the force of his hatred for the man. They had fought like a pair of bulls for dominance of the herd and the tactics that Duncan Alexander had used had won. Arthur Christy had said once, 'Nobody gives a damn these days whether it is moral or fair, all that counts is, will it work and can you get away with it?' For Duncan it had worked, and he had got away with it in the grandest possible style.

> As Managing-Director in charge of operations, Mr Nicholas Berg helped to build Christy Marine from a small coasting and salvage company into one of the five largest owners of cargo shipping operating anywhere in the world.
>
> After the death of Arthur Christy in 1968, Mr Nicholas Berg succeeded him as Chairman, and continued the company's spectacular expansion.
>
> At present, Christy Marine has in commission eleven bulk carriers and tankers in excess of 250,000 dead weight tons, and has building the 1,000,000 ton giant ultra-tanker *Golden Dawn*. It will be the largest vessel ever launched.

There it was, stated in the baldest possible terms, the labour of a man's lifetime. Over a billion dollars of shipping, designed, financed and built almost entirely with the energy and enthusiasm and faith of Nicholas Berg.

> Mr Nicholas Berg married Miss Chantelle Christy, the only child of Mr Arthur Christy. However, the marriage ended in divorce in September of last year and the former Mrs Berg has subsequently married Mr Duncan Alexander, the new Chairman of Christy Marine.

He felt the hollow nauseous feeling in his stomach again, and in his head the vivid image of the woman. He did not want to think of her now, but could not thrust the image aside. She was bright and beautiful as a flame – and, like a flame, you could not hold her. When she went, she took everything with her, everything. He should hate her also, he really should. Everything, he thought again, the company, his life's work, and the child. When he thought of the child, he nearly succeeded in hating her, and the newsprint shook in his hand.

He became aware again that five men were watching him, and without surprise he realized that not a flicker of his emotions had shown on his face. To be a player for fifteen years in one of the world's highest games of chance, inscrutability was a minimum requirement.

> In a joint statement issued by the new Chairman and incoming members of the Board, a tribute was paid.

Duncan Alexander paid the tribute for one reason, Nick thought grimly. He wanted the 100,000 Christy Marine shares that Nick owned. Those shares were very far from a controlling interest. Chantelle had a million shares in her own name, and there were another million in the Christy Trust, but insignificant as it was, Nick's holding gave him a voice in and an entry to the company's affairs. Nick had bought and paid for every one of those shares. Nobody had given him a thing, not once in his life. He had taken advantage of every stock option in his contract, had bartered bonus and salary for those options, and now those 100,000 shares were worth three million dollars, meagre reward for the labour which had built up a fortune of sixty million dollars for the Christy father and daughter.

It had taken Duncan Alexander almost a year to get those shares. He and Nicholas had bargained with cold loathing. They had hated each other from the first day that Duncan had walked into the Christy building on Leadenhall Street. He had come as old Arthur Christy's latest *Wunderkind*. The financial genius fresh from his triumphs as financial controller of International Electronics, and the hatred had been instant and deep and mutual, a fierce smouldering chemical reaction between them.

In the end Duncan Alexander had won, he had won it all, except the shares, and he had bargained for those from overwhelming strength. He had bargained with patience and skill, wearing his man down over the months. Using all Christy Marine's reserves to block and frustrate Nicholas, forcing him back step by step, taxing even his strength to its limits, driving such a bargain that at the end Nicholas was forced to bow and accept a dangerous price for his shares. He had taken as full payment the subsidiary of Christy Marine, Christy Towage and Salvage, all its assets and all its debts. Nick had felt like a fighter who had been battered for fifteen rounds, and was now hanging desperately to the ropes with his legs gone, blinded by his own sweat and blood and swollen flesh, so he could not see from whence the next punch would come. But he had held on just long enough. He had got Christy Towage and Salvage – he had walked away with something that was completely and entirely his.

Nicholas Berg lowered the newspaper, and immediately his officers attacked their breakfasts ravenously and there was the clatter of cutlery.

'There is an officer missing,' he said.

'It's only the Trog, sir,' Dave Allen explained.

'The Trog?'

'The Radio Officer, sir. Speirs, sir. We call him the Troglodyte.'

'I'd like all the officers present.'

'He never comes out of his cave,' Vinny Baker explained helpfully.

'All right,' Nick nodded. 'I will speak to him later.'

They waited now, five eager young men, even Vin Baker could not completely hide his interest behind the smeared lenses of his spectacles and the tough Aussie veneer.

'I wanted to explain to you the new set-up. The Chief has kindly read to you this article, presumably for the benefit of those who were unable to do so for themselves a year ago.'

Nobody said anything, but Vin Baker fiddled with his porridge spoon.

'So you are aware that I am no longer connected in any way with Christy Marine. I have now acquired Christy Towage and Salvage. It becomes a completely independent company. The name is being changed.' Nicholas had resisted the vanity of calling it Berg Towage and Salvage. 'It will be known as Ocean Towage and Salvage.'

He had paid dearly for it, perhaps too dearly. He had given up his three million dollars' worth of Christy shares for God alone knew what. But he had been tired unto death.

'We own two vessels. The *Golden Warlock* and her sister ship which is almost ready for her sea trials, the *Golden Witch*.'

He knew exactly how much the company owned on those two ships, he had agonized over the figures through long and sleepless nights. On paper the net worth of the company was around four million dollars; he had made a paper profit of a million dollars on his bargain with Duncan Alexander. But it was paper profit only, the company had debts of nearly four million more. If he missed just one month's interest payments on those debts – he dismissed the thought quickly, for on a forced sale his residue in the company would be worth nothing. He would be completely wiped out.

'The names of both ships have been changed also. They will become simply *Warlock* and *Sea Witch*. From now onwards "Golden" is a dirty word around Ocean Salvage.'

They laughed then, a release of tension, and Nick smiled with them, and lit a thin black cheroot from the crocodile-skin case while they settled down.

'I will be running this ship until *Sea Witch* is commissioned. It won't be long, and there will be promotions then.'

Nick superstitiously tapped the mahogany mess table as he said it. The dockyard strike had been simmering for a long time. *Sea Witch* was still on the ways, but costing interest, and further delay would prove him mortal.

'I have got a long oil-rig tow. Bight of Australia to South America. It will give us all time to shake the ship down. You are all tug men, I don't have to tell you when the big one comes up, there will be no warning.'

They stirred, and the eagerness was on them again. Even the oblique reference to prize money had roused them.

'Chief?' Nick looked across at him, and the Engineer snorted, as though the question was an insult.

'In all respects ready for sea,' he said, and tried simultaneously to adjust his trousers and his spectacles.

'Number One?' Nick looked at David Allen. He had not yet become accustomed to the mate's boyishness. He knew that he had held a master mariner's ticket for ten years, that he was over thirty years of age and that MacDonald had hand-picked him – he had to be good. Yet that fair unlined face and quick high colour under the unruly mop of blond hair made him look like an undergraduate.

'I'm waiting on some stores yet, sir,' David answered quickly. 'The chandlers have promised for today, but none of it is vital. I could sail in an hour, if it is necessary.'

'All right.' Nick stood up. 'I will inspect the ship at 0900 hours. You'd best get the ladies off the ship.' During the meal there had been the faint tinkle of female voices and laughter from the crew's quarters.

Nick stepped out of the saloon and Vin Baker's voice was pitched to reach him. It was a truly dreadful imitation of what the Chief believed to be a Royal Naval accent.

'0900, chaps. Jolly good show, what?'

Nick did not miss a step, and he grinned tightly to himself. It's an old Aussie custom; you needle and needle until something happens. There is no malice in it, it's just a way of getting to know your man. And once the boots and fists have stopped flying, you can be friends or enemies on a permanent basis. It was so long since he had been in elemental contact with tough physical men, straight hard men who shunned all subterfuge and sham, and he found the novelty stimulating. Perhaps that was what he really needed now, the sea and the company of real men. He felt his step quicken and the anticipation of physical confrontation lift his spirits off the bottom.

He went up the companionway to the navigation deck, taking the steps three at a time, and the doorway opposite his suite opened. From it emerged the solid grey stench of cheap Dutch cigars and a head that could have belonged to some prehistoric reptile. It too was pale grey and lined and wrinkled, the head of a sea-turtle or an iguana lizard, with the same small dark glittery eyes.

The door was that of the radio room. It had direct access to the main navigation bridge and was merely two paces from the Master's day cabin.

Despite appearances, the head was human, and Nick recalled clearly how Mac had once described his radio officer. 'He is the most anti-social bastard I've ever sailed with, but he can scan eight different frequencies simultaneously, in clear and morse, even while he is asleep. He is a mean, joyless, constipated son of a bitch – and probably the best radio man afloat.'

'Captain,' said the Trog, in a reedy petulant voice. Nick did not ponder the fact that the Trog recognized him instantly as the new Master. The air of command on some men is unmistakable. 'Captain, I have an "all ships signify".'

Nick felt the heat at the base of his spine, and the electric prickle on the back of his neck. It is not sufficient merely to be on the break line when the big wave peaks, it is also necessary to recognize your wave from the hundred others that sweep by.

'Co-ordinates?' he snapped, as he strode down the passageway to the radio room.

'72° 16′ south 32° 12′ west.'

Nick felt the jump in his chest and the heat mount up along his spine. The high latitudes down there in the vast and lonely wastes. There was something sinister and menacing in the mere figures. What ship could be down there?

The longitudinal co-ordinates fitted neatly in the chart that Nick carried in his mind, like a war chart in a military operations room. She was south and west of the Cape of Good Hope – down deep, beyond Gough and Bouvet Island, in the Weddell Sea.

He followed the Trog into the radio room. On this bright, sunny and windy morning, the room was dark and gloomy as a cave, the thick green blinds drawn across the ports; the only source of light was the glowing dials of the banked communication equipment, the most sophisticated equipment that all the wealth of Christy Marine could pack into her, a hundred thousand dollars' worth of electronic magic, but the stink of cheap cigars was overpowering.

Beyond the radio room was the operator's cabin, the bunk unmade, a tray of soiled dishes on the deck beside it.

The Trog hopped up into the swivel seat, and elbowed aside a brass shell-casing that acted as an ashtray and spilled grey flakes of ash and a couple of cold wet chewed cigar butts on to the desk.

Like a wizened gnome, the Trog tended his dials; there was a cacophony of static and electronic trash blurred with the sharp howl of morse.

'The copy?' Nick asked, and the Trog pushed a pad at him. Nick read off quickly.

> CTMZ. 0603 GMT. 72° 16′ S. 32° 12′ W. All ships in a position to render assistance, please signify. CTMZ.

He did not need to consult the R. T. Handbook to recognize that call-sign 'CTMZ'.

With an effort of will he controlled the pressure that caught him in the chest like a giant fist. It was as though he had lived this moment before. It was too neat. He forced himself to distrust his instinct, forced himself to think with his head and not his guts.

Beyond him he heard his officers' voices on the navigation bridge, quiet voices – but charged with tension. They were up from the saloon already.

'Christ!' he thought savagely. 'How do they know? So quickly?' It was as though the ship itself had come awake beneath his feet and trembled with anticipation.

The door from the bridge slid aside and David Allen stood in the opening with a copy of Lloyd's Register in his hands.

'CTMZ, sir, is the call sign of the *Golden Adventurer*. Twenty-two thousand tons, registered Bermuda 1975. Owners Christy Marine.'

'Thank you, Number One,' Nick nodded. Nicholas knew her well; he personally had ordered her construction before the collapse of the great liner traffic. Nick had planned to use her on the Europe-to-Australia run.

Her finished cost had come in at sixty-two million dollars, and she was a beautiful and graceful ship under her tall light alloy superstructure. Her accommodation was luxurious, in the same class as the *France* or the *United States*, but she had been one of Nick's few miscalculations.

When the feasability of operation on the planned run had shown up prohibitive in the face of rising costs and diminishing trade, Nick had switched her usage. It was this type of flexible and intuitive planning and improvisation that had built Christy Marine into the goliath she was now.

Nick had innovated the idea of adventure cruises – and changed the ship's name to *Golden Adventurer*. Now she carried rich passengers to the wild and exotic corners of the globe, from the Galapagos Islands to the Amazon, from the remote Pacific islands to the Antarctic, in search of the unusual.

She carried guest lecturers with her, experts on the environments and ecology of the areas she was to visit, and she was equipped to take her passengers ashore to study the monoliths of Easter Island or to watch the mating displays of the wandering albatross on the Falkland Islands.

She was probably one of the very few cruise liners that was still profitable, and now she stood in need of assistance.

Nicholas turned back from the Trog. 'Has she been transmitting prior to this signify request?'

'She's been sending in company code since midnight. Her traffic was so heavy that I was watching her.'

The green glow of the sets gave the little man a bilious cast, and made his teeth black, so that he looked like an actor from a horror movie.

'You recorded?' Nick demanded, and the Trog switched on the automatic playback of his tape monitors, recapitulating every message the distressed ship had sent or received since the previous midnight. The jumbled blocks of code poured into the room, and the paper strip printed out with the clatter of its keys.

Had Duncan Alexander changed the Christy Marine code? Nick wondered. It would be the natural procedure, completely logical to any operations man. You lose a man who has the code, you change immediately. It was that simple. Duncan had lost Nick Berg, he should change. But Duncan was not an operations man. He was a figures and paper man, he thought in numbers, not in steel and salt water.

If Duncan had changed, they would never break it. Not even with the Decca. Nick had devised the basis of the code. It was a projection that expressed the alphabet as a mathematical function based on a random six-figure master, changing the value of each letter on a progression that was impossible to monitor.

Nick hurried out of the stinking gloom of the radio room with the print-out in his hands.

The navigation bridge of *Warlock* was gleaming chrome and glass, as bright and functional as a modern surgical theatre, or a futuristic kitchen layout.

The primary control console stretched the full width of the bridge, beneath the huge armoured windows. The old-fashioned wheel was replaced by a single steel lever, and the remote control could be carried out on to the wings of the bridge on its long extension cable, like the remote on a television set, so that the helmsman could con the ship from any position he chose.

Illuminated digital displays informed the master instantly of every condition of his ship: speed across the bottom at bows and stern, speed through the water at bows and stern, wind direction and strength, together with all the other technical information of function and malfunction. Nick had built the ship with Christy money, and stinted not at all.

The rear of the bridge was the navigational area, and the chart-table divided it neatly with its overhead racks containing the 106 big blue volumes of the *Global Pilot* and as many other volumes of maritime publications. Below the table were the multiple drawers, wide and flat to contain the spread Admiralty charts that covered every corner of navigable water on the globe.

Against the rear bulkhead stood the battery of electronic navigational aids, like a row of fruit machines in a Vegas gambling hall.

Nick switched the big Decca Satellite Navaid into its computer mode and the display lights flashed and faded and relit in scarlet.

He fed it the six-figure control, numbers governed by the moon phase and date of dispatch. The computer digested this instantaneously, and Nick gave it the last arithmetical proportion known to him. The Decca was ready to decode and Nick gave it the block of garbled transmission – and waited for it to throw back gibberish at him. Duncan *must* have altered the code. He stared at the printout.

> Christy Main from Master of *Adventurer*. 2216 GMT. 72° 16′ S. 32° 05′ W. Underwater ice damage sustained midships starboard. Precautionary shutdown mains. Auxiliary generators activated during damage survey. Stand by.

So Duncan had let the code stand then. Nick groped for the croc-skin case of cheroots, and his hand was steady and firm as he held the flame to the top of the thin black tube. He felt the intense desire to shout aloud, but instead, he drew the fragrant smoke into his lungs.

'Plotted,' said David Allen from behind him. Already on the spread chart of the Antarctic he had marked in the reported position. The transformation was complete, the First Officer had become a grimly competent professional. There remained no trace of the high-coloured undergraduate.

Nick glanced at the plot, saw the dotted ice line far above the *Adventurer*'s position, saw the outline of the forbidding continent of Antarctica groping for the ship with merciless fingers of ice and rock.

The Decca printed out the reply:

Master of *Adventurer* from Christy Main. 2222 GMT. Standing by.

The next message from the recording tape was flagged nearly two hours later, but was printed out almost continuously from the Trog's recording.

Christy Main from Master of *Adventurer*. 0005 GMT. 72° 18′ S. 32° 05′ W. Water contained. Restarted mains. New course CAPE TOWN direct. Speed 8 knots. Stand by.

Dave Allen worked swiftly with parallel rulers and protractor.

'While she was without power she drifted thirty-four nautical miles, south-south-east – there is a hell of a wind or big current setting down there,' he said, and the other deck officers were silent and strained. Although none of them would dare crowd the Master at the Decca, yet in order of seniority they had taken up vantage points around the bridge best suited to follow the drama of a great ship in distress.

The next message ran straight out from the computer, despite the fact that it had been dispatched many hours later.

Christy Main from Master of *Adventurer*. 0546 GMT. 72° 16′ S. 32° 12′ W. Explosion in flooded area. Emergency shutdown all. Water gaining. Request your clearance to issue 'all ships signify'. Standing by.

Master of *Adventurer* from Christy Main. 0547 GMT. You are cleared to issue signify. Break. Break. Break. You are expressly forbidden to contract tow or salvage without reference Christy Main. Acknowledge.

Duncan was not even putting in the old chestnut, 'except in the event of danger to human life'.

The reason was too apparent. Christy Marine underwrote most of its own bottoms through another of its subsidiaries. The London and European Insurance and Finance Company. The self-insurance scheme had been the brain-child of Alexander Duncan himself when first he arrived at Christy Marine. Nick Berg had opposed the scheme bitterly, and now he might live to see his reasoning being justified.

'Are we going to signify?' David Allen asked quietly.

'Radio silence,' snapped Nick irritably, and began to pace the bridge, the crack of his heels muted by the cork coating on the deck.

'Is this my wave?' Nick demanded of himself, applying the old rule he had set for himself long ago, the rule of deliberate thought first, action after.

The *Golden Adventurer* was drifting in the ice-fields two thousand and more miles south of Cape Town, five days and nights of hard running for the *Warlock*. If he made the go decision, by the time he reached her, she might have effected repairs and restarted, she might be under her own command again. Again, even if she was still helpless, *Warlock* might reach her to find another salvage tug had beaten her to the scene. So now it was time to call the roll.

He stopped his pacing at the door to the radio room and spoke quietly to the Trog.

'Open the telex line and send to Bach Wackie in Bermuda quote call the roll unquote.'

As he turned away, Nick was satisfied with his own forethought in installing the satellite telex system which enabled him to communicate with his agent in Bermuda, or with any other selected telex station, without his message being broadcast over the open frequencies and monitored by a competitor or any other interested party. His signals were bounced through the high stratosphere where they could not be intercepted.

While he waited, Nicholas worried. The decision to go would mean abandoning the Esso oil-rig tow. The tow fee had been a vital consideration in his cash flow situation. Two hundred and twenty thousand sterling, without which he could not meet the quarterly interest payment due in sixty days' time – unless, unless . . . He juggled figures in his head, but the magnitude of the risk involved was growing momentarily more apparent – and the figures did not add up. He needed the Esso tow. God, how badly he needed it!

'Bach Wackie are replying,' called the Trog above the chatter of the telex receiver, and Nick spun on his heel.

He had appointed Bach Wackie as the agents for Ocean Salvage because of their proven record of quick and aggressive efficiency. He glanced at his Rolex Oyster and calculated that it was about two o'clock in the morning local time in Bermuda, and yet his request for information on the disposition of all his major competitors was now being answered within minutes of receipt.

For Master *Warlock* from Bach Wackie latest reported positions. *John Ross* dry dock Durban. *Woltema Wolteraad* Esso tow Torres Straits to Alaska Shelf –

That took care of the two giant Safmarine tugs; half of the top opposition was out of the race.

Wittezee Shell exploration tow Galveston to North Sea. *Grootezee* lying Brest –

That was the two Dutchmen out of it. The names and positions of the other big salvage tugs, each of them a direct and dire threat to *Warlock*, ran swiftly from the telex and Nicholas chewed his cheroot ragged as he watched, his eyes slitted against the spiralling blue smoke, feeling the relief rise in him as each report put another of his competitors in some distant waters, far beyond range of the stricken ship.

'*La Mouette*,' Nick's hands balled into fists as the name sprang on to the white paper sheet, '*La Mouette* discharged Brazgas tow Golfo San Jorge on 14th reported en route Buenos Aires.'

Nick grunted like a boxer taking a low blow, and turned away from the machine. He walked out on to the open wing of the bridge and the wind tore at his hair and clothing.

La Mouette, the seagull, a fanciful name for that black squat hull, the old-fashioned high box of superstructure, the traditional single stack; Nick could see it clearly when he closed his eyes.

There was no doubt in his mind at all. Jules Levoisin was already running hard for the south, running like a hunting dog with the scent hot in its nostrils.

Jules had discharged in the southern Atlantic three days ago. He would certainly have bunkered at Comodoro. Nick knew how Jules' mind worked, he was never happy unless his bunkers were bulging.

Nick flicked the stub of his cigar away, and it was whisked far out into the harbour by the wind.

He knew that *La Mouette* had refitted and installed new engines eighteen months before. With a nostalgic twinge, he had read a snippet in *Lloyd's List*. But even nine thousand horsepower couldn't push that tubby hull at better than eighteen knots, Nick was certain of that. Yet even with *Warlock*'s superior speed, *La Mouette* was better placed by a thousand miles. There was no room for complacency. And what if *La Mouette* had set out to double Cape Horn instead of driving north up the Atlantic? If that had happened, and with Jules Levoisin's luck it might just have happened, then *La Mouette* was a long way inside him already.

Anybody else but Jules Levoisin, he thought, why did it have to be him? And oh God, why now? Why now when I am so vulnerable – emotionally, physically and financially vulnerable. Oh God, why did it come now?

He felt the false sense of cheer and well-being, with which he had buoyed himself that morning, fall away from him like a cloak, leaving him naked and sick and tired again.

I am not ready yet, he thought; and then realized that it was probably the first time in his adult life he had ever said that to himself. He had always been ready, good and ready, for anything. But not now, not this time.

Suddenly Nicholas Berg was afraid, as he had never been before. He was empty, he realized, there was nothing in him, no strength, no confidence, no resolve. The depth of his defeat by Duncan Alexander, the despair of his rejection by the woman he loved, had broken him. He felt his fear turn to terror, knowing that his wave had come, and would sweep by him now, for he did not have the strength to ride it.

Some deep instinct warned him that it would be the last wave, there would be nothing after it. The choice was go now, or never go again. And he knew he could not go, he could not go against Jules Levoisin, he could not challenge the old master. He could not go – he could not reject the certainty of the Esso tow, he did not have the nerve now to risk all that he had left on a single throw. He had just lost a big one, he couldn't go at risk again.

The risk was too great, he was not ready for it, he did not have the strength for it.

He wanted to go to his cabin and throw himself on his bunk and sleep – and sleep. He felt his knees buckling with the great weight of his despair, and he hungered for the oblivion of sleep.

He turned back into the bridge, out of the wind. He was broken, defeated, he had given up. As he went towards the sanctuary of his day cabin, he passed the long command console and stopped involuntarily.

His officers watched him in a tense, electric silence.

His right hand went out and touched the engine telegraph, sliding the pointer from 'off' to 'stand by'.

'Engine Room,' he heard a voice speak in calm and level tones, so it could not be his own. 'Start main engines,' said the voice.

Seemingly from a great distance he watched the faces of his deck officers bloom with unholy joy, like old-time pirates savouring the prospect of a prize.

The strange voice went on, echoing oddly in his ears, 'Number One, ask the Harbour Master for permission to clear harbour immediately – and, Pilot, course to steer for the last reported position of *Golden Adventurer*, please.'

From the corner of his eye, he saw David Allen punch the Third Officer lightly but gleefully on the shoulder before he hurried to the radio telephone.

Nicholas Berg felt suddenly the urge to vomit. So he stood very still and erect at the navigation console and fought back the waves of nausea that swept over him, while his officers bustled to their sea-going stations.

'Bridge. This is the Chief Engineer,' said a disembodied voice from the speaker above Nick's head. 'Main engines running.' A pause and then that word of special Aussie approbation. 'Beauty!' – but the Chief pronounced it in three distinct syllables, 'Be-yew-dy!'

Warlock's wide-flared bows were designed to cleave and push the waters open ahead of her and in those waters below latitude 40°, she ran like an old bull otter, slick and wet and fast for the south.

Uninterrupted by any land-mass, the cycle of great atmospheric depressions swept endlessly across those cold open seas, and the wave patterns built up into a succession of marching mountain ranges.

Warlock was taking them on her starboard shoulder, bursting through each crest in a white explosion that leapt from her bows like a torpedo strike, the water coming aboard green and clear over her high foredeck, and sweeping her from stern to stern as she twisted and broke out, dropping sheer into the valley that opened ahead of her. Her twin ferro-bronze propellers broke clear of the surface, the slamming vibration instantly controlled by the sophisticated variable-pitch gear, until she swooped forward and the propellers bit deeply again, the thrust of the twin Mirrlees diesels hurtling her towards the slope of the next swell.

Each time it seemed that she could not rise in time to meet the cliff of water that bore down on her. The water was black under the grey sunless sky. Nick had lived through typhoon and Caribbean hurricane, but had never seen water as menacing and cruel as this. It glittered like the molten slag that pours down the dump of an iron foundry and cools to the same iridescent blackness.

In the deep valleys between the crests, the wind was blanketed so they fell into an unnatural stillness, an eerie silence that only enhanced the menace of that towering slope of water.

In the trough, *Warlock* heeled and threw her head up, climbing the slope in a gut-swooping lift, that buckled the knees of the watch. As she went up, so the angle of her bridge tilted back, and that sombre cheerless sky filled the forward bridge windows with a vista of low scudding cloud.

The wind tore at the crest of the wave ahead of her, ripping it away like white cotton from the burst seams of a black mattress, splattering custard-thick spume against the armoured glass. Then *Warlock* put her sharp steel nose deeply into it. Gouging a fat wedge of racing green over her head, twisting violently at the jarring impact, dropping sideways over the crest, and breaking out to fall free and repeat the cycle again.

Nick was wedged into the canvas master's seat in the corner of the bridge. He swayed like a camel-driver to the thrust of the sea and smoked his black cheroots quietly, his head turning every few minutes to the west, as though he expected at any moment to see the black ugly hull of *La Mouette* come up on top of the next swell. But he knew she was a thousand miles away still, racing down the far leg of the triangle which had at its apex the stricken liner.

'If she *is* running,' Nick thought, and knew that there was no doubt. *La Mouette* was running as frantically as was *Warlock* – and as silently. Jules Levoisin had taught Nick the trick of silence. He would not use his radio until he had the liner on his radar scan. Then he would come through in clear, 'I will be in a position to put a line aboard you in two hours. Do you accept "Lloyd's Open Form"?'

The Master of the distressed vessel, having believed himself abandoned without succour, would over-react to the promise of salvation, and when *La Mouette* came bustling up over the horizon, flying all her bunting and with every light blazing in as theatrical a display as Jules could put up, the relieved Master would probably leap at the offer of 'Lloyd's Open Form' – a decision that would surely be regretted by the ship's owners in the cold and unemotional precincts of an Arbitration court.

When Nick had supervised the design of *Warlock*, he had insisted that she look good as well as being able to perform. The master of a disabled ship was usually a man in a highly emotional state. Mere physical appearance might sway him in the choice between two salvage tugs coming up on him. *Warlock* looked magnificent; even in this cold and cheerless ocean, she looked like a warship. The trick would be to show her to the master of *Golden Adventurer* before he struck a bargain with *La Mouette*.

Nick could no longer sit inactive in his canvas seat. He judged the next towering swell and, with half a dozen quick strides, crossed the bridge deck in those fleeting moments as *Warlock* steadied in the trough. He grabbed the chrome handrail above the Decca computer.

On the keyboard he typed the function code that would set the machine in navigational mode, co-ordinating the transmissions she was receiving from the circling satellite stations high above the earth. From these were calculated *Warlock*'s exact position over the earth's surface, accurate to within twenty-five yards.

Nick entered the ship's position and the computer compared this with the plot that Nick had requested four hours previously. It printed out quickly the distance run and the ship's speed made good. Nick frowned angrily and swung round to watch the helmsman.

In this fiercely running cross sea, a good man could hold *Warlock* on course more efficiently than any automatic steering device. He could anticipate each trough and crest and prevent the ship paying off across the direction of the swells, and then kicking back violently as she went over, wasting critical time and distance.

Nick watched the helmsman work, judging each sea as it came aboard, checking the ship's heading on the big repeating compass above the man's head. After ten minutes, Nick realised that there was no wastage; *Warlock* was making as good a course as was possible in these conditions.

The engine telegraph was pulled back to her maximum safe power-setting, the course was good and yet *Warlock* was not delivering those few extra knots of speed that Nick Berg had relied on when he had made the critical decision to race *La Mouette* for the prize.

Nick had relied on twenty-eight knots against the Frenchman's eighteen, and he was not getting it. Involuntarily, he glanced out to the west as *Warlock* came up on the top of the next crest. Through the streaming windows, from which the spinning wipers cleared circular areas of clean glass, Nick looked out across a wilderness of black water, forbidding and cold and devoid of other human presence.

Abruptly Nick crossed to the R/T microphone.

'Engine Room confirm we are top of the green.'

'Top of the green, it is, Skipper.'

The Chief's casual tones floated in above the crash of the next sea coming aboard.

'Top of the green' was the maximum safe power-setting recommended by the manufacturers for those gigantic Mirrlees diesels. It was a far higher setting than top economical power, and they were burning fuel at a prodigious rate. Nick was pushing her as high as he could without going into the 'red' danger area above eighty per cent of full power, which at prolonged running might permanently damage her engines.

Nick turned away to his seat, and wedged himself into it. He groped for his cheroot case, and then checked himself, the lighter in his hand. His tongue and mouth felt furred over and dry. He had smoked without a break every waking minute since leaving Cape Town, and God knows he had slept little enough since then. He ran his tongue around his mouth with distaste before he returned the cheroot to his case, and crouched in his seat staring ahead, trying to work out why *Warlock* was running slow.

Suddenly he straightened and considered a possibility that brought a metallic green gleam of anger into Nick's eyes.

He slid out of his seat, nodded to the Third Officer who had the deck and ducked through the doorway in the back of the bridge into his day cabin. It was a ploy. He didn't want his visit below decks announced, and from his own suite he darted into the companionway.

The engine control room was as modern and gleaming as *Warlock*'s navigation bridge. It was completely enclosed with double glass to cut down the thunder of her engines. The control console was banked below the windows, and all the ship's functions were displayed in green and red digital figures.

The view beyond the windows into the main engine room was impressive, even for Nick who had designed and supervised each foot of the layout.

The two Mirrlees diesel engines filled the white-painted cavern with only walking space between, each as long as four Cadillac Eldorados parked bumper to bumper and as deep as if another four Cadillacs had been piled on top of them.

The thirty-six cylinders of each block were crowned with a moving forest of valve stems and con-rod ends, each enormous powerhouse capable of pouring out eleven thousand usable horsepower.

It was only custom that made it necessary for any visitor, including the Master, to announce his arrival in the engine room to the Chief Engineer. Ignoring custom, Nick slipped quietly through the glass sliding doors, out of the hot burned-oil stench of the engine room into the cooler and sweeter conditioned air of the control room.

Vin Baker was deep in conversation with one of his electricians, both of them kneeling before the open doors of one of the tall grey steel cabinets which housed a teeming mass of coloured cables and transistor switches. Nick had reached the control console before the Chief Engineer uncoiled his lanky body from the floor and spun round to face him.

When Nick was very angry, his lips compressed in a single thin white line, the thick dark eyebrows seemed to meet above the snapping green eyes and large slightly beaked nose.

'You pulled the over-ride on me,' he accused in a flat, passionless voice that did not betray his fury. 'You're governing her out at seventy per cent of power.'

'That's top of the green in my book,' Vin Baker told him. 'I'm not running my engines at eighty per cent in this sea. She'll shake the guts out of herself.' He paused and the stern was flung up violently as *Warlock* crashed over the top of another sea. The control room shuddered with the vibration of the screws breaking out of the surface, spinning wildly in the air before they could bite again.

'Listen to her, man. You want me to pour on more of it?'

'She's built to take it.'

'Nothing's built to run that hard, and live in this sea.'

'I want the over-ride out,' said Nick flatly, indicating the chrome handle and pointer with which the engineer could cancel the power settings asked for by the bridge. 'I don't care when you do it – just as long as it's any time within the next five seconds.'

'You get out of my engine room – and go play with your toys.'

'All right,' Nick nodded, 'I'll do it myself.' And he reached for the over-ride gear.

'You take your hands off my engines,' howled Vin Baker, and picked up the iron locking handle off the deck. 'You touch my engines and I'll break your teeth out of your head, you ice-cold Pommy bastard.'

Even in his own anger, Nick blinked at the epithet. When he thought about the blazing passions and emotions that seethed within him, he nearly laughed aloud. *Ice-cold*, he thought, so that's how he sees me.

'You stupid Bundaberg-swilling galah,' he said quietly, as he reached for the over-ride. 'I don't really care if I have to kill you first, but we are going to eighty per cent.'

It was Vin Baker's turn to blink behind his smeared glasses, he had not expected to be insulted in the colloquial. He dropped the heavy steel handle to the deck. It fell with a clang.

'I don't need it,' he announced, and tucked his spectacles into his back pocket and hoisted his trousers with both elbows. 'It will be more fun to take you to pieces by hand.'

It was only then that Nick realized how tall the engineer was. His arms were ridged with the lean wiry taut muscle of hard physical labour. His fists, as he balled them, were lumpy with scar tissue across the knuckles and the size of a pair of nine-pound hammers. He went down into a fighter's crouch, and rode the plunging deck with an easy flexing of the long powerful legs.

As Nicholas touched the chrome over-ride handle, the first punch came from the level of Baker's knees, but it came so fast that Nick only just had time to sway away from it. It whistled up past his jaw and scraped the skin from the outside corner of his eye, but he counter-punched instinctively, swaying back and slamming it in under the armpit, feeling the blow land so solidly that his teeth jarred his own head. The Chief's breath hissed, but he swung left-handed and a bony fist crushed the pad of muscle on the point of Nick's shoulder, bounced off and caught him high on the temple.

Even though it was a glancing blow, it felt as though a door had slammed in Nick's head, and resounding darkness closed behind his eyes. He fell forward into a clinch to ride the darkness, grabbing the lean hard body and smothering it in a bear hug as he tried to clear the singing darkness in his head.

He felt the Chief shift his weight, and was shocked at the power in that wiry frame, it took all his own strength to hold him. Suddenly and clearly he knew what was going to happen next. There were little white ridges of scar tissue half hidden by the widow's peak of flopping sandy hair on the Chief's forehead. Those scars from previous conflicts warned Nick.

Vin Baker reared back, like a cobra flaring for the strike, and then flung his head forward; it was the classic butt aimed for Nick's face and, had it landed squarely, it would have crushed in his nose and broken his teeth off level to the gums – but Nick anticipated, and dropped his own chin, tucking it down hard so that their foreheads met with a crack like a breaking oak branch.

The impact broke Nick's grip, and both of them reeled apart across the heaving deck, Vin Baker howling like a moon-sick dog and clutching his own head.

'Fight fair, you Pommy bastard!' he howled in outrage, and he came up short against the steel cabinets that lined the far side of the control room. The astonished electrician dived for cover under the control console, scattering tools across the deck.

Vin Baker lay for a moment gathering his lanky frame, and then, as *Warlock* swung hard over, rolling viciously in the cross sea, he used her momentum to hurl himself down the steeply tilting deck, dropping his head again like a battering ram to crush in Nick's ribs as he charged.

Nick turned like a cattle man working an unruly steer. He whipped one arm round Vin Baker's neck and ran with him, holding his head down and building up speed across the full length of the control room. They reached the armoured glass wall at the far end, and the top of Vin Baker's head was the point of impact with the weight of both their bodies behind it.

The Chief Engineer came round at the prick of the needle that Angel forced through the thick flap of open flesh on top of his head. He came round fighting drunkenly, but the cook held him down with one huge hairy arm.

'Easy, love.' Angel pulled the needle through the torn red weeping scalp and tied the stitch.

'Where is he, where is the bastard?' slurred the Chief.

'It's all over, Chiefie,' Angel told him gently. 'And you are lucky he bashed you on the head – otherwise he might have hurt you.' He took another stitch.

The Chief winced as Angel pulled the thread up tight and knotted it. 'He tried to mess with my engines. I taught the bastard a lesson.'

'You've terrified him,' Angel agreed sweetly. 'Now you take a swig of this and lie still. I want you in this bunk for twelve hours – and I might come and tuck you in.'

'I'm going back to my engines,' announced the Chief, and drained the medicine glass of brown spirit, then whistled at the bite of the fumes.

Angel left him and crossed to the telephone. He spoke quickly into it, and as the Chief lumbered off the bunk, Nick Berg stepped into the cabin, and nodded to the cook.

'Thank you, Angel.'

Angel ducked out of the cabin and left them facing each other. The Chief opened his mouth to snarl at Nick.

'Jules Levoisin in *La Mouette* has probably made five hundred miles on us while you have been playing prima donna,' said Nick quietly, and Vin Baker's mouth stayed open, although no sound came out of it.

'I built this ship to run fast and hard in just this kind of contest, and now you are trying to do all of us out of prize money.'

Nick turned on his heel and went back up the companionway to his navigation deck. He settled into his canvas chair and fingered the big purple swelling on his forehead tenderly. His head felt as though a rope had been knotted around it and twisted up tight. He wanted to go to his cabin and take something for the pain, but he did not want to miss the call when it came.

He lit another cheroot, and it tasted like burned tarred rope. He dropped it into the sandbox and the telephone at his shoulder rang once.

'Bridge, this is the Engine Room.'

'Go ahead, Chief.'

'We are going to eighty per cent now.'

Nick did not reply, but he felt the change in the engine vibration and the more powerful rush of the hull beneath him.

'Nobody told me *La Mouette* was running against us. No way that frog-eating bastard's going to get a line on her first,' announced Vin Baker grimly, and there was a silence between them. Something more had to be said.

'I bet you a pound to a pinch of kangaroo dung,' challenged the Chief, 'that you don't know what a galah is, and that you've never tasted a Bundaberg rum in your life.'

Nick found himself smiling, even through the blinding pain in his head.

'Be-yew-dy!' Nick said, making three syllables of it and keeping the laughter out of his voice, as he hung up the receiver.

Dave Allen's voice was apologetic. 'Sorry to wake you, sir, but the *Golden Adventurer* is reporting.'

'I'm coming,' mumbled Nick, and swung his legs off the bunk. He had been in that black death-sleep of exhaustion, but it took him only seconds to pull back the dark curtains from his mind. It was his old training as a watch-keeping officer.

He rubbed away the last traces of sleep, feeling the rasping black stubble of his beard under his fingers as he crossed quickly to his bathroom. He spent forty seconds in bathing his face and combing his tousled hair, and regretfully decided there was no time to shave. Another rule of his was to look good in a world which so often judged a man by his appearance.

When he went out on to the navigation bridge, he knew at once that the wind had increased its velocity. He guessed it was rising force six now, and *Warlock*'s motion was more violent and abandoned. Beyond the warm, dimly lit capsule of the bridge, all those elements of cold water and vicious racing winds turned the black night to a howling tumult.

The Trog was crouched over his machines, grey and wizened and sleepless. He hardly turned his head to hand Nick the message flimsy.

'Master of *Golden Adventurer* to Christy Main,' the Decca decoded swiftly, and Nick grunted as he saw the new position report. Something had altered drastically in the liner's circumstances. 'Main engines still unserviceable. Current setting easterly and increasing to eight knots. Wind rising force six from north-west. Critical ice danger to the ship. What assistance can I expect?'

There was a panicky note to that last line, and Nick saw why when he compared the liner's new position on the spread chart.

'She's going down sharply on the lee shore,' David muttered as he worked quickly over the chart. 'The current and wind are working together – they are driving her down on to the land.'

He touched the ugly broken points of Coatsland's shoreline with the tip of one finger.

'She eighty miles offshore now. At the rate she is drifting, it will take her only another ten hours before she goes aground.'

'If she doesn't hit an iceberg first,' said Nick. 'From the Master's last message, it sounds as though they are into big ice.'

'That's a cheerful thought,' agreed David, and straightened up from the chart.

'What's our time to reach her?'

'Another forty hours, sir,' David hesitated and pushed the thick white-gold lock of hair off his forehead, 'if we can make good this speed – but we may have to reduce when we reach the ice.'

Nick turned away to his canvas chair. He felt the need to pace back and forward, to release the pent-up forces within him. However, any movement in this heavy pounding sea was not only difficult but downright dangerous, so he groped his way to the chair and wedged himself in, staring ahead into the clamorous black night.

He thought about the terrible predicament of the liner's Captain. His ship was at deadly risk, and the lives of his crew and passengers with it.

How many lives? Nick cast his mind back and came up with the figures. The *Golden Adventurer*'s full complement of officers and crew was 235, and there was accommodation for 375 passengers, a possible total of over six hundred souls. If the ship was lost, *Warlock* would be hard put to take aboard that huge press of human life.

'Well, sir, they signed on for adventure,' David Allen spoke into his thoughts as though he had heard them, 'and they are getting their money's worth.'

Nick glanced at him, and nodded. 'Most of them will be elderly. A berth on that cruise costs a fortune, and it's usually only the oldsters who have that sort of gold. If she goes aground, we are going to lose life.'

'With respect, Captain,' David hesitated, and blushed again for the first time since leaving port, 'if her Captain knows that assistance is on the way, it may prevent him doing something crazy.'

Nick was silent. The Mate was right, of course. It was cruel to leave them in the despair of believing they were alone down there in those terrible icefields. The *Adventurer*'s Captain could make a panic decision, one that could be averted if he knew how close succour was.

'The air temperature out there is minus five degrees, and if the wind is at thirty miles an hour, that will make it a lethal chill factor. If they take to the boats in that —' David was interrupted by the Trog calling from the radio room.

'The owners are replying.'

It was a long message that Christy Marine were sending to their Captain. It was filled with those same hollow assurances that a surgeon gives to a cancer patient, but one paragraph had relevance for Nick:

'All efforts being made to contact salvage tugs reported operating South Atlantic.'

David Allen looked at him expectantly. It was the right humane thing to do. To tell them he was only eight hundred miles away, and closing swiftly.

Nervous energy fizzed in Nick's blood, making him restless and angry. On an impulse he left his chair and carefully crossed the heaving deck to the starboard wing of the bridge.

He slid open the door and stepped out into the gale. The shock of that icy air took his breath away and he gasped like a drowning man. He felt tears streaming from his eyes across his cheeks and the frozen spray struck into his face like steel darts.

Carefully he filled his lungs, and his nostrils flared as he smelt the ice. It was that unmistakeable dank smell, he remembered so well from the northern Arctic seas. It was like the body smell of some gigantic reptilian sea monster – and it struck the mariner's chill into his soul.

He could endure only a few seconds more of the gale, but when he stepped back into the cosy green-lit warmth of the bridge, his mind was clear, and he was thinking crisply.

'Mr Allen, there is ice ahead.'

'I have a watch on the radar, sir.'

'Very good,' Nick nodded, 'but we'll reduce to fifty per cent of power.' He hesitated, and then went on, 'and maintain radio silence.'

The decision was hard made, and Nick saw the accusation in David Allen's eyes before he turned away to give the orders for the reduction in power. Nick felt a sudden and uncharacteristic urge to explain the decision to him. He did not know why – perhaps he needed the Mate's understanding and sympathy. Instantly Nick saw that as a symptom of his weakness and vulnerability. He had never needed sympathy before, and he steeled himself against it now.

His decision to maintain radio silence was correct. He was dealing with two hard men. He knew he could not afford to give an inch of sea room to Jules Levoisin. He would force him to open radio contact first. He needed that advantage.

The other man with whom he had to deal was Duncan Alexander, and he was a hating man, dangerous and vindictive. He had tried once to destroy Nick – and perhaps he had already succeeded. Nick had to guard himself now, he must pick with care his moment to open negotiations with Christy Marine and the man who had displaced him at its head. Nick must be in a position of utmost strength when he did so.

Jules Levoisin must be forced to declare himself first, Nick decided. The Captain of the *Golden Adventurer* would have to be left in the agonies of doubt a little longer, and Nick consoled himself with the thought that any further drastic change in the liner's circumstances or a decision by the Master to abandon his ship and commit his company to the lifeboats would be announced on the open radio channels and would give him a chance to intervene.

Nick was about to caution the Trog to keep a particular watch on Channel 16 for *La Mouette*'s first transmission, then he checked himself. That was another thing he never did – issue unnecessary orders. The Trog's grey wrinkled head was wreathed in clouds of reeking cigar smoke but was bowed to his mass of electronic equipment, and he adjusted a dial with careful lover's fingers; his little eyes were bright and sleepless as those of an ancient sea turtle.

Nick went to his chair and settled down to wait out the few remaining hours of the short Antarctic summer night.

The radar screen had shown strange and alien capes and headlands above the sea clutter of the storm, strange islands, anomalies which did not relate to the Admiralty charts. Between these alien masses shone myriad other smaller contacts, bright as fireflies, any one of which could have been the echo of a stricken ocean liner – but which was not.

As *Warlock* nosed cautiously down into this enchanted sea, the dawn that had never been far from the horizon flushed out, timorous as a bride, decked in colours of gold and pink that struck splendorous splinters of light off the icebergs.

The horizon ahead of them was cluttered with ice, some of the fragments were but the size of a billiard table and they bumped and scraped down the *Warlock*'s side, then swung and bobbed in her wake as she passed. There were others the size of a city block, weird and fanciful structures of honeycombed white ice, that stood as tall as *Warlock*'s upperworks as she passed.

'White ice is soft ice,' Nick murmured to David Allen beside him, and then caught himself. It was an unnecessary speech, inviting familiarity, and before the Mate could answer, Nick turned quickly away to the radar-repeater and lowered his face to the eye-piece in the coned hood. For a minute he studied the images of the surrounding ice in the darkened body of the instrument, then went back to his seat and stared ahead impatiently.

Warlock was running too fast, Nick knew it; he was relying on the vigilance of his deck officers to carry her through the ice. Yet still this speed was too slow for his seething impatience.

Above their horizon rose another shoreline, a great unbroken sweep of towering cliff which caught the low sun, and glowed in emerald and amethyst, a drifting tableland of solid hard ice, forty miles across and two hundred feet high.

As they closed with that massive translucent island, so the colours that glowed through it became more hauntingly beautiful. The cliffs were rent by deep bays, and split by crevasses whose shadowy depths were dark sapphire, blue and mysterious, paling out to a thousand shades of green.

'My God, it's beautiful,' said David Allen with the reverence of a man kneeling in a cathedral.

The crests of the ice cliffs blazed in clearest ruby; to windward, the big sea piled in and crashed against those cliffs, surging up them in explosive bursts of white spray. Yet the iceberg did not dip nor swing or work, even in that murderous sea.

'Look at the lee she is making,' Dave Allen pointed. 'You could ride out a force twelve behind her.'

On the leeward side, the waters were protected from the wind by that mountain of sheer ice. Green and docile, they lapped those mysterious blue cliffs, and *Warlock* went into the lee, passing in a ship's length from the plunging rearing action of a wild horse into the tranquillity of a mountain lake, calm, windless and unnatural.

In the calm, Angel brought trays piled with crisp brown-baked Cornish pasties and steaming mugs of thick creamy cocoa, and they ate breakfast at three in the morning, marvelling at the fine pale sunlight and the towers of incredible beauty, the younger officers shouting and laughing when a school of five black killer whales passed so close that they could see their white cheek patterns and wide grinning mouths through the icy clear waters.

The great mammals circled the ship, then ducked beneath her hull, surging up on the far side with their huge black triangular fins shearing the surface as they blew through the vents in the top of their heads. The fishy stink of their breath pervaded the bridge, and then they were gone, and *Warlock* motored calmly along in the lee of the ice, like a holiday launch of day-trippers.

Nicholas Berg did not join the spontaneous gaiety. He munched one of Angel's delicious pies full of meat and thick gravy, but he could not finish it. His stomach was too tense. He found himself resenting the high spirits of his officers. The laughter offended him, now when his whole life hung in precarious balance. He felt the temptation to quell them with a few harsh words, conscious of the power he had to plunge them into instant consternation.

Nick listened to their carefree banter and felt old enough to be their father, despite the few years' difference in their ages. He was impatient with them, irritated that they should be able to laugh like this when so much was at stake – six hundred human lives, a great ship, tens of millions of dollars, his whole future. They would probably never themselves know what it felt like to put a lifetime's work at risk on a single flip of the coin – and then suddenly, unaccountably, he envied them.

He could not understand the sensation, could not fathom why suddenly he longed to laugh with them, to share the companionship of the moment, to be free of pressure for just a little while. For fifteen years, he had not known that sort of hiatus, had never wanted it.

He stood up abruptly, and immediately the bridge was silent. Every officer concentrating on his appointed task, not one of them glancing at him as he paced once, slowly, across the wide bridge. It did not need a word to change the mood, and suddenly Nick felt guilty. It was too easy, too cheap.

Carefully Nick steeled himself, shutting out the weakness, building up his resolve and determination, bringing all his concentration to bear on the Herculean task ahead of him, and he paused at the door of the radio room. The Trog looked up from his machines, and they exchanged a single glance of understanding. Two completely dedicated men, with no time for frivolity.

Nick nodded and paced on, the strong handsome face stern and uncompromising, his step firm and measured – but when he stopped again by the side windows of the bridge and looked up at the magnificent cliff of ice, he felt the doubts surging up again within him.

How much had he sacrificed for what he had gained, how much joy and laughter had he spurned to follow the high road of challenge, how much beauty had he passed along the way without seeing it in his haste, how much love and warmth and companionship? He thought with a fierce pang of the woman who had been his wife, and who had gone now with the child who was his son. Why had they gone, and what had they left him with – after all his strivings?

Behind him, the radio crackled and hummed as the carrier beam opened Channel 16, then it pitched higher as a human voice came through in clear.

'Mayday. Mayday. Mayday. This is the *Golden Adventurer*.'

Nick spun and ran to the radio room as the calm masculine voice read out the co-ordinates of the ship's position.

'We are in imminent danger of striking. We are preparing to abandon ship. Can any vessel render assistance? Repeat, can any vessel render assistance?'

'Good God,' David Allen's voice was harsh with anxiety, 'the current's got them, they're going down on Cape Alarm at nine knots – she's only fifty miles offshore and we are still two hundred and twenty miles from that position.'

'Where is *La Mouette*?' growled Nick Berg. 'Where the hell is she?'

'We'll have to open contact now, sir,' David Allen looked up from the chart. 'You cannot let them go down into the boats – not in this weather, sir. It would be murder.'

'Thank you, Number One,' said Nick quietly. 'Your advice is always welcome.' David flushed, but there was anger and not embarrassment beneath the colour. Even in the stress of the moment, Nick noted that, and adjusted his opinion of his First Officer. He had guts as well as brains.

The mate was right, of course. There was only one thing to consider now, the conservation of human life.

Nick looked up at the top of the ice cliff and saw the low cloud tearing off it, roiling and swirling in the wind, pouring down over the edge like boiling milk frothing from the lip of a great pot.

He had to send now. *La Mouette* had won the contest of silence. Nick stared up at the cloud and composed the message he would send. He must reassure the Master, urge him to delay his decision to abandon ship and give *Warlock* the time to close the gap, perhaps even reach her before she struck on Cape Alarm.

The silence on the bridge was deepened by the absence of wind. They were all watching him now, waiting for the decision, and in that silence the carrier beam of Channel 16 hummed and throbbed.

Then suddenly a rich Gallic accent poured into the silent bridge, a full fruity voice that Nick remembered so clearly, even after all the years.

'Master of *Golden Adventurer* this is the master of salvage tug *La Mouette*. I am proceeding at best speed your assistance. Do you accept Lloyd's Open Form "No cure no pay"?'

Nick kept his face from showing any emotion, but his heart barged wildly against his ribs. Jules Levoisin had broken silence.

'Plot his position report,' he said quietly.

'God! She's inside us,' David Allen's face was stricken as he marked *La Mouette*'s reported position on the chart. 'She's a hundred miles ahead of us.'

'No,' Nick shook his head, 'he's lying.'

'Sir?'

'He's lying. He always lies.' Nick lit a cheroot and when it was drawing evenly, he spoke again to his radio officer.

'Did you get a bearing?' and the Trog looked up from his radio direction-finding compass on which he was tracing *La Mouette*'s transmissions.

'I have only one co-ordinate, you won't get a fix –'

But Nick interrupted him, 'We'll use his best course from Golfo San Jorge for a fix.' He turned back to David Allen. 'Plot that.'

'There's a difference of over three hundred nautical miles.'

'Yes,' Nick nodded. 'That old pirate wouldn't broadcast an accurate position to all the world. We are inside him and running five knots better, we'll put a line over *Golden Adventurer* before he's in radar contact.'

'Are you going to open contact with Christy Main now, sir?'

'No, Mr Allen.'

'But they will do a deal with *La Mouette* – unless we bid now.'

'I don't think so,' Nick murmured, and almost went on to say, 'Duncan Alexander won't settle for Lloyd's Open Form while he is the underwriter, and his ship is free and floating. He'll fight for daily hire and bonus, and Jules Levoisin won't buy that package. He'll hold out for the big plum. They won't do a deal until the two ships are in visual contact – and by that time I'll have her in tow and I'll fight the bastard in the awards court for twenty-five per cent of her value –' But he did not say it. 'Steady as she goes, Mr Allen,' was all he said, as he left the bridge.

He closed the door of his day cabin and leaned back against it, shutting his eyes tightly as he gathered himself. It had been so very close, a matter of seconds and he would have declared himself and given the advantage to *La Mouette*.

Through the door behind him, he heard David Allen's voice. 'Did you see him? He didn't feel a thing – not a bloody thing. He was going to let those poor bastards go into the boats. He must piss ice-water.' The voice was muffled, but the outrage in it was tempered by awe.

Nick kept his eyes shut a moment longer, then he straightened up and pushed himself away from the door. He wanted it to begin now. It was in the waiting and the uncertainty which was eroding what was left of his strength.

'Please God, let me reach them in time.' And he was not certain whether it was for the lives or for the salvage award that he was praying.

Captain Basil Reilly, the Master of the *Golden Adventurer*, was a tall man, with a lean and wiry frame that promised reserves of strength and endurance. His face was very darkly tanned and splotched with the dark patches of benign sun cancer. His heavy moustache was silvered like the pelt of a snow fox, and though his eyes were set in webs of finely wrinkled and pouchy skin, they were bright and calm and intelligent.

He stood on the windward wing of his navigation bridge and watched the huge black seas tumbling in to batter his helpless ship. He was taking them broadside now, and each time they struck, the hull shuddered and heeled with a sick dead motion, giving reluctantly to the swells that rose up and broke over her rails, sweeping her decks from side to side, and then cascading off her again in a tumble of white that smoked in the wind.

He adjusted the life-jacket he wore, settling the rough canvas more comfortably around his shoulders as he reviewed his position once more.

Golden Adventurer had taken the ice in that eight-to-midnight watch traditionally allotted to the most junior of the navigating officers. The impact had hardly been noticeable, yet it had awoken the Master from deep sleep – just a slight check and jar that had touched some deep chord in the mariner's instinct.

The ice had been a growler, one of the most deadly of all hazards. The big bergs standing high and solid to catch the radar beams, or the eye of even the most inattentive deck watch, were easily avoided. However, the low ice lying awash, with its great bulk and weight almost completely hidden by the dark and turbulent waters, was as deadly as a predator in ambush.

The growler showed itself only in the depths of each wave trough, or in the swirl of the current around it, as though a massive sea-monster lurked there. At night, these indications would pass unnoticed by even the sharpest eyes, and below the surface, the wave action eroded the body of the growler, turning it into a horizontal blade that lay ten feet or more below the water level and reached out two or three hundred feet from the visible surface indications.

With the Third Officer on watch, and steaming at cautionary speed of a mere twelve knots, the *Golden Adventurer* had brushed against one of these monsters, and although the actual impact had gone almost unnoticed on board, the ice had opened her like the knife stroke which splits a herring for the smoking rack.

It was classic *Titanic* damage, a fourteen-foot rent through her side, twelve feet below the Plimsoll line, shearing two of her watertight compartments, one of which was her main engine room section.

They had held the water easily until the electrical explosion, and since then, the Master had battled to keep her afloat. Slowly, step by step, fighting all the way, he had yielded to the sea. All the bilge pumps were running still, but the water was steadily gaining.

Three days ago he had brought all his passengers up from below the main deck, and he had battened down all the watertight bulkheads. The crew and passengers were accommodated now in the lounges and smoking rooms. The ship's luxury and opulence had been transformed into the crowded, unhygienic and deteriorating conditions of a city under siege.

It reminded him of the catacombs of the London underground converted to air-raid shelters during the blitz. He had been a lieutenant on shore-leave and he had passed one night there that he would remember for the rest of his life.

There was the same atmosphere on board now. The sanitary arrangements were inadequate. Fourteen toilet bowls for six hundred, many of them seasick and suffering from diarrhoea. There were no baths nor showers, and insufficient power for the heating of water in the handbasins. The emergency generators delivered barely sufficient power to work the ship, to run the pumps, to supply minimal lighting, and to keep the communicational and navigational equipment running. There was no heating in the ship and the outside air temperature had fallen to minus twenty degrees now.

The cold in the spacious public lounges was brutal. The passengers huddled in their fur coats and bulky life-jackets under mounds of blankets. There were limited cooking facilities on the gas stoves usually reserved for adventure tours ashore. There was no baking or grilling, and most of the food was eaten cold and congealed from cans; only the soup and beverages steamed in the cold clammy air, like the breaths of the waiting and helpless multitude.

The desalination plants had not been in use since the ice collision and now the supply of fresh water was critical; even hot drinks were rationed.

Of the 368 paying passengers, only forty-eight were below the age of fifty, and yet the morale was extraordinary. Men and women who before the emergency could and did complain bitterly at a dress shirt not ironed to crisp perfection or a wine served a few degrees too cold, now accepted a mug of beef tea as though it were a vintage Château Margaux, and laughed and chatted animatedly in the cold, shaming with their fortitude the few that might have complained. These were an unusual sample of humanity, men and women of achievement and resilience, who had come here to this outlandish corner of the globe in search of new experience. They were mentally prepared for adventure and even danger, and seemed almost to welcome this as part of the entertainment provided by the tour.

Yet, standing on his bridge, the master was under no illusion as to the gravity of their situation. Peering through the streaming glass, he watched a work party, led by his First Officer, toiling heroically in the bows. Four men in glistening yellow plastic suits and hoods, drenched by the icy seas, working with the slow cold-numbed movements of automatons as they struggled to stream a sea-anchor and bring the ship's head up into the sea, so that she might ride more easily, and perhaps slow her precipitous rush down onto the rocky coast. Twice in the preceding days, the anchors they had rigged had been torn away by sea and wind and the ship's dead weight.

Three hours before, he had called his engineering officers up from below, where the risk to their lives had become too great to chance against the remote possibility of restoring power to his main engines. He had conceded the battle to the sea and now he was planning the final moves when he must abandon his command and attempt to remove six hundred human beings from this helpless hulk to the even greater dangers and hardships of Cape Alarm's barren and storm-rent shores.

Cape Alarm was one of those few pinnacles of barren black rock which thrust out from beneath the thick white mantle of the Antarctic cap, pounded free of ice like an anvil beneath the eternal hammering assault of storm and sea and wind.

The long straight ridge protruded almost fifty miles into the eastern extremity of the Weddell Sea, was fifty miles across at its widest point, and terminated in a pair of bull's horns which formed a small protected bay named after the polar explorer Sir Ernest Shackleton.

Shackleton Bay, with its steep purple-black beaches of round polished pebbles, was the nesting ground of a huge colony of chin-strap penguin, and for this reason was one of *Golden Adventurer*'s regular ports of call.

On each tour, the ship would anchor in the deep and calm waters of the bay, while her passengers went ashore to study and photograph the breeding birds and the extraordinary geological formations, sculptured by ice and wind into weird and grotesque shapes.

Only ten days earlier, *Golden Adventurer* had weighed anchor in Shackleton Bay and stood out into the Weddell Sea. The weather had been mild and still, with a slow oily swell and a bright clear sun. Now, before a force seven gale, in temperatures forty-five degrees colder, and borne on the wild dark sweep of the current, she was being carried back to that same black and rocky shore.

There was no doubt in Captain Reilly's mind – they were going to go aground on Cape Alarm, there was no avoiding that fate with this set of sea and wind, unless the French salvage tug reached them first.

La Mouette should have been in radar contact already, if the tug's reported position was correct, and Basil Reilly let a little frown of worry crease the brown parchment skin of his forehead and shadows were in his eyes.

'Another message from head office, sir.' His Second Officer was beside him now, a young man with the shape of a teddy bear swathed in thick woollen jerseys and marine blue top coat. Basil Reilly's strict dress regulations had long ago been abandoned and their breaths steamed in the frigid air of the navigation bridge.

'Very well.' Reilly glanced at the flimsy. 'Send that to the tug master.' The contempt was clear in his voice, his disdain for this haggling between owners and salvors, when a great ship and six hundred lives were at risk in the cold sea.

He knew what he would do if the salvage tug made contact before *Golden Adventurer* struck the waiting fangs of rock, he would override his owner's express orders and exercise his rights as Master by immediately accepting the offer of assistance under Lloyd's Open Form.

'But let him come,' he murmured to himself. 'Please God, let him come,' and he raised his binoculars and slowly swept a long jagged horizon where the peaks of the swells seemed black and substantial as rock. He paused with a leap of his pulse when something white blinked in the field of the glasses and then, with a little sick slide, realized that it was only a random ray of sunlight catching a pinnacle of ice from one of the floating bergs.

He lowered the glasses and crossed from the windward wing of the bridge to the lee. He did not need the glasses now, Cape Alarm was black and menacing against the sow's-belly grey of the sky. Its ridges and valleys picked out with gleaming ice and banked snow, and against her steep shore, the sea creamed and leapt high in explosions of purest white.

'Sixteen miles, sir,' said the First Officer, coming to stand beside him. 'And the current seems to be setting a little more northerly now.' They were both silent, as they balanced automatically against the violent pitch and roll of the deck.

Then the mate spoke again with a bitter edge to his voice, 'Where is that bloody frog?' And they watched the night of Antarctica begin to shroud the cruel lee shore in funereal cloaks of purple and sable, picked out with the ermine collars and cuffs of ice.

She was very young, probably not yet twenty-five years of age, and even the layers of heavy clothing topped by a man's anorak three sizes too big could not disguise the slimness of her body, that almost coltish elegance of long fine limbs and muscle toned by youth and hard exercise.

Her head was set jauntily on the long graceful stem of her neck, like a golden sunflower, and the profuse mane of long hair was sun-bleached, streaked with silver and platinum and copper gold, twisted up carelessly into a rope almost as thick as a man's wrist and piled on top of her head. Yet loose strands floated down on to her forehead and tickled her nose so that she pursed her lips and puffed them away.

Her hands were both occupied with the heavy tray she carried, and she balanced like a skilled horsewoman against the ship's extravagant plunging as she offered it.

'Come on, Mrs Goldberg,' she wheedled. 'It will warm the cockles of your tum.'

'I don't think so, my dear,' the white-haired woman faltered.

'Just for me, then,' the girl wheedled.

'Well,' the woman took one of the mugs and sipped it tentatively. 'It's good,' she said, and then quickly and furtively, 'Samantha, has the tug come yet?'

'It will be here any minute now, and the Captain is a dashing Frenchman, just the right age for you, with a lovely tickly moustache. I'm going to introduce you first thing.'

The woman was a widow in her late fifties, a little overweight and more than a little afraid, but she smiled and sat up a little straighter.

'You naughty thing,' she smiled.

'Just as soon as I've finished with this,' Samantha indicated the tray, 'I'll come and sit with you. We'll play some klabrias, okay?' When Samantha Silver smiled, her teeth were very straight and white against the peach of her tanned cheeks and the freckles that powdered her nose like gold dust. She moved on.

They welcomed her, each of them, men and women, competing for her attention, for she was one of those rare creatures that radiate such warmth, a sort of shining innocence, like a kitten or a beautiful child, and she laughed and chided and teased them in return and left them grinning and heartened, but jealous of her going, so they followed her with their eyes. Most of them felt she belonged to them personally, and they wanted all of her time and presence, making up questions or little stories to detain her for a few extra moments.

'There was an albatross following us a little while ago, Sam.'

'Yes, I saw it through the galley window –'

'It was a wandering albatross, wasn't it, Sam?'

'Oh, come on, Mr Stewart! You know better than that. It was *Diomedea melanophris*, the black-browed albatross, but still it's good luck. All albatrosses are good luck – that's a scientifically proved fact.'

Samantha had a doctorate in biology and was one of the ship's specialist guides. She was on sabbatical leave from the University of Miami where she held a research fellowship in marine ecology.

Passengers thirty years her senior treated her like a favourite daughter most of the time. However, in even the mildest crisis they became childlike in their appeal to her and in their reliance on her natural strength which they recognized and sought instinctively. She was to them a combination of beloved pet and den-mother.

While a ship's steward refilled her tray with mugs, Samantha paused at the entrance to the temporary galley they had set up in the cocktail room and looked back into the densely packed lounge.

The stink of unwashed humanity and tobacco smoke was almost a solid blue thing, but she felt a rush of affection for them. They were behaving so very well, she thought, and she was proud of them.

'Well done, team,' she thought, and grinned. It was not often that she could find affection in herself for a mass of human beings. Often she had pondered how a creature so fine and noble and worthwhile as the human individual could, in its massed state, become so unattractive.

She thought briefly of the human multitudes of the crowded cities. She hated zoos and animals in cages, remembering as a little girl crying for a bear that danced endlessly against its bars, driven mad by its confinement. The concrete cages of the cities drove their captives into similar strange and bizarre behaviour. All creatures should be free to move and live and breathe, she believed, and yet man, the super-predator, who had denied that right to so many other creatures, was now destroying himself with the same singlemindedness, poisoning and imprisoning himself in an orgy that made the madness of the lemmings seem logical in comparison. It was only when she saw human beings like these in circumstances like these that she could be truly proud of them – and afraid for them.

She felt her own fear deep down, at the very periphery of her awareness, for she was a sea-creature who loved and understood the sea – and knew its monumental might. She knew what awaited them out there in the storm, and she was afraid. With a deliberate effort she lifted the slump of her shoulders, and set the smile brightly on her lips and picked up the heavy tray.

At that moment the speakers of the public-address system gave a preliminary squawk, and then filtered the Captain's cultured and measured tones into the suddenly silent ship.

'Ladies and gentlemen, this is your Captain speaking. I regret to inform you that we have not yet established radar contact with the salvage tug *La Mouette*, and that I now deem it necessary to transfer the ship's company to the lifeboats.'

There was a sigh and stir in the crowded lounges, heard even above the storm. Samantha saw one of her favourite passengers reach for his wife and press her silvery-grey head to his shoulder.

'You have all practised the lifeboat drill many times and you know your teams and stations. I am sure I do not have to impress upon you the necessity to go to your stations in orderly fashion, and to obey explicitly the orders of the ship's officers.'

Samantha set down her tray and crossed quickly to Mrs Goldberg. The woman was weeping, softly and quietly, lost and bewildered, and Samantha slipped her arm around her shoulder.

'Come now,' she whispered. 'Don't let the others see you cry.'

'Will you stay with me, Samantha?'

'Of course I will.' She lifted the woman to her feet. 'It will be all right – you'll see. Just think of the story you'll be able to tell your grandchildren when you get home.'

Captain Reilly reviewed his preparations for leaving the ship, going over them item by item in his mind. He now knew by heart the considerable list he had compiled days previously from his own vast experience of Antarctic conditions and the sea.

The single most important consideration was that no person should be immersed, or even drenched by sea water during the transfer. Life expectation in these waters was four minutes. Even if the victim were immediately pulled from the water, it was still four minutes, unless the sodden clothing could be removed and heating provided. With this wind blowing, rising eight of the Beaufort scale at forty miles an hour and an air temperature of minus twenty degrees, the chill factor was at the extreme of stage seven, which, translated into physical terms, meant that a few minutes' exposure would numb and exhaust a man, and that mere survival was a matter of planning and precaution.

The second most important consideration was the physiological crisis of his passengers, when they left the comparative warmth and comfort and security of the ship for the shrieking cold and the violent discomfort of a life-raft afloat in an Antarctic storm.

They had been briefed, and mentally prepared as much as was possible. An officer had checked each passenger's clothing and survival equipment, they had been fed high-sugar tablets to ward off the cold, and the life-raft allocations had been carefully worked out to provide balanced complements, each with a competent crew member in command. It was as much as he could do for them, and he turned his attention to the logistics of the transfer.

The lifeboats would go first – six of them, slung three on each side of the ship, each crewed by a navigation officer and five seamen. While the great drogue of the sea-anchor held the ship's head into the wind and the sea, they would be swung outboard on their hydraulic derricks and the winches would lower them swiftly to the surface of a sea temporarily smoothed by the oil sprayed from the pumps in the bows.

Although they were decked-in, powered, and equipped with radio, the lifeboats were not the ideal vehicles for survival in these conditions. Within hours, the men aboard them would be exhausted by the cold. For this reason, none of the passengers would be aboard them. Instead, they would go into the big inflatable life-rafts, self-righting even in the worst seas and enclosed with a double skin of insulation. Equipped with emergency rations and battery-powered locator beacons, they would ride the big black seas more easily and each provide shelter for twenty human beings, whose body warmth would keep the interior habitable, at least for the time it took to tow the rafts to land.

The motor lifeboats were merely the shepherds for the rafts. They would herd them together and then tow them in tandem to the sheltering arms of Shackleton Bay.

Even in these blustering conditions, the tow should not take more than twelve hours. Each boat would tow five rafts, and though the crews of the motor boats would have to change, brought into the canopy of the rafts and rested, there should be no insurmountable difficulties; Captain Reilly was hoping for a tow-speed of between three and four knots.

The lifeboats were packed with equipment and fuel and food sufficient to keep the shipwrecked party for a month, perhaps two on reduced rations, and once the calmer shores of the bay had been reached, the rafts would be carried ashore, the canopies reinforced with slabs of packed snow and transformed into igloo-type huts to shelter the survivors. They might be in Shackleton Bay a long time, for even when the French tug reached them, it could not take aboard six hundred persons, some would have to remain and await another rescue ship.

Captain Reilly took one more look at the land. It was very close now, and even in the gloom of the onrushing night, the peaks of ice and snow glittered like the fangs of some terrible and avaricious monster.

'All right,' he nodded to his First Officer, 'we will begin.'

The mate lifted the small two-way radio to his lips. 'Foredeck. Bridge. You may commence laying the oil now.'

From each side of the bows, the hoses threw up silver dragon-fly wings of sprayed diesel oil, pumped directly from the ship's bunkers; its viscous weight resisted the wind's efforts to tear it away, and it fell in a thick coating across the surface of the sea, broken by the floodlights into the colour spectrum of the rainbow.

Immediately, the sea was soothed, the wind-riven surface flattened by the weight of oil, so the swells passed in smooth and weighty majesty beneath the ship's hull.

The two officers on the wing of the bridge could feel the sick, waterlogged response of the hull. She was heavy with the water in her, no longer light and quick and alive.

'Send the boats away,' said the Captain, and the mate passed the order over the radio in quiet conversational tones.

The hydraulic arms of the derricks lifted the six boats off their chocks and swung them out over the ship's side, suspended one moment high above the surface; then, as the ship fell through the trough, the oil-streaked crest raced by only feet below their keels. The officer of each lifeboat must judge the sea, and operate the winch so as to drop neatly onto the back slope of a passing swell – then instantly detach the automatic clamps and stand away from the threatening steel cliff of the ship's side.

In the floodlights, the little boats shone wetly with spray, brilliant electric yellow in colour, and decorated with garlands of ice like Christmas toys. In the small armoured-glass windows the officers' faces also glistened whitely with the strain and concentration of these terrifying moments, as each tried to judge the rushing black seas.

Suddenly the heavy nylon rope that held the cone-shaped drogue of the sea-anchor snapped with a report like a cannon shot, and the rope snaked and hissed in the air, a vicious whiplash which could have sliced a man in half.

It was like slipping the head halter from a wild stallion. *Golden Adventurer* threw up her bows, joyous to be freed of restraint. She slewed back across the scend of the sea, and was immediately pinned helplessly broadside, her starboard side into the wind, and the three yellow lifeboats still dangling.

A huge wave reared up out of the darkness. As it rushed down on the ship, one of the lifeboats sheared her cables and fell heavily to the surface, the tiny propeller churning frantically, trying to bring her round to meet the wave – but the wave caught her and dashed her back against the steel side of the ship.

She burst like a ripe melon and the guts spilled out of her; from the bridge they saw the crew swirled helplessly away into the darkness. The little locator lamps on their lifejackets burned feebly as fire-flies in the darkness and then blinked out in the storm.

The forward lifeboard was swung like a door-knocker against the ship, her forward cable jammed so she dangled stern upmost, and as each wave punched into her, she was smashed against the hull. They could hear the men in her screaming, a thin pitiful sound on the wind, that went on for many minutes as the sea slowly beat the boat into a tangle of wreckage.

The third boat was also swung viciously against the hull. The releases on her clamps opened, and she dropped twenty feet into the boil and surge of water, submerging completely and then bobbing free like a yellow fishing float after the strike. Leaking and settling swiftly, she limped away into the clamorous night.

'Oh, my God,' whispered Captain Reilly, and in the harsh lights of the bridge, his face was suddenly old and haggard. In a single stroke he had lost half his boats. As yet he did not mourn the men taken by the sea, that would come later – now it was the loss of the boats that appalled him, for it threatened the lives of nearly six hundred others.

'The other boats' – the First Officer's voice was ragged with shock – 'the others got away safely, sir.'

In the lee of the towering hull, protected from both wind and sea, the other three boats had dropped smoothly to the surface and detached swiftly. Now they circled out in the dark night, with their spotlights probing like long white fingers. One of them staggered over the wildly plunging crests to take off the crew of the stricken lifeboat, and they left the cracked hull to drift away and sink.

'Three boats,' whispered the Captain, 'for thirty rafts.' He knew that there were insufficient shepherds for his flock – and yet he had to send them out, for even above the wind, he thought he could hear the booming artillery barrage of high surf breaking on a rocky shore. Cape Alarm was waiting hungrily for his ship.

'Send the rafts away,' he said quietly, and then again under his breath, 'And God have mercy on us all.'

'Come on, Number 16,' called Samantha. 'Here we are, Number 16.' She gathered them to her, the eighteen passengers who made up the complement of her allotted life-raft. 'Here we are – all together now. No stragglers.'

They were gathered at the heavy mahogany doors that opened on to the open forward deck.

'Be ready,' she told them. 'When we get the word, we have to move fast.'

With the broadsiding seas sweeping the deck and cascading down over the lee, it would be impossible to embark from landing-nets into a raft bobbing alongside.

The rafts were being inflated on the open deck, the passengers hustled across to them and into the canopied interior between waves and then the laden rafts were lifted over the side by the clattering winches and dropped into the quieter waters afforded by the tall bulk of the ship. Immediately, one of the lifeboats picked up the tow and took each raft out to form the pitiful little convoy.

'Right!' the Third Officer burst in through the mahogany doors and held them wide. 'Quickly!' he shouted. 'All together.'

'Let's go, gang!' sang out Samantha, and there was an awkward rush out on to the wet and slippery deck. It was only thirty paces to where the raft crouched like a monstrous yellow bullfrog, gaping its ugly dark mouth, but the wind struck like an axe and Samantha heard them cry out in dismay. Some of them faltered in the sudden merciless cold.

'Come on,' Samantha shouted, pushing those ahead of her, half-supporting Mrs Goldberg's plump body that suddenly felt as heavy and unco-operative as a full sack of wheat. 'Keep going.'

'Let me have her,' shouted the Third Officer, and he grabbed Mrs Goldberg's other arm. Between them they tumbled her through the entrance of the raft.

'Good on you, love,' the officer grinned at Samantha briefly. His smile was attractive and warm, very masculine and likeable, his name was Ken and he was five years her senior. They would probably have become lovers fairly soon, Samantha knew, for he had pursued her furiously since she stepped aboard in New York. Although she knew she did not love him, yet he had succeeded in arousing her and she was slowly succumbing to his obvious charms and her own passionate nature. She had made the decision to have him, and had been merely savouring it up until then. Now, with a pang, she realized that the moment might never come.

'I'll help you with the others.' She raised her voice above the hysterical shriek of the wind.

'Get in,' he shouted back, and swung her brusquely towards the raft. She crept into the crowded interior and looked back at the brightly lit deck that glistened in the arc lamps.

Ken had started back to where one of the women had slipped and fallen. She sprawled helplessly on the wet deck, while her husband stooped over her, trying to lift her back to her feet.

Ken reached them and lifted the woman easily; the three of them were the only ones out on the open deck now, and the two men supported the woman between them, staggering against the heavy sullen roll of the waterlogged hull.

Samantha saw the wave come aboard and she shrieked a warning.

'Go back, Ken! For God's sake go back!' But he seemed not to hear her. The wave came aboard; over the windward rail like some huge black slippery sea-monster, it came with a deep silent rush.

'Ken!' she screamed, and he looked over his shoulder an instant before it reached them. Its crest was higher than his head. They could reach neither the raft, nor the shelter of the mahogany doors. She heard the clatter of the donkey-winch and the raft lifted swiftly off the deck, with a swooping tug in her guts. The operator could not let the rushing power of the wave crash into the helpless raft, throwing it against the superstructure or tearing its belly out on the ship's railing, for the frail plastic skin would rupture and it would collapse immediately.

Samantha hurled herself to the entrance and peered down. She saw the sea take the three figures in a black glittering rush. It cut them down, and swept them away. For a moment, she saw Ken clinging to the railing while the waters poured over him, burying his head in a tumbling fall of white and furious water. He disappeared and when the ship rolled sullenly back, shaking herself clear of the water, her decks were empty of any human shape.

With the next roll of the ship, the winch-operator high up in his glassed cabin swung the dangling raft outboard and lowered it swiftly and dexterously to the surface of the sea where one of the lifeboats circled anxiously, ready to take them in tow.

Samantha closed and secured the plastic door-cover, then she groped her way through the press of packed and terrified bodies until she found Mrs Goldberg.

'Are you crying, dear?' the elderly woman quavered, clinging to her desperately.

'No,' said Samantha, and placed one arm around her shoulders. 'No, I'm not crying.' And with her free hand, she wiped away the icy tears that streamed down her cheeks.

The Trog lifted his headset and looked at Nick through the reeking clouds of cigar smoke.

'Their radio operator has screwed down the key of his set. He's sending a single unbroken homing beam.'

Nick knew what that meant – they had abandoned *Golden Adventurer*. He nodded once but remained silent. He had wedged himself into the doorway from the bridge. The restless impatience that consumed him would not allow him to sit or be still for more than a few moments at a time. He was slowly facing up to the reality of disaster. The dice had fallen against him and his gamble had been with very survival. It was absolutely certain that *Golden Adventurer* would go aground and be beaten into a total wreck by this storm. He could expect a charter from Christy Main to assist *La Mouette* in ferrying the survivors back to Cape Town, but the fee would be a small fraction of the Esso tow fee that he had forsaken for this wild and desperate dash south.

The gamble had failed and he was a broken man. Of course, it would take months still for the effects of his folly to become apparent, but the repayments of his loans and the construction bills for the other tug still building would slowly throttle and bring him down.

'We might still reach her before she goes aground,' said David Allen sturdily, and nobody else on the bridge spoke. 'I mean there could be a backlash of the current close inshore which could hold her off long enough to give us a chance —' His voice trailed off as Nick looked across at him and frowned.

'We are still ten hours away from her, and for Reilly to make the decision to abandon ship, she must have been very close indeed. Reilly is a good man.' Nick had personally selected him to command the *Golden Adventurer*. 'He was a destroyer captain on the North Atlantic run, the youngest in the navy, and then he was ten years with P & O. They pick only the best —' He stopped talking abruptly. He was becoming garrulous. He crossed to the radarscope and adjusted it for maximum range and illumination before looking down into the eye-piece. There was much fuzz and sea clutter, but on the extreme southern edge of the circular screen there showed the solid luminous glow of the cliffs and peaks of Cape Alarm. In good weather they were a mere five hours' steaming away, but now they had left the shelter of that giant iceberg and were staggering and plunging wildly through the angry night. She could have taken more speed, for *Warlock* was built for big seas, but always there was the deadly menace of ice, and Nick had to hold her at this cautionary speed, which meant ten hours more before they were in sight of *Golden Adventurer*. – if she was still afloat.

Behind him, the Trog's voice crackled rustily with excitement. 'I'm getting voice – it's only strength one, weak and intermittent. One of the lifeboats is sending on a battery-powered transmitter.' He held his earphones pressed to his head with both hands as he listened.

'They are towing a batch of life-rafts with all survivors aboard to Shackleton Bay. But they've lost a life-raft,' he said. 'It's broken away from their tow-line, and they haven't got enough boats to search for it. They are asking *La Mouette* to keep a watch for it.'

'Is *La Mouette* acknowledging?'

The Trog shook his head. 'She's probably still out of range of this transmission.'

'Very well.' Nick turned back into the bridge. He had still not broken radio silence, and could feel his officers' disapproval, silent but strong. Again he felt the need for human contact, for the warmth and comfort of human conversation and friendly encouragement. He didn't yet have the strength to bear his failure alone.

He stopped beside David Allen and said, 'I have been studying the Admiralty sailing directions for Cape Alarm, David,' and pretended not to notice that the use of his

Christian name had brought a startled look and quick colour to the mate's features. He went on evenly, 'the shore is very steep-to and she is exposed to this westerly weather, but there are beaches of pebble and the glass is going up sharply again.'

'Yes, sir,' David nodded enthusiastically. 'I have been watching it.'

'Instead of hoping for a cross-current to hold her off, I suggest you offer a prayer that she goes up on one of those beaches and that the weather moderates before she is beaten to pieces. There is still a chance we can put ground tackle on her before she starts breaking up.'

'I'll say ten Hail Marys, sir,' grinned David. Clearly he was overwhelmed by this sudden friendliness from his silent and forbidding Captain.

'And say another ten that we hold our lead on *La Mouette*,' said Nick, and smiled. It was one of the few times that David Allen had seen him smile, and he was amazed at the change it made to the stern features. They lightened with a charm and warmth and he had not before noticed the clear green of Nick Berg's eyes and how white and even were his teeth.

'Steady as she goes,' said Nick. 'Call me if anything changes,' and he turned away to his cabin.

'Steady as she goes, it is, sir,' said David Allen with a new friendliness in his voice.

The strange and marvellous lights of the *Aurora Australis* quivered and flickered in running streams of red and green fire along the horizon, and formed an incredible backdrop for the death agonies of a great ship.

Captain Reilly looked back through the small portholes of the leading lifeboat and watched her going to her fate. It seemed to him she had never been so tall and beautiful as in these terrible last moments. He had loved many ships, as if each had been a wonderful living creature, but he had loved no other ship more than *Golden Adventurer*, and he felt something of himself dying with her.

He saw her change her action. The sea was feeling the land now, the steep bank of Cape Alarm, and the ship seemed to panic at the new onslaught of wave and wind, as though she knew what fate awaited her there.

She was rolling through thirty degrees, showing the dull red streak of her belly paint as she came up short at the limit of each huge penduluming arc. There was a headland, tall black cliffs dropping sheer into the turbulent waters and it seemed that *Golden Adventurer* must go full on to them, but in the last impossible moments she slipped by, borne on the backlash of the current, avoiding the cliffs and swinging her bows on into the shallow bay beyond where she was hidden from Captain Reilly's view.

He stood for many minutes more, staring back across the leaping wave-tops and in the strange unnatural light of the heavens his face was greenish grey and heavily furrowed with the marks of grief.

Then he sighed once, very deeply, and turned away, devoting all his attention to guiding his pathetic limping little convoy to the safety of Shackleton Bay.

Almost immediately it was apparent that the fates had relented, and given them a favourable inshore current to carry them up on to the coast. The lifeboats were strung out over a distance of three miles, each of them with its string of bloated and clumsy rafts lumbering along in its wake. Captain Reilly had two-way VHF radio contact with each of them, and despite the brutal cold, they were all in good shape and making steady and unexpectedly rapid progress. Three or four hours would be sufficient, he began to hope. They had lost so much life already, and he could not be certain that there would be no further losses until he had the whole party ashore and encamped.

Perhaps the tragic run of bad luck had changed at last, he thought, and he picked up the small VHF radio. Perhaps the French tug was in range at last and he began to call her.

'*La Mouette*, do you read me? Come in, *La Mouette* . . .'

The lifeboat was low down on the water and the output of the little set was feeble in the vastness of sea and ice, yet he kept on calling.

They had accustomed themselves to the extravagant action of the disabled liner, her majestic roll and pitch, as regular as a gigantic metronome. They had adjusted to the cold of the unheated interior of the great ship, and the discomfort of her crowded and unsanitary conditions.

They had steeled themselves and tried to prepare themselves mentally for further danger and greater hardship, but not one of the survivors in life-raft Number 16 had imagined anything like this. Even Samantha, the youngest, probably physically the toughest and certainly the one most prepared by her training and her knowledge and love of the sea, had not imagined what it would be like in the raft.

It was utterly dark, not the faintest glimmer of light penetrated the insulated domed canopy, once its entrance was secured against the sea and the wind.

Samantha realized almost immediately how the darkness would crush their morale and, more dangerously, would induce disorientation and vertigo, so she ordered two of them at a time to switch on the tiny locator bulbs on their life-jackets. It gave just a glimmering of light, enough to let them see each others' faces and take a little comfort in the proximity of other humans.

Then she arranged their seating, making them form a circle around the sides with all their legs pointing inwards, to give the raft better balance and to ensure that each of them had space to stretch out.

Now that Ken had gone, she had naturally taken command, and, as naturally, the others had turned to her for guidance and comfort. It was Samantha who had gone out through the opening into the brutal exposure of the night to take aboard and secure the tow-rope from the lifeboat. She had come in again half-frozen, shaking in a palsy of cold, with her hands and face numbed. It had taken nearly half an hour of hard massage before feeling returned and she was certain that she had avoided frost-bite.

Then the tow began, and if the movement of the light raft had been wild before, it now became a nightmare of unco-ordinated movement. Each whim of sea and wind was transmitted directly to the huddling circle of survivors, and each time the raft pulled away or sheered off, the tow-rope brought it up with a violent lurch and jerk. The wave crests whipped up by the wind and feeling the press of the land were up to twenty feet high, and the raft swooped over them and dropped heavily into the troughs. She did not have the lateral stability of a keel, so she spun on her axis until the tow-rope jerked her up and she spun the other way. The first of them to start vomiting was Mrs Goldberg and it spurted in a warm jet down the side of Samantha's anorak.

The canopy was almost airtight, except for the small ventilation holes near the apex of the roof, and immediately the sweetish acrid stench of vomit permeated the raft. Within minutes, half a dozen of the other survivors were vomiting also.

It was the cold, however, that frightened Samantha. The cold was the killer. It came up even through the flexible insulated double skin of the deck, and was transferred into their buttocks and legs. it came in through the plastic canopy and froze the condensation of their breaths, it even froze the vomit on their clothing and on the deck.

'Sing!' Samantha told them. 'Come on, sing! Let's do "Yankee Doodle Dandy", first. You start, Mr Stewart, come on. Clap your hands, clap hands with your neighbour.' She hectored them relentlessly, not allowing any of them to fall into that paralytic state which is not true sleep but the trance caused by rapidly dropping body temperature. She crawled among them, prodding them awake, popping barley sugar from the emergency rations into their mouths.

'Suck and sing!' she commanded them, the sugar would combat the cold and the sea-sickness. 'Clap your hands. Keep moving, we'll be there soon.'

When they could sing no more, she told them stories – and whenever she mentioned the word 'dog' they must all bark and clap their hands, or crow like the rooster, or bray like the donkey.

Samantha's throat was scratchy with singing and talking, and she was dizzy with fatigue and sick with cold, recognizing in herself the first symptoms of disinterest and lethargy, the prelude to giving up. She roused herself, struggling up into the sitting position from where she had slumped.

'I'm going to try and light the stove and get us a hot drink,' she sang out brightly. Around her there was only a mild stir and somebody retched painfully.

'Who's for a mug of beef tea —' she stopped abruptly. Something had changed. It took her a long moment to realize what it was. The sound of the wind had muted and the raft was riding more easily now, it was moving into a more regular rhythm of sweep and fall, without the dreadful jerk of the tow-rope snapping it back.

Frantically she crawled to the entrance of the raft, and with cold crippled fingers she tore at the fastenings.

Outside the dawn had broken into a clear cold sky of palest ethereal pinks and mauves. Although the wind had dropped to a faint whisper, the seas were still big and unruly, and the waters had changed from black to the deep bottle green of molten glass.

The tow-rope had torn away at the connecting shackle, leaving only a dangling flap of plastic. Number 16 had been the last raft in the line being towed by number three, but of the convoy, Samantha could now see no sign – though she crawled out through the entrance and clung precariously to the side of the raft, scanning the wave-caps about her desperately.

There was no sign of a lifeboat, no sight even of the rocky, ice-capped shores of Cape Alarm. They had drifted away, during the night, into the vast and lonely reaches of the Weddell Sea.

Despair cramped her belly muscles, and she wanted to cry out in protest against this further cruelty of fate, but she prevented herself doing so, and stayed out in the clear and frosty air, drawing it in carefully for she knew that it could freeze her lung tissue.

She searched and searched until her eyes streamed with the cold and the wind and concentration. Then at last the cold drove her back into the dark and stinking interior of the raft. She fell wearily among the supine and quiescent bodies, and pulled the hood of her anorak more tightly around her head. She knew it would not take long for them to start dying now, and somehow she did not care. Her despair was too intense, she let herself begin sinking into the morass of despondency which gripped all the others, and the cold crept up her legs and arms. She closed her eyes, and then opened them again with a huge effort.

'I'm not going to die,' she told herself firmly. 'I refuse to just lie down and die,' and she struggled up onto her knees. It felt as though she wore a rucksack filled with lead, such was the physical weight of her despair.

She crawled to the central locker that held all their emergency rations and equipment.

The emergency locator transmitter was packed in polyurethane and her fingers were clumsy with cold and the thick mittens, but at last she brought it out. It was the size of a cigar-box, and the instructions were printed on the side of it. She did not need to read them, but switched on the set and replaced it in its slot. Now for forty-eight hours, or until the battery ran out, it would transmit a DF homing-signal on 121,5 Mega Hertz.

It was possible, just possible, that the French tug might pick up that feeble little beam, and track it down to its source. She set it out of her mind, and devoted herself to the Herculean task of trying to heat half a mug of water on the small solid-fuel stove without scalding herself as she held the stove in her lap and balanced it against the raft's motion. While she worked, she searched for the courage and the words to tell the others of their predicament.

The *Golden Adventurer*, deserted of all human beings, her engines dead, but with her deck lights still burning, her wheel locked hard over, and the morse key in the radio room screwed down to transmit a single unbroken pulse, drifted swiftly down on the black rock of Cape Alarm.

The rock was of so hard a type of formation that the cliffs were almost vertical, and even exposed as they were to the eternal onslaught of this mad sea, they had weathered very little. They still retained the sharp vertical edges and the glossy polished planes of cleanly fractured faults.

The sea ran in and hit the cliff without any check. The impact seemed to jar the very air, like the concussion of bursting high explosive, and the sea shot high in a white fury against the unyielding rock of the cliff, before rolling back and forming a reverse swell.

It was these returning echoes from the cliff that held *Golden Adventurer* off the cliff. The shore was so steep-to that it dropped to forty fathoms directly below the cliffs. There was no bottom on which the ship could gut herself.

The wind was blanketed by the cliff and in the eerie stillness of air, she drifted in closer and closer, rolling almost to her limits as the swells took her broadside. Once she actually touched the rock with her superstructure on one of those rolls, but then the echo-wave nudged her away. The next wave pushed her closer, and its smaller weaker offspring pushed back at her. A man could have jumped from a ledge on the cliff on to her deck as she drifted slowly, parallel to the rock.

The cliff ended in an abrupt and vertical headland, where it had calved into three tall pillars of serpentine, as graceful as the sculptured columns of a temple of Olympian Zeus.

Again, *Golden Adventurer* touched one of those pillars, she bumped it lightly with her stern. It scraped paint from her side and crushed in her rail, but then she was past.

The light bump was just sufficient to push her stern round, and she pointed her bows directly into the wide shallow bay beyond the cliffs.

Here a softer, more malleable rock-formation had been eroded by the weather, forming a wide beach of purple-black pebbles, each the size of a man's head and water-worn as round as cannon balls.

Each time the waves rushed up this stony beach, the pebbles struck against each other with a rattling roar, and the brash of rotten and mushy sea ice that filled the bay susurrated and clinked, as it rose and fell with the sea.

Now *Golden Adventurer* was clear of the cliff, she was more fully in the grip of the wind. Although the wind was dying, it still had force enough to move her steadily deeper into the bay, her bows pointed directly at the beach.

Unlike the cliff shore, the bay sloped up gently to the beach and this allowed the big waves to build up into rounded sliding humps. They did not curl and break into white water because the thick layer of brash ice weighted and flattened them, so that these swells joined with the wind to throw the ship at the beach with smoothly gathering impetus.

She took the ground with a great metallic groan of her straining plates and canted over slowly, but the moving pebble beach moulded itself quickly to her hull, giving gradually, as the waves and wind thrust her higher and higher until she was firm aground; then, as the short night ended so the wind fell further, and in sympathy the swells moderated also and the tide drew back, letting the ship settle more heavily.

By noon of that day, *Golden Adventurer* was held firmly by the bows on the curved purple beach, canted over at an angle of 10°. Only her after end was still floating, rising and falling like a see-saw on the swell patterns which still pushed in steadily, but the plummeting air temperature was rapidly freezing the brash ice around her stern into a solid sheet.

The ship stood very tall above the glistening wet beach. Her upperworks were festooned with rime and long rapier-like stalactites of shining translucent ice hung from her scuppers and from the anchor fair-leads.

Her emergency generator was still running, and although there was no human being aboard her, her lights burned gaily and piped music played softly through her deserted public rooms.

Apart from the rent in her side, through which the sea still washed and swirled, there was no external evidence of damage, and beyond her the peaks and valleys of Cape Alarm, so wild and fierce, seemed merely to emphasize her graceful lines and to underline how rich a prize she was, a luscious ripe plum ready for the picking.

Down in her radio room, the transmitting key continued to send out an unbroken beam that could be picked up for five hundred miles around.

*

Two hours of deathlike sleep – and then Nick Berg woke with a wild start, knowing that something of direct consequence was about to happen. But it took fully ten seconds for him to realize where he was.

He stumbled from his bunk, and he knew he had not slept long enough. His skull was stuffed with the cottonwool of fatigue, and he swayed on his feet as he shaved in the shower, trying to steam himself awake with the scalding water.

When he went out on to the bridge, the Trog was still at his equipment. He looked up at Nick for a moment with his little rheumy pink eyes, and it was clear that he had not slept at all. Nick felt a prick of shame at his own indulgence.

'We are still inside *La Mouette*,' said the Trog, and turned back to his set. 'I reckon we have an edge of almost a hundred miles.'

Angel appeared on the bridge, bearing a huge tray, and the saliva jetted from under Nick's tongue as he smelled it.

'I did a little special for your brekker, Skipper,' said Angel. 'I call it "Eggs on Angel's Wings".'

'I'm buying,' said Nick, and turned back to the Trog with his mouth full and chewing. 'What of the *Adventurer*?'

'She's still sending a DF, but her position has not altered in almost three hours.'

'What do you mean?' Nick demanded, and swallowed heavily.

'No change in position.'

'Then she's aground,' Nick muttered, the food in his hand forgotten, and at that moment David Allen hurried on to the bridge still shrugging on his pea-jacket. His eyes were puffy and his hair was hastily wetted and combed, but spiky at the back from contact with his pillow. It had not taken him long to hear that the Captain was on the bridge. 'And in one piece, if her transmitter is still sending.'

'It looks like those Hail Marys worked, David.' Nick flashed his rare smile and David slapped the polished teak top of the chart table.

'Touch wood, and don't dare the devil.'

Nick felt his early despair slipping away with his fatigue, and he took another big mouthful and savoured it as he strode to the front windows and stared ahead.

The sea had flattened dramatically, but a weak and butter-yellow sun low on the horizon gave no warmth, and Nick glanced up at the thermometer and read the outside air temperature at minus thirty degrees.

Down here below 60° south, the weather was so unstable, caught up on the wheel of endlessly circling atmospheric depressions, that a gale could rise in minutes and drop to a flat calm almost as swiftly. Yet foul weather was the rule. For a hundred days and more each year, the wind was at gale-force or above. The photographs of Antarctica always gave a completely false impression of fine days with the sun sparkling on pristine snow fields and lovely towering icebergs. The truth was that you cannot take photographs in a blizzard or a white-out.

Nick distrusted this calm, and yet found himself praying that it would hold. He wanted to increase speed again, and was on the point of taking that chance, when the officer of the watch called a sharp alteration of course.

Ahead of them, Nick made out the sullen swirl of hidden ice below the surface, like a lurking monster, and as *Warlock* altered course to avoid it, the ice broke the surface. Black ice, striated with bands of glacial mud, ugly and deadly. Nick did not pass the order for the increase in speed.

'We should be raising Cape Alarm within the hour,' David Allen gloated beside him. 'If this visibility holds.'

'It won't,' said Nick. 'We'll have fog pretty soon,' and he indicated the surface of the sea, which was beginning to steam, emitting ghostly tendrils and eddies of seafret, as the difference between sea and air temperature widened.

'We'll be at the *Golden Adventurer* in four hours more.' David was bubbling with renewed excitement, and he slapped the teak table again. 'With your permission, sir, I'll go down and double-check the rocket-lines and tow equipment.'

While the air around them thickened into a ghostly white soup, and blotted out all visibility to a few hundred yards, Nick paced the bridge like a caged lion, his hands clasped behind his back and a black unlit cheroot clamped between his teeth. He broke his pacing every time that the Trog intercepted another transmission from either Christy Main, Jules Levoisin or Captain Reilly on his VHF radio.

At mid-morning, Reilly reported that he and his slow convoy had reached Shackleton Bay without further losses, that they were taking full advantage of the moderating weather to set up an encampment, and he ended by urging *La Mouette* to keep a watch on 121,5 Mega Hertz to try and locate the missing life-raft that had broken away during the night. *La Mouette* did not acknowledge.

'They aren't reading on the VHF,' grunted the Trog.

Nick thought briefly of the hapless souls adrift in this cold, and decided that they would probably not last out the day unless the temperature rose abruptly. Then he dismissed the thought and concentrated on the exchanges between Christy Main and *La Mouette*.

The two parties had diametrically changed their bargaining standpoints.

While *Golden Adventurer* was adrift on the open sea, and any salvage efforts would mean that the tug should merely put a rocket-line across her, pass a messenger wire to carry the big steel hawser and then take her in tow, Jules Levoisin had pressed for Lloyd's Open Form 'No cure no pay' contract.

Since the 'cure' was almost certain, 'pay' would follow as a matter of course. The amount of payment would be fixed by the arbitration of the committee of Lloyd's in London under the principles of international maritime law, and would be a percentage of the salved value of the vessel. The percentage decided upon by the arbitrator would depend upon the difficulties and dangers that the salvor had overcome. A clever salvor in an arbitration court could paint a picture of such daring and ingenuity that the award would be in millions of dollars.

Christy Main had been desperately trying to avoid a 'No cure no pay' contract. They had been trying to wheedle Levoisin into a daily hire and bonus contract, since this would limit the total cost of the operation, but they had been met by a Gallic acquisitiveness – right up to the moment when it became clear that *Golden Adventurer* had gone aground.

When that happened, the roles were completely reversed. Jules Levoisin, with a note of panic in his transmission, had immediately withdrawn his offer to go Lloyd's Open Form. For now the 'cure' was far from certain, and the *Adventurer* might already be a total wreck, beaten to death on the rocks of Cape Alarm, in which case there would be 'no pay'.

Now Levoisin was desperately eager to strike a daily hire contract, including the run from South America and the ferrying of survivors back to civilization. He was offering his services at $10,000 a day, plus a bonus of 2½% of any salved value of the vessel. They were fair terms, for Jules Levoisin had given up the shining dream of millions and he had returned to reality.

However, Christy Main, who had previously been offering a princely sum for daily hire, had just as rapidly withdrawn that offer.

'We will accept Lloyd's Open Form, including ferrying of survivors,' they declared on Channel 16.

'Conditions on site have changed,' Jules Levoisin sent back, and the Trog got another good fix on him.

'We are head-reaching on him handsomely,' he announced with satisfaction, blinking his pink eyes rapidly while Nick marked the new relative positions on the chart.

The bridge of *Warlock* was once again crowded with every officer who had an excuse to be there. They were all in working rig, thick blue boiler suits and heavy sea boots, bulked up with jerseys and balaclava helmets, and they watched the plot with total fascination, arguing quietly among themselves.

David Allen came in carrying a bundle of clothing. 'I've got working rig for you, sir. I borrowed it from the Chief Engineer. You are about the same size.'

'Does the Chief know?' Nick asked.

'Not exactly, I just borrowed it from his cabin –'

'Well done, David,' Nick chuckled. 'Please put it in my day cabin.' He felt himself warming more and more to the younger man.

'Captain, sir,' the Trog sang out suddenly. 'I'm getting another transmission. It's only strength one, and it's on 121.5 Mega Hertz.'

'Oh, shit!' David Allen paused in the entrance to the Captain's day cabin. 'Oh, shit!' he repeated, and his expression was stricken. 'It's that bloody missing life-raft.'

'Relative bearing!' snapped Nick angrily.

'She bears 280° relative and 045° magnetic,' the Trog answered instantly, and Nick felt his anger flare again.

The life-raft was somewhere out on their port beam, eighty degrees off their direct course to the *Golden Adventurer*.

The consternation on the bridge was carried in a babble of voices, that Nick silenced with a single black glance – and they stared at the plot in dismayed hush.

The position of each of the tugs was flagged with a coloured pin – and there was another, a red flag, for the position of the *Golden Adventurer*. It was so close ahead of them now, and their lead over *La Mouette* so slender, that one of the younger officers could not remain silent.

'If we go to the raft, we'll be handing it to the bloody frog on a plate.'

The words ended the restraint and they began to argue again, but in soft controlled tones. Nick Berg did not look up at them, but remained bowed over the chart, with his fist on the table-top bunched so fiercely that the knuckles were ivory white.

'Christ, they have probably all had it by now. We'd be throwing it all away for a bunch of frozen stiffs.'

'There is no telling how far off course they are, those sets have a range of a hundred miles.'

'*La Mouette* will waltz away with it.'

'We could pick them up later – after we put a line on *Golden Adventurer*.'

Nick straightened slowly and took the cheroot out of his mouth. He looked across at David Allen and spoke levelly, without change of expression.

'Number One, will you please instruct your junior officers in the rule of the sea.'

David Allen was silent for a moment, then he answered softly 'The preservation of human life at sea takes precedent over all other considerations.'

'Very well, Mr Allen,' Nick nodded. 'Alter 80° to port and maintain a homing course on the emergency transmission.'

He turned away to his cabin. He could control his anger until he was alone, and then he turned and crashed his fist into the panel above his desk.

Out on the navigation bridge behind him nobody spoke nor moved for fully thirty seconds, then the Third Officer protested weakly.

'But we are so close!'

David Allen roused himself, and spoke angrily to the helmsman.

'New course 045° magnetic.'

And as *Warlock* heeled to the change, he flung the armful of clothing bitterly onto the chart table and went to stand beside the Trog.

'Corrections for course to intercept?' he asked.

'Bring her on to 050°,' the Trog instructed, and then cackled without mirth. 'First you call him an ice-water pisser – now you squeal like a baby because he answers a Mayday.'

And David Allen was silent as the *Warlock* turned away into the fog, every revolution of her big variable-pitch propellers carrying her directly away from her prize, and *La Mouette*'s triumphant transmissions taunted them as the Frenchman raced across the last of the open water that separated her from Cape Alarm, bargaining furiously with the owners in London.

The fog seemed so thick that it could be chopped into chunks like cheese. From the bridge it was not possible to see *Warlock*'s tall bows. Nick groped his way into it like a blind man in an unfamiliar room, and all around him the ice pressed closely.

They were in the area of huge tabular icebergs again. The echoes of the great ice islands flared green and malevolently on the radar screen and the awful smell and taste of the ice was on every breath they drew.

'Radio Officer?' Nick asked tensely, without taking his eyes from the swirling fog curtains ahead.

'Still no contact,' the Trog answered, and Nick shuffled on his feet. The fog had mesmerized him, and he felt the shift of vertigo in his head. For a moment he had the illusion that his ship was listing heavily to one side, almost as though it were a space vehicle. He forcibly rejected the hallucination and stared fixedly ahead, tensing himself for the first green loom of ice through the fog.

'No contact for nearly an hour now,' David muttered beside him.

'Either the battery on the DF has run down, or they have snagged ice and sunk —' volunteered the Third Officer, raising his voice just enough for Nick to hear.

'- or else their transmitter is blanketed by an iceberg,' Nick finished for him, and there was silence on the bridge for another ten minutes, except for the quietly requested changes of course that kept *Warlock* zigzagging between the unseen but omnipresent icebergs.

'All right,' Nick made the decision at last. 'We'll have to accept that the raft has floundered and break off the search.' And there was a stir of reawakening interest and enthusiasm. 'Pilot, new course to *Golden Adventurer*, please, and we'll increase to fifty per cent power.'

'We could still beat the Frog.' Again speculation and rising hope buoyed the young officers. 'She could run into ice and have to reduce —' They wished misfortune on *La Mouette* and her Captain, and even the ship beneath Nick's feet seemed to regain its lightness and vibrancy as she turned back for a last desperate run for the prize.

'All right, David,' Nick spoke quietly. 'One thing is certain now, we aren't going to reach the prize ahead of Levoisin. So we are going to play our ace now —' he was about to elaborate, when the Trog's voice squeaked with excitement.

'New contact, on 121,5,' he cried, and the dismay on the bridge was a tangible thing.

'Christ!' said the Third Officer. 'Why won't they just lie down and die!'

'The transmission was blanked by that big berg north of us,' the Trog guessed. 'They are close now. It won't take long.'

'Just long enough to make certain we miss the prize.'

The berg was so big that it formed its own weather system about it, causing eddies and currents of both air and water, enough to stir the fog.

The fog opened like a theatre curtain, and directly ahead there was a heart-stopping vista of green and blue ice, with darker strata of glacial mud banding cliffs which disappeared into the higher layers of fog above as though reaching to the very heavens. The sea had carved majestic arches of ice and deep caverns from the foot of the cliff.

'There they are!'

Nick snatched the binoculars from the canvas bin and focused on the dark specks that stood out so clearly against the backdrop of glowing ice.

'No,' he grunted. Fifty emperor penguins formed a tight bunch on one of the flat floes, big black birds standing nearly as tall as a man's shoulder; even in the lens, they were deceptively humanoid.

Warlock passed them closely, and with sudden fright they dropped on to their bellies and used their stubby wings to skid themselves across the floe, and drop into the still and steaming waters below the cliff. The floe eddied and swung on the disturbance of *Warlock*'s passing.

Warlock nosed on through solid standing banks of fog and into abrupt holes of clear air where the mirages and optical illusions of Antarctica's flawed air maddened them with their inconsistencies, transforming flocks of penguins into herds of elephants or bands of waving men, and placing in their path phantom rocks and bergs which disappeared again swiftly as they approached.

The emergency transmissions from the raft faded and silenced, then beeped again loudly into the silence of the bridge, and seconds later were silent again.

'God damn them,' David swore quietly and bitterly, his cheeks pink with frustration. 'Where the hell are they? Why don't they put up a flare or a rocket?' And nobody answered as another white fog monster enveloped the ship, muting all sound aboard her.

'I'd like to try shaking them up with the horn, sir,' he said, as *Warlock* burst once more into sparkling and blinding sunlight. Nick grunted acquiescence without lowering his binoculars.

David reached up for the red-painted foghorn handle above his head, and the deep booming blast of sound the characteristic voice of an ocean-going salvage tug, reverberated through the fog, seeming to make it quiver with the volume of the sound. The echoes came crashing back off the ice cliffs of the bergs like the thunder of the skies.

Samantha held the solid-fuel stove in her lap using the detachable fibreglass lid of the locker as a tray. She was heating half a pint of water in the aluminium pannikin, balancing carefully against the wallowing motion of the raft.

The blue flame of the stove lit the dim cavern of plastic and radiated a feeble glow of warmth insufficient to sustain life. They were dying already.

Gavin Stewart held his wife's head against his chest, and bowed his own silver head over it. She had been dead for nearly two hours now, and her body had already cooled, the face peaceful and waxen.

Samantha could not bear to look across at them, she crouched over the stove and dropped a cube of beef into the water, stirring it slowly and blinking against the tears of penetrating cold. She felt thin watery mucus run down her nostrils and it required an effort to lift her arm and wipe it away on her sleeve. The beef tea was only a little above blood warmth, but she could not waste time and fuel on heating it further.

The metal pannikin passed slowly from mittened hand to numbed and clumsy hand. They slurped the warm liquid and passed it on reluctantly, though there were some who had neither the strength nor the interest to take it.

'Come on, Mrs Goldberg,' Samantha whispered painfully. The cold seemed to have closed her throat, and the foul air under the canopy made her head ache with grinding, throbbing pain. 'You must drink –' Samantha touched the woman's face, and cut herself off. The flesh had a putty-like texture and was cooling swiftly. It took long lingering minutes for the shock to pass, then carefully Samantha pulled the hood of the old woman's parka down over her face. Nobody else seemed to have noticed. They were all too far sunk into lethargy.

'Here,' whispered Samantha to the man beside her – and she pressed the pannikin into his hands, folding his stiff fingers around the metal to make certain he had hold of it. 'Drink it before it cools.'

The air around her seemed to tremble suddenly with a great burst of sound, like the bellow of a dying bull, or the rumble of cannon balls across the roof of the sky. For long moments, Samantha thought her mind was playing tricks with her, and only when it came again did she raise her head.

'Oh God,' she whispered. 'They've come. It's going to be all right. They've come to save us.'

She crawled to the locker, slowly and stiffly as an old woman.

'They've come. It's all right, gang, it's going to be all right,' she mumbled, and she lit the globe on her life-jacket. In its pale glow, she found the packet of phosphorus flares.

'Come on now, gang. Let's hear it for Number 16.' She tried to rouse them as she struggled with the fastenings of the canopy. 'One more cheer,' she whispered, but they were still and unresponsive, and as she fumbled her way out into the freezing fog, the tears that ran down her cheeks were not from the cold.

She looked up uncomprehendingly, it seemed that from the sky around her tumbled gigantic cascades of ice, sheer sheets of translucent menacing green ice. It took her moments to realize that the liferaft had drifted in close beneath the precipitous lee of a tabular berg. She felt tiny and inconsequential beneath that ponderous mountain of brittle glassy ice.

For what seemed an eternity, she stood, with her face lifted, staring upwards – then again the air resonated with the deep gut-shaking bellow of the siren. It filled the swirling fog-banks with solid sound that struck the cliff of ice above her and shattered into booming echoes, that bounded from wall to wall and rang through the icy caverns and crevices that split the surface of the great berg.

Samantha held aloft one of the phosphorus flares, and it required all the strength of her frozen arm to rip the igniter tab. The flare spluttered and streamed acrid white smoke, then burst into the dazzling crimson fire that denotes distress at sea. She stood like a tiny statue of liberty, holding the flare aloft in one hand and peering with streaming eyes into the sullen fog-banks.

Again the animal bellow of the siren boomed through the milky, frosted air; it was so close that it shook Samantha's body the way the wind moves the wheat on the hillside, then it went on to collide solidly with the cliff of ice that hung above her.

The working of sea and wind, and the natural erosion of changing temperatures had set tremendous forces at work within the glittering body of the berg. Those forces had found a weak point, a vertical fault line, that ran like an axe-stroke from the flattened tableland of the summit, five hundred feet down to the moulded bottom of the berg far below the surface.

The booming sound waves of *Warlock*'s horn found a sympathetic resonance with the body of the mountain that set the ice on each side of the fault vibrating in different frequencies.

Then the fault sheared, with a brittle cracking explosion of glass bursting under pressure, and the fault opened. One hundred million tons of ice began to move as it broke away from the mother berg. The block of ice that the berg calved was in itself a mountain, a slab of solid ice twice the size of Saint Paul's cathedral – and as it swung out and twisted free, new pressures and forces came into play within it, finding smaller faults and flaws so that ice burst within ice and tore itself apart, as though dynamited with tons of high explosive.

The air itself was filled with hurtling ice, some pieces the size of a locomotive and others as small and as sharp and as deadly as steel swords; and below this plunging toppling mass, the tiny yellow plastic raft bobbed helplessly.

'There,' called Nick. 'On the starboard beam.' The phosphorus distress flare lit the fog-banks internally with a fiery cherry red and threw grotesque patterns of light against the belly of lurking cloud. David Allen blew one last triumphant blast on the siren.

'New heading 150°,' Nick told the helmsman and *Warlock* came around handily, and almost instantly burst from the enveloping bank of fog into another arena of open air.

Half a mile away, the life-raft bobbed like a fat yellow toad beneath a glassy green wall of ice. The top of the iceberg was lost in the fog high above, and the tiny human figure that stood erect on the raft and held aloft the brilliant crimson flare was an insignificant speck in this vast wilderness of fog and sea and ice.

'Prepare to pick up survivors, David,' said Nick, and the mate hurried away while Nick moved to the wing of the bridge from where he could watch the rescue.

Suddenly Nick stopped and lifted his head in bewilderment. For a moment he thought it was gunfire, then the explosive crackling of sound changed to a rending shriek as of the tearing of living fibre when a giant redwood tree is falling to the axes. The volume of sound mounted into a rumbling roar, the unmistakeable roar of a mountain in avalanche.

'Good Christ!' whispered Nick, as he saw the cliff of ice begin to change shape. Slowly sagging outwards, it seemed to fold down upon itself. Faster and still faster it fell, and the hissing splinters of bursting ice formed a dense swirling cloud, while the cliff leaned further and further beyond its point of equilibrium and at last collapsed and lifted pressure waves from the green waters that raced out one behind the other, flinging *Warlock*'s bows high as she rode them and then nosed down into the troughs between.

Since Nick's oath, nobody had spoken on the bridge. They clutched for balance at the nearest support and stared in awe at that incredible display of careless might, while the water still churned and creamed with the disturbance and pieces of broken jagged ice, some the size of a country house, bobbed to the surface and revolved slowly, finding their balance as they swirled and bumped against each other.

'Closer,' snapped Nick. 'Get as close as you can.'

Of the yellow life-raft there was no longer any sign. Jagged shards of ice had ripped open its fragile skin and the grinding, tumbling lumps had trodden it and its pitiful human cargo deep beneath the surface.

'Closer,' urged Nick. If by a miracle anybody had survived that avalanche, then they had four minutes left of life, and Nick pushed *Warlock* into the still rolling and roiling mass of broken ice – pushing it open with ice-strengthened bows.

Nick flung open the bridge doors beside him and stepped out into the freezing air of the open wing. He ignored the cold, buoyed up by new anger and frustration. He had paid the highest price to make this rescue, he had given up his chance at *Golden Adventurer* for the lives of a handful of strangers, and now, at this last moment, they had been snatched away from him. His sacrifice had been in vain, and the terrible waste of it all appalled him. Because there was no other outlet for his feelings, he let waves of anger sweep over him and he shouted at David Allen's little group on the foredeck.

'Keep your eyes open. I want those people –'

Red caught his eye, a flash of vivid red, seen through the green water, becoming brighter and more hectic as it rose to the surface.

'Both engines half astern' he screamed. And *Warlock* stopped dead as the twin propellers changed pitch and bit into the water, pulling her up in less than her own length.

In a small open area of green water the red object broke out. Nick saw a human head in a red anorak hood, supported by the thick inflated life-jacket. The head was thrown back, exposing a face as white and glistening with wetness as the deadly ice that surrounded it. The face was that of a young boy, smooth and beardless, and quite incredibly beautiful.

'Get him,' Nick yelled, and at the sound of his voice the eyes in that beautiful face opened. Nick saw they were a misty green and unnaturally large in the glistening pale oval framed by the crimson hood.

David Allen was racing back, carrying life-ring and line.

'Hurry. God damn you.' The boy was still alive, and Nick wanted him. He wanted him as fiercely as he had wanted anything in his life, he wanted at least this one young life in return for all he had sacrificed. He saw that the boy was watching him. 'Come on, David,' he shouted again.

'Here!' called David, bracing himself at the ship's rail and he threw the life-ring. He threw it with an expert round arm motion that sent it skimming forty feet to where the hooded head bobbed on the agitated water. He threw it so accurately that it hit the bobbing figure a glancing blow on the shoulder and then plopped into the water alongside, almost nudging the boy.

'Grab it,' yelled Nick. 'Grab hold!'

The face turned slowly, and the boy lifted a gloved hand clear of the surface, but the movement was blunderingly unco-ordinated.

'There. It's right next to you,' David encouraged. 'Grab it, man!'

The boy had been in the water for almost two minutes already, he had lost control of his body and limbs, he made two inconclusive movements with the raised hand, one actually bumped the ring but he could not hold it and slowly the life-ring bobbed away from him.

'You bloody idiot,' stormed Nick. 'Grab it!' And those huge green eyes turned back to him, looking up at him with the total resignation of defeat, one stiff arm still raised – almost a farewell salute.

Nick did not realize what he was going to do until he had shrugged off his coat and kicked away his shoes; then he realized that if he stopped to think about it, he would not go.

He jumped feet first, throwing himself far out to miss the rail below him, and as the water closed over his head he experienced a terrified sense of disbelief at the cold.

It seized his chest in a vice that choked the air from his lungs, it drove needles of agony deep into his forehead, and blinded him with the pain as he rose to the surface again. The cold rushed through his light clothing, it crushed his testicles and his stomach was filled with nausea. The marrow in the bones of his legs and arms ached so that he found it difficult to force his limbs to respond, but he struck out for the floating figure.

It was only forty feet, but halfway there he was seized by a panic that he was not going to make it. He clenched his teeth and fought the icy water as though it was a mortal enemy, but it sapped away his strength with the heat of his body.

He struck the floating figure with one outflung arm before he realized he had reached him, and he clung desperately to him, peering up at *Warlock*'s deck.

David Allen had retrieved the ring by its line and he threw it again. The cold had slowed Nick down so that he could not avoid the ring and it struck him on the forehead, but he felt no pain, there was no feeling in his face or feet or hands.

The fleeting seconds counted out the life left to them as he struggled with the inert figure, slowly losing command of his own limbs as he tried to fit the ring over the boy's body. He did not accomplish it. He got the boy's head and one arm through, and he knew he could do no more.

'Pull,' he screamed in rising panic, and his voice was remote and echoed strangely in his own ears.

He took a twist of line around his arm, for his fingers could no longer hold, and he clung with the remains of his strength as they dragged them in.

Jagged ice brushed and snatched at them, but he held the boy with his free arm.

'Pull,' he whispered. 'Oh, for God's sake, pull!' And then they were bumping against *Warlock*'s steel side, were being lifted free of the water, the twist of line smearing the wet skin from his forearm, staining his sleeve with blood that was instantly dissolved to pink by sea water. He felt no pain.

With the other arm, he hung on to the boy, holding him from slipping out of the life-ring. He did not feel the hands that grabbed at him. There was no feeling in his legs and he collapsed face forward, but David caught him before he struck the deck and they hustled him into the steaming warmth of Angel's galley, his legs dragging behind him.

'Are you okay, Skipper?' David kept demanding, and when Nick tried to reply, his jaw was locked in a frozen rictus and great shuddering spasms shook his whole body.

'Get their clothes off,' grated Angel, and, with an easy swing of his heavily muscled shoulders, lifted the boy's body on to the galley table and laid it out face upwards. With a single sweep of a Solingen steel butcher's knife he spit the crimson anorak from neck to crutch and stripped it away.

Nick found his voice, it was ragged and broken by the convulsions of frozen muscles.

'What the hell are you doing, David? Get your arse on deck and get this ship on course for *Golden Adventurer*,' he grated, and would have added something a little more forceful, but the next convulsion caught him, and anyway David Allen had already left.

'You'll be all right.' Angel did not even glance up at Nick as he worked with the knife, ripping away layer after layer of the boy's clothing. 'A tough old dog like you – but I think we've got a ripe case of hypothermia here.'

Two of the seamen were helping Nick out of his sodden clothing, the cloth crackled with the thin film of ice that had already formed. Nick winced with the pain of returning circulation to half-frozen hands and feet.

'Okay,' he said, standing naked in the middle of the galley and scrubbing at himself with a rough towel. 'I'll be all right now, return to your stations.' He crossed to the kitchen range, tottering like a drunk, and welcomed the blast of heat from it, rubbing warmth into himself, still shaking and shuddering, his body mottled puce and purple with cold and his genitals shrunken and drawn up into the dense black bush at his crotch.

'Coffee's boiling. Get yourself a hot drink, Skip,' Angel told him, glancing up at Nick from his work. He ran a quick appreciative glance over Nick's body, taking in the wide rangy shoulders, the dark curls of damp hair that covered his chest, and the trim lines of hard muscle that moulded his belly and waist.

'Put lots of sugar in it – it will warm you the best possible way,' Angel instructed him, and returned his attention to the slim young body on the table.

Angel had put aside his camp airs, and worked with the brusque efficiency of a man who had been trained at his task.

Then suddenly he stopped and stood back for a moment. 'Would you believe! No fun gun!' Angel sighed.

Nick turned just as Angel spread a thick woollen blanket over the pale naked body on the table and began to massage it vigorously.

'You better leave us girls alone together, Skipper,' said Angel with a sweet smile and a twinkle of his diamond earrings, and Nick was left with the memory of a single fleeting glimpse of the stunningly lovely body of a young woman below the pale face and the thick sodden head of copper and gold hair.

Nick Berg was swaddled in a grey woollen blanket, over the boiler suit and bulk jerseys. His feet were in thick Norwegian trawlerman's socks and heavy rubber working boots. He held a china mug of almost boiling coffee in both hands, bending over it to savour the aroma of the steam. It was the third cup he had drunk in the last hour – and yet the shivering spasms still shook him every few minutes.

David Allen had moved his canvas chair across the bridge so he could watch the Trog and work the ship at the same time. Nick could see the loom of the black rock cliffs of Cape Alarm close on their port beam.

The morse beam squealed suddenly, a long sequence of code to which every man on the bridge listened with complete attention, but it needed the Trog to say it for them.

'*La Mouette* has reached the prize.' He seemed to take a perverse relish in seeing their expressions. 'She's beaten us to it, lads. 12½% salvage to her crew –'

'I want it word for word,' snapped Nick irritably, and the Trog grinned spitefully at him before bowing over his pad.

'*La Mouette* to Christy Main. *Golden Adventurer* is hard aground, held by ice and receding tides. Stop. Ice damage to plating appears to be below surface. Stop. Hull is flooded and open to sea. Stop. Under no circumstances will Lloyd's Open Form be acceptable. Emphasize importance of beginning salvage work immediately. Stop. Worsening weather and sea conditions. My final hire offer of $8000 *per diem* plus 2½% of salvaged value open until 1435 GMT. Standing by.'

Nick lit one of his cheroots and irrelevantly decided he must conserve them in future. He had opened his last box that morning. He frowned through the blue smoke and pulled the blanket closer around his shoulders.

Jules Levoisin was playing it touch and hard now. He was dictating terms and setting ultimatums. Nick's own policy of silence was paying off. Probably by now, Jules felt completely safe that he was the only salvage tug within two thousand miles, and he was holding a big-calibre gun to Christy Main's head.

Jules had seen the situation of the *Golden Adventurer*'s hull. If he had been certain of effecting salvage – no, even if there had been a fifty-fifty chance of a good salvage, Jules would have gone Open Form.

So Jules was not happy with his chances, and he had the shrewdest and most appraising eye in the salvage business. It was a tough one then. *Golden Adventurer* was probably held fast by the quicksand effect of beach and ice, and *La Mouette* could build up a mere nine thousand horse-power. It would mean throwing out ground-tackle, putting power on *Adventurer*'s pumps – the problems and solutions passed in review through Nick's mind. It was going to be a tough one, but *Warlock* had twenty-two thousand rated horsepower and a dozen other high cards.

He glanced at his gold Rolex Oyster, and he saw that Jules had set a two-hour ultimatum.

'Radio Officer,' he said quietly, and every man on the bridge stiffened and swayed closer, so as not to miss a word.

'Open the telex line direct to Christy Main, London, and send quote "Personal for Duncan Alexander from Nicholas Berg Master of *Warlock*. Stop. I will be alongside *Golden Adventurer* in one hour forty minutes. Stop. I make firm offer Lloyd's Open Form Contract Salvage. Stop. Offer closes 1300 GMT." '

The Trog looked up at him startled, and blinked his pink eyes swiftly.

'Read it back,' snapped Nick, and the Trog did it in a high penetrating voice and when he finished, waited quizzically, as if expecting Nick to cancel.

'Send it,' said Nick, and rose to his feet. 'Mr Allen,' he turned to David, 'I want you and the Chief Engineer in my day cabin right away.'

The buzz of excitement and speculation began before Nick had closed the door behind him.

David knocked and followed him three minutes later, and Nick looked up from the notes he was making.

'What are they saying?' Nick asked. 'That I am crazy?'

'They're just kids,' shrugged David. 'What do they know?'

'They know plenty, and they're right. I am crazy to go Open Form on a site unseen! But it's the craziness of a man with no other option. Sit down, David.

'When I made the decision to leave Cape Town on the chance of this job – that was when I did the crazy thing.' Nick could no longer keep the steely silence. He had to say it, to talk it out. 'I was throwing dice for my whole bundle. When I turned down the Esso tow, that was when I went on the line for the whole company, *Warlock* and her sister, the whole thing depended on the cash from the Esso tow —'

'I see,' muttered David, and his colour was pink and high, embarrassed by this confidence from Nick Berg.

'What I am doing now is risking nothing. If I lose now, if I fail to pull *Golden Adventurer* out of there, I have lost nothing that is not already forfeit.'

'We could have offered daily hire at a better rate than *La Mouette*,' David suggested.

'No. Duncan Alexander is my enemy. The only way I can get the contract is to make it so attractive, that he has no alternative. If he refuses my offer of Open Form, I will take him up before Lloyd's Committee and his own shareholders. I will make a rope of his own guts and hoist it around his neck. He has to go with me – whereas, if I had offered daily hire at a few thousand dollars less than *La Mouette* —' Nick broke off, reached for the box of cheroots on the corner of his desk, then arrested the gesture and swivelled in his chair at the heavy knock on the cabin door.

'Come!'

Vin Baker's overalls were pristine blue, but the bandage around his head was smeared with engine grease, and he had recovered all the bounce and swagger that Nick had banged out of him against the engine-room windows.

'Jesus!' he said. 'I hear you just flipped. I hear you blew your mind and jumped overboard – and when they fished you out, you up and went Open Form on a bomber that's beating herself to death on Cape Alarm.'

'I'd explain it to you,' offered Nick solemnly, 'only I don't know enough words of one syllable.' The Chief Engineer grinned wickedly at that and Nick went on quickly, 'Just believe me when I tell you that I'm playing with someone else's chips. I'm not risking anything I haven't lost already.'

'That's good business,' the Australian agreed handsomely, and helped himself to one of Nick's precious cheroots.

'Your share of 12½% of daily hire is peanuts and apple jelly,' Nick went on.

'Too right,' Vin Baker agreed, and hoisted at his waistline with his elbows.

'But if we snatch *Golden Adventurer* and if we can plug her and pump her out, and if we can keep her afloat for three thousand miles, there will be a couple of big "M's" – and that's beef and potatoes.'

'You know something,' Vin Baker grunted. 'For a Pommy, I'm beginning to like the sound of your voice.' He said it reluctantly and shook his head, as if he didn't really believe it.

'All I want from you now,' Nick told him, 'are your plans for getting power on to *Golden Adventurer*'s pumps and anchor-winch. If she's up on the beach, we will have to kedge her off and we won't have much time.'

Kedging off was the technique of using a ship's own anchor and power winch to assist the pull of the tug in dragging her off a stranding.

Vin Baker waved the cheroot airily. 'Don't worry about that, I'm here.' And at that moment the Trog put his head through the doorway again, this time without knocking.

'I have an urgent and personal for you, skipper.' He brandished the telex flimsy like a royal flush in spades.

Nick glanced through it once, then read it aloud:

'Master of *Warlock* from Christy Main. Your offer Lloyd's Open Form "No Cure No Pay" accepted. Stop. You are hereby appointed main salvage contractor for wreck of *Golden Adventurer*. ENDS.'

Nick grinned with that rare wide irresistible flash of very white teeth. 'And so, gentlemen, it looks as though we are still in business – but the devil knows for just how much longer.'

Warlock rounded the headland, where the three black pillars of serpentine rock stood into a lazy green sea, across which low oily swells marched in orderly ranks to push in gently against the black cliffs.

They came round to the sudden vista of the wide, ice-choked bay. The abandoned hulk of *Golden Adventurer* was so majestic, so tall and beautiful that not even the savage mountains could belittle her. She looked like an illustration from a child's book of fairy tales, a lovely ice ship, glistening and glittering in the yellow sunlight.

'She's a beauty,' whispered the Chief Engineer, and his voice captured the sorrow they all felt for a great ship in mortal distress. To every single man on the bridge of *Warlock*, a ship was a living thing for which at best they could feel love and admiration; even the dirtiest old tramp roused a grudging affection. But *Golden Adventurer* was like a lovely woman. She was something rare and special, and all of them, felt it.

For Nick Berg, the bond was much more deeply felt. She was child of his inspiration, he had watched her lines take shape on the naval architect's drawing-board, he had seen her keel laid and her bare skeleton fleshed out with lovingly worked steel, and he had watched the woman who had once been his wife speak the blessing and then smash the bottle against her bows, laughing in the sunlight while the wine spurted and frothed.

She was his ship, and now, as he would never have believed possible, his destiny depended upon her.

He looked away from her at last to where *La Mouette* waited in the mouth of the bay at the edge of the ice. In contrast to the liner, she was small and squat and ugly, like a wrestler with all the weight in his shoulders. Greasy black smoke rose straight into the pale sky from her single stack, and her hull seemed to be painted the same greasy black.

Through his glasses, Nick saw the sudden bustle of activity on her bridge as *Warlock* burst into view. The headland would have blanketed *La Mouette*'s radar and, with Nick's strict radio silence, this would be the first that Jules Levoisin knew of *Warlock*'s presence. Nick could imagine the consternation on her navigation bridge, and he noted wryly that Jules Levoisin had not even gone through the motions of putting a line on to *Golden Adventurer*. He must have been completely sure of himself, of his unopposed presence. In maritime law, a line on to a prize's hull bestowed certain rights, and Jules should have made the gesture.

'Get *La Mouette* in clear,' he instructed, and picked up the hand microphone as the Trog nodded to him.

'*Salut Jules, ça va?* You pot-bellied little pirate, haven't they caught and hung you yet?' Nick asked kindly in French, and there was a long disbelieving silence on Channel 16 before the fruity Gallic tones boomed from the overhead speaker.

'Admiral James Bond, I think?' and Jules chuckled, but unconvincingly. 'Is that a battle-ship or a floating whore-house? You always were a fancy boy, Nicholas, but what kept you so long? I expected to get a better run for my money.'

'Three things you taught me, *mon brave*: the first was to take nothing for granted; the second was to keep your big yap shut tight when running for a prize; and the third was to put a line on it when you got there – you've broken your own rules, Jules.'

'The line is nothing. I am arrived.'

'And I, old friend, am arrived also. But the difference is that I am Christy Main's contractor.'

'*Tu rigoles!* You are joking!' Jules was shocked. 'I heard nothing of this!'

'I am not joking,' Nick told him. 'My James Bond equipment lets me talk in private. But go ahead, call Christy Main and ask them – and while you are doing it, move that dirty old greaser of yours out the way. I've got work to do.' Nick tossed the microphone back to the Trog. 'Tape everything he sends,' he instructed, and then to David Allen, 'We are going to smash up that ice before it grabs too tight a hold on *Golden Adventurer*. Put your best man on the wheel.'

Nick was a man transformed, no longer the brooding, moody recluse, agonizing over each decision, uncertain of himself and reacting to each check with frustrated and undirected anger.

'When he starts moving – he really burns it up,' thought David Allen, as he listened to Nick on the engine-room intercom.

'I want flank power on both, Chief. We are going to break ice. Then I want you in full immersion with helmet, we are going on board her to take a peek at her engine room.' He swung back to David Allen. 'Number One, you can stand by to take command.' The man of action glorying in the end to inactivity, he almost seemed to dance upon his feet, like a fighter at the first bell. 'Tell Angel I want a hot meal for us before we go into the cold, plenty of sugar in it.'

'I'll ask the steward,' said David, 'Angel is no good at the moment. He's playing dolls with the lass you pulled out the water. God, he'll be dressing her up and wheeling her around in a pram —'

'You tell Angel, I want food – and good food,' growled Nick, and turned away to the window to study the ice that blocked the bay, 'or I'll go down personally and kick his backside.'

'He'd probably enjoy that,' muttered David, and Nick rounded on him.

'How many times have you checked out the salvage gear since we left Cape Town?'

'Four times.'

'Make it five. Do it again. I want all the diesel auxiliaries started and run up, then shut down for freezing and rigged to be swung out. I want to have power on *Adventurer* by noon tomorrow.'

'Sir.'

But before he could go, Nick asked, 'What is the barometric reading?'

'I don't know —'

'From now until the end of this salvage, you will know, at any given moment, the exact pressure and you will inform me immediately any variation over one millibar.'

'Reading is 1018,' David checked hastily.

'It's too high,' said Nick. 'And it's too bloody calm. Watch it. We are going to have a pressure bounce. Watch it like an eagle scout.'

'Sir.'

'I thought I asked you to check the gear.'

The Trog called out, 'Christy Main has just called *La Mouette* and confirmed that we are the main contractor – but Levoisin has accepted daily hire to pick up a full load of survivors from Shackleton Bay and ferry them to Cape Town. Now he wants to speak to you again.'

'Tell him I'm busy.' Nick did not take his attention from the ice-packed bay, then he changed his mind. 'No, I'll talk to him.' He took the hand microphone. 'Jules?'

'You don't play fair, Nicholas. You go behind the back of an old friend, a man who loves you like a brother.'

'I'm a busy man. Did you truly call to tell me that?'

'I think you made a mistake, Nicholas. I think you crazy to go Lloyd's Open on this one. That ship is stuck fast – and the weather! Did you read the met from Gough Island? You got yourself a screaming bastard there, Nicholas. You listen to an old man.'

'Jules I've got twenty-two thousand horses running for me —'

'I still think you made a mistake, Nicholas. I think you're going to burn more than just your fingers.'

'*Au revoir*, Jules. Come and watch me in the awards court.'

'I still think that's a whore-house, not a tug, you are sailing. You can send over a couple of blondes and a bottle of wine –'

'Goodbye, Jules.'

'Good luck, *mon vieux*.'

'Hey, Jules – you say "good luck" and it's the worst possible luck. You taught me that.'

'*Oui*, I know.'

'Then good luck to you also, Jules.' For a minute Nick looked after the departing tug. It waddled away over the oily swells, small and fat-bottomed and cheeky, for all the world like its Master – and yet there was something dejected and crestfallen about her going.

He felt a prick of affection for the little Frenchman, he had been a true and good friend as well as a teacher, and Nick felt his triumph softening to regret.

He crushed it down ruthlessly. It had been a straight, hard but fair run, and Jules had been careless. Long ago, Nick had taught himself that anybody in opposition was an enemy, to be hated and beaten, and when you had done so, you despised them. You did not feel compassion, it weakened your own resolve.

He could not quite bring himself to despise Jules Levoisin. The Frenchman would bounce back, probably snatching the next job out from under Nick's nose, and anyway he had the lucrative contract to ferry the survivors from Shackleton Bay. It would pay the costs of his long run southwards and leave some useful change over.

Nick's own dilemma was not as easily resolved. He put Jules Levoisin out of his mind, turning away before the French tug had rounded the headland and he studied the ice-choked bay before him with narrow eyes and a growing feeling of concern. Jules had been right – this was going to be a screaming bastard of a job.

The high seas that had thrown *Golden Adventurer* ashore had been made even higher by the equinoctial spring tides. Both had now abated and she was fast.

The liner's hull had swung also, so she was not aligned neatly at right angles to the beach. *Warlock* would not be able to throw a straight pull on to her. She would have to drag her sideways. Nick could see that now as he closed.

Still closer, he could see how the heavy steel hull, half filled with water, had burrowed itself into the yielding shingle. She would stick like toffee to a baby's blanket.

Then he looked at the ice, it was not only brash and pancake ice, but there were big chunks, bergie bits, from rotten and weathered icebergs, which the wind had driven into the bay, like a sheepdog with its flock.

The plunging temperatures had welded this mass of ice into a whole; like a monstrous octopus, it was wrapping thick glistening tentacles around *Adventurer*'s stern. The ice had not yet had sufficient time to become impenetrable, and *Warlock*'s bows were ice-strengthened for just such an emergency – yet Nick knew enough not to underestimate the hardness of ice. 'White ice is soft ice' was the old adage, and yet here there were big lumps and hummocks of green and striated glacial ice in the mass, like fat plums in a pudding, any one of which could punch a hole through *Warlock*'s hull.

Nick grimaced at the thought of having to send Jules Levoisin a mayday.

He spoke to the helmsman quietly. 'Starboard five – midships,' lining *Warlock* up for a fracture-line in the ice-pack. It was vital to come in at a right angle, to take the ice fully on the stem; a glancing blow could throw the bows off line and bring the vulnerable hull in contact with razor ice.

'Stand by, engine room,' he alerted them, and *Warlock* bore down on the ice at a full ten knots and Nick judged the moment of impact finely. Half a ship's length clear, he gave a crisp order.

'Both half back.'

Warlock checked, going up on to the ice as she decelerated, but still with a horrid rasping roar that echoed through the ship. Her bows rose, riding up over the ice. It gave with a rending crackle, huge slabs of ice up-ending and tumbling together.

'Both full back.'

The huge twin propellers changed their pitch smoothly into reverse thrust, and the wash boiled into the broken ice, sweeping it clear, as *Warlock* drew back into open water and Nick steadied her and lined her up again.

'Both ahead full,'

Warlock charged forward, checking at the last moment, and again thick slabs of white ice broke away, and grated along the ship's side. Nick swung her stern first starboard then port, deftly using the twin screws to wash the broken ice free, then he pulled *Warlock* out and lined up again.

Butting and smashing and pivoting, *Warlock* worked her way deeper into the bay, opening a spreading web of cracks across the white sheet of ice.

David Allen was breathless, as he burst on to the bridge.

'All gear checked and ready, sir.'

'Take her,' said Nick. 'She's broken it up now – just keep it stirred up.' He wanted to add a warning that the big variable-pitch propellers were *Warlock*'s most vulnerable parts, but he had a high enough opinion now of his mate's ability, so he went on instead, 'I'm going down now to kit up.'

Vin Baker was in the aft salvage hold ahead of him, he had already half finished the tray of rich food and Angel hovered over him, but, as Nick came down the steel ladder, he lifted the cover off another steaming tray.

'It's good,' said Nick, although he could hardly force himself to swallow. The nerves in his stomach were bunched up too tightly. Yet food was one of the best defences against the cold.

'Samantha wants to talk to you, skip.'

'Who the hell is Samantha?'

'The girl – she wants to thank you.'

'Use your head, Angel, can't you see I have other things on my mind?'

Nick was already pulling on the rubber immersion suit over a full-length woollen undersuit. He needed the assistance of a seaman to enter the opening in the chest of the suit.

He had already forgotten about the girl as they closed the chest opening of the suit with a double ring seal, and then over the watertight bootees and mittens went another full suit of polyurethane. Nick and Vin Baker looked like a pair of fat Michelin men, as their dressers helped them into the full helmets, with wrap-around visors, built-in radio microphones and breathing valves.

'Okay, Chief?' Nick asked, and Vin Baker's voice squawked too loudly into his headphones.

'Clear to roll.'

Nick adjusted the volume, and then shrugged into the oxygen rebreathing set. They were not going deeper than thirty feet, so Nick had decided to use oxygen rather than the bulky steel compressed-air cylinders.

'Let's go,' he said, and waddled to the ladder.

The Zodiac sixteen-foot inflatable dinghy swung overboard with the four of them in it, two divers and two picked seamen to handle the boat. Vin pushed one of them aside and primed the outboard himself.

'Come on, beauty,' he told it sternly, and the big Johnson Seahorse fired at the first kick. Gingerly, they began to feel their way through an open lead in the ice, with the two seamen poling away small sharp pieces that would have ripped the fabric of the Zodiac.

In Nick's radio headset, David Allen's voice spoke suddenly.

'Captain, this is the First Officer. Barometric pressure is 1021 – it looks like it's going through the roof.'

The pressure was bouncing, as Nick had predicted. What goes up, must come down – and the higher she goes, the lower she falls.

Jules Levoisin had warned him it was going to be a screamer.

'Did you read the last met from Gough Island?'

'They have 1005 falling, and the wind at 320° and thirty-five knots.'

'Lovely,' said Nick. 'We've got a big blow coming.' And through the visor of his helmet he looked up at the pale and beautiful sun. It was not bright enough to pain the eye, and now it wore a fine golden halo like the head of a saint in a medieval painting.

'Skipper, this is as close as we can get,' Vin Baker told him, and slipped the motor into neutral. The Zodiac coasted gently into a small open pool in the ice-pack, fifty yards from *Golden Adventurer*'s stern.

A solid sheet of compacted ice separated them, and Nick studied it carefully. He had not taken the chance of working *Warlock* in closer until he could get a look at the bottom here. He wanted to know what depth of water he had to manoeuvre in, and if there were hidden snags, jagged rock to rip through the *Warlock*'s hull, or flat shingle on which he could risk a bump.

He wanted to know the slope of the bottom, and if there was good holding for his ground-tackle, but most of all, he wanted to inspect the underwater damage to *Golden Adventurer*'s hull.

'Okay, Chief?' he asked, and Vin Baker grinned at him through the visor.

'Hey, I just remembered – my mommy told me not to get my feet wet. I'm going home.'

Nick knew just how he felt. There was thick sheet ice between them and *Adventurer*, they had to go down and swim below it. God alone knew what currents were running under the ice, and what visibility was like down there. A man in trouble could not surface immediately, but must find his way back to open water. Nick felt a claustrophobic tightening of his belly muscles, and he worked swiftly, checking out his gear, cracking the valve on his oxygen tank to inflate the breathing bag, checking the compass and

Rolex Oyster on his wrist and clipping his buddy line on to the Zodiac, a line to return along, like Theseus in the labyrinth of the Minotaur.

'Let's go,' he said, and flipped backwards into the water. The cold struck through the multiple layers of rubber and cloth and polyurethane almost instantly, and Nick waited only for the Chief Engineer to break through the surface beside him in a cloud of swirling silver bubbles.

'God,' Vin Baker's voice was distorted by the earphones, 'it's cold enough to crack the gooseberries off a plaster saint.'

Paying out the line behind him, Nick sank down into the hazy green depths, looking for bottom. It came up dimly, heavy shingle and pebble, and he checked his depth gauge – almost six fathoms – and he moved in towards the beach.

The light from the surface was filtered through thick ice, green and ghostly in the icy depths, and Nick felt unreasonable panic stirring deep in him. He tried to thrust it aside and concentrate on the job, but it flickered there, ready to burst into flame.

There was a current working under the ice, churning the sediment so that the visibility was further reduced, and they had to fin hard to make headway across the bottom, always with the hostile ceiling of sombre green ice above them, cutting them off from the real world.

Suddenly the *Golden Adventurer*'s hull loomed ahead of them, the twin propellers glinting like gigantic bronze wings in the gloom.

They moved in within arm's length of the steel hull and swam slowly along it. It was like flying along the outer wall of a tall apartment block, a sheer cliff of riveted steel plate – but the hull was moving.

The *Golden Adventurer* was hogging on the bottom, the stern dipping and swaying to the pulse of the sea, the heaving ground-swell that came in under the ice; her stern bumped heavily on the pebbly bottom, like a great hammer beating time to the ocean.

Nick knew that she was settling herself in. Every hour now was making his task more difficult and he drove harder with his swim fins, pulling slightly ahead of Vin Baker. He knew exactly where to look for the damage. Reilly had reported it in minute detail to Christy Main, but he came across it without warning.

It looked as though a monstrous axe had been swung horizontally at the hull, a clean slash, the shape of an elongated teardrop. The metal around it had been depressed, and the pain smeared away so that the steel gleamed as though it had been scoured and polished.

At its widest, the lips of the fifteen-foot rent gaped open by three feet or a little more, and it breathed like a living mouth – for the force of the ground-swell pushing into the gap built up pressure within the hull, then as the swell subsided the trapped water was forcibly expelled, sucking in and out with tremendous pressure.

'It's a clean hole,' Vin Baker's voice squawked harshly. 'But it's too long to pump with cement.'

He was right, of course, Nick had seen that at once. Liquid cement would not plug that wicked gash, and anyway, there wasn't time to use cement, not with weather coming. An idea began forming in his mind.

'I'm going to penetrate.' Nick made the decision aloud, and beside him the Chief was silent for long incredulous seconds, then he covered the edge of fear in his voice with,

'Listen, cobber, every time I've ever been into an orifice shaped like that, it's always meant big trouble. Reminds me of my first wife –'

'Cover for me,' Nick interrupted him. 'If I'm not out in five minutes –'

'I'm coming with you,' said the Chief. 'I've got to take a look at her engine room. This is good a time as any.'

Nick did not argue with him.

'I'll go first,' he said and tapped the Chief's shoulder. 'Do what I do.'

Nick hung four feet from the gash, finning to hold himself there against the current.

He watched the swirl of water rushing into the opening, and then gushing out again in a rash of silver bubbles. Then, as she began to breathe again, he darted forward.

The current caught him and he was hurled at the gap, with only time to duck his helmeted head and cover the fragile oxygen bag on his chest with both arms.

Raw steel snagged at his leg; there was no pain, but almost instantly he felt the leak of seawater into his suit. The cold stung like a razor cut, but he was through into the total darkness of the cavernous hull. He was flung into a tangle of steel piping, and he anchored himself with one arm and groped for the underwater lantern on his belt.

'You okay?' The Chief's voice boomed in his headphones.

'Fine.'

Vin Baker's lantern glowed eerily in the dark waters ahead of him.

'Work fast,' instructed Nick. 'I've got a tear in my suit.'

Each of them knew exactly what to do and where to go. Vin Baker swam first to the water-tight bulkheads and checked all the seals. He was working in darkness in a totally unfamiliar engine room, but he went unerringly to the pump system, and checked the valve-settings; then he rose to the surface, feeling his way up the massive blocks of the main engines.

Nick was there ahead of him. The engine room was flooded almost to the deck above and the surface was a thick stinking scum of oil and diesel, in which floated a mass of loose articles, most of them undefinable, but in the beam of his lantern Nick recognized a gumboot and a grease pot floating beside his head. The whole thick stinking soup rose and fell and agitated with the push of the current through the rent.

The lenses of their lanterns were smeared with the oily filth and threw grotesque shadows into the cavernous depths, but Nick could just make out the deck above him, and the dark opening of the vertical ventilation shaft. He wiped the filth from his visor and saw what he wanted to see and the cold was spreading up his leg. He asked brusquely, 'Okay, Chief?'

'Let's get the hell out of here.'

There were sickening moments of panic when Nick thought they had lost the line to the opening. It had sagged and wrapped around a steam pipe. Nick freed it and then sank down to the glimmer of light through the gash.

He judged his moment carefully, the return was more dangerous than the entry, for the raw bright metal had been driven in by the ice, like the petals of a sunflower – or the fangs in a shark's maw. He used the suck of water and shot through without a touch, turning and finning to wait for Vin Baker.

The Australian came through in the next rush of water, but Nick saw him flicked sideways by the current, and he struck the jagged opening a touching blow. There was instantly a roaring rush of escaping oxygen from his breathing bag, as the steel split it wide, and for a moment the Chief was obscured in the silver cloud of gas that was his life's breath.

'Oh God, I'm snagged,' he shouted, clutching helplessly at his empty bag, plummeting sharply into the green depths at the drastic change in his buoyance. The heavily leaded belt around his waist had been weighted to counter the flotation of the oxygen bag, and he went down like a gannet diving on a shoal of sardine.

Nick saw instantly what was about to happen. The current had him – it was dragging him down under the hull, sucking him under that hammering steel bottom, where he would be crushed against the stony beach by twenty-two thousand tons of pounding steel.

Nick went head down, finning desperately to catch the swirling body which tumbled like a leaf in high wind. He had a fleeting glimpse of Baker's face, contorted with terror and lack of breath, the glass visor of his helmet already swamping with icy water as the pressure spurted through the non-return valve. The Chief's headset microphone squealed once and then went dead as the water shorted it out.

'Drop your belt,' yelled Nick, but Baker did not respond; he had not heard, his headset had gone and instead he fought ineffectually in the swirling current, drawn inexorably down to brutal death.

Nick got a hand to him and threw back with all his strength on his fins to check their downward plunge, but still they went down and Nick's right hand was clumsy with cold and the double thickness of his mittens as he groped for the quick-release on the Chief's belt.

He hit the rounded bottom of the great hull with his shoulder, and felt them dragged under to where clouds of sediment blew like smoke from the working of the keel. Locked together like a couple of waltzing dancers, they swung around and he saw the keel, like the blade of a guillotine, rise up high above them. He could not reach the Chief's release toggle.

There were only micro-seconds in which to go for his one other chance. He hit his own release and the thick belt with thirty-five pounds of lead fell away from Nick's waist; with it went the buddy line that would guide them back to the waiting Zodiac, for it had been clipped into the back of the belt.

The abrupt loss of weight checked their downward plunge, and fighting with all the strength of his legs, Nick was just able to hold them clear of the great keel as it came swinging downwards.

Within ten feet of them, steel struck stone with a force that rang in Nick's eardrum like a bronze gong but he had an armlock on the Chief's struggling body, and now at last his right hand found the release toggle on the other man's belt.

He hit it, and another thirty-five pounds of lead dropped away. They began to rise, up along the hogging steel hull, faster and faster as the oxygen in Nick's bag expanded with the release of pressure. Now their plight was every bit as desperate, for they were racing upwards to a roof of solid ice with enough speed to break bone or crack a skull.

Nick emptied his lungs, exhaling on a single continuous breath, and at the same time opened the valve to vent his bag, blowing away the precious life-giving gas in an attempt to check their rise – yet still they went into the ice with a force that would have stunned them both, had Nick not twisted over and caught it on his shoulder and outflung arm.

They were pinned there under the ice by the cork-like buoyancy of their rubber suits and the remaining gas in Nick's bag.

With mild and detached surprise Nick saw that the lower side of the ice pack was not a smooth sheet, but was worked into ridges and pinnacles, into weird flowing shapes like some abstract sculpture in pale green glass. It was only a fleeting moment that he looked at it, for beside him Baker was drowning.

His helmet was flooded with icy water and his face was empurpled and his mouth contorted into a horrible rictus; already his movements were becoming spasmodic and unco-ordinated, as he struggled for breath.

Nick realized that haste would kill them both now. He had to work fast but deliberately – and he held Baker to him as he cracked the valve on his steel oxygen bottle, reinflating his chest bag.

With his right hand, he began to unscrew the breathing pipe connection into the side of Baker's helmet. It was slow, too slow. He needed touch for this delicate work.

He thought, 'This could cost me my right hand,' and he stripped off the thick mitten in a single angry gesture. Now he could feel – for the few seconds until the cold paralysed his fingers. The connection came free and while he worked, Nick was pumping his lungs like a bellows, hyperventilating, washing his blood with pure oxygen until he felt light-headed and dizzy.

One last sweet breath, and then he unscrewed his own hose connection; icy water flooded through the valve but he held his head at an angle to trap oxygen in the top of his helmet, keeping his nose and eyes clear, and he rescrewed his own hose into Baker's helmet with fingers that no longer had feeling.

He held the Chief's body close to his chest, embracing like lovers, and he cracked the last of the oxygen from his bottle. There was just sufficient pressure of gas left to expunge the water from Baker's helmet. It blew out with an explosive hiss through the valve, and Nick watched carefully with his face only inches from Baker's.

The Chief was choking and coughing, gulping and gasping at the rush of cold oxygen, his eyes watery and unseeing, his spectacles blown awry and the lenses obscured by sea water, but then Nick felt his chest begin to swell and subside. Baker was breathing again, 'which is more than I am doing,' Nick thought grimly – and then suddenly he realized for the first time that he had lost the guide line with his weight belt.

He did not know in which direction was the shore, nor which way to swim to reach the Zodiac. He was utterly disorientated, and desperately he peered through his half-flooded visor for sight of the *Golden Adventurer*'s hull to align himself. She was not there, gone in the misty green gloom – and he felt the first heave of his lungs as they demanded air. And as he denied his body the driving need to breathe, he felt the fear that had flickered deep within him flare up into true terror, swiftly becoming cold driving panic.

A suicidal urge to tear at the green ice roof of this watery tomb almost overwhelmed him. He wanted to try and rip his way through it with bare freezing hands to reach the previous air.

Then, just before panic completely obliterated his reason, he remembered the compass on his wrist. Even then his brain was sluggish, beginning to starve for oxygen, and it took precious seconds working out the reciprocal of his original bearing.

As he leaned forward to read the compass, more sea water spurted into his helmet, spiking needles of icy cold agony into the sinuses of his cheeks and forehead, making the teeth ache in his jaws, so he gasped involuntarily and immediately choked.

Still holding Baker to him, linked by the thick black umbilical cord of his oxygen hose, Nick began to swim out on the reciprocal compass heading. Immediately his lungs began to pump, convulsing in involuntary spasms, like those of childbirth, craving air, and he swam on.

With his head thrown back slightly he saw that the sheet of ice moved slowly above him; at times, when the current held them, it moved not at all, and it required all his self-control to keep finning doggedly, then the current relaxed its grip and they moved forward again, but achingly slowly.

He had time then to realize how exquisitely beautiful was the ice roof; translucent, wonderously carved and sculptured – and suddenly he remembered standing hand in hand with Chantelle beneath the arched roof of the Chartres cathedral, staring up in awe. The pain in his chest subsided, the need to breathe passed, but he did not recognize that as the sign of mortal danger, nor the images that formed before his eyes as the fantasy of a brain deprived of oxygen and slowly dying.

Chantelle's face was before him then, glowing hair soft and thick and glossy as a butterfly's wing, huge dark eyes and that wide mouth so full of the promise of delight and warmth and love.

'I loved you,' he thought. 'I really loved you.'

And again the image changed. He saw again the incredible slippery explosive liquid burst with which his son was born, heard the first querulous cry as he dangled pink and wet and hairless from the rubber-gloved hand, and felt again the soul-consuming wonder and joy.

'A drowning man –' Nick recognized at last what was happening to him. He knew then he was dying, but the panic had passed, as the cold had passed also, and the terror. He swam on, dreamlike, into the green mists. Then he realized that his own legs were no longer moving; he lay relaxed not breathing, not feeling, and it was Baker's body that was thrusting and working against him.

Nick peered into the glass visor still only inches from his eyes, and he saw that Baker's face was set and determined. He was gulping the pure sweet oxygen and gaining strength with each breath, driving on strongly.

'You beauty,' whispered Nick dreamily, and felt the water shoot into his throat, but there was no pain.

Another image formed before him, an Arrowhead-class yacht with spinnaker set, running free across a bright Mediterranean sea, and his son at the tiller, the dense tumble of curls that covered his small neat head fluttering in the wind, and the same velvety dark eyes as his mother's in the sun-tanned oval of his face as he laughed.

'Don't let her run by the lee, Peter,' Nicholas wanted to shout to his son, but the image faded into blackness. He thought for a moment that he had passed into unconsciousness, but then he realized suddenly that it was the black rubber bottom of the Zodiac only inches from his eyes, and that the rough hands that dragged him upwards, lifting him and tearing loose the fastening of his helmet, were not part of the fantasy.

Propped against the pillowed gunwale of the Zodiac, held by the two boatmen from falling backwards, the first breaths of sub-zero air were too rich for his starved lungs, and Nick coughed and vomited weakly down the front of his suit.

*

Nick came out of the shower cabinet. The cabin was thick with steam, and his body glowed dull angry red from the almost boiling water. He wrapped the towel around his waist as he stepped through into his night cabin.

Baker slouched in the armchair at the foot of his bunk. He wore fresh overalls, his hair stood up in little damp spikes around the shaven spot where Angel's cat-gut stitches still held the scabbed wound closed. One of the side frames of his spectacles had snapped during those desperate minutes below *Golden Adventurer*'s stern, and Baker had repaired it with black insulating tape.

He held two glasses in his left hand, and a big flat brown bottle of liquor in the other. He poured two heavy slugs into the glasses as Nick paused in the bathroom door, and the sweet, rich aroma smelled like the sugar-cane fields of northern Queensland.

Baker passed a glass to Nick, and then showed him the bottle's yellow label.

'Bundaberg rum,' he announced, 'the dinky die stuff, sport.'

Nick recognized both the offer of liquor and the salutation as probably the highest accolade the Chief would ever give another human being.

Nick sniffed the dark honey-brown liquor and then took it in a single toss, swirled it once around his mouth, swallowed, shuddered like a spaniel shaking off water droplets, exhaled harshly and said: 'It's still the finest rum in the world.' Dutifully he said what was expected of him, and held out his glass.

'The Mate asked me to give you a message,' said Baker as he poured another shot for each of them. 'Glass hit 1035 and now it's diving like a dingo into its hole – back to 1020 already. It's going to blow – is it ever going to blow!'

They regarded each other over the rims of the glasses.

'We've wasted almost two hours, Beauty,' Nick told him, and Baker blinked at the unlikely name, then grinned crookedly as he accepted it.

'How are you going to plug that hull?'

'I've got ten men at work already. We are going to fother a sail into a collision mat.'

Baker blinked again, then shook his head in disbelief. 'That's Hornblower stuff —'

'The *Witch of Endor*,' Nick agreed. 'So you can read?'

'You haven't got pressure to drive it home,' Baker objected. 'The trapped air from the engine room will blow it out.'

'I'm going to run a wire down the ventilation shaft of the engine room and out through the gash. We'll fix the collision mat outside the hull and winch it home with the wire.'

Baker stared at him for five seconds while he examined the proposition. A sail was fothered by threading the thick canvas with thousands of strands of unravelled oakum until it resembled a huge shaggy doormat. When this was placed over an aperture below a ship's waterline, the pressure of water forced it into the hole, and the water swelled the mass of fibre until it formed an almost watertight plug.

However, in *Golden Adventurer*'s case the damage was extensive and as the hull was already flooded, there was no pressure differential to drive home the plug. Nick proposed to beat that by using an internal wire to haul the plug into the gash.

'It might work.' Beauty Baker was noncommittal.

Nick took the second rum at a gulp, dropped the towel and reached for his working gear laid out on the bunk.

'Let's get power on her before the blow hits us,' he suggested mildly, and Baker lumbered to his feet and stuffed the Bundaberg bottle into his back pocket.

'Listen, sport,' he said. 'All that guff about you being a Pommy, don't take it too seriously.'

'I won't,' said Nick. 'Actually, I was born and educated in Blighty, but my father's an American. So that makes me one also.'

'Christ.' Beauty hitched disgustedly at his waist with both elbows. 'If there's anything worse than a bloody Pom, it's a goddamned Yank.'

Now that Nick was certain that the bottom of the bay was clean and free of underwater snags, he handled *Warlock* boldly but with a delicately skilful touch which David Allen watched with awe.

Like a fighting cock, the *Warlock* attacked the thicker ice line along the shore, smashing free huge lumps and slabs, then washing them clear with the propellers, giving herself space to work about *Golden Adventurer*'s stern.

The ominous calm of both sea and air made the work easier, although the vicious little current working below *Adventurer*'s stern complicated the transfer of the big alternator.

Nick had two Yokohama fenders slung from *Warlock*'s side, and the bloated plastic balloons cushioned the contact of steel against steel as Nick laid *Warlock* alongside the stranded liner, holding her there with delicate adjustments of power and rudder and screw pitch.

Beauty Baker and his working party, swaddled in heavy Antarctic gear, were already up on the catwalk of *Warlock*'s forward gantry, seventy feet above the bridge and overlooking *Adventurer*'s sharply canted deck.

As Nick nudged *Warlock* in, they dropped the steel boarding-ladder across the gap between the two ships and Beauty led them across in single file, like a troop of monkeys across the limb of a forest tree.

'All across,' the Third Officer confirmed for Nick, and then added, 'Glass has dropped again, sir. Down to 1005.'

'Very well,' Nick drew *Warlock* gently away from the liner's stern, and held her fifty feet off. Only then did he flick his eyes up at the sky. The midnight sun had turned into a malevolent jaundiced yellow, while the sun itself was a ball of dark satanic red above the peaks of Cape Alarm, and it seemed that the snowfields and glaciers were washed with blood.

'It's beautiful.' Suddenly the girl was beside him. The top of her head was on a level with his shoulder, and in the ruddy light, her thick roped hair glowed like newly minted sovereigns in red gold. Her voice was low and a little husky with shyness, and touched a chord of response in Nick, but when she lifted her face to him he saw how young she was.

'I came to thank you,' she said softly. 'It's the first chance I've had.'

She wore baggy, borrowed men's clothing that made her look like a little girl dressing up, and her face, free of cosmetics, had that waxy plastic glow of youth, like the polished skin of a ripe apple.

Her expression was solemn and there were traces of her recent ordeal beneath her eyes and at the corners of her mouth. Nick sensed the tension and nervousness in her.

'Angel wouldn't let me come before,' she said, and suddenly she smiled. The nervousness vanished and it was the direct warm unselfconscious smile of a beautiful child that has never known rejection. Nick was shocked by the strength of his sudden physical desire for her, his body moved, clenching like a fist in his groin, and he felt his heart pound furiously in the cage of his ribs.

His shock turned to anger, for she looked but fourteen or fifteen years of age; almost she seemed as young as his own son, and he was shamed by the perversity of his attraction. Since the good bright times with Chantelle, he had not experienced such direct and instant involvement with a woman. At the thought of Chantelle, his emotions collapsed in a disordered tangle, from which only his lust and his anger emerged clearly.

He cupped the anger to him, like a match in a high wind, it gave him strength again. Strength to thrust this aside, for he knew how vulnerable he still was and how dangerous a course had opened before him, to be led by this child woman. Suddenly he was aware that he had swayed bodily towards the girl and had been staring into her face for many long seconds, that she was meeting his gaze steadily and that something was beginning to move in her eyes like cloud shadow across the sunlit surface of a green mountain lake. Something was happening which he could not afford, could not chance – and then he realized also that the two young deck officers were watching them with undisguised curiosity, and he turned his anger on her.

'Young lady,' he said. 'You have an absolute genius for being in the wrong place at the wrong time.' And his tone was colder and more remote than even he had intended it.

Before he turned away from her, he saw the moment of her disbelief turn to chagrin, and the green eyes misted slightly. He stood stiffly staring down the foredeck where David Allen's team was opening the forward salvage hold.

Nick's anger evaporated almost at once, to be replaced by dismay. He realized clearly that he had completely alienated the girl and he wanted to turn back to her and say something gracious that might retrieve the situation, but he could think of nothing and instead lifted the hand microphone to his lips and spoke to Baker over the VHF radio.

'How's it going, Chief?'

There were ten seconds of delay, and Nick was very conscious of the girl's presence near him.

'Their emergency generator has burned out, it will need two days' work to get it running again. We'll have to take on the alternator,' Beauty told him.

'We are ready to give it to you,' Nick told him, and then called David Allen on the foredeck.

'Ready, David?'

'All set.'

Nick began edging *Warlock* back towards the liner's towering stern, and now at last he turned back to the girl. Unaccountably, he now wanted her approbation, so his smile was ready – but she had already gone, taking with her that special aura of brightness.

Nick's voice had a jagged edge to it as he told David Allen, 'Let's do this fast and right, Number One.'

Warlock nuzzled *Adventurer*'s stern, the big black Yokohama fenders gentling her touch, and on her foredeck the winch whined shrilly, the lines squealing in their blocks and from the open salvage hatch the four-ton alternator swung out. It was mounted on a sledge for easy handling. The diesel tanks were charged and the big motor primed and ready to start.

It rose swiftly, dangling from the tall gantry, and a dozen men synchronized their efforts, in those critical moments when it hung out over *Warlock*'s bows. A nasty freaky little swell lifted the tug and pushed her across, for the dangling burden was already putting a slight list on her, and it would have crashed into the steel side of the liner had not Nick thrown the screws into reverse thrust and given her a burst of power to hold her off.

The instant the swell subsided, he closed down and slid the pitch to fine forward, pressing the cushioned bows lightly back against *Adventurer*'s side.

'He's good!' David Allen watched Nicholas work. 'He's better than old Mac ever was.' Mackintosh, *Warlock*'s previous skipper, had been careful and experienced, but Nicholas Berg handled the ship with the flair and intuitive touch that even Mac's vast experience could never have matched.

David Allen pushed the thought aside and signalled the winchman. The huge dangling machine dropped with the control of a roosting seagull on to the liner's deck. Baker's crew leapt on it immediately, releasing the winch cable and throwing out the tackle, to drag it away on its sledge.

Warlock drew off, and when Baker's crew was ready, she went in to drop another burden, this time one of the high-speed centrifugal pumps which would augment *Golden Adventurer*'s own machinery – if Baker could get that functioning. It went up out of *Warlock*'s forward hold, followed ten minutes later by its twin.

'Both pumps secured.' Baker's voice had a spark of jubilation in it, but at that moment a shadow passed over the ship, as though a vulture wheeled above on wide-spread pinions, and as Nick glanced up he saw the men on the foredeck lift their heads also.

It was a single cloud seeming no bigger than a man's fist, a thousand or fifteen hundred feet above them, but it had momentarily obscured the lowering sun, before scuttling on furtively down the peaks of Cape Alarm.

'There is still much to do,' Nick thought, and he opened the bridge door and stepped out on to the exposed wing. There was no movement of air, and the cold seemed less intense although a glance at the glass confirmed that there were thirty degrees still of frost. No wind here, but high up it was beginning.

'Number One,' Nick snapped into the microphone. 'What's going on down there – do you think this is your Daddy's yacht?'

And David Allen's team leapt to the task of closing down the forward hatch, and then tramped back to the double salvage holds on the long stern quarter.

'I am transferring command to the stern bridge.' Nick told his deck officers and hurried back through the accommodation area to the second enclosed bridge, where every control and navigational aid was duplicated, a unique feature of salvage-tug construction where so much of the work took place on the afterdeck.

This time from the aft gantries, they lifted the loaded pallets of salvage gear on to the liner's deck, another eight tons of equipment went aboard *Golden Adventurer*. Then they pulled away and David Allen battened down again. When he came on to the bridge stamping and slapping his own shoulders, red-cheeked and gasping from the cold, Nick told him immediately.

'Take command, David, I'm going on board.' Nick could not bring himself to wait out the uncertain period while Beauty Baker put power and pumps into action.

Anything mechanical was Baker's responsibility, as seamanship was strictly Nick's, but it could take many hours yet, and Nick could not remain idle that long.

From high on the forward gantry, Nick looked out across that satiny ominous sea. It was a little after midnight now and the sun was half down behind the mountains, a two-dimensional disc of metal heated to furious crimson. The sea was sombre purple and the ice-bergs were sparks of brighter cherry red. From this height he could see that the surface of the sea was crenellated, a small regular swell spreading across it like ripples across a pond, from some disturbance far out beyond the horizon.

Nick could feel the fresh movement of *Warlock*'s hull as she rode this swell, and suddenly a puff of wind hit Nick in the face like the flit of a bat's wing, and the metallic sheen of the sea was scoured by a cat's-paw of wind that scratched at the surface as it passed.

He pulled the draw-string of the hood of his anorak up more tightly under his chin and stepped out on to the open boarding-ladder, like a steeplejack, walking upright and balancing lightly seventy feet above *Warlock*'s slowly rolling foredeck.

He jumped down on to *Golden Adventurer*'s steeply canted, ice-glazed deck and saluted *Warlock*'s bridge far below in a gesture of dismissal.

'I tried to warn you, dearie,' said Angel gently, as she entered the steamy galley, for with a single glance he was aware of Samantha's crestfallen air. 'He tore you up, didn't he?'

'What are you talking about?' She lifted her chin, and the smile was too bright and too quick. 'What do you want me to do?'

'You can separate that bowl of eggs,' Angel told her, and stooped again over twenty pounds of red beef, with his sleeves rolled to the elbows about his thick and hairy arms, clutching a butcher's knife in a fist like that of Rocky Marciano.

They worked in silence for five minutes, before Samantha spoke again.

'I only tried to thank him —' And again there was a grey mist in her eyes.

'He's a lower-deck pig,' Angel agreed.

'He is not,' Samantha came in hotly. 'He's not a pig.'

'Well, then, he's a selfish, heartless bastard – with jumped-up ideas.'

'How *can* you say that!' Samantha's eyes flashed now. 'He is not selfish – he went into the water to get me —'

Then she saw the smile on Angel's lips and the mocking quizzical expression in his eyes, and she stopped in confusion and concentrated on cracking the egg shells and slopping the contents into the mixing basin.

'He's old enough to be your father,' Angel needled her, and now she was really angry; a ruddy flush under the smooth gloss of her skin made the freckles shine like gold dust.

'You talk the most awful crap, Angel.'

'God, dearie, where did you learn that language?'

'Well, you're making me mad.' She broke an egg with such force that it exploded down the front of her pants. 'Oh, shit!' she said, and stared at him defiantly. Angel tossed her a dish-cloth, she wiped herself violently and they went on working again.

'How old is he?' she demanded at last. 'A hundred and fifty?'

'He's thirty-eight,' Angel thought for a moment, 'or thirty-nine.'

'Well, smart arse,' she said tartly, 'the ideal age is half the man's age, plus seven.'

'You aren't twenty-six, dearie,' Angel said gently.

'I will be in two years' time,' she told him.

'You really want him badly, hey? A fever of lust and desire?'

'That's nonsense, Angel, and you know it. I just happen to owe him a rather large debt – he saved my life – but as for wanting him, ha!' She dismissed the idea with a snort of disdain and a toss of her head.

'I'm glad,' Angel nodded. 'He's not a very nice person, you can see by those ferrety eyes of his –'

'He has beautiful eyes –' she flared at him, and then stopped abruptly, saw the cunning in his grin, faltered and then collapsed weakly on the bench beside him, with a cracked egg in one hand.

'Oh, Angel, you are a horrible man and I hate you. How can you make fun of me now?'

He saw how close she was to tears, and became brisk and businesslike.

'First of all, you better know something about him –' and he began to tell her, giving her a waspish biography of Nicholas Berg, embellished by a vivid imagination and a wicked sense of humour, together with a quasi-feminine love of gossip, to which Samantha listened avidly, making an occasional exclamation of surprise.

'His wife ran away with another man, she could be out of her mind, don't you think?'

'Dearie, a change is like two weeks at the seaside.'

Or asking a question. 'He owns this ship, actually owns it? Not just Master?'

'He owns this ship, and its sister, and the company. They used to call him the Golden Prince. He's a high flyer, dearie, didn't you recognize it?'

'I didn't –'

'Of course you did. You're too much woman not to. There is no more powerful aphrodisiac than success and power, nothing like the clink of gold to get a girl's hormones revving up, is there?'

'That's unfair, Angel. I didn't know a thing about him. I didn't know he was rich and famous. I don't give a damn for money –'

'Ho! Ho!' Angel shook his curls and the diamond studs flashed in his ears. But he saw her anger flare again. 'All right, dearie, I'm teasing. But what really attracts you is his strength and air of purpose. The way other men obey, and follow and fear him. The air of command, of power and with it, success.'

'I didn't –'

'Oh, be honest with yourself, love. It was not the fact he saved your life, it wasn't his beautiful eyes nor the lump in his jeans –'

'You're crude, Angel.'

'You're bright and beautiful, and you just can't help yourself. You're like a nubile little gazelle, all skittish and ready, and you have just spotted the herd bull. You can't help yourself, dearie, you're just a woman.'

'What am I going to do, Angel?'

'We'll make a plan, love, but one thing is certain. You're not going to trail around behind him, dressed like an escapee from a junk shop, breathing adoration and hero-worship. He's doing a job. He doesn't need to trip over you every time he turns. Play hard to get.'

Samantha thought about it for a moment. 'Angel, I don't want to play it that hard that I never get around to being got – if you follow me.'

Beauty Baker had the work in hand, well organized and going ahead as fast as even Nick, in his overwhelming impatience, could expect.

The alternator had been manhandled through the double doors into the superstructure on B deck, and it had been secured against a steel bulkhead and lashed down.

'As soon as I have power, we'll drill the deck and bolt her down,' he explained to Nick.

'Have you got the lines in?'

'I'll by-pass the main junction box on C deck, and I will select from the temporary box —'

'But you've identified the foredeck winch circuit, and the pumps?'

'Jesus, sport, why don't you go sail your little boat and leave me to do my work?'

On the upper deck one of Baker's gangs was already at work with the gas welding equipment. They were opening access to the ventilation shaft of the main engine room. The gas cutter hissed viciously and red sparks showered from the steel plate of the tall dummy smoke stack. The stack was merely to give the *Golden Adventurer* the traditional rakish lines, and now the welder cut the last few inches of steel plating. It fell away into the deep, dark cavern, leaving a roughly square opening six feet by six feet which gave direct access into the half-flooded engine room fifty feet below.

Despite Baker's advice, Nick took command here, directing the rigging of the winch blocks and steel wire cable that would enable a cable to be taken down into the flooded engine room and out again through that long, viciously fanged gash in the ship's side. When he looked at his Rolex Oyster again, almost an hour had passed. The sun had gone and a luminous green sky filled with the marvellous pyrotechnics of the *Aurora Australis* turned the night eerie and mysterious.

'All right, bosun, that's all we can do now. Bring your team up to the bows.'

As they hurried forward along the open foredeck, the wind caught them, a single shrieking gust that had them reeling and staggering and grabbing for support, then it was past and the wind settled down to nag and whine and pry at their clothing as Nick directed the work at the two huge anchor winches; but he heard the rising sea starting to push and stir the pack-ice, making it growl and whisper menacingly.

They catted the twin sea-anchors and with two men working over *Adventurer*'s side they secured collars of heavy chain to the crown of each anchor. *Warlock* would now be able to drag those anchors out, letting them bump along the bottom, but in the opposite direction to that in which they had been designed to drag, so that the pointed flukes would not be able to dig in and hold.

Then, when the anchors were out to the full reach of their own chains, *Warlock* would drop them, the flukes would dig in and hold. This was the ground-tackle which might resist the efforts of even a force twelve wind to throw *Golden Adventurer* further ashore.

When Baker had power on the ship, the anchor winches would be used to kedge *Golden Adventurer* off the bank. Nick placed much reliance on these enormously powerful winches to assist *Warlock*'s own engines, for even as they worked, he could feel through the soles of his feet how heavily grounded the liner was.

It was a tense and heavy labour, for they were working with enormous weights of dead-weight steel chain and shackles. The securing shackle which held the chain collar on the anchor crown alone weighed three hundred pounds and had to be manhandled by six men using complicated tackle.

By the time they had the work finished, the wind was rising force six, and wailing in the superstructure. The men were chilled and tired, and tempers were flashing.

Nick led them back to the shelter of the main superstructure. His boots seemed to be made of lead, and his lungs pumped for the solace of cheroot smoke, and he realized irrelevantly that he had not slept now for over fifty hours – since he had fished that disturbing little girl from the water. Quickly he pushed the thought of her aside, for it distracted him from his purpose, and, as he stepped over the door-sill into the liner's cold but wind-protected main accommodation, he reached for his cheroot-case.

Then he arrested the movement and blinked with surprise as suddenly garish light blazed throughout the ship – deck lights and internal lights, so that instantly a festival air enveloped her and from the loudspeakers on the deck above Nicholas' head wafted soft music as the broadcasting equipment switched itself in. It was the voice of Donna Summer, as limpid and ringing clear as fine-leaded crystal. The sound was utterly incongruous in this place and in these circumstances.

'Power is on!'

Nick let out a whoop and ran through to B deck. Beauty Baker was standing beside his roaring alternator and hugging himself with glee.

'Howzat, sport?' he demanded. Nick punched his shoulder.

'Right on, Beauty.' He wasted a few moments and a cheroot by placing one of the precious black tubes between Baker's lips and flashing his lighter. The two of them smoked for twenty seconds in close and companionable silence.

'Okay,' Nick ended it. 'Pumps and winches.'

'The two emergency portables are ready to start, and I'm on my way to check the ship's main pumps.'

'The only thing left is to get the collision mat into place.'

'That is your trick,' Baker told him flatly. 'You're not getting me into the water again, ever. I've even given up bathing.'

'Yeah, did you notice I'm standing upwind?' Nick told him. 'But somebody has got to go down again to pass the wire.'

'Why don't you send Angel?' Baker grinned evilly. 'Excuse me, cobber – I've got work to do.' He inspected the cheroot. 'After we've pulled this dog off the ground, I hope you will be able to afford decent gaspers.' And he was gone into the depths of the liner, leaving Nick with the one task he had been avoiding even thinking about. Somebody had to go down into that engine room. He could call for volunteers, of course, but then it was another of his own rules to never ask another man to do what you are afraid to do yourself.

'I can leave David to lay out the ground-tackle, but I can't let anybody else put the collision mat in.' He faced it now. He would have to go down again, into the cold and darkness and mortal danger of the flooded engine room.

The ground-tackle that David Allen had laid was holding *Golden Adventurer* handsomely, even in the aggravated swell which was by now pouring into the open mouth of the bay, driven on by the rising wind that was inciting it to wilder abandon.

David had justified Nick's confidence in the seamanlike manner in which he had taken the *Golden Adventurer*'s twin anchors out and dropped them a cable's length offshore, at a finely judged angle to give the best purchase and hold.

Beauty Baker had installed and test-run the two big centrifugals and he had even resuscitated two of the liner's own forward pump assemblies which had been protected by the watertight bulkhead from the sea break-in. He was ready now to throw the switch on this considerable arsenal of pumps, and he had calculated that if Nick could close that gaping rent in the hull, he would be able to pump the liner's hull dry and clean in just under four hours.

Nick was in full immersion kit again, but this time he had opted for a single bottle Drager diving-set; he was off oxygen sets for life, he decided wryly.

Before going down, he paused on the open deck with the diving helmet under his arm. The wind must be rising seven now, he decided, for it was kicking off the tops of the waves in bursts of spray and a low scudding sky of dirty grey cloud had blotted out the rising sun and the peaks of Cape Alarm. It was a cold dark dawn, with the promise of a wilder day to follow.

Nick took once glance across at *Warlock*. David Allen was holding her nicely in position, and his own team was ready, grouped around that ugly black freshly burned opening in *Adventurer*'s stack. He lifted the helmet on to his head, and while his helpers closed the fastenings and screwed down the hose connections, he checked the radio.

'*Warlock*, do you read me?'

Allen's voice came back immediately, acknowledging and confirming his readiness, then he went on, 'The glass just went through the floor, skipper, she's 996 and going down. Wind's force six rising seven and backing. It looks like we are fair in the dangerous quadrant of whatever is coming.'

'Thank you, David,' Nick replied. 'You warm my heart.'

He stepped forward, and they helped him into the canvas bosun's chair. Nick checked the tackle and rigging, that 'once-more-for-luck' check, and then he nodded.

The interior of the engine room was no longer dark, for Baker had rigged floodlights high above in the ventilation shaft, but the water was black with engine oil, and as Nick was lowered slowly down, with legs dangling from the bosun's chair, it surged furiously back and across like some panic-stricken monster trying to break out of its steel cage. That wind-driven swell was crashing into *Golden Adventurer*'s side and boiling in through the opening, setting up its own wave action, forming its own currents and eddies which broke and leaped angrily against the steel bulkheads.

'Slower,' Nick spoke into the microphone. 'Stop!'

His downward progress was halted ten feet above the starboard main engine block, but the confined surge of water broke over the engine as though it were a coral reef, covering it entirely at one instant, and then sucking back and exposing it again at the next.

The rush of water could throw a man against that machinery with force enough to break every bone in his body, and Nick hung above it and studied the purchases for his blocks.

'Send down the main block,' he ordered, and the huge steel block came down out of the shadows and dangled in the floodlights.

'Stop.' Nick began directing the block into position. 'Down two feet. Stop!'

Now waist-deep in the oily, churning water, he struggled to drive the shackle pin and secure the block to one of the main frames of the hull. Every few minutes a stronger surge would hurl the water over his head, forcing him to cling helplessly, until it relinquished its grip, and his visor cleared sufficiently to allow him to continue his task.

He had to pull out and rest after forty minutes of it. He sat as close as he could to the heat-exchangers of the running diesel engine of the alternator, taking warmth from them and drinking Angel's strong sweet Thermos coffee. He felt like a fighter between rounds, his body aching, every muscle strained and chilled by the efforts of fighting that filthy churned emulsion of sea water and oil, his flanks and ribs bruised from harsh contact with the submerged machinery. But after twenty minutes, he stood up again.

'Let's go,' he said and resettled the helmet. The hiatus had given him a chance to replan the operation, thinking his way around the problems he had found down there; now the work seemed to fall more readily into place, though he had lost all sense of time alone in the infernal resounding cavern of steel and he was not sure of the hour, or the phase of the day, when at last he was ready to carry the messenger out through the gap.

'Send it down,' he ordered into his headset, and the reel of light line came down, swinging and circling under the glaring floodlights to the ship's motion and throwing grotesque shadows into the far corners of the engine room.

The line was of finely plaited Dacron, with enormous strength and elasticity in relation to its thinness and lightness. One end was secured on the deck high above, and Nick threaded it into the sheave blocks carefully, so that it was free to run.

Then he clamped the reel of line on to his belt, riding it on his hip where it could be protected from snagging when he made the passage of the gap.

He realized then how close to final exhaustion he was, and he considered breaking off the work to rest again, but the heightened action of the sea into the hull warned him against further delay. An hour from now the task might be impossible, he had to go, and he reached for the reserve of strength and purpose deep inside himself, surprised to find that it was still there – for the icy chill of the water seemed to have penetrated his suit and entered his soul, dulling every sense and turning his very bones brittle and heavy.

It must be day outside, he realised, for light came through the gash of steel, pale light further obscured by the filthy muck of mixed oil and water contained in the hull.

He clung to one of the engine-room stringers, his head seven feet from the opening, breathing in the slow, even rhythm of the experienced scuba diver, feeling the ebb and flow through the hull, and trying to find some pattern in the action of the water. But it seemed entirely random, a hissing, bubbling ingestion followed by three or four irregular and weak inflows, then three vicious exhalations of such power that they would have windmilled a swimming man end over into those daggers of splayed steel. He had to choose and ride a middling-sized swell, strong enough to take him through smoothly, without the dangerous power and turbulence of those viciously large swells.

'I'm ready to go now, David,' he said into his helmet. 'Confirm that the work boat is standing by for the pick-up outside the hull.'

'We are all ready.' David Allen's voice was tense and sharp.

'Here we go,' said Nick, this was his wave now. There was no point in waiting longer.

He checked the reel on his belt, ensuring that the line was free to run, and watched the gash suck in clean green water, filled with tiny bright bubbles, little diamond chips that flew past his head to warn him of the lethal speed and power of that flood.

The inflow slowed and stopped as the hull filled to capacity, building up great pressures of air and water, and then the flow reversed abruptly as the swell on the far side subsided, and trapped water began to rush out again.

Nick released his grip on the stringer and instantly the water caught him. There was no question of being able to swim in that mill-race, all he could hope for was to keep his arms at his sides and his legs straight together to give himself a smoother profile, and to steer with his fins.

The accelerating speed appalled him as he was flung head first at that murderous steel mouth, he could feel the nylon line streaming out against his leg, the reel on his belt racing as though a giant marlin had struck and hooked upon the other end.

The rush of his progress seemed to leave his guts behind him as though he rode a fairground roller-coaster, and then a flick of the current turned him, he felt himself beginning to roll – and he fought wildly for control just as he hit.

He hit with a numbing shock, so his vision starred in flashing colour and light. The shock was in his shoulders and left arm, and he thought it might have been severed by that razor steel.

Then he was swirling, end over end, completely disorientated so he did not know which direction was up. He did not know if he was still inside *Golden Adventurer*'s hull, and the nylon line was wrapping itself around his throat and chest, around the precious air tubes and cutting off his air supply like a stillborn infant strangled by its own umbilical cord.

Again he hit something, this time with the back of his head, and only the cushioning of his helmet saved his skull from cracking. He flung out his arms and found the rough irregular shape of ice above him.

Terror wrapped him again, and he screamed soundlessly into his mask, but suddenly he broke out into light and air, into the loose scum of slush and rotten ice mixed with bigger, harder chunks, one of which had hit him.

Above him towered the endless steel cliff of the liner's side and beyond that, the low bruised wind-sky, and as he struggled to disentangle himself from the coils of nylon, he realized two things. The first was that both his arms were still attached to his body, and still functioning, and the second was that *Warlock*'s work boat was only twenty feet away and butting itself busily through the brash of rotten broken ice towards him.

*

The collision mat looked like a five-ton Airedale terrier curled up to sleep in the bows of the work boat, just as shaggy and shapeless, and of the same wiry, furry brown colour.

Nick had shed his helmet and pulled an Arctic cloak and hood over his bare head and suited torso. He was balanced in the stern of the work boat as she plunged and rolled and porpoised in the big swells; chunks of ice crashed against her hull, knocking loose chips off her paintwork, but she was steel-hulled, wide and sea-kindly. The helmsman knew his job, working her with calm efficiency to Nick's hand-signals, bringing her in close through the brash ice, under the tall sheer of *Golden Adventurer*'s stern.

The thin white nylon line was the only physical contact with the men on the liner's towering stack of decks, the messenger which would carry heavier tackle. However it was vulnerable to any jagged piece of pancake ice, or the fangs of that voracious underwater steel jaw.

Nick paid out the line through his own numbed hands, feeling for the slightest check or jerk which could mean a snag and a break-off.

With hand-signals, he kept the work boat positioned so that the line ran cleanly into the pierced hull, around the sheave blocks he had placed with such heart-breaking labour in the engine room, from there up the tall ventilation shaft, out of the burned square opening in the stack and around the winch, beside which Beauty Baker was supervising the recovery of the messenger.

The gusts tore at Nick's head so that he had to crouch to shield the small two-way radio on his chest, and Baker's voice was tinny and thin in the buffeting boom of wind.

'Line running free.'

'Right, we are running the wire now,' Nick told him. The second line was as thick as a man's index finger, and it was of the finest Scandinavian steel cable. Nick checked the connection between nylon and steel cable himself, the nylon messenger was strong enough to carry the weight of steel, but the connection was the weakest point.

He nodded to the crew, and they let it go over the side; the white nylon disappeared into the cold green water and now the black steel cable ran out slowly from the revolving drum.

Nick felt the check as the connection hit the sheave block in the engine room. He felt his heart jump. If it caught now, they would lose it all; no man could penetrate that hull again, the sea was now too vicious. They would lose the tackle, and they would lose *Golden Adventurer*, she would break up in the seas that were coming.

'Please God, let it run,' Nick whispered in the boom and burst of sea wind. The drum halted, made a half turn and jammed. Somewhere down there, the cable had snagged and Nick signalled to the helmsman to take the work boat in closer, to change the angle of the line into the hull.

He could almost feel the strain along his nerves as the winch took up the pull, and he could imagine the fibres of the nylon messenger stretching and creaking.

'Let it run! Let it run!' prayed Nick, and then suddenly he saw the drum begin to revolve again, the cable feeding out smoothly, and streaming down into the sea.

Nick felt light-headed, almost dizzy with relief, as he heard Baker's voice over the VHF, strident with triumph.

'Wire secured.'

'Stand by,' Nick told him. 'We are connecting the two-inch wire now.'

Again, the whole laborious, touchy, nerve-scouring process as the massive two-inch steel cable was drawn out by its thinner, weaker forerunner – and it was a further forty vital minutes, with the wind and sea rising every moment, before Baker shouted, 'Main cable secured, we are ready to haul!'

'Negative,' Nick told him urgently. 'Take the strain and hold.' If the collision mat in the bows hooked and held on the work boat's gunwale, Baker would pull the bows under and swamp her.

Nick signalled to his crew and the five of them shambled up into the bows, bulky and clumsy in their electric-yellow oilskins and work boots. With hand-signals, Nick positioned them around the shaggy head-high pile of the collision mat before he signalled to the helmsman to throw the gear in reverse and pull back from *Golden Adventurer*'s side.

The mass of unravelled oakum quivered and shook as the two-inch cable came up taut and they struggled to heave the whole untidy mass overboard.

There was nearly five tons of it and the weight would have been impossible to handle were it not for the reverse pull of the work boat against the cable. Slowly, they heaved the mat forward and outward, and the work boat took on a dangerous list under the transfer of weight. She was down at the bows and canting at an angle of twenty degrees, the diesel motor screaming angrily and her single propeller threshing frantically, trying to pull her out from under her cumbersome burden.

The mat slid forward another foot, and snagged on the gunwale, sea water slopped inboard, ankle-deep around their rubber boots as they strained and heaved at the reluctant mass of coarse fibre.

Some instinct of danger made Nick look up and out to sea. *Warlock* was lying a quarter of a mile farther out in the bay, at the edge of the ice, and beyond her, Nick saw the rearing shape of a big wave alter the line of the horizon. It was merely a forerunner of the truly big waves that the storm was running before her, like hounds before the hunter, but it was big enough to make *Warlock* throw up her stern sharply, and even then the sea creamed over the tug's bows and streamed from her scuppers.

It would hit the exposed and hampered work boat in twenty-five seconds, it would hit her broadside while her bows were held down and anchored by mat and cable. When she swamped, the five men who made up her crew would die within minutes, pulled down by their bulky clothing, frozen by the icy green water.

'Beauty,' Nick's voice was a scream in the microphone, 'heave all – pull, damn you, pull.'

Almost instantly the cable began to run, drawn in by the powerful winch on *Golden Adventurer*'s deck; the strain pulled the work boat down sharply and water cascaded over her gunwale.

Nick seized one of the oaken oars and thrust it under the mat at the point where it was snagged, and using it as a lever he threw all his weight upon it.

'Lend a hand,' he yelled at the man beside him, and he strained until he felt his vision darkening and the fibres of his back-muscles creaking and popping.

The work boat was swamping, they were almost knee-deep now and the wave raced down on on them. It came with a great silent rush of irresistible power, lifting the mass of broken ice and tossing it carelessly aside without a check.

Suddenly, the snag cleared and the whole lumpy massive weight of oakum slid overboard. The work boat bounded away, relieved of her intolerable burden, and Nick windmilled frantically with both arms to get the helmsman to bring her bows round to the wave.

They went up the wave with a gut-swooping rush that threw them down on to the floorboards of the half-flooded work boat, and then crashed over the crest.

Behind them the wave slogged into *Golden Adventurer*'s stern, and shot up it with an explosion of white and furious water that turned to white driven spray in the wind.

The helmsman already had the work boat pushing heavily through the pack-ice, back towards the waiting *Warlock*.

'Stop,' Nick signalled him. 'Back up.'

Already he was struggling out of his hood and oilskins, as he staggered back to the stern.

He shouted in the helmsman's face, 'I'm going down to check,' and he saw the disbelieving, almost pleading, expression on the man's face. He wanted to get out of there now, back to the safety of *Warlock*, but relentlessly Nick resettled the diving helmet and connected his air hose.

The collision mat was floating hard against *Golden Adventurer*'s side, buoyant with trapped air among the mass of wiry fibre.

Nick positioned himself beneath it, twenty feet from the maelstrom created by the gashed steel.

It took him only a few seconds to ensure that the cable was free, and he blessed Beauty Baker silently for stopping the winch immediately it had pulled the mat free of the work boat. Now he could direct the final task.

'She's looking good,' he told Baker. 'But take her up slowly, fifty feet a minute on the winch.'

'Fifty feet, it is,' Baker confirmed.

And slowly the bobbing mat was drawn down below the surface.

'Good, keep it at that.'

It was like pressing a field-dressing into an open bleeding wound. The outside pressure of water drove it deep into the gash, while from the inside the two-inch cable plugged it deeper into place. The wound was staunched almost instantly and Nick finned down, and swam carefully over it.

The deadly suck and blow of high pressure through the gap was killed now, and he detected only the lightest movement of water around the edges of the mat; but the oakum fibres would swell now they were submerged and, within hours the plug would be watertight.

'It's done,' said Nick into his microphone. 'Hold a twenty-ton pull on the cable – and you can start your pumps and suck the bitch clean.'

It was a measure of his stress and relief and fatigue that Nick called that beautiful ship a bitch, and he regretted the word as it was spoken.

Nick craved sleep, every nerve, every muscle shrieked for surcease, and in his bathroom mirror his eyes were inflamed, angry with salt and wind and cold; the smears of exhaustion that underlined them were as lurid as the fresh bruises and abrasions that covered his shoulders and thighs and ribs.

His hands shook in a mild palsy with the need for rest and his legs could hardly carry him as he forced himself back to *Warlock*'s navigation bridge.

'Congratulations, sir,' said David Allen, and his admiration was transparent.

'How's the glass, David?' Nick asked, trying to keep the weariness from showing.

'994 and dropping, sir.'

Nick looked across at *Golden Adventurer*. Below that dingy low sky, she stood like a pier, unmoved by the big swells that marched on her in endless ranks, and she shrugged aside each burst of spray, hard aground and heavy with the water in her womb. However, that water was being flung from her, in solid white sheets.

Baker's big centrifugals were running at full power, and from both her port and starboard quarters the water poured. It looked as though the flood gates had been opened on a concrete dam, so powerful was the rush of expelled water.

The oil and diesel mixed with that discharge formed a sullen, iridescent slick around her, sullying the ice and the pebble beach on which she lay. The wind caught the jets from the pump outlets and tore them away in glistening plumes, like great ostrich feathers of spray.

'Chief,' Nick called the ship. 'What's your discharge rate?'

'We are moving nigh on five hundred thousand gallons an hour.'

'Call me as soon as she alters her trim,' he said, and then glanced up at the pointer of the anemometer above the control panel. The wind force was riding eight now, but he had to blink his stinging swollen eyes to read the scale.

'David,' he said, and he could hear the hoarseness in his voice, the flat dead tone. It will be four hours before she will be light enough to make an attempt to haul her off, but I want you to put the main towing-cable on board her and make fast, so we will be ready when she is.'

'Sir.'

'Use a rocket-line,' said Nick, and then stood dumbly, trying to think of the other orders he must give, but his brain was blank.

'Are you all right, sir?' David asked with quick concern, and immediately Nick felt the prick of annoyance. He had never wanted sympathy in his life, and he found his voice again. But he stopped the sharp words that came so quickly to his lips.

'You know what to do, David. I won't give you any other advice.' He turned like a drunkard towards his quarters. 'Call me when you've done it, or if Baker reports alteration of trim – or if anything else changes, anything, anything at all, you understand.'

He made it to the cabin before his knees buckled and he dropped his terry robe as he toppled backwards on to his bunk.

At 60° south latitude, there runs only the sea-lane that circumnavigates the entire globe, unbroken by any land mass. This wide girdle of open water runs south of Cape Horn and Australasia and the Cape of Good Hope, and it has the fearsome reputation of breeding the wildest weather on earth. It is the meeting-ground of two vast air masses, the cold slumping Antarctic air, and the warmer, more buoyant airs of the sub-tropics. These are flung together by the centrifugal forces generated by the earth as it revolves on its own axis, and their movement is further complicated by the enormous torque of the coriolis force. As they strike each other, the opposing air masses split into smaller fragments that retain their individual characteristics. They begin to revolve upon themselves, gigantic whirlpools of tortured air, and as they advance, so they gain in strength and power and velocity.

The high-pressure system which had brought that ominously calm and silken weather to Cape Alarm, had bounced the pressure right up to 1035 millibars, while the great depression which pursued it so closely and swiftly had a centre pressure as low as 985 millibars. Such a sharp contrast meant that the winds along the pressure-gradient were ferocious.

The depression itself was almost fifteen hundred miles across its circumference, and it reached up to the high troposphere, thirty thousand feet above the level of the sea. The mighty winds it contained reached right off the maximum of the Beaufort scale of force twelve, gusting 120 miles an hour and more. They roared unfettered upon a terrible sea, unchecked by the bulwark of any land mass, nothing in their path, but the sudden jagged barrier of Cape Alarm.

While Nicholas Berg slept the deathlike sleep of utter exhaustion, and Beauty Baker tended his machines, driving them to their limits in an effort to pump *Golden Adventurer* free of her burden of salt water, the storm rushed down upon them.

When her knock was unanswered, Samantha stood uncertainly, balancing the heavy tray against the *Warlock*'s extravagant action as she rode the rising swells at the entrance to the bay.

Her uncertainty lasted not more than three seconds, for she was a lady given to swift decisions. She tried the door-latch and when it turned, she pushed it open slowly enough to warn anybody on the far side, and stepped into the Captain's day cabin.

'He ordered food,' she justified her intrusion, and closed the door behind her, glancing swiftly around the empty cabin. It had been furnished in the high style of the old White Star liners. Real rosewood panelling and the couch and chairs were in rich brown calf hide, polished and buttoned, while the deck was carpeted in thick shaggy wool, the colour of tropical forest leaves.

Samantha placed the tray on the table that ran below the starboard portholes, and she called softly. There was no reply, and she stepped to the open doorway into the night cabin.

A white terry robe lay in a heap in the centre of the deck, and she thought for one disturbing moment that the body on the bed was naked, but then she saw he wore a thin pair of white silk boxer shorts.

'Captain Berg,' she called again, but softly enough not to disturb him, and with a completely feminine gesture picked up the robe from the floor, folded it and dropped it over a chair, moving forward at the same time until she stood beside his bunk.

She felt a quick flare of concern when she saw the bruises which stood out so vividly on the smooth pale skin, and concern turned to dismay when she realized how he lay like a dead man, his legs trailing over the edge of the bunk and his body twisted awkwardly, one arm thrown back over his shoulder and his head lolling from side to side as *Warlock* rolled.

She reached out quickly and touched his cheek, experiencing a lift of real relief as she felt the warmth of his flesh and saw his eyelids quiver at her touch.

Gently she lifted his legs and he rolled easily on to his side, exposing the sickening abrasion that wrapped itself angrily across back and shoulder. She touched it with a light exploring fingertip and knew that it needed attention, but she sensed that rest was what he needed more.

She stood back and for long seconds gave herself over to the pleasure of looking at him. His body was fined down, he carried no fat on his belly or flanks; clearly she could see the rack of his ribs below the skin, and the muscles of his arms and legs were smooth but well-defined, a body that had been cared for and honed by hard exercise. Yet there was a certain denseness to it, that thickening of shoulder and neck, and the distinctive hair patterns of the mature man.

It might not have the grace and delicacy of the boys she had known, yet it was more powerful than that of even the strongest of the young men who had until then filled her world. She thought of one of them whom she had believed she loved. They had spent two months in Tahiti together on the same field expedition. She had surfed with him, danced and drunk wine, worked and slept sixty consecutive days and nights with him; in the same period they had become engaged to marry, and had argued, and parted, with surprisingly little regret on her part – but he had had the most beautiful tanned and sculptured body she had ever known. Now, looking at the sleeping figure on the bunk, she knew that even he would not have been able to match this man in physical determination and strength.

Angel had been right. It was the power that attracted her so strongly. The powerful, rangy body with the dark coarse hair covering his chest and exploding in flak bursts in his armpits – this, together with the power of his presence.

She had never known a man like this, he filled her with a sense of awe. It was not only the legend that surrounded him, nor the formidable list of his accomplishments that Angel had recounted for her, nor yet was it only the physical strength which he had just demonstrated while the entire crew of *Warlock*, she among them, had watched and listened avidly over the VHF relay. She leaned over him again, and she saw that even in repose, his jawline was hard and uncompromising, and the little creases and lines and marks that life had chiselled into his face, around the eyes at the corners of the mouth, heightened the effect of power and determination, the face of a man who dictated his own terms to life.

She wanted him, Angel was right, oh God, how she wanted him! They said there was no love at first sight – they had to be mad.

She turned away and unfolded the eiderdown from the foot of the bunk, spreading it over him, and then once again she stooped and gently lifted the fall of thick dark hair from his forehead, smoothing it back with a maternally protective gesture.

Although he had slept on while she lifted and covered him, strangely this lightest of touches brought him to the edge of consciousness and he sighed and twisted, then whispered hoarsely, 'Chantelle, is that you?'

Samantha recoiled at the bitter sharp pang of jealousy with which another woman's name stabbed her. She turned away and left him, but in the day cabin she paused again beside his desk.

There were a few small personal items thrown carelessly on the leather-bound blotter

– a gold money clip holding a mixed sheath of currency notes, five pounds sterling, fifty US dollars, Deutschmarks and francs, a gold Rolex Oyster perpetual watch, a gold Dunhill lighter with a single white diamond set in it, and a billfold of the smoothest finest calf leather. They described clearly the man who owned them and, feeling like a thief, she picked up the billfold and opened it.

There were a dozen cards in their little plastic envelopes, American Express, Diners, Bank American, Carte Blanche, Hertz No. 1, Pan Am VIP and the rest. But opposite them was a colour photograph. Three people: a man, Nicholas in a cable-stitch jersey, his face bronzed, his hair wind-ruffled; a small boy in a yachting jacket with a curly mop of hair and solemn eyes above a smiling mouth – and a woman. She was probably one of the most beautiful women Samantha had ever seen, and she closed the billfold, replaced it carefully, and quietly left the cabin.

David Allen called the Captain's suite for three minutes without an answer, slapping his open palm on the mahogany chart table with impatience and staring through the navigation windows at the spectacle of a world gone mad.

For almost two hours, the wind had blown steadily from the north-west at a little over thirty knots, and although the big lumpy seas still tumbled into the mouth of the bay, *Warlock* had ridden them easily, even connected, as she was, to *Golden Adventurer* by the main tow-cable.

David had put a messenger over the liner's stern, firing the nylon line from a rocket gun, and Baker's men had retrieved the line and winched across first the carrier wire and then the main cable itself.

Warlock had let the main cable be drawn out of her by *Adventurer*'s winches, slowly revolving off the great winch drums in the compartment under the tug's stern deck, out through the cable ports below the after navigation bridge where David stood controlling each inch of run and play with light touches on the controls.

A good man could work that massive cable like a fly-fisherman playing a big salmon in the turbulent water of a mountain torrent, letting it slip against the clutchplates, or run free, or recover slack, bringing it up hard and fast under a pull of five hundred tons – or, in dire emergency, he could hit the shear button, and snip through the flexible steel fibre, instantaneously relinquishing the tow, possibly saving the tug itself from being pulled under or being rushed by the vessel it was towing.

It had taken an hour of delicate work, but now the tow was in place, a double yoke made fast to *Golden Adventurer*'s main deck bollards, one on her starboard and one on her port stern quarters.

The yoke was Y-shaped, drooping over the high stern to join at the white nylon spring, three times the thickness of a man's thigh and with the elasticity to absorb sudden shock which might have snapped rigid steel cable. From the yoke connection, the single main cable looped back to the tug.

David Allen was lying back a thousand yards from the shore, holding enough strain on the tow-cable to prevent it sagging to touch and possibly snag on the unknown bottom. He was holding his station with gentle play on the pitch and power of the twin screws, and checking his exact position against the electronic dials which gave him his speed across the ground in both directions, accurate to within a foot a minute.

It was all nicely under control, and every time he glanced up at the liner, the discharge of water still boiled from her pump outlets.

Half an hour previously, he had been unable to contain his impatience, for he knew with a seaman's deep instinct what was coming down upon them out of the dangerous quadrant of the wind. He had called Baker to ask how the work on the liner was progressing. It had been a mistake.

'You've got nothing better to do than call me out of the engine room to ask about my piles, and the FA Cup final? I'll tell you when I'm ready, believe me, sonny, I'll call you. If you are bored, go down and give Angel a kiss, but for God's sake, leave me alone.'

Beauty Baker was working with two of his men in that filthy, freezing steel box deep down in the liner's stern that housed the emergency steering-gear. The rudder was right across at full port lock. Unless he could get power on the steering machinery, she would be almost unmanageable, once she was under tow, especially if she was pulled off stern first. It was vital that the big ship was responding to her helm when *Warlock* tried to haul her off.

Baker cursed and cajoled the greasy machinery, knocking loose a flap of thick white skin from his knuckles when a spanner slipped, but working on grimly without even bothering to lift the injury to his mouth to suck away the welling blood. He let it drop on to the spanner and thicken into a sticky jelly, swearing softly but viciously as he concentrated all his skills on the obdurate steel mass of the steering gear. He knew every bit as well as the First Officer what was coming down upon them.

The wind had dropped to a gentle force four, a moderate steady breeze that blew for twenty minutes, just long enough for the crests of the waves to stop breaking over on themselves. Then slowly, it veered north – and without any further warning, it was upon them.

It came roaring like a ravening beast, lifting the surface of the sea away in white sheets of spray that looked as though red-hot steel had been quenched in it. It laid *Warlock* right over, so that her port rail went under and she was flung up so harshly on her main cable that her stern was pulled down sharply, water pouring in through her stern scuppers.

It took David by surprise, so that she paid off dangerously before he could slam open the port throttle and throw the starboard screw into full reverser thrust. As she came up, he hit the call to the Captain's suite, watching with rising disbelief as the mad world dissolved around him.

Nick heard the call from far away, it only just penetrated to his fatigue-drugged brain, and he tried to respond, but it felt as though his body was crushed under an enormous weight and that his brain was slow and sluggish as a hibernating reptile.

The buzzer insisted, a tinny, nagging whine and he tried to force his eyes open, but they would not respond. Then dimly, but deeply, he felt the wild anguished action of his ship and the tumult that he believed at first was in his own ears, but was the violent uproar of the storm about the tug's superstructure.

He forced himself up on one elbow, and his body ached in every joint. He still could not open his eyes but he groped for the handset.

'Captain to the after bridge!' He could hear something in David Allen's voice that forced him to his feet.

When Nick staggered on to the after navigation bridge, the First Officer turned gratefully to him.

'Thank God you've come, sir.'

The wind had taken the surface off the sea, had stripped it away, tearing each wave to a shrieking fog of white spray and mingling it with the sleet and snow that drove horizontally across the bay.

Nick glanced once at the dial of the wind anemometer, and then discounted the reading. The needle was stuck at the top of the scale. It made no sense, a wind-speed of 120 miles an hour was too much to accept, the instrument had been damaged by the initial gusts of this wind, and he refused to believe it; to do so now would be to admit disaster, for nobody could salvage an ocean-going liner in wind velocities right off the Beaufort scale.

Warlock stood on her tail, like a performing dolphin begging for a meal, as the cable brought her up short and the bridge deck became a vertical cliff down which Nick was hurled. He crashed into the control panel and clung for purchase to the foul-weather rail.

'We'll have to shear the cable and stand out to sea.' David Allen's voice was pitched too high and too loud, even for the tumult of the wind and the storm.

There were men on board *Golden Adventurer*, Baker and sixteen others, Nick thought swiftly, and even her twin anchors could not be trusted to hold in this.

Nick clung to the rail and peered out into the storm. Frozen spray and sleet and impacted snow drove on the wind, coming in with the force of buckshot fired at point-blank range, cracking into the armoured glass of the bridge and building up in thick clots and lumps that defeated the efforts of the spinning 'clear vision' panels.

He looked across a thousand yards and the hull of the liner was just visible, a denser area in the howling, swirling, white wilderness.

'Baker?' he asked into the hand microphone. 'What is your position?'

'The wind's got her, she's slewing. The starboard anchor is dragging.' And then, while Nick thought swiftly, 'You'll not be able to take us off in this.' It was a flat statement, an acceptance of the fact that the destinies of Baker and his sixteen men were inexorably linked to that of the doomed ship.

'No,' Nick agreed. 'We won't be able to get you off.' To approach the stricken ship was certain disaster for all of them.

'Shear the cable and stand off,' Baker advised. 'We'll try to get ashore as she breaks up.' Then, with a hangman's chuckle, he went on, 'Just don't forget to come and fetch us when the weather moderates – that is if there is anybody to fetch.'

Abruptly Nick's anger came to the surface through the layers of fatigue, anger at the knowledge that all he had risked and suffered was now to be in vain, that he was to lose *Golden Adventurer*, and probably with her sixteen men, one of whom had become a friend.

'Are you ready to heave on the anchor winches?' he asked. 'We are going to pull the bitch off.'

'Jesus!' said Baker. 'She's still half flooded –'

'We will have a lash at it, cobber,' said Nick quietly.

'The steering-gear is locked, you won't be able to control her. You'll lose *Warlock* as well as –' but Nicholas cut Baker short.

'Listen, you stupid Queensland sheep-shagger, get on to those winches.' As he said it, *Golden Adventurer* disappeared, her bulk blotted out completely by the solid, white curtains of the blizzard.

'Engine room,' Nick spoke crisply to the Second Engineer. 'Disengage the override, and give me direct control of both power and pitch.'

'Control transferred to bridge, sir,' the Engineer confirmed, and Nick touched the shining stainless-steel levers with fingers as sensitive as those of a concert pianist. *Warlock*'s response was instantaneous. She pivoted, shrugging aside a green slithering burst of water which came in over her shoulder and thundered down the side of her superstructure.

'Anchor winches manned.' Beauty Baker's tone was almost casual.

'Stand by,' said Nick, and felt his way through that white inferno. It was impossible to maintain visual reference, the entire world was white and swirling, even the surface of the sea was gone in torn streamers of white; the very pull of gravity, that should have defined even a simple up or down, was confused by the violent pitch and roll of the deck.

Nick felt his exhausted brain begin to lurch dizzily in the first attacks of vertigo. Swiftly he switched his attention to the big compass and the heading indicator.

'David,' he said, 'take the wheel.' He wanted somebody swift and bright at the helm now.

Warlock plunged suddenly, so viciously that Nick's bruised ribs were brought in brutal contact with the edge of the control console. He grunted involuntarily with the pain. *Warlock* was feeling her cable, she had come up hard.

'Starboard ten,' said Nick to David, bringing her bows up into that hideous wind.

'Chief,' he spoke into the microphone, his voice still ragged with the pain in his chest. 'Haul starboard winch, full power.'

'Full power starboard.'

Nick slid pitch control to fully fine, and then slowly nudged open the throttles, bringing in twenty-two thousand horse-power.

Held by her tail, driven by the great wind, and tortured by the sea, lashed by her own enourmous propellers, *Warlock* went berserk. She corkscrewed and porpoised to her very limits, every frame in her hull shook with the vibration of her screws as her propellers burst out of the surface and spun wildly in the air.

Nick had to clench his jaws as the vibration threatened to crack his teeth, and when he glanced across at the forward and lateral speed-indicators, he saw that David Allen's face was icy white and set like that of a corpse.

Warlock was slewing down on the wind, describing a slow left-hand circle at the limit of the cable as the engine torque and the wind took her around.

'Starboard twenty,' Nick snapped, correcting the turn, and despite the rigour of his features, David Allen's response was instantaneous.

'Twenty degrees of starboard wheel on, sir.'

Nick saw the lateral drift stop on the ground speed-indicator, and then with a wild lurch of elation he saw the forward speed-indicator flicked into green. Its electronic digital read out, changing swiftly – they were moving forward at 150 feet a minute.

'We are moving her,' Nick cried aloud, and he snatched up the microphone.

'Full power both winches.'

'Both full and holding,' answered Baker immediately.

And Nick glanced back at the forward speed across the ground, 150, 110, 75 feet a minute, *Warlock*'s forward impetus slowed, and Nick realized with a slide of dismay that it was merely the elasticity of the nylon spring that had given them that reading. The spring was stretching out to its limit.

For two or three seconds, the dial recorded a zero rate of speed.*Warlock* was standing still, the cable drawn out to the full limit of her strength, then abruptly the dial flicked into vivid red; they were gong backwards, as the nylon spring exerted pressures beyond that of the twin diesels and the big bronze screws – *Warlock* was being dragged back towards that dreadful shore.

For another five minutes, Nick kept both clenched fists on the control levers, pressing them with all his strength to the limit of their travel, sending the great engines shrieking, driving the needles up around the dials, deep into the red 'never exceed' sectors.

He felt tears of anger and frustration scalding his swollen eyelids, and the ship shuddered and shook and screamed under him, her torment transmitted through the soles of his feet and the palms of his hands.

Warlock was held down by cable and power, so she could not rise to meet the seas that came out of the roaring whiteness. They tumbled aboard her, piling up on each other, so she burrowed deeper and more dangerously.

'For God's sake, sir,' David Allen was no longer able to contain himself. His eyes looked huge in his bone-white face. 'You'll drive her clean under.'

'Baker,' Nick ignored his Mate, 'Are you gaining?'

'No recovery either winch,' Beauty told him. 'she is not moving.'

Nick pulled back the stainless steel levers, the needles sank swiftly back around their dials, and *Warlock* reacted gratefully, shaking herself free of the piled waters.

'You'll have to shear the tow.' Baker's disembodied voice was muted by the clamour of the storm. 'We'll take our chances, sport.'

Beside him, David Allen reached for the red-painted steel box that housed the shear button. It was protected by the box from accidental usage; David Allen opened the box and looked expectantly, almost pleadingly at Nick.

'Belay that!' Nick snarled at him, and then to Baker, 'I'm shortening tow. Be ready to haul again, when I am in position.'

David Allen stared at him, his right hand still on the open lid of the red box.

'Close that bloody thing,' Nick said, and turned to the main cable controls. He moved the green lever to reverse, and felt the vibration in the deck as below him in the main cable room the big drums began to revolve, drawing the thick ice-encrusted cable up over *Warlock*'s stern.

Fighting every inch of the way like a wild horse on a head halter, *Warlock* was drawn in cautiously by her own winches, and the officers watched in mounting horror as out of the white terror of the blizzard emerged the mountainous ice-covered bulk of *Golden Adventurer*.

She was so close that the main cable no longer dipped below the surface of the sea, but ran directly from the liner's stern to the tug's massive fairleads on her stern quarter.

'Now we can see what we are doing,' Nick told them grimly. He could see now that much of *Warlock*'s power had been wasted by not exerting a pull on exactly the same plane as *Golden Adventurer*'s keel. He had been disoriented in the white-out of the blizzard, and had allowed *Warlock* to pull at an angle. It would not happen now.

'Chief,' he said. 'Pull, pull all, pull until she bursts her guts!' And again he slid the throttle handles fully home.

Warlock flung up against the elastic yoke, and Nick saw the water spurt from the woven fibres and turn instantly to ice crystals as it was whipped away on the shrieking wind.

'She's not moving, sir,' David cried beside him.

'No recovery either winch,' Baker confirmed almost immediately. 'She's solid!'

'Too much water still in her,' said David, and Nick turned on him as though to strike him to the deck.

'Give me the wheel,' he said, his voice cracking with his anger and frustration.

With both engines boiling the sea to white foam, and roaring like dying bulls, Nick swung the wheel to full port lock.

Wildly *Warlock* dug her shoulder in, water pouring on board her as she rolled, instantly Nick spun the wheel to full starboard lock and she lurched against the tow, throwing an extra ton of pressure on to it.

Even above the storm, they heard *Golden Adventurer* groan, the steel of her hull protesting at the weight of water in her and the intolerable pressure of the anchor winches and *Warlock*'s tow cable.

The groan became a crackling hiss as the pebble bottom gave and moved under her.

'Christ, she's coming!' shrieked Baker, and Nick swung her to full port lock again, swinging *Warlock* into a deep trough between waves, then a solid ridge of steaming water buried her, and Nick was not certain she could survive that press of furious sea. It came green and slick over the superstructure and she shuddered wearily, gone slow and unwieldy. Then she lifted her bows and, like a spaniel, shook herself free, becoming again quick and light.

'Pull, my darling, pull,' Nick pleaded with her.

With a slow reluctant rumble, *Golden Adventurer*'s hull began to slide over the holding, clinging bottom.

'Both winches recovering,' Baker howled gleefully, and *Warlock*'s ground speed-indicator flicked into the green, its little angular figures changing in twinkling electronic progression as *Warlock* gathered way.

They all saw *Golden Adventurer*'s stern swinging to meet the next great ridge of water as it burst around her. She was floating, and for moments Nick was paralysed by the wonder of seeing that great and beautiful ship come to life again, become a living, vital sea creature as she took the seas and rose to meet them.

'We've done it, Christ, we've done it!' howled Baker, but it was too soon for self-congratulation. As *Golden Adventurer* came free of the ground and gathered stern-way under *Warlock*'s tow, so her rudder bit and swung her tall stern across the wind.

She swung, exposing the enormous windage of her starboard side to the full force of the storm. It was like setting a main sail, and the wind took her down swiftly on the rocky headland with its sentinel columns that guarded the entrance to the bay.

Nick's first instinct was to try and hold her off, to oppose the force of the wind directly and he flung *Warlock* into the task, relying on her great diesels and the two anchors to keep the liner from going ashore again – but the wind toyed with them, it ripped the anchors out of the pebble bottom and *Warlock* was drawn stern first through the water, straight down on the jagged rock of the headland.

'Chief, get those anchors up,' Nick snapped into the microphone. 'They'll never hold in this.'

Twenty years earlier, bathing off a lonely beach in the Seychelles, Nick had been caught out of his depth by one of those killer currents that flow around the headlands of oceanic islands, and it had sped him out into the open sea so that within minutes the silhouette of the land was low and indistinct on his watery horizon. He had fought that current, swimming directly against it, and it had nearly killed him. Only in the last stages of exhaustion had he begun to think, and instead of battling it, he had ridden the current, angling slowly across it, using its impetus rather than opposing it.

The lesson he had learned that day was well remembered, and as he watched Baker bring *Golden Adventurer*'s dripping anchors out of the wild water he was driving *Warlock* hard, bringing her around on her cable so the wind was no longer in her teeth, but over her stern quarter.

Now the wind and *Warlock*'s screws were no longer opposed, but *Warlock* was pulling two points off the wind, as fine a course as Nick could judge barely to clear the most seaward of the rocky sentinels; now the liner's locked rudder was holding her steady into the wind – but opposing *Warlock*'s attempt to angle her away from the land.

It was a problem of simple vectors of force, that Nick tried to work out in his head and prove in physical terms, as he delicately judged the angle of his tow and the direction of the wind, balancing them against the tremendous leverage of the liner's locked rudder, the rudder which was dragging her suicidally down upon the land.

Grimly, he stared ahead to where the black rock cliffs were still hidden in the white nothingness. They were invisible, but their presence was recorded on the cluttered screen of the radar repeater. With both wind and engines driving them, their speed was too high, and if *Golden Adventurer* went on to the cliffs like this, her hull would shatter like a water melon hurled against a brick wall.

It was another five minutes before Nick was absolutely certain they would not make it. They were only two miles off the cliffs now, he glanced again at the radar screen, and they would have to drag *Golden Adventurer* at least half a mile across the wind to clear the land. They just were not going to make it.

Helplessly, Nick stood and peered into the storm, waiting for the first glimpse of black rock through the swirling eddies of snow and frozen spray, and he had never felt more tired and unmanned in his entire life as he moved to the shear button ready to cut *Golden Adventurer* loose and let her go to her doom.

His officers were silent and tense around him, while under his feet *Warlock* shuddered and buffeted wildly, driven to her mortal limits by the sea and her own engines, but still the land sucked at them.

'Look!' David Allen shouted suddenly, and Nick spun to the urgency in his voice.

For a moment he did not understand what was happening. He knew only that the shape of *Golden Adventurer*'s stern was altered subtly.

'The rudder,' shouted David Allen again. And Nick saw it revolving slowly on its stock as the ship lifted on another big sea.

Almost immediately, he felt *Warlock* making offing from under that lee shore, and he swung her up another point into the wind, *Golden Adventurer* answering her tow with a more docile air, and still the rudder revolved slowly.

'I've got power on the emergency steering gear now,' said Baker.

'Rudder amidships,' Nick ordered.

'Amidships it is,' Baker repeated, and now he was pulling her out stern first, almost at right angles across the wind.

Through the white inferno appeared the dim snow-blurred outline of the rock sentinels, and the sea broke upon them like the thunder of the heavens.

'God, they are close,' whispered David Allen. So close that they could feel the backlash of the gale as it rebounded from the tall rock walls, moderating the tremendous force that was bearing them down – moderating just enough to allow them to slide past the three hungry rocks, and before them lay three thousand miles of wild and tumultuous water, all of it open sea room.

'We made it. This time we really made it,' said Baker, as though he did not believe it was true, and Nick pulled back the throttle controls taking the intolerable strain off her engines before they tore themselves to pieces.

'Anchors and all,' Nick replied. It was a point of honour to retrieve even the anchors. They had taken her off clean and intact – anchors and all.

'Chief,' he said, 'instead of sitting there hugging yourself, how about pumping her full of Tannerax?' The anti-corrosive chemical would save her engines and much of her vital equipment from further sea-water damage, adding enormously to her salvaged value.

'You just never let up, do you?' Baker answered accusingly.

'Don't you believe it,' said Nick, he felt stupid and frivolous with exhaustion and triumph. Even the storm that still roared about them seemed to have lost its murderous intensity. 'Right now I'm going down to my bunk to sleep for twelve hours – and I'll kill anybody who tries to wake me.'

He hung the handmike on its bracket and put his hand on David Allen's shoulder. He squeezed once, and said:

'You did well – you all did very well. Now take her, Number One, and look after her.'

Then he stumbled from the bridge.

It was eight days before they saw the land again. They rode out the storm in the open sea, eight days of unrelenting tension and heart-breaking labour.

The first task was to move the two-cable to *Golden Adventurer*'s bows. In that sea, the transfer took almost 24 hours, and three abortive attempts before they had her head-on to the wind. Now she rode more easily, and *Warlock* had merely to hang on like a drogue, using full power only when one of the big icebergs came within dangerous range, and it was necessary to draw her off.

However, the tension was always there and Nick spent most of those days on the bridge, watchful and worried, nagged by the fear that the plug in the gashed hull would not hold. Baker used timbers from the ship's store to shore up the temporary patch, but he could not put steel in place while *Golden Adventurer* plunged and rolled in the heavy seas, and Nick could not go aboard to check and supervise the work.

Slowly, the great wheel of low pressure revolved over them, the winds changed direction, backing steadily into the west, as the epicentre marched on down the sea lane towards Australasia – and at last it had passed.

Now *Warlock* could work up towing speed. Even in those towering glassy swells of black water that the storm had left them as a legacy, she was able to make four knots.

Then one clear and windy morning under a cold yellow sun, she brought *Golden Adventurer* into the sheltered waters of Shackleton Bay. It was like a diminutive guide-dog leading a blinded colossus.

As the two ships came up into the still waters under the sheltering arm of the bay, the survivors came down from their encampment to the water's edge, lining the steep black pebble beach, and their cheers and shouts of welcome and relief carried thinly on the wind to the officers on *Warlock*'s bridge.

Even before the liner's twin anchors splashed into the clear green water, Captain Reilly's boat was puttering out to *Warlock*, and when he came aboard, his eyes were haunted by the hardship and difficulties of these last days, by the disaster of a lot command and the lives that had been ended with it. But when he shook hands with Nick, his grasp was firm.

'My thanks and congratulations, sir!'

He had known Nicholas Berg as Chairman of Christy Marine, and, as no other, he was aware of the magnitude of this most recent accomplishment. His respect was apparent.

'It's good to see you again,' Nick told him. 'Naturally you have access to my ship's communications to report to your owners.'

Immediately he turned back to the task of manoeuvring *Warlock* alongside, so that steel plate could be swung up from her salvage holds to the liner's deck; it was another hour before Captain Reilly emerged from the radio room.

'Can I offer you a drink, Captain?' Nick led him to his day cabin, and began with tact to deal with the hundred details which had to be settled between them. It was a delicate situation, for Reilly was no longer Master of his own ship. Command had passed to Nicholas as salvage master.

'The accommodation aboard *Golden Adventurer* is still quite serviceable, and, I imagine, a great deal warmer and more comfortable than that occupied by your passengers at present —' Nick made it easier for him while never for a moment letting him lose sight of his command position, and Reilly responded gratefully.

Within half an hour, they had made all the necessary arrangements to transfer the survivors aboard the liner. Levoisin on *La Mouette* had been able to take only one hundred and twenty supernumeraries on board his little tug. The oldest and weakest of them had gone and Christy Marine was negotiating for a charter from Cape Town to Shackleton Bay to take off the rest of them. Now that charter was unnecessary, but the cost of it would form part of Nick's claim for salvage award.

'I won't take more of your time.' Reilly drained his glass and stood. 'You have much to do.'

There were another four days and nights of hard work. Nick went aboard *Golden Adventurer* and saw the cavernous engine room lit by the eye-scorching blue glare of the electric welding flames, as Baker placed his steel over the wound and welded it into place. Even then, neither he nor Nick was satisfied until the new patches had been shored and stiffened with baulks of heavy timber. There was a hard passage through the roaring forties ahead of them, and until they had *Golden Adventurer* safely moored in Cape Town docks, the salvage was incomplete.

They sat side by side among the greasy machinery and the stink of the anti-corrosives, and drank steaming Thermos coffee laced with Bundaberg rum.

'We get this beauty into Duncan Docks – and you are going to be a rich man,' Nick said.

'I've been rich before. With me it never lasts long – and it's always a relief when I've spent the stuff.' Beauty gargled the rum and coffee appreciatively, before he went on, shrewdly. 'So you don't have to worry about losing the best goddamned engineer afloat.'

Nick laughed with delight. Baker had read him accurately. He did not want to lose this man.

Nick left him and went to see to the trim of the liner, studying her carefully and using the experience of the last days to determine her best points of tow, before giving his orders to David Allen to raise her slightly by the head.

Then there was the transfer from the liner's bunkers of sufficient bunker oil to top up *Warlock*'s own tanks against the long tow ahead, and Bach Wackie in Bermuda kept the telex clattering with relays from underwriters and Lloyd's, with the first tentative advances from Christy Marine; already Duncan Alexander was trying out the angles, manoeuvring for a liberal settlement of Nick's claims, without, as he put it, the expense of the arbitration court.

'Tell him I'm going to roast him,' Nick answered with grim relish. 'Remind him that as Chairman of Christy Marine I advised against underwriting our own bottoms – and now I'm going to rub his nose in it.'

The days and nights blurred together, the illusion made complete by the imbalance of time down here in the high latitudes, so that Nick could often believe neither his senses nor his watch when he had been working eighteen hours straight and yet the sun still burned, and his watch told him it was three o'clock in the morning.

Then again, it did not seem part of reality when his senior officers, gathered around the mahogany table in his day cabin, reported that the work was completed – the repairs and preparation, the loading of fuel, the embarkation of passengers and the hundred other details had all been attended to, and *Warlock* was ready to drag her massive charge out into the unpredictable sea, thousands of miles to the southernmost tip of Africa.

Nick passed the cheroot-box around the circle and while the blue smoke clouded the cabin, he allowed them all a few minutes to luxuriate in the feeling of work done, and done well.

'We'll rest the ship's company for twenty-four hours,' he announced in a rush of generosity. 'And take in tow at 0800 hours Monday. I'm hoping for a two speed of six knots – twenty-one days to Cape Town, gentlemen.'

When they rose to leave, David Allen lingered self-consciously. 'The wardroom is arranging a little Christmas celebration tonight, sir, and we would like you to be our guest.'

The wardroom was the junior officers' club from which, traditionally, the Master was excluded. He could enter the small panelled cabin only as an invited guest, but there was no doubt at all about the genuine warmth of the welcome they gave him. Even the Trog was there. They stood and applauded him when he entered, and it was clear that most of them had made an early start on the gin. David Allen made a speech which he read haltingly from a scrap of paper which he tried to conceal in the palm of one hand. It was a speech full of hyperbole, clichés and superlatives, and he was clearly mightily relieved once it was over.

Then Angel brought in a cake he had baked for the occasion. It was iced in the shape of '*Golden Adventurer*', a minor work of art, with the figures '12½%' picked out in gold on its hull, and they applauded him. That 12½% had significance to set them all grinning and exclaiming.

Then they called on Nick to speak, and his style was relaxed and easy. He had them hooting with glee within minutes – a mere mention of the prize money that would be due to them once they brought *Golden Adventurer* into Cape Town had them in ecstasy.

The girl was wedged into a corner, almost swallowed in the knot of young officers who found it necessary to press as closely around her as was possible without actually smothering her.

She laughed with a clear unaffected exuberance, her voice ringing high above the growl of masculine mirth, so that Nick found it difficult not to keep looking across at her.

She wore a dress of green clinging material, and Nick wondered where it had come from, until he remembered that *Golden Adventurer*'s passenger accommodation was intact and that earlier that morning, he had noticed the girl standing beside David Allen in the stern of the work boat as it returned from the liner, with a large suitcase at her feet. She had been to fetch her gear and she probably should have stayed aboard the liner. Nick was pleased she had not.

Nick finished his little speech, having mentioned every one of his officers by name and given to each the praise they deserved, and David Allen pressed another large whisky into his one hand and an inelegant wedge of cake into the other, and then left hurriedly to join the tight circle around the girl. It opened reluctantly, yielding to his seniority and Nick found himself almost deserted.

He watched with indulgence the open competition for her attention. She was shorter than any of them, so Nick saw only the top of that magnificent mane of sun-streaked hair, hair the colour of precious metal that shone as she nodded and tilted her head, catching the overhead lights.

Beauty Baker was on one side of her, dressed in a ready-made suit of shiny imitation sharkskin that made a startling contrast to his plaid shirt and acid-yellow tie; the trousers of the suit needed hoisting every few minutes and his spectacles glittered lustfully as he hung over the girl.

David Allen was close on her other side, blushing pinkly every time she turned to speak to him, plying her with cake and liquor – and Nick found his indulgence turning to irritation.

He was irritated by the presence of a tongue-tied fourth officer who had clearly been delegated to entertain him, and was completely awed by the responsibility. He was irritated by the antics of his senior officers. They were behaving like a troupe of performing seals in their competition for the girl's attention.

For a few moments, the tight circle around her opened, and Nick was left with a few vivid impressions. The green of her dress matched exactly the brilliant sparkling green of her eyes. Her teeth were very white, and her tongue as pink as a cat's when she laughed. She was not the child he had imagined from their earlier encounters; with colour touched to her lips and pearls at her throat, he realized she was in her twenties, early twenties perhaps, but a full woman, nevertheless.

She looked across the wardroom and their eyes met. The laughter stilled on her lips, and she returned his gaze. It was a solemn enigmatic gaze, and he found himself once again regretting his previous rudeness to her. He dropped his gaze from hers and saw now that under the clinging green material, her body was slim and beautifully formed, with a lithe athletic grace. He remembered vividly that one nude glimpse he had been given.

Although the green dress was high-necked, he saw that her breasts were large and pointed, and that they were not trussed by any undergarments; the young shapely flesh was as strikingly arresting as if it had been naked.

It made him angry to see her body displayed in this manner. It did not matter that every young girl in the streets of New York or London went so uncorseted, here it made him angry to see her do the same, and he looked back into her eyes. Something charged there, a challenge perhaps, his own anger reflected? He was not sure. She tilted her head slightly, now it was invitation – or was it? He had known and handled easily so many, many women. Yet this one left him with a feeling of uncertainty, perhaps it was merely her youth, or was it some special quality she possessed? Nicholas Berg was uncertain and he did not relish the feeling.

David Allen hurried to her with another offering, and cut off the gaze that passed between them, and Nick found himself staring at the Chief Officer's slim, boyish back, and listening to the girl's laughter again, sweet and high. But somehow it seemed to be directed tauntingly at Nick, and he said to the young officer beside him,

'Please ask Mr Allen for a moment of his time,' Patently relieved the officer went to fetch him.

'Thank you for your hospitality, David,' said Nick, when he came.

'You aren't going yet, sir?' Nick took a small sadistic pleasure in the Mate's obvious dismay.

He sat at the desk in his day cabin and tried to concentrate. It was the first opportunity he had had to consider the paper work that awaited him. The muted sounds of revelry from the deck below distracted him, and he found himself listening for the sounds of her laughter while he should have been composing his submissions to his London attorneys, which would be taken to the arbitrators of Lloyd's, a document and record of vital importance, the whole basis of his claim against *Golden Adventurer*'s underwriters. And yet he could not concentrate.

He swung his chair away from the desk and began to pace the thick sound-deadening carpet, stopping once to listen again as he heard the girl's voice calling gaily, the words unintelligible, but the tone unmistakable. They were dancing, or playing some raucous game which consisted of a great deal of bumping and thumping and shrieks of laughter.

He began to pace again, and suddenly Nick realized he was lonely. The thought stopped him dead again. He was lonely, and completely alone. It was a disturbing realization, especially for a man who had travelled much of life's journey as a loner. Before it had never troubled him, but now he felt desperately the need for somebody to share his triumph. Triumph it was, of course. Against the most improbable odds, he had snatched spectacular victory, and he crossed slowly to the cabin portholes and looked across the darkened bay to where *Golden Adventurer* lay at anchor, all her lights burning, a gay and festive air about her.

He had been knocked off his perch at the top of the tree, deprived of a life's work, a wife and a son – yet it had taken him only a few short months to clamber back to the top.

With this simple operation, he had transformed Ocean Salvage from a dangerously insecure venture, a tottering cash-starved, problem-hounded long chance, into something of real value. He was off and running again now, with a place to go and the means of getting there. Then why did it suddenly seem of so little worth? He toyed with the idea of returning to the revelry in the wardroom, and grimaced as he imagined the dismay of his officers at the Master's inhibiting intrusion.

He turned away from the porthole and poured whisky into a glass, lit a cheroot and dropped into the chair. The whisky tasted like toothpaste and the cheroot was bitter. He left the glass on his desk and stubbed the cheroot, before he went through on to the navigation bridge.

The night lights were so dim after his brightly lit cabin that he did not notice Graham, the Third Officer, until his eyes adjusted to the ruby glow.

'Good evening, Mr Graham.' He moved to the chart table and checked the log. Graham was hovering anxiously, and Nick searched for something to say.

'Missing the party?' he asked at last.

'Sir.'

It was not a promising conversational opening, and despite his loneliness of a few minutes previously, Nick suddenly wanted to be alone again.

'I will stand the rest of your watch. Go off and enjoy yourself.'

The Third Officer gawped at him.

'You've got three seconds before I change my mind.'

'That's jolly decent of you, sir,' called Graham over his shoulder as he fled.

The party in the wardroom had by now degenerated into open competition for Samantha's attention and approbation.

David Allen, wearing a lampshade on his head and, for some unaccountable reason, with his right hand thrust into his jacket in a Napoleonic gesture, was standing on the wardroom bar counter and declaiming Henry's speech before Agincourt, glossing over the passages which he had forgotten with a 'dum-de-dum'. However, when Tim Graham entered, he became immediately the First Officer. He removed the lampshade and inquired frostily.

'Mr Graham, am I correct in believing that you are officer of the watch? Your station at this moment is on the bridge –'

'The old man came and offered to stand my watch,' said Tim Graham.

'Good Lord!' David replaced his lampshade, and poured a large gin for his Third Officer. 'The old bastard must have come over all soft suddenly.'

Beauty Baker, who was hanging off the wall like a gibbon ape, dropped to his feet and drew himself up with rather unsteady dignity, hitched his trousers and announced ominously,

'If anybody calls the old bastard a bastard, I will personally kick his teeth down his throat.' He swept the wardroom with an eye that was belligerent and truculent, until it alighted on Samantha. Immediately it softened. 'That one doesn't count, Sammy!' he said.

'Of course not,' Samantha agreed. 'You can start again.'

Beauty returned to the starting point of the obstacle course, fortified himself with a draught of rum, pushed up his spectacles with a thumb and spat on his palms.

'One to get ready, two to get steady – and three to be off,' sang out Samantha, and clicked the stopwatch. Beauty Baker swung dizzily from the roof, clawing his way around the wardroom without touching the deck, cheered on by the entire company.

'Eight point six seconds!' Samantha clicked the watch, as he ended up on the bar counter, the finishing post. 'A new world record.'

'A drink for the new world champion.'

'I'm next, time me, Sammy!'

They were like schoolboys. 'Hey, watch me, Sammy!' But after another ten minutes, she handed the stopwatch to Tim Graham, who as a late arrival was still sober.

'I'll be back,' she lied, picked up a plate with a large untouched hunk of Angel's cake upon it and was gone before any of them realized it was happening.

Nick Berg was working over the chart-table, so intent that he was not aware of her for many seconds. In the dramatic lighting of the single overhead lamp, the strength of his features was emphasized. She saw the hard line of his jawbone, the heavy brow and the alert widely spaced set of his eyes. His nose was large and slightly hooked, like that of a plains Indian or a desert Bedouin, and there were lines at the corners of his mouth and around his eyes that were picked out in dark shadow. In his complete absorption with the charts and *Admiralty Pilot*, he had relaxed his mouth from its usual severe line. She saw now that the lips were full without being fleshy, and there was a certain sensitivity and voluptuousness there that she had not noticed before.

She stood quietly, enchanted with him, until he looked up suddenly, catching the rapt expression upon her face.

She tried not to appear flustered, but even in her own ears her voice was breathless.

'I'm sorry to disturb you. I brought some cake for Timmy Graham.'

'I sent him below to join the party.'

'Oh, I didn't notice him. I thought he was here.'

She made no move to leave, holding the plate in one hand, and they were silent a moment longer.

'I don't suppose I could interest you in a slice? It's going begging.'

'Share it,' he suggested, and she came to the chart-table.

'I owe you an apology,' he said, and was immediately aware of the harshness in his own voice. He hated to apologize, and she sensed it.

'I picked a bad moment,' she said, and broke off a piece of the cake. 'But this seems a better time. Thank you again, and I'm sorry for all the trouble I caused. I understand now that it nearly cost you the *Golden Adventurer*.'

They both turned to look out of the big armoured glass windows to where she lay.

'She is beautiful, isn't she?' said Nick, and his voice had lost its edge.

'Yes, she's beautiful,' Samantha agreed, and suddenly they were very close in the intimate ruddy glow of the night lights.

He began to talk, stiffly and self-consciously at first, but she drew him on, and with secret joy, she sensed him warming and relaxing. Only then did she begin to put her own ideas forward.

Nick was surprised and a little disconcerted at the depth of her view, and at her easy coherent expression of ideas, for he was still very much aware of her youth. Her had expected the giddiness and the giggle, the shallowness and uninformed self-interest of immaturity, but it was not there, and suddenly the difference in their ages was of no importance. They were very close in the night, touching only with their minds, but becoming each minute so much more closely involved in their ideas that time had no significance.

They spoke about the sea, for they were both creatures of that element and as they discovered this, so their mutual delight in each other grew.

From below came the faint unmelodious strains of Beauty Baker leading the ship's officers in a chorus of:

'- The working class can kiss my arse
I've got my 12½% at last!'

And at another stage in the evening, a very worried Tim Graham appeared on the bridge and blurted out,

'Captain, sir, Doctor Silver is missing. She's not in her cabin and we have searched —' He saw her then, sitting in the Captain's chair and his worry turned to consternation. 'Oh, I see. We didn't know – I mean we didn't expect – I'm sorry, sir. Excuse me, sir. Goodnight, sir.' And again he fled the bridge.

'Doctor?' Nick asked.

'I'm afraid so,' she smiled, and then went on to talk about the university, explaining her research project, and the other work she had in mind. Nicholas listened silently, for like all highly competitive and successful men, he respected achievement and ambition.

The chasm that he imagined existed between them shrank rapidly, so that it was an intrusion when the eight-to-twelve watch ended, and the relief brought other human presence to the bridge, shattering the fragile mood they had created around themselves, and denying them further excuse for remaining together.

'Goodnight, Captain Berg,' she said.

'Goodnight, Doctor Silver,' he answered reluctantly. Until that night, he had not even known her name, and there was so much more he wanted to know now, but she was gone from the bridge; as he entered his own suite, Nick's earlier loneliness returned, but with even more poignancy.

During the long day of getting *Golden Adventurer* under tow, the hours of trim and accommodation to the sea, until she was following meekly settling down to the long journey ahead, Nick thought of the girl at unlikely moments; but when he changed his usual routine and dined in the saloon rather than his own cabin, she was surrounded by a solidly attentive phalanx of young men, and, with a small shock of self-honesty, Nick realized that he was actually jealous of them. Twice during the meal, he had to suppress the sharp jibes that came to his lips, and would have plunged the unfortunate recipient into uncomprehending confusion.

Nick ate no desert and took coffee alone in his day cabin. He might have relished Beauty Baker's company, but the Australian was aboard *Golden Adventurer*, working on her main engines. Then, despite the tensions and endeavours of the day, his bunk had no attractions for him. He glanced at the clock on the panelled bulkhead above his desk and saw that it was a few minutes after eight o'clock.

On impulse he went through to the navigation bridge, and Tim Graham leapt guiltily to his feet. He had been sitting in the master's chair, a liberty which deserved at the least a sharp reprimand, but Nick pretended not to notice and made a slow round of the bridge, checking every detail from the cable tensions of the tow and power settings of *Warlock*'s engines, to the riding lights on both ships and the last log entry.

'Mr Graham,' he said, and the young officer stiffened to attention like the victim before a firing squad, 'I will stand this watch – you may go and get some dinner.'

The Third Officer was so thunderstruck that he needed a large gin before he could bring himself to tell the wardroom of his good fortune.

Samantha did not look up from the board but moved a bishop flauntingly across the front of David Allen's queen, and when David pounced on it with a gurgle of glee, she unleashed her rook from the rear file and said, 'Mate in three, David.'

'One more, Sam, give me my revenge,' pleaded David, but she shook her head and slipped out of the wardroom.

Nicholas became aware of the waft of her perfume. It was an inexpensive but exuberant fragrance – 'Babe', that was it, the one advertised by Hemingway's granddaughter. It suited Samantha perfectly. He turned to her, and it was only then that he was honest enough to admit to himself that he had relieved his Third Officer with the express intention of luring the girl up to the bridge.

'There are whales ahead,' he told her, and smiled one of those rare, irresistible smiles that she had come to treasure. 'I hoped you might come up.'

'Where? Where are they?' she asked with unfeigned excitement, and then they both saw the spout, a golden feather of spray in the low night sunlight two miles ahead.

'*Balaenoptera musculus*!' she exclaimed.

'I'll take your word for it, Doctor Silver, but to me it's still a blue whale.' Nick was still smiling, and she looked abashed for a moment.

'Sorry, I wasn't trying to dazzle you with science.' Then she looked back at the humpy, uninviting cold sea as the whale blew again, a far and ethereal column of lonely spray.

'One,' she said, 'only one.' And the excitement in her voice cooled. 'There are so few of them left now – that might be the last one we will ever see.'

'So few that they cannot find each other in the vastness of the ocean to breed.' Nick's smile was gone also, and again they talked of the sea, of their own involvement with it, their mutual concern at what man had done to it, and what he was still doing to it.

'When the Marxist government of Mozambique took over from the Portuguese colonists, it allowed the Soviets to send in dredges – not trawlers, but dredges – and they dredged the weed beds of Delagoa Bay. They actually *dredged* the breeding grounds of the Mozambique prawn. They took out a thousand tons of prawn, and destroyed the grounds for ever – and they drove an entire species into extinction in six short months.' Her outrage was in her voice as she told it.

'Two months ago the Australians arrested a Japanese trawler in their territorial waters. She had in her freezers the meat of 120,000 giant clams that her crew had torn from the barrier reef with crow bars. The clam population of a single coral reef would not exceed 20,000. That means they had denuded six oceanic reefs in one expedition – and they fined the Captain a thousand pounds.'

'It was the Japanese who perfected the "long line",' Nick agreed, 'the endless floating line, armed with specially designed hooks, and laid across the lanes of migration of the big pelagic surface-feeding fish, the tuna and the marlin. They wipe out the shoals as they advance – wipe them out to the last fish.'

'You cannot reduce any animal population beyond a certain point.' Samantha seemed much older as she turned her face up to Nick. 'Look what they did to the whales.'

Together they turned back to the windows, gazing out in hope of another glimpse of that gentle monster, doomed now to extinction, one last look at another creature that would disappear from the seas.

'The Japanese and the Russians again,' said Nick. 'They would not sign the whaling treaty until there were not enough blues left in the seas to make their killing an economic proposition. Then they signed it. When there were two or three thousand blue whales left in all the oceans, that is when they signed.'

'Now they will hunt the Fin and the Sei and the Minke to extinction.'

As they stood side by side staring into the bizarre sun-lit night, searching vainly for that spark of life in the watery wilderness, without thinking Nick lifted his arm; he would have placed it around her shoulders, the age-old protective attitude of man to his woman, but he caught himself at the last moment before he actually touched her. She had felt his movement and tensed for it, swaying slightly towards him in anticipation, but he stepped away, letting his arm fall and stooped over the radarscope. She only realized then how much she had wanted him to touch her, but for the rest of that evening he stayed within the physical limits which he seemed to have set for himself.

The next evening she declined the wardroom's importunate invitations, and after dinner waited in her own cabin, the door an inch ajar so she heard Tim Graham leave the bridge, clattering down the companionway with exuberance, relieved once more of his watch. The moment he entered the wardroom, Samantha slipped from her cabin and ran lightly up to the bridge.

She was with him only minutes after he had assumed the watch and Nick was amused by the strength of his pleasure. They grinned at each other like school children in a successful piece of mischief.

Before the light went, they passed close by one of the big tabular bergs, and she pointed out the line of filth that marked the white ice like the ring around a bathtub that had been used by a chimney sweep.

'Paraffin wax,' she said, 'and undissolved hydrocarbons.'

'No,' he said, 'that's only glacial striation.'

'It's crude oil,' she answered him. 'I've sampled it. It was one of the reasons I took the guide job on *Golden Adventurer*, I wanted first-hand knowledge of these seas.'

'But we are two thousand miles south of the tanker lanes.'

'The beach at Shackleton Bay is thick with wax balls and crude droplets, We found oil-soaked penguins on Cape Alarm, dead and dying. They hit an oil slick within fifty miles of that isolated shore.'

'I can hardly believe –' Nick started, but she cut across him.

'That's just it!' she said. 'Nobody wants to believe it. Just walk on by, as though it's another mugging victim lying on the sidewalk.'

'You're right,' Nick admitted grudgingly. 'Very few people really care.'

'A few dead penguins, a few little black tar balls sticking to your feet on the beach. It doesn't seem much to shout about, but it's what we cannot see that should terrify us. Those millions of tons of poisonous hydrocarbons that dissolve into the sea, that kill slowly and insidiously, but surely. That's what should really terrify us, Nicholas!'

She had used his given name for the first time, and they were both acutely aware of it. They were silent again, staring intently at the big iceberg as it passed slowly. The sun had touched it with ethereal pinks and dreaming amethyst, but that dark line of poisonous filth was still there.

'The world has to use fossil fuels, and we sailors have to transport them,' he said at last.

'But not at such appalling risks, not with an eye only to the profits. Not in the same greedy thoughtless grabbing petty way as man wiped out the whale, not at the cost of turning the sea into a stinking festering cesspool.'

'There are unscrupulous owners –' he agreed, and she cut across him angrily.

'Sailing under flags of convenience, without control, ships built to dangerous standards, equipped with a single boiler –' she reeled out the charges and he was silent.

'Then they waived the winter load-line for tankers rounding the Cape of Good Hope in the southern winter, to enable them to carry that extra fifty thousand tons of crude. The Agulhas Bank, the most dangerous winter sea in the world, and they send overloaded tankers into it.'

'That was criminal,' he agreed.

'Yet you were Chairman of Christy Marine, you had a representative on the Board of Control.'

She saw that she had made a mistake. His expression was suddenly ferocious. His anger seemed to crackle like electricity in the ruby gloom of the bridge. She felt an unaccountable flutter of real fear. She had forgotten what kind of man he was.

But he turned away and made a slow circuit of the bridge, elaborately checking each of the gauges and instruments, and then he paused at the far wing and lit a cheroot. She ached to offer some token of reconciliation, but instinctively she knew not to do so. He was not the kind of man who respected compromise or retreat.

He came back to her at last, and the glow of the cheroot lit his features so that she could see the anger had passed.

'Christy Marine seems like another existence to me now,' he said softly, and she could sense the deep pain of unhealed wounds. 'Forgive me, your reference to it took me off balance. I did not realize that you know of my past history.'

'Everybody on board knows.'

'Of course,' he nodded, and drew deeply on the cheroot before he spoke again. 'When I ran Christy Marine, I insisted on the highest standards of safety and seamanship for every one of our vessels. We opposed the Cape winter-line decision, and none of my tankers loaded to their summer-line on the Good Hope passage. None of my tankers made do with only one boiler, the design and engineering of every Christy Marine vessel was of the same standard as that ship there,' he pointed back at *Golden Adventurer*, 'or this one here,' and he stamped once on the deck.

'Even the *Golden Dawn*?' she asked softly, braving his anger again – but he merely nodded.

'*Golden Dawn*,' he repeated softly. 'It sounds such an absurdly presumptuous name, doesn't it? But I really thought of her as that, when I conceived her. The first million-ton tanker, with every refinement and safety feature that man has so far tested and proved. From inert gas scrubbers to independently articulated main tanks, not one boiler but four, just like one of the old White Star liners – she was really to be the golden dawn of crude oil transportation.

'However, I am no longer Chairman of Christy Marine, and I am no longer in control of *Golden Dawn*, neither her design nor her construction.' His voice was hollow, and in the dim light his eyes seemed shrunken into their cavities like those of a skull. 'Nor yet am I in control of her operation.'

It was all turning out so badly; she did not want to argue with him, nor make him unhappy. However, she had stirred memories and regrets within him, and she wished vainly that she had not disturbed him so. Her instinct warned her she should leave him now.

'Goodnight, Doctor Silver,' he nodded noncommittally at her sudden plea of tiredness.

'My name is Sam,' she told him, wishing that she could comfort him in some way, any way, 'or Samantha, if you prefer it.'

'I do prefer it,' he said, without smiling. 'Goodnight, Samantha.'

She was angry with both herself and him, angry that the good feeling between them had been destroyed, so she flashed at him:

'You really are old-fashioned, aren't you?' and hurried from the bridge.

The following evening she almost did not go up to him, for she was ashamed of those parting words, for having pointed up their age difference so offensively. She knew he was sufficiently aware of their differences, without being reminded. She had done herself harm, and she did not want to face him again.

While she was in the shower of the guest cabin, she heard Tim Graham come clattering down the stairs on the other side of the thin bulkhead. She knew that Nicholas had relieved him.

'I'm not going up,' she told herself firmly, and took her time drying and talcuming and brushing out her hair before she clambered naked and still pink from the hot water into her bunk.

She read for half an hour, a western that Beauty Baker had lent her, and it required all her concentration to follow the print, for her mind kept trying to wander. At last she gave an exclamation of self-disgust, threw back the blankets and began dressing.

His relief and pleasure, when she appeared beside him, were transparent, and his smile was a princely welcome for her. She was suddenly very glad she had come, and this night she effortlessly steered past all the pitfalls.

She asked him to explain how the Lloyd's Open Form contract worked, and she followed his explanations swiftly.

'If they take into consideration the danger and difficulties involved in the salvage,' she mused, 'you should be able to claim an enormous award.'

'I'm going to ask for twenty per cent of the hull value –'

'What is the hull value of *Golden Adventurer*?'

And he told her. She was silent a moment as she checked his mental arithmetic.

'That's six million dollars,' she whispered in awe.

'Give or take a few cents,' he agreed.

'But there isn't that much money in the world!' She turned and stared back at the liner.

'Duncan Alexander is going to agree with you.' Nick smiled a little grimly.

'But,' she shook her head, 'what would anybody do with that much money?'

'I'm asking for six – but I won't get it. I'll walk away with three or four millions.'

'Still, that's too much. Nobody could spend that much, not if they tried for a lifetime.'

'It's spent already. It will just about enable me to pay off my loans, launch my other tug, and to keep Ocean Salvage going for another few months.'

'You owe three or four million dollars?' She stared at him now in open wonder. 'I'd never sleep, not one minute would I be able to sleep —'

'Money isn't for spending,' he explained. 'There is a limit to the amount of food you can eat, or clothes you can wear. Money is a game, the biggest most exciting game in town.'

She listened attentively to it all, happy because tonight he was gay and excited with grand designs and further plans, and because he shared them with her.

'What we will do is this, we'll come down here with both tugs and catch an iceberg.'

She laughed. 'Oh, come on!'

'I'm not joking,' he assured her, but laughing also. 'We'll put tow-lines on a big berg. It may take a week to build up tow speed, but once we get it moving nothing will stop it. We will guide it up into the middle forties, catch the roaring forties and, just like the old wool clippers on the Australian passage, we will run our eastings down.' He moved to the chart table, selected a large-scale chart of the Indian Ocean and beckoned her to join him.

'You're serious.' She stopped laughing, and stared at him again. 'You really are serious, aren't you?'

He nodded, still smiling, and traced it out with his finger. 'Then we'll swing northwards, up into the Western Australian current, letting the flow carry us north in a great circle, until we hit the easterly monsoon and the north equatorial current.' He described the circle, but she watched his face. They stood very close, but still not touching and she felt herself stirred by the timbre of his voice, as though to the touch of fingers. 'We will cross the Indian Ocean to the east coast of Africa with the current pushing all the way, just in time to catch the south-westerly monsoon drift – right into the Persian Gulf.' He straightened up and smiled again.

'A hundred billion tons of fresh water delivered right into the dryest and richest corner of the globe.'

'But – but —' she shook her head, 'it would melt!'

'From a helicopter we spray it with a reflective polyurethane skin to lessen the effect of the sun, and we moor it in a shallow specially prepared dock where it will cool its own surrounds. Sure. it will melt, but not for a year or two and then we'll just go out and catch another one and bring it in, like roping wild horses.'

'How would you handle it?' she objected. 'It's too big.'

'My two tugs hustle forty-four thousand horses – we could pull in Everest, if we wanted.'

'Yes, but once you get it to the Persian Gulf?'

'We cut it into manageable hunks with a laser lance, and lift the hunks into a melting dam with an overhead crane.'

She thought about it. 'It could work,' she admitted.

'It will work,' he told her. 'I've sold the idea to the Saudis already. They are already building the dock and the dams. We'll give them water at one hundredth the cost of using nuclear condensers on sea water, and without the risk of radio-active contamination.'

She was absorbed with his vision, and he with hers. As they talked deep into the long watches of the night, they drew closer in spirit only.

Although each of them treasured those shared hours, somehow neither could bridge the narrow chasm between friendliness and real intimacy. She was instinctively aware of his reserves, that he was a man who had considered life and established his code by which to live it. She guessed that he did nothing unless it was deeply felt, and that a casual physical relationship would offer no attraction to him; she knew of the turmoil to which his life had so recently been reduced, and that he was pulling himself out of that by main strength, but that he was now wary of further hurt. There was time, she told herself, plenty of time – but *Warlock* bore steadily north by north-east, dragging her crippled ward up through the roaring forties; those notorious winds treated her kindly and she made good the six knots that Nick had hoped for.

On board *Warlock*, the attitude of the officers towards Samantha Silver changed from fawning adulation to wistful respect. Every one of them knew of the nightly ritual of the eight-to-midnight watch.

'Bloody cradle-snatcher,' groused Tim Graham.

'Mr Graham, it is fortunate I did not hear that remark,' David Allen warned him with glacial coldness – but they all resented Nicholas Berg, it was unfair competition, yet they kept a new respectful distance from the girl, not one of them daring to challenge the herd bull.

The time that Samantha had looked upon as endless was running out now, and she closed her mind to it. Even when David Allen showed her the fuzzy luminescence of the African continent on the extreme range of the radar-screen, she pretended to herself that it would go on like this – if not for ever, at least until something special happened.

During the long voyage up from Shackleton Bay, Samantha had streamed a very fine-meshed net from *Warlock*'s stern, collecting an incredible variety of krill and plankton and other microscopic marine life. Angel had grudgingly given her a small corner of his scullery in return for her services as honorary assistant under-chef and unpaid waitress, and she spent many absorbed hours there each day, identifying and preserving her specimens.

She was working there when the helicopter came out to *Warlock*. She looked up at the buffeting of the machine's rotors as they changed into fine pitch for the landing on *Warlock*'s heli-deck, and she was tempted to go up like every idle and curious hand on board, but she was in the middle of staining a slide, and somehow she resented the encroachment on this little island of her happiness. She worked on, but now her pleasure was spoiled, and she cocked her head when she heard the roar of the rotors as the helicopter rose from the deck again and she was left with a sense of foreboding.

Angel came in from the deck, wiping his hands on his apron and he paused in the doorway.

'You didn't tell me he was going, dearie.'

'What do you mean?' Samantha looked up at him, startled.

'Your boyfriend, darling. Socks and toothbrush and all.' Angel watched her shrewdly. 'Don't tell me he didn't even kiss you goodbye.'

She dropped the glass slide into the stainless steel sink and it snapped in half. She was panting as she gripped the rail of the upper deck and stared after the cumbersome yellow machine.

It flew low across the green wind-chopped sea, hump-backed and nose low, still close enough to read the operating company's name 'COURT' emblazoned on its fuselage, but it dwindled swiftly towards the far blue line of mountains.

Nick Berg sat in the jump seat between the two pilots of the big S. 58T Sikorsky and looked ahead towards the flat silhouette of Table Mountain. It was overlaid by a thick mattress of snowy cloud, at the south-easterly wind swirled across its summit.

From their altitude of a mere thousand feet, there were still five big tankers in sight, ploughing stolidly through the green sea on their endless odyssey, seeming to be alien to their element, not designed to live in harmony with it, but to oppose every movement of the waters. Even in this low sea, they wore thick garlands of white at their stubby rounded bows, and Nick watched one of them dip suddenly and take spray as high as her foremast. In any sort of blow, she would be like a pier with pylons set on solid ground. The seas would break right over her. It was not the way a ship should be, and now he twisted in his seat and looked back.

Far behind them, *Warlock* was still visible. Even at this distance, and despite the fact that she was dwarfed by her charge, her lines pleased the seaman in him. She looked good, but that backward glance invoked a pang of regret that he had been so stubbornly trying to ignore – and he had a vivid image of green eyes and hair of platinum and gold.

His regret was spiced by the persistent notion that he had been cowardly. He had left *Warlock* without being able to bring himself to say goodbye to the girl, and he knew why he had done so. He would not take the chance of making a fool of himself. He grimaced with distaste as he remembered her exact words, 'You really are old-fashioned, aren't you?'

There was something vaguely repulsive in a middle-aged man lusting after young flesh – and he supposed he must now look upon himself as middle-aged. In six months he would be forty years of age, and he did not really expect to live to eighty. So he was in the middle of the road.

He had always scorned those grey, lined, balding, unattractive little men with big cigars, sitting in expensive restaurants with pretty young girls beside them, the young thing pretending to hang on every pearl-like word, while her eyes focused beyond his shoulder – on some younger man.

But still, it had been cowardice. She had become a friend during those weeks, and she could hardly have been aware of the emotions that she had aroused in him during those long dark hours on *Warlock*'s bridge. She was not to blame for his unruly passions, in no way had she encouraged him to believe that he was more than just an older man, not even a father figure, but just someone with whom to pass an otherwise empty hour. She had been as friendly and cheerful to everyone else on board *Warlock*, from the Mate to the cook.

He really had owed her the common courtesy of a handshake and an assurance of the pleasure he had taken from her company, but he had not been certain he could restrict it to that.

He winced again as he imagined her horror as he blurted out some sort of declaration, some proposal to prolong their relationship or alter its structure into something more intimate, her disenchantment when she realized that behind the façade of the mature and cultured man, he was just as grimy an old lecher as the furtive drooling browsers in the porno-shops of Times Square.

'Let it go,' he had decided. No matter that he was probably in better physical shape now than he had been at twenty-five, to Dr Samantha Silver he was an old man – and he had a frightening vision of an episode from his own youth.

A woman, a friend of his mother's, had trapped the nineteen-year-old Nicholas alone one rainy day in the old beach house at Martha's Vineyard. He remembered his own revulsion at the sagging white flesh, the wrinkles, the lines of stria across her belly and breasts, and the *oldness* of her. She would then have been a woman of forty, the same as he was now, and he had done her the service she required out of some obligation of pity, but afterwards he had scrubbed his teeth until the gums bled and he had stood under the shower for almost an hour.

It was one of the cruel deceits of life that a person aged from the outside inwards. He had thought of himself in the fullness of his physical and mental powers, especially now after bringing in *Golden Adventurer*. He was ready for them to lead on the dragons and he would tear out their jugulars with his bare hands – then she had called him an old-fashioned thing, and he had realized that the sexual fantasy which was slowly becoming an obsession must be associated with the male menopause, a sorry symptom of the ageing process of which he had not been conscious until then. He grinned wryly at the thought.

The girl would probably hardly notice that he had left the ship, at the worst might be a little piqued by his lack of manners, but in a week would have forgotten his name. As for himself, there was enough, and more than enough to fill the days ahead, so that the image of a slim young body and that precious mane of silver and gold would fade until it became the fairy tale it really was.

Resolutely he turned in the jump seat and looked ahead. Always look ahead, there are never regrets in that direction.

They clattered in over False Bay, crossing the narrow isthmus of the Cape Peninsula under the bulk of the cloud-capped mountain, from the Indian Ocean to the Atlantic in under ten minutes.

He saw the gathering, like vultures at the lion kill, as the Sikorsky lowered to her roost on the heli-pad within the main harbour area of Table Bay.

As Nick jumped down, ducking instinctively under the still-turning rotors, they surged forward, ignoring the efforts of the Courtline dispatcher to keep the pad clear; they were led by a big red-faced man with a scorched-looking bald head and the furry arms of a tame bear.

'Larry Fry, Mr Berg,' he growled. 'You remember me?'

'Hello, Larry.' He was the local manager for Bach Wackie & Co, Nick's agents.

'I thought you might say a few words to the Press.' But the journalists swarmed around Nick now, demanding, importuning, jostling each other, their minions firing flash bulbs.

Nick felt his irritation flare, and he needed a deep breath and a conscious effort to control his anger.

'All right, lads and ladies.' He held up both hands, and grinned that special boyish grin. They were doing a tough job, he reminded himself. It couldn't be easy to be forced daily into the company of rich and successful men, grabbing for titbits, and being grossly underpaid for your efforts with the long-term expectation of ulcers and cirrhosis of the liver.

'Play the game with me and I'll play it with you,' he promised, and thought for a moment how it would be if they *didn't* want to speak with him, how it would be if they didn't know who he was, and didn't care.

'Where have you booked me?' he asked Larry Fry now, and turned back to them. 'In two hours' time I'll be in my suite at the Mount Nelson Hotel. You're invited, and there'll be whisky.'

They laughed and tried a few more half-hearted questions, but they had accepted the compromise – at least they had got the pictures.

As they went up the palm-lined drive to the gracious old hotel, built in the days when space included five acres of carefully groomed gardens, Nick felt the stir of memory, but he suppressed that and listened intently to the list of appointments and matters of urgency from which Larry Fry read. The change in the big man's attitude was dramatic. When Nick had first arrived to take command of *Warlock,* Larry Fry had given him ten minutes of his time and sent a deputy to complete the business.

Then Nick had been touched by the mark of the beast, a man on his way down, with as much appeal as a leper. Larry Fry had accorded him the minimum courtesy due the master of a small vessel, but now he was treating him like visiting royalty, limousine and fawning attention.

'We have chartered a 707 from South African Airways to fly *Golden Adventurer*'s passengers to London, and they will take scheduled commercial flights to their separate destinations from there.'

'What about berthing for *Golden Adventurer*?'

'The Harbour Master is sending out an inspector to check the hull before he lets her enter harbour.'

'You have made the arrangements?' Nick asked sharply. He had not completed the salvage until the liner was officially handed over to the company commissioned to undertake the repairs.

'Court are flying him out now,' Larry Fry assured him. 'We'll have a decision before nightfall.'

'Have the underwriters appointed a contractor for the repairs?'

'They've called for tenders.'

The hotel manager himself met Nicholas under the entrance portico.

'Good to see you again, Mr Berg.' He waived the registration procedures. 'We can do that when Mr Berg has settled in.' And then he assured Nick, 'We have given you the same suite.'

Nick would have protested, but already they were ushering him into the sitting-room. If it had been a room lacking completely in character or taste, the memories might not have been so poignant. However, unlike one of those soulless plastic and vinyl coops built by the big chains and so often offered to travellers under the misnomer of 'inns', this room was furnished with antique furniture, oil-paintings and flowers. The memories were as fresh as those flowers, but not as pleasing.

The telephone was ringing as they entered, and Larry Fry seized it immediately, while Nick stood in the centre of the room. It had been two years since last he stood here, but it seemed as many days, so clear was the memory.

'The Harbour Master has given permission for *Golden Adventurer* to enter harbour.' Larry Fry grinned triumphantly at Nick, and gave him the thumbs-up signal.

Nick nodded, the news was an anti-climax after the draining endeavours of the last weeks. Nick walked through to the bedroom. The wallpaper was a quietly tasteful floral design with matching curtains.

From the four-poster bed, Nick remembered, you could look out over the lawns. He remembered Chantelle sitting under that canopy, with a gossamer-sheer bed-robe over her creamy shoulders, eating thin strips of marmaladed toast and then delicately and carefully licking each slim tapered finger with a pink pointed tongue.

Nicholas had come out to negotiate the transportation of South African coal from Richards Bay, and iron ore from Saldanha Bay to Japan. He had insisted that Chantelle accompany him. Perhaps he had the premonition of imminent loss, but he had overridden her objections.

'But Africa is such a primitive place, Nicky, they have things that bite.'

And she had in the end gone with him. He had been rewarded with four days of rare happiness. The last four days ever, for though he did not then even suspect it, he was already sharing her bed and body with Duncan Alexander. He had never tired in thirteen years of that lovely smooth creamy body; rather, he had delighted in its slow luscious ripening into full womanhood, believing without question that it belonged to him.

Chantelle was one of those unusual women who grew more beautiful with time; it had always been one of his pleasures to watch her enter a room filled with other internationally acclaimed beauties, and see them pale beside his wife. And suddenly, for no good reason, he imagined Samantha Silver beside Chantelle – the girl's coltish grace would be transmuted to gawkiness beside Chantelle's poise, her manner as gauche as a schoolgirl's beside Chantelle's mature control, a warm lovable little bunny beside the sleekly beautiful mink –

'Mr Berg, London.' Larry Fry called from the sitting-room interrupting him, and with relief Nick picked up the telephone. 'Just keep going forward,' he reminded himself, and before he spoke, he thought again of the two women, and wondered suddenly how much that thick rich golden mane of Samantha's hair would pale beside Chantelle's lustrous sable, and just how much of the mother-of-pearl glow would fade from that young, clear skin –

'Berg,' he said abruptly into the telephone.

'Mr Berg, good morning. Will you speak to Mr Duncan Alexander of Christy Marine?'

Nick was silent for five full seconds. He needed that long to adjust to the name, but

Duncan Alexander was the natural extension of his previous thoughts. In the silence he heard the banging of doors and rising clamour of voices, as the journalists converged on the liquor-cabinet next door.

'Mr Berg, are you there?'

'Yes, ' he said, and his voice was steady and cool. 'Put him on.'

'Nicholas, my dear fellow.' The voice was glossy as satin, slow as honey, Eton and King's College, a hundred thousand pound accent, impossible to imitate, not quite foppish nor indolent, razor steel in a scabbard of velvet encrusted with golden filigree and precious stones – and Nicholas had seen the steel bared. 'It seems that it is impossible to hold a good man down.'

'But you tried, young Duncan,' Nick answered lightly. 'Don't feel bad about it, indeed you tried.'

'Come, Nicholas. Life is too short for recriminations. This is a new deck of cards, we start equal again.' Duncan chuckled softly. 'At least be gracious enough to accept my congratulations.'

'Accepted,' Nicholas agreed. 'Now what do we talk about?'

'Is *Golden Adventurer* in dock yet?'

'She has been cleared to enter. She'll be tied up within twenty-four hours – and you'd better have your cheque book ready.'

'I hoped that we might avoid going up before the Committee. There has been too much bitterness already. Let's try and keep it in the family, Nicholas.'

'The family?'

'Christy Marine is the family – you, Chantelle, old Arthur Christy – and Peter.'

It was the very dirtiest form of fighting, and Nick found suddenly that he was shaking like a man in fever and that his fist around the receiver was white with the force of his grip. It was the mention of his son that had affected him so.

'I'm not in that family any more.'

'In a way you will always be part of it. It is as much your achievement as any man's, and your son —'

Nick cut across him brusquely, his voice gravelly.

'You and Chantelle made me a stranger. Now treat me like one.'

'Nicholas—'

'Ocean Salvage as main contractor for the recovery of *Golden Adventurer* is open to an offer.'

'Nicholas —'

'Make an offer.'

'As bluntly as that?'

'I'm waiting.'

'Well now. My Board has considered the whole operation in depth, and I am empowered to make you an outright settlement of three-quarters of a million dollars.'

Nick's tone did not alter. 'We have been set down for a hearing at Lloyd's on the 27th of next month.'

'Nicholas, the offer is negotiable within reasonable limits —'

'You are speaking a foreign language,' Nick cut him off. 'We are so far apart that we are wasting each other's time.'

'Nicholas, I know how you feel about Christy Marine, you know the company is underwriting its own –'

'Now you are really wasting my time.'

'Nicholas, it's not a third party, it's not some big insurance consortium, it's Christy Marine –'

He used his name again, though it scalded his tongue.

'Duncan, you're breaking my heart. I'll see you on the 27th of next month, at the arbitration court.' He dropped the receiver on to its bracket, and moved across to the mirror, swiftly combing his hair and composing his features, startled to see how hard and bleak his expression was, and how fierce his eyes.

However, when he went through to the lounge of the suite, he was relaxed and urbane and smiling.

'All right, ladies and gentlemen. I'm all yours,' and one of the ladies of the press, blonde, pretty and not yet thirty but with eyes as old as life itself, took another sip of her whisky as she studied him, then murmured huskily, 'I wouldn't mind at all, duckie.'

Golden Adventurer stood tall and very beautiful against the wharf of Cape Town harbour, waiting her turn to go into the dry dock.

Globe Engineering, the contractors who had been appointed to repair her, had signed for her and legally taken over responsibility from *Warlock*'s First Officer. But David Allen still felt an immense proprietary pride in her.

From *Warlock*'s navigation bridge, he could look across the main harbour basin and see the tall, snowy superstructure glistening in the bright hot summer sunshine, towering as high as the giraffe-necked steel wharf cranes; and in gloating self-indulgence, David dwelt on a picture of the liner, wreathed in snow, half obscured by driving sleet and sea fume, staggering in the mountainous black seas off Antarctica. It gave him a solid feeling of achievement, and he thrust his hands deeply into his pockets and whistled softly to himself, smiling and watching the liner.

The Trog thrust his wrinkled head from the radio room.

'There's a call for you on the land-line,' he said, and David picked up the handset.

'David?'

'Yessir.' He drew himself to his full height as he recognized Nicholas Berg's voice.

'Are you ready for sea?'

David gulped, then glanced at the bulkhead clock. 'We discharged tow an hour and ten minutes ago.'

'Yes, I know. How soon?'

David was tempted to lie, estimate short, and then fake it for the extra time he needed. Instinct warned him against lying deliberately to Nicholas Berg.

'Twelve hours,' he said.

'It's an oil-rig tow, Rio to the North Sea, a semi-submersible rig.'

'Yessir,' David adjusted quickly, thank God he had not yet let any of his crew ashore. He had arranged for bunkering at 1300 hours. He could make it. 'When are you coming aboard, sir?'

'I'm not,' said Nick. 'You're the new Master. I'm leaving for London on the five o'clock flight. I won't even get down to shout at you. She's all yours, David.'

'Thank you, sir,' David stuttered, feeling himself flush hot scarlet.

'Bach Wackie will telex you full details of the tow at sea, and you and I will work out your own contract later. But I want you running at top economic power for Rio by dawn tomorrow.'

'Yessir.'

'I've watched you carefully, David.' Nick's voice changed, becoming personal, warmer. 'You're a damn good tug-man. Just keep telling yourself that.'

'Thank you, Mr Berg.'

Samantha had spent half the afternoon helping with the arrangements for taking off the remaining passengers from *Golden Adventurer* and embarking them in the waiting fleet of tourist buses which would distribute them to hotels throughout the city while they waited for the London charter flight.

It had been a sad occasion, farewell to many who had become friends, and remembering those who had not come back from Cape Alarm with them – Ken, who might have been her lover, and the crew of raft Number 16 who had been her special charges.

Once the final bus had left, with the occupants waving for the last time to Samantha, 'Take care, honey!' 'You come and visit with us now, hear?' she was as lonely and forlorn as the silent ship. She stood for a long time staring up the liner's high side, examining the damage where sea and ice had battered her – then she turned and picked her way dejectedly along the edge of the basin, ignoring the occasional whistle or ribald invitation from the fishermen and crew members of the freighters on their moorings.

Warlock seemed as welcoming as home, rakish and gallant, wearing her new scars with high panache, already thrusting and impatient at the restraint of her mooring lines. And then Samantha remembered that Nicholas Berg was no longer aboard her, and her spirits sagged again.

'God,' Tim Graham met her at the gangplank. 'I'm glad you got back. I didn't know what to do with your gear.'

'What do you mean?' Samantha demanded. 'Are you throwing me off the ship?'

'Unless you want to come with us to Rio.' He thought about that for a moment, and then he grinned, 'Hey, that's not a bad idea, how about it, old girl? Rio in Carnival time, you and me –'

'Don't get carried away, Timothy,' she warned him. 'Why Rio?'

'The Captain –'

'Captain Berg?'

'No, David Allen, he's the new skipper,' and she lost interest.

'When are you sailing?'

'Midnight.'

'I'd best go pack up.' She left him on the quarterdeck, and Angel pounced on her as she passed the galley.

'Where have you been?' He was in a flutter, all wrists and tossing hair, 'I've been beside myself, darling.'

'What is it, Angel?'

'It's probably too late already.'

'What is it?' She caught his urgency. 'Tell me.'

'He's still in town.'

'Who?' But she knew, they spoke of only one person in these emotional terms.

'Don't be dense, luv. Your crumpet.' She hated it when he referred to Nick like that, but now she let him go on. 'But he won't be very much longer. His plane leaves at five o'clock, he is making the local flight to Johannesburg, and connecting there for London.'

She stared at him.

'Well what are you waiting for?' Angel keened. 'It's almost four o'clock now, and it will take you at least half an hour to reach the airport.'

She did not move. 'But, Angel,' she almost wrung her hands in anguish, 'but what do I do when I get there?'

Angel shook his head and twinkled his diamonds in exasperation. 'Sweet merciful heavens, duckie.' Then he sighed. 'When I was a boy I had two guinea pigs, and they also refused to get it on. I think they were retarded, or something. I tried everything, even hormones, but neither of them survived the shots. Alas, their love was never consummated –'

'Be serious, Angel.'

'You could hold him down while I give him a hormone shot –'

'I hate you, Angel.' She had to laugh, even in her anxiety.

'Dearie, every night for the past month you have tried to set him on fire with your dulcet silvery voice – and we haven't even passed "GO" and collected our first $200 –'

'I know, Angel. I know.'

'It seems to me, sweetie, that it's time now to cut out the jawing and to ignite him with that magic little tinderbox of yours.'

'You mean right there in the departure lounge of the airport?' She clapped her hands with delight, then struck a lascivious pose. 'I'm Sam – fly me!'

'Hop, poppet there is a taxi on the wharf – he's been waiting an hour, with his meter running.'

There is no first-class lounge in Cape Town's DF Malan Airport, so Nicholas sat in the snake-pit, amongst the distraught mothers and their whining, sticky offspring, the harassed tourists loaded like camels with souvenirs and the florid-faced commercial travellers, but he was alone in a multitude; with unconscious deference they allowed him a little circle of privacy and he used the Louis Vuitton briefcase on his knee as a desk.

It occurred to him suddenly how dramatically the balance had swung in the last mere forty days, since he had recognized his wave peaking, but had almost not been able to find the strength for it.

A shadow passed across his eyes, and the little creased crowsfoot appeared between them as he remembered the physical and emotional effort that it had taken to make the 'Go' decision on *Golden Adventurer*, and he shivered slightly in fear of what might have happened if he had not gone. He would have missed his wave, and there would never have been another.

With a small firm movement of his head, he pushed that memory of fear behind him. He had caught his wave, and he was riding high and fast. Now it seemed that the fates were intent on smothering him with largesse: the oil-rig for *Warlock*, Rio to the Bravo Sierra field off Norway – then a back-to-back tow from the North Sea through Suez to the new South Australian field, would keep *Warlock* fully employed for the next six months. That was not all, the threatening dockyard strike at Construction Navale Atlantique had been smoothed over and the delivery date for the new tug had come forward by two months. At midnight the night before, a telephone call from Bach Wackie had awakened him to let him know Kuwait and Qatar were now also studying the iceberg-to-water project with a view to commissioning similar schemes; he would have to build himself another two vessels if they decided to go.

'All I need now is to hear that I have won the football pools,' he thought, and turned his head, started and caught his breath with a hiss, as though he had been punched in the ribs.

She stood by the automatic doors, and the wind had caught her hair and torn it loose from its thick twisted knot so that fine gold tendrils floated down on to her cheeks – cheeks that were flushed as though she had run fast, and her chest heaved so that she held one hand upon it, fingers spread like a star between those fine pointed breasts. She was poised like a forest animal that has scented the leopard, fearful, tremulous, but not yet certain in which direction to run. Her agitation was so apparent that he thrust aside his briefcase and stood up.

She saw him instantly, and her face lit with an expression of such unutterable joy, that he was halted in his intention of going towards her, while she in contrast wheeled and started to run towards him.

She collided with a portly, sweating tourist, nearly flooring him and shaking loose a rain of carved native curios and anonymous packets which clattered to the floor around him like ripe fruit.

He snarled angrily, then his expression changed as he looked at her. 'Sorry!' She stooped swiftly, picked up a packet, thrust it into his arms, hit him with her smile, and left him beaming bemusedly after her.

However, now she was more restrained, her precipitous rush calmed to that long-legged thrusting hip-swinging walk of hers, and the smile was a little uncertain as she pushed vainly at the loose streamers of golden hair, trying to tuck them up into the twisted rope on top of her head.

'I thought I'd missed you.' She stopped a little in front of him.

'Is something wrong?' he asked quickly, still alarmed by her behaviour.

'Oh no,' she assured him hurriedly. 'Not any more,' and suddenly she was awkward and coltish again. 'I thought,' her voice hushed, 'it was just that I thought I'd missed you.' And her eyes slid away from him. 'You didn't say goodbye –'

'I thought it was better that way.' And now her eyes flew back to his face, sparking with green fire.

'Why?' she demanded, and he had no answer to give her.

'I didn't want to –' How could he say it to her, without making the kind of statement that would embarrass them both?

Above them, the public address system squawked into life.

'South African Airways announces the departure of their Airbus flight 235 to Johannesburg. Will passengers please board at Gate Number Two.'

She had run out of time. 'I'm Sam – Fly Me! Please!' she thought, and felt the urge to giggle, but instead she said:

'Nicholas, tomorrow you'll be in London – in mid-winter.'

'It's a sobering thought,' he agreed, and for the first time smiled; his smile closed like a fist around her heart and her legs felt suddenly weak.

'Tomorrow or at least the day after, I'll be riding the long sea at Cape St Francis,' she said. They had spoken of that, on those enchanted nights. He had told her how he had first ridden the surf at Waikiki Beach long ago before the sport had become a craze, and it had been part of their shared experience, part of their love of the sea, drawing them closer together.

'I hope the surf's up for you,' he said. Cape St Francis was three hundred and fifty miles north of Cape Town, simply another beach and headland in a shoreline that stretched in unbroken splendour for six thousand miles, and yet it was unique in all the world. The young and the young-at-heart came in almost religious pilgrimage to ride the long sea at Cape St Francis. They came from Hawaii and California, from Tahiti and Queensland, for there was no other wave quite like it.

At the departure gate, the shuffling queue was shortening, and Nick stooped to pick up his briefcase, but she reached out and laid her hand on his biceps, and he froze.

It was the first time she had deliberately touched him, and the shock of it spread through his body like ripples on a quiet lake. Al the emotions and passions which he had so strenuously denied came tumbling back upon him, and it seemed that their strength had grown a hundredfold while under restraint. He ached for her, with a deep, yearning, wanting ache.

'Come with me, Nicholas,' she whispered, and his own throat closed so he could not answer. He stared at her, and already the ground hostesses at the gate were peering around irritably for their missing passenger.

She had to convince him and she shook his arm urgently, startled at the hardness of the muscle under her fingers.

'Nicholas, I really want,' she began, intending to finish, 'you to,' but her tongue played a Freudian trick on her, and she said, 'I really want you.'

'Oh God,' she thought, as she heard herself say it, 'I sound like a whore,' and in panic she corrected herself.

'I really want you to,' and she flushed, the blood came up from her neck, dark under the peach of her tan so the freckles glowed on her skin like flakes of gold-dust.

'Which one is it?' he asked, and then smiled again.

'There isn't time to argue.' She stamped her foot, feigning impatience, hiding her confusion, then added, 'Damn you!' for no good reason.

'Who is arguing?' he asked quietly, and suddenly, like magic, she was in his arms, trying to burrow herself deeper and deeper into his embrace, trying to draw all the man smell of him into her lungs, amazed at the softness and warmth of his mouth and the hard rasp of new beard on his chin and cheek, making little soft mewing sounds of comfort deep in her throat as she clung to him.

'Passenger Berg. Will passenger Berg please report to the departure gate,' chanted the public address.

'They're calling me,' Nicholas murmured.

'They can go right to the back of the queue,' she mumbled into his lips.

Sunlight was made for Samantha. She wore it like a cloak that had been woven especially for her. She wore it in her hair, sparkling like jewellery, she used it to paint her face and body in lustrous shades of burnt honey and polished amber, she wore it glowing in golden freckles on her cheeks and nose.

She moved in sunlight with wondrous grace, barefooted in the white sand, so that her hips and buttocks roistered brazenly under the thin green stuff of her bikini.

She sprawled in the sunlight like a sleeping cat, offering her face and her naked belly to it, so he felt that if he laid his hands against her throat he would feel her purr deep inside her chest.

She ran in the sunlight, light as a gull in flight, along the hard wet sand at the water's edge, and he ran beside her, tirelessly, mile after mile, the two of them alone in a world of green sea and sun and tall pale hot skies. The beach curved away in both directions to the limit of the eye, smooth and white as the snows of Antarctica, devoid of human life or the scars of man's petty endeavours, and she laughed beside him in the sunlight, holding his hand as they ran together.

They found a deep, clear rock pool in a far and secret place. The sunlight off the water dappled her body, exploding silently upon it like the reflections of light from a gigantic diamond, as she cast aside the two green wisps of her bikini, let down the thick rope of her hair and stepped into the pool, turning, knee-deep, to look back at him. Her hair hung almost to her waist, springing and thick and trying to curl in the salt and wind, it cloaked her shoulders and her breasts peeped through the thick curtains of it. Her breasts, untouched by the sun, were rich as cream and tipped in rose, so big and full and exuberant that he wondered that he had ever thought her a child; they bounced and swung as she moved, and she pulled back her shoulders and laughed at him shamelessly when she saw the direction of his eyes.

She turned back to the pool and her buttocks were white with the pinkish sheen of a deep-sea pearl, round and tight and deeply divided, and, as she bent forward to dive, a tiny twist of copper gold curls peeped briefly and coyly from the wedge where the deep cleft split into her tanned smooth thighs.

Through the cool water, her body was warm as bread fresh from the oven, cold and heat together, and when he told her this, she entwined her arms around his neck.

'I'm Sam the baked Alaska, eat me!' she laughed, and the droplets clung to her eyelashes like diamond chips in the sunlight.

Even in the presence of others, they walked alone; for them, nobody else really existed. Among those who had come from all over the world to ride the long sea at Cape St Francis were many who knew Samantha, from Florida and California, from Australia and Hawaii, where her field trips and her preoccupation with the sea and the life of the sea had taken her.

'Hey, Sam!' they shouted, dropping their boards in the sand and running to her, tall muscular men, burned dark as chestnuts in the sun. She smiled at them vaguely, holding Nicholas' hand a little tighter, and replied to their chatter absentmindedly, drifting away at the first opportunity.

'Who was that?'

'It's terrible, but I can't remember – I'm not even sure where I met him or when.' And it was true, she could concentrate on nothing but Nicholas, and the others sensed it swiftly and left them alone.

Nicholas had not been in the sun for over a year, his body was the colour of old ivory, in sharp contrast to the thick dark body hair which covered his chest and belly. At the end of that first day in the sun, the ivory colour had turned to a dull angry red.

'You'll suffer,' she told him, but the next morning his body and limbs had gone the colour of mahogany and she drew back the sheets and marvelled at it, touching him exploringly with the tip of her fingers.

'I'm lucky, I've got a hide like a buffalo,' he told her.

Each day he turned darker, until he was the weathered bronze of an American Indian, and his high cheek-bones heightened the resemblance.

'You must have Indian blood,' she told him, tracing his nose with her finger-tip.

'I only know two generations back,' he smiled at her. 'I've always been terrified to look further than that.'

She sat over him, crosslegged in the big bed and touched him, exploring him with her hands, touching his lips and the lobes of his ears, smoothing the thick dark curve of his eyebrows, the little black mole on his cheek, and exclaiming at each new discovery.

She touched him when they walked, reaching for his hand, pressing her hip against him when they stood, on the beach sitting between his spread knees and leaning back against his chest, her head tucked into his shoulder – it was as if she needed constant physical assurance of his presence.

When they sat astride their boards, waiting far out beyond the three-mile reef for the set of the wave, she reached across to touch his shoulder, balancing the board under her like a skilled horsewoman, the two of them close and spiritually isolated from the loose assembly of thirty or forty surf-riders strung out along the line of the long set.

This far out, the shore was a low dark green rind, above the shaded green and limpid blues of the water. In the blue distance, the mountains were blue on the blue of the sky and above them, the thunderheads piled dazzling silver, tall and arrogant enough to dwarf the very earth.

'This must be the most beautiful land in the world,' she said, moving her board so that her knee lay against his thigh.

'Because you are here,' he told her.

Under them, the green water breathed like a living thing, rising and falling, the swells long and glassy, sliding away towards the land.

Growing impatient, one of the inexperienced riders would move to catch a bad swell, kneeling on the board and paddling with both hands, coming up unsteadily on to his feet and then toppling and falling as the water left him, and the taunts and friendly catcalls of his peers greeted him as he surfaced, grinning sheepishly, and crawled back on to his board.

Then the ripple of excitement, and a voice calling, 'A three set!' the boards quickly rearranging themselves, sculled by cupped bare hands, spacing out for running room, the riders peering back eagerly over their dark burned shoulders, laughing and kidding each other as the wave set bumped up on the horizon, still four miles out at sea, but big enough so that they could count the individual swells that made up the set.

Running at fifty miles an hour, the swells took nearly five minutes, from the moment when they were sighted, to reach the line, and during that time Samantha had a little ritual of preparation. First, she hoisted the bottom of her bikini which had usually slipped down to expose a pair of dimples and a little of the deep cleft of her buttocks, then she tightened her top hamper, pulling open the brassiere of her costume and cupping each breast in turn, settling it firmly in its sheath of thin green cloth, grinning at Nick as she did it.

'You're not supposed to watch.'

'I know, it's bad for my heart.'

Then she plucked out a pair of hairpins and held them in her mouth as she twisted the wrist-thick plait of hair tighter until it hung down between her shoulder blades and pinned back the wisps over her ears.

'All set?' he called, and she nodded and answered,

'Ride three?'

The third wave in the set was traditionally the big one, and they let the first one swing them high and drop them again into its trough. Half the other riders were up and away, only their heads still visible above the peak of the wave, the land obscured by the moving wall of water.

The second wave came through, bigger, more powerful, but swooping up and over the crest and most of the other riders went on it, two or three tumbling on the steep front of water, losing their boards, dragged under as the ankle lines came up taut.

'Here we go!' exulted Samantha, and three came rustling, green and peaking, and in the transparent wall of water four big bottle-nosed porpoises were framed, in perfect motion, racing in the wave, pumping their flat delta-shaped tails and grinning that fixed porpoise grin of delight.

'Oh look!' sang Samantha. 'Just look at them, Nicholas!'

Then the wave was upon them and they sculled frantically, weight high on the board, the heart-stopping moment when it seemed the water would sweep away and leave them, then suddenly the boards coming alive under them and starting to run, tipping steeply forward, with the hiss of the waxed fibre-glass through the water.

Then they were both up and laughing in the sunlight, dancing the intricate steps that balanced and controlled the boards, lifted high on the crest, so they could see the sweep of the beach three miles ahead, and the ranks of other riders on the twin waves that had gone before them.

One of the porpoises frolicked with them on the racing crest, ducking under the flying boards, turning on its side to grin up at Samantha, so she stooped and stretched out a hand to touch him, lost her balance, and almost fell while the porpoise grinned at her mischievously and flipped away to rise fin up on her far side.

Now, out on their right hand, the wave was feeling the reef and starting to curl over on itself, the crest arching forwards, holding that lovely shape for long moments, then slowly collapsing.

'Go left,' Nick called urgently to her, and they kicked the boards around and danced up on to the stubby prows, bending at the knees to ride the hurtling craft, their speed rocketing as they cut across the green face of the wave, but behind them the arching wave spread rapidly towards them, faster than they could run before it.

Now at their left shoulders, the water formed a steep vertical wall, and, glancing at it, Samantha found the porpoise swimming head-high beside her, his great tail pumping powerfully, and she was afraid, for the majesty and strength of that wave belittled her.

'Nicholas!' she screamed, and the wave fanned out over her head, arcing across the sky, cutting out the sunlight, and now they flew down a long perfectly rounded tunnel of roaring water. The sides were smooth as blown glass, and the light was green and luminous and weird as though they sped through a deep submarine cavern, only ahead of them was the perfect round opening at the mouth of the tunnel – while behind her, close behind her, the tunnel was collapsing in a furious thunder of murderous white water, and she was as terrified and as exulted as she had ever been in her life.

He yelled at her, 'We must beat the curl,' and his voice was far away and almost lost in the roar of water, but obediently she went forward on her board until all her bare toes were curled over the leading edge.

For long moments they held their own, then slowly they began to gain, and at last they shot out through the open mouth of the tunnel into the sunlight again, and she laughed wildly, still high on the exultation of fresh terror.

Then they were past the reef and the wave firmed up, leaving the white water like lace on the surface far behind.

'Let's go right!' Samantha sang out to stay within the good structure of the wave, and they turned and went back, swinging across the steep face. The splatter of flung water sparkled on her belly and thighs, and the plait of her hair stood out behind her head like the tail of an angry lioness, her arms were extended and her hands held open, unconsciously making the delicate finger gestures of a Balinese temple dancer as she balanced; and miraculously the porpoise swam, fin up, beside her, following like a trained dog.

Then at last, the wave felt the beach and ran berserk, tumbling wildly upon itself, booming angrily, and churning the sand like gruel, and they kicked out of the wave, falling back over the crest and dropping into the sea beside the bobbing boards, laughing and panting at each other with the excitement and terror and the joy of it.

Samantha was a sea-creature with a huge appetite for the fruits of the sea, cracking open the crayfish legs in her fingers and sucking the white sticks of flesh into her mouth with a noisy sensuality, while her lips were polished with butter sauce, not taking her eyes from his face as she ate.

Samantha in the candlelight gulping those huge Knysna oysters, and then slurping the juice out of the shells.

'You're talking with your mouth full.'

'It's just that I've still got so much to tell you,' she explained.

Samantha was laughter, laughter in fifty different tones and intensities, from the sleepy morning chortle when she awoke and found him beside her, to the wild laughter yelled from the crest of a racing wave.

Samantha was loving. With a face of thundering innocence and the virginal, guileless green eyes of a child, she combined hands and a mouth whose wiles and wicked cunning left Nick stunned and disbelieving.

'The reason I ran away without a word was that I did not want to have your ravishment and violation on my conscience,' he shook his head at her disbelievingly.

'I wrote my PhD thesis in those subjects,' she told him blithely, using her forefinger to twist spit-curls in his sweat-dampened chest hairs. 'And what's more, buster, that was just the introductory offer – now we sign you up for a full course of treatment.'

Her delight in his body was endless, she must touch and examine every inch of it, exclaiming and revelling in it without a trace of self-consciousness, holding his hand in her lap and bending her head studiously over it, tracing the lines of his palm with her fingernail.

'You are going to meet a beautiful wanton blonde, give her fifteen babies and live to be a hundred and fifty.'

She touched the little chiselled lines around his eyes and at the corners of his mouth with the tip of her tongue, leaving cool damp smears of saliva on his skin.

'I always wanted a real craggy man all for myself.'

Then, when her examination became more intimate and clinical and he demurred, she told him severely, 'Hold still, this is a private thing between me and himself.'

Then a little later.

'Oh wow! He's real poison!'

'Poison?' he demanded, his manhood denigrated.

'Poison,' she sighed. 'Because he just slays me!'

In fairness, she offered herself for his touch and scrutiny, guiding his hands, displaying herself eagerly.

'Look, touch, it's yours – all yours,' wanting his approval, not able to give him sufficient to satisfy her own need to give. 'Do you like it, Nicholas? Is this good for you? Is there anything else you want, Nicholas, anything at all that I can give you?'

And when he told her how beautiful she was, when he told her how much he wanted her, when he touched and marvelled over the gifts she brought to him, she glowed and stretched and purred like a great golden cat so that when he learned that the Zodiacal sign of her birthday was Leo, he was not at all surprised.

Samantha was loving in the early slippery grey-pearl light of dawn, soft sleepy loving, with small gasps and murmurs and chuckles of deep contentment.

Samantha was loving in the sunlight, spread like a beautiful starfish in the fierce reflected sunlight of the sculptured dunes. The sand coated her body like crystals of sugar, and their cries rose together, high and ecstatic as those of the curious seagulls that floated above them on motionless white wings.

Samantha was loving in the green cool water, their two heads bobbing beyond the first line of breakers, his toes only just touching the sandy bottom and she twined about him like sea kelp about a submerged rock, clutching both their swim suits in one hand and gurgling merrily.

'What's good enough for a lady blue whale is good enough for Samantha Silver! Thar blows Moby Dick!'

And Samantha was loving in the night, with her hair brushed out carefully and spread over him, lustrous and fragrant, a canopy of gold in the lamplight, and she kneeling astride him in almost religious awe, like a temple maid making the sacrifice.

But more than anything else, Samantha was vibrant, bursting life – and youth eternal.

Through her, Nicholas recaptured those emotions which he had believed long atrophied by cynicism and the pragmatism of living. He shared her childlike delight in the small wonders of nature, the flight of a gull, the presence of the porpoise, the discovery of the perfect translucent fan of papery nautilus shell washed up on the white sand with the rare tentacled creature still alive within the convoluted interior.

He shared her outrage when even those remote and lonely beaches were invaded by an oil slick, tank washings from a VLCC out on the Agulhas current, and the filthy clinging globules of spilled crude oil stuck to the soles of their feet, smeared the rocks and smothered the carcasses of the jackass penguins they found at the water's edge.

Samantha was life itself, just to touch the warmth of her and to drink the sound of her laughter was to be rejuvenated. To walk beside her was to feel vital and strong.

Strong enough for the long days in the sea and sun, strong enough to dance to the loud wild music half the night, and then strong enough to lift her when she faltered and carry her down to their bungalow above the beach, she in his arms like a sleepy child, her skin tingling with the memory of the sun, her muscles aching deliciously with fatigue, and her belly crammed with rich food.

'Oh Nicholas, Nicholas – I'm so happy I want to cry.'

Then Larry Fry arrived; he arrived on a cloud of indignation, red-faced and accusing as a cuckolded husband.

'Two weeks,' he blared. 'London and Bermuda and St Nazaire have been driving me mad for two weeks!' And he brandished a sheath of telex flimsies that looked like the galley proofs for the *Encyclopaedia Britannica*.

'Nobody knew what had happened to you. You just disappeared.' He ordered a large gin and tonic from the white-jacketed bar-tender and sank wearily on to the stool beside Nick. 'You nearly cost me my job, Mr Berg, and that's the truth. You'd have thought I'd bumped you off personally and dumped your body in the bay. I had to hire a private detective to check every hotel register in the country.' He took a long, soothing draught of the gin.

At that moment, Samantha drifted into the cocktail lounge. She wore a loose, floating dress the same green as her eyes, and a respectful hush fell on the pre-luncheon drinkers as they watched her cross the room. Larry Fry forgot his indignation and gaped at her, his bald scorched head growing shining under a thin film of perspiration.

'Godstrewth,' he muttered. 'I'd rather feel that, than feel sick.' And then his admiration turned to consternation when she came directly to Nicholas, laid her hand on his shoulder and in full view of the entire room kissed him lingeringly on the mouth.

There was a soft collective sigh from the watchers and Larry Fry knocked over his gin.

'We must go now, today,' Samantha decided. 'We mustn't stay even another hour, Nicholas, or we will spoil it. It was perfect, but now we must go.'

Nicholas understood. Like him she had the compulsion to keep moving forward. Within the hour, he had chartered a twin-engined Beechcraft Baron. It picked them up at the little earth strip near the hotel and put them down at Johannesburg's Jan Smuts Airport an hour before the departure of the UTA flight for Paris.

'I always rode in the back of the bus before,' said Samantha, as she looked around the first-class cabin appraisingly. 'Is it true that up this end you can eat and drink as much as you like, for free?'

'Yes.' Then Nick added hastily, 'But you don't have to take that as a personal challenge.' Nicholas had come to stand in awe of Samantha's appetites.

They stayed overnight at the George V in Paris and caught the mid-morning TAT flight down to Nantes, the nearest airfield to the shipyards at St Nazaire, and Jules Levoisin was there to meet them at the Château Bougon field.

'Nicholas!' he shouted joyfully, and stood on tiptoe to buss both his cheeks, enveloping him in a fragrant cloud of eau de Cologne and pomade. 'You are a pirate, Nicholas, you stole that ship from under my nose. I hate you.' He held Nicholas at arm's length. 'I warned you not to take the job, didn't I?'

'You did, Jules, you did.'

'So why do you make a fool of me?' he demanded, and twirled his moustaches. He was wearing expensive cashmere and an Yves St Laurent necktie; ashore, Jules was always the dandy.

'Jules, I am going to buy lunch for you at La Rôtisserie,' Nicholas promised.

'I forgive you,' said Jules, it was one of his favourite eating-places – but at that moment Jules became aware that Nicholas was not travelling alone.

He stood back, took one long look at Samantha and it seemed that tricolors unfurled around him and brass bands burst into the opening bars of 'La Marseillaise'. For if dalliance was the national sport, Jules Levoisin considered himself veteran champion of all France.

He bowed over her hand, and tickled the back of it with his still black moustache. Then he told Nicholas, 'She is too good for you, *mon petit*, I am going to take her away from you.'

'The same way you did *Golden Adventurer*?' Nick asked innocently.

Jules had his ancient Citroën in the car park. It was lovingly waxed and fitted with shiny gew-gaws and dangling mascots. He handed Samantha into the front seat as though it was a Rolls Camargue.

'He's beautiful,' she whispered, as he scampered around to the driver's door.

Jules could not devote attention to both the road ahead and to Samantha, so he concentrated solely upon her, without deviating from the Citroën's top speed, only occasionally turning to shout, '*Cochon!*' at another driver or jerk his fist at them with the second finger pointed stiffly upwards in ribald salutation.

'Jules' great-grandfather charged with the Emperor's cavalry at Quatre Bras,' Nick explained. 'He is a man without fear.'

'You will enjoy La Rôtisserie,' Jules told Samantha. 'I can only afford to eat there when I find somebody rich who wishes a favour of me.'

'How do you know I want a favour?' Nick asked from the back seat, clinging to the door-handle.

'Three telegrams, a telephone call from Bermuda – another from Johannesburg,' Jules chuckled fruitily and winked at Samantha. 'You think I believe Nicholas Berg wants to discuss old times? You think I believe he feels so deeply for his old friend, who taught him everything he knows? A man who treated him like a son, and whom he blatantly robbed —' Jules sped across the Loire bridge and plunged into that tangled web of narrow one-way streets and teeming traffic which is Nantes; a way opened for him miraculously.

In the Place Briand, he handed Samantha gallantly from the Citroën, and in the restaurant he puffed out his cheeks and made little anxious little clucking and tut-tutting noises, as Nicholas discussed the wine list with the *sommelier* – but he nodded reluctant approval when they settled on a Chablis Moutonne and a Chambertin-Clos-de-Bèze, then he applied himself with equal gusto to the food, the wine and Samantha.

'You can tell a woman who is made for life and love, by the way she eats,' and when Samantha made wide lascivious eyes at him over her trout, Nicholas expected him to crow like a cockerel.

Only when the Cognac was in front of them, and both he and Nick had lit cheroots, did he demand abruptly:

'So, now, Nicholas, I am in a good mood. Ask me.'

'I need a Master for my new tug,' said Nick, and Jules veiled his face behind a thick blue curtain of cigar smoke.

They fenced like masters of épée all the way from Nantes to St Nazaire.

'Those ships you build, Nicholas, are not tugs. They are fancy toys, floating bordellos – all those gimmicks and gadgets —'

'Those gimmicks and gadgets enabled me to deal with Christy Marine while you still hadn't realized that I was within a thousand miles.' Jules blew out his cheeks and muttered to himself.

'Twenty-two thousand horsepower, *c'est ridicule!* They are over-powered —'

'I needed every single one of those horses when I pulled *Golden Adventurer* off Cape Alarm.'

'Nicholas, do not keep reminding me of that shameful episode.' He turned to Samantha. 'I am hungry, *ma petite*, and in the next village there is a *pâtisserie*,' he sighed and kissed his bunched fingers, 'you will adore the pastry.'

'Try me,' she invited, and Jules had found a soulmate.

'Those fancy propellers – variable pitch – ouf!' Jules spoke through a mouthful of pastry, and there was whipped cream on his moustache.

'I can make twenty-five knots and then slam *Warlock* into reverse thrust and stop her within her own length.'

Jules changed pace, and attacked from a new direction. 'You'll never find full employment for two big expensive ships like that.'

'I'm going to need four, not two,' Nick contradicted him. 'We are going to catch icebergs,' and Jules forgot to chew, as he listened intently for the next ten minutes. 'One of the beauties of the iceberg scheme is that all my ships will be operating right on the tanker lanes, the busiest shipping lanes in all the oceans —'

'Nicholas,' Jules shook his head in admiration, 'you move too fast for me. I am an old man, old-fashioned —'

'You're not old,' Samantha told him firmly. 'You're only just in your prime.' And Jules threw up both hands theatrically.

'Now you have a pretty girl heaping flattery on my bowed grey head,' he looked at Nicholas; 'is no trick too deceitful for you?'

*

It was snowing the next morning, a slow sparse sprinkling from a grey woollen sky, when they drove into St Nazaire from the little seaside resort of La Baule twenty-five kilometres up the Atlanti coast.

Jules had a small flat in one of the apartment blocks. It was a convenient arrangement, for *La Mouette*, his command, was owned by a Breton company and St Nazaire was her home port. It was a mere twenty-minute drive before they made out the elegant arch of the suspension bridge which crosses the estuarine mouth of the Loire River at St Nazaire.

Jules drove through the narrow streets of that area of the docks just below the bridge which comprises the sprawling ship-building yard of Construction Navale Atlantique, one of the three largest ship-building companies in Europe.

The slipways for the larger vessels, the bulk carriers and naval craft, faced directly on to the wide smooth reach of the river; but the ways for the small vessels backed on to the inner harbour.

So Jules parked the Citroën at the security gates nearest the inner harbour, and they walked through to where Charles Gras was waiting for them in his offices overlooking the inner basin.

'Nicholas, it is good to see you again.' Gras was one of Atlantique's top engineers, a tall stooped man with a pale face and lank black hair that fell to his eyebrows, but he had the sharp foxy Parisian features and quick bright eyes that belied the morose unsmiling manner.

He and Nicholas had known each other many years, and they used the familiar 'tu' form of address.

Charles Gras changed to heavily accented English when he was introduced to Samantha, and back to French when he asked Nicholas,

'If I know you, you will want to go directly to see your ship now, *n'est-ce pas?*'

Sea Witch stood high on her ways, and although she was an identical twin to *Warlock*, she seemed almost twice her size with her underwater hull exposed. Despite the fact that the superstructure was incomplete and she was painted in the drab oxide red of marine primer, yet it was impossible to disguise the symmetrically functional beauty of her lines.

Jules puffed, and muttered 'Bordello' and made remarks about 'Admiral Berg and his battleship', but he could not hide the gleam in his eye as he strutted about the uncompleted navigation bridge, or listened intently as Charles Gras explained the electronic equipment and the other refinements that made the ship so fast, efficient and manoeuvrable.

Nick realized that the two experts should be left alone now to convince each other; it was clear that although this was their first meeting the two of them had established immediate rapport.

'Come.' Nick quietly took Samantha's arm and they stepped carefully around the scaffolding and loose equipment, picking their way through groups of workmen to the upper deck.

The snow had stopped, but a razor of a wind snickered in from the Atlantic. They found a sheltered corner, and Samantha pressed close to Nick, snuggling into the circle of his arm.

High on her ways, *Sea Witch* gave them a sweeping view, through the forest of construction cranes, over the roofs of the warehouses and offices to the river slipways where the keels of the truly big hulls were laid down.

'You spoke about *Golden Dawn*,' Nick said. 'There she is.'

It took some moments for Samantha to realize she was looking at a ship.

'My God,' she breathed. 'It's so big.'

'They don't come bigger,' he agreed.

The structure of steel was almost a mile and a half long, three city blocks, and the hull was as tall as a five-storey building, while the navigation tower was another hundred feet higher than that.

Samantha shook her head. 'It's beyond belief. It looks like – like a city! It's terrifying to think of that thing afloat.'

'That is only the main hull, the tank pods have been constructed in Japan. The last I heard is that they are under tow direct to the Persian Gulf.'

Nick stared solemnly across the ship, blinking his eyes against the stinging wind.

'I must have been out of my mind,' he whispered, 'to dream up a monster like that.' But there was a touch of defiant pride in his tone.

'It's so big – beyond imagination,' she encouraged him to talk about it. 'How big *is* it?'

'It's not a single vessel,' he explained. 'No harbour in the world could take a ship that size, it could not even approach the continental United States, for that matter, there just is not enough water to float it.'

'Yes?' She loved to listen to him expound his vision, she loved to hear the force and power of his convictions.

'What you're seeing is the carrying platform, the accommodation and the main power source.' He held her closer. 'On to that, we attach the four tank pods, each one of them capable of carrying a quarter of a million tons of crude oil, each tank almost as large as the biggest ship afloat.'

He was still explaining the concept while they sat at lunch, and Charles Gras and Jules Levoisin listened as avidly as she did.

'A single rigid hull of those dimensions would crack and break up in heavy seas,' he took the cruet set and used it to demonstrate, 'but the four individual pods have been designed so that they can move independently of each other. This gives them the ability to ride and absorb the movement of heavy seas. It is the most important principle of ship construction, a hull must ride the water – not try to oppose it.'

Across the table, Charles Gras nodded lugubrious agreement.

'The tank pods hive on to the main hull, and are carried upon it like remora on the body of a shark, not using their own propulsion systems, but relying on the multiple boilers and quadruple screws of the main hull to carry them across the oceans.' He pushed the cruet set around the table and they all watched it with fascination. 'Then, when it reaches the continental shelf opposite the shore discharge site, the main hull anchors, forty or fifty, even a hundred miles offshore, detaches one or two or all of its pod tanks, and they make those last few miles under their own propulsion. In protected water and in chosen weather conditions, their propulsion systems will handle them safely. Then the empty pod ballasts itself and returns to hook on to the main hull.'

As he spoke, Nicholas detached the salt cellar from the cruet and docked it against Samantha's plate. The two Frenchmen were silent, staring at the silver salt cellar, but Samantha watched Nick's face. It was burned dark by the sun now, lean and handsome, and he seemed charged and vital, like a thoroughbred horse in peak of training, and she was proud of him, proud of the force of his personality that made other men listen when he spoke, proud of the imagination and the courage it took to conceive and then put into operation a project of this magnitude. Even though it were no longer his – yet his had been the vision.

Now Nicholas was talking again. 'Civilization is addicted to liquid fossil fuels. Without them, it would be forced into withdrawal trauma too horrible to contemplate. If then we have to use crude, let's pipe it out of the earth, transport and ship it with all possible precautions to protect ourselves from its side effects —'

'Nicholas,' Charles Gras interrupted him abruptly. 'When last did you inspect the drawings of *Golden Dawn*?'

Nick paused, taken in full stride and a little off balance. He frowned as he cast back, 'I walked out of Christy Marine just over a year ago.' And the darkness of those days settled upon him, making his eyes bleak.

'A year ago we had not even been awarded the contract for the construction of *Golden Dawn*.' Charles Gras twisted the stem of his wine glass between his fingers, and thrust out his bottom lip. 'The ship you have just described to us is very different from the ship we are building out there.'

'In what way, Charles?' Nick's concern was immediate, a father hearing of radical surgery upon his first-born.

'The concept is the same. The mother vessel and the four tank pods, but —' Charles shrugged, that eloquent Gallic gesture, 'it would be easier to show it to you. Immediately after lunch.'

'*D'accord*,' Jules Levoisin nodded. 'But on the condition that it does not interfere with the further enjoyment of this fine meal.' He nudged Nicholas. 'If you eat with a scowl on your face, *mon vieux*, you will grow yourself ulcers like a bunch of Loire grapes.'

Standing beneath the bulk of *Golden Dawn*, she seemed to reach up into that low grey snow-sky, like a mighty alp of steel. The men working on the giddy heights of her scaffolding were small as insects, and quite unbelievably as Samantha stared up at them a little torn streamer of wet grey cloud, coming up the Loire basin from the sea, blew over the ship, obscuring the top of her navigation bridge for a few moments.

'She reaches up to the clouds,' said Nick beside her, and the pride was in his voice as he turned back to Charles Gras. 'She looks good?' It was a question, not a statement. 'She looks like the ship I planned —'

'Come, Nicholas.'

The little party picked its way through the chaos of the yard. The squeal of power cranes and the rumble of heavy steel transporters, the electric hissing crackle of the huge automatic running welders combined with the roaring gunfire barrage of the rivetters into a cacophony that numbed the senses. The scaffolding and hoist systems formed an almost impenetrable forest about the mountainous hull, and steel and concrete were glistening wet and rimmed with thin clear ice.

It was a long walk through the crowded yard, almost twenty minutes merely to round the tanker's stern – and suddenly Nicholas stopped so abruptly that Samantha collided with him and might have fallen on the icy concrete, but he caught her arm and held her as he stared up at the bulbous stern.

It formed a great overhanging roof like that of a medieval cathedral, so that Nick's head was flung back, and the grip on her arm tightened so fiercely that she protested. He seemed not to hear, but went on staring upwards.

'Yes,' Charles Gras nodded, and the lank black hair flopped against his forehead. 'That is one difference from the ship you designed.'

The propeller was in lustrous ferro-bronze, six-bladed, each shaped with the beauty and symmetry of a butterfly's wing, but so enormous as to make the comparison laughable. It was so big that not even the bulk of *Golden Dawn*'s own hull could dwarf it, each separate blade was longer and broader than the full wingspan of a jumbo jet airliner, a gargantuan sculpture in gleaming metal.

'One!' whispered Nick. 'One only.'

'Yes,' Charles Gras agreed. 'Not four – but one propeller only. Also, Nicholas, it is fixed pitch.'

They were all silent as they rode up in the cage of the hoist. The hoist ran up the outside of the hull to the level of the main deck, and though the wind searched for them remorselessly through the open mesh of the cage, it was not the cold that kept them silent.

The engine compartment was an echoing cavern, harshly lit by the overhead floodlights, and they stood high on one of the overhead steel catwalks looking down fifty feet on to the boiler and condensers of the main engine.

Nick stared down for almost five minutes. He asked no questions, made no judgements, but at last he turned to Charles Gras and nodded once curtly.

'All right. I've seen enough,' he said, and the engineer led them to the elevator station. Again they rode upwards. It was like being in a modern office block – the polished chrome and wood panelling of the elevator, the carpeted passageways high in the navigation tower along which Charles Gras led them to the Master's suite and unlocked the carved mahogany doorway with a key from his watch chain.

Jules Levoisin looked slowly about the suite and shook his head wonderingly. 'Ah, this is the way to live,' he breathed. 'Nicholas, I absolutely insist that the Master's quarters of *Sea Witch* be decorated like this.'

Nick did not smile, but crossed to the view windows that looked forward along the tanker's main deck to her round blunt unlovely prow a mile and a quarter away. He stood with his hands clasped behind his back, legs apart, chin thrust out angrily and nobody else spoke while Charles Gras opened the elaborate bar and poured cognac into the crystal brandy balloons. He carried a glass to Nick who turned away from the window.

'Thank you, Charles, I need something to warm the chill in my guts.' Nick sipped the cognac and rolled it on his tongue as he looked slowly around the opulent cabin.

It occupied almost half the width of the navigation bridge, and was large enough to house a diplomatic reception. Duncan Alexander had picked a good decorator to do the job, and without the view from the window it might have been an elegant Fifth Avenue New York apartment, or one of those penthouses high on the cliffs above Monte Carlo, overlooking the harbour.

Slowly Nick crossed the thick green carpet, woven with the house device, the entwined letters C and M for Christy Marine, and he stopped before the Degas in its place of honour above the marble fireplace.

He remembered Chantelle's bubbling joy at the purchase of that painting. It was one of Degas' ballet pieces, soft, almost luminous light on the limbs of the dancers, and, remembering the unfailing delight that Chantelle had taken in it during the years, he was amazed that she had allowed it to be used on board one of the company ships, and that it was left here virtually unguarded and vulnerable. That painting was worth a quarter of a million pounds.

He leaned closer to it, and only then did he realize how clever a copy of the original it was. He shook his head in dismissal.

'The owners were advised that the sea air may damage the original,' Charles Gras shrugged, and spread his hands deprecatingly, 'and not many people would know the difference.'

That was typical of Duncan Alexander, Nicholas thought savagely. It could only be his idea, the sharp accountant's brain. The conviction that it was possible to fool all of the people all of the time.

Everybody knew that Chantelle owned that work, therefore nobody would doubt its authenticity. That's the way Duncan Alexander would reason it. It could not be Chantelle's idea. She had never been one to accept anything that was sham or dross; it was a measure of the power that he exerted over her, for her to go along with this cheap little fraud.

Nicholas indicated the forgery with his glass and spoke directly to Charles Gras.

'This is a cheat,' he spoke quietly, his anger contained and controlled, 'but it is harmless.' Now he turned away from it and, with a wider gesture that embraced the whole ship, went on, 'But this other cheat, this enormous fraud,' he paused to control the metallic edge that had entered his tone, going on quietly again, 'this is a vicious, murderous gamble he is taking. He has bastardized the entire concept of the scheme. One propeller instead of four – it cannot manoeuvre a hull of these dimensions with safety in any hazardous situation, it cannot deliver sufficient thrust to avoid collision, to fight her off a lee shore, to handle heavy seas.' Nick stopped, and his voice dropped even lower, yet somehow it was more compelling. 'This ship cannot, by all moral and natural laws, be operated on a single boiler. My design called for eight separate boilers and condensers, the standard set for the old White Star and Cunard Lines. But Duncan Alexander has installed a single boiler system. There is no back-up, no fail-safe – a few gallons of sea water in the system could disable this monster.'

Nicholas stopped suddenly as a new thought struck him. 'Charles,' his voice sharper still, 'the pod tanks, the design of the pod tanks. He hasn't altered that, has he? He hasn't cut the corners there? Tell me, old friend, they are still self-propelled, are they not?'

Charles Gras brought the Courvoisier bottle to where Nicholas stood, and when Nick would have refused the addition to his glass, Charles told him sorrowfully, 'Come, Nicholas, you will need it for what I have to tell you now.'

As he poured, he said, 'The pod tankers, their design has been altered also.' He drew a breath to tell it with a rush. 'They no longer have their own propulsion units. They are now only dumb barges that must be docked and undocked from the main hull and manoeuvred only by attendant tugs.'

Nicholas stared at him, his lips blanched to thin white lines. 'No. I do not believe it. Not even Duncan –'

'Duncan Alexander has saved forty-two million dollars by re-designing *Golden Dawn* and equipping her with only a single boiler and propeller.' Charles Gras shrugged again. 'And forty-two million dollars is a lot of money.'

There was a pale gleam of wintry sunlight that flickered through the low grey cloud and lit the fields not far from the River Thames with that incredible vivid shade of English green.

Samantha and Nicholas stood in a thin line of miserably cold parents and watched the pile of struggling boys across the field in their coloured jerseys; the light blue and black of Eton, the black and white of St Paul's, were so muddied as to be barely distinguishable.

'What are they doing?' Samantha demanded, holding the collar of her coat around her ears.

'It's called a scrum,' Nick told her. 'That's how they decide which team gets the ball.'

'Wow. There must be an easier way.'

There was a flurry of sudden movement and the slippery egg-shaped ball flew back in a lazy curve that was snapped up by a boy in the Etonian colours. He started to run.

'It's Peter, isn't it?' cried Samantha.

'Go it, Peter boy!' Nick roared, and the child ran with the ball clutched to his chest and his head thrown back. He ran strongly with the reaching co-ordinated stride of an older boy, swerving round a knot of his opponents, leaving them floundering in the churned mud, and angling across the lush thick grass towards the white-painted goal line, trying to reach the corner before a taller more powerfully built lad who was pounding across the field to intercept him.

Samantha began to leap up and down on the same spot, shrieking wildly, completely uncertain of what was happening, but wild with excitement that infected Nicholas.

The two runners converged at an angle which would bring them to the white line at the same moment, at a point directly in front of where Nick and Samantha stood.

Nick saw the contortion of his son's face, and realized that this was a total effort. He felt a physical constriction of his own chest as he watched the boy drive himself to his utmost limits, the sinews standing out in his throat, his lips drawn back in a frozen rictus of endeavour that exposed the teeth clenched in his jaw.

From infancy, Peter Berg had brought to any task that faced him the same complete focus of all his capabilities. Like his grandfather, old Arthur Christy, and his own father, he would be one of life's winners. Nick knew this instinctively, as he watched him run. He had inherited the intelligence, the comeliness and the charisma, but he bolstered all that with this unquenchable desire to succeed in all he did. The single-minded determination to focus all his talents on the immediate project. Nick felt the pressure in his chest swell. The boy was all right, more than all right, and pride threatened to choke him.

Sheer force of will had driven Peter Berg a pace ahead of his bigger, longer-legged adversary, and now he leaned forward with the ball held in both hands, arms fully extended, reaching for the line to make the touch-down.

He was ten feet from where Nick stood, a mere instant from success, but he was unbalanced, and the St Paul's boy dived at him, crashing into the side of his chest, the impact jarring and brutal, hurling Peter out of the field of play with the ball spinning from his hands and bouncing away loosely, while Peter smashed into the earth on both knees, then rolled forward head over heels, and sprawled face down on the soggy turf.

'It's a touch-down!' Samantha was still leaping up and down.

'No,' said Nick. 'No, it isn't.'

Peter Berg dragged himself upright. His cheek was streaked with chocolate mud and both his knees were running blood, the skin smeared open by the coarse grass.

He did not glance down at his injuries, and he shrugged away the St Paul boy's patronizing hand, holding himself erect against the pain as he limped back on to the field. He did not look at his father, and the moisture that filled his eyes and threatened to flood over the thick dark lashes were not tears of pain, but of humiliation and failure. With an overwhelming feeling of kinship, Nick knew that for his son those feelings were harder to bear than any physical agony.

When the game ended he came to Nicholas, all bloodied and mud-smeared, and shook hands solemnly.

'I am so glad you came, sir,' he said. 'I wish you could have watched us win.'

Nick wanted to say: 'It doesn't matter, Peter, it's only a game.' But he did not. To Peter Berg, it mattered very deeply, so Nicholas nodded agreement and then he introduced Samantha.

Again Peter shook hands solemnly and startled her by calling her, 'M'am.' But when she told him, 'Hi, Pete. A great game, you deserved to slam them,' he smiled, that sudden dazzling irresistible flash that reminded her so of Nicholas that she felt her heart squeezed. Then when the boy hurried away to shower and change, she took Nick's arm.

'He's a beautiful boy, but does he always call you "sir"?'

'I haven't seen him in three months. It takes us both a little while to relax.'

'Three months is a long time –'

'It's all tied up by the lawyers. Access and visiting-rights – what's good for the child, not what's good for the parents. Today was a special concession from Chantelle, but I still have to deliver him to her at five o'clock. Not five past five, five o'clock.'

They went to the Cockpit teashop and Peter startled Samantha again by pulling out her chair and seating her formally. While they waited for the best muffins in Britain to be brought to the table, Nicholas and Peter engaged each other in conversation that was stiff with selfconsciousness.

'Your mother sent me a copy of your report, Peter, I cannot tell you how delighted I was.'

'I had hoped to do better, sir. There are still three others ahead of me.'

And Samantha ached for them. Peter Berg was twelve years of age. She wished he could just throw his arms around Nicholas' neck and say, 'Daddy, I love you,' for the love was transparent, even through the veneer of public-school manners. It shone behind the thick dark lashes that fringed the boy's golden brown eyes, and glowed on the cheeks still as creamy and smooth as a girl's.

She wanted desperately to help them both, and on inspiration she launched into an account of *Warlock*'s salvage of *Golden Adventurer*, a tale with emphasis on the derring-do of *Warlock*'s Master, not forgetting his rescue of Samantha Silver from the icy seas of Antarctica.

Peter's eyes grew enormous as he listened, never leaving her face except to demand of Nicholas, 'Is that true, Dad?' And when the story was told, he was silent for a long moment before announcing, 'I'm going to be a tug captain when I'm big.'

Then he showed Samantha how to spread strawberry jam on her muffins in the correct way, and chewing together heartily with cream on their lips the two of them became fast friends, and Nicholas joined their chatter more easily, smiling his thanks to Samantha and reaching under the table to squeeze her hand.

He had to end it at last. 'Listen, Peter, if we are to make Lynwood by five –' and the boy sobered instantly.

'Dad, couldn't you telephone Mother? She might just let me spend the weekend in London with you.'

'I already tried that.' Nick shook his head. 'It didn't work,' and Peter stood up, his feeling choked by an expression of stoic resignation.

From the back of Nick's Mercedes 450 Coupé the boy leaned forward into the space between the two bucket seats, and the three of them were very close in the snug interior of the speeding car, their laughter that of old friends.

It was almost dark when Nicholas turned in through Lynwood's stone gateway, and he glanced at the luminous dial of his Rolex. 'We'll just make it.'

The drive climbed the hill in a series of broad even curves through the carefully tended woods, and the three-storied Georgian country house on the crest was ablaze with light in every window.

Nick never came here without that strange hollow feeling in the bottom of his stomach. Once this had been his home, every room, every acre of the grounds had its memories, and now, as he parked under the white columned portico, they came crowding back.

'I have finished the model Spitfire you sent me for Christmas, Dad.' Peter was playing desperately for time now. 'Won't you come up and see it?'

'I don't think so –' Nicholas began, and Peter blurted out before he could finish.

'It's all right, Uncle Duncan won't be here. He always comes down late from London on Friday nights, and his Rolls isn't in the garage yet.' Then, in a tone that tore at Nick like thorns, 'Please. . . . I won't see you again until Easter.'

'Go,' said Samantha. 'I'll wait here.' And Peter turned on her, 'You come too, Sam, please.'

Samantha felt herself infected by that fatal curiosity, the desire to see, to know more of Nick's past life; she knew he was going to demur further, but she forestalled him, slipping quickly out of the Mercedes.

'Okay, Pete, let's go.'

Nick must follow them up the broad steps to the double oaken doors, and he felt himself carried along on a tide of events over which he had no control. It was a sensation that he never relished.

In the entrance hall Samantha looked around her quickly, feeling herself overcome by awe. It was so grand, there was no other word to describe the house. The stair well reached up the full height of the three storeys, and the broad staircase was in white marble with a marble balustrade, while on each side of the hall, glass doors opened on to long reception rooms. But she did not have a chance to look further, for Peter seized her hand and raced her up the staircase, while Nick followed them up to Peter's room at a more sedate pace.

The Spitfire had place of honour on the shelf above Peter's bed. He brought it down proudly, and they examined it with suitable expressions of admiration. Peter responded to their praise like a flower to the sun.

When at last they descended the staircase, the sadness and restraint of parting was on them all, but they were stopped in the centre of the hall by the voice from the drawing-room door on the left.

'Peter, darling.' A woman stood in the open doorway, and she was even more beautiful than the photograph that Samantha had seen of her.

Dutifully Peter crossed to her. 'Good evening, Mother.'

She stooped over him, cupping his face in her hands, and she kissed him tenderly, then she straightened, holding his hand so he was ranged at her side, a subtle drawing of boundaries.

'Nicholas,' she tilted her head, 'you look marvellous – so brown and fit.'

Chantelle Alexander was only a few inches taller than her son, but she seemed to fill and light the huge house with a shimmering presence, the way a single beautiful bird can light a dim forest.

Her hair was dark and soft and glowing, and her skin and the huge dark sloe eyes were a legacy from the beautiful Persian noblewoman that old Arthur Christy had married for her fortune, and come to love with an obsessive passion.

She was dainty. Her tiny, narrow feet peeped from below the long, dark green silk skirt, and the exquisite little hand that held Peter's was emphasized by a single deep throbbing green emerald the size of a ripe acorn.

Now she turned her head on the long graceful neck, and her eyes took the slightly oriental slant of a modern-day Nefertiti as she looked at Samantha.

For seconds only, the two women studied each other, and Samantha's chin came up firmly as he looked into those deep dark gazelle eyes, touched with all the mystery and intrigue of the East. They understood each other instantly. It was an intuitive flash, like a discharge of static electricity, then Chantelle smiled, and when she smiled the impossible happened – she became more beautiful than before.

'May I present Dr Silver?' Nick began, but Peter tugged at his mother's hand.

'I asked Sam to see my model. She's a marine biologist, and she's a professor at Miami University –'

'Not yet, Pete,' Samantha corrected him, 'but give me time.'

'Good evening, Dr Silver. It seems you have made a conquest.' Chantelle let the statement hang ambiguously as she turned back to Nick. 'I was waiting for you, Nicholas, and I'm so glad to have a chance to speak to you.' She glanced again at Samantha. 'I do hope you will excuse us for a few minutes, Dr Silver. It is a matter of some urgency. Peter will be delighted to entertain you. As a biologist, you will find his guinea pigs of interest, I'm sure.'

The commands were given so graciously, by a lady in such control of her situation, that Peter went to take Samantha's hand and lead her away.

It was one of the customs of Lynwood that all serious discussion took place in the study. Chantelle led the way, and went immediately to the false-fronted bookcase that concealed the liquor cabinet, and commenced the ritual of preparing a drink for Nicholas. He wanted to stop her. It was something from long ago, recalling too much that was painful, but instead, he watched the delicate but precise movements of her hands pouring exactly the correct measure of Chivas Royal Salute into the crystal glass, adding the soda and the single cube of ice.

'What a pretty young girl, Nicholas.'

He said nothing. On the ornate Louis Quatorze desk was a silver-framed photograph of Duncan Alexander and Chantelle together, and he looked away and moved to the fireplace, standing with his back to the blaze as he had done on a thousand other evenings.

Chantelle brought the glass to him, and stood close, looking up at him – and her fragrance touched a deep nostalgic chord. He had first bought *Calèche* for her on a spring morning in Paris; with an effort he forced the memory aside.

'What did you want to speak to me about, is it Peter?'

'No. Peter is doing as well as we can hope for, in the circumstances. He still resents Duncan – but—' she shrugged, and moved away. He had almost forgotten how narrow was her waist, he would still be able to span it with both hands.

'It's hard to explain, but it's Christy Marine, Nicholas. I desperately need the advise of someone I can trust.'

'You can trust me?' he asked.

'Isn't it strange? I would still trust you with my life.' She came back to him, standing disconcertingly close, enveloping him with her scent and heady beauty. He sipped at the whisky to distract himself.

'Even though I have no right to ask you, Nicholas, still I know you won't refuse me, will you?'

She wove spells, he could feel the mesh falling like gossamer around him.

'I always was a sucker, wasn't I?'

Now she touched his arm. 'No, Nicholas, please don't be bitter. She held his gaze directly.

'How can I help you?' Her touch on his arm disturbed him, and, sensing this, she increased the pressure of her fingers for a moment, then lifted her hand and glanced at the slim white gold Piaget on her wrist.

'Duncan will be home soon – and what I have to tell you is long and complicated. Can we meet in London early next week?'

'Chantelle,' he began.

'Nicky, please.' *Nicky,* she was the only one who ever called him that. It was too familiar, too intimate.

'When?'

'You are meeting Duncan on Tuesday morning to discuss the arbitration of *Golden Adventurer*.'

'Yes.'

'Will you call me at Eaton Square when you finish? I'll wait by the telephone.'

'Chantelle –'

'Nicky, I have nobody else to turn to.'

He had never been able to refuse her – which was part of the reason he had lost her, he thought wryly.

*

There was no engine noise, just the low rush of air past the body of the Mercedes.

'Damn these seats, they weren't made for lovers,' Samantha said.

'We'll be home in an hour.'

'I don't know if I can wait that long,' Samantha whispered huskily. 'I want to be closer to you.'

And they were silent again, until they slowed for the weekend traffic through Hammersmith.

'Peter is a knockout. If only I were ten years old, I'd cash in my dolls.'

'My guess is he would swop his Spitfire.'

'How much longer?'

'Another half hour.'

'Nicholas, I feel threatened,' her voice had a sudden panicky edge to it. 'I have this terrible foreboding —'

'That's nonsense.'

'It's been too good – for too long.'

James Teacher was the head of Salmon Peters and Teacher, the lawyers that Nick had retained for Ocean Salvage. He was a man with a formidable reputation in the City, a leading expert on maritime law – and a tough bargainer. He was florid and bald, and so short that his feet did not touch the floorboards of the Bentley when he sat on the back seat.

He and Nick had discussed in detail where this preliminary meeting with Christy Marine should be held, and at last they had agreed to go to the mountain, but James Teacher had insisted on arriving in his chocolate-coloured Bentley, rather than a cab.

'Smoked salmon, Mr Berg, not fish and chips – that's what we are after.'

Christy House was one of those conservative smoke-stained stone buildings fronted on to Leadenhall Street, the centre of Britain's shipping industry. Almost directly opposite was Trafalgar House, and a hundred yard's further was Lloyd's of London. The doorman crossed the pavement to open Nicholas' door.

'Good to see you again, Mr Berg sir.'

'Hello, Alfred. You taking good care of the shop?'

'Indeed, sir.'

The following cab, containing James Teacher's two juniors and their bulky briefcases, pulled up behind the Bentley and they assembled on the pavement like a party of raiding Vikings before the gates of a medieval city. The three lawyers settled their bowler hats firmly and then moved forward determinedly in spearhead formation.

In the lobby, the doorman passed them on to a senior clerk who was waiting by the desk.

'Good morning, Mr Berg. You are looking very well, sir.'

They rode up at a sedate pace in the elevator with its antique steel concertina doors. Nicholas had never brought himself to exchange them for those swift modern boxes. And the clerk ushered them out on to the top-floor landing.

'Will you follow me, please, gentlemen?'

There was an antechamber that opened on to the board room, a large room, panelled and hung with a single portrait of old Arthur Christy on the entrance wall – fighting jaw and sharp black eyes under beetling white eyebrows. A log fire burned in the open grate, and there was sherry and Madeira in crystal decanters on the central table – another one of the old man's little traditions – that both James Teacher and Nick refused curtly.

They waited quietly, standing facing the door into the Chairman's suite. They waited for exactly four minutes before the door was thrown open and Duncan Alexander stepped through it.

His eyes flicked across the room and settled instantly on Nick, locking with his, like the horns of two great bull buffalo, and the room was very still.

The lawyers around Nick seemed to shrink back and the men behind Duncan Alexander waited, not yet following him into the antechamber, but all of them watched and waited avidly; this meeting would be the gossip of the City for weeks to come. It was a classic confrontation, and they wanted to miss not a moment of it.

Duncan Alexander was a strikingly good-looking man, very tall, two inches taller than Nick, but slim as a dancer, and he carried his body with a dancer's control. His face also was narrow, with the long lantern jaw of a young Lincoln, already chiselled by life around the eyes and at the corners of the mouth.

His hair was very dense and a metallic blond; though he wore it fashionably long over the ears, yet it was so carefully groomed that each gleaming wave seemed to have been sculptured.

His skin was smooth and tanned darker than his hair, sunlamp or skiing at Chantelle's lodge at Gstaad perhaps, and now when he smiled his teeth were dazzlingly white, perfect large teeth in the wide friendly mouth – but the eyes did not smile though they crinkled at the corners. Duncan Alexander watched from behind the handsome face like a sniper in ambush.

'Nicholas,' he said, without moving forward or offering a hand.

'Duncan,' said Nick quietly, not answering the smile, and Duncan Alexander adjusted the hang of his lapel. His clothes were beautifully cut, and the cloth was the finest, softest wool, but there were foppish little touches: the hacking slits in the tails of the jacket, the double-flapped pockets, and the waistcoat in plum-coloured velvet. Now he touched the buttons with his fingertips, another little distracting gesture, the only evidence of any discomfort.

Nicholas stared at him steadily, trying to measure him dispassionately, and now for the first time he began to see how it might have happened. There was a sense of excitement about the man, a wicked air of danger, the fascination of the leopard – or some other powerful predator. Nick could understand the almost irresistible attraction he had for women, especially for a spoiled and bored lady, a matron of thirteen years who believed there was still excitement and adventure in life that she was missing. Duncan had done his cobra dance, and Chantelle had watched like a mesmerized bird of paradise – until she had toppled from the branch – or that's how Nicholas liked to think it had happened. He was wiser now, much wiser and more cynical.

'Before we begin,' Nick knew that anger was seething to his still surface, must soon bubble through unless he could give it release, 'I should like five minutes in private.'

'Of course.' Duncan inclined his head, and there was a hurried scampering as his minions cleared the doorway into the Chairman's suite. 'Come through.'

Duncan stood aside, and Nick walked through. The offices had been completely redecorated, and Nick blinked with surprise, white carpets and furniture in chrome and perspex, stark abstract geometrical art in solid primary colours on the walls; the ceiling had been lowered by an eggcrate design in chrome steel and free-swivelling studio spotlights gave selected light patterns on wall and ceiling. It was no improvement, Nick decided.

'I was in St Nazaire last week.' Nicholas turned in the centre of the wide snowy floor and faced Duncan Alexander as he closed the door.

'Yes, I know.'

'I went over *Golden Dawn*.'

Duncan Alexander snapped open a gold cigarette case and offered it to Nick, then when he shook his head in refusal, selected one himself. They were special blend, custom-made for him by Benson and Hedges.

'Charles Gras exceeded his authority,' Duncan nodded. 'Visitors are not allowed on *Golden Dawn*.'

'I am not surprised you are ashamed of that death-trap you are building.'

'But you do surprise me, Nicholas.' Duncan showed his teeth again. 'It was your design.'

'You know it was not. You took the idea, and bastardized it. Duncan, you cannot send that,' Nick sought the word, 'monster on to the open sea. Not with one propulsion unit, and a single screw. The risk is too appalling.'

'I tell you this for no good reason, except perhaps that this was once your office,' Duncan made a gesture that embraced the room, 'and because it amuses me to point out to you the faults in your original planning. The concept was sound, but your soured the cream by adding those preposterous, shall we call them Bergean, touches. Five separate propulsion units, and a forest of boilers. It wasn't viable, Nicholas.'

'It was good, the figures were right.'

'The whole tanker market has changed since you left Christy Marine. I had to re-work it.'

'You should have dropped the whole concept if the cost-structure changed.'

'Oh no, Nicholas, I restructured. My way, even in these hard times, I will recover capital in a year, and with a five-year life on the hull there is two hundred million dollars' profit in it.'

'I was going to build a ship that would last for thirty years,' Nick told him. 'Something of which we could be proud –'

'Pride is an expensive commodity. We aren't building dynasties any more, we are in the game of selling tanker space.' Duncan's tone was patronizing, that impeccable accent drawn out, emphasizing the difference in their backgrounds. 'I'm aiming at a five-year life, two hundred million profit, and then we sell the hull to the Greeks or Japs. It's a one-time thing.'

'You always were a smash-and-grab artist,' Nick agreed. 'But it isn't like dealing in commodities. Ships aren't wheat and bacon, and the oceans aren't the orderly market floors.'

'I disagree, I'm afraid. The principles are the same – one buys, one sells.'

'Ships are living things, the ocean is a battleground of all the elements.'

'Come, Nicholas, you don't really believe that romantic nonsense.' Duncan drew a gold Hunter from his waist pocket, and snapped open the lid to read the dial, another of his affectations which irritated Nicholas. 'Those are very expensive gentlemen waiting next door.'

'You will be risking human life, the men who sail her.'

'Seamen are well paid –'

'You will be taking a monstrous risk with the life of the oceans. Wherever she goes *Golden Dawn* will be a potential –'

'For God's sake, Nicholas, two hundred million dollars is worth some kind of risk.'

'All right,' Nick nodded. 'Let's forget the environment, and the human life, and consider the important aspects – the money.'

Duncan sighed, and wagged that fine head, smiling as at a recalcitrant child.

'I have considered the money – in detail.'

'You will not get an A1 rating at Lloyd's. You will not get insurance on that hull – unless you underwrite yourself, the same way you did with *Golden Adventurer*, and if you think that's wise, just wait until I've finished with my salvage claim.'

Duncan Alexander's smile twisted slowly, and blood darkened his cheeks under the snow-tan. 'I do not need a Lloyd's rating, though I am sure I could get one if I wanted it. I have arranged continental and oriental underwriters. She will be fully insured.'

'Against pollution claims, also? If you burst that bag of crude on the continental shelf of America, or Europe, they'll hit you for half a billion dollars. Nobody would underwrite that.'

'*Golden Dawn* is registered in Venezuela, and she has no sister ships for the authorities to seize, like they did with the *Torrey Canyon*. To whom will they address the pollution bill? A defunct South American Company? No, Nicholas, Christy Marine will not be paying any pollution bills.'

'I cannot believe it, even of you.' Nick stared at him. 'You are cold-bloodedly talking about the possibility – no, the probability – of dumping a million tons of crude oil into the sea.'

'Your moral indignation is touching. It really is. However, Nicholas, may I remind you that this is family and house business – and you are no longer either family or house.'

'I fought you every time you cut a corner,' Nick reminded him. 'I tried to teach you that cheap is always expensive in the long run.'

'You taught me?' For the first time Duncan taunted him openly. 'What could you ever teach me about ships or money,' and he rolled his tongue gloating around the next words, 'or women?'

Nick made the first movement of lunging at him, but he caught himself, and forced himself to unclench his fists at his sides. The blood sang in his ears.

'I'm going to fight you,' he said quietly. 'I'm going to fight you from here to the Maritime Conference, and beyond.' He made the decision in that moment, he hadn't realized he was going to do it until then.

'A maritime conference has never taken less than five years to reach a decision restricting one of its members. By that time *Golden Dawn* will belong to some Japanese, Hong-Kong-based company – and Christy Marine will have banked two hundred million.'

'I'll have the oil ports closed to you –'

'By whom? Oil-thirsty governments, with lobbies of the big oil companies?' Duncan laughed lightly, he had replaced the urbane mask. 'You really are out of your depth again. We have bumped heads a dozen times before, Nicholas – and I'm still on my feet. I'm not about to fold up to your fine threats now.'

After that, there was no hope that the meeting in the panelled board room would lead to conciliation. The atmosphere crackled and smouldered with the antagonism of the two leading characters, so that they seemed to be the only persons on the stage.

They sat opposite each other, separated by the glossy surface of the rosewood table top, and their gazes seldom disengaged. They leaned forward in their chairs, and when they smiled at each other, it was like the silent snarl of two old dog wolves circling with hackles erect.

It took an enormous effort of self-control for Nicholas to force back his anger far enough to be able to think clearly, and to allow his intuition to pick up the gut-impressions, the subtle hints of the thinking and planning that were taking place across the table behind Duncan Alexander's handsome mask of a face.

It was half an hour before he was convinced that something other than personal rivalry and antagonism was motivating the man before him. His counter offer was too low to have any hope of being accepted, so low that it became clear that he did not want to settle. Duncan Alexander wanted to go to arbitration – and yet there was nothing he could gain by that. It must be obvious to everyone at the table, beyond any doubt whatsoever, that Nicholas' claim was worth four million dollars. Nicholas would have settled for four, even in his anger he would have gone for four – risking that an arbitration board might have awarded six, and knowing the delay and costs of going to litigation might amount to another million. He would have settled.

Duncan Alexander was offering two and a half. It was a frivolous offer. Duncan was going through the motions only. There was no serious attempt at finding a settlement. He didn't want to come to terms, and it seemed to Nicholas that by refusing to settle he was gaining nothing, and risking a great deal. He was a big enough boy to know that you never, but never, go to litigation if there is another way out. It was a rule that Nicholas had graven on his heart in letters of fire. Litigation makes only lawyers fat.

Why was Duncan baulking, what was he to gain by this obstruction? Nicholas crushed down the temptation to stand up and walk out of the room with an exclamation of disgust. Instead, he lit another cheroot and leaned forward again, staring into Duncan Alexander's steely grey eyes, trying to fathom him, needling, probing for the soft rotten spot – and thinking hard.

What had Duncan Alexander go gain from not settling now? Why did he not try with a low, but realistic offer – what was he to gain?

Then quite suddenly he knew what it was. Chantelle's enigmatic appeal for help and advice flashed back to him, and he knew what it was. Duncan Alexander wanted time. It was as simple as that. Duncan Alexander needed time.

'All right.' Satisfied at last, Nicholas leaned back in the deep leather-padded chair, and veiled his eyes. 'We are still a hundred miles apart. There will be only one meeting-ground. That's in the upper room at Lloyd's. It's set down for the 27th. Are we at least agreed on that date?'

'Of course.' Duncan leaned back also and Nicholas saw the shift of his eyes, the little jump of nerves in the point of his clenched jaws, the tightening of the long pianist's fingers that lay before him on the leather-bound blotter. 'Of course,' Duncan repeated, and began to stand up, a gesture of dismissal. He lied beautifully; had Nicholas not known he would lie, he might have missed the little tell-tale signs.

In the ancient lift, James Teacher was jubilant, rubbing his little fat hands together. 'We'll give him a go!' Nicholas glanced at him sourly. Win, lose or draw, James Teacher would still draw his fee, and Duncan Alexander's refusal to settle had quadrupled that fee. There was something almost obscene about the little lawyer's exultation.

'They are going to duck,' Nick said grimly, and James Teacher sobered slightly.

'Before noon tomorrow, Christy Marine will have lodged for postponement of hearing,' Nick prophesied. 'You'll have to use *Warlock* with full power on both to pull them before the arbitration board.'

'Yes, you're right,' James Teacher nodded. 'They had me puzzled, I sensed something –'

'I'm not paying you to be puzzled,' Nick's voice was low and hard. 'I'm paying you to out-guess and out-jump them. I want them at the hearing on the 27th, get them there, Mr Teacher.' He did not have to voice the threat, and in a moment, the exultation on James Teacher's rotund features had changed to apprehension and deep concern.

The drawing-room in Eaton Square was decorated in cream and pale gold, cleverly designed as a frame for the single exquisite work of art which it contained, the original of the group of Degas ballet-dancers whose copy hung in *Golden Dawn*'s stateroom. It was the room's centre-piece; cunningly lit by a hidden spotlight, it glowed like a precious jewel. Even the flowers on the ivory grand piano were cream and white roses and carnations, whose pale ethereal blossoms put the painting into stronger contrast.

The only other flash of brightness was worn by Chantelle, she had the oriental knack of carrying vivid colour without it seeming gaudy. She wore a flaming Pucci that could not pale her beauty, and as she rose from the huge shaggy white sofa and came to Nicholas, he felt the soft warm melting sensation in his stomach spreading slowly through his body like a draught of some powerful aphrodisiac. He knew he would never be immune to her.

'Dear Nicky, I knew I could rely upon you.' She took his hand and looked up at him, and still holding his hand she led him to the sofa, and then she settled beside him, like a bright, lovely bird alighting. She drew her legs up under her, her calves and ankles flashed like carved and polished ivory before she tucked the brilliant skirt around them, and lifted the Wedgwood porcelain teapot.

'Orange pekoe,' she smiled at him. 'No lemon and no sugar.'

He had to smile back at her. 'You never forget,' and he took the cup.

'I told you that you looked well,' she said, slowly and unselfconsciously studying him. 'And you really do, Nicholas. When you came down to Lynwood for Peter's birthday in June I was so worried about you. You looked terribly ill and tired – but now,' she tilted her head critically, 'you look absolutely marvellous.'

Now he should tell her that she was beautiful as ever, he thought grimly, and then they would start talking about Peter and their old mutual friends.

'What did you want to talk to me about?' he asked quietly, and there was a passing shadow of hurt in her dark eyes.

'Nicholas, you can be so remote, so –' she hesitated, seeking the correct word, 'so detached.'

'Recently someone called me an ice-cold Pommy bastard,' he agreed, but she shook her head.

'No. I know you are not, but if only –'

'The three most dangerous and inflammatory phrases in the English language,' he stopped her. 'They are "you always" ' and "you never" and "if only". Chantelle, I came here to help you with a problem. Let's discuss that – only.'

She stood up quickly, and he knew her well enough to recognize the fury in the snapping dark eyes and the quick dancing steps that carried her to the mantelpiece, and she stood looking up at the Degas with her small fists clenched at her sides.

'Are you sleeping with that child?' she asked, and now the fury was raw in her voice.

Nicholas stood up from the sofa.

'Goodbye, Chantelle.'

She turned and flew to him, taking his arm.

'Oh, Nicholas, that was unforgivable, I don't know what possessed me. Please don't go.' And when he tried to dislodge her hand. 'I beg you, for the first time ever, I beg you, Nicholas. Please don't go.'

He was still stiff with anger when he sank back on the sofa, and they were silent for nearly a minute while she regained her composure.

'This is all going so terribly badly. I didn't want this to happen.'

'All right, let's get on to safer ground.'

'Nicholas,' she started, 'you and Daddy created Christy Marine. If anything, it was more yours than his. The great days were the last ten years when you were Chairman, all the tremendous achievements of those years –'

He made a gesture of denial and impatience, but she went on softly.

'Too much of your life is locked up in Christy Marine, you are still deeply involved, Nicholas.'

'There are only two things I am involved with now,' he told her harshly. 'Ocean Salvage and Nicholas Berg.'

'We both know that is not true,' she whispered. 'You are a special type of man.' She sighed. 'It took me so long to recognize that. I thought all men were like you. I believed strength and nobility of mind were common goods on the market –' she shrugged. 'Some people learn the hard way,' and she smiled, but it was an uncertain, twisted little smile.

He said nothing for a moment, thinking of all that was revealed by those words, then he replied.

'If you believe that, then tell me what is worrying you.'

'Nicholas, something is terribly wrong with Christy Marine. There is something happening there that I don't understand.'

'Tell me.'

She turned her head away for a moment, and then looked back at him. Her eyes seemed to change shape and colour, growing darker and sadder. 'It is so difficult not to be disloyal, so difficult to find expression for vague doubts and fears,' she stopped and bit her lower lip softly. 'Nicholas, I have transferred my shares in Christy Marine to Duncan as my nominee, with voting rights.'

Nicholas felt the shock of it jump down his nerves and string them tight. He shifted restlessly on the sofa and stared at her, and she nodded.

'I know it was madness. The madness of those crazy days a year ago. I would have given him anything he asked for.'

He felt the premonition that she had not yet told him all and he waited while she rose and went to the window, looked out guiltily and then turned back to him.

'May I get you a drink?'

He glanced at his Rolex. 'The sun is over the yard-arm, what about Duncan?'

'These days he is never home before eight or nine.' She went to the decanter on the silver tray and poured the whisky with her back to him, and now her voice was so low that he barely caught the words.

'A year ago I resigned as executrix of the Trust.'

He did not answer, it was what he had been waiting for, he had known there was something else. The Trust that old Arthur Christy had set up was the backbone and sinews of Christy Marine. One million voting shares administered by three executors, a banker, a lawyer and a member of the Christy family.

Chantelle turned and brought the drink to him.

'Did you hear what I said?' she asked, and he nodded and sipped the drink before he asked,

'The other executors? Pickstone of Lloyd's and Rollo still?'

She shook her head and again bit her lip.

'No, it's not Lloyd's any more, it's Cyril Forbes.'

'Who is he?' Nick demanded.

'He is the head of London and European.'

'But that's Duncan's own bank,' Nick protested.

'It's still a registered bank.'

'And Rollo?'

'Rollo had a heart attack six months ago. He resigned, and Duncan put in another younger man. You don't know him.'

'My God, three men and each of them is Duncan Alexander – he has had a free hand with Christy Marine for over a year, Chantelle, there is no check on him.'

'I know,' she whispered. 'It was a madness. I just cannot explain it.'

'It's the oldest madness in the world.' Nick pitied her then; for the first time, he realized and accepted that she had been under a compulsion, driven by forces over which she had no control, and he pitied her.

'I am so afraid, Nicholas. I'm afraid to find out what I have done. Deep down I know there is something terribly wrong, but I'm afraid of the truth.'

'All right, tell me everything.'

'There isn't anything else.'

'If you lie to me, I cannot help you,' he pointed out gently.

'I have tried to follow the new structuring of the company, it's all so complicated, Nicholas. London and European is the new holding company, and – and —' her voice trailed off. 'It just goes round and round in circles, and I cannot pry too deep or ask too many questions.'

'Why not?' he demanded.

'You don't know Duncan.'

'I am beginning to,' he answered her grimly. 'But, Chantelle, you have every right to ask and get answers.'

'Let me get you another drink.' She jumped up lightly.

'I haven't finished this one.'

'The ice has melted, I know you don't like that.' She took the glass and emptied the diluted spirit, refilled it and brought it back to him.

'All right,' he said. 'What else?'

Suddenly she was weeping. Smiling at him wistfully and weeping. There was no sobbing or sniffing, the tears merely welled up slowly as oil or blood from the huge dark eyes, broke from the thick, arched lashes and rolled softly down her cheeks. Yet she still smiled.

'The madness is over, Nicholas. It didn't last very long – but it was a holocaust while it did.'

'He comes home at nine o'clock now,' Nicholas said.

'Yes, he comes home at nine o'clock.'

He took the linen handkerchief from his inner pocket and handed it to her.

'Thank you.'

She dabbed away the tears, still smiling softly.

'What must I do, Nicholas?'

'Call in a team of auditors,' he began, but she shook her head and cut him short.

'You don't know Duncan,' she repeated.

'There is nothing he could do.'

'He could do anything,' she contradicted him. 'He is capable of anything. I am afraid, Nicholas, terribly afraid, not only for myself, but for Peter also.'

Nicholas sat erect then.

'Peter. Do you mean you are afraid of something physical?'

'I don't know, Nicholas. I'm so confused and alone. You are the only person in the world I can trust.'

He could no longer remain seated. He stood up and began to pace about the room, frowning heavily, looking down at the glass in his hand and swirling the ice so that it tinkled softly.

'All right,' he said at last. 'I will do what I can. The first thing is to find out just how much substance there is to your fears.'

'How will you do that?'

'It's best you don't know, yet.'

He drained his glass and she stood up, quick with alarm.

'You aren't going, are you?'

'There is nothing else to discuss now. I will contact you when or if I learn anything.'

'I'll see you down.'

In the hall she dismissed the uniformed West Indian maid with a shake of her head, and fetched Nicholas' top coat from the closet herself.

'Shall I send for the car? You'll not get a cab at five o'clock.'

'I'll walk,' he said.

'Nicholas, I cannot tell you how grateful I am. I had forgotten how safe and secure it is to be with you.' Now she was standing very close to him, her head lifted, and her lips were soft and glossy and ripe, her eyes still flooded and bright. He knew he should leave immediately. 'I know it's going to be all right now.'

She placed one of those dainty ivory hands on his lapel, adjusting it unnecessarily with that proprietary feminine gesture, and she moistened her lips.

'We are all fools, Nicholas, every one of us. We all complicate our lives – when it's so easy to be happy.'

'The trick is to recognize happiness when you stumble on it, I suppose.'

'I'm sorry, Nicholas. That's the first time I've ever apologized to you. It's a day of many first times, isn't it? But I am truly sorry for everything I have ever done to hurt you. I wish with all my heart that it were possible to wipe it all out and begin again.'

'Unfortunately, it doesn't work that way.' With a major effort of will he broke the spell, and stepped back. In another moment he would have stooped to those soft red lips.

'I'll call you if I learn anything,' he said, as he buttoned the top of his coat and opened the front door.

Nicholas stepped out furiously with the cold striking colour into his cheeks, but her presence kept pace with him and his blood raced not from physical exertion alone.

He knew then, beyond all doubt, that he was not a man who could switch love on and off at will.

'You old-fashioned thing.' Samantha's words came back to him clearly – and she was right, of course. He was cursed by a constancy of loyalty and emotion that restricted his freedom of action. He was breaking one of his own rules now, he was no longer moving ahead. He was circling back.

He had loved Chantelle Christy to the limits of his soul, and had devoted almost half of his life to Christy Marine. He realized then that those things could never change, not for him, not for Nicholas Berg, prisoner of his own conscience.

Suddenly he found himself opposite the Kensington Natural History Museum in the Cromwell Road, and swiftly he crossed to the main gates – but it was a quarter to six and they were closed already. Samantha would not have been in the public rooms anyway, but in those labyrinthine vaults below the great stone building. In a few short days, she had made half a dozen cronies among the museum staff. He felt a stab of jealousy, that she was with other human beings, revelling in their companionship, delighting in the pleasures of the mind – had probably forgotten he existed.

Then suddenly the unfairness of it occurred to him, how his emotions of a minute previously had been stirring and boiling with the memories of another woman. Only then did he realize that it was possible to be in love with two different people, in two entirely different ways, at exactly the same time.

Troubled, torn by conflicting loves, conflicting loyalties, he turned away from the barred iron gates of the museum.

Nicholas' apartment was on the fifth floor of one of those renovated and redecorated buildings in Queen's Gate.

It looked as though a party of gypsies were passing through. He had not hung the paintings, not had he arranged his books on the shelves. The paintings were stacked against the wall in the hallway, and his books were pyramided at unlikely spots around the lounge floor, the carpet still rolled and pushed aside, two chairs facing the television set, and another two drawn up to the dining-room table.

It was an eating and sleeping place, sustaining the bare minima of existence; in two years he had probably slept here on sixty nights, few of them consecutive. It was impersonal, it contained no memories, no warmth.

He poured a whisky and carried it through into the bedroom, slipping the knot of his tie and shrugging out of his jacket. Here it was different, for evidence of Samantha's presence was everywhere. Though she had remade the bed that morning before leaving, still she had left a pair of shoes abandoned at the foot of it, a booby trap to break the ankles of the unwary; her simple jewellery was strewn on the bedside table, together with a book, Noel Mostert's *Supership*, opened face down and in dire danger of a broken spine; the cupboard door was open and his suits had been bunched up in one corner to give hanging space to her slacks and dresses; two very erotic and transparent pairs of panties hung over the bath to dry; her talcum powder still dusted the tiled floor and her special fragrance pervaded the entire apartment.

He missed her with a physical ache in the chest, so that when the front door banged and she arrived like a high wind, shouting for him, 'Nicholas, it's me!' as though it could possibly have been anyone else, her hair tangled and wild with the wind and high colour under the golden tan of her cheeks, he almost ran to her and seized her with a suppressed violence.

'Wow,' she whispered huskily. 'Who is a hungry baby, then.' And they tumbled on to the bed clinging to each other with a need that was almost desperation.

Afterwards they did not turn the light on in the room that had gone dark except for the dim light of the street lamps filtered by the curtains and reflected off the ceiling.

'What was that all about?' she asked, then snuggled against his chest, 'not that I'm complaining, mind you.'

'I've had a hell of a day. I needed you, badly.'

'You saw Duncan Alexander?'

'I saw Duncan.'

'Did you settle?'

'No. There was never really any chance.'

'I'm hungry,' she said. 'Your loving always makes me hungry.'

So he put on his pants and went down to the Italian restaurant at the corner for pizzas. They ate them in bed with a white Chianti from whisky tumblers, and when she was finished, she sighed and said:

'Nicholas, I have to go home.'

'You can't go,' he protested instantly.

'I have work to do – also.'

'But,' he felt a physical nausea at the thought of losing her, 'but you can't go before the hearing.'

'Why not?'

'It would be the worst possible luck, you are my fortune.'

'A sort of good-luck charm?' She pulled a face. 'Is that all I'm good for?'

'You are good for many things. May I demonstrate one of them?'

'Oh, yes please.'

An hour later Nick went for more pizzas.

'You have to stay until the 27th,' he said with his mouth full.

'Darling Nicholas, I just don't know —'

'You can ring them, tell them your aunt died, that you are getting married.'

'Even if I were getting married, it wouldn't lessen the importance of my work. I think you know that is something I will never give up.'

'Yes, I do know, but it's only a couple of days more.'

'All right, I'll call Tom Parker tomorrow.' Then she grinned at him. 'Don't look like that. I'll be just across the Atlantic, we'll be virtually next-door neighbours.'

'Call him now. It's lunchtime in Florida.'

She spoke for twenty minutes, wheedling and charming, while the blood-curdling transatlantic rumblings on the receiver slowly muted to reluctant and resigned mutterings.

'You're going to get me into trouble one of these days, Nicholas Berg,' she told him primly as she hung up.

'Now *there* is a happy thought,' Nick agreed, and she hit him with her pillow.

The telephone rang at two minutes past nine the next morning. They were in the bath together and Nicholas swore and went through naked and steaming and dripping suds.

'Mr Berg?' James Teacher's voice was sharp and businesslike. 'You were right, Christy Marine petitioned for postponement of hearing late yesterday afternoon.'

'How long?' Nicholas snapped.

'Ninety days.'

'The bastard,' grunted Nick. 'What grounds?'

'They want time to prepare their submission.'

'Block them,' Nick instructed.

'I have a meeting with the Secretary at eleven. I'm going to ask for an immediate preliminary hearing to set down and confirm the return date.'

'Get him before the arbitrators,' said Nick.

'Well get him.'

Samantha welcomed him back to the tub by drawing her knees up under her chin. Her hair was piled on top of her head, but damp wisps hung down her neck and on to her cheeks. She looked pink and dewy as a little girl.

'Careful where you put your toes, sir,' she cautioned him, and he felt the tension along his nerves easing. She had that effect on him.

'I'll buy you lunch at "Les A" if you can tear yourself away from your microscope and fishy-smelling specimens for an hour or two.'

'Les Ambassadeurs? I've heard about it! For lunch there I'd walk across London on freshly amputated stumps.'

'That won't be necessary, but you will have to charm a tribe of wild desert Sheikhs. I understand they are very sympathetic towards blondes.'

'Are you going to sell me into a harem – sounds fun, I've always fancied myself in baggy, transparent bloomers.'

'You, I'm not selling – icebergs, I am. I'll pick you up at the front gate of the museum at one o'clock sharp.'

She went with laughter and a great clatter and banging of doors and Nicholas settled at the telephone.

'I'd like to speak to Sir Richard personally, it's Nicholas Berg.' Sir Richard was at Lloyd's, an old and good friend.

Then he called and spoke to Charles Gras.

There were no new delays or threats to *Sea Witch*'s completion date.

'I am sorry for any trouble you had with Alexander.'

'*Cą ne fait rien*, Nicholas. Good luck at the hearing. I will be watching the *Lloyd's List*.' Nicholas felt a sense of relief. Charles Gras had risked his career to show him *Golden Dawn*. It could have been serious.

Then Nick spoke for nearly half an hour to Bernard Wackie of Bach Wackie in Bermuda. *Warlock* had reported on the telex two hours previously; she was making good passage with her oil-rig tow, would drop off at Bravo II on schedule and pick up her next tow as soon as she had anchored.

'David Allen is a good youngster,' Bernard told Nick. 'But have you got Levoisin for *Sea Witch*?'

'Jules is playing the prima donna, he has not said yes, but he'll come.'

'You'll have a good team, then. What's the latest date for *Sea Witch*?'

'End March.'

'The sooner the better, I've got contacts to keep both tugs running hard until the iceberg project matures.'

'I'm having lunch with the Sheikhs today.'

'I know. There's a lot of interest. I've got a good feeling. There is something big brewing, but they are a cagey bunch. The inscrutable smile on the face of the sphinx – when do we see you?'

'I'll come across just as soon as I've got Duncan Alexander into the arbitration court – end of the month, hopefully.'

'We've got a lot to talk about, Nicholas.'

Nick hesitated for the time it took to smoke the first cheroot of the day before he called Monte Carlo – for the call would cost him at least fifty thousand dollars, probably closer to seventy-five. The best is always the cheapest, he reminded himself, picked up the receiver and spoke to a secretary in Monte Carlo, giving his name.

While he waited for the connection he thought how his life was complicating itself once more. Very soon Bach Wackie would not be enough, there would have to be a London branch of Ocean Salvage, offices, secretaries, files, accounts, and then a New York branch, a branch in Saudi, the whole cycle again. He thought suddenly of Samantha, uncluttered and simple happiness, life without its wearisome trappings – then the connection was made and he heard the thin, high, almost feminine voice.

'Mr Berg – Claud Lazarus.' No other greeting, no expressions of pleasure at the renewal of contact. Nick imagined him sitting at his desk in the suite high above the harbour, like a human foetus – preserved in spirits, bottled on the museum shelf. The huge bald domed head, the soft putty-coloured rudimentary features, the nose hardly large enough to support the thick spectacles. The eyes distorted and startled by the lens, changing shape like those of a fish in an aquarium as the light moved. The body underdeveloped, as that of a foetus, narrow shoulders, seemingly tapering away to the bowed question mark of a body.

'Mr Lazarus. Are you in a position to undertake an indepth study for me?' It was the euphemism for financial and industrial espionage; Claud Lazarus' network was not limited by frontiers or continents, it spanned the globe with delicately probing tentacles.

'Of course,' he piped softly.

'I want the financial structuring, the lines of control and management, the names of the nominees and their principals, the location and inter-relationship of all the elements of the Christy Marine Group and London European Insurance and Banking Co. Group, with particular reference to any changes in structure during the previous fourteen months. Do you have that?'

'This is being recorded, Mr Berg.'

'Of course. Further, I want the country of registration, the insurers and underwriters of all bottoms traceable to their holdings.'

'Please continue.'

'I want an accurate estimate of the reserves of London and European Insurance in relations to their potential liability.'

'Continue.'

'I am particularly interested in the vessel *Golden Dawn* presently building at the yards of Construction Navale Atlantique at St Nazaire. I want to know if she has been chartered or has contracted with any oil company for carriage of crude and, if so, on what routes and at what rates.'

'Yes?' Lazarus squeaked softly.

'Time if of the essence – and, as always, so is discretion.'

'You need not have mentioned that, Mr Berg.'

'My contact, when you are ready to pass information, is Back Wackie in Bermuda.'

'I will keep you informed of progress.'

'Thank you, Mr Lazarus.'

'Good day, Mr Berg.'

It was refreshing not to have to pretend to be the bosom comrade of somebody who supplied essentials but nonetheless revolted him, Nick thought, and comforting to know he had the best man in the world for the job.

He looked at his watch. It was lunchtime, and he felt the quick lift of his spirits at the thought of being with Samantha.

Lime Street is a narrow alleyway, with tall buildings down each side of it, which opens off Leadenhall Street. A few yards from the junction, on the lefthand side as you leave the street of shipping, is the covered entrance to Lloyd's of London.

Nicholas stepped out of James Teacher's Bentley and took Samantha on his arm. He paused a moment, with a feeling of certain reverence.

As a seaman, the history of this remarkable institution touched him intimately. Not that the building itself was particularly old or venerable. Nothing now remained of the original coffee house, except some of the traditions: the caller who intoned the brokers' names like the offertory in the temple of some exotic religion, the stalls in which the underwriters conducted their business and the name and uniform of the institution's servants, the 'waiters' with brass buttons and red collar tabs.

Rather it was the tradition of concern that was enshrined here, the concern for ships and for all men who went down to the sea in those ships and did their business in great waters.

Perhaps later, Nicholas would find time to take Samantha through the Nelson rooms and show her the displays of memorabilia associated with the greatest of Britain's sailors, the plate and letters and awards. Certainly he would have her as lunch guest in the big dining-room, at the table set aside specifically for visiting sea captains.

But now there were more important considerations to demand all his attention. He had come to hear the verdict given on his future – within a few hours he would know just how high and how fast the wave of his fortune had carried him.

'Come,' he said to Samantha, and led her up the short flight of steps into the lobby, where there was a waiter alerted to receive them.

'We will be using the Committee Room today, sir.'

The earlier submissions by both parties had been heard in one of the smaller offices, leading off the high gallery above the vast floor of the exchange with its rows of underwriters' stalls. However, due to the extraordinary nature of this action, the Committee of Lloyd's had made a unique decision – to have their arbitrators give their findings and make their award in surroundings more in keeping with the importance of the occasion.

They rode up in silence, all of them too tense to make the effort of small-talk. and the waiter led them down the wide corridor, past the Chairman's suite of offices and through the double doors into the grandeur of the room designed by Adams for Bowood House, the country home of the Marquess of Lansdowne. It had been taken to pieces, panel by panel, floor, ceiling, fireplace and plaster mouldings, transported to London and re-erected in its entirety with such care and attention that when Lord Lansdowne inspected it, he found that the floorboards squeaked in exactly the same places as they had before.

At the long table, under the massive glittering pyramids of the three chandeliers, the two arbitrators were already seated. Both of them were master mariners, selected for their deep knowledge and experience of the sea, and their faces were toughened and leathery from the effects of sea and salt water. They talked quietly together, without acknowledging in any way the rows of quietly attentive faces in the rows of chairs facing them – until the minute hand of the antique clock on the Adams fireplace touched its zenith. Then the President of the court looked across at the waiter who obediently closed the double doors and stood to attention before them.

'This Arbitration Court has been set up under the Committee of Lloyd's and empowered to receive evidence in the matter between the Christy Marine Steamship Co. Ltd. and the Ocean Salvage and Towage Co. Ltd. This Court finds common ground in the following areas:

'Firstly, a contract of salvage under Lloyd's Open Form "No Cure No Pay" for the recovery of the passenger liner *Golden Adventurer*, a ship of 22,000 tons gross burden and registered at Southampton, exists between the parties.

'Secondly, that the master of the *Golden Adventurer* while steaming on a south-westerly heading during the night of December 16th at or near 72° 16′ south and 32° 12′ west –'

The President let no dramatics intrude on his assembly of the facts. He recounted it all in the driest possible terms, succeeding in making *Golden Adventurer*'s plight and the desperate endeavours of her rescuers sound boring. Indeed, his colleague seemed to descend into a condition of coma at the telling of it. His eyes slowly closed, and his head sagged gently sideways, his lips vibrating slightly at each breath – a volume not quite sufficient to make it a snore.

It took nearly an hour, with the occasional consultation of the ship's log books and a loose volume of handwritten and typed notes, before the President was satisfied that he had recounted all the facts, and now he rocked back in his chair and hooked his thumbs into his waistcoat. His expression became decisive, and while he surveyed the crowded room, his colleague stirred, opened his eyes, took out a white linen handkerchief and blew two sharp blasts, one for each nostril, like the herald angel sounding the crack of doom.

There was a stir of reawakened interest, they all recognized the moment of decision, and for the first time Duncan Alexander and Nicholas Berg looked directly at each other over the heads of the lawyers and company men. Neither of them changed expression, no smile nor scowl, but something implacable and clearly understood passed between them. They did not unlock their gaze, until the President began to speak again.

'Taking into consideration the foregoing, this Court is of the firm opinion that a fair and good salvage of the vessel was effected by the salvors, and that therefore, they are entitled to salvage awards commensurate with the services rendered to the owners and underwriters.'

Nicholas felt Samantha's fingers groping for his. He took her hand, and it was slim and cold and dry; he interlocked their fingers and laid their hands upon his upper thigh.

'This Court, in arriving at the value of the salvor's services, has taken into consideration, firstly, the situation and conditions existing on the site of operations. We have heard evidence that much of the work was carried out in extreme weather conditions. Temperatures of thirty degrees below freezing, wind forces exceeding twelve on the Beaufort scale, and extreme icing.

'We have also considered that the vessel *Golden Adventurer* was no longer under command. That she had been abandoned by her passengers, her crew and her Master. She was aground on a remote and hostile coast.

'We have further noted that the salvors undertook a voyage of many thousands of miles, without any guarantee of recompense, but merely in order to be in a position to offer assistance, should that have become necessary.'

Nicholas glanced across the aisle at Duncan Alexander. He sat at ease, as though he were in his box at Ascot. His suit was of sombre gunmetal grey, but on him it seemed flamboyant and the I Zingari tie as rakish as any of Cardin's fantasies.

Duncan turned that fine leonine head and looked directly at Nicholas again. This time Nicholas saw the deep angry glow in his eyes as when a vagrant breeze fans the coals of an open fire. Then Duncan turned his face back towards the President, and he balanced his thrusting square chin on the clenched, carefully manicured fingers of his right fist.

'Furthermore, we have taken into consideration the transportation of the survivors from the site of the striking, to the nearest port of succour, Cape Town in the Republic of South Africa.'

The President was summing up strongly in favour of Ocean Salvage. It was a dangerous sign; so often a judge about to deliver an unfavourable decision prefaced it by building a strong case for the loser and then tearing it down again.

Nicholas steeled himself, anything below three million dollars would not be sufficient to keep Ocean Salvage alive. That was the barest minimum he needed to keep *Warlock* afloat, and to put *Sea Witch* on the water for the first time. He felt the spasm of his stomach muscles as he contemplated his commitments – even with three million he would be at the mercy of the Sheikhs, unable to manoeuvre, a slave to any conditions they wished to set. He would not be off his knees even.

Nicholas squeezed Samantha's hand for luck, and she pressed her shoulder against his.

Four million dollars would give him a fighting chance, a slim margin of choice – but he would still be fighting hard, pressed on all sides. Yet he would have settled for four million, if Duncan Alexander had made the offer. Perhaps Duncan had been wise after all, perhaps he might yet see Nicholas broken at a single stroke.

'Three.' Nicholas held the figure in his head. 'Let it be three, at least let it be three.'

'This Court has considered the written reports of the Globe Engineering Co., the contractors charged with the repairing and refurbishing of *Golden Adventurer*, together with those of two independent marine engineering experts commissioned separately by the owners and the salvors to report on the condition of the vessel. We have also had the benefit of a survey carried out by a senior inspector of Lloyd's of London. From all of this, it seems apparent that the vessel sustained remarkably light damage. There was no loss of equipment, the salvors recovering even the main anchors and chains —'

Strange how that impressed a salvage court. 'We took her off, anchors and all,' Nick thought, with a stir of pride.

'Prompt anti-corrosion precautions by the salvors resulted in minimal damage to the main engines and ancillary equipment —'

It went on and on. Why cannot he come to it now? I cannot wait much longer, Nicholas thought.

'This Court has heard expert opinion and readily accepts that the residual value of the *Golden Adventurer*'s hull, as delivered to the contractors in Cape Town can be fairly set at twenty-six million US dollars or fifteen million, three hundred thousand pounds sterling, and in consideration of the foregoing, we are further of the firm opinion that the salvors are entitled to an award of twenty per cent of the residual hull value —'

For long cold seconds Nicholas doubted his hearing, and then he felt the flush of exultation burning on his cheeks.

'In addition, it was necessary to compute the value of the passage provided to the survivors of the vessel —'

It was six – six million dollars! He was clear and running free as a wild albatross sweeping across the oceans on wide pinions.

Nicholas turned his head and looked at Duncan Alexander, and he smiled. He had never felt so strong and vital and alive in his life before. He felt like a giant, immortal, and at his side was the vibrant young body pressing to him, endowing him with eternal youth.

Across the aisle, Duncan Alexander tossed his head, a gesture of dismissal and turned to speak briefly with his counsel who sat beside him. He did not look at Nicholas, however, and there was a waxen cast to his skin now as though it had a fine sheen of perspiration laid upon it, and the blood had drained away beneath the tan.

'Anyway, another few days and you'd probably have started to find me a boring dolly bird, or one of us would have had a heart attack.' Samantha smiled at him, a pathetic, lopsided little grin, nothing like her usual brilliant golden flashing smile. 'I like to quit while I'm still ahead.'

They sat close on the couch in the Pan Am Clipper Lounge at Heathrow.

Nicholas was shocked by the extent of his own desolation. It felt as though he were about to be deprived of the vital forces of life itself, he felt the youth and strength draining away as he looked at her and knew that in a few minutes she would be gone.

'Samantha,' he said. 'Stay here with me.'

'Nicholas,' she whispered huskily, 'I have to go, my darling. It's not for very long but I have to go.'

'Why?' he demanded.

'Because it's my life.'

'Make me your life.'

She touched his cheek, as she countered his offer.

'I have a better idea, give up *Warlock* and *Sea Witch* – forget your icebergs and come with me.'

'You know I cannot do that.'

'No,' she agreed, 'you could not, and I would not want you to. But, Nicholas, my love, no more can I give up my life.'

'All right, then, marry me,' he said.

'Why, Nicholas?'

'So I don't lose my lucky charm, so that you'd damn well have to do what I tell you.'

And she laughed delightedly and snuggled against his chest. 'It doesn't work like that any more, my fine Victorian gentleman. There is only one good reason for marrying, Nicholas, and that's to have babies. Do you want to give me a baby?'

'What a splendid idea.'

'So that I can warm the bottles and wash the nappies while you go off to the ends of the oceans – and we'll have lunch together once a month?' She shook her head. 'We might have a baby together one day – but not now, there is still too much to do, there is still too much life to live.'

'Damn it.' He shook his head. 'I don't like to let you run around loose. Next thing you'll take off with some twenty-five year-old oaf, bulging with muscles and –'

'You have given me a taste for vintage wine,' she laughed in denial. 'Come as soon as you can, Nicholas. As soon as you have done your work here, come to Florida and I'll show you my life.'

The hostess crossed the lounge towards them, a pretty smiling girl in the neat blue Pan Am uniform.

'Dr Silver? They are calling Flight 432 now.'

They stood and looked at each other, awkward as strangers.

'Come soon,' she said, and then she stood on tiptoe and placed her arms around his shoulders. 'Come as soon as you can.'

Nicholas had protested vigorously as soon as James Teacher advanced the proposition. 'I don't want to speak to him, Mr Teacher. The only thing I want from Duncan Alexander is his cheque for six million dollars, preferably guaranteed by a reputable bank – and I want it before the 10th of next month.'

The lawyer had wheedled and jollied Nicholas along. 'Think of the pleasure of watching his face – indulge yourself, Mr Berg, gloat on him a little.'

'I will obtain no pleasure by watching his face, off hand I can think of a thousand faces I'd rather watch.' But in the end Nicholas had agreed, stipulating only that this time the meeting should be at a place of Nicholas' choice, an unsubtle reminder of whose hand now held the whip.

James Teacher's rooms were in one of those picturesque. stone buildings in the Inns of Court covered with ivy, surrounded by small velvety lawns, bisected with paved walkways that connected the numerous blocks, the entire complex reeking with history and tradition and totally devoid of modern comforts. Its austerity was calculated to instil confidence in the clients.

Teacher's rooms were on the third floor. There was no elevator and the stairs were narrow, steep and dangerous. Duncan Alexander arrived slightly out of breath and flushed under his tan. Teacher's clerk surveyed him discouragingly from his cubicle.

'Mr who?' he asked, cupping his hand to one ear. The clerk was a man as old, grey and picturesque as the building. He even affected a black alpaca suit, shiny and greenish with age, together with a butterfly collar and a black string tie like that last worn by Neville Chamberlain as he promised peace in our time.

'Mr who?' and Duncan Alexander flushed deeper. He was not accustomed to having to repeat his name.

'Do you have an appointment, Mr Arbuthnot?' the clerk inquired frostily, and laboriously consulted his diary before at last waving Duncan Alexander through into the spartan waiting-room.

Nicholas kept him there exactly eight minutes, twice as long as he himself had waited in the board room of Christy Marine, and he stood by the small electric fire in the fireplace, not answering Duncan's brilliant smile as he entered.

James Teacher sat at his desk under the windows, out of the direct line of confrontation, like the umpire at Wimbledon, and Duncan Alexander barely glanced at him.

'Congratulations, Nicholas,' Duncan shook that magnificent head and the smile faded to a rueful grin. 'You turned one up for the books, you truly did.'

'Thank you, Duncan. However, I must warn you that today I have an impossible schedule to meet, I can give you only ten minutes.' Nicholas glanced at his watch. 'Fortunately I can imagine only one thing that you and I have to discuss. The tenth of next month, either a transfer to the Bermuda account of Ocean Salvage, or a guaranteed draft by registered airmail to Bach Wackie.'

Duncan held up his hand in mock protest. 'Come now, Nicholas – the salvage money will be there, on the due date set by the Court.'

'That's fine,' Nicholas told him, still smiling. 'I have no taste for another brawl in the debtors' court.'

'I wanted to remind you of something that old Arthur Christy once said –'

'Ah, of course, our mutual father-in-law.' Nicholas said softly, and Duncan pretended not to hear; instead he went on unruffled.

'He said, with Berg and Alexander I have put together one of the finest teams in the world of shipping.'

'The old man was getting senile towards the end.' Nicholas had still not smiled.

'He was right, of course. We just never got into step. My God, Nicholas, can you imagine if we had been working together, instead of against each other. You the best salt and steel man in the business, and I –'

'I'm touched, Duncan, deeply touched by this new and gratifying esteem in which I find myself held.'

'You rubbed my nose in it, Nicholas. Just as you said you would. And I'm the kind of man who learns by his mistakes, turning disaster to triumph is a trick of mine.'

'Play your trick now,' Nicholas invited. 'Let's see you turn six million dollars into a flock of butterflies.'

'Six million dollars and Ocean Salvage would buy you back into Christy Marine. We'd be on equal terms.'

The surprise did not show on Nicholas' face, not a flicker of an eyelid, not even a tightening of the lips, but his mind raced to get ahead of the man.

'Together we would be unstoppable. We would build Christy Marine into a giant that controlled the oceans, we'd diversify out into ocean oil exploration, chemical containers.' The man had immense presence and charm, he was almost – but not quite – irresistible, his enthusiasm brimming and overflowing, his fire flaring and spreading to light the dingy room, and Nicholas studied him carefully, learning more about him every second.

'Good God, Nicholas, you are the type of man who can conceive of a venture like the *Golden Dawn* or salvage a giant liner in a sub-zero gale, and I am the man who can put together a billion dollars on a wink and whistle. Nothing could stand before us, there would be no frontiers we could not cross.' He paused now and returned Nicholas' scrutiny as boldly, studying the effect of his words. Nicholas lit the cheroot he was holding, but his eyes watched shrewdly through the fine blue veil of smoke.

'I understand what you are thinking,' Duncan went on, his voice dropping confidentially. 'I know that you are stretched out, I know that you need those six big M's to keep Ocean Salvage floating. Christy Marine will guarantee Ocean Salvage outstandings, that's a minor detail. The important thing is us together, like old Arthur Christy saw it, Berg and Alexander.'

Nicholas took the cheroot from his mouth and inspected the tip briefly before he looked back at him.

'Tell me, Duncan,' he asked mildly, 'in this great sharing you envisage, do we put our women into the kitty also?'

Duncan's mouth tightened, and the flesh wrinkled at the corners of his eyes.

'Nicholas,' he began, but Nicholas silenced him with a gesture.

'You said that I need that six million badly, and you were right. I need three million of it for Ocean Salvage and the other three to stop you running that monster you have built. Even if I don't get it, I will still use it to stop you. I'll slap a garnishee order on you by ten minutes past nine on the morning of the eleventh. I told you I would fight you and *Golden Dawn*. The warning still stands.'

'You are being petty,' Duncan said. 'I never expected to see you join the lunatic fringe.'

'There are many things you do not know about me, Duncan. But, by God, you are going to learn – the hard way.'

Chantelle had chosen San Lorenzo in Beauchamp Place when Nicholas had refused to go again to Eaton Square. He had learned that it was dangerous to be alone with her, but San Lorenzo was also a bad choice of meeting-ground.

It carried too many memories from the golden days. It had been a family ritual, Sunday lunch whenever they were in town. Chantelle, Peter and Nicholas laughing together at the corner table. Mara had given them the corner table again.

'Will you have the *osso bucco*?' Chantelle asked, peeping at him over the top of her menu.

Nicholas always had the *osso bucco*, and Peter always had the *lasagne*, it was part of the ritual.

'I'm going to have a sole.' Nicholas turned to the waiter who was hovering solicitously. 'And we'll drink the house white.' Always the wine had been a Sancerre; Nicholas was deliberately down-grading the occasion by ordering the carafe.

'It's good.' Chantelle sipped it and then set the glass aside. 'I spoke to Peter last night, he is in the san with flu, but he will be up today, and he sent you his love.'

'Thank you,' he spoke stiffly, stilted by the curious glances from some of the other tables where they had been recognized. The scandal would fly around London like the plague.

'I want to take Peter to Bermuda with me for part of the Easter holidays,' Nicholas told her.

'I shall miss him – he's such a delight.'

Nicholas waited for the main course to be served before he asked bluntly, 'What did you want to speak to me about?'

Chantelle leaned towards him, and her perfume was light and subtle and evocative.

'Did you find out anything, Nicholas?'

'No,' he thought to himself. 'That's not what she wants.' It was the Persian in her blood, the love of secrecy, the intrigue. There was something else here.

'I have learned nothing,' he said. 'If I had, I would have called you.' His eyes bored into hers, green and hard and searching. 'That is not what you wanted,' he told her flatly.

She smiled and dropped her eyes from his. 'No,' she admitted, 'it wasn't.'

She had surprising breasts, they seemed small, but really they were too big for her dainty body. It was only their perfect proportions and the springy elasticity of the creamy flesh that created the illusion. She wore a flimsy silk blouse with a low lacey front, which exposed the deep cleft between them. Nicholas knew them so well, and he found himself staring at them now.

She looked up suddenly and caught his eyes, and the huge eyes slanted with a sly heart-stopping sexuality. Her lips pouted softly and she moistened them with the tip of her tongue.

Nick felt himself sway in his seat, it was a tell-tale mannerism of hers. That set of lips and movement of tongue were the heralds of her arousal, and instantly he felt the response of his own body, too powerful to deny, although he tried desperately.

'What was it?' He did not hear the husk in his voice, but she did and recognized it as readily as he had the flicker of her tongue. She reached across the table and took his wrist, and she felt the leap of his pulse under her fingers.

'Duncan wants you to come back into Christy Marine,' she said. 'And so do I.'

'Duncan sent you to me.' And when she nodded, he asked, 'Why does he want me back? God knows what pains the two of you took to get rid of me.' And he gently pulled his wrist from her fingers and dropped both hands into his lap.

'I don't know why Duncan wants it. He says that he needs your expertise.' She shrugged, and her breasts moved under the silk. He felt the tense ache of his groin, it confused his thinking. 'It isn't the true reason, I'm sure of that. But he wants you.'

'Did he ask you to tell me that?'

'Of course not.' She fiddled with the stem of her glass; her fingers were long and perfectly tapered, the painted nails set upon them with the brilliance of butterflies' wings. 'It was to come from me alone.'

Why do you think he wants me?'

'There are two possibilities that I can imagine.' She surprised him sometimes with her almost masculine appraisal. That was what made her lapse so amazing; as he listened to her now, Nicholas wondered again how she could ever have let control of Christy Marine pass to Duncan Alexander – then he remembered what a wild and passionate creature she could be. 'The first possibility is that Christy Marine owes you six million dollars, and he has thought up some scheme to avoid having to pay you out.'

'Yes,' Nicholas nodded. 'And the other possibility?'

'There are strange and exciting rumours in the City about you and Ocean Salvage – they say that you are on the brink of something big. Something in Saudi Arabia. Perhaps Duncan wants a share of that.'

Nicholas blinked. The iceberg project was something between the Sheikhs and himself, then he remembered that others knew. Bernard Wackie in Bermuda, Samantha Silver, James Teacher – there had been a leak somewhere then.

'And you? What are your reasons?'

'I have two reasons, Nicholas,' she answered. 'I want control back from Duncan. I want the voting rights in my shares, and I want my rightful place on the Trust. I didn't know what I was doing, it was madness when I made Duncan my nominee. I want it back now, and I want you to get it for me.'

Nicholas smiled, a bitter wintry smile. 'You're hiring yourself a gunman, just the way they do in the Western serials. Duncan and I alone on the deserted street, spurs clinking.' The smile turned to a chuckle, but he was thinking hard, watching her – was she lying? It was almost impossible to tell, she was so mysterious and unfathomable. Then he saw tears well in the depths of those huge eyes, and he stopped laughing. Were the tears genuine, or all part of the intrigue?

'You said you had two reasons.' And now his voice was gentler. She did not answer immediately, but he could see her agitation, the rapid rise and fall of those lovely breasts under the silk, then she caught her breath with a little hiss of decision and she spoke so softly that he barely caught the words.

'I want you back. That's the other reason, Nicholas.' And he stared at her while she went on. 'It was all part of the madness. I didn't realize what I was doing. But the madness is over now. Sweet merciful God, you'll never know how much I've missed you. You'll never know how I've suffered.' She stopped and fluttered one small hand. 'I'll make it up to you, Nicholas, I swear it to you. But Peter and I need you, we both need you desperately.'

He could not answer for a moment, she had taken him by surprise and he felt his whole life shaken again and the separate parts of it tumbled like dice from the cup of chance.

'There is no road back, Chantelle. We can only go forward.'

'I always get what I want, Nicholas, you know that,' she warned him.

'Not this time, Chantelle.' He shook his head, but he knew her words would wear away at him.

Duncan Alexander slumped on the luxurious calf-hide seat of the Rolls, and he spoke into the telephone extension that connected him directly with his office in Leadenhall Street.

'Were you able to reach Kurt Streicher?' he asked.

'I'm sorry, Mr Alexander. His office was unable to contact him. He is in Africa on a hunting safari. They did not know when to expect him back in Geneva.'

'Thank you, Myrtle.' Duncan's smile was completely lacking in humour. Streicher was suddenly one of the world's most industrious sportsmen – last week he had been skiing and was out of contact, this week he was in Africa slaughtering elephant, perhaps next week he would be chasing polar bears in the Arctic. And by then, it would be too late, of course.

Streicher was not alone. Since the salvage award on *Golden Adventurer*, so many of his financial contacts had become elusive, veritable will-o'-the-wisps skipping ahead of him with their cheque books firmly buttoned into their pockets.

'I shall not be back at the office again today,' he told his secretary. 'Please have my pending tray sent round to Eaton Square. I will work on it tonight, and do you think you could get in an hour earlier tomorrow morning?'

'Of course, Mr Alexander.'

He replaced the handset and glanced out of the window. The Rolls was passing Regent's Park, heading in the direction of St John's Wood; three times in the last six months he had taken this route, and suddenly Duncan felt that hot scalding lump deep under his ribs. He straightened up in his seat but the pain persisted, and he sighed and opened the rosewood liquor cabinet, spilled a spoonful of the powder into a glass and topped it with sodawater.

He considered the turbid draught with distaste, then drank it at a gulp. It left an aftertaste of peppermint on his tongue, but the relief was almost immediate. He felt the acid burn subside, and he belched softly.

He did not need a doctor to tell him that it was a duodenal ulcer, probably a whole bunch of them – or was that the correct collective noun, a tribe of ulcers, a convocation? He smiled again, and carefully combed his brazen waves of hair, watching himself in the mirror.

The strain did not show on his face, he was sure of that. The façade was intact, devoid of cracks. He had always had the strength, the courage to ride with his decisions. This had been a hard ride, however, the hardest of his life.

He closed his eyes briefly, and saw *Golden Dawn* standing on her ways. Like a mountain. The vision gave him strength, he felt it rising deep within him, welling up to fill his soul.

They thought of him only as a money-man, a paper man. There was no salt in his blood nor steel in his guts – that was what they said of him in the City. When he had ousted Berg from Christy Marine, they had shied off, watching him shrewdly, standing aside and waiting for him to show his guts, forcing him to live upon the fat of Christy Marine, devouring himself like a camel in the desert, running him thin.

'The bastards,' he thought, but it was without rancour. They had done merely what he would have done, they had played by the hard rules which Duncan knew and respected, and by those same rules, once he had shown his guts to be of steel, they would ply him with largesse. This was the testing time. It was so close now, two months still to live through – yet those sixty days seemed as daunting as the hard year through which he had lived already.

The stranding of *Golden Adventurer* had been a disaster. Her hull value had formed part of the collateral on which he had borrowed; the cash she generated with her luxury cruises was budgeted carefully to carry him through the dangerous times before *Golden Dawn* was launched. Now all that had altered drastically. The flow of cash had been switched off, and he had to find six million in real hard money – and find it before the 10th of the month. Today was the 6th, and time was running through his fingers like quicksilver.

If only he had been able to stall Berg. He felt a corrosive welling up of hatred again; if only he had been able to stall him. The bogus offer of partnership might have held him just long enough, but Berg had brushed it aside contemptuously. Duncan had been forced to scurry about in undignified haste, trying to pull together the money. Kurt Streicher was not the only one suddenly unavailable, it was strange how they could smell it on a man, he had the same gift of detecting vulnerability or weakness in others so he understood how it worked. It was almost as though the silver blotches showed on his hands and face and he walked the city pavements chanting the old leper's cry, 'Unclean, Beware, Unclean.'

With so much at stake, it was a piddling amount, six million for two months, the insignificance of it was an insult, and he felt the tension in his belly muscles again and the rising hot acid sting of his digestive juices. He forced himself to relax, glancing again from the window to find that the Rolls was turning into the cul-de-sac of yellow face-brick apartments piled upon each other like hen-coops, angular and unimaginatively lower middle class.

He squared his shoulders and watched himself in the mirror, practising the smile. It was only six million, and for only two months, he reminded himself, as the Rolls slid to a halt before one of the anonymous buildings.

Duncan nodded to his chauffeur as he held the door open and handed Duncan the pigskin briefcase.

'Thank you, Edward. I should not be very long.'

Duncan took the case and he crossed the pavement with the long, confident stride of an athlete, his shoulders thrown back, wearing his top coat like an opera cloak, the sleeves empty and the tails swirling about his legs, and even in the grey overcast of a March afternoon, his head shone like a beacon fire.

The man who opened the door to him seemed only half Duncan's height, despite the tall black Homburg hat that he wore squarely over his ears.

'Mr Alexander, shalom, shalom.' His beard was so dense and bushy black that it covered the starched white collar and white tie, regulation dress of the strict Hasidic Jew. 'Even though you come to me last, you still bring honour on my house,' and his eyes twinkled, a mischievous sparkling black under thick brows.

'That is because you have a heart of stone and blood like iced water,' said Duncan, and the man laughed delightedly, as though he had been paid the highest compliment.

'Come,' he said, taking Duncan's arm. 'Come in, let us drink a little tea together and let us talk.' He led Duncan down the narrow corridor, and halfway they collided with two boys wearing yamulka on their curly heads coming at speed in the opposite direction.

'Ruffians,' cried the man, stooping to embrace them briefly and then send them on their way with a fond slap on their backsides. Still beaming and shaking the ringlets that dangled out from under the black Homburg, he ushered Duncan into a small crowded bedroom that had been converted to an office. A tall old-fashioned pigeon-holed desk filled one wall and against the other stood an overstuffed horse-hair sofa on which were piled ledgers and box files.

The man swept the books aside, making room for Duncan. 'Be seated,' he ordered, and stood aside while a jolly little woman his size brought in the teatray.

'I saw the award court's arbitration on *Golden Adventurer* in *Lloyd's List*,' the Jew said when they were alone. 'Nicholas Berg is an amazing man, a hard act to follow – I think that is the expression.' He pondered, watching the sudden bloom of anger on Duncan's cheeks and the murderous expression in the pale eyes.

Duncan controlled his anger with an effort, but each time that somebody spoke that way of Nicholas Berg, he found it more difficult. There was always the comparison, the snide remarks, and Duncan wanted to stand up and leave this cluttered little room and the veiled taunts, but he knew he could not afford to, nor could he speak just yet for his anger was very close to the surface. They sat in silence for what seemed a long time.

'How much?' The man broke the silence at last, and Duncan could not bring himself to name the figure for it was too closely related to the subject that had just infuriated him.

'It is not a large amount, and for a short period – sixty days only.'

'How much?'

'Six million,' Duncan said. 'Dollars.'

'Six million is not an impossibly large amount of money, when you have it – but it is a great fortune when you do not.' The man tugged at the thick black bush of his beard. 'And sixty days can be an eternity.'

'I have a charter for *Golden Dawn*,' Duncan said softly. 'A ten-year charter.' He slipped the nine-carat gold catches on the slim, finely grained pigskin briefcase and brought out a batch of Xeroxed sheets. 'As you see, it is signed by both parties already.'

'Ten years?' asked the man, watching the papers in Duncan's hand.

'Ten years, at ten cents a hundred ton miles and a guaranteed minimum annual of 75,000 miles.'

The hand on the man's thick black beard stilled. '*Golden Dawn* has a burden of a million tons – that will gross a minimum of seventy-five million dollars a year.' With an effort he managed to disguise his awe, and the hand resumed its gentle tugging at the beard. 'Who is the charterer?' The thick eyebrows formed two thick black question marks.

'Orient Amex,' said Duncan, and handed him the Xeroxed papers.

'The El Barras field.' The man's eyebrows stayed up as he read swiftly. 'You are a brave man, Mr Alexander. But I never once doubted that.' He read on in silence for another minute, shaking his head slowly so that the ringlets danced on his cheeks. 'The El Barras field.' He folded the papers and looked up at Duncan. 'I think Christy Marine may have found a worthy successor to Nicholas Berg – perhaps the shoes are even a little small, maybe they will begin to pinch your toes soon, Mr Alexander.' He squirmed down in his chair thinking furiously, and Duncan watched him, hiding his trepidation behind a remotely amused half-smile.

'What about the environmentalists, Mr Alexander? The new American Administration, this man Carter is very conscious of environmental dangers.'

'The lunatic fringe,' said Duncan. 'There is too much invested already. Orient Amex have nearly a billion in the new cadmium cracking plants at Galveston, and three of the other oil giants are in it. Let them fuss, we'll still carry in the new cad-rich crudes.'

Duncan spoke with the force of complete conviciton. 'There is too much at stake, the potential profits are too large and the opposition is too weak. The whole world is sick of the doom-merchants, the woolly-headed sentimentalists,' he dismissed them with a short abrupt gesture, 'man has already adjusted to a little oil on the beaches, a little smoke in the air, a few less fish in the sea or birds in the sky, and he will go on adjusting.'

The man nodded, listening avidly. 'Yes,' he nodded. 'You are a brave man. The world needs men like you.'

'The important thing is a cadmium catalyst cracking system which breaks down the high carbon atoms of crude and gives back a 90% yield in low carbon instead of the 40% we hope for now. 90 % yield, double-double profits, double efficiency —'

'– and double danger.' The man smiled behind his beard.

'There is danger in taking a bath. You might slip and crack your skull, and we haven't invested a billion dollars in bathing.'

'Cadmium in concentrations of 100 parts to the million is more poisonous than cyanide or arsenic; the cad-rich crudes of the El Barras field are concentrated 2000 parts to the million.'

'That's what makes them so valuable,' Duncan nodded. 'To enrich crude artificially with cadmium would make the whole cracking process hopelessly uneconomic. We've turned what appeared to be a hopelessly contaminated oilfield into one of the most brilliant advances in oil refining.'

'I hope you have not under-estimated the resistance to the transportation of —'

Duncan cut him short. 'There will be no publicity. The loading and unloading of the crude will be conducted with the utmost discretion, and the world will not know the difference. Just another ultra-tanker moving across the oceans with nothing to suggest that she is carrying cad-rich.'

'But, just suppose the news did leak?'

Duncan shrugged. 'The world is conditioned to accept anything, from DDT to Concorde, nobody really cares any more. Come hell and high water, we'll carry the El Barras oil. Nobody is strong enough to stop us.'

Duncan gathered his papers and went on softly, 'I need six million dollars for sixty days – and I need it by noon tomorrow.'

'You are a brave man,' the man repeated softly. 'But you are finely stretched out. Already my brothers and I have made a considerable investment in your courage. To be blunt, Mr Alexander, Christy Marine has exhausted its collateral. Even *Golden Dawn* is pawned down to her last rivet – and the charter for Orient Amex does not change that.'

Duncan took another sheaf of papers, bound in a brown folder, and the man lifted an eyebrow in question.

'My personal assets,' Duncan explained, and the man skimmed swiftly through the typed lists.

'Paper values, Mr Alexander. Actual values are 50% of those you list, and that is not six million dollars of collateral.' He handed the folder back to Duncan. 'They will do for a start, but we'll need more than that.'

'What more is there?'

'Share options, stock options in Christy Marine. If we are to share risk, then we must have a share of the winnings.'

'Do you want my soul also?' Duncan demanded harshly, and the man laughed.

'We'll take a slice of that as well,' he agreed amiably.

It was two hours later that Duncan sank wearily into the leather-work of the Rolls. The muscles in his thighs trembled as though he had run a long way and there was a nerve in the corner of his eye that jumped as though a cricket was trapped beneath the skin. He had made the gamble, everything – Christy Marine, his personal fortune, his very soul. It was all at risk now.

'Eaton Square, sir?' the chauffeur asked.

'No,' Duncan told him. He knew what he needed now to smooth away the grinding, destroying tension that wracked his body, but he needed it quickly without fuss and, like the peppermint-tasting powder, like a medicine.

'The Senator Club in Frith Street,' he told the chauffeur.

Duncan lay face down on the massage table in the small green-curtained cubicle. He was naked, except for the towel, and his body was smooth and lean. The girl worked up his spine with strong skilled fingers, finding the little knots of tension in the sleek muscle and unravelling them.

'Do you want the soft massage, sir?' she asked.

'Yes,' he said and rolled on to his back. She lifted away the towel from around his waist. She was a pretty blonde girl in a short green tunic with the golden laurel leaf club insignia on the pocket, and her manner was brisk and business like.

'Do you want any extras, sir?' Her tone was neutral, and she began to unbutton the green tunic automatically.

'No,' Duncan said, 'No extras,' and closed his eyes, surrendering himself completely to the touch of her expert fingers.

He thought of Chantelle, feeling the sneaking guilt of the moment, but it was so seldom these days that he had the energy for her smouldering demanding Persian passions. He did not have the strength for her, he was drained and weary, and all he wanted was the release, swift and simple. In two months' time it would be different, he would have the strength and energy to pick the world up in his bare hands and shake it like a toy.

His mind was separated from his body, and odd disconnected images flitted across the red darkness of his closed eyelids. He thought again how long it had been since last he and Chantelle had made love together, and he wondered what the world would say if they knew of it.

'Nicholas Berg left a big empty place in his bed also,' they would say.

'The hell with them,' Duncan thought, but without the energy for real anger.

'The hell with all of them.' And he gave himself up to the explosion of light that burst against his eyelids and the dark, but too fleeting, peace that followed it.

Nicholas lay back in the rather tatty old brown leather armchair which was one of James Teacher's concessions to creature comfort and he stared at the cheap hunting prints on the faded wallpaper through a thin fug of cheroot smoke. Teacher could have afforded a decent Gaugin or a Turner, but such vulgar display was frowned on in the Inns of Court. It might lead prospective clients to ponder the amount of the fees that they were to be charged.

James Teacher replaced the telephone and stood up behind his desk. It did not make much difference to his height.

'Well, I think we have covered all the entrances to the warren,' he announced cheerfully, and he began to tick off the items on his fingers. 'The sheriff of the South African supreme court will serve notice of attachment on the hull of *Golden Adventurer* at noon local time tomorrow. Our French correspondent will do the same on *Golden Dawn* –' He spoke for three minutes more, and, listening to him, Nicholas reluctantly admitted to himself that he earned the greater proportion of his enormous fees.

'Well, there it is, Mr Berg. If your hunch is correct –'

'It's not a hunch, Mr Teacher. It's a certainty. Duncan Alexander has his backside pinched in the doorway. He's been rushing round the City like a demented man looking for money. My God, he even tried to stall me with that incredible offer of a partnership. No, Mr Teacher, it's not a hunch. Christy Marine is going to default.'

'I cannot understand that. Six millions is peanuts,' said James Teacher. 'At least it's peanuts to a company like Christy Marine, one of the healthiest shipping owners.'

'It was, a year ago,' Nicholas agreed grimly. 'But since then, Alexander has had a clear run, no checks, it's not a public company, he administers the shares in the Trust.' He drew on his cheroot. 'I'm going to use this to force a full investigation of the company's affairs. I'm going to have Alexander under the microscope and we'll have a close look at all his pimples and warts.'

Teacher chuckled and picked up the telephone at the first ring. 'Teacher,' he chuckled, and then laughed out loud, nodding, 'Yes,' and 'Yes!' again. He hung up and turned to Nicholas, his face bright red with mirth, fat and round as the setting sun.

'I have a disappointment for you, Mr Berg.' He guffawed. 'An hour ago a transfer was made to the credit of Ocean Salvage in Bermuda by Christy Marine.'

'How much?'

'Every penny, Mr Berg. In full and final payment. Six million and some odd dollars in the legal currency of the United States of America.'

Nicholas stared at him, uncertain as to which of his emotions prevailed – relief at having the money, or disappointment at being prevented from tearing Duncan Alexander to shreds.

'He's a high roller and very fast on his feet,' said Teacher. 'It wouldn't pay to underestimate a man like Duncan Alexander.'

'No, it would not,' Nicholas agreed quietly, knowing that he had done so more than once and each time it had cost him dearly.

'I wonder if your clerk could find out from British Airways when the next flight leaves for Bermuda?'

'You are leaving so soon? Will it be in order to mark my brief and send it direct to Bach Wackie in Bermuda?' Teacher asked delicately.

Bernard Wackie in person was waiting for Nicholas beyond the customs barrier. He was tall and lean and alert, burned by the sun dark as a stick of chew tobacco, and dressed in open-neck shirt and cotton trousers.

'Nicholas, it's good to see you.' His handshake was hard and dry and cool. He was under sixty and over forty, it was impossible to get nearer to his age. 'I'm taking you directly to the office, there is too much to discuss. I don't want to waste time.' And he took Nicholas' arm and hurried him through burning sunlight into the shivery cold of the Rolls air-conditioning.

The car was too big for the island's narrow winding roads. Here ownership of automobiles was restricted to one per family unit, but Bernard made the most of his rights.

He was one of those men whose combination of energy and brilliance made it impossible for him to live in England and to subject himself to the punitive taxes of envy.

'It's hard to be a winner, in a society dedicated to the glorification of the losers,' he had told Nicholas, and had moved his whole operation to this taxless haven.

To a lesser man it would have been suicide, but Bernard had taken over the top floor of the Bank of Bermuda building, with a magnificent view across Hamilton Harbour, and had fitted it out with a marine operations room and a communications system the equal of NATO Command.

From it, he offered a service so efficient, so personally involved, so orientated to every single facet of ship ownership and operation, that not only had his old clients followed him, but others had come flocking.

'No taxes, Nicholas,' he smiled. 'And look at the view.' The picturesque buildings of Hamilton town were painted in candy colours, strawberries and limes, plum and lemon – and across the bay the cedar trees stood tall in the sunlight, and the yachts from the pink-painted clubhouse spread multicoloured sails across green waters. 'It's better than London in winter, isn't it?'

'The same temperature,' said Nicholas, and glanced up at the air-conditioning.

'I'm a hot-blooded man,' Bernard explained, and when his tall nubile secretary entered to his ring, bearing the Ocean Salvage files like a high priestess carrying the sacrament, Bernard fell into an awed silence, concentrating all his attention on her pneumatic bosoms; they bounced and strained against the laws of gravity as though filled with helium.

She flashed a dazzling, painted smile at Nicholas as she placed the files on Bernard's desk, and then she left with her perfectly rounded buttocks under the tightly tailored skirt, swinging and dancing to a distant music. 'She can type too,' Bernard assured Nick with a sigh, and shook his head as if to clear it. He opened the top file.

'Right,' he began. 'The deposit from Christy Marine –'

The money had come in, and only just in time. The next instalment on *Sea Witch* was already forty-eight hours overdue and Atlantique were becoming highly agitated.

'Son of a gun,' said Bernard. 'You would not think six million was an easy sum of money to get rid of, would you?'

'You don't even have to try,' Nick agreed. 'It just spends itself.' Then with a scowl, 'What's this?'

'They've invoked the escalation clause again, another 3+106%.' *Sea Witch's* builders had included a clause that related the contract price to the index cost of steel and the Union labour rates. They had avoided the threatened dockyard strike by capitulating to Union demands, and now the figures came back to Nicholas. They were big fat ugly figures. The clause was a festering canker to Nicholas, draining his strength and money.

They worked on through the afternoon, paying, paying and paying. Bunkers and the other running costs of *Warlock*, interest and capital repayments on the debts of Ocean Salvage, lawyers' fees, agents' fees, the six million whittled away. One of the few payments that gave Nicholas any pleasure was the 12½% salvage money to the crew of *Warlock*. David Allen's share was almost thirty thousand dollars, Beauty Baker another twenty-five thousand – Nick included a note with that cheque, 'Have a Bundaberg on me!'

'Is that all the payments?' Nicholas asked at last.

'Isn't it enough?'

'It's enough.' Nick felt groggy with jet-lag and from juggling with figures. 'What's next?'

'Good news, next.' Bernard picked up the second file. 'I think I've squared Esso. They hate you, they have threatened never to use your tugs again, but they are not going to sue.' Nicholas had breached contract when he deserted the Esso tow and ran south for *Golden Adventurer*; the breach of contract suit had been hanging since then. It was a relief to have it aside, Bernard Wackie was worth every penny of his hire.

'Okay. Next?'

It went on for another six unbroken hours, piled on top of the jet-lag that Nicholas had accumulated across the Atlantic.

'You okay?' Bernard asked at last. Nicholas nodded, though his eyes felt like hard-boiled eggs, and his chin was dark and raspy with beard.

'You want something to eat?' Bernard asked, and then Nick shook his head and realized that it was dark outside. 'Drink? You'll need one for what comes next.'

'Scotch,' Nicholas agreed, and the secretary brought the tray through, and poured the drinks in another respectful hush.

'That will be all, Mr Wackie?'

'For now, honey.' Bernard watched her go, and then saluted Nicholas with his glass.

'I give you the Golden Prince!' And when Nicholas scowled, he went on swiftly, 'No, Nicholas, I'm not shafting you. It's for real. You've done it again. The Sheikhs are fixing to make you an offer. They want to buy you out, clean, take over the whole show, liabilities, everything. Of course, they'll want you to run it for them – two years, while you train one of their own men. A hell of a salary,' he went on crisply, and Nicholas stared at him.

'How much?'

'Two hundred grand, plus 2½% profits.'

'Not the salary,' Nicholas told him. 'How much are they offering for the company?'

'They are Arabs, the first offer is just to stir the pot a little.'

'How much?' Nicholas asked impatiently.

'The sum of five was delicately mentioned.'

'What do you think they'll go to?'

'Seven, seven and half – eight, perhaps.'

Through the fuzz of fatigue, far off like a lantern in the window on a winter's night, Nicholas saw the vision of a new life, a life such as Samantha had shown him. A life uncluttered, uncomplicated, shorn of all but joy and purpose.

'Eight million dollars clear?' Nicholas' voice was husky, and he tried to wipe away the fatigue from his stinging eyelids with thumb and forefinger.

'Maybe only seven,' Bernard demurred, 'but I'd try for eight.'

'I'll have another drink,' Nicholas said.

'That's a splendid idea,' Bernard agreed, and rang for his secretary with an anticipatory sparkle in his eyes.

Samantha wore her hair in twin braids down her back, and hacked-off denim pants which left her long brown legs bare and exposed a pale sliver of tight round buttock at each step as she walked away. She had sandals on her feet and sun-glasses pushed up on top of her head.

'I thought you were never coming,' she challenged Nick as he stepped through the barrier at Miami International. He dropped his bag and fielded her rush against his chest. She clung to him and he had forgotten the clean, sun-drenched smell of her hair.

She was trembling with a suppressed eagerness like a puppy, and it was only when a small quivering sob shook her shoulders that he realized she was weeping.

'Hey now!' He lifted her chin, and her eyes were flooded. She snuffled once loudly.

'What's the trouble, little one?'

'I'm just so happy,' Samantha told him, and deeply Nicholas envied the ability to live so near the surface. To be able to cry with joy seemed to him at that moment to be the supreme human accomplishment. He kissed her and she tasted salty with tears. With surprise he felt a choke deep in his own throat.

The jaded airport crowds had to open and trickle around the two of them like water around a rock, and they were oblivious to it all.

Even when they came out of the building into the Florida sunlight, she had both arms around his waist, hampering his stride, as she led him to her vehicle.

'Good God!' exclaimed Nicholas, and he shied when he saw it. It was a Chevy van, but its paintwork had been restyled. 'What's that?'

'It's a masterpiece,' she laughed. 'Isn't it?' It was rainbowed, in layers of vibrant colour and panels of fantastic landscapes and seascapes.

'You did that?' Nick asked, and he took his dark glasses from his breast pocket, and inspected the seagulls and palm trees and flowers through them.

'It's not that bad,' she protested. 'I was bored and depressed without you. I needed something to brighten my life.'

One of the panels depicted the translucent green of a curling wave, and on the face of the wave a pair of human figures on Hawaii boards and a graceful dolphin shape flew in formation together. Nick leaned closer and barely recognized the male figure as himself; each detail of the features had been rendered with loving attention, and he came out of it looking something between Clark Gable and Superman – only a little more glamorous.

'From memory,' she said proudly.

'It's tremendous,' he told her. 'But I've got bigger biceps, and I'm more beautiful.'

Despite the wild choice of colour and the romantic style, he realized she had real talent.

'You don't expect me to ride in that – what if one of my creditors saw me!'

'Get your mind out of its stiff collar and blue suit, mister. You have just signed on for the voyage to never-never land by way of the moon.'

Before she started the engine she looked at him seriously out of those great shining green eyes.

'How long, Nicholas?' she asked. 'How long have we got together this time?'

'Ten days,' he told her. 'Sorry, but I must be back in London by the 25th. There is a big one coming up, *the* big one. I'll tell you about it.'

'No.' She covered her ears with both hands. 'I don't want to hear about it, not yet.'

She drove the Chevy with careless unforced skill, very fast and efficiently, acknowledging the homage of other male drivers with a grin and a shake of her braids.

When she slipped off highway 95 and parked in the lot of a supermarket, Nicholas raised an eyebrow.

'Food,' she explained, and then with a lascivious roll of her eyes, 'I reckon to get mighty hungry later.'

She chose steaks, a bag full of groceries and a jug of California Riesling, and would not let him pay. 'In this town, you are my guest.'

Then she paid the toll and took the Rickenbacker causeway across the water to Virginia Key.

'That's the marine division of the University of Miami and that's my lab at the top of the jetty, just beyond that white fishing boat – see it?'

The low buildings were crowded into a corner of the island, between the seaquarium and the wharves and jetties of the University's own little harbour.

'We aren't stopping,' Nicholas observed.

'Are you kidding?' she laughed at him. 'I don't need a controlled scientific environment for the experiment I am about to conduct.'

And with no diminution of speed, the Chevy flew across the long bridge between Virginia Key and Key Biscayne, and three miles on, she turned off sharply left on a narrow dirt track that twisted through a lush tropical maritime forest of banyan and palmetta and palm, and ended at a clapboard shack just above the water.

'I live close to the shop,' Samantha explained, as she clattered up on to the screened porch, her arms full of groceries.

'This is yours?' Nicholas asked. He could just make out the tops of big blocks of condominiums on each side; they were incompletely screened by the palms.

'Pa left it to me. He bought it the year I was born,' Samantha explained proudly. 'My ground stretches from there to there.'

A few hundred yards, but Nicholas realized the value of it. Everybody in the world wants to live on the water, and those condominiums were pressing in closely.

'It must be worth a million.'

'There is no price on it,' she said firmly. 'That's what I tell those awful sweaty little men with their big cigars. Pa left it to me and it's not for sale.'

She had the door open now, bumping it with her denim-clad backside.

'Don't just stand there, Nicholas,' she implored him. 'We've only got ten days.'

He followed her into the kitchen as she dumped her load into the sink, and whirled back to him.

'Welcome by my house, Nicholas,' and then as she slid her arms around his waist, jerked his shirt tails out of his belt and slid her hands up his bare back, 'You'll never know just how welcome. Come, let me show you around – this is the living-room.'

It had spartan furniture, with Indian rugs and pottery, and Samantha's chopped-off denims were discarded in the centre of the floor along with Nicholas' shirt.

'And this – surprise! surprise! – is the bedroom.' She dragged him by one hand, and under the short tee-shirt her bottom reminded him of a chipmunk with its cheeks stuffed with nuts, chewing vigorously.

The tiny bedroom overlooked the beach. The sea breeze fluffed out the curtains and the sound of the low surf breathed like a sleeping giant, a deep regular hiss and sigh that filled the air around them.

The bed was too big for the room, all ornate antique brass, with a cloudy soft mattress and an old-fashioned patchwork quilt in a hundred coloured and patterned squares.

'I don't think I could have lived another day without you,' she said, and unwound the thick plaits of her hair. 'You came like the cavalry, in the very nick of time.'

He reached up and took the golden tresses of hair, winding them thickly around his wrist, twining them in his fingers, and he pulled her gently down beside him.

Suddenly Nick's life was uncluttered and simple again. Suddenly he was young and utterly carefree again. The petty strivings, the subterfuge, the lies and the cheating did not exist in this little universe that encompassed a tiny wooden shack on the edge of the ocean, and a huge brass bed that clanged and rattled and banged and squeaked with the wholesale, the completely abandoned happiness that was the special miracle called Samantha Silver.

Samantha's laboratory was a square room, built on piles over the water, and the soft hum of the electric pumps blended with the slap of the wavelets below and the burble and blurp of the tanks.

'This is my kingdom,' she told him. 'And these are my subjects.'

There were almost a hundred tanks, like the small glass-sided aquaria for goldfish, and suspended over each of them was a complicated arrangement of coils and bottles and electric wiring.

Nick sauntered across to the nearest of the tanks and peered into it. It contained a single large salt-water clam; the animal was feeding with the double shells agape, the pink soft flesh and frilly gills rippling and undulating in the gentle flow of pumped and filtered sea water. To each half of the shell, thin copper wires were attached with blobs of polyurethane cement.

Samantha came to stand beside him, touching, and he asked her,'What's happening?'

She touched a switch and immediately the cylindrical scroll above the tank began to revolve slowly and a stylus, after a few preliminary jerks and quivers, began to trace out a regular pattern on the paper scroll, a trough and double peak, the second a fraction lower than the first, and then the trough again.

She said, 'He's wired and bugged.'

'You're a member of the CIA,' he accused.

And she laughed. 'His heart-beat. I'm passing an electric impulse through the heart – the heart is only a millimetre across – but each spasm changes the resistance and moves the stylus.' She studied the curve for a moment. 'This fellow is one very healthy cheerful *Spisula solidissima*.'

'Is that his name?' Nick asked. 'I thought he was a clam.'

'One of fifteen thousand bivalves who use that common generic,' she corrected.

'I had to pick an egghead,' said Nicholas ruefully. 'But what's so interesting about his heart?'

'It's the closest and cheapest thing to a pollution metre that we have discovered so far – or rather,' she corrected herself without false modesty, 'that I have discovered.'

She took his hand and led him down the long rows of tanks. 'They are sensitive, incredibly sensitive to any contamination of their environment, and the heart-beat will register almost immediately any foreign element or chemical, organic or otherwise, in such low concentrate that it would take a highly trained specialist with a spectroscope to detect otherwise.'

Nicholas felt his mild attention changing and growing into real interest as Samantha began to prepare samples of common pollutants on the single bench against the forewall of the cluttered little laboratory.

'Here,' she held up one test tube, 'aromatic carbons, the more poisonous elements of crude petroleum – and here,' she indicated the next tube, 'mercury in a concentration of 100 parts to the million. Did you see the photographs of the human vegetables and the Japanese children with the flesh falling off their bones at Kiojo? That was mercury. Lovely stuff.'

She picked up another tube. 'PCB, a by-product of the electrical industry, the Hudson River is thick with it. And these, tetrahydrofurane, cyclohexane, methylbenzene – all industrial by-products but don't let the fancy names throw you. One day they will come back to haunt us, in newspaper headlines, as THF or CMB – one day there will be other human cabbages and babies born without arms or legs.' She touched the other tubes.

'Arsenic, old-fashioned Agatha Christie vintage poison. And then here is the real living and breathing bastard daddy of them all – this is cadmium; as a sulphide so it's easily absorbed. In 100 parts to the million it's as lethal as a neutron bomb.'

While he watched, she carried the tray of tubes across to the tanks and set the ECG monitors running. Each began to record the normal double-peaked heart beat of a healthy clam.

'Now,' she said, 'watch this.'

Under controlled conditions, she began to drip the weak poisoned solutions into the reticulated water systems, a different solution to each of the tanks.

'These concentrations are so low that the animals will not even be aware of trauma, they will continue to feed and breed without any but long-term indications of systemic poisoning.'

Samantha was a different person, a cool quick-thinking professional. Even the white dust-coat that she had slipped over her tee-shirt altered her image and she had aged twenty years in poise and authority as she passed back and forth along the row of tanks.

'There,' she said, with grim satisfaction as the stylus on one recording drum made a slightly double beat at its peak and then just detectably flattened the second peak. 'Typical aromatic carbon reaction.'

The distorted heart-beat was repeated endlessly on the slowly turning drum, and she passed on to the next tank.

'See the pulse in the trough, see the fractional speeding up of the heart spasm? That's cadmium in ten parts to the million, at 100 parts it will kill all sea life, at five hundred it will kill man slowly, at seven hundred parts in air or solution it will kill him very quickly indeed.'

Nicholas' interest became total fascination, as he helped Samantha record the experiments and control the flow and concentration in the tanks. Slowly they increased the dosage of each substance and the moving stylus dispassionately recorded the increasing distress and the final convulsions and spasmodic throes that preceded death.

Nicholas voiced the tickle of horror and revulsion he felt at watching the process of degeneration.

'It's macabre.'

'Yes.' She stood back from the tanks. 'Death always is. But these organisms have such rudimentary nervous systems that they don't experience pain as we know it.' She shuddered slightly herself and went on. 'But imagine an entire ocean poisoned like one of these tanks, imagine the incredible agonies of tens of millions of sea birds, of the mammals, seals and porpoises and whales. Then think of what would happen to man himself —' Samantha shrugged off her white dust-coat.

'Now I'm hungry,' she announced, and then looking up at the fibreglass panels in the roof, 'No wonder! It's dark already!'

While they cleaned and tidied the laboratory, and made a last check of the pumps and running equipment, Samantha told him, 'In five hours we have tested over a hundred and fifty samples of contaminated water and got accurate indications of nearly fifty dangerous substances – at a probable cost of fifty cents a sample.' She switched out the lights 'To do the same with a gas spectroscope would have cost almost ten thousand dollars and taken a highly specialized team two weeks of hard work.'

'It's a hell of a trick,' Nicholas told her. 'You're a clever lady – I'm impressed, I really am.'

At the psychedelic Chevy van she stopped him, and in the light of the street lamp looked up at him guiltily.

'Do you mind if I show you off, Nicholas?'

'What does that mean?' he asked suspiciously.

'The gang are eating shrimps tonight. Then they'll sleep over on the boat and have the first shot at fish tagging tomorrow – but we don't have to go. We could just get some more steaks and another jug of wine.' But he could see she really wanted to go.

She was fifty-five foot, an old purse-seiner with the ungainly wheelhouse forward looking like a sentry box or an old-fashioned pit latrine. Even with her coat of new paint, she had an old-fashioned look.

She was tied up at the end of the University jetty, and as they walked out to her, so they could hear the voices and the laughter coming up from below decks.

'*Tricky Dicky*,' Nicholas read her name on the high ugly rounded stern.

'But we love her,' Samantha said, and led him across the narrow, rickety gangplank. 'She belongs to the University. She's only one of our four research vessels. The others are all fancy modern ships, two-hundred-footers, but the *Dicky* is our boat for short field trips to the gulf or down the Keys, and she's also the faculty clubhouse.'

The main cabin was monastically furnished, bare planking and hard benches, a single long table, but it was as crowded as a fashionable discotheque, packed solid with sunburned young people, girls and boys all in faded jeans and tee shirts, impossible to judge sexes by clothing or by the length of their sun-tortured and wind-tangled hair.

The air was thick with the rich smell of broiling gulf shrimps and molten butter, and there were gallon jugs of California wine on the table.

'Hey!' Samantha shouted above the uproar of voices raised in heated dispute and jovial repartee. 'This is Nicholas.'

A comparative silence descended on the gathering, and they looked him over with the curious veiled group hostility of any tribe for an interloper, an intruder in a closed and carefully guarded group. Nick returned the scrutiny calmly, met each pair of eyes, while realizing that despite the affected informality of their dress and some of the wildly unkempt hairstyles and the impressive profusion of beards, they were an elite group. There was not a face that was not intelligent, not a pair of eyes that was not alert and quick, and there was that special feeling of pride and self-confidence in all of them.

At the head of the table sat a big impressive figure, the oldest man in the cabin, perhaps Nick's age or a little older, for there were silver strands in his beard and his face was lined and beaten by sun and wind and time.

'Hi, Nick,' he boomed. 'I won't pretend we've never heard of you. Sam has given us all cauliflower ears —'

'You cut that out, Tom Parker,' Samantha stopped him sharply, and there was a ripple of laughter, a relaxation of tension and a casual round of greetings.

'Hi, Nick, I'm Sally-Anne.' A pretty girl with china-blue eyes behind wire-framed spectacles put a heavy tumbler of wine into his hand.

'We are short of glasses, guess you and Sam will have to share.'

She slid up along the bench and gave them a few inches of space and Samantha perched in Nicholas' lap. The wine was a rough fighting red, and it galloped, booted and spurred across his palate but Samantha sipped her share with the same relish as if it had been a '53 Château Lafitte, and she nuzzled Nicholas' ear and whispered:

'Tom is prof of the Biology Department, he's a honey. After you – he's my most favourite man in the world.'

A woman came through from the galley, carrying a huge platter piled high with bright pink shrimps and a bowl of molten butter. There was a roar of applause for her as she placed the dishes in the centre of the table, and they fell upon the food with unashamed gusto.

The woman was tall with dark hair in braids and a strong capable face, lean and supple in tight breeches, but she was older than the other women and she paused beside Tom Parker and draped one arm across his shoulders in a comfortable gesture of long-established affection.

'That's Antoinette, his wife.' The woman heard her name and smiled across at them, and with dark gentle eyes she studied Nicholas and then nodded and made the continental 'O' of thumb and forefinger at Samantha, before slipping back into the galley.

The food did not inhibit the talk, the lively contentious flow of discussion that swung swiftly from banter to deadly seriousness and back again, bright trained informed minds clicking and cannoning off each other with the crispness of ivory billiard balls, while at the same time buttery fingers ripped the whiskered heads off the shrimps, delving for the crescent of sweet white flesh, then leaving greasy fingerprints on the wine tumblers.

As each of them spoke, Samantha whispered their names and credentials. 'Hank Petersen, he's doing a PhD on the Bluefin Tuna – spawning and a trace of its migratory routes. He's the one running the tagging tomorrow.

'That's Michelle Rand, she's on loan from UCLA, and she's porpoises and whales.'

Then suddenly they were all discussing indignantly a rogue tanker captain who the week before had scrubbed his tanks in the middle of the Florida straits and left a thirty-mile slick down the Gulf Stream. He had done it under cover of night, and changed course as soon as he was into the Atlantic proper.

'We finger-printed him,' Tom Parker like an angry bear, 'we had him made, dead in the cross hairs.' Nick knew he was talking of the finger-printing of oil residues, the break-down of samples of the slick under gas spectroscopy which could match them exactly to the samples taken by the Coast Guard from the offender's tanks. The identification was good enough to bear up in an international court of law. 'But the trick is getting the son-of-a-bitch into court.' Tom Parker went on. 'He was fifty miles outside our territorial waters by the time the Coast Guard got to him, and he's registered in Liberia.'

'We tried to cover cases like that in the set of proposals I put up to the last maritime conference.'

Nick joined the conversation for the first time. He told them of the difficulties of legislating on an international scale, of policing and bringing to justice the blatant transgressors; then he listed for them what had been done so far, what was in process and finally what he believed still should be done to protect the seas.

He spoke quietly, succinctly, and Samantha noticed again, with a swell of pride, how all men listened when Nicholas Berg talked. The moment he paused, they came at him from every direction, using their bright young minds like scalpels, tearing into him with sharp lancing questions. He answered them in the same fashion, sharp and hard, armed with total knowledge of his subject, and he saw the shift in the group attitude, the blooming of respect, the subtle opening of ranks to admit him, for he had spoken the correct passwords and they recognized him as one of their own number, as one of the élite.

At the head of the table, Tom Parker sat and listened, nodding and frowning, sitting in judgement with his arm around Antoinette's slim waist and she stood beside him and played idly with a curl of thick wiry hair on the top of his head.

Tom Parker found fish forty miles offshore where the Gulf Stream was setting blue and warm and fast into the north. The birds were working, falling on folded wings down the backdrop of cumulonimbus storm clouds that bruised the horizon. The birds were bright, white pinpoints of light as they fell, and they struck the dark blue water with tiny explosions of white spray, and went deep. Seconds later they popped to the surface, stretching their necks to force down another morsel into their distended crops, before launching into flight again, climbing in steep circles against the sky to join the hunt again. There were hundreds of them and they swirled and fell like snowflakes.

'Anchovy,' grunted Tom Parker, and they could see the agitated surface of the water under the bird flock where the frenzied bait-fish churned. 'Could be bonito working under them.'

'No,' said Nick. 'They are blues.'

'You sure?' Tom grinned a challenge.

'The way they are bunching and holding the bait-fish, it's tuna,' Nick repeated.

'Five bucks?' Tom asked, as he swung the wheel over, and *Tricky Dicky's* big diesel engine boomed as she went on to the top of her speed.

'You're on,' Nick grinned back at him, and at that moment, they both saw a fish jump clear. It was a brilliant shimmering torpedo, as long as a man's arm. It went six feet into the air, turned in flight and hit the water again with a smack they heard clearly above the diesel.

'Blues,' said Nick flatly. 'Shoal blues – they'll go twenty pounds each.'

'Five bucks,' Tom grunted with disgust. 'Son of a gun, I don't think I can afford you, man,' and he delivered a playful punch to the shoulder which rattled Nick's teeth, then he turned to the open window of the wheelhouse and bellowed out on to the deck, 'Okay, kids, they are blues.'

There was a scramble and chatter of excitement as they rushed for lines and tagging poles. It was Hank's show, he was the bluefin tunny expert, he knew as much about their sex habits, their migratory routes and food chains as any man living, but when it came to catching them, Nick observed drily, he could probably do a better job as a blacksmith.

Tom Parker was no fisherman either. He ran down the shoal, charging *Tricky Dicky* through the centre of it, scattering birds and fish in panic – but by sheer chance one of the gang in the stern hooked in, and after a great deal of heaving and huffing and shouted encouragement from his peers, dragged a single luckless baby bluefin tuna over the rail. It skittered and jumped around the deck, its tail hammering against the planking, pursued by a shrieking band of scientists who slid and slipped in the fish slime, knocked each other down and finally cornered the fish against the rail. The first three attempts to affix the plastic tag were unsuccessful, Hank's lunges with the dart pole becoming wilder as his frustration mounted. He almost succeeded in tagging Samantha's raised backside as she knelt on the deck trying to cradle the fish in both arms.

'You do this often?' Nicholas asked mildly.

'First time with this gang,' Tom Parker admitted sheepishly. 'Thought you'd never guess.'

By now the triumphant band was solicitously returning the fish to the sea, the barbed dart of the plastic tag embedded dangerously near its vitals; and if that didn't eventually kill it, the rough handling probably would. It had pounded its head on the deck so heavily that blood oozed from the gill covers. It floated away, belly up on the stream, oblivious of Samantha's anguished cries of:

'Swim, fish, get in there and swim!'

'Mind if we try it my way?' Nick asked, and Tom relinquished command without a struggle.

Nicholas picked the four strongest and best co-ordinated of the young men, and gave them a quick demonstration and lecture on how to handle the heavy handlines with the Japanese feather lures, showing them how to throw the bait, and the recovery with an underhand flick that recoiled the line between the feet. Then he gave each a station along the starboard rail, with the second member of each team ready with a tagging pole and Hank Petersen on the roof of the wheel-house to record the fish taken and the numbers of the tags.

They found another shoal within the hour and Nicholas circled up on it, closing steadily at good trolling speed, helping the feeding tuna bunch the shoal of frenzied anchovy on the surface, until he could lock *Tricky Dicky*'s wheel hard down starboard and leave her to describe her own sedate circles around the shoal. Then he hurried out on to the deck.

The trapped and surrounded fish thrashed the surface until it boiled like a porridge of molten, flashing silver; through it drove the fast dark torpedoes of the hungry tuna.

Within minutes Nick had his four fishermen working to the steady rhythm of throwing the lures into the frothing water, almost instantly striking back on the line as a tuna snatched the feathers, and then swinging hand over head, recovering and coiling line fast with minimum effort, swinging the fish out and up with both hands and then catching its streamlined body under the left armpit like a quarter back picking up a long pass, clamping it there firmly, although the cold firm silver bullet shape juddered and quivered and the tail beat in a blur of movement. Then he taught them to slip the hook from the jaw, careful not to damage the vulnerable gills, holding the fish firmly but gently while the assistant pressed the barbed dart into the thick muscle at the back of the dorsal fin. When the fish was dropped back over the side, there were so few after-affects that it almost immediately began feeding again on the packed masses of tiny anchovies.

Each plastic tag was numbered and imprinted with a request in five languages to mail it back to University of Miami with details of date and place of capture, providing a valuable trace of the movements of the shoals in their annual circumnavigation of the globe. From their spawning grounds somewhere in the Caribbean they worked the Gulf

Stream north and east across the Atlantic, then south down and around the Cape of Good Hope with an occasional foray down the length of the Mediterranean Sea – although now the dangerous pollution of that landlocked water was changing their habits. From Good Hope east again south of Australia to take a gigantic swing up and around the Pacific, running the gauntlet of the Japanese long-liners and the California tunny men before ducking down under the terrible icy seas of the Horn and back to their spawning grounds in the Caribbean.

They sat up on the wheelhouse as the *Dicky* ran home in the sunset, drinking beer and talking. Nicholas studied them casually and saw that they possessed so many of the qualities he valued in his fellow humans; they were intelligent and motivated, they were dedicated and free of that particular avarice that mars so many others.

Tom Parker crumpled the empty beer can in a huge fist as easily as if it had been a paper packet, fished two more from the pack beside him and tossed one across to Nick. The gesture seemed to have some special significance and Nicholas saluted him with the can before he drank.

Samantha was snuggled down in luxurious weariness against his shoulder, and the sunset was a magnificence of purple and hot molten crimson. Nicholas thought idly how pleasant it would be to spend the rest of his life doing things like this with people like these.

Tom Parker's office had shelves to the ceiling, and they were sagging with hundreds of bottled specimens and rows of scientific papers and publications.

He sat well back in his swivel chair with ankles crossed neatly in the centre of the cluttered desk.

'I ran a check on you, Nicholas. Damned nerve, wasn't it? You have my apology.'

'Was it an interesting exercise?' Nicholas asked mildly.

'It wasn't difficult. You have left a trail behind you like a –' Tom sought for a comparison, 'like a grizzly bear through a honey farm. Son of a gun, Nicholas, that's a hell of a track record you've got yourself.'

'I've kept busy,' Nicholas admitted.

'Beer?' Tom crossed to the refrigerator in the corner that was labelled 'Zoological Specimens. DO NOT OPEN.'

'It's too early for me.'

'Never too early,' said Tom and pulled the tag on a dewy can of Millers and then picked up Nicholas' statement. 'Yes, you have kept busy. Strange, isn't it, that around some men things just happen.'

Nicholas did not reply, and Tom went on. 'We need a man around here who can *do*. It's all right thinking it out, then you need the catalyst to transform thought and intention into action.' Tom sucked at the can and then licked the froth off his moustache. 'I know what you have done. I've heard you speak, I've seen you move, and those things count. But most important of all, I know you care. I've been watching you carefully, Nick, and you really care, down deep in your guts, the way we do.'

'It sounds as though you're offering me a job, Tom.'

'I'm not going to horse around, Nick, I *am* offering you a job.' He waved a huge paw, like a bunch of broiled pork sausages. 'Hell, I know you're a busy man, but I'd like to romance you into an associate professorship. We'd want a little of your time when it came to hassling and negotiating up in Washington, we'd call for you when we needed real muscle to put our case, when we need the right contacts, somebody with a big reputation to open doors, when we need a man who knows the practical side of the oceans and the men that use them and abuse them.

'We need a man who is a hard-headed businessman, who knows the economics of sea trade, who has built and run tankers, who knows that human need is of paramount importance, but who can balance the human need for protein and fossil fuels against the greater danger of turning the oceans into watery deserts.' Tom lubricated his throat with beer, watching shrewdly for some reaction from Nicholas, and when he received no encouragement, he went on more persuasively. 'We are specialists, perhaps we have the specialist's narrow view; God knows, they think of us as sentimentalists, the lunatic fringe of doomsayers, long-haired intellectual hippies. What we need is a man with real clout in the establishment – shit, Nicholas, if you walked into a Congressional committee they'd really jerk out of their geriatric trance and switch on their hearing-aids.' Nicholas was silent still and Tom was becoming desperate. 'What can we offer in return?' I know you aren't short of cash, and it would be a lousy twelve thousand a year, but an associate professorship is a nice title. We start out holding hands with that. Then we might start going steady, a full professorship – chair of applied oceanology, or some juicy title like that which we'd think up. I don't know what else we can offer you, Nick, except perhaps the warm good feeling in your guts when you're doing a tough job that has to be done.' He stopped again, running out of words, and he wagged his big shaggy head sadly.

'You aren't interested, are you?' he asked.

Nick stirred himself. 'When do I start?' he asked, and as Tom's face split into a great beaming grin, Nick held out his hand. 'I think I'll take that beer now.'

The water was cool enough to be invigorating. Nick and Samantha swam so far out that the land was almost lost in the lowering gloom of dusk, and then they turned and swam back side by side. The beach was deserted; in their mood, the lights of the nearest condominiums were no more intrusive than the stars, the faint sound of music and laughter no more intrusive than the cry of gulls.

It was the right time to tell her, and he did it in detail beginning with the offer by the Sheikhs to buy out Ocean Salvage and Towage.

'Will you sell?' she asked quietly. 'You won't, will you?'

'For seven million dollars clear?' he asked. 'Do you know how much money that is?'

'I can't count that far,' she admitted. 'But what would you do if you sold? I cannot imagine you playing bowls or golf for the rest of your life.'

'Part of the deal is that I run Ocean Salvage for them for two years, and then I've been offered a part-time assignment which will fill any spare time I've got left over.'

'What is it?'

'Associate Professor at Miami University.'

She stopped dead and dragged him around to face her.

'You're having me on!' she accused.

'That's a start only,' he admitted. 'In two years or so, when I've finished with Ocean Salvage, there may be a full chair of applied oceanology.'

'It's not true!' she said, and took him by the arms, shaking him with surprising strength.

'Tom, wants me to ram-rod the applied aspects of the environmental research. I'll trouble-shoot with legislators and the maritime conference, a sort of hired gun for the Green-Peacers –'

'Oh Nicholas, Nicholas!'

'Sweet Christ!' he accused. 'You're crying again.'

'I just can't help it.' She was in his arms still wet and cold and gritty with beach sand. She clung to him, quivering with joy. 'Do you know what this means, Nicholas? You don't, do you? You just don't realize what this means.'

'Tell me,' he invited. 'What does it mean?'

'What it means is that, in future, we can do everything together, not just munch food and go boom in bed – but everything, work and play and, and *live* together like a man and woman should!' She sounded stunned and frightened by the magnitude of the vision.

'The prospect daunts me not at all,' he murmured gently, and lifted her chin.

They washed off the salt and the sand, crowding together into the thick, perfumed steam of the shower cubicle and afterwards they lay together on the patchwork quilt in the darkness with the sound of the sea as background music to the plans and dreams they wove together.

Every time they both descended to the very frontiers of sleep, one of them would think of something vitally important and prod the other awake to say it.

'I've got to be in London on Tuesday.'

'Don't spoil it all, now,' she murmured sleepily.

'And then we're launching *Sea Witch* on the 7th April.'

'I'm not listening,' she whispered. 'I've got my fingers in my ears.'

'Will you launch her – I mean break the bottle of bubbly and bless her?'

'I've just taken my fingers out again.'

'Jules would love it.'

'Nicholas, I cannot spend my life commuting across the Atlantic, not even for you. I've got work to do.'

'Peter will be there, I'll work that as a bribe.'

'That's unfair pressure,' she protested.

'Will you come?'

'You know I will, you sexy bastard. I wouldn't miss it for all the world.' She moved across the quilt and found his ear with her lips. 'I am honoured.'

'Both of you are sea witches,' Nick told her.

'And you are my warlock.'

'Sea witch and warlock,' he chuckled. 'Together we will work miracles.'

'Look, I know it's terribly forward of me, but seeing that we are both wide awake, and it's only two o'clock in the morning, I would be super ultra-grateful if you could work one of your little miracles for me right now.'

'It will be a great pleasure,' Nick told her.

*

Nicholas was early, he saw as he came out of the American Consulate and glanced at his Rolex, so he moderated his pace across the Place de la Concorde, despite the gentle misty rain that settled in minute droplets on the shoulders of his trench coat.

Lazarus was at the rendezvous ahead of him, standing under one of the statues in the corner of the square closest to the French Naval headquarters.

He was heavily muffled against the cold, dressed all in sombre blue with a long cashmere scarf wound around his throat and a dark blue hat pulled down so low as to conceal the pale smooth bulge of his forehead.

'Let's find a warm place,' Nick suggested, without greeting the little man.

'No,' said Lazarus, looking up at him through the thick distorting lenses of his spectacles. 'Let us walk.' And he led the way through the underpass on to the promenade above the embankment of the Seine, and set off in the direction of the Petit Palais.

In the middle of such an inclement afternoon they were the only strollers, and they walked in silence three or four hundred yards while Lazarus satisfied himself absolutely of this, and while he adjusted his mincing little steps to Nick's stride. It was like taking Toulouse-Lautrec for a stroll, Nick smiled to himself. Even when Lazarus began speaking, he kept glancing back over his shoulder, and once when two bearded Algerian students in combat jackets overtook them, he let them get well ahead before he went on.

'You know there will be nothing in writing?' he piped.

'I have a recorder in my pocket,' Nick assured him.

'Very well, you are entitled to that.'

'Thank you,' murmured Nick dryly.

Lazarus paused, it was almost as though a new reel was being fitted into the computer, and when he began talking again, his voice had a different timbre, a monotonous almost electronic tone, as though he was indeed an automaton.

First, there was a recital of share movements in the thirty-three companies which make up the Christy Marine complex, every movement in the previous eighteen months.

The little man reeled them off steadily, as though he were actually reading from the share registers of the companies. He must have had access, Nicholas realized, to achieve such accuracy. He had the date, the number of the shares, the transferor and transferee, even the transfer of shares in Ocean Salvage and Towage to Nicholas himself, and the reciprocal transfer of Christy Marine stock, was faithfully detailed, confirming the accuracy of Lazarus' other information. It was all an impressive exhibition of total knowledge and total recall, but much too complicated for Nicholas to make any sense of it. He would have to study it carefully. All that he would hazard was that somebody was putting up a smokescreen.

Lazarus stopped on the corner of the Champs Elysées and the rue de la Boetie. Nicholas glanced down at him and saw his shapeless blob of a nose was an unhealthy purplish pink in the cold, and that his breathing had coarsened and laboured with the exertion of walking. Nick realized suddenly that the little man was probably asthmatic, and as if to confirm this, he took a little silver and turquoise pill-box from his pocket and slipped a single pink capsule into his mouth before leading Nicholas into the foyer of a movie house and buying two tickets.

It was a porno movie, a French version of *Deep Throat* entitled *Gorge Profonde*. The print was scratched and the French dubbing was out of synchronization. The cinema was almost empty, so they found two seats in isolation at the rear of the stalls.

Lazarus stared unblinkingly at the screen, as he began the second part of his report. This was a detailed breakdown of cash movements within the Christy Marine Group, and Nick was again amazed at the man's penetration.

He drew a verbal picture of the assemblage of enormous sums of money, marshalled and channelled into orderly flows by a master tactician. The genius of Duncan Alexander was as clearly identifiable as that flourishing signature with the flamboyant 'A' and 'X' which Nicholas had seen him dash off with studied panache. Then suddenly the cash-flow was not so steady and untroubled, there were eddies and breaks, little gaps and inconsistencies that nagged at Nicholas like the false chimes of a broken clock. Lazarus finished this section of his report with a brief summation of the Group's cash and credit position as at a date four days previously and Nicholas realized that the doubts were justified. Duncan had run the Group out along a knife-edge.

Nicholas sat hunched down in the threadbare velvet seat, both hands thrust into the pockets of his trench-coat, watching the incredible feats of Miss Lovelace on the screen, without really seeing them, while beside him Lazarus took an aerosol can from his pocket, screwed a nozzle on to it and noisily sprayed a fine mist down his own throat. It seemed to relieve him almost immediately.

'Insurance and marine underwriting of vessels owned by the Christy Marine Group of companies.' He began again with names and figures and dates, and Nicholas picked up the trend. Duncan was using his own captive company, London and European Insurance and Banking, to lead the risk on all his vessels, and then he was reinsuring in the marketplace, spreading part of the risk, but carrying a whacking deductible himself, the principle of self-insurance that Nicholas had opposed so vigorously, and which had rebounded so seriously upon Duncan's head with the salvage of *Golden Adventurer*.

The last of the vessels in Lazarus' recital was *Golden Dawn*, and Nicholas shifted restlessly in his seat at the mention of the name, and almost immediately he realized that something strange was taking place.

'Christy Marine did not apply for a Lloyd's survey of this vessel.' Nicholas knew that already. 'But she has been rated first class by the continental surveyors.' It was a much easier rating to obtain, and consequently less acceptable than the prestigious 'A1 at Lloyd's'.

Lazarus went on, lowering his voice slightly as another patron entered the almost deserted cinema and took a seat two rows in front of them.

'And insurance has been effected outside Lloyd's.' The risk was led by London and European Insurance. Again, Duncan was self-insuring, Nicholas noted grimly, but not all of it. 'And further lines were written by —' Lazarus listed the other companies which carried a part of the risk, with whom Duncan had re-insured. But it was all too thin, too nebulous. Again, only careful study of the figures would enable Nicholas to analyse what Duncan was doing, how much was real insurance and how much was bluff to convince his financiers that the risk was truly covered, and their investment protected.

Some of the names of the re-insurers were familiar, they had been on the list of transferees who had taken stock positions in Christy Marine.

'Is Duncan buying insurance with capital?' Nicholas pondered. Was he buying at desperate prices. He must have cover, of course. Without insurance the finance houses, the banks and institutions which had loaned the money to Christy Marine to build the monstrous tanker would dig in against Duncan. His own shareholders would raise such hell – No, Duncan Alexander had to have cover, even if it was paper only, without substance, a mere incestuous circle, a snake eating itself tail first.

Oh, but the trail was so cleverly confused, so carefully swept and tied up, only Nicholas' intimate knowledge of Christy Marine made him suspicious, and it might take a team of investigators years to unravel the tortured tapestry of deceit. In the first instant, it had occurred to Nicholas that the easiest way to stop Duncan Alexander was to leak his freshly gleaned suspicions to Duncan's major creditors, to those who had financed the building of *Golden Dawn*. But immediately he realized that this was not enough. There were no hard facts, it was all inference and innuendo. By the time the facts could be exhumed and laid out in all their putrefaction for autopsy, *Golden Dawn* would be on the high seas, carrying a million tons of crude. Duncan might have won sufficient time to make his profit and sell out to some completely uncontrollable Greek or Chinaman, as he had boasted he would do. It would not be so simple to stop Duncan Alexander, it was folly to have believed that for one moment. Even if his creditors were made aware of the flimsy insurance cover over *Golden Dawn*, were they too deeply in already? Would they not then accept the risks spreading them where they could, and simply twist the financial rope a little tighter around Duncan's throat. No, it was not the way to stop him, Duncan had to be forced to remodify the giant tanker's hull, forced to make her an acceptable moral risk, forced to accept the standard Nicholas had originally stipulated for the vessel.

Lazarus had finished the insurance portion of his report and he stood up abruptly, just as Miss Lovelace was about to attempt the impossible. With relief, Nick followed him down the aisle and into the chill of a Parisian evening, and they breathed the fumes that the teeming city exhaled as Lazarus led him back eastwards through the VIIIe Arrondissement with those little dancing steps, while he recited the details of the charters of all Christy Marine's vessels, the charterer, the rates, the dates of expiry of contract; and Nicholas recognized most of them, contracts that he himself had negotiated, or those that had been renewed on expiry with minor alterations to the terms. He was relying on the recorder in his pocket, listening only with the surface layer of his mind, pondering all he had heard so far from this extraordinary little man – so that when it came he almost did not realize what he was hearing.

'On 10th January Christy Marine entered a contract of carriage with Orient Amex. The tenure is ten years. The vessel to be employed is the *Golden Dawn*. The rate is 10 cents US per hundred ton miles with a minimum annual guaranteed usage of 75,000 nautical miles.'

Nicholas registered the trigger word *Golden Dawn* and then he assimilated it all. The price, ten cents per hundred ton miles, that was wrong, high, much too high, ridiculously high in this depressed market. Then the name, Orient Amex – what was there about it that jarred his memory?

He stopped dead, and a following pedestrian bumped him. Nicholas shouldered him aside thoughtlessly and stood thinking, ransacking his mind for buried items of information. Lazarus had stopped also and was waiting patiently, and now Nicholas laid a hand on the little man's shoulder.

'I need a drink.'

He drew him into a brasserie which was thick with steam from the coffee machine and the smoke of Caporal and Disque Bleu, and sat him at a tiny table by the window overlooking the sidewalk.

Primly, Lazarus asked for a Vittel water and sipped it with an air of virtue, while Nicholas poured soda into his whisky.

'Orient Amex,' Nicholas asked, as soon as the waiter had left. 'Tell me about it.'

'That is outside my original terms of reference,' Lazarus demurred delicately.

'Charge me for it,' Nicholas invited, and Lazarus paused as the computer reels clicked in his mind, then he began to speak.

'Orient Amex is an American-registered company, with an issued capital of twenty-five million shares at a par value of ten dollars —' Lazarus recited the dry statistics. 'The company is presently undertaking substantial dry-land exploration in Western Australia and Ethiopia, and offshore exploration within the territorial waters of Norway and Chile. It has erected a refinery at Galveston in Texas to operate under the new atomic catalyst cracking process, first employed at its pilot plant on the same site. The plant is projected for initial operation in June this year, and full production in five years.'

It was all vaguely familiar to Nicholas, the names, the process of cracking the low-value high-carbon molecules, breaking up the carbon atoms and reassembling them in volatile low-carbon molecules of high value.

'The company operates producing wells in Texas, and in the Santa Barbara offshore field, in Southern Nigeria, and has proven crude reserves in the El Barras field of Kuwait, which will be utilized by the new cracking plant in Galveston.'

'Good God,' Nicholas stared at him. 'The El Barras field – but it's cadmium-contaminated it's been condemned by —'

'The El Barras field is a high cadmium field, naturally enriched with the catalyst necessary for the new process.'

'What are the cadmium elements?' Nicholas demanded.

'The western area of the El Barras field has sampled at 2,000 parts per million, and the north and eastern anticline have sampled as high as 42,000 parts per million.' Lazarus recited the figures pedantically. 'The American and Nigerian crudes will be blended with the El Barras crudes during the revolutionary cracking process. It is projected that the yield of low-carbon volatiles will be increased from 40% to 85% by this process, making it five to eight times more profitable, and extending the life of the world's known reserves of crude petroleum by between ten and fifteen years.'

As he listened, Nicholas had a vivid mental image of the stylus in Samantha's laboratory recording the death throes of a cadmium-poisoned clam. Lazarus was talking on dispassionately. 'During the cracking process, the cadmium sulphide will be reduced to its pure metallic, non-toxic form, and will be a valuable by-product, reducing the costs of refining.'

Nicholas shook his head in disbelief, and he spoke aloud. 'Duncan is going to do it. Across two oceans, a million tons at a time, in that vulnerable jerry-built monster of his, Duncan is going to do what no other shipowner has ever dared to do – he's going to carry the cad-rich crudes of El Barras!'

From the balcony windows of his suite in the Ritz, Nicholas could look out across the

Place Vendôme at the column in the centre of the square with its spiral bas-relief made from the Russian and Austrian guns and commemorating the little Corsican's feats of arms against those two nations. While he studied the column and waited for his connection, he did a quick calculation and realized that it would be three o'clock in the morning on the eastern seaboard of North America. At least he would find her at home. Then he smiled to himself. If she wasn't at home, he'd want to know the reason why.

The telephone rang and he picked it up without turning away from the window.

There was a confused mumbling and Nicholas asked, 'Who is this?'

'It's Sam Silver – what's the time? Who is it? Good God, it's three o'clock. What do you want?'

'Tell that other guy to put his pants on and go home.'

'Nicholas!' There was a joyous squeal, followed immediately by a crash and clatter that made Nicholas wince and lift the receiver well away from his ear.

'Oh damn it to hell, I've knocked the table over. Nicholas, are you there? Speak to me, for God's sake!'

'I love you.'

'Say that again, please. Where are you?'

'Paris. I love you.'

'Oh,' her tone drooped miserably. 'You sound so close. I thought —' Then she rallied gamely. 'I love you too – how's himself?'

'On the dole.'

'Who is she?'

'Dole is unemployment insurance – welfare —' He sought the American equivalent. 'I mean he is temporarily unemployed.'

'Great. Keep him that way. Did I tell you I love you, I forget?'

'Wake up. Shake yourself. I've got something to tell you.'

'I'm awake – well, almost anyway.'

'Samantha, what would happen if somebody dumped a million tons of 40,000 parts concentration of cadmium sulphide in an emulsion of aromatic Arabian crude into the Gulf Stream, say thirty nautical miles off Key West?'

'That's a freaky question, Nicholas. For three in the morning, that's a bomber.'

'What would happen?' he insisted.

'The crude would act as a transporting medium,' she was struggling to project a scenario through her sleepiness, 'it would spread out on the surface to a thickness of quarter of an inch or so, so you'd end up with a slick of a few thousand miles long and four or five hundred wide, and it would keep going.'

'What would be the results?'

'It would wipe out most of the marine life on the Bahamas and on the eastern seaboard of the States, no, correct that – it would wipe out all marine life, that includes the spawning grounds of the tuna, the freshwater eels and the sperm whale, and it would contaminate —' she was coming fully awake now, and a stirring horror altered her tone. 'You're macabre, Nicholas, what a sick thing to think about, especially at three in the morning.'

'Human life?' he asked.

'Yes, there would be heavy loss,' she said. 'As sulphide, it would be readily absorbed and in that concentration it would be poisonous on contact, fishermen, vacationers, anybody who walked on a contaminated beach.' She was truly beginning to realize the enormity of it. 'A large part of the population of the cities on the east coast – Nicholas, it could amount to hundreds of thousands of human beings, and if it was carried beyond America on the Gulf Stream, the Newfoundland Banks, Iceland, the North Sea, it would poison the cod fisheries, it would kill everything, man, fish, bird and animal. Then the tail of the Gulf Stream twists around the British Isles and the north continent of Europe – but why are you asking me this, what kind of crazy guessing game is this, Nicholas?'

'Christy Marine has signed a ten-year contract to carry one million ton loads of crude from the El Barras field on the South Arabian Gulf to the Orient Amex refinery in Galveston. The El Barras crude has a cadmium sulphide constituent of between 2,000 and 40,000 parts per million.'

Now there was trembling outrage in her voice as she whispered, 'A million tons! That's some sort of genocide, Nicholas, there has probably never been a more deadly cargo in the history of seafaring.'

'In a few weeks' time *Golden Dawn* will run down her ways at St Nazaire – and when she does, the seeds of catastrophe will be sewn upon the oceans.'

'Her route from the Arabian Gulf takes her around Good Hope.'

'One of the most dangerous seas in the world, the home of the hundred-year wave,' Nicholas agreed.

'Then across the southern Atlantic —'

'– and into the bottle-neck of the Gulf Stream between Key West and Cuba, into the Devil's Triangle, the breeding ground of the hurricanes —'

'You can't let them do it, Nicholas,' she said quietly. 'You just have to stop them.'

'It won't be easy, but I'll be working hard on it this side, there are a dozen tricks I am going to try, but you have to take over on your side,' he told her. 'Samantha, you go get Tom Parker. Get him out of bed, if necessary. He has to hit Washington with the news, hit all the media – television, radio and the press. A confrontation with Orient Amex, challenge them to make a statement.'

Samantha picked up the line he was taking. 'We'll get the Green-Peacers to picket the Orient Amex refinery in Galveston, the one which will process the cadmium crudes. We'll have every environmental agency in the country at work – we'll raise a stink like that of a million corpses,' she promised.

'Fine,' he said. 'You do all that, but don't forget to get your chubby little backside across here for the launching of *Sea Witch*.'

'Chubby obese, or chubby nice?' she demanded.

'Chubby beautiful,' he grinned. 'And I'll have room service ready to send up the food, in a front-end loader.'

Nicholas sat over the telephone for the rest of the day, having his meals brought up to the suite, while he worked systematically down the long list of names he had drawn up with the help of the tape-recording of Lazarus' report.

The list began with all those who it seemed had loaned capital to Christy Marine for the construction of *Golden Dawn*, and then went on to those who had written lines of insurance on the hull, and on the pollution cover for the tanker.

Nicholas dared not be too specific in the summation he gave to each of them, he did not want to give Duncan Alexander an opportunity to throw out a smoke-screen of libel actions against him. But in each case, Nicholas spoke to the top men, mostly men he knew well enough to use their christian names, and he said just enough to show that he knew the exact amount of their involvement with Christy Marine, to suggest they re-examine the whole project, especially with regard to *Golden Dawn*'s underwriting and to her contract of carriage with Orient Amex.

In the quiet intervals between each telephone call, or while a name was tracked down by a secretary, Nicholas sat over the Place Vendôme and carefully re-examined himself and his reasons for what he was doing.

It is so very easy for a man to attribute to himself the most noble motives. The sea had given Nicholas a wonderful life, and had rewarded him in wealth, reputation and achievement. Now it was time to repay part of that debt, to use some of that wealth to protect and guard the oceans, the way a prudent farmer cherishes his soil. It was a fine thought, but when he looked below its shining surface, he saw the shape and movement of less savoury creatures, like the shadows of shark and barracuda in the depths.

There was pride. *Golden Dawn* had been his creation, the culmination of a lifetime's work, it was going to be the laurel crown on his career. But it had been taken from him, and bastardized – and when it failed, when the whole marvellous concept collapsed in disaster and misery, Nicholas Berg's name would still be on it. The world would remember then that the whole grandiose design had originated with him.

There was pride, and then there was hatred. Duncan Alexander had taken his woman and child. Duncan Alexander had wrested his very life from him. Duncan Alexander was the enemy, and by Nicholas's rules, he must be fought with the same single-mindedness, with the same ruthlessness, as he did everything in his life.

Nicholas poured himself another cup of coffee and lit a cheroot; brooding alone in the magnificence of his suite, he asked himself the question:

'If it had been another man in another ship who was going to transport the El Barras crudes – would I have opposed him so bitterly?'

The question needed no formal reply. Duncan Alexander was the enemy.

Nicholas picked up the telephone, and placed the call he had been delaying. He did not need to look in the red calf-bound notebook for the number of the house in Eaton Square.

'Mrs Chantelle Alexander, please.'

'I am sorry, sir. Mrs Alexander is at Cap Ferrat.'

'Of course,' he muttered. 'Thank you.'

'Do you want the number?'

'That's all right, I have it.' He had lost track of time. He dialled again, this time down to the Mediterranean coast.

'This is the residence of Mrs Alexander. Her son Peter Berg speaking.'

Nicholas felt the rush of emotion through his blood, so that it burned his cheeks and stung his eyes.

'Hello, my boy.' Even in his own ears his voice sounded stilted, perhaps pompous.

'Father,' undisguised delight. 'Dad, how are you – sir? Did you get my letters?'

'No, I didn't, where did you send them?'

'The flat – in Queen's Gate.'

'I haven't been back there for,' Nicholas thought, 'for nearly a month.'

'I got your cards, Dad, the one from Bermuda and the one from Florida. I just wrote to tell you —' and there was a recital of schoolboy triumphs and disasters.

'That's tremendous, Peter. I'm really proud.'

Nicholas imagined the face of his son as he listened, and his heart was squeezed – by guilt, that he could do so little, could give him so little of his time, squeezed by longing for what he had lost. For it was only at times such as these that he could admit how much he missed his son.

'That's great, Peter —' The boy was trying to tell it all at the same time, gabbling out the news he had stored so carefully, flitting from subject to subject, as one thing reminded him of another. Then, of course, the inevitable question:

'When can I come to you, Dad?'

'I'll have to arrange that with your mother, Peter. But it will be soon. I promise you that.' Let's get away from that, Nick thought, desperately. 'How is *Apache*? Have you raced her yet these holidays?'

'Oh yes, Mother let me have a new set of Terylene sails, in red and yellow. I raced her yesterday.' *Apache* had not actually been placed first in the event, but Nicholas gained the impression that the blame lay not on her skipper but rather on the vagaries of the wind, the unsporting behaviour of the other competitors who bumped when they had the weather gauge, and finally the starter who had wanted to disqualify *Apache* for beating the gun. 'But,' Peter went on, 'I'm racing again on Saturday morning —'

'Peter, where is your mother?'

'She's down at the boathouse.'

'Can you put this call through there? I must speak to her, Peter.'

'Of course.' The disappointment in the child's voice was almost completely disguised. 'Hey, Dad. You promised, didn't you. It will be soon?'

'I promised.'

'Cheerio, sir.'

There was a clicking and humming on the line and then suddenly her voice, with its marvellous timbre and serenity.

'C'est Chantelle Alexander qui parle.'

'C'est Nicholas ici.'

'Oh, my dear. How good to hear your voice. How are you?'

'Are you alone?'

'No, I have friends lunching with me. The Contessa is here with his new boyfriend, a matador no less!'

The 'Contessa' was an outrageously camp and wealthy homosexual who danced at Chantelle's court. Nicholas could imagine the scene on the wide paved terrace, screened from the cliffs above by the sighing pines and the rococo pink boathouse with its turrets and rusty-coloured tiles. There would be gay and brilliant company under the colourful umbrellas.

'Pierre and Mimi sailed across from Cannes for the day.' Pierre was the son of the largest manufacturer of civil and military jet aircraft in Europe. 'And Robert —'

Below the terrace was the private jetty and small beautifully equipped yacht basin. Her visitors would have moored their craft there, the bare masts nodding lazily against the sky and the small Mediterranean-blue wavelets lapping the stone jetty. Nicholas could hear the laughter and the tinkle of glasses in the background, and he cut short the recital of the guest list.

'Is Duncan there?'

'No, he's still in London – he won't be out until next week.'

'I have news. Can you get up to Paris?'

'It's impossible, Nicky.' Strange how the pet name did not jar from her. 'I must be at Monte Carlo tomorrow, I'm helping Grace with the Spring Charity –'

'It's important, Chantelle.'

'Then there's Peter. I don't like to leave him. Can't you come here? There is a direct flight at nine tomorrow. I'll get rid of the house guests so we can talk in private.'

He thought quickly, then, 'All right, will you book me a suite at the Negresco?'

'Don't be silly, Nicky. We've thirteen perfectly good bedrooms here – we are both civilized people and Peter would love to see you, you know that.'

The Côte d'Azur was revelling in a freakish burst of early spring weather when Nicholas came down the boarding ladder at Nice Airport, and Peter was waiting for him at the boundary fence, hopping up and down and waving both hands above his head like a semaphore signaller. But when Nicholas came through the gate he regained his composure and shook hands formally.

'It's jolly good to see you, Dad.'

'I swear you've grown six inches,' said Nicholas, and on impulse stooped and hugged the child. For a moment they clung to each other, and it was Peter who pulled away first. Both of them were embarrassed by that display of affection for a moment, then quite deliberately Nicholas placed his hand on Peter's shoulder and squeezed.

'Where is the car?'

He kept his hand on the child's shoulder as they crossed the airport foyer, and as Peter became more accustomed to this unusual gesture of affection, so he pressed closer to his father, and seemed to swell with pride.

Characteristically, Nicholas wondered what had changed about him that made it easier for him to act naturally towards those he loved. The answer was obvious, it was Samantha Silver who had taught him to let go.

'Let go, Nicholas.' He could almost hear her voice now.

The chauffeur was new, a silent unobtrusive man, and there were only the two of them in the back seat of the Rolls on the drive back through Nice, and along the coast road.

'Mother has gone across to the Palace. She won't be back until dinner time.'

'Yes, she told me. We've got the day to ourselves,' Nicholas grinned, as the chauffeur turned in through the electric gates and white columns that guarded the entrance to the estate. 'What are we going to do?'

They swam and they played tennis and took Peter's Arrowhead-class yacht *Apache* on a long reach up the coast as far as Menton and then raced back, gull-winged and spinnaker set on the wind with the spray kicking up over the bows and flicking into their faces. They laughed a lot and they talked even more, and while Nicholas changed for dinner, he found himself caught up in the almost post-coital melancholy of too much happiness – happiness that was transitory and soon must end. He tried to push the sadness aside, but it persisted as he dressed in a white silk roll-neck and double-breasted blazer and went down to the terrace room.

Peter was there before him, early as a child on Christmas morning, his hair still wet and slicked down from the shower and his face glowing pinkly from the sun and happiness.

'Can I pour you a drink, Dad?' he asked eagerly, already hovering over the silver drinks tray.

'Leave a little in the bottle,' Nicholas cautioned him, not wanting to deny him the pleasure of performing this grown-up service, but with a healthy respect for the elephantine tots that Peter dispensed in a sense of misplaced generosity.

He tasted the drink cautiously, gasped, and added more soda. 'That's fine,' he said, Peter looked proud, and at that moment Chantelle came down the wide staircase into the room.

Nicholas found it impossible not to stare. Was it possible she had grown more lovely since their last meeting, or had she merely taken special pains this evening?

She was dressed in ivory silk, woven gossamer fine, so it floated about her body as she moved, and as she crossed the last ruddy glow of the dying day that came in from the french windows of the terrace, the light struck through the sheer material and put the dainty line of her legs into momentary silhouette. Closer to him, he saw the silk was embroidered with the same thread, ivory on ivory, a marvellous understatement of elegance, and under it the shadowy outline of her breasts, those fine shapely breasts that he remembered so well, and the faint dusky rose suggestion of her nipples. He looked away quickly and she smiled.

'Nicky,' she said, 'I'm so sorry to have left you alone.'

'Peter and I have had a high old time,' he said.

She had emphasized the shape and size of her eyes, and the planes of the bone structure of her cheeks and jawline, with a subtlety that made it appear she wore no make-up, and her hair had a springing electrical fire to it, a rich glowing sable cloud about the small head. The honeyed ivory of her skin had tanned to the velvety texture of a cream-coloured rose petal across her bare shoulders and arms.

He had forgotten how relaxed and gracious she could be, and this magnificent building filled with its treasures standing in its pine forest high above the darkening ocean and the fairylights of the coast was her natural setting. She filled the huge room with a special glow and gaiety, and she and Peter shared an impish sense of fun that had them all laughing at the old well-remembered jokes.

Nicholas could not sustain his resentment, could not bring himself to dwell on her betrayal in this environment, so the laughter was easy and the warmth uncontrived. When they went through to the small informal dining-room, they sat at the table as they had done so often before; they seemed to be transported back in time to those happy almost forgotten years.

There were moments which might have jarred, but Chantelle's instinct was so certain that she could skirt delicately around these. She treated Nicholas as an honoured guest, not as the master of the house; instead she made Peter the host. 'Peter darling, will you carve for us?' and the boy's pride and importance was almost overwhelming, although the bird looked as though it had been caught in a combine-harvester by the time he had finished with it. Chantelle served food and wine, a chicken stuffed in Creole style and a petit Chablis, that had no special associations from the past; and the choice of music was Peter's. 'Music to develop ulcers by,' as Nicholas remarked aside, to Chantelle.

Peter fought a valiant rearguard action to delay the passage of time, but finally resigned himself when Nicholas told him, 'I'll come and see you up to bed.'

He waited while Peter cleaned his teeth with an impressive vigour that might have continued beyond midnight if Nicholas had not protested mildly. When at last he was installed between the sheets, Nicholas stooped over him and the boy wrapped both arms around his neck with a quiet desperation.

'I'm so happy,' he whispered against Nicholas' neck and when they kissed he crushed Nicholas' lips painfully with his mouth – then, 'Wouldn't it be fabulous if we could be like this always?' he asked. 'If you didn't have to go away again, Dad?'

Chantelle had changed the wild music to the muted haunting melodies of Liszt, and as he came back into the room she was pouring cognac into a thin crystal balloon.

'Did he settle down?' she asked, and then answered herself immediately. 'He's exhausted, although he doesn't know it.'

She brought him the cognac and then turned away and went out through the doors on to the terrace. He followed her out, and they stood at the stone balustrade side by side. The air was clear but chill.

'It's beautiful,' she said. The moon paved a wide silver path across the surface of the sea. 'I always thought that the highway to my dreams.'

'Duncan,' he said. 'Let's talk about Duncan Alexander,' and she shivered slightly, folding her arms across her breasts and grasping her own naked shoulders.

'What do you want to know?'

'In what terms did you give him control of your shares?'

'As an agent, my personal agent.'

'With full discretion?'

She nodded, and he asked next, 'Did you have an escape clause? In what circumstances can you reclaim control?'

'The dissolution of marriage,' she said, and then shook her head. 'But I think I knew that no court would uphold the agreement if I wanted to change it. It's too Victorian. Anytime I want to I could simply apply to have the appointment of Duncan as my agent set aside.'

'Yes, I think you're right,' Nicholas agreed. 'But it might take a year or more, unless you could prove malafides, unless you could prove he deliberately betrayed the trust of agency.'

'Can I prove that, Nicky?' She turned to him now, lifting her face to him. 'Has he betrayed that trust?'

'I don't know yet,' Nicholas told her cautiously, and she cut in.

'I've made a terrible fool of myself, haven't I?' He kept silent, and she went on tremulously, 'I know there is no way I can apologize to you for – for what I did. There is no way that I can make it up to you, but believe me, Nicholas – please believe me when I tell you, I have never regretted anything so much in all my life.'

'It's past, Chantelle. It's over. There is no profit in looking back.'

'I don't think there is another man in the world who would do what you are doing now, who would repay deceit and betrayal with help and comfort. I just wanted to say that.'

She was standing very close to him now, and in the cool night he could feel the warmth of her flesh across the inches that separated them, and her perfume had a subtlely altered fragrance on that creamy skin. She always wore perfume so well, the same way she wore her clothes.

'It's getting cold,' he said brusquely, took her elbow and steered her back into the light, out of that dangerous intimacy. 'We still have a great deal to discuss.'

He paced the thick forest-green carpet, quickly establishing a beat as regular as that of a sentry, ten paces from the glass doors, passing in front of where she sat in the centre of the wide velvet couch, turning just before he reached the headless marble statue of a Greek athlete from antiquity that guarded the double oaken doors into the lobby, and then back in front of her again. As he paced, he told her in carefully prepared sequence all that he had learned from Lazarus.

She sat like a bird on the point of flight, turning her head to watch him, those huge dark eyes seeming to swell larger as she listened.

It was not necessary to explain it to her in layman's language, she was Arthur Christy's daughter, she understood when he told her how he suspected that Duncan Alexander had been forced to self-insure the hull of *Golden Dawn* and how he had used Christy stock to buy re-insurance, stock that he had probably already pledged to finance construction of the vessel.

Nicholas reconstructed the whole inverted pyramid of Duncan Alexander's machinations for her to examine, and almost immediately she saw how vulnerable, how unstable it was.

'Are you certain of all this?' she whispered, and her face was drained of all its lustrous rose tints.

He shook his head. 'I've reconstructed the Tyrannosaurus from a jawbone,' he admitted frankly. 'The shape of it might be a little different, but one thing I am certain of is that it's a big and dangerous beast.'

'Duncan could destroy Christy Marine,' she whispered again. 'Completely!' She looked around slowly, at the house – at the room and its treasures, the symbols of her life. 'He has risked everything that is mine, and Peter's.'

Nicholas did not reply, but he stopped in front of her and watched her carefully as she absorbed the enormity of it all.

He saw outrage turn slowly to confusion, to fear and finally to terror. He had never seen her even afraid before – but now, faced with the prospect of being stripped naked of the armour which had always protected her, she was like a lost animal, he could even see that flutter of her heart under the pale swelling flesh of her bosom, and she shivered again.

'Could he lose everything, Nicholas? He couldn't, could he?' She wanted assurance, but he could not give it to her, all he could give her was pity. Pity was the one emotion, probably the only one, she had never aroused in him, not once in all the years he had known her.

'What can I do, Nicholas?' she pleaded. 'Please help me. Oh God, what must I do?'

'You can stop Duncan launching *Golden Dawn* – until the hull and propulsion has been modified, until it has been properly surveyed and underwritten – and until you have taken full control of Christy Marine out of his hands again.' And his voice was gentle, filled with his compassion as he told her.

'That's enough for one day, Chantelle. If we go on now, we will begin chasing our tails. Tonight you know what could happen, tomorrow we will discuss how we can prevent it. Have you a Valium?'

She shook her head. 'I've never used drugs to hide from things.' It was true, he knew, that she had never lacked courage. 'How much longer can you stay?'

'I have a seat on the eleven o'clock plane. I have to be back in London by tomorrow night – we'll have time tomorrow morning.'

The guest suite opened on to the second-floor balcony which ran along the entire front of the building overlooking the sea and the private harbour. The five main bedrooms all opened on to this balcony, an arrangement from fifty years previously when internal security against kidnapping and forcible entry had been of no importance.

Nicholas determined to speak to Chantelle about that in the morning. Peter was an obvious target for extortion, and he felt the goose bumps of horror rise on his arms as he imagined his son in the hands of those degenerate monsters who were everywhere allowed to strike and destroy with impunity. There was a price to pay these days for being rich and successful. The smell of it attracted the hyenas and vultures. Peter must be better protected, he decided.

In the sitting-room, there was a well-stocked liquor cabinet concealed behind mirrors, nothing so obvious and resoundingly middle-class as a private bar. The daily papers, in English, French and German were set out on the television table, *France Soir, The Times, Allgemeine Zeitung,* with even an airmail version of the *New York Times*.

Nicholas flipped open *The Times* and glanced quickly at the closing prices. Christy Marine common stock was at £5.32p, up 15p on yesterday's prices. The market had not sniffed corruption – yet.

He pulled off his silk roll-neck, and even though he had bathed three hours previously, the tension had left his skin feeling itchy and unclean. The bathroom had been lavishly redecorated in green onyx panels and the fittings were eighteen-carat gold, in the shape of dolphins. Steaming water gushed from their gaping mouths at a touch. It could have been vulgar, but Chantelle's unerring touch steered it into Persian opulence instead.

He showered, turning the setting high so that the stinging needles of water scalded away his fatigue and the feeling of being unclean. There were half a dozen thick white terry towelling robes in the glass-fronted warming cupboard, and he selected one and went through into the bedroom, belting it around his naked waist. In his briefcase there was a draft of the agreement of sale of Ocean Salvage and Towage to the Sheikhs. James Teacher and his gang of bright young lawyers had read it, and made a thick sheaf of notes. Nicholas must study these before tomorrow evening when he met them in London.

He took the papers from his case and carried them through into the sitting-room, glancing at the top page before dropping them carelessly on to the low coffee table while he went to pour himself a small whisky, heavily diluted. He brought the drink back with him and sprawled into the deep leather armchair, picked up the papers and began to work.

He became aware of her perfume first, and felt his blood quicken uncontrollably at the fragrance, and the papers rustled in his hand.

Slowly he lifted his head. She had come in utter silence on small bare feet. She had removed all her jewellery and had let down her hair brushing it out on to her shoulders.

It made her seem younger, more vulnerable, and the gown she wore was cuffed and collared in fine soft lace. She moved slowly towards his chair, timorous and for once uncertain, the eyes huge and dark and haunted, and when he rose from the armchair, she stopped and one hand went to her throat.

'Nicholas,' she whispered, 'I'm so afraid, and so alone.' She moved a step closer, and saw his eyes shift, his lips harden, and she stopped instantly.

'Please,' she pleaded softly, 'don't send me away, Nicky. Not tonight, not yet. I'm afraid to be alone – please.'

He knew then that this had been going to happen, he had hidden the certainty of it from himself all that evening, but now it was upon him, and he could do nothing to avoid it. It was as though he had lost the will to resist, as though he stood mesmerized, his resolve softening and melting like wax in the candle flame of her beauty, of the passions which she commanded so skilfully, and his thoughts lost coherence, began to tumble and swirl like storm surf breaking on rock.

She recognized the exact instant when it happened to him, and she came forward silently, with small gliding footsteps, not making the mistake of speaking again and pressed her face to his bare chest framed in the collar of his robe. The thick curling hair was springing over hard flat muscle, and she flared her nostrils at the clean virile animal smell of his skin.

He was still resisting, standing stiffly with his hands hanging at his sides. Oh, she knew him so well. The terrible conflict he must suffer before he could be made to act against that iron code of his own. Oh, she knew him, knew that he was as sexual and physical an animal as she was herself, that he was the only man who had ever been able to match her appetites. She knew the defences he had erected about himself, the fortressing of his passions, the controls and repressions, but she knew so well how to subvert these elaborate defences, she knew exactly what to do and what to say, how to move and touch. As she began now, she found the deliberate act of breaking down his resistance excited her so swiftly that it was pain almost, agony almost, and it required all her own control not to advance too swiftly for him, to control the shaking of her legs and the pumping of her lungs, to play still the hurt and bewildered and frightened child, using his kindness, the sense of chivalry which would not allow him to send her away, in such obvious distress.

Oh God, how her body churned, her stomach cramped with the strength of her wanting, her breasts felt swollen and so sensitive that the contact of silk and lace was almost too painfully abrasive to bear.

'Oh, Nicky, please – just for a moment. Just once, hold me. Please, I cannot go on alone. Just for a moment, please.

She felt him lift his hands, felt the fingers on her shoulders, and the terrible pain of wanting was too much to bear, she could not control it – she cried out, it was a soft little whimper, but the force of it shook her body, and immediately she felt his reaction. Her timing had been immaculate, her natural womanly cunning had guided her. His fingers on her shoulders had been gentle and kindly, but now they hooked cruelly into her flesh.

His back arched involuntarily, his breath drummed from his chest under her ear, a single agonized exhalation like that of a boxer taking a heavy body punch. She felt his every muscle come taught, and she knew again the frightening power, the delirious giddy power she could still wield. Then, at last, joyously, almost fearfully, she experienced the great lordly lift and thrust of his loins – as though the whole world had moved and shifted about her.

She cried out again, fiercely, for now she could slip the hounds she had held so short upon the leash, she could let them run and hunt again. They had been too long denied, but now there was no longer need for care and restraint.

She knew exactly how to hunt him beyond the frontiers of reason, to course him like a flying stag, and his fingers tangled frantically in the foaming lace at her throat as he tried to free her tight swollen breasts. She cried out a third time, and with a single movement jerked open the fastening at his waist, exposing the full hard lean length of his body, and her hands were as frantic as his.

'Oh, sweet God, you're so hard and strong – oh sweet God, I've missed you so.'

There was time later for all the refinements and nuances of love, but now her need was too cruel and demanding to be denied another moment. It had to happen this instant before she died of the lack.

Nicholas rose slowly towards the surface of sleep, aware of a brooding sense of regret. Just before he reached consciousness, a dream image formed in his sleep-starved brain, he relived a moment from the distant past. A fragment of time, recaptured so vividly as to seem whole and perfect. Long ago he had picked a deep-sea trumpet shell at five fathoms from the oceanic wall of the coral reef beyond the Anse Baudoin lagoon of Praslin Island. It was the size of a ripe coconut and once again he found himself holding the shell in both cupped hands gazing into the narrow oval opening, around which the weed-furred and barnacle-encrusted exterior changed dramatically, flaring into the pouting lips and exposing the inner mother-of-pearl surfaces that were slippery to the touch, a glossy satin sheen, pale translucent pink, folded and convoluted upon themselves, shading darker into fleshy crimsons and wine purples as the passage narrowed and sank away into the mysterious lustrous depths of the shell.

Then abruptly, the dream image changed in his mind. the projected opening in the trumpet shell expanded, articulating on jaw-hinges and he was gaping into the deep and terrible maw of some great predatory sea-creature, lined with multiple rows of serrated triangular teeth – sharklike, terrifying, so he cried out in half sleep, startling himself awake, and he rolled quickly on to his side and raised himself on one elbow. Her perfume still lingered on his skin, mingled with the smell of his own sweat, but the bed beside him was empty, though warm and redolent with the memory of her body.

Across the room, the early sun struck a long sliver of light through a narrow chink in the curtains. It looked like a blade, a golden blade. It reminded him instantly of Samantha Silver. He saw her again wearing sunlight like a cloak, barefoot in the sand – and it seemed that the blade of sunlight was being driven up slowly under his ribs.

He swung his feet off the wide bed and padded softly across to the gold and onyx bathroom. There was a dull ache of sleeplessness and remorse behind his eyes and as he ran hot water from the dolphin's mouth into the basin, he looked at himself in the mirror although the steam slowly clouded the image of his own face. There were dark smears below his eyes and his features were gaunt, harsh angles of bone beneath drawn skin.

'You bastard,' he whispered at the shadowy face in the mirror. 'You bloody bastard.'

They were waiting breakfast for him, in the sunlight on the terrace under the gaily coloured umbrellas. Peter had preserved the mood of the previous evening, and he ran laughing to meet Nicholas.

'Dad, hey Dad.' He seized Nicholas' hand and led him to the table.

Chantelle wore a long loose housegown, and her hair was down on her shoulders, so soft that it stirred like spun silk in even that whisper of breeze. It was calculated, Chantelle did nothing by chance; the intimately elegant attire and the loose fall of her hair set the mood of domesticity – and Nicholas found himself resisting it fiercely.

Peter sensed his father's change of mood with an intuitive understanding beyond his years, and his dismay was a palpable thing, the hurt and reproach in his eyes as he looked at Nicholas; and then the chatter died on his lips and he bent his head studiously over his plate and ate in silence.

Nicholas deliberately refused the festival array of food, took only a cup of coffee, and lit a cheroot, without asking Chantelle's permission, knowing how she would resent that. He waited in silence and as soon as Peter had eaten he said:

'I'd like to speak to your mother, Peter.'

The boy stood obediently.

'Will I see you before you leave, sir?'

'Yes.' Nicholas felt his heart wrung again. 'Of course.'

'We could sail again?'

'I'm sorry, my boy. We won't have time. Not today.'

'Very well, sir.' Peter walked to the end of the terrace, very erect and dignified, then suddenly he began to run, taking the steps down two at a time, and he fled into the pine forest beyond the boathouse as though pursued, feet flying and arms pumping wildly.

'He needs you, Nicky,' said Chantelle softly.

'You should have thought about that two years ago.'

She poured fresh coffee into his cup. 'Both of us have been stupid – all right, worse than that. We've been wicked. I have had my Duncan, and you have had that American child.'

'Don't make me angry now,' he warned her softly. 'You've done enough for one day.'

'It's as simple as this, Nicholas. I love you, I have always loved you – God, since I was a gawky schoolgirl,' she had never been that, but Nicholas let it pass, 'since I saw you that first day on the bridge of old *Golden Eagle*, the dashing ship's captain —'

'Chantelle. All we have to discuss is *Golden Dawn* and Christy Marine.'

'No, Nicholas. We were born for each other, Daddy saw that immediately, we both knew it at the same time – it was only a madness, a crazy whim that made me doubt it for a moment.'

'Stop it, Chantelle.'

'Duncan was a stupid mistake. But it's unimportant —'

'No, it's not unimportant. It changed everything. It can never be the same again, besides —'

'Besides, what? Nicky, what were you going to say?'

'Besides, I am building myself another life now. With another very different person.'

'Oh God, Nicky, you aren't serious?' She laughed then, genuine amusement, clapping her hands delightedly. 'My dear, she's young enough to be your daughter. It's the forty syndrome, the Lolita complex.' Then she saw his real anger, and she was quick, retrieving the situation neatly, aware that she had carried it too far.

'I'm sorry, Nicky. I should never have said that.' She paused, and then went on. 'I will say she's a pretty little thing, and I'm sure she's sweet – Peter liked her.' She damned Samantha with light condescension, and then dismissed her as though she were merely a childlike prank of Nicholas', a light and passing folly of no real significance.

'I understand, Nicholas, truly I do. However, when you are ready, as you will be soon, then Peter and I and Christy Marine are waiting for you still. This is your world, Nicholas.' She made a gesture which embraced it all. 'This is your world, you will never really leave it.'

'You are wrong, Chantelle.'

'No.' She shook her head. 'I am very seldom wrong, and on this I cannot be wrong. Last night proved that, it is still there – every bit of it. But let's discuss the other thing now, *Golden Dawn* and Christy Marine.'

Chantelle Alexander lifted her face to the sky and watched the big silver bird fly. It climbed nose high, glinting in the sunlight, twin trails of dark unconsumed fuel spinning out behind it as the engines howled under the full thrust. With the wind in this quarter, the extended centreline of the main Nice runway brought it out over Cap Ferrat.

Beside Chantelle, only an inch or two shorter than she was, Peter stood and watched it also and she took his arm, tucking her small dainty hand into the crook of his elbow.

'He stayed such a short time,' Peter said, and overhead the big airbus turned steeply on to its crosswind leg.

'We will have him with us again soon,' Chantelle promised, and then she went on. 'Where were you, Peter? We hunted all over when it was time for Daddy to go?'

'I was in the forest,' he said evasively. He had heard them calling, but Peter was hidden in the secret place, the smuggler's cleft in the yellow rock of the cliff; he would have killed himself rather than let Nicholas Berg see him weeping.

'Wouldn't it be lovely if it was like the old times again?' Chantelle asked softly, and the boy stirred beside her, but unable to take his gaze from the aircraft, 'Just the three of us again?'

'Without Uncle Duncan?' he asked incredulously, and high above them the aircraft, with a last twinkle of sunlight, dove deeply into the banks of cumulus cloud that buttressed the northern sky. Peter turned at last to face her.

'Without Uncle Duncan,' he demanded again, 'but that's impossible.'

'Not if you help me, darling.' She took his face in her cupped hands. 'You will help me, won't you?' she asked, and he nodded once, a sharply incisive gesture of assent; she leaned forward and kissed him tenderly on the forehead.

'That's my man,' she whispered.

'Mr Alexander is not available. May I take a message?'

'This is Mrs Alexander. Tell my husband that it's urgent.'

'Oh, I'm terribly sorry, Mrs Alexander.' The secretary's voice changed instantly, cool caution becoming effusive servility. 'I didn't recognize your voice. The line is dreadful. Mr Alexander will speak to you directly.'

Chantelle waited, staring impatiently from the study windows. The weather had changed in the middle of the morning with the cold front sweeping down off the mountains, and now icy wind and rain battered at the windows.

'Chantelle, my dear,' the rich glossy voice that had once so dazzled her, 'is this my call to you?'

'It's mine, Duncan. I must speak to you urgently.'

'Good,' he agreed with her. 'I wanted to speak to you also. Things are happening swiftly here. It's necessary for you to come up to St Nazaire next Tuesday, instead of my joining you at Cap Ferrat.'

'Duncan –'

But he went on over her protest, his voice as full of self-confidence, as ebullient as she had not heard it in over a year.

'I have been able to save almost four weeks on *Golden Dawn*.'

'Duncan, listen to me.'

'We will be able to launch on Tuesday. It will be a make-shift ceremony, I'm afraid, at such short notice.' He was inordinately proud of his own achievement. It annoyed her to hear him. 'What I have arranged is that the pod tanks will be delivered direct to the Gulf from the Japanese yards. They are towing them in their ballast with four American tugs. I will launch the hull here, with workmen still aboard her, and they will finish her off at sea during the passage around Good Hope, in time for her to take on her tanks and cargo at El Barras. We'll save nearly seven and a half million –'

'Duncan!' Chantelle cried again, and this time something in her tone stopped him.

'What is it?'

'This can't wait until Tuesday, I want to see you right away.'

'That's impossible,' he laughed, lightly, confidently. 'It's only five days.'

'Five days is too long.'

'Tell me now,' he invited. 'What is it?'

'All right,' she said deliberately, and the vicious streak of Persian cruelty was in her voice. 'I'll tell you. I want a divorce, Duncan, and I want control of my shares in Christy Marine again.'

There was a long, hissing crackling silence on the line, and she waited, the way the cat waits for the first movement of the crippled mouse.

'This is very sudden.' His voice had changed completely, it was bleak and flat, lacking any timbre or resonance.

'We both know it is not,' she contradicted him.

'You have no grounds.' There was a thin edge of fear now. 'Divorce isn't quite as easy as that, Chantelle.'

'How is this for grounds, Duncan?' she asked, and there was a spiteful sting in her voice now. 'If you aren't here by noon tomorrow, then my auditors will be in Leadenhall Street and there will be an urgent order before the courts —'

She did not have to go on, he spoke across her and there was a note of panic in his voice. She had never heard it before. He said, 'You are right. We do have to talk right away.' Then he was silent again, collecting himself, and his voice was once more calm and careful when he went on, 'I can charter a Falcon and be at Nice before midday. Will that do?'

'I'll have the car meet you,' she said, and broke the connection with one finger. She held the bar down for a second, then lifted her finger.

'I want to place an international call,' she said in her fluent rippling French when the operator answered. 'I do not know the number, but it is person to person. Doctor Samantha Silver at the University of Miami.'

'There is a delay of more than two hours, madame.'

'*J'attendrai*,' she said, and replaced the receiver.

The Bank of the East is in Curzon Street, almost opposite the White Elephant Club. It has a narrow frontage of bronze and marble and glass, and Nicholas had been there, with his lawyers, since ten o'clock that morning. He was learning at first hand the leisurely age-old ritual of oriental bargaining.

He was selling Ocean Salvage, plus two years of his future labour – and even for seven million dollars he was beginning to wonder if it was worth it – and it was not a certain seven millions either. The words tripped lightly, the figures seemed to have no substance in this setting. The only constant was the figure of the Prince himself, seated on the low couch, in a Savile Row suit but with the fine white cotton and gold-corded headdress framing his dark handsome features with theatrical dash.

Beyond him moved a shadowy, ever-changing background of unctuous whispering figures. Every time that Nicholas believed that a point had been definitely agreed, another rose-pink or acid-yellow Rolls-Royce with Arabic script number-plates would deposit three or four more dark-featured Arabs at the front doors and they would hurry through to kiss the Prince on his forehead, on the bridge of his nose and on the back of his hand, and the hushed discussion would begin all over again with the newcomers picking up at the point they had been an hour previously.

James Teacher showed no impatience, and he smiled and nodded and went through the ritual like an Arab born, sipping the little thimbles of treacly coffee and watching patiently for the interminable whisperings to be translated into English before making a measured counter proposal.

'We are doing fine, Mr Berg,' he assured Nicholas quietly. 'A few more days.'

Nicholas had a headache from the strong coffee and the Turkish tobacco smoke, and he found it difficult to concentrate. He kept worrying about Samantha. For four days he had tried to contact her. He had to get out for a while and he excused himself to the

Prince, and went down to the Enquiries Desk in the Bank's entrance hall and the girl told him,

'I'm sorry, sir, there is no reply to either of those numbers.'

'There must be,' Nicholas told her. One number was Samantha's shack at Key Biscayne and the other was her private number in her laboratory.

She shook her head. 'I've tried every hour.'

'Can you send a cable for me?'

'Of course, sir.'

She gave him a pad of forms and he wrote out the message.

'Please phone me urgently, reverse charges to –' he gave the number of the Queens Gate flat and James Teacher's rooms, then he thought with the pen poised, trying to find the words to express his concern, but there were none.

'I love you,' he wrote. 'I really do.'

Since Nicholas's midnight call to tell her of the carriage of cad-rich crude petroleum, Samantha Silver had been caught up in a kaleidoscope whirl of time and events.

After a series of meetings with the leaders of the Green-Peacers, and other conservation bodies in an effort to publicize and oppose this new threat to the oceans, she and Tom Parker had flown to Washington and met with a deputy director of the Environmental Protection Agency and with two young senators who spearheaded the conservation lobby – but their efforts to go further had been frustrated by the granite walls of big oil interest. Even usually co-operative sources had been wary of condemning or speaking out against Orient Amex's new carbon-cracking technology. As one thirty-year-old Democrat senator had pointed out, 'It's tough to try and take a shot at something that's going to increase the fossil fuel yield by fifty per cent.'

'That's not what we are shooting at,' Samantha had flared, bitter with fatigue and frustration. 'It's this irresponsible method of carrying the cad-rich through sensitive and highly vulnerable seaways we are trying to prevent.' But when she presented the scenario she had worked out, picturing the effects on the north Atlantic deluged with a million tons of toxic crude, she saw the disbelief in the man's eyes and the condescending smile of the sane for the slightly demented.

'Oh God, why is common sense the hardest thing in the world to sell?' she had lamented.

She and Tom had gone on to meet the leaders of Green-Peace in the north, and in the west, and they had given advice and promises of support. The Californian Chapter counselled physical intervention as a last resort, as some of their members had successfully interposed small craft between the Russian whalers and the breeding Minkes they were hunting in the Californian Gulf.

In Galveston, they met the young Texans who would picket the Orient Amex refinery as soon as they were certain the ultra-tanker had entered the Gulf of Mexico.

However, none of their efforts were successful in provoking confrontation with Orient Amex. The big oil company simply ignored invitations to debate the charges on radio or television, and stone-walled questions from the media. It's hard to stir up interest in a one-sided argument, Samantha found.

They managed one local Texas television show, but without controversy to give it zip, the producer cut Samantha's time down to forty-five seconds, and then tried to date her for dinner.

The energy crisis, oil tankers and oil pollution were joyless subjects. Nobody had ever heard of cadmium pollution, the Cape of Good Hope was half a world away, a million tons was a meaningless figure, impossible to visualize, and it was all rather a bore.

The media let it drop flat on its face.

'We're just going to have to smoke those fat cats at Orient Amex out into the open,' Tom Parker growled angrily, 'and kick their arses blue for them. The only way we are going to do that is through Green-Peace.'

They had landed back at Miami International, exhausted and disappointed, but not yet despondent. 'Like the man said,' Samantha muttered grimly, as she threaded her gaudy van back into the city traffic flow, 'we have only just begun to fight.'

She had only a few hours to clean herself up and stretch out on the patchwork quilt before she had to dress again and race back to the airport. The Australian had already passed through customs and was looking lost and dejected in the terminal lobby.

'Hi, I'm Sam Silver.' She pushed away fatigue, and hoisted that brilliant golden smile like a flag.

His name was Mr Dennis O'Connor and he was top man in his field, doing fascinating and important work on the reef populations of Eastern Australian waters, and he had come a long way to talk to her and see her experiments.

'I didn't expect you to be so young.' She had signed her correspondence 'Doctor Silver' and he gave the standard reaction to her. Samantha was just tired and angry enough not to take it.

'And I'm a woman. You didn't expect that either,' she agreed. 'It's a crying bastard, isn't it? But then, I bet some of your best friends are young females.'

He was a dinky-die Aussie, and he loved it. He burst into an appreciative grin, and as they shook hands, he said, 'You are not going to believe this, but I like you just the way you are.'

He was tall and lean, sunburned and just a little grizzled at the temples, and within minutes they were friends, and the respect with which he viewed her work confirmed that.

The Australian had brought with him, in an oxygenated container, five thousand live specimens of *E. digitalis*, the common Australian water snail, for inclusion in Samantha's experimentation. He had selected these animals for their abundance and their importance in the ecology of the Australian inshore waters, and the two of them were soon so absorbed in the application of Samantha's techniques to this new creature that when her assistant stuck her head through and yelled, 'Hey, Sam, there's a call for you,' she shouted back, 'Take a message. If they're lucky I'll call them back.'

'It's international, person to person!' and Samantha's pulse raced; instantly forgotten was the host of spiral-coned sea snails.

'Nicholas!' she shouted happily, spilled half a pint of sea water down the Australian's trouser leg and ran wildly to the small cubicle at the end of the laboratory.

She was breathless with excitement as she snatched up the receiver and she pressed one hand against her heart to stop it thumping.

'Is that Doctor Silver?'

'Yes! It's me.' Then correcting her grammar, 'It is she!'

'Go ahead, please,' said the operator, and there was a click and pulse on the line as it came alive.

'Nicholas!' she exulted. 'Darling Nicholas, is that you?'

'No.' The voice was very clear and serene, as though the speaker stood beside her, and it was familiar, disconcertingly so, and for no good reason Samantha felt her heart shrink with dread.

'This is Chantelle Alexander, Peter's mother. We have met briefly.'

'Yes.' Samantha's voice was now small, and still breathless.

'I thought it would be kind to tell you in person, before you hear from other sources – that Nicholas and I have decided to remarry.'

Samantha sat down jerkily on the office stool.

'Are you there?' Chantelle asked after a moment.

'I don't believe you,' whispered Samantha.

'I'm sorry,' Chantelle told her gently. 'But there is Peter, you see, and we have rediscovered each other – discovered that we had never stopped loving each other.'

'Nicholas wouldn't –' her voice broke, and she could not go on.

'You must understand and forgive him, my dear,' Chantelle explained. 'After our divorce he was hurt and lonely. I'm sure he did not mean to take advantage of you.'

'But, but – we were supposed to, we were going to –'

'I know. Please believe me, this has not been easy for any of us. For all our sakes –'

'We had planned a whole life together.' Samantha shook her head wildly, and a thick skein of golden hair came loose and flopped into her face, she pushed it back with a combing gesture. 'I don't believe it, why didn't Nicholas tell me himself? I won't believe it until he tells me.'

Chantelle's voice was compassionate, gentle. 'I so wanted not to make it ugly for you, my child, but now what can I do but tell you that Nicholas spent last night in my house, in my bed, in my arms, where he truly belongs.'

It was almost miraculous, a physical thing, but sitting hunched on the hard round stool Samantha Silver felt her youth fall away from her, sloughed off like a glittering reptilian skin. She was left with the sensation of timelessness, possessed of all the suffering and sorrow of every woman who had lived before. She felt very old and wise and sad, and she lifted her fingers and touched her own cheek, mildly surprised to feel that the skin was not dried and withered like that of some ancient crone.

'I have already made the arrangements for a divorce from my present husband, and Nicholas will resume his position at the head of Christy Marine.'

It was true, Samantha knew then that it was true. There was no question, no doubt, and slowly she replaced the receiver of the telephone, and sat staring blankly at the bare wall of the cubicle. She did not cry, she felt as though she would never cry, nor laugh, again in her life.

Chantelle Alexander studied her husband carefully, trying to stand outside herself, and to see him dispassionately. She found it easier now that the giddy insanity had burned away.

He was a handsome man, tall and lean, with those carefully groomed metallic waves of coppery hair. Even the wrist that he shot from the crisp white cuff of his sleeve was covered with those fine gleaming hairs. She knew so well that even his lean chest was covered with thick golden curls, crisp and curly, as fresh lettuce leaves. She had never been attracted by smooth hairless men.

'May I smoke?' he asked, and she inclined her head. His voice had also attracted her from the first, deep and resonant, but with those high-bred accents, the gentle softening of the vowel sounds, the lazy drawling of consonants. The voice and the patrician manner were things that she had been trained to appreciate – and yet, under the mannered cultivated exterior was the flash of exciting wickedness, that showed in the wolfish white gleam of smile, and the sharp glittering grey steel of his gaze.

He lit the custom-made cigarette with the gold lighter she had given him – her very first gift, the night they had become lovers. Even now, the memory of it was piquant, and for a moment she felt the soft melting warmth in her lower belly and she stirred restlessly in her chair. There had been reason, and good reason for that madness, and even now it was over, she would never regret it.

It had been a period in her life which she had not been able to deny herself. The grand sweeping illicit passion, the last flush of her youth, the final careless autumn that preceded middle age. Another ordinary woman might have had to content herself with sweaty sordid gropings and grapplings in anonymous hotel bedrooms, but not Chantelle Christy. Her world was shaped by her own whims and desires, and, as she had told Nicholas, whatever she desired was hers to take. Long ago, her father had taught her that there were special rules for Chantelle Christy, and the rules were those she made herself.

It had been marvellous, she shivered slightly at the lingering sensuality of those early days, but now it was over. During the past months she had been carefully comparing the two men. Her decision had not been lightly made.

She had watched Nicholas retrieve his life from the gulf of disaster. On his own, stripped naked of all but that invisible indefinable mantle of strength and determination, he had fought his way back out of the gulf. Strength and power had always moved her, but she had over the years grown accustomed to Nicholas. Familiarity had staled their relationship for her. But now her interlude with Duncan had freshened her view of him, and he had for her all the novel appeal of a new lover – yet with the proven values and qualities of long intimate acquaintance. Duncan Alexander was finished, Nicholas Berg was the future.

But, no, she would never regret this interlude in her life. It had been a time of rejuvenation, she would not even regret Nicholas' involvement with the pretty American child. Later, it would add a certain perverse spice to their own sexuality, she thought, and felt the shiver run down her thighs and the soft secret stirring of her flesh, like the opening of a petalled rosebud. Duncan had taught her many things, bizarre little tricks of arousal, made more poignant by being forbidden and wicked. Unfortunately Duncan relied almost entirely on the tricks, and not all of them had worked for her – the corners of her mouth turned down with distaste as she remembered; perhaps it was just that which had begun the curdling process.

No, Duncan Alexander had not been able to match her raw, elemental sexuality and soaring abandon. Only one man had ever been able to do that. Duncan had served a purpose, but now it was over. It might have dragged on a little longer, but Duncan Alexander had endangered Christy Marine. Never had she thought of that possibility; Christy Marine was a fact of her life, as vast and immutable as the heavens, but now the foundations of heaven were being shaken, his sexual attraction had staled, she might have forgiven him that, but not the other.

She became aware of Duncan's discomfort. He twisted sideways in his chair, crossing and uncrossing his long legs, and he rolled the cigarette between his fingers, studying the rising spiral of blue smoke to avoid the level, expressionless gaze of her dark fathomless eyes. She had been staring at him, but seeing the other man. Now, with an effort, she focused her attention on him.

'Thank you for coming so promptly,' she said.

'It did seem rather urgent.' He smiled for the first time, glossy and urbane – but with fear down there in the cool grey eyes, and his tension was betrayed by the clenched sinew in the point of his jaw.

Looking closely, as she had not done for many months, she saw how he was fined down. The long tapered fingers were bony, and never still. There were new harder lines to his mouth, and a frown to the set of his eyes. The skin at the corners cracked like oil paint into hundreds of fine wrinkles that the deep brown snow-tan hid from a casual glance. Now he returned her scrutiny directly.

'From what you told me yesterday –'

She lifted her hand to stop him. 'That can wait. I merely wanted to impress you with the seriousness of what is happening. What is really of prime importance now is what you have done with control of my shares and those of the Trust.'

His hands went very still. 'What does that mean?'

'I want auditors, my appointed auditors, sent in –'

He shrugged. 'All this will take time, Chantelle, and I'm not certain that I'm ready to relinquish control.' He was very cool, very casual now and the fear was gone.

She felt a stir of relief, perhaps the horror story that Nicholas had told her was untrue, perhaps the danger was imaginary only. Christy Marine was so big, so invulnerable.

'Not just at the moment, anyway. You'd have to prove to me that doing so was in the best interest of the company and of the Trust.'

'I don't have to prove anything, to anyone,' she said flatly.

'This time you do. You have appointed me –'

'No court of law would uphold that agreement.'

'Perhaps not, Chantelle, but do you want to drag all this through the courts – at a time like this?'

'I'm not afraid, Duncan.' She stood up quickly, light on her feet as a dancer, the lovely legs in loose black silk trousers, soft flat shoes making her seem still smaller, a slim gold chain emphasizing the narrowness of the tiny waist. 'You know I'm afraid of nothing.' She stood over him, and pointed the accuser's finger. The nails tipped in scarlet the colour of fresh arterial blood. 'You should be the one to fear.'

'And precisely what is it you are accusing me of?'

And she told him, reeling off swiftly the lists of guarantees made by the Trust, the transfer of shares and the issues of new shares and guarantees within the Christy Marine group of subsidiaries, she listed the known layering of underwriting cover on *Golden Dawn* that Nicholas had unearthed.

'When my auditors have finished, Duncan darling, not only will the courts return control of Christy Marine to me, but they will probably sentence you to five years at hard labour. They take this sort of thing rather seriously, you know.'

He smiled. He actually smiled! She felt her fury seething to the surface and the set of her eyes altered, colour tinted the smooth pale olive of her cheeks.

'You dare to grin at me,' she hissed. 'I will break you for that.'

'No,' he shook his head. 'No, you won't.'

'Are you denying —' she snapped, but he cut her off with a raised hand, and a shake of that handsome arrogant head.

'I am denying nothing, my love. On the contrary, I am going to admit it – and more, much more.' He flicked the cigarette away, and it hissed sharply in the lapping blue wavelets of the yacht basin. While she stared at him, struck speechless, he let the silence play out like a skilled actor as he selected and lit another cigarette from the gold case.

'For some weeks now I have been fully aware that somebody was prying very deeply into my affairs and those of the company.' He blew a long blue feather of cigarette smoke, and cocked one eyebrow at her, a cynical mocking gesture which increased her fury, but left her feeling suddenly afraid and uncertain. 'It didn't take long to establish that the trace was coming from a little man in Monte Carlo who makes a living at financial and industrial espionage. Lazarus is good, excellent, the very best. I have used him myself, in fact it was I who introduced him to Nicholas Berg.' He chuckled then, shaking his head indulgently. 'The silly things we do sometimes. The connection was immediate. Berg and Lazarus. I have run my own check on what they have come up with and I estimate that even Lazarus could not have uncovered more than twenty-five per cent of the answers.' He leaned forward and suddenly his voice snapped with a new authority. 'You see, Chantelle dear, I am probably one of the best in the world myself. They could never have traced it all.'

'You are not denying then —' She heard the faltering tone in her own voice, and hated herself for it. He brushed her aside contemptuously.

'Be quiet, you silly little woman, and listen to me. I am going to tell you just how deeply you are in – I am going to explain to you, in terms that even you can understand, why you will not send in your auditors, why you will not fire me, and why you will do exactly what I tell you to do.'

He paused and stared into her eyes, a direct trial of strength which she could not meet. She was confused and uncertain, for once not in control of her own destiny. She dropped her eyes, and he nodded with satisfaction.

'Very well. Now listen. I have put it all – everything that is Christy Marine – it is all riding on *Golden Dawn*.'

Chantelle felt the earth turn giddily under her feet and the sudden roaring rush of blood in her ears. She stepped back and the stone parapet caught the back of her knees. She sat down heavily.

'What are you talking about?' she whispered. And he told her, in substantial detail, from the beginning, how it had worked out. From the laying of *Golden Dawn*'s keel in the times of vast tanker tonnage demand. 'My calculations were based on demand for tanker space two years ago, and on construction costs of that time.'

The energy crisis and collapse in demand for tankers had come with the vicious rise in inflation, bloating the costs of construction of *Golden Dawn* by more than double.

Duncan had countered by altering the design of the gigantic tanker. He had reduced the four propulsion units to one, he had cut down the steel structuring of the hull reinforcement by twenty per cent, he had done away with elaborate safety functions and fail-safe systems designed by Nicholas Berg, and he had cut it too fine. He had forfeited the Al Lloyd's rating, the mark of approval from the inspectors of that venerable body; without the insurance backing of that huge underwriting market, he had been forced to look elsewhere to find the cover to satisfy his financiers. The premiums had been crippling. He had to pledge Christy Marine stock, the Trust stock. Then the spiralling cost of production had overtaken him again and he needed money and more money. He had taken it where he could find it, at rates of interest that were demanded, and used more Christy stock as collateral.

Then the insurance cover had been insufficient to cover the huge increase in the cost of the ultra-tanker's hull.

'When luck runs out —' Duncan shrugged eloquently, and went on. 'I had to pledge more Christy stock, all of it. It's all at risk, Chantelle, every single piece of paper, even the shares we retrieved from your Nicholas – and even that wasn't enough. I have had to write cover through front companies, cover that is worthless. Then,' Duncan smiled again, relaxed and unruffled, almost as though he was enjoying himself, 'then, there was that awful fiasco when *Golden Adventurer* went up on the ice, and I had to find six million dollars to pay the salvage award. That was the last of it, I went out for everything then, all of it. The Trust, the whole of Christy Marine.'

'I'll break you,' she whispered. 'I'll smash you. I swear before God —'

'You don't understand, do you?' He shook his head sorrowfully, as though at an obtuse child. 'You cannot break me, without breaking Christy Marine and yourself. You are in it, Chantelle, much much deeper than I am. You have everything, every penny, this house, that emerald on your finger, the future of your brat – all of it is riding on *Golden Dawn*'.

'No.' She closed her eyes very tightly, and there was no colour in her cheeks now.

'Yes. I'm afraid it's yes,' he contradicted. 'I didn't plan it that way. I saw a profit of 200 millions in it, but we have been caught up in circumstances, I'm afraid.'

They were both silent, and Chantelle swayed slightly as the full enormity of it overwhelmed her.

'If you whistle up your hounds now, if you call in your axemen, there will be plenty for them to work on,' he laughed again, 'buckets of dung for us all to wallow in. And my backers will line up to cancel out, *Golden Dawn* will never run down her ways – she is not fully covered, as I explained to you. It all hangs on a single thread, Chantelle. If the launching of *Golden Dawn* is delayed now, delayed by a month – no, by a week even, it will all come tumbling down.'

'I'm going to be sick,' she whispered thickly.

'No, you are not.' He stood up and crossed quickly to her. Coldly he slapped her face, two hard open-handed back and forth blows, that snapped her head from side to side, leaving the livid marks of his fingers on her pale cheeks. It was the first time ever that a man had struck her, but she could not find the indignation to protest. She merely stared at him.

'Pull yourself together,' he snarled at her, and gripped her shoulders fiercely, shaking her as he went on. 'Listen to me. I have told you the worst that can happen. Now, I will tell you the best. If we stand together now, if you obey me implicitly, without question, I will pull off one of the greatest financial coups of the century for you. All it needs is one successful voyage by *Golden Dawn* and we are home free – a single voyage, a few short weeks, and I will have doubled your fortune.' She was staring at him, sickened and shaken to the core of her existence. 'I have signed an agreement of charter with Orient Amex, that will pull us out from under a single voyage, and the day *Golden Dawn* anchors in Galveston roads and sends in her tank pods to discharge, I will have a dozen buyers for her.' He stepped back, and straightened the lapels of his jacket. 'Men are going to remember my name. In future when they talk of tankers, they are going to talk of Duncan Alexander.'

'I hate you,' she said softly. 'I truly hate you.'

'That is not important.' He waved it away. 'When it is over, I can afford to walk away – and you can afford to let me go. But not a moment before.'

'How much will you make from this, if it succeeds?' she asked, and she was recovering, her voice firmer.

'A great deal. A very great deal of money – but my real reward will be in reputation and achievement. After this, I will be a man who can write his own ticket.'

'For once, you will be able to stand comparison with Nicholas Berg. Is that it?' She saw she had scored immediately, and she pressed harder, trying to wound and destroy. 'But you and I both know it is not true. *Golden Dawn* was Nicholas' inspiration and he would not have had to descend to the cheat and sham –'

'My dear Chantelle–'

'You will never be, could never be the man Nicholas is.'

'Damn you.' Suddenly he was shaking with anger, and she was screaming at him.

'You're a cheat and a liar. For all your airs, you're still a cheap little barrow-boy at heart. You're small and shoddy –'

'I've beaten Nicholas Berg every time I've met him.'

'No, you haven't, Duncan. It was I who beat him for you –'

'I took you.'

'For a while,' she sneered. 'Just for a short fling, Duncan dear. But when he wanted me he took me right back again.'

'What do you mean by that?' be demanded.

'The night before last, Nicholas was here, and he loved me in a way you never could. I'm going back to him, and I'll tell the world why.'

'You bitch.'

'He is so strong, Duncan. Strong where you are weak.'

'And you are a whore.' He half turned away, and then paused. 'Just be at St Nazaire on Tuesday.' But she could see he was hurt, at last she had cut through the carapace and touched raw quick nerves.

'He loved me four times in one night. Duncan, magnificent soaring love. Did you ever do that?'

'I want you at St Nazaire, smiling at the creditors on Tuesday.'

'Even if you succeed with *Golden Dawn*, within six months Nicholas will have your job.'

'But until then you'll do exactly what I say.' Duncan braced himself, a visible effort, and began to walk away.

'You are going to be the loser, Duncan Alexander,' she screamed after him, her voice cracking shrilly with frustration and outrage. 'I will see to that – I swear it to you.'

He subdued the urge to run, and crossed the terrace, holding himself carefully erect, and the storm of her hatred and frustration burst around him.

'Go into the streets where you belong, into the gutter where I found you,' she screamed, and he went up the stone staircase and out of her sight. Now he could hurry, but he found his legs were trembling under him, his breath was ragged and broken, and there was a tight knot of anger and jealousy turning his guts into a ball.

'The bastard,' he spoke aloud. 'That bastard Berg.'

'Tom? Tom Parker?'

'That's right, who is this, please?' His voice was so clear and strong, although the Atlantic Ocean separated them.

'It's Nicholas, Nicholas Berg.'

'Nick, how are you?' the big voice boomed with genuine pleasure. 'God, I'm glad you called. I've been trying to reach you. I've got good news. The best.'

Nicholas felt a quick lift of relief.

'Samantha?'

'No, damn it,' Tom laughed. 'It's the job. Your job. It went up before the Board of Governors of the University yesterday. I had to sell it to them hard – I'll tell you that for free – but they okayed it. You're on, Nick, isn't that great?'

'It's terrific, Tom.'

'You're on the Biology faculty as an associate, it's the end of the wedge, Nicholas. We'll have you a chair by the end of next year, you wait and see.'

'I'm delighted.'

'Christ, you don't sound it,' Tom roared. 'What's bugging you, boy?'

'Tom, what the hell has happened to Samantha?'

And Nicholas sensed the mood change, the silence lasted a beat too long, and then Tom's tone was guileless.

'She went off on a field trip – down the Keys, didn't she tell you?'

'Down the keys?' Nicholas' voice rose with his anger and frustration. 'Damn it, Tom. She was supposed to be here in France. She promised to come over for the launching of my new vessel. I've been trying to get in touch with her for a week now.'

'She left Sunday,' said Tom.

'What is she playing at?'

'That's a question she might want to ask you sometime.'

'What does that mean, Tom?'

'Well, before she took off, she came up here and had a good weep with Antoinette – you know, my wife. She plays den mother for every hysterical female within fifty miles, she does.'

Now it was Nicholas' turn to be silent, while the coldness settled on his chest, the coldness of formless dread.

'What was the trouble?'

'Good God, Nick, you don't expect me to follow the intimate details of the love life —'

'Can I speak to Antoinette?'

'She isn't here, Nick. She went up to Orlando for a meeting. She won't be back until the weekend.'

The silence again.

'All that heavy breathing is costing you a fortune, Nicholas. You're paying for this call.'

'I don't know what got into Sam.' But he did. Nicholas knew – and the guilt was strong upon him.

'Listen, Nick. A word to the wise. Get your ass across here, boy. Just as soon as you can. That girl needs talking to, badly. That is, if you care about it.'

'I care about it,' Nicholas said quickly. 'But hell, I am launching a tug in two days' time. I've got sea trials, and a meeting in London.'

Tom's voice had an air of finality. 'A man's got to do what he's got to do.'

'Tom, I'll be across there as soon as I possibly can.'

'I believe it.'

'If you see her, tell her that for me, will you?'

'I'll tell her.'

'Thanks, Tom.'

'The governors will want to meet you, Nicholas. Come as soon as you can.'

'It's a promise.'

Nicholas cradled the receiver, and stood staring out of the windows of the site office. The view across the inner harbour was completely blocked by the towering hull of his tug. She stood tall on her ways. Her hull already wore its final coat of glistening white and the wide flaring bows bore the name *Sea Witch* and below that the port of registration, 'Bermuda'.

She was beautiful, magnificent, but now Nicholas did not even see her. He was overwhelmed by a sense of imminent loss, the cold premonition of onrushing disaster. Until that moment when he faced the prospect of losing her, he had not truly known how large a part that lovely golden girl had come to play in his existence, and in his plans for the future.

There was no way that Samantha could have learned of that single night of weakness, the betrayal that still left Nicholas sickened with guilt – there must be something else that had come between them. He bunched his right fist and slammed it against the sill of the window. The skin on his knuckles smeared, but he did not feel the pain, only the bitter frustration of being tied down here in St Nazaire, weighed down by his responsibilities, when he should have been free to follow the jack-o'-lantern of happiness.

The loudspeaker above his head gave a preliminary squawk, and then crackled out the message, 'Monsieur Berg. Will Monsieur attend upon the bridge?'

It was a welcome distraction, and Nicholas hurried out into the spring sunshine. Looking upwards, he could see Jules Levoisin on the wing of the bridge. His portly figure foreshortened against the open sky, like a small pugnacious rooster, he stood facing the electronics engineer who was responsible for the installation of *Sea Witch*'s communications system, and Jules' cries of 'Sacré bleu' and 'Merde' and 'Imbécile' carried clearly above the cacophony of shipyard noises.

Nicholas started to run as he saw the engineer's arms begin to wave and his strident Gallic cries blended with those of *Sea Witch*'s new Master. It was only the third time that Jules Levoisin had become hysterical that day, however it was not yet noon. As the hour of launching came steadily closer, so the little Frenchman's nerves played him tricks, he was behaving like a prima ballerina awaiting the opening curtain. Unless Nicholas reached the bridge within the next few minutes, he would need either a new Master or a new electronics engineer.

Ten minutes later, Nicholas had a cheroot in each of their mouths. The atmosphere was still tense but no longer explosive, and gently Nick took the engineer by the elbow, placed his other arm around Jules Levoisin's shoulders and led them both back into the wheelhouse.

The bridge installation was complete, and Jules Levoisin was accepting delivery of the special equipment from the contractors, a negotiation every bit as traumatic as the Treaty of Versailles.

'I myself authorized the modification of the MK IV transponder,' Nicholas explained patiently. 'We had trouble with the same unit on *Warlock*. I should have told you, Jules.'

'You should have,' agreed the little Master huffily.

'But you were perceptive to notice the change from the specification,' Nicholas soothed him, and Jules puffed out his chest a little and rolled the cheroot in his mouth.

'I may be an old dog, but I know all the new tricks.' He removed the cheroot and smugly blew a perfect smoke ring.

When Nicholas at last left them chatting amiably over the massed array of sophisticated equipment that lined the navigation area at the back of the bridge, they were paging him from the site office.

'What is it?' he asked, as he came in through the door.

'It's a lady,' the foreman indicated the telephone lying on the littered desk below the window.

'Samantha,' Nick thought, and snatched up the receiver.

'Nicky.' He felt the shock of quick guilt at the voice.

'Chantelle, where are you?'

'In La Baule.' The fashionable resort town just up the Atlantic coast was a better setting for Chantelle Alexander than the grubby port with its sprawling dockyards. 'Staying at the Castille. God, it's too awful. I'd forgotten how awful it was.'

They had stayed there together, once long ago, in a different life it seemed now.

'But the restaurant is still quite cute, Nicholas. Have lunch with me. I must speak to you.'

'I can't leave here.' He would not walk into the trap again.

'It's important. I must see you.' He could hear that husky tone in her voice, imagine clearly the sensuous droop of the eyelids over those bold Persian eyes. 'For an hour, only an hour. You can spare that.' Despite himself, he felt the pull of temptation, the dull ache of it at the base of his belly – and he was angry at her for the power she could still exert over him.

'If it's important, then come here,' he said brusquely, and she sighed at his intransigence.

'All right, Nicholas. How will I find you?'

The Rolls was parked opposite the dockyard gates and Nicholas crossed the road and stepped through the door that the chauffeur held open for him.

Chantelle lifted her face to him. Her hair was cloudy dark and shot with light like a bolt of silk, her lips the colour of ripe fruit, moist and slightly parted. He ignored the invitation and touched her cheek with his lips before settling into the corner opposite her.

She made a little moue, and slanted her eyes at him in amusement. 'How chaste we are, Nicky.'

Nicholas touched the button on the control console and the glass soundproof partition slid up noiselessly between them and the chauffeur.

'Did you send in the auditors?' he asked.

'You look tired, darling, and harassed.'

'Have you blown the whistle on Duncan?' he avoided the distraction. 'The work on *Golden Dawn* is still going ahead. The arc lights were burning over her all night and the talk in the yards is that she is being launched at noon tomorrow, almost a month ahead of schedule. What happened, Chantelle?'

'There is a little bistro at Mindin, it's just across the bridge —'

'Damn it, Chantelle. I haven't time to fool around.'

But the Rolls was already gliding swiftly through the narrow streets of the port, between the high warehouse buildings.

'It will take five minutes, and the Lobster Armoricaine is the local speciality – not to be confused with Lobster Américaine. They do it in a cream sauce, it's superb,' she chatted archly, and the Rolls turned out on to the quay. Across the narrow waters of the inner harbour humped the ugly camouflaged mounds of the Nazi submarine pens, armoured concrete so thick as to resist the bombs of the R.A.F. and the efforts of all demolition experts over the years since then.

'Peter asked me to give you his love. He has got his junior team colours. I'm so proud.'

Nicholas thrust his hands deep into his jacket pockets and slumped down resignedly against the soft leather seat.

'I am delighted to hear it,' he said.

And they were silent then until the chauffeur checked the Rolls at the toll barrier to pay before accelerating out on to the ramp of the St Nazaire bridge. The great span of the bridge rose in a regal curve, three hundred feet above the waters of the Loire River. The river was almost three miles wide here, and from the highest point of the bridge there was an aerial view over the dockyards of the town.

There were half a dozen vessels building along the banks of the broad muddy river, a mighty forest of steel scaffolding, tall gantries and half-assembled hulls, but all of it insignificant under the mountainous bulk of *Golden Dawn*. Without her pod tanks, she had an incomplete gutted appearance, as though the Eiffel Tower had toppled over and somebody had built a modernistic apartment block at one end. It seemed impossible that such a structure was capable of floating. God, she was ugly, Nick thought.

'They are still working on her,' he said. One of the gantries was moving ponderously along the length of the ship like an arthritic dinosaur, and at fifty paces the brilliant blue electric fires of the welding torches flickered; while upon the grotesquely riven hull crawled human figures reduced to antlike insignificance by the sheer size of the vessel.

'They are still working,' he repeated it as an accusation.

'Nicholas, nothing in this life is simple –'

'Did you spell it out for Duncan?'

'- except for people like you.'

'You didn't confront Duncan, did you?' he accused bitterly.

'It's easy for you to be strong. It's one of the things that first attracted me.'

And Nicholas almost laughed aloud. It was ludicrous to talk of strength, after his many displays of weakness with this very woman.

'Did you call Duncan's cards?' he insisted, but she put him off with a smile.

'Let's wait until we have a glass of wine –'

'Now,' he snapped. 'Tell me right now. Chantelle, I haven't time for games.'

'Yes, I spoke to him,' she nodded. 'I called him down to Cap Ferrat, and I accused him – of what you suspected.'

'He denied it? If he denies it, I now have further proof –'

'No, Nicholas. He didn't deny a thing. He told me that I knew only the half of it.' Her voice rose sharply, and suddenly it all spilled out in a torrent of tortured words. Her composure was eroded swiftly away as she relived the enormity of her predicament. 'He's gambled with my fortune, Nicholas. He's risked the family share of Christy Marine, the Trust shares, my shares, it's all at risk. And he gloated as he told me, he truly gloried in his betrayal.'

'We've got him now.' Nicholas had straightened slowly in his seat as he listened. His voice was grimly satisfied and he nodded. 'That's it. We will stop the *Golden Dawn*, like that –' he hammered his bunched fist into the palm of the other hand with a sharp crack. 'We will get an urgent order before the courts.'

Nicholas stopped suddenly and stared at her. Chantelle was shaking her head slowly from side to side. Her eyes slowly filled, making them huge and glistening, a single tear spilled over the lid and clung in the thick dark lashes like a drop of morning dew.

The Rolls had stopped now outside the tiny bistro. It was on the river front, with a view across the water to the dockyards. To the west the river debouched into the open sea and in the east the beautiful arch of the bridge across the pale blue spring sky.

The chauffeur held open the door and Chantelle was gone with her swift birdlike grace, leaving Nicholas no choice to follow her.

The proprietor came through from his kitchen and fussed over Chantelle, seating her at the window and lingering to discuss the menu.

'Oh, let's drink the Muscadet, Nicholas.' Shc had always had the most amazing powers of recovery, and now the tears were gone and she was brittle and gay and beautiful, smiling at him over the rim of her glass. The sunlight through the leaded window panes danced in the cool golden wine and rippled on the smoky dark fall of her hair.

'Here's to us, Nicholas darling. We are the last of the great.' It was a toast from long ago, from the other life, and it irritated him now but he drank it silently and then set down the glass.

'Chantelle, when and how are you going to stop Duncan?'

'Don't spoil the meal, darling.'

'In about thirty seconds I'm going to start becoming very angry.'

She studied him for a moment, and saw that it was true. 'All right then,' she agreed reluctantly.

'When are you going to stop him?'

'I'm not, darling.'

He stared at her. 'What did you say?' he asked quietly.

'I'm going to do everything in my power to help him launch and sail the *Golden Dawn*.'

'You don't understand, Chantelle. You're talking about risking a million tons of the most deadly poison –'

'Don't be silly, Nicky. Keep that heroic talk for the newspapers. I don't care if Duncan dumps a million tons of cadmium in the water supply of greater London, just as long as he pulls the Trust and me out of the fire.'

'There is still time to make the modifications to *Golden Dawn*.'

'No, there isn't. You don't understand, darling. Duncan has put us so deeply into it that a delay of a few days even would bring us down. He has stripped the cupboard bare, Nicky. There is no money for modifications, no time for anything, except to get *Golden Dawn* under way.'

'There is always a way and a means.'

'Yes, and the way is to fill *Golden Dawn*'s pod tanks with crude.'

'He's frightened you by –'

'Yes,' she agreed. 'I am frightened. I have never been so frightened in my life. Nicky. I could lose everything – I am terrified. I could lose it all.' She shivered with the horror of it. 'I would kill myself if that happened.'

'I am still going to stop Duncan.'

'No, Nicky. Please leave it, for my sake – for Peter's sake, it's Peter's inheritance that we are talking about. Let *Golden Dawn* make one voyage, just one voyage – and I will be safe.'

'It's the risk to an ocean, to God alone knows how many human lives, we are talking about.'

'Don't shout, Nicky. People are looking.'

'Let them look. I'm going to stop that monster.'

'No, Nicholas. Without me, you cannot do a thing.'

'You best believe it.'

'Darling, I promise you, after her first voyage we will sell *Golden Dawn*. We'll be safe then, and I can rid myself of Duncan. It will be you and I again, Nicky. A few short weeks, that's all.'

It took all his self-control to prevent his anger showing. He clenched his fists on the starched white tablecloth, but his voice was cool and even.

'Just one more question, Chantelle. When did you telephone Samantha Silver?'

She looked puzzled for a moment as though she was trying to put a face to a name. 'Samantha, oh, your little friend. Why should I want to telephone her?' And then her expression changed. 'Oh, Nicky, you don't really believe I'd do that? You don't really believe I would tell anybody about it, about that wonderful –' Now she was stricken, again those huge eyes brimmed and she reached across and stroked the fine black hairs on the back of Nicholas' big square hand. 'You don't think that of me! I'm not that much of a bitch. I don't have to cheat to get the things I want. I don't have to inflict unnecessary hurt on people.'

'No,' Nicholas agreed quietly. 'You'd not murder more than a million or poison more than a single ocean at a time, would you?' He pushed back his chair.

'Sit down, Nicky. Eat your lobster.'

'Suddenly I'm not hungry.' He stripped two one-hundred-franc notes from his money clip and dropped them beside his plate.

'I forbid you to leave,' she hissed angrily. 'You are humiliating me, Nicholas.'

'I'll send your car back,' he said, and walked out into the sunlight. He found with surprise that he was trembling, and that his jaws were clenched so tightly that his teeth ached.

The wind turned during the night, and the morning was cold with drifts of low, grey, fast-flying cloud that threatened rain. Nicholas pulled up his collar against the wind and the tails of his coat flogged about his legs, for he was exposed on the highest point of the arched bridge of St Nazaire.

Thousands of others had braved the wind, and the guard-rail was lined two and three deep, all the way across the curve of the northern span. The traffic had backed up and half a dozen gendarmes were trying to get it moving again; their whistles shrilled plaintively. Faintly the sound of a band floated up to them, rising and falling in volume as the wind caught it, and even with the naked eye Nicholas could make out the wreaths of gaily coloured bunting which fluttered on the high cumbersome stern tower of *Golden Dawn*.

He glanced at his wristwatch, and saw it was a few minutes before noon. A helicopter clattered noisily under the grey belly of cloud, and hovered about the yards of Construction Navale Atlantique on the gleaming silver coin of its rotor.

Nicholas lifted the binoculars and the eyepieces were painfully cold against his skin. Through the lens, he could almost make out individual features among the small gathering on the rostrum under the tanker's stern.

The platform was decorated with a Tricolour and a Union Jack, and as he watched the band fell silent and lowered their instruments.

'Speech time,' Nicholas murmured, and now he could make out Duncan Alexander, his bared head catching one of the fleeting rays of sun, a glimmer of coppery gold as he looked up at the towering stern of *Golden Dawn*.

His bulk almost obscured the tiny feminine figure beside him. Chantelle wore that particular shade of malachite green which she so dearly loved. There was confused activity around Chantelle, half a dozen gentlemen assisting in the ceremony she had performed so very often. Chantelle had broken the champagne on almost all of Christy Marine's fleet; the first time had been when she was Arthur Christy's fourteen-year-old darling – it was another of the company's many traditions.

Nicholas blinked, believing for an instant that his eyes had tricked him, for it seemed that the very earth had changed its shape and was moving.

Then he saw that the great hull of *Golden Dawn* had begun to slide forward. The band burst into the 'Marseillaise', the heroic strains watered down by wind and distance, while *Golden Dawn* gathered momentum.

It was an incredible, even a stirring sight, and despite himself, Nicholas felt the goose-bumps rise upon his forearms and the hair lift on the back of his neck. He was a sailor, and he was watching the birthing of the mightiest vessel ever built.

She was grotesque, monstrous, but she was part of him. No matter that others had bastardized and perverted his grand design – still the original design was his and he found himself gripping the binoculars with hands that shook.

He watched the massive wooden-wedged arresters kick out from under that great sliding mass of steel as they served to control her stern-first rush down the ways. Steel cable whipped and snaked upon itself like the Medusa's hair, and *Golden Dawn*'s stern struck the water.

The brown muddy water of the estuary opened before her, cleaved by the irresistible rush and weight, and the hull drove deep, opening white-capped rollers that spread out across the channel and broke upon the shores with a dull roar that carried clearly to where Nicholas stood.

The crowd that lined the bridge was cheering wildly. Beside him, a mother held her infant up to watch, both of them screaming with glee.

While *Golden Dawn*'s bows were still on the dockyard's ways her stern was thrusting irresistibly a mile out into the river; forced down by the raised bows it must now be almost touching the muddy bottom for the wave was breaking around her stern quarters.

God, she was huge! Nicholas shook his head in wonder. If only he had been able to build her the right way, what a ship she would have been. What a magnificent concept!

Now her bows left the end of the slips, and the waters burst about her, seething and leaping into swirling vortices.

Her stern started to rise, gathering speed as her own buoyancy caught her, and she burst out like a great whale rising to blow. The waters spilled from her, creaming and cascading through the steelwork of her open decks, boiling madly in the cavernous openings that would hold the pod tanks when she was fully loaded.

Now she came up short on the hundreds of retaining cables that prevented her from driving clear across the river and throwing herself ashore on the far bank.

She fought against this restraint, as though having felt the water she was now eager to run. She rolled and dipped and swung with a ponderous majesty that kept the crowds along the bridge cheering wildly. Then slowly she settled and floated quietly, seeming to fill the Loire River from bank to bank and to reach as high as the soaring spans of the bridge itself.

The four attendant harbour tugs moved in quickly to assist the ship to turn its prodigious length and to line up for the roads and the open sea.

They butted and backed, working as a highly skilled team, and slowly they coaxed *Golden Dawn* around. Her sideways motion left a mile-wide sweep of disturbed water across the estuary. Then suddenly there was a tremendous boil under her counter, and Nicholas saw the bronze flash of her single screw sweeping slowly through the brown water. Faster and still faster it turned, and despite himself Nicholas thrilled to see her come alive. A ripple formed under her bows, and almost imperceptibly she began to creep forward, overcoming the vast inertia of her weight, gathering steerage way, under command at last.

The harbour tugs fell back respectfully, and as the mighty bows lined up with the open sea she drove forward determinedly.

Silver spouts of steam from the sirens of the tugs shot high, and moments later, the booming bellow of their salute crashed against the skies.

The crowds had dispersed and Nicholas stood alone in the wind on the high bridge and watched the structured steel towers of *Golden Dawn*'s hull blending with the grey and misted horizon. He watched her turn, coming around on to her great circle course that would carry her six thousand miles southward to Good Hope, and even at this distance he sensed her change in mood as she steadied and her single screw began to push her up to top economic speed.

Nicholas checked his watch and murmured the age-old Master's command that commenced every voyage.

'Full away at 1700 hours,' he said, and turned to trudge back along the bridge to where he had left the hired Renault.

It was after six o'clock and the site office was empty by the time Nicholas got back to *Sea Witch*. He threw himself into a chair and lit a cheroot while he thumbed quickly through his address book. He found what he wanted, dialled the direct London code, and then the number.

'Good afternoon. This is the *Sunday Times*. May I help you?'

'Is Mr Herbstein available?' Nicholas asked.

'Hold on, please.'

While he waited, Nicholas checked his address book for his next most likely contact, should the journalist be climbing the Himalayas or visiting a guerrilla training camp in Central Africa, either of which were highly likely – but within seconds he heard his voice.

'Denis,' he said. 'This is Nicholas Berg, how are you? I've got a hell of a story for you.'

Nicholas tried to bear the indignity of it with stoicism, but the thick coating of pancake make-up seemed to clog the pores of his skin and he moved restlessly in the make-up chair.

'Please keep still, sir,' the make-up girl snapped irritably; there was a line of unfortunates awaiting her ministrations along the bench at the back of the narrow room. One of them was Duncan Alexander and he caught Nicholas' eye in the mirror and raised an eyebrow in a mocking salute.

In the chair beside him, the anchor-man of 'The Today and Tomorrow Show' lolled graciously; he was tall and elegant with dyed and permanently waved hair, a carnation in his button-hole, a high camp manner and an ostentatiously liberal image.

'I've given you the first slot. If it gets interesting, I'll run you four minutes forty seconds, otherwise I'll cut it off at two.'

Denis Herbstein's Sunday article had been done with high professionalism, especially bearing in mind the very short time he had to put it together. It had included interviews with representatives of Lloyd's of London, the oil companies, environmental experts both in America and England, and even with the United States Coast Guard.

'Try to make it tight and hard,' advised the anchorman. 'Let's not pussyfoot around.' He wanted sensation, not too many facts or figures, good gory horror stuff – or a satisfying punch-up. The *Sunday Times* article had flushed them out at Orient Amex and Christy Marine; they had not been able to ignore the challenge for there was a question tabled for Thursday by a Labour member in the Commons, and ominous stirrings in the ranks of the American Coast Guard service.

There had been enough fuss to excite the interest of 'The Today and Tomorrow Show'. They had invited the parties to meet their accuser, and both Christy Marine and Orient Amex had fielded their first teams. Duncan Alexander with all his charisma had come to speak for Christy Marine, and Orient Amex had selected one of their directors who looked like Gary Cooper. With his craggy honest face and the silver hairs at his temple he looked like the kind of man you wanted flying your airliner or looking after your money.

The make-up girl dusted Nicholas' face with powder.

'I'm going to invite you to speak first. Tell us about this stuff – what is it, cadmium?' the interviewer checked his script.

Nicholas nodded, he could not speak for he was suffering the ultimate indignity. The girl was painting his lips.

The television studio was the size of an aircraft hangar, the concrete floor strewn with thick black cables and the roof lost in the gloomy heights, but they had created the illusion of intimacy in the small shell of the stage around which the big mobile cameras cluttered like mechanical crabs around the carcass of a dead fish.

The egg-shaped chairs made it impossible either to loll or to sit upright, and the merciless white glare of the arc lamps fried the thick layer of greasy make-up on Nicholas' skin. It was small consolation that across the table Duncan looked like a Japanese Kabuki dancer in make-up too white for his coppery hair.

An assistant director in a sweatshirt and jeans clipped the small microphone into Nicholas' lapel and whispered,

'Give them hell, ducky.'

Somebody else in the darkness beyond the lights was intoning solemnly, 'Four, three, two, one – you're on!' and the red light lit on the middle camera.

'Welcome to The Today and Tomorrow Show,' the anchor-man's voice was suddenly warm and intimate and mellifluous. 'Last week in the French ship-building port of St Nazaire, the largest ship in the world was launched – ' In a dozen sentences he sketched out the facts, while on the repeating screens beyond the cameras Nicholas saw that they were running newsreel footage of *Golden Dawn*'s launching. He remembered the helicopter hovering over the dockyard, and he was so fascinated by the aerial views of the enormous vessel taking to the water that when the cameras switched suddenly to him, he was taken by surprise and saw himself start on the little screen as the interviewer began introducing him, swiftly running a thumbnail portrait and then going on:

'Mr Berg has some very definite views on this ship.'

'In her present design and construction, she is not safe to carry even regular crude petroleum oil,' Nicholas said. 'However, she will be employed in the carriage of crude oil that has been contaminated by cadmium sulphide in such concentrations as to make it one of the more toxic substances in nature.'

'Your first statement, Mr Berg, does anyone else share your doubts as to the safety of her design?'

'She does not carry the A1 rating by the marine inspectors of Lloyd's of London,' said Nicholas.

'Now can you tell us about the cargo she will carry – the so-called cad-rich crudes?'

Nicholas knew he had perhaps fifteen seconds to draw a verbal picture of the Atlantic Ocean turned into a sterile poisoned desert; it was too short a time, and twice Duncan Alexander interjected, skilfully breaking up the logic of Nicholas' presentation and before he had finished, the anchor-man glanced at his watch and cut him short.

'Thank you, Mr Berg. Now Mr Kemp is a director of the oil company.'

'My company, Orient Amex, last year allocated the sum of two million U.S. dollars as grants to assist in the scientific study of world environmental problems. I can tell you folks, right now, that we at Orient Amex are very conscious of the problems of modern technology – ' He was projecting the oil-company image, the benefactors of all humanity.

'Your company's profit last year, after taxation, was four hundred and twenty-five million dollars,' Nicholas cut in clearly. 'That makes point four seven per cent on environmental research – all of it tax deductible. Congratulations, Mr Kemp.'

The oil man looked pained and went on: 'Now we at Orient Amex,' plugging the company name again neatly, 'are working towards a better quality of life for all peoples. But we do realize that it is impossible to put back the clock a hundred years. We cannot allow ourselves to be blinded by the romantic wishful thinking of *amateur* environmentalists, the weekend scientists and the doomcriers who —'

'Cry *Torrey Canyon*,' Nicholas suggested helpfully, and the oil man suppressed a shudder and went on quickly.

' – who would have us discontinue such research as the revolutionary cadmium cracking process, which could extend the world's utilization of fossil fuels by a staggering forty per cent and give the world's oil reserves an extended life of twenty years or more.'

Again the anchor-man glanced at his watch, cut the oil man off in mid-flow and switched his attention to Duncan Alexander.

'Mr Alexander, your so-called ultra-tanker will carry the cad-rich crudes. How would you reply to Mr Berg?'

Duncan smiled, a deep secret smile. 'When Mr Berg had my job as head of Christy Marine, the *Golden Dawn* was the best idea in the world. Since he was fired, it's suddenly the worst.'

They laughed, even one of the cameramen out beyond the lights guffawed uncontrollably, and Nicholas felt the hot red rush of his anger.

'Is the *Golden Dawn* rated A1 at Lloyd's?' asked the anchor-man.

'Christy Marine has not applied for a Lloyd's listing – we arranged our insurance in other markets.'

Even through his anger Nicholas had to concede how good he was, he had a mind like quicksilver.

'How safe is your ship, Mr Alexander?'

Now Duncan turned his head and looked directly across the table at Nicholas.

'I believe she is as safe as the world's leading marine architects and naval engineers can make her.' He paused, and there was a malevolent gleam in his eyes now, 'So safe, that I have decided to end this ridiculous controversy by a display of my personal confidence.'

'What form will this show of faith take, Mr Alexander?' The anchor-man sensed the sensational line for which he had been groping and he leaned forward eagerly.

'On *Golden Dawn*'s maiden voyage, when she returns from the Persian Gulf fully laden with the El Barras crudes, I and my family, my wife and my step-son, will travel aboard her for the final six thousand miles of her voyage – from Cape Town on the Cape of Good Hope to Galveston in the Gulf of Mexico.' As Nicholas gaped at him wordlessly, he went on evenly, 'That's how convinced I am that *Golden Dawn* is capable of performing her task in perfect safety.'

'Thank you.' The anchor-man recognized a good exit line, when he heard one. 'Thank you, Mr Alexander. You've convinced me – and I am sure you have convinced many of our viewers. We are now crossing to Washington via satellite where —'

The moment the red 'in use' light flickered out on the television camera, Nicholas was on his feet and facing Duncan Alexander. His anger was fanned by the realization that Duncan had easily grandstanded him with that adroit display of showmanship, and by the stabbing anxiety at the threat to take Peter aboard *Golden Dawn* on her hazardous maiden voyage.

'You're not taking Peter on that death trap of yours,' he snapped.

'That's his mother's decision,' said Duncan evenly. 'As the daughter of Arthur Christy, she's decided to give the company her full support,' he emphasized the word 'full'.

'I won't let either of you endanger my son's life for a wild public-relations stunt.'

'I'm sure you will try to prevent it,' Duncan nodded and smiled, 'and I'm sure your efforts will be as ineffectual as your attempts to stop *Golden Dawn*.' He deliberately turned his back on Nicholas and spoke to the oil man. 'I do think that went off rather well,' he said, 'don't you?'

James Teacher gave a graphic demonstration of why he could charge the highest fees in London and still have his desk piled high with important briefs. He had Nicholas' urgent application before a Judge-in-Chambers within seventy-two hours, petitioning for a writ to restrain Chantelle Alexander from allowing the son of their former marriage, one Peter Nicholas Berg, aged twelve years, to accompany her on an intended voyage from Cape Town in the Republic of South Africa to Galveston in the state of Texas aboard the bulk crude-carrier *Golden Dawn*, and/or to prevent the said Chantelle Alexander from allowing the child to undertake any other voyage aboard said vessel.

The Judge heard the petition during a recess in the criminal trial of a young post-office worker standing accused of multiple rape. The judge's oak-panelled book-lined chambers were overcrowded by the two parties, their lawyers, the judge's registrar and the considerable bulk of the judge himself.

Still in his wig and robes from the public court, the judge read swiftly through the written submission of both sides, listened attentively to James Teacher's short address and the rebuttal by his opposite number, before turning sternly to Chantelle.

'Mrs Alexander.' The stern expression wavered slightly as he looked upon the devastating beauty which sat demurely before him. 'Do you love your son?'

'More than anything else in this life.' Chantelle looked at him steadily out of those vast dark eyes.

'And you are happy to take him on this journey with you?'

'I am the daughter of a sailor, if there was danger I would understand it. I am happy to go myself and take my son with me.'

The judge nodded, looked down at the papers on his desk for a moment.

'As I understand the circumstances, Mr Teacher, it is common ground that the mother has custody?'

'That is so, my lord. But the father is the child's guardian.'

'I'm fully aware of that, thank you,' he snapped acidly. He paused again before resuming in the measured tones of judgement, 'We are concerned here exclusively with the welfare and safety of the child. It has been shown that the proposed journey will be made during the holidays and that no loss of schooling will result. On the other hand, I do not believe that the petitioner has shown that there exists reasonable doubts about the safety of the vessel on which the voyage will be made. It seems to be a modern and sophisticated ship. To grant the petition would, in my view, be placing unreasonable restraint on the child's mother.' He swivelled in his chair to face Nicholas and James Teacher. 'I regret, therefore, that I see insufficient grounds to accede to your petition.'

In the back seat of James Teacher's Bentley, the little lawyer murmured apologetically. 'He was right, of course, Nicholas. I would have done the same in his place. These domestic squabbles are always —'

Nicholas was not listening. 'What would happen if I picked up Peter and took him to Bermuda or the States?'

'Abduct him!' James Teacher's voice shot up an octave, and he caught Nicholas' arm with genuine alarm. 'I beg of you, dismiss the thought. They would have the police waiting for you – God!' Now he wriggled miserably in his seat. 'I can't bear to think of what might happen. Apart from getting you sent to gaol, your former wife might even get an order restraining you from seeing your boy again, she could get guardianship away from you. If you did that, you could lose the child, Nicholas. Don't do it. Please don't do it!'

Now he patted Nicholas' arm ingratiatingly. 'You'd be playing right into their hands.' And then with relief he switched his attention to the briefcase on his lap.

'Can we read through the latest draft of the agreement of sale again?' he asked. 'We haven't got much time, you know.' Then, without waiting for a reply, he began on the preamble to the agreement which would transfer all the assets and liabilities of Ocean Salvage and Towage to the Directors of the Bank of the East, as nominees for parties unnamed.

Nicholas slumped in the far corner of the seat, and stared thoughtfully out of the window as the Bentley crawled in the traffic stream out of the Strand, around Trafalgar Square with it wheeling clouds of pigeons and milling throngs of tourists, swung into the Mall and accelerated down the long straight towards the Palace.

'I want you to stall them,' Nicholas said suddenly, and Teacher broke off in the middle of a sentence and stared at him distractedly.

'I beg your pardon?'

'I want you to find a way to stall the Sheikhs.'

'Good God, man.' James Teacher was utterly astounded. 'It's taken me nearly a month – four hard weeks to get them ripe to sign,' his voice choked a little at the memory of the long hours of negotiation. 'I've written every line of the agreement in my own blood.'

'I need to have control of my tugs, I need to be free to act —'

'Nicholas, we are talking about seven million dollars.'

'We are talking about my son,' said Nicholas quietly. 'Can you stall them?'

'Yes, of course I can, if that's what you truly want.' Wearily James Teacher closed the file on his lap. 'How long?'

'Six weeks – long enough for *Golden Dawn* to finish her maiden voyage, one way or the other.'

'You realize that this may blow the whole deal, don't you?'

'Yes, I realize that.'

'And you realize also that there isn't another buyer?'

'Yes.'

They were silent then, until the Bentley pulled up before the Bank building in Curzon Street, and they stepped out on to the pavement.

'Are you absolutely certain?' Teacher asked softly.

'Just do it,' Nicholas replied, and the doorman held the bronze and glass doors open for them.

Bermuda asserted its calming influence over Nicholas the moment he stepped out of the aircraft into its comfortable warmth and clean, glittering sunlight. Bernard Wackie's gorgeous burnt-honey-coloured secretary was there to welcome him. She wore a thin cotton dress the colour of freshly cut pineapple and a flashing white smile.

'Mr Wackie's waiting for you at the Bank, sir.'

'Are you out of your mind, Nicholas?' Bernard greeted him. 'Jimmy Teacher tells me you blew the Arabs out of the window. Tell me it's not true, please tell me it's not true.'

'Oh, come on, Bernard,' Nicholas shook his head and patted him consolingly on the shoulder, 'your commission would only have been a lousy point seven million, anyway.'

'Then you did it!' Bernard wailed, and tried to pull his hand out of Nicholas' grip. 'You screwed it all up.'

'The Sheikhs have been screwing us up for over a month, Bernie baby. I just gave them a belt of the same medicine, and do you know what? They loved it. The Prince sat up and showed real interest for the first time. For the first time we were speaking the same language. They'll still be around six weeks from now.'

'But why? I don't understand. Just explain to me why you did it.'

'Let's go into the plot, and I'll explain it to you.'

In the plot Nicholas stood over the perspex map of the oceans of the globe, and studied it carefully for fully five minutes without speaking.

'That's *Sea Witch*'s latest position, she's making good passage?'

The green plastic disc that bore the tug's number was set in mid-Atlantic.

'She reported two hours ago,' Bernie nodded, and then with professional interest, 'How did her sea trials go off?'

'There were the usual wrinkles to iron out, that's what kept me in St Nazaire so long. But we got them straight – and Jules has fallen in love with her.'

'He's still the best skipper in the game.'

But already Nicholas' attention had switched halfway across the world.

'*Warlock*'s still in Mauritius,' his voice snapped like a whip.

'I had to fly out a new armature for the main generator. It was just bad luck that she broke down in that Godforsaken part of the world.'

'When will she be ready for sea?'

'Allen promises noon tomorrow. Do you want to telex him for an update on that?'

'Later.' Nicholas wet the tip of a cheroot carefully, without taking his eyes off the plot, calculating distances and currents and speeds.

'*Golden Dawn*?' he asked, and lit the cheroot while he listened to Bernard's reply.

'Her pod tanks arrived under tow at the new Orient Amex depot on El Barras three weeks ago.' Bernie picked up the pointer and touched the upper bight of the deep Persian Gulf. 'They took on their full cargoes of crude and lay inshore to await *Golden Dawn*'s arrival.'

For a moment, Nicholas contemplated the task of towing those four gigantic pod tanks from Japan to the Gulf, and then he discarded the thought and listened to Bernard.

'*Golden Dawn* arrived last Thursday and, according to my agent at El Barras, she coupled up with her pod tanks and made her turn around within three hours.' Bernard slid the tip of the pointer southwards down the eastern coast of the African continent. 'I have had no report of her since then, but if she makes good her twenty-two knots, then she'll be somewhere off the coast of Mozambique, or Maputo as they call it now, and she should double the Cape within the next few days. I will have a report on her then, she'll be taking on mail as she passes Cape Town.'

'And passengers,' said Nicholas grimly; he knew that Peter and Chantelle were in Cape Town already. He had telephoned the boy the night before and Peter had been wildly elated at the prospect of the voyage on the ultra-tanker.

'It's going to be tremendous fun, Dad,' his voice cracking with the onset of both excitement and puberty. 'We'll be flying out to the ship in a helicopter.'

Bernard Wackie changed the subject, now picking up a sheaf of telex flimsies and thumbing swiftly through them.

'Right, I've confirmed the standby contract for *Sea Witch*.' Nicholas nodded, the contract was for Jules Levoisin and the new tug to stand by three offshore working rigs, standard exploration rigs, that were drilling in the Florida Bay, that elbow of shallow water formed by the sweep of the Florida Keys and the low swampy morass of the Everglades. 'It's ridiculous to use a twenty-two-thousand-horsepower ocean-going tug as an oil rig standby,' Bernard lowered the file, and could no longer contain his irritation, 'Jules is going to go bananas sitting around playing nursemaid. You are going to have a mutiny on your hands – and you'll be losing money. The daily hire won't cover your direct costs.'

'She will be sitting exactly where I want her,' said Nicholas, and switched his attention back to the tiny dot of an island in the middle of the Indian Ocean. 'Now *Warlock*.'

'Right. *Warlock*.' Bernie picked up another file. 'I have tendered for a deep-sea tow.'

'Cancel it,' said Nicholas. 'Just as soon as Allen has repaired his generator, I want him running top of the green for Cape Town.'

'For Cape Town – top of the green?' Bernard stared at him. 'Christ, Nicholas. What for?'

'He won't be able to catch *Golden Dawn* before she rounds the Cape, but I want him to follow her.'

'Nicholas, you're out of your mind – do you know what that would cost?'

'If *Golden Dawn* gets into trouble he'll be only a day or two behind her. Tell Allen he is to shadow her all the way into Galveston roads.'

'Nicholas, you're letting this whole thing get out of all proportion. It's become an obsession with you, for God's sake!'

'With her superior speed, *Warlock* should be up with her before she enters the –'

'Listen to me, Nicholas. Let's think this all out carefully. What are the chances of *Golden Dawn* suffering structural failure or crippling breakdown on her maiden voyage – a hundred to one against it? It's that high?'

'That's about right.' Nicholas agreed. 'A hundred to one.'

'What is it going to cost to hold one ocean-going salvage tug on standby, at a lousy fifteen hundred dollars a day – and then to send another halfway around the world at top of the green?' Bernard clasped his brow theatrically. 'It's going to cost you a quarter of a million dollars, if you take into consideration the loss of earnings on both vessels – that's the very least it's going to cost you. Don't you have respect for money any longer?'

'Now you understand why I had to stall the Sheikhs,' Nicholas smiled calmly. 'I couldn't shoot their money on a hundred-to-one chance – but it's not their money yet. It's mine. *Sea Witch* and *Warlock* aren't their tugs, they are mine. Peter isn't their son, he's mine.'

'You're serious,' said Bernard incredulously. 'I do believe you are serious.'

'Right,' Nicholas agreed. 'Damned right, I am. Now get a telex off to David Allen and ask him for his estimated time of arrival in Cape Town.'

Samantha Silver had one towel wrapped around her head like a turban. Her hair was still wet from the luxurious shampooing it had just received. She wore the other towel tucked under her armpits, making a short sarong of it. She still glowed all over from the steaming tub and she smelled of soap and talcum powder.

After a long field trip, it took two or three of these soakings and scrubbings to get the salt and the smell of the mangroves out of her pores, and the Everglades mud from under her nails.

She poured the batter into the pan, the oil spitting and crackling with the heat and she sang out, 'How many waffles can you eat?'

He came through from the bathroom, a wet towel wrapped around his waist, and he stood in the doorway and grinned at her. 'How many have you got?' he asked. She had still not accustomed her ear to the Australian twang.

He was burned and brown as she was, and his hair was bleached at the ends, hanging now, wet from the shower, into his face.

They had worked well together, and she had learned much from him. The drift into intimacy had been gradual, but inevitable. In her hurt, she had turned to him for comfort, and also in deliberate spite of Nicholas. But now, if she turned her head away, she would not really be able to remember his features clearly. It took an effort to remember his name – Dennis, of course, Doctor Dennis O'Connor.

She was detached from it all, as though a sheet of armoured glass separated her from the real world. She went through the motions of working and playing, of eating and sleeping, of laughing and loving, but it was all a sham.

Dennis was watching her from the doorway now, with that slightly puzzled expression, the helpless look of a person who watches another drowning and is powerless to give aid.

Samantha turned away quickly. 'Ready in two minutes,' she said, and he turned back into the bedroom to finish dressing.

She flipped the waffles on to a plate and poured a fresh batch of batter.

Beside her, the telephone rang and she sucked her fingers clean and picked it up with her free hand.

'Sam Silver,' she said.

'Thank God. I've been going out of my mind. What happened to you, darling?'

Her knees went rubbery under her, and she had to sit down quickly on one of the stools.

'Samantha, can you hear me?'

She opened her mouth, but no sound came out.

'Tell me what's happening –' She could see his face before her, clearly, each detail of it so vividly remembered, the clear green eyes below the heavy brow, the line of cheek-bone and jaw, and the sound of his voice made her shiver.

'Samantha.'

'How is your wife, Nicholas?' she asked softly – and he broke off. She held the receiver to her ear with both hands, and the silence lasted only a few beats of her heart, but it was long enough. Once or twice, in moments of weakness during the last two weeks, she had tried to convince herself that it was not true. That it had all been the viciousness of a lying woman. Now she knew beyond any question that her instinct had been correct. His silence was the admission, and she waited for the lie that she knew would come next.

'Would it help to tell you I love you?' he asked softly, and she could not answer. Even in her distress, she felt the rush of relief. He had not lied. At that moment it was the most important thing in her life. He had not lied. She felt it begin to tear painfully, deep in her chest. Her shoulders shook spasmodically.

'I'm coming to get you,' he said into the silence.

'I won't be here,' she whispered, but she felt it welling up into her throat, uncontrollably. She had not wept before, she had kept it all safely bottled away – but now, the first sob burst from her, and with both hands she slammed the telephone back on to its cradle.

She stood there still, shaking wildly, and the tears poured down her cheeks and dripped from her chin.

Dennis came into the kitchen behind her, tucking his shirt into the top of his trousers, his hair shiny and wet with the straight lines of the comb through it.

'Who was that?' he asked cheerfully, and then stopped aghast.

'What is it, love?' He started forward again, 'Come on now.'

'Don't touch me, please,' she whispered huskily, and he stopped again uncertainly. 'We are fresh out of milk,' she said without turning. 'Will you take the van down to the shopping centre?'

By the time Dennis returned, she was dressed and she had rinsed her face and tied a scarf around her head like a gypsy. They chewed cold, unappetizing waffles in silence, until she spoke.

'Dennis, we've got to talk –'

'No,' he smiled at her. 'It's all right, Sam. You don't have to say it. I should have moved on days ago, anyway.'

'Thanks,' she said.

'It was Nicholas, wasn't it?'

She regretted having told him now, but at the time it had been vitally necessary to speak to somebody.

She nodded, and his voice had a sting to it as he went on.

'I'd like to bust that bastard in the mouth.'

'We levelled the score, didn't we?' she smiled, but it was an unconvincing smile, and she didn't try to hold it.

'Sam, I want you to know that for me it was not just another quick shack job.'

'I know that.' Impulsively she reached out and squeezed his hand. 'And thanks for understanding – but is it okay if we don't talk about it any more?'

Peter Berg had twisted round in his safety straps, so that he could press his face to the round perspex window in the fuselage of the big Sikorsky helicopter.

The night was completely, utterly black.

Across the cabin, the Flight Engineer stood in the open doorway, the wind ripping at his bright orange overalls, fluttering them around his body, and he turned and grinned across at the boy, then he made a windmilling gesture with his hand and stabbed downwards with his thumb. It was impossible to speak in the clattering, rushing roar of wind and engine and rotor.

The helicopter banked gently and Peter gasped with excitement as the ship came into view.

She was burning all her lights; tier upon tier, the brilliantly lit floors of her stern quarters rose above the altitude at which the Sikorsky was hovering, and, seeming to reach ahead to the black horizon, the tank deck was outlined with the rows of hooded lamps, like the street-lamps of a deserted city.

She was so huge that she looked like a city, there seemed to be no end to her, stretched to the horizon and towering into the sky.

The helicopter sank in a controlled sweep towards the white circular target on the heliport, guided down by the engineer in the open doorway. Skilfully the pilot matched his descent to the forward motion of the ultra-tanker, twenty-two knots at top economical – Peter had swotted the figures avidly – and the deck moved with grudging majesty to the scend of the tall Cape rollers pushing in unchecked from across the length of the Atlantic Ocean.

The pilot hovered, judging his approach against the brisk north-westerly cross-wind, and from fifty feet Peter could see that the decks were almost level with the surface of the sea, pressed down deeply by the weight of her cargo. Every few seconds, one of the rollers that raced down her length would flip aboard and spread like spilled milk, white and frothy in the deck lights, before cascading back over the side.

Made arrogant and unyielding by her vast bulk, the *Golden Dawn* did not woo the ocean, as other ships do. Instead, her great blunt bows crushed the swells, churning them under or shouldering them contemptuously aside.

Peter had been around boats since before he could walk, he too was a sea-creature. But though his eye was keen, it was as yet un-schooled, so he did not notice the working of the long wide deck.

Sitting beside Peter on the bench seat, Duncan Alexander knew to look for the movement in the hull. He watched the hull twisting and hogging, but so slightly, so barely perceptibly, that Duncan blinked it away, and looked again. From bows to stern she was a mile and a half long, and in essence she was merely four steel pods held together by an elaborate flexible steel scaffolding and driven forward by the mighty propulsion unit in the stern. There was small independent movement of each of the tank pods, so the deck twisted as she rolled, and flexed like a long-bow as she took the swells under her. The crest of these swells were a quarter of a mile apart. At any one time, there were four separate wave patterns beneath *Golden Dawn*'s hull, with the peaks thrusting up and the troughs allowing the tremendous dead weight of her cargo to push downwards; the elastic steel groaned and gave to meet these shearing forces.

No hull is ever completely rigid, and elasticity had been part of the ultra-tanker's original design, but those designs had been altered. Duncan Alexander had saved almost two thousand tons of steel, by reducing the stiffening of the central pillar that docked the four pods together, and he had dispensed with the double skins of the pods themselves. He had honed *Golden Dawn* down to the limits at which his own architects had baulked; then he had hired Japanese architects to rework the designs. They had expressed themselves satisfied that the hull was safe, but had also respectfully pointed out that nobody had ever carried a million tons of crude petroleum in a single cargo before.

The helicopter sank the last few feet and bumped gently on to the insulated green deck, with its thick coat of plasticized paint which prevented the striking of spark. Even a grain of sand trodden between leather sole and bare steel could ignite an explosive air and petroleum gas mixture.

The ship's party swarmed forward, doubled under the swirling rotor. The luggage in its net beneath the fuselage was dragged away and strong hands swung Peter down on to the deck. He stood blinking in the glare of deck lamps and wrinkling his nose to the characteristic tanker stench. It is a smell that pervades everything aboard one of these ships, the food, the furniture, the crew's clothing – even their hair and skin.

It is the thin acrid chemical stench of under-rich fumes vented off from the tanks. Oxygen and petroleum gas are only explosive in a mixture within narrow limits: too much oxygen makes the blend under-rich and too much petroleum gas makes it over-rich, either of which mixtures are non-explosive, non-combustible.

Chantelle Alexander was handed down next from the cabin of the helicopter, bringing an instant flash of elegance to the starkly lit scene of bleak steel and ugly functional machinery. She wore a cat-suit of dark green with a bright Jean Patou scarf on her head. Two ship's officers closed in solicitously on each side of her and led her quickly away towards the towering stern quarters, out of the rude and blustering wind and the helicopter engine roar.

Duncan Alexander followed her down to the deck, shook hands quickly with the First Officer.

'Captain Randle's compliments, sir. He is unable to leave the bridge while the ship is in the inshore channel.'

'I understand.' Duncan flashed that marvellous smile. The great ship drew almost twenty fathoms fully laden and she had come in very close, as close as was prudent to the mountainous coastline of Good Hope with its notorious currents and wild winds. However, Chantelle Christy must not be exposed to the ear-numbing discomfort of the helicopter flight for a moment longer than was necessary, and so *Golden Dawn* had come in through the inner channel, perilously close to the guardian rocks of Robben Island that stood in the open mouth of Table Bay.

Even before the helicopter rose and circled away towards the distant glow of Cape Town city under its dark square mountain, the tanker's great blunt bows were swinging away towards the west, and Duncan imagined the relief of Captain Randle as he gave the order to make the offing into the open Atlantic with the oceanic depths under his cumbersome ship.

Duncan smiled again and reached for Peter Berg's hand.

'Come on, my boy.'

'I'm all right, sir.'

Skilfully Peter avoided the hand and the smile, containing his wild excitement so that he walked ahead like a man, without the skipping energy of a little boy. Duncan Alexander felt the customary flare of annoyance. No more, than that – bare anger at this further rejection by Berg's puppy. They went in single file along the steel catwalk with the child leading. He had never been able to get close to the boy and he had tried hard in the beginning. Now Duncan stopped his anger with the satisfying memory of how neatly he had used the child to slap Berg in the face, and draw the fangs of his opposition.

Berg would be worrying too much about his brat to have time for anything else. He followed Chantelle and the child into the gleaming chrome and plastic corridors of the stern quarters. It was difficult to think of decks and bulkheads rather than floors and walls in here. It was too much like a modern apartment block, even the elevator which bore them swiftly and silently five storeys up to the navigation bridge helped to dispel the feelings of being shipborne.

On the bridge itself, they were so high above the sea as to be divorced from it. The deck lights had been extinguished once the helicopter had gone, and the darkness of the night, silenced by the thick double-glazed windows, heightened the peace and isolation. The riding lights in the bows seemed remote as the very stars, and the gentle lulling movement of the immense hull was only just noticeable.

The Master was a man of Duncan Alexander's own choosing. The command of the flagship of Christy Marine should have gone to Basil Reilly, the senior captain of the fleet. However, Reilly was Berg's man, and Duncan had used the foundering of *Golden Adventurer* to force premature retirement on the old sailor.

Randle was young for the responsibility, just a little over thirty years of age, but his training and his credentials were impeccable, and he was an honours graduate of the tanker school in France. Here top men received realistic training in the specialized handling of these freakish giants in cunningly constructed lakes and scale-model harbours, working thirty-foot models of the bulk carriers that had all the handling characteristics of the real ships.

Since Duncan had given him the command, he had been a staunch ally, and he had stoutly defended the design and construction of his ship when the reporters, whipped up by Nicholas Berg, had questioned him. He was loyal, which weighed heavily, tipping the balance for Duncan against his youth and inexperience.

He hurried to meet his important visitors as they stepped out of the elevator into his spacious, gleaming modern bridge, a short stocky figure with a bull neck and the thrusting heavy jaw of great determination or great stubbornness. His greeting had just the right mixture of warmth and servility, and Duncan noted approvingly that he treated even the boy with careful respect. Randle was bright enough to realize that one day the child would be head of Christy Marine. Duncan liked a man who could think so clearly and so far ahead, but Randle was not quite prepared for Peter Berg.

'Can I see your engine room, Captain?'

'You mean right now?'

'Yes.' For Peter the question was superfluous. 'If you don't mind, sir,' he added quickly. Today was for doing things and tomorrow was lost in the mists of the future. Right now, would be just fine.

'Well now,' the Captain realized the request was deadly serious, and that this lad could not be put off very easily, 'we go on automatic during the night. There's nobody down there now – and it wouldn't be fair to wake the engineer, would it? It's been a hard day.'

'I suppose not.' Bitterly disappointed, but amenable to convincing argument, Peter nodded.

'But I am certain the Chief would be delighted to have you as his guest directly after breakfast.'

The Chief Engineer was a Scot with three sons of his own in Glasgow, the youngest of them almost exactly Peter's age. He was more than delighted. Within twenty-four hours, Peter was the ship's favourite, with his own blue company-issue overalls altered to fit him and his name embroidered across the back by the lascar steward, 'PETER BERG'. He wore his bright yellow plastic hard hat at the same jaunty angle as the Chief did, and carried a wad of cotton waste in his back pocket to wipe his greasy hands after helping one of the stokers clean the fuel filters – the messiest job on board, and the greatest fun.

Although the engine control room with its rough camaraderie, endless supplies of sandwiches and cocoa and satisfying grease and oil that made a man look like a professional, was Peter's favourite station, yet he stood other watches.

Every morning he joined the First Officer on his inspection. Starting in the bows, they worked their way back, checking each of the pod tanks, very valve, and every one of the heavy hydraulic docking clamps that held the pod tanks attached to the main frames of the hull. Most important of all they checked the gauges on each compartment which gave the precise indication of the gas mixtures contained in the air spaces under the main deck of the crude tanks.

Golden Dawn operated on the 'inert' system to keep the trapped fumes in an over-rich and safe condition. The exhaust fumes of the ship's engine were caught, passed through filters and scrubbers to remove the corrosive sulphur elements and then, as almost pure carbon dioxide and carbon monoxide, they were forced into the air spaces of the petroleum tanks. The evaporating fumes of the volatile elements of the crude mingled with the exhaust fumes to form an over-rich, oxygen-poor, and unexplosive gas.

However, a leak through one of the hundreds of valves and connections would allow air into the tanks, and the checks to detect this were elaborate, ranging from an unceasing electronic monitoring of each tank to the daily physical inspection, in which Peter now assisted.

Peter usually left the First Officer's party when it returned to the stern quarters, he might then pass the time of day with the two-man crew in the central pump room.

From here the tanks were monitored and controlled, loaded and offloaded, the flow of inert gas balanced, and the crude petroleum could be pushed through the giant centrifugal pumps and transferred from tank to tank to make alterations to the ship's trim, during partial discharge, or when one or more tanks were detached and taken inshore for discharge.

In the pump room was kept a display that always fascinated Peter. It was the sample cupboard with its rows of screw-topped bottles, each containing samples of the cargo taken during loading. As all four of *Golden Dawn*'s tanks had been filled at the same off-shore loading point and all with crude from the same field, each of the bottles bore the identical label.

EL BARRAS CRUDE
BUNKERS 'C'
HIGH CADMIUM

Peter liked to take one of the bottles and hold it to the light. Somehow he had always expected the crude oil to be treacly and tarlike, but it was thin as human blood and when he shook the bottle, it coated the glass and the light through it was dark red, again like congealing blood.

'Some of the crudes are black, some yellow and the Nigerians are green,' the pump foreman told him. 'This is the first red that I've seen.'

'I suppose it's the cadmium in it,' Peter told him.

'Guess it is,' the foreman agreed seriously; all on board had very soon learned not to talk down to Peter Berg, he expected to be treated on equal terms.

By this time it was mid-morning and Peter had worked up enough appetite to visit the gallery, where he was greeted like visiting royalty. Within days, Peter knew his way unerringly through the labyrinthine and usually deserted passageways. It was characteristic of these great crude-carriers that you might wander through them for hours without meeting another human being. With their huge bulk and their tiny crews, the only place where there was always human presence was the navigation bridge on the top floor of the stern quarters.

The bridge was always one of Peter's obligatory stops.

'Good-morning, Tug,' the officer of the watch would greet him. Peter had been christened with his nickname when he had announced at the breakfast table on his first morning:

'Tankers are great, but I'm going to be a tug captain, like my dad.'

On the bridge the ship might be taken out of automatic to allow Peter to spell the helmsman for a while, or he would assist the junior deck officers while they made a sun shot as an exercise to check against the satellite navigational Decca; then, after socializing with Captain Randle for a while, it was time to report to his true station in the engine.

'We were waiting on you, Tug,' growled the Chief. 'Get your overalls on, man, we're going down the propeller shaft tunnel.'

The only unpleasant period of the day was when Peter's mother insisted that he scrub off the top layers of grease and fuel oil, dress in his number ones, and act as an unpaid steward during the cocktail hour in the elaborate lounge of the owner's suite.

It was the only time that Chantelle Alexander fraternized with the ship's officers and it was a painfully stilted hour, with Peter one of the major sufferers – but the rest of the time he was successful in avoiding the clinging restrictive rulings of his mother and the hated, fiercely but silently resented presence of Duncan Alexander, his step-father.

Still, he was instinctively aware of the new and disturbing tensions between his mother and Duncan Alexander. In the night he heard the raised voices from the master cabin, and he strained to catch the words. Once, when he had heard the cries of his mother's distress, he had left his bunk and gone barefooted to knock on the cabin door. Duncan Alexander had opened it to him. He was in a silk dressing-gown and his handsome features were swollen and flushed with anger.

'Go back to bed.'

'I want to see my mother,' Peter had told him quietly.

'You need a damned good hiding,' Duncan had flared. 'Now do as you are told.'

'I want to see my mother.' Peter had stood his ground, standing very straight in his pyjamas with both his tone and expression neutral, and Chantelle had come to him in her nightdress and knelt to embrace him.

'It's all right, darling. It's perfectly all right.' But she had been weeping. After that there had been no more loud voices in the night.

However, except for an hour in the afternoon, when the swimming-pool was placed out of bounds to officers and crew, while Chantelle swam and sunbathed, she spent the rest of the time in the owner's suite, eating all her meals there, withdrawn and silent, sitting at the panoramic windows of her cabin, coming to life only for an hour in the evenings while she played the owner's wife to the ship's officers.

Duncan Alexander, on the other hand, was like a caged animal. He paced the open decks, composing long messages which were sent off regularly over the telex in company code to Christy Main in Leadenhall Street.

Then he would stand out on the open wing of *Golden Dawn*'s bridge, staring fixedly ahead at the northern horizon, awaiting the reply to his last telex, chafing openly at having to conduct the company's business at such long remove, and goaded by the devils of doubt and impatience and fear.

Often it seemed as though he were trying to forge the mighty hull onwards, faster and faster into the north, by the sheer power of his will.

In the north-western corner of the Caribbean basin, there is an area of shallow warm water, hemmed in on one side by the island chain of the great Antilles, the bulwark of Cuba and Hispaniola, while in the west the sweep of the Yucatan peninsula runs south through Panama into the great land-mass of South America – shallow warm trapped water and saturated tropical air, enclosed by land-masses which can heat very rapidly in the high hot sun of the tropics. However, all of it is gently cooled and moderated by the benign influence of the north-easterly trade winds – winds so unvarying in strength and direction that over the centuries, sea-faring men have placed their lives and their fortunes at risk upon their balmy wings, gambling on the constancy of that vast moving body of mild air.

But the wind does fail; for no apparent reason and without previous warning, it dies away, often merely for an hour or two, but occasionally – very occasionally – for days or weeks at a time.

Far to the south and east of this devil's spawning ground, the *Golden Dawn* ploughed massively on through the sweltering air and silken calm of the doldrums, northwards across the equator, changing course every few hours to maintain the great circle track that would carry her well clear of that glittering shield of islands that the Caribbean carries, like an armoured knight, on its shoulder.

The treacherous channels and passages through the islands were not for a vessel of *Golden Dawn*'s immense bulk, deep draught and limited manoeuvrability. She was to go high above the Tropic of Cancer, and just south of the island of Bermuda she would make her westings and enter the wider and safer waters of the Florida Straits above Grand Bahamas. On this course, she would be constricted by narrow and shallow seaways for only a few hundred miles before she was out into the open waters of the Gulf of Mexico again.

But while she ran on northwards, out of the area of equatorial calm, she should have come out at last into the sweet cool airs of the trades, but she did not. Day after day, the calm persisted, and stifling still air pressed down on the ship. It did not in any way slow or affect her passage, but her Master remarked to Duncan Alexander:

'Another corker today, by the looks of it.'

When he received no reply from his brooding, silent Chairman, he retired discreetly, leaving Duncan alone on the open wing of the bridge, with only the breeze of the ship's passage ruffling his thick coppery hair.

However, the calm was not merely local. It extended westwards in a wide, hot belt across the thousand islands and the basin of shallow sea they enclosed.

The calm lay heavily on the oily waters, and the sun beat down on the enclosing land-masses. Every hour the air heated and sucked up the evaporating waters; a fat bubble like a swelling blister began to rise, the first movement of air in many days. It was not a big bubble, only a hundred miles across, but as it rose, the rotation of the earth's surface began to twist the rising air, spinning it like a top, so that the satellite cameras, hundreds of miles above, recorded a creamy little spiral wisp like the decorative-icing flower on a wedding cake.

The cameras relayed the picture through many channels, until at last it reached the desk of the senior forecaster of the hurricane watch at the meteorological headquarters at Miami in Southern Florida.

'Looks like a ripe one,' he grunted to his assistant, recognizing that all the favourable conditions for the formation of a revolving tropical storm were present. 'We'll ask Airforce for a fly-through.'

At forty-five thousand feet the pilot of the US Airforce B52 saw the rising dome of the storm from two hundred miles away. It had grown enormously in only six hours.

As the warm saturated air was forced upwards, so the icy cold of the upper troposphere condensed the water vapour into thick puffed-up silver clouds. The boiled upwards, roiling and swirling upon themselves. Already the dome of cloud and ferociously turbulent air was higher than the aircraft.

Under it, a partial vacuum was formed, and the surrounding surface air tried to move in to fill it. But it was compelled into an anti-clockwise track around the centre by the mysterious forces of the earth's rotation. Compelled to travel the long route, the velocity of the air mass accelerated ferociously, and the entire system became more unstable, more dangerous by the hour, turning faster, perpetuating itself by creating greater wind velocities and steeper pressure gradients.

The cloud at the top of the enormous rising dome reached an altitude where the temperature was thirty degrees below freezing and the droplets of rain turned to crystals of ice and were smeared away by upper-level jet-streams. Long beautiful patterns of cirrus against the high blue sky were blown hundreds of miles ahead of the storm to serve as its heralds.

The US Airforce B52 hit the first clear-air turbulence one hundred and fifty miles from the storm's centre. It was as though an invisible predator had seized the fuselage and shaken it until the wings were almost torn from their roots, and in one surge, the aircraft was flung five thousand feet straight upwards.

'Very severe turbulence,' the pilot reported. 'We have vertical wind speeds of three hundred miles an hour plus.'

The senior forecaster in Miami picked up the telephone and called the computer programmer on the floor above him. 'Ask Charlie for a hurricane code-name.'

And a minute later the programmer called him back. 'Charlie says to call the bitch "Lorna".'

Six hundred miles south-west of Miami the storm began to move forward, slowly at first but every hour gathering power, spiralling upon itself at unbelievable velocities, its high dome swelling upwards now through fifty thousand feet and still climbing. The centre of the storm opened like a flower, the calm eye extended upwards in a vertical tunnel with smooth walls of solid cloud rising to the very summit of the dome, now sixty thousand feet above the surface of the wind-tortured sea.

The entire mass began to move faster, back towards the east, in a directly contrary direction to the usual track of the gentle trade winds. Spinning and roaring upon itself, devouring everything in its path, the she-devil called 'Lorna' launched itself across the Caribbean Sea.

Nicholas Berg turned his head to look down upon the impressive skyline of Miami Beach. The rampart of tall elegant hotel buildings followed the curve of the beach into the north, and behind it lay the ugly sprawled tangle of urban development and snarled highways.

The Eastern Airlines direct flight from Bermuda turned on to its base leg and then on to final approach, losing height over the beach and Biscayne Bay.

Nicholas felt uncomfortable, the nagging of guilt and uncertainty. His guilt was of two kinds. He felt guilty that he had deserted his post at the moment when he was likely to be desperately needed.

Ocean Salvage's two vessels were out there somewhere in the Atlantic, *Warlock* running hard up the length of the Atlantic in a desperate attempt to catch up with *Golden Dawn*, while Jules Levoisin in *Sea Witch* was now approaching the eastern seaboard of America where he would refuel before going on to his assignment as standby tug on the exploration field in the Gulf of Mexico. At any moment, the Master of either vessel might urgently need to have his instructions.

Then there was *Golden Dawn*. She had rounded the Cape of Good Hope almost three weeks ago. Since then, even Bernard Wackie had been unable to fix her position. She had not been reported by other craft, and any communications she had made with Christy Main must have been by satellite telex, for she had maintained strict silence on the radio channels. However, she must rapidly be nearing the most critical part of her voyage when she turned west and began her approach to the continental shelf of North America and the passage of the islands into the Gulf. Peter Berg was on board that monster, and Nicholas felt the chill of guilt. His place was at the centre, in the control room of Bach Wackie on the top floor of the Bank of Bermuda building in Hamilton town. His post was there where he could assess changing conditions and issue instant commands to co-ordinate his salvage tugs.

Now he had deserted his post, and even though he had made arrangements to maintain contact with Bernard Wackie, still it would take him hours, perhaps even days, to get back to where he was needed, if there was an emergency.

But then there was Samantha. His instincts warned him that every day, every hour he delayed in going to her would reduce his chances of having her again.

There was more guilt there, the guilt of betrayal. It was no help to tell himself that he had made no marriage vows to Samantha Silver, that his night of weakness with Chantelle had been forced upon him in circumstances almost impossible to resist, that any other man in his position would have done the same, and that in the end the episode had been a catharsis and a release that had left him free for ever of Chantelle.

To Samantha, it had been betrayal, and he knew that much was destroyed by it. He felt terrible aching guilt, not for the act – sexual intercourse without love is fleeting and insignificant – but for the betrayal and for the damage he had wrought.

Now he was uncertain, uncertain as to just how much he had destroyed, how much was left for him to build upon. All that he was certain of was that he needed her, more than he had needed anything in his life. She was still the promise of eternal youth and of the new life towards which he was groping so uncertainly. If love was needing, then he loved Samantha Silver with something close to desperation.

She had told him she would not be there when he came. He had to hope now that she had lied, he felt physically sick at the thought that she meant it.

He had only a single Louis Vuitton overnight valise as cabin luggage so he passed swiftly through customs, and as he went into the telephone booths, he checked his watch. It was after six o'clock, she'd be home by now.

He had dialled the first four digits of her number before he checked himself.

'What the hell am I phoning for?' he asked himself grimly. 'To tell her I'm here, so she can have a flying start when she runs for the bushes?'

There is nothing so doomed as a timid lover. He dropped the receiver back on its cradle, and went for the Hertz desk at the terminal doors.

'What's the smallest you've got?' he asked.

'A Cougar,' the pretty blonde in the yellow uniform told him. In America, 'small' is a relative term. He was just lucky she hadn't offered him a Sherman tank.

The brightly painted Chevy van was in the lean-to shelter under the spread branches of the ficus tree, and he parked the Cougar's nose almost touching its tail-gate. There was no way she could escape now, unless she went out through the far wall of the shed. Knowing her, that was always a possibility, he grinned mirthlessly.

He knocked once on the screen door of the kitchen and went straight in. There was a coffee pot beside the range, and he touched it as he passed. It was still warm.

He went through into the living room, and called:

'Samantha!'

The bedroom door was ajar. He pushed it open. There was a suit of denims, and some pale transparent wisps of underwear thrown carelessly over the patchwork quilt.

The shack was deserted, he went down the steps of the front stoop and straight on to the beach. The tide had swept the sand smooth, and her prints were the only ones. She had dropped her towel above the high-watermark but he had to shade his eyes against the ruddy glare of the lowering sun before he could make out her bobbing head – five hundred yards out.

He sat down beside her towel in the fluffy dry sand and lit a cheroot.

He waited, while the sun settled in a wild, fiery flood of light, and he lost the shape of her head against the darkening sea. She was half a mile out now, but he felt no urgency, and the darkness was almost complete when she rose suddenly, waist-deep from the edge of the gentle surf, waded ashore and came up the beach, twisting the rope of her hair over one shoulder to wring the water from it.

Nicholas felt his heart flop over and he flicked the cheroot away and stood up. She halted abruptly, like a startled forest animal, and stood completely still, staring uncertainly at the tall, dark figure before her. She was so young and slim and smooth and beautiful.

'What do you want?' she faltered.

'You,' he said.

'Why? Are you starting a harem?' Her voice hardened and she straightened; he could not see the expression of her eyes, but her shoulders took on a stubborn set.

He stepped forward and she was rigid in his arms and her lips hard and tightly unresponsive under his.

'Sam, there are things I'll never be able to explain, I don't even understand them myself, but what I do know very clearly is that I love you, that without you my life is going to be flat and plain goddamned miserable —'

There was no relaxation of the rigid muscles. Her hands were still held stiffly at her sides and her body felt cold and wet and unyielding.

'Samantha, I wish I were perfect – I'm not. But all I am sure of is that I can't make it without you.'

'I couldn't take it again. I couldn't live through this again,' she said tightly.

'I need you. I am certain of that,' he insisted.

'You'd better be, you son of a bitch. You cheat on me one time more and you won't have anything left to cheat with – I'll take it off clean, at the roots.' Then she was clinging to him. 'Oh God, Nicholas, how I hated you, and how I missed you – and how long you took to come back,' and her lips were soft and tasted of the sea.

He picked her up and carried her up through the soft sand. He didn't trust himself to speak, it would be so easy to say the wrong thing now.

*

'Nicholas, I've been sitting here waiting for your call.' Bernard Wackie's voice was sharp and alert, the tension barely contained. 'How soon can you get yourself back here?'

'What is it?'

'It is starting to pop. I've got to hand it to you, baby, you've got a nose for it. You smelled this coming.'

'Come on, Bernie!' Nicholas snapped.

'This call is going through three open exchanges,' Bernie told him. 'You want chapter and verse, or did nobody ever tell you that it's a tough game you are in? There is a lot of competition cluttering up the scene. The cheese-heads have one lying handy.' Probably *Wittezee* or one of the other big Dutch tugs, Nicholas thought swiftly. 'They could be streaming a towing wire within a couple of days. And the Yanks are pretty hot numbers, McCormick has one stationed in the Hudson River.'

'All right,' Nick cut through the relish with which Bernie was detailing the threat of hovering competition.

'There is a direct flight at seven tomorrow morning – if I can't make that, I'll connect with the British Airways flight from Nassau at noon tomorrow. Meet me,' Nick ordered.

'You shouldn't have gone running off,' said Bernard Wackie, showing amazing hindsight. Before he could deliver any more pearls of wisdom, Nicholas hung up on him.

Samantha was sitting up in the centre of the bed. She was stark naked, but she hugged her knees to her chest with both arms, and under the gorgeous tangle of her hair her face was desolate as that of a lost child and her green eyes haunted.

'You're going again,' she said softly. 'You only just came, and now you're going again. Oh God, Nicholas, loving you is the toughest job I've ever had in my life. I don't think I have got the muscle for it.'

He reached for her quickly and she clung to him, pressing her face into the thick pad of coarse dark hair that covered his chest.'

'I have to go – I think it's *Golden Dawn*,' he said, and she listened quietly while he told it to her. Only when he finished speaking did she begin to ask the questions which kept them talking quietly, locked in each other's arms in the old brass bed, until long after midnight.

She insisted on cooking his breakfast for him, even though it was still dark outside and she was more than half asleep, hanging on to the range for support and turning up the early morning radio show so that the music might shake her awake.

'Good morning, early birds, this is W.W.O.K. with another lovely day ahead of you. A predicted 85° at Fort Lauderdale and the coast, and 80° inland with a 10% chance of rain. We've got a report on hurricane "Lorna" for you also. She's dipping away south, towards the lesser Antilles – so we can all relax, folks – relax and listen to Elton John.'

'I love Elton John,' Samantha said sleepily. 'Don't you?'

'Who is he?' Nicholas asked.

'There! I knew right away we had a lot in common.' She blinked at him owlishly. 'Did you kiss me good morning? I forget.'

'Come here,' he instructed. 'You're not going to forget this one.'

Then, a few minutes later, 'Nicholas, you'll miss your plane.'

'Not if I cut breakfast.'

'It would have been a grotty breakfast anyway.' She was coming awake fast now.

She gave him the last kiss through the open window of the Cougar. 'You've got an hour – you'll just about make it.'

He started the engine and still she held on to the sill.

'Nicholas, one day we will be together – I mean all the time, like we planned? You and me doing our own thing, our own way? We will, won't we?'

'It's a promise.'

'Hurry back,' she said, and he gunned the Cougar up the sandy driveway without looking back.

There were eight of them crowded into Tom Parker's office. Although there was only seating for three, the others found perches against the tiered shelves with their rows of biological specimens in bottles of formaldehyde or on the piles of reference books and white papers that were stacked against the walls.

Samantha sat on the corner of Tom's desk, swinging her long denim-clad legs, and answered the questions that were fired at her.

'How do you know she will take the passage of the Florida Straits?'

'It's an educated guess. She's just too big and clumsy to thread the needle of the islands.' Samantha's replies were quick. 'Nicholas is betting on it.'

'I'll go along with that then,' Tom grunted.

'The Straits are a hundred miles wide —'

'I know what you're going to say,' Samantha smiled, and turned to one of the other girls. 'Sally-Anne will answer that one.'

'You all know my brother is in the Coast Guard – all traffic through the Straits reports to Fort Lauderdale,' she explained. 'And the coastguard aircraft patrol out as far as Grand Bahama.'

'We'll have a fix on her immediately she enters the Straits – we've got the whole U.S. Coast Guard rooting for us.'

They argued and discussed for ten minutes more, before Tom Parker slapped an open palm on the desk in front of him and they subsided reluctantly into silence.

'Okay,' he said. 'Do I understand the proposal to be that this chapter of Green-Peace intercepts the tanker carrying cad-rich crudes before it enters American territorial waters and attempts to delay or divert the ship?'

'That's exactly it,' Samantha nodded, and looked about her for support. They were all nodding and murmuring agreement.

'What are we trying to achieve? Do we truly believe that we will be able to hold up the delivery of toxic crudes to the refinery at Galveston? Let's define our objectives,' Tom insisted.

'In order for evil men to triumph it is necessary only that good men do nothing. We are doing something.'

'Bullshit, Sam,' Tom growled. 'Let's cut down on the rhetoric – it's one of the things that does us more harm than good. You talk like a nut and you discredit yourself before you have begun.'

'All right,' Samantha grinned. 'We are publicizing the dangers, and our opposition to them.'

'Okay,' Tom nodded. 'That's better. What are our other objectives?'

They discussed that for twenty minutes more, and then Tom Parker took over again.

'Fine, now how do we get out there in the Straits to confront this vessel – do we put on our water-wings and swim?'

Even Samantha looked sheepish now. She glanced around for support, but the others were studying their fingernails or gazing with sudden fascination out of the windows.

'Well,' Samantha began, and then hesitated. 'We thought —'

'Go on,' Tom encouraged her. 'Of course, you weren't thinking of using University property, were you? There is actually a law in this country against taking other people's ships – it's called piracy.'

'As a matter of fact —' Samantha gave a helpless shrug.

'And as a senior and highly respected member of the faculty, you would not expect me to be party to a criminal act.'

They were all silent, watching Samantha, for she was their leader, but for once she was at a loss.

'On the other hand, if a party of graduate researchers put in a requisition, through the proper channels, I would be quite happy to authorize an extended field expedition across the Straits to Grand Bahama on board the *Dicky*.'

'Tom, you're a darling,' said Samantha.

'That's a hell of a way to speak to your Professor,' said Tom, and scowled happily at her.

'They came in on the British Airways flight from Heathrow yesterday afternoon. Three of them, here is a list of the names,' Bernard Wackie slid a notepad across the desk, and Nicholas glanced at it quickly.

'Charles Gras – I know him, he's Chief Engineer at Construction Navale Atlantique,' Nicholas explained.

'Right,' Bernard nodded. 'He gave his occupation and employer to Immigration.'

'Isn't that privileged information?'

Bernard grinned. 'I keep my ear to the ground,' and then he was deadly serious again. 'All right, so these three engineers have a small suitcase each and a crate in the hold that weighs three hundred and fifty kilos, and it's marked "Industrial Machinery".'

'Don't stop now,' Nicholas encouraged him.

'And there is an S61N Sikorsky helicopter sitting waiting for them on the tarmac. The helicopter has been chartered direct from London by Christy Marine of Leadenhall Street. The three engineers and the case of machinery are shuttled aboard the Sikorsky so fast that it looks like a conjuring trick, and she takes off and egg-beats for the south.'

'Did the Sikorsky pilot file a flight-plan?'

'Sure did. Servicing shipping, course 196° magnetic. ETA to be reported.'

'What's the range of the 61N – 500 nautical miles?'

'Not bad,' Bernard conceded. '533 for the standard, but this model has long-range tanks, she's good for 750. But that's one way, not the return journey. The helicopter hasn't returned to Bermuda yet.'

'She could refuel aboard – or, if they aren't carrying avgas, she could stay on until final destination,' Nicholas said. 'What else have you got?'

'You want more?' Bernard looked aghast. 'Doesn't anything ever satisfy you?'

'Did you monitor the communications between Bermuda Control, the chopper, and the ship she was servicing?'

'Nix,' Bernard shook his head. 'There was a box-up.' He looked shamefaced. 'It happens to the best of us.'

'Spare me the details. Can you get information from Bermuda Control of the time the chopper closed her flight-plan?'

'Jesus, Nicholas, you know better than that. It's an offence to listen in on the aviation frequencies, let alone ask them.'

Nicholas jumped up, and crossed swiftly to the perspex plot. He brooded over it, leaning on clenched fists, his expression smouldering as he studied the large-scale map.

'What does all this mean to you, Nicholas?' Bernard came to stand beside him.

'It means that a vessel at sea, belonging to the Christy Marine fleet, has requested its head office to send machinery spares and specialist personnel by the fastest possible means, without regard to expense. Have you figured the air freight on a package of 350 kilos?'

Nicholas straightened up and groped for the crocodile-skin cheroot case.

'It means that the vessel is broken down or in imminent danger of breakdown somewhere in an area south-west of Bermuda, within an arc of four hundred and fifty miles – probably much closer, otherwise she would have requested service from the Bahamas, and it's highly unlikely they would have operated the chopper at extreme range.'

'Right,' Bernard agreed. Nicholas lit his cheroot and they were both silent a moment.

'A hell of a small needle in a bloody big haystack,' said Bernard.

'You let me worry about that,' Nicholas murmured, still without taking his eyes from the plot.

'That's what you are paid for,' Bernard agreed amiably. 'it's *Golden Dawn*, isn't it?'

'Has Christy Marine got any other vessels in the area?'

'Not as far as I know.'

'Then that was a bloody stupid question.'

'Take it easy, Nicholas.'

'I'm sorry.' Nicholas touched his arm. 'My boy's on that pig.' He took a deep draw on the cheroot, held it a moment, and then slowly exhaled. His voice was calm and business-like, as he went on:

'What's our weather?'

'Wind at 060° and 15 knots. Cloud three eighths stratocumulus at four thousand feet. Long-range projection, no change.'

'Steady trade winds again,' Nicholas nodded. 'Thank God for all small mercies.'

'There is a hurricane warning out, as you know, but on its present position and track, it will blow itself out to sea a thousand miles south of Grand Bahama.'

'Good,' Nicholas nodded again. 'Please ask both *Warlock* and *Sea Witch* to report their positions, course, speed and fuel-conditions.'

Bernard had the two telex flimsies for him within twenty minutes.

'*Warlock* has made a good run of it,' Nicholas murmured, as the position of the tug was marked on the plot.

'She crossed the equator three days ago,' said Bernard.

'And *Sea Witch* will reach Charleston late tomorrow,' Nicholas observed. 'Are any of the opposition inside us?'

Bernard shook his head. 'McCormick has one in New York and *Wittezee* is halfway back to Rotterdam.'

'We are in good shape,' Nicholas decided, as he balanced the triangles of relative speeds and distances between the vessels.

'Is there another chopper available on the island to get me out to *Warlock*?'

'No,' Bernard shook his head. 'The 61N is the only one based on Bermuda.'

'Can you arrange bunkering for *Warlock*, I mean immediate bunkering – here in Hamilton?'

'We can have her tanks filled an hour after she comes in.'

Nicholas paused and then made the decision. 'Please telex David Allen on *Warlock*, TO MASTER WARLOCK FROM BERG IMMEDIATE AND URGENT NEW SPEED TOP OF THE GREEN NEW COURSE HAMILTON HARBOUR BERMUDA ISLAND DIRECT REPORT EXPECTED TIME OF ARRIVAL ENDS.'

'You're going to run, then?' Bernard asked. 'You are going to run with both your ships?'

'Yes,' Nicholas nodded. 'I'm running with everything I've got.'

Golden Dawn wallowed with the dead heavy weight of one million tons of crude oil. Her motion was that of a waterlogged hulk. Broadside to the set of the swells, her tank decks were almost awash. The low seas broke against her starboard rail and the occasional crest flopped over and spread like pretty patches of white lace-work over the green plastic-coated decks.

She had been drifting powerlessly for four days now.

The main bearing of the single propeller shaft had begun to run hot forty-eight hours after crossing the equator, and the Chief Engineer had asked for shut-down to inspect the bearing and effect any repairs. Duncan Alexander had forbidden any shut-down, over-riding the good judgement of both his Master and Chief Engineer, and had only grudgingly agreed to a reduction in the ship's speed.

He ordered the Chief Engineer to trace any fault and to effect what repairs he could, while under reduced power.

Within four hours, the Chief had traced the damaged and leaking gland in the pump that force-lubricated the bearing, but even the running under reduced power setting had done significant damage to the main bearing, and now there was noticeable vibration, jarring even *Golden Dawn*'s massive hull.

'I have to get the pump stripped down or we'll burn her clear out,' the Chief faced up to Duncan Alexander at last. 'Then you'll *have* to shut down and not just a couple of hours either. It will take two days to fit new bearing shells at sea.' The Chief was pale and his lips trembled, for he knew of this man's reputation. The engineer knew that he discarded those who crossed him, and he had the reputation of a special vindictiveness to hound a man until he was broken. The Chief was afraid, but his concern for the ship was just strong enough.

Duncan Alexander changed direction. 'What was the cause of the pump failure in the first place? Why wasn't it noticed earlier? It looks like a case of negligence to me.'

Stung at last, the Chief blurted out, 'If there had been a back-up pump on this ship, we could have switched to secondary system and done proper maintenance.

Duncan Alexander flushed and turned away. The modifications he had personally ordered to *Golden Dawn*'s design had excluded most of the duplicated back-up systems; anything that kept down the cost of construction had been ordered.

'How long do you need?' He stopped in the centre of the owner's stateroom and glared at his engineer.

'Four hours,' the Scot replied promptly.

'You've got exactly four hours,' he said grimly. 'If you haven't finished by then you will live to regret it. I swear that to you.'

While the engineer stopped his engines, stripped, repaired and reassembled the lubrication pump, Duncan was on the bridge with the Master.

'We've lost time, too much time,' he said. 'I want that made up.'

'It will mean pushing over best economic speed,' Captain Randle warned carefully.

'Captain Randle, the value of our cargo is 85 dollars a ton. We have on board one million tons. I want the time made up.' Duncan brushed his objection aside. 'We have a deadline to meet in Galveston roads. This ship, this whole concept of carrying crude is on trial, Captain. I don't have to keep reminding you of that. The hell with the costs, I want to meet the deadline.'

'Yes, Mr Alexander,' Randle nodded. 'We'll make up the time.'

Three and a half hours later, the Chief Engineer came up to the bridge.

'Well?' Duncan turned on him fiercely as he stepped out of the elevator.

'The pump is repaired, but –'

'What is it, man?'

'I've got a feeling. We ran her too long. I've got a nasty feeling about that bearing. It wouldn't be clever to run her over 50% of power, not until it's been taken down and inspected –'

'I'm ordering revolutions for 25 knots,' Randle told him uneasily.

'I wouldn't do that, man,' the Chief shook his head mournfully.

'Your station is in the engine room,' Duncan dismissed him brusquely, nodded to Randle to order resumption of sailing, and went out to his customary place on the open wing of the bridge. He looked back over the high round stern as the white turbulence of the great propeller boiled out from under the counter and then settled in a long slick wake that soon reached back to the horizon. Duncan stood out in the wind until after dark, and when he went below, Chantelle was waiting for him. She stood up from the long couch under the forward windows of the stateroom.

'We are under way again.'

'Yes,' he said. 'It's going to be all right.

The engine control was switched to automatic at nine o'clock local time that night. The engine room personnel went up to dinner, and to bed, all except the Chief Engineer. He lingered for another two hours shaking his head and mumbling bitterly over the massive bearing assembly in the long narrow shaft tunnel. Every few minutes, he laid his hand on the massive casting, feeling for the heat and vibration that would warn of structural damage.

At eleven o'clock, he spat on the steadily revolving propeller shaft. It was thick as an oak trunk and polished brilliant silver in the stark white lights of the tunnel. He pushed himself up stiffly from his crouch beside the bearing.

In the control room, he checked again that all the ship's systems were an automatic, and that all circuits were functioning and repeating on the big control board, then he stepped into the elevator and went up.

Thirty-five minutes later, one of the tiny transistors in the board blew with a pop like a champagne cork and a puff of grey smoke. There was nobody in the control room to hear or see it. The system was not duplicated, there was no back-up to switch itself in automatically, so that when the temperature of the bearing began to rise again, there was no impulse carried to the alarm system, no automatic shut-down of power.

The massive shaft spun on while the over-heated bearing closed its grip upon the area of rough metal, damaged by the previous prolonged running. A fine sliver of metal lifted from the polished surface of the spinning shaft, and curled like a silver hair spring, was caught up and smeared into the bearing. The whole assembly began to glow a sullen cherry red and then the oxide paint that was daubed on the outer surfaces of the bearing began to blister and blacken. Still the tremendous power of the engine forced the shaft around.

What oil was still being fed between the glowing surfaces of the spinning shaft and the shells of the bearing turned instantly thin as water in the heat, then reached its flash point and burst into flame and ran in little fiery rivulets down the heavy casting of the main bearing, flashing the blistered paintwork alight. The shaft tunnel filled with thick billows of stinking chemical-tainted smoke, and only then did the fire sensors come to life and their alarms repeated on the navigation bridge and in the quarters of Master, First Officer and Chief Engineer.

But the great engine was still pounding along at 70% of power, and the shaft still turned in the disintegrating bearing, smearing heat-softened metal, buckling and distorting under unbearable strains.

The Chief Engineer was the first to reach the central console in the engine control room, and without orders from the bridge he began emergency shut-down of all systems.

It was another hour before the team under the direction of the First Officer had the fire in the shaft tunnel under control. They used carbon dioxide gas to smother the burning paint and oil, for cold water on the heated metal would have aggravated the damage done by heat distortion and buckling.

The metal of the main bearing casting was still so hot when the Chief Engineer began opening it up, that it scorched the thick leather and asbestos gloves worn by his team.

The bearing shells had disintegrated, and the shaft itself was brutally scored and pitted. If there was distortion, the Chief knew it would not be detected by eye. However, even a buckling of one ten thousandth of an inch would be critical.

He cursed softly as he worked, making the obscenities sound like a lullaby; he cursed the manufacturers of the lubricating pump, the men who had installed and tested it, the damaged gland and the lack of a back-up system, but mostly he cursed the stubbornness and intractability of the Chairman of Christy Marine whose ill-advised judgement had turned this functionally beautiful machinery into blackened smoking twisted metal.

It was mid-morning by the time the Chief had the spare bearing shells brought up from stores and unpacked from their wood shavings in the wooden cases; but it was only when they came to fit them that they realized that the cases had been incorrectly stencilled. The half-shells that they contained were obsolete non-metric types, and they were five millimetres undersized for *Golden Dawn*'s shaft; that tiny variation in size made them utterly useless.

It was only then that Duncan Alexander's steely urbane control began to crack; he raged about the bridge for twenty minutes, making no effort to think his way out of the predicament, but abusing Randle and his engineer in wild and extravagant terms. His rage had a paralysing affect on all *Golden Dawn*'s officers and they stood white-faced and silently guilty.

Peter Berg had sensed the excitement and slipped up unobtrusively to watch. He was fascinated by his step-father's rage. He had never seen a display like it before, and at one stage he hoped that Duncan Alexander's eyeballs might actually burst like over-ripe grapes; he held his breath in anticipation, and felt cheated when it did not happen.

At last, Duncan stopped and ran both hands through his thick waving hair; two spikes of hair stood up like devil's horns. He was still panting, but he had recovered partial control.

'Now sir, what do you propose?' he demanded of Randle, and in the silence Peter Berg piped up.

'You could have new shells sent from Bermuda – it's only three hundred miles away. We checked it this morning.'

'How did you get in here?' Duncan swung round. 'Get back to your mother.'

Peter scampered, appalled at his own indiscretion, and only when he left the bridge did the Chief speak.

'We could have spares flown out from London to Bermuda —'

'There must be a boat —' Randle cut in swiftly.

'Or an aircraft to drop it to us —'

'Or a helicopter —'

'Get Christy Main on the telex,' snapped Duncan Alexander.

It was good to have a deck under his feet again, Nicholas exulted. He felt himself coming fully alive again.

'I'm a sea-creature,' he grinned to himself. 'And I keep forgetting it.'

He looked back to the low silhouette of the Bermuda islands, the receding arms of Hamilton Harbour and the flecking of the multi-coloured buildings amongst the cedar trees, and then returned his attention to the spread charts on the navigation table before him.

Warlock was still at cautionary speed. Even though the channel was wide and clearly buoyed, yet the coral reef on each hand was sharp and hungry, and David Allen's full attention was on the business of conning *Warlock* out into the open sea. But as they passed the 100 fathom line, he gave the order to his deck officer,

'Full away at 0900 hours, pilot,' and hurried across to join Nicholas.

'I didn't have much of a chance to welcome you on board, sir.'

'Thank you, David. It's good to be back.' Nicholas looked up and smiled at him. 'Will you bring her round on to 240° magnetic and increase to 80% power?'

Quickly David repeated his order to the helm and then shifted from one foot to the other, beginning to flush under the salt-water tan.

'Mr Berg, my officers are driving me mad. They've been plaguing me since we left Cape Town – are we running on a job – or is this a pleasure cruise?'

Nicholas laughed aloud then. He felt the excitement of the hunt, a good hot scent in the nostrils, and the prospect of a fat prize. Now he had *Warlock* under him, his concern for Peter's safety had abated. Whatever happened now, he could get there very fast. No, he felt good, very good.

'We're hunting, David,' he told him. 'Nothing certain yet —' he paused, and then relented, 'Get Beauty Baker up to my cabin, tell Angel to send up a big pot of coffee and a mess of sandwiches – I missed breakfast – and while we are eating, I'll fill both of you in.'

Beauty Baker accepted one of Nicholas' cheroots.

'Still smoking cheap,' he observed, and sniffed at the four-dollar cheroot sourly, but there was a twinkle of pleasure behind the smeared lenses of his spectacles. Then, unable to contain himself, he actually grinned.

'Skipper tells me we are hunting, is that right?'

'This is the picture —' Nicholas began to spell it out to them in detail, and while he talked, he thought with comfortable self-indulgence, 'I must be getting old and soft – I didn't always talk so much.'

Both men listened in silence, and only when he finished did the two of them begin bombarding him with the perceptive penetrating questions he had expected.

'Sounds like a generator armature,' Beauty Baker guessed, as he puzzled the contents of the wooden case that had been flown out to *Golden Dawn*. I cannot believe that *Golden Dawn* doesn't carry a full set of mechanical spares.'

While Baker was fully preoccupied with the mechanics of the situation, David Allen concentrated on the problems of seamanship. 'What was the range of the helicopter? Has it returned to base yet? With her draught, she must be heading for the Florida Straits. Our best bet would be to shape a course for Matanilla Reef at the mouth of the Straits.'

There was a peremptory knock on the door of the guest cabin, and the Trog stuck his grey wrinkled tortoise head through. He glanced at Nicholas, but did not greet him. 'Captain, Miami is broadcasting a new hurricane alert. "Lorna" has kicked northwards, they're predicting a track of north north-west and a speed over the ground of twenty knots.'

He closed the door and they stared at each other in silence for a moment.

Nicholas spoke at last.

'It is never one single mistake that causes disaster,' he said. 'It is always a series of contributory errors, most of them of small consequence in themselves – but when taken with a little bad luck —' he was silent a moment and then, softly, 'Hurricane "Lorna" could just be that bit of bad luck.'

He stood up and took one turn around the small guest cabin, feeling caged and wishing for the space of the Master's suite which was now David Allen's. He turned back to

Beauty Baker and David Allen, and suddenly he realized that they were hoping for disaster. They were like two old sea wolves with the scent of the prey in their nostrils. He felt his anger rising coldly against them, they were wishing disaster on his son.

'Just one thing I didn't tell you,' he said. 'My son is on *Golden Dawn*.'

The immense revolving storm that was code-named 'Lorna' was nearing full development. Her crest was reared high above the freezing levels so she wore a splendid mane of frosted white ice particles that streamed out three hundred miles ahead of her on the jet stream of the upper troposphere.

From one side to the other, she now measured one hundred and fifty miles across, and the power unleashed within her was of unmeasurable savagery.

The winds that blew around her centre tore the surface off the sea and bore it aloft at speeds in excess of one hundred and fifty miles an hour, generating precipitation that was as far beyond rain as death is beyond life. Water filled the dense cloud-banks so that there was no clear line between sea and air.

It seemed now that madness fed upon madness, and like a blinded and berserk monster, she blundered across the confined waters of the Caribbean, ripping the trees and buildings, even the very earth from the tiny islands which stood in her path.

But there were still forces controlling what seemed uncontrollable, dictating what seemed to be random, for, as she spun upon a spinning globe, the storm showed the primary trait of gyroscopic inertia, a rigidity in space that was constant as long as no outside force was applied.

Obeying this natural law, the entire system moved steadily eastwards at constant speed and altitude above the surface of the earth, until her northern edge touched the land-mass of the long ridge of land that forms the greater Antilles.

Immediately another gyroscopic law came into force, the law of precession. When a deflecting force is applied to the rim of a spinning gyro, the gyro moves not away from, but *directly towards* that force.

Hurricane 'Lorna' felt the land, and, like a maddened bull at the flirt of the matador's cape, she turned and charged towards it, crossing the narrow high strips of Haiti in an orgy of destruction and terror until she burst out of the narrow channel of the Windward Passage into the open beyond.

Yet still she kept on spinning and moving. Now, barely three hundred miles ahead of her, across those shallow reefs and banks prophetically named 'Hurricane Flats' after the thousands of other such storms that had followed the same route during the memory of man, lay the deeper waters of the Florida Straits and the mainland of the continental United States of America.

At twenty miles an hour, the whole incredible heaven-high mass of crazed wind and churning clouds trundled northwestwards.

Duncan Alexander stood under the bogus Degas ballet dancers in the owner's stateroom. He balanced easily on the balls of his feet and his hands were clasped lightly behind his back, but his brow was heavily furrowed with worry and his eyes darkly underscored with plum-coloured swollen bags of sleeplessness.

Seated on the long couch and on the imitation Louis Quatorze chairs flanking the fireplace, were the senior officers of *Golden Dawn* – her Captain, Mate and Chief Engineer, and in the leather-studded wing-backed chair across the wide cabin sat Charles Gras, the engineer from Atlantique. It seemed as though he had chosen his seat to keep himself aloof from the owner and officers of the crippled ultra-tanker.

He spoke now in heavily accented English, falling back on the occasional French word which Duncan translated quickly. The four men listened to him with complete attention, never taking their eyes from the sharp pale Parisian features and the foxy bright eyes.

'My men will have completed the re-assembly of the main bearing by noon today. To the best of my ability, I have examined and tested the main shaft. I can find no evidence of structural damage, but I must emphasize that this does not mean that no damage exists. At the very best, the repairs must be considered to be temporary.' He paused and they waited, while he turned deliberately to Captain Randle. 'I must urge you to seek proper repair in the nearest port open to you, and to proceed there at the lowest speed which will enable you efficiently to work the ship.'

Randle twisted uncomfortably in his seat, and glanced across at Duncan. The Frenchman saw the exchange and a little steel came into his voice.

'If there is structural distortion in the main shaft, operation at speeds higher than this may result in permanent and irreversible damage and complete breakdown. I must make this point most forcibly.'

Duncan intervened smoothly. 'We are fully burdened and drawing twenty fathoms of water. There are no safe harbours on the eastern seaboard of America, that is even supposing that we could get permission to enter territorial waters with engine trouble. The Americans aren't likely to welcome us. Our nearest safe anchorage is Galveston roads, on the Texas coast of the Gulf of Mexico – and then only after the tugs have taken off our pod tanks outside the 100–fathom line.'

The tanker's First Officer was a young man, probably not over thirty years of age, but he had so far conducted himself impeccably in the emergencies the ship had encountered. He had a firm jaw and a clear level eye, and he had been the first into the smoke-filled shaft tunnel.

'With respect, sir,' and they all turned their heads towards him, 'Miami has broadcast a revised hurricane alert that includes the Straits and southern Florida. We would be on a reciprocal course to the hurricane track, a directly converging course.'

'Even at fifteen knots, we would be through the Straits and into the Gulf with twenty-four hours to spare,' Duncan stated, and looked to Randle for confirmation.

'At the present speed of the storm's advance – yes,' Randle qualified carefully. 'But conditions may change –'

The Mate persisted. 'Again, with respect, sir. Our nearest safe anchorage is the lee of Bermuda Island –'

'Do you have any idea of the value of this cargo?' Duncan's voice rasped. 'No, you do not. Well, I will inform you. It is $85,000,000. The interest on that amount is in the region of $25,000 a day.' His voice rose a note, again that wild note to it. 'Bermuda does not have the facilities to effect major repairs –'

The door from the private accommodation opened silently and Chantelle Alexander stepped into the stateroom. She wore no jewellery, a plain pearl silk blouse and a simple dark woollen skirt, but her skin had been gilded by the sun and she had lightly touched her dark eyes with a make-up that emphasized their size and shape. Her beauty silenced them all and she was fully aware of it as she crossed to stand beside Duncan.

'It is necessary that this ship and her cargo proceed directly to Galveston,' she said softly.

'Chantelle –' Duncan began, and she silenced him with a brusque gesture of one hand.

'There is no question about the destination and the route that is to be taken.'

Charles Gras looked to Captain Randle, waiting for him to assert the authority vested in him by law. But when the young Captain remained silent, the Frenchman smiled sardonically and shrugged a world-weary dismissal of further interest. 'Then I must ask that arrangements be made for my two assistants and myself to leave this ship immediately we have completed the temporary repairs.' Again Gras emphasized the word 'temporary'.

Duncan nodded. 'If we resume our sailing when you anticipate, and even taking into consideration the low fuel condition of the helicopter, we will be within easy range of the east coast of Florida by dawn tomorrow.'

Chantelle had not taken her eyes from the *Golden Dawn*'s officers during this exchange, and now she went on in the same quiet voice.

'I am quite prepared to accept the resignation of any of the officers of this ship who wish to join that flight.'

Duncan opened his mouth to make some protest at her assumption of his authority, but she turned to him with a small lift of the chin, and something in her expression and the set of her head upon her shoulders reminded him forcibly of old Arthur Christy. There was the same toughness and resilience there, the same granite determination; strange that he had not noticed it before.

'Perhaps I have never looked before,' he thought. Chantelle recognized the moment of his capitulation, and calmly she turned back to face *Golden Dawn*'s officers.

One by one, they dropped their eyes from hers; Randle was the first to stand up.

'If you will excuse me, Mrs Alexander, I must make preparations to get under way again.'

Charles Gras paused and looked back at her, and he smiled again, as only a Frenchman smiles at a pretty woman.

'Magnifique!' he murmured, and lifted one hand in a graceful salute of admiration before he stepped out of the stateroom.

When Chantelle and Duncan were alone together, she turned to him slowly, and she let the contempt show in her expression.

'Any time you feel you have not got the guts for it, let me know, will you?'

'Chantelle –'

'You have got us into this, me and Christy Marine. Now you'll get us out of it, even if it kills you.' Her lips compressed into a thinner line and her eyes slitted vindictively. 'And it would be nice if it did,' she said softly.

*

The pilot of the Beechcraft Baron pulled back the throttles to 22″ of boost on both engines, and slid the propellers into fully fine pitch, simultaneously beginning a gentle descending turn towards the extraordinary-looking vessel that came up swiftly out of the low early morning haze that spilled over from the islands.

The same haze had blotted the low silhouette of the Florida coast from the western horizon, and even the pale green water and shaded reefs of little Bahamas Bank were washed pale by the haze, and partially obscured by the intermittent layer of stratocumulus cloud at four thousand feet.

The Baron pilot selected 20° of flap to give the aircraft a nosedown attitude which would afford a better forward vision, and continued his descent down through the cloud. It burst in a brief grey puff across the windshield before they were out into sunlight again.

'What do you make of her?' he asked his co-pilot.

'She's a big baby,' the co-pilot tried to steady his binoculars. 'Can't read her name.'

The enormously wide low bows were pushing up a fat sparkling pillow of churning water, and the green decks seemed to reach back almost to the limits of visibility before rising sheer into the stern quarters.

'Son of a gun,' the pilot shook his head. 'She looks like the vehicle-assembly building on Cape Kennedy.'

'She does too,' agreed his co-pilot. The same square unlovely bulk of that enormous structure was repeated in smaller scale by the navigation bridge of the big ship. 'I'll give her a call on 16.' The co-pilot lowered his binoculars and thumbed the microphone as he lifted it to his lips.

'South-bound bulk carrier, this is Coast Guard November Charlie One Fife Niner overhead. Do you read me?'

There was the expected delay; even in confined and heavily trafficked waters, these big bastards kept a sloppy watch and the spotter fumed silently.

'Coast Guard One Fife Niner, this is *Golden Dawn*. Reading you fife by fife. Going up to 22.'

Two hundred miles away the Trog knocked over the shell-casing, spilling damp and stinking cigar butts over the deck, in his haste to change frequency to channel 22 as the operator on board *Golden Dawn* had stipulated, at the same time switching in both the tape recorder and the radio direction-finder equipment.

High up in *Warlock*'s fire-control tower, the big metal ring of the direction-finding aerial turned slowly, lining up on the transmissions that boomed so clearly across the ether, repeating the relative bearing on the dial of the instrument on the Trog's cluttered bench.

'Good morning to you, *Golden Dawn*,' the lilting Southern twang of the coastguard navigator came back. 'I would be mightily obliged for your port of registry and your cargo manifest.'

'This ship is registered Venezuela.' The Trog dexterously made the fine tuning, scribbled the bearing on his pad, ripped off the page and darted into *Warlock*'s navigation bridge.

'*Golden Dawn* is sending in clear,' he squeaked with an expression of malicious glee.

'Call the Captain,' snapped the deck officer, and then as an afterthought, 'and ask Mr Berg to come to the bridge.'

The conversation between coastguard and ultra-tanker was still going on when Nicholas burst into the radio room, belting his dressing-gown.

'Thank you for your courtesy, sir,' the coastguard navigator was using extravagant Southern gallantry, fully aware that *Golden Dawn* was outside United States territorial waters, and officially beyond his government's jurisdiction. 'I would appreciate your port of final destination.'

'We are en route Galveston for full discharge of cargo.'

'Thank you again, sir. And are you apprised of the hurricane alert in force at this time?'

'Affirmative.'

From *Warlock*'s bridge, David Allen appeared in the doorway, his face set and flushed.

'She must be under way again,' he said, his disappointment so plain that it angered Nicholas yet again. 'She is into the channel already.'

'I'd be obliged if you would immediately put this ship on a course to enter the Straits and close with her as soon as is possible,' Nicholas snapped, and David Allen blinked at him once then disappeared on to his bridge, calling for the change in course and increase in speed as he went.

Over the loudspeaker, the coastguard was being politely persistent.

'Are you further apprised, sir, of the up-date on that hurricane alert predicting storm passage of the main navigable channel at 1200 hours local time tomorrow?'

'Affirmative.' *Golden Dawn*'s replies had become curt.

'May I further trouble you, sir, in view of your sensitive cargo and the special weather conditions, for your expected time of arrival abeam of the Dry Tortugas Bank marine beacon and when you anticipate clearing the channel and shaping a northerly course away from the predicted hurricane track?'

'Stand-by.' There was a brief hum of static while the operator consulted the deck officer and then the *Golden Dawn* came back, 'Our ETA Dry Tortugas Bank beacon is 0130 tomorrow.'

There was a long pause now as the coastguard consulted his headquarters ashore on one of the closed frequencies, and then:

'I am requested respectfully, but officially, to bring to your attention that very heavy weather is expected ahead of the storm centre and that your present ETA Dry Tortugas Bank leaves you very fine margins of safety, sir.'

'Thank you, coastguard One Fife Niner. Your transmission will be entered in the ship's log. This is *Golden Dawn* over and out.'

The coastguard's frustration was evident, clearly he would have loved to order the tanker to reverse her course. 'We will be following your progress with interest, *Golden Dawn*. Bon voyage, this is coastguard One Fife Niner over and out.'

Charles Gras held his blue beret on with one hand, while with the other he lugged his suitcase. He ran doubled up, instinctively avoiding the ear-numbing clatter of the helicopter's rotor.

He threw his suitcase through the open fuselage door and then hesitated, turned and scampered back to where the ship's Chief Engineer stood at the edge of the white-painted helipad target on *Golden Dawn*'s tank deck.

Charles grabbed the Engineer's upper arm and leaned close to shout in his ear.

'Remember, my friend, treat her like a baby, like a tender virgin – if you have to increase speed, do so gently – very gently.' The Engineer nodded, his sparse sandy hair fluttering in the down-draught.

'Good luck,' shouted the Frenchman. '*Bonne chance*!' He slapped the man's shoulder. 'I hope you don't need it!'

He darted back and scrambled up into the fuselage of the Sikorsky, and his face appeared in one of the portholes. He waved once, and then the big ungainly machine rose slowly into the air, hovered for a moment and then banked away low over the water, setting off in its characteristic nose-down attitude for the mainland, still hidden by haze and distance.

Dr Samantha Silver, dressed in thigh-high rubber waders and with her sleeves rolled up above the elbows, staggered under the weight of two ten-gallon plastic buckets of clams as she climbed the back steps of the laboratory building.

'Sam!' down the length of the long passageway, Sally-Anne screamed at her. 'We were going to leave without you!'

'What is it?' Sam dumped the buckets with relief, slopping salt water down the steps.

'Johnny called – the anti-pollution patrol bespoke *Golden Dawn* an hour ago. She's in the Straits, she was abeam Matanilla reef when they spotted her and she will be abeam of Biscayne Key before we can get out there, if we don't leave now.'

'I'm coming.' Sam hefted her heavy buckets, and broke into a rubber-kneed trot. 'I'll meet you down on the wharf – did you call the TV studio?'

'There's a camera team on the way,' Sally-Anne yelled back as she ran for the front doors. 'Hurry, Sam – fast as you like!'

Samantha dumped the clams into one of her tanks, switched on the oxygen and as soon as it began to bubble to the surface, she turned and raced from the laboratory and out of the front doors.

Golden Dawn's deck officer stopped beside the radarscope, glanced down at it idly, then stooped with more attention and took a bearing on the little glowing pinpoint of green light that showed up clearly inside the ten-mile circle of the sweep.

He grunted, straightened, and walked quickly to the front of the bridge. Slowly, he scanned the green wind-chopped sea ahead of the tanker's ponderous bows.

'Fishing boat,' he said to the helmsman. 'But they are under way.' He had seen the tiny flash of a bow wave. 'And they are right in the main navigational channel – they must have seen us by now, they are making a turn to pass us to starboard.' He dropped the binoculars and let them dangle against his chest. 'Oh thank you.' He took the cup of cocoa from the steward, and sipped it with relish as he turned away to the chart-table.

One of the tanker's junior officers came out of the radio room at the back of the bridge.

'Still no score,' he said, 'and only injury time left now,' and they fell into a concerned discussion of the World Cup soccer match being played under floodlights at Wembley Stadium on the other side of the Atlantic.

'If it's a draw then it means that France is in the –'

There was an excited shout from the radio room, and the junior officer ran to the door and then turned back with an excited grin. 'England has scored!'

The deck officer chuckled happily. 'That will wrap it up.' Then with a start of guilt he turned back to his duties, and had another start, this time of surprise, when he glanced into the radarscope.

'What the hell are they playing at!' he exclaimed irritably, and hurried forward to scan the sea ahead.

The fishing boat had continued its turn and was now bows on.

'Damn them. We'll give them a buzz.' He reached up for the handle of the foghorn and blew three long blasts, that echoed out mournfully across the shallow greenish water of the Straits. There was a general movement among the officers to get a better view ahead through the forward bridge windows.

'They must be half asleep out there.' The deck officer thought quickly about calling the Captain to the bridge. If it came to manoeuvering the ship in these confined waters, he flinched from the responsibility. Even at this reduced speed, it would take *Golden Dawn* half an hour and seven nautical miles to come to a stop; a turn in either direction would swing through a wide arc of many miles before the ship was able to make a 90° change of course – God, then there was the effect of the wind against the enormously exposed area of the towering stern quarters, and the full bore of the Gulf Stream driving out of the narrows of the Straits. The problems of manoeuvering the vessel struck a chill of panic into the officer – and the fishing boat was on collision course, the range closing swiftly under the combined speeds of both vessels. He reached for the call button of the intercom that connected the bridge directly to the Captain's quarters on the deck below, but at that moment Captain Randle came bounding up the private staircase from his day cabin.

'What is it?' he demanded. 'What was that blast on the horn?'

'Small vessel holding on to collision course, sir.' The officer's relief was evident, and Randle seized the handle of the foghorn and hung on to it.

'God, what's wrong with them?'

'The deck is crowded,' exclaimed one of the officers without lowering his binoculars. 'Looks as though they have a movie camera team on the top deck.'

Randle judged the closing range anxiously; already the small fishing vessel was too close for the *Golden Dawn* to stop in time.

'Thank God,' somebody exclaimed. 'They are turning away.'

'They are streaming some sort of banner. Can anybody read that?'

'They are heaving-to,' the deck officer yelled suddenly. 'They are heaving-to right under our bows.'

Samantha Silver had not expected the tanker to be so big. From directly ahead, her bows seemed to fill the horizon from one side to the other, and the bow wave she threw up ahead of her creamed and curved like the set of the long wave at Cape St Francis when the surf was up.

Beyond the bows, the massive tower of her navigation bridge stood so tall it looked like the skyline of the Miami beach, one of those massive hotel buildings seen from close inshore.

It made her feel distinctly uneasy to be directly under that on-rushing steel avalanche.

'Do you think they have seen us?' Sally-Anne asked beside her, and when Samantha heard her own unease echoed by the pretty girl beside her, it steeled her.

'Of course they have,' she announced stoutly so that everyone in the small wheelhouse could hear her. 'That's why they blew their siren. We'll turn aside at the last minute.'

'They aren't slowing down,' Hank Petersen, the helmsman, pointed out huskily, and Samantha wished that Tom Parker had been on board with them. However, Tom was up in Washington again, and they had taken the *Dicky* to sea with a scratch crew, and without Tom Parker's written authorization. 'What do you want to do, Sam?' And they all looked at her.

'I know a thing that size can't stop, but at least we're going to make them slow down.

'Are the TV boys getting some stuff?' Samantha asked, to delay the moment of decision. 'Go up, Sally-Anne, and check them.' Then to the others, 'You-all get the banner ready, we'll let them get a good look at that.'

'Listen, Sam.' Hank Petersen's tanned intelligent face was strained. He was a tunny expert, and was not accustomed to handling the vessel except in calm and uncluttered waters. 'I don't like this, we're getting much too close. That thing could churn us right under, and not even notice the bump. I want to turn away now.' His voice was almost drowned by the sudden sky-crashing blast of the tanker's foghorns.

'Son of a gun, Sam, I don't like playing chicken-chicken with somebody that size.'

'Don't worry, we'll get out of their way at the last moment. All right!' Samantha decided. 'Turn 90° to port, Hank. Let's show them the signs, I'm going to help them on deck.'

The wind tore at the thin white canvas banner as they tried to run it out along the side of the deckhouse, and the little vessel was rolling uncomfortably while the TV producer was shouting confused stage directions at them from the top of the wheelhouse.

Bitterly Samantha wished there was somebody to take command, somebody like Nicholas Berg – and the banner tried to wrap itself around her head.

The *Dicky* was coming around fast now, and Samantha shot a glance at the oncoming tanker and felt the shock of it strike in the pit of her stomach like the blow of a fist. It was huge, and very close – much too close, even she realized that.

At last she managed to get a turn of the thin line that secured the banner around the stern rail – but the light canvas had twisted so that only one word of the slogan was readable. 'POISONER', it accused in scarlet, crudely painted letters followed by a grinning skull and crossed bones.

Samantha dived across the deck and struggled with the flapping canvas; above her head the producer was shouting excitedly; two of the others were trying to help her; Sally-Anne was screaming 'Go back! Go back!' and waving both arms at the great tanker. 'You poison our oceans!'

Everything was becoming confused and out of control, the *Dicky* swung ahead into the wind and pitched steeply, the person next to her lost his footing and knocked painfully into Samantha, and at that moment she felt the change of the engine beat.

Tricky Dicky's diesel had been bellowing furiously as Hank opened the throttle to its stop, using full power to bring the little vessel around from under the menace of those steel bows.

The smoking splutter of the exhaust pipe that rose vertically up the side of the deckhouse, had made all speech difficult – but now it died away, and suddenly there was only the sound of the wind.

Even their own raised voices were silenced, and they froze, staring out at *Golden Dawn* as she bore down on them without the slightest check in her majestic approach.

Samantha was the first one to recover, then she ran across the plunging deck to the wheelhouse.

Hank Petersen was down on his knees beside the bulkhead, struggling ineffectually with the conduit that housed the controls to the engine room on the deck below.

'Why have you stopped?' Samantha yelled at him, and he looked up at her as though he were mortally wounded.

'It's the throttle linkage,' he said. 'It's snapped again.'

'Can't you fix it?' and the question was a mockery. A mile away, *Golden Dawn* came down on them – silent, menacing, unstoppable.

For ten seconds Randle stood rigid, both hands gripping the foul weather rail below the sill of the bridge windows.

His face was set, pale and finely drawn, as he watched the stern of the wallowing fishing boat for the renewed churning of its prop.

He knew that he could not turn nor stop his ship in time to avoid collision, unless the small vessel got under way immediately, and took evasive action by going out to starboard under full power.

'Damn them to hell,' he thought bitterly, they were in gross default. He had all the law and the custom of the sea behind him; a collision would cause very little damage to *Golden Dawn*, perhaps she would lose a little paint, at most a slightly buckled plate in the reinforced bows – and they had asked for it.

He had no doubts about the object of this crazy, irresponsible seamanship. There had been controversy before the *Golden Dawn* sailed. He had read the objections and seen the nut-case environmentalists on television. The scarlet-painted banner with the ridiculously melodramatic Jolly Roger made it clear that this was a boatload of nutters attempting to prevent *Golden Dawn* entering American waters.

He felt his anger boiling up fiercely. These people always made him furious. If they had their way, there would be no tanker trade, and now they were deliberately threatening him, placing him in a position which might prejudice his own career. He already had the task of taking his ship through the Straits ahead of the hurricane. Ever moment was vital – and now there was this.

He would be happy to maintain course and speed, and to run them down. They were flaunting themselves, challenging him to do it – and, by God, they deserved it.

However, he was a seaman, with a seaman's deep concern for human life at sea. It would go against all his instincts not to make an effort to avoid collision, no matter how futile that effort would be. Then beside him one of his officers triggered him.

'There are women on board her – look at that! Those are women!'

That was enough. Without waiting for confirmation, Randle snapped at the helmsman beside him.

'Full port rudder!'

And with two swift paces he had reached the engine room telegraph. It rang shrilly as he pulled back the chromed handle to 'Full Astern'.

Almost immediately, the changed beat came up through the soles of his feet, as the great engine seven decks below the bridge thundered suddenly under all emergency power, and the direction of the spinning main propellor shaft was abruptly reversed.

Randle spun back to face ahead. For almost five minutes, the bows held steady on the horizon without making any answer to the full application of the rudder. The inertia of a million tons of crude oil, the immense drag of the hull through water and the press of wind and current held her on course, and although the single ferro-bronze propeller bit deeply into the green waters, there was not the slightest diminution of the tanker's speed.

Randle kept his hand on the engine telegraph, pulling back on the silver handle with all his strength, as though this might arrest the great ship's forward way through the water.

'Turn!' he whispered to the ship, and he stared at the fishing boat that still lay, rolling wildly, directly in *Golden Dawn*'s path. He noticed irreleventLy that the tiny human figures along the rear rail were waving frantically, and that the banner with its scarlet denunciation had torn loose at one end and was now whipping and twisting like a Tibetan prayer flag over the heads of the crew.

'Turn,' Randle whispered, and he saw the first response of the hull; the angle between the bows and the fishing boat altered, it was a noticeable change, but slowly accelerating and a quick glance at the control console showed a small check in the ship's forward speed.

'Turn, damn it, turn.' Randle held the engine telegraph locked at full astern, and felt the sudden influence of the Gulf Stream current on the ship as she began to come across the direction of flow.

Ahead, the fishing boat was almost about to disappear from sight behind *Golden Dawn*'s high blunt bows.

He had been holding the ship at full astern for almost seven minutes now, and suddenly Randle felt a change in *Golden Dawn*, something he had never experienced before.

There was harsh, tearing, pounding vibration coming up through the deck. He realized just how severe that vibration must be, when *Golden Dawn*'s monumental hull began to shake violently – but he could not release his grip on the engine telegraph, not with that helpless vessel lying in his track.

Then suddenly, miraculously, all vibration in the deck under his feet ceased altogether. There was only the calm press of the hull through the water, no longer the feel of the engine's thrust, a sensation much more alarming to a mariner than the vibration which had preceded it, and simultaneously, a fiery rash of red warning lights bloomed on the ship's main control console, and the strident screech of the full emergency audio-alarm deafened them all.

Only then did Captain Randle push the engine telegraph to 'stop'. He stood staring ahead as the tiny fishing boat disappeared from view, hidden by the angle from the navigation bridge which was a mile behind the bows.

One of the officers reached across and hit the cut-out on the audio-alarm. In the sudden silence every officer stood frozen, waiting for the impact of collision.

Golden Dawn's Chief Engineer paced slowly along the engine-room control console, never taking his eyes from the electronic displays which monitored all the ship's mechanical and electrical functions.

When he reached the alarm aboard, he stopped and frowned at it angrily. The failure of the single transistor, a few dollars' worth of equipment, had been the cause of such brutal damage to his beloved machinery. He leaned across and pressed the 'test' button, checking out each alarm circuit, yet, while he was doing it, recognizing the fact that it was too late. He was nursing the ship along, with God alone knew what undiscovered damage to engine and main shaft only kept in check by this reduced power setting – but there was a hurricane down there below the southern horizon, and the Chief could only guess at what emergency his machinery might have to meet in the next few days.

It made him nervous and edgy to think about it. He searched in his back pocket, found a sticky mint humbug, carefully picked off the little pieces of lint and fluff before tucking it into his cheek like a squirrel with a nut, sucking noisily upon it as he resumed his restless prowling up and down the control console.

His on-duty stokers and the oilers watched him surreptitiously. When the old man was in a mood, it was best not to attract attention.

'Dickson!' the Chief said suddenly. 'Get your lid on. We are going down the shaft tunnel again.'

The oiler sighed, exchanged a resigned glance with one of his mates and clapped his hard-hat on his head. He and the Chief had been down the tunnel an hour previously. It was an uncomfortable, noisy and dirty journey.

The oiler closed the watertight doors into the shaft tunnel behind them, screwing down the clamps firmly under the Chief's frosty scrutiny, and then both men stooped in the confined headroom and started off along the brightly lit pale grey painted tunnel.

The spinning shaft in its deep bed generated a high-pitched whine that seemed to resonate in the steel box of the tunnel, as though it was the body of a violin. Surprisingly, the noise was more pronounced at this low speed setting, it seemed to bore into the teeth at the back of the oiler's jaw like a dentist's drill.

The Chief did not seem to be affected. He paused beside the main bearing for almost ten minutes, testing it with the palm of his hand, feeling for heat or vibration. His expression was morose, and he worried the mint humbug in his cheek and shook his head with foreboding before going on up the tunnel.

When he reached the main gland, he squatted down suddenly and peered at it closely. With a deliberate flexing of his jaw he crushed the remains of the humbug between his teeth, and his eyes narrowed thoughtfully.

There was a thin trickle of seawater oozing through the gland and running down into the bilges. The Chief touched it with his finger. Something had shifted, some balance was disturbed, the seal of the gland was no longer watertight – such a small sign, a few gallons of seawater, could be the first warning of major structural damage.

The Chief shuffled around, still hunched down beside the shaft bed, and he lowered his face until it was only inches from the spinning steel main shaft. He closed one eye, and cocked his head, trying once again to decide if the faint blurring of the shaft's outline was real or merely his over-active imagination, whether what he was seeing was distortion or his own fears.

Suddenly, startlingly, the shaft slammed into stillness. The deceleration was so abrupt that the Chief could actually see the torque transferred into the shaft bed, and the metal walls creaked and popped with the strain.

He rocked back on to his heels, and almost instantly the shaft began to spin again, but this time in reverse thrust. The whine built up swiftly into a rising shriek. They were pulling emergency power from the bridge, and it was madness, suicidal madness.

The Chief seized the oiler by the shoulder and shouted into his ear, 'Get back to control – find out what the hell they are doing on the bridge.'

The oiler scrambled away down the tunnel; it would take him ten minutes to negotiate the long narrow passage, open the watertight doors and reach the control room and as long again to return.

The Chief considered going after him, but somehow he could not leave the shaft now. He lowered his head again, and now he could clearly see the flickering outline of the shaft. It wasn't imagination at all, there was a little ghost of movement. He clamped his hands over his ears to cut out the painful shriek of the spinning metal, but there was a new note to it, the squeal of bare metal on metal and before his eyes he saw the ghost outline along the edge of the shaft growing, the flutter of machinery out of balance, and the metal deck under his feet began to quiver.

'God! They are going to blow the whole thing!' he shouted, and jumped up from his crouch. Now the deck was juddering and shaking under his feet. He started back along the shaft, but the entire tunnel was agitating so violently that he had to grab the metal bulkhead to steady himself, and he reeled drunkenly, thrown about like a captive insect in a cruel child's box.

Ahead of him, he saw the huge metal casting of the main bearing twisting and shaking, and the vibration chattered his teeth in his clenched jaw and drove up his spine like a jack hammer.

Disbelievingly he saw the huge silver shaft beginning to rise and buckle in its bed, the bearing tearing loose from its mountings.

'Shut down!' he screamed. 'For God's sake, shut down!' but his voice was lost in the shriek and scream of tortured metal and machinery that was tearing itself to pieces in a suicidal frenzy.

The main bearing exploded, and the shaft slammed it into the bulkhead, tearing steel plate like paper.

The shaft itself began to snake and whip. The Chief cowered back, pressing his back to the bulkhead and covering his ears to protect them from the unbearable volume of noise.

A sliver of heated steel flew from the bearing and struck him in the face, laying open his upper lip to the bone, crushing his nose and snapping off his front teeth at the level of his gums.

He toppled forward, and the whipping, kicking shaft seized him like a mindless predator and tore his body to pieces, pounding him and crushing him in the shaft bed and splattering him against the pale metal walls.

The main shaft snapped like a rotten twig at the point where it had been heated and weakened. The unbalanced weight of the revolving propeller ripped the stump out through the after seal, as though it were a tooth plucked from a rotting jaw.

The sea rushed in through the opening, flooding the tunnel instantly until it slammed into the watertight doors – and the huge glistening bronze propeller, with the stump of the main shaft still attached, the whole unit weighing one hundred and fifty tons, plummeted downwards through four hundred fathoms to embed itself deeply in the soft mud of the sea bottom.

Freed of the intolerable goad of her damaged shaft, *Golden Dawn* was suddenly silent and her decks still and steady as she trundled on, slowly losing way as the water dragged at her hull.

Samantha had one awful moment of sickening guilt. She saw clearly that she was responsible for the deadly danger into which she had led these people, and she stared out over the boat's side at the *Golden Dawn*.

The tanker was coming on without any check in her speed; perhaps she had turned a few degrees, for her bows were no longer pointed directly at them, but her speed was constant.

She was achingly aware of her inexperience, of her helplessness in this alien situation. She tried to think, to force herself out of this frozen despondency.

'Life-jackets!' she thought, and yelled to Sally-Anne out on the deck, 'The life-jackets are in the lockers behind the wheelhouse.'

Their faces turned to her, suddenly stricken. Up to this moment it had all been a glorious romp, the old fun-game of challenging the money-grabbers, prodding the establishment, but now suddenly it was mortal danger.

'Move!' Samantha shrieked at them, and there was a rush back along the deck.

'Think!' Samantha shook her head, as though to clear it. 'Think!' she urged herself fiercely. She could hear the tanker now, the silken rustling sound of the water under its hull, the sough of the bow wave curling upon itself.

The *Dicky*'s throttle linkage had broken before, when they had been off Key West a year ago. It had broken between the bridge and the engine, and Samantha had watched Tom Parker fiddling with the engine, holding the lantern for him to see in the gloomy confines of the smelly little engine room. She had not been certain how he did it, but she remembered that he had controlled the revolutions of the engine by hand – something on the side of the engine block, below the big bowl of the air filter.

Samantha turned and dived down the vertical ladder into the engine room. The diesel was running, burbling away quietly at idling speed, not generating sufficient power to move the little vessel through the water.

She tripped and sprawled on the greasy deck, and pulled herself up, crying out with pain as her hand touched the red-hot manifold of the engine exhaust.

On the far side of the engine block, she groped desperately under the air filter, pushing and tugging at anything her fingers touched. She found a coil spring, and dropped to her knees to examine it.

She tried not to think of the huge steel hull bearing down on them, of being down in this tiny box that stank of diesel and exhaust fumes and old bilges. She tried not to think of not having a life-jacket, or that the tanker could tramp the little vessel deep down under the surface and crush her like a matchbox.

Instead, she traced the little coil spring to where it was pinned into a flat upright lever. Desperately she pushed the lever against the tension of the spring – and instantly the diesel engine bellowed deafeningly in her ears, startling her so that she flinched and lost the lever. The diesel's beat died away into the bumbling idle and she wasted seconds while she found the lever again and pushed it hard against its stops once more. The engine roared, and she felt the ship picking up speed under her. She began to pray incoherently.

She could not hear the words in the engine noise, and she was not sure she was making sense, but she held the throttle open, and kept on praying.

She did not hear the screams from the deck above her. She did not know how close the *Golden Dawn* was, she did not know if Hank Petersen was still in the wheelhouse conning the little vessel out of the path of the onrushing tanker – but she held the throttle open and prayed.

The impact when it came was shattering, the crash and crackle of timbers breaking, the rending lurch and the roll of the deck giving to the tearing force of it.

Samantha was hurled against the hot steel of the engine, her forehead striking with such a force that her vision starred into blinding white light; she dropped backwards, her body loose and relaxed, darkness ringing in her ears, and lay huddled on the deck.

She did not know how long she was unconscious, but it could not have been for more than a few seconds; the spray of icy cold water on her face roused her and she pulled herself up on to her knees.

In the glare of the single bare electric globe in the deck above her, Samantha saw the spurts of water jets through the starting planking of the bulkhead beside her.

Her shirt and denim pants were soaked, salt water half blinded her, and her head felt as though the skull were cracked and someone was forcing the sharp end of a bradawl between her eyes.

Dimly she was aware that the diesel engine was idling noisily, and that the deck was sloshing with water as the boat rolled wildly in some powerful turbulence. She wondered if the whole vessel had been trodden under the tanker.

Then she realized it must be the wake of the giant hull which was throwing them about so mercilessly, but they were still afloat.

She began to crawl down the plunging deck. She knew where the bilge pump was, that was one thing Tom had taught all of them – and she crawled on grimly towards it.

Hank Petersen ducked out of the wheelhouse, flapping his arms wildly as he struggled into the life-jacket. He was not certain of the best action to take, whether to jump over the side and begin swimming away from the tanker's slightly angled course, or to stay on board and take his chances with the collision which was now only seconds away.

Around him, the others were in the grip of the same indecision; they were huddled silently at the rail staring up at the mountain of smooth rounded steel that seemed to blot out half the sky. Only the TV cameraman on the wheelhouse roof, a true fanatic oblivious of all danger, kept his camera running. His exclamations of delight and the burr of the camera motor blended with the rushing sibilance of *Golden Dawn*'s bow wave. It was fifteen feet high, that wave, and it sounded like wild fire in dry grass.

Suddenly the exhaust of the diesel engine above Hank's head bellowed harshly, and then subsided into a soft burbling idle again. He looked up at it uncomprehendingly, now it roared again, fiercely, and the deck lurched beneath him. From the stern he heard the boil of water driven by the propeller, and the *Dicky* shrugged off her lethargy and lifted her bows to the short steep swell of the Gulf Stream.

A moment longer Hank stood frozen, and then he dived back into the wheelhouse and spun the spokes of the wheel through his fingers, sheering off sharply, but still staring out through the side glass.

The *Golden Dawn*'s bows filled his whole vision now, but the smaller vessel was scooting frantically out to one side, and the tanker's bows were swinging majestically in the opposite direction.

A few seconds, more and they would be clear, but the bow wave caught them and Hank was flung across the wheelhouse. He felt something break in his chest, and heard the snap of bone as he hit, then immediately afterwards there was the crackling rending tearing impact as the two hulls came together and he was thrown back the other way, sprawling wildly across the deck.

He tried to claw himself upright, but the little fishing boat was pitching and cavorting with such abandon that he was thrown flat again. There was another tearing impact as the vessel was dragged down the tanker's side, and then flung free to roll her rails under and bob like a cork in the mill race of the huge ship's wake.

Now, at last, he was able to pull himself to his feet, and doubled over, clutching his injured ribs, he peered dazedly through the wheelhouse glass.

Half a mile away, the tanker was lazily turning up into the wind, and there was no propeller wash from under her counter. Hank staggered to the doorway, and looked out. The deck was still awash, but the water they had taken on was pouring out through the scuppers. The railing was smashed, most of it dangling overboard and the planking was splintered and torn, the ripped timber as white as bone in the sunlight.

Behind him, Samantha came crawling up the ladder from the engine room. There was a purple swelling in the centre of her forehead, she was soaking wet and her hands were filthy with black grease. He saw a livid red burn across the back of one hand as she lifted it to brush tumbled blonde hair out of her face.

'Are you all right, Sam?'

'Water's pouring in,' she said. 'I don't know how long the pump can hold it.'

'Did you fix the motor?' he asked.

Samantha nodded. 'I held the throttle open,' she said, and then with feeling, 'but I'll be damned to hell if I'll do it again. Somebody else can go down there, I've had my turn.'

'Show me how,' Hank said, 'and you can take the wheel. The sooner we get back to Key Biscayne, the happier I'll be.'

Samantha peered across at the receding bulk of *Golden Dawn*.

'My God!' she shook her head with wonder. 'My God!' We were lucky!'

'Mackerel skies and mares' tails,
Make tall ships carry short sails.'

Nicholas Berg recited the old sailor's doggerel to himself, shading his eyes with one hand as he looked upwards.

The cloud was beautiful as fine lacework; very high against the tall blue of the heavens it spread swiftly in those long filmy scrolls. Nicholas could see the patterns developing and expanding as he watched, and that was a measure of the speed with which the high winds were blowing. That cloud was at least thirty thousand feet high, and below it the air was clear and crisp – only out on the western horizon the billowing silver and the blue thunderheads were rising, generated by the land-mass of Florida whose low silhouette was still below their horizon.

They had been in the main current of the Gulf Stream for six hours now. It was easy to recognize this characteristic scend of the sea, the short steep swells marching close together, the particular brilliance of these waters that had been first warmed in the shallow tropical basin of the Caribbean, the increased bulk flooding through into the Gulf of Mexico and there heated further, swelling in volume until they formed a hillock of water which at last rushed out through this narrow drainhole of the Florida Straits, swinging north and east in a wide benevolent wash, tempering the climate of all countries whose shores it touched and warming the fishing grounds of the North Atlantic.

In the middle of this stream, somewhere directly ahead of *Warlock*'s thrusting bows, the *Golden Dawn* was struggling southwards, directly opposed to the current which would clip eighty miles a day off her speed, and driving directly into the face of one of the most evil and dangerous storms that nature could summon.

Nicholas found himself brooding again on the mentality of anybody who would do that; again he glanced upwards at the harbingers of the storm, those delicate wisps of lacey cloud.

Nicholas had sailed through a hurricane once, twenty years ago, as a junior officer on one of Christy Marine's small grain carriers, and he shuddered now at the memory of it.

Duncan Alexander was a desperate man even to contemplate that risk, a man gambling everything on one fall of the dice. Nicholas could understand the forces that drove him, for he had been driven himself – but he hated him now for the chances he was taking. Duncan Alexander was risking Nicholas' son, and he was risking the life of an ocean and of the millions of people whose existence was tied to that ocean. Duncan Alexander was gambling with stakes that were not his to place at hazard.

Nicholas wanted one thing only now, and that was to get alongside *Golden Dawn* and take off his son. He would do that, even if it meant boarding her like a buccaneer. In the Master's suite, there was a locked and sealed arms cupboard with two riot guns, automatic 12 gauge shotguns and six Walther PK.38 pistols. *Warlock* had been equipped for every possible emergency in any ocean of the world, and those emergencies could include piracy or mutiny aboard a vessel under salvage. Now Nicholas was fully prepared to take an armed party on board *Golden Dawn*, and to take his chances in any court of law afterwards.

Warlock was racing into the chop of the Gulf Stream and scattering the spray like startled white doves, but she was running too slowly for Nicholas and he turned away impatiently and strode into the navigation bridge.

David Allen looked up at him, a small frown of preoccupation marring the smooth boyish features.

'Wind is moderating and veering westerly,' he said, and Nicholas remembered another line of doggerel:

'When the wind moves against the sun
Trust her not for back she'll run.'

He did not recite it, however, he merely nodded and said:

'We are running into the extreme influence of Lorna. The wind will back again as we move closer to the centre.'

Nicholas went on to the radio room and the Trog looked up at him. It was not necessary for Nicholas to ask, the Trog shook his head. Since that long exchange with the coastguard patrol early that morning, *Golden Dawn* had kept her silence.

Nicholas crossed to the radarscope and studied the circular field for a few minutes; this usually busy seaway was peculiarly empty. There were some small craft crossing the main channel, probably fishing boats or pleasure craft scuttling for protection from the coming storm. All across the islands and on the mainland of Florida the elaborate precautions against the hurricane assault would be coming into force. Since the highway had been laid down on the spur of little islands that formed the Florida Keys, more than three hundred thousand people had crowded in there, in the process transforming those wild lovely islands into the Taj Mahal of ticky-tacky. If the hurricane struck there, the loss of life and property would be enormous, it was probably the most vulnerable spot on a long exposed coastline. For a few minutes, Nicholas tried to imagine the chaos that would result if a million tons of toxic crude oil was driven ashore on a littoral already ravaged by hurricane winds. It baulked his imagination, and he left the radar and moved to the front of the bridge. He stood staring down the narrow throat of water at a horizon that concealed all the terrors and desperate alarms that his imagination could conjure up.

The door to the radio shack was open and the bridge was quiet, so that they all heard it clearly; they could even catch the hiss of breath as the speaker paused between each sentence, and the urgency of his tone was not covered by the slight distortion of the VHF carrier beam.

'Mayday! Mayday! Mayday! This is the bulk oil carrier *Golden Dawn*. Our position is 79° 50′ West 25° 43′ North.'

Before Nicholas reached the chart-table, he knew she was still a hundred miles ahead of them, and, as he pored over the table, he saw his estimate confirmed.

'We have lost our propeller with main shaft failure and we are drifting out of control.'

Nicholas' head flinched as though he had been hit in the face. He could imagine no more dangerous condition and position for a ship of that size – and Peter was on board.

'This is *Golden Dawn* calling the United States Coast Guard service or any ship in a position to afford assistance –'

Nicholas reached the radio shack with three long strides, and the Trog handed him the microphone and nodded.

'*Golden Dawn*, this is the salvage tug *Warlock*. I will be in a position to render assistance within four hours –'

Damn the rule of silence, Peter was on board her.

'– Tell Alexander I am offering Lloyd's Open Form and I want immediate acceptance.'

He dropped the microphone and stormed back on to the bridge, his voice clipped and harsh as he caught David Allen's arm.

'Interception course and push her through the gate,' he ordered grimly. 'Tell Beauty Baker to open all the taps.' He dropped David's arm and spun back to the radio room.

'Telex Levoisin on *Sea Witch*. I want him to give me a time to reach *Golden Dawn* at his best possible speed,' and he wondered briefly if even the two tugs would be able to control the crippled and powerless *Golden Dawn* in the winds of a hurricane.

Jules replied almost immediately. He had bunkered at Charleston, and cleared harbour six hours previously. He was running hard now and he gave a time to *Golden Dawn*'s position for noon the next day, which was also the forecast time of passage of the Straits for hurricane Lorna, according to the meteorological up-date they had got from Miami two hours before, Nicholas thought as he read the telex and turned to David Allen.

'David, there is no precedent for this that I know of – but with my son on board *Golden Dawn* I just have to assume command of this ship, on a temporary basis, of course.'

'I'd be honoured to act as your First Officer again, sir,' David told him quietly, and Nicholas could see he meant it.

'If there is a good salvage, the Master's share will still be yours,' Nicholas promised him, and thanked him with a touch on the arm. 'Would you check out the preparations to put a line aboard the tanker?'

David turned to leave the bridge, but Nicholas stopped him. 'By the time we get there, we will have the kind of wind you have only dreamed about in your worst nightmares – just keep that in mind.'

'Telex,' screeched the Trog. '*Golden Dawn* is replying to our offer.'

Nicholas strode across to the radio room, and read the first few lines of message as it printed out.

OFFER CONTRACT OF DAILY HIRE FOR TOWAGE THIS VESSEL FROM PRESENT POSITION TO GALVESTON ROADS

'The bastard,' Nicholas snarled. 'He's playing his fancy games with me, in the teeth of a hurricane and with my boy aboard.' Furiously he punched his fist into the palm of his other hand. 'Right!' he snapped. 'We'll play just as rough! Get me the Director of the U.S. Coast Guard at the Fort Lauderdale Headquarters – get him on the emergency coastguard frequency and I will talk to him in clear.'

The Trog's face lit with malicious glee and he made the contact.

'Colonel Ramsden,' Nicholas said. 'This is the Master of *Warlock*. I'm the only salvage vessel that can reach *Golden Dawn* before passage of Lorna, and I'm probably the only tug on the eastern seaboard of America with 22,000 horsepower. Unless the *Golden Dawn*'s Master accepts Lloyd's Open Form within the next sixty minutes, I shall be obliged to see to the safety of my vessel and crew by running for the nearest anchorage – and you're going to have a million tons of highly toxic crude oil drifting out of control into your territorial waters, in hurricane conditions.'

The Coast Guard Director had a deep measured voice, and the calm tones of a man upon whom the mantle of authority was a familiar garment.

'Stand by, *Warlock*, I am going to contact *Golden Dawn* direct on Channel 16.'

Nicholas signalled the Trog to turn up the volume on Channel 16 and they listened to Ramsden speaking directly to Duncan Alexander.

'In the event your vessel enters United States territorial waters without control or without an attendant tug capable of exerting that control, I shall be obliged under the powers vested in me to seize your vessel and take such steps to prevent pollution of our waters as I see fit. I have to warn you that those steps may include destruction of your cargo.'

Ten minutes later the Trog copied a telex from Duncan Alexander personal to Nicholas Berg accepting Lloyd's Open Form and requesting him to exercise all dispatch in taking *Golden Dawn* in tow.

'I estimate we will be drifting over the 100-fathom line and entering U.S. territorial waters within two hours,' the message ended.

While Nicholas read it, standing out on the protected wing of *Warlock*'s bridge, the wind suddenly fluttered the paper in his hand and flattened his cotton shirt against his chest. He looked up quickly and saw the wind was backing violently into the east, and beginning to claw the tops of the Gulf Stream swells. The setting sun was bleeding copiously across the high veils of cirrus cloud which now covered the sky from horizon to horizon.

There was nothing more that Nicholas could do now. *Warlock* was running as hard as she could, and all her crew were quietly going about their preparations to pass a wire and take on tow. All he could do was wait, but that was always the hardest part.

Darkness came swiftly but with the last of the light, Nicholas could just make out a dark and mountainous shape beginning to hump up above the southern horizon like an impatient monster. He stared at it with awful fascination, until mercifully the night hid Lorna's dreadful face.

The wind chopped the Gulf Stream up into quick confused seas, and it did not blow steadily, but flogged them with squally gusts and rain that crackled against the bridge windows with startling suddenness.

The night was utterly black, there were no stars, no source of light whatsoever, and *Warlock* lurched and heeled to the patternless seas.

'Barometer's rising sharply,' David Allen called suddenly. 'It's jumped three millibars – back to 1005.'

'The trough,' said Nicholas grimly. It was a classic hurricane formation, that narrow girdle of higher pressure that demarcated the outer fringe of the great revolving spiral of tormented air. 'We are going into it now.'

And as he spoke the darkness lifted, the heavens began to burn like a bed of hot coals, and the sea shone with a sullen ruddy luminosity as though the doors of a furnace had been thrown wide.

Nobody spoke on *Warlock*'s bridge, they lifted their faces with the same awed expressions as worshippers in a lofty cathedral and they looked up at the skies.

Low cloud raced above them, cloud that glowed and shone with that terrible ominous flare. Slowly the light faded and changed, turning a paler sickly greenish hue, like the shine on putrid meat. Nicholas spoke first.

'The Devil's Beacon,' he said, and he wanted to rationalize it to break the superstitious mood that gripped them all. It was merely the rays of the sun below the western horizon catching the cloud peaks of the storm and reflected downwards through the weak cloud cover of the trough – but somehow he could not find the right words to denigrate that phenomenon that was part of the mariner's lore, the malignant beacon that leads a doomed ship on to its fate.

The weird light faded slowly away leaving the night even darker and more foreboding than it had been before.

'David,' Nicholas thought quickly of something to distract his officers, 'have we got a radar contact yet?' and the new Mate roused himself with a visible effort and crossed to the radarscope.

'The range is very confused,' he said, his voice still subdued, and Nicholas joined him at the screen.

The sweeping arm lit a swirling mass of sea clutter, and the strange ghost echoes thrown up by electrical discharges within the approaching storm. The outline of the Florida mainland and of the nearest islands of the Grand Bahamas bank were firm and immediately recognizable. They reminded Nicholas yet again of how little sea-room there was in which to manoeuver his tugs and their monstrous prize.

Then, in the trash of false echo and sea clutter, his trained eye picked out a harder echo on the extreme limits of the set's range. He watched it carefully for half a dozen revolutions of the radar's sweep, and each time it was constant and clearer.

'Radar contact,' he said. 'Tell *Golden Dawn* we are in contact, range sixty-five nautical miles. Tell them we will take on tow before midnight.' And then, under his breath, the old sailor's qualifications, 'God willing and weather permitting.'

The lights on *Warlock*'s bridge had been rheostatted down to a dull rose glow to protect the night vision of her officers, and the four of them stared out to where they knew the tanker lay.

Her image on the radar was bright and firm, lying within the two mile ring of the screen, but from the bridge she was invisible.

In the two hours since first contact, the barometer had gone through its brief peak as the trough passed, and then fallen steeply.

From 1005 it had crashed to 900 and was still plummeting, and the weather coming in from the east was blustering and squalling. The wind mourned about them on a forever rising note, and torrential rain obscured all vision outside an arc of a few hundred yards.

Even *Warlock*'s twin searchlights, set seventy feet above the main deck on the summit of the fire-control gantry, could not pierce those solid white curtains of rain.

Nicholas groped like a blind man through the rain fog, using pitch and power to close carefully with *Golden Dawn*, giving his orders to the helm in a cool impersonal tone which belied the pale set of his features and the alert brightness of his eyes as he reached the swirling bank of rain.

Abruptly another squall struck *Warlock*. With a demented shriek, it heeled the big tug sharply and shredded the curtains of rain, ripping them open so that for a moment Nicholas saw *Golden Dawn*.

She was exactly where he had expected her to be, but the wind had caught the tanker's high navigation bridge like the mainsail of a tall ship, and she was going swiftly astern.

All her deck and port lights were burning, and she carried the twin red riding lights at her stubby masthead that identified a vessel drifting out of control. The following sea driven on by the rising wind piled on to her tank decks, smothering them with white foam and spray, so that the ship looked like a submerged coral reef.

'Half ahead both,' Nicholas told the helmsman. 'Steer for her starboard side.'

He closed quickly with the tanker, staying in visual contact now; even when the rain mists closed down again, they could make out the ghostly shape of her and the glow of her riding lights.

David Allen was looking at him expectantly and Nicholas asked, 'What bottom?' without taking his eyes from the stricken ship.

'One hundred sixteen fathoms and shelving fast.' They were being blown quickly out of the main channel, on to the shallow ledge of the Florida littoral.

'I'm going to tow her out stern first,' said Nicholas, and immediately David saw the wisdom of it. Nobody would be able to get up into her bows to secure a tow-line, the seas were breaking over them and sweeping them with ten and fifteen feet of green water.

'I'll go aft —' David began, but Nicholas stopped him.

'No, David. I want you here – because I'm going on board *Golden Dawn*.'

'Sir,' David wanted to tell him that it was dangerous to delay passing the towing cable – with that lee shore waiting.

'This will be our last chance to get passengers off her before the full hurricane hits us,' said Nicholas, and David saw that it was futile to protest. Nicholas Berg was going to fetch his son.

From the height of *Golden Dawn*'s towering navigation bridge, they could look directly down on to the main deck of the tug as she came alongside.

Peter Berg stood beside his mother, almost as tall as she was. He wore a full life-jacket and a corduroy cap pulled down over his ears.

'It will be all right,' he comforted Chantelle. 'Dad is here. It will be just fine now.' And he took her hand protectively.

Warlock staggered and reeled in the grip of wind as she came up into the tanker's lee, rain blew over her like dense white smoke and every few minutes she put her nose down and threw a thick green slice of sea water back along her decks.

In comparison to the tug's wild action, *Golden Dawn* wallowed heavily, held down by the oppressive weight of a million tons of crude oil, and the seas beat upon her with increasing fury, as if affronted by her indifference. *Warlock* edged in closer and still closer.

Duncan Alexander came through from the communications room at the rear of the bridge. He balanced easily against *Golden Dawn*'s ponderous motion but his face was swollen and flushed with anger.

'Berg is coming on board,' he burst out. 'He's wasting valuable time. I warned him that we must get out into deeper water.'

Peter Berg interrupted suddenly and pointed down at *Warlock*.

'Look!' he cried.

Until that moment, the night and the storm had hidden the small huddle of human shapes in the tug's high forward tower. They wore wet, glistening oilskins and their life-jackets gave them a swollen pregnant look. They were lowering the boarding gantry into the horizontal position.

'There is Dad!' Peter shouted. 'That's him in front.'

At the extremity of her roll, *Warlock*'s boarding gantry touched the railing of the tanker's quarter deck, ten feet above the swamped tank deck – and the leading figure on the tug's upperworks ran out lightly along the gantry, balanced for a moment high above the roaring, racing green water and then leapt across five feet of open space, caught a hand hold and then pulled himself over *Golden Dawn*'s rail.

Immediately the tug sheered off and fell in fifty yards off the tanker's starboard side, half hidden in the rain mists, but holding her station steadily, despite all the wind's and the sea's spiteful efforts to separate the two vessels.

The whole manoeuvre had been performed with an expertise which made it seem almost casual.

'Dad's carried a line across,' Peter said proudly, and Chantelle, looking down, saw that a delicate white nylon thread was being hove in by two seamen on the tanker's quarter deck, while from the tug's fire-control tower a canvas bosun's chair was being winched across.

The elevator doors slid open with a whine and Nicholas Berg strode on to the tanker's bridge. His oilskins still ran with rainwater that splattered on to the deck at his feet.

'Dad!' Peter ran to meet him and Nicholas stooped and embraced him fiercely before straightening; with one arm still about his son's shoulders, he confronted Chantelle and Duncan Alexander.

'I hope both of you are satisfied now,' he said quietly, 'but I for one don't rate our chances of saving this ship very highly, so I'm taking off everybody who is not needed on board to handle her.'

'Your tug,' burst out Duncan, 'you've got 22,000 horse-power, and can –'

'There is a hurricane on its way,' said Nicholas coldly, and he shot a glance at the roaring night. 'This is just the overture.' He turned back to Randle. 'How many men do you want to keep on board?'

Randle thought a moment. 'Myself, a helmsman, and five seamen to handle the tow-lines and work the ship.' He paused and then went on, 'And the pump room personnel to control the cargo.'

'You will act as helmsman, I will control the pump room, and I'll need only three seamen. Get me volunteers,' Nicholas decided. 'Send everybody else off.'

'Sir,' Randle began to protest.

'May I remind you Captain, that I am salvage master, my authority now supersedes yours.' Nicholas did not wait for his reply. 'Chantelle,' he picked her out, 'take Peter down to the quarter deck. You'll go across first.'

'Listen here, Berg,' Duncan could no longer contain himself, 'I insist you pass the towing cable, this ship is in danger.'

'Get down there with them,' Nicholas snapped. 'I'll decide the procedures.'

'Do as he says, darling,' Chantelle smiled up at her husband vindictively. 'You've lost. Nicholas is the only winner now.'

'Shut up, damn you,' Duncan hissed at her.

'Get down to the afterdeck,' Nicholas' voice cracked like breaking ice.

'I'm staying on board this ship,' said Duncan abruptly. 'It's my responsibility. I said I'd see it out and by God I will. I am going to be here to make sure you do your job, Berg.'

Nicholas checked himself, studied him for a long moment, and then smiled mirthlessly. 'Nobody ever called you a coward,' he nodded reluctantly. 'Other things – but not a coward. Stay if you will, we might need an extra hand,' Then to Peter, 'Come, my boy.' And he led him towards the elevator.

At the quarterdeck rail, Nicholas hugged the boy, holding him in his arms, their cheeks pressed tightly together, and drawing out the moment while the wind cannoned and thrummed about their heads.

'I love you, Dad.'

'And I love you, Peter, more than I can ever tell you – but you must go now.'

He broke the embrace and lifted the child into the deep canvas bucket of the bosun's chair, stepped back and windmilled his right arm. Immediately, the winch party in *Warlock*'s upperworks swung him swiftly out into the gap between the two ships and the nylon cable seemed as fragile and insubstantial as a spider's thread.

As the two ships rolled and dipped, so the line tightened and sagged, one moment dropping the white canvas bucket almost to the water level where the hungry waves snatched at it with cold green fangs, and the next, pulling the line up so tightly that it hummed with tension, threatening to snap and drop the child back into the sea, but at last it reached the tug and four pairs of strong hands lifted the boy clear. For one moment, he waved back at Nicholas and then he was hustled away, and the empty bosun's chair was coming back.

Only then did Nicholas become aware that Chantelle was clinging to his arm and he looked down into her face. Her eyelashes were dewed and stuck together with the flying raindrops. Her face ran with wetness and she seemed very small and childlike under the bulky oilskins and life-jacket. She was as beautiful as she had ever been but her eyes were huge and darkly troubled.

'Nicholas, I've always needed you,' she husked. 'But never as I need you now.'

Her existence was being blown away on the wind, and she was afraid.

'You and this ship are all I have left.'

'No, only the ship,' he said brusquely, and he was amazed that the spell was broken.

That soft area of his soul which she had been able to touch so unerringly was now armoured against her. With a sudden surge of relief, he realized he was free of her, for ever. It was over; here in the storm, he was free at last.

She sensed it – for the fear in her eyes changed to real terror.

'Nicholas, you cannot desert me now. Oh Nicholas, what will become of me without you and Christy Marine?'

'I don't know,' he told her quietly, and caught the bosun's chair as it came in over *Golden Dawn*'s rail. He lifted her as easily as he had lifted his son and placed her in the canvas bucket.

'And to tell you the truth, Chantelle, I don't really care,' he said, and stepping back, he windmilled his right arm. The chair swooped out across the narrow water, swinging like a pendulum in the wind. Chantelle shouted something at him but Nicholas had turned away, and was already going aft in a lurching run to where the three volunteers were waiting.

He saw at a glance that they were big, powerful, competent-looking men.

Quickly Nicholas checked their equipment, from the thick leather gauntlets to the bolt cutters and jemmy bars for handling heavy cable.

'You'll do,' he said. 'We will use the bosun's tackle to bring across a messenger from the tug – just as soon as the last man leaves this ship.'

Working with men to whom the task was unfamiliar, and in rapidly deteriorating conditions of sea and weather, it took almost another hour before they had the main cable across from *Warlock* secured by its thick nylon spring to the tanker's stern bollards – yet the time had passed so swiftly for Nicholas that when he stood back and glanced at his watch, he was shocked. Before this wind they must have been going down very fast on the land. He staggered into the tanker's stern quarters, and left a trail of sea water down the passageway to the elevators.

On the bridge, Captain Randle was standing grim-faced at the helm, and Duncan Alexander snapped accusingly at him.

'You've cut it damned fine.' A single glance at the digital print-out of the depth gauge on the tanker's control console bore him out. They had thirty-eight fathoms of water under them now, and the *Golden Dawn*'s swollen belly sagged down twenty fathoms below the surface. They were going down very swiftly before the easterly gale winds. It was damned fine, Nicholas had to agree, but he showed no alarm or agitation as he crossed to Randle's side and unhooked the hand microphone.

'David,' he asked quietly, 'are you ready to haul us off?'

'Ready, sir,' David Allen's voice came from the speaker above his head.

'I'm going to give you full port rudder to help your turn across the wind,' said Nicholas, and then nodded to Randle. 'Full port rudder.'

'Forty degrees of port rudder on,' Randle reported.

They felt the tiny shock as the tow-cable came up taut, and carefully *Warlock* began the delicate task of turning the huge ship across the rising gusting wind and then dragging her out tail first into the deeper water of the channel where she would have her best chance of riding out the hurricane.

*

It was clear now that *Golden Dawn* lay directly in the track of Lorna, and the storm unleashed its true nature upon them. Out there upon the sane and rational world, the sun was rising, but here there was no dawn, for there was no horizon and no sky. There was only madness and wind and water, and all three elements were so intermingled as to form one substance.

An hour – which seemed like a lifetime – ago, the wind had ripped away the anemonmeter and the weather-recording equipment on top of the navigation bridge, so Nicholas had no way of judging the wind's strength and direction.

Out beyond the bridge windows, the wind took the top off the sea; it took it off in thick sheets of salt water and lifted them over the navigation bridge in a shrieking white curtain that cut off visibility at the glass of the windows. The tank deck had disappeared in the racing white emulsion of wind and water, even the railing of the bridge wings six feet from the windows was invisible.

The entire superstructure groaned and popped and whimpered under the assault of the wind, the pressed aluminium bulkheads bulging and distorting, the very deck flexing and juddering at the solid weight of the storm.

Through the saturated, racing, swirling air, a leaden and ominous grey light filtered, and every few minutes the electrical impulses generated within the sixty-thousand-foot-high mountain of racing, spinning air released themselves in shattering cannonades of thunder and sudden brilliance of eye-searing white lightning.

There was no visual contact with *Warlock*. The massive electrical disturbance of the storm and the clutter of high seas and almost solid cloud and turbulence had reduced the radar range to a few miles, and even then it was unreliable. Radio contact with the tug was drowned with buzzing squealing static. It was possible to understand only odd disconnected words from David Allen.

Nicholas was powerless, caged in the groaning, vibrating box of the navigation bridge, blinded and deafened by the unleashed powers of the heavens. There was nothing any of them could do.

Randle had locked the ultra-tanker's helm amidships, and now he stood with Duncan and the three seamen by the chart-table, all of them clinging to it for support, all their faces pale and set as though carved from chalk.

Only Nicholas moved restlessly about the bridge; from the stern windows where he peered down vainly, trying to get a glimpse of either the tow-cable and its spring, or of the tug's looming shape through the racing white storm, then he came forward carefully, using the foul-weather rail to steady himself against the huge ship's wild and unpredictable motion, and he stood before the control console, studying the display of lights that monitored the pod tanks and the ship's navigational and mechanical functions.

None of the petroleum tanks had lost any crude oil and in all of them the nature of the inert gas was constant, there had been no ingress of air to them; they were all still intact then. One of the reasons that Nicholas had taken the tanker in tow stern first was so that the navigation tower might break the worst of wind and sea, and the fragile bloated tanks would receive some protection from it.

Yet desperately he wished for a momentary sight of the tank deck, merely to reassure himself. There could be malfunction in the pump control instruments, the storm could have clawed one of the pod tanks open, and even now *Golden Dawn* could be bleeding her poison into the sea. But there was no view of the tank decks through the storm, and

Nick stooped to the radarscope. The screen glowed and danced and flickered with ghost images and trash – he wasn't too certain if even *Warlock*'s image was constant, the range seemed to be opening, as though the tow-line had parted. He straighten up and stood balanced on the balls of his feet, reassuring himself by the feel of the deck that *Golden Dawn* was still under tow. He could feel by the way she resisted the wind and the sea that the tow was still good.

Yet there was no means of telling their position. The satellite navigational system was completely blanketed, the radio waves were distorted and diverted by tens of thousands of feet of electrical storm, and the same forces were blanketing the marine radio beacons on the American mainland.

The only indication was the ship's electronic log which gave Nicholas the speed of the ship's hull through the water and the speed across the sea bottom, and the depth finder which recorded the water under her keel.

For the first two hours of the tow, *Warlock* had been able to pull the ship back towards the main channel at three and a half knots, and slowly the water had become deeper until they had 150 fathoms under them.

Then as the wind velocity increased, the windage of *Golden Dawn*'s superstructure had acted as a vast mainsail and the storm had taken control. Now, despite all the power in *Warlock*'s big twin propellers, both tug and tanker were being pushed once more back towards the 100–fathom line and the American mainland.

'Where is *Sea Witch*?' Nicholas wondered, as he stared helplessly at the gauges. They were going towards the shore at a little over two knots, and the bottom was shelving steeply. *Sea Witch* might be the ace that took the trick, if she could reach them through these murderous seas and savage winds, and if she could find them in this wilderness of mad air and water.

Again, Nicholas groped his way to the communications room, and still clinging to the bulkhead with one hand he thumbed the microphone.

'*Sea Witch. Sea Witch*. This is *Warlock*. Calling *Sea Witch*.'

He listened then, trying to tune out the snarl and crackle of static, crouching over the set. Faintly he thought he heard a human voice, a scratchy whisper through the interference and he called again and listened, and called again. There was the voice again, but so indistinct he could not make out a single word.

Above his head, there was a tearing screech of rending metal. Nicholas dropped the microphone and staggered through on to the bridge. There was another deafening banging and hammering and all of them stood staring up at the metal roof of the bridge. It sagged and shook, there was one more crash and then with a scraping, dragging rush, a confused tangle of metal and wire and cable tumbled over the forward edge of the bridge and flapped and swung wildly in the wind.

It took a moment for Nicholas to realise what it was.

'The radar antennae!' he shouted. He recognized the elongated dish of the aerial, dangling on a thick coil of cable, then the wind tore that loose also, and the entire mass of equipment flapped away like a giant bat and was instantly lost in the teeming white curtains of the storm.

With two quick paces, he reached the radarscope, and one glance was enough. The screen was black and dead. They had lost their eyes now, and, unbelievably, the sound of the storm was rising again.

It boomed against the square box of the bridge, and the men within it cowered from its fury.

Then abruptly, Duncan was screaming something at Nicholas, and pointing up at the master display of the control console. Nicholas, still hanging on to the radarscope, roused himself with an effort and looked up at the display. The speed across the ground had changed drastically. It was now almost eight knots, and the depth was ninety-two fathoms.

Nicholas felt icy despair clutch and squeeze his guts. The ship was moving differently under him, he could feel her now in mortal distress; that same gust which had torn away the radar mast had done other damage.

He knew what that damage was, and the thought of it made him want to vomit, but he had to be sure. He had to be absolutely certain, and he began to hand himself along the foul-weather rail towards the elevator doors.

Across the bridge the others were watching him intently, but even from twenty feet it was impossible to make himself heard above the clamorous assault of the storm.

One of the seamen seemed suddenly to guess his intention. He left the chart-table and groped his way along the bulkhead towards Nicholas.

'Good man!' Nicholas grabbed his arm to steady him, and they fell forward into the elevator as *Golden Dawn* began another of those ponderous wallowing rolls and the deck fell out from under their feet.

The ride down in the elevator car slammed them back and forth across the little coffin-like box, and even here in the depths of the ship they had to shout to hear each other.

'The tow cable,' Nicholas yelled in the man's ear. 'Check the tow cable.'

From the elevator they went carefully aft along the central passageway, and when they reached the double storm doors, Nicholas tried to push the inner door open, but the pressure of the wind held it closed.

'Help me,' he shouted at the seaman, and they threw their combined weight against it. The instant that they forced the jamb open a crack, the vacuum of pressure was released and the wind took the three-inch mahogany doors and ripped them effortlessly from their hinges, and whisked them away, as though they were a pair of playing cards – and Nicholas and the seaman were exposed in the open doorway.

The wind flung itself upon them, and hurled them to the deck, smothering them in the icy deluge of water that ripped at their faces as abrasively as ground glass.

Nicholas rolled down the deck and crashed into the stern rail with such jarring force that he thought his lungs had been crushed, and the wind pinned him there, and blinded and smothered him with salt water.

He lay there helpless as a new-born infant, and near him he heard the seaman screaming thinly. The sound steeled him, and Nicholas slowly dragged himself to his knees, desperately clutching at the rail to resist the wind.

Still the man screamed and Nicholas began to creep forward on his hands and knees. It was impossible to stand in that wind and he could move only with support from the rail.

Six feet ahead of him, the extreme limit of his vision, the railing had been torn away, a long section of it dangling over the ship's side, and to this was clinging the seaman. His weight driven by the wind must have hit the rail with sufficient force to tear it loose, and now he was hanging on with one arm hooked through the railing and the other arm twisted from a shattered shoulder and waving a crazy salute as the wind whipped it about. When he looked up at Nicholas his mouth had been smashed in. It looked as though he had half chewed a mouthful of black currants, and the jagged stumps of his broken front teeth were bright red with the juice.

On his belly, Nicholas reached for him, and as he did so, the wind came again, unbelievably it was stronger still, and it took the damaged railing with the man still upon it and tore it bodily away. They disappeared instantly in the blinding white-out of the storm, and Nicholas felt himself hurled forward towards the edge. He clung with all his strength to the remaining section of the rail, and felt it buckle and begin to give.

On his knees still he clawed himself away from that fatal beckoning gap, towards the stern, and the wind struck him full in the face, blinding and choking him. Sightlessly, he dragged himself on until one outstretched arm struck the cold cast iron of the port stern bollard, and he flung both arms about it like a lover, choking and retching from the salt water that the wind had forced through his nose and mouth and down his throat.

Still blind, he felt for the woven steel of *Warlock*'s main tow wire. He found it and he could not span it with his fist – but he felt the quick lift of his hopes.

The cable was still secured. He had catted and prevented it with a dozen nylon strops, and it was still holding. He crawled forward, dragging himself along the tow-cable, and immediately he realized that his relief had been premature. There was no tension in the cable and when he reached the edge of the deck it dangled straight down. It was not stretched out into the whiteness, to where he had hoped *Warlock* was still holding them like a great sea anchor.

He knew then that what he had dreaded had happened. The storm had been too powerful, it had snapped the steel cable like a thread of cotton, and *Golden Dawn* was loose, without control, and this wild and savage wind was blowing her down swiftly on to the land.

Nicholas felt suddenly exhausted to his bones. He lay flat on the deck, closed his eyes and clung weakly to the severed cable. The wind wanted to hurl him over the side, it ballooned his oilskins and ripped at his face. It would be so easy to open his fingers and to let go – and it took all his resolve to resist the impulse.

Slowly, as painfully as a crippled insect, he dragged himself back through the open, shattered doorway into the central passageway of the stern quarters – but still the wind followed him. It roared down the passageway, driving in torrents of rain and salt water that flooded the deck and forced Nicholas to cling for support like a drunkard.

After the open storm, the car of the elevator seemed silent and tranquil as the inner sanctum of a cathedral. He looked at himself in the wall mirror, and saw that his eyes were scoured red and painful-looking by salt and wind, and his cheeks and lips looked raw and bruised, as though the skin had been rasped away. He touched his face and there was no feeling in his nose nor in his lips.

The elevator doors slid open and he reeled out on to the navigation bridge. The group of men at the chart-table seemed not to have moved, but their heads turned to him.

Nicholas reached the table and clung to it. They were silent, watching his face.

'I lost a man,' he said, and his voice was hoarse and roughened by salt and weariness. 'He went overboard. The wind got him.'

Still none of them moved nor spoke, and Nicholas coughed, his lungs ached from the water he had breathed. When the spasm passed, he went on.

'The tow-cable has parted. We are loose – and *Warlock* will never be able to re-establish tow. Not in this.'

All their heads turned now to the forward bridge windows, to that impenetrable racing whiteness beyond the glass, that was lit internally with its glowing bursts of lightning.

Nicholas broke the spell that held them all. He reached up to the signal locker above the chart-table and brought down a cardboard packet of distress flares. He broke open the seals and spilled the flares on to the table. They looked like sticks of dynamite, cylinders of heavily varnished waterproof paper. The flares could be lit, and would spurt out crimson flames, even if immersed in water, once the self-igniter tab at one end was pulled.

Nicholas stuffed half a dozen of the flares into the inner pockets of his oilskins.

'Listen,' he had to shout, even though they were only feet away. 'We are going to be aground within two hours. This ship is going to start breaking up immediately we strike.'

He paused and studied their faces; Duncan was the only one who did not seem to understand. He had picked up a handful of the signal flares from the table and he was looking inquiringly at Nicholas.

'I will give you the word; as soon as we reach the twenty-fathom line and she touches bottom, you will go over the side. We will try and get a raft away. There is a chance you could be carried ashore.'

He paused again, and he could see that Randle and his two seamen realized clearly just how remote that chance was.

'I will give you twenty minutes to get clear. By then, the pod tanks will have begun breaking up —' He didn't want this to sound melodramatic and he searched for some way to make it sound less theatrical, but could think of none. 'Once the first tank ruptures, I will ignite the escaping crude with a signal flare.'

'Christ!' Randle mouthed the blasphemy, and the storm censored it on his lips. Then he raised his voice. 'A million tons of crude. It will fireball, man.'

'Better than a million-ton slick down the Gulf Stream,' Nicholas told him wearily.

'None of us will have a chance. A million tons. It will go up like an atom bomb.' Randle was white-faced and shaking now. 'You can't do it!'

'Think of a better way,' said Nicholas and left the table to stagger across to the radio room. They watched him go, and then Duncan looked down at the signal flares in his hand for a moment before thrusting them into the pocket of his jacket.

In the radio room, Nicholas called quietly into the microphone. 'Come in, *Sea Witch* – *Sea Witch*, this is *Golden Dawn*.' And only the static howled in reply.

'*Warlock*. Come in, *Warlock*. This is *Golden Dawn*.'

Something else went in the wind, they heard it tear loose, and the whole superstructure shook and trembled. The ship was beginning to break up, it had not been designed to withstand winds like this.

Through the open radio room door, Nicholas could see the control console display. There were seventy-one fathoms of water under the ship, and the wind was punching her, flogging her on towards the shore.

'Come in, *Sea Witch*,' Nicholas called with quiet desperation. 'This is *Golden Dawn*. Do you read me?'

The wind charged the ship, crashing into it like a monster, and she groaned and reeled from the blow.

'Come in, *Warlock*.'

Randle lurched across to the forward windows, and clinging to the rail he bowed over the gauges that monitored the condition of the ship's cargo. Checking for tank damage.

'At least he is still thinking.' Nicholas watched him, and above the Captain's head, the sounding showed sixty-eight fathoms.

Randle straightened slowly, began to turn, and the wind struck again.

Nicholas felt the blow in his stomach, it was a solid thing, like a mountain in avalanche, a defeaning boom of sound and the forward bridge window above the control console broke inwards.

It burst in a glittering explosion of glass shards that engulfed the figure of Captain Randle standing directly before it. In a fleeting moment of horror, Nicholas saw his head half severed from his shoulders by a guillotine of flying glass, then he crumpled to the deck and instantly the bright pulsing hose of his blood was diluted to spreading pale pink in the torrent of wind and blown water that poured in through the opening, and smothered the navigation bridge.

Charts and books were ripped from their shelves and fluttered like trapped birds as the wind blustered and swirled in the confines of glass and steel.

Nicholas reached the Captain's body, protecting his own face with an arm crooked across it, but there was nothing he could do for him. He left Randle lying on the deck and shouted to the others.

'Keep clear of the windows.'

He gathered them in the rear of the bridge, against the bulkhead where stood the Decca and navigational systems. The four of them kept close together, as though they gained comfort from the close proximity of other humans, but the wind did not relent.

It poured in through the shattered window and raged about the bridge, tearing at their clothing and filling the air with a fine mist of water, flooding the deck ankle deep so that it sloshed and ran as the tanker rolled almost to her beam ends.

Randle's limp and sodden body slid back and forth in the wash and roll, until Nicholas left the dubious security of the after bulkhead, half-lifted the corpse under the arms, and dragged it into the radio room and wedged it into the radio operator's bunk. Swift blood stained the crisply ironed sheets, and Nicholas threw a fold of the blanket over Randle and staggered back into the bridge.

Still the wind rose, and now Nicholas felt himself numbed by the force and persistence of it.

Some loose material, perhaps a sheet of aluminium from the superstructure, or a length of piping ripped from the tank deck below, smashed into the tip of the bridge like a cannon ball and then flipped away into the storm, leaving a jagged rent which the wind exploited, tearing and worrying at it, enlarging the opening, so that the plating flapped and hammered and a solid deluge of rain poured in through it.

Nicholas realized that the ship's superstructure was beginning to go; like a gigantic vulture, soon the wind would begin stripping the carcass down to its bones.

He knew he should get the survivors down nearer the water line, so that when they were forced to commit themselves to the sea, they could do so quickly. But his brain was numbed by the tumult, and he stood stolidly. It needed all his remaining strength merely to brace himself against the tearing wind and the ship's anguished motion.

In the days of sail, the crew would tie themselves to the main mast, when they reached this stage of despair.

Dully, he registered that the depth of water under the ship was now only fifty-seven fathoms, and the barometer was reading 955 millibars. Nicholas had never heard of a reading that low; surely it could not go lower, they must be almost at the centre of the revolving hurricane.

With an effort, he lifted his arm and read the time. It was still only ten o'clock in the morning, they had been in the hurricane for only two and a half hours.

A great burning light struck through the torn roof, a light that blinded them with its intensity, and Nicholas threw up his hands to protect his eyes. He could not understand what was happening. He thought his hearing had gone, for suddenly the terrible tumult of the wind was muted, fading away.

Then he understood. 'The eye,' he croaked, 'we are into the eye,' and his voice resounded strangely in his own ears. He stumbled to the front of the bridge.

Although the *Golden Dawn* still rolled ponderously, describing an arc of almost forty degrees from side to side, she was free of the unbearable weight of the wind and brilliant sunshine poured down upon her. It beamed down like the dazzling arc lamps of a stage set, out of the throat of a dark funnel of dense racing swirling cloud.

The cloud lay to the very surface of the sea, and encompassed the full sweep of the horizon in an unbroken wall. Only directly overhead was it open, and the sky was an angry unnatural purple, set with the glaring, merciless eye of the sun.

The sea was still wild and confused, leaping into peaks and troughs and covered with a thick frothy mattress of spindrift, whipped into a custard by the wild winds. But already the sea was subsiding in the total calm of the eye and *Golden Dawn* was rolling less viciously.

Nicholas turned his head stiffly to watch the receding wall of racing cloud. How long would it take for the eye to pass over them, he wondered.

Not very long, he was sure of that, half an hour perhaps – an hour at the most – and then the storm would be on them again, with its renewed fury every bit as sudden as its passing. But this time, the wind would come from exactly the opposite direction as they crossed the hub and went into the far side of the revolving wall of cloud.

Nicholas jerked his eyes away from that racing, heaven-high bank of cloud, and looked down on to the tank deck. He saw at a single glance that *Golden Dawn* had already sustained mortal damage. The forward port pod tank was half torn from its hydraulic coupling, holding only by the bows and lying at almost twenty degrees from the line of the other three tanks. The entire tank deck was twisted like the limb of an arthritic giant, it rolled and pitched out of sequence with the rest of the hull.

Golden Dawn's back was broken. It had broken where Duncan had weakened the hull to save steel. Only the buoyancy of the crude petroleum in her four tanks was holding her together now. Nicholas expected to see the dark, glistening ooze of slick leaking from her; he could not believe that not one of the four tanks had ruptured, and he glanced at the electronic cargo monitor. Loads and gas contents of all tanks were still normal. They had been freakishly lucky so far, but when they went into the far side of the hurricane he knew that *Golden Dawn*'s weakened spine would give completely, and when that happened it must pinch and tear the thin skins of the pod tanks.

He made a decision then, forcing his mind to work, not certain how good a decision it was but determined to act on it.

'Duncan,' he called to him across the swamped and battered bridge. 'I'm sending you and the others off on one of the life-rafts. This will be your only chance to launch one. I'll stay on board to fire the cargo when the storm hits again.'

'The storm has passed,' suddenly Duncan was screaming at him like a madman. 'The ship is safe now. You're going to destroy my ship – you're deliberately trying to break me.' He was lunging across the heaving bridge. 'It's deliberate. You know I've won now. You are going to destroy this ship. It's the only way you can stop me now.' He swung a clumsy round arm blow. Nicholas ducked under it and caught Duncan around the chest.

'Listen to me,' he shouted, trying to calm him. 'This is only the eye –'

'You'd do anything to stop me. You swore you would stop me –'

'Help me,' Nicholas called to the two seamen, and they grabbed Duncan's arms. He bucked and fought like a madman, screaming wildly at Nicholas, his face contorted and swollen with rage, sodden hair flopping into his eyes. 'You'd do anything to destroy me, to destroy my ship –'

'Take him down to the raft deck,' Nicholas ordered the two seamen. He knew he could not reason with Duncan now, and he turned away and stiffened suddenly.

'Wait!' he stopped them leaving the bridge.

Nicholas felt the terrible burden of weariness and despair slip from his shoulders, felt new strength rippling through his body, recharging his courage and his resolution – for a mile away, from behind that receding wall of dreadful grey cloud, *Sea Witch* burst abruptly into the sunlight, tearing bravely along with the water bursting over her bows and flying back as high as her bridgework, running without regard to the hazard of sea and storm.

'Jules,' Nicholas whispered.

Jules was driving her like only a tugman can drive a ship, racing to beat the far wall of the storm.

Nicholas felt his throat constricting and suddenly the scalding tears of relief and thankfulness half-blinded him – for a mile out on *Sea Witch*'s port side, and barely a cable-length astern of her, *Warlock* came crashing out of the storm bank, running every bit as hard as her sister ship.

'David,' Nicholas spoke aloud. 'You too, David.'

He realized only then that they must have been in radar contact with him through those wild tempestuous hours of storm passage, hovering there, holding station on *Golden Dawn*'s crippled bulk and waiting for their first opportunity.

Above the wail and crackle of static from the overhead loud-speaker boomed Jules Levoisin's voice. He was close enough and in the clear eye the interference allowed a readable radio contact.

'*Golden Dawn*, this is *Sea Witch*. Come in, *Golden Dawn*.'

Nicholas reached the radio bench and snatched up the microphone.

'Jules.' He did not waste a moment in greeting or congratulations. 'We are going to take the tanks off her, and let the hull go. Do you understand?'

'I understand to take off the tanks,' Jules responded immediately.

Nicholas' brain was crisp and clear again, he could see just how it must be done. '*Warlock* takes off the port tanks first – in tandem.'

In tandem, the two tanks would be strung like beads on a string, they had been designed to tow that way.

'Then you will take off the starboard side –'

'You must save the hull.' Duncan still fought the two seamen who held him. 'Goddamn you, Berg. I'll not let you destroy me.'

Nicholas ignored his ravings until he had finished giving his orders to the two tug masters. Then he dropped the microphone and grabbed Duncan by the shoulders. Nicholas seemed to be possessed suddenly by supernatural strength, and he shook him as though he were a child. He shook him so his head snapped back and forth and his teeth rattled in his head.

'You bloody idiot,' he shouted in Duncan's face. 'Don't you understand the storm will resume again in minutes?'

He jerked Duncan's body out of the grip of the two seamen and dragged him bodily to the windows overlooking the tank deck.

'Can't you see this monster you have built is finished, finished! There is no propeller, her back is broken, the superstructure will go minutes after the wind hits again.'

He dragged Duncan round to face him, their eyes were inches apart.

'It's over, Duncan. We will be lucky to get away with our lives. We'll be luckier still to save the cargo.'

'But don't you understand – we've got to save the hull – without it –' Duncan started to struggle, he was a powerful man, and quickly he was rousing himself, within minutes he would be dangerous – and there was no time, already *Warlock* was swinging up into her position on *Golden Dawn*'s port beam for tank transfer.

'I'll not let you take off –' Duncan wrenched himself out of Nicholas' grip, there was a mad fanatic light in his eyes.

Nicholas swivelled; coming up on to his toes and swinging from the shoulders he aimed for the point of Duncan's jaw, just below the ear and the thick sodden wedge of Duncan's red-gold sideburns. But Duncan rolled his head with the punch, and the blow glanced off his temple, and *Golden Dawn* rolled back the other way as Nicholas was unbalanced.

He fell back against the control console, and Duncan drove at him, two running paces like a quarter-back taking a field goal, and he kicked right-legged for Nicholas' lower body.

'I'll kill you, Berg,' he screamed, and Nicholas had only time to roll sideways and lift his leg, scissoring it to protect his crotch. Duncan's kick caught him in the upper thigh. An explosion of white pain shot up into his belly and numbed his leg to the thigh, but he used the control console and his good leg to launch himself into a counter-punch, hooking with his right again, under the ribs – and the wind went out of Duncan's lungs with a whoosh as he doubled. Nicholas transferred weight smoothly and swung his left fist up into Duncan's face. It sounded like a watermelon dropped on a concrete floor, and Duncan was hurled backwards against the bulkhead, pinned there for a moment by the ship's roll. Nicholas followed him, hobbling painfully on the injured leg, and he hit him twice more. Left and right, short, hard, hissing blows that cracked his skull backwards against the bulkhead, and brought quick bright rosettes of blood from his lips and nostrils.

As his legs buckled, Nicholas caught him by the throat with his left hand and held him upright, searching his eyes for further resistance, ready to hit again, but there was no fight left in him.

Nicholas let him go, and went to the signal locker. He snatched three of the small walkie-talkie radios from the radio shelves and handed one to each of the two seamen.

'You know the pod tank undocking procedures for a tandem tow?' he asked.

'We've practised it,' one of them replied.

'Let's go,' said Nicholas.

It was a job that was scheduled for a dozen men, and there were three of them. Duncan was of no use to them, and Nicholas left him in the pump control room on the lowest deck of *Golden Dawn*'s stern quarter, after he had closed down the inert gas pumps, sealed the gas vents, and armed the hydraulic releases of the pod tanks for undocking.

They worked sometimes neck-deep in the bursts of green, frothing water that poured over the ultra-tanker's foredeck. They took on board and secured *Warlock*'s main cable, unlocked the hydraulic clamps that held the forward pod tank attached to the hull and, as David Allen eased it clear of the crippled hull, they turned and lumbered back along the twisted and wind-torn catwalk, handicapped by the heavy seaboots and oilskins and the confused seas that still swamped the tank-deck every few minutes.

On the after tank, the whole laborious energy-sapping procedure had to be repeated, but here it was complicated by the chain coupling which connected the two half-mile-long pod tanks. Over the walkie-talkie. Nicholas had to co-ordinate the efforts of his seamen to those of David Allen at the helm of *Warlock*.

When at last *Warlock* threw on power to both of her big propellers and sheered away from the wallowing hull, she had both port pod tanks in tow. They floated just level with the surface of the sea, offering no windage for the hurricane winds that would soon be upon them again.

Hanging on to the rail of the raised catwalk Nicholas watched for two precious minutes with an appraising professional eye. It was an incredible sight, two great shiny black whales, their backs showing only in the troughs, and the gallant little ship leading them away. They followed meekly, and Nicholas' anxiety was lessened. He was not confident, not even satisfied, for there was still a hurricane to navigate – but there was hope now.

'*Sea Witch*,' he spoke into the small portable radio. 'Are you ready to take on tow?'

Jules Levoisin fired the rocket-line across personally. Nicholas recognized his portly but nimble-figure high in the fire-control tower, and the rocket left a thin trail of snaking white smoke high against the backdrop of racing, grey hurricane clouds. Arching high over the tanker's tank-deck, the thin nylon rocket-line fell over the catwalk ten feet from where Nicholas stood.

They worked with a kind of restrained frenzy, and Jules Levoisin brought the big graceful tug in so close beside them that glancing up Nicholas could see the flash of a gold filling in Jules' white smile of encouragement. It was only a glance that Nicholas allowed himself, and then he raised his face and looked at the storm.

The wall of cloud was slippery and smooth and grey, like the body of a gigantic slug, and at its foot trailed a glistening white slimy line where the winds frothed the surface of the sea. It was very close now, ten miles, no more, and above them the sun had gone, cut out by the spiralling vortex of leaden cloud. Yet still that open narrow funnel of clear calm air reached right up to a dark and ominous sky.

There was no hydraulic pressure on the clamps of the starboard forward pod tank. Somewhere in the twisted damaged hull the hydraulic line must have sheared. Nicholas and one of the seamen had to work the emergency release, pumping it open slowly and laboriously by hand.

Still it would not release, the hull was distorted, the clamp jaws out of alignment.

'Pull,' Nicholas commanded Jules in desperation. 'Pull all together.' The storm front was five miles away, and already he could hear the deadly whisper of the wind, and a cold puff touched Nicholas' uplifted face.

The sea boiled under *Sea Witch*'s counter, spewing out in a swift white wake as Jules brought in both engines. The tow-cable came up hard and straight; for half a minute nothing gave, nothing moved – except the wall of racing grey cloud bearing down upon them.

Then, with a resounding metallic clang, the clamps slipped and the tank slid ponderously out of its dock in *Golden Dawn*'s hull – and as it came free, so the hull, held together until that moment by the tanks' bulk and buoyancy, began to collapse.

The catwalk on which Nicholas stood began to twist and tilt so that he had to grab for a handhold, and he stood frozen in horrified fascination as he watched *Golden Dawn* begin the final break-up.

The whole tank deck, now only a gutted skeleton, began to bend at its weakened centre, began to hinge like an enormous pair of nutcrackers – and caught between the jaws of the nutcracker was the starboard after pod tank. It was a nut the size of Chartres Cathedral, with a soft liquid centre, and a shell as thin as the span of a man's hand.

Nicholas broke into a lurching, blundering run down the twisting, tilting catwalk, calling urgently into the radio as he went.

'Shear!' he shouted to the seamen almost half a mile away across that undulating plane of tortured steel. 'Shear the tandem tow!'

For the two starboard pod tanks were linked by the heavy chain of the tandem, and the forward tank was linked to *Sea Witch* by the main tow-cable. So *Sea Witch* and the doomed *Golden Dawn* were coupled inexorably, unless they could cut the two tanks apart and let *Sea Witch* escape with the forward tank which she had just undocked.

The shear control was in the control box halfway back along the tank deck, and at that moment the nearest seaman was two hundred yards from it.

Nicholas could see him staggering wildly back along the twisting, juddering catwalk. Clearly he realized the danger, but his haste was fatal, for as he jumped from the catwalk, the deck opened under him, gaping open like the jaws of a steel monster and the seaman fell through, waist deep, into the opening between two moving plates, then as he squirmed feebly, the next lurch of the ship's hull closed the plates, sliding them across each other like the blades of a pair of scissors.

The man shrieked once and a wave burst over the deck, smothering his mutilated body in cold, green water. When it poured back over the ship's side there was no sign of the man, the deck was washed glisteningly clean.

Nicholas reached the same point in the deck, judged the gaping and closing movement of the steel plate and the next rush of sea coming on board, before he leapt across the deadly gap.

He reached the control box, and slid back the hatch, pressing himself into the tiny steel cubicle as he unlocked the red lid that housed the shear button. He hit the button with the heel of his hand.

The four heavy chains of the tandem tow lay between the electrodes of the shear mechanism. With a gross surge of power from the ship's generators and a flash of blue electric flame, the thick steel links sheared as cleanly as cheese under the cutting wire – and, half a mile away, *Sea Witch* felt the release and pounded ahead under the full thrust of her propellers, taking with her the forward starboard tank still held on main tow.

Nicholas paused in the opening of the control cubicle, hanging on to the sill for support and he stared down at the single remaining tank, still caught inextricably in the tangled moving forest of *Golden Dawn*'s twisting, contorting hull. It was as though an invisible giant had taken the Eiffel Tower at each end and was bending it across his knee.

Suddenly there was a sharp chemical stink in the air, and Nicholas gagged on it. The stink of crude petroleum oil gushing from the ruptured tank.

'Nicholas! Nicholas!' The radio set slung over his shoulder squawked, and he lifted it to his lips without taking his eyes from the *Golden Dawn*'s terrible death throes.

'Go ahead, Jules.'

'Nicholas, I am turning to pick you up.'

'You can't turn, not with that tow.'

'I will put my bows against the starboard quarterdeck rail, directly under the forward wing of the bridge. Be ready to jump aboard.'

'Jules, you are out of your head!'

'I have been that way for fifty years,' Jules agreed amiably. 'Be ready.'

'Jules, drop your tow first,' Nicholas pleaded. It would be almost impossible to manoeuvre the *Sea Witch* with that monstrous dead weight hanging on her tail. 'Drop tow. We can pick up again later.'

'You teach your grandfather to break eggs,' Jules blithely mangled the old saying, giving it a sinister twist.

'Listen Jules, the No. 4 tank has ruptured. I want you to shut down for fire. Do you understand? Full fire shut down. Once I am aboard, we will put a rocket into her and burn off cargo.'

'I hear you, Nicholas, but I wish I had not.'

Nicholas left the control cubicle, jumped the gaping, chewing gap in the decking and scrambled up the steel ladder on to the central catwalk.

Glancing over his shoulder, he could see the endlessly slippery grey wall of racing cloud and wind; its menace was overpowering, so that for a moment he faltered before forcing himself into running back along the catwalk towards the tanker's stern tower half a mile ahead.

The single remaining seaman was on the catwalk a hundred yards ahead of him, pounding determinedly back towards the pick-up point. He also had heard Jules Levoisin's last transmission.

A quarter of a mile across the roiling, leaping waters, Jules Levoisin was bringing *Sea Witch* around. At another time Nicholas would have been impressed by the consummate skill with which the little Frenchman was handling his ship and its burdensome tow, but now there was time and energy for one thing only.

The air stank. The heavy fumes of crude oil burned Nicholas' pumping lungs, and constricted his throat. He coughed and gasped as he ran, the taste and reek of it coated his tongue and seared his nostrils.

Below the catwalk, the bloated pod-tank was punctured in a hundred places by the steel lances of the disintegrating hull, pinched and torn by moving steel girders, and the dark red oil spurted and dribbled and oozed from it like the poisonous blood from the carcass of a mortally wounded dragon.

Nicholas reached the stern tower, barged in through the storm doors to the lowest deck and reached the pump control room.

Duncan Alexander turned to him, as he entered, his face swollen and bruised where Nicholas had beaten him.

'We are abandoning now,' said Nicholas. '*Sea Witch* is taking us off.'

'I hated you from that very first day,' Duncan was very calm, very controlled, his voice even, deep and cultured. 'Did you know that?'

'There's no time for that now.' Nicholas grabbed his arm, and Duncan followed him readily into the passageway.

'That's what the game is all about, isn't it, Nicholas, power and wealth and women – that's the game we played.'

Nicholas was barely listening. They were out on to the quarter-deck, standing at its starboard rail, below the bridge, the pick-up point that Jules had stipulated. *Sea Witch* was turning in, only five hundred yards out, and Nicholas had time now to watch Jules handle his ship.

He was running out the heavy tow-cable on free spool, deliberately letting a long bight of it form between the tug and its enormous whalelike burden, and he was using the slack in the cable to cut in towards *Golden Dawn*'s battered, sagging hulk. He would be alongside for the pick-up in less than a minute.

'That was the game we played, you and I,' Duncan was still talking calmly. 'Power and wealth and women –'

Below them *Golden Dawn* poured her substance into the sea in a slick, stinking flood. The waves, battering against her side, churned the oil to a thick filthy emulsion, and it was spreading away across the surface, bleeding its deadly poison into the Gulf Stream to broadcast it to the entire ocean.

'I won,' Duncan went on reasonably. 'I won it all, every time –' He was groping in his pockets, but Nicholas hardly heard him, was not watching him. ' – until now.'

Duncan took one of the self-igniting signal flares from his pocket and held it against his chest with both hands, slipping his index finger through the metal ring of the igniter tab.

'And yet I win this one also, Nicholas,' he said. 'Game, set and match.' And he pulled the tab on the flare with a sharp jerk, and stepped back, holding it aloft.

It spluttered once and then burst into brilliant sparkling red flame, white phosphorescent smoke billowing from it.

Now at last Nicholas turned to face him, and for a moment he was too appalled to move. Then he lunged for Duncan's raised hand that held the burning flare, but Duncan was too fast for him to reach it.

He whirled and threw the flame in a high spluttering arc, out over the leaking, stinking tank-deck.

It struck the steel tank and bounced once, and then rolled down the canted oil-coated plating.

Nicholas stood paralysed at the rail staring down at it. He expected a violent explosion, but nothing happened, the flare rolled innocently across the deck, burning with its pretty red twinkling light.

'It's not burning,' Duncan cried. 'Why doesn't it burn?'

Of course, the gas was only explosive in a confined space, and it needed spark. Out here in the open air the oil had a very high flashpoint, it must be heated to release its volatiles.

The flare caught in the scuppers and fizzled in a black pool of crude, and only then the crude caught. It caught with a red, slow, sulky flame that spread quickly but not explosively over the entire deck, and instantly, thick billows of dark smoke rose in a dense choking cloud.

Below where Nicholas stood, the *Sea Witch* thrust her bows in and touched them against the tanker's side. The seaman beside Nicholas jumped and landed neatly on the tug's bows, then raced back along *Sea Witch*'s deck.

'Nicholas,' Jules' voice thundered over the loudhailer. 'Jump, Nicholas.'

Nicholas spun back to the rail, and poised himself to jump.

Duncan caught him from behind, whipping one arm around his throat, and pulling him backwards away from the rail.

'No,' Duncan shouted. 'You're staying, my friend. You are not going anywhere. You are staying here with me.'

A greasy wave of black choking smoke engulfed them, and Jules' magnified voice roared in Nicholas' ears.

'Nicholas, I cannot hold her here. Jump, quickly, jump!'

Duncan had him off-balance, dragging him backwards, away from the ship's side, and suddenly Nicholas knew what he must do.

Instead of resisting Duncan's arm, he hurled himself backwards and they crashed together into the superstructure – but Duncan bore the combined weight of both their bodies.

His armlock around the throat relaxed slightly and Nicholas drove his elbow into Duncan's side below the ribs, then wrenched his body forward from the waist, reached between his own braced legs and caught Duncan's ankles. He straightened up again, dragging Duncan off his feet and the same instant dropped backwards with his full weight on to the deck.

Duncan gasped and his arm fell away, as Nicholas bounced to his feet again, choking in the greasy billows of smoke, and he reached the ship's side.

Below him, the gap between *Sea Witch*'s bows and the tanker's side was rapidly widening and the thrust of the sea and the drag of the tug pulled them apart.

Nicholas vaulted on to the rail, poised for an instant and then jumped. He struck the deck and his teeth cracked together with the impact; his injured leg gave under him and he rolled once, then he was up on his hands and knees.

He looked up at *Golden Dawn*. She was completely enveloped now in the boiling column of black smoke. As the flames heated the leaking crude, so it burned more readily. The bank of smoke was shot through now with the satanic crimson of high, hot flame.

As *Sea Witch* sheered desperately away, the first rush of the storm hit them, and for a moment it smeared the smoke away, exposing the tanker's high quarterdeck.

Duncan Alexander stood at the rail above the roaring holocaust of the tank-deck. He stood with his arms extended, and he was burning, his clothing burned fiercely and his hair was a bright torch of flame. He stood like a ritual cross, outlined in fire, and then slowly he seemed to shrivel and he toppled forward over the rail into the bubbling, spurting, burning cargo of the monstrous ship that he had built – and the black smoke closed over him like a funeral cloak.

As the crude oil escaping from the pierced pod tank fed the flames, so the heat built up swiftly, still sufficient to consume only the volatile aromatic spirits which constituted less than half the bulk of the cargo.

The heavy carbon elements, not yet hot enough to burn, boiled off in that solid black column of smoke, and as the returning winds of the hurricane raced over the *Golden Dawn* once more, so that filthy pall was mixed with air and lifted into the cloud bank of the storm, rising first a thousand, then ten, then twenty thousand feet above the surface of the ocean.

And still *Golden Dawn* burned, and the temperatures of the gas and oil mixture trapped in her hull rocketed steeply. Steel glowed red, then brilliant white, ran like molten wax, and then like water – and suddenly the flashpoint of heavy carbon smoke in a mixture of air and water vapour was reached in the womb of this mighty furnace.

Golden Dawn and her entire cargo turned into a fireball.

The steel and glass and metal of her hull disappeared in an instantaneous explosive combustion that released temperature like those upon the surface of the sun. Her cargo, a quarter of a million tons of it, burned in an instant, releasing a white blooming rose of pure heat so fierce that it shot up into the upper stratosphere and consumed the billowing pall of its own hydrocarbon gas and smoke.

The very air burst into flame, the surface of the sea flamed in that white fireball of heat and even the clouds of smoke burned as the oxygen and hydrocarbon they contained exploded.

Once an entire city had been subjected to this phenomena of fireball, when stone and earth and air had exploded, and five thousand German citizens of the city of Cologne had been vaporized, and that vapour burned in the heat of its own release.

But this fireball was spawned by a quarter of a million tons of volatic liquids.

'Can't you get us further away?' Nicholas shouted above the thunder of the hurricane. His mouth was only inches from Jules Levoisin's ear.

They were standing side by side, hanging from the overhead railing that gave purchase on this wildly pitching deck.

'If I open the taps I will part the tow wire,' Jules shouted back.

Sea Witch was alternately standing on her nose and then her tail. There was no forward view from the bridge, only green washes of sea water and banks of spray.

The full force of the hurricane was on them once more, and a glance at the radarscope showed the glowing image of *Golden Dawn*'s crippled and bleeding hull only half a mile astern.

Suddenly the glass of the windows was obscured by an impenetrable blackness, and the light in *Sea Witch*'s navigation bridge was reduced to only the glow of her fire-lights and the electronic instruments of her control console.

Jules Levoisin turned his face to Nicholas, his plump features haunted by green shadows in the gloom.

'Smoke bank,' Nicholas shouted an explanation. There was no reek of the filthy hydrocarbon in the bridge, for *Sea Witch* was shut down for fire drill, all her ports and ventilators sealed, her internal air-conditioning on a closed circuit, the air being scrubbed and recharged with oxygen by the big Carrier unit above the main engine room. 'We are directly down wind of the *Golden Dawn*.'

A fiercer rush of the hurricane winds laid *Sea Witch* over on her side, the lee rail deep under the racing green sea, and held her there, unable to rise against the careless might of the storm for many minutes. Her crew hung desperately from any hand hold, the irksome burden of her tow helping to drag her down further; the propellers found no grip in the air, and her engines screamed in anguish.

But *Sea Witch* had been built to live in any sea, and the moment the wind hesitated, she fought off the water that had come aboard and began to swing back.

'Where is *Warlock*?' Jules bellowed anxiously. The danger of collision preyed upon him constantly, two ships and their elephantine tows manoeuvring closely in confined hurricane waters was nightmare on top of nightmare.

'Ten miles east of us.' Nicholas picked the other tug's image out of the trash on the radarscope. 'They had a start, ahead of the wind –'

He would have gone on, but the boiling bank of hydrocarbon smoke that surrounded *Sea Witch* turned to fierce white light, a light that blinded every man on the bridge as though a photograph flashlight had been fired in his face.

'Fireball!' Nicholas shouted, and, completely blinded, reached for the remote controls of the water cannons seventy feet above the bridge on *Sea Witch*'s fire-control tower.

Minutes before, he had aligned the four water cannons, training them down at their maximum angle of depression, so now as he locked down the multiple triggers, *Sea Witch* deluged herself in a pounding cascade of sea water.

Sea Witch was caught in a furnace of burning air, and despite the torrents of water she spewed over herself, her paintwork was burned away in instantaneous combustion so fierce that it consumed its own smoke, and almost instantly the bare scorched metal of her exposed upperworks began to glow with heat.

The heat was so savage that it struck through the insulated hull, through the double glazing of the two-inch armoured glass of her bridge windows, scorching and frizzling away Nicholas' eyelashes and blistering his lips as he lifted his face to it.

The glass of the bridge windows wavered and swam as they began to melt – and then abruptly there was no more oxygen. The fireball had extinguished itself, consumed everything in its twenty seconds of life, everything from sea level to thirty thousand feet above it, a brief and devastating orgasm of destruction.

It left a vacuum, a weak spot in the earth's thin skin of air, it formed another low pressure system smaller, but much more intense, and more hungry to be filled than the eye of hurricane Lorna itself.

It literally tore the guts out of that great revolving storm, setting up counter winds and a vortex within the established system that ripped it apart.

New gales blew from every point about the fireball's vacuum, swiftly beginning their own dervish spirals and twenty miles short of the mainland of Florida, hurricane Lorna checked her mindless, blundering charge, fell in upon herself and disintegrated into fifty different willy-nilly squalls and whirlpools of air that collided and split again, slowly degenerating into nothingness.

On a morning in April in Galveston roads, the salvage tug *Sea Witch* dropped off tow to four smaller harbour tugs who would take the *Golden Dawn* No. 3 pod tank up the narrows to the Orient Amex discharge installation below Houston.

Her sister ship *Warlock*, Captain David Allen commanding, had dropped off his tandem tow of No. 1 and No. 2 pod tanks to the same tugs forty-eight hours previously.

Between the two ships, they had made good salvage under Lloyd's Open Form of three-quarters of a million tons of crude petroleum valued at $85.50 U.S. a ton. To the prize would be added the value of the three tanks themselves – not less than sixty-five million dollars all told, Nicholas calculated, and he owned both ships and the full share of the salvage award. He had not sold to the Shiekhs yet, though for every day of the tow from the Florida Straits to Texas, there had been frantic telex messages from James Teacher in London. The Sheikhs were desperate to sign now, but Nicholas would let them wait a little longer.

Nicholas stood on the open wing of *Sea Witch*'s bridge and watched the four smaller harbour tugs bustling importantly about their ungainly charge.

He lifted the cheroot to his lips carefully, for they were still blistered from the heat of the fireball – and he pondered the question of how much he had achieved, apart from spectacular riches.

He had reduced the spill from a million to a quarter of a million tons of cad-rich crude, and he had burned it in a fireball. Nevertheless, there had been losses, toxins had been lifted high above the fireball. They had spread and settled across Florida as far as Tampa and Tallahassee, poisoning the pastures and killing thousands of head of domestic stock. But the American authorities had been quick to extend the hurricane emergency procedures. There had been no loss of human life. He had achieved that much.

Now he had delivered the salvaged pod tanks to Orient Amex. The new cracking process would benefit all mankind, and nothing that Nicholas could do would prevent men carrying the cad-rich crudes of El Barras across the oceans. But would they do so in the same blindly irresponsible manner that Duncan Alexander had attempted?

He knew then with utter certainty that it was his appointed life's work, from now on, to try and ensure that they did not. He knew how he was to embark upon that work. He had the wealth that was necessary, and Tom Parker had given him the other instruments to do the job.

He knew, with equal certainty, who would be his companion in that life's work – and standing on the fire-scorched deck of the gallant little vessel he had a vivid image of a golden girl who walked forever beside him in sunlight and in laughter.

'Samantha.'

He said her name aloud just once, and suddenly he was very eager to begin.